ZODIAC ACADEMY

SORROW AND STARLIGHT

CAROLINE PECKHAM
SUSANNE VALENTI

Zodiac Academy
Earth Cavern
Pitball Stadium
Saturn Auditorium
Uranus Infirmary
Aqua House
Lunar Leisure
Neptune Tower
Water Lagoon
The Shimmering Springs

Terra House
Asteroid Place
The Howling Meadow
King's Hollow
The Orb
Mars Laboratory
The Wailing Wood
Earth Observatory
Venus Library
Mercury Chambers
Aer House
Aer Cove
Fire Arena

Sorrow and Starlight
Zodiac Academy #8

Interior Formatting & Design by Wild Elegance Formatting
Map Design by Fred Kroner

Sorrow and Starlight/Caroline Peckham & Susanne Valenti – Alternate ed.
ISBN-13 - 978-1-914425-60-8

This book is dedicated to all those who have drowned in the depths of loss, with memories clutched in your fist like fragments of the sun. May you be brave enough to peer between your fingers, so they might shine again.

WELCOME TO SOLARIA

Note to all Fae: Lesser Orders will be sent to the Nebula Inquisition Centres if seen using Order gifts aggressively. All traitors of the crown will be sentenced to death in the palace amphitheatre, and their executions will be televised as a warning to insurgents.

King Lionel Acrux has pledged to make Solaria powerful once more and has vowed upon the stars to protect the loyal, honourable Fae of the nation at any cost.

The King's United Nebular Taskforce will be watching.

All hail the Dragon King

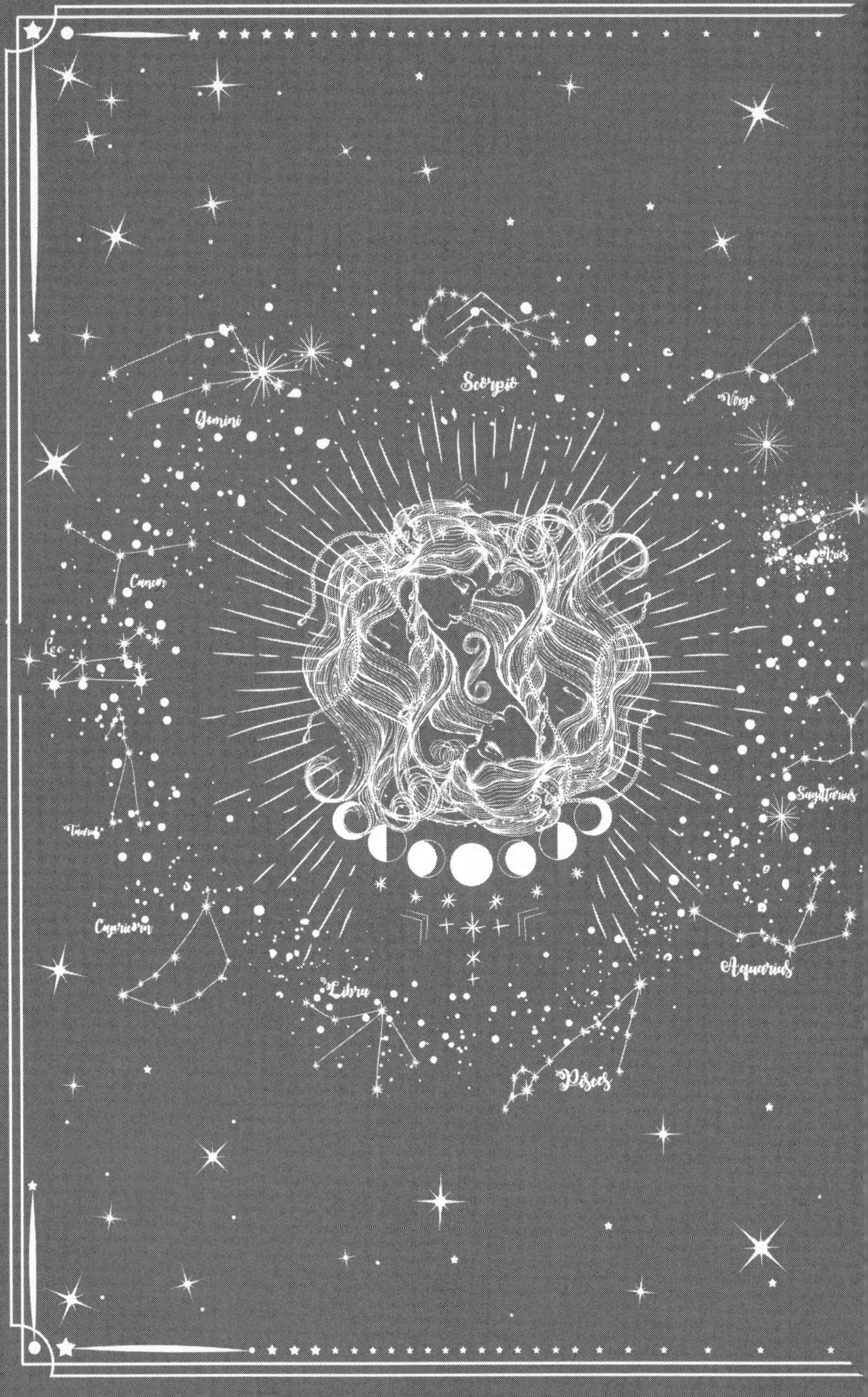
Scorpio
Gemini
Virgo
Cancer
Leo
Sagittarius
Taurus
Capricorn
Aquarius
Libra
Pisces

DARCY

CHAPTER ONE

Pain splintered through my chest as I climbed the rocky mountain, my body still taking the form of the monstrous beast which bound me to Lavinia's curse.

I was holding onto my own mind with everything I had left, but the Shadow Beast's desires were surrounding each of my thoughts and snuffing them out like a raging storm against a flickering flame. Its presence was crushing, suffocating, and so powerful it felt like it was carving fissures into the depths of what made me…*me*.

A scream tore from my throat as I called on my power in an effort to take charge of this creature that had stolen ownership of my flesh, but it came out as a tremendous roar which shook the entire mountainside. My magic lay quiet inside me, not responding to my plea, like it no longer belonged to me at all.

I could feel the beast's desire to go back, to return to the battle and sate the bloodlust raking at the centre of my throat, demanding more carnage. It was a command that held me hostage, like the fiercest Coercion I'd ever known. But still, I held on, thinking of my sister back there, and of the man I loved with every furious beat of my heart. I wouldn't hurt them. Not ever.

Somehow, I managed to keep increasing the distance between me and the battlefield, hating that I was abandoning everyone, yet knowing my presence would only make it worse.

Blood stained my muzzle, and the scent of death was vile and intoxicating at once. I was two opposing creatures housed within one body, and I feared I wasn't strong enough to dominate the one that didn't belong here.

What if I was merging into this being, becoming a monster? And when it was done with me, it would spit me back out and leave me barren, Darcy Vega just a memory cast to the wind.

The hollow space in my chest where my magic usually lived echoed dully as I tried to encourage even a scrap of it to my aid.

There was nothing. I was empty, and the fear that I was becoming mortal tangled with every other terror inside of me until it nearly ripped me apart. This was worse than anything else Lavinia could have done to me; she was taking my soul, cleaving it from my chest and burning it to ash. The Shadow Beast was fuelled by her desires, and she wanted me ruined.

Exhaustion was rattling my bones, begging me to stop running and rest my aching muscles. I'd climbed high into the mountains now and cold air swept around me, the snow-cloaked peaks above me almost within reach.

The closest mountaintop was damaged where the fallen star had streaked through the sky and slammed into it, boulders and rocks strewn across the side of it, disappearing into a ravine somewhere ahead of me.

I didn't know why I'd chased it out here into the depths of nowhere, but it had been like a beacon calling my name, urging me on, helping me to maintain some shred of control over my own destiny and giving me something to aim for.

My heart pounded dangerously fast, and my breaths fell so heavily it felt like my lungs were going to burst. But I refused to stop in case my will faltered, and the Shadow Beast managed to turn us around and take me back to the battlefield.

I ran into a thick group of pine trees, climbing a steep hill that seemed never ending, the glittering stars peeking through the dark canopy above like they were trying to get a better look at me.

I finally crested the hill, spilling out of the trees and finding myself at a dead end, my paws skidding to a halt on the black rocks lining the edge of an ominously dark lake.

The large body of water was surrounded by gunmetal grey cliff faces that towered up around it in a half-moon like a giant bowl, one side of it shattered from the impact of the fallen star. The lake should have been still, seeing as there was no river of water pouring into it to create a stir, but the surface was rippling as if something had caused it to move, and there was a strange metallic scent hanging in the air too.

The ground beneath my paws was wet and I sensed an energy in the atmosphere which brought a sharpness to my mind that I'd been so desperately trying to reclaim. Although it was a bitter, agonising thing to endure, because with that clarity came grief, the type that made my heart feel like it was bleeding.

Geraldine.

Countless had fallen to the teeth and claws of this Shadow Beast. This monster. *Me.* Including one of the best friends I'd ever had the fortune to know.

As my emotions poured through me, the shift rippled down my spine, the black fur of the Shadow Beast receding into my skin, and I suddenly hit the ground on my knees in my Fae form.

My reflection shone back at me from the surface of the lake, revealing the shadows which clung to my hair. They floated around me like Lavinia's, as black as the night sky. A dress of deepest shadow coiled around me too, ever moving and changing, covering my body. It felt like damp fingers were clinging to me, caressing my skin. The sensation was both abhorrent and laced with pleasure, the call of the shadows whispering in my ear. But that wasn't the worst of it, because my eyes weren't mine at all. They were obsidian, no hint of green, and more terrible than that, no silver rings, the mark of my Elysian mating to Orion erased.

I buckled forward, slashing a hand through my reflection as a sob tore from my throat and sorrow consumed me. I was a monstrosity.

I'd killed so many people. Good people. People who deserved to return to their families after finding victory on that battlefield and vanquishing the evil which had come to claim our freedom. It wasn't right that they'd been stolen so violently from this world.

"I'm sorry," I croaked, knowing it was pointless. Just words spoken into the wind, and words had never had the power to turn back time.

The loss of Geraldine was tearing me apart as my mind turned over my vicious attack on her, how her blood had tasted in my mouth. I shuddered as a desperate sob left me and I clutched my hands to my chest as my heart felt like it was trying to fight its way out and escape me. I wanted to escape me too.

I sat there for so long in the depths of my despair, that my tears turned cold against my cheeks, the freezing air gusting against me, shifting through the shadows hugging my body and the icy water lapping up against my knees.

Despite the time that had passed, the lake was still rippling and shifting in that unnatural way which said something had disturbed it. I didn't care what it was, even if another monster lurked in its depths. There was no greater monster than the one I'd become tonight on that battlefield, one which slept within me now, waiting to return at any moment. The terror of losing myself to it again was a torture in itself. Did I even have any control over the beast at all, or was it waiting for Lavinia to command it into action once again?

Shadows danced around me, licking my skin in the way they did the Shadow Princess, and I shrank from their touch as they tried to lure me in. The whispers of the lost souls within them trying to calm me, baiting me as they offered me solace from my pain. But I wasn't going to let them steal that from me. It was the only thing tying me to myself right now, and I was sure the Shadow Beast would possess me again if I let the darkness have its way.

I lifted my hands, trying to draw magic to my fingertips, wanting to cast the strongest chains of iron my earth magic could conjure and tether myself here so I could never return to hurt my friends.

No power sparked within me, not a glimmer of magic to be seen. My Phoenix was silent too, and not in a way that said it was sleeping; no, it was...gone. Taken by the Shadow Beast which held me captive and perhaps devoured from existence entirely.

My tears stopped falling, replaced by a grief so potent it went far beyond tears. It was the type of grief I wasn't sure I could come back from, the loss of the world as I knew it, and the hopeless fear that those I loved could be laying lifelessly back there somewhere, their souls beyond the Veil, leaving me far behind. I couldn't even return to check if they were safe, because I was the very danger that I feared would find them.

There was only one thing I could do, and I doubted it would help at all, but I could try.

"*Please*." I turned my gaze to the stars, knowing they had the power to change all of this if only they cared to. I'd never begged them for anything, but I was down on my knees now and I desperately hoped they were listening, that I could make them care even if it was only for a moment. Maybe a moment was all I needed to change the world. "Let them live. Let them escape death. Let them have another day. Give us one more chance."

The stars glittered quietly, and I could have sworn I felt them turning their gaze to me, though what they saw, I didn't know. Probably just a broken girl who was as meaningless as dust to them. But this dust could think and feel and *love*, and I was done being tossed around in the tides of fate. I wanted to be heard, and most of all I wanted to steal the reins from their almighty hands and steer all our fortunes towards the light.

"Release me from this curse!" I screamed so loud it tore at my throat. "Return my powers. Give me the chance to fight and I'll give you something to watch from your perches up there. I'll give you blood, vengeance, and an end to the false king and his shadow queen that will sate your need for entertainment," I spat, rage flooding through me as they watched with hushed indifference.

Were they amused by me? Was I just a puppet in a play I didn't know I was a part of? Was it all some pastime they liked to indulge in up there? A game for their sick enjoyment, the Fae stuck below them following a script that had been written for us the moment we were born.

Maybe we were never meant to win, maybe this was a tragedy, and I was in the final act, moving towards an inevitable end along with everyone I loved. Maybe I never really had a choice in how this would go.

I hung my head, the stars' silence like a dismissal that told me all I needed to know about how much they cared for my predicament. Despair was all I had left to me, a noxious companion who breathed agony into my lungs. The further I fell into it, the more the shadows coiled and tightened beneath my skin like chains. They whispered soft promises to me of escape that seemed far too tempting now that the hopelessness was setting in. All I had to do was let go and the darkness would take this pain away. Bliss awaited me in their arms, I just had to give in…

The Shadow Beast roused inside me and with every passing second, it became harder to keep it at bay. Its thirst for blood was unending, an eternal void that would drink up every drop it could find, and it didn't care who it belonged to.

Somewhere in the recesses of my mind, I heard Lavinia speaking to me softly, *"It's over, Princess. Give in to the shadows, they've already won."*

My fingers clenched as the shadows wound around me, seeping out from my skin to embrace me like an old friend. Maybe she was right. Maybe everyone I loved was gone and I was responsible for it. I'd turned the tide of the battle in favour of Lionel's army, and I'd caused everything that had happened after. It was all my fault.

Death was branded on me now, my hands turned murderous against my will. But I should have been strong enough to fight back, I should have found a way to stop this, I should have seen the signs. I was a Phoenix, one of the rarest and most powerful Orders to exist, and more than that, I was the daughter of the Savage King. How could I have been so useless when it had counted? How had all that power slipped from my grasp so easily? Shouldn't I have been strong enough to defeat the Shadow Beast before it had gotten its claws into me this deep?

No, in the end, I'd been too weak to stop it.

I'd failed my parents. I'd failed Tory, Lance…*Geraldine.*

A tremor ran through me as I took in the blood on my fingers and clogged under my nails, a noise of anguish leaving me as I tried to scrub it away. When that didn't work, I shoved them into the icy lake and tried to wash it off, the shadows releasing their hold a little as the pain came back to me in floods. *I'm so sorry, Geraldine.*

Tears blurred my vision and dripped into the water as I worked desperately to get the blood off my hands, whilst knowing I would never truly be clean of it.

A silvery light seemed to grow deep in the water, and I blinked to clear my eyes, my lips parting as the light grew brighter in the obsidian depths of the lake.

I fell still as a huge rock was illuminated at the base of the deep water, and I thought of the falling star which had torn through the sky during the battle, the one I had chased to this lonely corner of the world.

My breaths became shallower and though logically I knew I should withdraw my hands from the water, my instincts told me the opposite. There was something so familiar about that silver light and the way it pulsed through the lake, setting the hairs rising along the back of my neck.

The water shifted before me until I could no longer see the fallen star, the silver glow spreading out until it created a mirror-like sheen just beyond the tips of my fingers. I flexed my hands, already reaching for it as the shadows withdrew and I sensed the presence responsible for this magic. My heart twisted in hope, the need for some small respite from my grief consuming me as my skin prickled with awareness, and I drew in a shuddering breath.

"Mom?" I whispered with a pang of longing in my voice.

My fingers connected with the silvery glow and it moved at my touch, twisting into two beautiful silver wings. It was her, I was sure of it. I'd know her anywhere now.

She gazed at me through that light and my heart fractured with how much I needed to be closer to her. Logically, I knew she wasn't really there, that this was just a vision or memory left for me to uncover, but she felt closer than ever before as I reached for her within the lake.

"This surely won't work," a deep male voice spoke from afar, and the wings shifted once more until they became a perfectly clear mirror submerged in the water. Or maybe a window was closer to the truth, because I saw my mother looking back at me through it, her full lips tilting in sadness.

She wore a navy gown that hugged her body and was encrusted with jewels around her waist, her dark hair twisted up into a delicate style. She looked regal, breath-taking, so wise and yet she was still so young. She had many years of life left before her, but she'd never gotten to see even half of it. It hurt me to look at her, to feel the love in her gaze while never having truly felt it at all when I needed her most. So much had been stolen from all of us, our family ripped apart and the lives we should have known together destroyed before they had ever really begun.

She was standing in what looked like a bedchamber, with an enormous four poster behind her and an arching window beyond that showing a night sky.

I frowned, waiting for the memory to play out like it always had in the past, but my mother continued to gaze right at me. It must have been an illusion, but I was so desperate to be close to her that I let myself pretend she really could see me. Though shame washed over me as my sins wrapped around me like a cloak, the blood tarnishing my body an admission of my crimes.

"Hello, darling," she said softly, and I froze, sure this was impossible.

"Can you see me?" I breathed in disbelief, wanting to shrink into the shadows so she couldn't see the truth of me.

"Yes, we both can." She ushered someone closer, and my father stepped into view a little hesitantly, making my heartbeat stutter.

Hail Vega was an imposing figure, his strong features cast in shadow as he leaned forward, a hand on my mom's shoulder like he was half tempted to draw her back, protective, yet supportive at once. It wasn't hard to see why he had so easily been called savage when taking in his huge frame and the power which practically emanated from him, but there was so much more in his expression too. A softness around his eyes, though his stubbled jaw was locked in a stubborn position which reminded me so much of Tory that I almost broke into a sob as I took it in. I was beginning to get a sense of where she got her cynical streak from. He wore an expensive black jacket and pants, his ebony hair pushed back and his green eyes staring directly into mine, assessing me just as I was him.

"How is this possible?" I asked, heat rising along my cheeks at the intensity of their gazes.

Maybe death had come for me, and this was me passing beyond the Veil. I wasn't even opposed to it if everyone I loved was waiting for me there.

"I'm *seeing* you in the future and casting a vision of that future here within the mirror for us to look at. This is a memory of us for you, but for us, it is real. It is the now," she explained, though that only made my mind twist up in knots.

"Merissa," my father whispered, his gaze fixed on my face in terror and hope. "Can I truly speak with her?"

"Yes, but remember what I told you," my mother said, her features turning grave.

"What did you tell him?" I asked and she looked back at me with pain in her eyes.

"That we are speaking to you at a time of great need. I cannot *see* all of what ails you, and I must ask you not to speak of it, for our timelines are delicate, and we should not be crossing the barrier of them at all."

"Gwendalina," my father said, taking me in with purest love, the kind I had only ever felt from Hamish Grus, and I suddenly realised how deeply Geraldine's father cared for me and Tory. Because this was a father's love I was seeing, I'd just never recognised it before. It left me shaken and yearning, wanting to dive into its warmth.

My father's throat rose and fell as he scraped a hand over his face, the shock on his features clear. "Is it safe for you to talk right now?"

"Yes, I think so," I said, hardly able to believe I was really talking to him at all, our words coming together across eras, the past and the present colliding. "But…"

"What is it?" he asked, the concern in his voice making me long for the embrace of a father I would never truly feel the touch of.

"I've killed so many people," I admitted, shame slicing into my flesh. But I could sense the importance of this meeting, the risk my mother was taking to carve out this moment for us across the years, and I had to be honest, if nothing else. "My enemy has turned me into a weapon."

"Then whatever you have done, it is not your fault," Merissa said fiercely, and my gaze met the perfectly brown colour of her eyes, making my heart thunder furiously. "Do not blame yourself, promise me this."

I tried to make the words cross my lips, but I couldn't. They would be a lie.

"You need to get somewhere safe," my father urged, like he could sense the trouble I was in. "Merissa, can you *see* what she needs to do? Where is her sister?"

"Can you *see* her? Is she okay? Is she alive?" I blurted, realising my mom's gifts could give me the answers I desperately craved. Though suddenly I feared the reply she was about to give me with all my heart. My twin had been left to fight back on the battlefield, and I should have been with her until the end. If I ever got to return to her in this world as someone whole, I would never, ever leave her side again.

Merissa's expression darkened, all light leaving it, and panic swept through me in waves.

"She lives," she confirmed, and relief crashed through me in a torrent so fierce, it made me sag forward.

"And Lance?" I asked, my voice cracking with fear. Losing my mate would break me, I almost couldn't take the seconds that passed as my mother's eyes glazed, her gifts seeking him out.

Please, please.

"Yes, he is alive. For now," she revealed and though those last words struck a chord of terror in me, the first ones were enough to heal some of the fractured pieces of my soul. "I cannot say more, for it will shift the hand of fate. Listen closely, darling, you must listen now."

I nodded, my throat clogging up as my father moved nearer to her and the two of them observed me with so much love in their eyes that it hurt to know I had never had a chance to experience it.

"You must harness this darkness that lives in you," Hail said. "You cannot break, and you must never, ever give up. For if you do, all will be lost."

"My magic is gone, how can I fight?" I asked in dismay.

"Gone?" Hail rasped, already shaking his head at the impossibility of it. "But how?"

"Hush," Mom cut in. "Do not answer that, Gwendalina. It is not for us to know. Your fates are fragile."

I nodded and my father carved his fingers through his hair anxiously, looking to Merissa for an answer, seeming as desperate for one as I was.

My mother looked broken for a moment, her hand moving to her heart like it pained her, and as her eyes glazed, her expression made me fear she *saw* something terrible in my future.

"It is the greatest gift to meet you," Hail said quietly. "I see your mother in your features, but I'm there too…" He reached for me, his fingers pressing to the glass of the mirror he could see me through, and I touched my fingers to his, feeling nothing but cold water, but sensing him through the connection of my mother's Sight somehow.

He smiled, light touching his eyes and despite the terror of my reality, my own lips lifted to mirror his, knowing this moment was as fleeting as a flash of lightning. If only I could bottle it and keep it forever.

Merissa blinked out of her vision and stepped a little closer to me, her eyes welling with tears that she didn't let fall.

"You can find a way through this," she said. "There are many dark paths, but I *see* glimmers of hope."

"But there are no guarantees?" I begged, and she shook her head, making my father turn to her in desperation.

"There must be something you can tell her, something more," he pressed, taking her hand, his eyes pleading.

"I cannot say more on this," she said, bowing her head in apology.

"Will I be mortal?" I rasped and Merissa looked to me again, her lower lip trembling as she fought to hold her composure.

"Your future from here is difficult to *see*. I'm sorry, my love, I cannot rule out that you will become mortal," she said with a look of distress, the truth like a knife slashing across my throat.

"*No*," my father boomed. "There must be a way to avoid a fate so grave."

My mother's eyes unfocused again as she searched for more answers and my father left her side, moving towards the mirror so that he was all I could see.

Hail swallowed hard, then raised his chin, the ferocity of a king falling over him. "Gwendalina, I wish I could walk through this glass and be there for you in this moment. But know this, you are a Vega. Your blood is royal and more powerful than anything you can imagine. You can move the sky if you want it enough, but you must banish all doubt from your heart, because it will steal that power from you. Do you understand me?"

I swallowed the razor-sharp lump in my throat as I nodded, my eyes carving along every line of his face as I worked to memorise him like this, as a man who really saw me, who was looking me in the eye and sharing a real moment with me.

"I'm scared," I admitted. "I'm so scared of what I'm becoming."

His jaw tightened and his right hand curled into a fist. "I know what it is like to fear such a thing," he said quietly, like the admission left him raw. "But you are stronger than me, than your mother. You, your sister and your brother are remarkable, you truly have no idea. I swear you can defeat whatever it is that plagues you."

"Dad," I croaked, opening my mouth to tell him everything I knew of how Lionel had twisted my father's mind against himself, how every bad thing he had ever done was not his fault. But my mother snapped out of her vision and swept forward urgently.

"It is time to go, darling. Fate is changing. We love you. There is hope, know this. Do not forget it." She kissed her hand, holding it out towards me as the vision of them began to fade.

Panic set in as I felt their presence leaving me behind in the cold and dark.

"Wait," I gasped.

"Just a moment longer," my father begged, but my mother shook her head sadly and he turned to gaze at me in those final moments between us which were flittering away so rapidly.

"We love you, Roxanya and Gabriel to the depths of our hearts," he said fiercely, the words resounding through the fabric of my being, stitching together some long broken thing.

"Always and forever," my mom confirmed, and tears welled in my eyes.

"I love you too. Please stay," I pleaded, but the vision was already fading.

"Remember to own your actions. When wielding a weapon greater than any should call their own, only the strength of your heart can guide it, only the power of your will can contain it. Know yourself and own every piece of who you are. I am sure you won't ever fail the way I have," my father called to me.

The two of them drank me in for a final second, then the silver light vanished, and I was left with bright spots dancing in my vision. The water became a menacingly dark pool beneath me once again, and I stared into the abyss, willing them back into existence. But they were gone.

I pulled my frozen hands from the water, tipping my head back to the sky, finding the moon had risen high enough to crest the mountain peak to my right.

The quiet pressed in, and I sat back on my heels as I held onto my parents' words, taking comfort in knowing that Tory and Lance still lived. But the loneliness and the weighted silence was enough to leave me feeling like the smallest creature on earth.

My father had told me to rely on the strength of my heart, but the lump of pounding muscle trapped within my chest was a ravaged, broken thing, stained with so much sin that I knew it would never be clean again. The Shadow Beast had seen to that, the curse upon me twisting all the good I'd once claimed as my own and making it as irrelevant as sand clinging to a shore. The tide of shadows would seek it out again soon enough, sweeping those scattered grains into a maelstrom of chaos which I had no hope of defeating. Bit by bit, those pieces would be stolen away and I was afraid of what would remain of me once they were gone. Perhaps nothing at all.

As the night hung heavily around me, the stars seemed to whisper among themselves in the black sky, and as they made their plans and plotted our fates, I was encased in a deep and terrible fear, that the worst was yet to come.

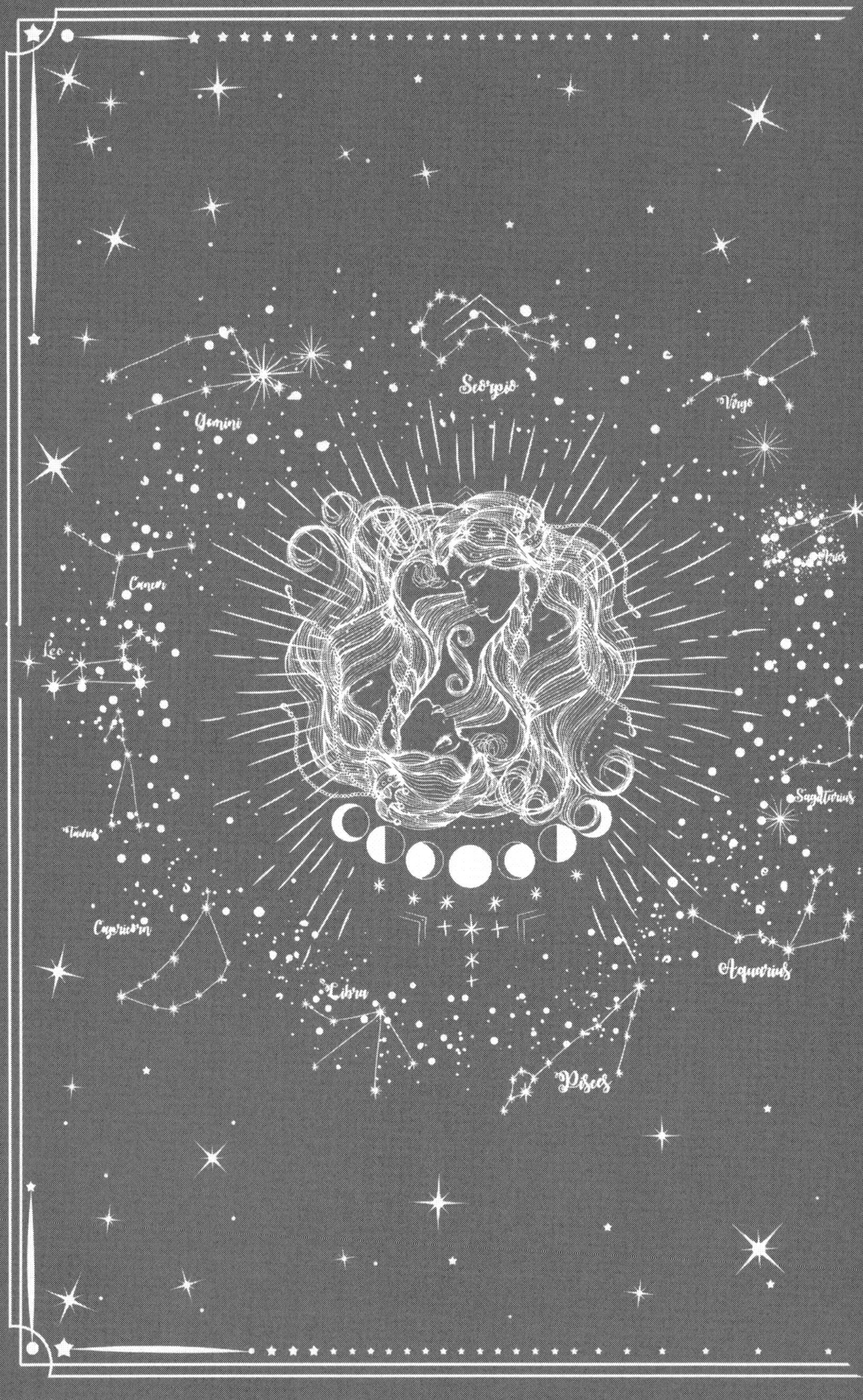
Scorpio
Virgo
Gemini
Cancer
Leo
Sagittarius
Taurus
Capricorn
Aquarius
Libra
Pisces

Tory

CHAPTER TWO

Grief had paralysed me for so long that time had lost meaning. My body had become numb where I remained kneeling in the blood and filth of the battlefield, my forehead pressed to the silent chest of the man I loved.

Darius was still beneath me and the sun steel blade which had punctured his heart lay in the dirt beside us, stained with our blood while my hand steadily dripped more red onto his icy skin.

The sobs had turned to tears and the tears had slipped into silence until there was nothing but him and me, both cold and empty where we lay in the devastation left behind by the battle.

Hours had passed, countless time slipping away while my heart split apart and fractured into a thousand un-linkable pieces. Every soft part of me had hardened into this violent shell of the girl I had been with Darius.

My wings lay over us, casting the two of us within a coffin made of golden feathers, and I had no desire to rise from it without him to stand with me. But even as I lay there, shivering and feeling more hopeless than I had ever felt before, there was one, single thing which kept me here on this cursed earth. One thing which stayed my hand when I thought to take that blade and drive it through my own heart, so that I could make the pain inside it stop and follow my one great love into the beyond.

Darcy was out there somewhere.

My other half. My soul. My twin.

So in the hours that had passed since my tears had dried upon my cheeks, I'd forced myself to think of her. In the time it had taken for me to fall apart, break open and accept the loss of my heart's one greatest desire, I'd kept her in my mind.

She needed me. No matter how damaged and broken the remains of me were.

I cupped Darius's jaw in my hand and found his cold lips for the final time, kissing him softly and exhaling my love for him into the air which surrounded us, as I forced myself to release him.

"Your soul is bound to mine," I breathed against his mouth, even though I knew he was no longer there to hear my words, but a dark and unknown energy seemed to stir the air itself at that vow. "And I won't rest until I make every star in the heavens fall for trying to cleave us apart."

The cut on my hand burned with raw energy at my words, magic stirring within my blood despite the fact I was tapped out. The blast I'd used to destroy the Nymphs had taken everything from me, every last drop of my energy, and I was left without it in a battlefield which had now become nothing more than a graveyard.

I stood, though every muscle in my body protested the movement after so long spent kneeling over the corpse of the man I had bound myself to in every way. He was mine and I was his. That wouldn't change even with the shadow of death hanging between us, keeping us apart. *There is only him.* Endlessly. Always.

I blinked against the darkness that surrounded me, my eyes aching from so many shed tears. My breath left me in a cloud of vapour which rose then dispersed as I took in the devastation of the battlefield and worked to get my bearings.

I picked up my sword, the weight of it heavier than anything I had ever lifted before, failure clinging to the metal as the devastation of our defeat tainted the air surrounding us. It was soaked with the blood of Fae and Nymphs alike, countless enemies slain at my hand, but it wasn't enough. I'd become the warrior Queen Avalon had trained me to be, I'd raced into war with my sister at my side and the power of all that was good and right behind us, but it had been for nothing. All it had gained us was death and destruction, our army decimated beneath the power of evil.

That wasn't how these stories were supposed to go. Shouldn't we have vanquished the monster who plagued this kingdom? Shouldn't all have been set right in the world and some infinite reign of peace and prosperity begun with the dawn?

The cut on my palm burned as my grip tightened on the hilt of my sword, the pain centring me in that moment, reminding me that I was still alive, no matter how wretched and pointless that life might be. I was cold. Perpetually cold in a way I knew would never leave me, the fire which had been my love for Darius Acrux no longer heating my veins.

I looked down at the sword, drowning in how pointless it all seemed now; hating him and loving him, fighting against the crown I'd been born to claim, then fighting for it in turn. None of it had come to anything if this was the fate we'd been dealt.

My jaw tightened at the thought and I refused it, tarot cards shifting through my mind as if I could truly see them while I shuffled the deck, casting out any which didn't fall in our favour, determined to draw only those I wanted. The Chariot flashed through my mind and stuck there as I drew in a long breath. Vengeance, war, triumph. I would accept no other fate than that from now on.

I forced my eyes to open once more, uncertain when I'd even allowed them to close, and I sheathed my sword in the filthy, bloodstained scabbard which still hung from my hip.

Numb.

I felt nothing at all as I took in the charred and blackened ground which was all that remained of the Nymphs who had been taken out by my blast of power, their bodies cast to shadow in death, leaving a battlefield littered with only Fae behind. It was almost as if the Nymphs had never been here, even though the deaths they'd caused proved their presence all too keenly.

I was trembling, my body spent, energy sapped, and all I wanted was to sink back down and lay beside Darius once more, give in to the exhaustion that was swamping me, and just let go of everything. But I knew I couldn't do that. I didn't have the luxury of being able to let my grief consume me.

My sister was out there somewhere. She needed me. I could feel it in my bones. I just didn't know where to begin my search for her. I thought on those terrifying moments from the battle, of her losing control of her fate to the curse Lavinia had forced upon her, and of Orion racing after her as she managed to run from this place. They had to be together now. They had to be alright.

Shivers wracked my body, and I swallowed a lump in my throat as I tried to take stock of where I was, working out my position on the battlefield as I got my bearings without once raising my eyes to the watchful stars.

Let them watch. I wouldn't do them the favour of looking back. I would only turn my eyes to them when their time came, and they would feel the wrath of the creature

I had become when I did so.

I curled my right hand into a fist, the sharp bite of pain from the deep cut on my palm giving me something to focus on besides the agony in my heart, then I set my eyes on the far side of the battlefield where I was sure I had last seen Darcy. Though between the chaos of the fight and the wreckage left in its wake, it was hard to be sure of anything. Echoes of what I'd just survived were pressing in on me from all around, the bloodshed, the screams, the death; but I forced them out again, sinking into that numbness as I focused on the only thing that mattered now. Darcy.

"I'll be back," I murmured to Darius, though I knew he neither heard me nor cared what happened to his body anymore. But I wasn't going to leave him there, laying in the mud for the crows to find, like he was nothing.

I flexed my wings, wanting to fly, but the weight of them seemed more likely to press me into the dirt than lift me from the ground. I banished them instead, a heavy sigh escaping me as my Order form retreated and I was left fully in my Fae form once more.

My boots felt leaden as I walked across the battlefield, trying not to look at the broken, bloody bodies or focus on what I was stepping on as I walked. There was nothing but death to be found here. No point in me trying to hunt for survivors. I could feel that in the weight of the air and the pressure of the silence. Death had come to this place and feasted well.

The words of the prophecy which had appeared to me spun through my head, like a chant that refused to abandon me as it was committed to memory, and I knew in my soul that my brother had sent me those words. They mattered. They were likely the key to everything. Though they made little sense to me.

When all hope is lost, and the darkest night descends,
remember the promises that bind.
When the dove bleeds for love, the shadow will meet the warrior.
A hound will bay for vengeance where the rift drinks deep.
One chance awaits. The king may fall on the day the Hydra bellows in a spiteful palace.

I hunted for meaning in those words, but they made no sense to my aching mind and I banished the memory of them, giving up for now and concentrating on the only thing I needed in this stars-forsaken world.

On and on I walked across the battlefield, my heart heavy and my thoughts focused on my sister. She needed me. This pain, this heartache, this grief, I could bear it for her. And as my mind shifted from the need to find my other half to what else I had to do with the breaths I still drew, I knew for certain that I'd been left in this darkest of places for one reason only. Lionel Acrux would die by my hand. Whatever cost it took.

My head lifted suddenly, almost of its own accord as I looked between dismembered bodies, rebels' faces left in eternal screams of agony as they died for a cause which they would never now learn the fate of.

I blinked at the horror surrounding me, unable to feel anything other than rage and a desperate desire to burn the entire world for all it had taken from us this night.

Something caught my eye in the mud as I made to turn away and I stilled before stepping closer to it, my breath catching in my throat as I spotted the necklace my sister had worn day and night for months now.

The Imperial Star seemed so innocent as it lay there, speckled with blood and muck, filled with limitless power which was utterly unattainable while that monster sat upon my father's throne. It was still hidden within the intricate silver amulet, hanging from the chain that had once belonged to Darius, a piece from his closely guarded trove.

I picked it up, my fingers trembling with a mixture of fatigue, cold, and fear for my twin as I raised my eyes to the horizon where dawn was just beginning to colour the sky with the slightest hint of blue. This weapon which promised so much power, so much help, had done nothing at all to aid us when we needed it most.

I had half a mind to hurl the thing away, cast it into the ruin of battle and let it lay forgotten and abandoned here just like it had abandoned us. What good was a weapon which only bowed to the will of a reigning monarch? What was the point of the damn thing if it wouldn't relinquish its power to fight against a tyrant?

I gripped the amulet which disguised the star in my fist, the blood from my star-sworn wound marking it as I gritted my teeth against the overwhelming urge to throw it the fuck away and cast it into damnation.

"Fuck you," I hissed at the thing, the power trapped within it throbbing in time with the painful pounding of my own pulse in that unhealing wound.

The air shifted around me as I gripped it so tightly that the pain was near blinding, welcoming the agony as punishment for my survival amid so much loss. A whisper stirred the silence, words spoken in some language I didn't know tracing a shiver down my spine while the power of the Imperial Star thrummed in time with them.

I drew in a shaky breath, calling on that hidden power within it, summoning it to me, beckoning it to rise and fall to my command. The power surged inside the amulet, heating my skin, and for a moment, I thought it was going to yield to me, to submit to my power. But just as I began to believe that fate might finally be turning in our favour, the energy in the Star ebbed and faded again, like a wave crashing against a cliff, unable to rise to the top.

I wanted to scream at that refusal, at the knowledge of the power I held and yet couldn't summon. Yet another twisted joke of the fucking stars at my expense. My muscles tensed as the urge to hurl it away from me became near overwhelming and I cursed the lump of rock for its obnoxious refusal, wondering if it would be better to destroy it than keep the fucking thing, better to rid the world of its potential. But I had no idea how to do that and certainly had no way of attempting it in this barren wasteland.

With a will of effort, I clasped the Imperial Star around my own neck and took up the burden of guarding it myself. It was the least I could do for my other half.

"Where are you?" I breathed to the still air surrounding me, my soul aching with the need to find my twin.

Fear took my heart captive as I hunted the dead space all around me for some sign of my sister, but there was nothing at all left here aside from me. And I wasn't certain I even counted anymore.

A gleam of bright metal drew my eyes between the corpse of a broken red Dragon and a rebel whose face was still set in a battle snarl, his hand gripping his sword despite the gaping wound in his chest and the lack of soul remaining in his body.

I took a step towards it and reached for the sword, my fingers closing around the hilt of the cold and lifeless blade as I recognised the weapon my sister had created for the man she loved.

I tugged the blade free of the dirt, my eyes moving over every speck of blood and gore which marked it, before I turned to search the faces of all the dead who lay on this bloody battlefield.

I wasn't certain there was any space left within me for more grief, and I released a heavy breath as I failed to spot Orion among the dead. It meant nothing. I knew that. In all of this carnage, my failure to spot a body gave no guarantees of that person's survival and my throat thickened at the thought of everyone I might have lost tonight.

My skin prickled like tiny fingers were poking and prodding at me, the eyes of the stars a weight upon my soul and the call of fate thickening the air.

I turned my back on the sensation, my lip curling at the thought of dancing to that tune. I was done being a pawn that the stars could tug and pull whichever way they pleased. The call of fate meant nothing to me if this was the life they'd chosen for me. I refused it as harshly as I refused them, and they were soon going to learn how hot my fire could burn in vengeance.

Blood ran between my fingers and dripped against the already bloodstained dirt beneath my boots as I fought against the bone-deep exhaustion in my flesh and forced myself to walk on. The oath I'd made to the stars with the sun steel blade was buzzing inside my veins, the deep cut still bleeding just as the pain inside me only seemed to grow sharper by the second.

I didn't want to look at the devastation I passed through, but I made myself do it, made myself look into the face of every fallen rebel, made myself remember each and every one of them. They had come here because they believed in this fight. They had given their lives because they had wanted to deny this destiny too. I wouldn't spit on their sacrifice by turning my eyes from it. Each face I looked upon, every chest ruptured by the probes of our enemies registered and stuck within my memory. This place was little more than a graveyard now, and I was nothing but a spirit tethered to it while hunting out the release of my own death.

I wasn't sure how far I walked nor how many faces I looked upon before my boots scuffed against hard stone instead of bloody soil.

I paused, my attention falling on a scrap of red fabric as it fluttered in a breeze I hadn't even noticed, a piece of it lifting and tumbling over the toe of my boot.

My throat thickened as I recognised the expensive lace of the dress I'd worn to marry the man who now lay dead out on that battlefield. The man who I had stolen back from the stars only to have them spit in my face as they tore him away again so much more permanently than before. Married and widowed in the same day.

The agony within my soul threatened to pull me from my feet and make me crumple where I was. I could lay there. Drop down on that dirt and let the crows have me. I could follow him away from this agony and into the beyond. It was such a sweet and simple answer, such a quiet relief to think of it.

My grip tightened on the sword I'd claimed from the depths of the battlefield as I considered it, climbing back up to that hill where I'd left the body of the man I burned for and taking that step to follow him. It would be so easy. And didn't I deserve easy after all I'd suffered through in this world?

The whispering of the stars built around me again as they looked on, their watchful, hateful eyes urging me this way and that, like my fate was nothing more than a game to them.

But despite every reason I had to yearn for the soft embrace of that final release, I made no move to lift the sword in my grip any higher than it was. I wouldn't give the stars or Lionel Acrux such an easy answer to the end of this fight.

I walked on, uncertain what I was even searching for anymore, knowing that there was nothing left here besides death. The Nymphs had seen to that surely enough. They had spilled across the battlefield searching out any Fae who might have stood some chance of recovery, ending them with a probe to the heart long before any aid could find them.

I stumbled to a halt as I spotted a wide ring of rock ahead of me, two bodies lying before the yawning mouth of the cave which marked the entrance to The Burrows beyond.

My heart stilled as I recognised them, their faces pale in death and still linked hands telling me they had been together until the end.

I dropped to my knees beside the body of the woman who had become so important to me. She had been the closest thing to a parent I had ever really known, and I hadn't ever told her that. I hadn't told her how much I'd needed the kind of love she offered me so simply, or how much she had come to mean to me in the time we'd spent together. She had become something to me which I'd only ever dared to dream of in the most secret corners of my heart.

Catalina Acrux had been my family and now she lay dead alongside the man she'd finally found love with upon a battlefield of slain Fae who I should have been able to lead to victory.

"I'm sorry," I choked out. For her, for Hamish, for Darius and for every Fae who had placed their faith in the hope of something better, only to die here beneath the wrath of the monster who had stolen our throne from us. "I'm so...fuck..."

I had no tears left to offer, my heart already shattered beyond repair as I took in this loss, and my grief welled endlessly. They'd deserved so much more than this, than me.

I stared at them for so long that it took me several minutes to feel the pulse within my flesh as my magic reserves were fuelled, but only with the barest hint of a spark.

I sucked in a breath as I raised my head, finding a tiny fire burning along the edge of what I assumed had once been a part of the tunnels. The wooden beam was blackened and the fire almost burned out, but the embers remained on that final edge, an offering to a girl who hungered for nothing more than death now.

I reached out on instinct, the tiny kindling of my magic taking root within me and latching on to that flame, stoking it without thought, making it flicker and burn then blaze.

The fire grew and grew as I threw some small measure of my power into it, the heat forcing me to notice the gnawing cold setting into my limbs even as the strength of the flames began to recharge my magic faster and faster.

There was nothing for me in this place. But Hamish and Catalina had made a stand here. They'd died to stop someone from passing them at this point, and I knew in my soul that person had been Lionel. They had held him off so that he couldn't get into The Burrows, and I knew the plan had been to cave those tunnels in. Which meant that there were likely still rebels out there, perhaps even some of the people I loved.

And that gave me a goal.

I pushed to my feet, my magic reaching out to Catalina and Hamish, vines crawling across them, binding them softly and cushioning their bodies with care while ice spread up and around them, encasing them as they were, preserving them in this final moment of sacrifice where they had given everything to save all they could.

I wouldn't leave the people who had led this rebellion out here in this wasteland. I wouldn't leave them after they had given their lives for those courageous Fae and their belief in two untested queens. Let alone leaving the mother of the man I loved or the father of my truest friend.

I pushed more magic into the fire as I worked, building and building it while it stoked the furnace in my soul, recharging my power with every ember and feeding me the one thing I needed to make this world burn in payment for what had been taken from me.

Death. That was all that was left to me now. I was cast adrift in my grief and swallowed whole by my rage. There had never been a creature born of such fury as me, let alone one so powerful and vengeful. The stars would regret gifting me with this power by the time I was done. They wouldn't whisper my name any longer; they would scream it while I ripped them apart for all they had done to poison what little good I had ever claimed for my own.

I turned my gaze back across the battlefield towards the ravaged hill where Darius's body lay, that burn rolling down my throat and into my blood, finding its way to each and every piece of me and taking root.

I wouldn't leave him here either, no more than I would say goodbye. Because this wasn't goodbye. I would never utter that word to the keeper of my heart, and I would never relinquish the promise I'd made to him with the blood cut from my veins mixed with his own, which I'd taken from the wound that had stolen him from me.

I had never wanted to be a queen. But now a crown of flames would ignite like a funeral pyre upon my brow, and my one and only decree would be to seek out the end to all who had crossed me, and make them scream as they were forced to bow at my feet.

Scorpio
Gemini
Virgo
Cancer
Leo
Sagittarius
Taurus
Capricorn
Aquarius
Libra
Pisces

ORION

CHAPTER THREE

Lavinia dragged me through the vast halls of The Palace of Souls, the shadow collar around my neck tethered to her by a leash of darkness. It was glacial and unforgiving against my skin, like the noose of a hangman.

My teeth ground together, and my heart thumped to a painful beat as I started to process everything that had happened tonight. The loss of Darius was suffocating me, the memory of him laying so still on the ground tearing a rift through my chest. He was my best friend, and I loved him more deeply than he had ever really known. We were brothers, raised together and meant to live life side by side. Even when he'd told me about the deal he'd made with the stars for a year of life, I'd been determined to believe there was a way for him to avoid death. But it had come for him even sooner than he'd planned, and now I was left without him, and it was like I'd had a piece of my lifeforce stolen away forever. They'd given him a year, but that didn't grant him immortality for that time and he'd known it. Now even that short span of time had been cut off early, leaving him with so much less than he deserved from fate.

Beyond that, my fear over Blue left me with an anchor weighing down my heart. She was alone out there, and though I knew she would be fighting the grip of the beast with every scrap of power she possessed, I couldn't be sure it was enough. Not when the curse ran so deep and was nourished by all the strength of Lavinia's shadows.

All of that tangled with my fear for everyone else I'd lost sight of during the battle, and I was breaking with every step I took, wondering if I'd just made the gravest mistake of my life by offering myself up to the Shadow Princess.

Darcy would be destroyed by my decision, and I'd abandoned everyone who remained to pick up the pieces of Lionel's destruction. Had Tory survived? And what about Gabriel and his family?

I was sick with the anxiety of it all, but as I followed the Shadow Princess deeper into the palace that had once belonged to the Savage King, numbness began to set in. The kind of emptiness that came after intense trauma. I remembered falling into this very same pit of despair after I lost Clara the first time. It was a void that sucked away all hope in the world and chipped away at the last glimmers of light in my soul, devouring them one by one until all that remained was a desolate space where nothing could grow.

As my thoughts found Blue again, I held onto the single thing that remained to me; paying this debt to Lavinia to break my mate's curse.

I had to make it through this for her. My final light. The girl who was worth a thousand years in hell. I'd wait that long and more if I could be sure I would one day return to her, and that she would be safe, protected from all the darkness of the world. She may have been capable of fighting in battles and destroying those who opposed her, but she deserved a life of peace and endless smiles. Our happiness was a flower that had bloomed and withered before I'd barely had a moment to breathe in its sweet scent. I had to find a way to buy her an eternal summer where it could bloom once again.

"You're very quiet back there, little hunter," Lavinia called. "Are you trying to mourn your friends in peace? Because I assure you there will be no peace between these walls."

"I have nothing to say to you," I growled, and she twisted her head to look back at me, the angle of her neck unnatural. Her eyes were two sunken pits of black, and dark veins rippled and shifted beneath her skin as the shadows writhed within her. My neck prickled just looking at her, my hatred for her a venomous creature that spat poison in my chest.

"I knew the taste of love once, a very long time ago. Love exposes you; it makes you a fool," she hissed.

"Then I am a fool," I said hollowly.

"*My* fool," she said, a smile gripping her mouth before she turned away again and led me on.

There was a din of noise in the palace which I couldn't ignore, my Vampire hearing not allowing me to turn my attention from it. The closer we got, the worse it became and dread filled me as I recognised it for what it was. Rebels had been captured and were being tortured somewhere deep within this place, their screams colouring the inside of my skull red.

It was hard to believe this was the same palace I'd visited when Darcy and Tory had stayed here, a sanctuary where I'd known joy for a time, though those days seemed so fleeting now. I wished I'd held onto them tighter, but more than that, I wished I'd taken all those I loved and run somewhere far beyond Solaria to a haven where Lionel could never touch us. The other kingdoms were not all welcoming though. To the south, Voldrakia was a savage kingdom, and across the ocean to the east, The Waning Land was a war-torn world where Elementals were divided, and dictators controlled their people. No, on reflection, I never really would have run; Solaria was my home, and I would fight for it until there was nothing left to fight for.

As I drew nearer to the sounds of screams, a voice caught my ear which set my heart thrashing.

"I'll never give you what you want," Gabriel spat. "No pain in this world will force me to reveal a single vision of mine."

"We shall see," Lionel answered, and I acted on instinct, shooting forward with the speed of my Order.

"Gabriel!" I bellowed in terror for him as Lavinia yanked me back with the shadows so ferociously that I was thrown to the floor.

My throat burned as the shadows choked me, squeezing tight so blood pounded in my ears before finally loosening enough for me to breathe again.

"The Seer?" She gasped excitedly, clapping her hands before dragging me to my feet and towing me along after her. "Daddy has done well."

By the stars, no. *How could this night get any worse?*

Panic warred through me as she led me up a flight of stairs and I found Gabriel there on his knees before Lionel as he choked the air out of his lungs.

"Stop!" I shouted as Lavinia held me close with the shadows, preventing me from going to my Nebula Ally. It physically pained me that I was helpless to this, and it felt like the final blow of an already devastating defeat.

Lionel looked over at me with intrigue, his eyebrows arching as he took in his queen's captive. Two glittering, lilac Pegasus wings with a rainbow sheen were lying on the floor behind him and my stomach knotted in horror as I recognised them as Xavier's.

My hands shook as I wondered who was even left alive after the battle, and violence made my muscles tighten with the need for vengeance.

"Lance Orion." Lionel smiled cruelly, stalking closer and I bared my teeth at him, my fangs extending in a threat of death I wished I could deliver. "Well done, Lavinia. Hand him to me. I shall have Vard extract his memories then execute him myself."

I could barely feel the strike of those words, death seeming so small a threat when aimed at me. It was the people I loved who mattered. Like Gabriel who continued to thrash on the floor, clawing at his throat as he fought to get in a breath of air, but Lionel held it all within his control.

"Release him," I commanded, my words measured and rippling with power, but Lionel took no interest in me.

"Come, Lavinia. Hand him to me." Lionel waved a hand impatiently. He was still flecked with blood, painted in the deaths he'd delivered tonight, and it was clear his appetite wasn't close to sated.

"No," Lavinia said simply just as Lionel's hand fell on my arm, gripping tight, the monster in his eyes growing hungry for more blood.

Lionel frowned, turning to the wraith at my side in confusion. "No?" he questioned like he had never heard the word in his life.

"This one is mine. He made a deal with me." She yanked on my collar with the gifts of her dark power, and I was pulled from Lionel's grip into hers. A chew toy for two rabid dogs to snarl over.

Lavinia tiptoed up to run her tongue along my cheek and I winced from the icy touch of it, though I didn't resist it either. I couldn't now that I was bound to her. It was the price of the deal I'd made. My body was hers, and I was only just starting to truly appreciate how horrifying that reality was.

The words of the Death bond rang inside my head like the toll of fate itself. *"Your body will be willingly mine for three moon cycles, and when that time is up, I shall release Darcy Vega from her curse."*

Keyword, fucking 'willingly'.

I looked to my Nebula Ally as his face turned blue and my pulse pounded more furiously.

"Let him go," I snarled but again Lionel acted as if I hadn't spoken, his gaze set on Lavinia.

"What deal? That was not part of the plan," he hissed.

"I tied the Vega's curse to her one true love," Lavinia said, amusement lacing her tone. "Now he's agreed to pay the price with three months of torture. Isn't it perfect, Daddy?"

"Why would you agree to such a thing when you could kill him instead?" Lionel demanded in a thunderous voice, his lack of control over the situation clearly irking him. His eyes flashed green, his irises transforming into two reptilian slits as heat radiated from him.

"Because the torment of the Vega girl's Elysian Mate is a far greater punishment than any other I could offer her. He has agreed that he is mine, body and soul." She smiled that wild, unhinged smile of hers and there was no humanity in it at all.

"Lionel," I snapped, jerking forward to try and go to Gabriel who was twitching as he started to pass out.

Lionel's eyes whipped onto me, and he struck me in the gut with a punch of air magic that sent me doubling over and wheezing for breath. "Do not address me so informally. I am your king. The ruler of Solaria and you are nothing but dirt muddying my palace floors."

"It was you, wasn't it?" I gritted out, emotion filling my words as my heart ripped open and bled. "You killed Darius."

The pain of his loss came crashing in on me like stormy waves hitting the shore, and I didn't know how I would ever recover from it. He was my pillar of certainty when the rest of the world was crumbling, the man who had stood by me after I'd lost everything. He had been one of the few things in this world worth waking up for after I lost Clara, and it had nothing to do with Lionel's Guardian bond, it was because Darius was a brother chosen for me by fate. He was one of the only good things in this forsaken world the stars had offered me, and now they'd taken him away without even offering me a chance to say goodbye.

Lionel's lips slid into a mocking slant. "Yes. My worthless, traitor son is dead. And now we know who the greatest Dragon who ever lived is. Though there was hardly any doubt bef-"

I was on him in the next heartbeat, my fists slamming into his ribs and my fangs tearing into the skin of his shoulder as I sought out the magic I needed to kill him, but before I could taste a drop of blood, Lavinia yanked my leash tight, forcing me back behind her where I crashed to the floor on my knees.

"Down, boy," she scalded teasingly as the empty well in my chest was left pining for magic and my need for that bastard's demise went abhorrently unanswered.

Lionel staggered back a step, lifting a hand to heal the torn flesh of his shoulder and running a palm over his ribs where a satisfying crunch had marked a break I felt only mildly appeased by. The moment he was healed, he lunged for me, but Lavinia stepped into his way with a wild laugh, and the Dragon King bore down on her with a snarl lighting his features in a blood red death.

"Move. Aside. The boy is overdue his end at my hand. He has defied me one too many times, and I will make him suffer before I cast him to ash," he spat. "He is as useless as his father was."

"My father was not useless," I hissed, getting to my feet, and Lionel scoffed.

"The man destroyed himself with dark magic. He had little purpose in this life, and what he had to offer, I took willingly whenever I wanted. Just like I took your mother whenever I wanted her."

I didn't care what he said about Stella, but my father was another matter. "He was ten times the Fae you are," I hurled at him, holding the truth back about his death, and the steppingstones he'd laid for the Zodiac Guild. I wasn't going to give Lionel any reason to sift through my memories and hunt out that knowledge. I couldn't be sure Lavinia would protect me from that if her king insisted on it.

"There is no Fae greater than I. I am the greatest Dragon who ever lived," he said in a voice that quavered with the determination behind those words.

"I will grant my pet all the suffering he is owed, my King," Lavinia said in a sultry voice, stepping forward to caress his arm. "Let me handle it. I will make him scream and scream for you."

A tense beat of silence passed, and smoke plumed from Lionel's nostrils, but he finally backed down, clearly liking the idea of what Lavinia was offering.

"Very well," he muttered, turning away from us, and hatred spewed through me.

"Darius Vega is the greatest Dragon who ever lived," I spoke loud and clear, making Lionel fall deathly still.

"What did you just call him?" he asked venomously, danger thick in the air.

"He married Tory. She is more powerful than him, so that made him a Vega," I said, relishing this final blow I could land to him, feeling Darius's defiance humming through the air and knowing Lionel could feel it too.

His shoulders tightened and he looked back at Lavinia with fury making his lower lip quiver. "Do as you will to him, Lavinia. Peel the flesh from his bones and carve his heart from his chest, but ensure that I am there to watch when it is time for him to die."

"Of course, my King," Lavinia said, looking to me and pressing a finger to her lips that spoke of a secret I hadn't realised we were sharing. It seemed that Lionel wouldn't be finding out about the details of our deal, and that my death was not on the cards once it played out.

Relief rushed through me as Lionel finally released Gabriel from his magic and my friend gasped down a lungful of oxygen from his position on the floor. Lionel dragged him to his feet by his hair and threw him into the hands of two Dragon cronies waiting obediently down the hall, their bulky frames wrapped in the navy robes of his pathetic Dragon Guild. "Take him to the Royal Seer's chamber."

They dragged my friend away and Gabriel looked back at me, our eyes locking and fear tangling with my blood as I saw a thousand terrible fates shining in his irises. He shook his head as if in apology, and I wished I could convince him he had nothing to be sorry for.

"There's hope yet, Orio," he called. "Have faith in the flames!"

One of the Dragons punched him to silence him, then he was dragged around a corner, and I didn't know if I would ever see him again. I didn't know if he'd spoken those words just to comfort me, or if there was really truth in them. The flames? Did he mean the twins?

I wanted to believe he could *see* a way out of this, but after everything, it was hard to take any solace in a word like hope.

"My King," a man appeared running along the hall, bowing low. He had bright red hair and large teeth, his eyes downcast as he approached Lionel. "Can I assist you at all? Are you well after battle? How can I be of service?"

"Stop blabbering and pick up my disgusting second son's wings, Horace." Lionel pointed to the severed Pegasus wings on the floor and Horace's eyes widened before he hauled them into his arms.

"Praise the king and all his might," he stammered as he struggled to keep his hold on their awkward weight.

"Hang them in the dining hall," Lionel commanded, smiling smugly to himself, and walking off down the corridor. "I want them displayed as a trophy. A reminder to all of what I do to rebels and lesser Fae scum alike."

"As you wish, sire," Horace said before hurrying away with them, a trail of blood which sparkled with glitter marking the tiles as he dragged the wings along in his king's wake.

I was left shaking, thinking of Gabriel, and not knowing what to do. Because there was nothing I *could* do, no path in front of me but the one I'd bound myself to now. I was helpless to a callous destiny, and I could hardly breathe for how stifling the world suddenly was. There was too much loss, too many people I loved torn away from me, and now I was alone with nothing but blood and suffering awaiting me.

Remember Blue. Stay strong for her.

Lavinia drew me back down the corridor, humming an eerie tune to herself as her shadowy hair danced around her shoulders.

My ears were already adjusting to the distant din of screams deep in the palace and I felt the hopelessness of this place closing in on me on all sides. The Palace of Souls was living up to its name tonight, for there were countless souls trapped here, and I had no idea how many would be released to the stars by dawn. I thought of Gabriel's family, of Catalina, Hamish, Geraldine…and then my mind turned to the Heirs and how they had never shown up at the battle. Were they safe? Would they return to The Burrows and find themselves drowning in the grief of all those who'd been killed?

The Shadow Princess led me down the beautiful corridors of the palace until we entered the huge throne room with its vaulted ceiling and unwelcoming ambience. The blue stained-glass windows sat high up above, letting in an icy light in vertical shafts.

The Hydra throne took centre stage at the heart of it, the tall back of the seat splitting into a monstrous bouquet of Hydra heads, their scaly necks twisting together like serpents. It was a towering reminder of the king who had once been housed within these walls. And as I thought of all the bad feeling I'd once held towards him, regret weighed heavily on my soul. Lionel had been the shadow hanging over the Vegas all this time, a snake lurking in plain sight who had injected its poison in secret, one drip at a time until the whole kingdom had been polluted. If only someone had discovered his treason and stopped him sooner.

Lavinia guided me past a cage of black night iron that stood against one wall, leading me along a corridor and into a chamber through a heavy metal door. It swung shut behind me, and I took in the room full of torture devices set in a circle around a raised stone platform where two metal manacles hung on chains attached to the ceiling.

"Do you like it, pet? Lionel gifted me this space and I feel I've done beautiful work," Lavinia crooned like she was showing me a playhouse.

Dread slithered down my spine as I sensed a familiar, cloying energy from each of the torture devices, from blades to whips and saws, all held the oppressive aura of the shadows about them.

Lavinia placed a hand against my back, encouraging me towards the platform where my fate awaited. "Kneel up there for me, pet. Hands in the air."

I swallowed the lump in my throat, raising my chin and walking willingly forward, though my legs weighed me down like they were made of lead. As I stepped onto the platform and knelt, I thought of Blue and held her there in my mind before raising my hands above my head. She was the greatest gift I'd ever received, but all gifts had a price. I should have known my debt to the stars wasn't yet paid. But if anyone deserved this sacrifice from me, it was Blue. She loved me with the fury of a night storm, and I was going to honour that love down to every last raindrop.

Lavinia slinked up behind me, pulling my shirt off and tossing it aside. My fangs were still out, my need for blood already making my mind sink into the more animal part of my nature. Though I had no idea when I'd be getting my next feed or if she would allow me to feed at all. It was probably the least of my concerns, but without magic, I would be driven to insanity. I not only had to recharge it, I had to use it or else succumb to madness. Was that to be my destiny too?

Lavinia locked the manacles over my wrists and yanked the chain taut in a winch that forced me to stand again. I felt the power of the metal around my wrists shutting me off from using magic even if I'd had any to cast.

Lavinia trailed a sharp fingernail down the length of my spine before circling around the platform, examining me. "Pretty, pretty."

I turned my mind to the girl who was worth a thousand bloody deaths. Three moon cycles, that was all, and the clock was already ticking down. I'd return to her soon, and she would be free of the curse when I did so. That was enough to dip my will in molten iron and harden it into an unbreakable thing.

I stared at my possessor, anxious to start so that I could move closer to the end. "Do your worst."

"Such big words from a lonely man on the losing side of my king's war," she purred, moving to pick up a blade that glinted with dark magic. "But I will not do my worst, Lance Orion. No, I will do my absolute best."

She threw the blade at me, and it drove deep into my side, making me cry out in agony. I felt the kiss of some wicked power, but it didn't call to me like it had when I was cut with a draining dagger. This time, the souls trapped within the shadows were screaming, and it seemed as though they were being tortured too, all of their pain amplifying mine tenfold.

Lavinia rushed toward me in a blur of shadow, yanking the blade out and making blood rush hot and fast down my side. Before I could recover, she'd stabbed me again, then again, choosing her targets carefully so death didn't come for me.

I gritted my teeth through the torture for all the good it did me, my mind spiralling deep down into the shadows with every strike she made, and each visit there was worse than the reality I was facing. For all I could hear were screams, and all I could feel were knives carving me up from the inside out.

Through all the darkness and the pain, I started losing my grip on Blue, like she was being wrenched away from me with every burning cut of Lavinia's knife. The shadows were taking me, laying a claim that spoke of Lavinia's deal, owning me completely and marking me as hers.

For the first time since I'd offered myself to Darcy Vega under the stars, I feared that I really could be taken from her, that I could be twisted and carved up, altered irreversibly by this torment. Because it wasn't just my flesh it damaged, the dark power imbued in Lavinia's weapon was severing the chords that tied me to my soul. The part of me that made me who I was.

If that was destroyed, then would my mate even want me anymore? If I became a shell of a man with nothing to offer the girl who deserved the universe, what would happen to us? Would I even be a match for her in the eyes of the stars?

I pushed those fears aside, knowing there was only one reason I was here, and that whatever was lost in the process was out of my control now. Through this suffering I might be destroyed, but she would be saved. So I would be a willing sacrifice on the altar of our love.

Scorpio
Gemini
Virgo
Aries
Cancer
Leo
Sagittarius
Taurus
Capricorn
Aquarius
Libra
Pisces

JUSTIN

CHAPTER FOUR

My eyes stung like a swarm of bees had taken up residence beneath my eyelids, and they would only be quieted by me closing them.

Oh, what a fate that had befallen me. I was a dust mote cast awry on a breeze, and as I battled my way through the second day of my aerial escape, I had to wonder if the stars had forgotten about me altogether.

The parachute my queen had constructed for me from great leaves cast from her earth magic still held true, despite a few holes which had been punched into it by the wild magic of the creatures who chased me.

The Nymphs crowded below me, a swarm of them like a moving forest of rot far beneath my feet, their gnarled features twisted with bloodlust as they chased me over rough and barren terrain. Waiting.

They were waiting for exhaustion to claim me and drag me down to their clutches as they kept up this hunt. There must have been fifty of them down there, a host large enough to easily take out a small town. And though I feared for my own mortality, any time I had spied lights or signs of civilisation on the horizon, I had tugged on the vines which supported me and turned away from such salvation. I wouldn't lead this hoard of monsters towards innocent Fae, no matter the cost that incurred for myself.

I was living on borrowed time, uncertain what hope I could even muster with the small amount of magic lingering in my veins thanks to the trusty nummy pouch I had strapped to my chest.

My momsy had always made sure I carried it with me at all times, the little leather pouch containing the leaves of aconite my Cerberus form required to replenish my power. I slipped a leaf from the pouch as I thought on her soft face and stern words. *"Never leave the nest without a nummy pouch."*

That ethos had served me well through the haunting hours of my escape, keeping my power replenished just enough to allow me to craft a flame above my head, the heat of which kept my parachute aloft and my heart still beating. The only other magic I dared waste these final dregs of my power on was the odd wakefulness spell, though I hadn't cast one in over six hours now.

The exhaustion from the battle was pressing in on me like a weighted blanket, urging my tired bones to rest despite the peril I found myself trapped in. The memory of Roxanya Vega shooting me into the sky, like a star bound for the heavens, played over and over within my mind. My queen had valued my life enough to save it when certain death had loomed all around us, valued my sorry soul highly enough to craft this method of escape for me while she fought gallantly on. What fate had befallen her now? What destiny had I been forced to abandon my sovereign to?

Shame tugged at my gut even as the undeniable honour of fighting at her side in that battle gave me the strength to carry on, to lead these heathens far from hapless, innocent Fae with the last of my strength.

I had succumbed to sleep once and jerked awake just in time to stop my descent onto the probes of the vicious creatures below me. Adrenaline and fear unlike any I had ever experienced had jerked me back to consciousness as their screeches lit the air. A blast of fire magic had torn from me just before their deathly rattles could block my ability to cast at all – the heat sending my parachute skyward once more while the exertion of power ate away at my measly reserves.

The Nymphs hungered for my end just as I hungered for the power I would need to strike at them, to go down fighting for the good of Solaria like I had sworn I would do if my fate called me to. But I had lost that strength along with my weapons when my lady sent me skyward to save this unfortunate A.S.S. man.

And so I waited. The small flame flickering and burning on above me, keeping me aloft while I scanned the horizon for the only hope I could still cling to. Clouds. I just needed to find some cloud cover and perhaps I could give the Nymphs the slip. Perhaps I could get free of their relentless pursuit. Perhaps I could evade them, refill my magic and live on to re-join the army of my ladies and fight another day.

I didn't allow my thoughts to linger on my nummy pouch. Only three aconite leaves left now. I was running out of time. And all around me, nothing but blue sky stretched in every direction as if the stars themselves had abandoned me too.

A day so full of grief and loss had no right to shine so brightly, and yet here it was, filling the world with light when all that should have remained in the wake of that battle was darkness.

Onwards I would flounder, to the edge of the world and beyond, and perhaps if I was lucky a cloud may yet appear, but as that blue abyss stretched ever yonder before me, I gave in to the reality I had been dealt. Master Masters would die this day, at the gnarled fingers of my enemies I would meet my end. Yet I held on to the sweet scent upon the air and the chance my queen had given me with this method of escape. One nummy leaf at a time, I would munch my way towards my destiny and face it head on when the time came.

Scorpio
Gemini
Virgo
Cancer
Leo
Sagittarius
Taurus
Capricorn
Aquarius
Libra
Pisces

GERALDINE

CHAPTER FIVE

Pain that cut so fiercely, I felt the salt of it seeping into the wounds that lay within the fabric of my darn soul.

Grief so poisonous, that my body was likely to give out from the toxic depths of it which burned me to my very core.

Agony so wild, it seared the scales from my behind and flayed me upon a writhing eel of doom.

And rage so furious that I felt the horns of hell jabbing into my bosom out of the dark.

The bells of war tolled in my veins with every pump of my furious heart, and the scorch of wildfire raged through my nether regions like an inferno burning tirelessly on, never to be sated by anything but death. Death to the Dragoon who had stolen so much from us in this true and gallant war. Death to the soulless shadow wench who had spilled into our world like a plague of decay from whence she should have stayed. Death to the army of cretinous, bark-skinned lombardos who stomped across valley and glen, fighting the bad fight. And death to the heinous hag who had stolen my dear Angelica into the nevermore.

I would rain my vengeance down upon them all in the name of everything that had been taken from me, and what I might still lose.

Let my life be the price if that was what it took to reset the balance. The scales had been unduly tipped, the heavens in disarray. This was not what the Monks of Mallakin had spoken of in their sacred scrolls. Nay, they had hailed the stars as just and fair, claiming they kept an equilibrium of good and evil, of right and wrong.

But where was the justice in this? Where was the hand of fate and honour? Why had the heavens abandoned us when all we sought was a world where true and gallant Fae could live in harmony, ruled over by the bounteous and most elegant reign of my true queens?

A cry burst from my cracked and bleeding lips as some rapscallion once again fought to heal me, and I batted my arms like flailing wollyhoppers in an attempt to get them gone.

"Wolfsbane!" I gasped, my throat a roar and bloodied thing that cast my normally lyrical voice across a field of glass on its way between my parted jaw.

A pause, a lull in their ministrations while yet more agony tumbled through my body, biting into me with the sickly promise of my demise from the poison of the beast which had tried to tear me asunder.

My lady. My sweet and genteel lady, now nothing but a tufty haired beast of shadow, blinded by the darkest of powers and turned against her own truest friend by a cruel and horrorsome twist of destiny. Where was she now? My Darcy gal? Galloping through brush and brindle on a mission of isolation to save her soul?

Run fast with the wind beneath your clawsome paws, my hungry beast lady. Find your nirvana and the end to this most woe-filled curse.

A true and eternal agony sliced deep within me, my back arching against the hard surface I lay upon, my eyes scrunched shut from the world, keeping it out while I refused to face it. I may have been in untold pain, but I knew the weight of grief awaiting me beyond this poisonous torture would be far worse than any physical boon to bear. I thought of my angelic Angelica and that nasty narghoul Mildred who had slain her in her prime. Oh, what a cruel, undeserving fate. I would smite that blaggard of a Dragoon the moment I had my chance.

A hand grasped my jaw and I thrashed like a hairy beluga stranded on the shore, the sun scorching my blubbery behind and pebbles digging into my rumpus while I flipped and flopped.

But the hand did not release me, the grip tight and unrelenting until I was forced to part my lips and the sweet, wholly lethal taste of the plant I needed for my entire magical existence swept over my tongue.

I munched down on the aconite leaves like the hungriest caterpillar ever to have been born beneath the light of an uncaring sky. I munched like a pot-bellied pig at a trough, my belly never full, always wanting. I munched like a munch-maker whose only purpose in this accursed world was to chomp and chomp and chomp.

Then I swallowed. More leaves brushed my lips and I snaffed those rascals down too. And more. More still.

I scoffed them all, rousing the beast within, the dormant creature who had been howling three beauteous notes in unison at the very bottom of my empty, grieving soul.

The shift came upon me fast, my enormous, brindle, three headed canine Order form emerging from my skin. The shift made my breast plate ping from my bountiful begonias so hard that the healer who had been working on me cried out as one pointed nip-tip caught him in the eye and knocked him upon his buttocks.

I flipped over, my shifted form too large to fit on the stone table they had laid me upon, and my four paws making the rocky floor shudder as I landed on them.

I lifted my three heads in a mournful howl which echoed off of the stone walls surrounding us, grief and hurt colliding within me even as the power of my Order form finally began to fix what had been working to destroy me.

A Cerberus held the most lethal of toxins in our fangs, one bite enough to end any manner of monster, and our blood ran thick with the power it took to resist such poison too.

My stomach cramped and spasmed, my spine arching and another howl echoing on as the three voices of my three heads all wove a song of grieving so beautifully that I could feel my heart cracking in two.

The constellation of my kind was no doubt burning brightly somewhere in the skies above me as I called on the gifts of my Order, fighting against the shadow rot which was festering in my bones.

I began to shudder with violence untold, and though there were voices speaking around me, I had no ears to hear them.

My howling song ended, and I slumped to my belly, panting heavily while my body worked to do what it knew how to through nothing other than instinct.

For vast hours, I lay there in my grief, while the magic that had been born to me healed that which should have killed me.

Why was I being spared such a fate when so many courageous and noble Fae had lost their lives on that field of bloodshed and carnage?

A shuddering breath huffed from my lungs, and I emerged from the pit of slumber which had yawned with wide jaws in anticipation of my demise.

Not today, you nefarious wraith. I shall not yield to you this day.

I cracked open an eye, finding myself in a stone room, the walls a brackish sandy colour, painted with effigies from the Fae of old. The air here was stale, though the decorations told of a once beautiful room, perhaps a temple to the stars or something of the sort. I wasn't certain.

I had wind-tossed memories of being hauled through dark tunnels carved away into the depths of the earth, then up and out of the ground, across field and through forest, over rivers and between dales. The retreating rebels had made a desperate dash for freedom indeed, unable to do more than press what healing magic they could spare into the worst of the injured, while abandoning the dead as they ran ever on.

Escape was all that had fuelled them, retreat and the urgent, desperate need to be able to fight another day.

I had fallen in and out of consciousness, vaguely aware of time and distance passing through the agony of the poison tearing through my veins, while those able to had worked to hide our passage.

I could only assume that whatever they had done had worked now that I found myself in this place of cold stone, that the rebels had found some small salvation and a place to rest a while in their retreat. They had finally been gifted the time needed to try and heal me, and I assumed that meant others in desperate need of healing were getting treatment too, but what of the battle? What of my queens and all we had fought for?

Low groans made me lift one of my three canine heads and I opened the rest of my eyes too, the room coming into clearer focus through the three sets of eyes I now trained on it, my outer heads turning to take it all in.

Star signs were marked upon the sand-coloured walls in faded paint, tarot images too, with swirling script notating the bottom of each, spelling out either a poem or a long-forgotten prophecy. This place was old, forgotten, a relic of a time passed.

My central head turned towards the door beyond the stone table I had lain upon, my blood coating it, drying and as tacky as the spittle of a wasp.

I inhaled deeply, scenting death and decay on the air, too many bodies packed tight into a small space.

I rose to my feet.

The spike of pain that lanced through me at the movement was no little thing, but I pushed aside any inclination to rest further as another groan met with all six of my sensitive ears.

I recognised Xavier's voice. My gallant gelding, crying out in agony so pure it cut me to my core.

I was moving on silent paws before the thought fully emerged, the memory of that sweet, horsey fellow cut down and bleeding on the battlefield searing into my mind as I hurried to the aid of my dear stepbrother.

The doorway did not allow for the enormity of my Cerberus form, so I shifted, a gasp of pain parting my lips like a drop of dew sliding from a mulberry bush before I forced my shaking Fae legs on.

A dusty corridor beckoned me along it, faint light peering in through glassless windows, their thin openings meant to allow blasts of magic out while the thick walls helped keep any returning fire at bay. Old indeed was this place.

Naked as the dawn, I staggered closer to those pain-filled groans, a hand braced against the smooth stone as I went, the orange glow of firelight beckoning me closer.

I fell completely still as I reached that gaping doorway, my eyes tracing over the dying man who lay on yet another stone table there, three rebels using healing magic on him over and over again while both Tyler and Sofia watched on, tears glistening on their cheeks.

Another pain-tinged groan escaped sweet Xavier's mouth, but he wasn't awake, his eyes closed as his body began to relent under the threat of those obsidian shadows.

"By the might of the heavens above, sky have mercy," I murmured, my voice catching on a bout of hysterical sobs which would do no Fae any favours.

"You're up," Sofia gasped in surprise as she took me in. "They said your Order gifts were healing you, but they thought it would take days-"

"There is no time for lollygagging," I snapped, swiping the back of my hand across my face to remove tears and snot. This was no moment for falling apart like a dandelion clock on a windy morn.

I strode into the room, my begonias bouncing even as another bout of unspeakable pain ripped through me from the inside out. But I ignored it. Ignored everything aside from the sweet, carrot-loving colt who needed my aid.

"Someone needs to find a Basilisk," I commanded.

"The last Basilisk in Solaria was killed six years ago," replied a man I neither knew nor cared to find out more about as he withdrew his hand from Xavier's side. "And there is nothing else that can save him. I'm afraid it's-"

I slapped him clean around the chops with a spray of water cast into the shape of a fish, snarling at him with the ferocity of what I was. A hell beast intent on a fate which I refused to turn from. Xavier Acrux would not die here on this table, the bleeding wounds from his missing wings and gauntness of his face the only things left of him beyond this moment.

"Then find him some Basilisk antivenom that was bottled before such a death," I snarled. "Go and ask the Oscuras for it, if you don't already know, that is where you need look. They hold all manner of treasures in their possession, and will no doubt be able to find you this."

"Geraldine?" Sofia asked, a touch of hope in her watery gaze as she looked to me like I might just have the answer to this riddle. My poor, pale, Pegasus pal looked so anguished over her dear Dom, that I knew her love for Xavier Acrux ran as deep as the ocean gullies of Galgadon.

"If you wish to do more than wet the weeds with your tears sweet Sofia, please go and help that fellow search. I will do all I can to aid my dear brother until you return with what he requires."

I shifted before she could respond, dropping my central head low and releasing a canine whine before I lapped at the shadow-cursed wound which had torn Xavier Acrux to shreds. There was power in the saliva of a Cerberus. Power against poisons and toxins, though not so much as a Basilisk possessed. But I would get him through the time it took to find the cure he so desperately required.

Sofia and Tyler hurried from the room at a galloping gait, their need to save their sweet stallion filling them with purpose as they tore away in search of the cure he so desperately required. I dropped onto my haunches, my body sagging with my own pain as I fought the damning poison of the shadows from within my own blood, but I ignored such irksome nonsense in favour of helping my kin, my sweet stepbrother.

The night wore on while I lay with Xavier, tirelessly lending him what aid I could through my gifts, and though he didn't wake, his brow softened, and his moans of pain lessened. All three sets of my ears remained locked on the solid beat of his heart, and as it steadied a little, I found some semblance of strength, of belief.

He would survive this. I would make it so, no matter the path the stars had tried to lay out for him.

A great clamour of noise interrupted my silent vigil, and I raised my heads with a ferocious snarl, making the three huge men in the doorway pause as they beheld me.

"It's okay, carina," Dante Oscura murmured, raising a hand clad in gold rings as a symbol of peace between us. He was a bulked-up beast of a Dragon Shifter with his dark hair dishevelled and the olive tone of his Faetalian ancestry still laced with blood. It saddened me to find his youthful, handsome face drawn with anguish by the woes of battle. "I've brought what you need."

"Let them pass, Geraldine," Sofia begged, and I caught sight of her blonde head hidden behind the wall of muscular males who had entered.

There was no room for them to approach Xavier while I remained in Cerberus form, so I shifted, my eyes as glassy as a ghoul's mirror as I stepped aside for the tattooed man and the Lion Shifter to pass me.

"Here," Sofia added in a soft voice, holding out a green cloak which I donned with little fanfare to hide my voluptuous nudity.

"You have the antivenom?" I inquired, fatigue lining every one of my words.

"We do," the man coated in Disney tattoos growled, a grim set to his features as he looked upon poor Xavier. His brown hair was tied into a knot upon the crest of his head, and he licked his lips as he moved closer to my stepbrother, almost as if he could taste the pain in the air.

I opened my mouth to say more but a great cry went up from beyond the confines of the walls which held us, my heart leaping in reverent hope as I caught a single sentence between the clamouring which was enough to ignite that most desperately needed of things in me: hope.

"The queen returns!"

I was running from the room which held dear Xavier before I could hear any more, hurrying down more ancient corridors and cold stone passages in the hunt for a way out of here to where the shouts only grew louder.

I whirled around a corner just in time to see a large Minotaur woman in shifted form pull open a heavy wooden door, and I sprinted for the sight of the stars revealed beyond it.

"My lady!" I cried as I was met with a crowd, the direction they were all surging towards making it clear where one of my queens now stood.

I barked a warning to make them all move, many of them falling back beneath my fierceness like lily livers on a May morn, but still too many barrelled into my way, blocking me from her.

I threw my hands up, my magic now blooming thanks to all the aconite I had devoured, and I knocked a path through the centre of the crowd with a blast of water which I regretted not one bit.

I sprinted through that gap, my cloak billowing wide and revealing my naked body to any who cared to turn an eye my way, but I didn't have time to care for such things as my gaze fell on a bloody, battle warn warrior where she stood at the top of the hill ahead of me.

Ruins lay all around us, some broken while others remained standing, able to house the wounded as they were. I recognised this as an ancient place of worship, though the once revered hillside was now strewn with blood-splattered soldiers. The light of the slowly setting sun gilded our queen in gold and orange, and for a moment I could have sworn an angel stood before her as the light blazed off the burnished bronze colour of her wings.

"Lady Tory!" I yelled, noting the onyx colour of her hair beneath the blood and grime that was matted in it, and she turned cold, empty eyes my way.

Her beauteous face was hollow, gaunt, devoid of that wild glow I had always loved so dearly in her.

The crowd was falling to a hush now, sidling back to make space around her, their backs pressing to the crumbling walls of the ruins the rebels were using for shelter.

I felt it then. A severing of something vital within me. Before my gaze even fell from the utter, broken grief in her green eyes to take in the three huge objects which lay behind her.

Three coffins carved of ice.

"No," I breathed, begging the stars for it not to be so as my bare feet stumbled over cold, hard ground towards my queen.

Tory said nothing and I knew it wasn't for lack of wanting to, but more for lack of words which could encompass the awful reality hurtling towards me second by agonising second.

I couldn't bear to look inside those ice coffins, couldn't bear to see who she had transported here in their eternal slumber in such a way, couldn't bear to face the cost of this battle we had lost so brutally.

"Please," I begged the stars once more, but as my bare toes brushed against the first of the frozen coffins, I was nothing but a slave to fate as my eyes fell to take in the face of the man who lay trapped in death within.

The ice casket encasing my father glistened like the dewberries of Nor, beautiful and ruinous at once. All of it splintered within my vision, fracturing into a thousand flickering Faeflies in my eyes as my tears welled and began to drip down my cheeks like two never-ending rivers.

I blinked a butterfly's blink, and it all became clear once more, the cold clutch of grief holding onto my heart and squeezing with all the strength of a Dragon's talon coiled around it.

"I'm sorry, Geraldine," Tory said, her voice an empty urn.

Beside Daddy, lay the sweet, beautiful Lady Catalina in her crystalised crypt, as exquisite in death as she had been in life. There they rested, quiet, silenced forevermore upon this plane. Beyond them, in his deep and timeless sleep was my Queen Tory's dear love, her fierce and gallant man brought to the gates of the stars by his monstrous flesh and blood. Her dear Dragoon, Darius.

They had passed beyond the Veil, where no man nor woman could ever tread in life. Gone.

My heart withered, bleeding and forever weeping for them all. My darling Daddy with his courage and his hope, his kind words all lost to the wind, nothing but memories for me to capture like moths to keep in jars, to be treasured and defended always.

I had thought my Mama's loss would be the end of me. Grief felt like dying, and I had been so sure I'd been following her into oblivion once she had passed on from this world, her fire blown out by the breath of the heavens.

But Daddy had held my hand and been there for me in a way only a parent can. With bravery deeper than all the oceans of the world, and with a tenderness that eased my pain and bathed my aching soul in molten love. I'd had him through the worst time of my life, but now no one was here but me as I stood on the shores of loss once again, with the tide receding and the last of the goodbyes lapping at my feet.

I, Geraldine Gundellifus Gabolia Gundestria Grus, was alone, and I felt as though I was standing upon a spinning compass, directionless, true north abandoning me to the chaos of a circling needle. For where did I go from here?

I moved closer, feet shuffling and hesitant as I shifted so I would be able to look upon his face. It was still, and the claws in my chest released a little at the sight of peace resting lightly on his features. Yes, death it seemed, had been kind, pulling him gently into its arms. He had not fought it, I could see that, and I was glad to discover he had walked willingly into the stars' embrace. He was unscathed apart from the deep stab wound to his chest that had surely equalled his end.

The beauty that was Catalina mirrored his serenity, a cut to her throat the mark of her own demise, and if I wasn't mistaken, their hands seemed to extend toward one another's as if even now they wished to unite, to never be parted. I offered them that wish with ease, standing back to work my magic and allow my water Element to take over as I combined their casket into one entity, their hands sliding over one another's.

A sharp inhale came at my back, and I turned, a lump as hard as knotweed rising in my throat as I met the gaze of poor, dear Xavier. He was pale faced, still weak from the wounds inflicted upon him, but it seemed as though the Basilisk antivenom had done its job. He would heal in time, though not of this grief. That, I knew, would never die.

"Xavier, I..." Tory started, but words failed her. Failed all of us, truly.

The tears continued to run along my cheeks in steady streams and I let them fall as they wished to, knowing keeping them inside was akin to jabbering with a deadly danzerdile of the northern rivers. Holding grief within only made it boil, bubble and spit until it burned its way out, so it was better to let it flow free and face it head on. Pain was meant to be felt, just as all emotions were. And as my Daddypops always said, *"We must feel the bad as deeply as the sea, for then we are able to feel the joy as high as the moon."*

"Xavier, I am so gravely sorry for your loss. Your mother was a star descended from the sky, come to shine upon us, she was so cherished by us all, by me, by my father. Her mark at The Burrows will never be forgotten, and I have been as privileged as the pilgrims of the Yunetide to know her. As for Darius-" I choked on the name, a desperate sob escaping me and climbing into a wail.

Xavier broke before me, a house one moment, a ruin the next. He staggered towards his brother's frozen tomb, rearing over it and crying quietly against the ice.

"It's my fault," he croaked. "He drew our father away from me. I should have killed that bastard before this could have happened."

Tory shook her head, looking like she wanted to say something to contradict the blame he was casting down upon himself, but instead her head hung and her gaze moved back to the coffins. She was steel, hard and cold and unmovable in her grief. It had destroyed her, this loss. I could see that, see the way it had carved something vital from her soul and left her barren without it, unable to so much as feel the wind on her cheeks as the pain in her took precedent over all.

I flung myself at the boy who had been made a man before my eyes within The Burrows, this Acrux who had been forced to hide his Order, who had lived in a house of fear and distress while his mother was kept in servitude to the monster of the manor. I wrapped my arms around him, and he turned into me, burying his face against my shoulder, while our grief spilled out, unravelling like twine before knitting itself into a bond of devastation that created a true kinship between us.

"I don't want to go on without them. I don't want to be here with them gone," he sobbed, the muscles of his arms crushing the wind out of me, but I let it fly away to the breeze. I could go without breath for a dear friend, a brother born of our parents' love for one another, and now our shared hurt in our family members' passing too.

"It feels like that now, indeed, sweet Pegasus," I whispered, reaching a hand up to brush my fingers through his dark hair. "It may even feel worse for a time, but this pain we must bear, because there are others left here who love us to the sun and beyond, others who need us to keep moving forward towards the hills of hope."

"I don't want to," he growled stubbornly. "I don't want to let go. I want to turn back time. I want to kill my father, I want to fucking kill him!"

He yanked free of my arms, fire igniting in one hand, while sharpened icicles grew on the other. His breathing was heavy and furious, his shoulders rigid before he cast away the magic and doubled over, the agony taking him once more.

I moved to sit upon the ground with him, my own heart cleaved apart by the macabre scythe of death. Tory was silent, unmoving iron as she stood in the wake of all this death, as if her body was frozen by the hand of time.

I reached a hand towards her in offering, but she didn't even seem to notice it, unable to fall here with us, something cracked apart and bleeding so deeply within her that tears were useless now. I knew better than to push her, so I simply tightened my grip on the brother I had claimed for my own.

Silence descended on the three of us and Xavier tucked his knees to his chest, his face buried in them while I started to hum the tune played at my mother's funeral. Shaylin's Lullaby. A song of goodbyes and morrows yet to come. It was sad and soothing at once, a paradox of hope and sorrow, the two meeting within the rhythm like two ladybirds upon a falling leaf.

"Take my hand and find me here. I live in the wind and grass, my dear. So when you need me, call my name. You'll feel me close within the rain. For I, for I, for I, will wait beyond the Veil for you. But please, my love, don't wait for me. My time is done, my seeds are sown. So live a life of joy and love, and I'll be watching up above. The greatest show has just begun, my seat is taken, my song is sung. I'll smile with every smile you take, I'll laugh with you when times are great. So live for me, and live for you. I'll see you in the star's lagoon...I'll see you in the star's lagoon."

My hand had found Xavier's somewhere during the song and as the final words slipped from my tongue, my tears dried against my cheeks and we sat there, the silence a relief. For no more needed to be said. The chimes of the Gorgon clock were tolling, but this pain would be chiselled away into a treasure eventually. One we could place gently within a casket in our chests, to take out and cry over whenever we needed. But for now, our grief was a roughened stone with edges that made us bleed inside. It was bleak, it was agony, it was the cruel and unforgiving way of death.

I raised my eyes to Tory, noting the blood dripping slowly from some wound on her hand as she watched us.

Broken.

My queen, my lady, my dear friend had been broken by all she had now survived, and as I looked into that darkness in her eyes, I had the terrifying feeling that there was nothing on this earth that could ever fix her again.

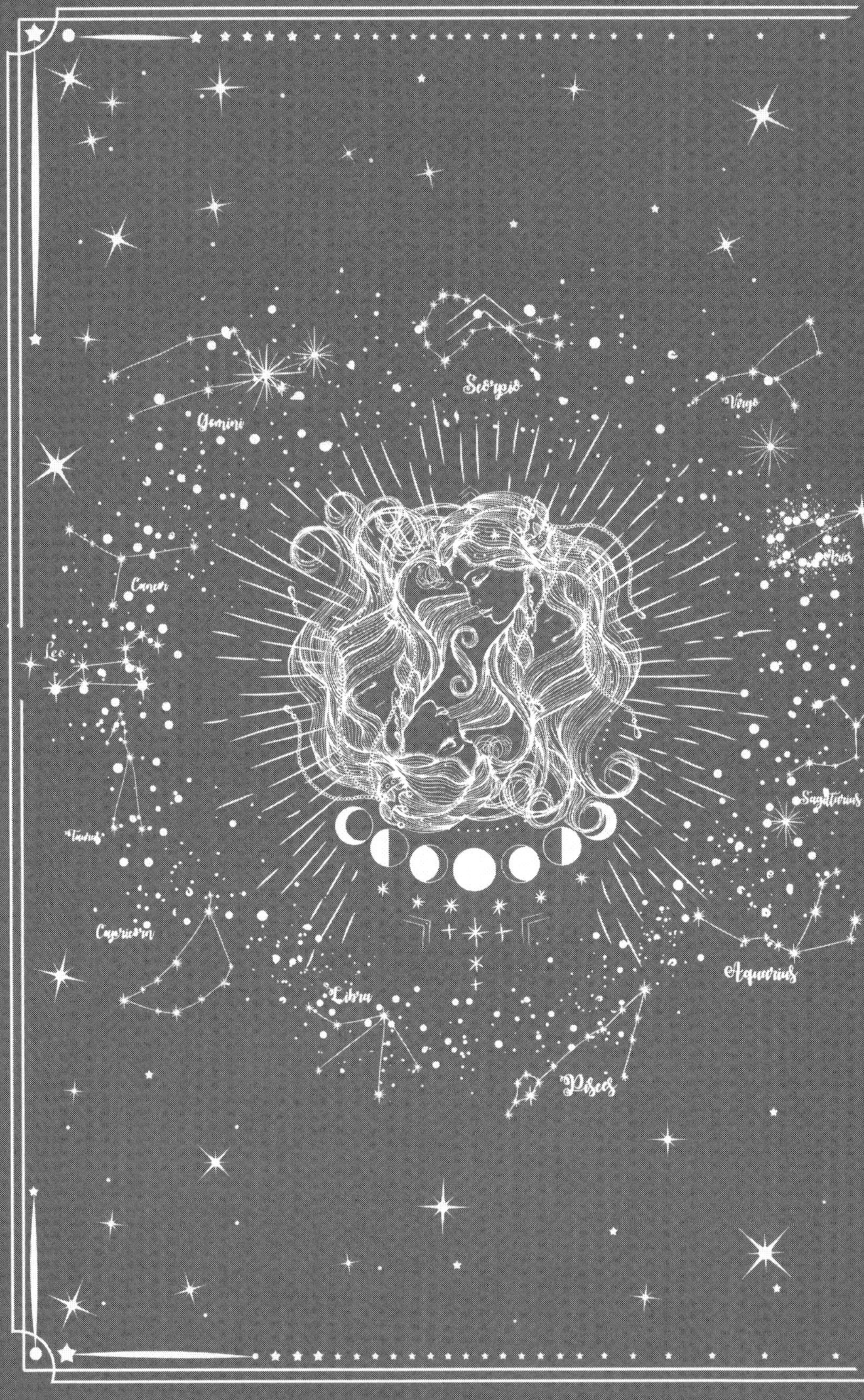

Scorpio
Gemini
Virgo
Cancer
Leo
Sagittarius
Taurus
Capricorn
Aquarius
Libra
Pisces

TORY

CHAPTER SIX

The ruins the rebels had made into a temporary camp were situated on the eastern side of a lonely mountain no more than fifty miles from the site of the battlefield where we'd all lost so much. I'd heard some of them call it Mount Lyra, and some actually believed this place held an old magic gifted by the Lyra constellation, making it a haven capable of soothing the souls of the weary. My soul felt anything but soothed though.

In the hours that had passed since my arrival, I'd been told far more about the crumbling stone buildings and the Fae of old who used to come here to worship the sunrise around two thousand years ago than I had any interest in knowing. I had to assume my silence had caused the rush of words to tumble from the rebel who'd told me about the colony of Harpies who had once circled the skies here while singing a welcome to the sun each and every morning in a language long since forgotten.

I hadn't even looked up at the Fae who'd spent his time telling me about such distant things while the rebels had created a funeral procession around me, a ceaseless line of them passing the coffins I'd returned with and saying goodbye to the Fae housed in them.

My feet felt fused to the spot where I stood, my eyes riveted on the cold and empty form of the man I loved while people he neither knew nor cared for wept over his loss.

The air was so thick with grief that it felt like a fog pressing down on my shoulders, the weight of it palpable and yet somehow entirely outside of me.

These people hadn't known the Fae they sobbed over, had never felt the warmth of their love the way I had, and yet their pain over losing them was undeniable.

Xavier and Geraldine had remained by my side when the rebels embarked upon this endless farewell, but after a few hours, Xavier had practically collapsed, the mixture of his heartache and still-healing wounds getting the better of him. He had returned inside to one of the few chambers which still stood with four walls and a roof where the healers were working on those with the worst injuries.

Much to her dismay, Tyler had insisted Geraldine go with him to rest too and despite her wailing back to me to simply command her presence by my side, I hadn't done so. I hadn't said a word.

On and on the procession continued with Fae casting small tokens using their magic, everything from flowers to figures of ice and tiny everflames in every colour now flickering in the space surrounding the coffins.

They spoke to me too, words of condolence and pledges of allegiance to the true queens. They bowed, curtsied, swore oaths which I felt far from worthy of, and breathed constant wishes for Darcy's safe return to us soon.

All the while my mind stuck and spun, fragments of the battle darkening my thoughts one after another as I fought to figure out every piece which had gone so horribly wrong and why.

The pain in my soul was a void I couldn't face. The heartache and grief a yawning chasm just waiting to swallow me whole. But not yet. Darcy needed me. Orion was missing too. The Heirs still hadn't returned from whatever hell had unfolded for them and Gabriel…my brow pinched as I thought of the message my brother had sent me.

I knew it had been him. I'd felt the kiss of his power, so familiar to my own while I knelt in the blood of the man I'd taken for my husband, and I'd read those words.

The same words which now echoed through my mind in a voice that could only belong to my brother, begging me to find meaning in them and understand what he needed me to do.

"Tory?" a familiar voice made me focus my attention on the man standing before me and I blinked as I took in Dante Oscura, his clothes torn and stained from battle, though he seemed unscathed beyond that, already healed of any wounds he'd gained. "Your people are waiting for your orders," he said softly but firmly, like he was trying to remind me of what was expected of me.

My eyes shifted to the coffin where Hamish Grus now lay with Catalina, the man who had led the rebels with such efficiency and care, now forever adrift beyond the Veil. As I lifted my gaze beyond the coffin, I noticed something I'd either been ignoring or had been too distracted by my own thoughts to notice.

The rebels extended away from me down the mountainside, their eyes trained on me in their silence as they watched the procession finish and waited for me to… what? Were they really seeking orders? Or words of encouragement? Did they expect answers or praise on a battle well fought but lost? Was I supposed to rally them or console them?

The truth was, I didn't know how to do any of this. I was just a lost princess who had grown up in the wrong place and now stood before them after losing almost everything I held closest. I was broken. I could feel the reality of that deep within the cracks which had shattered through me after all that had been destroyed on the battlefield. But I was still standing here before them.

I drew my gaze back to Dante and nodded, watching as he withdrew, and I was left standing before my people alone as the sun began to set behind the mountain at my back.

Silence spread so thickly that it stalled the air in my lungs as thousands of faces stared back at me, some I recognised, but many I didn't. I wasn't sure what I was even supposed to tell them, but I knew that turning my back on them now would break what little resolve they clung to.

So I drew in a deep breath and raised my chin as I began to speak, the silence letting my words carry to every Fae who cared to listen.

"Glory is an accolade coveted by so many," I said, my voice rough from lack of use but strong all the same. "It is what a lot of us expected to claim when we faced our enemies on the battlefield at last, and yet it is not what many of you feel you found. What glory can be found in defeat after all?"

The silence stretched and stretched, and I began to wonder what I'd even been thinking by trying to speak to them now, with no preparation and no thought to where I was going with this. But it was too late for me to back out so I just pressed on, speaking from the shattered remains of my heart and hoping it might resonate with even one of the Fae listening on with rapt attention.

"What glory can be found when standing shoulder to shoulder with men and women you don't even know while united against oppression and persecution? What glory can be found when standing firm against a tide of tyranny so all-encompassing that you feel like a grain of sand trying to resist an entire ocean? What glory is there in seeing Fae you love cut down and butchered by monsters weaving shadows and creatures born of darkness? What glory can you claim when you fight against a leash which has already tightened around your throat? When laws are written against your rights and a false king dons a crown and no one manages to knock it from his over-inflated head?"

My heart was thrashing in my chest as I spoke, the words an outpouring of every injustice I had faced along with my sister from the moment we set foot back in Solaria.

"What glory is there in fighting a losing battle? In standing with blade in hand and magic burning fiercely through you, against a force far bigger than your own, without fear ever once making you flinch? When even the stars won't help us, and the night turns dark with shadows? What glory is there then, I ask you?"

Wide eyes looked to me with such a need for that answer that it set a fire of fury blazing through every fibre of my being and I gripped the pommel of my sword as I raised my voice in answer to my own question.

"Every one of you standing before me and every Fae who fell on that battlefield fighting by our sides knows the answer to that question. Because we don't need glory. We only need to know that we are fighting for what is right. We are fighting for freedom from oppression and the end of a tyrant. We are standing up and saying no more. And Lionel Acrux may have sat his scaley ass on my father's throne, but he is nothing but a serpent perched on a pretty seat. I don't bow to him or his false crown. Do you?"

A deafening roar of defiance met my question, and a brutal smile curved my lips as I saw that need to fight rising in them once more.

"No war is won in a single battle," I went on. "No kingdom claimed with one fight. And though we may have bled for our cause on that field of chaos and carnage, they bled for it too. We cut them in that fight. We made them bleed for us and a thousand tiny cuts can kill just as surely as a single blow to the heart. So I say we keep cutting Lionel Acrux and his shadow bitch bride in every way we can. We cut and slice and carve them up and we keep fighting and fighting them until the bitter end, when I know in my soul that we will claim more glory than any of us ever dared wish for!"

I drew my sword, the last rays of the setting sun catching on the polished metal between the bloodstains that still marked it, making it flash like a beacon above my head.

The rebels roared for a glory that was yet to come as they drew their weapons too, punching the air and chanting in defiance as they all swore to keep fighting this war. Not because they knew we would win. But because they knew it was the right thing to do.

I turned and strode away from them, keeping my chin high as I walked, not allowing my eyes to turn towards the coffin which contained Darius Acrux, the man I had hated and loved so eternally.

This is not our end.

I had no way of making that oath into reality, but the still-bleeding wound on my palm ached with that promise, the slice of the sun steel blade which had caused it not allowing it to heal over as my other wounds had.

I welcomed the pain of it though, some touch of reality to keep me from the darkest of the ideas which were circling inside my mind.

"Your Highness," a man murmured as I stepped into the ruins of this place of worship and began to walk down a stone hall which must have been beautiful in its time, though the old carvings had faded long ago. "A room has been prepared for you, if you would care to follow me?"

I nodded once, needing some semblance of solitude while I worked on the plan that was forming in my mind.

"Are we safe here?" I asked, my voice rough, flat, hard.

"For now," he agreed. "There are wards and spells in place to keep prying eyes from seeking us out. The beacon which led you to find us was specifically designed for a member of your bloodline and no other. No one else would have felt the pull you did which drew you back to us, my Queen." I nodded, my memory of flying here with the coffins in tow a blur of pain and grief, but I had known where to fly to, had felt the power he spoke of and followed it here. "Diversions have been cast for miles around by some of our most gifted Fae and there are protection spells of every kind surrounding us. We can make use of these ruins for now, rest, heal, gather our strength."

He didn't go on, but I heard the rest of what he didn't want to say directly. We couldn't stay here permanently. We needed somewhere truly safe to regroup, gather more Fae to our cause, come up with a new plan to strike back at our enemies.

I paused, looking behind me to the open land beyond the entrance to the ruins, the hateful stars rising in the darkening sky.

"Who betrayed us?" I asked, turning back to the passageway and continuing on, trying to ignore the feeling of eyes on my back even though I'd just seen for myself that no one followed us.

"I..." the man winced and I frowned at him, noting the lines around his eyes, the dried blood on his neck and the hollow look in his pale eyes. "We don't know, Your Majesty."

He hung his head and I blew out a breath, wondering how safe we really could be in this place while whoever had sold us out to Lionel might still be lurking among us.

"No one leaves," I said firmly. "No one uses an Atlas – can something be done to ensure that?"

"A magical charge can be sent through the entire camp at the exact voltage needed to destroy any such items which anyone here might have been hiding. Would you like me to set some aside for use by your inner circle?"

"Yes," I decided. "Give a selection to Tyler Corbin. He can work on making sure they're secure before we consider distributing them again."

He nodded in agreement before going on. "The wards are currently stopping anyone from coming or going and the earth and water Elementals can see to the issue of food, water, clothing-"

"Good." I upped my pace, satisfied that we were safe enough here for now and done with the questions which rattled through my too-tender thoughts. I couldn't offer more than that to him or anyone else here.

I could tell what was expected of me, what the rebels needed, and yet that wasn't what I was going to do. I wasn't going to take Hamish's place at the head of this group. I wasn't going to be the one who led the rebels to their next hideout and planned what battles we may face or how best to strike back. At least not right away. There were things I had to do, things which I didn't have time to spend discussing with anyone, and things which I refused to bow out of just because I was a figurehead at the prow of this army.

The rebels had been busy since their arrival here, and though I knew it wasn't safe for us to linger in this place for long, they had surrounded the mountain refuge with enough protection while working to recuperate to set any urgent fears at bay.

There were Fae who needed healing and the remains of an army to be fed and cared for. Another day or two here was necessary, after that...well, I'd worry about after if we made it that far.

I was relieved to find that no one was allowed to leave this place, fear of the traitor who had betrayed our position to Lionel still hanging thick in the air. But so long as no one could leave, I was as confident as I could be that the rebels would be safe here for the time they needed before a new plan would have to be put together.

The rebel man led me to a room which looked like it had once been used for star gazing, the space entirely circular and the roof a glass dome overhead. In the centre of the space, a large bath had been created out of earth magic, milky water already steaming in the copper tub with flowers floating on its surface that perfumed the air.

A bed had been created for me too, some clean clothes found from the stars only knew where and laid out on it. There was food waiting as well, bread and fruit sitting beside a pitcher of cold water, calling out to my empty stomach. The earth Elementals had been kept busy with the task of feeding this army since our arrival, and I knew I was damn lucky to have been gifted anything that required baking, but the thought of food seemed like the least appealing prospect I could imagine.

"Is there anything else you need?" the man asked.

I shook my head, my fingers moving to the straps securing my armour, beginning to unbuckle it automatically. I felt like a machine, running on empty but unable to stop moving, following the motions of my body while not really registering any of them. I was here and somewhere utterly else at once, and I didn't think there was enough of me left to try and reunite those pieces, even if I'd had half a mind to attempt it.

He bowed and left the chamber as I continued to undress, dropping the heavy, bloodied metal to the floor piece by piece before tugging my underclothes free and climbing into the bath.

The water was hotter than I expected, my skin tingling as it tried to scald me, but I made no attempt to cool it as I simply sank deeper into its embrace, dropping my head beneath the surface and exhaling slowly as the filth of the battle was washed from my skin.

I flicked up an air shield surrounding me as I remained submerged, hiding from the world and all it had to offer in the cloudy water, even if I knew I couldn't remain there forever. But I wanted to. I wanted to drift away in that water and forget…everything.

I used my air magic to stay there, breathing beneath the surface and holding onto thoughts of my sister while I fought the urge to shatter entirely. I'd hoped she might be here when I returned, but now I didn't even know where to begin hunting for her, her fate as murky as the water I was hiding in and my fear for her consuming me even as I clung to the belief that she was still alive with all I had.

My mind ticked over the message Gabriel had sent me as I tried to piece it together, working to find meaning in the words I knew had to hold great importance. It was one of the few clear things left to me, though the confusion I felt at the prophecy he'd gifted me meant the task held as little meaning as everything else.

A presence knocked against the shield I'd left intact around myself and I pushed upright suddenly, sucking down fresh air as I swiped my black hair out of my face, blinking through the water cascading over my lashes as I took in the two huge figures in the room.

"Forgive the intrusion, bella," Dante Oscura growled as my gaze collided with his, sparks of his Storm Dragon's electricity meeting with the wave of heat that had tumbled from me on instinct before both our magic fell still once again.

My gaze flicked from him to Leon Night who stood at his side, the Lion Shifter looking graver than I had ever seen him, his luscious blonde hair tangled and unkempt, his eyes dark with the battle he'd survived.

"What is it? Are we under attack?" I demanded.

They waved me off quickly before I could rise from my bath, and I looked between them in confusion as Dante cleared his throat.

"Darius Acrux is a loss all of us will bear with great sadness," Dante murmured softly and something akin to a knife twisted through my heart at the sudden change to our conversation and the sound of that name. "His sacrifice for this cause will go down in the history of Solaria and never be forgotten. A morte e ritorno."

I fisted my right hand, blood oozing from it as the wound there continued to bleed, the cut from the sun steel blade a constant ache which I refused to even try to heal.

Leon's gaze moved to my fist where I'd perched it on the side of the tub and his golden eyes seemed to burn with understanding.

"That cut is to remember him?" he asked, and I could feel the power of his Lion Charisma pushing at me as his gifts encouraged me to open up, to lean on him for some kind of relief and support, but I didn't give in to the urge to do so.

"It's to remember the oath I made with his blood and mine, to the stars who sat by and watched this fate play out," I growled low in the back of my throat.

"You want it to scar?" Dante asked and I nodded, admitting to the reason that I'd made no attempt to heal the wound, though I knew a cut made with sun steel would likely scar regardless. "I can help you close it while maintaining the scar," he added in offering, extending a hand to me.

I only hesitated a moment before raising my fist and letting him take it. Water dripped across the floor of the chamber as Dante turned my hand over and uncurled my fingers, his dark eyes flickering at the sight of the deep and jagged wound there.

"You may have to withdraw your Phoenix for this to work," he murmured, the air crackling as he called on his gifts, and my pulse began to hammer in my chest at the thought of feeling the strength of that power again.

Lionel had so loved to torture me with lightning born of this man, watching with sick pleasure as my body bucked and burned from the inside out, agony coursing through me. I feared the kiss of that power more than I wanted to admit. But I feared the loss of that scar even more than that.

With a force of will, I pulled my Phoenix back, allowing his gifts the chance to burn my skin as I drew in a deep breath and felt the static rising all around us.

"Per amore e sacrificio," Dante murmured in Faetalian, brushing two fingers along the bleeding wound on my palm, the power of his lightning burning into my flesh and crackling between us.

I sucked in a sharp breath, my spine arching at the blazing kiss of his power as it fought to bring up some of my worst memories. But I refused to let them surface, instead focusing on the memory of eyes as dark as sin itself, and the love of a man I had barely begun to claim as my own, the echo of his touch escaping me all too soon.

Dante released me and I sagged back in the bath, milky water sloshing over the edge. I withdrew my hand and looked at the scar which now adorned my palm. The skin was raised and reddened, tiny lines spreading out from it across my hand where the electricity had spread away from the wound just a little. It looked like a tree locked forever in winter. Spiny branches spreading out from a trunk which was thick and rough with age. It was raw, savage, beautiful. And it cut through both my heart and lifelines, defying any foretold expectations fate may have had for me, leaving me free to set my own destiny from this moment on.

"Thank you," I breathed as I examined the scar, the pain of it fading to nothing as I allowed my own magic to sooth the lingering ache, then lifted my eyes to look between them once more. "But you didn't come here to heal my hand."

Dante gave me the ghost of a smile as he shook his head. "We need to know where Gabriel is."

My gaze travelled from him to Leon, his golden eyes swirling as their fear for my brother's safety weighed down on them.

"Lost," I breathed, knowing it wasn't what they had wanted to hear and feeling that flicker of shock and fear as it hit them like it was yet another stab to my own soul.

"How?" Dante demanded, his Faetalian accent thick as electricity once again crackled in the air and a note of thunder rumbled through the heavens overhead.

I glanced up at the sky through the glass roof as the clouds converged to steal all sight of the stars, exhaling in relief as the weight of their stares were lifted from me.

"I don't know," I admitted, the pain in my voice clear. "But he sent me a message while I knelt grieving on the battlefield. A prophecy thick with the familiarity of his magic which tasted of goodbye."

If I'd had any tears left in me, I knew one would have rolled down my cheek at those words to drop into the water I still sat in.

"No way," Leon said firmly. "Gabe wouldn't leave us. Not in a million, billion years."

"Tell us the prophecy," Dante demanded, and Leon began to pace.

"When all hope is lost, and the darkest night descends, remember the promises that bind. When the dove bleeds for love, the shadow will meet the warrior. A hound will bay for vengeance where the rift drinks deep. One chance awaits. The king may fall on the day the Hydra bellows in a spiteful palace."

We looked at each other for several long seconds, each of us willing the other to understand something in those words that could help us.

But there was nothing.

"We're leaving," Leon said firmly. "Heading back to the battlefield to search for our brother. He will have left us something there, some way to find him. Gabe loves his twisty word games, we'll figure it out."

"Don't call him Gabe," Dante muttered and the two of them exchanged a brief, terrified look before turning their gazes back to me. "We'll leave now."

I nodded, my heart pounding at the thought of even more people abandoning me, but I knew it was for the best. They could focus on Gabriel. They could figure out what had happened to him, find him…something.

"Tell whoever is controlling the wards that I said you can leave," I said, knowing the rebels would only relax that rule on my orders. I wasn't worried about either of them being the one who had betrayed us anyway, and if there was any chance they could find Gabriel, I wasn't going to get in their way. "If there's anything you need of me, simply ask," I breathed as they turned to leave.

"Kill that Dragon asshole if you can," Leon called back to me as they strode away. "That would be all kinds of handy."

A choked laugh that may have been a sob escaped me as I was left there, alone in the scalding water which prickled my skin, only the Phoenix in me stopping it from burning.

I leaned back, my eyes on the glass roof as rain began to fall from the thunder clouds gathering under the might of Dante's power, and I watched the storm build above me, lightning flashing and thunder booming while feeling entirely powerless beneath it.

Hours passed and the camp went quiet while the storm raged on, rebels finding what rest they could while fear and uncertainty crept in all around us.

But I wasn't powerless.

I was Roxanya Vega.

I stood abruptly, water sloshing from my body then rising off of me in a cloud of steam as I strode for the clothes laid out for me.

I pulled on the black jeans and navy crop top that left room for my wings, ignoring the ridiculous dress which looked fit for a coronation beside them. I had no need of finery where I was headed.

We may have been running from the so-called Dragon King, but I wasn't going to take this defeat lying down.

The people I loved were out there and they needed me. More than I could bear were lost or unaccounted for, but I knew where three of them had been headed before the battle.

And the Heirs had still not returned.

Flames caught and licked beneath my skin, hungry to dole out death and pain for all I'd endured, and I fell into that rampant need for revenge like a ravaged soul hungering for life.

The fire had replenished my magic to its brim, and I was itching for a fight. This would be the start of the end, and I wasn't ever going to back down again.

I strapped my dagger to my belt, the one which had taken Darius from me. It was now destined to remain at my side until I saw that twist of fate unravelled and Lionel's life force spilling from the wound I inflicted upon him with it.

The storm raged on as I stepped outside, but the drops of rain couldn't so much as touch me as the heat of my Phoenix burned them from existence well before they reached my head.

I tipped my face to the sky and unleashed my flaming wings, turning south and setting my destination firmly within my mind.

"My lady!" Geraldine's voice was probably the only one which could have made me pause and I turned to look as she ran for me, her eyes wide and full of wrath. "You mean to retrieve the three rapscallions from the clutches of whatever kept them from battle?" she demanded, and I had to wonder if she had a touch of The Sight to have realised my destination so easily.

Her hair, which had been a bland and forgettable colour before, had been dyed a deep, blood red, the furious set to her features letting me know that it was a promise of its own, to see the blood of her enemies spilled in payment for the losses she'd suffered in that battle. It suited her, the colour matching with the fire which burned unwaveringly within her soul, bright and brutal and wholly her.

"I do," I agreed.

"Then I am coming with you. My Maxy boy awaits me, and I shall bay for vengeance on behalf of my dear Daddy while ripping the throats from our enemies as we retrieve him."

The fire in her eyes brokered no arguments, and I found my chest compressing with relief as I gazed into the eyes of my dearest friend.

"Well then," I said, extending my hand to her as I wrapped her in my air magic and leashed her to me. "It sounds like it's time for us to hunt."

Scorpio
Gemini
Virgo
Cancer
Leo
Sagittarius
Taurus
Capricorn
Aquarius
Libra
Pisces

SETH

CHAPTER SEVEN

The ground circled like a treadmill beneath my feet, forcing me to run until my lungs felt ready to rip open. I was bound to the altar of black stone outside the Acrux Manor, the moonlight burning down on my back, recharging my magic before it was swiftly sucked out of me again by the rift. The chains of shadow that dragged at my power made my head spin with weakness, and my legs ached with the exertion of running without rest.

The dark and churning portal of the rift in front of me was like a gateway to hell, calling me to a place where I was sure my essence would be torn clean from my body. The pull of countless hungry souls within that void were begging to claim me, and their call was so damn tempting, it was nearly impossible to resist.

The rift seemed to suck more violently at my power and my eyes darkened, my feet stumbling heavily.

"Seth, hold on," my mom called to me, and I blinked hard to clear my vision, finding her across the altar tethered alongside the other Councillors. "Stay strong. You're an Alpha."

I swallowed the sharp, jagged thing in my throat and nodded to her, not wanting to show weakness as my family looked to me. They needed me to be strong, and I could do anything for my pack. I straightened my spine and ran on, ignoring the pain and locking away any signs of vulnerability deep down in that iron chest within me. The place I'd only ever let a few people see the inside of.

Caleb was on my left, kneeling on the ground as he fed from a man's neck, the hunger in him so keen his eyes were almost red with it. The man began to fall still, his features pale and his efforts to fight back fading.

"Cal!" I called to him as he came close to killing the Fae in his grasp, his fingers biting into his victim's shoulders and his grip unyielding. The nameless man was going limp, his eyes beginning to flutter shut while Caleb was still lost to the madness of the bloodlust, the rift making him weak to the bane of his Order.

"Caleb!" I bellowed louder, stumbling on the shifting ground as I tried to get to him, but the chains that shackled me to the stone altar kept me from stepping off of the enchanted treadmill.

Caleb looked up, his eyes finding mine as blood dripped from his mouth and some clarity finally awakened in the depths of his blazing blue eyes.

"Seth," he said, his voice rough and hard. He looked like he wanted to reach out to me, panic etched into his features as he saw the pain in my movements. But we couldn't save each other any more than we could save ourselves.

The Nymphs moved in, dragging the half-conscious man away from him as the rift latched onto Caleb's new power and began to drain it as fast as he had claimed it. His brow pinched as the bloodlust rushed in once more, trying to steal away his mind and provoke the beast in him.

"Stay with me," I pleaded, knowing I couldn't do this without him. This, life, anything.

"I'm trying," he swore, his shoulders trembling as his muscles tightened and he struggled to hold onto his power. The rift was merciless, taking everything from us, and I didn't know how much longer we could last like this.

"Mom," Caleb rasped in concern, and I looked to Melinda, but she was in her own hell, feeding from another victim while Caleb's younger brother Hadley fed on them too.

Sweat raced down my back and my muscles roared in protest as I continued to run, and the only thing that gave me any strength at all was needing to survive this for the people I loved.

Max's features were twisted in anguish, his power fuelled by the fear and panic coiling through the air like poisonous gas. My brother was fighting against the shadows which stole away his magic, but it was no good. Opposite me, my mom, Athena and Grayson were all being fed on by the rift, and the exhaustion in their expressions left me almost barren of hope.

My dad and younger siblings were nowhere to be seen, but I knew they were here, locked away somewhere, the threat of them being next forcing all of us to keep going, keep fighting, but every second that passed only made it harder to do so.

How long could we all go on like this for? There was no way we could survive it forever.

I tried to seek out that place in me which was always full of light. Time and again, I could bring levity to the darkest of situations, but now...I couldn't find anything but a dying ember that had no fuel left to stoke it.

"Cal," I panted as he gazed up at me through hooded eyes, his breaths falling heavily from his chest. "I don't see a way out of this one."

"We always get out," he rasped, though his words were tinted with doubt. Oh man, I'd fucked up big time when it came to him. Was this really how we went out of the world? I was meant to have eternity to figure shit out with him, but now it felt like there was a ticking clock above my head and we were down to our final seconds.

"What if we don't this time?" I voiced my deepest terror and his throat bobbed as another Fae was dragged towards him, the girl kicking and fighting the strength of the Nymphs, but it was a losing battle.

Caleb's eyes trailed to her, the need for more blood making his jaw tick and his shoulders tighten. He wouldn't be able to resist it once they cut her, no matter how strong he was; Vampires were always a slave to this one thing in the end.

I knew now might be my last chance to say everything I'd been holding back on saying to Caleb, but between the cries for help, the terror sizzling through the atmosphere and the hopelessness that was descending on us all like a dark cloud, I couldn't form the words I needed. I didn't want his final memory of me to be some selfish declaration. I wanted him to think of every good moment we'd shared and all the life we'd lived together, even if it wasn't enough. Even if all our plans and dreams for the future died here and now with us, at least we had the good times. At least we had years of laughter and joy in between all the pressures we'd faced together. Me, him, Max and Darius. It had always been the four of us, and it would be the same when we ended up beyond the Veil.

"We always went on adventures together," I gritted out as I fought to keep breathing, though my lungs felt like they were close to bursting.

Caleb nodded firmly. "We'd never leave each other behind."

"Death was always gonna be the last one we faced. And if it's now, then that's far sooner than I wanted. Fuck, I thought we had forever. I thought the four of us were invincible when I was a kid, pretty sure I still felt that way until now."

"It's not over yet," Caleb gritted out, giving me a fierce look that commanded me not to give up. "Darius knows where we are. He'll come back."

"I know. But just in case the stars have other plans, then I want you to know I'm fucking privileged to get to face it with you," I said heavily, and his expression contorted as he saw my acceptance of what was coming for us.

"Maybe there's more adventures waiting for us beyond the stars," he murmured as the girl was shoved down in front of him, her arm slit open with a silver blade.

Caleb's pupils dilated and he fell on the wound ravenously, unable to fight the pull of his Order. My gaze turned to Max, and I found him watching me with all-knowing eyes, a goodbye forged upon his face. By the moon, I loved that face, every inch of it. He was one of the best friends I'd ever had. He was the glue that held us all together, the one who made everything alright. And it had nothing to do with his Siren gifts. It was him. Purely him. His loyalty knew no bounds, and he would walk from one end of this universe to the other for his brothers. His family. I'd damn well do the same for him too.

He nodded to me, no words needing to pass between us. It was an acknowledgement of all we'd ever been to one another, and a promise to follow each other into whatever came after death.

I looked up to the stars as my legs threatened to buckle, seeing no mercy for me in their sparkling eyes. But the moon always had mercy for me, so I looked to her instead and felt her mourning her wolves who stood too far away for her to help. Then I tipped my head back and howled, releasing all the sorrow of the world into that sound as it was echoed by my family.

I felt a shift in the world that set a shiver tracking along my spine, a sense of knowledge filling me as if the stars were offering me a glimpse of our future.

The end was coming. I could feel it everywhere.

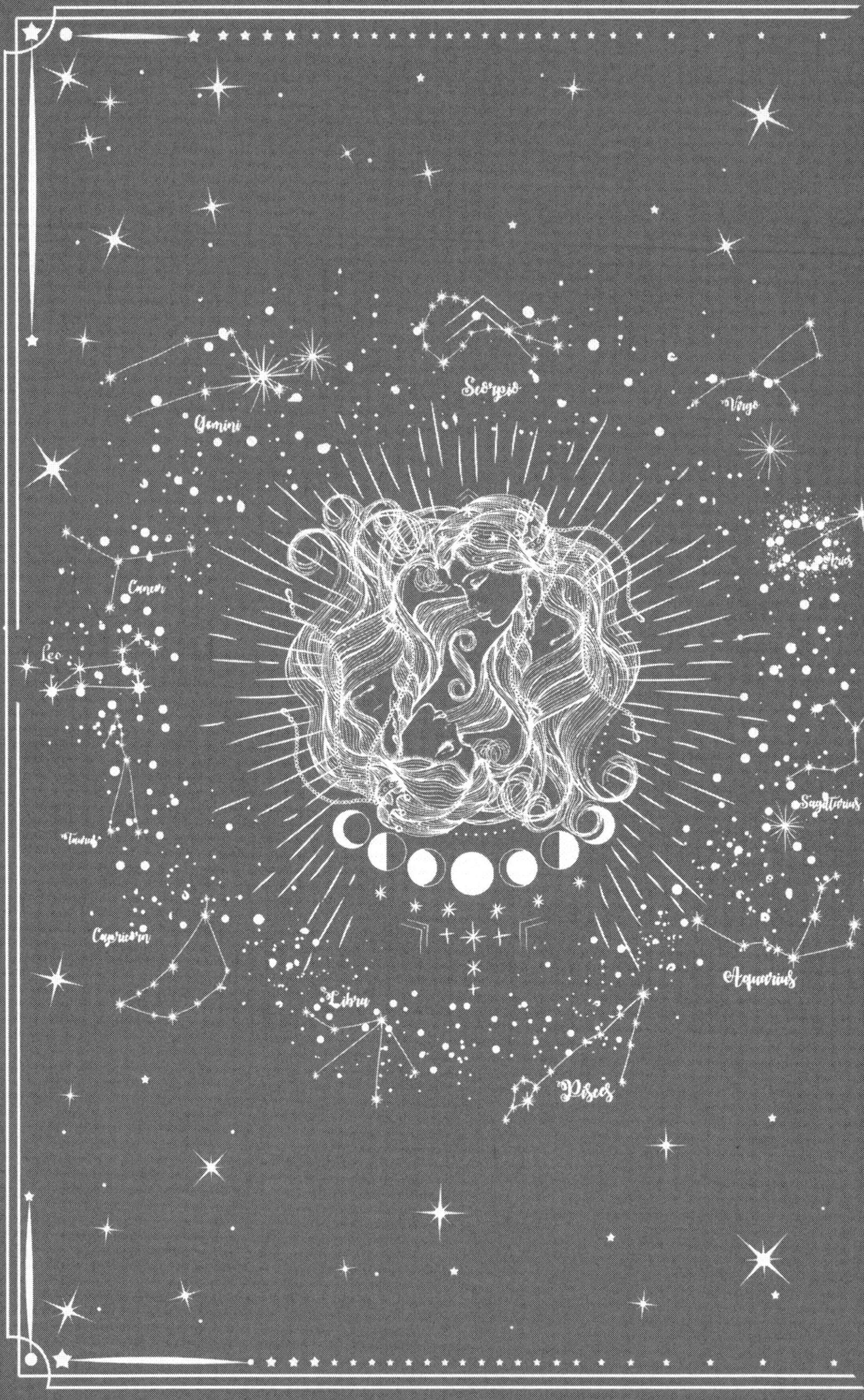
Scorpio
Gemini
Virgo
Cancer
Aries
Leo
Sagittarius
Capricorn
Aquarius
Libra
Pisces

TORY

CHAPTER EIGHT

The wind was harsh against my cheeks, the flames of my wings the only thing fighting off the freezing chill of it as I flew both me and Geraldine ever southward.

We'd left the storm behind, the crash of thunder long since faded into the distance and the depth of night enveloping us as we flew.

"Yonder, my Queen!" Geraldine bellowed, her arm outstretched before her as she pointed to some spot on the horizon which I wasn't able to make out. Maybe that was the gifts of her canine eyesight, or just her instincts, but I wasn't going to question her either way.

I'd thought on all the ways I would take on whatever awaited us at Lionel Acrux's manor before giving in to the reality of what I'd already known anyway.

I was too angry for subtle, too full of rage for calm, I had no patience for clever, nor the time for caution.

I was fury given wings, grief given strength and power given life.

Whoever awaited us in that place would be better off running than trying to stand against the hell I brought with me now.

I beat my wings harder, the air magic which held Geraldine in its grasp hurling her along at my speed while I threw my power into the invisible ties that bound us.

Acrux Manor loomed on the horizon just as the sun began to rise, the blinding light of the new day giving me cover as I swung us around to approach with its blazing rays at my back.

"Oh, in the valley of the fruit of my loins, sweet Petunia shall rise and claim her salmon," Geraldine called, drawing her flail into her hand and beginning to swing it in preparation of a fight.

I lifted us higher, casting a vision enhancing spell on my eyes as I took in the sprawling grounds of the Acrux family home beneath us, the enormous manor house squatting like a spider at the centre of it.

The wards were still in place surrounding it, but I kept us high above them, hiding in the eye of the dawning sun. We looked down at the group of figures who were clustered in a garish courtyard to the rear of the property, stone Dragons standing around the horrors taking place beneath us.

"What is that?" I gasped, my eyes falling on a ribbon of darkness which pulsed and hummed with the shadows at the centre of the space, the Fae surrounding it looking like worshipers at some ungodly altar.

"Oh my petals," Geraldine breathed, her voice almost lost to the wind buffeting us as I used my magic to create a platform of air she could stand on at my side. "A rift."

My heart free-fell as that realisation struck me, the figures surrounding that dark abyss no longer looking like worshippers as I took in the reality of what they were. Slaves.

"The Heirs," I hissed, my attention flicking between the people who were shackled to that vile thing by chains of iron and magic. I spotted Caleb first, his golden hair plastered to his scalp and blood colouring his chin and shirt. Beside him, Seth ran on a rolling mound of earth, other Wolves who I belatedly recognised as his mom and siblings trapped on similar magical contraptions too.

"What tangled tentacles have you gotten yourself coiled in, Maxy Boy?" Geraldine growled, her Cerberus rattling in her words like the beast inside of her wished to break free. Max was kneeling before a group of Nymphs who were torturing helpless Fae, his face a picture of distress as his Siren powers fed on their pain.

My lip peeled back in a snarl as I took in everything I could about the scene below us; the captives, the Nymphs, the darkness surrounding each and every one of them.

"What say you, my Queen?" Geraldine demanded as she swung her flail in furious moves, the spiked ball passing around and around above her head, between her legs and in figure eights all around her body while she limbered up for the fight.

My eyes darted back and forth over every man, woman and beast in that courtyard, and a feral smile twisted my lips as I decided.

"When the opportunity presents itself can you shield everyone who counts with your water magic?" I asked, looking to my greatest friend and Geraldine's eyes sparked with a wild, depraved kind of excitement as her blood red hair whipped out behind her in the wind.

"By golly, I'd say I can, milady."

"Good."

Without another word, I drew my sword and dropped from the sky like a stone, Geraldine right beside me, propelled along by the air magic which bound us as one.

"For honour and death and the true queens!" Geraldine cried, her words lost to the wind as we hurtled down so fast that the world became nothing but a blur around us.

I held my sword up, Phoenix fire bursting along the length of it as the power of the wards hummed beneath us and as I swung it with a furious cry, a bird of red and blue flames erupted from its tip.

Power exploded from me as I threw everything I had into the blast, striking the wards with the might of the hammer of Thor.

The noise they made as they shattered was something akin to a tidal wave breaking apart the sky. All eyes beneath us turned upward as the power of the Acrux line, which had stood unchallenged for far too long, buckled and broke beneath the might of a Vega.

Down we plummeted, a battle cry escaping me while Geraldine howled with a trio of voices, baying for a vengeance we both needed more than life itself.

Magic poured from me as I slammed into the ground, tiles and earth shattering beneath me as my power took the force of my landing and I came to a halt in a crouch with the tip of my sword piercing the stone at my feet.

Geraldine landed to my right, flail swinging and magic building all around her as she raised her other hand defensively. An echoing beat of silence fell as everyone just stared in shock at our arrival.

"Long live the true queens," Geraldine hissed, and I felt myself smiling a cruel and wicked smile as I raised my flame-coated sword and prepared to fight.

Seth, Caleb, Max, the Councillors and the Spares were all on their knees or running on treadmills cast from the earth itself, surrounding an altar of onyx stone which sat so heavily on the flagstones that cracks spread from it in every direction as though it had fallen from a great height before landing here.

I briefly cast my eyes over all of them, taking in the cuts to their wrists where both blood and magic poured endlessly towards the twisting, swirling vortex of shadows standing above that soulless stone.

They looked back at me in a mixture of awe and horror, no doubt fearing that my magic would join with theirs if the surrounding Nymphs and enemy Fae got their way. But there was no chance of that. I'd come here to reunite with my friends, and I would gladly end any who stood between us.

"Gerry," Max gasped, staring at her in wonder even as he fought to get the word past his cracked lips. "*Run.*"

"Not on your nelly," she scoffed, flail swinging as she set her eyes on the Nymphs closest to her and took off with a bark of challenge.

A flash of movement caught my eye and I lurched aside, the lessons the Phoenix queen had taught me making my reflexes sharper than ever as the thin blade hurtled towards me. A wall of heat flared out from my skin, melting it from existence in the blink of an eye just as my gaze met with Vard's.

The Seer stared at me in horror from his one remaining eye as I hefted my sword and ran at him with a battle cry.

Vard shrieked an order for the Nymphs to attack and before I could close in on him, I found myself surrounded by four of the creatures at once, their bark-covered limbs reaching for me as their rattles drowned out thought and magic alike.

The weight of their power crashed into me, but I didn't buckle beneath it, calling on my Phoenix as my entire body was gilded in the flames of my Order form, and my sword swung with precise lethality.

Black blood sprayed the tiles as the first Nymph's head came crashing to the ground, and I leapt through the smoke that erupted from its corpse to tackle the next, my blade puncturing its heart before it even realised I was upon it.

"The needle!" Caleb cried from somewhere behind me, but I couldn't spare him a glance as I parried a strike from one Nymphs' probes and kicked the second in the chest hard enough to send it crashing to the ground.

More of them were rushing for me already, but I simply ran into the fray, fire blazing so brightly all around me that any who got too close were cast to ash, while others drew weapons of their own to fight me.

"The binding needle!" Caleb yelled again as I spun beneath the outstretched blade of one Nymph, before slicing my sword across the backs of another's knees.

My head snapped around at that, the words puncturing the frenzied bloodlust I'd fallen into and making me pause.

The hesitation cost me too much. Pain flared along my back as a Nymph swung a war hammer into my spine, but the shield of air I held tight to my skin took the brunt of the blow, leaving me free to turn and impale the beast upon my sword.

"What ho, my lady?" Geraldine cried as she leapt overhead on a column of water, her flail circling savagely and crashing into the skull of a Nymph who had been charging for her.

"Close that rift," I commanded her, unable to turn and hunt for the needle myself as five more Nymphs charged me at once.

The press of their power weighed my magic down heavily, but I gritted my teeth, sinking deeper into the might of my Order and throwing a blast of air magic away from me which sent them all flying.

The Heirs and their families cried out as the power collided with them too, but the chains securing them to the ground ensured they went nowhere despite the force of it.

I needed to get the Nymphs and Lionel's followers away from the Heirs and their families, draw them far enough from here for Geraldine to shield our people while I blasted every last one of our enemies with Phoenix fire and watched them burn. But every time I tried to lead them away from the rift, they herded me back towards it, their numbers forcing me closer than I could afford to be if I was ever going to unleash that power.

So it looked like I'd be cutting them down one by one.

As my blade swung again and my muscles burned with the force required to cleave flesh and bone, I found myself not minding that so much.

I wanted to feel this. I wanted an outlet for the fury in me. So if I had to carve my way through every single creature who had sworn allegiance to Lionel Acrux before making it to him, then I would do so. And I didn't give a fuck what fate had to say on the subject.

Scorpio
Virgo
Gemini
Aries
Cancer
Leo
Sagittarius
Taurus
Capricorn
Aquarius
Libra
Pisces

GERALDINE

CHAPTER NINE

I swung the Flail of Unending Celestial Karma into the face of a shrieking Nymph, casting him to ash, his smoky innards becoming his outtards as he floated away on the breeze.

I hollered my victory, warbling it high and true for all to hear.

Caleb was making one hell of a racket, jerking his chin yonder and crying, "The binding needle!" while that rapscallion of a hound, Seth, howled along with him.

"Get it, Gerry!" my dear, sweet ocean boy called to me, and I ran toward him, flail a-swinging. Oh bless my moonstones, I had missed him something fierce.

My queen was striking down enemies left and right, her glorious Phoenix fire cutting through barky flesh and barky bone, killing our enemies in a rain of might and murder I would never forget. My heart had been weeping not hours ago for my dear Daddy, but now I could put that pain to action, to howl to the dawn and cry vengeance to the sky.

"For Daddy dearest!" I swore, leaping over Maxy boy's head, and slamming my flail into the chest of another nefarious Nymph, turning it to shadow before my very eyes as my feet hit the ground.

"There," Caleb urged, his fangs glinting like the seas of Noonbar and his gallant blue eyes full of an unbridled desperation.

I saw what he spoke of at last, a binding needle perched upon the ground, discarded and forgotten. Great gandergeese! Its power could save our fellows from the rift that fed on their souls.

I did a roly-poly across the ground, avoiding the swipe of a Nymph's probes and snatching the binding needle into my grasp.

"Hoorah!" I bleated.

"Yes – go on, Geraldine," Seth called while he ran upon a never-ending wheel of stone beneath his feet. I gripped his arm to pull myself skyward, leaping onto his shoulders and springing lithely from them onto the altar of doom as he cursed my kickers.

I kept myself well back from the rift which sucked and sapped at my skin like a yowling ghoul of Caloop out for my blood. But not this day. No, for this day was a day of victory and cunning. We would outwit the false king, and free our merry men from his grasp.

Tory moved like a viper, striking left and right, ducking the fierce blows of her assailants before driving her gleaming sword into their chests. I was so dazzled by her display, that I almost didn't move in time as a Nymph heaved a deck chair into its hold and threw it at my noggin.

But oh-ho! I did move. Like a lily pad on the back of a jiffy frog, I ducked, and the chair went crashing to the ground somewhere yonder, Hadley Altair crying out in alarm as it darn near hit him where he was chained with the rest.

A spear of ice and malice saw the Nymph dead, shadows spiralling for the sky before it could hurl so much as an insult my way and I grinned at another bloody victory to my tally.

"Never fear, young brother of the Callyfang!" I called to Hadley. "I am your rescuer, your knightess in gleaming breastplate!"

I rolled up my sleeves, facing the wild and hungry rift and lifting the binding needle into the air.

"I am Geraldine Gundellifus Gabolia Gundestria Grus, and I shall return these shadows from whence they came in the name of my father and his love for Catalina!" I began to knit the rift closed, my hips rocking and swaying, my knees bending and flexing as I put all I had into the rhythm of my task.

The Heirs and their families were cheering me on while the marvellous Phoenix queen tore through the ranks of our foes, and I worked to free our friends from this wicked void.

My gaze fell on my Maxy boy, and my heart was clad in sun steel as I focused on this valiant man who had proved he was not a cad, but a gentleFae with the deepest ocean of love in his heart.

I would claim him this day, and nevermore would I seek the loins of another codfish. For he was my one true salmon, and the rivers of our destiny were wide and flowing toward an eternal horizon. It was time to bathe in our estuary and sup upon the freshwater, and may all those who opposed us perish on my flail.

Scorpio
Gemini
Virgo
Aries
Cancer
Leo
Sagittarius
Taurus
Capricorn
Aquarius
Libra
Pisces

MAX

CHAPTER TEN

My body quaked with the effort of trying to resist the call of the shadows as Gerry shouted at the top of her lungs, "Out with the darkness and in with the light! All shall burn beneath my lady's might!"

Tory was locked in battle with the Nymphs to our right, holding them back through fury and violence alone. I scrambled up onto my knees as I turned my head towards her, craning my neck to watch as Phoenix fire blazed from her body and her enemies fell all around her.

More were coming though. I could feel the dark rot of their emotions churning the air as they raced our way from somewhere beyond the manor walls, their bloodlust and sick thirst choking me as my gifts wrapped around them and I forced myself to start counting.

"The Vega line runs true," Melinda Altair breathed from her position across the altar, and I could hear the awe in her voice as she watched one of the girls who had been born to sit upon the throne fight with such incredible power.

"There are around fifty Nymphs headed this way," I yelled, and Caleb's head snapped around as he looked to me to confirm my words.

His jaw and chest were covered with the blood of the Fae he'd been forced to feed from, and the haunted look in his eyes let me know how close to the surface that monstrous part of him resided, the hope there fading at my announcement.

"How long?" Seth panted as the rock beneath his feet continued to rotate, forcing him to run even though the sun had now fully crested the horizon, the Fae who had been in charge of the magic now caught up in the fight.

"Five minutes," I said, cringing away from the presence closing in on us and drawing the power of my gifts back to me. "If we're lucky."

"Luck has nothing to do with this roll of the dice, sweet salamander," Geraldine cooed as she drove the binding needle into the fabric of the world itself and tugged, that slice of hell growing smaller with every pull of her arm as she fought to seal the rift.

Sweat lined her brow and the set of her jaw was more than enough to tell me how hard she was fighting to channel the dark magic and end that thing, her own power waning with the effort required to do it.

She was magnificent. Blood splattered and furious, a queen in no need of a crown, her hair a river of blood red, come here like some avenging angel, fighting against hopeless odds without so much as a flinch of fear.

"If you can't close it in time, you have to run, Gerry," I begged her. "If those Nymphs arrive before you can-"

"I do not recall asking for the advice of a doubtful dogfish," she ground out. "Nor do I recall you having the heart of a cowardly lionfish, Maxy boy. Tell me, did the rift suck out your heart of ice alongside siphoning away your power, or are you simply going all wet in the whistle over me in particular?"

I could feel my father's eyes on me as I shook my head, but I didn't care. It didn't matter anymore anyway, not when I could feel our end closing in on us and the only ray of light I cared to look upon was the woman standing up on that black altar before me.

"Nothing in this world could break me the way you can, Gerry," I admitted roughly. "Nothing could make me falter or blink other than the need to protect you. I can't watch them lash you to this thing with us. It would rip the last pieces of me free of my body and destroy them more certainly than anything else."

Geraldine's cheeks darkened with a blush as she fought to push the binding needle into the edge of the rift once more, the last foot of it pulsing and bulging like a living thing that was fighting to resist its end.

"Then I suggest you turn your efforts from trying to dissuade me and focus instead on cheering me on," she replied. "For my feet are now soldered to this spot, my will iron and my focus fixed like a flan on a Friday. I shall not yield this position to any but death, and if its dark minions come calling for old Grussy, I shall fight them to the bitter end while seeing this most precious of tasks fulfilled. My queen bid me here, and here I shall stand, even if the great wide yonder comes to gobble me up."

"Geraldine," I snarled, my gifts reaching for her as I fought to make her see reason.

A cry of pain had us all turning our eyes towards Tory as a Nymph managed to get around her defences, and blood poured from a slice which had been carved down her side beneath her arm.

The Nymph which had struck her exploded in a blaze of blue and red flames just as Tory slapped a hand to her side and froze the wound solid before the whip of shadows spiralling from the rift towards her could make contact. She cursed at the pain, but it worked, the shadows recoiling once more to feast on those of us still tethered to it, but it was as if the scent of her blood on the air had awoken the most beastly nature of every Nymph who remained.

The Nymphs shrieked as they lunged at her, no longer seeming to have any care for self-preservation as they converged around her recklessly, probes extended and rattles filling the air with such potency that my own magic guttered and died within my chest.

We lost sight of her in the throng of creatures, Seth howling balefully while Caleb roared her name.

"Gobble, gobble, gobble!" Geraldine bellowed, the binding needle flashing in the light of the breaking dawn as she drove it in and out of the air faster than before. Sweat glistened on her skin, her limbs trembling with fatigue, and as I sent my Siren power towards her, I felt the press of her exhaustion crashing into me like a solid force.

"Let me in!" I demanded.

I pressed my gifts at her, offering what little strength I had and begging her to accept it as the chains which held me cut into my flesh and made me bleed even more.

The shadows latched onto those wounds as they formed, my magic pouring from me faster than it had before. The rift guzzled at it greedily, even though only a few drops of it remained.

Geraldine relented, her mental barriers falling, and my gifts broke into the ocean of her mind like I'd jumped from a clifftop to descend into the purest blue sea.

I threw my strength into her, not caring one bit for my own needs and giving all of what I had to her, begging the stars to offer us just a few more seconds so she might finish this like she'd sworn to.

I couldn't allow for any other fate. Not for her. She was my everything.

My vision blurred, a sea of pastel coloured fish swimming all around my head as I lost myself within Geraldine's mind and felt my hold on my own body slipping. It didn't matter. Not while she was still fighting on. I gave and gave, pressing every bit of strength left from me into her so that she might do this, even as I heard the next wave of Nymphs come crashing out into the courtyard.

"Oh fuck," Seth said and the hopeless tone to his voice told me all I needed to know about the legion which had just arrived.

A flare of power brushed against mine, as familiar as a summer breeze and ten times as powerful. My father's Siren spell, his gifts scorching a path alongside my own towards the girl who fought to free us as the Nymphs closed in.

She wasn't going to stop. Not even to defend herself. The rift was almost closed, and I knew that she would sacrifice her own life to see it shut if that was what it took.

My terror at the mere thought of that set something blazing not just within me but within the power that had joined mine. With a surge of our gifts, both me and my father gave that beautiful girl every bit of strength we still possessed.

"Who comes to take down the last pillar of the Grus empire?" Geraldine roared as she drove the binding needle into the air one last time. "Who presumes to defy the will of the true queens? Come forth and rip me from this rock of shadow and whisperings if you so dare, but know this – I fight in the name of all that is, was and will be. And you, shall. Not. Smite. Me!"

The needle plunged into the void between worlds for one final time, snapping the rift closed with a brutal finality that sent me and all of us who had been tethered to it crashing to the ground, releasing us at last.

I cracked my eyes open to stare up at Geraldine as three Nymphs leapt for her, but she rocketed towards the sky on a pillar of water before they managed to so much as brush the toes of her boots with their probes.

The Nymphs screeched, unleashing their rattles as Geraldine took a pouch from her pocket and stuffed a handful of aconite into her mouth before ripping through her clothes as she shifted and fell from the sky right into the midst of the hellish creatures. Her armour shot away from her in every direction, Athena yelling in fright as the pointed breastplate damn near impaled her. Hadley caught hold of her, yanking her tight to his side and kicking the piece of armour away from her like it had been *him* it had almost taken out.

Four mighty paws hit the ground with a rattle that made the tiles beneath me tremble and Geraldine bayed like a bloodhound on the heels of a fresh kill with all three of her mighty heads.

She ripped into the Nymphs, black blood spraying from three sets of jaws while her huge paws swiped and kicked, sending even more of them tumbling away from her.

The sound of shattering glass made me whip around and my eyes widened as I took in the forms of three frozen Nymphs. Tory carved her way free of their bodies by shattering another of their companions, her dark eyes blazing in a way that made my heart skip a beat.

Her green gaze took in the empty patch of air which had held the rift and she smiled in a feral, terrifying way that instantly made me think of the Savage King who had sired her.

"Now, Geraldine!" she cried, the voice of a queen breaking over the sound of battle.

My girl lifted her three bloodstained heads to howl her agreement and she broke into a run, making the Nymphs scatter and fall back from the altar, the monsters heading towards Tory and away from us.

I managed to summon the strength to push myself to my feet, the cut to my wrist still dripping blood, though I barely even noticed it as I watched the powerful beast that was the girl I loved racing our way.

Geraldine took a running jump, soaring over our heads and I spun to watch her as she shifted in mid-air, landing straight in the centre of the stone altar in her Fae form, butt naked and releasing a warrior's cry.

Magic exploded from her in a wave of water that crashed past everyone who was chained to the altar, surrounding us and the Fae who had been chained and tortured to feed me and the other Sirens, before solidifying into a dome of ice that shimmered with power all around us.

The explosion that followed a moment later nearly knocked me from my feet, the ground bucking, heat blazing over the shield that protected us and making water drip down onto our heads as the ice began to melt beneath the onslaught of fire.

With a shuddering gasp, Geraldine maintained the shield for a few more seconds before stumbling to her knees, the water washing away in a great wave as it melted, revealing the princess of flames who stood among a pile of ash beyond it.

My lips parted as I took in the destruction that Tory had woven with her power, not a Nymph in sight and the closest wall of the enormous manor house which had stood at our backs reduced to rubble too.

Flames licked at the rooms which had been exposed by the damage to the building and for several long moments, all any of us could do was stare at the girl in the epicentre of that blast.

Tory Vega stared back at us with her chest heaving and blood still frozen to her side from that massive wound. More cuts and bruises were revealed across her skin as she released her hold on her Phoenix and the fire guttered from her body, her wings disappearing with it, leaving the girl I knew standing in place of the creature of legend we had all just witnessed wielding power beyond all measure.

"Stars save us all," Antonia Capella murmured, her eyes moving to the blue sky overhead as if she might see through the rising dawn to the glimmering entities above.

The crunch of bare feet moving across broken debris made me turn again, finding Geraldine striding towards me with her body on full display to anyone who cared to glance her way and a look in her eyes which could set the world alight once more.

"Gerry, where are your-" I began, but she cut me off as she caught hold of the back of my neck and propelled me against her body. Her other arm banded around my spine and before I'd fully realised what was happening, I found her dipping me backwards as she claimed my mouth with her own, and I clung to her like a damn barnacle on the hull of a ship.

Any protests I may have wanted to make died on my tongue at the taste of that kiss though, my heart skipping and racing and damn near galloping its way through my chest. I gave in to the call of her, her song more powerful than even the lure of the greatest Sirens on earth.

Geraldine kissed me like she owned me, and in that moment, and likely all other moments too, she did. I was her creature for better or worse and she had come for me in the dark when I needed her most.

Geraldine released me suddenly, setting me back on my feet and slapping me so hard my face whirled to the side, the sting of her palm marking my skin as I swore at her and stumbled back a step.

"What the fuck was that for?"

"For getting yourself tangled up in this hilly holly and leaving me to wonder if I would ever set eyes upon your salacious face again, that's what, you wandering kipper."

"Gerry," I ground out, reaching for her but instead of letting me take her hand, she took hold of the chains which bound me and severed them with the force of her earth magic.

I rubbed at the point where the manacle had held me, and she stalked away to free Seth next. He leapt at her, licking her face and making me swear louder as I stalked towards them, pulling my shirt off as I approached.

"Thank you, Batty Betty," he exhaled, squeezing her hard enough to make her yip.

"Yes, yes, that's quite enough wilting and welping. Now let me see what I can do for you all, I'm a little low on power though," she said breathlessly while batting him off. "But I'll heal what I can when I've had a moment to recover."

"Put this on," I snarled, thrusting the shirt into her face while she sighed loudly like I was nothing but a burden set on this world to torment her.

"You and your worries about my wandering petunia will be the end of me one of these days," she grouched, though she took the shirt and shrugged it on before moving to free Caleb next.

Seth dove on him, hugging him tight and licking Caleb's cheek. I ran over to them, and Seth yanked me into the fold of their arms, all of us clinging to one another, the power of our unit missing just one vital piece. Seth whimpered anxiously, still pawing at Caleb's golden curls and nuzzling my neck.

"I thought we were goners. Real, for true goners," Seth said.

"We can't die," Cal said a little breathlessly. "We're Bitey C, Wolfman, and Fish Fury."

"You remembered," Seth gasped.

"Of course I fucking remembered." Caleb scruffed Seth's long hair and I managed an actual laugh, shoving Seth in the shoulder.

Geraldine tried to leave us to it, and I stalked after her, but she shrugged me off, moving to release everyone else while I just trailed her like a whipped little bitch. But if destiny was kind enough to allow me to be her whipped bitch, then I was all for it. I was hers in any way she would take me and damn the consequences.

When she broke the shackles from my father's limbs, he almost collapsed, his arms crashing around me as he hauled me close and choked out a laugh that was half sob.

"I thought I was going to die while knowing you would follow me beyond the Veil," he breathed, his grip unyielding as I gave into the warmth of his embrace and held him in return.

"I never should have agreed to you staying in Lionel's company for so long," I ground out in reply, hating myself for not insisting on him joining us at The Burrows before this came to pass.

"Since when do I run my choices by you?" Dad joked as he pulled back, his palm encompassing my cheek as he looked me over.

"Perhaps you should in future," I replied steadily, and he nodded in solemn agreement as he looked around to check on the other Councillors as they were released from their bonds too.

"Where's Ellis?" I asked, my sister's absence prickling at me just as it had since I'd first noticed it. But it had been hard to so much as hold onto my own name while tethered to that rift, let alone ask questions about the only Spare missing from this circus of depravity.

"Some of the family members were kept inside as further motivation for us to cooperate," Dad said, but I felt a touch of his discomfort as he said the words, the taste of a lie hanging between us.

"But you don't think she's with them?" I pressed.

Dad sighed, his shoulders slumping as he shook his head. "They wanted me to believe that she and your stepmother were being held with Melinda and Antonia's husbands and younger children, but I felt the smugness coming from Linda when she was led inside. The feeling of accomplishment and the…excitement. I fear they have truly thrown their lot in with Lionel and helped with this ruse to trap us here."

I blew out a shallow breath, some small part of me disappointed at that news even if it didn't surprise me. Linda could go to hell for all I cared; I hoped she burned for her choice to ally with that son of a bitch. But Ellis… My sister may have been a brat and more ambitious than her abilities really allowed for, but she was still my blood at the end of the day. What would it mean for her fate now that she had chosen to align herself on the other side of this war?

"So," Dad said, a quirk to his lips and the shift in his mood alerting me to the object of his attention as I glanced over my shoulder towards Geraldine. "It's the Grus girl then, is it?"

"Yeah," I replied as I watched Geraldine bark orders at anyone close enough to follow them, her upper lip curling back in a canine snarl of distaste as she picked up her breast plate which had landed in a puddle of black blood. "It is."

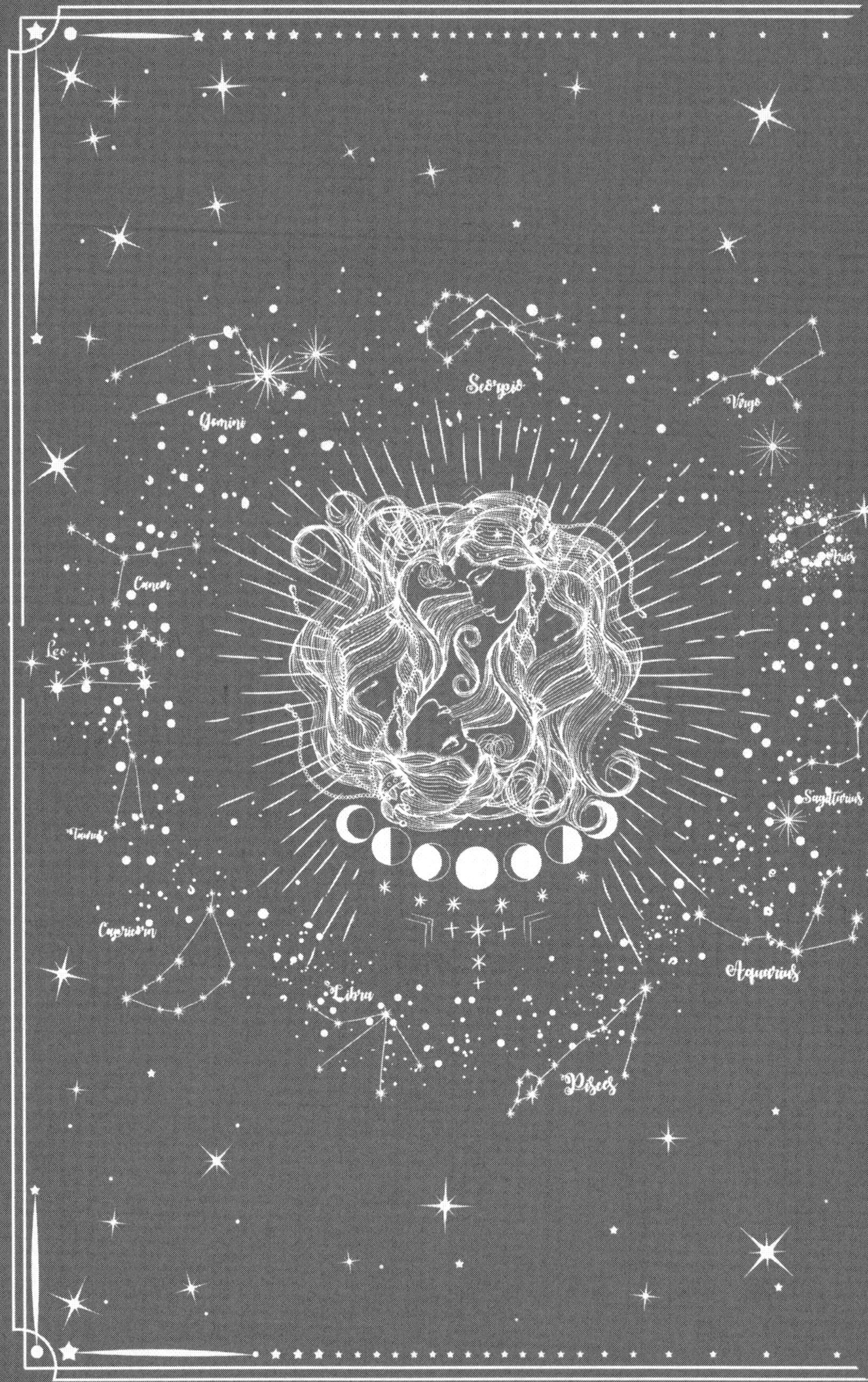

Scorpio
Gemini
Virgo
Cancer
Aries
Leo
Sagittarius
Taurus
Capricorn
Aquarius
Libra
Pisces

TORY

CHAPTER ELEVEN

I knelt among the ashes of the Nymphs and Fae who had been fighting me, my breaths heavy as the adrenaline which had kept me fighting on still danced in my limbs, my heart racing to an erratic pace.

Through a curtain of dark hair, I watched Geraldine free the Heirs and their families, offering them healing magic while replenishing her own by chewing on some aconite leaves she'd had in her pocket. Relief found me in some distant way as I watched them all rise on unsteady feet, casting aside the shackles which had been binding them to their doom.

I leaned on my sword, the tip pressing heavily into the flagstones beneath me as it took my weight. It might have been the only thing keeping me from collapsing entirely at that point.

I let my eyes shutter, darkness welcoming me and instantly pressing images of chaos through my mind as I relived the worst of the things that haunted me through brief moments. Where was Darcy? Gabriel? Orion?

My hands shook where I gripped the sword, pain threatening to swallow me whole alongside my fear for the three of them as I saw Darius lying on that hilltop again, coloured with blood, his soul passed over.

"Fuck," I hissed, the word barely sliding between my teeth.

I gripped the hilt of my sword tighter, feeling the ridge of the scar which now marked my palm and bound me to the oath I'd made him and the stars. I just had no idea how I was supposed to honour it.

I turned my mind from grief and gave myself over to the anger that sustained me now. Nothing would get done if I remained a crumpled wreck on this broken floor.

I took a hand from my sword and moved it to the jagged wound running down my side, the ice I'd used to seal it forming blood-soaked crystals across my skin and clothes.

I pressed my fingers against the wound, sucking in a sharp breath at the pain shooting through me, my spine arching involuntarily as my thoughts snapped together with a little more focus. That was a pain I could handle, one solid and real and so much less ruinous than what I was battling inside of myself.

"You're hurt," Caleb's voice brought me back into the moment, and I withdrew my fingers from the wound.

"A little," I admitted.

Even I could hear the raw edge to my voice, the dark that was creeping in to contaminate my soul.

I expelled a shuddering breath and rose, pushing my weight down on my sword as I did so before swiping my hair away from my face and looking into the dark blue eyes of my friend.

Caleb looked like shit, his eyes haunted and cheeks hollow. Blood stained his chin, the front of his shirt was torn and dishevelled, and his normally pristine blonde curls were a mess of tangles and knots. But he was alive.

I threw my arms around him as the reality of that sunk in. One less name on my list of the lost. Three less in fact. And as Seth bounded over and threw his arms around the two of us with a bark of relieved laughter, I let myself hold them tight, my wound singing with pain as they crushed me between them, my heart feeling lighter than it had since I left that battlefield behind.

We broke apart too soon, the press of urgency driving us into action as I turned to face the manor. Lionel's pride and joy. This soulless monstrosity of a house which had always felt so cold and barren whenever I'd visited it. It had never been a home. Not to Catalina or Xavier or…*him.*

This place had been a prison of the worst design. I doubted even all that Darius had shared with me, and what Catalina had implied, came close to a full account of the horrors Lionel Acrux had inflicted upon the three of them while they were trapped here with him.

"I'm going to burn it down," I announced, flames igniting in my hands at the thought, an empty kind of pleasure lighting within me just as fast.

"Wait." Caleb took hold of my arm with a shot of Vampire speed, his fearful tone making me pause. "My father is in there somewhere. Or at least, I think he is. My little sisters too and Seth's dad and younger siblings, Max's step-mom and-"

"I don't think we'll find Linda in there," Max's deep voice carried to us in a low rumble as he moved to join us.

I reached out on instinct, the warmth of his skin enveloping mine as he took my hand without hesitation.

A look passed between us which said more than words might convey, but as I felt his gifts reaching out for my emotions, I slammed a mental wall of thickest iron into place to keep him locked out.

Max frowned in surprise, his gifts withdrawing out of respect for my privacy while his dark eyes filled with questions I couldn't answer now. I didn't even have the words to answer them anyway. The words which would break them just as surely as the truth of them had broken me.

Darius is dead.

I withdrew my hand and blew out a breath, reminding myself of the reasons I had to stay upright, moving forward, fighting. I had people who needed me and an oath to fulfil.

I ground my jaw, glancing first at Caleb who looked utterly shattered and in no state to go racing around Acrux Manor in search of anyone, then at Max, who looked in a similar state of exhaustion, but who at least wouldn't have to move to hunt for the rest of the Heirs' families.

I wouldn't tell them about Darius yet, not while we needed to focus on escaping this place before Lionel could show up. I had no doubt someone would get word to him of my attack on his home soon enough, and as much as I ached for a taste of his blood, I knew I wouldn't win that battle today.

"Can you find the rest of your families with your gifts?" I asked Max, my fingers moving to the edge of that jagged wound again and pressing down.

Pain thickened my throat with a cry I refused to let out, focusing my mind. I swallowed thickly as Max closed his eyes and reached out with his gifts to find Caleb's dad and the others through emotion alone.

"They're inside," he confirmed. "In the west tower, scared but unhurt, so far as

I can tell."

"Are they being guarded?" I asked and he frowned a moment before shaking his head.

"I guess whoever had been in charge of that came out here to fight. Either that or they ran."

I nodded and turned towards the half-destroyed wall of the house which would serve as our entrance point, then fell still as I found myself face to face with the three Councillors who had stood at the side of my enemy for so many years.

Tension filled the air between us as the seconds stretched. It spoke of the rivalry I'd held against their sons since the moment Darcy and I had arrived in Solaria, and the strength of the power that each of us possessed.

It almost seemed as though one of us should bow, though whether that was me or them, I couldn't tell, and my spine remained ramrod straight in defiance of such a thought.

"When you dropped from the sky like that, I could have sworn I was looking at your mother," Melinda Altair broke the silence, and a lump thickened my throat at yet another Fae who I should have had in my life but had been stolen from me by fate. Or more accurately, by Lionel Acrux.

She was wearing what had once been a white pants and shirt combo, her feet bare and blood coating her jaw and clothes. I had never once seen so much as a coil of her blonde hair out of place before that moment, and I blinked as I took her in, seeing past that perfect facade she usually let the world see and looking at the woman who stood beneath the mask. Her eyes burned with a fierceness which let me know we were more than alike in our hatred of Lionel Acrux, and I found my resentment toward her and her years of alliance with our shared enemy softening just a little.

"We carry the souls of those we love closest in times of need," I replied, the words feeling unlike my own, yet I supposed they were true all the same.

"Thank you," Antonia Capella said softly, her earthy brown eyes roaming over me curiously while shining with gratitude so clearly that I couldn't deny it. There was something extremely lupine in the way she held herself, her eyes blazing with the silver irises of her Wolf and her teeth bared like she expected an attack at any moment, but I felt no shred of animosity from her, just that urgent desire for vengeance that she and the others now shared.

I wasn't sure I was worthy of her gratitude, and I certainly didn't feel capable of a reply without spilling every secret I was hoarding between us right now. About the battle we'd lost, the grief we all faced, the brother who the men at my back didn't even realise was dead yet.

I blinked hard, inclining my head just a little in acknowledgement of her thanks before turning towards the manor once more.

"We can't linger here," I said simply. "Lionel will find out what's happened to his precious mansion soon and none of you look ready for a fight."

"I'll go and get Dad out," Caleb said firmly, shooting away with his mom and brother before any of us could protest the idea of us splitting up.

I bit my tongue on my irritation over that.

"What ho, my lady?" Geraldine called as she strode over to join us, stomping into the space between Antonia Capella, Tiberius Rigel, and me as if it had been a void just waiting for a powerhouse to step in and claim it.

She was buckling her armour back on, the straps securing it spelled to quick release when she shifted, meaning it all went back onto her body smoothly. Even if the shirt and pants beneath it had been reduced to half-shredded tatters which revealed a whole lot of ass cheek and side boob. The shirt Max had given her to wear slapped him in the face as he began to protest the exposed skin she was now flaunting, and he cursed as she commanded him to cover his own 'nippoleons' if he was so opposed to anyone seeing any.

"Do you have enough stardust to get us out of here?" Seth asked, leaning in to nuzzle the side of my face like he just couldn't help himself.

I allowed it, seeing as I'd actually missed the mutt and his boundary-crossing bullshit. Hard to believe I ever would have felt that way about the asshole who had cut my sister's hair off, but there it was.

"No," I replied, wincing at the truth of that fact. "Maybe we could take a few of the cars from the garage…" My voice trailed off as I considered that, the idea of me riding one of Darius's motorbikes both seriously tempting and utterly unthinkable.

"If Lionel comes for us, a few cars won't be much use in outrunning him," Max murmured. "Where are we heading anyway? What happened with the fight at The Burrows? What-"

"This isn't the time for lollygagging, you simpering salamander," Geraldine interrupted before I could force some words out, lies or poor attempts at explanations wouldn't get us far here and I didn't want to make them face the truth until they had the time and space to process it. "There is much to tell you." Her voice cracked but she forged on. "But the moment is not nigh. We must focus on our escape from this rotten cesspit of a household, and we can fill you in on all you need know after the fact. Though I do have to wonder what form of transportation we should take. For without the aid of stardust, I fear the great Dragoon will indeed come a-hunting for us before long. But of course, I have no doubt you could end the foul beast in such a battle if you needed to, my Queen."

"Not if he brings an army with him," I muttered, my brow furrowing at the problem before I remembered something Darius had told me. On one of those endless nights where we'd filled each other in on every detail of ourselves and the rot of our upbringings, he'd once said that beneath Acrux Manor, his father held a trove of Dragon treasure greater than any other in the land, filled with gems and jewels and every form of valuable item you could imagine, including a hoard of stardust…

"I have an idea," I announced suddenly, only realising that I'd spoken over Tiberius and Antonia as the two of them both turned somewhat shocked expressions my way. But if they were going to expect me to simper and grovel like every other Fae they were used to dealing with, then they were all kinds of wrong about that. "Wait here, get everyone ready to leave. I'll be back as soon as I can with our way out of here."

I didn't bother to wait for a response, turning and striding across the heaped rubble which had once been the rear wall to this section of the manor, making my way inside.

Seth bounded after me with the energy of a puppy despite all he'd just endured, and I glanced at him as he moved to nudge me lightly, knocking his shoulder against mine.

"Remember that time I peed on you?" he sighed nostalgically. "Who would have thought we'd end up here, Wolfman and Bitchy Flame Eyes striding into yet another adventure side by side with Fish Fury and Batty Betty bringing up the rear-"

"Remember the time I punched you in the dick because of that time you peed on me?" I asked in return, and he frowned in confusion just before I swung my fist towards his crotch.

Seth leapt back with a howl of surprise before breaking a laugh which made my heart hurt. It was so tempting to let him draw me into his nonsense, to let myself pretend things were okay for a little while before the truth came for them. But I just didn't have it in me. Neither the effort it would take to pretend, nor the strength it would take to keep the weight of what I really felt from them.

He cast a subtle air shield around his junk as I turned away. His power obviously hadn't all been consumed by the rift before he'd been released from it.

I opened the door on the other side of the destroyed room and headed into one of the ostentatious hallways lining this place, while Seth bounced on the balls of his feet as he kept pace with me.

Geraldine and Max said nothing behind us, and I was starting to get the feeling that Max could already tell something was gravely wrong, even with my mental shields keeping him firmly out of my head. He just understood that now wasn't the time to ask.

A warm hand pressed to my side and I looked around at Geraldine as a flare of healing magic swept into me, stealing the pain of that wound as her power roamed free within my skin.

My heart sank as she took that distraction from me, the physical pain having been a welcome reprieve from the agony raging within my soul, but I simply patted her hand in thanks and said nothing about it. She took a chocolate bar from her pocket and offered it to me, but I shook my head, the thought of eating entirely unappealing.

"I thought you didn't have any snacks to spare?" Seth sniped and she scoffed.

"Nay, not for the riff-raff. This is queenly chocolate of the grandest kind."

I left them bickering over the so-called royal snacks and headed straight to the grand entrance hall then moved to the hidden panel beyond the stairs that Darius had told me about. The hum of Lionel's power hung all around it, the urge to leave and go somewhere else filling me as his concealment spells pushed at my mental defences, but I'd expected that.

I pushed back with my own power, forcing my will against the spells until they shattered before flicking my fingers at the hidden door and simply blasting it from its hinges.

A stairway spiralled away beneath us, the steps and banister lined with gold, tapestries and paintings hanging from the stone walls, each depicting a green Dragon in various states of puffed up splendour.

I led the way inside, a flame igniting on the tip of my finger which I used to score a smouldering line through each and every priceless piece of art that bastard had commissioned of himself.

Down and down we walked, the press of stone and earth surrounding us making the hairs along the back of my neck stand on end.

"Deep into the belly of the beast we delve, where ninnyhobbins hide and bombadills dwell," Geraldine cooed from the rear of our group, and though I had no idea what those things were, the haunting tone of her voice made me wary of them.

At last, the stairs came to a halt and just as Darius had described, a huge golden door stood blocking the way on, a wheel marking the lock which barred our passage and hid countless treasures beyond it.

"How are we supposed to get through that?" Seth asked in a hushed voice. "It looks thicker than my cock on a full moon."

"Surely nothing is thicker than that," Max replied with mock horror and Seth grinned.

"Only this door," he said seriously.

"I am well versed in magical locks," Geraldine interrupted their jokes. "Perhaps I can break through those and then we can think up some way to crack the physical locks too…"

She trailed off as she looked over the immense door, clearly realising it would take far too long to do any of that, but I wasn't going to give up there.

"I was a thief long before I set foot in Solaria," I said simply. "And nothing has ever stopped me from claiming my prize before."

With little more than a thought, I summoned the essence of my soul from where it had been lurking and my Order form sprang up within me, lighting a fire across my flesh and coaxing my blazing wings into place along my spine.

"Darius once told me that this door had been crafted to withstand all known powers in Solaria – even Dragon fire itself. It's eight inches thick and completely impenetrable. But I'm willing to bet that the Fae who built it didn't account for the possibility of Phoenixes arising in Solaria."

I took a step forward and pressed my hand to the centre of the door as I finished my explanation, the cold, hard metal resisting for several seconds before melting away like butter cut by a hot knife.

I grinned darkly, stepping up to the door with my wings flaring on either side of me, willing the flames to burn, melt, destroy as I stepped forward and seared a hole into existence before me.

There were magical locks in place on the door too, but all of them had been focused around the idea of someone trying to open it, not carving a hole straight through the centre of it, so none of them were so much as triggered by my actions as I walked through molten metal until I found myself standing in the centre of Lionel Acrux's most prized possessions.

"Ho-ly fuck nuts," Seth breathed from behind me.

I withdrew from my Order form, banishing the flames and turning to look at him through the perfect silhouette of a Phoenix which had now been melted into that impenetrable door. When Lionel found this place empty of all he coveted most, there would be no doubt whatsoever over who had done this.

Good.

I raised my hand and cast ice at the door, cooling it enough to allow the three of them to pass inside too, then turning to look around at the treasure trove awaiting us.

I threw a handful of Faelights out from my fingertips to illuminate the echoing space, and Max released a low whistle at the heaps of gold, diamonds and riches sweeping out before us, piled against the walls, and stacked on shelves. It was more money than I'd even known existed in the world and here it was, ripe for the picking.

"I spy a snallywaffer," Geraldine called, hurrying past us towards a shelf lined with velvet bags of stardust, taking a pinch out to show us.

I moved to grab a bag too, looking around at the myriad of treasures with my heart pumping hard in my chest.

"Can we use stardust to send this back to the rebels?" I asked hopefully.

I'd broken the wards surrounding this place when we arrived, so we'd be able to use stardust to get in and out. An army was damn expensive after all, and what better way to reward those who fought for us than with a piece of treasure straight from the lair of the Dragon we'd fought against. If that didn't help bolster their spirits after the loss we'd faced, then I didn't know what would.

"Certainly, my Queen," Geraldine said. "It is as simple as transporting oneself – you simply toss the stardust over the object in question and tell the stars where to take it. Poof!"

She threw a scattering of stardust at the closest heap of treasure, and it disappeared in a twinkling flash which had an almost real smile lifting my lips.

I snatched a pouch of stardust and quickly began tossing it over the treasure in the room, sending it on the wings of the stars to the camp we'd left up in the mountains.

Seth whooped excitedly as Geraldine and I worked our way through the huge vault as quickly as we could, sending every heap of gold, priceless piece of jewellery and valuable bauble out of that room and into the heart of the rebel camp.

It took less time than it should have, each piece of treasure blinking out of existence, shooting across the kingdom until nothing was left but a few pouches of stardust in an empty vault with a ruined door.

"Come on, we need to leave before his scaly ass shows up here," I urged, turning for the door, but Geraldine ran back, a dagger in her hand as she made it to the rear wall and hastily carved a message into the stone there.

Long live the true queens.

I smiled wolfishly at the note left for Lionel Asscrux and grabbed the last of the stardust – all we'd need to transport us and the others out of here – and headed for the stairs. But that smile turned to ice as it splintered across my lips, a sucker punch to my heart damn near making me double over right there and then as I thought of Darius and imagined his booming laugh while he took part in this carnage with me.

He deserved to have been here, to have ransacked this hell he'd been born into and to have stolen the hoard of his piece of shit father.

Lionel was going to fucking lose it when he realised his entire treasure trove was gone, but it felt like a wasp stinging the paw of a bear. I needed more, had to hit him harder.

Max gave me a wary look as some of the crushing pain inside of me escaped, and

I braced my hand against the wall, turning my eyes from his as I shut him out again. It wasn't safe here, there wasn't time for this, but as my hand heated the concrete wall so much that it cracked beneath my palm, an idea struck me with the clarity I needed to pull myself together.

"You go ahead and get everyone ready to leave," I said, my wings flaring at my spine, fire rippling along the bronze feathers as I fell more deeply into my Order form, and the others moved past me. "I'm going to make this place burn."

Seth howled wildly as flames burst to life in my hands, and the three of them broke into a run the moment they stepped out onto the stairs.

I trailed my fingers along the walls as I stalked after them, my magic singing to the flames and urging them to grow and grow and grow, every inch of my flesh igniting while I called on the power of my Phoenix to keep my feet moving one at a time.

I bathed in the heat of the fire as it engulfed me, breathing in the smoke, and caressing the flames while walking through the rooms of the manor house one by one and watching them all burn. My fingers scored through portraits and tapestries while trailing lines of orange and gold raced from me to consume every piece of furniture, every curtain, every carpet. The gold adornments hanging on the walls and encrusting the bannisters bled as they melted, molten liquid spilling like rain down the walls and across the floors.

I thought of every horrific story Darius had shared with me about his upbringing, of every punch and kick, every lesson and punishment. I thought of the man who had been forged within this hell, his heart brave and true despite all he had endured.

I thought of him as I walked through room after room and the heat of the flames burned the tears from my cheeks as if they weren't even falling at all. The only pause I made was to gather things from his old bedroom, treasured photos of him with the Heirs and Xavier as they grew up, a few of him and Catalina too. They were the only hint of joy that had been found in this place, and I left everything else to the flames as I headed further into the house.

The thundering boom of the roof cracking beneath my power loosened the knot in my chest, just enough to let me breathe. I closed my eyes as I felt the ghost of him beside me, the man I loved come to witness the destruction of this nightmare.

Either my mind was splitting apart with my grief, or I was simply hallucinating from the smoke inhalation, but I could have sworn I felt the brush of his lips against my neck, his powerful body pressing to my back as his arms encircled me.

"I'll burn it all if that's what it takes," I breathed as the sensation faded, my chest an empty, hollow thing once more, that feeling fading to nothing and forcing me to admit it had never been there at all.

But when I stepped out into the cool light of day with the heat of the fire igniting my very core, I smiled up at the sky. For him. The man who I loved so fiercely and who I felt so close to me then, like he was watching me burn the world down and cheering me on as I did it.

Caleb had returned with the missing members of the Heirs' families, his and Seth's dads and their younger siblings clinging to their moms. A small group of the Fae who had been tortured to feed power to those tethered to the rift lingered just behind them, shuffling closer as Geraldine ordered them all to prepare for travel.

I strode towards them, banishing the fire from my body as I approached, ignoring the looks of awe, wonder and fear which my shifted form drew, and nodding to my friends as they looked to me to see if we were done here.

As I stepped into their midst, Geraldine threw a handful of stardust over our assembled group, and I knew that by the time Lionel Acrux arrived at the place he had once called home, he would find nothing but embers and a golden vault door with a Phoenix-shaped hole melted straight through the heart of it.

Geraldine's message awaited him beyond it, alongside the slight change I had made to the wording for his benefit.

Long live the motherfucking Queens.

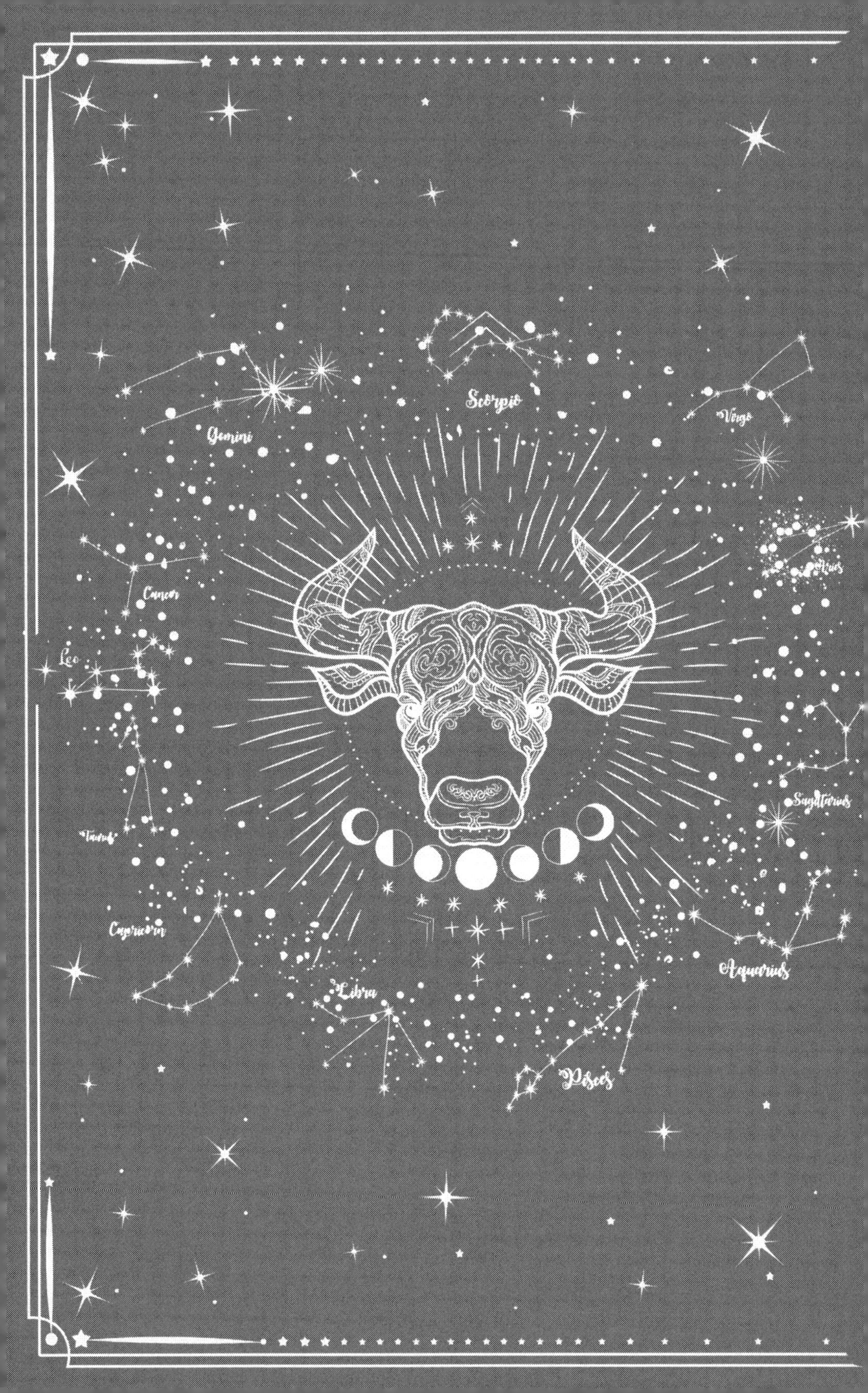

Scorpio
Gemini
Virgo
Leo
Sagittarius
Capricorn
Aquarius
Libra
Pisces

CALEB

CHAPTER TWELVE

The stars swirled around us in a vortex, my mind spinning with them as they transported us across land and space before spitting us back out again onto a harsh, windswept mountainside.

Lionel's treasure was laid out all around us, the heaps of gold sparkling in the light of the rising sun warming my back, and I looked around at my family and friends in disbelieving relief.

We were safe. Alive.

A clamour of voices drew my attention up the mountain towards the ruins there, crumbling pale brown stone structures peeking out from between an endless sea of tents cast from earth magic, the leaves and vines making them up blending in with the grassy ground surrounding them.

"I can feel their emotions from here," Max said and one glance at him told me that he'd already recovered his magic from the emotions of those surrounding us. He caught the train of my thoughts as my fangs prickled and held his wrist out obligingly, letting me drink from him and sating the ache in my chest.

I tried not to think of the Fae I'd been forced to feed from alongside that rift, of how brutally and deep I'd drunk. I'd been lost to the worst of my nature, and I didn't want to teeter that close to the edge for a single moment more.

"The Queens' Army have worked tirelessly to set up this camp," Geraldine sighed, looking towards them as I released my hold on Max and stepped back.

"What-" I began, but Tory cut me off as she spoke.

"We lost the battle," she said, her eyes on the ruins too, the wind tugging her hair away from her face and tossing it behind her. She didn't look at any of us as she spoke and there was a brittle, aching tone to her voice which made my heart stall in my chest. She'd kept this from us until now, wanted us here before she delivered this devastating news, and fear bit into me as I thought of all the people I knew who had been in The Burrows when that fight broke out.

"What happened?" I begged, glancing at Max whose face paled as he took in the emotions of the rebels camping close by. There were hundreds of tents, thousands, but not nearly enough to contain the force we'd commanded at The Burrows.

"We fought hard, but there were so many Nymphs and..." Tory trailed off. "We lost too many people."

"My sweet Papa and his Lady Love gave their lives to let our army retreat," Geraldine declared, her voice catching and tears spilling freely down her cheeks as a mixture of pride and grief crossed her features.

"Fuck, Gerry." Max had his arms around her within a heartbeat, the pain he felt over that loss crashing into me, even as my own sorrow made words feel impossible.

"Catalina," my mom breathed, a hand moving to her heart as Dad took hold of her hand and squeezed tightly.

Antonia released a sorrowful howl and Seth and the rest of their family joined in, even the youngest of the pups who were barely past the age of two, their pain colouring the air as my lungs constricted with the weight of that declaration. The twins, Athena and Grayson, clutched onto each other and my younger brother Hadley gazed at them with pain sweeping through his expression.

But as I turned my attention back to Tory, that weight seemed to triple, quadruple, the threat of it crushing me entirely because she'd turned her hollow gaze on me, and even though she didn't seem to have the words to say what was haunting her, I *knew*.

I felt it. I felt the emptiness in the world and the echoing void which would never be filled, its arms open wide as it beckoned me close, and I shook my head as I fought the urge to back away.

I shot towards her, gripping her arms so tightly I was likely bruising her, but I needed her to tell me it wasn't true. I needed some other explanation for him not being here now to greet us, for him not coming with her to close the rift and save our sorry asses.

"Where is he?" I demanded, my voice so loud it forced everyone's attention onto me.

Tory's green eyes swum with emotion and I looked into them deep, finding nothing but pain and darkness there. Loss and sorrow.

"No," I denied, shaking my head fiercely as I released her and took a step back like I could run from the answer I'd just demanded from her.

A cry escaped Max's lips as he felt the truth, sensed it in her emotions. He dropped to his knees with a roar of agony so potent that it burst from him and crashed into all of us, the grief of it almost knocking me from my feet.

"No," I snarled again, a fissure rupturing through me as I turned from the truth in those green eyes, turned from my friends and family, looking towards the camp which stretched away up the mountainside above me.

It wasn't true. There was no world that I could conceive of without him in it. The four of us were blood-bound brothers, we would remain that way until the end of our days which would not come any time soon.

Seth howled again at my back and the pain in that single, unbroken note was like claws ripping through my fucking soul.

"*No*," I damn near shouted it before I broke into a run, shooting away from them with the speed of my gifts as I sped up the hill and into the camp. He would be there, waiting for me, that smug and cocky grin on his face which always seemed to be taunting death and danger, daring them to try and take a bite of him. He was immovable, impenetrable, an utterly indestructible entity and I wouldn't hear any truth other than that.

I shot through tents and crowds of rebels, shoving Fae aside when they made it into my path and ignoring their cries of outrage as I bellowed his name, demanding he emerge from wherever he was hiding and tell me this was some sick joke.

"Darius!" I yelled, my throat splintering with the force of that single demand while the campsite blurred past me so fast it was hard for me to even focus on the faces I passed. But none of them were him. None held that swagger, that arrogance, that damn immortal presence which couldn't possibly have been torn from this world.

I shot out into a clearing which had been set between towering rocks, an infinite view of the plains beyond laid out before it and the sky wide open above.

Two ice caskets lay in the centre of that space, one twice as wide as the other, built to accommodate more than one person. Tombs for fallen warriors so precious that someone had brought them all this way rather than leaving them behind on the battlefield with the rest of the dead.

I skidded to a halt at the foot of them, unable to see the faces of those who lay within. Unable to face this bitter truth, though I already felt it right down to the core of me.

The wind seemed to cry out for this loss as it howled between the rocks surrounding the coffins, causing the sea of flowers and everflames, tokens of memorial and thanks which decorated the floor to shift back and forth within the grip of that wind.

My feet began moving without my permission, stumbling over each other as I closed in on the closest casket of unmelting ice.

I lifted a shaking hand and reached for it, my already numb fingers skimming over the frozen block of ice as I closed in on the head of it, on the reality which was racing towards me like a freight train, the blare of a horn droning through my skull, warning me to run while I remained tethered in place, unable to do so.

My gaze finally fell on the face of my brother within that ice, his features still and empty, his body bloody and battle-worn, his battle axe at his side and his fisted hand so close to it that it was almost as though he would reach out and take it up once more. But he wouldn't. Never again. Even the strength of his powerful body couldn't break through this wretched twist of fate. My life yawned out before me, void of this man and all he was to me.

My knees buckled.

I hit the ground hard, a sob rising in my chest before a roar of agony burned from my lungs, rattling through to the core of me and yet doing nothing at all to ease the weight of the pain that threatened to crush me beneath it.

I dropped my head forward, pressing my forehead to the pane of frozen ice dividing us, leaning towards the man who owned a portion of my soul. A grief so endless that I couldn't even comprehend it rushed in on me from all sides.

I broke beneath the hateful sky, surrounded by tokens of sorrow from strangers who had never even known the beauty and strength of the man who lay dead here now. I broke into a thousand pieces which I knew would never again fix back into a whole.

Another powerful sob choked me as I dug my fingers into the ice, my gifted strength threatening to crack it open as though I could rip him from within it and wake him up, return him to us, to where he belonged.

I begged the stars in silent, hopeless anguish to change this spiteful fate. I begged each of them by name, listing every heavenly being and constellation that held even the slightest tie to Darius's birth to change their minds on his death, but not a single one of them listened, if they even heard me at all.

A rush of feet over grass approached me, the world crashing down all around me while I remained in place, unable to think or breathe.

A broken howl filled the air as Seth joined me in my destruction. The thump of his knees hitting the ground beside mine resounded through my body, but I was unable to tear my eyes from Darius's lifeless face in that coffin of ice.

Max joined us too, the despairing sound that escaped him echoed by the grief tumbling from his body on the wings of his Siren gift, soaring free of him and pouring over the entire mountainside as he collapsed down on my other side.

No words passed between us as we knelt there, our pain too raw and brutal to put into words as our love for our fallen brother broke each and every one of us beyond repair.

Their shoulders pressed to mine as we sought each other out in our darkest hour, and through the haze of my wracking sobs and the tightness in my chest which threatened to draw me into death's embrace too, I felt the blaze of our power connecting.

The maelstrom of magic which merged between the three of us writhed like a tempestuous storm, crashing against the barriers of our skin and roaring for freedom from the pain it found within us.

Where my palm met with the frozen earth beneath me, it found that outlet, pouring from me in an unformed rush like it was desperate for release, the echoes of power remaining inside us following our escape from that rift, all racing away from me in a frantic pattern and sinking into the ground beneath us.

A rumble passed through the clearing beside the tomb of the man we all loved so dearly, and a tree began to grow beyond the ice coffin. Up and up it shot while our tears hit the soil and were absorbed into its creation, the bark twisting and growing into an unnatural and yet familiar shape as a Dragon of legend grew from the ground, one wing spread wide and passing over our heads.

Golden leaves sprung from its branches, and blossom sparkled beneath the force of the sun beating down on us, gilding every bough.

We relinquished every drop of our combined magic into the soil, our bodies trembling from the rush of power as it escaped us like water raging down a storm drain.

The tree grew and grew until it was the exact size of the enormous beast who had once resided within the man now lying dead in its shadow. The outstretched wing curved over both coffins protectively, the beast's wooden face set in a firm and unyielding expression as it watched over this most precious treasure.

And there, beneath the wing of that wooden creature, curved over a casket of ice which held the worst truth any of us had ever faced, we broke. The four Celestial Heirs no more, a future we had been groomed for our entire lives torn from beneath our feet, and our brotherhood shattered in the most unthinkable way.

Hours we knelt there. Countless hours where none of us could find a single word or summon the strength to rise from our vigil. My skin was numb from the press of the cold coffin I'd fallen apart over, and I was filled with a hopelessness which had taken root so deeply within me that I couldn't even make myself care about anything anymore.

Firm hands took hold of us as the stars spun above, the murmured voices of our parents tumbling over me and cascading away again as they tugged us from our grieving and pressed healing magic into our skin.

I leaned into the embrace of my mom, her arms banding around me so tightly that I knew she felt this agony too. I wasn't even sure if I'd walked or been carried inside, the warmth of a fire thawing my frozen skin as she sat me down on a bed which had been cast into place within a room that looked like anything but a bedroom, the stone walls painted with ancient markings of worship.

I didn't care. I let her pull blankets over me and run her fingers through my hair, the numbness sinking beneath my skin keeping me from so much as thanking her.

Distantly, I heard Geraldine murmuring sweet words of sorrow to Max as she led him to another room, and the hazy press of sleep washed over me, the power of Tiberius's Siren gifts taking hold of my mind.

I didn't try to fight him off, made no attempt to cling to wakefulness as my pain ate into me and devoured pieces which I knew would never return.

A body hit the bed beside me, Seth's earthy scent offering the smallest measure of comfort as I rolled towards him, my hand finding his, our fingers winding together and our faces turning towards each other on the soft pillows.

I pressed my forehead to his as Tiberius guided me into sleep, and even though the world had just fallen apart beneath me and cut me adrift into an endlessly dark sky, I found myself tethered by my grip on Seth's hand, one tiny point of light amid a sea of misery.

It was impossible to know how long we slept, the room we'd been given holding stone walls with no windows, and the lack of sound coming from beyond it making it obvious that someone had cast a silencing bubble around us to let us claim as much rest as we needed.

I didn't open my eyes though. I didn't so much as move while I lay there, my forehead still pressed to Seth's, his fingers still gripping mine tightly.

"We should…move, get up…something," Seth breathed, seeming to know I was awake despite my lack of reaction to the fact.

"Why?" My voice was gruff, the word rasping from a throat thick with agony which didn't wish to hold the burden of words.

Seth sighed and I opened my eyes, finding him watching me with the same pain that had broken me glistening in their depths. His long hair was pushed away from his face, the braids along the shorn side of his head falling loose of the magic which had held them in place.

"Darius," he began, wincing at the name which drove a dagger through my heart, before forcing himself to go on. "Darius would want us to keep fighting. To help the rebels regroup and-"

I shot to my feet, abandoning him in the bed as I crossed the room in a blur of motion, carving a hand through my matted curls and shaking my head.

"No," I growled, turning my back on him, and refusing those words. I couldn't just get up and go on as if nothing had changed, as if his death made no difference to any of it.

"Cal." The crack in Seth's voice made me turn to look at him.

He rose too, his fists balling at his sides as he took me in, the catastrophic loss between us needing no words, though he'd clearly decided to voice them anyway.

"What?" I bit out, my anger irrational and unstoppable.

I knew he didn't deserve any of it, but it was like I'd lost my grip on some leash within me, my emotions needing an outlet beyond agony, and rage was the simplest way forward.

"I know," he said with the echo of a whimper to his words. "You know that. You know how deeply this cuts me, and I wish there was any other way that fate could have played out but…"

"But what?" I demanded.

My fangs were aching with my need for blood, and I had to fight to keep them from snapping out and ripping into his throat. I knew it would be pointless anyway, his magic gone just as mine was, but it didn't stop the hunger that rose in me as he dared to take another step closer.

Seth's jaw tightened and I could see that same anger mirrored in his eyes, but as he spoke, I realised that it wasn't aimed at the stars or Lionel or injustice of this destiny the way mine was at all.

"He made that deal," Seth growled, betrayal written into the tightness of his posture as he held my eye and spoke those tainted words. "He bargained with the stars and gave up his own life in the process. He chose this. He chose to do this to us, even though he knew what it would do to us. He gave up on-"

I slammed into him so fast that he didn't even have a moment to block the blow before my fist crashed into his face and sent him stumbling back.

Seth's lip split from the strike, red blood staining his mouth and making the monster in me snarl with starvation as my eyes locked onto that bead of red.

He took advantage of the distraction his blood caused me and launched himself at me, his shoulder colliding with my gut as he threw me back against the wall and sent bits of crumbling masonry cascading down on us from the ancient ruin.

"Take it back," I snarled as I threw my weight into him, hurling him from his feet and landing on top of him as I swung another punch at his jaw.

"No," Seth spat, furiously. "I won't. He made that deal with the stars and bought himself a single year with it. He didn't even give us the chance to change his fate. He wasted that time, letting the clock run down on his life without giving the people who loved him the option of fighting it. He kept it secret just like he always kept his secrets from us." Seth's fist crashed into my ribs.

He flipped me onto my back and straddled me, his long hair spilling down towards me as he gave me a Wolf's snarl.

"I hate him for it," he choked out, and I lost it.

A ferocious growl parted my lips, and I threw my gifted strength into him, sending him tumbling off of me and slamming into the wall behind him.

I was on my feet in less than a second, fury pulsing wildly through my veins as I bellowed at him. "Darius gave everything for this war! He gave everything for love and the hope of destroying the man who made his life hell for every moment that we knew him. And we just stood by and did nothing. We knew what Lionel was doing to him in that fucking manor. For years we knew, even if he couldn't tell us outright, and we did *nothing*."

A strangled noise escaped me as the guilt I felt over that threatened to consume me, but Seth's fury matched my own and his was aimed squarely at the brother we had both lost.

"He never wanted our help. Never once even tried to ask for it. Always the fucking martyr, always standing between that monster and the world like he'd been waiting to die for us all his entire life regardless of any deal he made with the stars."

"That's not fair," I hissed.

"Not fair is him leaving us here without him!" Seth shouted, thumping the wall, and causing more gravel to tumble from it to the floor. "He should have fought that fate," he growled. "He should have told us, should have let us help him. But instead, he embraced it. He let Tory love him, let us believe in a future he knew we would never get to claim and walked towards his death like a willing sacrifice while damning the consequences. He's gone now. Passed through the Veil to the peace that awaits there and where are we? Left broken in the ruins left by his end, left grieving and bleeding from a wound which will never heal."

"He didn't expect to die on that battlefield," I said, my voice cracking. "He didn't expect to leave us yet. He thought he still had more time. He thought-"

"What difference does it make?" Seth asked, his eyes flashing silver as his Wolf paced beneath his skin. "Christmas is weeks away. He knew this end was coming, and he knew the stars offered no guarantees. They gave him a year, but they didn't give him immortality for that time. He knew that and yet he walked willingly towards death all the same, just like he would have done even if his time hadn't been running out. Because this sacrifice was acceptable to him, this destruction of us was a price that he was willing to pay because our pain didn't matter to-"

I slammed into him so fast that I had barely even registered the movement myself, my fangs snapping free and plunging into his throat before he could so much as raise a hand in defence against me.

The taste of his blood washed over my tongue and my snarl deepened as I drank from him, my hand encircling his throat and pinning him to the wall at his back, my fingers squeezing tight as I cut off his air.

Seth fisted his hand in my hair, growling viciously as I drank from him despite the lack of magic in his veins. It didn't matter though, the monster in me was hungry and the violence he'd invoked in me demanded this taste of him.

Seth's muscles bunched as his grip on my hair tightened and with a furious snarl, he wrenched me back, ripping my teeth from his flesh and tearing his skin wide open in the process.

Blood ran freely down his neck, staining his shirt and racing over my fingers where I still gripped his throat.

"Fuck you, Cal," he choked out around the tightness of my hold.

I bared my teeth at him, wanting his pain, his anger, anything at all other than facing the abyss of Darius's loss which waited with open jaws, hungering for me with every passing second.

"Fuck you, Seth," I snarled right back.

A moment hung in the silence that followed those words, one tainted with something so bleak and heart breaking that neither of us dared move. We just stared at each other, the heat of his blood warming my frozen fingers and my pulse falling into rhythm with the thumping beat I could feel beneath the tightness of my grip on his jugular.

My mouth was on his before I could think of anything else, my tongue breaching the barrier of his lips as I shoved him back against the wall, endless nights of fantasising about the taste of him, the feel of him all rushing into me and making me act without thought or reason.

I knew how this ended. Knew it didn't mean the same thing to him as it did to me, but right now, I didn't care. I was so lost in the sea of this pain that I just needed to feel something else. Even if I knew it wasn't real, that his heart didn't ache for mine the way mine beat only for his. Even if the words he'd thrown at me in this room made me want to destroy him, and the anger I felt towards him for them wasn't abating one bit.

I didn't care.

Seth groaned as I kissed him harder, his fist tightening in my hair like he sought to take ownership of me while my grip on his throat reminded him which of us was truly in charge here.

His free hand dug into the ruined fabric of my shirt and he tore at it as my tongue rode over his, the fabric parting beneath the force of his attack on it. I let him shove it from my left arm, leaving it hanging from my right where I refused to relinquish my hold on his throat.

Mine. In here, right now, he was mine, and I didn't care what that meant for after. I didn't care that this wasn't the same for him as it was for me because he was submitting to it, giving me what I craved and letting me fall for this pretty lie while I worked to bury myself in it.

I broke our kiss and the rough stubble of Seth's jaw grazed over my lips while I worked my way down to his neck, licking at his skin and savouring the taste of him while my cock hardened in my pants and a growl of longing built in my chest.

Seth tried to push against me, working to assert his own dominance with a growl as he yanked on my hair so hard that my mouth was ripped from his skin, and I was forced to meet the vortex taking place within his deep brown eyes.

"You want to fuck so you can feel something else?" he asked me icily, the question seeming so simple and so weighted all at once.

I licked my lips, tasting his blood on them as I panted in his hold, my cock throbbing with need and my blood pumping so hard it was difficult to hear around the whooshing of my pulse within my skull.

I was sure he could see it, this need in me for him, the vulnerability which I'd been fighting so hard to hide from him ever since the last time we'd been in a position like this, and he'd told me it meant nothing to him. What would he do if I admitted that this wasn't nothing to me? Would he push me away? Remind me that that wasn't the way he worked? That I was just another notch to add to his bedpost?

"Isn't that what you do?" I replied darkly. "Fuck your feelings away so that you don't have to deal with them?"

Seth's gaze shuttered at those words and a growl rolled through his body, my fingers buzzing with the feeling of it where I still gripped his throat possessively.

"Yeah," he spat bitterly. "That's what I do. I just want to make sure we're clear on that before you go making any dumb decisions like falling in love with me."

Something burrowed into my chest at those words, sharp claws tearing through whatever part of me was left whole in the wake of losing Darius, but I forced the feeling aside. I didn't need more pain. I needed something else.

I forced a hollow laugh and tightened my hold on him until his breath was cut off again, pushing him back against the wall as I used my free hand to unbuckle his belt and open his fly.

"How about we stop talking and you just come for me like a good pup," I growled, my eyes on his as I pushed his boxers down and took the straining length of his cock into my hand.

Seth snarled at me as I began to stroke him, my thumb smearing precum all around the head of his shaft as I watched his pupils dilate at my touch.

I held him like that for several more seconds, watching the concoction of pleasure and pain blend together in his eyes, refusing to let him draw breath until he gave me an answer.

Seth glared at me defiantly and I began to draw my hand away as doubt crept in, but before I could release my hold on his dick, he sagged back against the wall and nodded, the ire in his expression melting into something unreadable as he gave himself up to me.

I let him breathe and he sucked in air, watching me hungrily as I teased his cock with my hand, a groan escaping me as the lust in his eyes set me alight.

"Use me then, Cal," Seth panted in submission, the want in him peeling me open and making me come undone for him. "Take me and use me and make me forget all the shit in this world for a little while. I'll be a good pup for you if that's what you need. Just promise you'll be rough with me while I'm yours. My heart can't take tender right now."

We stared at each other as I nodded my agreement to that, to fucking without feeling and forgetting everything else. I could do that. I could try.

I slammed into him again, taking his words seriously and letting my need to dominate run through me as I used the power of my gifts to press him back against the wall while I took a kiss from him which I wanted more than I'd ever dare tell him.

Seth growled into my mouth, his Alpha instincts refusing to let him submit easily even after he'd asked me to take charge, but I was more than willing to meet him in that battle.

My teeth sank into his lower lip, and he moaned as I sucked on it, tasting his blood from the punch I'd landed on him earlier before sinking my fangs in and making him hiss with pain.

I pumped his cock in my hand as I sucked harder, driving him back against the wall and moving my hand from his throat to grip his shirt instead.

I ripped the material from his body just as he had done to me, revealing the hard planes of his muscular chest before running my hand over every ridge and line. I wanted to commit every bit of this to memory, wanted to lock it all away so that the next time I thought of him while I was fucking my own hand, I could be certain of my fantasy.

Seth drove his hips forward as I continued to work his cock in my fist and I snarled at him in warning as I maintained control, kissing him deeply once again as I pumped him harder, faster.

His body shuddered where I pressed myself against him, his hand moving to my belt as he worked to free my cock too, but despite the bone deep ache I felt for his touch, I smacked his hand aside.

"When I make you come for me, I want to fuck that filthy mouth of yours again, Seth Capella," I snarled in his ear, my hand rolling down the solid length of his cock before caressing his balls then pushing back further until I ran a finger over his ass, making his cheeks clench.

Want built in me as he groaned at that touch, the thought of me burying my cock inside him so tempting that I could have come at the mere thought of it.

I drew my hand back and Seth whimpered as I slowly dragged my fingers back up his shaft to the tip. I leaned in to lick the blood from his still bleeding neck, my tongue rolling in slow circles over his skin as I thought about taking him into my mouth to finish him instead of using my hand.

I wanted to. Had thought about it over and over again in the dead of night, aching to know what he would taste like, how it would feel to bring a Fae as powerful as him to ruin from my knees. But hesitation gripped me even as the fantasy taking place within my mind begged me to try it.

Seth's hips pumped into my hand as I ran my fist up and down, his fingers grasping my forearm as I felt him moving towards the edge. He was so fucking close, all because of me and knowing that had me moving my hand faster, kissing him harder, crushing him against the wall and making him submit to this.

I could feel him clinging to the edge as he panted into my mouth, and just as his determination began to crumble, I broke our kiss and looked him dead in the eye.

"Come for me," I growled, my voice a low command which he couldn't refuse as he came hot and heavy in my fist.

Seth groaned loudly and I swallowed that sound as I kissed him again, my hand guiding him through his climax as his cum spilled through my fingers and onto the floor beside us.

I broke our kiss suddenly and Seth's lips parted in lust as I sucked on my fingers and groaned at the taste of him there. It was salty and earthy and wholly him, and I was pretty certain I'd just found a rival to his blood for my favourite taste in the entire world.

"Fucking…fuck…" Seth panted, and I nodded as I shrugged the tattered remains of my shirt from my arm before moving with a flash of speed and yanking his hair into my grip.

My blood was pumping too fast, the need in me for him so potent that I was drunk on it. I wanted him more than I had ever wanted any girl, and the way I felt when we were together like this was so foreign and exhilarating that I wasn't convinced my need for it could ever be sated.

"On your knees," I demanded, tugging on his hair hard enough to make him hiss, but a groan followed the noise, making it more than clear that he liked it. "I've been dreaming about that mouth of yours and I need to feel it again."

Seth sucked in a sharp breath at those words but instead of giving in to my demand, he yanked against my hold on his hair and took my mouth with his instead.

My heart leapt as he kissed me, his hands moving to cup my face between them as the passion in it rose and rose, his tongue wrapping around mine and his hold on me tightening like he didn't ever want to let me go.

Just as I began to feel like I was losing all sense of myself entirely in that kiss, Seth jerked back, his molten eyes on mine and a dare in them that set my skin burning with desire unlike any other.

"If you want me on my knees for you, Caleb," he said low and deep. "Then you'd better put me there. You'd better make me take your cock like a good pup. You'd better make me taste every damn drop of you and use me like you promised me you wanted to."

Any restraint I'd been clinging to snapped at those words and I gave into that demand with no resistance whatsoever.

I growled at Seth as I took hold of his shoulders and shoved him to his knees before me.

Seth snarled right back, glaring up at me in challenge as I slowly wrapped the length of his brown hair around my fist and released my cock from my pants.

I licked my lips as I looked at him down there, running my hand up and down my length as I stared at his mouth and tugged on his hair enough to tilt his head back.

Defiance flared in his eyes as he watched me jerk myself off before him, the tip of my cock a bare inch from his lips as I released a low groan and made no attempt to move it closer, simply stroking and teasing myself.

Seth drew in a shuddering breath as he watched me, sucking his bottom lip between his teeth and looking so fucking hot that I knew I'd have been happy to just finish myself like this, to spill myself over him and mark him as mine even if he didn't take me into that sinful mouth of his.

"Tell me how much you want me," I commanded, my heart hammering to a rampant tune as I pumped my cock so close to that mouth.

Seth hesitated for a moment, his eyes moving from my dick to meet my gaze and my heart leapt as we looked at one another like that.

"Too much," he breathed. "I want you too fucking bad and I can't help it. Can't stop it. I'm yours to do whatever you want with. I'm *your* fucking Wolf, Cal, and the thought of making you mine is too much to bear."

"You want it that bad?" I panted, his words pushing into my overrun mind and falling to ash against the lust which was set to consume me at any moment.

"Yes." He nodded, licking his lips. "So give it to me."

I groaned loudly as I finally gave in, thrusting my hips forward and sinking my cock between his lips, making him take me all the way to the base.

Our eyes remained locked the entire time, and I knew I was already done for as I looked down at that perfect sight. I gave up on restraint, on making this last and savouring it. He had offered me a respite from the pain that had crippled me, and I was beyond the point of holding back now.

My fingers knotted in his hair, and I began to fuck his mouth hard and fast, the perfection of his lips and tongue worshipping me too much to resist as I gripped him tightly and took what I needed from him. He was so good at this, so skilled it was like he was made to pleasure me.

Faster and faster, I pounded into his mouth, a purely male sound escaping me as I lost control entirely and gave in to the speed of my gifts. I did as he'd begged of me and I wasn't gentle as I took from him, fucking his mouth until I was coming down his throat and his name was bursting from my lips like a prayer and a curse combined.

Seth groaned as if my release had been just as good for him as it was for me, and he swallowed down every drop of me with a glint of hunger in his eyes which made me feel like he had barely even begun with me.

I staggered back a step, panting heavily as he rose to his feet while I tugged my pants back up again.

I could already feel the pain of grief pushing in on me. That stolen moment fading all too soon and the things he'd said about Darius rousing some embers of anger in me once again.

"So that's it then?" Seth asked, righting his own pants as he glared at me like he wanted me to say something. "You got what you needed?"

"Did you?" I asked in return, the taste of him still lingering on my tongue and my cock practically solid again already as I thought over what we'd done. I wanted more but the tightness of his posture told me he didn't anymore, even if I could see how hard he was through the tightness of his jeans.

"Oh yeah," he replied scathingly. "You know me, fucking is like breathing for me. It was really a toss-up between sucking your cock or going to find myself a drink and I wasn't all that thirsty, so…"

"So?" Words burned on the back of my tongue, but I didn't know how to form them, and I was pretty certain he didn't *want* me to form them. We'd just lost our brother and whatever the fuck that had been was the least of our problems, but still…

Seth tightened his jaw and gave me the most aggressive peace sign I had ever seen in my life.

"Right," I said as something akin to a lead weight dropped through the hollow remains of my chest. "I guess I'll catch you later then."

I returned the fucking peace sign, feeling like a damn idiot, not to mention all kinds of used. But that was what he'd offered me, wasn't it? He'd said we should use each other to forget for a little while and we had. So peace to that.

I turned and shot from the room before I could say something that would restart our argument from earlier, knowing in my soul that Darius wouldn't want us turning on each other over him. But every step I took away from that room felt heavier, every inch like a mile I would never be able to cross again, and as I ran into a wide room filled with the Councillors, Tory, Xavier and Geraldine, I had to wonder what the fuck I'd been thinking when I'd agreed to something so empty with the one person I cared for more than anyone else in this damn world.

It took me a few seconds to realise that everyone seated around the large, round table was now looking at me expectantly, and I cleared my throat as I took in the tension in the room, the subtle divide.

My mom was sitting to the left of the table between Antonia and Tiberius, their unity and ease with each other clear from everything about their posture to the small looks they exchanged. To the right of the table, Tory sat on a chair which was bigger than all the others with vines curving up and over the back of it, forming a design which looked suspiciously like a crown just above her head. I didn't need to look at Geraldine to know who was responsible for that little bit of earth magic, but a single glance her way showed her sitting as upright as a lamppost at Tory's right hand, her chin set with defiance and eyes blazing with passion.

Xavier also sat towards the right of the table, though his was the chair which stood closest to the middle, like he was aiming to bridge the gap between the various powers in the room. His gaze shifted to mine and I bowed my head in acknowledgment of his loss, the grief we shared. Xavier nodded in reply and though his eyes were bloodshot and several days' worth of stubble coated his jaw, he seemed determined to take part in whatever this was without descending into the darkness of that pain.

"Caleb," Mom greeted me warmly, her eyes shining with love and concern, though I knew she wouldn't address those feelings now. She had been playing these games for long enough to know when the time for such things were appropriate and when politics had to come first. I'd always been able to tell which mode she was in from a single word or expression, and it looked like this meeting was going to take precedent over all else for now.

"Is this a private meeting?" I asked, though I had no intention of leaving.

"Stay," Tory replied, speaking in place of my mom, and drawing the attention of the Councillors who bristled at the command in her tone. But I knew her well enough to understand there was no real command there at all, simply an offer.

I circled the table and took a chair for myself, only realising that I'd chosen the exact centre of the divide as my ass hit the seat and I found myself positioned as a bridge between the two groups. A fact that none of them missed. My mom arched a brow at my bare chest but said nothing on my state of undress, presumably because she was expecting an extra ally in the room now.

"We were discussing the best course of action from here," Tiberius answered my unvoiced question. "Plans for our movements and where best to strike back-"

"And it has been pointed out more than once that there is no need for any command from a pack of gandergeese here," Geraldine cut him off. "The rebellion has and always will be members of the Almighty Sovereign Society, followers of the true queens and servants to the crown-"

"A crown which now sits upon the brow of a usurper," Antonia growled.

"It matters not where a trinket rests, whether it be upon the scaley slapper chaps of that most loathsome of cretins or down a dump shoot, covered in Griffin poop. The crown itself is an ideal and title which cannot be bandied about like a parcel at a children's soiree. There is no doubt as to the true owners of such a headpiece, and you should all be taking the knee as you sit before one of those fine and beauteous ladies – not ruffling feathers like rats in a hen coop!"

"Solaria does not recognise the leadership of Roxanya or Gwendalina Vega," Tiberius replied easily. "And neither do we. The three of us are honour bound and blood sworn to serve, protect and lead our people, so that is what we intend to do."

They kept up that back and forth, Geraldine throwing all kinds of weird and wild names at the Councillors while they adamantly insisted on maintaining rule among the rebels regardless of their loyalties to the Vegas. All the while they argued, Tory said nothing, even Xavier offered a word here and there, implying that he stood with his sister-in-law on this, despite the fact it was clear that my mom and the others were looking to him to take up the fourth place in their ring of power now that Lionel had betrayed them, and Darius was no longer able to take it himself.

I looked to the girl who had been my friend, lover, enemy and so much in between, but I struggled to recognise much of the person who lived within those deep green eyes now. Her fingers traced a pattern over the solid tabletop, and I cocked my head to look at what she had burned into the wood there. A sea of stars sitting high above a mountaintop, the scene wreathed in a dark circle surrounded by markings which made my brow furrow. Runes. It was hard to see them all from my position, but I recognised a few, reading their meaning and shivering as a chill passed down my spine.

Runes held symbolic meaning which could change in divination depending on a number of factors, but from the combination she had etched into the wood, I guessed at the intention behind them and stilled.

Gebo for sacrifice, Naudhiz for resistance, Perthro for fate, Uruz for power, and Eihwaz for rebirth.

Were they meant as predictions or promises?

Tory's eyes snapped up to meet mine and something glimmered there, defiance in the darkness which made a creeping sense of foreboding crawl up my spine.

"Where is Gwendalina anyway?" Antonia barked and the chord which had loosely formed between me and Tory snapped as her eyes shifted straight to Seth's mom, fire flaring in her palm for a moment as she swiped it over the table and destroyed the image she'd been drawing there.

"That is what I intend to focus on," she replied coolly, no question over whether or not that would be permissible, just a statement from a queen.

"We have all studied the reports from the battle," my mom said. "There has been no trace of her since the fighting began. So far as I can glean, the entire flank of the army where she fought was wiped out by some monstrous creature under Lavinia's command. You have to have considered the possibility that she fell-"

"She did not," Tory said in a low, dangerous voice while Geraldine gasped and threw a hand to her head like the mere suggestion might be enough to steal her from consciousness.

"How can you be certain?" Tiberius demanded, his gifts reaching out across the table, probing towards her emotions, but I didn't have to be a Siren to be able to tell that Tory had crushed that attempted intrusion with a mental wall built of solid iron.

"I simply am," Tory replied.

My mom and the other Councillors exchanged doubtful looks, and I spoke up before any of them could try to counter her claim.

"I imagine you're more than overwhelmed with all the information you've gathered since returning here, but there's another fact you should know," I said, wincing a little at the reaction I knew these words would earn. "Orion and I ended up in a bit of a situation several months ago. One involving another of those shadow rifts. He was in danger of being ripped through it, his soul dragged back to whatever dark hell they occupy. So to stop that from happening…well…" I cleared my throat, fighting off the feeling of being a little kid trying to own up to being bad in front of my mom. "We accidentally formed a coven."

Tiberius paled and Antonia gasped loudly, my mom simply staring at me blankly like she was trying to figure out what I'd just said while denying the words I'd spoken clear as day.

"I'm only bringing it up because I know the tales of the covens of old, and I know that if Orion were dead, I would have felt the ripping of that bond from my soul. I have felt no such thing, meaning-"

"His shameless brutishness lives!" Geraldine gasped, placing a hand to her heart in thanks for that confirmation, and Tory's shoulders fell just a fraction in relief at my words too. "And if that is so, then I know beyond the wiggle of a worm's waggle bottom that he is with his Darcy love. That together they must be fighting the cur-" Tory cut her a look and she swerved midsentence "-ious call of fate," she finished awkwardly, looking around the room at anything except the people who sat on the far side of the table.

I frowned as I tried to figure out what she'd just hidden from them, but my mom and the others didn't even seem to have noticed, their ire focused on me as the news of what I'd done sank in.

"Caleb, this is beyond some minor mistake," Mom hissed, her knuckles blanching as she curled her hand into a fist on top of the table. "We can't simply overlook something so dangerous. You've gone against the oaths that were formed after the blood wars, betrayed the trust of the people in all Vampires – especially considering who you are and the power of your position. I don't think you understand the seriousness of-"

"My sister and I pardoned them of all implied or real punishments that might have been expected for their bond," Tory interrupted, though they definitely hadn't done that, and I wouldn't have recognised their power to do so anyway. "If you have an issue with it, then perhaps you should take that up with me."

The challenge hung in the air, an offer I could tell Tory wouldn't back down from. She was hungry for a fight, hunting for an outlet for all the pain and fury she was keeping contained so deeply within her. She may have been hiding it convincingly from the world, but to those who knew her well enough, that agony was clear to see in the vacancy of her eyes.

"No more fighting," Xavier said firmly, his fist slamming down on the table and making Geraldine gasp dramatically. "Hasn't there been enough of that already? Haven't we seen enough blood spill the last few days?"

When silence met his outburst, I found myself nodding my agreement. A time would come for this challenge, but it wasn't now. Not with Darcy and Orion missing and the fate of everyone in this camp in peril for every moment we lingered here.

"We need to prepare the rebels to move," Tory said after a beat of silence let the tension in the air simmer down. "We can debate the location later. Geraldine can fill you in on everything else you need to know until then."

The girl who could be queen stood, turning from the room despite the protests of my mom and the other Councillors, not even giving a shit as she turned her back on them and offered up that insult before striding from the room.

Mom's furious eyes fixed on me before the door had even swung closed behind her and I shot to my feet too, muttering some vague apology before I sped away after Tory and escaped that particular lecture. For now, at least.

Geraldine spoke loudly before any of them could protest, my gifts picking up her words through the heavy door as she started telling them about the Atlas Tyler had just finished making untraceable and the fact that the rebels needed to be getting news stories out into the world again as soon as possible, to counter the bile spilled by that rag of a newspaper, The Celestial Times, in favour of the false king.

It sounded like the plans for that were already well underway and I didn't hang around to hear any more about it.

Tory had already made it to the end of the ancient stone corridor by the time I reached her, and she didn't even flinch as I appeared in her path, catching her arm to halt her.

"What was that about back there?" I asked, and we both knew I wasn't talking about the discussion she'd been having but the marks she'd burned into the table.

Tory drew in a slow breath as she looked up at me, moving to take my hand in hers and place my fingertips against the jagged line of a scar now marking her palm. I looked down at it, the brand of lightning seared into her skin humming with an unfamiliar power as I touched it.

"I don't accept this fate," she said simply. "I refuse it, and I refuse the guidance of the stars over my life."

"What does that mean?" I asked, my brows drawing together as I looked down at her hand between us and the heat of a furnace burning within her skin warmed me.

"I cursed them," she replied simply, like there was anything simple about that idea. "Each and every one of them. I cursed them and I swore to rip my fate from their clutches no matter the cost to me or my soul. I'll see them burn, Caleb. And I'll find him again in this life or the next before I'm done."

My lips parted in denial of that insane claim, but there was something about the power of that vow which stopped any protest I may have made in its tracks and made me do something unthinkable instead.

I took her scarred hand and placed it over my heart, against my bare skin, dropping my forehead to press against hers as I let her feel that unending grief in me too, let her feel how deeply I shared in her pain.

"Then I offer myself to you," I swore in a low and steady voice, whispering my next words because they felt so important. "In any way that I can be of service to you in fulfilling that vow, I offer it. Through blood, duty, honour, or sacrifice, I am yours to command in pursuit of this end."

Tory released a shuddering breath and a single tear fell from her eye, rolling down her cheek before splashing against the back of her burning hot hand where it lay over my heart.

"There isn't a depth I won't fall to for this," she warned me, and I nodded.

"Then I'm ready to fall at your side."

I wasn't certain if it was intentional or not, but magic flared between us where our entwined hands lay against my heart, that promise becoming binding as the stars took note of it; and whether we sought their approval or scorned it, it didn't matter now.

It was done.

Scorpio
Gemini
Virgo
Aries
Cancer
Leo
Taurus
Sagittarius
Capricorn
Aquarius
Libra
Pisces

LIONEL

CHAPTER THIRTEEN

I travelled through stardust towards my manor house, Lavinia's dark form twisting in a blur of shadow in my periphery. I materialised on the lawn, needing to check in on Vard and the rift he was watching over, but the moment my boots hit the grass, a raging fire came into view before me. My manor was burning with all the chaos of Phoenix fire, the red and blue flames devouring what was left of my precious abode. Liquid gold was spewing like lava from the ruins, every golden decoration in my house destroyed by the Vega whore.

An earth-shattering roar poured from my lungs, and I lost control entirely, my Dragon exploding from my flesh and shredding my clothes. I took off into the sky as Lavinia shrieked, turning into smoke beside me and travelling at my side. I wheeled over the house with urgency, the heat of the flames washing over me as rage consumed me. I was hunting for the Vega girl and her accomplices, desperate to capture them and kill them for this. And I would not rest until I saw them torn apart for this.

"No!" Lavinia cried as we flew over the altar of black stone down in the courtyard at the back of my abode, all of my prisoners vanished and the rift nowhere to be found. The ex-Councillors were now free to try and challenge my rule, just as they had the night I had captured them. But I had seen their treachery coming, had been prepared for it, awaited it.

They had shown up here at my manor just as Stella had opened the new rift, and exactly as Vard had predicted, they began protesting my latest decisions, arguing over the Nebular Inquisition Centres and my great plans for this kingdom. I was done. I didn't need them biting at my ankles, threatening me with their power and banding together with their bullshit attempts to placate me. Lavinia had wanted them for her rift anyway, and though I was loathed to offer up any more power to my wife than necessary, it had been an obvious solution to the problem of the Councillors and their offspring.

All it had taken was a few threats to their smallest children to force them to bare themselves to my power. Antonia's youngest pups had screamed so easily at the kiss of my knife to their throats, and all three of the Councillors had submitted then. Weak. Such abhorrent weakness to sacrifice themselves in place of some squalling brats who would likely never even rise to their full power regardless.

Lavinia and I had subdued them along with the Spares, binding them to the rift without so much as a blast of magic from anyone. And the rest of their useless families had served as a good incentive for them to keep feeding their powers into the rift, to continue struggling on through fatigue and the loss of hope. Yes, Vard had done well with his predictions for once. He had even managed to creep into the minds of the traitorous scum who had once sworn their allegiance to me and had found Melinda's cunning little way to contact her oldest son. That had been the icing on the cake, luring the Heirs here with her crystal, hearing that they had also fallen prey to my plans and were immobilised upon the onyx altar.

But now, all of that, every piece had been shattered beyond my worst imaginings, that Vega bitch stealing in here in the dead of night and incinerating my beautiful manor. I didn't know how she had managed such a thing while suffering the weight of her defeat on the battlefield, but there was no denying it as I circled my beautiful home, a growl of purest rage and horror echoing away across the scorched grounds. And where were any of my Nymphs? Where was Vard? Anyone at all who could have sent word of this attack?

I circled back over the house, landing on the singed lawn before what had once been my entrance hall, the ground shuddering beneath my weight before I shifted back into a man. Lavinia materialised before me, picking up my jade green robe from the ground, the clasp destroyed when I had shifted but the length of it intact. I snatched it from her hold, throwing it around my shoulders before marching up to the inferno that coiled towards the sky, consuming everything within it.

I reached towards it, trying to take hold of the flames to put them out, but they flared even hotter, making me jerk back my hand with a curse of fury.

I turned to my manor, the huge wooden doors groaning as they succumbed to the flames and fell from their hinges with a deafening boom which resounded through me to my core.

"No!" I bellowed in furious defiance as I ran forward, climbing over them and forging a passage inside.

"My King – it is not safe!" Lavinia yelled after me, but my mind was pinned on my most valuable treasures in my vault. I had to get to them and pull them from the depths of this cursed fire that was working to devour everything I had claimed for my own.

The heat of those flames fell over me from the stairs, the portrait of me in my Dragon form at the top of it melting beneath the intensity of the fire. Everything was burning, the fire hungrily destroying the stairs and the golden bannisters nothing but melted pools of metal spreading across the tiles, tainted and ravaged, their value lost.

I let out a cry of anguish as I ran deeper into my house, fire spewing from every doorway, and I only avoided it all by the luck of the stars and the strength of the air shield I'd erected around myself, though even that couldn't fully douse the heat of that fire.

I moved fast through my house, hurrying downstairs with my mind set on my treasure as I wound through the halls.

I finally made it to my vault and stopped dead in my tracks, finding the carved-out shape of a Phoenix burned right through the centre of the door.

Horror splintered through me as I stared at the impossibility of that reality. That door was impenetrable, both the metal itself and the spells I had used to seal it in place. But as my heart raced in fierce denial of what I was seeing before me, I realised what she had done, how she had bypassed the magic by destroying the centre of the door and how very easily she had managed this act of horror.

I stumbled forward, blinking against the smoke as I looked into the cavernous space which should have been heaped high with all of my most valued treasure. A Dragon's trove was his soul, the most important thing in all the world to him and mine was…gone.

She'd taken everything, the entirety of the treasure I housed in that safe, every heirloom and jewel, every single piece.

Smoke billowed across the room and something caught my eye on the far wall, my feet tripping over each other as I stumbled towards it, the glimmer it gave off making me salivate at the thought of her missing something, of there being something left, a single piece...

The shining gold which had lured me in so temptingly blazed brighter as I closed in on it and my blood itself began to boil as I took in the golden, shimmering words cast there on my wall and emblazoned with the fire of a Phoenix itself.

Long live the motherfucking Queens.

Anger exploded from me in a torrent, panic and horror colliding in the depths of my being as I read that taunt and felt the fullness of this blow against all I was and all I cared for.

I roared so loudly the ceiling shook, and suddenly it broke apart, a Dragon statue carved from jade crashing towards me. I cast air, throwing it away from me, turning and running from this place as the entire building began to fall, like it had been waiting for that exact moment, wanting me to read that message before it succumbed to the terrible power of my enemy.

I moved with speed, blasting debris out of my path and scrambling up the hidden stairs on my hands and knees, the stone burning my palms even through my shield. Never had I been forced to fear a flame before that moment, never had my own Element turned on me like this, betraying me.

I made it back to the burning entranceway, crawling across the floor, coughing and cursing as the hem of my cloak caught fire, my bare knees bleeding on the broken tiles.

I was trembling with rage and an emotion which I refused to admit came even close to fear as that fire burned hotter and hotter, my skin blistering, smoke clouding my vision, my air magic barely withstanding the force of it.

I clambered over the shattered front doors, my foot catching on something sharp and making me hiss as I fell, rolling across smouldering wood and the ruin of my once perfect manor house.

The second my back hit the singed grass, the walls crashed down behind me, bricks slamming into my air shield and pinging off of it as a plume of dust billowed into the sky.

I lay there on my back, panting and bleeding, burns blistering my exposed skin where the cloak had spilled open, unable to cover me, and just stared at the ruin which now lay where my home had once been. Where my treasure had once resided.

Horror paralysed me as I absorbed this impossible truth, my heart thundering in my chest and my hatred for the Vegas so potent that it ran through every piece of me like poison, promising them the worst of deaths once I had them in my grasp.

How could this have happened? I had left almost a hundred Nymphs guarding this place, along with that piece of shit who claimed he was my Royal Seer. How could his Sight have missed such a thing coming this way? How could he have failed so spectacularly?

"VARD!" I boomed at the top of my voice, the ground quaking beneath me from my ferocity.

To my right, a garden shed stood beneath an oak tree, the door swinging open and revealing a cowering, snivelling Vard within its shadowy depths.

"F-Forgive me, s-sire. The Vega girl was here."

I launched myself to my feet and stormed towards him, fury tangling with my blood as my gaze locked on my prey and the need to release it consumed me.

Vard shrank away to try and escape, tripping over some plant pots and crashing down onto the floor in the back of the shed. Fire lit in my palms as I stepped into the small space, my huge form taking up the entire doorway as I glared down at this insolent, pathetic creature who was supposed to be the Royal Seer.

"And did you not *see* her coming?" I demanded.

"I-I-I-" he stammered.

"Did you, or did you not *see* her coming?!" I bellowed.

"I *saw* her as she landed, sire," he blurted.

"You mean when she arrived?" I snapped, smoke spilling from my lips.

"Y-yes," he whimpered.

I stepped deeper into the shed, the wooden floor groaning beneath my weight as Vard tried to scramble backwards away from me, knocking more plant pots off the shelves which bounced off of his head.

"All I know is that the rift is gone and so are every one of the prisoners I had here feeding it," I hissed, hearing Lavinia wail somewhere behind me in response to that. "And my worthless Seer has been hiding in a garden shed for the stars only know how fucking long without summoning me here!"

While Vard babbled out some non-response, my mind ticked over the knowledge that Lavinia was weakened again, no rift in place to feed her. She would have been greatly strengthened by it, but she could no longer harness never-ending power now that it was closed. The rift being gone was not an entirely bad thing. In fact, I needed to find a way to regain control over her, to remain the more powerful one in our arrangement.

This certainly levelled the playing field a little. Though I had no Guardians now, and I was still not strong enough to control her, especially with this damn shadow hand attached to me.

I reached down, my fist locking around Vard's throat as fire blazed in my palm. He screamed like a dying animal as I picked him fully off the floor and threw him with all my might through the back wall of the shed.

Vard bounced across the grass beyond the shed and I followed through the hole he'd created with his body, shattering more of the wood as I forced my shoulders through and stalked him like prey.

"Please, my King," he begged, trying to get up, but I stamped down on his leg, hearing bone snap under the impact.

Lavinia appeared at my side, licking her lips and smiling at his pain. "More, my King. Make the one-eyed man pay."

"No – please! Remember what I did for you – remember that I was the one who led you to the rebels' hideout. My Seer gifts have proved themselves valuable beyond all bounds," Vard panted.

I paused, considering those words. It was true. He had come to me the night of the battle, wailing about what he had perceived of their location, locking it down despite all the magic those vagrants had used to conceal themselves. It had surpassed all realm of my imagination in what I believed him capable of, and I could not deny it now. Though that did not excuse him from punishment.

I stamped down on the other leg, leaving that broken too, the heat of my anger like hellfire in my chest. I wanted his death, a long, drawn-out suffering to assuage my fury, but Vard had made himself too valuable. Not just with the odd vision he supplied that was incredibly advantageous to me, but with his other gifts too.

I was having no luck breaking Gabriel Nox's mind, and he was impervious to Dark Coercion for reasons that I was sure had to do with those fucking Vegas. So I needed a Cyclops powerful enough to break into his head and pull out the visions he was keeping there. Vard was capable of it, but I would make him suffer before I healed his deplorable form and dragged him back to the palace.

"You have greatly displeased your king." I gripped his shirt in my fist, hauling him halfway up towards me before slamming a fire coated fist against his jaw, bones snapping and pain singing in the air. I was driven on by the heat of the Phoenix flames at my back, picturing the Vegas in the place of Vard as I showed him no mercy.

Lavinia urged me on, her own anger sharp now that the rift was closed, and I let her play with him too when I was done, standing back to watch her torture him with the shadows. A dark hunger was falling over me, and my mind twisted onto Gwendalina Vega.

"Lavinia," I said, prowling towards her, and she smiled at me in that wild way of hers.

"Yes, my King?"

"I have to get my hands on those Vegas. We must send out every member of our army today and hunt them down," I commanded, my blood spiking with adrenaline at the thought of capturing them.

"Of course. But – oh! I can do better than that. I think I can summon the Vega I cursed. Now that she has fallen deep into the trap of the beast, I can control her almost entirely. Would that please you, Daddy?"

"You can summon her?" I gasped eagerly.

"Yes, I believe so," she said excitedly.

"Then return to the palace and do so." I cast a look back at the devastation which had once been my manor and forced myself to feel nothing but purest rage at what had been done to it. "There's nothing more for us here." A thrill scored through my veins at the vengeance I was going to seek so soon, at the thought of having a Vega at my mercy at last.

"I'll speak with my Nymphs first and seek out any whispers in the shadows which may point us in the direction of the rebels."

I almost bit back at her, wanting the Vega girl brought to the palace as a priority, but I had to think of the war. If there were leads to the rebels, then I needed them soon before the trails went cold. Besides, they had my treasure now, and I ached with the need to retrieve it more than I would ever admit.

"Very well," I agreed. "Report back to me immediately if you discover anything of use."

"Of course, Daddy." She ran a hand down my bare chest, hunger in her dark eyes which roused some semblance of lust in me as I looked at her. She was beautiful, and willing, perhaps it was time I took my queen back to my bed and reminded her of the power of a Dragon. Perhaps with her weakened from the rift, I could do so fully again, asserting my dominance over her body in the way I should. I watched her go as she rushed away into the trees, darkness shrouding her as she went, and my gaze turned to the path leading to the border of my property and onto Stella's land.

I ran my tongue across my teeth, glancing down at Vard as he whimpered, figuring he would live long enough for me to go and speak with her. Surely she had heard the commotion here? Was she not home?

I stepped over Vard, and his fingers brushed my ankle. "Please, sire," he groaned, blood leaking from his mouth.

I jerked my leg out of his grip, my foot hitting him in the face before I continued heading along the path, fire coiling between my hands.

"Do not heal yourself of these wounds until I deign to do so or you shall sorely regret it," I spat at him before striding away.

When I made it to the porch of Stella's house, I found the door ajar and light spilling out over my feet. I pushed it open, raising my hands and drawing a tight air shield around me in case I might find some enemies within those walls. I would relish the chance to kill a few rats.

I moved down the hall and dropped my hands as I found Stella unconscious on the floor by the hatch in the wall which hid the way into the basement where she kept her dark magic equipment.

I crouched down, pushing her onto her back and frowning at the beauty of her. Perhaps I never should have brought the Shadow Princess into our lives; perhaps I should have allowed Stella to stay at my side during my takeover of the kingdom. She was certainly more amenable, easily controlled, and I had always enjoyed her body.

Now that Clara's soul had left her, Lavinia was a cold, unfeeling thing who neither bowed to me nor pleasured me the way I liked. I may have wondered at being able to dominate her again now, but Stella had always known just how to do so without any need for me to work at it.

I brushed my fingers over Stella's throat, waking her from the sleeping spell that was cast upon her, and I choked away her inhale as she woke.

"My King," she croaked as I squeezed, my bicep bulging as I held back my strength.

How easily I could simply snap her neck; it was that kind of power I craved over the Fae around me. Utter dominion, complete control. And after all I had lost this day, how good it would feel to simply snuff out a life.

"What. Happened?" I hissed, smoke pluming from my lips and making her cough.

I only increased the pressure on her throat, my blood pounding with the need to do something to prove my might. Vard's punishment had not been enough. I craved death.

"The rebels came," she said in a strangled voice, clasping my hand to try and pull it off her, though she didn't cast magic against me. She knew my moods, perhaps better than anyone left alive now, and she had found ways to temper them in the past. I wondered if she was still capable of that.

"Yes, I am aware," I bit out. "They have destroyed my home, and all the prisoners are gone. The blame is falling heavily on Vard, but unfortunately, I need him alive for other purposes. You, however, I am questioning the worth of."

"Lionel," she rasped, her eyes wide and full of fear.

I revelled in that fear, drinking it in and enjoying the kick it gave to my ego. I was the King, the most powerful Fae in existence, and this was the way all Fae should look at me. It was time I got Lavinia back under control and ensured she started looking at me like this too.

"I'm sorry," Stella said, reaching for my face and caressing my cheek. "Forgive me."

It wasn't her softness that stayed my hand, but something in me relented, and I decided not to kill her. She was a constant in my life, a reminder of all I had been through to gain power. Perhaps she had purpose yet.

My fingers loosened until she could breathe properly again, and I rose to my feet, finding myself eye to eye with a mirror on the wall. Ash had settled in my hair from the fire, and I had a rattled look about me that I didn't much like. The burns marring my skin simply added insult to the injustice of this attack and I sneered at them as I took them in, healing them away with a flash of magic. I was feeling more and more out of control since Lavinia had forced me to impregnate her with that monstrous shadow creature, which had thankfully been destroyed before I'd had to endure much of its company. I knew at any moment, she could come to me again and command I give her another, and there was nothing I could do to stop her from forcing me to agree.

I swiped a palm over my face, marking it with soot and blood, realising my hand was shaking. I curled it into a fist, crushing the weakness from my bones. *I will not falter.*

Stella got to her feet beside me, taking hold of my arm and drawing my attention to her.

"You're afraid," she said, her voice softening. "Talk to me."

"I am no such thing," I barked, and she flinched as I spun towards her, expecting a strike. I was tempted, but I kept my hands from her.

Afraid? The Dragon King does not feel fear.

A spark of defiance flared in her eyes. "Remember when we used to talk of these days, of you sitting on the throne and the kingdom a place of glory?"

I remained still as she moved into my personal space, tiptoeing up to whisper in my ear. "It doesn't look the way I hoped. I think you've lost your way."

The emotion in her voice made me pause, and I pressed her back, darkness dripping through me.

"And what would you have it look like?" I asked. "I won my first battle and crushed the enemy thoroughly. I have captured the greatest Seer alive, and tonight I will execute a Vega."

I had been taken aback by Vard's vision of the truth which he had perceived after I'd commanded that the portraits of the Vegas be pulled from the walls. One in particular had caught my eye as the servants had taken it down, of Hail and Merissa coddling the infant boy they'd claimed as their ward. It had always seemed strange to me, but when Vard had seen the truth of who he was, my suspicions were finally justified.

It had all become so obvious. Merissa's bastard-born son - a true blooded son and not some waif they'd taken pity on at all. I had thought him dead after my Nymphs had come to kill them all those years ago, but it seemed the Seer queen had made certain that all of her children escaped my wrath that night. That explained everything. Why his Sight was so great. Where his unwavering allegiance to those Vega brats had come from, and why he had been so certain of his devotion to them. But now he belonged to me.

"I always thought I'd be there to soak in your victories, Lion. But I guess I was just another steppingstone on your journey to domination," she said coldly, retreating like she was done with me, but I knew she wasn't. It was there plain to see in her eyes how much she wanted me, she was just bitter I had turned my back on her for so long. I could claim her again, and I would savour the challenge of it too.

"Is this meant to be some grand rejection of me?" I asked, my tone bland and proving I was unaffected by her charade. She had always been good at putting on a show for others, but for me, she crumbled. And she would do so again. I only had to push the right buttons.

Her eyes welled with tears and there it was; the truth behind the mask. "Maybe it is. Maybe I'm done waiting for you to fulfil all the promises you once made to me."

I hounded towards her, and she backed up, raising her chin, and holding eye contact with me like she expected me to attack her. It seemed she didn't mind risking being consumed by my flames, and that awoke a thrill in me.

"And what were those promises, Stella?"

"Don't insult me by acting like you don't remember," she snarled. "You and I were so close once, you confided in me about everything. Now, I look at you and I'm not sure I ever knew you at all."

"No…it isn't that," I said, moving closer until her back hit the wall and I stole all the air between us, taking up the entirety of her vision and keeping her there in my trap. My eyes shifted to green, reptilian slits and her throat bobbed as she fought to hold her nerve. "You always knew the depths of my power, Stella. You saw the darkness in me and my need to conquer and rise, but you cannot face it now that I am king, and I am able to unleash it all. You aren't able to handle my deepest fury or my unimaginable strength, so now you are running from me." I lifted a finger, stroking it along the length of her jaw before tucking a lock of black hair behind her ear. The way she parted her lips and let out a quiver of a breath revealed her want for me. "I am too much for you."

"I'm the only one who could ever handle you," she insisted as her will broke, her dark eyes flaring with desire. "But I deserved better. I waited for you year after year, I married a man I didn't love because you commanded it, I have offered you counsel in dark magic, I have been there for you through everything, and now you offer me nothing."

"Lavinia kills any woman I go near," I said, a growl rumbling in my chest as I admitted that fucking vulnerability. I lowered my voice to a whisper as I went on, "She is no queen of mine. I will rid myself of her when the time is right." I simply had to figure out how to do that first, and I had conquered greater challenges in the past.

Stella's eyes widened, hope flashing in them. "And then?"

I knew what she wanted me to say, and it was so terribly easy to weave the lie for her. I did not want a queen at all. But right now, I did want warm flesh and the pretty moans of a Fae who was obsessed with me.

"Then, and only then, perhaps you and I can come to a better arrangement," I said.

I waited for her to swallow the vague promise as easily as honey laced with poison, but hesitation crossed her features then she shook her head.

"Liar," she breathed, and anger sparked hot beneath my flesh. "You're lying now, just like you lied when you swore I'd be there when you came to rule."

She took my hand, placing it against her pounding heart as if I should be able to read something from it.

I snatched my hand back, rearing forward and throwing her against the wall.

"You *are* here," I barked, done with this game. "And you are *mine*."

I lifted her up, spreading her legs wide for me and she gasped, leaning in to kiss me as her will collapsed, crumbling for me as easily as always. My head turned so she met the corner of my mouth, and I shoved her skirt up her thighs, the warmth of her skin a delight after knowing only the icy touch of Lavinia's for so long.

"Oh, Lion, have you missed me?" she moaned, arching her back and clinging to my neck in encouragement.

"I missed this." I dropped my robe, ripping her panties off and driving myself into her hot wetness, bracing myself against the wall as she cried out. I fucked her without mercy, the power of my thrusts driving us hard into the wall until plaster was showering down around us.

Finally, I had a release for this ferocious energy tearing through my body, and it was her. A true ally who knew her place beneath her king. She was a reminder of my power, and I fed on it like flames devouring gasoline. *Yes*, I was the Dragon King, the greatest Fae in the land.

I was already primed to explode, and I came with a roar as I pinned her there with the full weight of my body, my palms burning holes in her wallpaper as my fire magic spilled out of me.

As the relief of the outlet settled over me, my mind immediately turned to more important things.

I jerked out of her as I thought of my treasure and what had been lost to me this day, the need to protect all of my remaining assets demanding I act fast.

I picked up my robe, donning it as Stella panted against the wall, holding herself up as she sagged there, ravaged and no doubt satisfied beyond all bounds.

"You will bring your things to the palace and stay there from now on," I commanded.

"I am not safe in the company of Lavinia. If she learns of our relationship, she will-"

"Relationship?" I scoffed. "You are privileged to service your king." I strode to the door and her next words fell over me, shaky and dipped in far more emotion than I cared to deal with.

"You loved me once," she whimpered.

I glanced back at her with a sneer at that word, that disgustingly weak notion. "Your emotions will be your downfall, Stella. Find a way to harness them or I will retract my offer. If you come to the palace, you will do so with your eyes wide open to what our arrangement will be. The only relationships you and I have are of business and fucking. Each play by the same rules, and it is emotion that ruins both. You, of course, will continue to covet me, love me even - if you believe in such things - but understand that I have never and will never return such...sentiments."

I strode out the door, her sob following me, and some ghost of a memory reminded me of a time when we had spent our days at Zodiac Academy together, plotting and cavorting, and even laughing at times. She had been an interesting distraction once, but my plans had outgrown her. Maybe there had been a time when I had felt something in my heart for her, but I had learned a long time ago that there was no reward in loving someone.

I had felt such affections for my father once when I was young and naïve. I'd tried to gain his favour, but he had always focused his efforts into Radcliff, his eldest son, the Heir. And eventually, I had learned that the only way to be noticed in this life and taken seriously, was to prove my power. When Radcliff had died, Father had seen me then. He had been forced to acknowledge my superiority once I was finally given the opportunity to prove myself. I did not blame him for his initial preference, in fact, I had seen merit in it myself when I had sired my own sons. Darius had always shown more prowess than Xavier, and so he was where my resources had been placed. It was pragmatic and did away with foolish concepts like coddling your spawn. This life was harsh, and you didn't thrive in it without stepping on some spines. It was not a place for runts.

My parenting methods may have seemed cruel to weaker-minded Fae, but my father had been a wise man who had proved how much more could be achieved in life when power was placed above all else. I had taken his skills and combined them with the charisma I had learned from Radcliff. I had watched him closely, observed how Fae would do anything for him because of his charm, and I knew if I could mimic that behaviour, then I would be unstoppable.

My brother may have been strong, but I was smart. I cut down enemies in their sleep, took revenge without anyone knowing of my involvement. And over time, my strength grew to match that of my brother's, and now outshone it entirely. Between all of my skills, I was a master of power in every manner that mattered. How my brother and father would envy me now as they watched from the stars, this man with all the reins of fate in his grip.

Stella was my final reminder of those times when I had been scaling the ladder of my ascension. She was a leftover from my past and now she could not even begin to comprehend the magnificent plans I had for Solaria. Fucking her again had relieved me of the small pull I'd felt towards her tonight. From now on, I would keep her in my court as a consultant of dark magic, and whenever I wanted my cock sucked or a warm body to sink into, I could access her with ease. Stella would have her slice of power that way, and she had best be damn grateful for it too. I would just have to make sure Lavinia never learned of our trysts.

I returned to my manor grounds and peeled Vard's shattered, twitching body off the grass, healing him before shifting into my Dragon form and clutching him in my talons. I took off into the sky, vengeance rushing through me as I flew above the burning remains of my abode.

I would answer Roxanya Vega's attack with an attack of my own. Her sister's blood would paint me red by the time I was done, and I would ensure her death was broadcast live to the world.

First, I would head to the city of Celestia and hold a meeting with the Dragon Guild to demand they relinquish much of their treasure to me – although the priceless items I had lost could never be truly replaced. I would hunt Roxanya to the ends of the earth to retrieve my treasure.

At least I had something to look forward to in the meantime, because when I returned to The Palace of Souls tonight, a Vega would be waiting for me, and it would be time for me to destroy one of the most powerful creatures in this world and half the threat against me.

This was my kingdom, and I would assert my dominance in blood again and again until no one dared defy me. Once upon a time, I had twisted Hail Vega into a creature of violence who everyone in Solaria feared, and I had seen the effectiveness of that. It was time I truly donned his crown and took his title upon myself. For it had always been me behind his greatness anyway. I was the Dragon Lord, Lionel Acrux, and I was the true Savage King.

Scorpio
Gemini
Virgo
Aries
Cancer
Leo
Sagittarius
Taurus
Capricorn
Aquarius
Libra
Pisces

MILTON

CHAPTER FOURTEEN

Good morning, Sagittarius.
The stars have spoken about your day!
The wind is wild, and the seas are stormy as darkness clouds your night, never seeming to give way to sunrise. But take heed, a light may soon be shining through the dark to illuminate the way on, if only you can find it for yourself. An unexpected alliance with an Aries may fall into your lap today, an adversary turned friend if you can open your heart to such a path. Beware the chime of the morning bell and seek peace in the company of those you trust above all. Remember, the sun always shines brightest after a storm.

I frowned at the words displayed on my Atlas, still uncertain of their meaning even at this late stage of the day as I feigned attention in my Cardinal Magic class, counting the minutes until we were released for dinner. Professor Highspell perched on the edge of her desk with her pencil skirt riding up to dangerous heights. She smiled in delight as Tricia Buttram squirmed beneath her attention, trying to remember some facts about the Corona Borealis constellation.

I snorted as she spluttered for something to say about the constellation which was linked to my Order form, and Highspell's eyes snapped to me in my seat at the back of the room where the so-called lesser Orders like us had to sit.

"Mr Hubert?" she asked, arching a brow which warned of punishment if she caught me doing anything other than paying attention to her and her dull as fuck lesson. "I suppose you know a little more about this subject?"

I nodded, waiting for her to actually ask me for the information before offering it out. She would give me detention for speaking out of turn at the very least, and I didn't want to spend a single second more than I had to in her company.

"Then please, enlighten us," she swept a hand out, indicating the rest of the class who had all turned to look my way, more than a few of them seeming grateful to have avoided her attention and left it to me.

I raised my chin, my eyes moving beyond the overtly sexual teacher to the board behind her where she'd written the name of the constellation in swirling script, and I rattled off what I knew.

"Corona Borealis also known as The Northern Crown or Woomera, the

Boomerang, lies in the sky between Boötes and Hercules, and is the most closely linked constellation to the Minotaur Order. It contains four stars with known planets and the brightest star it claims is Alphecca-"

"Yes, yes." Highspell flicked a hand at me to stop me mid-sentence and I fought to keep my features still as I fell silent and leaned back in my chair. "The cow constellation, or mud clogged field of the sky as I like to call it." She tittered to herself, but everyone else in the room stayed silent. If that was her idea of a joke, then it was no wonder the bitch had no friends. "I want you all to study the Corona Borealis constellation before our next class and write me an essay titled: Ten things that make this constellation less powerful than most. Extra points for descriptions of the Order linked to this particular formation of the stars and eloquent examples of their weaknesses and their strengths – they are lesser for a reason, but it is always worth noting the ways that such cunning beasts can undermine the hard work and resilience of our great land, so no corner cutting."

Her blood red lips pulled into a wide smile as she met my gaze, daring me to say a word to defend my kind. She sneered just slightly as her attention slipped to my nose ring, the symbol of my position as a full bull, able to create a herd of my own. Bernice, the only one of my prospective cows in this class shifted in her seat, one of her braids slipping over her shoulder to kiss the dark skin of her cheek.

I held Highspell's stare. I wasn't a fool. I wasn't going to waste my breath on defiant outbursts which would only land me in detention, or worse. This game we were playing wasn't worth risking for petty pride, so I dropped my eyes to the desk before me in what Highspell would assume was submission, or shame over my Order, or whatever the fuck else she cared to believe, and I bit down on my tongue so hard that it bled.

The bell sounded the end of class, but no one moved, all of us waiting for Highspell to officially dismiss us.

Mildred Canopus raised her hand from the row of fancy desks at the front of the classroom, her back ramrod straight as she waited for permission to speak.

"Yes, Mildred?" Highspell asked without looking at her, her attention instead fixed on Gary Jones in the front row as she ran her tongue over her bottom lip.

He was a Manticore, a powerful fire Elemental and pure-blooded for the last four generations, so he had been quickly selected for his position at the front of the class. I knew he didn't want it though, he was as much of a prisoner to this system as the rest of us. Gary looked down at his desk as though urging it to turn into a black hole to swallow him up, and I actually pitied my friend for his position as one of the favoured Orders. Or at least I did until I reminded myself about dinner coming up next and my stomach rumbled loudly.

"Is it acceptable to list the best ways to kill a Minotaur in our essays?" Mildred asked, a cruel glint in her squinty eyes as she turned a pencil over between her fingers.

"Such as?" Highspell inquired lightly.

"They moo real loud when you blast them with Dragon Fire," Mildred said, drawing a chuckle from a few of the King's United Nebular Taskforce as she went on, and I found myself sitting up in my chair, my hand moving to grip the edge of my desk as if it might be able to stop me from doing anything dumb like leaping to my feet and ripping that bitch apart right there in the middle of the classroom. She'd been boasting loudly about her part in the battle the king had won against the rebels ever since returning to the academy this morning, and if I had to listen to one more fucked-up story from her experience in the fight, then I was sure I was going to snap.

"And they taste just like braised beef too," Mildred finished.

"By the stars," Frank muttered to the left of the room, his face paling with horror and he wasn't even my kind.

I glanced at Bernice who had fallen as still as a statue, her hands shaking where she clasped them in her lap, the urge to shift written all over her beautiful features, but if she did that, she was as good as dead.

Every student still attending Zodiac Academy had been hauled through an inquisition, more than a few never returning from their bout with the FIB interrogators, their fates unknown. I knew that the supposed lesser Orders like the two of us who had kept our place were only really here for the sake of appearances. There had been several bullshit articles published about our ongoing attendance here, claiming that even lesser Fae could still have a place within Solaria so long as we could prove our loyalty to the crown, that we were innocent of treachery and were able to overcome the failures of our Orders.

It was bullshit. Utter fucking bullshit, but I didn't care because I was still here, witness to it all, close enough to see exactly what was happening all around us and able to do something about it whether they knew it or not.

"It's not worth trying to swallow the horns though," Mildred said lightly. "I got one caught in my throat and damn near choked on the thing."

More's the fucking pity.

Bernice was trembling more noticeably now, her hot-headed temper rising, words no doubt burning like bile in her throat as she fought to hold them in.

I released my hold on my desk and dropped my hands into my own lap, subtly casting an illusion so that Bernice would feel the gentle stroke of my palm along her spine. She stiffened at the touch, her gaze cutting to mine and connecting.

I offered her a look of solidarity, silently reminding her that we'd be out of here soon, safe perhaps, able to do…something. Or at least I hoped so.

Bernice blew out a breath, her fingers unclenching as she got control of her Order form and nodded subtly, but I kept that illusion going, slowly caressing her, easing her worries just a little.

"During the battle, my uncle Fredrick and I actually managed to herd five of them together while chasing them from the skies," Mildred was saying, her chest puffed up as she spoke, her tongue darting out to lick at her hairy upper lip. "It was exhilarating, the way they mooed and ran, a little stampede of death appearing before them as they trampled their own allies in their attempt to escape us-"

"Fascinating," Highspell purred, her gaze boring into me, but I kept mine fixed on the desk, refusing to give her the excuse she was looking for to punish me, some sign of defiance, some indication that I felt anything at all for the demise of those rebels. "But unfortunately, we can't condone the deaths of the lesser Orders unless of course they are found guilty of crimes such as betraying the crown or allying with the Vega trash. So, let's say no to adding a section on the best ways to kill them, and instead focus on how you might look out for a trap they could lay with their cunning and conniving ways for the essay. Dismissed."

Highspell waved a hand at the door, and it swung open as she finally released us from the torment of her classes on prejudiced bullshit.

I waited in my seat as the higher Orders left first, the front rows emptying quickly while Gary practically ran from the room to escape the predatory looks Highspell was throwing his way.

So far as I knew, she hadn't actually touched any of the students she drooled over, but she was clearly fine with making them as uncomfortable as physically possible.

Mildred stood so suddenly that she knocked her chair over, not even bothering to pick it up as she strode from the room, the other K.U.N.Ts swarming around her as she went, Marguerite Helebor pursing her lips as she ended up at the back of the group.

Only when they had all gone did the rest of us grab our bags and stand too, the second-class citizens forced to offer up every privilege to those the false king deemed more worthy than us.

I slipped between the mass of bodies, taking Bernice's hand as we headed out of the room in the middle of the crowd, neither of us daring so much as a word with so many witnesses lingering close, but her fingers tightened around mine. She was a beautiful girl, fiery and full of passion, which was a lot of what had drawn me to her when I began to think about building my herd after earning my nose ring, but we hadn't made anything between us official yet. She was one of my prospective cows, but only in the sense of us considering forming an official herd, my hand surrounding hers the most physical we had gotten with each other.

I'd wanted more, thought about it on more than one occasion, but it wasn't that simple. We were in the midst of a war, our families and entire Order were at constant risk of persecution, and of being snatched in the night and dragged away to a Nebular Inquisition Centre, never to be seen again for nothing more than the crime of being born to our kind. Crossing that line with her or any of my potential cows felt like a risk we shouldn't take.

Opening our hearts to each other like that could so easily end in tragedy if the things we were up to were discovered, and I didn't want to risk anyone loving me when I was almost certain I would end up dead before long. It wasn't fair.

We made our way across the quiet campus to The Orb, my gaze following the higher Orders as they strutted inside, claiming gourmet meals, and situating themselves in the best seats around the room.

To the right of the door, a line was already forming made up of the lesser Orders. We had to wait until everyone else had been fed before we could enter the room, and once we claimed our much less satisfactory meal, we were expected to sit in the small courtyard outside the main building on hard picnic benches left open to the elements.

I said nothing about the injustice of it as we waited in line, my eyes meeting those of a few other Fae in silent acknowledgement of the secret we shared.

My eyes moved to the sky as I traced my thumb over the back of Bernice's hand, the sun setting in the distance and the first stars igniting as it retreated. They watched us, but if they even noticed our plight, they did nothing about it.

Eventually, we trailed into The Orb, moving to the counter to the right of the huge golden dome and collecting our trays of plain rice and peas. I said nothing as I took it, ignoring the smells of the delicious food being consumed by the other Orders in the room and grabbing a couple of grass and kale smoothies from the refrigerator as I headed outside to the shitty dining area reserved for us.

Bernice sat beside me, glaring down at her basic meal with fire in her dark eyes and I dropped my hand to her thigh, squeezing lightly before leaning close to speak in her ear.

"I have some chocolate for after," I murmured, the scent of her fresh skin drawn into my lungs as my lips brushed the shell of her ear.

"You went into town?" she hissed, turning that wild glare on me instead as she took in my words, the movement placing our lips mere inches apart.

"There's no rule against me doing so," I replied, a note of firmness to my tone as she frowned at me.

Bernice flicked a silencing bubble around us before she went on, her eyes darting to the people sitting at the tables surrounding ours for a moment, but they were in the same position as us, and I wasn't afraid of what any of them might report to the teachers. I was simply having a conversation with my potential cow. There weren't any rules against that.

"No, but there are Nymphs patrolling the streets of Tucana and my mom warned me that Minotaurs, Sphinxes and Tiberian Rats are going missing every day."

"We know that," I said but she shook her head.

"I'm not talking about the ones who are taken to those fucked-up camps. I mean Fae who just disappear, their bodies never found. Rumour has it that the Nymphs have been given permission to prey on our kind so long as they keep it subtle and-"

"I didn't see any Nymphs while I was there," I told her, though that wasn't entirely true; I had seen some in the distance at the far end of a long street before I ducked into the store to grab what I wanted. "And I'm not doing anything wrong by spending my money on decent food. There aren't any rules against us buying our own food and I have more than enough auras to do so. I'm not going to eat this shit day in day out without any respite from its blandness."

"I just don't think chocolate bars are worth risking your life for," Bernice hissed, knocking my hand from her thigh irritably, but I caught her jaw in my grip as she made to look away from me, forcing her to hold my gaze.

“I didn’t just go there for chocolate,” I breathed, the secret I’d been keeping all day burning a hole in my chest as it fought to break free, but I didn’t dare mention it here.

Bernice’s full lips parted in surprise, my attention fixing on them briefly before I forced myself to release her, and we both fell silent as we ate our bland meals.

We hung around for a while, taking care to look casual when we finally got to our feet and wandered away up the path which led towards the Uranus Infirmary and Aqua House beyond. Anyone who noticed us would simply see a pair of Minotaurs headed towards Water Territory, nothing suspicious about that, no reason to take any particular notice of it.

I cast subtle magic around us as we strolled on, the back of my hand brushing against hers more than once, a slight thrill going through me at the contact each time.

We rounded the infirmary, moving into the deep shadow cast by the beautiful building and my magic coiled around us as those shadows darkened further. The concealment spell rose to give us cover, the shadows so thick that I couldn’t even see my own face within them as Bernice slid her hand into mine.

I found the wall with my free hand, my fingers carving a line along the cold stone as I felt my way down it, my magic reaching out with a careful caress until finally, it curled around the face of the stone gargoyle I’d been hunting for.

I ran my fingers over its rocky features, cresting its head before finding a spot right between its stumpy stone wings and pressing firmly until I felt something give.

I kept the shadows close to us as we stepped through the new opening in the stone wall, and we stayed silent until we were inside, the subtle grinding of stone letting me know that the secret entrance was once again closed behind us.

I let the concealment spells drop away and strode down the narrow corridor, Bernice falling a step behind me when it became too narrow for us to walk side by side.

The path was familiar now, but I still got a prickle of tension running through me every time I walked it. What we were doing was so risky, but not doing anything had to be worse.

I finally made it to the heavy wooden door at the far end of the stone passage and I touched my hand to it, allowing a pulse of my power to pass into it and prove who I was before it opened for me. It immediately slammed shut behind me, making Bernice do the same thing before she was allowed through, and I blinked at the orange glow of the firelight illuminating this place.

I glanced towards the fireplace, smiling at Gary as he beckoned me over to join him on the couch there, around twenty other Fae already making themselves comfortable in the large room. The walls were built of exposed bricks, deep arches carved into them all around us, the concrete floor well-worn with years of use, yet this space had been wholly unoccupied when we’d found it and made it ours. The door which led up into the main part of the building would be as carefully sealed as the one Bernice and I had entered through now, and I could feel the power of the wards and silencing bubbles protecting our hideout still in effect all around us.

“You haven’t heard?” Gary asked me in a rough voice, and I braced myself for more harrowing news from the war as I sat opposite him on the grey couch.

“Heard what?” I asked, making room for Bernice as she joined us.

Gary hesitated, his eyes dark with a grief I had come to know and expect far too much of during the last year, and I waited on his words with a cold kind of dread.

“Lionel killed Darius during the battle,” Gary breathed, and it was like the entire world fell still around me as I took in those words, trying to make sense of them.

“You can’t be serious?” Bernice gasped as Gary hung his head like he couldn’t bear watching the truth of that declaration sink into us.

“They’ve finally released a full account of the battle – stuffed full of biased bullshit in favour of the fucking king of course, but Darius’s name was listed there, right at the top.”

“No,” I breathed, yanking my Atlas from my pocket and opening it up, hitting the button for The Celestial Times app and trying not to flinch as I read over the article.

Darius Acrux Named Among the Executed Traitors in The Battle of The Great King's Rise, by Gus Vulpecula.

On this grand and triumphant day, following the glorious triumph against the rebels who sought to undermine our noble new king, a full account of the battle has now come to light.

King Lionel Acrux, the first of his line and most adamant supporter of the strength of the Fae, has given this humble reporter a harrowing and touching account of the battle he so valiantly led against the terrorists who have set themselves against the crown, seeking to sow discord and unrest in our wonderful kingdom.

Eyes weighed down with the mass of a thousand suns and gleaming with the power of a truly awe-inspiring Fae, he told me himself of the awful task he had to fulfil for the safety of his people. He spoke with a heavy and true heart about the moment when he was forced to end the life of his traitorous son, Darius Acrux, for the greater good of our nation.

I couldn't bear to read another word of that ass-licking bullshit, and I switched my Atlas off as the backs of my eyes began to burn.

Darius and I had had our rift, but I had never stopped supporting him, or loving him as the true friend I had always been to him. He may never have held me as one of his closest companions, but I'd been in his inner circle, I'd gotten to know and admire the man he was growing into and had been holding out hope for him to be the one to destroy his father for the sake of all of Solaria.

"He killed his own son," Bernice breathed, the horror in her words slipping beneath my skin and festering there. "Who else might even stand a chance against him now? Who the hell is going to be able to stop that Orderist piece of shit from destroying our entire kingdom now that Darius is..."

"The Vegas are more powerful than Lionel Acrux," I said firmly, raising my voice as I looked around the gathered group. The Undercover A.S.S.

We had been meeting like this for months now, working against the injustices taking place at the academy, swapping information, and doing what little we could to defy the rules that had been forced upon us, but it didn't feel like nearly enough. Especially not now.

Our numbers were growing slowly, but we had to be careful. Most of us were so-called lesser Orders, but some, like Gary were just good Fae who hated this segregation shit just as much as the rest of us and wanted to do something to defy it. "We need to hold on. The queens are coming for their crown, they're growing into their strength. They'll end this, sooner or later they'll-"

"Darius trained his entire life and still fell at the hands of that monster," Frank breathed from the back of the room, the rest of Seth Capella's old pack gathered close around him. "The Vegas could take decades to grow into the fullness of their power, to learn to wield it the way they'd have to in order to reclaim the throne from that son of a bitch. We don't have that long to wait. We'll all be dead long before they can-"

"Enough," I mooed, shoving to my feet and scraping my foot across the floor in challenge. "If any of us here were cowards, then we wouldn't be in this room, clinging to the Undercover A.S.S. with all we have. I'm sure as fuck not going to run scared now. I'm in this because it's the right thing to do. I understand the risks, just as you all do, and I know what will happen to me if I'm caught, but I won't stop, I won't back down and I won't let the death of Darius Acrux cast fear into my heart. He was a good man despite the way his father raised him, and he gave his life fighting for the rights of all of us. I won't disrespect that sacrifice by turning from his cause now."

A low cheer went up among the group and I expelled a breath from my nose, nodding in satisfaction.

"I finally got the package we've all been waiting for today," I said, pulling the smartphone from my pocket and looking at its dark screen.

"Are you sure its untraceable?" Alice asked in a low voice, her hand moving to grip Frank's knee like she was hoping the other Wolf might be able to offer us that reassurance.

"It came from Portia Silverstone herself. She left the rebel stronghold so that she could focus on reporting the truth from the front lines, and she needs Fae like us to help her break that news. I met her in the back of Andromeda Place. She says she's trying to get in contact with Tyler Corbin so that they can collaborate on stories and get the truth out there. If we want to expose all the fucked-up Orderist shit going on in this place, then she can help us do it."

"The moment that exposé is released, they'll start hunting for us," Bernice murmured, a fact more than a warning. "We'll have to be ready."

"We'll need cover stories in place," I agreed. "And our mental shields need to be bulletproof. Is everyone still practicing regularly?"

Everyone nodded and I glanced towards Elijah Indus who puffed his chest up as he shifted as if on command, his two eyes merging into one as his Cyclops Order took over and he beckoned some of the Wolf pack closer to practice.

It was a difficult art to evade their invasion without them realising it. Like locking your secrets behind a door, then disguising that door as something that wouldn't draw any attention, hiding your feelings about what lay beyond it with memories from another time.

We'd been working on it tirelessly, Elijah testing our abilities so that if and when we fell under investigation, we'd be ready. We couldn't risk anyone exposing us. So far, we had mostly just been helping any students who came under suspicion, aiding them in escaping the school before the inquisitors showed up – though we'd only been successful in helping two of them escape entirely. But if we followed through with our plan to share footage from within the school walls, to reveal the fucked-up teaching methods taking place here, then we needed to be beyond suspicion. We had to be unbreakable. And I wouldn't risk taking so much as a single photograph until I was confident we were ready.

Even just meeting like this, with so many different Orders in one place, could see us sent to detention, or worse. And with the punishments Nova allowed the K.U.N.Ts to dole out getting harsher by the day, who knew what we might face if we were discovered?

I relaxed back into my chair as conversation started up around me. Even with the devastating news of Darius's death hanging in the air, I could tell that everyone was relieved to be stealing this time to talk freely, mix with other Orders and just be something close to normal.

Drinks were passed around and a couple of Fae slunk away into dark corners, tugging their partners with them as they took the opportunity to be together without having to fear watchful eyes spying them mixing with other Orders. The moans started up quickly, though most were hidden within silencing bubbles to give some semblance of privacy.

No one commented on it.

I accepted a beer as Gary tossed it to me, shifting in my seat while not looking at Bernice. I could feel her eyes on me though, feel her gaze moving over my face, lingering on my bull's nose ring.

I gave in and turned to her, finding her bottom lip captured between her teeth and I reached out to grasp her chin, tugging it free.

"Keep looking at me like that and we'll end up doing something we swore we wouldn't," I murmured, my blood heating at the liquid brown of her eyes.

"Maybe I'm starting to think differently about that promise," she said quietly. "Maybe I'm thinking that life is too short and can be stolen so briefly. So why deny ourselves anything in the time we have?"

I swallowed the lump in my throat as I considered that, considered *her.* She was my little bovine, one of my potential herd, and yet there was nothing official in those titles yet. She didn't wear my bell around her neck. But the way she was looking at me made me wonder if she wanted me to offer her that. Made me think about buying her the finest golden bell and hanging it from a beautifully decorated choker that I could wrap around her throat. If she accepted that from me, then that would be it. She would truly be my heifer, the first official member of the herd a bull of my stature could claim.

I felt Gary watching us from across the small table, but he may as well have not been there at all as I reached out and ran a finger from one side of her throat to the other, just where that choker would sit if I offered it to her.

Bernice blinked those big brown eyes of hers and my cock stiffened at the thought of it, of me and her…

"Mooove over," Ranjeep said loudly as she appeared beside us, twisting her fingers into her long hair which was brushed to a bright sheen. The movement of her hand beside her huge breasts drew my attention to them as I glanced up at her in surprise, the moment between Bernice and I shattering.

"I didn't think you were coming tonight," I said, shifting back to make room for her as she dropped into the space which hadn't really existed between me and Bernice.

Ranjeep was another of my potential herd, though she was much more forthright in telling me that she wanted to make it official sooner rather than later. She'd shown me cow bell brochures more than once and made plenty of comments about what an attentive herd member she would make once she committed herself to her bull. But Minotaur herds were complicated things. Sometimes they were polyamorous, generally a group of females with one male, though there could be solo gender herds or even mixed groups so long as there was an acceptance of the dominant bull. Sometimes they weren't sexual in nature at all, or they could be formed from a monogamous couple and their subsequent children. Generally, we spent our teens and early adulthood testing different styles of herding, figuring out the best fit for us before settling down and offering up cow bells a bit later on in life. My potential herd had started to form around me since I'd become worthy of my nose ring, but none of us were under any obligation to stay as a herd permanently. It was simply a starting point to help us figure out how we might fit into herd life before any long-term decisions were made.

I still had no idea what path I wanted. My cock had no objections to the notion of polyamory, but I would only choose that path if I felt certain I could offer the emotional support to each member of my herd in that situation equally too.

Ranjeep, on the other hand, seemed to have already decided what she wanted.

"Ah!" Bernice cursed as Ranjeep smacked into her while making herself comfortable. "You nearly took my eye out with those fucking udders!"

"Don't be jealous, sweety, green isn't your colour," Ranjeep laughed, her eyes moving quickly back to me.

"Your colour will be red in a moment if you don't watch your fucking mouth," Bernice growled, and I swiped a hand down my face. Cow politics were enough to give me a headache at the best of times, but right now, I didn't have the energy to mediate.

"How about I sit in the middle?" I suggested, grabbing Ranjeep around the waist and tugging her over my lap before she had the chance to answer.

She mooed excitedly as I moved her over my crotch, wriggling her ass against me and making it even harder to focus my thoughts.

I dropped her into my seat and took her place in the middle, taking the phone Portia had given me from my pocket once more and praying to the stars for mercy as I switched it on.

The screen flashed with a loading bar just as a thump sounded at the door, and every undercover A.S.S. member in the room lurched around in fright.

I was on my feet in a moment, switching the phone off again as I drew fire magic into my hands, fear rippling through me.

"Milton?" a girl shouted from beyond the door, and I stilled in horror as I recognised Marguerite Helebor's voice. "You have to run!" she cried. "Mildred is on the hunt and she's on your trail. I know you're all in there, please, listen to me!"

"Shit," I cursed, grabbing Bernice and Ranjeep and hauling them to their feet as everyone began running towards the hidden exit behind the fireplace. The earth Elementals among us had spent weeks carving it for this purpose.

"If she's alone, we could take her out," Gary suggested, glancing around at the space as it emptied out, but I shook my head.

"She said Mildred is onto us. We can't risk it. All of you need to go, I'll make sure there's nothing out of place here. I'll take the fall if someone has to."

"Milton, no," Bernice gasped, gripping my arm and tugging me towards the fireplace just as the door was blasted from the other side, the spells strengthening it barely holding as Marguerite hurled her fire against it.

Seth's old pack and Elijah darted into the hidden tunnel next, the last of our group racing away while we remained. Ranjeep would have to cave the tunnel in as she went, the last earth Elemental left to do it, but we had time, we could make it, we could-

The door broke apart and I threw my hands up, a shield of heated energy rising between us and Marguerite where she was revealed alone in the doorway beyond.

Her bloodshot eyes were wild as she looked between me and the others, her chest heaving as though she had sprinted the entire way here just to beat Mildred.

"The K.U.N.Ts are coming," she hissed. "*Run*."

I had no idea why she was helping us, but the frantic panic in her eyes was more than enough to force me into action, and I shoved the others towards the hidden passage as quickly as I could.

"Why?" I asked as I backed into the gloom beyond the fire, Marguerite's grief-stricken eyes meeting mine with a hollowness which gave me my answer before she even spoke the words.

"Because I loved him," she said simply. "And that bastard killed him. Now go."

Ranjeep threw her hands out, the hole in the wall closing with the aid of her magic, and we all turned and broke into a sprint, the tunnels caving in at our backs as we went.

We raced away into the darkness as fast as our legs could carry us, Gary casting a Faelight to light the way on while the three of us simply shifted into our Minotaur forms. Running in darkened passageways was what we were built for after all, and as we sprinted away into the dark and escaped a horrendous fate, I was left with one single thought in my mind: Marguerite Helebor had just risked everything to save us. So it looked like the Undercover A.S.S. had just bagged themselves a K.U.N.T.

Scorpio
Gemini
Virgo
Aries
Cancer
Leo
Sagittarius
Taurus
Capricorn
Aquarius
Libra
Pisces

DARCY

CHAPTER FIFTEEN

The cold bit deep into my bones and the darkness licked at the inside of my flesh, trying to coax me into it as always. The Shadow Beast was stirring, urging me to shift, and I knew I'd be far warmer if I gave into it and allowed it to take over. But if I let it take my body, then it might take my mind too, and I couldn't risk that. So instead, I faced the cold, huddled naked against a wall within a cave I'd found to one side of the lake.

Snow had fallen freshly on the ground outside and the howling wind sometimes sounded like a monster ready to come feast on my bones. But I was already in the clutches of a monster, one far more terrible than the wind.

I replayed the memory of my parents in my mind, seeking comfort in their words, the way their love had shone on me like rays of the sun. They had felt so close, as if I could reach out and touch them, yet we'd been separated by years of time that none of us could cross with all the magic in the world. The image of their faces was one of the few things sustaining me, along with thoughts of those I loved.

I shivered, the shadows cloaking my body offering some defence against the cold, the whispers within them never faltering as they offered me sanctuary in their embrace.

I had to do something. I couldn't stay here and starve, though even the thought of leaving the mountain came with a rush of fear for everyone I loved. I was the danger, and I could never go near them again if it put them at risk.

I tried to ignore the hunger ripping at my stomach, knowing that starvation alone was going to kill me if I stayed here too long, but maybe it was better to die than put my loved ones in peril again. Though I would never willingly put my sister or my mate through that. I just didn't know what to do, or how to protect them.

Bile rose in my mouth as the memories of the Shadow Beast sifted through my mind, its hunger for a kill as it hunted down the rebels in the night, the taste of blood in my mouth as their screams were silenced for good.

I clawed my fingers into my shadow-stained hair, burying my face against my knees. But before the suffocating guilt and grief could claim me like it had so many times, a glimmer of silver light in my periphery made me lift my head, a frown pulling at my brow as I watched it dance and flutter across the rocky cave walls.

It was coming from the lake, and all of my thoughts abandoned me as I rose to my feet, my body draped in silver as the flickering reflection of the water shimmered around me.

In the depths of the lake, something was shining, glowing as bright as the moon far, far down at its base.

The air fell unnaturally still, and the cold slipped from my skin as I walked barefoot out of the cave to the water's edge beneath the waning moon, the shadows wrapping around me in a gown of darkness.

There was a song in the air, or that was the easiest way to describe it. It wasn't of this world, more like I was hearing it through the veil of an entirely different universe. One I didn't belong to.

I gazed down into the water, realising it was the fallen star glowing brighter at its heart, and I was certain that the strange, beautiful sound was coming from it, luring me towards it.

The glacial water lapped over my toes, and I blinked, pulling myself out of the trance that was trying to hold onto me. Nothing good could come from following some ethereal music into a dark lake.

I backed up, but the song grew louder inside my head and my gaze locked on the fallen star once more, glimmering and making the entire body of water sparkle. My lips parted in awe at the beauty, and as the power around me intensified, rolling deep into the belly of my bones, I was lost to its call.

I strode into the lake, following the sound, not feeling the icy clutch of the water, although a small part of me was aware I could freeze out here. But that seemed so inconsequential somehow…

I waded deeper, the water lapping up around my waist and the shadows coiling tight around my body like a second skin as I walked further and further.

This was madness in its truest form, but the part of me that should have cared was locked down, like I was no longer afraid of anything, least of all the hallowed power writhing in this lake.

Suddenly, the bottom dropped away beneath my feet, and I gazed down at the fallen star far below me as I treaded water to stay afloat.

"Daughter of the flames," it whispered to me, summoning me with a force no one in this world could have resisted. It was like the summons that had come from the midst of that star had come from me too, as well as every other divine being in the universe. I was made of the magic it sung, every fibre of my body recognising it from a time inconceivably long ago when my existence had been nothing but a farfetched possibility.

I took a huge breath and dove down, kicking hard as I swam straight for the bottom of the lake, bubbles streaming from my lips as I went, my gaze never faltering from the fallen star.

The lake was even deeper than I'd realised, but there was no turning back now, and no part of me wanted to retreat either. I swam furiously towards the god-like being waiting in the water for me, not knowing what fate it was going to hand me, a curse, or a gift, or perhaps nothing at all. All I knew was that it felt like I was approaching the edge of the world, and at any second, I might drop off of it, my essence scratched from reality like it had never existed at all. And still, I wasn't afraid.

The star was far larger than it had appeared from the surface, at least ten times my size, its surface glittering like rhinestones, the silver light it emitted bright enough to cut through the gloom all around me. I reached for it, unblinking and totally enraptured by its beauty, the pressure of the water making my ears pop, my lungs beginning to ache for air. But nothing could turn me from this path. Not death, nor the promise of life. This was something far beyond the realm of both those things, and at the same time, it embodied them too.

My fingers grazed its beautiful surface and the water shifted around me in an instant. My feet hit the rocky lakebed as the water withdrew, creating an orb of air which surrounded me and the star. Two entities, one who would be here on this earth for barely a scrap of a moment, and the other timeless beyond all bounds, who had seen the solar system itself formed from matter and magic.

Water dripped from my hair and naked skin, the shadows slithering away inside me like snakes, and I could no longer hear the voices within them. They seemed to go to sleep in my chest beside the Shadow Beast, leaving me bare and alone. But my nakedness didn't matter. It was as if this star saw only my soul, the rest of me insignificant.

The air pulsed and hummed with an intense magic that made my bones vibrate, and my heart hammered at the immensity of the power I was witnessing.

"It is time for my release," the star whispered within my head, soft and light like feathers against my temples.

"What do you mean?" I asked, stunned as I took a step closer, my fingers burning to touch its gleaming surface once more. It was the most breath-taking being I'd ever seen, like a living diamond that held a soul. It was an impossible thing to behold, but I couldn't deny its truth.

The air stirred around me, and it almost sounded like a sigh, the silver light of the star dimming then brightening once more.

"All stars fall. My time has come," it said, and I swallowed against the lump in my throat.

"I don't understand," I said, shaking my head in confusion.

The air hummed again, and I felt the kiss of its untold magic sliding over my skin, warming me through to my core. It was like being bathed in molten love, the emotion rising in my chest and ebbing out into every corner of my limbs.

"I remember now..."

"What do you remember?" I whispered.

"You are shadow cursed, a mortal you shall soon be."

I winced from those words, the pure certainty of them cutting me deep. "Is there a way to stop it?"

"The fates are still being woven, thread by thread."

"Then stop weaving them," I demanded, my anger starting to rise as I thought of the battle, of all that had been lost. I remembered myself at last, and my wrath against the stars, of all they had stolen from us. "Aren't you in control of fate? Don't *you* decide all of this? Why are you so cruel?"

The power of the place intensified, trying to keep me calm, but my mind was sharpening now, and I held tightly onto what I knew about these beings. The stars cursed us at every turn, they were the ones who had done this, who had Starcrossed Tory and Darius, who had offered me Orion, only to tear us apart by a twisted curse, who had let so many good people die under their watch in a battle we should have won. This creature, as beautiful and divine as it clearly was, was my enemy. And I wasn't going to do anything it asked of me.

"Cruelty is a construct of Fae, not us. When we are perched within the sky, we are neither good nor bad. We see all, we offer answers, we guide and gift, but we may take and destroy if the choices made below us invoke it."

"So what have me and my sister done to deserve the fates you've offered us? What paths have we chosen that have made you curse us and the people we love?" I hissed, anger flaring hotly beneath my skin, and for a second, I could have sworn I felt a spark of fire magic within me.

"Fate is unbalanced. The wrath of Clydinius wove your woes."

"Who is Clydinius?" I pressed, feeling I was on the cusp of some answer that could change everything.

"Clydinius wants you to keep the broken promise, warrior of the Vega line."

"What is the promise?" I gasped, moving forward in desperation as those words circled in my head. The ones the Imperial Star had spoken too. "I'll keep it. Just tell me what it is. How can I fix what I have no knowledge of?"

"It is time for my end. My death is the gift of Fae, a gift all stars offer in their demise. It is why magic lives in your world, for my magic is your magic." The light grew brighter and brighter, blinding me until I had to throw up a hand and shut my

eyes against the glow of it. It spread into everything, flowing into the rocks, the water, me. I could feel the soul of this star spreading and shattering, the essence of it pouring out into every corner of the world.

There was so much power, it made the ground tremble beneath me, and the sky far above began to sing. I was witnessing something that was bound with nature, the four Elements seeming to burn in the air around me, everything crackling, sparkling, shining. I was nearly thrown from my feet by the shockwave of it, but the star's power held me in place, and my head fell back as all that magic tumbled through me like I was nothing but a ghost in its path.

I cried out, the purest form of ecstasy setting my skin alight and making my mind spark with memories. Long, long ago memories of our sun being birthed into existence, of the planets settling into place around it, then of Earth flourishing from a barren wasteland to luscious, fruitful lands; a gift like no other. I saw the mortal realm, Fae realm, and Shadow realm all at once, overlapping as if they were the same, and yet divided by magic and divine intervention. And as the first Fae emerged, the stars were placed around to guard us, their full power residing only in our realm, where the beings who dwelled there were capable of wielding it too. The stars took up their shapes within the constellations, but it seemed like they weren't the only power here, like there was some other, higher force at play I couldn't comprehend.

I fathomed it all in an intangible way that wasn't like any memory I had experienced before, it was happening now, then, always, past, present, future, all of time rushing together as the first fates were spun. I was on the cusp of grasping something, understanding the drive behind these fates and what it was all for, when the power evaporated, and I stumbled to my knees.

It was gone and I was abandoned, panting on the rocky lakebed with a sense of nirvana washing over me, still trembling from the experience. The star's light began to dim before my eyes, leaving me with a quiet, empty rock with no presence inside it at all. Tears slid silently down my cheeks, and I lifted my hand to touch them, not knowing if they were of joy or sadness, or somewhere in between.

Before I could even begin to process what I'd just witnessed, a voice filled my head, loud and commanding, the authority in it ringing right down to my soul and binding it in steel ropes.

"Come to me." Lavinia's summoning resounded through my skull and the shadows seemed to screech inside my ears, pouring back out of me to bind around my skin.

The light of the star faded entirely, and the water rushed in around me before I had a chance to draw in a single breath.

I was plunged into darkness at the base of the lake and panic slammed into my chest as my heart beat to a frantic tune. I started swimming for the surface, kicking and kicking as I carved my way through the inky blackness of the lake, not knowing how far I still had to go or if I was getting anywhere near the air I so desperately craved.

My lungs screamed and my limbs froze, the weight of the water pressing me down like it was trying to drown me in its depths and claim me for its own.

My pulse thundered in my ears as I thought of Tory and Lance and Gabriel, of the people who would never find me in this watery grave if I didn't make it out. I'd disappear as if I'd never existed, sink away to the bottom of this black pool to become a pile of lonely bones.

I kicked harder, the determination to find them all again fuelling my muscles, and suddenly my head broke through the surface and I gasped down a crisp lungful of air.

"Come to me," Lavinia's voice beckoned me again and the yanking in my chest told me the Shadow Beast was rising to her call.

"No," I growled, gritting my teeth as I swam for the water's edge, trying to fight the pull of her summoning.

But the moment my feet hit the rocks in the shallows, Lavinia's power fell over me and the shift rippled down my spine.

In moments, I was a towering, furry black beast once more, a roar spilling from my lips as I took off across the mountain and into the trees. I was falling away into the darkness of the creature's mind, and as hard as I tried to hold on, it was a losing battle.

The Shadow Beast raced down the mountainside, and I was cast into the gulf of its power, drifting away into a cavernous void I feared I'd never awake from.

When I finally regained consciousness, I was looking through the Shadow Beast's eyes as I climbed the steps that led to the door of The Palace of Souls. The towering walls of my ancestors' home looked less welcoming under a murky sky, the taint of the Shadow Princess and her wicked king drenching the air.

I pressed my will out against the Shadow Beast's, fighting to reclaim control from it, a furnace of resilience igniting in me at the sight of this building which should have belonged to me and my sister. I ached to seize it back from the monsters who had taken up residence in its walls. This was Vega territory, and if I ever got the chance to defend it, I'd damn well do so.

I reached the palace doors and shivered as they opened, finding Lavinia waiting there for me, her eyes as sharp as two razors and as dark as the trenches of the sea.

She stepped forward, the shadows dancing around her, and I felt them tighten on me as she reached up to brush her fingers over the fur of my shoulder.

"Hello, little Princess," she said mockingly. "Welcome home. I have a surprise for you."

She turned her back on me and I was immediately drawn after her, fighting to hold onto my conscious thoughts as the Shadow Beast tried to greedily swallow me down again and take over everything I was. But I wasn't going to let go, not if I could help it. The fear of what Lavinia would make me do was enough to keep me here for now.

I followed her through the luxurious halls of my family's palace, finding changes in the decoration that made my skin crawl. Paintings of my mother and father had been replaced with countless artworks of Dragons, and the one who featured in them the most was Lionel, his jade green form staring down at me from every angle of these corridors with a smug hubris to his features. Anger burned hot in the centre of my chest and the Shadow Beast fed on it like a meal, its own rage rising to meet mine.

Lavinia led me through to the throne room where shafts of moonlight poured through the stained-glass windows above and severed the darkness. The shadow bitch turned to me, looking me dead in the eye, seeming particularly excited about something. I had the sense I really didn't want to know what it was.

"Shift," she commanded, and the shadows rippled through me, forcing me to do as she bid before I could even try and hold them back.

The Shadow Beast fell away, leaving me as a girl standing before a monster, shadow cloaking both of our bodies, my hair a mirror of hers. I was shorter than her, but apart from that, we looked like we were birthed of the same thing now, and I despised it.

I immediately tried to lunge at her, a shriek of hatred tearing from my throat, but she bound me in place with lashes of shadow, her head cocking to one side as she appraised me.

"There is fire in you yet," she commented. "I wonder how long you can hold onto it for. The Shadow Beast is hungry." At her words, I felt the evil creature sinking its teeth into some vital piece of my essence, weakening me as it fed on all the parts of me that made me Fae.

"Why did you bring me here?" I asked in a hiss, my disgust with her clear on my face. There was nothing more she could take from me now, she had me captured with my magic in the clutches of her Shadow Beast, so what more was there to claim from me?

"To suffer, of course." She smiled, beckoning me after her and I held my head high as I followed, my bare feet pressing to the cold flagstones, the shadows the only thing concealing my nudity.

I passed an empty cage of black night iron and frowned at it before following her to the back exit from the throne room and down a corridor to a wide metal door. She unlocked it, guiding me inside and my world fell apart before my eyes, every ounce of oxygen in my lungs crushed from existence and leaving me desolate.

"Lance!" I ran to him, my scream rending the air apart.

He was on his knees, chained at the heart of the room while his hands were secured above his head by manacles.

Blood raced down his flesh, dripping to the floor around him from lacerations across his body.

I dropped down before him and gripped his face in my hands, desperate to see life in his eyes, the thought of losing him too awful to consider. I couldn't go on without him. He was the epitome of the most reckless, soul-bursting love I had ever known. We were star bound, but more than that, we had fought for each other through laws and battlelines, blood and tears. We were meant to remain together, there was no alternative. I was done losing him and done with all the monsters who kept lurking at our door. Lance Orion was mine, on this plane and every other, and he was *not* going to be stolen from me now.

Terror made my heart thrash, but as he released a low groan and his eyes flickered open a crack, I buckled forward in relief, an agonised sob heaving from my chest. Though finding him like this, tortured and made to suffer by our enemies was almost as devastating as finding him dead.

"Blue?" he murmured, only half conscious, his blood still running down into a circuit of drains around the chamber.

"I'm here, I've got you." I trembled as I pressed my hands to his shoulders and Lavinia drifted closer at my back, watching me intently with a sickly smile on her face.

I tried to bring magic to my fingertips, determined to heal him, but the well of power in my chest had nothing to give.

"Please, please," I begged of the stars.

Orion's eyes fell closed, his head lolling, and my heart thrashed all over again. He was on the brink of death, and I could almost feel the Veil parting for him, the stars about to pull him away from me forever.

"No!" I cried, cursing myself as I failed him in his most urgent moment of need, no magic coming to my aid, the shadows thickening until I could barely breathe.

Lavinia was pouring all of her power into me to keep me subdued, leaving me useless, able to do nothing but witness Orion's death.

"He's only got a few more moments of life in him," Lavinia said in a mocking voice.

"Hang on," I begged, tugging furiously on that well of power in me again as I refused to submit to the curse, and for a second, I could have sworn there was a flicker of magic, blazing some of the shadows aside and promising Orion life.

Lavinia shoved me forcefully before I could attempt to heal him, releasing him from the chains so he slumped down at her feet, though magic blocking cuffs still remained locked around his wrists.

"Get away from him!" I commanded, lurching forward but a web of shadows snatched me back by the waist, yanking me tight to the wall to keep me from going to him.

I thrashed and struggled to get free, fear burrowing into my core as Lavinia produced a key and slid it into the manacle on his right wrist. Then she slapped him hard enough to make his head wheel sideways and he groaned as he came back to consciousness.

"Lance, I'm here. Stay with me," I called, my heart frenzied with fear, but it was like he couldn't even hear me.

She gripped his hand, pressing it firmly to his chest.

"Heal yourself," she said idly, and my lips parted in confusion as she allowed him to do that, green light flooding from his palm and knitting over the wounds on his body.

I fought to get to him, panic slashing across my heart as the shadows dragged me back and the Shadow Beast dug its claws in beneath my skin.

When Orion was almost healed, I yelled to him, "Fight her!", praying he was strong enough to turn his magic against her.

His attention focused on me, and terror fell over his features like he was only just realising I was truly there. But his eyes were heavily lidded, and that terror melted away again before it could take a real grip.

"Darcy…" he murmured.

He'd managed to heal most of his injuries, but there were still marks and bruises on his flesh left from her torture, like she wanted to leave him branded.

"I'm here," I said. "What's she done to you?"

"Arm up, pet," Lavinia ordered, and he offered his wrist to her as simply as that.

She snapped the magic-blocking cuff back in place, making me stiffen in horror.

I couldn't understand why he was complying with her, letting himself be shackled once more. It didn't make any sense.

"Lance? What's going on?" I begged, but he wouldn't look at me.

"Please," he spoke to Lavinia quietly like I wasn't even in the room, his voice a distant thing that sounded as though it had been dragged up from the depths of his chest. "Send her away from here."

His words shredded my heart, and I shook my head in refusal of them, even though neither of them were paying any attention to me now. He wasn't himself. Something wasn't right. He was barely even reacting to me being here.

"That would entirely defeat the purpose of our little deal, pet." Lavinia ran her hand over his hair and disgust snaked down my spine.

"Get your hands off of him," I snarled, and she turned to look at me as a ferocious, protective fury flooded over me in blistering waves.

"What have you done?" I breathed at Orion, my voice lost to fear, but his eyes remained on the floor like he couldn't bear to look my way, or maybe that he didn't even care to.

"He has done what he needs to save his Vega princess," Lavinia said, her voice lilting with amusement.

"Lance?" I refused to take my eyes off of him, ignoring the horrid woman in the room who had us bound in her dark power like the puppet master of our destiny. I needed to hear this from the man I loved, not the bitch who had cursed me.

"Tell her, pet," Lavinia encouraged, brushing her fingers through his hair possessively.

I jerked forward with a growl of warning, my teeth bared, but it only seemed to make her smile grow.

"Get your filthy paws away from him," I spat venomously.

"Hush now, let him answer," Lavinia said with a smirk.

Orion released a sigh that seemed so full of defeat it carved a hole in my chest. There was some twisted magic at play here, something Lavinia had done to subdue him, there had to be.

"She bound my blood to your curse. I'm the answer to breaking it," he revealed.

My throat tightened and I looked from him to Lavinia, my breaths coming heavier, my mind splintering and soul cracking. "What does that mean?"

"It means he is *mine*," she said, watching me closely and drinking in the moment my heart shattered within the cage of my chest.

"For three moon cycles," Orion added hollowly like that made it any better. Maybe it did, but I couldn't focus on anything but the ringing in my ears and the potent rage building inside me.

"You can't do this," I refused, turning to Lavinia. "I'll pay the price. This is my curse, not his. If you want my blood, my suffering, then have it." I offered her my wrists, ready to be chained in his place as I jutted my chin up, but she didn't seem remotely interested in that offer.

"It must be him," she said, her eyes alight with this wicked game of hers. "Besides, we made a Death bond on it, didn't we, pet?"

"No," I gasped.

Orion gave me a look that broke through the darkness in his eyes, filled with an apology that could never undo this, because it confirmed everything she had said, and broke my heart in turn.

"I'll leave you to fill in the details," Lavinia said, leaning down and gripping Orion's throat where a collar of shadow sat against his skin.

Everything stilled, ice sliding the full length of my spine as she pressed her mouth to his. I expected him to flinch away, to fight back against her abhorrent touch, but as she deepened that kiss and slid her tongue between his lips, I watched in a state of torturous shock as he let her, the only sign of his distress a crease on his brow and his hands balling into tight fists. Something twisted sharply in the centre of my stomach and malice took over everything I was down to the roots of my being, stealing away what little was left of my sanity.

"Stop!" I yelled, fighting wildly, blood pounding furiously through my veins.

My soul was wounded by seeing my mate do that with another woman, and not just any woman, *her*. This creature born of darkness who held our fates so tightly in her grip.

"I'll kill you, I'll fucking kill you!" I swore on every entity who cared to listen, marking this monster's death as *mine*.

Lavinia released him, her nails having torn crescent-shaped gouges into his neck, and I could do nothing but struggle against my shadow restraints as she turned to me with a savage smile lighting her features. Then she leaned down and whispered something in Orion's ear that made his face pale before she stood upright and swept past me out the door, throwing me a vicious look of satisfaction as she went.

Disgust made my throat thick, and I couldn't stop shaking as I stared at Orion, his gaze now on the bloody floor beneath him like he couldn't bear to look at me again.

The silence deepened and tears seared the backs of my eyes from witnessing the man I loved more than life itself being forced into subservience. I was so, so angry that he had allowed this, but I was broken by seeing him like that too, and I simply didn't know how to fix any of it.

"How could you agree to this? How could you enter into a Death bond with her?" I asked, finding my voice at last, the cracks in it giving away my rage.

He finally looked at me, and all I saw was a man forced right up to the edge of his breaking point, suspended there on the fringe of oblivion. Darkness clung to him in a way I could see in his eyes, and even as those silver rings glittered at me from his irises, they seemed dimmer somehow.

A primal feeling took root in me, and I was sure of just one thing in that moment; I had to find a way to save him.

"It was the only way to break the curse," he said. "I had to offer myself to her in flesh, bone, or blood. Knowing I would free you within three months and that I would be free too…it seemed like the answer we needed, even if it isn't the one we wanted."

After everything that had happened at the battle, I'd thought things couldn't get much worse. But how wrong I'd been. I should have known that everything could get so much fucking worse. It always did.

"What are the terms of this deal?" I hissed, yanking against my shadow restraints again in an effort to get to him, but they wouldn't release me.

"I must willingly give her my body in any way she wants it."

A chill swept through me that made me fall still, my blood freezing over in my veins.

"Lance, please tell me you haven't- that she hasn't-" I couldn't even finish that sentence, the way she'd kissed him making me think of how much worse this could have already been. Had she raped him? Taken his body under the terms of this fucking deal?

"No," he said firmly, a vow of truth in his eyes. "She hasn't done anything but torture me. Until that kiss." He shuddered, his muscles bunching in resistance to the mere memory of it, and I was glad to see he wasn't entirely under her control. He seemed to be coming back to me a little more, strength returning to his posture.

"What else has she done?" I pushed. "I can see this is more than torture. You're looking at me like you don't really see me." My voice broke on those last words and his gaze sharpened a little more, his wrists tugging against his shackles like he wanted to get to me, but there was something holding him at bay which went beyond chains.

"It's the dark magic in the weapons she uses against me," he said thickly. "It makes it hard to…feel. It will wear off. I just need to rest."

I nodded, seeing his exhaustion, and how profoundly he had been affected by Lavinia's torture. It was intolerable.

"What did she whisper to you before she left?" I asked through shaking lips, though I wasn't sure if it was fear or anger that was making me tremble most.

"*Blue*," he begged.

"Tell me," I demanded, my body thawing as a fiery rage was stoked in me instead.

"She said…" His throat bobbed and his eyes moved to the wall beyond me, resignation falling over him. "That perhaps there are deeper ways to make you suffer than making me bleed."

A blinding wrath took hold of me, making the Shadow Beast roar inside my chest. This was too much. I could have weathered my curse, but Lavinia had made sure to link it to the man I loved, knowing that hurting him hurt me more than anything she could do to me.

A scream of anger left me, and I yanked more fiercely on my restraints, murder calling my name. I would rip her head from her shoulders, I'd spill every drop of her blood and wipe her from existence.

The shift came upon me in a wave and my skin split apart, giving way to the feral beast who embodied my curse. My roar joined with the monster's and for once, I relished its fury, because I had it in my control right now and I could wield it however I wanted.

I hounded forward, ready to tear Orion free of his chains, but he shook his head at me as he realised my intention.

"I can't run from her," Orion said in earnest. "I have to uphold the deal, or I'll die."

I howled at that reality, turning and throwing my full weight at the metal door, the thing flying open upon impact.

"Darcy!" Orion cried.

In the next heartbeat, I was racing through the throne room on a quest for blood. Lavinia's, Lionel's. Everyone who had wronged us would die the moment I was upon them.

I charged through the halls in search of my prey, the Shadow Beast tugging at my mind as it tried to regain control, but I wasn't letting go this time. I'd wield this animal against the creature who had cursed me with it and wipe her from the face of the earth in payment for her touching my mate.

I turned into a corridor where silver chandeliers sparkled above and arching windows towered up to my left, the moonlight pooling across the floor like a river of liquid silver.

Lavinia shot into view at the far end of the passage, startled as she found me there.

"*Stop*," she hissed, the command ringing through me, but I managed to resist it as I thought of Orion bleeding for her, of this witch's mouth on his, and I charged forward in a bid for death.

She raised her hands and ropes of shadow shot towards me, trying to bind my limbs, but I tore through every strand of dark power she cast. She had captured my mate, bound him to her will, and I would not stand idly by to see her torture him. She had no claim on him, he was mine. And I would place myself between him and the stars if I had to. I was going to twist fate myself and shape it into something good that could never be taken from us.

My bellow tore through the air as Lavinia backed up a step, working harder to bind my limbs in shadow, but I saw the moment of doubt in her. The fear that she couldn't stop me, and it fed my vengeful hunger.

When I was close enough, I leapt at her, huge paws outstretched and claws as sharp as sun steel promising to tear her to pieces. I had burned her in Phoenix Fire at the battle, and she had risen like the undead before my eyes. But this time, I would leave nothing of her. I'd destroy her with the very thing she was made of. Shadow and death.

"Stop!" she commanded in my mind, but I fought off the desire to obey once more.

She screamed as she hit the ground beneath me and I ripped into her shoulder with my teeth, aiming for her head but missing as she wheeled aside, her body contorting unnaturally. My claws raked down the centre of her chest, spilling blackish blood and making her wails pitch higher. I caught her neck between my jaws and bit down, ready to end this, to tear her head clean from her body and destroy the rest of her too. But her hands grasped at my throat, and she yanked sideways with unimaginable power, making pain spike through me.

"You are mine! Do as your queen commands you!" Her voice exploded inside my skull and this time, the magic she used found its way to my soul.

The Shadow Beast gained an inch of control over me, and my jaw loosened around Lavinia's throat. I fought as hard as I could to keep her down, but Lavinia's will pressed into me, and it was like drowning in a murky sea. I couldn't find a way out, every direction dark and everlasting.

"Shift," she hissed, and the Shadow Beast slid away into my skin, leaving me on top of her with my muscles tense and my body unable to move.

Her wounds healed over before my eyes, her brow creasing in concentration as she held me under her power.

"Keep your hands off of my mate," I warned, my palms pressed to the floor either side of her as I fought to move.

The shadows were crawling through my skin, trapping me, and there was nothing I could do when she pulled on them like puppet strings, making me roll off of her onto my back. She rose to her feet, the shadows gathering around her feet and climbing up her body to caress her, healing her wounds as she sneered down at me.

"*Feed*," she growled, and the Shadow Beast started feasting on the very core of me.

I screamed, the pain like knives carving along the inside of my bones as the Shadow Beast fed on whatever magic remained in me, the crux of what made me Fae.

I writhed against the stone-cold floor, power fading from my limbs, and that strength I'd just felt disappearing along with it. The Shadow Beast gorged itself until it felt like there was nothing left of me to take, a horrible emptiness sinking into my chest that not even the shadows wanted to touch.

The pain subsided until I was abandoned by everything, curled on the floor, my ear pressed to the flagstones and my eyes squeezed shut.

Make it stop. Please take this reality away.

Long fingers wrapped in my hair and Lavinia started dragging me along by it with inhuman strength, my body limp and lifeless.

My fingers skimmed along the floor, and I swear I heard the palace groaning around me, the walls seeming to quiver in anguish of the fallen Vega within them. But maybe that was just the wild imaginings of a half dead girl who was barely even Fae anymore.

I was vaguely aware of Orion shouting my name from somewhere nearby and I cracked my eyes, finding two Nymphs corralling him into the night iron cage in the throne room.

Lavinia tossed me in with him, my back smacking against the far wall before I hit the floor like a rag doll. The clang of the cage door shutting filled my ears the same moment Orion pulled me into his arms, turning me over and seeking out life in me. His eyes were frantic, like he'd suddenly woken up from the dark magic she'd tainted him with, and his hand cupped my face in panicked movements.

I squinted up at him under heavy lashes, trying to speak, but the weight of the shadows wouldn't let me.

"What have you done to her?!" Orion barked at Lavinia.

"It is the curse, pet," Lavinia spat, her rage still sharp. "And you had better keep her well behaved because the curse will move along far quicker if I have to encourage the beast to feed more often. She will be mortal in a few weeks if this is how she behaves. Three moon cycles is an awfully long time for such an advanced curse, Lance Orion. Are you sure she will survive it?"

"You fucking bitch," he snarled, his fangs on show.

Lavinia's voice drew closer, though I couldn't see her from the angle I was lying at. "You look hungry, Vampire. Was the servant's blood I gave you today not enough? Will you drink the blood of your mate and take what little magic remains in her? Perhaps the Shadow Beast is not the only monster she should fear tonight."

She took hold of his arm and shadows slid from her body, creeping over his skin, and lapping at the bruises and cuts still marking his bare chest. He groaned, trying to pull away but his head fell forward in the next moment, a harsh breath leaving him and washing over me.

"That's it. Let the shadows in. They only want to play," Lavinia purred, then the slap of her bare feet drifted away alongside the heavy footfalls of the Nymphs as they followed her.

Orion tightened his hold on me, but didn't look down again, his hair in his eyes as he breathed slower, trying to regain control. His fangs were out and a tightness to his expression told me he was working hard against the urge to feed too.

"I won't bite you. I wouldn't," he swore, his voice flatter than before, like the shadows were taking hold again.

An ounce of strength returned to me, enough for me to lift my hand and graze my fingers over the stubble on his jaw which was beginning to thicken to a beard.

"Look at me."

He hesitated a beat longer before doing as I asked, and my muscles relaxed as those familiar dark eyes met mine.

"I'm sorry I failed," I whispered.

He caught my hand, drawing it gently to his mouth and kissing my palm, his gaze flickering with hunger. "I love you for trying. But please understand that this promise I've made must be fulfilled. If I break it, I will die."

"And what about her? What if she breaks it?" I asked, trying to sit up but he growled a little, tightening his grip on me, and it was so good to be in his arms again that I just let him hold me.

"Then she will die," he said, a frown on his brow.

"So maybe we can find a way to make her break it," I said hopefully and a little more light entered his eyes, that veil of dark power drawing back again.

"Yeah, maybe, Blue," he said. But that small light extinguished again as he stared at me, and I sensed a weight on him that was heavier than the sun and moon combined.

"What happened at the battle? Did you see who got out?" I asked, terror thickening my throat.

He shook his head marginally and pain swept through his features, his jaw ticking as he refused to meet my gaze again.

"I only know of two fates," he said quietly. "Gabriel is here. Lionel captured him."

"Oh god," I exhaled, fear for my brother welling fast. Even the mere fact of his capture told me a lot about how badly the battle must have gone – for the greatest Seer of our generation to have been caught in a trap of fate like that, there must have been pure carnage taking place around him, clouding the sight of his own destiny.

"He's still alive at least," he said, and I took comfort in that small fact, though it still broke me to think of what he was probably going through as Lionel's prisoner.

"And the other fate?" I asked, but Orion didn't look at me, pain splintering through his eyes. "Lance?" I whispered, sensing he was about to tell me something awful, something that would shatter my heart into even more pieces, but I needed to know all the same.

He hesitated for several more heartbeats, like voicing his next words would cause him immeasurable pain.

"Darius didn't make it."

"No," I gasped, sitting bolt upright, refusing that fact with every fibre of my being. Because Darius Acrux was one of the strongest people I knew, he was a warrior, a creature as powerful as a deity. And more than that, he was my friend, and my sister's star-bound mate, her husband. "No, no, please. It can't be true."

"I saw his body," he said, his voice breaking as agony spilled into his eyes. "Lionel killed him. He's gone."

Those words undid me, and I came apart in his arms, the two of us clinging to each other as if nothing else existed but our grief. It sat between us like a freezing lump of ice, and the only warmth came from the places our bodies touched.

I couldn't contain the hurt I felt over losing the man I'd come to love as deeply as a brother, and it was only stoked by the pain I knew my twin was feeling out there somewhere. I should have been with her through this. I couldn't stand the thought of her facing this alone.

I yearned to be with Tory more strongly than I ever had in my life, and the torment that caused me was unimaginable. She might as well have been an entire universe away for how impossible it was to reach her now. She was no doubt suffering under the weight of a grief so fierce, it must have felt like the sky was falling down on her.

The guilt I already felt over everything I'd done multiplied tenfold. I'd turned the tide of the battle, the Shadow Beast in me had made sure the rebels had lost.

Was it my fault Darius lay dead? Would he still be here if only I'd been strong enough to fight off the grip of the curse?

I doubled forward, consumed by it all and crumbling completely.

I'm so sorry, Tor.

Scorpio
Virgo
Gemini
Cancer
Aries
Leo
Sagittarius
Taurus
Capricorn
Aquarius
Libra
Pisces

ORION

CHAPTER SIXTEEN

A Dragon's roar roused me from the nightmarish daydream I'd fallen into. Flashbacks of the battle had been flitting through my mind like a little house of horrors contained in my head, and I wasn't sure I was ever going to truly escape those awful memories.

Lionel's sudden presence in the palace made the walls shiver, like they were recoiling from his touch. There was old magic in this place, and something about it was loyal to the Vegas, revolted by his presence and rebelling against him.

I looked down at Darcy in my arms, exhaustion having stolen her away into sleep for an hour, or perhaps it was two. The creases on her brow told me all I needed to know about how restful that slumber was. She hadn't spoken a single word to me after I'd told her about Darius, descending into a pit of despair so deep I didn't know how to pull her out of it. I felt helpless, fucking useless in fact. How was I ever going to make things okay again?

I was falling into that despair myself, thoughts of Darius binding themselves to the recesses of my mind, playing on repeat.

"Come on, hurry up," Darius urged as I ran after him down one of the darker corridors in this corner of Acrux Manor.

I'd never been here before, Uncle Lionel usually made us stay in the eastern wing as far away from his office as possible. One time, my dad had pointed out that he could just use a silencing bubble, and the look Darius's dad had given him had reminded me he held a beast inside him that was capable of eating Fae whole. My dad never acted like he noticed though. But that was because my dad was a badass.

I followed Darius through a door, and he shot me a mischievous look back over his shoulder that spelled trouble. And that was our favourite thing in the world.

I slipped in after him and my mouth fell open at the pile of treasure standing in that room, heaped there like a miniature mountain.

"The Dragon Guild sent it as a gift for my birthday," Darius said with a stupid look on his face.

"You sure you're gonna Emerge as a Dragon?" I teased and Darius frowned, looking like the sky might fall if he didn't.

"Of course. Look at me." He thumped his chest which was far wider than any eight-year-old's I'd met before. He might have been younger than me by a few years,

but our friendship had always been encouraged since we were kids. I'd seen him take his first steps, had caught him when he'd fallen, and he'd always been one of the best friends I'd ever had. I couldn't explain it, but it was like we were meant to be friends, and it made me think of something Aunt Catalina had told me once – back when she'd seemed a bit nicer. "Nebular Allies are the most precious of friends. They are rarer than gold, and far more valuable."

That was before she'd gone all weird, sort of cold and distant. I didn't really like her anymore; she gave me the creeps. I hated the way she looked at me vacantly, yet always wanted to be close to me and my family, like she wanted to say something interesting, but she didn't have the brain power to manage it.

Darius kicked off his shoes and dove headfirst into the gold, all of it cascading down beneath his weight. "I know I'll be a Dragon because this feels so good."

I edged closer, aware of the way Dragons could be about their gold and not wanting to overstep the line, but he sat up, beckoning me into it. I knew the weight of what he was offering, and wondered if we really might be Nebular Allies, because his trust in me right now was limitless.

I kicked off my shoes and dove into it beside him, the two of us laying back and wriggling deeper into the coins, our laughter carrying up to the ceiling.

"You're so rich, man," I said, picking up one of the coins and twisting it around to admire it in the light. He stole it from my fingers, possessiveness in his eyes and I snorted, shoving to my feet, and getting out of his precious gold pile.

He met my gaze, his jaw grinding like he was conflicted on something, then he shoved himself up too and jogged down the pile of gold.

"Look at this," he encouraged, and I followed him over to a cabinet full of trinkets. He took out a little book no bigger than his palm, the planets coloured crimson on the jet-black cover.

"Is that a Blood Tome?" I gasped, reaching for it on instinct and Darius let me take it.

"Yeah, it's rare as hell, right? It's from the early years of the blood ages."

I flicked it open in excitement, finding a handwritten note scrawled in the top corner of it.

For you, my dearest friend and lifelong companion. Our blood was made to spill on each other's battlefields.

I closed the book a little unwillingly and offered it back to Darius.

He folded his arms with a serious look. "It's yours. Keep it."

I shook my head, trying to make him take it back. "If your dad found out-"

"He won't. That book's been sitting there untouched for years," Darius said. "Besides, it's meant for a friend. And that's what you are."

I sensed the magnitude of what he was offering me and couldn't help but give in. It was a token of our friendship to each other, and it felt wrong to refuse it. And I decided there and then that we were Nebular Allies, whether the stars agreed or not, I didn't really care. I was gonna look out for him, and he would look out for me. And that was all there was to it.

"Darius?" a deep voice boomed through the halls, making my heart quake for a second before I realised it was just his father calling for him.

Darius winced, pressing his lips together and not answering.

"Darius!? The other Heirs are here," Lionel urged, the use of magic making his voice radiate throughout the house.

Darius's expression lifted as we moved around the pile of gold to the door, slipping out of the room as I tucked the book into my pocket.

We made it to the entrance hall where Seth, Max, and Caleb were waiting, pushing and shoving each other in some game that captured my interest. Lionel was there and he smiled at Darius, directing him over to the Heirs. He jogged to them, immediately falling into their game and my heart urged me to join them, but my feet remained in place.

"Hey, Lance," Seth said, waving at me and I waved back, stepping forward as Max smiled at me too and Caleb looked me over with intrigue.

Darius turned, beckoning me over, and I took another step.

Lionel moved into my way, bracing a hand on my shoulder and I looked up at him in surprise.

"Your mother is waiting for you at home. It's time to go, Lance," he said, guiding me past the Heirs to the door.

"No, let him stay," Darius demanded, but Lionel was already ushering me outside and closing the door in my face. It felt like a wall, not a door.

I knew the Heirs needed to bond, to have their 'special time' together. Mom had explained that to me a hundred times. My role in Darius's life was different, something that could never mix with the Heirs. I had to keep our secrets of dark magic, and ensure the Heirs never found out about that, but I'd never felt like I was missing out on something until now.

I thought of the book in my pocket, and the heavy weight in my chest eased. Nothing was going to change our bond. Darius and I were friends regardless of what relationships he had with the Heirs. It was me and him, and nothing and no one would ever come between us.

I drew myself out of that memory, having almost forgotten about that day, remembering how fucking naïve I'd been. Something had been waiting to tear us apart all this time after all, I'd just never thought it would be death.

I sighed, an uncomfortable feeling stirring between the sinews of my grief-stricken heart. I could hardly recall wanting to befriend the Heirs, but that feeling was momentarily rekindled, and I wondered if I might have been a part of their group in some way if we'd just been normal kids living normal lives. Regardless, it wasn't to be. And probably never would have been anyway. It was just a pretty mirage of an idea, long lost to the ravening of time.

Although my body felt heavy, the dark magic imbued in the weapons Lavinia used to torture me had finally relinquished me from its grip. It was harder to break free of it than it had been the first time, and I had the terrible feeling it was only going to get worse.

Now that my mind was sharp again, it came with so much fear for the girl who lay in my lap. No matter how good it felt to have her close again, I needed her as far away from here as possible. She wasn't safe between these walls, but she was going to be trapped in this reality unless I could find a way to get her out.

I tucked a lock of inky, shadow-bound hair behind her ear and at my touch, the shadows receded from it, the lock of hair becoming blue all over once again and making my heart jolt.

"Darcy." I shook her lightly, hope sparking in me.

Her eyes fluttered open and for the briefest of seconds I thought I might find them returned to their normal green hue with that endless band of silver ringing them, linking her eternally to me. But that was a fool's hope. They were as black as night.

"Look." I drew the lock of hair forward, but it was drenched in shadow once more before she could see, and my heart dipped in disappointment.

"What is it?" she asked, her eyes still ringed red from the tears she'd cried over Darius.

Breaking that news to her had been one of the worst things I'd ever had to do, and I was sure it had left a fresh wound on my heart too.

"It was blue for a moment," I said, and she frowned, turning another piece of hair over in her palm.

It swirled between her fingers as the shadows clung to it and I couldn't help but examine her further, the way that dark power hugged her body, moving over her like it was bound to her skin. I wanted to rip the shadows from her and free her from Lavinia's curse, but the only way I could do that was by fulfilling my promise and paying the debt.

Just three moon cycles. That's all.

She shifted away from me, drawing her knees to her chest, and grinding her jaw.

"I wish you didn't have to see me like this," she murmured, and a growl rose in my throat. "I'm poison."

"I'd love you in any form, poisonous or otherwise," I said, reaching for her, but she recoiled from me further, and hurt slashed through me. "Look at me," I commanded, but she didn't. "*Blue*."

"I killed so many people," she whispered, her gaze on the stone floor. "Geraldine," her voice cracked. My heart crushed at that girl's name. She'd saved my life, and it seemed she had paid the ultimate price for it. She hadn't deserved to be torn from this world so soon.

"And maybe Darius would still be here too if it wasn't for me," Darcy added.

Anger rose sharply in me at those words. I got to my feet, towering over her and she finally looked at me, seeming so damn small that it was like she was a ghost of her former self.

"Lavinia is to blame for every kill by your hand, and Darius is dead because of Lionel Acrux. Not you."

She looked away again, but I wasn't having it. I pulled her to her feet, tugging her close to me by the wrists, but she wriggled free of my hold and moved to stand against the wall, her head falling forward and a swathe of black hair tumbling down to curtain her face. I wasn't going to let her retreat from me though. She had to see the truth, because I refused to let her take the blame for any of this.

"Darcy Vega," I growled, boxing her in against the wall at the back of the cage and taking hold of her chin, making her look at me. Her eyes were so deathly black, they made my heart thump unevenly with how eerily similar they were to Lavinia's now, but that wasn't going to make me withdraw from her. I knew who she was down to her roots, and I needed to remind her of it so that she'd come back to me. "You are not the actions of that beast. It is not you. It's a curse that forces your hand. Do you blame me for when Lavinia harnessed the shadows in my flesh and made me drive a blade into you?" It was up there with the worst memories of my life, the night we had gone to my family home all those moons ago.

"Of course not," she muttered, trying to jerk her chin out of my grip, but I wouldn't let go. "This is different. I should have been strong enough to fight the Shadow Beast off before it ever got as far as it did. I'm supposed to be some all-powerful Phoenix but look at me now. I'm nothing."

"You are everything," I said firmly, and she tried to push past me, but I slammed my palms to the wall either side of her, not letting her go. "And you will not run from me."

"How can you even stand to look at me?" she hissed. "I'm a monster. I look like *her*. Like Lavinia." She winced as if she wanted to cringe away from her own skin and a frown furrowed my brow.

"Listen to me, Blue. I loved you when your soul shone with all the starlight in the night sky, and I'll love you now when your soul is the blackest you've ever known. I will love you whole and I'll love you in pieces. It doesn't matter, light or dark, I am here. That is what mates are for. It's what I'm made to be for you by the stars themselves, so stop trying to shut me out."

Her lips parted to answer that, her cheeks tinting with colour and the reminder of her blood set my pulse racing, my fangs prickling with need. Lavinia had given me a few meagre mouthfuls of some weak Fae's blood earlier today, but I was starving for a real drink. Darcy's magic was in the grip of the Shadow Beast though, and I didn't know what power was even left in her now. I certainly wasn't going to take any more of it from her.

"I'm sorry," she said. "It's just…when you look at me like that, I feel so goddamn undeserving of it after everything I've done. Darius was your best friend-"

"And he loved you like a sister. He will be watching us now, cursing you out for feeling this way. And knowing Darius, he'll be busy blaming himself for his failure.

He won't be thinking for a single moment that you were responsible for his end." A sharp knife was stabbing itself repeatedly into my chest as I spoke about my friend, the knowledge that I would never see him in this life again too agonising to truly accept.

Fuck...Darius. I didn't even get to say goodbye.

Tears welled in her eyes, and I caught them on my thumb as they fell, wiping them away.

"What about Geraldine?" she breathed, her lower lip quivering.

The loss of her weighed over me and I leaned down to rest my forehead to Darcy's.

"It's not your fault," I promised, and she looked into my eyes, trying to soak in my belief in those words, though I wasn't sure it helped. I hated to think that Geraldine Grus was gone. That girl was one of a kind. I respected her and her unwavering loyalty to the Vegas, even if we hadn't always seen eye to eye in the past.

Lionel's booming voice sounded right next to us as if he were in this very cage, making both of us jump violently.

"Do you realise how much treasure I have lost, Lavinia?! Rare coins and gemstones that are now in the filthy hands of disgusting lesser Fae. And now I have been stuck at the Court of Solaria all day and half the night to try and prepare a final attack on those fucking rebels who have vanished off the face of the earth."

"By the fucking stars," I cursed, realising the sound was coming from the wall itself, but how was that possible?

Darcy and I shifted closer to the cold bricks, the volume of his words lowering as if the palace was offering us a secret, carrying his voice right here for us to listen in on.

"I must make a stand," he went on. "With the Heirs and Councillors free, and presumably gone to join with that orphaned whore, that puts the rebels in a stronger position again."

I shared a look of hope with Darcy at the news that Caleb, Seth, and Max were okay. To hear my coven brother was safe made me feel all the better. And to my surprise, I was really fucking relieved about the others too.

"You control the press, Daddy, you can have them write a story about your greatness. They can tell the world what wicked, vile creatures those Vegas are," Lavinia's crooning voice carried to us next.

"It is not good enough," Lionel spat. "Don't you understand? The Phoenixes are stronger than I ever imagined, and now the rebels' strength is bolstered once more by the most powerful bloodline in Solaria. I must make a statement in blood and death. I must show them what I am capable of."

"Of course, my King. What will you do?" Lavinia asked excitedly.

"You know what I must do," he snarled. "I will show the world what the Dragon King can do to Phoenixes. Has Gwendalina Vega arrived?"

"Yes, but-" Lavinia started but Lionel cut over her.

"Finally," he breathed in excitement. "I have one of my greatest enemies right here in the palace. I will have the world watch while I behead her alongside her Elysian Mate. I will prove I am far superior to the Vega line in a show of power and brutality. And I will make her bow before she bleeds."

My spine straightened and I turned to Darcy with a vow in my eyes that I wouldn't let that happen, and she gave me the same look right back. Though how I could protect her, I didn't know.

"My King," Lavinia said gently. "They are under my control. I am afraid I cannot allow it."

"Allow it?" Lionel hissed venomously. "It is not your place to *allow* me anything! I am the power here. I am the ruler of Solaria."

"And I am owed a debt from the Vega and her mate because Queen Avalon banished me to the Shadow Realm all those years ago."

"You've had your fun. I will make sure they both suffer intensely before the end, and Roxanya Vega can watch her sister die on television; what better vengeance is there than that?"

"Daddy, wait," Lavinia gasped, and all fell quiet, though I knew in my bones that they were headed this way.

Panic darted through me, and I looked to Darcy in alarm. I had to get her out of here.

I grabbed two bars of the cage, trying to bend them apart with the strength of my Order, my muscles tensing fiercely. But the night iron was built to withstand far more power than I possessed right now, and I cursed as I turned, looking desperately around me for an answer.

Darcy caught my arm, looking up at me through pitch black eyes. "I'll fight."

"And what if Lavinia stops you again?" I demanded, my eyes turning to the wall at the back of the cage.

I threw myself against it at full force, slamming my fists into the huge blocks of stone and working to break through them, my knuckles splitting and blood spilling. I had to get her out. She had to run from here and never come back.

The doors to the throne room were shoved wide, slamming into the walls and sending an echoing boom reverberating through the space.

I twisted around, planting myself in front of Darcy, my fangs bared and a promise of death in my eyes as Lionel Acrux prowled towards us with intent.

"Stay back," I warned.

Lavinia drifted along behind him, her feet just grazing the floor as she used her shadows to levitate, her eyes moving from me to Darcy curiously.

"We have a deal!" I bellowed, pointing at her.

"Daddy is very angry," she said, blinking innocently at me. "He needs a little outlet."

Lionel swept toward me wearing smart pants and a white shirt that was unbuttoned at the throat, his hair dishevelled and the look of a madman about him.

Darcy growled, stepping to my side and facing him head on, darkness swirling around her.

"Unlock the cage, Lavinia. And keep Lance under control," Lionel commanded.

"No," I gasped, reaching for Darcy, but Lavinia flicked her fingers, chains of shadow lashing around me and yanking me away from my mate.

"It's okay," Blue whispered, though this was the fucking opposite of okay.

The door was wrenched open by the Shadow Princess's power and Darcy raised her hands as she narrowed her eyes on Lionel.

He hesitated, lifting his chin as he studied her, seeming wary.

"Is her magic subdued?" he muttered to Lavinia like the fucking coward he was.

"You unFae piece of shit," I spat, but Lionel ignored me.

"Yes, my King. She cannot fight you. Come here, little beastie," Lavinia purred, and her command had Darcy stepping out of the cage.

I could sense her fighting it from the tension in her spine, but it was clear she was losing the battle, and the most stifling kind of fear stole away my ability to breathe.

"Blue!" I called in desperation, but she didn't look back. And as Lionel Acrux walked closer to my Elysian Mate with the wrath of death in his eyes, I felt the stars turning our way, like they knew something terrible was about to happen, and they had no mind to stop it.

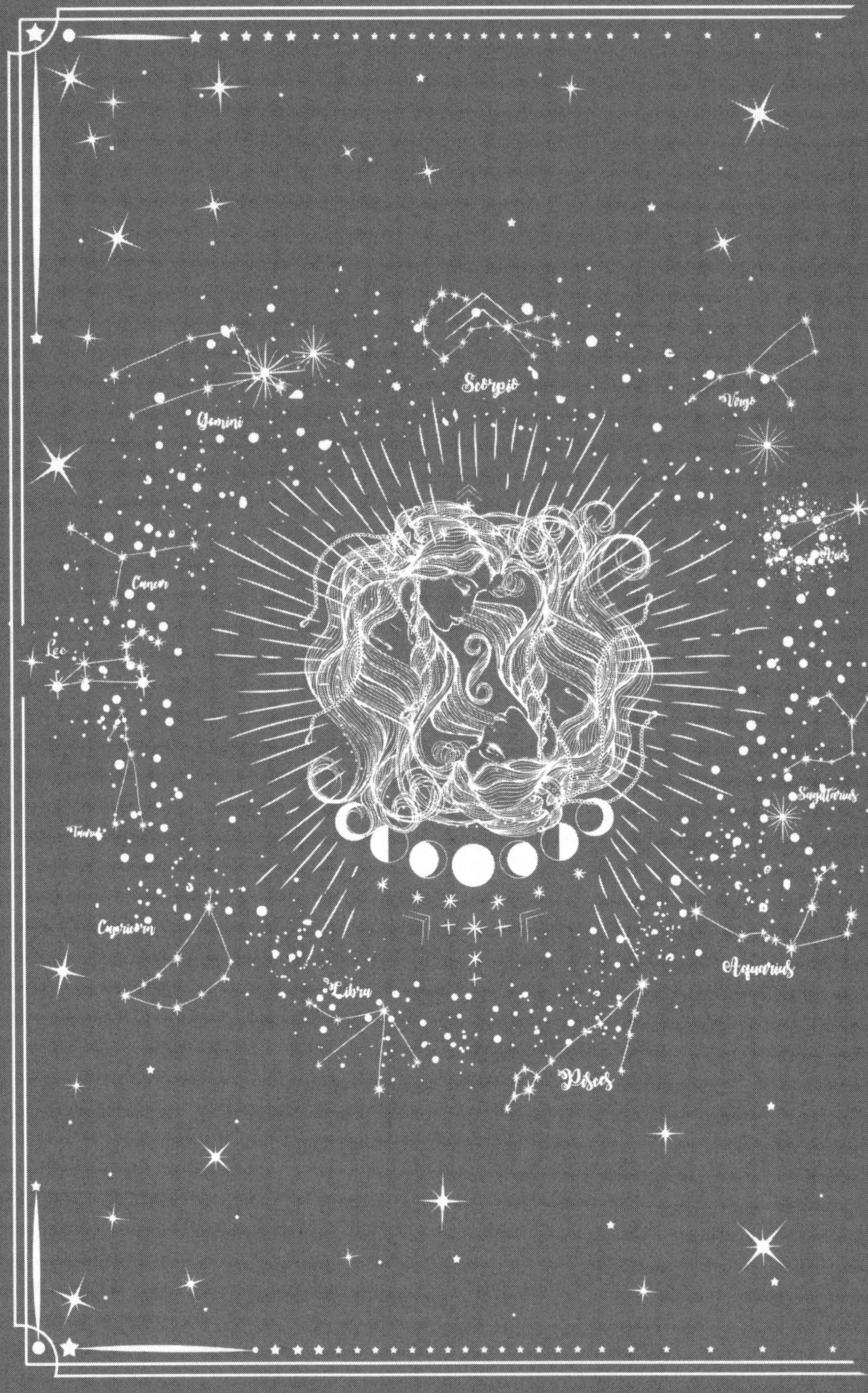
Scorpio
Gemini
Virgo
Leo
Sagittarius
Capricorn
Aquarius
Libra
Pisces

DARCY

CHAPTER SEVENTEEN

"Get away from her!" Orion roared. "We had a deal, you cannot kill her or-" Lavinia silenced him with a whip of shadow wrapping around his mouth and terror danced through my veins.

I came to a halt in front of Lionel, my hands still raised, but no power sparking in them as I desperately tried to draw magic to the edges of my skin. The eyes of the monster who had caused everyone I loved so much pain gazed deep into my own, smoke slipping from his nostrils and heat radiating from his chest. He was a huge man, at least three times my size when you accounted for all that muscle, but the real danger in him didn't lie in his bulk, it was the power in his veins and the merciless cruelty he ruled with.

"Is she quite under your control, Lavinia?" Lionel asked again.

"Fully, my King. Her magic is being devoured by the Shadow Beast, there is little of it left at all and my creature has already stolen her Order form away from her. She's basically a mortal."

Lionel grinned, his smile taking up all of my vision, the savagery in it promising my suffering. I didn't give him the satisfaction of trying to run, defiance flaring in my eyes as I held his gaze.

"Good," he purred. "Mortals can burn."

I gritted my teeth, trying to tear magic from my well of power, but the Shadow Beast wouldn't relinquish it. Lavinia was right, I was powerless, and there was no chance of me defending myself.

"Have your false queen order the Shadow Beast to return my magic so I can fight you one on one. Face me like Fae and find out which of us really deserves my father's throne," I demanded.

"You don't know the meaning of being Fae," he said coldly. "You mother hid you in the mortal world and you were raised with the weakness of their kind burrowing into your soul. You reek of their powerlessness, their pathetic, pointless existence, and the only claim you have is the watery blood of the Vega line in your veins. But your father's power does not run true in you, his merger with a half-breed whore is clear proof of that."

"Don't you *dare* speak about my mother like that," I snapped.

"I will speak of trash as it deserves to be spoken of. Your father's failings allowed fate to collude in *my* favour. Me. A man of true worth. The dominion of purity and real power is clear for all to see now, and the world will watch you fall, the shroud finally falling from their eyes as you are revealed to them for the pathetic creature you are in your final moments."

He raised his hand and air magic wrapped around me, binding my arms to my sides as he lifted me above him and lit a fire beneath me that licked my bare feet. I had no magic and no way to escape. Orion shouted out to me through his gag, his fear for me pulling at my heartstrings. I didn't want him to watch me die, to see me as some weak, almost mortal creature being snuffed from this world without ever being given the chance to fight. But what could I do?

I swallowed my screams for as long as I could, but as the flames rose higher, climbing my legs and tasting my flesh, they ripped free of my lungs, filling the whole room, and echoing back to me from every surface.

Orion fought desperately to get to me, but for every shadow bind he broke through, Lavinia cast another in its place.

Lionel slid his Atlas from his pocket, tossing it to Lavinia who caught it out of the air and did a twirl. "Record this for the press. Let them see what their king does to traitors, let them see that I am far greater than any Phoenix who ever lived."

"All they'll see is a coward who can't face me with my true power intact," I spat as I swallowed back my screams. "I'm cursed by your queen; she's the one who has made it even possible for you to face me!"

Lionel sneered, the fire burning hotter at my feet and making more screams pitch from chest.

Orion struggled furiously against Lavinia's shadow tethers, roaring against his gag in desperation. My heart broke for him, and I wished I could have one last, peaceful moment with him in this life, but it looked like the stars were done with us, our story speeding towards a violent conclusion.

Before the flames could climb any higher, Lionel whipped his hand sideways and I was launched through the air, slamming onto the tiled floor and skidding across it, my head hitting the throne.

Pain exploded through my skull and my vision swum from the impact. The scent of burnt skin filled my nose and I struggled to get up as the Shadow Beast kept me subdued, Lavinia's shadows running so deep that I couldn't find any power of my own to latch onto. If I could only dig it out...

"I've waited so very long for this moment," Lionel growled as he closed in on me, a keen buzz of excitement in his voice. "You and your sister have been an irritation for far too long. And now you are going to be the first to be crushed by a power far superior to you."

"Have Lavinia release me from the beast," I demanded once again. "Then we will find out who is truly more powerful."

"*Quiet*." His boot impacted with my ribs, and I gasped, having hardly a second to recover before he did it again and again. Bone cracked under the sheer strength of his strikes, and I bit down on my tongue, trying not to give him the satisfaction of knowing how much pain I was in. But the maddened delight in his eyes told me he knew, and he was nearly salivating over it.

With every kick, something shifted in me, power crackling in the deepest regions of my bones. It was there for a fleeting second, and I grabbed onto it, trying to pull it from the grip of the Shadow Beast, clenching my teeth with the effort.

Give it back to me!

With a furious, determined wrench inside me, something gave way and magic tore into my veins. I sent it spiralling out of me before the Shadow Beast could get close to it again, casting every drop of it from my body in an explosion of power. The Element of air blasted from me in a storm, and Lionel was thrown across the room with a yell of shock that made hope flutter in my chest.

I twisted my fingers, hurriedly casting shards of deadly ice blades beneath him as he fell. I could finish this, make it quick and bloody even though he deserved far more than that in death. But at least he would be gone.

He caught himself with a gust of his own air power at the last second, the spikes pressing lightly to his back. I forced them to grow with a surge of hatred cleaving my chest open, but he whipped himself away from them on a breeze that planted him on his feet, a wall of fire billowing out from him and consuming my ice.

I shoved myself upright, hands raised as I ripped more magic from the Shadow Beast's hold, but the little I gained wouldn't mould into what I wanted, my hold on it slippery and faltering despite my desperate need for its cooperation.

"Lavinia!" Lionel barked. "Get hold of her this instant."

"Of course, my King," Lavinia purred, stepping forward and stirring a maelstrom into the shadows housed within my body. "*Feed.*"

A scream poured from me as the Shadow Beast started devouring my magic away, its teeth ripping me apart from the inside out.

I retreated around the throne as fast as I could move, dropping down behind it and clasping my chest in agony. The curse fell upon me deeper than ever, and blackness was all I could see. I tried to fight back but the strength of it was unimaginable.

I had to get a grip. This was my chance to finish the monsters in this room, and I couldn't let it pass me by. *Please stars, give me one more fucking chance, if nothing else.*

I wasn't sure if I was going crazy from the dark power that had me in its grip, but I felt something shift where my arm was braced against the back of the throne, and my hand slid into a small, hidden alcove. My fingers fell on cold, engraved metal and I turned it over in my palm, realising it was a small knife, hidden there for who knew how long by some stranger whose choice may just have become my salvation. The handle was made of two silver wings wrapping around a crimson garnet gemstone.

I quickly tightened my grasp, pulling it close to my body just as Lionel rounded the throne, looking down at me in disgust.

My limbs were heavy, and I felt horribly, undeniably mortal as the Shadow Beast finished its feast and I was left panting beneath the stare of the false king.

"Is it done?" he asked Lavinia without taking his eyes from me.

"She will not fight back again," she promised.

"UnFae asshole," I rasped.

"There is no shame in wielding another's power as my own." Lionel reached down, his fingers knotting in my hair and yanking so that I was forced to look up at him.

I kept the knife hidden against the inside of my wrist as he leaned over me, sensing the air shield that sat tight against his skin and would block any physical attack I made.

"If you're so big and powerful, then why have you still got a shield up against me? I'm just a mortal in the grip of your shadow bitch, right? You must be really fucking scared of me if you can't even let your defences down now," I mocked him and his grip on my hair tightened as he cracked my skull back against the throne with blinding strength, making my vision spin and my ears ring.

"You're less than mortal; you're nothing." He shoved me to the floor, forcing my cheek to grind against the tiles, his weight pressing down through his shoulders. He leaned close, whispering cruel words into my ear. "Your mother was a foreign whore, and your father was a weak-minded Fae who was only great because of me. And I killed them both. I watched the strength fade from their limbs, their magic drained by the Nymphs I brought to their door. I was always the true power in this palace, and now the world knows it too. I will crush you as I crushed them, and then I will hunt down your sister and eradicate the last of the Vega line."

I cried out at the pain bursting through my cheek, fire flaring under his palm and the colossal weight of him bearing down on my skull.

"That's enough, Daddy," Lavinia called. "You've had your fun."

She cast whips of shadow towards us as if to hold him back, but Lionel threw up a wall of air around him, her dark power stopped in its tracks. His eyes flashed jade green with his Dragon, and he bared his teeth, releasing the shield of air that sat against his skin with a smirk. "I am afraid of nothing. Least of all a powerless girl with no fight left in her."

"I'd rather be a powerless girl than a lonely man in an empty palace. I fought this war for a future I could share with everyone I loved. If you win, you'll have nothing and no one. Even if I die, there'll be people waiting for me in the afterlife, but who do you have?"

"I do not need anyone when I have all the power and gold in the world," he taunted like he was so damn fortunate and I was nothing but an ignorant child.

"You're a void because you've never felt love," I hissed.

"I do not need love," he scoffed. "Catalina learned the cost of love when she offered it to some royalist scum. And the two of them paid the ultimate price when I ripped them from this world in blood and glory."

Pain splintered through my chest at his words, to know that he had killed them in battle. "You're a fool to scoff at love. It's the only thing that can fill the void in you. You try to fill that space with all the riches and control you can possess, but it will never be enough. Only family is capable of that. And you cast yours aside. I love your sons, and I love Catalina; they're the greatest treasures you ever had, and you lost them. Thank the stars you did, because they escaped the monster who tried to bend them to his will. They cut out all the pieces of you that were left in them too. They're free of you now. Dead or alive. They're fucking free. And you can never take that away from them. So live your hollow life, and enjoy your hollow death. At least wherever I end up, there'll be warm arms waiting to greet me."

"The stars will offer me a golden throne among them when I leave this world," he snarled.

"I'd choose love over any throne," I breathed, the pressure in my head causing me unbearable agony.

"And that is why I rule the world and you do not."

"One kingdom, not the world," I reminded him, and a bellow of anger left him.

He took his hand from my face, lifting it up and curling it into a fist as he readied to drive it down against my skull, fire coating his knuckles and the power of air swirling around it too. I knew I wouldn't survive the attack, the finality of my death gleaming in his eyes as clear as day.

Orion was crying out to me through the gag, his love and fear for me crashing through the air, lending me the strength I needed for my final act.

Despite the pain ricocheting through my body, I managed to move. And I had to move fast. I twisted up onto my knees, launching myself at Lionel with a yell of purest hatred spilling from my lips.

The blade was ready in my hand, destined for his eye, one true, furious stab enough to finish him if I drove it deep enough.

Lionel reared back in alarm and my aim was thrown off, the blade sinking into the fleshy meat of his throat instead. Shock crossed his features and I drove the blade deeper, pressing all of my strength into it and carving it through skin and cartilage in a bid to cut some vital artery.

His magic blasted into me, a ferocious wind sending me flying towards the back of the room, where I hit the floor hard and skidded across it in a tangle of limbs.

I slammed into the wall and a snap sounded, all of my pain stolen away as a terrible numbness flowed along my spine.

"Blue!" Orion yelled through his gag, breaking through his binds only to be snared by fresh ones once again.

I tried to get up but found I couldn't move, paralysed by my injures. I was just able to lift my head to look at Lionel, finding him on his knees by the throne as he ripped the knife from his neck and began to heal the bloody wound.

Failure sank deep into my chest, and I cursed him, the stars, and the Shadow Beast that kept my magic subdued.

"Are you well, my King?" Lavinia cooed as Lionel choked on his own blood, working frantically to fix the damage I'd done.

When he got to his feet, the knife was gripped in his hand, blood staining his shirt red, splashes of it dripping everywhere as he strode towards me with a Dragon's growl in his chest.

Lavinia rushed up behind him, her shadows still tearing at his air shield as she tried to get closer to him.

"Enough - she is mine. You cannot kill her," she commanded, but he wasn't listening.

I looked to Orion, wanting him to be the last thing I saw as the monster came for me. The hurt in his eyes made me bleed inside as he fought his restraints and couldn't get free.

"I love you," I mouthed, the words not finding their way past my lips, and he shook his head in utter refusal of the goodbye I was offering.

Lionel grabbed my hair, wrenching me upright and holding me to his chest while pressing the knife to my throat. "I'll place your head on a spike on the palace wall for all to see," he whispered in my ear. "Now scream for me until you cannot scream anymore."

The blade slit my skin and I couldn't even struggle, the damage he'd caused too much for a mortal body to recover from. It was over, and now he was going to make a vicious, bloody spectacle of my death.

I tried to be brave in the face of the unimaginable pain I was about to endure, thinking of my sister and how desperately I wanted to see her face again one last time, of Gabriel and all the days that had been stolen from us, which we'd never be able to make up for now. I thought of Seth and the friendship we'd found together against all odds, the white Wolf who had made me a part of his pack, of Caleb and Max who had drawn me into their circle of safety, of Xavier, Sofia and Tyler who had created light within the dark, and of all those who had been taken from us too soon. Geraldine, Diego...Darius. I hoped to see them when the Veil parted and let me step beyond it.

Finally, my thoughts fell on Lance Orion. The fierce, protective keeper of my heart. I had known the furthest depths of love with him, I'd experienced devotion unlike anything I had ever imagined before, and we had protected each other for as long as we could.

My only comfort was in knowing that my family would one day find me in whatever form I took outside this life, because they were a part of my soul.

My twin was my other half.

My brother my wings of guidance.

My mate my soul-bound love.

I could let go of this world, so long as I knew we would all be together again one day. I just wished it could have been in this life, not the next.

I waited for death, but death didn't come. It took three eternal beats of silence for me to realise Lavinia had broken down Lionel's air shield and his arms were made rigid by the power of the shadows, holding him back as the knife hovered against my neck.

"Release me!" Lionel bellowed and the whole palace shook from the ferocity of the noise.

"You cannot have her death while she is bound to the curse. I have deals to uphold," Lavinia growled. "You had your playtime with her, now you must let her go. If you need a kill, there are still rebels in the amphitheatre dungeon."

"I am your ruler," Lionel snarled, his arms shaking as they clung to me, fighting the intensity of her power, but he couldn't get free. "You will release me this instant."

"I will do as I please." Lavinia flicked a finger, a coil of shadow plucking the knife from Lionel's hand and relieving me of the pressure against my neck.

It was drawn to her side, and she bound it in place there, caressing the weapon as she claimed it for herself.

Lionel was forced to release me, his huge body dragged away from me by the shadows and without him holding me up, I crumpled to the floor again as broken as an old doll. I tasted blood in my mouth, but I didn't care because it only reminded me that I was still here, impossibly alive.

I turned my head enough to watch Lionel be dragged towards the throne room doors, curses spilling from his lips as he battled Lavinia's power but he couldn't get free. "Unhand me!"

Lavinia drifted after him, weaving left and right through the air. "You still owe me an Acrux heir, my King, have you forgotten that?"

A tense pause passed and when Lionel spoke again, it was with an inflection of fear I had never heard in his voice before. "No, I have not forgotten. There is little time for such…pleasures these days."

She pressed him back against the arching wooden doors, tracing a finger under his chin.

"You never play with me anymore," she said with a pout. "You don't look at me the way he looks at her."

"Who looks at who? What are you talking about?" Lionel demanded, though there was an undeniable quaver in his voice that made my heart race. Holy shit, was the asshole Dragon afraid of Lavinia?

"The Vampire and his Vega," she spat, fury lining her words. "If you love me, then why do you not touch me anymore?"

"We are at war, Lavinia," his voice softened to something sickeningly placating, his muscles bulging against the shadow restraints around his arms. "There has not been time. Now, why don't you have some fun with our prisoners while I check to see that Stella is on her way here? She can make a new rift within these walls, somewhere the rebels will never reach, something to strengthen you again."

Silence stretched for a moment before Lavinia replied, the air bound with a tension so thick that I could taste it. Their allegiance was not the thing of unbreakable dominion which Lionel had been trying so hard to pretend it was. Their hunger for power was the only true thing binding them to one another along with Lavinia's insistent desire to claim what had been promised to her so very long ago. An Acrux king, and an all-powerful Heir.

But what would happen if she lost faith in those desires? What might happen if she opened her eyes to the way Lionel was using her for his own good? I may have hated the shadow bitch, but there was one thing about her which could just be the key to taking that bastard down, because as insane and awful as she was, she held more power than him. She could win if they were ever pitted against one another, and if there was some way to get her to do so, then all the better for us. One less psychotic tyrant for us to take down ourselves.

"Very well," she agreed finally, but I could tell she wasn't entirely placated by his words, some lingering disquiet rooted within her.

"Opening a rift takes time, remember?" Lionel added and there was something so sickeningly sweet about his tone as he worked to soothe her, a mask slipping over his features which made me wonder if he had manipulated our father in much the same way. "You will have to be patient."

"I can be patient, Daddy." Lavinia floated up to kiss Lionel on the lips, his relief a palpable thing as she gave in to the lure of his words, but then she opened the doors and tossed him through them like a sack of shit before slamming them shut in his face and locking them tight.

I tried to move, my muscles trembling as Orion called to me in terror through his gag. I opened my mouth to assure him I was alive, but I was finding it harder and harder to do anything at all. My heart was slowing to a dull thud and as I stared at my mate, the world grew dimmer. Had he just witnessed what I had? Would he be able to find a way to use that to help win this war? Because as a seeping coldness crept through my body like a dark tide, I began to think that perhaps I hadn't avoided death after all.

The love I held for that man blazed through the centre of my being, hotter than the deepest regions of the sun.

I would love him here and now, tomorrow and always. Wherever I went, wherever the stars took me, that love would never die. Even if I did.

Scorpio
Gemini
Virgo
Cancer
Leo
Sagittarius
Taurus
Capricorn
Aquarius
Libra
Pisces

ORION

CHAPTER EIGHTEEN

My shouts of fear were muffled by the gag, the shadows never relenting as they tethered me in place.

Darcy was unmoving on the floor, her limbs twisted awkwardly and burns covering her body.

She was leaving me, and the moment she vanished, I'd vanish too. There was no life without her. She was the centre of my existence, my saviour, my warrior, my sunshine.

The heated burn of the Death bond I'd made with Lavinia began to drive into my palm, my heart thumping to a frantic beat.

Lavinia let out a gasp as she felt it too, her hand going to her own heart and I realised that Darcy's passing would make our vows void, the Death bond would claim us. And there was so much goddamn relief in knowing that, because if Blue was leaving me now, then I was so fucking glad I was going with her. And the shadow bitch would at least fall too.

Lavinia ran toward me with wild eyes, throwing out a hand and releasing me from my shadow binds and gag. She wrenched the door to the cage open, producing a key and unlocking the cuff on my right wrist, a clatter sounding as it hit the floor.

"Heal her!" Lavinia screeched.

I was already running with the speed of my Order, moving faster than the wind before I fell to my knees beside my sweet, broken girl. Pulling her into my arms, I placed my hands to her skin and desperately sought out the hum of magic deep within her. I needed to find that source of power for this to work. I couldn't heal a mortal, so she had to still be Fae.

"Please, Blue. Please stay with me. I've got you." I closed my eyes, pushing my magic into her flesh and casting it as far as it could reach as I hunted for the fiery blaze of power that lived in this perfect creature. I didn't have much to work with, but what I did have, I gave to her.

"Hurry up!" Lavinia cried, and I squeezed my eyes harder to block her out.

There, at the very edges of her being was the last of Darcy's power, swirling like embers in smoke. I drove my magic into hers, offering her everything I had to give, healing her as fast as I possibly could.

"Take everything," I commanded. "Take it all, Darcy Vega."

Slowly, she began to heal, the burns on her legs fading first before the soft snap of bones fusing together reached me. I winced every time I found another broken part of her, offering her more and more of my magic in a torrent of power.

I was shaking, my mind beginning to splinter as I teetered on the edge of chaos. I couldn't bear what I'd witnessed, couldn't unsee the way Lionel had beaten her and taken her to the edge of death in the most unFae of fights. It was insufferable to me, and my fangs were aching with the need to tear Lionel's throat out for what he'd done to her. If I ever got my way, I would spend day after day torturing him for this. I'd make him scream as she had screamed and pay him back tenfold for each mark he'd left on her.

At last, she woke, stirring in my arms and curling into me. She was so small; it was hard to believe sometimes that she was one of the most powerful beings in existence. I lowered my head, kissing her cheek, her temple, her hair.

Her eyes fluttered open, her fingers brushing my stubble as confusion crossed her features, and for a moment I could have sworn there was a glint of silver in them, but my imagination must have been playing tricks on me, because they were pitch black now.

"Did we die?" she whispered.

"No, beautiful," I said heavily, emotion burning a hole in my chest. "We're still here."

I feared she might be sad about that, like she'd given up on the world, but then a small smile lifted the corner of her lips and I twitched one back in return.

"Thank fuck," I breathed, my heart rate levelling out and the Death bond releasing its grip on me. There was fight in us yet.

Lavinia sighed dramatically as the Death bond relieved her of its threat, but I didn't look her way, my eyes trailing over Darcy as I made sure I'd healed every last cut and break.

"Well, well, what drama that was for the little lovers. And such a romantic ending; someone should really write it into a storybook," Lavinia said icily, and my head whipped around, my fangs baring instinctively in a warning for her to stay the fuck away. She slinked over to the throne and threw herself onto it with a huff.

"It's ugly, this throne. I wanted Queen Avalon's throne. It was so pretty, all red and made of rubies. This one doesn't like me, it prods and pokes my back like it wants me to get off."

She shifted further onto it, then whipped a finger in our direction, a coil of shadow snatching my magic-blocking cuff and sending it flying onto my wrist, the metal snapping shut with a harsh finality and cutting off access to my Elements. Not that I had any power left.

Darcy rose from my lap, leaving me on my knees, her gaze settling on Lavinia, a dark strength about her that set my pulse pounding. She'd just been beaten to the brink of death, and resilience still lived in her. Trying to snuff out her light had only made it blaze brighter than ever.

She looked down at me, offering me her hand and I wrapped mine around hers, our bond alight. I rose to stand at her side, the two of us glaring at our captor, all the injustice of the universe making the air thicken in my lungs.

"Come here, pets," Lavinia summoned us, stroking the dagger at her hip which held the garnet gemstone in its hilt. "The time for storybook moments is over."

My fingers wound through Blue's and my muscles tensed in anticipation of a fight, but Lavinia just sighed, looking between us with narrowed eyes, beckoning us closer again.

I glanced at Darcy, and she gave me a nod before we walked forward together, cautiously approaching the throne to stand before Lavinia.

The Shadow Princess cocked her head to one side as she examined us, her lips pursing before she pushed to her feet and closed in on us like a wraith of darkness.

I held Darcy's hand tighter, my back straightening as I stepped forward to keep Lavinia's eyes on me.

"Look at that, how he tries to draw the attention onto him." She clucked her tongue, moving past me to Darcy and stroking her fingers through my girl's hair, the strands so thick with shadows that there wasn't a lick of blue in sight. "Lucky, lucky little Princess. What makes you so special, hm? Even Daddy has a fascination with you Vegas. Vega this and Vega that." She tutted, her soulless eyes landing on me again. "And look at this man you've caught in your thrall. So loyal, so adoring. The perfect mate. Well maybe I shall have some fun with this mate of yours; why should you have all the good things?"

Darcy's features twisted with hatred as she stared at the psycho who had cursed her. "It's me you want punished, so why not have your fun with me like your lizard king did?" she offered.

I growled, stepping forward threateningly as I snared Lavinia's gaze.

"You know the deal. If you want blood, then it's mine that gets spilled," I insisted. There was no way in hell I was going to let Darcy be tortured again. Once had been enough to fracture my sanity, and I wasn't sure I'd ever recover from it. This wasn't how this was supposed to go. She was never meant to come here. The price of the curse was my pain, not hers.

"Lance," Darcy hissed, shooting me a furious look as she pulled her hand from mine. "Don't say that."

Lavinia grinned that mad grin of hers as she looked between us, sweeping closer to me and running a hand up my arm before laying her head on my shoulder.

"Perhaps enough blood has been spilled today. There are other ways we can have some fun…" She trailed her hand up under my shirt, her ice-cold fingers caressing my skin, and if I'd thought this day was already a living nightmare that couldn't get any worse, then the stars were apparently taking that as a challenge.

I fought off the demanding urge to attack Lavinia, force her to the ground and never let her lay her disgusting hands on me again. But the Death bond ensured I remained in place, her willing little pet.

"Get away from him!" Darcy leapt forward with a savage look on her face, her hands outstretched, but no magic sparked in them, though for a second, I swear I could have seen hellfire blazing in her eyes.

Lavinia whipped out an arm and bands of shadow wrapped around Darcy, throwing her to the floor and holding her there. She fought furiously to get free, crying out as Lavinia slithered her hand down to my waistband and a shudder of disgust ran over me.

"Tell her to stop - make her stop!" Darcy screamed and I looked to her in agony.

Her pain made me act and I raised a hand to grip Lavinia's wrist, but the immediate burn of the Death bond made my heart hammer with an urgency that spoke of an imminent death.

"He will die if he is not willing," Lavinia explained, licking her lips as she goaded Darcy. "So what will it be, little Princess? Will you see your mate die for you all because you cannot bear to watch him offer me his body?" Her taunting made me so full of violence, it took everything in me not to attack her and try to break her neck. But even if I could manage it, the curse wouldn't release Blue, and I would die for breaking my vow to Lavinia.

"Please," Darcy said in a voice brimming with emotion. "Take anything from me, but not from him. Release him from this promise. It's my pain you want, so have it."

"But his pain causes you a far deeper torture than I could ever slice into your skin," Lavinia purred and my grip on her wrist firmed, even as my heart thundered more furiously in my chest, and I struggled to catch my breath. Death was coming for me if I resisted much longer.

My free hand went to my chest as pain splintered through my heart, my breaths heaving and darkness brushing the edges of my vision.

"The Death bond will take him then," Lavinia sighed in exaggerated disappointment.

"Let her go, Lance," Darcy gasped in panic and my fingers came loose of Lavinia's arm, the threat of the Death bond ceasing in an instant.

Lavinia smiled in victory, gripping my waistband and pushing her hand beneath it. I cringed, but the feel of her horrid skin against mine never came, a glow of silver brightening my eyes and a spark of power flourishing down my body. Lavinia yelped, snatching her hand back as if she'd been burned, looking at me in fearful confusion as she backed up a step. And I was wholly fucking confused myself.

"What have you got down there?" she demanded, stepping back further as that silver glow glittered over my skin. "Why are you glowing? What is happening?" The shadows gathered around her defensively, but whatever power this was, I couldn't wield it. It was a part of me, and yet not, at the same time.

"You can't have him like that," Darcy said in realisation, relief coating her words. "It's the Elysian Mate bond. Lance, your eyes… they're burning silver."

Whispers rushed through my head and the voice of the stars themselves trickled through my mind, their power rattling through the centre of me. *"A gift, Libra, son of the hunter, for there must be a balance. A light to counter the dark. Your bond will be safeguarded with starlight from this day forward."*

I turned my hands over, admiring the silver light, relief diving through me in a blaze. Were the stars actually protecting me for once? Go fucking figure. But what did they mean about a balance?

Lavinia's lips peeled back, and she rushed towards me with a shriek of anger. She grabbed my arm, assuring herself she could do so, and the silver light faded away beneath her touch.

"Curse the stars," she spat, a leash of shadow whipping from her palm and latching onto the collar around my throat. She yanked it tight, dragging me toward the torture chamber beyond the throne room, forcing Darcy to follow with the might of her dark power. "No matter. If I cannot fuck you, then I will make you bleed instead."

"No!" Darcy screamed, fighting as hard as she could to get free of Lavinia's control, but all I felt was relief at knowing the shadow bitch couldn't lay any claim on my body beyond the strike of a weapon.

A wild laugh left me as she forced me into the manacles on the platform in her chamber, down on my knees for her like making me submit meant anything at all. There was only one woman I had ever bowed to, and Lavinia was not her.

She tied Darcy down in front of me with chains of shadow, and she fought desperately to get to me, crying out for Lavinia not to hurt me.

"It's okay, beautiful," I promised her through a crazed smile that made her pause, her eyes searching mine as she took in this renewed strength in me. "She can't have anything more from me than pain. I'm all yours. She can't touch my soul; it'll be whole and waiting for you when this is over. So let me bleed for you, my Queen. It would be a fucking honour."

The first strike of the whip hit my back, the dark magic imbued in it diving deep into the cut she tore into my flesh. A roar left me, and Darcy's gaze locked on Lavinia, a promise of vengeance within her eyes that made her look like a fierce, transcendent creature of destruction. And I knew that somehow, someday, she would deliver our captor her end. I'd make damn sure of it.

Lavinia had left me in the cage in the throne room, still bleeding from her torture, although she'd had Lionel's butler, Horace, heal me just enough so I wouldn't die. That was one of the few times he actually acknowledged I existed outside of escorting me to the bathroom and shouting at me to hurry up with my shower. The clothes he gave me whenever I washed were from the new King Acrux merchandise line, and I swear he took pleasure in seeing me wear them. The shirts were emblazoned with jade Dragons and K.U.N.T. slogans, and I often discarded them instead of degrading myself by wearing them.

Horace hadn't healed me well this time. There were still lacerations down my back and across my chest that were burning with the aftershock of the shadows, the pain making me drift in and out of consciousness. The dark power of Lavinia's torture devices had laid a heavy blanket over my thoughts and emotions, stealing me away into their embrace, but I fought it as hard as I could for the sake of my girl.

I preferred it when I was awake, finding Blue there waiting for me, whispering words of encouragement, her kisses pressing to my torn flesh and making me feel new again even though I remained in ruins. But I always lost my grip on her, returning to nightmares where the darkness of the shadows bled into my bones, and I fell so deep into the black that I wasn't sure I would ever come out of it. That was where the real danger lay, because sometimes I tumbled so far into the shadows that I started to lose my grip on who I was and why I was there. But so far, I always found my way back.

When I returned to reality again, I found Darcy beside me, still awake as she watched over me, though exhaustion was written into her features. She opened her mouth to speak, but instead she gasped, her entire body turning to black smoke.

I reached for her in fright, her voice carrying to me from that dark cloud. "She summoned me."

She disappeared between the bars, Lavinia stealing her away for who knew what purpose. I could only be certain it was nothing good.

"Blue!" I shouted.

The word echoed back to me from the vaulted ceiling of the throne room, and no answer came in reply.

She was gone.

I waited for her to return with anxiety cutting me to ribbons, the hard floor serving me no comfort and every small movement I made sending fresh waves of pain skittering over my skin. It was tolerable enough when I reminded myself what was at stake, but with my mate back in Lavinia's clutches, it was difficult to find any of that strength I'd felt earlier in the torture chamber.

The pain was descending again, the shadows writhing under my skin and dragging me back into them. I didn't want to return to the dark, but I didn't have any control over it, the lingering effect of Lavinia's weapons still present in my soul. I was tossed between the shadows hour after hour, tortured within my own mind, their pain my pain, their anguish my anguish.

Where am I?

What am I searching for in this dark and immortal sea of blackness?

I finally felt Darcy's hand wrapping around mine once more, bringing me back from oblivion and anchoring me in my own body. She was who I searched for, and I could never, ever lose sight of that when the shadows tried to make me forget.

I squeezed her fingers, needing her closer. I knew this was torture for her too, and that she was never going to forgive me for the vow I'd made with the Shadow Princess, but there was no other choice to make in the face of her destruction. I'd told her straight that I would always place myself between her and danger whenever I could, so here we were. And it wasn't forever.

"What has she done to you?" a female voice spoke that didn't belong to my mate, then healing magic washed into my skin, followed by a kiss of power that peeled away the worst of the shadows inside me.

My eyes cracked open as the pain subsided and I rasped down a breath at the relief I was being offered, though it was soured by who I found there giving it to me.

"Come to gloat?" I asked icily, dragging my hand from my mother's through the bars of my prison and pushing myself up to sit against the back wall. It had been her hand after all, not Darcy's.

Tears ran down Stella's cheeks in two little rivers and she had the gall to choke on a sob too. She didn't look like her usual self, wearing navy sweatpants and a white t-shirt, the type of casual outfit I was pretty sure I had never seen on her in all my life.

"Of course not." Her eyes widened and I realised she was taking in the silver rings that adorned my eyes. "I heard about your Mating, but seeing it now is just..."

She trailed off, shaking her head in awe. "Is she good to you?"

"She's every good thing I forgot existed in this world."

Stella nodded, more tears spilling from her eyes as if this was all so fucking hard for her to bear witness to. Poor little Stella and her lost dreams. Boo fucking hoo.

"You're so like him..." She searched my features with an ache in her expression. "It's so difficult to look at you these days. All I see is Azriel looking back at me, judging me like he always did."

"He knew what you were," I muttered, unsure why I was even bothering to entertain a conversation with her.

"And what am I?" she asked in a shaky voice.

"You're Lionel's little lap dog."

"No, baby boy, it's not like that."

"Then what is it like?" I drawled, wondering what lies she planned on weaving for me now. Wasn't she tired of all these games? I certainly was.

"Lionel and I...we had history. We were together once, you know? When we were studying at Zodiac Academy. I was a foolish girl in love with him, with his power. The stronger he became, the more I fell into his shadow, but that didn't even break my heart. It broke when he arranged for me to marry another man."

My jaw tightened. "Dad deserved better than you."

"Yes," she agreed instantly. "He did. And I gave him better than me. I gave him you and Clara."

"And now two out of three of us are dead."

She winced, a sob leaving her throat as she clung to the bars. "I never wanted this."

"What did you want when you crawled into Lionel's bed again then, Stella? And what was it you expected when you tried to make me fall in line, when you allowed Clara to Guardian bond herself to that monster?"

"I didn't know she did that," she begged. "I thought he loved me. After your father died, Lionel comforted me. He was there for me, and over time my high school love for him returned. Or maybe it never really went away. He had his pure-blooded heirs by then, so I thought...maybe he would want me again as I wanted him. I thought we could all be a family."

"You mean you thought you'd just replace my father after he was done serving both of your purposes," I snapped, fury making my blood heat.

"It wasn't like that. After a while, I came to love Azriel. We weren't perfect but it was there for a time. It was born of you and your sister. There wasn't anything we wouldn't have done for you both."

"Well congratulations, Stella. I hope you're happy with your life choices. You can save the tears for someone who actually gives a fuck though. I'm not buying them."

"You're still my child," she rasped, reaching for me, but I shifted away so she couldn't touch me again and grief marred her features. "I meant to protect you. Truly I did. What is it Lavinia wants from you? Why is she keeping you alive?"

"I'm paying the price to break the curse on my mate. She asked for the debt to be paid in blood, flesh, or bone. My blood is bound to the curse, so those were my options. I can bear any pain or torment, but I vowed to my mate that I would not die, so I will suffer instead and one day we will both be free."

"You can't do this," Stella gasped.

"It's already done. I can endure anything for her."

She shook her head, some dawning comprehension in her eyes. "Please, Lance. As your mother, I'm begging you. I'll speak to Lionel. I'll have him order Lavinia to release you."

"Where is this even coming from? I'm your disappointment. You disowned me a long time ago, don't act like you're some loving mother now. I'm not going to swallow your lies."

"Why would I lie? What would it gain me? I may have been angry with you, baby, and I was hurt when you turned your back on me, but we are still Orions, you and me. Do you know why I kept his surname after he died?"

"To keep up the pretence that you loved him?" I shrugged, not really caring.

"No, it's because that name binds me to my children. After everything that's happened, I have never stopped loving you or her." She paused as the loss of Clara hung between us and I felt that long-lived grief pulling at my heart again, reminding me of the fresher loss I'd faced. Darius. Was he with my sister now? Looking down from above, cursed to watch us all suffer until we one day joined him in the stars? I couldn't stand the grief it caused me, knowing he was gone, that my best friend was lost and had taken so much light with him in his passing.

"My surname isn't Columba anymore. I'm not a dove, I'm a hunter. An Orion. I am your family whether you want me or not."

"You are no Orion," I snarled. "Family loves without condition. I've forged my own family through determination, sacrifice, and dedication. They aren't my blood, but they are bound to me deeper than you will ever be. You don't just get to love me and expect that to be enough. True love is built on everything that exists outside of the word. It's showing up when you're needed, no matter the inconvenience. It's knowing someone, *truly* knowing them, and accepting everything they are even where you differ or clash. It's making effort despite the differences, it's apologies when they're owed and forgiveness even when it feels impossible. And it took me so fucking long to become a man capable of those things, in part because of you. But mostly because of *him*. This false king you claim to love. A man who stole everything away from me and is still keen to take more. If you can love a monster unconditionally then that makes you a monster too. So don't you dare, don't you fucking dare come to me on your knees, begging for forgiveness, because you won't find it. You're not a part of my family, and there's nothing here for you in my heart but hate."

"Please, you don't understand. I've lost everything too."

"The difference is, you're the reason you lost it all. You're the one who pushed away the light and embraced the dark, Stella. I may be tainted, and I won't ever claim to have a pure soul, but I've owned every single one of my sins and never tried to make out that I was anything but what I am. You've spent so long convincing yourself that your actions are justified, that maybe you really believe it. But I know the truth of you. You're corrupted by power and greed, and of course you love Lionel Acrux, because he is the epitome of those things. My father was worth far more than your superficial love ever could have offered him. He was brave and honourable, and he sacrificed himself so that the entire kingdom might have a chance at fighting this malevolent fate we've all been handed. You could never have loved him how he deserved to be loved, because he embodies all the things you are not. But *I* love him. I love him from the depths of my heart, so profoundly that I know he can feel it beyond the boundaries of our world."

"What do you mean he sacrificed himself?" Stella scoffed in confusion. "Azriel died in a dark magic accident."

I didn't correct her, wanting to, but knowing that might just lead to her ordering a Cyclops Interrogation on me. "I found a note he left for me, and in those words, he said he knew what you were. He knew what you'd become. He wasn't just your pawn, he was a piece on the chessboard himself, and he was well aware that you were playing for the other side."

"Stop," she begged, trying to deny the reality I was brutally painting for her.

"He probably even knew you'd stand before me one day and would still expect me to find a scrap of love in my heart for you. But there's nothing here, Stella. And now you know you've lost Lionel too, and you're all alone with nothing but your insufferable self for company. You think you can come crawling to me now and fake that you care? You think that I'll seek comfort from you after everything you've done?"

"You can forgive me, just give me a chance," she croaked, and I saw the fear in her eyes of being all alone in the big, wide world, where everything she had put her faith in had abandoned her.

"No. And I hope you live a long, arduous life all alone, with no one but yourself for company, because there's no greater curse that I could wish on you but that."

"Baby, please. You're my boy. My little hunter. I love you. I know things have been difficult, but I'll make it right. I'll get you out of here."

"And then what? Sign me up to your Acrux fan club?" I sneered.

"No," she whispered, inching closer and tightening the silencing bubble around us. "I'll free you and find a way to return you to your friends. You and your mate. You and Dar-"

"Don't you dare speak her name," I snarled viciously. "I'm in this cage for her. I'm here to break the fucking curse your shadow queen put on her. I'm not going anywhere."

"What is the curse?" she asked through a whimper, and I didn't know why I indulged her, perhaps because I wanted her to know the lengths I'd go to for someone I really loved. For someone who would do the same for me, unlike she ever had. And maybe in part, I did it just to see if she really did care what became of me. Or if the lie of her love ran as deep as I believed it to.

"She's bound to a Shadow Beast. A fucking monster that's draining her power and will leave her wasted and mortal when it's done with her. So Lavinia will torture me in any way she sees fit for three moon cycles before she frees Darcy from it. I would rather there was a chance for us than give up and accept the fate the stars seem so fucking insistent upon offering us. I owe her that. And I can bear any pain to the ends of the earth and back for Darcy, but regardless, I entered a Death bond with Lavinia to ensure I don't fight it."

"No." Stella stilled in horror at those final words, her hand going to her mouth as it trembled, and fat tears spilled down her cheeks.

She was shaking her head and for once, her expression didn't look stitched into place. She looked worn and broken and all too fucking real. She looked horribly familiar too, and memories stirred within me from my childhood. This woman who had loved me and Clara behind closed doors when her theatrics weren't needed. Because it was just us. And for an uncomfortable moment, that expression made me falter.

She cried in a way that wasn't loud or for attention. It was quiet and full of pain as she hid her face in her hands and broke to pieces in front of me.

I remained silent, not knowing what to say, doubting myself for being sucked into what could easily just be another charade. But something told me this was the real deal, and I had no clue how to respond to it.

Stella reached through the bars, hunting for my hand and I was so stunned when she took it, clinging to me as she continued to sob and shudder, that I simply let her do it.

"You and Clara were the best thing I ever had," she croaked as she managed to compose herself a little and look me in the eye. "I wasted so much time being elsewhere as you got older, plotting and scheming, working out how you could both fit into this world Lionel and I were creating. I got lost in dreams of the future we were building. And for every inch of power I claimed, the deeper I fell into that fantasy land. I thought that once I seized the world with Lionel, everything would slide into place, but instead it's shattered into a million pieces. Lionel holds no love for me, and now I look back at the trail behind me after all these years and I'm finally seeing the destruction I left in my wake. The worst thing of all is that I see that same destruction staring back at me from your eyes. My son hates me, and though you're still here on this earth, I have lost you as permanently as I have lost my daughter."

More tears rolled down her cheeks as grief tore her expression apart, and I felt that same grief slicing into me over my sister, a wound never to be healed. The only real thing that Stella and I had in common now.

"I can see that there is no apology deep enough to fix us," she breathed, a dark acceptance veiling her eyes. "It's like you say - words mean nothing. I've failed in loving you. And now it's too late to be the mother I should have been. You're all grown up and full of sharp pieces because of me. The stars have offered you an Elysian Mate only to demand a terrible sacrifice from you. An unimaginable sacrifice." She squeezed my hand, looking at me in despair.

"You may not be mine any longer, but you are Azriel's son through and through. I know he is watching you from beyond the Veil, and he's been there even when I have not. He's the man I should have loved as devotedly as I have loved Lionel, but I never would have deserved his love in return."

I took my hand from hers, letting my walls slide firmly back into place between us, seeing the agony it caused her and not caring at all. She rose to her feet, trembling before turning and hurrying away, but I spoke my last words loud enough for her to hear.

"No," I agreed. "You wouldn't have."

The night wore on and I didn't let sleep take me again, worry carving chasms in my chest as I waited for Darcy to return.

Where the fuck had Lavinia taken her? What was she making her do? What new sins would haunt her after tonight?

Now I was healed, I had the energy to pace, walking up and down in front of the bars, testing their strength here and there. Perhaps I should have stolen a drink from Stella, but the idea of having that vile woman's blood in my mouth made my stomach churn.

The conversation we'd had kept circling in my mind, riling me up. If she was truly feeling guilty after everything, then that was her burden to bear, and I wasn't going to show kindness or empathy. She'd shown me none when I needed her most, when Clara had been killed and Lionel had stolen my future away by binding me to Darius.

I paused in my pacing, my hands curling around the bars and my eyes lifting to the vast, arching ceiling of the throne room above while picturing the sky far beyond it.

"Darius, if you're watching all of this, then I really hope the stars have told you their plans, that this is all just a storm that's about to clear up so I can see blue sky again. And if that's true, is there any chance you could send me a sign?"

Silence.

Grief welled in me, my fists tightening on the bars, my fear for Blue pressing down on me too. I felt so fucking helpless in this cage, but I had no other option. Darcy had to be saved, and I had to find a way to get her back to Tory, because together those two were the only answer Solaria had now.

Three moon cycles. That's all. The grains of sand are already counting down within the hourglass of our fate.

A dark swirl of smoke rushed through the throne room and relief pounded through me as it slipped into the cage and Darcy materialised before me, the shadows wrapping around her body and shielding her nakedness.

I grabbed hold of her, checking her over and she squeezed my arms in reassurance.

"I'm fine," she promised, though the way her throat bobbed told me something had happened.

"What did she make you do?"

"She gave me to Vard. He sifted through my memories," she said, a flash of power in her eyes. "I shielded a lot of them, like you taught me, and gave him enough to believe he'd *seen* everything."

"Good girl."

Her eyes drifted down me and her lips parted. "You're healed." She brushed her fingers over the place where one of the worst wounds had been on my side. "How?"

"Stella," I answered in a low voice. "She came looking for forgiveness. I'm not sure if she's had a jolt of conscience or if she's up to some game, but I sent her away regardless."

Darcy eyes sparked with protectiveness for me at the mention of my heartless mother. "I'm sorry."

"For what?"

"For how she treats you. For the fact that you should have had a mother who stood by you your whole life."

I brushed a lock of hair away from her shoulder and the shadows receded from it, letting me see the blue hiding beneath. I didn't mention it this time though, afraid it would disappear again the moment I pointed it out.

"She was an okay mother once. And I had my dad too. You're the one who grew up alone when you should have had the whole world placed at your feet."

"I *saw* a vision of my parents on the mountain," she revealed, a crease forming between her brows. "They could speak to me like they saw me. It was a vision for them in the past, but it was real for me." She touched her heart as if it hurt her and I took hold of her hand, kissing her knuckles softly.

She leaned into me with a sigh, her hands brushing up my chest and the warmth of her fell against me. I wrapped her in my arms, and she tiptoed up until our mouths met in a slow, aching kiss that drove out some of the darkness in my chest.

"What will happen if I turn mortal?" she whispered as our lips broke apart and I pressed forward, claiming her mouth again, murmuring my answer between kisses.

"You won't."

She drew back again. "Will your mate rings fade too? Or will you be stuck pining for a mortal you can rarely visit?"

"*Blue*," I growled, furious that she would even voice such a future. "I will save you."

"What if it's already too late?" she said in fear.

"Then I will find a way to tear my own magic from my flesh and join you in the mortal world," I said, the words falling easily from my tongue. "Where you go, I will follow. Have I not made that clear enough to you yet?" I bit her lower lip and my fangs extended, the bloodlust rising and making me pull back so I could think clearer.

She gripped my arms, tilting her head to one side in an offering and my throat ached with need.

"No," I gritted out.

"Do it," she demanded. "I hate seeing you like this. You need to feed. Besides, if you latch onto the well of power in me, you'll know if there's anything still there or if the Shadow Beast has taken it all. Since Lavinia made it feed again, I can't feel any power at all."

Her desperation to know the answer to that broke my resolve, or maybe I was just fucking weak because I was dying to taste her on my tongue, and I was at the brink of insanity.

I lunged forward, clutching her hard against me and driving my fangs into her exposed neck with a groan. Her blood coated my mouth, the sweetness of sunshine dampened by the darkness of the shadows. I tried to connect with the well of her magic, a growl of frustration leaving me when it didn't automatically flow to me. There were shadows deep within her, concealing my way to that power, but as I pressed my will against them, demanding they part for me, I finally found it. Her magic hit my tongue and I lost my fucking mind, driving her against the cage bars as I stole it for myself, the intense, fiery power of her pouring through me.

She gasped, feeling it too, and her body grew hotter against me, like living fire was sparking in her skin.

She didn't have a whole lot to spare, so despite how difficult it was to pull away, I finally managed it, easing my fangs from her skin, and raising a hand to run my thumb over the pinprick marks, wishing I could heal her, but the magic-blocking cuffs I wore kept the power I'd stolen subdued. Still, without the hunger burning at the base of my throat, I could think clearer at last.

"It's still there," I confirmed, and she nodded, hope dancing in her eyes. It was such a fucking relief to have some good news that the two of us smiled.

"You're Fae, Blue, and you're going to damn well stay that way." I kissed her, picking her up and she latched her legs around my waist. She gripped the back of my neck, kissing me again, her smiles feeding me the strength of an army.

We were going to get through this. We just had to hold on.

"Today was fucking devastating, beautiful," I said. "But you know what keeps playing on repeat in my mind?"

"What?" she asked, drawing me closer and fisting her hands in my hair.

"The way you looked when you drove that blade into Lionel's throat," I said, pressing her harder against the bars and gripping the smooth backs of her bare thighs, the shadows retreating wherever I touched her.

She bit her lip, her head falling back to rest against the bars and a wild laugh leaving her. "If only I'd struck his eye like I'd planned, maybe he'd be dead and gone at last."

"If you had full access to your magic and Order, you would have destroyed him, Blue. He's a fucking coward who can't face you like Fae, and if he ever did, he knows he'd lose," I said fiercely, and she dropped her head to look at me.

"You always have so much faith in me."

"You're a queen destined to rule. I knew that the first moment I saw you."

"You spent a long time denying it," she jibed, and I smirked.

"I like to think that me being your asshole professor drove you to greatness."

"Oh, do you now?" she prodded my cheek and my grin only widened, this small moment of peace expanding around us, reminding me of the time I'd taken her to the bottom of the Acrux swimming pool. This was our little bubble of light, and no darkness could get in. It was purely ours, even if it was woefully temporary.

"Yeah, that and all the fun we had sneaking around campus together," I said, letting those memories fill me up to the brim.

"I miss those days," she said quietly, her smile falling, and my heart fell with it.

"We'll have them again," I insisted.

"I really, really want to believe that," she said, her fingers tightening in my hair.

I brushed my hand up her side and she shivered, leaning into me. "I feel so fragile in your arms. I never felt like that before. I'm so close to mortal, I can't stand it."

I kissed her gently and she tugged my hair, forcing our mouths to part as fury blazed in her eyes.

"Don't treat me like I'm breakable. I want you to remind me I'm Fae, that I'm shatterproof."

"Is that an order?" I asked in low tone, growing hard between her thighs at the power in her words.

"Yes, it's an order," she said passionately, and I didn't need any more encouragement than that. "Don't you dare hold back on me."

I gripped her hips then spun her around with the speed of my Order, crushing my chest to her back to pin her in place against the bars and taking her hair in my fist. I tugged her head sideways so I had access to her ear, grazing my teeth along the shell of it and a sigh of desire left her.

"This is a bad idea. I'm angry, Blue, so fucking angry at the world. I've got a whole lot of pent-up energy in my veins that I want to let out."

"I can handle it," she growled. "Show me the devil in you."

The mayhem in me flooded out and I let it take over, needing an outlet and wanting it to be her. If she craved the dark in me, she could have it, along with every sin I had to offer. She may have been a creature of sweetness and light, but she held her own vices too, and they complimented my own perfectly.

I twisted us around, lowering her to the floor with my speed, catching her head before it hit the tiles and pushing her legs apart with my knees.

"Yes," she sighed, reaching for me and I watched as the shadows evaporated from her skin, baring her to me entirely.

I took a moment to admire all that bronze flesh and the way she writhed for me, aching for my touch. I cocked my head to one side, loving that I was the sole Fae on this earth allowed to have her like this.

"Just for me," I said in a gruff voice, urging a confirmation from her.

"Only you," she swore, playing with her breasts and making my cock so hard, it was almost impossible to hold back any longer. "You're my saviour, my felon, my sinister knight. And if you don't touch me this second, I'll go mad."

I tasted my lower lip, pressing my knees harder into her inner thighs, rearing over her and spreading her wide for me, my hands laying on the cold tiles either side of her. "Look at me. And don't stop looking until I'm finished with you. Forget this place. It's just us, beautiful. You and me."

She nodded and I reached between us to shove my pants down just enough to free my aching cock and guiding it against her soaked core. I smiled as she gasped, holding her in suspense and savouring the heat of her as the head of my dick throbbed with need. Her eyes remained locked on mine and my heart rampaged for her as I thrust inside her, driving myself into her tight body as far as I could go and clamping my hand down over her mouth as she cried out.

She bit down on my palm, and I started fucking her in deep, firm thrusts, bracing one arm above her head and pinning her to the floor. My hunger for her spilled everywhere and a waterfall of blue suddenly pooled out around her as the shadows fell away from her hair.

I took my hand from her mouth, admiring her beauty as her body gripped mine and the world faded to nothing around us.

"When we get out of here, I'm going to have you like this every damn day," I said heavily. "Because I spent too much time at the academy being cautious, letting time slip by where I didn't see you at all. We're gonna fuck, and laugh, and love each other, and I'm gonna make you smile from the moment you wake up in the morning to your last moments of wakefulness at night."

I ground my hips, circling them as I pushed deeper inside her and she moaned, arching her back and clinging to my arms.

"I want that more than anything," she breathed.

"We're gonna make it to that future, beautiful."

Her legs knotted around me, and I scooped her up, flipping us over with a burst of speed and clasping her ass as she straddled me. I enjoyed the view as I fucked her from beneath, watching her breasts bounce and bathing in the sounds of the sultry noises leaving her. She met every thrust with a grind of her hips, giving to me as I gave to her, and we found a heady rhythm between us. She started to shatter for me, legs shaking and her breaths coming in ragged waves, but as tempting as it was to feel her explode around me, I was more tempted to taste her climax instead.

I used my strength to drag her up to kneel over my face, and one long stroke of my tongue had her crying out in delight. She braced herself on the floor as I found her clit and started teasing her, sucking and licking while her hips rocked in time with my mouth, and I brought her to the edge of oblivion before drawing her away from it again. I squeezed her ass in a bruising grip, feasting on her and drowning in the sound of her perfect moans until I finally allowed her to come on my tongue, growling my victory against her pussy.

She went limp as her orgasm shuddered through her and I lifted her up by the hips, placing her over my cock and driving deep into her with a flash of my Order speed, before she'd even realised I'd switched positions again.

"*Lance*," she gasped, her hands slamming to my chest to catch herself, and I laughed darkly as I gripped her hips and fucked her through the last waves of her climax, making her ride me just how I liked it.

She clenched tight around my shaft, and I groaned in pleasure at the feel of her, so close to finishing too but wanting to prolong this for as long as I could.

She found her strength again and lowered over me, grinding her clit against my pubic bone as we started fucking in a slower, more intense rhythm, her gaze remaining locked with mine. She writhed against me, chasing another release, and I stroked my fingers between her shoulder blades, making her shiver in pleasure.

She fell into her second orgasm, her pussy so wet and pulsing around me that it took every ounce of concentration I had not to follow her to ruin.

I fucked her in lazy thrusts, slow and hard, the tight buds of her nipples grinding into my chest as she continued to pant in ecstasy. I stretched out her climax with every drive of my cock until she collapsed against my chest, her heated breaths rushing over my skin and her blue hair tumbling around my neck.

I didn't let her rest for long, rolling us back over and holding her down, taking control of her body and lifting her hips as I started fucking her for my own release. My muscles tensed all over as I channelled every drop of rage and injustice into my thrusts, claiming my mate and casting out all darkness in my flesh in the face of her. This princess who owned me down to my bones, and who I would love to the edges of eternity.

I came with a roar, thrusting in to the hilt and finishing inside her as my fingers bit into the flesh of her hips, keeping her still for me. She reared up, kissing me hard, and I melted into that kiss, pleasure, fire, and fucking brimstone washing over me. Her tongue stroked mine and I was lost to her, possessed by the way she loved me and drowning in the beauty of the starlight which bound us.

My weight settled over her and I held her in my arms, wanting to keep the shadows from claiming her for as long as possible.

"I never thanked you for offering yourself up to break the curse," she whispered, her mouth falling against the space below my ear as she curled herself into the arc of my body. "I hate you for it, but I love you for it too. I love you so much, I don't know how my heart contains it all."

Her words wrapped around me, reminding me that the stars had chosen me for this girl, and as unworthy as I felt of her love, I couldn't deny that I was made for her. So it had to be true that I could be enough for her, even if it took me the rest of my life to prove it. However long that may be.

Scorpio
Gemini
Virgo
Cancer
Leo
Sagittarius
Taurus
Capricorn
Aquarius
Libra
Pisces

LEON

CHAPTER NINETEEN

"Gaaaaabe!" I called into the wind. "Gaaaaaaabe!"

A storm was crackling in the air as Dante fought to keep a tether on his powers, and my long, thick mane of blonde hair was starting to stand up on end from the static.

The battlefield was a churned-up land of mud and death, and the quiet that hung over us made me shudder. Fear was a tangled knot in my chest, and I couldn't let my mind drift to the worst-case scenario that Gabriel was lying dead among the bodies somewhere. We'd been searching for him day and night, scouring the bodies one after the other, but there were so many of them to check that it was an endless task.

Rosalie was leading the Oscura Wolves back and forth across the ground in shifted form, their noses to the ground as they tried to scent some trace of him. The rest of our family were digging, using earth and air magic, to shift as much soil as they could and hunt the ground beneath us, searching the ruins of The Burrows in desperation.

Dante and I had scoured the land up here three times over, and I was starting to think we should head underground too. I turned to him, finding him standing with his back to me, his eyes on the horizon and tension in the set of his broad shoulders. He carved a hand over his dark hair and sparks of electricity tumbled off of him, a Dragon's rage rising in his skin.

"If he was here, he'd *see* us. He'd call for us, or leave some sign," Dante said as I moved up behind him, my heart as heavy as a lump of lead.

I rested my hand on his shoulder and electricity flowed freely into my body, making me growl, but I pushed through it even as all my hair stood fully on end, reaching for the sky.

"He could be trapped. Maybe he can't get to us because he's out of magic. Maybe we should start tunnelling like the others are. We can't give up," I insisted.

He spun towards me, forcing my hand off of him, his eyes flashing like a sea storm. "I would never give up on him, fratello. A morte e ritorno. Even if he is dead, we shall return him to us and give him the greatest burial a Fae has ever known."

Pain struck me in the heart at him even voicing that thought. "He's not dead," I growled, my Lion raising its head in my chest. There was no way I was giving that possibility airtime. It could fuck right off and bury itself up a duck's ass.

I fell to my knees, shoving my hands into the dirt and starting to dig. I only had a fire Element, but I didn't need earth to get underground. I'd dig my way to the other side of the world for Gabriel.

"Gaaaabe!" I cried into the hole I was opening up. My fingers dragged over something hard, and black hair peeked through the mud around it. I gasped, trying to dig deeper into the earth in case it was him. "Gabe? Gabe hold on!"

I cleared the mud, and a charred skull came loose in my hand, black hair still sticking up from the top of it, the rest of it all burnt away by fire.

"Gabriel?!" I looked into the empty eye sockets of the skull, then to that black tuft of hair on its head, stroking it as grief welled in me. "What if this is Gabe?" I cried and Dante dropped down in the mud beside me, reaching for the skull.

I didn't let him touch it, hugging it to my chest and cradling it softly as I sobbed.

"Shh, shh, I've got you Gabe. We can fix this. We can put you back together dude," I promised.

Dante pressed his air Element into the soil, carving out the ground and digging up the rest of the body. In seconds, we'd know the truth, we'd see a piece of his clothes, his sword still valiantly in his hand. Oh man, I just knew he died valiantly.

"Ga-hay-hay-be," I cried, rubbing my face on the skull as tears ran down my cheeks. I couldn't say goodbye. He was one of the best Fae I knew. My winged friend, my angel man.

Dante eased Gabe's body from the ground, laying down the pile of bones which still had tattered, burnt clothes clinging to its shoulders. He tugged off a scrap of red material which was branded with the crest of the Dragon Guild and my sobs immediately died in my throat.

"It's not Gabriel," Dante confirmed with a sigh of relief before I realised I was hugging some gross, dead creep.

"Ergh!" I slammed the skull down on a rock, then again and again and again, pieces of bone shattering beneath the force. "Double, triple, quadruple die, you devil dick," I snarled through my teeth.

I didn't stop until the skull was in fifty pieces and there was nothing left of it to destroy, but then I realised a piece of its hair was stuck on my finger and I shook my hand with a scream.

It flicked from my hand, slapping Dante in the face and he fell back onto his ass with a curse. The hair landed on his knee, and he kicked out his leg to send it fluttering down onto the mud. I burned it with a flash of fire and breathed out a sigh of relief, subtly wiping my hands off on Dante's sleeve.

"Let's start digging," Dante said darkly, moving to stand and splitting the dirt apart with his air Element. I used the power of fire to harden the walls of the muddy tunnel he was creating, and although we definitely weren't as efficient as an earth Elemental would be, we made steady progress, descending into the dark.

When we were ten feet deep and tunnelling along nicely, I cast Faelights around us, wanting to conserve my fire Element in case we came under attack. What if Lionel came back with an even bigger army? What if the first battle had been the pre-battle to a bigger battle? A battle of doom.

"Let's hurry," I whispered.

"Wait, did you hear that?" Dante said, pressing his ear to the muddy wall ahead of us.

My stomach growled loudly, and I pressed a hand to it. "That's just me, bro."

"No, it's not that."

My stomach growled louder. "Pretty sure it is. I could hardly eat breakfast this morning, I was so worried about Gabe. I only had three dry bagels with butter and jelly on top and two Poptarts. Not even the good kind of Poptarts. They were unbranded, Dante. And I didn't have any cereal – you know how I love cereal."

"Get over here, Leone," he barked, and I hurried forward, pressing my ear to the wall too and gazing at my best friend with hope chasing my heart around my chest.

There was a musical whistling noise coming from somewhere beyond it and I gasped.

"Do you think it's Gabriel? Maybe he got hit on the head and he's lost all memory of who he was, and now he identifies as a bird, and we'll find him in there with his wings out and his eyes all cuckoo as he tries to communicate to us in bird language."

"Your imagination scares me sometimes," Dante murmured, then pressed his hand to the wall.

"We're coming, Gabe!" I called then formed my lips into an O, whistling to him in case that was all he understood now.

Dante cut a hole through the wall, and I blasted a swirl of fire around it to harden it, but the tremor that ran through the ceiling told me this place was not stable at all. I sent my Faelights ahead of us and we stepped into a small section of the rebels' passages, all the ways on now collapsed and rubble lying everywhere.

The whistling was coming from a large pile of rocks, and I gasped as I spotted a thin, metal pipe sticking out of it. I hurried forward, dropping to my knees and throwing bricks and huge stones aside as I dug Gabe free.

"I'm coming, I'm here, I got you dude." I cleared the area around the pipe, the wind from the frantic whistling puffing against my face, and I wrinkled my nose at the strange scent coming from it. "What the-"

"Dalle stelle," Dante cursed as he moved closer and I gazed at what I'd unveiled in shock, my mind not able to decipher the leathery, orange-toned skin.

It was definitely part of a body, some spandex torn open around it and the silver pipe clutched between what looked like-

"Is that a bare ass?" Dante whispered, confirming my worst fears as the pipe continued to whistle and the air expelled from it puffed into my mouth.

"Ah!" I reared backwards, spitting on the ground and wiping my tongue over and over against my sleeve. "Why is there a whistling ass in that pile of rocks?!"

I picked up a stone, lunging at it in a bid to kill it for the ass-flavoured air which I would never forget the taste of. Dante knocked me back, wielding his air Element and unveiling the man within the rocks.

He was on his knees, ass up and pretty much naked apart from the slip of spandex that was wrapped around his cock and balls.

"I'll kill you, you ass whistling monster!" I dove forward, but Dante knocked me back again, looking me in the eye.

"He's on our side, fratello. That's Brian Washer."

"I don't care who he is, his ass whistled in my mouth," I snapped.

"He might have seen Gabriel," Dante hissed, and I clenched my teeth, fighting back the fire in me and nodding stiffly as I gave in. But if he didn't think I was going to hold a grudge for the rest of time for this, he didn't know me at all.

"Help," Washer whimpered, still in the same awkward position on his knees, cuts and bruises lining his body, ass pointed at us like it wanted to catch my eye.

Dante took pity on him, leaning down and pressing a hand to his shoulder to heal him.

Washer started flexing his hips, rocking back and forth, making the ass whistle go off sporadically.

"What the hell is that?" I pointed at the pipe and Washer peeled himself off the ground at last, reaching back to pluck it from his ass crack. "I ran out of magic, you see? But I found this teeny weenie pipe among the debris, and I couldn't reach my mouth to make a noise with it to hail attention this way. So I did what any desperate fellow would do and-"

"Why didn't you just shout for help?" I demanded.

"That's far less efficient. I am well trained in survival one-oh-one. Now." He held out his hand to Dante. "I must shake the hands of my saviours. Goodness, you are a strapping man…oh - I know who you are."

"Dante Oscura," Dante said anyway, briefly shaking his hand. "We need to know what you've seen down here. We're looking for someone."

"Of course," Washer said, holding his hand out to me and I hissed at him like a cat in refusal.

He placed his hands on his hips, rocking side to side as he limbered up. My gaze slipped down to his Speedos and I inhaled sharply as I spotted a smooth, waxed ball hanging out one side of it.

"So, did you see anyone else down here?" Dante pushed.

I tugged on his sleeve, trying to get his attention and draw it to the ball that was looking me right in the eye.

"*Dante*," I whispered subtly.

"Ohhh, yes," Washer said in a warbling tone. "I saw the man himself. The big, puffed-up Dragon Lord, that false king. I was here among the rubble already, knocked out by all those naughty rocks that had fallen on my head. But as I woke, I heard a terrible, terrible voice."

"What did he say?" Dante asked while I tried to give the tanned, leathery dude in front of me the heads up that his shiny nut was hanging out with us.

Washer didn't seem to pick up my expressive eye movements though, instead barrelling on with his story.

"He said, 'The dead queen's bastard son, and it looks like he's all out of magic'," Washer relayed ominously, and my gaze finally snapped up from his ball to his face.

"Gabe," I gasped, sharing a look of fear with Dante. "What happened next?"

"Well, my boy, he said something about needing a new Seer, then there was a bit of a kafuffle, a twinkle of stardust and I believe the king took whoever the poor fellow was prisoner."

"It was our Gabriel," I said in despair.

"No," Dante growled, electricity exploding from his body, and I stepped back instinctively while Washer got a blast to the chest, sending him flying onto his ass, his legs spread wide and twitching under the onslaught of his power.

"Gabriel? As in Gabriel Nox?" Washer balked. "Are you saying he was Merissa's son? That he is the half-brother of the Vega twins?"

"Yeah, duh," I said, and Dante rounded on me

"That was a secret, Leone."

"Ohhh," I said in guilty realisation. "Well, it's still a secret, right bro?" I looked to Washer. "Or I'll smash your nuts in with a hammer. Nuts that might be more accessible than you even realise."

"Of course. I shall solemnly vow that I will never utter the truth," Washer promised, holding out a hand to strike the deal, but I grimaced at it. Dante took the bullet, moving forward and making the star promise with him.

"Come on, Dante, we have to tell the others." I lunged at my Dragon friend, dragging him nose to nose with me by the shirt. "We have to go after Gabe. We have to rescue him."

Dante's face paled with terror. "Let's gather everyone and get back to the rebels."

I nodded, fury falling over me and making the beast in me stand to attention. No one took a member of our family and got away with it. I'd grown up in the roughest city in Solaria, I'd survived gang fights, psychotic, power-hungry Fae trying to rule my life and everyone else's, and I was *not* going to let a small-dicked Dragon steal away my Gabe and live to tell the tale.

Scorpio
Gemini
Virgo
Cancer
Leo
Sagittarius
Taurus
Capricorn
Aquarius
Libra
Pisces

JUSTIN

CHAPTER TWENTY

Exhaustion held me tight in its fist, but I didn't care, it no longer mattered because I'd made it! A cloud hung ahead of me at last, the final leaves from my nummy pouch and drops of water from my flask lining my groaning stomach, gifting me a touch of magic for my escape.

I had been a dead man, whispering my farewells to the stars and beyond as I awaited my end, expecting the small spark holding me aloft to gutter out soon and mark my descent into the awaiting probes of the creatures below.

But my salvation had crested the horizon and the dark rain cloud there called me forth with a wry grin and promise of freedom. In the depths of those clouds, I could lose them, hide myself from deadly probes and live to fight another day once I made it to some distant safe haven.

I kicked my legs as if I was running through the air itself, then hastily tightened the straps around me, hard enough to make my skin tingle with pins and needles, but I ignored the sensation and leaned towards that cloud with determination.

A wild laugh spilled from me as the first tendrils of grey brushed against me, and I cast one final look down at the Nymphs who had been chasing me, shaking my fist at them and calling out.

"There'll be no feasting on my flames tonight you blaggards! So take that and stuff it up your jumper!"

My cheeks flushed pink at the foul words as they escaped my lips, but there it was, the brute in me awoken and set free for all the world to see.

The wind picked up at my back and I swept forward quickly, pushing a touch more magic into the flame above my head so the hot air made me rise into the belly of the cloud, lost to the Nymphs below and safe at long last.

Water droplets formed on my cheeks as they condensed against my skin and I opened my mouth wide, licking at the air itself to gain myself a drink.

It had been a long, hard week. But here I was, Justin Masters, Master of the Nymphs and now Captain Cloud Cruiser too. Perhaps someone would write a bard about my daring escape upon my return. Perhaps my dear Grussy would be the one to weave the sonnet.

Something in my chest constricted as I gave that some real thought, my mind returning to that blood-soaked battlefield, my queen throwing me aloft and remaining to fight alone after all others around us were lost.

It had seemed so hopeless, but I had seen the fire burning in her eyes, seen the fury and determination, and I couldn't believe that such ferocious power could have guttered out.

My queens were out there somewhere. And I would return to them just as soon as I made it beyond this cloud and found a way back to civilisation.

The first hour within the belly of the cloud passed quickly enough, my thirst eventually sated by the droplets of rain I'd managed to steal from it and my clothes slowly soaking through until even my bones felt heavy with the cold.

But even that couldn't dampen my mood. No sir-ee.

Two more hours dragged on, the shivers wracking my body intensifying to the point of pain, my teeth chattering and clattering like they were playing a tune all of their own until finally, I had to give in.

I took a steadying breath and banished the flame which had been burning above my head for so long, keeping me aloft and alive within this parachute of salvation while I drifted hopelessly above a sea of death.

I began to descend instantly, my parachute buffeted by the wind which had been guiding the cloud across the sky and pushing me north.

The thick layer of cloud thinned out below me, the ground calling my name as I dropped lower and lower, the last of my energy fleeing as I held on to consciousness by pure force of will. Perhaps I might find a warm bed to rest upon once I landed. Perhaps some kind Fae would offer aid to a fellow fresh from war and in need of some charitable resilience.

I dipped beneath the cloud at last, drawing in a breath through my still-chattering teeth and looking out at the lush green landscape below.

I had travelled over a forest during my time within the cloud, a mountain looming in the distance which drew my eye.

I knew that mountain, had studied it in foraging club and even taken a trip out to it on a grub gathering expedition with my forage chums. There were ruins there of an old temple dedicated to the worship of the planets and beyond. Mount Lyra.

I could find shelter there, perhaps find some scrummy lichen for food and rest a while before setting out on my quest to return to my queens.

At last, my luck was changing, and just in time too now that my magic had well and truly gone and my return to the ground was inevitable.

But just as I began to give in to the sweet and wholesome call of the earth beneath me, my toes passed beyond the outskirts of the forest and a screech straight from my nightmares sent a spike of terror coursing through my heart like a spear.

No.

My eyes widened in horror as I looked down and found the Nymphs pouring from beneath the trees at my feet, their wild cries and violent desires colouring the air around me until I was choking on it.

I didn't know if they had somehow been able to keep track of me through the cloud cover, had followed the direction of the wind or had simply made a lucky guess, but it mattered not now.

I was totally out of magic, not even a snuff of it left to ignite a flame to carry me skyward once more. I had nothing left. Nothing but guts and gusto, and as I dragged my eyes from them towards that mountainside once again, I found myself diving into those parts of me.

It seemed as if I was destiny-bound to face this path. And if that was the case, then I would do so upon two feet with my sword in hand.

I reached up and tugged on the vine securing the righthand side of the parachute above me, forcing the thing to turn me towards those ruins where Fae of old had worshipped the sun in all its glory. It was as good a place as any for a final stand, and with a bit of luck, I could find myself a narrow spot to place my feet and force them to face me one at a time.

I had no illusions about the way my fate would turn in the face of so many foes, but I would aim to take as many of them as I could into the after with me.

The Nymphs yowled in hungry victory again and I darn near soiled my britches.

So this was it. Destiny had come calling for my soul. What a dastardly end to endure.

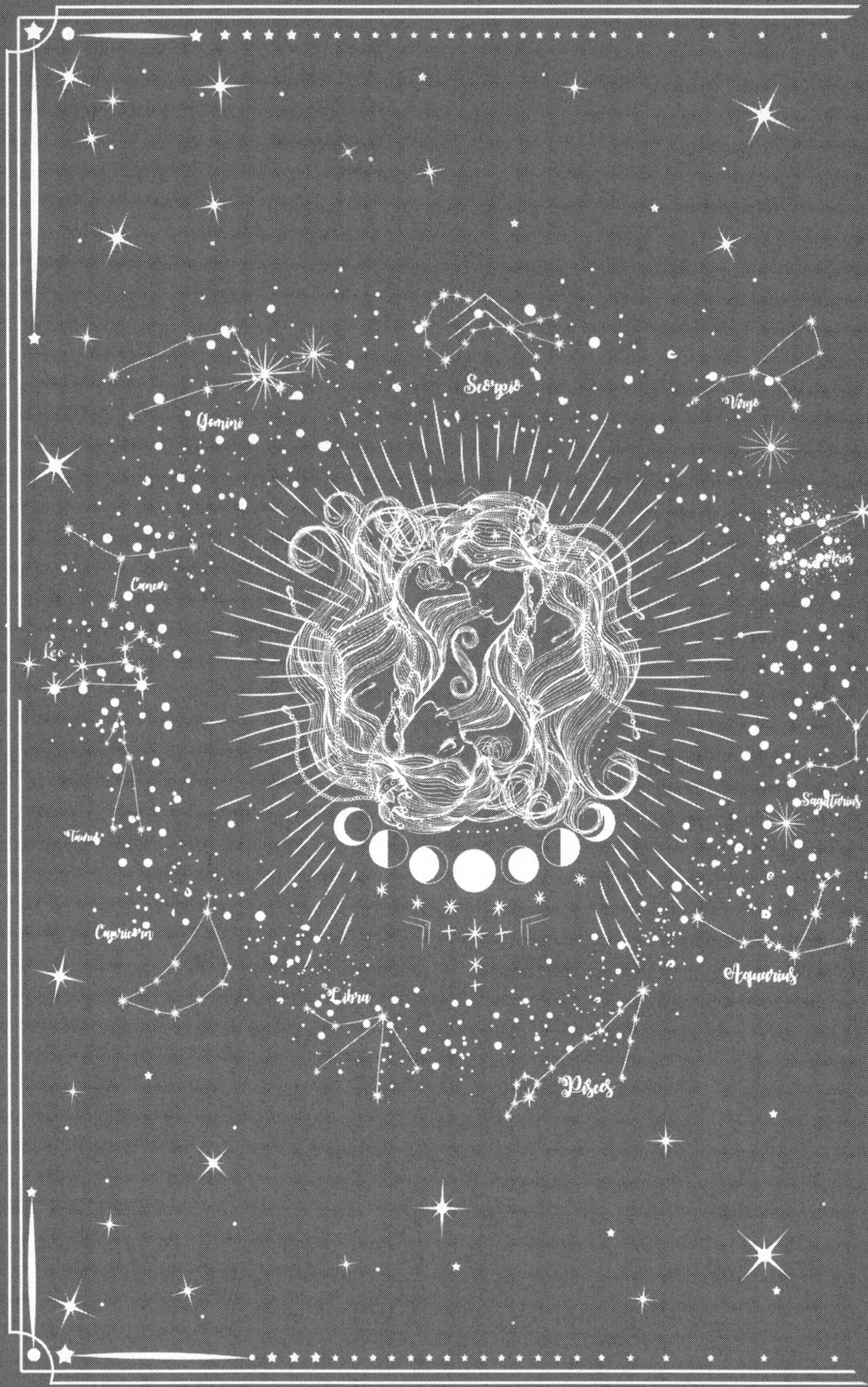
Scorpio
Gemini
Virgo
Cancer
Aries
Leo
Sagittarius
Taurus
Capricorn
Aquarius
Libra
Pisces

TORY

CHAPTER TWENTY ONE

The grass was soft beneath my fingers, the cool wind brushing my cheeks while drops of rain fell through the branches of the magical tree above me, parting the golden leaves that coated the wooden wing of the Dragon who kept watch over the people laid to rest here.

My chest was tight and aching, my cheeks dry, though my eyes burned with the pain of the reality I lay within.

"Where is she?" I breathed, my fingers brushing against the ice of the coffin to my left, my head turning that way as I looked to him for an answer I knew I wouldn't get.

It was a certain kind of agony coming here, lying with him without truly being with him at all. There was no answer, no sense of him in the heavy presence that accompanied the cold body in those walls of ice. He wasn't here. He wasn't anywhere anymore.

The pain in my chest sharpened, the ache of my reality cutting deep as always and still I didn't cry. I wasn't sure I had any tears left in me.

"God, I wish I could hate you the way I used to," I hissed, my fist closing against the ice then crashing against it, sending a spiderweb of cracks through the side of the casket before they crystalised and hardened once more.

I was losing control. The power within me was a rampant, violent thing and it burned so hot all the time that I felt like I was in an endless battle to contain it. One I couldn't even decide if I wanted to win or lose.

I pushed myself to my feet, unable to lay with the body that wasn't him any longer, and striding away without once looking back.

The shattered pieces of me cut deeper with every step, like I was abandoning him or failing him with each moment that passed without me doing anything which would help me keep the promise I'd made to him.

I drew in a deep breath then screamed at the top of my lungs as I looked out over the mountainside towards the sky beyond, a deep and roiling rain cloud pouring its contents over everything and reducing the view to a blur of nothing.

The silencing bubble surrounding me kept the sound from travelling beyond my own personal destruction, but the action did little to soothe anything inside of me.

I was wasting time and I didn't know which way to turn to stop it. My sister was out there somewhere, needing me and lost in the dark, and I had no idea how to even begin the hunt for her.

My mind tossed every thought or idea I'd had since the battle around and around, but it never threw up anything which seemed in any way likely to help me find her.

I needed Gabriel to *see* a way for me to do this, to tell me what path to take while I struggled to think of a single one which could even come close to setting me on the path I had sworn to follow.

Where are you, Darcy?

I turned and stalked inside the crumbling ruins without looking towards the huge camp the rebels had erected as a temporary home in the wake of our defeat. I knew there were eyes on me, watching, waiting, expecting. But I had no answers for them and even less hope. We couldn't stay here much longer either, the pressure of that decision weighing heavily on my shoulders even though I had never asked for the burden of carrying it.

The absence of sound from the central worshipping chamber where we'd set up something of a war council let me know that a silencing bubble was already in place around the room. No doubt the ex-Councillors were in there debating everything to within an inch of its life. I swear they and Geraldine would argue what colour the grass was if they ever ran out of subjects to talk to death. And none of it was getting us anywhere. Days had passed with no decisions really being made beyond providing for the people who were waiting on more important choices beyond these walls.

I knew I should have been weighing in more but between the loss of Darcy and Gabriel, my grief over Darius, and the unfulfilled promise which still lay scarred across my palm, I couldn't find it in me to sit for hours and argue with them over every small decision.

Four heavily armed rebels stood to attention in the passageway leading to the war council, one of them shifted into his Centaur form, his huge body only just fitting in the space and his head brushing the roof. I assumed he was using his gifts to help him keep watch too, but I doubted any form of magic or Order gift would be of much help to any of us if Lionel and his army found us now, licking our wounds and lost in the wilds.

The rebels bowed as I approached, a woman silently opening the door for me and the people inside all turned to look as I joined them.

My gaze swept over the empty places at the round table, the two throne-like chairs beside Geraldine, one for me and one for Darcy, despite her ongoing absence. Another place which I assumed was intended for Orion and one for Gabriel too. The three Councillors sat to the left, united as one, the way they had every time I'd been summoned to this chamber to listen to their plans and ideas for an army which wasn't theirs to command. They were too used to being in control, and I knew it was up to me to put them in their place, but I hadn't made any attempt to do so. Yet.

The three Heirs sat together in the chairs between their parents and Xavier, who lingered close to Geraldine's side, their allegiance more tenuous than it had been before. It was hard to remember the feeling of us all being united, working as one against Lionel and Lavinia, when right now all I could see was that line in the sand. The one that had pushed them to be our enemies from the moment we'd first laid eyes on them.

There was no chair left vacant for Darius.

I stilled, a lump rising in my throat as my hands curled into fists at my sides, fire racing along my limbs and begging to be set loose.

"We were expecting you an hour ago," Tiberius clipped, his eyes scouring over me from the black crop top to the ripped jeans, a single raised eyebrow casting judgement as he adjusted the cuff of his crisp blue shirt. The earth Elementals within the camp had been producing their own cotton to spin yarn, weaving all manner of clothing for the needs of our army, especially those of us at the top of the food chain. It hadn't escaped my notice that most of the rebels themselves wore simple, plain shirts and pants while much more effort had gone into the creation of outfits for the people in this room.

Geraldine herself had crafted me several obnoxious gowns before I'd firmly begged her to just give me something I could feel normal in. I hadn't been up for playing the role of pampered princess before the world had fallen apart at my feet, and I wasn't going to start pretending now.

"A queen arrives at precisely the right moment, no matter the preferences of her subjects," Geraldine quipped, and the corner of my lips quirked in amusement.

"As you well know, most of the people in this room do not recognise Roxanya and Gwendalina Vega as our monarchs," Tiberius replied firmly.

I shrugged as I forced my feet to move, heading for the chair which was clearly a throne and dropping into it with as much arrogance and contempt as any king or queen of old may have held.

"If that's the case, then why do you care so much for my timekeeping?" I drawled.

"Because certain members of this group refused to so much as begin discussions of anything vital until you had arrived," Tiberius said tersely, the weight of his irritation colouring the air and I arched a brow at him as his emotions pressed at mine.

"Are you unable to control your Order form or are you purposefully trying to rile every person in this room with your gifts?" I asked.

"I think we would do better to question your capabilities of controlling *your* gifts after witnessing that outburst of them at the Acrux Manor," he replied in a level tone.

"A controlled outburst," I pointed out. "A control which I have never once let slip the way you're allowing your power to burst from its dam right now. If I had, then there would likely be a lot of dead corpses smouldering in my wake at all times."

Caleb coughed a laugh which he tried to hide at a hard look from his mother, but Seth's lips hitched with amusement too and some of the unease I'd felt over the power dynamic in the room shifted. Perhaps the lines weren't drawn as clearly as they seemed to be, though I had to admit that I felt outnumbered sitting alongside Geraldine while facing all six of them – Xavier I wasn't certain on yet.

Tiberius clicked his tongue and the feeling of his irritation disappeared so suddenly that it felt like a slap of cold water to my cheek.

Melinda Altair stayed silent throughout the exchange, but there was a glimmer in her dark blue eyes which hinted at amusement and made me feel about one percent less hostile towards her.

"My stepmother and sister have sided with Lionel," Max said in a low voice, seeming to want to excuse his father's behaviour and I nodded in understanding. Caleb had already filled me in on that fact, and I guessed I could cut Tiberius a little slack considering the weight of the betrayal he must have been feeling.

"Is that how you were captured?" I asked curiously. "Did they sell you out?"

The Councillors exchanged looks before Tiberius nodded. "I believe so. We had already come to the decision to publicly denounce Lionel as our king and join the rebellion, we were just working to secure our families' safety before making our position clear to the citizens of Solaria. We came together with the intention of fleeing his wrath and finding you, but before Melinda could send a message to you to tell you we were coming, we were summoned to Acrux Manor, our families used as bait to draw us there. We suspected a trap, but Lavinia used her shadows to poison our own bodies against us and choke the very air from our lungs the moment we arrived. We awoke with our blood and magic spilling into that fucking thing outside Lionel's home."

"Do you know how they managed to open another rift?" I asked. "We were under the impression that the rifts occurred naturally, through some power from the other side punching its way through the fabric of the worlds. We'd closed them all and didn't think any more could be created."

The ex-Councillors exchanged loaded looks, seeming to silently communicate the desire to answer or not between themselves before finally replying.

"Stella Orion was there crafting dark magic," Antonia said. "She had a knife unlike anything I have ever seen before, the blade cast of moonlight and shadow combined. It looked to me as though the cost of wielding such a thing was steep though – the bitch was half dead when she was hauled away to rest, as Lionel put it. Maybe the stars will have been favouring us and we'll find out she died to pay the price of creating that heinous thing."

"The stars," I scoffed, hatred burning hotly through to my core. "They don't favour anything aside from their own twisted cruelty."

Geraldine gasped at my side, a hand going to her heart at the blasphemy, but I ignored it. I was pretty sure the stars had gotten the memo about my intentions towards them when I'd cursed them with the blood of the man I loved.

"Yeah, fuck the stars," Seth growled. "We can make our own destiny."

"Which is?" Antonia questioned, though I could already tell that she and the other Councillors had their own ideas on that.

Everyone looked to me expectantly and though Geraldine's eyes shone with belief and adoration, I knew the only reason the three people across the table from me were giving me the opportunity to speak first was because they knew full well, I had no answer to that question.

"So…" I began, but I really had nothing. We needed a plan, but as of yet, nothing viable had come to mind. We were all eager to strike back at Lionel, but until we could secure the rebels in a safe and sustainable location, we couldn't even begin readying them for battle again. Then we'd need to get back to recruiting, building our decimated army back up and doing whatever the hell else we could to bolster our power. Not to mention the fact that I only had a few points of focus I intended to act on right now. "My sis-"

The doors banged open violently and we all looked around in surprise, magic flaring in fists and weapons pulled from sheaths in anticipation of an attack.

But the Dragon who stood there wasn't a scaly green sack of shit, just a wild, dark-haired Faetalian with electricity crackling from his skin and fury in his eyes.

"Did you find him?" I demanded, shoving to my feet so fast that my not-a-throne was knocked to the ground behind me with a clatter.

"Yes and no," Dante growled, tugging a man out from behind him.

I sucked in a breath at the sight of Washer standing there, near naked with one testicle hanging out the side of his tiny half shredded Speedos, a look of haunted horror in his eyes as he stumbled towards me.

His skin was charred across the left side of his exposed chest and the iridescent blue of his scales were shining over his body. His hazel-coloured hair was slicked back and wet, his face clean despite the rest of him being marked with the muck of battle, and I had to assume he'd used his magic to clean that much of himself at least.

For once, I couldn't feel a single flicker of his gifts trying to push against my mental shields, no hint of him trying to claim some of my magic via my emotions. Pain as raw as mine probably wasn't desirable anyway, even if I was one of the most powerful Fae alive.

"Tell her what you told us," Dante commanded, Leon stepping up beside him and giving me a little wave of greeting.

"My Queen," Washer gasped, dropping to one knee, and lowering his head before me while the anticipation set my bones shaking.

"Spit it out," I demanded, having no patience for royalist bullshit.

"The false king captured Gabriel Nox," he replied. "I was trapped beneath fallen stone, my magic squeezed from every orifice to the point of utter demise. I had to feed on the pain of the dying Fae in the dirt around me, and I managed to create just enough water magic that I could sup upon it day after day. But by the end I was wrung out, my juices spurted free, not even a teeny weeny-"

"Where did Lionel take him?" I growled, striding around the table and gripping Washer's arm as I tugged him to his feet.

Blood marked his bare skin, and his eyes were haunted as he looked at me, letting me know that he'd more than suffered for his allegiance to our cause, but he stood here now before me, and I needed the answer he held.

"I don't know for certain. But he said he needed a new Seer," Washer breathed, pity filling his expression as understanding hit me, my mind whirling with those words and horror seeping into me.

I made a move to step away but paused at the look of trauma lurking on Washer's face.

"Thank you," I breathed, my grip on his arm turning into a reassuring squeeze. "You don't know how much I appreciate you telling me this and...I'm glad you survived."

Washer's face crumpled and I sucked in an alarmed breath as he threw his arms around me, embracing me tightly.

"I felt them dying all around me," he breathed into my ear. "They were afraid and in pain, but all of them, each and every one, was proud to be fighting this fight for you and your sister. For a better world."

His words eased a burden which had been pressing down on my soul ever since I'd been forced to accept the utter defeat that we'd faced on that battlefield, the shame I felt whenever I looked to the rebels who had placed so much hope on mine and Darcy's shoulders, only to have been brought to a loss when it counted.

I would have returned the hug he was giving me for those words – had I not remembered that he was one scrap of Lycra short of naked and I did not want his teeny weeny getting so much as another moment of time this close to my body.

I pushed Washer back firmly, nodding at him in gratitude for his words and keeping my eyes well away from that exposed testicle as I called out for someone to get him some food, a bath, and a set of thick and lumpy clothing.

"Gabriel would never give Lionel Acrux a prophecy, no matter what he threatened him with," Dante said firmly, taking a seat at my end of the table while Geraldine quickly righted my chair and beckoned me back to it.

"No," I agreed, frowning as I thought that over, knowing that Lionel would understand that too. And with a sickening sense of realisation, I found myself knowing what he would do to overcome that problem. "But Gabriel can't shut off his access to visions, can he? Not entirely."

"He tries not to *see* some things," Leon agreed as he came to sit beside me on the throne intended for Darcy, as if he hadn't even realised it wasn't meant for him. "Like he doesn't like to *see* visions of my sex life, but they still force their way in. Unless of course that's because he really does want to *see* them. But then I'd imagine he'd get performance anxiety so he probably doesn't want to know how many times I can make-"

"Not relevant, Leone," Dante growled, giving him a kick beneath the table which Leon cried out at.

I ignored his continued cursing and forced myself to think back on the time I'd spent as a captive of Lionel Acrux. The times he'd forced his way into my mind and destroyed my mental barriers, before letting Vard use his Cyclops invasion to examine the thoughts within my skull at his leisure and twist them to his own fucked up designs.

"Lionel will put him into the Royal Seer's chair," I said, knowing it in my soul. "He'll force him to have powerful visions whether he wants to or not and he'll use Vard to pluck the truth of them from his mind."

Silence followed my words as the weight of the truth fell over everyone, the reality of the weapon that Lionel had gained when he took Gabriel sinking in on us with terrifying clarity.

"Is Gabriel truly that gifted?" Melinda asked, her fearful eyes moving to Caleb then back to me for confirmation.

"He's the most powerful Seer of our time," Xavier murmured hopelessly, and my jaw tightened at the defeat in the room.

"That's a mighty high claim," Tiberius scoffed and I straightened.

"It's no claim. Gabriel is my brother. My mother's son. She brought him to the palace with her when she arrived here to marry my father and they hid his identity, claiming he was their ward until after they could produce legitimate heirs. They never got the chance to tell the world the truth of his heritage, and when they were killed, my mother entrusted Ling Astrum to hide him from Lionel's wrath. Gabriel is the greatest Seer of our generation and I can only assume that Lionel discovered that fact somehow and decided to steal him for his own benefit," I said plainly, sick of all the lies and secrets. I was proud to call Gabriel my brother and I wanted the whole world to know exactly who he was.

"By the stars," Melinda breathed, the three ex-Councillors exchanging concerned looks over that revelation.

"He's also one powerful stronzo who will fight tooth and claw to keep his famiglia safe," Dante said firmly. "Which means he won't let that motherfucker into his head easily."

"He's been captive for days now," Antonia replied. "If Lionel is determined to break through his defences, then it is only a matter of time. Even the most powerful of Fae cannot hold out forever."

"I'm going to go break him out of there then," I announced, making a move to rise once more, but Geraldine caught my wrist in an iron grip and held me in place.

"Your sweet flappy featherman sent you a message, did he not, my Queen?" she asked, and it took me a moment to understand what she was saying before I nodded my head in agreement. "A message which may hold the key to this conundrum. A gift from the heavens themselves." My jaw tightened at the mention of those fucking stars, and she hurried on. "Perhaps there is an answer in those words? He must have sent them to you with his final moments before capture. They must be important indeed-"

"A part of it has come to pass already," I admitted, having realised the truth of it after we rescued the Heirs from Lionel's manor.

"Tell us," Max demanded, and I did so, repeating the words of the prophecy for all of them to hear.

"A hound bays for vengeance where the rift drinks deep," Geraldine repeated in understanding, her eyes watering with tears. "He *saw* me. Little old nothing me."

"Don't be ridiculous, Geraldine, of course he *saw* you. You're one of the most important people in this whole damn kingdom," I replied, and she beamed with pride, wafting at her eyes to try and banish the tears which began to fall regardless.

"What promises have you made?" Tiberius asked me and I raised my chin as I answered.

"Vengeance, death, to find my family and to refuse the fate dealt to me and my husband."

"Husband?" Antonia gasped, and Geraldine's cries of pride turned into a wail of anguish at the news.

I, however, turned to stone beneath the weight of that question, ice spilling through me, but I refused to release the flood of emotions threatening to break free.

"Darius became a Vega the morning of the battle," Xavier murmured in explanation, grief making his voice catch as he spoke. "I've never seen him as happy as he was when he took those vows."

Words were spoken then, about me, to me, I wasn't even sure because there was nothing but a ringing in my head growing louder and louder, a tidal wave of suppressed emotions rising up to try and breach the dam I'd so hastily built around them. I closed my eyes, drawing in a slow breath through my nose as I blocked them all out, started plugging the holes in that dam and forcing the tide to stay back, refusing to face it even though I knew I was only delaying the inevitable with this denial.

The ruby pendant hanging around my neck seemed to heat against my skin as I battled to keep control of myself, my fingers moving to touch it, and I could have sworn I felt an imposing shadow moving over me. A shiver ran down my spine, the scent of smoke and cedar filling my lungs as I inhaled, and I swear I could almost feel-

The door banged open again, and I expelled the breath I'd been holding as my eyes snapped to Rosalie Oscura who was swaggering into the room like she owned the damn place. She inclined her head to me the smallest amount but ignored the Councillors entirely before setting a heavy wooden box hewn from earth magic onto the table in front of me.

"We found all of that while searching the ruins of The Burrows," she explained, her eyes flicking to her cousin then back to me again. "One of my pack has a touch of The Sight – nothing to write to the moon about, but enough to tell her that this stuff is important. I figured that meant I could interrupt this 'too important for everyone to attend' meeting."

I snorted in amusement as electricity crackled off of Dante, letting me know who had tried to keep her out of here clearly enough.

"We should discuss that issue further," Antonia Capella muttered, her eyes moving over the latest additions to the room, and I gave her a level stare as I replied.

"I have no problem with them joining these meetings," I said firmly. "My trust for them is implicit."

Antonia looked inclined to argue about me offering gang members and criminals a place at the royal war council, but Geraldine slammed a gavel she'd cast from nothing down on the table with a loud crack that made everyone flinch.

"My queen has spoken. I shall make a note to the minutes confirming the newest members of her court and their places at this grand table."

The Councillors looked like they wanted to argue that, but Caleb hissed at them to leave it and surprisingly, they backed down.

Rosalie arched an amused brow at me before carrying on as if there had been no interruption.

"There's a bunch of Dragon treasure that belonged to Darius too – we left that in your room for you."

My heart twisted at the gesture, no words coming to my lips to convey how much I appreciated that act. Darius had loved that damn gold almost as much as he'd loved me, and the thought of it laying buried beneath a battlefield forevermore had been eating at me constantly, despite knowing I couldn't spare the time to recover it myself.

"I told you, Rosa," Dante growled in the low tone of an Alpha. "That I don't want you getting too mixed up in all of this."

"I'm already on the run with the rebellion, stronzo. I don't think forcing me out of meetings with the queens is going to keep me any safer than I would be if I attended." Her attention moved back to me, and she cocked her head in question. "Where's the other one anyway? The entire camp is curious as fuck to know where she's run off to."

"Rosa, that's enough," Dante barked, and she rolled her eyes at him but backed away a step, leaving the box in front of me.

"Darcy will return soon," I said in a commanding tone, like that might be enough to make it the truth, and to the credit of everyone in the room, none of them questioned me on that.

"There. You have your answer, now go check on my son for me and tell his mama that I'll be back to see them shortly." Dante waved Rosalie from the room, and she retreated with a mocking bow, leaving me to look into the box of items she'd delivered.

Geraldine leapt to her feet as I reached for it, swiping it away from me. "You should not sully your hands on such menial work as sorting through these scraps and trinkets, my lady," she gasped, taking on the job of looking through it herself, and I let her as I turned my attention back to the others.

"If the prophecy refers to my promises, then all I can say is I have no intention of forgetting a single one of them. Aside from that, I don't know what the dove might be referring to, do any of you?" I asked.

Frowns and muttering gave way to shaking heads and I sighed in frustration. Fucking prophecies. I swear they were created with the sole intention of sowing insanity into the minds of those who worked to solve their riddles. What good was it to me to figure out the meaning to the words after they'd come to pass?

A loud thump made everyone at the table flinch as the Phoenix-crafted weapons which belonged to the Heirs all slammed down into the middle of the table, Geraldine clearly having found them in the box.

"A bunch of merry whop snaffers for the unbelievers," Geraldine muttered, her attention still on the box as she rummaged.

"Oh, sweet," Seth cooed as he snatched his clawed gauntlets from the table, putting them on and grinning as the flames of red and blue ignited across his knuckles at his command.

"What are those?" Melinda asked curiously, watching her son as Caleb picked up his twin daggers, a smirk on his lips.

"Gifts from the true Queens to those who fight at their backs," Geraldine said dismissively.

"At their backs?" Tiberius growled, taking Max's metal bow from him, and inspecting it.

"Beside them," Caleb corrected, but it did little to wipe the looks of suspicion from their parents' faces.

"It seems like we've missed a lot during these months," Melinda murmured slowly.

"Since when were your own claws not enough without help, pup?" Antonia asked Seth pointedly, and he pouted.

"By the stars, Mom, don't rain on my parade. You never minded using that Medusa mirror to help you do your makeup, so why are you judging my flame claws?" Seth demanded.

"I'm simply questioning the way it would look to the press if they find out you are using weapons forged from the flames of your competitors to the throne in battle. Surely you can see how it could be portrayed as a weakness if-"

"It indeed is a weakness by comparison," Geraldine agreed loudly. "One which these bothersome barracudas would do well to admit to now. They neither hold the power nor beauty of the true-"

"Can we just focus on the prophecy?" I asked loudly, seeing the descent of this conversation coming from a mile off and needing it to stop.

Luckily, they all seemed to realise that this was more important right now, but I could tell the issue of the weapons would be addressed between the Heirs and their parents later as I moved on to the final unsolved piece of the puzzle.

"The king may fall on the day the Hydra bellows in a spiteful palace…"

There were a few moments of silence before Tiberius sucked in a sharp breath and slapped a hand down on the table, a jolt of excitement slamming into all of us as his gifts escaped their leash once more.

"There is a tradition in The Palace of Souls, started years ago by one of the old kings…I forget which, but that's beside the point. Every year during the Hydrids meteor shower, at the height of the celestial event, a celebration was held at the palace where we would all gather. But the year Hail brought your mother back from Voldrakia, Merissa used her magic to alter the throne because the meteor shower was linked to his Order form. It was a gift for her husband. When the meteor shower is at its fullest, magic awakes and sets the throne roaring with the voice of the creature itself – it was quite the extravagant surprise the first time we all heard it, let me tell you."

"It made my heart damn near leap out of my chest," Antonia agreed with a faint smile at the memory.

My heart began to gallop at those words, at the possibility they presented. "The king may fall," I repeated hopefully. "The Palace of Souls has been locking Lionel out of countless rooms ever since he claimed it for his own. That sounds pretty fucking spiteful to me."

"When is the peak of the meteor shower?" Seth asked excitedly, the desire to see Lionel fall hyping him up so he was practically bouncing in his seat.

"Twelve days, eighteen hours and seven minutes from this very moment," Geraldine cried. Fuck knew how she knew that so accurately, but I damn well trusted her when it came to nonsense royal traditions.

"That isn't long enough to ready the army for another battle and raise more rebels to our cause to bolster their numbers," Antonia pointed out.

"It doesn't take an army to kill a king," I said coldly, the need for revenge rising in me so powerfully that I was more than tempted to ignore the fucking prophecy and simply head for the palace to kill him now.

"Gabriel sent you that message for a reason," Dante said, seeming to see that desire in me even as I realised he was right. "He knows that is when you will have a real chance at success, bella."

Twelve more days. How was I supposed to wait twelve days to end this? How was I supposed to wait when I knew what Gabriel would be facing at the hands of that monster for every moment I delayed? But I did trust my brother. I trusted his gifts and I knew that he wouldn't have wasted his last bit of magic on sending me that prophecy if it wasn't vital that I followed it. The bit about the rift had come to pass and we'd rescued half the people in this room thanks to that, so I had to trust in what he was telling me.

"What are we supposed to do for twelve more days?" Max asked. "Gabriel could break within that time and Lionel will be upon us in a matter of moments if he does. He could literally arrive in the next breath and we're just sitting here, scratching our asses while we wait for him to pounce."

"We need to move in the ways of the wilds," Leon said mysteriously before anyone else could voice an idea. "Be as unpredictable as the sea, as tricksome as the wind, as ever changing as the seasons, and as cunning as a Lion."

Xavier frowned. "Aren't foxes usually the-"

"Shhh." Leon pressed a finger to his mouth as he silenced him. "Gabriel will *see* you questioning that and tell Lionel. You're being so damn obvious, little Pego-dude."

"How am I-" Xavier began, but Leon echoed his words a fraction of a second behind him as though trying to convince everyone that he'd *seen* him speak them before he did.

"See?" Leon said, looking between us all. "So obvious. I've spent years mastering the art of thwarting Gabe's gifts. I can keep us safe from them while we wait for the time to strike."

"How?" I asked, needing an answer to that because Max was right, we were sitting ducks here and we needed to do something to change that from being the case.

"We should head out to sea," Leon said with a firm nod.

"To sea?" Melinda frowned. "We are miles from the coast and-"

"And you wouldn't have expected that? I know. But now that I know and you know, Gabe knows too. See, it's already fucked. But it won't be because when we get to the sea, we will carve an island from the land. Some say it will be carved into the shape of a regal and cunning Lion Shifter. Some say that would make this plan work even better. But don't decide now or he will *see*."

"This doesn't sound like much of a plan," Caleb muttered but Seth shushed him aggressively.

"Yes, it does. It makes perfect sense. We all head out to sea and then we float aimlessly, sometimes shooting magic one way or another at random to move us, other times following the whims of the waves-"

"Nothing is as wild and unpredictable as water," Tiberius agreed proudly, like being one of the most powerful water wielders in our kingdom made him responsible for every drop of it in the ocean.

"Your Majesty, if I might say something!" Geraldine cried, leaping from her seat onto the table and looking to me to allow her to speak, though she already held the attention of the entire room.

"You don't need my permission," I said, my mouth lifting a little at her theatrics.

"Well, my lady, I think this Lion is cunning indeed, smarter perhaps than any faithful feline I have met afore!" she hollered, and Leon sat up straighter in his seat, looking smug as fuck while Dante snorted under his breath. "We can go this way and that – yonder and to far-flung places not even the grabooling of the gracious sea could predict."

"That might actually work," I admitted, despite how insane it sounded, and as the discussion around the table focused on that idea, I found myself relaxing a little. We had a plan for the rebels. Some semblance of one at least. And without that burden left on my shoulders, I could focus on what I needed to do with the days before we headed to The Palace of Souls to kill the false king.

Geraldine jumped back down into her seat beside me, continuing the process of emptying the box Rosalie had given me and my heart stalled as I took in the priceless trove of treasures that her pack member had recovered for us.

There were the stones that Orion had found for the Zodiac Guild, and the books he'd been using to research them, alongside the diary his father had left him. The Map of Espial laid beside them, the night iron spyglass with its gruesome shadow eye still locked in place, waiting for someone to use it at leisure. Diego's gross soul hat was there too, grandma and co presumably intact within, though I wasn't going to be putting the thing on my head to check. A few more of Orion's books were there and some other trinkets I didn't care to sift through right now.

"We should act randomly at all times," Seth said, getting caught up in the plan. "Never let anyone predict our next moves so Gabriel can't *see* us at all. We'll be invisible to the false king." He stood up, smashing his chair against the wall and Leon whooped, jumping up and starting to do burpees. Antonia and Tiberius tried to calm them down, but chaos was clearly breaking out and I had no intention of trying to stop it.

I reached for the map as Geraldine continued to examine the contents of the box, my fingers tracing over the ever-changing details as the whole of Solaria was spread out before me.

"Is there a way to use this to find someone?" I asked Geraldine in a low voice, ignoring the others as they continued to discuss the details involved in moving our army to the coast so that we could enact the plan. Antonia was still trying to get Leon and Seth to sit down but they were busy getting everyone else riled up.

"Alas, the magic doesn't work as such," Geraldine replied sadly, brushing her fingers over the magical ink like she wished it wasn't so. "I assumed you have tried a simple locating spell already?"

I nodded, worry for my sister consuming me as I looked down at the map with my hope fading.

"Anyone with powerful shields would be impossible to find that way," she said softly.

"Or anyone being held captive or…dead." I didn't believe that last guess could be true, but it had been so long without a word and every second that passed left me tied up in knots which were getting harder and harder to deny. I felt her in my soul, was certain she lived, but if that was true, then where was she? Why not send me a message or something to prove that she was alive and well? There had to be some way.

"Perhaps…" Geraldine glanced around nervously, then leaned in close, a silencing bubble surrounding the two of us at a flick of her fingers before she cupped a hand around her mouth too, ensuring there was no chance of anyone other than me discerning her words – though no one was paying attention to us considering Seth was now ripping up the notes Melinda had made during this meeting while Leon threatened to burn them with his fire Element too. "I have heard legend of powerful magic which could circumvent such things as shields, no matter their power."

"What magic?" I demanded instantly and she cringed, as though fighting an inner battle with herself over telling me or not, but I knew Geraldine and she would never deny a request from her queen, no matter her thoughts on it.

"Dark magic," she breathed.

"We can't risk using the shadows," I said dismissively, disappointment warring through me but she shook her head, beckoning me closer as she went on in a conspiratorial tone.

"Dark magic is much more than just communing with shadows. There are old ways. Ways that were used by Fae long ago before they learned how to fully Awaken their powers with the blessing of the stars. I don't know much about it aside from the fact that it comes at a cost. And you know I would never suggest such a thing, but... but...my sweet summer child with the bluest hair..."

Geraldine choked back a sob and I gripped her hand, squeezing it tightly.

"Where would I find out more about this magic?" I asked, wondering what else I might be able to learn of the old ways. It certainly seemed to me that wielding power which predated the blessing of the stars might be of use when fulfilling my promise to destroy them.

Geraldine's eyes fell to the map, her finger pressing down on the Library of the Lost for the briefest of moments before she rolled it up tightly and tossed it back in the box, dispelling the silencing bubble and acting as if she had never said a single word to me about any of it.

My thoughts twisted with that information as I processed it, wondering if she could be right, if I might find a way to locate Darcy using the knowledge in that library.

Geraldine continued to pack the contents of the box away and I looked around at the others. I blinked in surprise at Leon as he held the night iron spy glass up to the light and examined it with interest.

"How did you get that?" I asked him as he began to tap the end of it in his palm, making the shadow eye bounce grossly inside it.

"Best thief in the whole of Solaria," he said simply, pointing at himself before tapping the spy glass in his palm again. "What's this thing for anyway?"

"We used it to see the rifts on the map of espial and close them all," I explained.

Geraldine gave a pterodactyl screech so loud that I almost fell out of my damn chair, silence falling in the room as everyone stared at her in alarm and she hastily got to her feet before explaining herself.

"I have just had an idea. What if we could make use of the shadow eye which we took from the face of that cretin, Vard?"

"Make use of it how?" Xavier asked.

"Perhaps – and I can't be certain – but perhaps, if one of us were to take out our own eye and place the shadow eye into our face instead, we may be able to use it to *see* the shadows, much as the previous owner of that foul creation once did to serve the false king. If so, we may be able to *see* what Lavinia is doing with the shadows and thus report back about everything we learn, giving ourselves a major advantage over our enemy at every turn!"

"Who the fuck would volunteer to have that thing put in their face?" Caleb asked in disgust as he recoiled from the table.

"I volunteer myself!" Geraldine cried, pulling her grandma's eye scoop from her pocket, and tipping her head back to the roof as she prepared to pluck her own eye from her face to make room for the shadow thing.

"What the fuck are you doing?!" Max roared as he lunged for her, and I jumped to my feet as I fought to get the eye scoop away from her too.

"No Geraldine!" I cried. "No fucking way!"

She fought against us as we tried to take the scoop, calling out about willingly sacrificing everything for our cause while I insisted I didn't want her to, and Max lost his shit entirely.

"Ah, it's slimy," Leon gasped from behind me, and I glanced around to look at him, finding the shadow eye free of the spy glass and crawling over his hand, heading towards his arm as it began an ascent towards his face. "What's it doing?"

"It's searching for your eye so that it may devour it and take up residence within your skull," Geraldine replied simply like that wasn't horrifying as hell.

"Ah!" Leon shook his hand wildly and the eye shot off of it, flying across the table and slapping straight into Seth's face where it grabbed hold of his cheek and instantly started wriggling towards his eye instead.

Seth howled in horror, leaping forward and slamming into Tiberius as he tried to get up to help him.

I yelled for Seth to grab it even as the thing made it over his cheek bone and the wild flailing of his arms did nothing to knock it off.

"Hold still!" Caleb roared and Seth did so, half a second before Caleb punched him with a fist coated in stone.

Seth howled in agony as something definitely broke in his face and he fell to the ground before Caleb shot closer and yanked him upright again.

I shoved my way past the others to inspect the damage, taking in the burst shadow eye across Seth's cheek and the broken eye socket that Caleb had given him for good measure.

"Is it gone?" Seth pleaded and I nodded in confirmation, taking his hand and healing him while he looked from me to Caleb whose face was a mixture of shock and relief.

"Looks like no one will be using the shadow eye then," I said, not a single part of me upset over that fact.

"Then I think we should get back to planning our next move," Melinda said calmly, not even seeming to have been ruffled by the chaos of the shadow eye being splattered across Seth's face and I had to admit, I quite liked her.

Scorpio
Virgo
Gemini
Cancer
Aries
Leo
Sagittarius
Taurus
Capricorn
Aquarius
Libra
Pisces

SETH

CHAPTER TWENTY TWO

Everyone filed out of the room as the meeting finally ended and I drifted into Caleb's way, wanting to catch his attention, unsure exactly what I was going to say exactly, only that I definitely needed to say something.

I could lead with a 'thank you for saving me from the creepy shadow eye'- though had he seriously had to punch me in the fucking face with a stone hand? That shit seemed personal.

The tension between us was unbearable, but I didn't know how to fix it. Was I supposed to just walk right up to him and say, *hey man, maybe we should talk about how you made me come so hard I nearly blacked out the other night?*

Or, hey bro, remember how I said we were BFF BJ buddies, well I'm actually so in love with you that I wanna tattoo your name on my cock, and I know you won't ever feel that way about me, but hooking up with you is slowly breaking my heart because I know I can never truly, really have you.

Dammit, I needed Darcy here to tell me what to say. Where even was she? Tory had been cagey as hell about her in that meeting. My moon senses were telling me something was up, and I was going to find out what it was. Just as soon as I spoke to Cal…

I moved into his way as he went to leave, but the motherfucker shoulder checked me, stalking past me with Tory at his side. Rage simmered in my chest, turning my heart from solder to coldest steel. *Fine. Have it your way, asshole.*

The room emptied out and I flexed my fingers, a storm of air swirling between them as the echoing silence drew in around me. Alone, that was me. Just a pup on a mountain with no one to snuggle him.

I sank onto a chair, clasping my head in my hands as my thoughts fell on Darius and the grief I'd been disguising as anger spilled out of me in one long, mournful howl. I pressed my mouth to my arm, suffocating the sound away so no one heard me. Max would come offering me comfort, and I couldn't face him or anyone else right now. I just wanted to remain furious at Darius, because the second I let the mask slip, I was gonna have to feel it all. The loss, the pain, the grief. I didn't want it. I wasn't strong enough to survive it. But despite how much I tried to escape it, I still fell into a chasm of despair that I doubted I'd ever escape from.

"Seth? I'm still here." Xavier's voice made me jump and my fist snapped out in the direction it came from, slamming into a wall of ice he cast to block the blow. My knuckles split apart on its surface, and I savoured the pain, standing and throwing my fists into it again and again until it crumbled to crushed ice at my feet.

Beyond it, Xavier was revealed, his eyes heavy with shadows and a dejected look about him that made me wonder if he would ever smile again.

I stepped through the hole I'd made in the ice and wrapped my arms around him, drawing him tight to my chest. "I'm so sorry, Xavier."

"Not your fault," he grunted, not hugging me back, but that didn't mean I was going to let go. Everyone needed a hug now and again. I was a hug master, and people always needed hugs most when they refused them. It was their way of trying to resist the emotions that hugs brought on, especially in the aftermath of so much loss. But that pain had to come out one way or another, better it was shared in the arms of someone who loved you.

We stood like that until time turned to grains of sand at our feet and I finally released him, hunting his expression for some sign of resilience but there was little there except grief.

"I don't care what the Councillors say, I'll never take his place as an Heir," he said, his eyes darkening and revealing the pressure they were clearly placing him under. It was a fucking joke to put him through that while he was still struggling through losing his family, but then again, I wasn't surprised. I'd seen my mom and the other Heirs' parents act in the name of duty all my life, and politics rarely took emotion into account.

"I know, man," I said gently.

"He's only been gone for a few turns of the earth and all they care about is their precious power balance being restored, the future and all the fucking horse shit they think is still a possibility." He stamped his foot. "Even if there was some small chance of us defeating Lionel now and the Council regaining power, I would *die* before I stepped into my brother's place."

I noticed how he called his father by his name, like he was rejecting all ties to him and refusing the word that made them family. I understood that on a soul-deep level. Real family were the people who earned their place in your life, not the ones who demanded things of you just because you were tethered to them by blood.

"If there's anything you ever need-" I started but the door cracked open and Sofia's golden head slipped through followed by Tyler's, the two of them gazing at Xavier with longing in their eyes.

"Are you finished with your meeting?" Sofia asked hopefully.

Xavier glanced at me, and I stepped back, nodding toward the door.

"See you later," I murmured, painting on the falsest of smiles - I was real gifted at that. Not letting people see the hurt in me, that I needed company right now more than I needed anything else in the world.

Xavier squeezed my arm then trotted over to Sofia and Tyler, his two herd mates pulling him through the door and surrounding him in affection, whinnying softly as they went. I watched them go through the open door and the fires burning in the sconces on the walls all went out as Xavier's magic left with him.

I was alone in the dark and suddenly I could taste snowflakes on my tongue and feel the pressing walls of an ice-cold cave closing in on me. The Forging I'd been forced to endure as a pup was so far in the past, yet it always came back to me in moments like this. When I felt frighteningly alone.

I didn't have a pack among the rebels, the Oscura Wolves all too deep in their own clan for me to take part in that. There were other Wolves who'd come to me, offering to form a group with me, but I'd rejected them all because I'd already had the best pack I could imagine. I'd had the Heirs, Darcy, Tory, Orion, even crazy-ass Geraldine Grus. They were my family, and some of the best times of my life had happened in The Burrows. It shouldn't have taken losing everything to realise that.

It all seemed so fucked now. Darius was gone, Tory was heartbroken, Orion and Darcy were lost, and Max was trying to forge this new, sweet thing he had going with

Geraldine amidst a world of despair. Then there was Caleb. The man who had become the centre of every thought, every dream, every nightmare I experienced day after day.

The truth was, my Order demanded the closeness of a pack around me when I was suffering. I needed to be wrapped in the arms of Fae I loved, and frankly if I was getting all the things that would make me feel better, I also wanted someone to tickle my tummy and call me a good boy. The problem was that, that someone couldn't be just anyone anymore. The person I wanted to comfort me was the one person I couldn't have. And I didn't want to crawl into anyone else's arms but his. So instead, I rejected the world, rejected all the instincts of my Order and I drowned in this pain. That was what this felt like, sinking so deep into a torturous pool of unrequited feelings that I couldn't breathe.

I missed King's Hollow. I missed when things were simple, but mostly I missed a time that didn't even exist. A place where all of the people I loved were safe, where we weren't at war with each other or a false king, and where my best friend was as fiercely in love with me as I was with him. Yeah, I was selfish. I should have wished that none of this had ever happened between Cal and I, that we'd stayed friends and never muddied the water of that friendship. But there was no denying the truth that if the moon and stars offered me one, unconditional wish, it would always be him.

I sighed, moving to the door, lingering in the shadows as I clogged up the bloody holes in my heart over Darius and cloaked my pain with rage.

My hand curled into a fist and I strode out of the room, needing an outlet of carnage. I felt like a cruel Heir again, hunting the halls of Zodiac Academy for a Vega to toy with, and a small voice in the back of my head reminded me how well that had ended. Darcy wasn't here to call me out on my bullshit, Darius wasn't here to keep me in line, Professor Orion wasn't around to drag me into detention, and no one else was going to stop me.

I rounded a sharp corner in the ruins and slammed straight into Rosalie Oscura. I barked, expecting her to flinch and submit to me as the superior Alpha, but she lifted her chin and growled low in her throat in a challenge. And maybe I really did fancy beating her down to release some of this energy in me.

"Oh hey, didn't see you there, cucciolo stupido." She went all innocent on me, batting her lashes, but there was a mocking in it that had my eyes narrowing.

"What did you just call me?" I growled.

"It means…friend." She shrugged, stepping sideways to head past me but I darted into her way.

"Why did it have the word stupid in it then?" I pressed, hungry for a fight with one of my kind. I could use the reminder that I was the strongest Werewolf in this kingdom.

"Did it?" She frowned like she couldn't remember then clapped me on the arm. "If you're looking for Caleb, he went to the old bell tower with Tory."

"Who says I'm looking for Caleb?" I said defensively.

"You did," she said.

"No I didn't," I balked.

"Not with words, obviously," she said. "With your stupidi occhi da cucciolo."

"My what?" I demanded. She was pissing me off now.

"Look." She took my arm, pulling me over to a glassless window that looked out over the ruins running down the mountainside, pointing to the belltower where the sun glinted off the ancient bronze metal of the bell at its peak.

"What am I looking at?" I muttered.

"This." She leapt up onto the window ledge and sprang out of it, casting vines of earth magic and swinging away from me before landing on a half-crumbled balcony far below. "See you later, dumb puppy!"

I growled, stalking away from the window, and heading along in the vague direction of the belltower. It wasn't like I was actually going to go there. I could walk in that direction though. I could walk anywhere I liked. Caleb wasn't king of the ruins. Maybe I just fancied a trip up the belltower. Maybe I just liked the view from up there.

It had nothing to do with him. Nothing at all.

The grass coating the mountainside was long and swayed in the endless cool breeze, its soft tendrils swishing around my knees as I stalked through it, every step sounding my approach loudly enough for a Vampire to hear with ease. There was snow further up the mountain and the scent of that cold air sweeping down from its peak stung my nose, reminding me of those days in the wilderness, of the things I'd survived to bring me to this point. It was maddening in a way, the memories of being so helpless and so alone pressing in until my mind was spinning with them and my chest ached with the need for comfort.

When I arrived at the belltower, I gazed up at the rustic walls, the old reddish stone still mostly intact, ancient carvings near unrecognisable after years of corrosion from the wind.

I headed inside, walking up the tightly curling stairway, casting a silencing bubble around me. Not that I was trying to stop Caleb and Tory from detecting my approach or anything…

I made it to the top of the tower and peered out from the final stone steps that led onto the veranda beneath the giant bell which hung there.

Caleb and Tory stood arm to arm, looking out over the mountainside, talking within a silencing bubble of their own. They were facing the opposite direction to the way I'd come, so they probably had no idea I was here. That anyone was here. And something in my gut twisted like knotweed as Caleb dropped his arm over her shoulders and drew her close.

Tory wasn't a hugger. I knew that from first-hand experience of trying to get snuggles out of her, but the way she melted into him and rested her head to his chest had my lungs refusing to work.

He spoke to her in soft murmurs, affection pouring from his eyes. I tried to lip read what he was saying and could have sworn I saw him say, 'I've got you, sweetheart.'

They had a past together, and now they were shattering over Darius's death and the obvious arms for them to fall into were each other's. It wasn't Max she'd brought up here, not Gerry, not me. It was him. The man she had sought out plenty of times before, because they had a connection. Maybe one I'd long underestimated until now.

A lump thickened in my throat and my pulse pounded unevenly in my ears. My world was caving in, the ground collapsing beneath my feet. I'd been such a fucking idiot. I'd been Caleb's easy lay when he'd been breaking, the Werewolf who never caught feelings for the Fae he fucked. The one who could be emotionless with anyone he took to his bed. I was the obvious answer to his curiosity too. He wanted to know what it was like to be with a guy, so why not pick Seth Capella? He wasn't going to catch feelings, he wasn't going to make it awkward, he wasn't going to tell anyone either because he was a loyal friend. He was just Seth.

Tory lifted her head, speaking to him and I read the words, trying to decipher them from her perfect lips. Lips my lips could never rival. "*Your dick is so hard, Caleb.*"

Okay, so maybe that wasn't what she'd said, but that was all I could see right now. His huge, throbbing, perfect dick, and I didn't want it anywhere near anyone else unless it was sleeping contentedly in his pants dreaming of me.

I didn't want to fall into a pit of jealousy, I didn't want to focus on this when Darius was in a coffin, growing eternally colder by the second. It should have been the last thing on my mind. Tory was heartbroken, Caleb too. I just hadn't expected to see them here breaking together, finding something in their shattered pieces to clutch onto. And it was each other.

My eyes traced the loving smile his lips painted for her, and I captured that moment in my mind, knowing I would rewrite it later, with me in her place.

I moved back down a step as my heart crumpled like a ball of paper in a tight fist, planning to leave when a cry from above made me pause. I squinted toward the sun above the mountain ahead and Caleb's head snapped in that direction too, probably hearing some faraway words within that cry which I couldn't perceive.

A small shadow was cast over the mountainside and I spotted the source of it in the sky; a man tethered to a parachute made of leaves, his legs wheeling through the air as he descended towards us.

Tory dropped the silencing bubble around them, and I dropped mine too, hurrying up onto the veranda, crossing beneath the huge bronze bell above.

Caleb's eyes whipped onto me in an instant, and I raised my chin, showing no sign of the acidic envy I was feeling. Just chilled out, ever-smiling Seth Capella.

"Who is that?" I asked, looking to the sky again.

"I think it's…Justin," Tory said in shock. "Shit, do you think he's been stuck in that thing since the battle?"

"Why is he even in it at all?" I asked and Tory grimaced.

"He saved my life, but then we were surrounded by Nymphs, and I knew I needed to be able to fight without having to worry about accidentally burning him to a crisp. So, I sort of…made a parachute for him, shot him into the air and totally forgot about it until just now. I may be an asshole."

My surprise was overridden by the sound of Justin's voice, and I looked back to him as he drew closer.

"Hide the children!" he cried, pulling on the vines of his parachute to guide himself towards us. "The enemy advances!"

I climbed up onto the low wall at the edge of the veranda, squinting towards the horizon, but the sun was blinding. "What enemy?"

"What-ho!" Geraldine appeared with Max from one of the ruined buildings down below, spotting Justin as he sailed towards the belltower.

"Milady!" Justin cried. "The dastards approach from yonder!"

"Yonder?" she gasped. "From whence did you come, you bucktailed barklouse?"

"Over the bracken hills and the whistling woodlands," Justin called.

"Can someone speak a language I understand and point me at an enemy so I can kill it?" I yelled and Tory fisted her hand in the back of my shirt, pulling herself up beside me on the wall.

"Hang on, I speak semi-fluent *ASS*," she said as Justin came floating down to the belltower. His parachute caught on the spire above the bell, and he jerked to a halt, hanging down beside us from his harness and fighting to get free of it.

Caleb whipped out a finger, cutting the binds with magic and letting Justin crash down on his ass before picking him up and planting him firmly on his feet.

"Where's the enemy?" he demanded.

Justin lifted a trembling finger, pointing in the direction of the forest at the foot of the mountain and I turned, following his line of sight just as a cloud drifted over the sun so I could see clearer. Nymphs. Rivers of them, all bursting from the thick trees and running up the mountain, splitting apart and taking different paths so they weren't all bunched together as a single target.

"Fuck nuts," I breathed, adrenaline zipping through my blood and bringing on a hunger for war.

The camp for the rebels was spread out between us and them, a few cries going up from the earth grown tents as some of them spotted the Nymphs too, and my stomach clenched with fear for them.

"Avast!" Geraldine cried from below.

"We'll get the weapons!" Max shouted. "Alert the rebels!"

He and Geraldine took off running towards the central part of the ruins where most of us had been sleeping and I spun around, my eyes falling on the bell.

I cast a powerful wind, throwing it at the bell and making it ring with a deafening sound that carried all across the ruins to alert the rebels immediately.

"I have no power, I shall seek out a store of Aconite so that I may recharge and join the fight. I'll warn as many rebels as I can on my way," Justin said, running off into the stairwell without another word and I had to hand it to him for finding that reserve of energy because the poor bastard looked like shit.

"Caleb, power share with me!" Tory shouted over the din of the bell. "We need to stop as many of the Nymphs from making it to the rebels as we can." She offered him her hand and he slapped his into it, stepping up onto the wall at her side.

I ground my jaw, turning for the stairs to leave them to their little power sharing battle date, but Caleb called out to me, halting me in my tracks.

"We need you, Seth." He offered me his free hand and I hesitated by the stairs, part of me wanting to leave out of spite, but I shook off that thought and remembered what was really important here. We were under attack. I had to protect the people I still had left in the world, and that included him and Tory.

I moved to join them, jumping back onto the wall and clapping my hand into his. His fingers slid between mine and I shared a look with him that could only have lasted a single breath but felt like it lasted a whole lifetime. I saw a fate where we survived this war, and I woke each day with him by my side, felt his mouth on mine whenever I craved it, and he stood at my side always, two kings of the world.

But then I blinked, and reality slapped me around the ear.

"Create a wall of thorns, vines, trees, anything you can to block their path. We can take it in turns to cast and use the full force of our combined power for each move we make," Tory said, and she gasped as her magic merged with Caleb's.

Caleb released a noise that was almost sexual as her power poured into his, and jealousy burned hot in my flesh. I threw all of my power into the place where Caleb's hand connected with mine and he let it in all at once. I sent so much furious, stormy power his way, that he literally moaned, and a smirk lifted my lips.

He sent his own magic flowing back into me, followed by the fiery power of Tory's and it was his turn to smirk as I gasped, the earthy fury of his power tumbling through my body alongside the flaming glory of a Vega.

"Fuck," I exhaled.

"I need a free hand to cast," Caleb said, slipping his hand from Tory's and she pushed her hand up the back of his shirt to press her palm to his skin there instead. Could have rolled his sleeve back and touched his arm, but whatever Trevor. I wasn't the touching police. If the touching police were here, they might have a thing or two to say about it, but that wasn't anything to do with me.

I ground my teeth, not thinking about the magic flowing between them through that more intimate spot. I yanked my gaze away, turning to the Nymphs streaming up the mountainside while rebels rallied below, the strongest of them forming a line just beyond the tents while the children ran for the safety of the ruins. I raised my free hand, anger splintering through my chest as my gaze locked on our enemies. I had a furious, merciless monster in me to let out, and they had picked the wrong day to come knocking at our door.

I took the lead, wielding the earth of the mountain, caging Nymphs in a tangle of thick, thorny vines, strangling them in the grip of my magic. The huge, twisted knot of vines grew out fast across the mountainside as Caleb and Tory fuelled my cast, creating a mighty barrier to slow them down.

I bared my teeth as a line of Nymphs broke through before I could close the gaps, and I focused on the ground beneath them, the whole mountain beginning to quake from our god-like power. Boulders as big as cars began to fall from the base of the ruins, crashing down among the mass of Nymphs and ripping through their ranks. It was hell on earth, a glorious rain of destruction that felt so fucking good. I'd have no mercy here. I'd watch them all fall and make them scream as they went out of this world.

The rebels who had been rallied ran towards the mountain base with Geraldine and Max heading the way forward, preparing to fight the moment a Nymph made it to the edge of the ruins.

But between me, Caleb and Tory, our calamitous power was keeping them at bay.

I spotted the Councillors among the masses, calling out orders and trying to form their own plan of attack, but the rebels kept looking our way instead, waiting for a signal from the Vega princess.

Caleb's fingers tightened on mine, drawing on my power and I gave him everything as he took over, setting a furious earthquake rocking through the mountain, a huge fissure opening up behind our vines so Nymphs were sent hurtling into its depths.

I whooped, tugging on the combined magic and turning my attention to the power of air as I threw a raging wind at the Nymphs who were still standing, forcing them into that void.

We offered our power to Tory next, and she twisted her fingers, flames bursting out all along the vines, making the Nymphs shriek as they burned in her fire.

Max and Geraldine locked hands at the forefront of the rebels, and suddenly the mountain was trembling for a whole different reason as water came pouring out of Max's hands and rushing down the mountain before them. The glorious devastation made my jaw fall slack and I watched in fascination as we let our Elements loose, working together in a unit which felt impossibly right, though I could feel the absence of the others now more than ever, the Fae who should have been here guiding their power with us.

The wave slammed into the Nymphs, washing them away, their bark-covered limbs sticking out of the water as they tried to swim, but were lost to the violent Element as it swallowed them whole.

The moment the wave hit the vines, Geraldine and Max turned it to ice, freezing every last one of our enemies who still lived, creating an impenetrable barrier.

"*Yes*," I growled, my heart thumping manically in my chest.

A few beats of silenced passed as we all stopped casting magic, waiting for another enemy to appear, but all that remained were Nymphs twitching in the ice. It was a beautiful victory, something we all star-damned needed after our defeat, and even if it was only a tiny win in the grand scheme of things, it still felt so good.

A cheer went up from the rebels and the Councillors looked from Max and Geraldine to us up on the belltower. My chest puffed up as my mom's eyes fell on me, but my heart sank when I didn't find pride or gratitude there. She was hella pissed off.

Her gaze slipped to Tory beyond me, taking in the way the three of us were holding onto each other, sharing power.

She turned her back on me, heading away in the direction of the Nymphs, while Tiberius frowned and muttered some words to Melinda – the only one of them who was smiling. A little whine left my throat, but I swallowed it down, rejecting the feelings of dismissal and disappointment Mom had cast my way.

Tiberius stalked off after my mom, striding down the hillside with the rebels, swords drawn as they moved to finish off any Nymph who still lived.

Melinda looked to her son and Caleb dropped my hand in an instant, his power leaving my body just as abruptly and I missed it immediately. His mom kissed her fingers, holding them out toward him in a gesture of love before heading off after the others. I was relieved for him, and though I was jealous of that pride Melinda had shone his way, I'd never begrudge him of it.

Max and Geraldine came hurrying back through the crowd and Tory plucked them up with a gust of air, guiding them to the top of the belltower before jumping down from the wall to join them. Caleb hopped down after her while I lingered in place, pushing my hands into my pockets.

"Well grab a grape and call it a date," Geraldine said, slapping her thigh. "That was a jolly good show. My lady Tory, did you see those devilish danderkoots tumbling into that ravine? What fun!"

"We should go finish the fun," Tory said darkly, glancing over her shoulder to look at the rebels making their way down the mountain. "There'll be plenty still alive."

"Ohhhh, by my cockles, you do have a streak of savagery in your lady waters, does she not, Maxy boy?" Geraldine elbowed him, but I noticed Max's gaze was set firmly on me.

I stood up straighter, realising I hadn't been shielding my inner emotions and my gaze had been firmly set on Caleb. I locked that pining shit down fast, veiling it with anger and baring my teeth at Max in a warning to stay of my head. The last thing I needed was him figuring out that I was hopelessly in love with my best friend and fucking up the last remnants of the Heirs.

"I'm up for a kill too. Come on, Tory." I turned and stepped off of the wall, casting a bridge of air beneath my feet and stalking across it, creating a straight path down the mountain.

Tory followed me, instead choosing to fly as she set her wings free at her back, the bronze feathers glinting beautifully in the sunlight.

"Do you have to do that?" I snipped at her.

"Do what?" she muttered.

"Be so…feathery."

"Feathery?" she echoed dryly. "What's your deal, Seth?"

I glanced over my shoulder, finding Caleb following on my air bridge with Geraldine and Max behind him. I bet he loved all those feathers brushing his face, touching his golden hair. Were they really going to bury their grief over Darius in each other while she wrapped her wings around him and held him like a baby duckling?

"I don't have a deal," I growled.

"Right. Whatever," she said, shutting down and I glanced at her, feeling like an asshole. She'd lost her star-bound mate, I didn't wanna be the dick who made her life even more difficult than it was right now.

"Sorry," I murmured, and she shrugged like she didn't care about my apology, about anything. "We'll find Darcy," I said, knowing that was the only thing that could bring any kind of light back to Tory now. And fuck, I was worried about my little blue-haired bestie too.

Tory frowned then flew a little closer. "I told Caleb on the belltower, and Geraldine told Max earlier, so…"

"What?" I asked anxiously, not liking being the last to know whatever she was about to say.

Tory flicked a silencing bubble around us, and dread cornered my heart and prodded it with a sharp stick. "You know the Shadow Beast from the battle everyone keeps talking about?"

"Yeah…"

"Well," Tory swallowed, pain crossing her features. "It was Darcy."

Confusion knitted my brows together and I shook my head dumbly. "What was Darcy?"

"The Shadow Beast," Tory pressed.

"I don't understand."

"It's Lavinia's curse," Tory said thickly. "Darcy was the one killing those people in The Burrows. Darcy was the one who shifted into that beast at night and fucking ate people. And Darcy was the one who was forced to turn against her own people in the battle, rip through our ranks and kill again and again and again. That fucking Shadow Beast was one of the most powerful monsters I've ever seen. And it has hold of her."

I stopped walking, a cold, horrid shock sliding down my spine and holding me there. I shook my head mutely again while Tory beat her wings in place, hovering before me and looking me dead in the eye.

"You can't tell a single soul, Seth Capella. No one outside of our group. If the rebels find out it was her, they might not understand. And the Councillors, they could-"

"Want her dead," I finished in a rasp. "They'll want her dead if she poses a threat against us like that."

Tory nodded, terror making her cheeks pale as she laid a hand on my shoulder. "I believe when she regained some control, she ran to protect us, and that Orion is with her keeping her safe. Either that, or he managed to drag her away from the battle somewhere."

"So we can't go looking for her?" I asked with a sad whimper, horrified about what she must be going through.

"We'll find her. But she can't come back to the rebels until we can figure out how to get that fucking monster out of her."

"Orion will know how," I said firmly. "He knows everything."

"If he's still alive," she replied gravely then turned and flew away from me, dropping her silencing bubble as she went. I was left standing there in the air, a fresh wound added to my heart and a feeling of complete helplessness to Darcy's curse. I realised Tory hadn't even made me do a star vow with her to keep this secret, and my heart squeezed tight in my chest at her trust in me.

I tipped my head back, a howl of anguish leaving me, and Caleb came to my side.

"She told you?" he guessed.

"Is anything ever going to be okay again?" I whispered, not wanting to voice it too loud in case the stars listened in and took it as a challenge to make things worse.

Caleb let out a low sigh, his head falling forward and a few curls tumbling into his eyes. "I don't know, Seth."

He shot away from me, catching up with Tory and slowing on my path of air to walk beside her.

"Not to worry, Jimbob," Geraldine said as she caught up, clapping me on the shoulder hard enough to send me stumbling forward a step. "All will be right in the end." She continued on, singing a song about broken warriors and some long-forgotten war, though there was a warbling tone to her voice that spoke of her own persistent grief.

Max joined us and I hung my head as I walked on, dragging my feet, my body feeling like it was slowly turning into a lump of used up coal.

"Are you gonna talk about it or pretend I can't feel all that emotion you're bottling up?" Max murmured.

"There's only one emotion. I'm ragey."

"You are desperately sad too," he said.

"Fine. There's a sprinkling of sadness. But that's it."

"And you're lonely."

"I'm not lonely," I hissed. "I don't get lonely. I have all of you."

"Yeah, which is why I can't quite figure out the root of that one. But I think I'm starting to get it."

"There's nothing to get, Max." I knocked my shoulder hard into his, trying to make him drop it. "Of course my emotions are fucked, I'm trying to process all this shit."

"No, you're not, you're trying to bury it. Don't you think you're getting too old to keep hiding away from everything real about you?"

"Oh, so now I'm not real," I scoffed. "Thanks for the pep talk, Max. Why don't you go hang out with your new royalist girlfriend? That's where you really wanna be right now anyway." I gestured for him to walk ahead of me, but he didn't go anywhere, his dark eyes boring into mine.

"Just because I love her, doesn't mean I love you any less. I'm not abandoning you by wanting her."

I let out a doggish whine, glancing at him and trying to confirm that from his expression. "Promise?" I whispered, brushing a hand over the braids that ran along the side of my head.

"I swear it."

"Everything's changing," I said. "Are we even gonna be the Heirs once this war is over? It was always the four of us, now it's three, and I don't know how much longer I can hold onto you and Cal."

"We're not going anywhere," he said.

"You can't promise that," I snarled. "Darius promised the same thing once. Besides, if we win this war and actually survive it, we aren't going to be *us* anymore. Everyone will head off to build their own lives, to find their happy place. And she's your happiness. You'll get married and have babies, and Caleb will want that too eventually. Who do you think he's going to pick?"

My gaze whipped to him and Tory, and I knew it was just my overactive imagination running on hyper drive, but I could see how this played out. We'd all grieve Darius month after month, then year after year, while she found comfort in Caleb, and he found comfort in her. Eventually, they'd create something good out of the ruins of their loss, and maybe they'd decide that was enough to fill the voids in them. I was pretty sure he'd loved her before, or at least come close; what if that had never gone away?

"Seth, please talk to me," Max said, drawing my attention back to him. "I won't judge anything you say. You know I've always got your back."

"I dunno what you mean," I muttered, locking away those emotions I felt towards Caleb, refusing to let Max's Siren gifts get a read on them. He could never know this secret, because it meant nothing. Unrequited love that I would smother with a pillow until it stopped kicking.

We made it to the frozen vines where the rebels were killing any living Nymphs in our trap and I carried us all down to the ground on the bridge of air, jumping onto the rocky ground and setting my gaze on a Nymph about to break free of the ice it was encased in.

The Nymph cut through the snare of vines with its probes and the ice came down in a shower of shards as the monster came running forward to intercept me, a screech of hate tearing from its throat. With a surge of energy, I raised my hands, casting a rough metal sword in my hand, preferring to do this one on one. I needed to stretch my muscles and feel the song of a kill in my veins.

The Nymph tried to grab hold of me, but I ducked its probes, swinging my blade and carrying myself to its chest on a gust of air. I slammed the sword in deep and the Nymph turned to smoke and ash before my eyes.

I released my hold on the air beneath me, dropping to the ground with a thud and running toward the head of another Nymph sticking out of the ice. It looked almost dead, but I lopped its head off to finish the job, a howl of anger leaving me as I thought of Darius.

Die for him, motherfucker.

The rebels were finishing the last of them, and my gaze fell on a Nymph they hauled from the ice as he shifted into his Fae-like form, naked as he was tossed to the ground at the feet of my mother. He was a slim man with a gaunt face and black, thinning hair.

"Wait – please!" he cried, his voice touched with an accent. "I wish to speak with the Vega Queens. I am not your enemy."

I glanced back in the direction Tory had taken, but she was busy finishing off Nymphs of her own with Geraldine. Caleb met my eye and Max jogged forward with a frown on his brow as my mother raised a hand to silence the Nymph for good.

"I think he's telling the truth," Max said as he felt the Nymph's emotions.

"Wait," I called to my mother a second before she could cast a killing blow.

I moved forward, holding my roughly forged sword out and pressing it under the Nymph's chin as he gazed up at me in fear. "What's your name?"

"Miguel Polaris," he said.

"Did you know Diego?" I asked in surprise and he nodded quickly, grief filling his eyes.

"He was my son," he croaked. "Please, have mercy. I can help you with your cause."

I lowered the sword and my mother stepped closer.

"He's our enemy, pup," she warned.

"I'm not a pup," I growled, shrugging her off.

I slammed the sword into the earth beside Miguel's head and he winced in fright. Then I shed my shirt, offering it to him before making him a pair of pants out of leaves.

"Seth," Mom hissed, stepping closer and whispering to me. "This isn't the time to try and prove the size of your wee willy winky-"

"Go," I barked at her, an Alpha tone ringing through the word, and she flinched, almost submitting before she bared her teeth and growled in anger.

By the moon, I can't believe she brought my winky into this.

"I am still your Alpha," she snapped. "Do not speak to me as if you are in charge."

"I won't submit," I said, lifting my chin and we stared at each other, the urge to shift trickling through me, and I wondered if the day had finally come when I was going to challenge her.

Max pressed a hand to my arm, sending a flow of calming energy into me and I took a breath.

"Not now, brother," he said quietly. "Keep your head."

I glanced at Caleb who was looking at me with heat in his eyes, his gaze falling to my naked chest briefly before he cleared his throat and leaned down to pull Miguel to his feet. He created metal cuffs, locking them in place at the base of the Nymph's spine.

"We'll ask Tory if he's worth keeping," he said.

"You cannot truly think it is appropriate to seek council from a Vega, Caleb," my mom said in horror.

"Holy shit, is that a falling star?" Caleb gasped, pointing to the sky and Mom whipped around to look.

Caleb shot away with Miguel in his arms, and I snorted a laugh, exchanging a grin with Max.

"Argh, that boy," Mom said with a huff as she realised what he'd done. "Go round him up, Seth."

I headed away from her with Max, having zero intention of doing what she said but happy to use the opportunity to escape.

Caleb tossed Miguel at Tory's feet as he reached her, and her brows lifted in surprise. Max and I broke into a jog to catch up to them and when we made it there, Tory was frowning.

"How can we trust you?" she demanded of Miguel.

"Let me prove it. If you still have my son's hat-"

"I'm not letting you near that," Tory said. "You'll send some sort of shadow soul hat message and tell Lavinia where we are."

"Lavinia," Miguel spat on the ground at her name. "She is a plague. The shadows are her prisoner."

"By the goolads of Gragoria!" Geraldine cried from somewhere to my left and I realised she'd hacked a path through the vines with her flail. "I. Shall. Smite. You. Oh. Ghoulish. Foe. Of. Mine." She spoke with every strike of her flail against the vines, fighting to get deeper towards a Nymph who was tangled in the thorns. "Hear my name and hear it well – for it shall follow you into the evernight!" She swung her flail into its chest, finishing it off with the merciless blow and it shrieked as it died.

Geraldine came running back to join us, wiping a line of sweat from her brow, before swinging the handle of her flail up to rest on her shoulder.

Miguel looked up at her from the ground in awe. "I know of you. The Nymphs call you Sentina Laquorian. It means the Sentinel of the Royals in the shadow language of old."

"Who is this swine in the muck?" She raised her flail. "I shall clobber his nefarious clout-trapper for you, my Queen." She brought her flail down and Miguel flinched, but Tory caught hold of Geraldine's weapon with a vine, keeping it from falling on the Nymph.

I bounced from foot to foot in excitement, unsure if death was in the air or something even more thrilling.

"He's Diego's father," Tory explained.

Geraldine gasped dramatically, throwing the back of her hand to her forehead. "Our gentle, hatted friend. What kind of father were you to he?" She demanded of Miguel. "Speak loud and clear, for these next words might be the last farthings that ever fall from your penny purse."

Miguel swallowed tightly. "Not the one I wished I could be, Sentina," he choked out, bowing his head to her in shame. "I was held in the power of the shadows. My… *wife* Drusilla kept me under her control, and I was subdued for many years, a walking pawn at her and her brother's side. I was under Drusilla's control until Gwendalina

Vega cast her to dust and broke the dark spell which kept me as her prisoner. She freed me. And I shall do anything to repay that debt, anything to make up for what happened to my boy, my Diego."

"Her name is Darcy," Tory growled, and Miguel mumbled a string of apologies.

"So what, pray tell," Geraldine hissed. "Are you doing among the masses of an enemy army? If you are as pious as you plead, then why have we discovered you in the midst of these rapscallions?" She began pacing back and forth in front of him, leaving her flail hanging from Tory's vines as she clasped her hands behind her back. It was pretty damn entertaining to watch, and Max looked like he was in danger of poking Miguel's eye out with his boner over his girl's interrogation.

"I've been hiding among them, if I had tried to escape, they would have killed me," Miguel said.

"Oh – ho! So you were there when we fought the Nymphs in battle? Did you stand shoulder to shoulder with them, nary a word of complaint as you took up arms and stood against us, you cuttlefish of a fellow?"

"I fought in the battle, yes," he blurted. "But I did not kill a single Fae. In fact, I led those monstrous Nymphs to their deaths whenever I could. They are twisted up by Lavinia's power, they covet her like some dark goddess, but she is no such thing." He spat on the ground again. "She is the reason we suffer in the dark. She is the reason for all the chaos in the shadows. She is-"

"Silence!" Geraldine crowed and I sniggered, nudging Max beside me, but he was slack-jawed and unblinking as he watched her.

I looked to Caleb, trying to catch his eye but he was firmly looking at Geraldine even though I knew he could feel my eyes on him. *Hmph.*

"You are but a whelk at a dolphin's door," Geraldine proclaimed, pointing from Miguel to Tory. "How are we to believe these preposterous tittling tales?"

I snorted at the word tittling, but no one else joined in. Tough crowd.

"I lost a father, a mother, and a brother upon that battlefield," Geraldine lamented, pain lacing every one of her words and darkness fell over us all like a cloak.

Tory backed up, looking like she wanted to disappear from the world, and I half expected her to take off and fly away into the sky, only Caleb took hold of her arm and kept her there. Of course he did. Because he was her anchor now. Her rock in a stormy sea. And that didn't hurt. Not even a little.

"Ow," Max breathed, looking to me as he felt my pain, and I snatched it away from him again.

"I can nary lose another," Geraldine croaked, taking a moment to contain herself as she held her fist to her mouth and squeezed her eyes shut.

"Gerry," Max said softly, moving to her side.

She sighed, patting his arm before turning back to Tory. "I say we behead this loathsome creature and be done with this dalliance. What say you, my Queen?"

Tory gazed down at Miguel with a frown, mulling over what to do. "He helped us once before. He gave us the information about Vard's shadow eye through Diego's hat."

"That is not enough to prove his innocence, my lady. He could have been trying to wandangle us, to lure us into trusting him before. He brought an army of Nymphs to our door," Geraldine said passionately.

Tory looked to Max. "What can you feel?"

"It feels like the truth to me," Max said thoughtfully. "Though that doesn't confirm it. I'd have to look deeper to be sure. It could take some time. I'd need to hear him speak more about his time in Lionel's army."

"We have to move!" Leon's voice made us all turn, weapons and hands raising defensively. He was running towards us down the mountainside with a backpack on, weaving left and right between the tents. "We're being far too predictable." He picked up a rock, throwing it at an unsuspecting rebel and it bounced off the guy's head, his cry of pain cutting the air. "Pack your bags, or burn your bags, for the love of the stars, don't tell me what you're gonna do with your bags dudes, we just need to go!"

"Is Lionel coming?" a woman asked him in panic and Leon grabbed hold of her, shaking her as he shouted in her face.

"He will if you keep acting predictably, Mindy," he yelled.

"My name isn't Mindy," she said in confusion, and he tossed her over his shoulder, slapping another guy around the face before pointing directly at Tory. "You know the plan. We need to go. Give the order, but don't be predictable about it."

"Where will we go?" someone lamented from the crowd and Tiberius Rigel muscled his way forward to see what the commotion was.

"To the sea of course," Leon said, tossing the woman he had hold of into the arms of Tiberius. "Like we planned. But we have to choose a beach at random."

"Calm down, you're causing a panic," Tiberius commanded.

I tossed away my makeshift sword, unbuckling my pants. "Fuck it, let's go."

"My lady? The rebels will not move unless you give the order," Geraldine said and Tory shrugged, taking off into the sky on her wings. She pressed a hand to her throat, casting an amplifying spell that carried her voice up the mountainside.

"Let's go! Gather supplies and get ready to leave," she called, and the rebels finally listened, hurrying to obey.

"Shift into your Order forms, run for the sea!" Leon shouted and an answering roar sounded as Dante shifted from somewhere along the barrier of thorns and ice before taking off into the sky with a muscular man and a petite woman holding a baby on his back.

"Follow your queen!" Geraldine bayed before tearing her shirt and bra off, her huge tits springing free and Max cursed, trying to cover her up while she knocked him aside with a swing of her hip. "You're acting too predictably, you tantalising trout."

"Yeah, Maxy boy," I taunted as Geraldine leapt forward, shifting into her Cerberus form and picking up Miguel with one of her three mouths, while taking her flail into another. Miguel wailed in fright as Geraldine charged off down the hill after Tory, and the rebels followed with hollers of passion, roars, neighs and howls all colliding together as many of them shifted.

The Councillors cried out to people, trying to restore order, but none of them were listening, half of them leaping and twirling about the place as they followed Leon's lead while the rest raced after the Vega princess.

"I'm going after Gerry," Max said, but I caught his arm.

"That's predictable. Go dive onto that Griffin's back and fly away with him." I pointed to the white Griffin who was preparing to take off, clawing at the ground with the eagle talons on its front legs. I shoved Max in that direction, and he hesitated only a moment before giving into the madness descending around us and leaping onto the Griffin's back, shouting 'yah!'. The Griffin bucked angrily, but Max held on as it flexed its wings and sailed into the sky.

"This is crazy," Caleb breathed, and I rounded on him as I yanked my belt off, whipping him hard across the chest. "Ah, motherfucker!"

"Gotta be random, Cal," I taunted.

He lunged at me, but I moved before he could catch me, whipping his ass with the belt.

"Give me that," he growled, darting forward with a blur of Vampire speed and taking hold of the belt. I didn't let go of the other end, wrapping it around his wrists, lashing it tight with a skill only an orgy pro could achieve, smirking as I captured him.

"You can't beat me at being unpredictable," I challenged.

"It's not a game," he said. "It's life or death."

"Sounds like the best kind of game to me." I reeled him closer by the belt, knowing he could have just burned it away by now, but for some reason he hadn't.

The thundering of footfalls sounded around us, and no one was paying us any attention at all.

"I bet you'll never guess what I'm about to do," I said.

"Go on. Surprise me," he said dryly, the anger between us still a potent thing. "Though the only thing you could really do that would surprise me right now would be to apologise for being a prick about Darius. But you won't, because you can't ever admit when you're wrong."

His words scalded me and I released a Wolfish growl. "Oh yeah, Cal? Well how about *this*?" I carved the ground out from beneath us into a huge chasm, the two of us falling fast and slamming into the mud at the bottom. I was on him in the next second, punching him in the side and he kicked out at me, using his Vampire strength to snap the belt in two.

"I liked that belt," I huffed, punching him again.

He shot to his feet, kicking me in the side and I wheezed as I was thrown onto my back. He was on top of me in the next second, strangling me as mud coated us and I tore at his shirt until it was half ripped off of him.

"Ha-ppy now?" I forced out around the pressure in my throat.

"Happy?" he barked, coming nose to nose with me as his hair fell into his eyes and he blocked out the sunlight from far above. "Right now, I can't even see a glimmer of happiness in my future."

A whine slid through my lips at those words, and he released me, his breaths coming heavily as he rested his hands either side of my head.

"Oh, you'll find your glimmer. Your feathery little glimmer," I said icily, then shoved him off of me. I got to my feet, trampling his chest and preparing to launch myself out of the hole on a gust of air. But a probed hand shot out of the mud wall to my right and I yelped in surprise, my ass hitting the ground as a Nymph clawed its way out of the earth like a fucking zombie, clearly buried here by our earlier attack. I brought my hands up to cast magic and blast the thing into death, but its rattle filled the air, locking down my power in my chest.

I cursed, about to shift into my Wolf form, but Caleb shot forward with a flash of speed, kicking the Nymph's head again and again before it died under his vicious attack and finally turned to ash. Caleb dropped down beside me, his hand going to my ankle and healing the bloody cut I hadn't even realised the Nymph had given me.

"I had it," I said, meaning for it to come out as a growl, but the words were weakened by the concern in his eyes.

"I know," he muttered. "But I wanted revenge for what it did to you. You're my… Source. It makes me protective." He didn't look at me, his thumb carving over my ankle in soft strokes even though he'd already healed the skin. I wasn't sure anyone had ever taken care of me like that while I'd still been able to do so myself.

"If I'm still your Source, why haven't you had a drink from me in days?" I asked, my voice rough as Caleb let go of my ankle and looked to me with his jaw ticking.

"Because sometimes your blood makes me…" He trailed off and I mentally filled in the end of that sentence. *Makes you wanna casually fuck your best friend, before you prance off with someone you could have real feelings for.*

"Got it." I shoved to my feet, going stone cold on him.

I cast air beneath me, carrying myself out of the hole and I continued down the mountainside on my little breeze, feeling all the things. Mostly the bad things. But then there was the unmistakable tingling in my ankle and that burning way he'd looked at me when he'd healed me.

Fuck, maybe I was destined to pine for a man who would never want me. But moments like that made me think the suffering was worth it. So I'd keep drowning until I got another one.

Scorpio
Gemini
Virgo
Aries
Cancer
Leo
Sagittarius
Taurus
Capricorn
Aquarius
Libra
Pisces

XAVIER

CHAPTER TWENTY THREE

I ran among the rebels as we headed south across the land, a bag strapped to my back containing some of the few supplies the rebels had salvaged from The Burrows.

"Shift, Xavier!" Sofia called out to me from Tyler's back, riding his silver Pegasus form, his wings tucked tight to his side. "We'll stay with you."

Other flying Orders were already sweeping overhead, their shadows rushing by, feathers rustling as they went. I clenched my jaw, pretending I hadn't heard her, my back prickling and reminding me that I would never fly again.

I hadn't shifted since the battle, and had only been able to recharge my magic by flying through the clouds on Sofia's back. I'd done so once, feeling like a vital part of me had been stripped away, too ashamed to do it more than that. I wasn't a Pegasus anymore, I was just a horse with a horn, and I didn't need all the rebels looking at me with pity while in my Order form.

The urge to shift had been my biggest challenge though, it was a need that ran deep and couldn't be cut out. Now I was cantering along the ground on two feet, that desire was stronger than it had ever been, the animal in me demanding to come out.

Sofia steered Tyler closer to me and I looked up at her fierce expression, the way the wind was tearing through her blonde pixie cut hair, her body moving perfectly in time with Tyler's. She wore one of the plain khaki jumpsuits that the earth Elementals had been making for everyone, a belt cinching it in tight around her narrow waist, and a sparkling pink Pegobag strapped to her back.

"At least ride with me," she said, reaching for me, but I champed my teeth at her fingers, and she retracted her hand with a pout.

Tyler neighed in frustration, and I ran stubbornly on, trying to overtake him but he easily outpaced me in his Pegasus form. I had a rush of blazing energy contained in my chest and it needed an outlet. I wanted to Dom Tyler down and prove I was the top Pegasus, but without my wings, how was I ever going to be that again?

A Harpy whooshed over me so low that she kicked me in the head, and I neighed in fury, scowling after her as the sound of her laughter carried back to me. My cheeks flushed hot I was filled with the need to shift, take to the sky and make her pay for that. But I wasn't able to do that anymore.

Seth came bounding past us in his enormous white Werewolf form, weaving left and right through the rebels at random while howling wildly. Caleb shot after him in a blur, throwing punches at his friend's flanks, their game seeming a little intense.

Max fell from the sky, leaping off of a Griffin's back and landing on Seth's, taking him by surprise and nearly knocking him over. Max howled like a madman and Seth echoed it, picking up speed as Caleb raced along at his side. I watched them go, thinking of my brother and how he should have been a part of that group.

The loss of him left me raw and I worked hard to force that thought from my mind, knowing that if I dwelled on it now, I'd break all over again.

"Hey, Xavier!" Seth's younger sister Athena called to me as she shot into view on Hadley Altair's back, her arms and legs wrapped around him.

Hadley's Vampire fangs were out, and he had a glint of excitement in his eyes as he looked to me. He was so like Caleb in ways, but his dark features gave him a brooding look that matched his personality to a T. Athena's purple-streaked, black hair fluttered in the wind as she jumped from Hadley's back and began running at my side instead, leaving Hadley gazing after her.

"We're gonna have a race," she said. "Hadley's not allowed to use his tornado legs. Do you guys wanna play?"

"Hell yes!" Sofia called and Tyler neighed in agreement.

"I'm good," I clipped.

Athena's twin brother Grayson ran into view in his Wolf form which resembled a giant husky – just the same as his sister's. He snapped playfully at Hadley's ass, making him curse as he worked to avoid his sharp teeth and he shot forward to keep up with us.

"Come on, Xavier," Athena urged. "The winner gets to dare the loser to do whatever they want." She moved closer to me, lowering her voice as she whispered. "You don't even have to win, I just wanna thrash Hadley so I can make him my bitch boy again."

"I can hear you, Athena," Hadley growled.

"You know why I agreed to play with you, leech," Athena tossed back. "Every single one of our interactions is purely for the enjoyment of me proving I'm superior to you in every way." She smirked as she saw that jibe rile him up, his eyes flickering darkly.

"Then you should have learned how wrong you are by now, Capella," he bit out.

Sometimes it seemed like those two were obsessed with each other, and other times it was like they wanted to murder one another. I guessed it was a power thing. But when I thought of how my own power play with Tyler had turned out, I wondered if there might be something more brewing between them.

Athena punched me in the arm, and I cursed. "Get me back, come on, Xavier."

"Yeah, get her Xavier," Sofia cheered and Tyler whinnied his encouragement.

"No," I grunted.

"Fine," Athena said lightly, darting past me and punching Sofia in the leg instead, making her neigh in surprise. "I punched your mare, what are you gonna do about it?" She darted behind Tyler who kicked a hind hoof at her, but Athena was fast, sprinting around him and avoiding the blow, her laughter carrying back to me and setting my pulse hammering.

"I'll get her." Sofia leapt to her feet on Tyler's back with a vengeful fire in her eyes that was hot as fuck, but I was her Dom and I wanted to be the one who put Athena in her place now.

"I'm racing," I announced. "I'll beat you to the sea, Athena!"

She laughed, flipping me the finger before leaping forward and shifting into her black and grey Wolf form, making her brother Grayson howl as he ran to join her.

"Hey – you can't use your Order if I can't," Hadley snapped, but Athena was already gone. He cursed, running on, looking like he really wanted to use his speed, but was stubborn enough to stick to the rules, even if they did put him at a disadvantage.

I took my pack from my shoulders and tossed it to Sofia as she sat back down on Tyler.

"Are you gonna shift?" she asked, a smile lighting her up and making her literally glow.

This decision was making her happy, and that was enough to solidify it as I shifted mid-run, letting my clothes tear to shreds. My four hooves hit the ground and a neigh fell from my lips like a battle cry, echoed by Sofia and Tyler as I charged forward and took the lead.

Lilac glitter tumbled from my mane, the wind rushing over me and making me feel more alive than I had in days. Darius's death had left my heart numb, but right now I was awake again, seeking out something good beyond all the tragedy, if only for a moment.

On instinct, I tried to flex my wings and a mournful whinny left me when I felt the empty space they should have filled. I galloped on, my gaze set on Athena and Grayson's fluffy tails up ahead, and I put on a burst of speed.

I was faster than the wind, the most powerful Pegasus stallion of my generation, and I easily caught them and soon led Tyler past them too.

A line of Minotaurs barred our way forward, all in their shifted forms, horns curling up from the bulls' heads and the cows mooing to the sky. I nosed my way between them, sending glitter tumbling over them, then leaping over a family of Teumessian Fox Shifters.

I was well in the lead of the race, and as the rebels tore across the rocky land, I spotted a glimmer of sunlight dancing on the sea in the distance.

Tory's wings were a blazing beacon of fire, trailing embers through the sky to mark our path and guide everyone on ahead of us all. It felt so good to be doing something at last, taking action even if it was as simple as finding a sanctuary for everyone. It definitely beat sitting around in the ruins waiting for my father to find us.

The ground was trembling from the hoards of us all migrating across it at speed, and there was a sense of hope among us that I hadn't felt since before the battle.

The Oscura Wolves all howled to the sky, a river of fur and sharp teeth rushing along ahead of us, and I raced straight into them, weaving through their ranks and earning myself a few snaps at my ankles.

The instinct to fly away from their jaws made me stumble and Tyler nearly crashed into me before I righted myself, heat flooding up my neck and shame washing over me. I was just a flightless horse now. I didn't even know what you called a horse that had a horn and no wings. I'd never heard of such a thing.

I looked to the sky, aching to join the other flying Orders up there, wheeling this way and that through the air. It was my favourite place in the world to be, and now I would only experience it second hand. I'd never flap my wings and follow the current of a breeze, and there was a grief in that which I could never have prepared for.

What made it worse was that I'd spent so long having to hide my Order in Lionel's manor that I'd missed out on countless times when I could have been flying. Now, he'd taken away something that made me what I was, and it was so fucking unfair. But it was the least of what he'd taken really. I couldn't even truly process the loss of my mom and my brother. I kept expecting them to show up, to walk through the nearest door, greeting me the way they always had.

But I would never get to experience that again. They were gone. And I didn't think I would ever really move on without them. The pain was too present and seemed to grow sharper than it did duller.

Sofia and Tyler did everything they could to comfort me, but there was no comfort in violent deaths handed out by the man who had sired me. He had stripped everything that he could from me, and I was left with a hatred that filled me to the brim and made happiness feel like a long-forgotten memory that would never resurface.

I whinnied as that pain poured out once again, impossible to contain now that it was unleashed. I reared up, my hooves striking the back of an Oscura Wolf who yelped and leapt out of my way. Tyler cantered fast to keep up, the sound of his hooves echoing mine as he kept pace with me with Sofia on his back.

I charged on, moving as quickly as my hooves would allow and knocking anyone aside who dared step into my way. I gnashed my teeth at the Wolves' legs as they had done to me, and they parted for me so I could gallop my way through the centre of them.

The huge shadow of Dante's Storm Dragon form swept overhead, and a furious wind was brought along with him, pressing against our backs and driving our feet forward even faster. Static hung in the air as it crackled off of his scales and it set adrenaline pounding through my blood.

I was moving almost as fast as the flying Orders above, my hooves feeling weightless, like they could lift off the ground and launch me into the sky. But it was just a mirage, because as my shoulder blades flexed in yearning for my wings, no wind took me into its hold.

I whinnied and Tyler echoed the sound in recognition of my longing, Sofia's fingers brushing my back as they kept to my side.

The ground began to slope down beneath my hooves and my gaze settled on the glistening sea beyond a long, sandy beach.

I was among the first to make it onto the beach, panting as I came to a halt and shifting back into my Fae form. Sofia tossed me some clothes from her pack, and I pulled on the jumpsuit, kicking my feet into some slippers made of leaves which didn't feel at all sturdy and looked kind of dumb. But whatever.

Athena and Grayson made it to the beach, skidding to a halt and falling into a tussle with each other, sending sand spraying up everywhere and flicking me in the face. I sighed, turning to look at the sea while Tory Vega circled down to perch on the shoulder of the huge brindle Cerberus that was Geraldine.

She scratched behind Geraldine's ear and her hind leg started kicking, her tail wagging furiously and sending more sand flying into my face.

I huffed, moving away from them, folding my arms, and waiting for the rest of the rebels to arrive. Hadley appeared, trying to shove his way past the Minotaurs who were mooing and chattering together, snarling as he broke through and ran to meet us.

"How come you all got to use your Order forms, but I didn't? That makes the game void," he snapped at Athena, and she dove on him in her Wolf form, trying to knock him to the ground. He shot away before she could pin him, spinning around and grabbing hold of the back of her neck by the scruff and squeezing tight enough to make her go limp.

"Gotcha," he laughed as her front paws kicked, but she couldn't get out of his hold.

She shifted, suddenly standing there naked with Hadley's hand locked around the back of her neck, but when she jerked forward to get free, he didn't let go.

"You agreed to the rules, leech. Xavier won, so what's the dare for Hadley?" she called to me.

Hadley's eyes dropped to Athena's bare ass, his grip on her clearly loosening as he got distracted because she yanked herself free, twirling around and slapping him as she went.

"Bitch," he growled, lunging forward to catch her again and hitting an air shield.

She laughed loudly, flipping him off with two middle fingers as he worked to break through the barrier.

"I dare you to be nice to Athena for a week," I said, and Hadley whirled on me.

"What?" he snapped.

"You two would get along if you stopped being so competitive," I said with a shrug, knowing there was more to their relationship than they let on to the world.

I'd seen it myself. And I'd seen what had happened to my brother when he'd continued acting like he hated Tory Vega for so long. He could have had so much more happiness in his life if he'd just…if he'd…

My mind spiralled into a vortex of misery, and I turned away from them, walking towards Tory and Geraldine.

Tory jumped down to land on the sand before me, and with one look I could tell she knew where my mind was. She nodded a little, sadness filling her eyes before she moved forward and toed my foot with her boot.

"Are you okay about leaving him behind?" I asked, my voice rough. I'd visited the shrine made for Darius, Mom and Hamish just this morning, casting fresh flowers to lay around them, and talking to them all as if they could hear me. I wasn't ready for another goodbye, but at least I knew I could find this place when it was safe to return.

"He's not there," she said darkly, her eyes moving to the mountain we'd left them all on before she pressed a hand to her heart. "He's here."

I nodded, my throat thickening and blocking all oxygen from entering my airway.

"Cast with me?" she offered, and I nodded, relieved to do anything but remain in this moment of agony.

"What do you want me to cast?" I asked.

"We're going to carve ourselves an island from this land and float out to sea."

My ears pricked up at that and I looked back at the hilly landscape we'd travelled across and the green grass hugging its slopes. The rebel army covered the land for as far as I could see, the remaining thousands of them all racing towards us, a mass of colourful feathers, scales, fur and fangs.

"How big?" I asked.

"Let's say…as far as that hill with the tree at the top." She pointed it out in the distance, several miles away from here.

A frown creased her brow as she began to cast, the ground trembling beneath us before the land beyond the hill began to fracture. A gigantic crack formed all through the valleys and hills and I raised my hands, pouring all of my focus into this task and working to rip that fracture wider. It felt good, really damn good to let my magic free like that. There was relief in the outlet, just untethering the almighty power that lived in me and watching it work to split the very ground apart.

More and more earth Elementals rushed to help us, Caleb and Seth standing shoulder to shoulder as they cast together while Geraldine shifted out of her Cerberus form to join in, standing naked and proud at Tory's side.

The chasm ran deeper and deeper, a roaring noise filling the air as we cleaved the land apart and created a huge island for us to take as our own.

As the crack met with the sea and cliffs at the far ends of our view, the beach began to crumble under our ferocious power, Max and his father ran to the water line, sending the sea surging into the chasm we'd made. It rushed in fast, and the ground shifted beneath our feet as it rose out of the waves and our newly made island rode out upon them. Everyone cheered as an enormous wave exploded up from the edge of the beach and washed over us all, the island setting sail with a fanfare of cheers and cries of support from the rebels.

"I henceforth declare this island the Rebels' Undying-"

"Wait," Seth said, holding up a hand as he hurried over barefoot and in sweatpants, his eyes alight with the excitement. "I think we should vote on the name-"

"Nonsense," Geraldine scoffed dismissively.

"Guys, just think about it, this name will go down in history and Geraldine has a track record of calling herself an ass – on purpose! Do we really want to risk-"

"You are not even a sworn-in member of the court of the true Queens," Geraldine chastised. "And I am known for my wonderous and most apt namings of all things."

"Just let her do it, Seth," Max murmured, and Seth whined in protest, but I didn't bother to join the debate – none of us here were going to win in an argument with Geraldine when it came to this anyway so what was the point?

"The choice is yours, my Queen," Geraldine said, looking to Tory who didn't even seem to be listening.

"About the name thing?" she asked and Seth tried turning the puppy dog eyes on her, but she didn't seem to notice. "I don't care."

"Then I shall carry the burden of naming it for you, Your Majesty," Geraldine gushed, raising her voice as Seth tried to protest again. "I hereby declare this island, the Rebels' Undying Mighty Province!" she boomed, amplifying her voice with a spell that reverberated off of every hill we'd claimed for our new sanctuary.

"R.U.M.P.?" Seth demanded furiously. "So now we're all just asses on the rump?

I told you she'd do this. I said that she'd-"

"Pish posh, Seth Capella, green does not become you. Perhaps once you bend the knee upon this fine land of R.U.M.P. and become a true member of the A.S.S. you shall stop attention seeking so blatantly."

The ex-Councillors shared a look at the name too, but no one listened when they tried to object, the rebels already breaking into a celebration that no one could stop.

"Where to?" Seth asked Tory, much to the disapproving glare of his mother.

"Anywhere and everywhere," she said. "We'll keep it as random as we can."

"I'm gifted at that," he said with a grin before raising his hands and casting a tremendous wind that pushed the island far out into the sea.

I moved back from the edge of the beach, breathing in the fresh, briny air and hoping that this place really could remain a secret from Lionel. Because most of the people I cared for in the world were right here on this floating lump of land, and I didn't intend on losing another one of them to this war.

Scorpio
Gemini
Virgo
Cancer
Aries
Leo
Sagittarius
Taurus
Capricorn
Aquarius
Libra
Pisces

GABRIEL

CHAPTER TWENTY FOUR

I *saw* infinite outcomes, all of them drenched in blood and housed in agony. The sleep deprivation was taking its toll on me. I couldn't control where my visions went, my mind slipping too closely to those I loved even as I tried with all my strength to keep from looking their way.

The worst part of my ever-weakening state was that I *saw* my own future. The fate that was looming at my back and towering over me, engulfing me in its shadow. There was no way to escape it, no path I could perceive that would stop Lionel Acrux from gaining access to my visions through the use of his Cyclops servant, Vard. As soon as my mental defences fell, he would make it into my head and pick through every vision I had foreseen within these walls. I would hide what I could, but there would be no way to conceal all of it and with access to my visions, only the worst could come of Lionel's plans.

The only small mercy I had was that Lionel Acrux couldn't crack into my head with Dark Coercion, and it had been a fucking pleasure to see him lose his mind over that. The power of the Phoenixes thwarting him once again was a beautiful damn thing and I thanked the stars for the Phoenix kiss which marked my ring finger, protecting me from becoming little more than a vessel bound to his will.

I bucked against the restraints binding me to the glass throne at the heart of the Royal Seer's Chamber, finding my way back to the present moment for a second, a snapshot of walls lined with portraits of Seers from years past, my own mother's eyes cast in paint watching me suffer through every moment of this, before the intensity of my own Sight dragged me away again, this place designed too perfectly to keep me *seeing*.

The cuffs on my wrists held my magic at bay, even if I'd had any power left to use, so I had no defences to draw on, I was simply a slave to The Sight.

This ability of mine could be a curse in life. I'd had to bear witness to countless deaths, *seeing* my wife and family all succumb to bloody fates time and again, whilst trying to think clearly enough to find a way to avoid it. But ever since this war had started, those visions had increased significantly, and the burden of this gift had become greater than it ever had before. My family and the rebels had been relying on me, and I'd failed them, unable to *see* Lionel's destructive plan before it was far too late. And now I was trapped here, about to be wielded as a weapon against them.

A fate flickered through my mind of me trying to cave my own skull in on the glass throne, throwing my head back against it until I could no longer be used as Lionel's instrument to bring about death on everyone I held dear.

My pulse quickened as I *saw* those attempts fail, then of my neck being strapped tight to the seat and a chain cinched around my forehead too. Immobilised. No, that wasn't my answer. And I was relieved by that, not wanting to leave this world yet; there was so much life to live if only I could find a way for us all to claim it. As my mind slipped that way, I fought to hold back the visions, but my energy waned and I fell into the future the stars offered me.

I *saw* an island of land floating in the ocean and my heart clenched with need as I *saw* the faces of the people I adored. They were still alive, exhaustion in their eyes, but determination too. Fate wheeled left and right, changing before my eyes so I couldn't perceive their location or the direction they were taking, and I thanked the fucking stars that they were acting at random. They could be anywhere in the oceans of the world, and I couldn't find them, so long as they didn't make any mistakes, any solid plans.

They were safe, for now.

My mind skipped onto Orion and though his fate was somewhat shrouded in shadow because of Lavinia, I felt his pain and *saw* the lacerations on his body as he lay in a cage in the throne room. I could feel the fight in him and knew my friend could withstand the torture he was being subjected to, but with each passing day that slipped by in my mind's eye, he grew emptier, colder. It seemed Lavinia was attacking some part of him that was deeper than his flesh, and anxiety burned through my veins as I watched him beginning to fade. His determination turning to acceptance, then to numbness then finally…nothing. He was carved out from the inside, the fire of his being dulled down to barely more than a flickering flame, and I couldn't *see* a way back from it.

"Brother," I sighed, desperate to reach him through the fabric of the present and the future, to give him the hope I *saw* fading out of existence in his eyes.

I turned my gaze to Darcy as I had many times before, but only darkness was offered. Nothing had changed. Whatever had happened to her was something steeped in shadow, something I was unable to *see* an answer to. And maybe that was a blessing in disguise.

A hand slid tight around my throat and a needle stuck in my neck before something icily cold plunged into my veins. I jerked back into the present moment, finding Vard before me, pocketing the syringe he'd just injected me with and releasing me.

"Hello, Seer," he said, and my gaze was drawn to his left eye socket, which was empty thanks to Geraldine.

"Get on with it," Lionel's sharp tone sounded beyond him, but Vard took up my entire view, from the grisly black hair that hung lankly down to his shoulders, to the hungry smirk on his lips that made me feel like fresh meat before a wolf. But I was no meal for him to devour, I'd fight with what strength I had left, though even as I thought it, exhaustion swept through me, diving ever deeper.

"What have you given me?" I demanded, but I suddenly realised what it was as I lost my connection to my Harpy Order.

"Just a little Order suppressant," Vard said.

"I can't go much longer without recharging my magic," I said breathlessly, my muscles shaking from the exertion of using my Sight for such a prolonged time. I needed to lay in a sunrise and let my power replenish, I needed sleep to let my mind rest from all it had perceived. It was too much. It was going to kill me if this didn't stop soon.

"Do it," Lionel commanded, ignoring my words, and Vard's empty eye socket slid towards his other eye, the two meeting in the middle and merging into one large orb at the centre of his face. Though there was damage to it on the side where he'd lost his shadow eye. It was bloodshot and filled with ugly red and blue veins that seemed to cause him discomfort as he blinked.

He reached for me, his palm pressing to the centre of my forehead, and I forced a mental block up against him on instinct, but it was a brittle thing now, already subjected to so many attempts to break it that I realised my time was up.

I held on for as long as I could, the rush of his power crashing against my mental shields, a roar leaving me as I gave every last scrap of energy in my body to this one task. It was no good though. Like water bursting through a dam, my walls came tumbling down and Vard got into my head, his power sweeping through me greedily and a grunt of satisfaction leaving him as he took charge of my thoughts.

I tried to hide any visions that contained those I loved, but he was ready for me, latching onto them every time I made those attempts and forcing them to the forefront of my mind. I watched in horror as he took them, stealing them into his own mind and muttering, "Yes, yes, yes," as he kept taking everything I had foreseen, sucking it into him like some horrid vacuum hollowing out my head.

"*Stop*," I snarled, fighting against my restraints, but there was nothing I could do. Nausea fell over me and I started to tremble in the grasp of his power as he took and took and took.

"Finally," Lionel said in relief, his eager voice closer than before. "Take everything, Vard. Leave no vision behind."

"But it could kill him, sire. He is already waning," Vard said just as a seizure took over me, my limbs going rigid and shockwaves of pain exploding through my limbs.

"I said take it all," Lionel snapped. "If you kill him, I will tear out your liver and feed it to you. Is that motivation enough?"

"Y-yes, sire," Vard stammered in fear, his power pressing deeper into my head.

I felt death coming with him, starlight glimmering in my periphery. All I had to do was turn into it and I could step beyond the Veil. I was losing consciousness fast, that starlight brightening and the whispers of the celestial beings who ruled me drawing nearer.

Take heart, son of fate.

The stars' voice was gifted to me along with a sliver of strength that I latched onto with the last of my energy, not knowing why they cared to offer me anything at all now. But I wasn't going to question it when I hovered on the brink of death.

Somewhere between the pain and the dark, I found life again. My eyes cracked open, and I had no idea how much time had passed, only that Vard was now on his knees, his bulging Cyclops eye wide and his mouth agape as he watched my visions play out for him. Lionel's hand was on my shoulder, healing magic rushing from him into me and despite desperately needing it, I flinched away from him with a curse.

"Can you see the rebels' location?" Lionel asked eagerly.

"They are on an island, sire," Vard said excitedly. "But...oh."

"What is it?" Lionel hissed.

"They are moving at random, sending the island this way and that to evade prediction," Vard said, flinching in preparation of a strike that didn't come. "Perhaps Gabriel will perceive more in time though."

Lionel clucked his tongue, moving to stand in front of me and gazing coldly down at me. "Well I can't have you go mad, Gabriel. So I have an opportunity for you this morning. The sun is due to rise in just under an hour. Fortunately, that is the exact time I have planned a celebration for the press."

"No," I gasped as I *saw* what he meant.

"Yes." His lips curled up cruelly. "Some of the rebels we captured have been quite useless to the crown. Their minds held very few helpful memories, and as traitors, there are only two fates left for them. The more promising subjects have been selected for a special...*project* we are undertaking. I will have you brought to the amphitheatre for the executions of the rest as a thank you for your service to your king." He turned away from me, grabbing Vard's shoulder and dragging him out of the room, the door snapping shut behind them.

My head dropped forward, my breaths coming heavily and my heart weighing down my chest. I'd failed everyone. Perhaps I should have killed myself before Lionel took me, because if they could find a way to wield my visions against my family, I was the reason they might find themselves in early graves.

I released a bellow of anguish, my muscles bulging against my restraints as murder sang my name. If only I could *see* a way to killing that monstrous fucking Dragon. If only the stars would give me an answer that would see him dead before he could rip that same vision from my head and learn of his demise in time for him to stop me.

"Give me a chance. I'll die for it if I have to. One fucking chance," I demanded of the stars, but they were deathly quiet.

The door opened again, and two large Dragon Shifters ducked through it in their Fae forms, moving to untie me and drag me along. I didn't bother to try and fight them, too weak to do anything but let them pull me through the luxurious corridors of the palace until eventually we stepped outside.

The sky was paling with the oncoming dawn, and I looked up at the stars as they began to fade from the night sky, watching quietly from their nest of darkness. I'd once been told that the stars were unbiased, that they only punished us if we invoked their wrath, but I couldn't pinpoint what it was that I'd done to deserve this. The only comfort I had was that there had been times in my life where things had seemed incredibly hopeless, and somehow the stars had offered me light in the end. Were there still paths before me that could offer us salvation? Or was I on the final road available to me, all lights around me flickering out until I was left in obscurity?

I was taken to the amphitheatre, its high, curving stone walls towering above me through the gloom before I was hauled through a wooden door at its base.

The cold swept over me, the air damp and the way forward lit with fiery torches on the walls. Somewhere beyond the dank passage I was in, prisoners were screaming and praying to the stars, the sound of our approach rousing them. My heart tripled its pace as we passed a corridor and I caught a glimpse of rebels locked in cells, cuffed hands reaching through the bars and wild, fearful eyes meeting mine. But I had nothing to offer them, no safe haven to give.

"Where is my wife?" a man screamed in demand. "Her name is Mary! They took her – where did they take her?"

A flash of bright lights and wicked magic speared through my mind, a woman tied to a table, begging for mercy. It was gone as quickly as it appeared, bile coating my tongue in its wake and my limbs trembling as the vision faded.

I was taken up a flight of stone steps, then out into the wide ring of sand at the centre of the amphitheatre, stone seats circling up around it.

The Dragons dragged me over to a cage of night iron at one side of the ring, unlocking it and pushing me inside. My legs gave out and I fell to the ground as the door clanged shut behind me, and they left me there alone.

The bed of sand beneath me was so soft, and the days of being kept awake to weaken my mind fell upon me all at once. I crashed into sleep, letting it guide me away on silver wings, so familiar to me that I wanted to curl up in their silken feathers forever.

"I love you, Gabriel. You're my little star, my guiding light."

The words felt like a long-forgotten memory stirring from the recesses of my mind, and they gave me the comfort of a boy in the arms of a loving Fae, because some part of me knew who they belonged to. My mother.

Blood.

Just as the dawn had arrived, the Nymphs had drained the rebels dry. Eight of them in total. Men and women, courageous Fae who had died to the cheers of a crowd and a press team recording every minute of it, live streaming it to drive fear into the hearts of anyone in the kingdom who might dare go against their king.

The rebels had been made to suffer, forced to fight the Nymphs hand to hand, and some of their limbs had been ripped off before they were given the reprieve of death. Their magic had been stolen by the Nymphs, the huge creatures fighting to claim the hearts of the strongest Fae among them, and I'd winced away from the final moments of the bloodbath.

I'd had to watch it all from the cage at the ring's edge, and the smug looks Lionel threw my way told me he was enjoying making me watch.

There was only a small measure of relief in the feeling of sanity that had been returned to me because of the newly risen sun, magic swelling in my chest at last. It wasn't like it was much good to me with the cuffs on my wrists, but it drove back the madness in my mind and let me think more clearly again.

Lionel sat up straight on his throne with Lavinia at his side, several large Dragon Shifters around him with magic flickering threateningly in their palms. Mildred was among them, wearing a silver breast plate, her chin tilted up and her undercut jaw grinding threateningly. Lionel wasn't taking any chances anymore, and I had no doubt he was sitting within a firm air shield, and plenty of other defensive spells too.

The crowd applauded as the Nymphs finished their squabbling and started dragging the bodies away into the underground chambers of the amphitheatre, leaving bloody trails behind them in the sand.

Lionel got to his feet, brushing his fingers over his throat to cast an amplifying spell before he spoke.

"Our victory runs deep. Today, we continue our celebrations while the last remnants of the enemy rebels run scared into the wilds. But rest assured, I, your mighty king, will hunt them down. I shall not sleep until every last insurgent is crushed and Solaria is safe once more. And to ensure the protection of the people from the traitors who remain at large, I am passing a new law. The rebels are comprised of the lesser Orders in the most part, from Pegasuses to Minotaurs, Tiberian Rats, Sphinxes, Heptian Toads, Experian Deer Shifters and many others. It is my duty to restrict their power until the threat of the insurgents can be eradicated. So, any Fae under the classification of a lesser Order will now require a permit to shift or use their Order gifts in public. Any lesser Fae found using their Order forms aggressively will be arrested without question."

A knot of horror formed in my chest at him using the rebels as an excuse to control more Fae, to strip away the rights of people he saw as less than him. It made me sick. And he was a fucking liar too because the rebels were made up of every kind of Order, and they were all willing to die to secure each other's rights.

"All hail the King!" Lavinia cried, rising to her feet and hugging Lionel's arm as her words were echoed in a fierce roar around the amphitheatre.

Lionel and his entourage slipped away through a door behind his throne and magic sparked against it as it shut, a telling sign that no one could follow.

The rest of the crowd started to leave, filing out of the stadium, some jeering me as they walked by, while others refused to meet my eye. A pale faced toddler met my gaze as his mother carried him in her arms, and my jaw ground at the idea of bringing a child to such a bloody event. I missed my own child with all I was and knew I could never subject him to the atrocities I'd witnessed here today.

It was a relief when the crowd was gone, the silence a blessing after so long stuck in the Royal Seer's Chamber, forced to endure more visions than I ever had at once. When I was that deep in The Sight, sometimes it didn't feel like I was me anymore. I was just a vessel for the stars to channel their perpetual plans, the possibilities of fate cycling through my mind, a thousand mysteries for me to decipher.

The responsibility of it all left me drained. I knew I might be holding vital answers, potential paths that could help my sisters win this war. The task of figuring out which roads could lead them to an advantage rested firmly on my shoulders. But right now, all I wanted to do was close my eyes and never have another vision again.

I rested my forehead against the bars, my hands curling around them as I bathed in the silence, certain it wouldn't last much longer. I didn't need my gifts to predict that Lionel was not even close to done with torturing me for visions he could use against my family and Solaria as a whole.

I blinked my eyes open at the sound of approaching footsteps, finding Orion being led across the sand by two large men in navy robes, his hands cuffed and a collar of shadow around his neck, but there was a look of relief in his gaze as he spotted me. He wore a tight white t-shirt with the symbol of a jade green Dragon on his chest, the words 'Just a Guy Who Loves His Dragon King' arching over it.

One of the men unlocked my cage, swinging the door wide before promptly turning away, heading back through a heavy metal door, and locking it tight behind them, leaving us alone. I glanced around in confusion, calling upon The Sight despite how wrecked my mind still felt, but when I sensed no danger, I rushed forward and wrapped my Nebula Ally in my arms.

He clasped me tight, a weighted sigh leaving him. "Hey Noxy."

"By the stars, Orio, are you alright?" I asked, drawing back but keeping hold of his shoulders as I searched his expression.

The Sight slammed into me, and I winced as I *saw* him bloody and bruised, laying on the stone floor of a cage, a vision that had plagued me since I'd arrived at the palace. I couldn't *see* anything more than that for him, not even who caused it, which led me to draw the conclusion that Lavinia was responsible.

"Well, I'm wearing this cunt of a t-shirt and it's not even the right size. So I'd say I've seen better days," he said, clasping my arm as he frowned. "What hell are they offering you?"

"They want my visions, of course," I muttered. "They've taken all I've *seen*. I held up my mental shields for as long as I could, but I…" I dropped my gaze as guilt stole through me and Orion gripped my arm tighter.

"You did all you could."

A lump rose in my throat as I nodded vaguely, knowing that was true, but it did nothing to ease the pressure in my chest. I looked around at the high walls surrounding the sandy ring, and when I looked to the future to *see* if we could escape that way, I *saw* us being captured by the Dragon guards posted in the grounds. I didn't have access to my Order thanks to Vard injecting me with Order suppressant, so I couldn't fly us out.

A vision snapped through my mind of Orion biting my wrist and my brows lifted.

"You're here to feed on me," I said in realisation.

"It must be more than that…" He glanced around the blood-stained ground, the quiet all too pressing.

I called on my gifts again and took a step back as I sensed the truth in what I *saw*. "Lionel believes I might perceive more of your fate, to *see* whether you have some plot against him while you're here, or any plans you may have to escape that he can thwart."

Orion's shoulders dropped. "Well, I guess this is my lucky day," he said dryly. "I have neither." His eyes sparked in realisation of something, and he looked to me in shock. "Wait, you don't know that Darcy is here, do you? You can't *see* her."

"She's here?" I gasped, lurching closer to him. "What's happened to her?"

Orion's face became grave and he started to recount the curse and how the Shadow Beast had taken possession of my sister in the battle, turning the tide against us by forcing her to fight against her own people. It killed me to know Darcy had gone through that, and now Orion was offering himself as a sacrifice to save her from this atrocious fate.

"I'll stay here until the three moon cycles are up," he finished darkly. "I have no plan except that, but with every passing day, I fear the Shadow Beast lays a deeper claim on her. On her magic too."

I turned my Sight towards my sister's future, but there was nothing I could grasp. It was murky, draped in shadow. If there was any chance of her coming through the other side of it, then I was useless to predict it.

"Thank you," I said thickly. "For doing this for her. Though I wish there was another way."

"Me too, brother," he said, and a cold wind swept around us as we stood together, shackled to the darkest of destinies.

"I'm so sorry about Darius," I said. The moment I'd *seen* the truth, my heart had broken for Tory, and sadness had engulfed me.

Orion's features flinched in pain, and he nodded sadly, saying nothing, though his desolate expression said everything.

"Have you *seen* the others? Are they safe?" he asked.

"Yes, I've *seen* them. They're together, though thankfully I can't *see* the direction they're taking or their plans. My family are well versed in how to avoid me predicting their moves when they want to, so I hope they're teaching all the rebels to keep every decision random."

"Leon will be great at that," Orion said, cracking half a smile and I mirrored him, releasing a breath of amusement.

"He'll be driving everyone mad with his acts of randomness," I said.

"He'll take it way too far," Orion agreed, and my chest lightened a little.

"Let's hope they all have a plan to strike at Lionel that I will never *see* coming. I would dearly love to be surprised by the sight of his head suddenly exploding, or a spear puncturing his chest."

A door opened on the other side of the amphitheatre and Lionel appeared in all his finery, his jade green robes sweeping around his body as he strode towards us, head held high and a gleaming golden sword at his hip.

Vard scampered along in his wake and three huge Dragon Shifters in their Fae forms walked at his back, towering over him and casting long shadows in the morning sun.

My spine straightened and Orion moved to stand at my side defensively, though without our magic we were pretty much fucked if things turned nasty.

"Did you enjoy the show?" Lionel asked smugly as he came to stand in front of us.

Neither of us answered and he regarded us coldly.

"Well then, I shall cut straight to the point. Lance, I have your mate just beyond those doors, chained and at my mercy." Lionel pointed to the tall wooden doors at the far end of the arena.

Orion strode forward in a threatening stance and Lionel's hand whipped out, slamming into the centre of his chest to stop him in his tracks.

"Let her go," Orion snarled, his fangs bared in warning.

"One more move, and I'll give the order for her to be killed." Lionel sneered. "And I'll make sure she's back in her Fae form, naked and begging on her knees before she dies at my hand. Lavinia is not here to stop me this time."

The words made him snap, and Orion threw himself at Lionel with a growl tearing from his throat and a bid for murder in his eyes. He hit an air shield and in the next second Lionel drew his sword, the morning light catching on the gold before he slammed it through the centre of my friend's chest.

I shouted out in terror, lurching forward to catch Orion as Lionel yanked the blade back out, leaving a gaping, bloody hole behind it.

"By the stars," Lionel exhaled. "I've wanted to do that for such a long time."

Blood spilled from Orion's mouth, his knees hitting the sand and the weight of him taking me down with him. He fell onto his back across my knees, and I clasped the wound on his chest, desperate for the magic in my veins that I couldn't harness.

"Hold on," I gasped in panic, fear and pain blossoming through me unbearably fast.

"Free. Her," he managed to say, his eyes blazing at me in a furious demand for me to agree. I was already nodding, feeling this goodbye coming upon me too quick, the shock of it leaving me raw. His eyes turned to the sky and stars glittered within them as they claimed his soul, stealing him away from me before I'd even had a chance to say goodbye…

I blinked and the vision faded, finding Orion in front of me again, solidly there, still alive.

"Fuck," I breathed, fearful of the vision I'd just witnessed.

"What?" he asked, just as the door opened at the end of the amphitheatre and Lionel appeared with his jade green robes sweeping around his body as he strode towards us, that gleaming gold sword at his hip a promise of what was to come if I couldn't change the hand of fate.

"Do as I say, unless you wish to die here and now," I hissed at my friend, and he nodded quickly, trusting my visions and my ability to change what I had *seen.*

Vard hurried along in Lionel's wake and three Dragon Shifters walked at his back.

My spine straightened and Orion moved to stand at my side defensively, just like I'd *seen* him do before.

"Did you enjoy the show?" Lionel asked smugly as he came to stand in front of us.

Neither of us answered and he regarded us coldly.

"Well then, I shall cut straight to the point. Lance, I have your mate just beyond those doors, chained and at my mercy." Lionel pointed to the tall wooden doors at the far end of the pit of sand and I readied myself for what was to come.

Orion strode forward in a threatening stance and Lionel's hand whipped out, slamming into the centre of his chest to stop him in his tracks.

"Let her go," he snarled, his fangs glinting.

"One more move, and I'll give the order for her to be killed." Lionel sneered. "And I'll make sure she's back in her Fae form, naked and begging on her knees before she dies at my hand. Lavinia is not here to stop me this time."

"Orio, stand down," I barked, grabbing his arm to draw him away and his muscles tightened as he held himself back from his impulse to attack. He glanced around at me, and I gave him a firm look that spoke of the terrible fate that awaited him if he didn't listen.

He retreated, returning to my side, his fingers flexing as he ached for magic and a kill that neither of us were going to get today.

"Good boy," Lionel said mockingly, fate shifting and a breath of relief escaping me as Orion's future spilled out ahead of him once more, no longer cut short here and now.

Lionel snapped his fingers and a pair of high wooden doors groaned as they opened at the far end of the arena. A beast of shadow was dragged out of it by chains around its throat, four Nymphs hauling it onto the sand as it fought to get free of them.

Orion lurched forward, shouting my sister's name and sending my heart into a riot as I realised this was the monstrous creature she was bound to, that this monster was her. This was her curse, and it was a terrifying thing to behold.

"I'll do whatever you want, just let her go," Orion begged in earnest, catching on to the threat in the air.

"First of all, I want you to kneel for me," Lionel said slowly, savouring the power he held over us all as he gestured to the ground at his feet.

Orion's muscles bunched but I gave him a look that told him to get fucking moving and he didn't hesitate any longer, dropping down on his knees before Lionel.

Darcy roared, thrashing against her restraints and I met her gaze, finding her soul right there in the beast's eyes. She was present, not lost to the Shadow Beast as Orion had described during the battle. Maybe she could fight this yet.

I gave her a look, trying to convey that I would do everything in my power to protect her and her mate, and I stepped closer behind Orion.

"You will sift through his fates, Gabriel," Lionel instructed. "And Vard will syphon your visions from you while you do so. You will leave no stone unturned; I wish to see every fate in his future."

Orion shuddered and I took a moment to *see* what might happen if I refused, finding myself holding a bleeding, dying Orion once more and deciding there was no other option but for me to do this.

"I'm sorry, Orio," I murmured, and he let his head hang forward, ready for me to do what I had to. Vard hurried forward, slicking his tongue across his lips like this was whetting his appetite.

The Cyclops touched the back of my head and I shut my eyes, praying I wasn't going to find anything in Orion's mind that could give Lionel more ammo for his war.

The first thing I felt were my friend's mental shields but they began to bend, allowing me in. But before I could begin to *see* into his future, a bubble of thought slipped into my vision. Its edges were almost undetectable, and I quickly created a path through my own mind that Vard's Cyclops Invasion could not touch. It was delicate, complex shielding, and I had to focus hard to keep it separate from him. Carefully, I let part of my mind slip into that thought, keeping the rest of it from Vard's clutches.

"If I see *anything that can help us, I'll place it here and keep it from Vard,"* I spoke to Orion through the connection of our minds.

The pressure of casting such complicated magic was high, and I wasn't sure I could manage it only that Orion and I already had a close connection which would help us work together in this.

"Get on with It," Vard snarled impatiently.

I let the first vision rush in, *seeing* Orion in agony after some terrible torture as I had countless times since I'd arrived in the palace. I let Vard have that, grimacing at the awful knowledge of what Orion had been going through and was still yet to suffer through. The next visions were much the same, but many futures were wrapped in darkness, impossible for me to see at all. Then, among the pain, the cold, hard floor of the throne room and the torment my Nebula Ally had to endure, a glint of something different caught my mind's eye, and like a cat before a shard of light, I leapt towards it.

I continued to feed Vard the images of blood and terror while carving this other vision out and feeling Orion's mind shielding it too, offering it extra protection from the hungry Cyclops at my back.

When it was safe within a pocket in my head, I let it play out, watching as Orion slipped into the walls of the palace and delved deep, deep down beneath it through a secret passage. At its end was a bright silver door with a huge coat of arms at its centre, the Vega crest twinkling with age old magic.

I *saw* Orion beyond that door, and inside were countless treasures, a long-forgotten throne, and answers to something I couldn't fathom but which was endlessly important. The lasting moments in the visions showed Orion with a book in his hands, the cover woven from bronze feathers, and the look of hope in his eyes gave me more hope than I'd had in weeks. When this moment arose, I could sense the time he would have to find his way in and out of that mysterious place before anyone came searching for him. Hours. Three at least.

I focused hard and passed the vision to Orion, the grip of his mind taking it from me while I worked to pass Vard more visions of my Nebula Ally beaten and bloody. I could *see* his anticipation over getting into those tunnels, his desire to find me and break me free.

"You cannot free me this way. The tunnels do not lead to me."

I sent those words through to him as a vision of their own, then released my grip on his mind and stepped backwards with a jerk, knocking into Vard, sending him crashing onto the sand with a curse.

"My bad. I didn't *see* you there," I muttered.

"Very funny," he spat, shoving to his feet while Lionel looked to him impatiently.

"Well?" he demanded.

"Nothing, sire," Vard snivelled, brushing sand from his knees. "Lance Orion's future holds only suffering."

"Good." Lionel stepped forward, clapping Orion mockingly on the cheek. "Let me tell you this, Lance...the moment Lavinia leaves an opening for me to kill the Vega girl, I will execute her so viciously that you will beg me to kill you after. And I *will* grant that request, do you hear me?" He raised a finger, pressing it to Orion's heart and my friend snarled as Lionel scored a target there with fire, singing a hole in his t-shirt and leaving a reddened burn in his wake.

"Yeah, I hear what you're saying loud and clear," Orion said. "You're Lavinia's little bitch."

"How *dare* you speak to me that way?" Lionel hissed, raising a hand to strike him with magic, and a vision of death crossed my eyes that had me momentarily bound in terror.

"What are you doing, Daddy?" Lavinia came flying down over the high walls of the amphitheatre on a cloud of darkness, descending from the sky and drawing Lionel's attention to her as she came to hover beside him. He jerked away from her, and my muscles tensed with the instinct to fight. "You're not playing with my toys without me, are you?"

She landed in front of Orion, cocking her head to one side, and caressing his arm like she was petting him. He remained in place, but his muscles went rigid, and a growl rolled from my throat in response, drawing her death-black eyes to me.

"Hello, little Seer. Are you jealous of the attention your pretty friend is getting? I can always make room for you in my playroom too." She reached for me, but Lionel lunged forward, yanking me to his side possessively.

"Take Lance. Do what you want with him. I have work to attend to." Lionel tossed me into the arms of his Dragon guards.

I looked back at Orion in fear as Lavinia lashed a whip of shadow to the collar at his throat, then to Darcy in the form of the Shadow Beast as she continued to fight against her restraints.

Vard scampered after us and the Dragons forced me towards the exit. As I was hauled away from Darcy and Orion, I held onto the knowledge that I'd given my friend a vision that could hopefully be of some help, though how he would have a chance to get into those passages, I couldn't yet *see*. But perhaps that meant Darcy held the answers, for her fate was shrouded in shadow, and maybe this time, that darkness in her would let in some light.

Scorpio
Gemini
Virgo
Cancer
Aries
Leo
Sagittarius
Taurus
Capricorn
Aquarius
Libra
Pisces

TORY

CHAPTER TWENTY FIVE

Geraldine had been up half the night wielding her earth magic plus Max's power - which he'd donated to her cause through some kind of bagel-based bribery if I was understanding her correctly. An entire night and morning had passed while I did nothing beyond sitting on a rock at the far edge of the island we'd ripped from the edge of Solaria, staring out into the depths of the inky water surrounding us on all sides.

A flame burned beside me, an ever-present companion to my solitude as I let my power recharge and occasionally sent a blast of magic into the sea to change our trajectory at random. But while I'd sat there wallowing in the distance growing between me and my sister with every passing moment, Geraldine had been hard at work. And as the brightest rays of sunlight had spilled down onto me marking the zenith of the sun's arc, she'd come running towards me in her Cerberus form, barking a command for me to join her while her tail wagged in a frenzied way, giving me no choice but to agree.

She'd even given me a ride back here, the lolloping gait of her enormous canine form bringing a breath of laughter to my lips despite all I had to wallow over. As we crested a hill near the centre of the huge island, my breath caught in my lungs and Geraldine finally fell still.

"What…how?" I breathed, sliding from her back and landing beside her so that she could shift and give me the answer to that question.

Geraldine returned to her Fae form, a broad smile on her mouth as she set her bare feet on the grass and planted her fists on her hips.

"My lady, may I present the R.U.M.P. Castle, the crown jewel upon the head of Solaria, the wandering castle to the true queens and the seat upon which you shall sit while guiding the home to the rebellion during the War of Shadows and Heartache."

"I thought you were calling it the War of the Reborn?" I muttered, remembering that small fact, but Geraldine swiped a flippant hand through the air.

"It's a work in progress," she explained, gesturing for me to focus on the view ahead, and I stilled as I really took it in.

My lips parted at the castle she had created in the dead of night, turrets of stone and ice carved above an enormous drawbridge that crossed a moat filled with flowing water, which I seriously doubted had been there before.

There were flowers blooming in deepest red and midnight blue up the sides of the stunning building, their petals shifting in a breeze I couldn't feel, making them look like living flames as they danced with the motion.

The building had nothing on the size of The Palace of Souls, looking more homely than imposing, though I guessed it would still house plenty of Fae.

"There aren't words for this," I said in a low voice as Geraldine took my arm and drew me forward, marching at a fierce pace.

As we closed in on the drawbridge, Max stepped out of the trees, his jaw ticking as he threw a wall of water up around us, blocking us from view. He stepped straight through it a moment later, bone dry despite the torrent he had just carved his way through and holding out a dress for Geraldine to put on.

"Oh you nibleberry nagfish," she sighed as she took the thing from him and tugged it on. It was white and a bit on the small side for Geraldine's voluptuous curves, meaning her tits were practically exploding from it and her nipples were still visible through the material.

"No," Max snarled, lifting his hands to try and cover her again but she knocked him aside with an impatient huff, casting two shells of ice over her boobs to cover them a bit better while rolling her eyes at him.

"Honestly, Maxy boy, anyone would think you are afraid I might wander from your dingle dangler at any given moment with the way you go on," she sighed, wafting him out of her path and tugging me along with her through the wall of water.

It took little more than a thought for me to keep the water from touching my skin as I walked with her, and I couldn't help but think back to our first lesson on water magic when Darcy and I had found such simple control of our power so challenging.

"After much nattering from the rabble, I was coerced into creating some additional sleeping space down here for some of the lower ranking members of your court and our wafsome allies," Geraldine explained as we crossed the drawbridge and stepped into the entranceway of the castle.

Max tried to follow us inside, but Geraldine barked at him to remain yonder while she escorted me around my new abode and threw her magic at the drawbridge mechanism to make it slam in his face while he shouted his objections at us from beyond it.

Geraldine sighed like she was some long-suffering wife, pinching the bridge of her nose between her thumb and forefinger, then casting a silencing bubble to block out Max's shouts. She gave me a rueful smile and patted my arm before tugging me further inside.

The beauty of the place extended within, ice carvings of Phoenixes decorating the stone walls, depicting Darcy and me in scenes that I remembered surviving through battle and bloodshed, the entire thing seeming so much more impressive than it had felt at the time. Honestly, I just felt like I was faking my way through this game of power and politics most days, but in the images Geraldine had rendered of the two of us, we looked regal, beautiful, confident and impressive. Like we really were queens.

Geraldine batted away every attempt I made at complimenting the work she'd done on this place, telling me repeatedly that it was little more than a cow shed with a flower on top of it and still required much more work. But if this was a cow shed, then I had definitely grown up in a pig pen, or maybe a cesspit.

She led me towards a short corridor to the left of the central entry hall which was half hidden beneath the grand staircase, knocking open a door and revealing a plain, unadorned room within. It looked about the same size as my dorm back at Zodiac Academy, had a basic wooden bed with a scattering of straw for a mattress and the floor was just hard-packed dirt. It almost seemed as though it couldn't be a part of the same building that we'd entered a few moments ago.

"What's this for?" I asked curiously.

"This is Melinda Altair's chamber," Geraldine explained with a shrug. "There's one for each of the shamed and denounced former Councillors and their family members down here."

"All of their family members?" I asked, looking at the squat space and trying not to snort in amusement. "Even the Heirs?"

"What precisely are those three dongleberries heirs to anymore?" Geraldine asked me curiously, turning us around and drawing me away from the dark and forgotten corridor she'd crafted for the use of the non-royalists in our company. I doubted they would happily sleep in those rooms, they'd probably just use their own magic to make a counter-castle that was even bigger than this one. "There is no Celestial Council anymore, they hold no claim to the throne through bloodline or weight of their own power. Some might say they are shamed beyond all reproach, have come crawling for pity at the feet of the true queens and are lucky to even be allowed to step foot upon the R.U.M.P. at all."

"Are you 'some'?" I asked in faint amusement, and she winked at me.

"Maybe I am. Though perhaps I should be forced to bed down there with the rabble too after so shamefully linking myself to that scandalous sealion out there," she mused.

"Max?" I asked and she nodded gravely, her brow furrowed.

"I have so tried to tempt my Lady Petunia away from his fine hose. But alas, her mind is set upon him and…I fear my heart may have followed in her wake."

I tugged her to a halt at the foot of an enormous frozen staircase and turned to face her, taking her hands in mine as I looked into her deep blue eyes.

"Geraldine," I said firmly. "If Max is it for you, then let him be it. This war, this doubt and uncertainty we live in has only confirmed one thing to me, and that's how brief life can be and how quickly it can be stolen from us at any point in time. So don't waste any more of it simply because he hasn't knelt for me and Darcy. I don't give a fuck about that anyway." I swallowed against a lump in my throat as I forced the next words past my lips. "Darius never knelt for me either, but I didn't want him to. Not in the end. All I really wanted was for him to be mine, and I had far less of that than I might have done if I'd just accepted what he was to me sooner."

Geraldine's lower lip wobbled, and she reached for me like she was going to embrace me, but I shook my head, hardening that wall of ice and fire surrounding my shattered heart as I refused to feel any of it.

"I don't want pity," I said firmly, my hatred for the stars rising like lava through the core of me. "I just want you to go out there and grab that fish boy by the balls and tell him he's yours, bad choices in politics be damned."

"I…" Geraldine glanced towards the drawbridge like she might be about to do precisely that, but she raised her chin and gave me a rueful grin instead. "I may just do that, my lady, but I think I'll allow him to flounder out there a touch longer before I do."

I snorted and let her lead me on through the castle she'd spent the entire night building. There was a room laid out for war councils, a round table far grander than the one we'd used back at the ruins, ready with a map of Solaria at the heart of it and murals of a dismembered jade green Dragon hanging on every wall. Then there was a huge kitchen, a dining hall fit for a medieval banquet with a high table presiding over the others, two huge chairs carved with mine and Darcy's names at the centre of it.

Upstairs there were two more floors, one set up with far grander rooms which Geraldine declared would be used by the members of our court, a group she reminded me needed selecting officially as I looked at the four poster beds and lavishly decorated spaces.

"I thought our inner circle was pretty clear," I pointed out as she continued the tour. "There's you-"

Geraldine squealed and fell to her knees at my offhanded remark. I had my damn sword in hand and a fistful of fire before I realised she was just overwhelmed and bowing to me, sobbing all over my boots and thanking me relentlessly for the great honour I had bestowed upon her.

"Get up," I begged her, sheathing my sword, and grabbing her arm as I heaved her to her feet. "You can't seriously have doubted that we'd want you by our sides through all of this?" I asked incredulously as tears and snot ran freely down her face and she seemed in real danger of hyperventilating.

"You…mean to take…little old me…as one of your chosen…most honoured… most beloved-"

"Yes, Geraldine," I said, helping her out as her sobs made it almost impossible to make out her words, and she flung herself at me, squeezing me so tightly I feared for the integrity of my ribcage as she fell apart entirely.

"Who else might we send an official word to, to confirm their place among your court?" she managed to ask me, though she was still trembling so violently that I didn't dare release her.

"Err, I dunno," I hedged, though my mind instantly went to Xavier. I had to wonder if he would even want to accept a position like that from me, knowing the ex-Councillors had plans for him to join their circle as the Fire Lord, but he was my family. One of the few members I had left now, and I knew I needed to offer this to him even if he chose not to accept it. Though for now I decided to keep that to myself. "I guess Sofia and Tyler," I said, giving Geraldine an answer.

"Oh yes!" she cried, releasing me so fast that I almost fell over.

She whipped a hand beside her, and a scroll appeared there with a fucking quill to match, all cast from her magic so quickly that they almost seemed to fall from the air itself.

"I shall make a list of positions that need to be assigned," she announced. "Do you have anyone in particular in mind to help manage your army? We need a true and stalwart gal or gander to take on the role of liaising with the people and making sure that their voices are heard. I, of course, will gladly assist in such a role as my sweet papa would have wanted, but with my duties to fight and remain at your side, I think it might be prudent to attach someone else to the role too. Someone who has experience in commanding authority and whose loyalty is unwavering and unquestionable. Someone who can be trusted to convey the true, honest needs and wants of your people so that they might best be served. Can you think of any such a noble Fae?"

"I'm pretty sure the person you're describing doesn't actually exist," I said, frowning as I tried to think of someone who could do the things she'd described, though one name came to mind and stuck there like a wet leaf clinging to an unwilling frog.

"Oh, that cannot be, my lady, the stars have always had a guiding hand in…" she trailed off at the look which darkened my features with the mention of the stars, and I sighed.

"We need someone used to leading groups of people, yes?"

"Indeed."

"Someone who publicly denounced Lionel and fought against him when they could have easily pretended submission and stayed out of this war?"

"That would be most preferable," she agreed, and I winced a little at the name which was the only one that came to mind.

"Well… I think Washer pretty much fits that bill."

Geraldine's mouth parted in what might have been shock, or horror, or some combination of the two, but when it came down to it, if we ignored the Speedos and overly tactile behaviour, Washer was actually half decent. He had bowed to us and thrown his lot in with us, even though it meant losing his job and his relationship falling apart. He was used to commanding groups of unruly students too, so he had experience in managing people, and with his Siren gifts, he'd be able to sense any needs the rebels had without even having to wait for the issues to be brought to him.

"I shall have an order sent to the wigglesome worm himself post haste," she said firmly. "As you say, he has indeed proven himself a fine and worthy candidate – even if his attire often leaves a lot to be desired."

"Yeah, maybe we should get him an official uniform," I suggested. "Something buttoned up to the neck and baggy on the ass."

Geraldine's eyes sparkled with that idea, and she wrote it down, the words glaring back at me from the page.

A.S.S. costume for Washer.

I supressed a shudder at the mental image those words conjured in my mind, reassuring myself that the uniform itself would most definitely be modest and sensible – not a nipple or wandering ball sack in sight.

"Alright then, now we're rolling," she said, giving me a nudge to get me climbing the next staircase which led up to the highest level of the castle. "Who else would you like to be officially enrolled into your court?"

"Dante Oscura and his family have been loyal to us from the moment we met them," I said as I thought on it. "I doubt they'll want to serve the crown long-term if we win this war, but I value their input enough to want them with us while it lasts at least."

"Say no more, my Queen, I shall see it done."

Geraldine wrote their names down then stuffed the scroll into her cleavage before hurrying the last few steps to the huge doors awaiting us at the top. She grasped the handles and threw the doors wide at once, light spilling through them from an enormous suite of private rooms intended for me and Darcy.

I didn't have words for the beauty of what she'd created as I strode between the bedrooms and stunning bathing area, my heart full of gratitude for her doing this for us as well as awe over her talent.

"Geraldine, this is-"

"I know it is nothing in the face of all you have abandoned at your true home in The Palace of Souls," she interrupted me as I stepped into the room she'd designed for me, finding my few possessions already there and a fire lit in the hearth.

The room was big but still cosy, the walls decorated in red and black roses which crept up and over the bed then hung down over it, a delicate scent coating the air. There was a large copper bathtub beneath a window formed with ice standing on a slightly raised area to my right, and a desk for me to sit at too. My clothes had been placed in a walk-in closet to the left of the space and Geraldine started telling me her plans to create more garments as soon as possible.

I nodded along, feeling somehow detached from the girl who was being shown around this place, the room I would now own, the bed I would occupy alone without a single thing here belonging to the man I should have shared it with.

"There is a training area on the roof with targets and practice dummies, all manner of things for you to train with, whether with weapon or magic, should you so wish," Geraldine was saying, but I was finding it hard to hear her.

I unbuckled my scabbard and dropped my sword onto the desk before sinking down on the edge of the bed and staring at the roses adorning the walls. The flowers in Darcy's room were pink and blue, Geraldine had already explained to me, and I nodded vacantly, trying not to see blood in the deep red of the roses before me.

"Where's Darius's treasure?" I blurted, interrupting something she'd been saying about magical targets, my fingers curling into the softness of the bed sheets with a grip that was far too tight and not tight enough.

"I…think that it was being transported by a herd of Minotaurs…" Geraldine seemed to realise that I was on the verge of cracking because she stopped mid-sentence and raised her chin. "I will fetch it now, sweet lady love of mine. Forgive me, I should have thought, I was distracted but I should have thought to make sure it was here. I shall gladly flay the skin from my bosom in penance for my failure this day. I shall scoop both eyes from my skull and drop them in a lagoon. I shall scald the skin from my fingers and allow a rat to eat the remains of-"

"Don't do any of those things," I said as firmly as I could manage, shaking my head even as screams rang in the confines of my skull. "It isn't important. Just forget about it. I just need a few minutes."

My grip on the bedding tightened until I could feel my fingernails trying to puncture the skin of my palms through it. Geraldine opened and closed her mouth several times before bowing so low that her nose brushed the ground, then she fled the room.

The second the door closed, a silencing bubble burst from me and I released a scream so loud that I was surprised the entire building didn't come falling down on top of my head.

This was all wrong. I shouldn't have been here, sitting in a castle surrounded by beautiful things while my sister was missing. While Darius lay cold and alone on the side of some forgotten mountain.

I'd let the others talk me into leaving him there to rest alongside Hamish and Catalina. I'd let them convince me it was the right place for him, beneath the open sky, surrounded by such strong magic that no one but those of us who had cast it would be able to find them again.

But now I was here, and I was alone, sitting on the edge of a bed meant for two, a band of metal on my finger binding me to a man who would never again look me in the eyes and call me his.

I pushed off of the bed and slumped to the floor, my fingers taking hold of my hair and tearing at it as I dropped my forehead to my knees and fell into the deep hole within me.

The walls I'd been building so forcefully were cracking, the weight of all I tried to hold back within them pressing out too powerfully.

I would die from this pain. Slowly but surely, it would consume me and rot everything good I had ever claimed for my own. And I couldn't even say I cared about that anymore.

I screamed again, fire igniting across my body as my wings burst from my back and sent the bed screeching across the floorboards behind me.

I managed to hold onto the power of the flames just enough to stop them from burning this beautiful castle to the ground, but I let it have me. Hotter and hotter I blazed until the glow from my own flesh was too much and I was forced to close my eyes against the power of it.

I was fury incarnate, a raging void that craved nothing but death and an end to all things.

Lionel Acrux's face flashed through my mind, and I burned him up too, watching him scream as the skin melted from his bones and the fire in me consumed those as well until he was nothing but ash, then not even that. A simple stain on the map of the world where he had once stood tall and dared call himself king.

The ruby pendant which hung from my neck seemed to heat beyond even the power of the flames, a pulse sounding within it as though the heart of it had come alive, beating to a rhythm I knew as intimately as my own pulse. Like he was there, his chest pressed to mine, our souls linked as one, reaching for each other even through the barrier of the Veil.

Could he see me? Was he watching me break for him with knowing eyes, wondering where the girl he had fallen for had gone in the wake of his end?

The door banged against the wall as it was thrown open, the sound of gold and jewels hitting the floor making me look up from my own personal pit of despair as Caleb dropped the huge chest of treasure to the floor and let the pieces scatter everywhere.

He said nothing as he moved to sit before me on the floor, his fangs snapping out as he let me see the monster in him too, no sign from him that the fire I was wielding frightened him. No sign that he believed I was as close to losing control of it as I felt.

"You need to keep moving," he said to me in a low voice, his eyes dark and full of the same pain which was blinding me. "You need to be doing something real, not sitting in a castle tower, waiting for the world to come find you."

I choked out a laugh or maybe it was a sob, the sound so fucking hopeless that it was impossible to tell.

"I thought I was supposed to be leading an army?" I replied hollowly.

"No one said you have to stay sitting here to do it. What about that promise you made? What about Darcy?"

A rush of longing ran through me at the mention of my sister's name and with a force of pure will, I banished my Phoenix.

Caleb arched an eyebrow at me, his gaze dropping to my body for half a heartbeat. I realised with a flash of irritation that I'd been even closer to losing control than I'd thought as I found my clothes missing and the wooden floor beneath me scorched and blackened by the heat of my flames. I brushed a hand over my hair, thankful to find that at least had survived.

"Don't go blushing on me now, pretty boy. It's not like you haven't seen it all before," I ground out as I stood, turning my ass to him, and striding towards the closet with intent. Because he was right. I didn't have to sit around in this fancy castle and Geraldine had already given me a place to start.

I ignored the beautiful gowns hanging on the rail, pushing them aside and finding the practical clothes I needed before tugging on a black crop top and a pair of matching sweatpants. I looked about as queenly as the street thief I'd been before I came to this fucking kingdom, and I was more than okay with that.

I brushed my fingers over the two necklaces hanging at my throat. The ruby from Darius was still warm to the touch, though there was no echo of a pulse lingering within it. Had I imagined that it had been there at all? But even as I wondered that, the scent of him seemed to wrap around me, that smoke and cedar rolling along the back of my tongue and making me think of all the kisses we'd shared from brutal to tender and everything in between. I shifted my fingers from the necklace he had given me to the Imperial Star which my sister should have worn, the thing thrumming with hidden power too.

I pushed my power into the star, wondering if it might submit to me now, when I needed it most, but there was no answering call to my magic, nothing to say that it even knew I was there, knocking on the sealed door which contained its incredible power.

I exhaled through my nose, releasing my grip on the necklaces and focusing on the task I had decided upon.

I kicked on a pair of sneakers and pulled my hair into a high ponytail before expelling a deep breath and striding back into the bedroom.

Caleb was leaning against the door, casually flicking through something on a shiny new Atlas and I frowned at the item as he glanced up at me.

"Tyler got done working on a bunch of these for the trustworthy rebels to have," he explained, taking another from his pocket and tossing it to me. "They've been shielded with magic to make sure they can't be traced, so they're safe to use. I assume we'll be leaving, so we're going to need to be able to call someone for a location to stardust back to when we're done."

I dropped the Atlas into my pocket, noticing the bed had been moved back into position and now mostly covered the blackened patch of flooring, hiding all the evidence that remained of me losing my shit.

I stepped over the treasure which was still spread across the floor, not making any attempt to move it, simply taking reassurance in the fact that it was here, safe, like he would want it to be.

The urge to count each and every piece tugged at me, and I looked over my shoulder sharply, almost expecting to see him there, bitching about the golden trinkets which were scattered across my floor and threatening to beast-out if it wasn't all carefully counted and polished immediately. I shook my head to dispel it of the ghost I was imagining, knowing that no spirit would ever be enough to fill the void in me even if I did find one lurking close to me.

Caleb tossed me a pouch of stardust, then held out a hand for me, and I moved towards him, letting him lift me into his arms and looping an arm around his neck.

"You know where we're going?" he confirmed as he tightened his grip on me.

"Yeah," I agreed because it was the only faint hope of a plan I had, and it was all I'd been able to think about since the moment Geraldine had suggested it. I'd held back out of some vague sense of responsibility to the people on this island, but that wasn't what I needed to be responsible for. I had to focus on the things I required to stand any chance of victory and the first of those goals was clear. Darcy.

"Okay then." Caleb shot into motion.

My stomach swooped as he raced us out of the castle past a group of Fae who I couldn't even hope to recognise at the speed we were travelling, then away across the open green land which made up the centre of the island we'd cleaved from Solaria.

The cold bit at us mercilessly as he moved faster than the wind and I found myself clinging to him for dear life as the world became a blur all around us while he raced for the edge of the wards where we would be able to disappear into the clutches of the stars.

In no time at all, he had made it to the clifftop on the western side of the island, the point where the land had once been attached to Solaria now nothing but an unforgiving drop into the depths of the ocean below.

Caleb didn't slow as he ran for it, leaping straight from the edge and into the void beyond.

We began to fall, the water rushing up towards us at speed, the motion reminding me of a time long ago when we'd done this very thing before, when our problems had seemed so big and yet now seemed so incredibly small in hindsight.

I took a pinch of stardust from the bag he'd given me and tossed it over our heads just before we could hit the water.

The world twisted all around us, the stars looking on with their greedy eyes, and I was really tempted to flip them all off and tell them to get fucked. But even as I thought of it, they spat us back out again and we appeared on a lush hillside, a mountainous terrain sweeping out around us in an endless sea of green.

We were still falling as we appeared, but a gust of my air magic caught us and set Caleb down on his feet before he released me too, both of us looking around in confusion at the yawning, empty space which surrounded us.

"There's nothing here," Caleb muttered, turning to take in the wild and untainted landscape we found ourselves in.

Everything here was a deep and vibrant green, the rolling mountains painted in the colour, and the air so fresh that breathing it in felt like waking up more fully than I had in weeks. There were no roads or paths, no signs at all of inhabitants beyond the lone eagle I spotted soaring through the low clouds above our heads. The air felt thick with moisture, rain oncoming or recently passed and the silence was of the heavy, unrelenting kind which I had never once known while growing up in a bustling city. There was peace here, untainted and unfractured, just a natural, endless peace which set my body at ease in a purely organic way.

"There's the lake," I pointed out, drawing Caleb's attention to the still water which spread out in a bowl between the mountains at his back.

Caleb turned to look at the steely grey expanse and together we started walking towards it, our boots treading on springy moss as we followed the impossibly green hillside down to where it met with the water's edge.

The world was still here, harmony encompassing every bit of the surrounding landscape in a way that was alien and yet alluring all at once. It was as if nothing resided here beyond the solitude and wilderness, this oasis of calm lost within a world I knew was fraught with war and suffering.

Even our soft footsteps on the mossy ground sounded loud here, the silence stretching between us as we maintained it, not wanting to taint the serenity we'd discovered with unnecessary words.

We fell still as we made it to the lakeshore, the toes of my boots crunching in the slate-coloured gravel marking the water's edge.

A few heartbeats passed, but nothing happened, no one came to greet us the way Darcy had described to me, no island sat in the centre of the water nor grew from the depths of that mirror-like pane of glass.

"Maybe there's no one home," Caleb mused, bending down to claim a piece of slate from the ground before throwing it out into the lake.

The stone skipped five times, ripples arcing out in its wake before it sank into the icy depths and was lost.

We watched in silence as the ripples spread across the surface, the disturbance eerie in this too calm place and yet still, nothing happened.

"I am Roxanya Vega," I called out, the loudness of my voice a harsh break to the peace. "Daughter of the Savage King and the Greatest Seer of their generation. I wish to gain entry to the Library of the Lost."

Nothing replied to my request beyond the echoes of my own voice resounding from the mountains that surrounded us and I sighed.

"Do we head back?" Caleb asked me uncertainly, but I shook my head.

"I came here to visit a fucking library. And I'm not leaving until I've checked out some books."

I took his hand, and he didn't protest as I drew him with me towards the lake, air magic circling us as we strode straight into the water, carving a path through it with the arrowhead of air that surrounded us and descending beneath the surface.

A flick of my fingers sent flares of Phoenix fire tumbling away through the blackness of the water ahead, lighting the way on as we strode towards the centre of the lake where I knew the library was hidden.

"What if they still refuse to open the door when we find it?" Caleb asked curiously, no concern in his voice.

"Then I'll break in," I replied with a shrug. "I'm beyond the point of niceties. Darcy needs me, and the only hope I have of finding her is locked within their precious sanctuary. If they don't want to help me with that, then that makes them my enemies. And my enemies are forming a nasty habit of ending up as soot."

"Savage," he commented, the corner of his lips twitching with approval.

"Whatever it takes."

Deeper and deeper we delved into the lake, the weight of the water above us pressing down with impossible intensity on the roof of my air shield, but I didn't falter, simply pushing more power into it to reinforce it as we went.

The light of the flares I shot out ahead of us lit up shoals of small fish which darted away from the invasion of their underwater kingdom, their scales flashing silver as they fled.

"Look." Caleb jerked his chin to draw my attention to our right and I fell still as I spotted several huge, nameless shadows circling just out of sight, the silt at the bottom of the lake billowing up to disguise their bodies as they moved.

I flicked my fingers towards them, Phoenix fire tumbling away from us in an attempt to illuminate them, but the dark swallowed the flames before I could see more than a flash of scales.

"Do you think those things guard the library?" I asked, my heart leaping as an enormous, red tentacle was revealed for a second before it whipped out of sight into the cloud of silt.

"Or they're just hungry," Caleb suggested, taking his twin daggers from his belt, and igniting the fire which was imbued into the metal, readying for an attack.

I pursed my lips, considering the beasts tailing us before turning away from them and continuing towards the heart of the lake.

"Let them come for us if they dare," I challenged. "I could do with a good fight."

"Feeling bloodthirsty?" Caleb asked as he turned his back to the creatures too, matching my pace and striding on at my side.

"That's pretty much all I feel now," I agreed.

There was a pause before he replied, an acknowledgement of the man we had both loved and lost, a ripple in our reality which would never smooth out.

"Good."

I could feel the monsters drawing closer to us as we walked, their eyes roaming down my spine, sizing me up, stalking me in the dark, but I didn't look back again.

I wasn't some prey to be hunted and I had to think they knew that too, or they would have attacked by now.

My senses were on high alert for an ambush though, the fire in my veins pulsing in time with the pounding of my heart, sending adrenaline skittering through me. I got off on that feeling, the urge for survival, the desire to fight. It was the one thing that let me know I even wanted to live anymore, the automatic reactions of my body which was stubbornly determined to keep fighting even if inside I felt like I was crumbling.

I was so focused on the monsters hunting us in the dark that I almost didn't notice the stone and silt of the lakebed giving way to the firmness of rock beneath my boots.

I fell still, looking down at the circle of stone surrounding us and releasing a low breath as I took in the glimmering constellations which were carved into an ancient-looking zodiac wheel with a sun symbol at the centre of it.

"Is this it?" Caleb asked as he looked down at it too. "The door?"

My lips parted on a reply but just as I started to speak, a rush of water crashed into the back of my air shield, the attack coming so fast and so violently that my magic almost buckled beneath the force of it as those enormous tentacles crashed into the hardened shell encasing us.

"Fuck," I cursed, whirling towards the monster as it shot to our right, orbiting us in a haze of silt that hid most of its enormous body from view.

I wrenched my arm back, a spear forming in my hand as my earth magic flared and I hurled it towards the monster with a cry of effort, the sharp tip puncturing my air shield as I allowed the smallest hole to pierce it for that purpose alone.

The spear flew true, but the creature moved with ungodly speed, whirling away from us, and evading my attack just as another resounding crash slammed into my air shield from behind.

I whipped around, magic burning a path through the centre of me. My eyes widened at the sight of the giant, green pincer as it snapped against the walls of my air magic, the power vibrating and threatening to buckle with every sharp strike as a second monster attacked us too.

"What the fuck are these things?" I hissed, my muscles bunching as I fought to hold them off, throwing more power into my shield and bracing as the pincer snapped at it again.

"There are all kinds of monsters lurking in the corners of this world," Caleb replied, his head turning to look just as a third creature launched its attack to our left.

A glimmering golden horn - which looked like it could have belonged to a Pegasus on Faeroids - drove into my shield, and a beast with a shark-like body and a mouth full of wicked, sharp teeth charged us ferociously. "Didn't you read the tale of Joseph and the Long Horned Ergut when you were a kid?"

"Who the fuck is Joseph?" I hissed.

The thing I was assuming was a Long Horned Ergut whirled away from us into the depths of the water. I wasn't dumb enough to think it was giving up on us though, and I poured even more magic into my shield just as I spotted the glimmer of that lethal-looking horn turning back towards us once more.

"Joseph was a kid who went searching for treasure in the depths of the dark pool beyond his family home," Caleb said, rolling his eyes at me like I should know that.

"Is this some fairy tale shit?" I asked. "Did he put on his little red riding hood and defeat this thing, because if he did, I'd appreciate you skipping to that bit and giving me a few pointers."

"Little Red Riding Hood was an Orderist piece of shit murderer who killed her grandma when she found out she was a Werewolf and not a Medusa like she'd believed," Caleb said, looking disgusted. "We know your pretty little mortal versions of the stories too, but all Fae know that nothing is ever as simple as once upon a time."

My concentration faltered at that weird as fuck version of the story every mortal grew up with, but I was distracted again when the pincer beast thing snapped its claws against my defences.

The shield rippled and almost collapsed beneath the might of the attack, and I swore loudly as I poured more magic into it, launching a spear gilded in Phoenix fire the monster's way, making it retreat with a scream of pain.

The Long Horned Ergut wasn't deterred though, and I was forced to throw both hands out in its direction, the impossibly sharp horn slamming into my shield with the force of a hammer against an anvil.

Cracks spiderwebbed across my shield, lake water trickling in through them. I gasped and fought to patch the holes again, Caleb's hand finding mine as he offered me his power too.

I instantly dropped my mental shields, the roaring rush of his magic tumbling into me like the charge of some powerful beast itself, and the shield protecting us glimmered as it was reinforced.

"Okay then, tell me how Joseph killed the Long-Horned thing," I gritted out, another spear forming in my free hand while I twisted my head to look for the other monsters in the gloom surrounding us.

"He didn't," Caleb said, frowning at me. "He found its cavern, stole one of its eggs and when the Long Horned Ergut discovered him, it ripped him apart and swallowed the pieces. His family never discovered what happened to him, and the moral of the story was to never venture into the dark places of this world without being prepared for the beasts that lurk there."

I gaped at him, my magic vibrating as the tentacles lashed against my shield from behind, and the third beast reminded us that it was still very much here too.

"What the fuck kind of kids story is that?"

"The only kind that matters," he replied with a shrug. "What did you expect? A happy ending?"

"Yes, I expected a happy fucking ending," I snarled. "I expected a tale where the beast was defeated, the treasure was claimed, and everyone lived happily ever after."

Caleb broke a merciless laugh. "I suggest you stop believing in nonsense like that, Princess," he said, his voice low and rough. "That's not the way Faery tales go. The endings are always brutal and bloody, and no one walks away from them unscathed. Especially not the main characters."

My eyes moved to the monsters around us once more, my power threatening to buckle at any given moment, a brutal fate awaiting us if it did.

"Well fuck that," I hissed. "I'm fighting on the side of once upon a time, and I'm gonna walk away from this a hero, just like the mortal stories promised."

"Good luck with that," Caleb snorted, and I took that as a challenge as I drew on my magic and prepared to show him exactly what I meant.

Out of the corner of my eye, the enormous tentacles whipped back, preparing for another strike just as the Long Horned Ergut charged at us again.

The moment it struck, I threw my air magic out, widening my shield to encompass both of them within it, a wild shriek of panic escaping the thing that looked like a giant squid as it crashed down in the waterless area, its tentacles flailing wildly and almost knocking Caleb from his feet.

He reacted fast, shooting around it before leaping towards its head, the blazing daggers in his grip primed for a killing blow as my focus was stolen by the Long Horned Ergut.

The thing was hideous without the shroud of the silt from the lakebed to shield it, its enormous mouth gnashing wildly as it tried to heave its body towards me and swallow me whole.

I offered the monster a feral grin, ignoring the crash of weight against the far edge of my shield from the giant crab thing and casting another spear into my hand as I ran for it, my gaze fixing on the one, bulbous eye on this side of its horned head.

A roar escaped my lungs as I launched the spear with all my strength, hurling it straight for that eye and following it with a blast of fire magic destined for its brain.

But instead of piercing the flesh of the creature's eyeball, I watched in shock as a silvery, opaque eyelid snapped across the eye half a heartbeat before the spear could make contact with it.

Even the sharpened point of my weapon stood no chance against whatever that eyelid was made of, and I cursed as it bounced off, the fireball I'd sent after it flaring across its scaley skin and extinguishing too.

The only thing my attack seemed to achieve was to piss the monster off, and I was forced to turn and run as it threw its weight towards me, its huge body slamming into the muddy lakebed right where I'd just been.

I cast blades of ice into my hands as I continued running, hurling them at the beast one after another, hoping to stall it, though the cuts they made in its scaley hide seemed to do little more than anger it.

With a surge of energy, my wings burst free of my back, fire erupting over my body as I took off towards the higher regions of our air pocket beneath the lake, soaring above the tentacled squid thing just as it managed to wrap Caleb in one of its snake-like appendages.

I threw a blast of Phoenix fire at the limb and the squid screamed as it was forced to release him.

Caleb instantly took the chance I'd given him, and with a flash of speed and whirl of his flaming blades, he sliced the belly of the creature wide open, bluish-green blood spraying across the muddy lakebed as it roared in anguish.

I beat my wings hard, flying for the very top of my air shield, glancing back over my shoulder as I felt the Long Horned Ergut lunging after me, the air shifting as it heaved its bulk upwards like a shark beaching itself in search of a meal.

I threw my arms wide, my head falling back as I tucked my wings in tight and flipped over backwards, the hot breath of the monster licking up my spine and its jaws snapping shut just shy of my heels.

I dove down, air rushing behind me to make me move faster while I drew my sword and plummeted towards the monster's back.

The Long Horned Ergut shrieked as I landed on it, my feet slipping on its wet scales, but I kept my footing and plunged my sword down into its spine with a bellow of effort.

The creature thrashed and roared as my sword was buried right up to the hilt, its greyish blood spilling all over my hands, making it even harder for me to hold my position.

I flapped my flaming wings to help me balance, my pulse thundering as adrenaline crashed through me and I lost myself to this feeling. The fight for my life woke me up and made everything seem so much sharper than it had since the moment my world had imploded, and the people I loved most in this star-cursed life of mine had been lost to me.

I gritted my teeth and wrenched my sword to the right, the monster screaming with a deafening finality as its body went rigid then lax beneath me.

I leapt away as it began to fall to one side, beating my wings to get airborne again and ripping my sword free in a spray of blood. It fell to the silt at the bottom of the lake, finally releasing its hold on the brutal existence it had claimed.

I expelled a wicked laugh, swiping a hand over my face to clear the blood from my eyes and turning to see how Caleb was doing against the giant squid.

But as my gaze fell on him still fighting a ferocious battle with the creature, I found one huge tentacle whipping my way, the suckers along its edge pulsing as they sheared through the air straight for me.

I sucked in a sharp breath and raised my arms to shield myself, but I wasn't fast enough, and the full force of that monstrous limb collided with me hard enough to blast the wind from my lungs and send me flying.

I was hurled across the open space and I banished my wings, my eyes widening in fear as the edge of my air shield loomed ahead of me as solid as a brick wall.

I screamed in terror, throwing a hand out, and the shield blinked out of existence less than a second before I would have been plastered all over it like roadkill.

I crashed into the murky water of the lake, my scream turning into a stream of bubbles which raced away to the distant surface.

I kicked hard, trying to turn myself around while I lost all sense of direction, and the only sound I could hear was the thrashing of my own pulse against my eardrums.

I spread my fingers wide, and sparks burst from them, illuminating the dark water before me. The crab creature lunged for me, its beaky mouth gaping and gleaming with razor sharp teeth.

Horror came for me, that mouth wide enough to swallow me whole, moving so fast that I could do little more than flinch before those teeth snapped shut around me and I was drawn into the jaws of the beast.

For three horrifying seconds I was frozen, my hands curled around my head, limbs tucked tight to my chest as I waited for my end to take me before realising it hadn't quite come yet.

I was crouched on a thick, lumpy tongue, rows of endless teeth surrounding me, a churning, clacking grinding noise starting up in its throat. I may have been breathing for the moment, but I got the horrifying sensation that death was fast approaching, as I found myself trapped within the cage of its mouth.

The song of my Phoenix hummed through my veins, fire lighting in the depths of my soul and burning right through me until my flesh began to glow with the strength of it, every drop of my magic and Order gifts rushing to help me. The teeth and tongue of the crab's mouth were lit up around me, the monster beginning to chew as it nudged me towards those churning teeth.

A flash of blinding light burst from me, and I had no choice but to close my eyes against it, fire blooming in an explosion of red and blue as I let every drop of my power explode from me at once.

For a single moment the water dissolved, silence reigning as I cracked my eyes open and looked up towards the sky which I glimpsed between the walls of water which were forced to part beneath the intensity of my fire.

I sucked in a desperate breath, my eyes wide as I took in the lumps of bloodied crab meat hurtling back down towards me just as the lake water rushed back in to fill the void my fire had created.

The water collided with me, tossing me through its depths so fast that I lost all hope of figuring out which way was up, and memories of a frozen swimming pool stole through my mind for several hopeless seconds.

I thought of *him*, of the man I wasn't allowed to think of, the one who I hated so very, very much and had ended up loving so deeply that the loss of him had destroyed me entirely. The memory of him was like a burn that wouldn't heal, the pain of it constant and flaring into agony with little to no provocation. It stole my breath, stole my capacity to go on and it left me with nothing at all aside from the desire to douse the fire that had caused it before I headed into the flames myself and begged for them to end me too.

Perhaps that was my fate, to die here in the frozen water like I could have done so many times before, first when that car had crashed with me trapped inside it, and then when he had trapped me in that pool. Wouldn't it all be so much easier if I just gave in to that fate now?

My back hit something hard and rough, my hand snapping out on instinct to grip the mound of stone which lay on the lakebed, some small piece of me still fighting despite the desperate, morbid turn of my thoughts.

A vibration echoed through the stone as I clung to it, my head turning to look at it just as it parted, a door appearing within it and a man I knew reaching out and grabbing my arm.

Caleb's blonde curls were plastered to his scalp, water dripping down his face and a scowl set firmly on his features as he yanked me into a pocket of air he'd managed to trap at the bottom of the lake with his earth magic.

I fell to my knees as he sealed us into the small space once more, the water lapping over my hands while I coughed and trembled at his feet.

"Happily ever after my ass," he muttered and it was so fucking funny that I laughed.

Here I was, this broken, brutal thing, a princess without a crown hunting for a lost girl at the ends of the earth, while monsters tried to eat me and all hope was well and truly lost, yet still I fought to live another day. Eternally fighting and hurting and hoping that this might just be a bump in the road, an agony I had to endure before the end. But what end could there possibly be that could offer me any light now?

The ground trembled beneath me, and I squinted in the dim light of the flame Caleb had conjured for us to see by. The submerged island topped with a cluster of zodiac stones lay all around me under the foot of water I knelt in.

My stomach dipped as the ground began to rise, the sensation not unlike being inside an elevator. We broke through the surface of the lake and the zodiac wheel beneath us locked into place at the centre of an island, the cold air sweeping in around us and I released my air shield, gazing up at the cloudy sky.

Caleb offered me my sword and I took it from him without managing to summon the energy to ask how he'd found it amid that chaos.

"I killed the giant squid," he said in a low voice. "But I think you might have me beat with two monsters to my one, sweetheart."

"Sounds like a pretty good end to a story if ever I heard one," I said as I sat back on my feet and tried to slow the frantic beating of my heart. "Unless of course we're about to be eaten by whatever is making the ground move beneath us."

"Nah," Caleb replied, cocking his head to one side as he used his gifts to listen to something beyond my range of hearing. "I can hear people talking. I think we just found the door to the library at last."

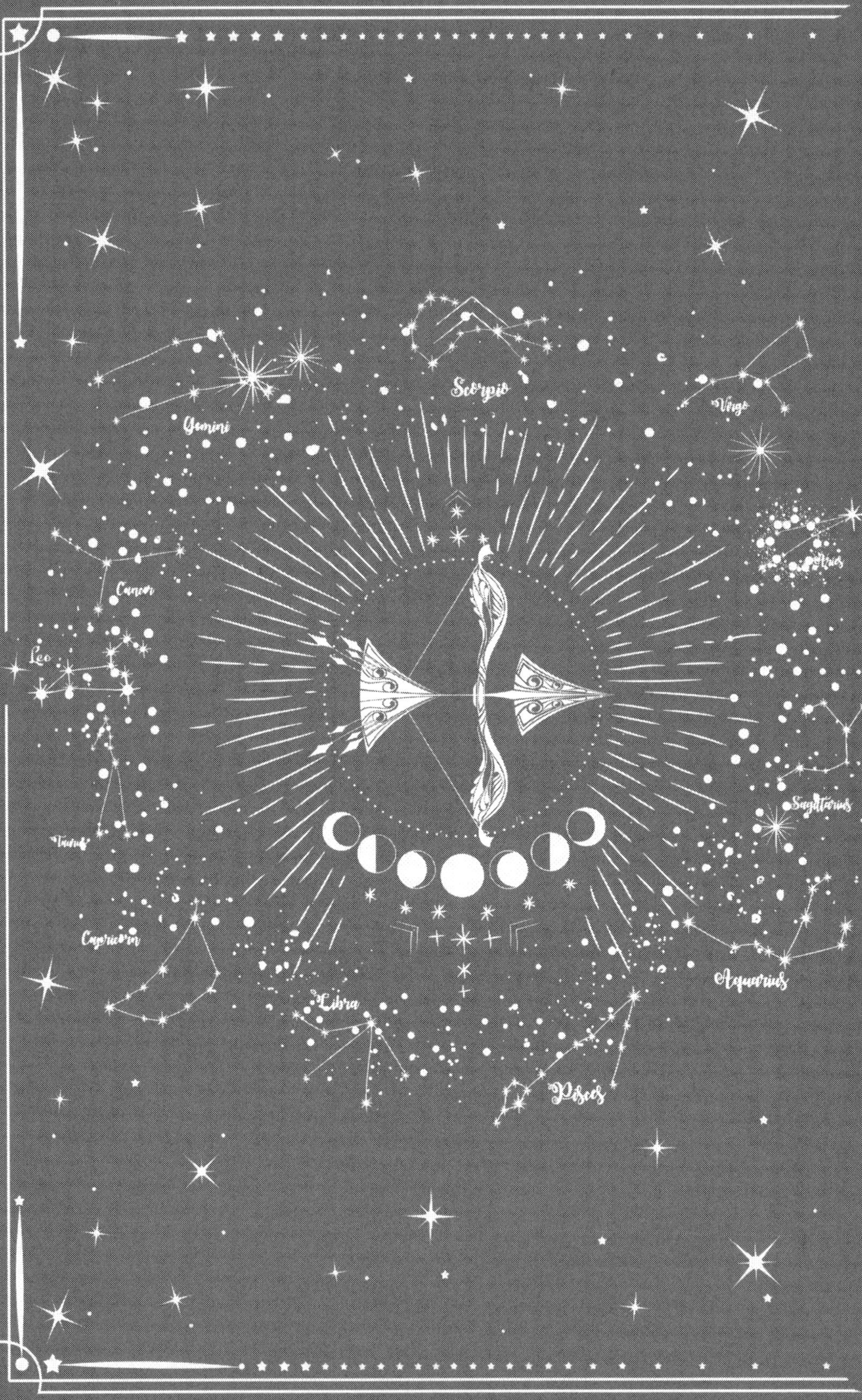
Scorpio
Gemini
Virgo
Aries
Cancer
Leo
Sagittarius
Taurus
Capricorn
Aquarius
Libra
Pisces

XAVIER

CHAPTER TWENTY SIX

Rain pattered the window of my room in the R.U.M.P. Castle, and I watched the droplets tumbling down the glass while sitting on a window seat with my back to the wall. I mentally picked two droplets to race to the bottom of the pane, my eyes following the one I was banking on to win. But of course, it came last and I sighed. No matter how many times I'd played this silent game, I somehow always picked the loser.

Geraldine had given us one of the finest rooms on the second level of the palace, and there was a basket of bagels waiting outside our door each morning with handwritten notes from her. She always addressed them 'to my sweet Pega-brother.' I felt like an asshole because firstly, I rarely ate any of the food she left for me, Sofia, and Tyler, and secondly…I hadn't offered her anything to help with her grief.

She was rising at the stars only knew what time to bake those bagels fresh and bring them to me daily, leaving little sympathy notes to help me through my grief, and what had I given her in return? Nothing. And honestly, I didn't feel capable of anything. The hours of the day were on repeat, each one dragging its heels towards the next. My pain never eased or changed within those passing minutes, the weight of it never heavier or lighter. It just was. Like a woeful creature had crawled into my chest and made a home there.

I'd thought grief would be louder than this. It felt like there should have been people screaming, thousands of fists hammering at the walls, thunder cracking through the sky. But if anything, things were quieter. More still.

I gazed down at one of the training arenas that was being built by earth Elementals, watching the rebels work in the drizzling rain.

The atmosphere on the island was dark and rife with pain, people moving like zombies from one work post to another, eyes reddened by lack of sleep and loss of tears, faces gaunt, like something vital had been carved from the centre of them. I was them and they were me. There was no distinguishing us. We were meant to be the lucky ones, the survivors who'd made it through battle. But I had the sinking feeling that the dead were luckier than us. Being left behind while members of our families and friends passed on forever was an unending curse of unfathomable pain.

"Xavier?" Sofia said gently, perching on the window seat beside me and drawing her knees to her chest.

I could feel her eyes on me, but couldn't turn my head to look at her, my mind hooked on racing raindrops again. The one I chose didn't even make it to the bottom, swept away on the wind, while the other slid smoothly down to secure its win. Another loss. *Figures*.

"Tyler's worked out a way to pick up a signal on his Atlas to access outside news," Sofia said, continuing as if I was listening raptly.

"I'm a ghost," Tyler called excitedly from the bed across the room. "I can see everything out in the world, but no one can see me. There's a bunch of stuff coming out of Zodiac Academy. There's students in there fighting back!"

"That's great," I said, my voice void of emotion, though I really was glad he had been able to keep The Daily Solaria going since the battle. The people of the kingdom needed to know the truth more than ever now.

Sofia shifted closer, her fingers brushing mine as she tried to capture my attention.

"Is there anything I can do?" she whispered, and my heart wrenched.

I was an asshole. Hardly able to give her anything, only the barest hints of affection. I wanted to, but I also didn't. Because it seemed wrong to let myself feel anything but the agony of my loss. I didn't want to disrespect my mom or Darius or Hamish like that. They deserved to have people sit and suffer over their deaths, not move on and act as if the world could happily keep turning without them. Even if it could, I didn't want it to.

Any time I indulged in kisses or held Sofia and Tyler too long, guilt plagued me because those things made me feel better. And I had no right to feel better. I didn't want to smile again, because smiling meant I wasn't sad anymore, and I should suffer for as long and as deeply as possible. Though I was certain no amount of grieving would ever set the balance of the world right again. They weren't coming back, and I had the awful feeling that I wasn't either.

"No." I remembered to answer Sofia, unsure how long I'd left that question hanging, only that I'd lost three more raindrop races on the window.

Sofia whinnied softly, pain lacing that noise and she moved forward, resting her head on my shoulder. She smelled so sweet, like candy apples and sugarcanes, and as she looked up at me, I saw tears rolling down her cheeks, pink glitter sparkling within them.

Her pain made my thoughts sharpen and I swam up from the depths of my stupor, reaching out to wipe her tears away with my thumb.

"Don't cry, little mare," I said.

"I want to help," she begged. "Let me help."

I brushed my thumb along her lower lip, staining her mouth with the glitter of her tears and frowning at my girl, wishing I could see her smile again. When I'd been at my loneliest, trapped in the nightmare of Acrux Manor, Sofia had been my escape. She'd been there for me when the walls seemed too close, and the pounding of my father's footfalls had driven a sliver of dread into my heart. She had been my shining fantasy, and I'd loved her before I'd even met her. To see her here now, weeping for me, made me want to try for her. If this beautiful creature was cursed to love a zombie, then I needed to find a way to restart my heart.

"Asshole," Tyler growled, and I looked over at him, finding his brow creased, his eyes set on the Atlas resting on his knees.

"What is it?" Sofia asked.

Tyler glanced at us, his jaw ticking and his hand going to his light brown hair, fisting it tightly. "That piece of shit Gus Vulpecula has been printing all kinds of lies about the rebels. And he did another article on the battle."

"Let's see it then," I muttered, pushing to my feet.

Tyler took his Atlas and shoved it under his ass, shaking his head. "Nah, man. It's fucked. Don't worry about it."

His cagey bullshit only made me more determined to see it and I strode over to the wide bed, made with three people in mind with a headboard that had a rainbow carved into it.

"Give it here," I commanded, pulling the Dom card on him, but he resisted still, not handing it over. "Tyler."

"No," he said, rising to his feet and barring my way to the bed where the Atlas lay waiting. "Leave it, Xavier."

My chest crashed into his and I stamped my foot in warning. "Move."

Tyler held it out, his eyes locked on mine and the furious pounding of his heart echoing through his body into my own.

"I'm trying to protect you," he said in a low voice.

"I can handle Vulpecula's propaganda," I said through clenched teeth.

Tyler held out a second longer before his eyes dropped and his head bowed in submission. He stepped aside and I moved forward, grabbing the Atlas and looking down at the news article on the screen for The Celestial Times.

New information arises surrounding the King's magnificent victory against the rebels!

Reports from the noble Dragons who fought at King Lionel's side have been painting a wondrous picture of glory after insurgents made a callous call for war against the crown.

Our king, in a kind and humble manner, arrived at the battlefield in an attempt to find a peaceful solution to the violence that has been running rife through the kingdom due to the rebels' nasty agenda. However, his arrival was greeted with instantaneous attack, and our king was forced to meet his enemies head on. Witnesses stated they saw his own son Darius Acrux attack his father from behind in a vicious, unFae act that almost could have seen the king's end, if only he were not twice as strong as his former Heir.

Darius Acrux's widow, and most esteemed Dragon, Mildred Canopus, had this to say on the matter:

"Darius turned to the dark side, corrupted by the Vega whore and jealous of his father's ascension to power, turning against his own family in a bid to seize it from our great king. His violence knew no end, and I watched as he led the traitor army with the Vega twins at his side and a wickedness in his eyes. His envy was obvious to everyone watching, and even as his adoring father tried to reason with him, Darius would hear no word of it. In fact, I heard him say 'I want your throne and to have the kingdom do my bidding', then King Lionel was forced to battle with his own flesh and blood, given no choice but to put him down. It must have been a terrible sacrifice for the king to make, but in the end, he showed his strength as the greater Fae and did what had to be done in the name of Solaria."

More witnesses have come forward, painting a picture of Darius Acrux's descent into madness after he and the other former Heirs were tempted to the dark side by Roxanya and Gwendalina Vega. The famed historian, Norman Gimplight, has uncovered new findings about the Phoenix Orders, confirming their abilities in manipulation and corruption that would have you shuddering in fear.

It is clear to see that Darius was a victim of such powers, and it caused his obsession with his father's greatness to deepen until the man we once knew and loved, was lost.

It seems that in recent times, there was a far murkier side to the once Fire Heir that none of us could have known existed, and it coincided with the Vegas' return to the Fae realm. There can be no coincidence about it, their influence ran deep upon he and the other former Heirs from day one, and

Gimplight has confirmed that there is no cure to the taint of their power.

In the wake of Darius Acrux's death, witnesses are coming forward in their droves now that they are no longer afraid of his wrath against them. It is apparent that he threatened many of the students at Zodiac Academy into keeping dark secrets about him, and the truth behind the mask is a frightening thing indeed.

Honey Highspell, a professor of Cardinal Magic at Zodiac Academy, had this to say of his behaviour:

"Darius Acrux was brash in class, often arriving with bloodstains on his clothes and a wrath about him that frightened many of my students. And though I had my suspicions that he was terrorising his fellow classmates, when I asked around to try and confirm it, there was a sense of fear among my students that worried me deeply and no one dared to speak up. I feared for my own life at times, waking in the night and finding golden eyes peering at me through the window of my chalet in the teachers' residence. He wanted me in a way I couldn't fathom, perhaps sexually, perhaps more."

As a fellow student at Zodiac Academy, Mildred Canopus had this to add:

"I heard rumours of something called the blood ring, where Darius Acrux brought his victims somewhere on the school grounds. One night, I snuck out of my bedroom and followed Darius into The Wailing Wood. And that's when I saw them. Seth Capella, Caleb Altair and Max Rigel, all teamed up with their ringleader Darius against one Fae. It made me almost vomit with how unFae it was."

With much effort, I managed to track down a Fae who was a victim of the Heirs' brutality regularly, who was brave enough to make this statement. To protect himself, the Weasel Shifter wishes to remain anonymous.

"I was dragged out of bed in the middle of night by Darius Acrux and brought to the woods where he and the other Heirs proceeded to beat me. They laughed while they did it. And Darius kept saying he was the true king – it was really weird. He also said he was going to bring all of his friends to the palace to stab King Lionel while he was sleeping. It was so unFae. I think about it a lot."

All in all, I think we can agree that the king's eldest son was a far more sinister character than we were led to believe, and the likelihood that this darkness came directly from the Phoenix twins is a truly disturbing one. I am saddened to think of his dear, devoted fans learning of this news in the wake of his death, but I cannot shield you from the truth any longer. It is my duty to bring you the facts as I uncover them, and I shall not let my own devastation over the Fire Heir's real nature quiet my voice. Together, we shall overcome this grave news and move forward into a better world.

All hail the King.
-Gus Vulpecula

Great news! The esteemed choreographer, Janobee Moonbeam, is already working closely with the marvellous composer, Danith Aquanti, to create a ballet based around the battle and King Lionel's victory. Tickets will be made available in the spring – sign up to our newsletter now and receive a ten percent discount!

Comments:

Seliene Ardon: Well, I for one am glad the truth has come out at last. Those Heirs always seemed off to me. I can sense a bad apple from a mile away, and I always knew something like this would happen #dingdongtheDragonsdead #hoorah #iknewit #toldyouso

Kass Bruinier: Good for you Gus! You're a wonderful, brave man. Thank you for all the good you do by spreading the truth. #Gusforagoldengibbonaward #thefoxyfoxdoesitagain #thetruthwillout

Kirsteen Oliver: This is utter horseshit! Darius wasn't unFae and neither are the Heirs. The Vega twins don't have corruption powers it's all propaganda! #justiceforDarius #longlivetheVegaqueens #SavageQueens

Kylie Gibbons: Does anyone know if the ballet will be held at the Sunshine Theatre? I hope not because the last time I went there the seats were sticky and the food tasted like ground mealworms. Fine if you're a Woodpecker Shifter, but I'm a sturdy Manticore. They never replied to my email about it either. #terribleservice #sturdyManticore #letspetitionfortheballettobeheldatthepalace

Oriane Steiner: Round up the Heirs and burn them, I say! Back in my day, a good old Dragon burning was the way to deal with insurgents. The kids these days have it too easy, they don't know the meaning of consequences. #burnthemall #Iloveagoodburning #nothingwrongwithabitofaburning #burningislearning

Sam Greene: Hello? I'm trying to contact my son Peter. Peter? Are you here??

Kenna Red: This is a comment thread for a newspaper, there ain't no Peter here.

Peter Bamchamp: Hello, my name is Peter. Are you looking for me?

Sam Greene: No. I'm looking for my son. Peter??? Hello???

Kate Gaetano: I once knew a guy called Darius who was also an asshole – figures #dicksofafeathercocktogether

Josh Medley: I know two Sandras, one of them is a saint, the other is a total dickwad – you can't just tar all Dariuses with the same traitor brush #insanity #notallDariusesarethesame

Kate Gaetano: You don't even know me, why are you in this thread??? #allDariusesareevil #fact

Josh Medley: I'll be on this thread if I want to be on this thread and I happen to know a guy called Darren who is actually really nice #notallDisequal

Kate Gaetano: Everyone knows that Darrens are nice! That was never even up for debate #Darrensforlife #DeathtoallDariuses

Darius Cumcount: I, as a Darius, would have you know that I am actually a really chipper fella #noneedtospreadlies

Admin: This thread has been closed for utter bullshit

Brown Cow: There isn't a sane Fae in this kingdom who believes any of the crap you're printing. Darius Acrux died fighting for the rights of the Fae who he had committed his life to protecting. He was a true and honest man and he fought to bring down a tyrant. We all know the truth which hides beneath the bullshit of these lies, and the citizens of this kingdom are just waiting for the word to rise up and end this reign of tyranny once and for all. #longlivethetruequeens #Dariusdiedahero #noFaeislesser #thepeoplearewaiting #deathtoLionelAcrux #dontbealiaraboutPhoenixfire #dontblametheVegaflame

I stared at the article, my grip tightening on Tyler's Atlas as a sneer pulled my lip back, the comment from Brown Cow disappearing before my eyes as some admin asshole no doubt deleted it. I released a furious neigh, tossing the Atlas down onto the bed and stamping my foot in fury.

"I'll kill him," I declared. "I'll rip his tail off and strangle him with it."

"Woah," Tyler breathed to Sofia. "Xavier's gone dark. It's hot."

Sofia whinnied softly, trotting to my side, and tugging me around to look at her. She was a tiny thing, but she was powerful in her own right, and all that power demanded my attention from her now.

"Not everyone's going to swallow Gus Vulpecula's lies. Tyler is still getting articles out to The Daily Solaria. The people who want the truth will find it."

"I'll write one now to counter this," Tyler said, and I glanced over at him, nodding in thanks, though my heart was still racing from reading that bullshit printed about my brother.

I turned back to Sofia, my brows lowering. "I just can't stand the thought that so many people will take this as fact. They'll think Darius was a monster."

"Lionel is the monster," Sofia said firmly. "We'll prove Darius and the Heirs innocent, and Darcy and Tory too."

My father's name sent a sickening tug through my chest, and I whirled away from Sofia, picking up an iridescent glass lamp from the nightstand and hurling it at the wall. It exploded into glittering fragments, and my heart thumped keenly at seeing it break. It gave me an outlet I so desperately needed, but it wasn't enough, not even close.

"I wanna destroy something," I said, my hands fisting tightly and magic rising to the edges of my skin. "I want the world to look like it looks inside my head."

"Why didn't you say so?" Tyler said, a note of scheming to his voice. "I'll be back in ten minutes." He grabbed his Atlas then ran out of the room, leaving me frowning after him.

"I'm gonna jump in the shower." Sofia squeezed my hand then slipped away from me, pulling off her clothes as she went until she was fully naked, disappearing into the ensuite.

My cock twitched to attention, and I fought the urge to go after her. We hadn't had sex since before the battle, and this was the first time I'd even had half a mind to lose myself in my favourite girl in the world. But it felt selfish too. Like putting aside my grief to claim something good for myself.

I dropped onto the bed, kicking my feet up and releasing a heavy breath that came from the depths of my lungs. When Sofia returned, she was wrapped in a fluffy towel woven from moss, her short blonde hair hanging wet down to her chin.

She walked to the closet and my eyes tracked her the whole way. She always moved on her tiptoes when she was barefoot, like a little pixie. Apparently, her mom had called her Tiptoe when she was a toddler. I hoped I got a chance to meet her family someday; they were in hiding out in Solaria somewhere, and Sofia had only managed to get them a few messages.

She'd invited them to join the rebels, but they were with a growing herd which had a bunch of young foals who needed protecting. It was best they stayed away until the fighting was over. If it ever came to an end.

Sofia dropped her towel and a knot rose in my throat as she picked out some pants and a plain white t-shirt some of the rebels had provided us with. The earth Elementals had been working hard to produce clothes and food for the masses, and there was still work going on to divide up the items that had been salvaged from The Burrows. Tyler had been selected to be given an Atlas so he could keep getting news stories out, but I was yet to get hold of one myself.

Sofia rummaged for some underwear, and I found myself on my feet, my eyes riveted to the smooth sheen of her skin and the droplets running from the wet hair at the nape of her neck, all the way down the length of her spine. I came up behind her, picking one of those droplets in my mind and deciding that if I won this race, I'd give in to this want in me. I'd let myself quiet the chaos and I'd remind Sofia how much I loved her.

The droplet charted a path along the soft ridges of her spine, and the one I'd chosen to race against it slowed its pace. Impossibly, my droplet made it to the base of her spine first and I reached out to circle my fingers over that very spot, making Sofia gasp in surprise.

"Xavier," she said breathily.

"Between all these goodbyes, I forgot to remind you that I love you," I said quietly, and her skin began to shimmer at my words. "I'm sorry I've been so distant."

I trailed my finger up the length of her spine, making her shiver before I gripped the back of her neck and turned her to face me, stepping closer.

"You don't have to be sorry," she said, her chest heaving as I continued to move into her personal space, admiring the way she glimmered just for me. "You've gone through hell."

"And you haven't?" I asked.

"Not like you," she said.

I took the clothes from her fingers, tossing them aside. "You've been there for me, while I haven't been there for you. I've been a shit Dom."

"No," she said firmly.

"You and Tyler deserve better," I pressed. "I'm not going to let our herd fall apart, little mare. I promise."

The door opened and I straightened, finding Tyler returning with a glint of some plot in his eyes. His gaze fell on us, and he kicked the door shut at his back, his expression falling into something far more heated.

"What have you been up to?" I asked.

"I'll show you in a minute. It looks like you're busy right now," he said, stepping closer before halting and looking to me. "Do you want me here?"

"Always. You're a part of us," I said, my heart ticking a little faster. "Unless either of you want to find another herd, which…I'll understand. I'm a wingless Dom now, I know I'm not exactly your best option anymore."

"Don't say that," Sofia growled.

Tyler snorted angrily, practically cantering over to us and gripping my arm. "You're our Dom. That's never going to change; I swear Xavier."

My pulse pounded more evenly, and I released a breath of relief. "Alright. Well, be a good Sub, Tyler, and get on your knees for our girl."

"Yes, boss," he said through a smirk, dropping down and I cast vines with my earth Element, curling them around the backs of her thighs and spreading them for her, creating a tree stump beneath her ass so she could perch there. I admired the gemstones gilding the skin around her pussy, loving the way they sparkled.

Tyler moved in, licking her clit and drawing a moan from her lips, and I dropped my hand to the back of his head, keeping eye contact with her while applying pressure to encourage him. She deserved to feel something good that had nothing to do with the darkness clouding our world. Both of them did.

I leaned in, swallowing her next moan as I sank my tongue between her soft lips, kissing her slow and deep. She tasted sweeter than candy and was far more appetising.

I drew her legs wider with my vines, dropping down to my knees too and muscling in next to Tyler, needing to taste even more of her. He rolled his head to one side, giving me access to her pussy and I leaned in, licking her with him. I groaned from the sugary sweetness washing over my tastebuds, wanting more as Tyler's tongue met mine and we kissed each other between pleasuring her.

It wasn't long before she was rocking her hips, her hands sinking into our hair and a whinny of purest ecstasy leaving her as she came for us, her thighs shuddering.

I released her from my vines, giving her a moment to recover and turning my attention to Tyler, taking hold of his shirt and pulling it over his head. He gripped my shirt too, a question in his eyes as he asked permission and I nodded, letting him pull it off of me. He reared forward, kissing my neck and nipping at my ear, making me curse in pleasure as the bulk of him pressed against me.

I knocked him back before I could get carried away with him, rising to my feet and scooping Sofia into my arms. She bit her lip, looking hungry for me as I lay her on the bed, pressing her arms out into the sheets with her fingers knotting in the material.

"Tyler," I beckoned him, and he trotted to my side, his cock straining against his jeans.

I turned to him, unbuttoning them for him and moving my mouth to his ear. "Take them off and start fucking our girl. I want her glowing, Ty. Can you do that for me?"

"Yes, Dom." He turned towards me, kissing me hard before dropping his pants eagerly, kicking them off with his shoes and climbing onto the bed. I wanted to run my fingers over the diamond that sat at the top of his cock, and all the rhinestones fanning out from it in a tempting pattern, but more than that, I wanted to watch every one of those stones press against our girl's skin.

Sofia wrapped her arms around him as he pressed her into the bed, lining himself up with her slick core, their eyes locked and smiles dancing at the corner of their mouths. Damn, it felt so good to see them smile like that. It had been too long. I should have told them to claim each other before this, but they wouldn't have done so without my approval, and now I wanted to make up for not thinking of their needs sooner.

I moved to the end of the bed and Sofia's fingers dug into Tyler's back as he held her in suspense.

"Watching?" Tyler asked me, his smirk spreading wider.

"Uh huh. Stop keeping her waiting," I murmured, and he drove himself inside her with a punishing thrust.

She cried out, her neck arching back and her legs tangling around him as he started fucking her to a tormentingly slow beat. It was like music was thrumming through the air as my eyes hooded and I watched them find that torturously slow rhythm between them, hypnotised by their bodies joining and finding something so pure between the friction of their skin.

My own cock was begging for attention, but I denied myself anything, taking in the two of them claiming each other and seeing the light return to their eyes. It stole away some of my pain, and made me feel one percent less of an asshole for how distant I'd been with them. I had to be better. They needed me to be better. And for them, I was pretty sure I could do anything.

"Roll over," I commanded when I couldn't resist them any longer, and Tyler moved onto his back, bringing Sofia with him so she was riding him.

She started to glow, her hips rolling in time with his as they created a beautiful cadence between them once more, their love for each other as clear as a rainbow in the sky. I walked around the bed, dropping my pants, moving onto the mattress behind Sofia and pressing a hand to her back so she lowered over Tyler, their bodies drawn flush together.

"Is she glowing enough for you yet?" Tyler asked over her shoulder and I realised his skin was gleaming too in the way only our kind could show happiness.

"You're both pleasing the hell out of me," I said, and they whinnied in unison, delighted by my praise. I almost smiled at that, but the muscles needed for smiling felt frozen and heavy, so I gave up on trying and shifted my knees between Tyler's.

I slicked my hard length with my water Element, running my thumb over the gemstones pierced through it in the colours of the rainbow. Then I reached between Sofia's cheeks and got her ready for me, my fingers soaked with a thick lube I made with my magic.

I shifted into position behind her and eased myself inside as Tyler slowed his pace, letting her adjust to the feeling of me filling her this way. She moaned as she took every inch of me and I kissed the back of her neck before starting to fuck her in that same heady rhythm they'd been moving to before.

Tyler met my pace so naturally, it was like we were made for this. And maybe we were. The three of us destined to come together, chosen by some celestial being somewhere in the universe. Or maybe we were a happy accident that had nothing to do with stars or suns or moons. We just were.

I kissed Tyler over Sofia's shoulder and Sofia turned her head so she could join the kiss too, our tongues meeting as I closed my eyes and lost myself to the rapture of them. Time ceased to exist, and I fell into a river of pleasure, captivated by the carnal movements of our bodies, finding it easy to give into the trance they wrapped me in. It was slow, intense, and star-damned enchanting, built of nothing but love. And I never wanted it to end.

Sofia came once more with a shiver that seemed to echo into Tyler and me, our bodies hugged close together, pressing her between us. The heat of their skin was a pleasure in its own, my body having felt so void of anything, like I was one of those ice-forged caskets that encased my family. I winced as that thought invaded my head, focusing again and fighting to keep the grief from stealing into me once more.

"I can't hold on," Tyler rasped, looking to me like he was asking for permission to come.

"Wait," I commanded, pressing my hands either side of both of them and thrusting forward, Sofia's tight body building me towards climax I was desperate to reach.

"Glow for us, Dom," Sofia panted, and I felt that urge rising. I wanted to. For them. I wanted that sensation of euphoria to wash over me and share in their light, but I didn't know if I could. The cold hand of grief was sweeping over me again, and my thoughts were starting to scatter.

"Fucking hell," Tyler said as he held off on finishing.

I found my way back to them and blocked all else out, continuing to take my time enjoying them, knowing as soon as it was over, the darkness would rush back in. I was once again focused on them and nothing else, but my body still wouldn't relax enough to let me finish and bask in the afterglow with them.

"Xavier," Tyler begged, his jaw tight and I champed my teeth at him in an order to wait.

I ground my hips down on Sofia's round ass, driving in deep once more and my mind started flashing with unwanted thoughts, the battle, blood, death.

I forced my eyes shut, trying to maintain a grip on the present moment, but it was like the floodgates were opening and I wasn't strong enough to keep it all out.

I cursed as Tyler's fingernails bit into my arm and a sigh of defeat left me as I realised I couldn't finish this.

"Come," I told him, and he drove hard inside Sofia, climaxing with a groan.

I pulled out of her, heading away from them at a fast speed, leaving them glowing in ecstasy on the bed.

"Xavier?" Sofia called after me, but I slammed the door to the bathroom, locking it and stepping into the shower.

I turned the water on, letting it run freezing cold all over me and staring at the stone wall, my teeth grinding together hard. My chest was tight, like pythons were winding between my ribs, cinching around my lungs until I couldn't breathe.

Tyler and Sofia called out to me, and I cast a silencing bubble so I couldn't hear them anymore, needing to fall into oblivion on my own. I didn't want them to watch me crack, didn't want their words of pity.

I stood there until time was a blur and I was frozen through to the bone, my fingers turning blue and every part of me numb.

I stepped out of the shower, wrapping a towel around my waist, casting the silencing bubble away and opening the door. They were sitting at the base of it, Sofia wearing my shirt while Tyler had pulled on some sweatpants.

"Are you o-" Sofia started but I spoke over.

"Clean up," I ordered, ushering them into the bathroom and pulling the door closed behind them.

I tugged my towel free, using it to scrub at my soaked hair and heading to the closet to grab some clothes. I dressed quickly then sat waiting on the bed for them to return. I only grunted in answer when they did and both of them pulled on clothes, sharing looks of concern over me.

"I've got a surprise ready for you, Xavier," Tyler said. "Come with us, and I'll show you."

I shrugged, rising to my feet, not meeting their gazes as I followed them from the room, but I let Sofia take my hand.

Tyler guided us out of the palace and across the drizzly landscape of the island down one of the newly laid paths. He slowed before a roughly-built shed and led me inside, glancing back at me with a hopeful grin.

I entered a room with plain wooden furniture all around the space, and I frowned in confusion.

“What is this?” I muttered.

Tyler moved forward, casting a huge sledgehammer into his grip with his earth Element and handing it to me. “You wanna destroy something? Go nuts. I built it to be ruined.”

My eyebrows arched in surprise, and I looked down at the sledgehammer in my hands, the opportunity to smash everything in here seriously tempting.

“I can break it all?” I confirmed and Tyler nodded.

“Every last bit. Even the walls if you want, bro,” he said.

“Fuck it.” I moved towards a chair, not needing to be told twice, but Sofia hurried forward, stepping in front of me.

“Wait.” She raised a hand, brushing her fingers over my eyes and casting an illusion. I inhaled sharply as the interior of the shed changed to mirror my father’s office instead. I’d shown her photos of this place on my phone, and she’d even remembered to add the little green Dragon paperweight on the desk that was an exact replica of the asshole who’d sired me.

Sofia stepped aside and I moved forward with a thirst for vengeance. I raised the sledgehammer and swung it down at that paperweight with a roar of hatred leaving me. It smashed beneath my might and the desk cracked in two.

A savage sort of smile pulled at my mouth, and I swung the hammer at photographs of Lionel on the walls and his favourite fucking treasures kept safe in cabinets. I broke it all, watching it cascade around me in pieces, the outside finally looking how it felt inside my head.

It was a world of ruin and devastation, a place where everything around me was broken, fractured, half of what it once was. This was my mind spilling out and finally finding an outlet for the maddening pain within. It was destruction in its purest form. My shattered reality. And at last, it existed beyond my mind too.

“Cast an illusion of him in his chair, Sofia,” I encouraged, and she flicked her fingers, showing me my father right before me, his expression smug like he was fresh back from war, counting his victories.

A cry left me that was pure animal, and I swung my sledgehammer at him, striking right between his eyes. Sofia did a beautiful job of letting me see the blood pour, the light dying in his cold, unfeeling gaze and his death rushing in like the wings of the stars.

It may not have been real, but for a second it felt like it was. And my heart sung from the violent delivery of his death. I could almost scent his blood in the air, and I hungered for it like I was a carnivore placed on this earth to make this man my prey.

“One day,” I whispered to the image of his bloody corpse. “I will stand above you, and you will beg for a mercy I won’t offer. I’ll reap the pain from you that you offered my family, and revel in the moment your heart stops beating. The clock is ticking, old man.”

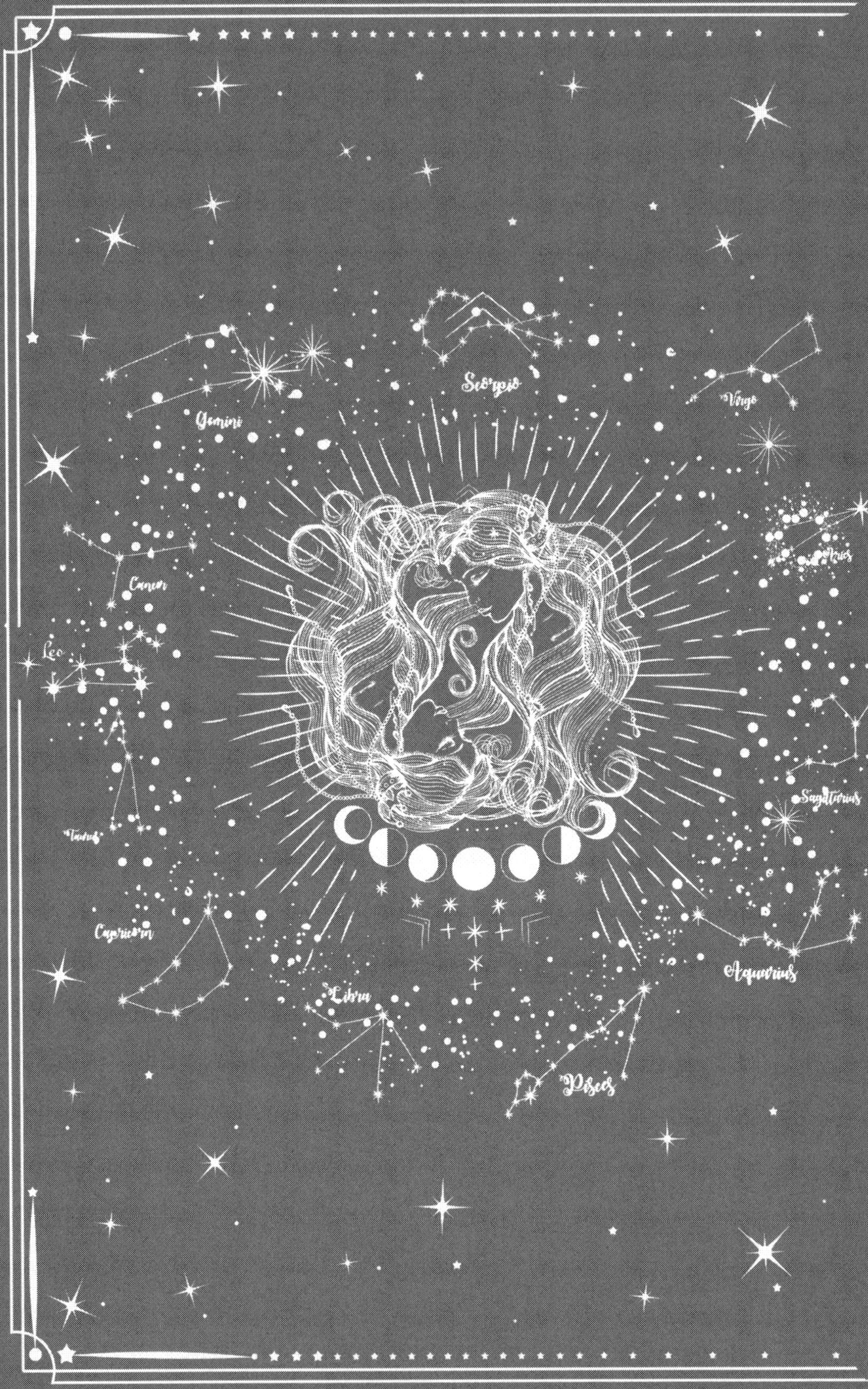
Scorpio
Gemini
Virgo
Aries
Cancer
Leo
Sagittarius
Taurus
Capricorn
Aquarius
Libra
Pisces

TORY

CHAPTER TWENTY SEVEN

I wouldn't have called myself the master of dramatic arrivals by any means, but I had to admit that the sight of me on my knees covered in lake water, blood, and gore, panting through my exhaustion and clinging to a sword as if it was the only thing capable of keeping me upright in this world, was likely an all-time low.

We'd had to get out of the way while the stone zodiac wheel beneath us slid sideways underground, and another stone platform raised in its place.

The people standing on top of it were struggling to contain their expressions as they took me in, and I blew out a breath as I gave in to the inevitability of this not going all that well from the get-go.

With a surge of effort, I forced myself to summon some energy as I pressed the tip of my sword into the wet ground beside me and used it to leverage myself to my feet.

A single glance in Caleb's direction let me know that the asshole had used his speed and fire magic to not only dry himself off, but to stow his weapons away and straighten out his clothes too, meaning he looked the epitome of unruffled perfection.

"Bastard," I hissed so low that no one but a Vampire would be able to hear it and the corner of his lips twitched the tiniest amount, just as a lump of monster guts fell from my hair to land on my boot with a wet slap.

"You could have simply knocked," the girl standing before us said, her head tilting to one side, causing her braids to tumble over one shoulder as she inspected us with rapt interest.

"Take a picture, it'll last longer," I quipped, my heart leaping as one of the guys behind her actually did, and I was half blinded by the fucking flash on his camera.

"The Library of the Lost isn't just some cock-handed vacation destination," a watery eyed man said in a wavering yet unyielding tone from the back of the group of four. "As head librarian, I wish for you to know that despite your lineage or anything of the sort, the gift of knowledge is not one which can be claimed by birth right alone. You do not get to simply stomp up here willy-nilly and demand access to our tomes. Only the worthy are invited to peruse our pages and so, until a time when you have been deemed such or the stars guide you to our door on the wings of fate, I'm afraid you will have to leave."

"Leave?" Caleb asked, his entitlement showing in the way he blinked in confusion, like the word held no meaning to him whatsoever and he'd never heard it before.

I sheathed my sword, an act which may have seemed friendly, except for the look of violence that passed across my eyes as I set a heavy gaze on them.

"Look," I began, picking a lump of tentacle from my arm and tossing it to the floor just in front of the librarians' feet. "I've had one hell of a time recently. I've been captured and tortured, brutalised and traumatised. I've been married and widowed, fought and defeated. And to top it all off, I have been without the other half of my soul for over a week now. To put it lightly, I've reached my limit. So I've come a long way in search of this place and the knowledge you hold here. I've made that journey – and helped you out with what I would call a considerable monster infestation in your lake by the way – and now I'm standing here before you, covered in fuck knows what, my power depleted and my tether on my temper running dangerously short. I have absolutely no intention of letting you simply shut that door in my motherfucking face. So, I'm posing that you need to think again on the subject of that invitation."

The librarians all paled, the girl who stood in front of them giving the older a man a pointed look and hissing something which sounded like 'See?', though with the amount of water that still resided in my ears, I wasn't certain on that.

"Those *monsters*, as you call them, were the three ancient guardians of this place," the Minotaur in shifted form at the back of the group mooed, stomping his foot angrily.

I arched a brow as I glanced towards the water where the decapitated head of the giant squid was spinning in a slow circle beside the upturned belly of the Long Horned Ergut, whose blood was slowly colouring the water all around it. There weren't enough bits of the demon crab left to really be called a body, but half a claw was perched on top of the Virgo constellation stone beside me.

"Oh," Caleb said, exchanging a look with me where we both silently admitted we may have fucked up a little there. "Whoops."

"They did try to eat us," I explained with half a shrug. "So, this situation is kinda on them. If they were as well trained as you claim, then-"

"They weren't trained," the girl interrupted. "They were simply brought here to act as a further protection surrounding the library from those who were not invited. Bloodthirsty monsters prowling the lake is pretty off-putting… At least to most people."

"Thank fuck for that. You had me thinking I'd gone and killed your pets for a moment there," I said, flashing my teeth at them in a way that couldn't really be called a smile.

"No one can tame the monsters of legend," Cameraman piped up.

"Good to know you aren't all as dumb as you look then. Because I just so happen to be one of those so-called monsters, so I guess the question is whether or not you'll be offering me that invitation, because option B involves me burning my way inside with Phoenix fire."

"You make a wonderful politician," Caleb drawled as the librarians all recoiled in horror at my words.

"Miss Vega-" the old librarian began, but I cut him off.

"I tend to go by my royal titles these days. Haven't you been hearing reports of the war being waged in your kingdom?"

Caleb stepped in. "This might be a good moment for me to interrupt the Savage King's daughter before she insults every one of you so thoroughly that any sympathy you may have been convinced to feel is long since forgotten. The things she told you are true, we have faced loss and pain beyond what any Fae should have to face in their lifetime and still we fight on, knowing we might face plenty more of that in time. We fight because, as I hope you would agree, the alternative is far worse. Lionel Acrux is determined to rule with tyranny and persecution, destroying all knowledge that doesn't suit his agenda and forcing the people of this kingdom to submit in all the ways that count. We are on the side of freedom and equality, and we have come here in desperate need, seeking access to your library in the fleeting hope that it may help us win that fight in the end. So we beg you, implore you actually, to open your doors to us and offer us that slim chance." Caleb pressed a hand to his heart and dammit, I had to admit he had the whole political bullshit down, especially as the enraged faces before us turned thoughtful and pragmatic.

"Very well," the old man said eventually, though I didn't miss the unimpressed look he shot me as another lump of fish guts fell out of my hair. "Though I will have to ask you to clean up before you are allowed near the texts. There are volumes here which date back through the millennia, knowledge which has been lost to the modern world resides in parchment and ink, preserved here for fate to serve up again in times of need and searching. What we protect here is precious beyond the realms of any other treasure."

"Got it," I agreed, flicking my fingers and sending a flood of water magic over my body, using a combination of that and earth to remove every unsanitary piece of lake muck and dead monster from my body. Another flick of my hand sent fire magic tearing through me, and within moments I was dry and clean, though there was little to be done for the huge tear in the side of my crop top.

My body was bruised and battered, but I didn't heal myself beyond making sure I wasn't bleeding on anything, preferring the bit of physical pain to the ever-present emotional void eating away at my insides.

The old man eyed me, hunting for any bit of grime I may have missed, but I was as clean as a whistle, and eventually he nodded to the Minotaur in some form of confirmation because the next second, the island beneath our feet began to descend again.

This time though, the island didn't sink into the water. Instead, we moved onto the stone zodiac wheel and descended into a magical tube which was crystal clear.

We travelled down through the lake and deeper still, the sight of the library revealed below us, cavernous and stretching out in every direction. I didn't want to be impressed by it with the group of angry librarians observing my expression, but damn, it was hard not to be.

Each of the four immense walls around us held giant carved effigies of beautiful women's faces which represented the Elements. The one for earth was covered in moss, stunning flowers and delicate magical butterflies dancing along the grass fronds of her eyelashes; the fire carving had blazing blue eyes and rivers of magma swirling within the rock to highlight her features; the air monument had white clouds floating around it, her hair seeming to move despite it being clearly carved from stone; finally, the water Elemental face had frost glittering across her cheekbones and lips, and a furious waterfall poured all the way down to a river far below. Bridges of glass, stone and wood curved over the winding river, a mish-mash maze of bookshelves standing in nearly every space available below us.

Caleb straightened as he took it in, that arrogant slouch giving way to wonder as his mouth slackened and his eyes roamed over the books which were stacked and laid out in every direction as far as the eye could see.

"This place is… I don't have words," he breathed, and the librarians all smiled at the praise while I just stared at the endless rows of tomes and scrolls, wondering how the fuck I was ever supposed to find what I needed in this palace of knowledge.

As if sensing the question consuming me, the girl stepped closer, a hesitant smile on her full lips.

"I'm Laini," she said softly. "I greeted your sister when she visited us."

"From what I heard, that one had better manners," the old man muttered as he turned away from us and headed down a set of golden steps towards a huge desk sitting at the base of the waterfall where it flooded into the river.

"She is better than me in all the ways that matter," I agreed with him, though he was too far from me to hear.

The flash of the camera went off again and I scowled at the man who had taken the shot, subtly suggesting with flames in my eyes that he fuck the hell off.

"Sorry about Dave," Laini cringed as she waved him and his camera away. "It's his duty to record history as it happens. He documents basically everything, but when your sister visited us, he was bed-bound with dick rot, so he missed her."

"Dick rot?" I choked in surprise and Dave glared at Laini before turning and hurrying away from us.

"Yeah. I'm pretty sure it was dick rot." She nodded seriously. "Anyway, he hasn't shut up about missing the chance to document a visit from one of the first Phoenixes to arise in a thousand years, so I think he's determined not to miss out a second time."

"Well tell him if he flashes that camera in my face one more time, I'll be melting it to his nosey chops," I said, knowing full well that Dick Rot Dave could hear me and not caring.

"Maybe try not threatening the people who just agreed to help us, yeah, sweetheart?" Caleb suggested softly as he took a step closer to me and I banished a harsh breath before nodding.

He got it. Knew how fucked up I was inside and how close to the edge I was all the damn time at the moment. Fury was my preferred method of coping, but the chaos of my inner turmoil was a fickle thing, and I couldn't be certain of the ways it would lash from me when it got too much to handle.

"If you're looking for anything specific, Arnold here can help you find it," Laini went on like I hadn't just threatened someone's face with melted plastic, her unflinching disposition easily likeable.

I turned to the Minotaur she'd gestured towards, and he inclined his head proudly, waiting for me to make my request of him. His head was that of a bull's, with large, curling horns and a wide bovine nose. The rest of his body was more human, though it was covered with brown fur and his legs ended in hooves instead of feet.

"I need a way to track someone using old magic. A way that circumvents any measures that have been taken to protect themselves or shield me from finding them, like mental walls or identity concealing spells. I was told there's dark magic that can be used that way."

"Dark magic is a potent thing," Arnold said in a low, warning tone but I just shrugged.

"I didn't ask for your opinion on it, just for the spell in question."

"Messing with the shadows is dangerous-"

"No," I interrupted. "No shadows. Not a single fucking shadow. I need old magic, the kind that predates shadows and possibly even the harnessing of the Elements. The kind no one uses or protects themselves against anymore. Is there something like that here?"

Laini and Arnold exchanged a cautious look, but I just raised my chin in certainty.

"Before the Awakening was gifted to our kind by the stars, there were types of magic among our ancestors," Laini said softly. "But they came at a cost. The kind that is paid in blood and portions of your soul. There is a reason why they were cast aside and forgotten in favour of wielding the Elements via the Awakening."

"I understand that, but I'm still asking for information on that power. Do you hold it here or not?" I glanced at the vast walls of bookshelves stretching out around us, knowing in my soul that if they didn't have that knowledge here then I wouldn't find it anywhere.

"I'll take you to it," Arnold said simply. "Follow me."

He took off at a trot, Laini waving goodbye, her eyes dark with caution as we strode after the Minotaur, following him towards a dim passageway which led further into the depths of the library.

We walked across a bridge that spanned a small stream towards a huge door, the colour of it so black that it seemed to suck the light from the rest of the room, pulling every shadow in this place to it and keeping them close.

Arnold ran his hand over what I assumed were magical locks, the dark metal glowing beneath his palm before he drew the door wide.

"We keep everything on dark magic in the labyrinths. They are heavily warded against stardust or outside influence," he said in a low voice which almost gave way to a moo as his bovine lips curled around the words. "You must stay with me at all times;

only the Minotaurs know these paths, anyone else who wanders down here will end up eternally lost in the maze beneath. It is death to leave my side."

I nodded, already knowing about this from Darcy's account of her time here, and Caleb moved to walk beside me as we followed Arnold into the dark.

The doors boomed close behind us, stealing the light and Caleb cast a Faelight above our heads to see by. Arnold broke into a fast trot, not bothering to look back and check we were still with him. Apparently, it was up to us to make sure we didn't lose him down here and he wasn't going to give any attempt to make that easy for us.

Arnold kept up a punishing pace and after a few minutes, Caleb offered to carry me so we could move with his speed, letting me jump up onto his back while he shot along through the dark and encouraged the Minotaur to move even faster.

Dark passages loomed all around us, so many twists and turns in the tunnels that it was impossible to keep track of where we'd been or where we were going. Sometimes I heard distant bells and once I could have sworn screams echoed back to us from a staircase we passed, but Arnold didn't react to any of it.

"Are there people lost down here?" I asked him as he ran down yet another passageway, his head lowered while he charged, smoke billowing from his nostrils. "Or prisoners?"

"You can't trust anything you see or hear in this place," Arnold replied gravely. "Nothing but the written word, and even then, you should use caution. There are malignant things lurking in these dark passages, cruel and cunning creatures which are always hungry and would like nothing more than to lead you to their door."

"Sounds cosy," I muttered, and Caleb snorted in amusement.

Eventually, Arnold turned into a tunnel which widened into a yawning staircase that delved away into the earth, the air rising from it dank and unwelcoming.

"It has been a long time since anyone ventured into those depths," Arnold said, his hoofed foot scraping at the stone floor. "And for good reason too. The knowledge you seek is down there and down there alone. There is no other way to access it but within the chamber beneath."

"You're not coming with us?" Caleb asked as he lowered me to the floor and Arnold shook his head.

"I will remain here until you return. Or until it becomes clear that you have met your end within."

"Well, that's just great," I muttered, calling on my Phoenix as I gazed down those stairs.

There was something unholy about the dark that awaited us there, something that sang to me in an unheard voice and lured me closer with promises of a death so sweet that I might just step into the arms of oblivion willingly if only I was allowed to enter it.

I met Caleb's navy blue eyes, but neither of us bothered with any pointless sentiments like questioning what the fuck we were doing here. We both knew that we would be crossing that threshold if it was what it took to find Darcy. And now that I was here, I was beginning to wonder if there might be more to this place than just discovering that one forgotten spell. Perhaps there might be other uses for the old magic which we hadn't considered. And if it came down to a question of cost, then I already knew I would pay whatever it took to see the end of Lionel's rule. I'd already lost almost everything anyway.

We stepped over the threshold as one, our movements synchronised as we headed down, down, down. The staleness of the air gave way to the scent of something impossibly old the lower we descended, both musty and powerful, ancient beyond words.

The darkness grew around us as we went, the Faelight above us seeming smaller and smaller, its illumination struggling to pierce the utter blackness which tried to press in on all sides. We instinctively moved closer to one another, our arms brushing as we continued without our steps so much as faltering. We were on this path now and there was no question of turning from it.

My boots echoed on the flagstones as I finally reached the base of the stairs, water stirring in a small puddle at my feet and making me frown. What kind of books could survive in the damp for who knew how long?

I squinted into the darkness, a soft call seeming to wrap its tongue around my name and tug. I couldn't even say for certain if it was real in any sense of the word, but I couldn't resist the pull of it regardless.

My boots splashed softly through the puddle coating the floor as we let the darkness call us forward, and I couldn't help but rest my hand on the pommel of my sword, wanting to feel the realness of the steel while surrounded by so much ethereal strangeness.

I stopped sharply, my head turning to the left without me having planned it and I blinked as I found an alcove there, an ancient text hanging beneath a stone archway set into the wall, the words looking like they'd been branded onto the thick material containing them.

I stepped closer and Caleb kept with me, his presence the one thing reminding me that we were still here, flesh and bone and not a part of this unreal space which felt like it lay somewhere between life and death. The words written there were not in any language or alphabet I had ever seen before, and I frowned as I was forced to wonder if everything down here would be written with such words. If so, then this trip was destined to fail because I didn't have the faintest clue how to read so much as a single symbol in that language.

"Those are runes," Caleb pointed out, his finger tracing the edge of the brown material where they'd been marked alongside the words.

"Any chance you can read the rest of it?" I asked and he cocked his head as he studied the text.

"I don't think that's even a language," he said unhelpfully. "More like a…code. Something which could only hold meaning to someone with the key."

I huffed out a frustrated breath, wondering where the hell I was supposed to find the key to a code which was likely written thousands of years ago.

A thin, rectangular, sapphire blue stone was set into the wall beneath the text, something about it making me give it a closer look the moment my attention fell to it.

I wasn't sure if it was instinct or intuition or just a dumb idea, but I reached for the stone, my fingers brushing against it and feeling the unnatural warmth residing within.

At the touch of my fingers, the stone slipped free of its position on the wall, and I caught it automatically, turning it over in my palm before holding it up to the fabric above, trying to look through it to the coded words there.

Instead of unravelling the text, the warmth in the stone flared and I gasped as visions pierced my skull of long forgotten Fae in some unrecognisable place. They worshipped and sacrificed in the name of dark magic, claiming untold power through unspeakable acts and raw brutality.

A man with a knife piercing his chest.

Three women drinking vials of blood while someone screamed beyond them.

A Medusa cutting the head from one of her own serpents with an agonising cry.

A mother begging for the life of her child.

A flare of blinding power as a Dragon was chained to a stone table, bellowing in fear as its throat was slit, blood spilling into channels carved into the stone beneath it to collect every drop.

A man walking through realms as if the walls between them were nothing but vapour, stealing mortals to sacrifice in the name of claiming more power.

Two Werewolves leaping into a raging fire while a crowd of masked Fae screamed their approval and their howls of agony ripped the air apart.

My grip on the stone loosened, the urge to hurl it away from me a potent thing as I started to think we wouldn't find anything here but memories of a time best left forgotten. But just before it could tumble from my fingers, the vision changed again, and my breath caught in my throat.

The realm walker, his skin painted in blood which wasn't his, markings drawn onto his flesh in that deep and scorching red, striding through the passage between realms which no living soul should be able to cross. The Veil parted like oil around him as he stepped through, his jaw gritting and muscles tensing with pain as he forced the unknown realm to allow him entry despite his still beating heart. The power of the stars ate at him as he forced the divide to part for him, ripping at his strength and fighting against his will, but he didn't falter, determination burning through him until, with one final step and a ring of power which almost knocked me from my feet, he passed beyond.

He was panting, bleeding and had a hollow look in his eyes which made it more than clear that doing so had been anything but easy, the bloody marks now burned into his skin, but still, he'd made it. Waiting for him on the other side were a woman and a child, their faces full of joy as they ran to embrace him, and he collapsed into their arms as he held them again. His family. Reunited by dark magic in spite of the rules the stars had laid out for them.

The blue stone tumbled from my fingers and fell to the floor where it sank into the puddle at my feet, that unholy light within it blinking out.

"Did you *see* that?" I breathed, unable to lift my eyes to meet Caleb's in case he hadn't, and I would be left to question every bit of those memories alone.

"Yeah," he replied roughly, the back of his hand brushing against mine like he wasn't sure if he should offer me comfort or not.

"He travelled beyond the Veil," I whispered, afraid of speaking too loud in case the stars were listening and would *see* every impossible wish I held in my broken heart and fight even harder to keep me from them.

"It looked like it took almost everything from him to do so," Caleb replied. "And I doubt he had what it would take to make the journey once again in reverse. Seems like death would have been a simpler way to access his family."

I nodded slowly, accepting the truth of those words, and wondering what would happen to a living soul who had trapped themselves on the other side like that. I doubted it would be anything pleasant. Yet he'd done it. For some unfathomable reason, that Fae had crossed over without using the bridge of death to do so.

"I would give anything to speak with him one last time, Tory," Caleb said, knowing my mind was on that one soul in particular who had been dragged to the other side before his time, forced to abandon the life he had only just claimed for himself after suffering through misery at the hands of his father for far too long. "But I don't think that's the way to do it. There's a reason why we can't access that realm, and I think it's about more than simply keeping the living and the dead apart. I also doubt that realm walker ever returned."

He had no way of knowing that, but I nodded because I felt the truth of it too. It had taken so much for him to cross through, his power devoured by whatever it was that divided here and there. I couldn't imagine any way that he might have returned. But then the question of why he went at all remained, because if his only desire was to reunite with his loved ones, then death would have been a far simpler answer than all he endured to arrive with them while his heart remained beating.

I reached for the brown fabric holding those coded memories, my fingers drifting over the runes marked along its edges as I worked to memorise them. I already knew that runes were among the oldest form of divination and magical tools, and I'd been drawn towards the power of them since I'd cursed the stars, wanting to focus on forms of divination that didn't wholly rely on their favour to offer clarity. Not that I could say I'd gleaned much from them. My mother's gifts had clearly skipped me altogether in that regard.

"As a side note," Caleb added, watching me paint my fingers down the edge of the waxy brown fabric as I studied the next rune. "I'm around ninety percent certain that those markings have been made on skin. Likely the hide of some murdered Fae in their shifted form."

I yanked my hand away from the waxy fabric with a cry of disgust and turned to him in horror. "Why would you think that?" I hissed.

"Because there's a plaque just there which says so." He pointed to the bit of metal which claimed the gross skin scroll was likely over two thousand years old from the time of the Vampire blood ages.

I cut a look at Caleb, my gaze moving to his mouth where his fangs were currently hidden away, his pretty boy looks and polished appearance hard to marry with a race of Fae who had terrorised the entire kingdom and ruled it with fear and bloodshed.

"Did your mom lose her shit about the whole coven thing?" I asked in a low voice as I stepped away from the alcove and turned down the passageway once more. "Is it really so bad?"

"Yes and no," Caleb said, shrugging one shoulder. "She's pissed about it. My dad too. But they heard me out and understand that it wasn't exactly intentional. They think I should stay away from Orion if he returns."

"For how long?" I asked.

"Forever." Caleb blew out a breath and shook his head. "I didn't argue but I also know it isn't going to happen. Even if his life and mine weren't so wrapped up with all of yours to make it pretty much impossible, the connection I feel to him wouldn't be so easily ignored. We'll have to be careful though, especially when it comes to hunting. So long as we don't engage in the hunt together there really shouldn't be any issue. Neither of us are looking to return Solaria to the rule of blood and carnage."

"I think your mom and the other Councillors need to get used to the idea that they aren't the ones in charge anymore," I said, but before Caleb could reply, a rush of wind made us both spin towards a narrow opening on our left, a groan passing through it either from the movement of the air or something...*else.*

"Why do I get the feeling you want to go in there?" Caleb asked as I took a step closer to the narrow gap.

"Because I'm a fearless badass and you know it," I suggested but he just snorted.

"More like reckless to the point of idiocy, but sure, let's squeeze through a creepy gap in a wall where anything could be waiting to drag us into the depths of this place, never to be seen again."

"That's the spirit." I slapped him on the arm then moved closer to the gap, directing a Faelight through it and squinting against the brightness of it while my eyes adjusted.

"I'm just glad we didn't have to fight any lake monsters on the way in here and end up down here with our magic half depleted," Caleb added, and I shrugged as I drew my sword and let the flames ignite along the length of it, my Phoenix preening at the heat of them and my power beginning to swell instantly.

"I'm good," I commented, turning myself sideways as I began to push my body into the gap between the cold stone walls and move through it. "Sucks to suck though."

"Was that a shitty Vampire joke?" Caleb asked and I almost smiled.

"No."

We kept going, the walls getting tighter and tighter against both my back and my chest as I shimmied along, claustrophobia making my breaths shallow. I started to wonder if I would even be able to make it through to the other side at all.

I swallowed a lump in my throat and kept going, the fire from my sword guiding me on, giving me strength with every step.

At last, I forced my way out of the gap, stumbling a step as I found myself in another chamber, this one wide and laid out with five ancient tomes on stone pedestals set in a random pattern around the room. I sent several more Faelights up to hang around the room, illuminating the corners of the space as whispering seemed to stir the air and a shiver tracked down my spine.

There was no door here, no official way in, and the crack which I'd forced my way through seemed too unnatural to have been here originally, almost like some huge power had erupted in this place and forced the opening into existence. And if that was the case, then it meant that at some point, long ago, someone had sealed these books and the knowledge within them inside this chamber, intending to keep them hidden away, down here where no one could find them.

I almost leapt out of my damn skin as a grinding noise started at my back and I turned to glare at Caleb. He was using his earth Element to carve the stone of the narrow gap I'd just forced myself through, widening the passageway and then walking through it with a smug look on his face that reminded me of all the times I'd wanted to punch him.

"It seemed kinda dumb to force myself through that tiny crevice when I could just do that," he explained with an innocent shrug, and I decided not to comment on the fact that I hadn't even thought to do the same.

I stepped further into the chamber, the floor heavy with dust here, no water making its way through the gap behind us, even after Caleb had widened it.

"This place feels old," I breathed, unsure if that word could even come close to the enormity of time I felt spreading out around us here.

The Faelights flickered as if affected by some wind I couldn't feel, and my gaze moved to the walls where carvings sat crumbling along the brickwork, the subjects hard to make out amid the cobwebs covering them.

I stepped forward, a shiver running down my spine as I crossed some invisible threshold, a breath of magic on my skin.

I moved towards the closest book, the cover a deep, blood red, the material thick and carved with runes, flames, and the triangular symbol for fire. Three zodiac constellations were marked with rubies on the front of it. Leo, Aries, and Sagittarius, the fire signs.

Caleb crossed the space behind me, and I turned from looking at the book to see him approaching a similar one bound in a deep forest green material, the Taurus, Virgo, and Capricorn signs marked on it in emeralds, along with images of plants and runes too.

"These feel...alive," Caleb breathed, his hand skimming along the spine of the book as if he could sense some inner pulse calling out to him from within its pages.

"Should we open them?" I asked, knowing it was insane to question doing so after coming all this way in search of knowledge, but there was something about the five books which set my teeth on edge, something about opening their pages which seemed so very final. Once we did it, we would never be able to undo it again.

Caleb didn't answer, his attention slipping to the dark grey bound book for air, marked with diamonds, then the midnight blue, sapphire inlaid tome for water. "Why are there five?" he asked.

I turned slowly to look at the last book, the one on the pedestal standing at the furthest point of the room, the pitch-black cover which bound it seeming to draw light into it and shroud it in darkness.

"Shadows?" I questioned, taking a step towards it but Caleb shot into my path and halted me with a raised hand.

"Look at the marks on the floor," he murmured, pointing and drawing my attention to the lines which looked like veins of midnight amid the dust that had gathered there. I blinked at them then sucked in a breath, recognising the shape from countless places, though I had never heard a single teacher at Zodiac Academy refer to it as if it held any true power.

"A pentagram," I said, toeing the edge of the closest line with my boot. "With a book at each corner. But why?"

"There are legends, the kind of thing mostly forgotten but mentioned in kids' stories from time to time," Caleb said. "But I've heard people say that long ago, the Elements were always portrayed on a pentagram like this, with one lost power sitting at its helm, a power no one spoke of for fear of waking it again."

"The kind of power we could use to topple a false king?" I asked, knowing his words had been intended to raise fear in me while finding myself filled with hope instead.

"It could be dangerous, Tory," Caleb warned but I shrugged.

"Danger doesn't get to have anything to do with it. My sister needs me; Solaria needs *us*. I won't flinch from a creepy book all forgotten in the dark."

Caleb held my gaze for several seconds, his hesitation melting away at those words and a ferocity taking its place which reminded me that he was one of the most powerful Fae in this entire kingdom.

"Whatever it takes," he said in a low voice, and I swear the lightning-touched scar on my palm tingled at those words.

"No matter the cost," I agreed and together we moved towards the final book.

A lump formed in my throat as I approached it, a heaviness filling the air which left a strange taste on the back of my tongue.

The watchful eyes of a thousand lost souls seemed to fall upon my back as I closed that short span of distance, a low clicking noise registering on the edge of my attention. Something moved in the darkness beyond this chamber, but none of it took my attention from the cloying darkness surrounding that fifth book.

The tome seemed to be warning us away, energy buzzing through the air and the echoes of long-dead screams sounding on the edge of my hearing, but I didn't slow. I couldn't afford to. Not while my sister was missing, Lionel was on the throne, and our people were on the run, at risk of falling prey to him at any given moment. We had taken too great of a hit in that battle, and we needed a weapon to wield against him so that we might be able to turn the tide of this war.

My fingers brushed against the Imperial Star at my throat, the weight of it taunting me with the endless possibilities it contained, coupled with the fact that no one could currently wield it aside from the monster we were set to destroy.

The deep thump of power contained within the Imperial Star pulsed against my fingertips, summoning me closer, making promises it couldn't fulfil. I wanted to curse it along with the stars for taunting us with salvation while refusing to hand it to us.

I ground my jaw and moved my grip from the Imperial Star to the heavy weight of the ruby necklace Darius had gifted me, the stone heating with hidden fire, and I drew in a long breath. A breath seemed to brush against my neck, in that curve where it met with my shoulder, precisely where he had taken to kissing me in the mornings when he woke, his body pressing to my spine as he reeled me into the net of him. Not that I had ever tried to escape. Not once we had finally chosen each other. A prickle of sensation rose up the side of my neck, marking my skin with butterfly soft kisses that I could have sworn were trailed with that stubble he never quite shaved off. A sigh escaped me, longing and heartache merging as the ghost of him faded once more, his intention unclear.

He'd tell me not to do this. Tell me not to do anything that could end badly or risk my life. But then the asshole would have just done it himself, taking on the risks regardless of the cost that losing him would place on everyone he left behind if it failed.

"Do you think he knew he'd die on that battlefield?" I asked.

We stopped before the book and Caleb stilled in that unnatural way only Vampires could manage, almost like he had turned to stone at the mention of the man whose death had destroyed us both.

"I don't think he would have willingly left any of us unless it was the only choice remaining to him. And the one that would save those he loved," he said slowly.

"This doesn't feel like he saved me," I replied, releasing my hold on the ruby pendant bitterly, severing any imagined connection I felt to Darius's spirit through it and slamming those walls back up around my heart before I could feel any more of the agony which was threatening to consume me. "It feels like he destroyed me one final time. Like this was all some big joke, leading up to the annihilation of everything I was and ever could have been."

"You're still you, Tory," Caleb said, reaching for my hand but I shrugged the contact off and reached for the book instead.

"No. I'm not. I'm just an echo left behind, a malignant spirit set on revenge, and I'm far beyond the point of salvation. Which means there isn't anything in this book I won't use if that's what it takes to right the wrongs which have been done against me and mine. Do you understand?"

There was a threat there, a promise of its own as I drew that line, letting him know that I wasn't going to back out of anything we found here now. There was no boundary containing me, no leash on my need for revenge. No matter what we found in this book, I wouldn't be turned from the idea of using it if I could do so to keep the promises I'd made while kneeling in the blood of the man I loved and cursing the stars themselves.

Caleb's gaze was steady as he looked back at me, and I knew then that I wasn't the only one who had gone beyond the point of salvation. Losing Darius was a burden neither of us could bear without reparation, and there would be no morality or fear which might hold us back now.

Whatever we found in that book, in this place, we would use it and damn the consequences.

I willed the Faelight above us to shine brighter and brighter, the blaze hurting my eyes before it grew enough to illuminate the single word marking the black leather of the book which stood at the top of the pentagram.

Ether.

"The fifth Element," I breathed, my eyes moving over dark and twisted runes, the likes of which I hadn't even seen before. In place of Elemental images, the book was covered in twisting patterns which almost seemed like a path or puzzle, my gaze automatically following one to the next, a never-ending trail that held no heart.

I reached for the book, the sound of something shifting across the rocks at my back almost making me turn, but I couldn't tear my eyes from the dark power before me. It was hauntingly intoxicating, a wealth of knowledge and power unlike anything I had ever encountered before.

Our answers lay within those pages, I knew it down to the depths of my soul, but they might just have held our damnation too.

I raised my chin and thought of my sister, lost somewhere out there in the wastelands of this world. She needed me and I wouldn't back down now, so without another thought, I reached for the cover of the Book of Ether and opened it.

A cold wind collided with my spine as the book fell open, a scream rising in my throat then choking out as the power in my veins was ripped away, burning out in a flashfire that left me completely tapped out. It all happened so quickly that I almost fell to my knees from the brutality of its destruction.

I clung to the dais before me, Caleb panting heavily at my side as the same thing happened to him. I couldn't help but look behind us, scanning the walls and the open passageway at our backs for any signs of something coming for us in our newly vulnerable state.

"What the fuck was that?" Caleb asked, his fangs glinting in the faint light as his Order form was released.

"I don't know. But if this book can command that much power with something as simple as opening it, then I have to think we're looking in the right place."

Caleb nodded slowly, his eyes darting around the room too and I was reassured as he turned back to the book. If his Vampire senses hadn't revealed anything to worry about, then I was confident I could turn my attention the Book of Ether and unveil its secrets.

The first page held nothing beyond the symbol of the pentagram, the power humming from the ominous shape making a shiver dart through me as I carefully turned the page again.

Ether is the epitome of all magics. It's power great, and influence vast. Those who dare tap into the call of this purest form of magic should heed this warning:

No prize comes without a cost. Blood shall spill, spirits shall splinter, and all shall behold the one-eyed demon of fate before the end.

"That sounds promising," I muttered, turning the page again and finding a table of contents which listed things from omens to bloodletting, soul walking to the power of the true name, curses, hexes, bone magic, blood magic, the power of chaos, to the corruption of fate. So many magics, most of which I had never heard of and beyond.

I found a chapter titled 'to find a lost soul' and quickly flipped the pages to locate it.

The book fell open but the chapter I'd been seeking wasn't the one I found. Instead, staring up at me was an image of two Fae standing on either side of what looked like a pane of glass or a mirror, their faces torn with grief as they reached for one another. In the second image, the Fae to the left was cutting their arm open, the blood spilling onto a collection of rune-marked bones and other items which were hard to recognise in the drawing. But in the third image, the thing that had been dividing the two Fae had cracked apart, not broken, not enough for anything more than their voices to pass through, but it was enough for that much and the look of relief on their faces set my heart racing.

I flipped back a page and looked to the title there. *Conversing with the dead.*

My lips parted as I began to read more, my eyes drinking in each and every word while Caleb fell deathly still at my side.

A strange scraping, rattle stole through the air.

The power of conversing with the dead is one of the more sought-after forms of necromancy, the ability both often one of deepest desire and most potent grief, but it is not an act that many Fae can complete.

Most commonly, a séance is the key to achieving such a gift, but it must be noted that such power should not be wielded lightly.

First off, a spirit board will likely be needed to help translate the words of those beyond the Veil. Such an item is best crafted from the wood of a Necrolis Tree, the power of its wood imbued with ether from the casting Fae to help create a bridge.

My heart thundered like the galloping hooves of a wild stallion as I read on, but it began to sink the further I went, the book explaining the way the board could be used to get simple answers such as yes or no most effectively, needing more power and the addition of blood magic to access full words which would be spelled out letter by letter. The chances of gleaning so much as a full sentence were bleak and there were multiple mentions of the pitfalls of such magic. For one, the Fae wielding it needing to bleed the entire time the connection was in place, and worse than that, malignant spirits took the place of the intended Fae on the other side more often than not. They would play games and send messages of either hope or despair in an attempt to lure the Fae wielding the magic to linger too long and bleed out while casting it.

It became clear that the practice would offer up little more than yes or no answers even if a connection with the departed soul was created. I wouldn't even be able to hear his voice.

My fist slammed down on the plinth beside the book as frustration and disappointment bit into me, and Caleb sighed as he came to the same conclusion that I had. Spirit boards weren't the answer to us finding Darius again in any form. If there even was a way to contact him in the beyond, then this wasn't it.

"Fuck," I hissed, turning the pages aggressively to find the one I'd been hunting for in the first place.

To Find a Lost Soul.

When encountering this magic for the first time, one must be aware of the pitfalls involved with soul walking. This magic is not for the weak of heart and can be more dangerous than it first seems.

First, to seek out a missing soul, the Fae casting the magic must have a deep and intimate knowledge of the one they seek. A blood relation or mate is the best and only real option, unless one wishes to risk the perils of being cast adrift in the in-between.

I scanned several more paragraphs which gave a more in-depth description of the way the magic would work. First, I was going to have to find a bone of my enemy and carve it with the true name of the Fae I sought. Then there was a whole bit on tethering my lifeforce to a subject of immovable value so that I could find my way back again because to achieve this magic, my soul was literally going to be walking out of my damn body and shifting across the world to search out the one I was hunting for. On top of that, I would need to harness the energy of the sun at its highest point in the day.

It looked complicated and damn difficult, plus there were a ton of warnings about not lingering outside the confines of my flesh and never attempting to soul walk beyond the Veil unless I was seeking the true death.

All in all, it sounded pretty full-on and all kinds of terrifying, but I wasn't put off in the least. If I could use that power to find my sister, then there was nothing in this world which would keep me from doing so.

Caleb didn't protest when I said as much to him, only suggesting we should stop by the battlefield on our way back home to gather the bones of our enemies for the spell.

I nodded grimly, knowing I should have left it at that, the book having already given us the knowledge we'd come here for, but I couldn't help myself as I began to turn more pages, one after another, drinking in the words and twisted magic awaiting me there.

There were other kinds of necromancy beyond the spirit board, almost all aimed at conversing with the dead, though some referred to raising dead bodies. The momentary excitement I felt over those chapters was quickly quelled by the facts as I read more. The things the book talked about raising were nothing beyond shells, no part of the Fae who had once resided within them lingering. They were simply mindless skeletons with some lingering magic in their bones which could be used for simple things like protecting particular items or guarding against unwanted trespassers, much like the dead in The Everhill Graveyard who had been awakened when we had gone there without permission in the dead of night.

Just as I felt like screaming at the whole damn world for teasing me with possibilities which weren't anywhere close to becoming reality, I turned one more page and my eyes fell on a footnote beneath the description of a spell on the corruption of fate.

Even a destiny mapped out by the stars and drawn into reality by time itself can often be changed. Fate is not the master of this world. Only ether commands the true power, and those who learn to master its call can learn to master the world itself and all those who exist within it.

My lips parted on Caleb's name as I pointed towards the sentence, but in the next heartbeat, a swell of unnatural power drove into us again and the Faelights all blinked out.

That scraping, clawing noise ground against the stones at our backs, and I whirled towards it, the dark pressing in so thickly that I couldn't even see my hand before my face, let alone anything else.

The sound of the book slamming shut behind me sent an echo reverberating right down to my core. I worked to summon magic to my command, despite already knowing that it had all been stripped away from me and a pit of dread lodged itself within me as I felt the empty bowels of my power in reply.

"We are the Keepers of the Lost Knowledge," a voice of nightmares spoke from the dark, a horrible clacking sound punctuating each word. "And you have trespassed where you are not welcome."

Scorpio
Gemini
Virgo
Cancer
Aries
Leo
Sagittarius
Taurus
Capricorn
Aquarius
Libra
Pisces

CALEB

CHAPTER TWENTY EIGHT

My fangs snapped out as I squinted into the darkness, my gifted vision barely managing to pick apart the shadows at all in this place of endless night, but there was something there in the dark, something shifting across the wall with a body that writhed unnaturally.

"What is it?" Tory hissed at my side, drawing her sword even though she couldn't see shit either, but as the Phoenix fire burst to life along the length of it, the room flared into sudden and all too real focus.

The thing on the wall wasn't alone, more and more of them creeping out of cracks which had seemed like nothing but dark shadows around the edges of this forgotten chamber but now proved themselves to be doorways designed for things unlike any creature I had ever known to walk this earth.

Their bodies were a matte black, overlapping armoured plates coating their length, the things moving like centipedes while clinging to walls and ceilings with overly long legs that bent at unnatural angles, knees turning back on themselves. But their faces weren't like any insect, their deep green eyes blazing with intelligence and seeming almost Fae. Their jaws were something born of a twisted fantasy, a gaping mouth of sharp and rotting teeth that hung slack, saliva dripping onto the dark floor as they surveyed their meals.

"What do you want?" I demanded, drawing my twin daggers, and igniting the flames on them at my command while trying to keep my eyes on the monsters circling us.

Without our magic, we were at one hell of a disadvantage, but if we could keep them distracted for just a little longer then Tory would be able to use the fire from our weapons to recharge at least some of her power.

"To fulfil the task left to us by the Mother," one hissed from my left and I fought to hide my repulsion as drool slid from its fangs to the floor. "To protect the knowledge here from Fae who would seek to abuse it for selfish gains."

"We aren't looking to abuse anything," Tory said firmly, her chin held high as she met the monstrous eyes of the one directly in front of us. "I am a Vega princess and Caleb is an Heir to the Celestial Council. Solaria is in desperate need of the magic hidden inside these books."

The creatures all began to clack their teeth, and it took me a moment to realise they were speaking to one another, their movements growing faster as they riled themselves up. I glanced between them where they continued to crawl across the walls surrounding us.

A faint glow drew my attention to the pentagram we stood within, the lines of it coming alive with some ancient power while the beasts circled us.

"They can't cross those lines," I breathed for Tory's ears alone and she nodded in understanding as one of the creatures came close to a glimmering line then skuttled away again with a hiss of pain.

"The Mother hid this knowledge from your kind," one of the monsters said suddenly, making me turn towards it on our right. "Hid it from those who abused it time and again. It is to remain lost."

"And if we refuse to leave it here?" Tory demanded, causing those rotting teeth to clatter together as the creatures hissed and snapped in rage.

"Then we will show you how very hungry we are," one rasped.

"I get the feeling you intend to show us that regardless of our choices concerning the books," I pointed out and something akin to laughter filled the air.

"You know of the books' existence," one breathed from the ceiling directly above our heads. "That knowledge cannot leave this place."

"Well, that makes this conversation somewhat pointless," Tory muttered, her fingers twisting subtly to throw a silencing bubble over the two of us. "How fast are you feeling?" she asked, her focus locked on the monsters as they swarmed around us.

"Lightning," I replied, eyeing the creatures as they circled us, knowing as well as they did that we couldn't hide within the confines of the pentagram for long. The magic which pulsed along the lines of it was already flickering and I was willing to bet that after a few thousand years, its power was burning low. "We probably have another minute at best before the pentagram falls."

"I'll make a bag for the books then jump on your back, you throw them all into it and I'll blast them with fire to create a path to the exit for you to shoot us through," Tory said, her hand already moving as she cast a large bag from thick leaves, the monsters clacking and yowling as they saw what she was doing.

"I hope that Minotaur can run fast," I muttered, knowing we were going to need his help to find our way back out of the Labyrinth once we made it to the upper level again.

"Let's focus on not dying in this chamber first then worry about the speed his hooves can move if we don't die before we get back to him," Tory suggested, and I swear the thought of us dying down here in this pit had her dark eyes glimmering with excitement.

"You're a fucking psychopath, you know that?" I muttered and she flashed me a grin that was all bloodlust for a fight.

"Says the apex predator."

Tory tossed me the bag and I stowed one of my daggers before snatching it from mid-air as she sheathed her sword then leapt onto my back.

I shot into motion as the creatures screamed in horror, realising what we were doing while still powerless to stop us from beyond the magical barrier created by the pentagram.

I grabbed the book on ether first, the weight of it notable beyond what I would have expected even with how big the fucking thing was. I tossed it into the bag, cringing a little at how roughly I was handling it and knowing that somewhere in the world, Orion had just shuddered in horror. The book on fire went in next, then water and air, the bag feeling like it was weighted with fucking rocks and the leaves which had gone into its creation groaning at the strain of holding them.

My fingers brushed the edge of the earth book just as a shudder of power rumbled through the room and the light gleaming from the pentagram fell apart on a breath of unnatural wind.

The creatures screamed as they lunged at us, shadows of deepest black dancing across the walls in their wake as the light from my lone dagger was all we had left to see by.

I was forced to dart aside as they lunged for me, hopping over one then almost tripping on another before a hot slice of pain cut into my thigh as one of them managed to swipe at me with its razor-sharp pincers.

I swore loudly and a blast of flame erupted over my shoulder as Tory unleashed her magic, the creature screaming as it was caught in the fire, its body curling in on itself while the armoured plates of its back locked together to protect it from the flames.

The other monsters lurched away, shielding their eyes with their grossly bent limbs as the flare of light momentarily blinded them.

I lunged for the earth book, hurling it into the bag and shooting towards the exit as the creatures recovered and came for us again.

Tory cried out in pain as one of them swung a pincer at us and the hot splatter of her blood on my cheek told me it had found flesh.

"Fuck, that hurts," she hissed, letting me know that she wasn't mortally wounded as I shot for the exit with her still clinging on tight to my back.

Fire tore from her palm as she aimed for the passage leading back out into the underground library, the creatures throwing themselves aside or curling in on their own bodies in defence to the flames.

I shot between them and hurtled out into the damp chamber, a flash of dizziness making me stumble as I turned a corner, and I swore as I almost crashed into a wall at breakneck speed.

The creatures howled behind us as they took chase and my pulse hammered wildly in chest as my feet began to slow.

"My Phoenix is fading!" Tory cried as I ran on, my gifted speed coming and going so that one moment we raced through the passages and the next I was stumbling at Fae speed.

"They must have had some kind of Order suppressant in their pincers," I cursed, spotting the stairs we needed ahead of us and staggering on, managing another flash of speed which hurled us up several flights before I almost fell face first against the wall as my gifts slipped away again.

"Let me down," Tory commanded, but I shook my head and forced myself to focus, baring my fangs and shooting us on once more.

The sound of those things chasing us wasn't nearly far enough away and I knew if we had to run at our normal Fae speed, they'd catch us in no time.

"I can hold on a little longer," I gritted out even as pain radiated through my mouth and my fangs began to retract.

We shot up the stairs once more, but I tripped over the final one, the two of us crashing to the ground and tumbling across the stone floor where we re-joined the Labyrinth, my dagger and the bag of books sliding away across the stone floor.

"That motherfucking bovine cunt!" I roared as I shoved myself to my feet and hunted the dark passageway for any sign of Arnold, the asshole who had promised to wait right here for us and had apparently given up on that promise at the earliest opportunity.

Tory got up too, her eyes whipping left and right in search of the Minotaur, but it was clear that he had been gone a while. I didn't know if the shrieks of those monsters down in the dark had scared him off or if the motherfucker had abandoned us the second we'd descended those stairs, but it didn't matter now. We were fucked.

"There's no escaping a Minotaur's labyrinth, Tory," I said as she threw a hand out towards the stairs and blocked them off with a wall of rock, the screams of the monsters beyond it cutting off abruptly.

"You need to bite me," she snapped, whirling towards me and ignoring what I'd said entirely.

"No," I barked, a flash of memory spearing through me as I remembered what I'd done to her the last time I'd bitten her. The sound of her spine breaking as she fell from the roof of King's Hollow, the utter fury and betrayal in Darius's eyes as he realised what I'd done and had commanded me never to come near her with my fangs again. I couldn't bite her. I wouldn't.

"Stop giving me that fucking look and bite me before you lose contact with your Vampire entirely. You're no use to either of us if you have no access to your Order form and no magic to fight with."

"Tory, I can't. I swore an oath to Darius after I hurt you before. You know I can't-"

She punched me so hard, my fucking head wheeled to one side, and I tasted my own blood.

"Don't throw his fucking name at me and talk about promises you made to him. He promised me he'd fight for me. He promised he wouldn't fucking leave. And look what he did. So don't go keeping promises to that asshole which will end up getting the both of us killed, when he broke every oath he ever swore by dying on that fucking battlefield and leaving me all on my own."

The raw pain and heartache in her green eyes ripped at something deep inside of me, but as the weight of several huge bodies collided with the wall of rock beside me, I knew this wasn't the time to dwell on that. And even if I didn't believe in half the things she'd just said or even believe that she meant them herself, I did know one thing. Darius had made me swear that oath to protect the woman who stood before me. And he would want me to do anything I could to protect her now too. Which meant I needed to be able to fight.

My fangs throbbed with pain again and I knew we were almost out of time, my Vampire retreating into the dark recesses of my mind as the venom from those fucking pincers delved under my skin and banished it.

With a snarl of frustration, I lunged for her, my fingers knotting in her hair as her head fell back in submission and my teeth broke the soft skin of her throat with a violence that I should have subdued.

Tory hissed as I drank from her, this bite nothing like the ones we'd once shared, a gap of space dividing our bodies which neither of us felt any urge to close. The power of her blood still overwhelmed me the way it always had, but the intoxication I'd once felt at the taste of her was missing, an ache for something dipped in moonlight burning in my chest as I took what I needed to replenish my power.

My fangs throbbed as I fought against the venom which was trying to force them to retract and I gulped her blood down greedily, taking as much as I could before the suppressant won out and my fangs were banished.

I released her instantly and Tory raised a hand to pile more rocks against the wall beside us as it rattled violently once again.

"This way," she commanded, breaking into a sprint while I threw the bag full of books onto my back, retrieved my dagger and chased after her, already uncertain of the way in this maze of tunnels.

Flames coated Tory's hands as she sprinted on ahead of me, both lighting the way and regenerating her power as we raced down tunnel after tunnel.

A resounding boom in the distance made it clear that the creatures had forced their way through the barricade and my pulse raced as I glanced back in that direction, magic building in my palms.

We took a set of stairs up a level before a few more turns revealed a dead end, and we were forced to double back again.

The clacking, grinding sound of the creatures racing over the stone walls was so much closer when we reached the bottom of the stairs again that I expected them to be on us at any moment.

Tory threw another wall of stone up at our backs and I added my power to hers, reinforcing it before we charged on, but no matter how many twists and turns we took, no exit revealed itself.

"I can't believe we survived all we have only to end up lost in a fucking labyrinth and eaten by a bunch of mutated centipedes," I swore, and the sounds of pursuit grew closer again, our end closing in on us no matter how fast we ran.

"Fuck that," Tory growled, sprinting around another bend before cursing so loudly that I knew it was a dead end before I even turned it myself.

"Shit," I agreed, putting my back to the wall at her side and casting spears of wood and stone to grow from every wall of the tunnel just as the first of the beasts launched themselves around the corner.

I glanced at Tory as she bared her teeth at the monsters, whips cast from thorny vines coiling from her fists as she prepared to fight to the death at my side, a fire lit behind us making the blood from the bite on her throat gleam deepest red.

"We don't die here," she said, a queen's command and for once, I had no problem following it.

"Agreed."

Chaos erupted all around us as the Guardians of the Lost Knowledge attacked us at full force, countless insectile bodies leaping for us, those grotesque teeth bared for our throats as they screamed out in desire for our deaths.

Tory flicked her whips, the vines binding two of the beasts tightly, the thorns digging into scaled flesh before bursting alight and making them scream in agony.

I threw the spears I'd cast from the walls at them, dark blue blood spraying the brickwork as they were impaled upon them, their screams of pain colouring the air and making my ears ring in the confined space.

Tory threw her hands out and sent a tornado of fire and air magic at them, their wails of agony letting us know how much they hated the flames, and I turned my power to fire too.

The monsters screamed louder as they tried to run from us, but I curled my fist and slammed it against the wall sending earth magic ricocheting through the walls themselves, seeking out the monsters as they raced away before throwing a wall of steel into place to trap them in this tunnel.

"Let's end this," I snarled, pouring all of my power into the flames again, filling the entire passageway with them as the heat threatened to burn us alive too.

Tory gritted her teeth and ice grew at our backs, air swirling up and over us, circling past the ice over and over again as she protected us from the flames and we set the entire world on fire before us, not relenting for even the briefest of moments until the screams of those monsters fell to nothing.

My power guttered out as the last of the screams sounded and the flames fell away, revealing the charred, skeletal bodies of the beasts in a tunnel lined with nothing but soot.

The two of us stood there for several long minutes, panting and staring at the bodies of the dead creatures from our position lost in a fucking Minotaur's labyrinth, which we were likely to stay lost in for a long fucking time.

"What are we supposed to do now?" I asked, glancing up at the stone roof which curved above our heads, towards the world which awaited us up there.

"Well, I'm not staying down in some fucking tunnel for god knows how long," Tory replied, and I snorted in amusement as she raised her hands and started breaking the damn roof apart right above our heads.

The entire world seemed to shake and rattle around us as she gritted her teeth, the flames burning hotter to stoke her power as she built it to greater heights, the magic of the labyrinth fighting against her in an attempt to stop what she was trying to do. This place was built to withstand the force of any Fae fool enough to try and carve their way free of it. But Tory wasn't just any Fae. She was a Vega, the most powerful bloodline in known history and a Phoenix too, her magic endless while that fire burned at her back and her will iron as she forced the laws of magic and nature to bend to her will.

The roof above our heads cracked apart with an almighty boom, debris tumbling down onto us and colliding with a shield she'd already thrown up to protect us.

I adjusted the weight of the bag on my back as she lifted us with air magic and we rose into the tunnel she was carving above us, heading higher and higher until finally some light spilled down to reveal the golden halls of the pristine library.

The world continued to groan and shudder in protest to her power, and I tried to hide my awe at the incredible magic as she forced a labyrinth built of ancient magic to crumble at her will.

A scream of purest horror greeted us as Tory shot us up through the library and deposited us, bloodstained, filthy and dripping fuck knew what onto a beautiful cream carpet in the middle of a huge chamber filled with golden bookshelves.

The librarian who hadn't wanted to let us into this place stood there, a hand on his chest and a silent scream on his lips as he sagged against a shame-faced Minotaur called Arnold.

"Thanks so much for your hospitality," Tory said brightly, striding past them towards the exit where she gave a gobsmacked Laini a salute and struck the call button for the elevator which would return us to ground level at last. "We'll be sure to visit again soon."

"By the light of the ever-waning moon," the librarian breathed, and I tossed him a wicked grin as Arnold continued to try and hold him upright.

"Oh, and Arnold?" Tory added, backing into the elevator which had arrived behind us. "If I ever see your cowardly, abandoning face again, I'm gonna cut your horns off and shove them up your ass. Got it?"

Arnold mooed weakly and I gnashed my teeth at him to back up that promise right as the doors closed to the sound of the librarian protesting us leaving with a bag full of books.

"Bite me," I called in challenge but if he replied again, the answer was lost as the elevator soared up through the lake towards the fresh air above.

"Tell me you kept hold of your Atlas in that madness so we can get back to the rebels," I begged of Tory as we stepped out of the elevator and found ourselves on the island sat in the middle of the lake, bits of dead lake monster still floating in the dark water surrounding us. "Because we still haven't got use of our Order forms and I seem to have lost mine somewhere when you attacked those monsters-"

"Don't blame me for that dude, that was fully the crab thing's fault."

"Either way, we're looking a hell of a lot like a pair of mortals on a camping trip in the near future, unless you still have yours?" We needed someone to give us the current location of the floating island or we'd be stranded here with countless hours having passed since we'd left.

"We could start walking?" she suggested half-heartedly and I sighed, the idea of camping out in the middle of nowhere about as appealing as taking a bath in that lake as I glanced at those monster lumps floating in the water once more. "Or we could call for a location?" Tory flashed her Atlas at me with a taunting look and I cursed her as she hit dial on Geraldine's number.

"Don't forget we need to stop for a bone of your enemy on the way back," I said, grimacing at that lovely idea.

"Your dating game has really picked up recently, you know that?" she said sweetly and the memory of our utter failure of a date flashed through my mind, making my grimace deepen.

"You really would have preferred grave robbing and fighting those monsters to karaoke and sushi, wouldn't you?" I asked and her eyes flashed with what looked like amusement for a moment as she shrugged.

"Definitely."

I rolled my eyes just as Geraldine answered the call, her gushing voice spilling from the speaker as the truth of that statement settled in me, and I found nothing but amusement in it. Tory Vega was one hell of a friend to take on a night out, but our destiny had never been meant to merge in the way I had once thought it might, and I found that there was no sting left to that truth anymore, no lingering hurt or resentment. Me and her were a train wreck waiting to happen as a couple, but as friends we worked out pretty damn well.

Tory managed to end her call with Geraldine fairly quickly, and I looked to her in expectation as she took the stardust from her pocket.

"They're just doing something with Xavier that apparently can't wait. She'll let us know once she's carved out a landing spot for us between the wards," she explained, and I nodded, my eyes moving over the silent, picturesque landscape that surrounded us.

"Wanna sit and enjoy the view?" I offered.

Tory's eyes tracked across the vibrantly green landscape, but she shook her head. "Silence isn't good for me right now."

I resisted the urge to hug her, knowing she didn't want that, not here, not while she was fighting so hard to remain unbroken through all of this.

"Wanna go find some bones of your enemies then instead?"

Her lips twitched with amusement, but she just pulled a shard of bone from her pocket, holding it out to me.

"I took it from those things that tried to kill us down there. They certainly seemed to think we were their enemies, so..."

"Savage," I snorted, and she returned the bone to her pocket with a shrug.

"I'm not wasting any more time."

"Well, unfortunately for you, we can't head back until we hear from Geraldine, so either sit your ass down and enjoy the view with me while we wait or start walking if you need to keep moving. Lady's choice."

Tory looked inclined to start walking, but I had to assume she saw the pointlessness in that and dropped down to sit on the damp grass instead, her chin raised as she looked out over the stunning view.

I joined her on the ground, the bag of stolen books sitting between us with an air of power radiating from them that neither of us spoke on.

Silence stretched and a cool wind blew between the mountains, giving our grief a moment to rise up and have its way once more.

"It feels like I've lost a limb," I murmured, my throat thickening as I looked across the mountainous landscape, imagining a golden Dragon tearing across that sky, tumbling through the clouds.

Tory didn't reply but she shifted closer to me, her head falling against my shoulder as she took my hand in hers. I could feel the ridge of the scar cut into her palm where her skin pressed to mine, and I could have sworn a note of power radiated from the oath she'd carved into her skin.

"I made a promise to the stars to end them for this failure," she said in a low voice, the cold certainty in her words making the hairs along the back of my neck stand on end. "And I intend to keep it."

Silence fell away from us once more and I could feel the echoes of her words spilling out over the sky and beyond, the certainty and power of that oath she'd made, and the knowledge that she wouldn't stop until she saw it fulfilled. If there was a single Fae in Solaria capable of making the stars themselves tremble with their wrath, then I knew it was Tory Vega. And not even the might of the heavens would save them when that time came.

Scorpio
Gemini
Virgo
Aries
Cancer
Leo
Taurus
Sagittarius
Capricorn
Aquarius
Libra
Pisces

SETH

CHAPTER TWENTY NINE

"I don't know about this," Xavier said as we sat out by the fire pit, smoke coiling up towards the twilight sky.

"Nonsense, you nincompoop," Geraldine exclaimed as she helped Sofia and Tyler strap Xavier into a glittery lilac harness around his chest. They'd convinced him to strip down to his boxers, ready to shift and Sofia and Tyler were also in their underwear, putting on their own harnesses which were attached to Xavier's between them by four thick straps.

"I feel like an idiot," Xavier muttered.

"It'll be fine once we're up there," Tyler said firmly. "Just give it a shot."

Xavier stamped his foot in annoyance but didn't refuse it any more than that.

"This is gonna be shit show," Max muttered to me from my right.

I'd spent some time crafting the log seats out here, so they were comfy as hell with a lining of moss on them too, and I had my feet kicked up on a little loggy pouffe. But as comfy as I was, I wasn't in the best of moods. Caleb and Tory still hadn't returned, and my mind was chasing visions of them together in that deep, dark library, seeking solace in each other's arms. What was taking so fucking long? Geraldine had taken a call not long ago, but had cast a silencing bubble and gone all incognito about it since, sending Justin and a couple of other Asses off with some job in mind. She always did shit like that, acting as if me, Caleb and Max weren't worthy of hearing the plans of the mighty A.S.S. And it pissed me the hell off.

"Righto, are you ready, my stout stallion?" Geraldine clapped Xavier on the arm, and he huffed a breath then nodded.

Sofia undid her bra, wriggling out of it and tossing it away before her and her two Pega-men dropped their underwear and revealed a whole host of glittery rocks and shiny encrustings on their Ds and her P.

I'd always quite liked the idea of a dijazzle and wondered if my cock would appreciate a little makeover. *I wonder if there was anything true to that rumour about Cal having the hots for Pegasuses…*

The three of them shifted and the harnesses stretched out around their bodies to accommodate their new size. Sofia had had the idea to use the same magic as the Tempa Pego-bags to make it easier for them to shift in and out of their Order forms while wearing the harness. It had quick release buckles too for when they landed.

Seemed like a solid idea, only Xavier was pouting like someone had pissed in his pancake mix. Even in Pegasus form, his lips were pursed and his eyes all angry-like.

"Go on, Xavier," Max encouraged, the air filling with a buzz of excitement as he fed it to all of us.

Xavier looked a little brighter as he absorbed Max's gifts and Geraldine moved around to smack him on the rump.

"Yah!" she cried, and Xavier kicked his hind legs at her, making her dive out of the way and do a forward roll before rising stylishly back to her feet.

It made me think of her signature Pitball moves and a whine left my throat as I thought of that game and how I was never going to get to play it again with all of my friends.

Max reached out to brush his fingers over my arm and I let him steal away some of my pain, before pressing some happies into me.

"Thanks, man," I murmured.

"Any time," he said. "I can go a little deeper if you like?"

"No," I said quickly. Any deeper, and he'd find my secret feelings for Caleb, but I hated the way my friend frowned at me, as if he knew I was hiding stuff from him.

"Love you, bro," I added, and his face softened.

"Love you too, asshole," he said.

The Pegasuses walked forward, turning in a large circle until they were facing downhill away from the firepit, their tails swishing and muscles twitching in anticipation of the flight.

"Go on, Xavier," Geraldine hooted. "Fly to the nevermore and beyond!"

Xavier neighed, rearing up and flicking his head so his beautiful lilac mane fluttered in the wind, then he charged forward, leading the way. Tyler and Sofia raced along beside him, their wings stretching out either side of them, flapping in preparation of take-off.

"Go, Xavier!" I howled in excitement.

They started lifting into the sky, Tyler and Sofia rising fast while the harness attached to Xavier went taut between them, and he was hoisted off the ground with his horsey legs wheeling through the sky.

Sofia whinnied happily to Xavier, but Darius's little brother slowly stopped kicking his legs, hanging there like a limp dick instead as he sailed overhead.

"Give it some gusto, dear brother!" Geraldine called to him, but Xavier's features had fallen flat, his long face looking sullen as hell while Sofia and Tyler flew back and forth in the sky above.

"He looks like he's about to be fed to a T-rex," I said to Max who burst out laughing just as Xavier was flown overhead again, his horsey pout deepening.

"What in the world…" My mom appeared with Tiberius Rigel, the two of them watching the strange display in confusion.

Geraldine bustled her way over to them, grabbing Tiberius's hand and pulling him closer.

"Good day to you and your cockles, Tiberius. Look, I have been wanting to say this to you for a finnywag or two, but there has been much ado about war and politics that has taken the front seat of our caddy wagon. So hear me now. I know you and my father stood upon separate cliffs which bordered a desolate sea, but I must say that you have sired a fine salmon, and I have decided I wish to form something of a trout truce with you. We can put our whelks aside for the sake of mine and Maxy boy's pimpersnapping, at least outside of the war councils and such, what say you?"

Tiberius frowned, looking to Max then back to Geraldine. "I'm terribly sorry, my dear, but I have no idea what you just said."

"Oh-ho! You are quite the devil dancing with a dandelion," Geraldine laughed, slapping Tiberius on the chest. "You have such wit about your warthole. Shall we sup together this eve? Or perhaps upon the morrow if this night doesn't suit? It would be best for us to get to know each other on a more personable level, to forge a bond that can transcend our animosity towards one another. Of course, I won't promise to shut my tripper trapper when it comes to my loyalties, and no doubt your tongue will dance the dinglehop in my direction whenever a debate arises, but Maxy and I have found fertile ground to plant our neutral begonias in, and I do not see any reason why we cannot do the same. So what say you, does a supper suit or is a tiffin more appetising to your belly box?"

"I, er…" Tiberius looked lost for words and Max shoved to his feet.

"She'd like dinner with us, Dad," Max explained, moving to slip his arm around Geraldine's waist. My mom made a face that said she was concerned about my friend's new relationship with a royalist.

It got my hackles rising, because I was so sick of all this 'us and them' bullshit. The royals versus the Heirs. I knew all of that might be relevant again one day if we ever got a chance to seize the throne, but I was tired of battles and I definitely didn't want to go back to war with the Vegas and their friends. And yeah, okay, so maybe that made me a hypocrite considering all the shit I'd done in the past to try and get rid of the twins, but like, why couldn't everyone just get along now? If anything made alliances more important than ever, it was war. We'd put our Heir hats back on if we ever killed the lizard king. Simple.

"Of course," Tiberius said, smiling kindly at Geraldine. "How about dinner tomorrow?"

Xavier swooped over our heads again, eyes narrowed and expression flat even though Sofia and Tyler were working hard to give him the ride of his life.

Mom walked over to me, cocking her head as she took in the way I was slumped in my chair.

"You could go and speak with some of the rebels, start talking them around and gaining some favour among them," she suggested.

"And why would I do that?" I asked, folding my arms.

"Politics, Seth," she clipped. "Have you forgotten everything I taught you? You need to become a leader among these people. It's important you show your face, and that you're seen helping with the new building sites. I've been working on the construction of a nursery on the eastern side of the island, perhaps you could head over there and offer a hand?"

"You mean slap on a fake smile and go win some allegiance with my charm," I corrected dryly, not looking at her, but she stepped firmly into my line of sight.

"I know you're still grieving, pup," she said gently. "But it really is time to start thinking of the future again. We must rebuild what has been lost. If you don't want to get involved in public relations today, then perhaps you'll spend some time speaking to Xavier once he's let down from that humiliating harness?"

Xavier flew over us again just at that moment, his head hanging in shame as he heard my mom speak those words.

"Now look what you've done," I hissed, pointing at sad little Xavier in the sky. "Sure, it's embarrassing. Demeaning even-"

Xavier whinnied woefully, apparently hearing me say that as he sailed by again. Damn, horse ears were more sensitive than I'd realised.

"But the guy deserves to fly around up there as much as he likes, kicking his little hooves and remembering what it was like to soar through the clouds before he lost his wings," I went on, pushing to my feet and looking down at my mom. She was tall, but I was taller. "Maybe we all deserve to remember the good times. Maybe *I* want a go in that harness."

"You wouldn't dare," she gasped.

"I would. I'd go up in that harness and I wouldn't care how shameful, mortifying, embarrassing, and reputation-shattering it looked," I said proudly, hearing Xavier neigh mournfully again in response to my words.

Xavier started biting at the harness to get free of it, whinnying angrily at Sofia and Tyler, but they didn't seem able to hear him. He shifted back into his Fae form like he thought that might release him, but instead he flipped upside down in the harness, naked as a new-born with his arms flailing and his bejewelled cock flapping in the wind.

"Argh!" he cried out, wheeling left and right as Tyler and Sofia continued to fly around in huge circles, not noticing the carnage unfolding beneath them while they focused on staying airborne.

Xavier grappled with the harness, managing to unstrap one side of it, which only made him hang more awkwardly, the whole thing slipping down to snag around his ass. He flopped forward, ass now high in the air and his hands reaching desperately for the other buckle which had twisted around to sit at the base of his spine.

"Someone should help him," I said, shaking my head sadly.

"*You* should help him," Mom insisted, and I realised she was right, lifting my hand and casting a gust of air to try and twist him upright again. Woops. Totally could have helped out sooner. My brain was so frazzled today. It kept hanging out in the little world I'd made up called Calaria, where Caleb was all smitten with me, kissing me and calling me a good pup while fondling my balls.

I cast my magic a tiny bit too powerfully as I got distracted by my thoughts, sending Xavier into a wild tailspin instead of steadying him, and he cried out in fury as he went spinning past my head like an ass tornado.

I quickly righted the magic, holding him still and flicking the buckle open to free him with the power of air. He tumbled out of it, and I caught him on a little cloud, carrying him down to land at my side and leaving the fluffy cloud in place to cover his junk. His cheeks were bright red, and he looked ready to dig a hole for himself and disappear, or maybe punch me in the face, I wasn't quite sure.

"There you go, bud," I said, patting his shoulder and he shrugged me off with a snort of rage.

"You asshole," he snapped.

"Yeah, I, er, have to take the blame for that one for sure," I said, giving him a guilty look. "But on the plus side, you looked great up there. Really cool."

He gave me a flat look that said he knew that was most obvious lie I'd ever told, and he had a point.

"Xavier, that was quite…something," Mom said, smiling brightly, her voice coated in false enthusiasm.

I looked at her, seeing so much of myself in her mannerisms. The phony smiles that were painted on so thickly, you couldn't see through them at all. The only reason I could was because she'd taught me that skill, and I knew her well enough to sense when she was being fake. I was sick of always having to act like everything was perfect, like I was this brave, happy, always optimistic figure head that people relied on to keep their own spirits high. But what about *my* spirits? What about when they were obliterated and every forced smile I jammed into my cheeks chipped off a fresh, juicy piece of my soul?

For my entire life, every action I took was carefully monitored, the reactions I got from news articles demanding more or less of my personality, until there were times when I didn't even know who I was when I was standing on the stage of the world. The only times when I'd been free of that was in the company of the Heirs, and more recently the Vegas and my new friends. I wasn't ready to go back to correcting every move I made that might piss off the masses. Fuck the masses. They could wait until I was done grieving.

Xavier turned away, grabbing his clothes as he went and stalking off up the track that led back to the R.U.M.P. castle, the cloud still hovering around his ass.

"Go after him," Mom encouraged. "And try to talk him into taking Darius's place and stepping up into the position of Fire Lord. I know it's hard but we're at war. It's time he took up his role in it."

Rage slashed through my chest, and I growled at her, showing the Alpha in me.

"He doesn't want Darius's place. Leave it empty, who cares?" I sniped.

"You are not yourself," she snarled, casting a silencing bubble around us in case any nosey rebel might be near enough to hear us. Like I gave a fuck anymore. "We got word today that Linda Rigel has been given a position as 'High Councillor' in the new court Lionel is setting up."

I blanched at that little snippet of information, looking over at Max and his dad who looked to be talking seriously in a silencing bubble, no doubt discussing what this meant too. Max's stepmom was a royal bitch and we all knew that, so I doubted he was too shocked by the additional betrayal, but it had to sting, especially for his dad.

"When did they announce that?" I asked, my curiosity captured despite myself.

"Just this morning – look." Mom took the Atlas she'd been given from her pocket and held it out for me to see as she opened up the article from The Celestial Times, but before I could read it, a pop-up blocked the screen instead.

Good day and a wet Wednesday to you, Libra, the stars have spoken about your day! Today is a great day to clean out the nooks and crannies which have been stuffed full of woe of late. Delve deep into the gaping chasm of your soul and pound those worrisome thoughts right out of you. A dip in the sea is just the ticket to see you slippery and salacious once more, and don't forget that you can always dump on a friend if the load gets to be too much. A handsome Pisces would be more than happy for you to dump on them if you need a release – even a teeny weeny dump can leave you feeling as wet as a whistle precisely when you need it most. But don't forget, the best secrets are those held closest to your heart, for a traitor still lurks among our ranks and we must all be at our most cunning to lick that lurker out!

"What the fuck kind of horoscope is that?" I asked, my nose wrinkling as I read it over again and Mom growled low in the back of her throat as she dismissed it.

"That Vega girl offered Brian Washer a position as a general in her army," Mom muttered irritably. "And the first thing he thought to do with his new title was to start up a daily horoscope for the rebels. He's been reading tarot cards and sending out nonsense like this all day. I intend to have a stern word with him about it when I next see him."

"Good luck with that," I muttered, because if Washer and his teeny weeny had decided to do this, then I knew there was about as much chance of my mom convincing him to stop as there was of a Lionel revealing himself to be a secret Worm Shifter in his next press release.

I closed the horoscope down and turned my attention to the article Mom had opened up instead.

A New Dawn for the Celestial Council.

Today has dawned another rioting success in the newly risen kingdom of Solaria under the wise and powerful rule of our great king. As many of us rejoice in the ascension of the most powerful Fae in Solaria, and a return to the rule of a king at last, we are finally beginning to see how this new and prosperous reign will look over the coming years.

Linda Rigel has today been announced as High Councillor – the position granted to her after a brave and selfless act of devotion to the king when she informed him of the treason being plotted by the former High Councillors – her now estranged husband and suspected sexual deviant Tiberius Rigel along with Melinda Altair – check out page six for more on the torture chamber found in her basement - and Antonia Capella – see page twelve for an exposé on the cult she called her pack and the debased activities they had been performing in secret.

Linda Rigel, seeing her chance to escape the tyranny which had been taking place in her own home, spoke bravely about the women Tiberius used to have brought to him on a regular basis, his son Max one of many bastards he has sired over the years, though the only one Tiberius allowed to live beyond conception.

As a survivor of this ruthless household and adamant supporter of the crown, Linda had been trying without success to escape her husband's control for years, and with the help of our powerful and benevolent king, she finally managed to do so. In a twist of fate which will likely delight the population as a whole, Lionel Acrux has rewarded her years of constant, quiet loyalty to him with the most illustrious position as head of his new Council.

In a spin on tradition, Lionel has decided that no further High Councillors shall be appointed, instead Linda Rigel will head up his court and help run the day-to-day tasks required of a kingdom so that he may continue to rule with a just and firm hand, seeking out the insurgents who seek to undermine him at every turn, making Solaria into the great kingdom we all know and trust he can return it to.

All hail the King.
-Gus Vulpecula

Skye Marie: I always knew Tiberius Rigel was shifty – he was at a pie eating contest once and told the entire room that he didn't even like pie when he was offered a piece #shiftynopieguy #canttrustaFaewhowonteatpie #ibetheeatsquiche

BigGriff99: I for one am elated to see a new face in politics. I can't wait to see what she brings to the table and am excited to hear her plans on taxes for Griffins when the issue of street turd taxation is next brought up in Council #dontpersecuteusforneedingtopoop #whyshouldipaymoreforevacuatingmybackdoor #freedomtodump #itsalsoaratdeterrent

Brandy May: @BigGriff99 It's Griffins like you who give the rest of us a bad name – I have never and will never take a public dump and I for one am horrified at not only the prospect of having to pay the Griffin turd tax, but that Fae of my Order have taken to public shitting so often that it is now necessary to actually discuss this as an option #forshame #imallforonthespotfines #notallGriffinsdoit

BigGriff99: @Brandy May I'll have you know that our kind have been dumping in public for over six thousand years – it is a part of our culture and heritage, and I can only assume that you are not pure blooded if you don't understand that #poopingrights #illploptilidrop

Telisha Mortensen: LINDA RIGEL IS A TWUNT

an admin removed this comment

Kristen Cannell: Oh I am sure Linda Rigel will make a fine High Councillor! After our king's new law stating lesser Fae needing a permit to shift in public, I am over the moon that I no longer have to watch my neighbour Mr Grunnet shift into his disgusting Heptian Toad form whenever it rains, sitting in the gutter like a slimy turd opposite my lovely porch. It makes my beautiful Lioness skin crawl. #nomoretoadintheroad #antiamphibian

Jeremy Grunnet: Damn you, Kristen! You're the one who reported me to the authorities, weren't you?? #fuckyourporch #lowlyLion

BigGriff99: There's nothing wrong with a slimy turd in the gutter #itsmyrighttoshite

Lejla Asoli: I'm glad we have a High Councillor, but did it have to be Linda Rigel?? When she laughs, it sounds like a goat choking on a chipmunk. I'd know. That's how I lost my dear Chippy. It brings back terrible memories, but will she answer my emails about building a statue in his honour? Of course not. #insensistiveSiren #buildastatueforChippy

Brown Cow: Solaria is being run into the ground by that prejudiced, Orderist, asshole sitting on the Vega throne! Don't listen to the lies printed in this drivel. Read The Daily Solaria for the truth! #jointherebellion #thisbrowncowwillshowyouhow #themoooovementiscoming #allhailtheVegaqueens

an admin removed this comment

"Well, you always said Linda was a prick, so I guess you must feel validated in that opinion now," I said, handing my mom's Atlas back to her.

"Seth Capella, do not use that potty mouth with me," she snapped, clipping me around the ear with a strike of air magic so swift I didn't see it coming in time to block it. "Do you not understand what news like this means? Lionel is creating a foothold within the kingdom, he is setting up his court, and the people need to see us solidifying ours in response if we stand any chance of convincing them that we are the better option. And when I say us, I mean just that – the Celestial Council as it should be with Xavier taking up the place as Fire Lord. The Vegas mean well, but they are severely underprepared for the task of ruling even if they were able to claim that position from us – which I do not believe they can. It is vital that we re-establish ourselves as the power in this army. We must recruit. We must start to spread word across Solaria to-"

"Good luck with all that. I'm out." I turned away from her, stalking up the track in the direction Xavier had taken, a heavy mood falling over me. All I wanted was the last remnants of the people I loved to be safe. I wanted Lionel gone, sure, but I didn't want to rush into another battle unprepared. I refused to watch another person I loved die, and I wasn't going to start rallying the troops ready to lead more people to a bloody end before we were ready for battle again. No fucking way.

I stalled as the air glimmered in front of the castle and Caleb and Tory materialised from the stardust, with a large bag made of leaves and something hopeful in their eyes.

Relief flooded me at finding them safe and I broke into a run, colliding with them the moment I got there and pulling them both into a chokehold of a hug.

"Argh, you're on my foot, Seth," Tory cursed, ducking out of my grip while I tried to hold onto Cal, but he batted me off too, backing up.

I looked between them with a whimper in my throat, needing more than that small little snuggle. I needed a mega snuggle. Blankets, movies, candles, the works. But their eyes said I wasn't gonna be getting that any time soon.

"So? What did you find out?" I asked.

"We found a way to locate Darcy, but I can't do the spell until midday tomorrow," Tory said, and hope bubbled in my chest. "I wanna go hide these books before your parents spy them and start asking questions."

"I'll take them to your room. I think I can feel my Order starting to wake up, hopefully it won't be much longer." Caleb took all the books into his arms then jogged away into the castle.

I opened my mouth to ask Tory a stream of questions, but then my gaze fell onto two bloody pinprick marks on her neck. A bite. A Vampire bite. A *Caleb* bite.

I froze, coldness pouring down my spine as Tory lifted a hand, her fingers brushing over that mark as she realised what I was looking at, healing it away. But I'd seen it. It was branded to the inside of my skull now, right to the backs of my eye sockets.

"I gotta go," I muttered, turning, and marching off across the grass.

Darius had made Caleb promise he'd never feed from her again after he'd hunted her and knocked her off the roof of King's Hollow. He'd broken his word to him. He'd fucking bitten her. He'd drunk her blood, and when? For what? They'd been in a dusty old library, what possible reason could he have had for drinking from her?

They've been fucking.

I saw red. Blinding, burning red.

I was done pining, done whimpering, and spending every night alone in a cold bed thinking of my best friend. I needed to remind the world what Seth Capella was capable of, that he was a tempest housed in the flesh of Fae.

I spotted Justin Masters out taking a stroll on the path and bared my teeth as I claimed him as my first victim. I sent a barrage of air into his back, sending him flying off of the path with a yelp of fright before I buried him in five feet of soil and left only his head poking out.

"Why?!" he wailed as I stalked past him, not giving him an answer.

Because during my time at Zodiac, no one had questioned why I did shit. I was one of the most powerful Fae at the academy, a volatile Aquarius ruled by chaotic forces like Uranus, but it was my Libra rising sign that was fucking me up. Ruled by fucking Venus with her wily ways, cursing me to love a man who would never love me back.

I shoved my hands into my pockets, marching on, my eyes falling on a hill up ahead where a huge nest was being constructed by Leon, Dante, and some tattooed guy I was pretty sure was called Carson. There were other people there too, earth Elementals casting beautiful sticks and offering them to Leon who either approved them with a nod or shook his head violently and tossed them away – or sometimes he smacked its maker around the head with it.

The nest was beautiful, bent into the shape of a falcon, its wings parted at its back to allow entrance inside.

"Hey dude," Leon called to me. "Wanna help us? We could use another decent earth Elemental over here."

"We don't need shit. Stop recruiting every asshole who walks by," Carson grunted, tugging his long hair up into a topknot and offering me an unwelcoming scowl. He cast a long stick in his hands and encrusted it with jewels that glittered like starlight. Dante took it from him, cocking his head with intrigue, the Dragon in him making his eyes spark possessively.

"I'm not gonna fight you for every stick I make, Infer-" He coughed hard like he'd just breathed in a bug. "-nal asshole." Carson yanked it back out of his grip and moved to fix it onto the leg of the falcon while Dante's skin crackled with electricity.

"I'm good," I muttered, shrugging and walking on, but Leon jogged down the hill to get into my way.

"Aren't you all intrigued by what we're doing, dude?" he asked hopefully, golden eyes sparkling. "It's so cunning. The most cunning idea I've ever had."

"It was my idea, stronzo," Dante called.

"It was a joint idea," Leon said, waving a hand at him and turning back to me. "Mostly mine," he whispered.

"All you've done is shout orders at us and been a pain in the ass," Carson said, standing upright as he finished fixing a new stick to the underside of the nest.

Leon laughed like the guy was joking and I made a move to step past him again. He leapt into my way with the agility of a cat despite the huge size of him.

"It's to distract Gabe," he announced. "Because his Harpy brain is obsessed with nests, isn't it great? When he tries to *see* us, all he'll *see* is this amazing nest and he'll go all pigeon brain on it, cooing happily while he examines every bit of it. We've hidden all kinds of fancy sticks inside it, so it'll keep his mind super distracted, and he won't be able to *see* too much of our war plans."

"That's dumb. No way is that gonna work," I said, folding my arms.

"Pfft. It'll work. This nest is like the best Harpy porno ever made. It doesn't matter how hard he tries to resist it, his brain is gonna tiptoe back here to look at it with lube in one hand and tissues in the other. Besides he won't want to look away – he'll understand the cunningness of my most cunning plan and keep looking at this, so if Lionel sneaks into his head for a peek at our future all he gets is the nest. It's pure genius."

"Well good luck with that," I grumbled, darting past him before he could stop me again and hurrying on down the path.

I turned around the base of the next hill and my gaze settled on Rosalie Oscura in her silver Wolf form, laying on her back as she soaked in the last of the sun. A cruel smile twisted my lips, and I tugged my shirt over my head, tossing it away before dropping my sweatpants and kicking off my socks and shoes too. I was dying for a fight. And she was the answer.

I ran forward, letting the shift ripple through me, and howling as my four enormous white paws hit the ground and sent a tremor rocking through the hillside.

Rosalie looked my way lazily peeking out from under one floppy ear that pricked up as she spotted me.

Her eyes narrowed as I padded forward, my lips peeling back in a snarl.

Fight me.

A growl rolled out of her throat, and she shoved herself upright, engaging me as her hackles raised. We started to circle one another, assessing the threat. She was the biggest Alpha Wolf I'd ever met, her size almost matching mine, and defeating her was just the kind of victory I needed today.

A group of rebels noticed our interaction, gathering to watch, but I didn't let my focus falter from her. It had been too long since I'd asserted myself as an Alpha. I was going to remind the world of my power, and let Rosalie pay the price of that. This girl with her knowing eyes, and little looks in my direction whenever she was close by. Like she held some information I could never understand, and it was time she learned not to rile me.

I leapt forward with a snarl, claws outstretched as I collided with her and she swiped me hard across the side, sending me crashing to the ground. I'd gotten my claws into her flank too though, and I was back on my paws in seconds, snapping at her throat. She lurched backwards, trying to avoid my attack, but I pressed forward, my paws smashing into her chest and knocking her to the ground.

I was on her in the next second, barking in fury as I went for her throat again, but her legs kicked me back and she managed to wriggle free and gain her feet once more. Rosalie was forced to run, and I got a mouthful of fur as my teeth closed over the tip of her tail.

She howled angrily, twisting around and coming back in for another strike, but I was ready when she swiped her claws at my eyes, ducking low and driving myself forward.

My teeth finally closed around her neck, and I forced her to the ground, my paws crashing down on her shoulder to keep her in place. She thrashed like a wild thing, and I tightened my grip, a growl of warning in my throat as I told her to submit to me. My heart hammered with adrenaline, the call of a hunter running through my veins and urging me on towards my victory.

She snarled, gnashing her teeth in refusal and my bite deepened until she yelped.

Come on. Give up. Yield to me.

Rosalie managed to get a paw between us, tearing her claws across my face and my jaws unlocked, the pain of the attack making me release her with a whine.

Blood ran down my cheek and she leapt away from me again, forcing me to take chase up the hill. I followed her with fury fuelling my muscles, wanting to make her pay for the cuts gouged into my face.

She didn't keep fleeing like a pup as I expected though, she turned back at the crest of the steep hill, jumping into the air and coming down on me like a ton of bricks, teeth and claws ripping into fur and flesh.

The collision sent us rolling back down the hill and I bit every piece of her I could as we spun in a tornado of silver and white fur, unable to see where my attacks were landing only that blood was starting to taint the air.

I clamped my teeth down on the tip of her fluffy tail with a surge of triumph. *I've got you now, Rosalie.*

I bit down harder, and a yelp left me as I realised it was my own tail I had hold of, and I quickly released it before anyone noticed.

We landed at the base of the hill with a tremendous thud and the crowd gasped as I lay on top of Rosalie, our paws twisted together. She didn't move, her eyes closed and her body eerily still.

My heart began to thrash as I nosed her cheek, trying to wake her, but she still didn't move.

Panic washed over me in a tidal wave, and I whimpered in fright, pushing to my feet above her and nosing her side. *Get up, Rosalie. Please, get up.*

I couldn't face any more death. What had I done? Had I really killed her just for the sake of securing myself a pointless win?

I yapped like a terrified pup, nosing her again and the crowd broke out in worried mutters. Blackness sank deep into my head, death seeming to follow me everywhere these days, and now it had come for me again all because I'd needed an outlet for my anger.

I shifted back into my Fae form, kneeling at her side and pressing my fingers into her fur until I found skin, readying healing magic as quickly as I could.

But before I could even begin to heal her, she leapt upright, her tail wagging and a bark of amusement tearing from her throat. She ran the pad of her tongue right up the centre of my bloody face then trotted off with her tail held high, pushing through the crowd and leaving me staring after her, in the grass, naked on my knees. Like a fucking idiot.

"Goodness me, what fun," Washer called from the crowd, stepping to the front of it in his Speedos, his hands on his hips and his leathery chest looking freshly waxed.

He came jogging over, and his Siren gifts got a hold on me before I could escape. He latched onto the rage inside me, then picked apart the humiliation, and started to find his way to the worst emotion of all that sat beneath it, the jet fuel poured on the fire of all other emotions. Love.

I blocked him out fast, my mental barriers slamming into place and making him pout.

"I can help with all those knots deep inside you, my boy. Let me get myself in there to do some untangling. It will take a teeny-weeny bit of pushing and pulling, thrusting and ramming, but if you let me have full access to your darkest regions, I will give you so much relief, I assure you."

"I don't want your relief," I hissed, shoving to my feet, and heading across the grass to fetch my clothes.

Blood was sticking to my skin from the wounds on my body, and I pressed a hand to my chest to heal them all.

"Holy shit," breathed a teen girl among the rebels, looking to her friends as they admired my body. "He's a savage."

I tugged my clothes back on, twisting around and finding Washer standing right behind me, our chests knocking together.

I pressed my shoulders back, my teeth baring. "Get out of my way."

"You really do need to take a breath, Mr Capella," he said in a low, concerned voice. "Come on, breathe with me now. In and out, in and out." He started squatting in front of me, his arms raising and lowering with every breath he took. "I can stand behind you if you like and guide you through the movements hip to hip."

Air blasted out of my hands the same moment a bark spilled from my lips and Washer was sent sky high with a cry of alarm. The crowd broke out in more mutters as I prowled towards them, most of them darting aside, but I barged into anyone who didn't.

"He touched me," one of the teen girls squealed in excitement. "Look, I have his blood all over my ear!"

Washer suddenly came racing out of the sky on a slide of ice he'd cast beneath him, and he went splashing into a pond some of the water Elementals had created, a whoop of joy carrying from him.

I set my gaze on the stone building that had been built as a makeshift observatory, where everything we'd had left of our arcane supplies had been brought. I knew what I was gonna do. I'd demand answers from the stars, find a way to rip this love from my chest so it wouldn't torment me anymore. Then I'd be back to myself, and I wouldn't lose Caleb as my friend. I'd make a deal with the moon, or the sun, or maybe Venus herself. One of those celestial beings had to be feeling generous today, and I was sure as shit gonna take advantage of them.

I wrenched open the wooden door, stepping into the dark, circular chamber that rose to a glass roof above. Shelves all around the edges of the room held the last of our tarot decks, crystals, scrying bowls, pendants, and books on the divine arts. There were a couple of Fae at the table in the middle of the space and I snapped my fingers to get their attention before pointing to the door.

"I'm actually in the middle of a reading," one of the men squeaked.

"And I'm about to be in the middle of ripping your face off and making a hat out of it," I hissed.

He placed down the tarot card in his hand which was 'Death' and nodded quickly, running for the door with his friend. There was a bottle of bourbon on the table which they'd been sharing, and I growled, knowing for sure it must have once belonged to Orion. It was his favourite brand. The Silver Circle.

I shoved the door shut and grabbed the bottle, drinking from the neck in a long guzzle. The burn trailed all the way down my throat into my stomach and I revelled in the way it melted some of my anxiety, but hated the way it reminded me of my moon friend. Where was he? Was he still alive, still protecting Darcy with every breath he took?

Had to be. That was his thing. He wouldn't leave her ever, and as much as I missed them, I had to keep believing they were going to find their way back to us one day soon. *Just make it really, really soon, guys.*

I placed it down, heading to the shelves and grabbing a book on planetary astrology, dumping it on the desk along with a pen and paper.

I dropped onto a seat, collecting the tarot cards scattered on the desk and shuffling them back into a fresh deck.

"Come on then, stars. Let's have it out. What's in my future, huh? More bullshit?" I aggressively pulled cards from the deck at random, placing them down before me and scoffing at the sight. The Lovers lay right next to The Chariot, both of which were upside down, hinting to a disharmony in love and a lack of control.

"Yeah, ya think?" I barked, drawing the next card, laughing humourlessly as I slammed down The Hermit on the table which was upside down too.

"Loneliness," I spat bitterly. "Where are the answers in this? This is just stating my star-damned, everyday life. Why don't you give me something helpful for once?"

I drew the next card finding The Hanged Man looking back at me. "Sacrifice," I murmured, placing it down and feeling an ominous atmosphere closing in around me.

I grabbed the bottle of bourbon, taking another deep swig and thinking of Orion and Darcy again. Were they okay? Had Darcy gotten control of her curse? But if she had, then why hadn't she come to find us?

I swallowed heavily, drinking on and reading through the book on planets until there was nothing but dregs in the bottle and my head was swimming.

I turned to a page with a large picture of Venus on it and slammed my finger down on her face.

"*You.* You're the one who caused this. You had no right. I was doing just fine before you made me fall for him. Why'd you have to go and be such a bitch about it? Why couldn't you let me fall for someone who could love me back? Or better yet, why couldn't you let *him* be able to love me back?"

I grabbed the pen on the table, writing across the page on her stupid Venus face.

Venus is a dirty, conniving, skank bitch who invented unrequited love and thinks it's funny to fuck with Fae emotions whenever she likes.

"I'm gonna come up there," I slurred, looking to the darkening sky through the glass roof above, Venus smirking back at me from her position in the sky, her glow positively mocking. *Whore.* "I'm gonna bring the moon with me and we're gonna fuck you up."

I shoved to my feet, heading to the shelves to find something to help me. There had to be some spell I could do that would make this agony go away. I knew it wasn't just this agonising pining for Caleb either, it was all of it. The grief was driving me to insanity, and every time my mind slipped too close to Darius, I was sure I was going to break into a million fragments of childhood memories, pacts made and delivered, friendship forged from the deepest love in the universe.

"Yah!" I lunged at Darius with the awesome wooden stick I'd found among the dead leaves.

It smacked down on his shoulder, breaking in two. He was getting big, those arms looking too large on his ten-year-old body. But it was clear what he was becoming. When he filled out all over, he was going to get that fierce Dragon look about him that his dad had.

His dad kinda gave me the heebies sometimes. He was always grumpy, looking at us as if we were taking up too much of his time. I'd padded up his fancy staircase in my pup form when I was younger, dripping mud all over it, my white coat completely sodden with filth after Max had pushed me in the pond and I'd clambered my way out up a steep, mucky bank. Uncle Lionel had gone craaaaazy on my butt, then Darius had come running in after me and demanded I go home so that he could deal with the situation. There had been this awful kind of tension in the air and Lionel had asked Darius if he was certain he wanted to take on the responsibility for my actions. Darius had shoved me out of the door, holding his chin high as he confirmed that he did.

I'd always felt awkward around his dad after that, though Darius had only shrugged off my questions over what had happened after I'd left, telling me not to worry about it. Luckily Lionel was always working and we rarely saw him even when we hung out here at Acrux Manor. Especially because we mostly liked to play outside in the woods.

Darius launched himself at me with a laugh, taking me to the ground and a second later Max and Caleb bundled in too, crushing me at the bottom of the pile. We were all soon playfighting, laughing and rolling in the leaves while snowflakes began to fall, the promise of winter making my heart stutter. I thought of the mountain my parents had left me on during the Forging and pushed myself to sit upright, a whine leaving me.

Darius sat up next, slinging an arm around my shoulders even though he wasn't often very touchy.

"Forget the mountain," he said, like he knew. He always knew.

I smiled, looking at him and nuzzling his face.

"You're not ever gonna be alone again," he swore, and my smile reached as high as the moon.

I winced out of the memory, remembering how I'd believed those words that day, so certain nothing could tear the four of us apart. We had seemed so immortal back then. I couldn't remember a time without them, and I had foolishly assumed there would be no time to come where they didn't exist. I'd lost Darius now, popping that illusion and forcing me to consider the possibility that I could lose more of them. There was no enduring that.

I found a bottle of moon-charged water and yanked the cap off, drinking it down, all of it. It was for potions, but I didn't give a fuck, I just needed the pain to stop. The moon always had the answers, and the immediate buzz I got in my veins did a great job of numbing some of my wounds.

I found an Atlas sitting in a portable speaker and my eyebrows arched. I clumsily tapped on the screen, wondering if the motherfucker who owned it had any decent music on there. Thankfully, they seemed to have some taste, and I pressed play on Bones by Imagine Dragons, the music thundering through the air and filling up my soul.

I gave up on trying to find a spell for my needs, and decided to invent one myself, grabbing a couple of fire crystals, a black-wick candle, a banishing stone, and some ground lilarock.

I melted some of the candle with a fire crystal, mixing the hot wax with the rock until it made a thick, inky liquid. Then I shed my shirt, painting the Taurus constellation over my heart and feeling a kiss of magic against my skin. This was gonna be fiiiiine. It was definitely gonna work.

The constellation that represented Caleb prickled against my heart and I lifted the banishing stone as the heavy pounding of the music filled me up, then I pressed it directly against the mark that was hardening against my skin. There was definitely good logic in this. I was going to use the stone to banish my love for Caleb, sending it anywhere else but in my heart where it constantly tortured me. Maybe I'd send it into a potato then smash that potato up with a hammer and kick the pieces into the sea. That oughta do it.

The banishing stone met my skin and pain exploded along my chest. The mark was devoured by the stone, and I gasped as the power of the spell sank into my body, deeper and deeper. I didn't know what was going to happen, and I was half aware that this might just kill me, but it was too late now.

A tearing sensation circled my nipple and I looked down, gaining some good sense and tugging the stone away from my skin. My nipple went with it, perched there on that rock, while my skin was left smooth where it had been.

"Ah!" I yelped in panic, pressing the stone back to my skin. "Give it back, you nipple stealing rock of doom!"

The door opened and Caleb, fucking Caleb of all people, walked in, finding me there with one missing nipple, standing among the mess I'd made making my nipple-stealing spell.

"Get out," I rasped, but he only kicked the door shut, shooting towards me in concern.

He looked down at the stone in my hand and the nipple it had taken from me, a curse leaving his lips.

"Are you drunk?" he snapped, snatching the stone from my grip.

I didn't answer, leaving him to head away from me to the shelves, grabbing a binding crystal and some kiffer salt before returning to me just as fast. His hand slammed to my chest, knocking me flat onto the table at my back and leaning over me, holding the banishing stone over the place where my nipple should have been.

Why did everything I do lately make stuff so much worse?

He murmured a spell under his breath, using the binding stone to knit my nipple back onto my skin before dipping his fingers in the kiffer salt and rubbing it over it. His touch sent lightning tearing through me, and my nipple hardened under his fingers, making me knock his hand away fast, his touch sending aftershocks rippling through my skin.

I shoved myself upright to sit on the edge of the table, nose to nose with him when he didn't move aside. His breath was hot against my mouth and it tasted like a sin I wanted to commit.

"What are you doing, Seth?" Caleb asked in a low tone, like he was angry with me, or maybe he was worried about me. It was hard to tell when my mind was full of alcohol and my body was falling into the madness of being this close to him.

"I was trying out a new spell," I muttered.

"What spell?"

"It doesn't matter," I snarled.

"Why are you so angry at me all the time? We used to talk about shit," he said.

"Because you keep pissing me off." I tried to get up, but he gripped my arm and used his Vampire strength to keep me in place.

"Talk to me," he commanded.

"You bit Tory," I spat, the truth pouring out like I'd never had a chance to hold it back.

His eyes widened in surprise. "Are you…jealous?" he asked.

"No," I lied quickly, heat rising in my veins. "Of course I'm not. Why would I be jealous? It's just the principle of it all."

"What principle?" he demanded.

"You broke your promise to Darius," I said in fury, sitting up straighter. "You swore you'd never bite her again, and now he's dead and cold in a coffin, and you think it's fine for you to just disregard any promises that passed between you two."

Caleb's eyes shuttered and he dropped his head in shame, stepping back. "It wasn't like that. We were in trouble. I needed magic and she insisted…I had to."

"Yeah, whatever." I dropped down from the desk, turning my back on him and picking up the tarot cards which I'd been forced to sit on while he stuck my nipple back onto my body. I subtly plucked one from my ass where it had gotten stuck, The Lovers laughing at me as I shoved the card into the deck and shuffled.

"I didn't want to break that promise," he went on.

"Uh huh," I said dismissively.

"*Seth,*" he snarled.

"Wanna do a reading? Let's find out your truth, Cal," I said coldly, moving to the other side of the table and dropping onto a seat. He looked to me with narrowed eyes, and I took the liberty to carry on.

I pulled out a card, turning it over and finding Justice reversed.

"Dishonesty," I announced, flicking the card at him with a gust of air so it slapped him in the face. "Sounds like you're lying about something, Cal. Maybe you're lying to your best friend. Who can say? Maybe you're hiding something like, oh I dunno – let's ask the cards."

I whipped another one out and surprise, surprise there were The Lovers. I cast it away from me, so it slapped him in the face again and he cursed in anger. "A secret love affair perhaps. That would be quite the scandal. I wonder who it could be?"

"You can't draw conclusions like that, you're not even letting me pull the cards myself and you're just guessing random shit based on them," he hissed, but I barrelled on.

"It's not me, Caleb. It's the cards. I'm not saying any of this. Oh look, Death," I announced, sending it flying towards him again, but this time his hand came up to block it, but I was fast, making it slap him in the ear instead. "Death of an old relationship, maybe? A lifelong friend cast aside? Could be that, for sure."

"What are you going on about?" he huffed.

"You tell me," I barked.

I went to draw another card, but Caleb leaned forward, snatching them from my fist and tossing them into the air, a rain of fate and destiny showering down on us as we glared at each other.

The Wheel of Fortune came fluttering down to land on his shoulder and I picked it up with a lump in my throat.

"Inevitability," I whispered.

"You're drunk, and you're rambling," Caleb said, pushing a hand through his hair and knocking The Chariot out of his curls where it stood upright, signifying a sense of control, but as it cascaded down to land in front of me, it lay upside down. *Losing control, chaos, willpower crumbling.*

I looked up at him from my seat, the turmoil in me rising to the surface of my skin, begging to come out.

"Talk to me," he said in a low voice, leaning down and bracing a hand on my bare shoulder. Skin to skin contact with him was like a drug, and I was his hopeless addict. I fractured there and then beneath him, the alcohol loosening my tongue and letting out some of my truth.

"Sometimes I dream of waking up and finding everyone gone. I'm in the dark and it's cold, so fucking cold. There's frost in my veins and I can feel the loss of you all. But what if one day I wake up and realise it's not a nightmare anymore? It's *real*." I grabbed hold of Caleb, feeling the solidness of him to assure myself he was still there, and he drew me to my feet, pulling me close. When I spoke again, my voice was a raspy whisper of desperation, "If you have to go, please be the last one. Please stay until the end. I can't lose you. Not you."

"I'm not going anywhere, Seth," he vowed, unblinking as he stared me straight in the eye. "I am not. Going. Anywhere."

I sagged against him, loving him through to my bones. His promise wasn't binding; life was too volatile for certainty, but it meant a hell of a lot that he voiced it anyway, because I knew the heart of Caleb Altair, and he had never let me down yet.

"It's not fair," I exhaled, my hands fisted in his shirt and my head bowed so he couldn't read my expression.

"What's not fair?" he asked, his breath stirring my hair and making my heartbeat skitter.

"All of it," I cursed, my fingers curling tighter. He wasn't pulling away, but I wasn't letting go either. I just needed to be close to him for a second. My skin was starved of contact and my Order needs were polluted by my desire for his hands to be the ones to sate those needs. "Did you ever think it would come to this? Because I didn't. I was stupidly optimistic. I really thought we'd win this war. I should have known better. I always did look at things with blind positivity, but I'm running out of reasons to feign ignorance now."

"Seth..."

I chanced a look up at him, my throat tight and not letting in a single scrap of air.

"Don't let this war change you," he said. "Your optimism is one of my favourite things about you."

"One of?" I snagged onto that breadcrumb of attention. I was pathetic for it, but I didn't give a fuck. Caleb had implied there was more, so I'd be getting it if I could.

"I envy the way you feel everything so sharply, even when you try to disguise your pain in rage," he said.

"But doesn't that make me weak, Cal? I feel weak. I can't contain this pain. It pours out of me like I'm filled with holes. But you're always so strong. You don't have cracks, let alone holes."

"Your pain is the most admirable strength I know. I keep mine inside because I don't know how to express it outside of words, but you're the opposite. You bleed with your actions, and I'm one of the few people in the world who can read your anger and hate for what it really is."

"What is it?" I asked, because hell if I knew.

"Love."

That word was a curse upon my soul, and I flinched away from him, withdrawing. "I can't do this anymore," I whispered to myself, scraping a hand down my face. "Lie to me, Cal. Tell me it will all be okay, even as the walls crumble and the earth shatters beneath our feet. Lie to me so good that I don't feel it when our world falls to ruin."

His brow creased and he pushed a lock of my hair behind my ear, the simple touch meaning everything to me. "It will all be okay."

He said it with so much certainty that I really did believe it for a second, unsure if it was actually a lie or just a truth he was banking on. It helped either way.

"But not if you keep starving yourself of your Order needs," he said darkly. "Why don't you turn to your family?"

"I'm supposed to be strong for them. I don't want them seeing me like this," I breathed shamefully.

"You can't keep sleeping alone and staying away from people. You need the touch of other Fae," he urged, his hand pressing to my spine, and I shivered with want.

"Don't, Cal," my plea was weak, sounding more like I was begging for the exact opposite.

"You need this," he said firmly. "And you're my Source. I always protect my Source."

His knuckles traced the length of my spine, and I felt my resolve cracking and falling to ruin. I could practically hear Venus laughing at me, making me yearn for this man who wasn't meant for me.

"Come on. You'll stay with me tonight," he said, and I realised night must have fallen some time ago while I was lost to this place.

He took my hand, guiding me to the door, but our fingers parted the moment it opened, like we were both quietly acknowledging the fact that it meant more than it should have, and no one was allowed to witness it.

"I hate this place," I sighed. "I miss King's Hollow."

Caleb frowned at me then scooped me into his arms in a blur of motion, speeding across the island at the full capacity of his Order gifts, stealing the breath from my lungs. He placed me down and I stumbled dizzily, a throaty laugh leaving my chest as he grinned.

We were at the base of a large oak tree on the edge of the island, the sea crashing against the shore to our left. Caleb began to wield his earth Element, building a treehouse that was like a small version of King's Hollow, with a single ladder running up to a little arching doorway.

When he was done, he jerked his head in an offering and I hurried forward, scaling the ladder, and stepping into the beautiful room he'd built. A large wooden bed with a thick mattress of springy moss lay to one side of a stone fireplace and when Caleb entered behind me, he raised a hand, casting a fire into the hearth. Heat spread quickly into the space, and I glanced back to find Caleb locking the door and pulling his shirt off. His body belonged to a creature not of this world, one that went beyond all magic I knew and captivated me deeper than any power the stars possessed.

"Lie down," he commanded, and I cocked my head to one side.

"Sometimes I think you forget I'm an Alpha too," I said, and he smirked, closing in on me.

"I think you like being bossed around," he said, pressing a hand to my chest and shoving me onto the bed and by the stars, my heart leapt like it just wanted to prove him right. "On your front."

I moved up the bed and lay on my stomach, confused as fuck but drunk-happy too now that I was getting this treatment from him. A little birdy in the back of my head was squawking at me though, telling me I was just going to feel like shit again in the morning. But the morning was a wandering doom, too far off to cause me issues right now and the night…well the night was making me promises which I had no hope of even trying to deny as my entire world was filled up by the powerful presence of Caleb Altair.

Caleb moved to straddle my back, his fingers kneading at my shoulders, massaging my skin in firm strokes. I groaned at how good that felt, his hands working over every inch of me and feeding the demands of my Order.

He pushed my hair away from the back of my neck, his thumbs rolling over the top of my spine in a perfect way. He didn't hold back on using his strength, digging deep into my muscles and driving out any kinks and knots he found.

His fingers grazed lower, working into the muscles around my shoulder blades before he painted out a crescent moon between them, making my cock immediately hard. *Fuck, how was I ever going to get up from this bed without him seeing that?*

"Are you still planning on getting a tattoo here?" he asked and a beat later his mouth pressed to that very spot.

"Cal," I said breathlessly, grinding my hips into the mattress.

"Answer me," he insisted, and I cursed him in a growl.

"Yes," I said, and his mouth dragged over my skin again like he was rewarding me for obeying him. "Now answer me something."

"Ask away," he whispered, his breath on my back driving me wild.

His mouth travelled lower and his hands ran down my sides, his thumbs massaging as he went and sending a quiver of delight through me.

"Whose blood do you prefer, mine or Tory's?" I asked and he laughed against my skin, his fangs suddenly grazing me.

"Her blood is a head rush for sure," he admitted, and I swallowed a jealous growl, remaining silent. "But yours…" He reared up over me, his palm pressing to the mattress beside my head and his body crushing me down into the bed. I loved the weight of him, the way he never held back his power with me, the two of us so perfectly, equally matched in strength that we could always handle anything the other offered.

His mouth ran over my neck and my fingers fisted tightly in response to his fangs dragging over my sensitive skin.

"You taste like the earth and sky colliding, but it's more than that. There's moonlight in you, and it calls to me like a song in the night. You're my Source and nothing is going to change that. I don't want to claim anyone else, this is mine and it's all I crave." His fangs drove into my neck and my back arched, the kiss of pain making me even harder and sending my thoughts scattering to the wind.

Me and him, this thing between us, it was getting to be more than I could take. But if I had no choice in desiring him then maybe I needed to surrender to it, and let it run its course. I would stop swimming upstream and let the river of this all-engulfing love claim me into its rapids. It would end with me dashed against the rocks, but I was going to enjoy the ride before I reached that unavoidable end.

He fed deep, pinning me down and growling every time I shifted beneath him. I felt him hardening against my ass, his cock driving against me through the fabric of his sweatpants and my breaths came heavier. It was just his obsession with my blood, or maybe he wanted to use me again for an outlet. But then hadn't Tory given him that?

He drew his fangs free of me, sitting back fast and starting to massage me more aggressively, his body angled so I couldn't feel his arousal anymore, but we both knew the truth, even if neither of us would voice it.

He massaged me until my muscles were jelly and peace was coming for me, the kind I hadn't felt in so, so long.

Caleb rolled down to lay next to me, casting a woven sheet of leaves over us and I turned onto my side, grateful for the cover so it wouldn't give away how fucking hot that had gotten me.

"What do you need?" he asked softly. "Do whatever it is your Order wants."

I glanced at his bare chest, then shifted forward, curling into him and pulling him tight against me. His arms wrapped around me, and I nuzzled against his cheek, our stubble raking together and feeling so star-damned good, all I wanted to do was turn my head and steal a hungry kiss from his mouth. But holding him close and feeling his muscles tighten around me was enough of a gift for tonight, and I wasn't going to do anything stupid that might send him running from here.

So I shut my eyes and breathed in his sharp, masculine scent, finding some clarity in why I had fallen for him so hopelessly. He was Caleb Altair. The most protective, loyal Fae who knew every piece of me and never flinched from it. Of course I'd fallen for him. Just like The Wheel of Fortune card had predicted. It was inevitable.

Scorpio
Gemini
Virgo
Cancer
Leo
Sagittarius
Taurus
Capricorn
Aquarius
Libra
Pisces

MAX

CHAPTER THIRTY

The tiny bedroom I'd been given in the back corner of the R.U.M.P. Castle was big enough for little more than my bed alone, which seemed extra insulting seeing as I'd given every drop of my magic to Gerry while she created the damn thing.

In all honesty, I had been more caught up in the feeling of power sharing with her than concentrating on what she was doing with her magic, so I was at least a little to blame, but this shit wasn't going to work for me.

I wrenched my bedroom door open, having every intention of hunting her down and demanding a better room, but the door slammed into the edge of my bed and got itself wedged there with the force I used.

I cursed, tugging on the thing but somehow managing to wedge it further, the wood groaning in protest as I yanked on it again.

I braced a foot against the bed and heaved on it, putting my weight into the motion. The door sprung free, and I flew backwards into the hall, slamming down on my ass with a torrent of cursing.

"Well, that's one way to peel an onion," Justin Masters said from somewhere above me, and I swore louder as I shoved to my feet and whirled on him.

"What did you say?" I snarled, my gifts whipping from me and throwing a strong dose of terror his way, but his mental walls were firm and waiting, so the attack did little more than make him flinch.

"It isn't every day a slop-headed ninny falls at my feet, is all," he replied with a shrug before turning and striding away from me like this was already over.

"Have you spoken to Gerry?" I demanded as I fell into step with him uninvited.

"What business is that of yours?" Justin asked, glancing at me from the corner of his eye and puffing his chest up a little. I had a good foot on the asswipe and at least fifty pounds of muscle, so it wasn't exactly intimidating.

"Because me and her have a good thing going and I want to be sure that you're clear that whatever you thought you had with her is done now."

Justin scoffed lightly but said nothing as he tried to up his pace, heading towards the banquet hall where the scent of freshly baked bagels was calling to us like a summons.

"Spit it out," I growled, grabbing him by the collar and forcing him to face me.

Justin set his feet, a canine growl peeling his lips back which I replied to by hissing like a cat. That seemed to make him realise he was losing his grip on his ever-so-carefully controlled persona, and he pressed his mouth closed into a thin line.

"Say it," I insisted when he seemed inclined towards silence. "I can see the words twisting around inside that skull of yours and I can feel your contempt like the stench of a fart on the air, so there's no point in holding back."

"Fine," Justin said haughtily, knocking my hand from his collar and straightening out the wrinkle I'd left there before raising his chin and looking me dead in the eye. "You, Max Rigel, are simply a dalliance in the water of Geraldine's youth," he said and to my utter outrage, I felt a note of pity coming from him as he surveyed me. "You are brash and uncouth, pig-headed, arrogant and utterly unwavering in your self-righteousness. Yet you are tall and muscular and no doubt talented in the ways of pleasuring women, so for now, my sweet flower has allowed her head to be turned from those less desirable traits in favour of using you to those ends. It is abundantly clear to all but you. Every fine member of the A.S.S. watches you pant over her like a dog in heat, and we smile at the power she wields so flippantly over a man who believes himself to be untouchable. She may not wish to fulfil her arrangement to wed me any longer, and though it is a shame, my family have always and will always serve the crown. My marriage will only ever be to the benefit of the Vegas, one way or another, and I am more than content with that, whomever my bride shall be. Geraldine too has dedicated her life into their service, and she may have cut off her betrothal to me, but that doesn't mean anyone in the entire kingdom believes for one moment that she will now turn to you when she decides she is ready to take a husband. The uncouth water Heir who is clinging to his title and wishy-washy claim to the throne which all but he and his little pals already know will never see the shadow of his pert buttocks descending upon it. It's sad, really, that you can't see that too. But amusing, nonetheless."

My muscles were locked so tightly and my jaw grinding so violently that I did nothing at all as Justin turned and strode away from me, heading into the banquet hall where Geraldine was no doubt leading the newly formed Vega court in all manner of royalist nonsense.

I turned my attention inwards as I closed my eyes, expelling a long breath through my nose and using my own gifts to quell a lot of the rage I was feeling before I ended up hounding after Justin and plastering his well-groomed head to the newly built castle walls.

When I was confident that I could control myself again, I opened my eyes and drifted towards the door to the banquet hall, magic curling around me as I went, hiding me in shadows and concealing my presence from anyone who might turn my way.

I leaned my shoulder against the newly carved wood of the door and peered inside.

The hall had been laid out with five long tables which stretched towards the door where I stood and a top table on a dais presided over all of them at the far end of the huge room. There was a raging fire in the grate behind the two throne-like chairs which had been crafted specifically for the Vegas to sit their royal asses on, but Tory wasn't there to sit on hers and Darcy was…well, fuck knew where Darcy was. I was worried about her, I knew that much.

Geraldine was standing close to the top table, her shrewd expression combing over the gathered rebels. They were her closest allies, the biggest advocates of the Vega line and the most avid supporters of Tory and Darcy reclaiming the throne. Sofia and Tyler were pointing out something on his Atlas, no doubt another article he was readying to send to the press, reminding Solaria that we were all still here, still fighting, even if it was easy to feel forgotten while we floated across the sea at random, far from the places we had all once called home.

There was no place for me or the other Heirs set aside. Even my father and Seth and Caleb's moms were left to sit at one of the five tables, though as I watched them, I could tell they were plotting ways to regain their hold on their power. I just didn't think it mattered what they did here, not surrounded by this group of royalists. None of them would be won away from the Vegas, none of them had any interest in supporting our claim to the throne.

"Chip chop!" Geraldine cried and I trained my attention on her, casting an amplification spell her way and focusing on everything she was saying to the Fae around her. "The army won't just organise themselves. I need reports on the new barracks and any issues which have arisen since we set sail on this here island of destiny."

The group of Fae closest to her all began calling out reports on how the relocation for the rebels was going, giving facts and figures about the housing being erected all over the island in strategic positions. More of them started offering reports on the progress being made to shield and ward our new stronghold, others letting her know how work was going with food production, clothing manufacturing etc.

Washer was one of the most vocal amongst them, a pen scratching away before him as he noted down everything that was said and drew out a map of the island. Geraldine looked over his shoulder, giving notes on improvements and telling him that she would bring it to the true queens for approval once everything was ship-shape.

I cast my gifts over the Fae surrounding her, searching for any signs of deception or betrayal, but there was nothing. The search for whoever had given our location to Lionel when he attacked The Burrows had turned up nothing, and now we were all left wondering if there might still be a traitor amongst our ranks or if whoever it was had died or fled during the battle. I didn't know and the thought haunted me endlessly, but we were taking precautions. The Atlases which were now being handed out more freely between the rebels had all been given hardware which scanned any outgoing messages and restricted access to the outside world. In addition to that, only a very few, specially selected Fae had been allowed to go on trips to the mainland to gather essential supplies, the wards surrounding our hiding place preventing anyone from leaving without permission via both stardust and physically. We were doing all we could to protect ourselves and I just had to hope it would be enough. We needed time to regroup, bolster our numbers and plan our retaliation on Lionel as soon as possible.

When Geraldine seemed satisfied by all she had seen, she moved along to the next table where Justin the asshole now sat prim and proper with a napkin draped across his lap as he cut a bagel into bite sized pieces with a knife and fork like a fucking heathen.

Geraldine began to question the Fae surrounding him about the scouting missions she'd clearly had them all out on, cross-referencing their reports on possible rebel strongholds within the kingdom as well as noting down any Nebular Inquisition Centres and their locations.

Justin chimed in with a bunch of information about the land he'd travelled over while stuck in that parachute and to my disgust, the Fae surrounding him simpered, marvelling at his tenacity while he endured the elements in his legendary plight of escape and daring. It sounded to me like the idiot had just been lucky not to die while he hung around up there in a diaper forged of leaves which Tory had used to save his scrawny ass when he'd gotten in her way on the battlefield. No one was asking him where he'd been shitting all those days, were they? Oh no, no one wondered how many times he'd had to piss himself up there. But now Geraldine was talking about a statue being erected in his honour or a tapestry of his bold escapades being woven for the royal palace.

My irritation with Justin aside, I couldn't help but realise what was going on here. What me and the other Heirs had so blatantly neglected while licking our wounds and wallowing in our grief over our lost brother.

The war was still raging. And Geraldine and the A.S.S. hadn't wasted a single moment despite facing their own losses and pain. They were gathering intelligence, rallying for the next strike. It was…humiliating. My whole fucking life I'd been trained to take charge, taught how to lead, and prepared for any eventuality. And yet when our people had needed us most, needed leadership and guidance and someone to stand up tall and tell them that we wouldn't break, I hadn't done a damn thing.

Geraldine had orchestrated this, and Tory had stepped up, she'd rallied the rebels after their defeat, and was clearly overseeing all of these plans as Gerry moved them into action. They were no doubt holding more war councils too, plotting, figuring out what Lionel was up to.

Not to mention the fact that Tory had headed out to that library and returned with several books on forgotten magic, more plans burning in her green eyes even as she broke apart over all she'd lost.

Fuck.

I took a step away from the banquet hall, feeling unwelcome there despite the bounty of bagels which made my stomach growl with need. I wasn't going to just sit on my ass and eat. I needed to do something real. Needed to help with the war effort and stop wallowing like the entitled little bitch Justin clearly thought I was. I needed to step up and show Geraldine that I could be the man she chose long term, that I wasn't just some fling from her youth, a nothing mistake she'd use and forget.

I turned sharply and strode away from the delicious scent of food, heading for the impressive staircase in the centre of the castle and striding up it at a fast pace.

No one paid me much attention until I turned towards the next staircase which led up to the top floor, the private royal suites which I was willing to bet were about a million times nicer than the room I'd been given down in the dregs of this place. Geraldine hadn't even had the decency to warn me about the size of my room, simply assigning some low-level Ass member to lead me there and informing me that I was blessed to be welcomed into the abode of the true queens. It was bullshit. And I was going to call it out just as soon as I proved to her that I was worth more than some suit stuffing, napkin-wielding douchebag called Justin.

I made a move to pass the guards standing watch at the foot of the stairs to the royal chambers, but they instantly swarmed into action, a wall of ice blocking my way as the four of them shifted into defensive stances.

"You do not have free access to the true queen," one of them said firmly, a dare in his eyes which was just begging for me to punch it away, but I held myself in check.

"She'll want to see me," I ground out, waiting for one of them to go confirm that claim, but none of them moved.

"As of yet, we have heard no signs to suggest that Her Highness has awoken. You are free to wait here until such a time as she does. Aside from that, we are under strict orders not to disturb her slumber."

I narrowed my eyes at them, then cast an amplifying spell and tipped my head back as I roared Tory's name at the top of my lungs. All four of the guards cried out and clapped their hands over their ears, but before any of them could get any dumb ideas about fighting me, a reply called down from above.

"Let him through," Tory said. "He'll only start crying a river of tears if you don't and flood the whole building."

The guards reluctantly shifted aside, and I stalked past them, offering death glares and a clear challenge for any and all of them to seek me out later if they wanted a real fight. The averted eyes and slight dips to their heads let me know that none of them were going to take me up on that, and I took the minor ego boost in my stride as I headed on up the stairs at last.

I pushed the door open to Tory's room, arching a brow as I found her there, cross-legged on the floor in nothing but an oversized black t-shirt and her panties, her dark hair tied in a messy knot on top of her head.

There was a plate of untouched food by the door which looked like last night's dinner and an almost empty bottle of tequila beside it, which I assumed was the option she'd gone for instead.

She had made a kind of nest out of a heap of coins and jewels from Darius's treasure trove to sit in and there were five ancient-looking books open to various pages around her.

"Well," I said slowly, taking in the hastily scribbled and crossed out notes on the crumpled bits of paper that littered the floor. "You look like shit."

“Why thank you,” she replied sarcastically, swigging from the bottle of tequila while holding my eye in a challenge for me to mention it. “You’re looking your own kind of tragically bereft yourself. Wanna sit?”

She indicated the heap of coins beside her and despite the fact that it looked anything but comfortable, I found the reminder of Darius soothing in a way I hadn’t expected and carefully stepped past the books to take the spot she’d offered.

Tory lifted a book out of my way as I got comfortable, the deep blue cover awakening my interest as she turned it over in her hands, then dumped it in my lap.

“Here, give yourself a book boner. It’ll make you think of Orion.”

I arched a brow doubtfully, but as I took in the beautiful decoration on the front of the book which depicted my most powerful Element in all its forms, I had to admit that a chill ran over me.

I opened the book carefully, almost reverently as I sensed the age of the tome and read the introduction with interest.

All things begin and end with the Element of water, it is life just as it is death, power, and purity. It is both ambivalent and altruistic. Beware the power of washing your soul clean in its icy depths, for once you have taken the plunge into the life of aqua, you will never again be the same.

I frowned as I took in the truth of those words, turning a few more pages and finding spells and incantations unlike anything I had ever learned before describing how to harness the power of water. If I was reading it correctly, it didn’t even matter which star sign you possessed. If you wanted to wield the Element and were willing to pay the price of doing so, then there were ways here that could make it happen – even if the effects were short-lived and to serve a sole purpose.

“This is…I’ve heard the odd thing about the way magic was tamed before the Awakening was discovered, but I never knew they could do so much,” I said, turning pages listed with instructions for all forms of water magic, including some I had never even considered before. “To give life…” I read aloud and Tory snatched the book from me before I could go on.

Her eyes scanned the page, a tendril of hope pouring from her and brushing against my senses, feeding my power, but as she skimmed down the page, despair took its place until she finally dropped the book into her lap.

“This is for imbuing land with self-replenishing water so that crops can grow through drought,” she huffed, a flash of anger hitting me before she reined it in again. No…she didn’t rein it in, she hid it from me, letting me feel a touch of pain and despair but shielding that rage, like she knew it was the most potent and powerful emotion she was experiencing right now and didn’t want me stealing that from her.

I reached out and took her hand, the strength of my gifts growing as I maintained that contact and forced her to look at me.

“You’re not coping,” I told her, though it was clear she knew that already.

“There is no coping with this,” she replied, a burst of anger hitting me again, and this time she didn’t bother to conceal it. “All I have is this rage in me. I need to find my sister, kill that Dragon son of a bitch and then…well then there isn’t anything left for me unless…”

Her eyes moved over the ancient books surrounding us, and a hopeless kind of need tainted the air, making me tighten my hold on her hand and offer her some reassurance.

“You’re trying to find a way to bring him back?” I asked softly, wishing with all I had that there was some way to do such a thing while knowing in my soul that it was impossible. “Tory, in the entire history of our world, in all the years that have passed and with all the losses Fae have endured, none have ever found a way to return the dead to us.”

“Don’t,” she hissed. “Don’t try to explain it to me like I’m some silly mortal trying to figure out how magic works. I know what you’re saying, I understand it.

But that doesn't mean I'm giving up on him. I *can't* give up on him, don't you get that? He is everything to me, and the stars stole him away. I don't believe for one second that they couldn't bring him back if that was what they wanted. But they won't, because they only interfere with our lives when it amuses them to do so. They only get involved when it comes to love or hate, and all the things they should have no dominion over in the first place. They gifted Fae this magic so that they could use it like puppet masters pulling on our strings, forcing us to worship them in the heavens above, and yet all the while they do nothing to help us when we need it most. They offered him death in exchange for my life. That means they gave me life when their fate had chosen death for me instead. So they can either give him his life back too, or they can find out what I will do to them in payment for that sacrifice."

Tory reached out for the onyx black book behind her, the cover etched with a word that was at once unfamiliar and yet resounded deep within me like an old friend greeting me from another lifetime. *Ether.*

"What is that?" I asked.

"This is the power we gave up when the stars began Awakening our kind. Not the power they gifted us. Not the power they can control. This is wild, free, and untouched by them or their ideas of fate. It's the true fifth Element and they hold no dominion over it. And this is what I will use to destroy everyone and everything who has tried to take so very much from me."

I almost reached for the book, but something deep within me warned against it, some intuition or knowledge lodged in the depths of my bones.

"I thought the shadows were the fifth Element?" I asked, eyeing her warily as I took in the certainty in her, the promise carved into her hand.

"No," she scoffed. "More lies passed down through time, either intentionally or through poor translation. The shadows were never meant to be a part of this world, our realm and the shadow realm divided just as we are from the humans you named mortal – another half-truth that alludes to immortality in Fae kind and was only used to scare the humans when the first rifts were created between our realm and theirs, before we used magic to make them forget about us or cast us as characters in fairy tales which they no longer believe in. So if that's the case, then I'm thinking the shadows never were the fifth element at all and this-" she tapped the title of the book, "-was the true name for it. This was what they used to capture the shadows and bind them to whatever desire they wanted, this was the power that make wielding them possible in the first place."

"Who told you the shadows were never meant to be a part of this world?" I asked with a frown.

"Queen Avalon told us all kinds of stories like that while we were training with her. She was…well she was a total bitch, if I'm being honest. Stuffed full of just as much Order supremacy bullshit as Lionel is, and pretty much a tyrant in her own time. Of course, she painted herself out to be some benevolent creature, but over time, we saw between the lines of her stories, noticed the prejudices she spoke with. She persecuted anyone she deemed less worthy of life than her, the Nymphs most of all."

"Our people and the Nymphs have been at war for as long as anyone can remember. Fae are prey to them. There's no changing that fact, and it makes sense that a Fae queen of old would have wanted to eradicate them," I pointed out.

Tory chewed on her bottom lip, her fingers trailing over the cover of the book as she considered my words.

"Darcy doesn't believe they're simply soulless monsters set on preying on all of us. Miguel claims he's on our side, though no one has managed to get much more out of him than that since he was captured. And despite the lies and the deceptions, Diego died to save my sister in the end. I know he wasn't perfect but…"

"But what?" I pressed.

"I don't know. But I do know that we're missing something here, something vital, something which Darcy would want me to think about. It's why I won't let anyone execute Miguel, there's too many what ifs. And I think Darcy will want to talk to him too, and I think she might be the one who can figure out the truth in all of this. I don't want to blindly follow the guidance of the stars and I don't want to blindly follow a path laid out by past royals either. The past should be where we learn from our mistakes, the future is open to all new possibilities."

Her attention dropped back to the Book of Ether in her lap and I tensed as I took in the determination in her.

"I don't think you should be playing with that, Tory," I murmured, but she just gave a humourless laugh.

"Playing is exactly what I've been doing up until now. Playing with the Elements they offered me and toying with the flames of my Order. But this right here is where things will get real. And I won't back down. So I suggest you don't get in my way."

She held my gaze with an unbreakable will, and I could feel her decision to see this through burning in the air as brightly as her Phoenix ever could. She wouldn't be turned from this path. There was no backing out of it, and quite frankly, I wasn't sure there was a Fae alive powerful enough to stop her anyway.

"Okay," I agreed heavily, nodding in acceptance of the vow she was so desperate to keep. "I'm with you. If you think there's a way to change this fate, then fuck knows I would give anything for that to be true. So whatever you need, whatever it takes, I'm in."

"Good."

We spent another hour looking through the books, Tory mainly giving the tome on ether her attention while I tried to get my head around the very different ways that Fae used to wield power. There wasn't a single spell in any of the books that was simple, all of them requiring various items, sacrifices, incantations, or the like to work at all and even then, the power was short-lived. But despite that, from the numerous warnings and often terrifying depictions accompanying the various magics, there was great power in this form of summoning. The risks seemed to outweigh the benefits to me for the most part though, and even as I continued leafing through the books, reading page after page, helping Tory to make notes on anything that looked like it might be promising, I found myself wanting to avoid that kind of power.

"There are notes here on the shadows, but it's like they were barely even relevant to dark magic when this kind of power was in use," Tory said suddenly, snapping the Book of Ether shut. "I don't get it. Orion used blood and bone magic, but he mostly used the shadows whenever I saw him wielding the dark powers. How could something so prevalent now have been so irrelevant back then?"

"Maybe they hadn't figured out how to use the shadows when these books were written?" I suggested, closing the air book too.

"If there was no mention of them at all then I'd believe that, but they do come up from time to time, in a way that is practically dismissive. There was one line…" She started hunting through the loose notes littering the floor around us before snatching one out triumphantly and holding it up for me to take.

I read the copied sentence with a frown as I tried to understand its meaning.

Shadows are powerful in their own right, but they are of another realm and are the magic of Unemph, so are wielded best by their kind alone.

"I mean, that word kinda sounds like Nymph to me. You think that's who they're talking about? The Nymphs wielding the shadows? Didn't Diego's grandma knit herself into a shadow hat or some shit? Seems like it adds up to me." I shrugged but couldn't help the smug grin tugging at the corner of my lips when Tory's irritation at herself reached me alongside her excitement over that possible answer.

Tory got to her feet and found a pair of sweatpants, pulling them on and turning her back to me as she switched the oversized shirt for a white crop top, then kicked on a pair of sneakers. I stood too, watching as she moved to grab a small bag from the desk beside the door, then took a lethal-looking dagger and dropped both things into her pocket.

"You just carry concealed weapons these days, do you?" I teased her and she looked over her shoulder at me, something dark flickering in her green eyes.

For a brief moment, I was in her head, locked up at Lionel's mercy, her Order suppressed, her magic kept in check by the Guardian bond he'd forced on her. The memories faded as fast as they'd come, my connection to her severing as both of us drew away from it, and she shrugged.

"I have a whole list of reasons for wanting to have plenty of ways to defend myself at all times," she said. "But this dagger has its own purpose for later."

She didn't give me an explanation of what that was, and I had to hurry to match her pace as she headed out the door.

We exited the royal chambers, my stomach rumbling from the breakfast I'd missed out on and my jaw ticking as I thought about fucking Justin and his stupid fucking face. I was going to smack that face the next time I laid my eyes on him. Then we'd see if he was still so star-damned smug.

"Is that my lady?" a cry drew my attention, and I half turned to look around for Geraldine, but Tory caught my arm and yanked on it, forcing me to move faster as we headed for the drawbridge.

"I love Gerry, but if she checks up on my eating habits one more time, I'm going to scream," she hissed, her pace practically a trot as guards moved aside to let us out and we moved over the drawbridge.

I glanced down at Tory, taking in the sharpness of her cheekbones and the haunted expression in her ferocious gaze. I could tell why Geraldine was fussing.

"Maybe you should eat a bit more," I suggested. "It's never a good idea to get too hung-"

"One more word, Max Rigel, and I'll kick you in the balls and leave you wheezing on the floor while I go talk to Miguel alone," she said, her fingernails biting into my arm painfully, making me want to snatch it away.

Instead, I aimed soothing magic towards her, subtly weaving a little hunger into the emotions too, but she just clicked her tongue and shut me out, releasing my arm and striding away towards the newly built jail on the far side of the island.

I would have tried to argue further, but I could already tell that it wouldn't get me anywhere. Besides, the fact that she hadn't just shifted and flown on ahead of me told me she didn't actually want to leave me behind at all. Despite the walls she was now maintaining to keep me out of her head, I knew how alone she was feeling.

"Coowee!" Geraldine called from behind us, and I resisted the urge to turn her way as I jogged to catch up to Tory.

"You do realise she isn't going to give up, don't you?" I asked as I fell into step with her again, and the corner of Tory's lips twitched in amusement.

"I know."

We walked another ten steps or so before a Tarzan yell reached my ears, and I was forced to turn and look at Geraldine who was swinging across the terrain with a vine wrapped around her waist and a platter full of buttery bagels balanced on an outstretched hand.

"My ladyyyy!" Geraldine called and Tory broke a rueful grin as she turned too, folding her arms in some attempt to look irritated while we waited for Geraldine to land.

The vines snapped her skyward before releasing her and she flipped over, somehow keeping every single bagel on that platter before landing solidly in front of us and bowing to Tory.

"Oh good, I caught you," Geraldine panted, her chest rising and falling heavily, drawing more than a little of my attention. Her crimson hair was plastered to her forehead where beads of perspiration lined her brow from the chase she'd embarked on to catch us.

"Were you looking for me?" Tory asked innocently, and if I hadn't been with her the entire time, I swear I would have believed she'd had no idea. No wonder that girl had never been charged with anything in the mortal realm.

"Oh, you cheeky cherub, you know I was," Geraldine laughed, planting her free hand on her hip and offering Tory the platter. "And I know that you do not feel the pangs of hunger while the cloud of grief gathers close around you, but I would be failing in my duties if I did not attempt to tempt you with some buttery goodness on a fine morn such as this. You know you must eat to maintain your strength, and I would be a narry nubby of a friend if I didn't look out for you in this time of war, strife, and need."

"Fine," Tory gave in, reaching for a bagel and taking a big bite which made Geraldine sigh with relief.

"I also haven't eaten on this nerry morn," I pointed out, eyeing the bagels while Geraldine gave me little more than a cursory glance.

"What on earth are you gabbering about, you slothsome seabeast?" she asked, frowning at me like I'd just spoke Martian or something.

"I just…would like a bagel. Please," I said, my stomach punctuating that request by growling loudly enough for all of us to hear.

"These are royal bagels," Geraldine laughed like I'd been joking, wafting me away. "Baked with royal tums in mind, the fluffiest and butteriest of their kind. Not the flotsam fish stew more suited to one such as you."

"Gerry," I ground out, the mountain of bagels whispering to me. "There are about fifty bagels there. Tory couldn't possibly eat all of them even if she wanted to. What are you planning to do with all the ones she doesn't eat if no one else can have any?"

Geraldine stared at me with those beguiling blue eyes of hers, blinked once, looked at the bagels, then burst out laughing again.

I assumed that was my cue to take one and reached for it, but she snapped at my fucking fingers like a dog guarding a chew toy, and I was forced to snatch them away again.

Tory barked a laugh as she turned towards the jail once more, striding ahead of us and leaving me to start bickering with Geraldine over the fate of the fucking baked goods she was hoarding like a Dragon with treasure.

By the time we made it to the squat wooden building, I'd been hit over the head with a bagel, called at least eighteen different types of fish-based insults, and was pretty certain I would be getting laid tonight too. It was all fucking confusing, and I was still grumbling about being hungry while Tory hadn't even bothered to take a second bagel after eating the first.

The guards who were on duty outside the wooden jailhouse all leapt to attention as they spotted Tory, the five of them bowing low even when she forcefully told them not to.

"Geraldine, can you tell them?" Tory asked in exasperation when they refused to rise without her permission. Tory in turn refused to give them permission to rise, based on the fact that she didn't want to have the power to tell them to do any such thing.

"Well, my lady, it is a bit of a conundrum. They wish to honour you by bowing, and yet you take the bowing as something of an insult, which in turn makes them want to placate and honour you more, so they bow lower, but then you do not appear appeased by that, so then they have no choice but to bow even lower and-"

"I'm just gonna go on in and leave this shit show to play out without me," Tory interrupted her. "But if we can avoid more of this going forward, then that would be great."

She rolled her eyes at the guards who were practically laying in the mud at this point, their confusion and desperate desire to please her filling the air. Tory grabbed a couple more bagels from the platter then told Geraldine to offer the rest to the guards once they managed to get themselves up off the floor, jerking her chin to me in a command for me to follow her inside.

"You know you're not my queen, don't you?" I growled as I stalked after Tory. "And I wanted some of those bagels you just handed out to the rabble-"

"Shh." Tory pushed one of the bagels she'd just taken into my mouth, cutting off my rant, then handing me the other. "You're really bitchy when you're hangry."

I would have argued with her about that, but I gave in to the demands of my stomach and chewed instead, the sound of Geraldine consoling the confused rebels following us into the darkness of the small building.

No real effort had been made in here to make it comfortable; it was just a wooden box with a single window allowing a minimal amount of light inside. The only thing within the building was the huge night iron cage containing the one and only Nymph we had taken captive after the attack on the ruins.

Tory created a torch with her earth magic, lighting it with a spark of fire and plunging the other end into the ground beside us, the dirt supporting it as the flickering flames illuminated Miguel in his cage.

My gifts flared as I tried to get a sense of the Nymph, figuring out his motivations and any plots he might be concealing, but all I could perceive from him was this endless kind of relief, a lot of sadness, and a spark of hope which flared brighter as he took in his visitors.

"You came," he said, pushing to his feet from the dirt where he'd been lying. He brushed off his clothes and tried to flatten the mess of thinning dark hair on his head, embarrassment tumbling from him as he looked from Tory to me.

"We have questions," Tory said simply, her eyes moving over the cold cage and her lips tightening. "Sit."

A flick of her fingers had three stools growing from the ground itself, two on our side of the bars for us and one inside for him to use.

Miguel dropped onto the stool with a sigh, wringing his hands in his lap as he fought the desire to speak, respect and humility adding to the mixture of emotions I could feel from him. He was making no attempt to shield any of it from me, and I wasn't sure if he was even capable of doing so. Either way, I relaxed, sensing no threat or signs of deceit here.

"I've been researching dark magic," Tory said, subtle as a bull, like always. "Old magic. The kind that predates the Awakening of our kind."

"Si. The Nymphs have been servants of the dark for a long time," Miguel said, nodding. "Though it was only ever called dark by your kind. At least it was once the shadows were tainted."

"Tainted how?"

"La Princesa de las Sombras."

"English, please," I grunted, and his eyes flicked to me, a flinch of fear coating my tongue as his emotions shifted once more.

"Sorry." Miguel dipped his head. "They were tainted by the Shadow Princess. Lavinia. When she was banished to their realm and her curse bled into it."

"So you're saying that before she entered the shadow realm, things were different? How?" I asked.

Miguel hesitated, fear and uncertainty wrapping around me like a silk glove stroking its way down my cheek.

"I want to be honest with you," he said. "But…there is more than just my life at stake here. There are others who I need to protect."

"Others who don't wish to follow Lavinia?" Tory asked, scooting forward on her stool, and I could tell she'd guessed right by the shift in Miguel's emotions.

He nodded. "Do you swear you won't hurt them? They have never hunted Fae, never stolen magic. The few of them who have any of your power were gifted it just as our kind were in the days of old. By willing Fae already at death's door, those waiting to walk beyond the Veil, ready to part with their power."

I frowned, wondering why even a dying Fae would ever agree to a Nymph taking their magic from them, but Tory spoke before I could.

“I won’t ever attack anyone who doesn’t first strike at me or this kingdom,” she swore, a ring of authority to those words. “My sister and I have no taste for war or death beyond fighting for the freedom everyone deserves from tyranny.”

Miguel wrung his hands again, his emotions roiling as he came to some decision, and he pushed to his feet, clinging to the night iron bars as if they caused him no discomfort at all. And maybe if his claims about not wielding the shadows were true, then they didn’t.

“My son trusted you. He loved you. You gave him a family when he couldn’t claim one at home,” his voice cracked, and I could sense Tory’s discomfort. She hadn’t been as close to Diego as Darcy had, but I knew their friendship had been real enough, even if it had been a little fraught at times. “And I think he would have wanted me to tell you this. He would have wanted me to trust you too.”

“Trust me with what?” Tory asked, and I leaned closer as I felt the importance of this revelation rising in the room.

“I was born in a secluded part of the kingdom, hidden from all outsiders through years of careful and diligent work. We broke our allegiance with others of our kind when we decided to resist the call of la Princesa de las Sombras. We saw through the lies she was spinning and came to understand the taint she had placed upon the shadows we had once loved and wielded so dearly. So we left them, six entire tribes of Nymphs left and hid ourselves away from those who wished to continue down her path. We worked to cleanse a small portion of the shadows of her vile corruption so that we could use them without her input, so that we wouldn’t be polluted by her desires and become maddened with the need to steal magic from Fae. There are even Fae who live among us peacefully. They have married our kind and live full lives with us, giving up their power only when death comes calling at their door and even then, they only do so if they wish it.”

“I need to learn more about the magic you possess,” Tory said. “I need to use everything that I possibly can to bring Lionel down. Can you teach me?”

“Tory,” I warned her in a low growl, but she shot me a dark look, telling me all too clearly to back off, and I gritted my teeth as I waited for Miguel’s reply.

“I don’t know much of the old magics,” he admitted. “But I could give you some guidance in handling the shadows – though your kind cannot wield them in the ways we can.”

“Is there anyone who would know more about the old Fae way of casting? Anyone who I could ask in your hidden village?” she pushed.

Miguel froze, his eyes moving between the two of us warily. “Their location is a secret which has been guarded for almost a thousand years-”

“But let’s say it wasn’t. Let’s say your people were here with us now. Let’s say they really wanted to deal with Lavinia and reclaim the shadows from her. Would there be someone among them who might have the answers I seek? Would there be a chance that the rest of them might be rallied into an army to fight on our side of this war?”

“Tory,” I barked, shoving to my feet as disgust filled me at the thought of that. “You can’t seriously be suggesting an alliance with some of the Nymphs?”

She turned her dark eyes on me with a warning flaring in them, but I refused to let her push ahead with this madness.

“You’re forgetting that you aren’t actually a queen,” I growled. “You can’t offer up alliances with anyone, let alone our sworn enemies.”

“I’m simply asking a question,” she replied icily, turning back to look at Miguel. “Is there a chance?”

Miguel looked from her to me with hesitation written into every piece of his being. His fear clung to the walls and rolled down them in a thick and cloying fog which was impossible to ignore, but piercing through that terror, a single beam of emotion drew my attention. Hope.

“Perhaps,” he breathed, and I swear the entire world spun on its axis as the stars peered closer to listen to that one, impossible word.

Silence hung between all of us, filled with tension, mistrust, and that aching hope.

"We need to go," Tory said suddenly, lifting her head to look through the window to the sky beyond.

I followed her gaze to see the sun moving closer to its zenith, the midday light brightening the sky to a stunning shade of blue.

"I'll leave you to think about that offer and return to discuss it further," she said to Miguel, a flick of her fingers growing a bed of soft moss with warm blankets for him, then a small, wooden shelter to add some privacy to his shitting bucket. Lastly, she cast a stone bowl filled with heated water for him to wash in and a smaller one with chilled water to drink from.

I'll make sure someone brings you some food," she added, and Miguel's eyes widened in shock and gratitude at the kindness. It didn't surprise me though; the Vegas had suffered in hunger and coldness. She wouldn't want anyone else to endure the same, even if they might turn out to be her enemy.

Tory strode from the room without bothering to check if I was actually following her or not, and I trotted along in her wake, the words Justin had tossed at me earlier ringing in my skull.

I wasn't just some side piece to the ascension of the Vegas. But I had to admit that Tory was stepping into the role of ruler without so much as a flicker of hesitation, her actions strong and decisive, even if they were touched with harshness in the wake of all she'd lost.

We headed out of the jail and across the open plain beyond, ignoring the guards as they bowed again, no sign of Gerry anywhere, much to my disappointment.

My stride lengthened so that we walked together and I was no longer trailing behind, but Tory didn't show any indication that she had even noticed the difference.

There was a hill to the south of the island, and we headed up its steep sides until we made it to the top where Seth, Caleb, and Geraldine had already gathered.

"Have you got everything?" Caleb asked, looking to her, and Tory nodded, her eyes moving from him to the sun above which was almost at its highest point.

"We need to hurry," she said.

"Is anyone going to explain this to me?" Seth asked, cocking his head like a pup, and Geraldine sighed like a long-suffering mother.

"At the height of the sun, our dear and magnanimous lady shall use the powers of old to transport her wandering soul to the location of her other half, walking the path between life and death while bound to a single, flickering flame. Once the sun doth wane and the effigy burns out, she shall return to herself here, and lo, we shall at last have the answer to our dearest Darcy's location."

"Okay, so eighty percent of that made no sense," Seth said as Tory took the small bag from her pocket and placed it on the floor beside the dagger. "But I think there were mentions of a wandering soul which sounds a whole lot like death to me."

The coldness creeping through me had nothing to do with the chilled wind sweeping around us and everything to do with the truth in his words. I couldn't help but agree with him.

"Are you really sure about messing with this stuff, Tory?" I asked, eyeing her cautiously as she flicked her fingers at the ground and burned a perfect pentagram through the grass right at the apex of the hill. "I don't think Darius would have wanted you to risk-"

"That's the thing about dying," Tory hissed venomously. "You give up the chance to want anything at all."

"We could just stop you from doing this," Seth piped up, moving closer to me as he seemed to agree with my feelings on the subject. It felt like spitting on Darius's grave to ignore the risks here and let his mate take part in untested magic which would quite literally involve her soul departing from her body.

"Do you really think so?" Tory challenged, a slight shimmer in the air between us making it clear that she'd placed a shield there so fast I hadn't even noticed her casting it.

"Yeah," Seth growled, rising to the challenge and taking a step closer. "I think we can. And for another thing-"

"Leave it," Caleb growled, shooting around to place himself between us and Tory, his fangs flashing in the light as he bared them at us.

My heart stilled in shock, then free-fell inside my chest to splatter all over the floor in a bloody mess as I found myself standing off against him like that, my friend standing in defence of a Vega over his brothers.

"Caleb, what the fuck?" I growled, but he didn't back down, and as I reached for his emotions with my gifts, I found him determined and unyielding, even if standing against us like that was hurting him too.

"She needs to figure out this magic. And I swore an oath to help her do it. I believe she can, and I agree with her on the Darius point. If he'd wanted a say in what she did, he should have stuck around to voice his own opinion."

The words struck me like a blow, and if I hadn't been able to feel how much it hurt him to speak them, I likely would have beat his fucking head in for them.

I looked to Geraldine as she casually swung her flail in one hand, moving to stand at Caleb's side, a half-raised eyebrow inviting us to press on with this challenge.

"You really think this is the right thing?" Seth asked, a whimper in the back of his throat as he cocked his head towards Tory who was now cross-legged on the floor, various herbs sprouting from the ground around her under the guidance of her earth magic.

"I think it's the only thing we have right now which might give us an edge. Which might, change our shitty fucking fates," Caleb said and with those words I felt the truth of him. He had bought into Tory's way of thinking about this untested power. He believed in her pointless quest to try and shift what had already come to pass, to force a different destiny upon us and the man we'd all lost.

"Caleb," I said slowly, the aggression falling from my posture as I felt the weight of my own loss crashing down on me. "I don't believe..."

I shook my head, glancing to Tory again before expelling a breath. She was her own woman. She understood the risks in what she was attempting by wielding this ancient power, and I could feel how deeply determined she was to go through with this insane plan. She was going to immerse herself in the use of ether regardless of anything anyone else had to say on the subject. And she was right, we couldn't stop her.

Even if we succeeded now, we wouldn't be able to keep her from this path without restraining her day and night, and I had no intention of doing any such thing to her after all she'd suffered at Lionel's hands, even if I knew that Darius would have hated this.

"Okay," I agreed at last. "We won't stand against you."

I glanced to Seth for confirmation, and he gave a low growl which voiced his discomfort before nodding firmly in agreement.

"Jolly good." Geraldine pranced away as if facing off against me meant absolutely nothing in the grand scheme of her day, and I resisted the urge to pout as I gave Tory's actions my attention.

She now held a roughly fashioned corn doll in her grip, the thing looking weirdly feminine despite its stuffing sticking out all over the place. Its chest remained open, and Tory carefully picked a sprig of vervain and pushed it into the doll. Next, she added chamomile and then some sweet marjoram before taking the dagger and cutting off a small lock of her own hair to press into the chest of the creepy looking thing.

"Vervain for aiding astral workings," Geraldine breathed as she began to walk in a slow circle around the edge of the pentagram where Tory worked. "And to induce the psychic ability to part one's soul from their flesh. Chamomile to capture the gifts of the sun and borrow its almighty power when it is at its highest peak. Sweet marjoram to call on her one true love – for what greater love is there than that of two sisters?"

"You're making this whole thing sound very romantic," I muttered, eyeing Tory warily as she took a lapis lazuli crystal from her bag next, the deep blue stone filled with pure golden swirls which made my breath catch. It was a priceless piece, one she'd no doubt taken from Darius's treasure, and the thought of him losing his shit over that both amused me and sent a twinge of sadness through my soul.

"The lapis lazuli is the epitome of wisdom, intuition and clarity, it will help keep her wandering soul on track to find the answer she seeks," Geraldine said in that creepy tone, and I found myself glad that this ritual was taking place in full daylight as a shiver ran down my spine.

"Stop making this weird, Geraldine," Seth complained. "I already don't like it, and you're making it all kinds of freaky."

Tory took her dagger and lifted it over the stone, her brow furrowing in concentration as she etched two runes into the flawless face of it.

"Fehu for luck and Dagaz for awareness," Geraldine cooed mysteriously, and I reached for Seth as he whimpered in protest, offering him some reassuring energy to help combat Geraldine's insistence on dramatics.

Tory pushed the lapis lazuli into the corn doll's chest then pinched the opening closed, sealing everything inside it as she positioned herself in the centre of the pentagram.

I held my breath as she turned the blade around and slit her finger open on it, her blood spilling over the doll and sizzling as some magic began to take hold already.

The pentagram burned into the ground started glowing, seeming to suck light from the air itself as Tory tipped her head back to the sky and spoke a set of words which were strange and unruly, the power of them lashing against the air itself and making it hard to breathe.

The moment she stopped, the doll she held burst into flames, a scream escaping it as everything it contained was consumed by the fire in a flash of heat hot enough to scorch my cheeks.

A blast of power exploded from the thing as it fell apart into nothing but ash, and Tory gasped as it hit her, her body lifting from the floor, spine arching backwards unnaturally.

"Tory!" I yelled, trying to move closer to her, but there was a potent energy surrounding the pentagram which I couldn't cross, the power of it crackling painfully against my skin as I tried.

"It's working!" Geraldine gasped as Tory's eyes flew open and her unseeing gaze stared up at the sky.

The power that held her vanished suddenly and she fell to the floor with a thump, her body completely still as her wide-open eyes looked at nothing at all and I felt the loss of her in everything around us.

"No," I begged, trying to force my way past the power of the pentagram but finding it impenetrable even as I threw my magic at it.

Seth howled as he tried to help me, Caleb's face paling with each second that passed without her so much as breathing.

She was gone. Utterly gone. The only other time I had felt such a lack of someone was in death. Even a Fae who was shielding their emotions from me gave off a signature I could read, a flicker of self that allowed me to know they were there. But not Tory. There was nothing left of her here with us beyond the empty body which was shielded from our help by the pentagram she'd drawn.

"No, no, no, no." Seth fought to get to her, the idea of losing another member of our group clearly on the brink of breaking him.

Caleb shook his head, refusing it, as if he was still holding onto the vague hope that she could return to us, but what if he was wrong?

"I knew this was a bad idea!" I yelled as I slammed my fist into the wall of power once again, ice shattering across the edge of it before melting then evaporating entirely, my water destroyed as if it were nothing at all.

A shuddering breath forced me to still and the power holding me back disappeared as if it had never been at all.

Geraldine shrieked at a pitch so high I was pretty sure she'd shattered my eardrums. By the time I took my hands from shielding my ears, I found her prostrate on the floor before a dazed-looking Tory who was blinking at all of us like she hardly recognised where she was.

"Did you find her?" Seth begged while Geraldine garbled on about the undeniable power of the true queens.

"Yes," Tory panted, and the look of horror on her face told me the answer before she even spoke it, her hands tightening to fists and fear dancing in her eyes. "And Orion was with her too. Lionel has them."

Scorpio
Virgo
Gemini
Aries
Cancer
Leo
Sagittarius
Taurus
Capricorn
Aquarius
Libra
Pisces

MILTON

CHAPTER THIRTY ONE

Tension lined every inch of my posture, a bead of sweat rolling down my temple as I sat up straight and looked dead ahead.

The Orb was deathly quiet as the entire school sat to attention, a hum of concern settling over us while we waited, the only sound the ticking of the large clock hanging on the wall. I glanced at it, specifically at the minute hand which had just shifted past the six-minute marker, all of us still waiting, and no one daring to say a word.

My eyes met Gary's across the room, a flicker of concern and determination passing between us. It was too late to back out now. Everything was in place, the magic cast to hide the involvement of the Undercover A.S.S. and nothing left besides the time between now and our strike landing.

Lionel Acrux was here. We'd been told at dinner last night that our esteemed king was coming to speak with us, to rally us in this time of unease and reassure us about the threat posed by the rebels.

We were just one stop on a long list of press appointments he had today, political posturing designed to make everyone believe he was this kind, magnanimous leader, concerned about the citizens of his kingdom. I'd already caught a couple of minutes from the live stream of him visiting a hospital this morning, kissing babies on the head, and claiming to bless them. If it had been my baby he'd come to kiss, I think I would have hurled myself and the child out of the window before allowing his poisonous mouth anywhere near it.

Seven minutes past ten.

If this went on much longer, then our plan might execute itself before he even arrived to feel the effects of it.

Bernice shifted in her seat a little way from me, biting her bottom lip as she felt my attention on her.

We hadn't sat together. None of us were very close to each other, keeping our distance and maintaining the ruse that we were sticking to our Order segregation. I was positioned at the far back of the room, surrounded by the other Minotaurs as we waited on the false king's tardy arrival. The Tiberian Rats sat to our right, a line of division set between our seats and theirs, no one daring to so much as look at it while we continued our silent waiting game.

Eight minutes past.

I resisted the urge to wipe my sweaty palms on my trousers, remaining utterly still as my gaze tracked towards the door, the one most likely to be Lionel's entry point to this room, and I found Marguerite Helebor watching me with stern interest from her position standing beside it.

She had a shiny K.U.N.T. badge pinned to her lapel, her red hair tumbling down around her face in that overly styled way she always preferred, and her uniform clung to her figure in crisp perfection. The epitome of student piety and a devoted servant to the king.

Except she wasn't. Nothing had come of the hunt for us when she'd warned us to flee. Whatever had happened which had led to the K.U.N.T. raid on our meeting place, she'd hidden us from discovery. I had so many questions for her, more than I could count, which had been keeping me up at night ever since that brief moment where she'd saved our asses.

Like how had she known I was there? Had anyone tipped them off to our whereabouts, or had one of the other K.U.N.T.s like Mildred been the one to figure it out and decide to come after us?

We hadn't all met up since that night, too spooked to risk it, instead swapping information and making plans one on one, passing notes in the corridors or simply exchanging looks of solidarity.

I had managed to send footage and information out to Portia using the phone she'd given me though. We'd evaded suspicion so far too, the K.U.N.Ts hunting us all over the academy but not once coming close to discovering who we were.

We were still here. We were still fighting.

And now a real opportunity had dropped in our laps, and we were risking our damn lives to see it come to fruition – I just hoped to fuck that it did so while the Dragon asshole was in the room because if he didn't turn up within the next minute, the entire thing would go off without him here.

We could die for this. I knew it. All of us knew it. If we were caught, we'd be taken to one of his Nebular Inquisition Centres and tortured or executed or at the very least, left to rot away inside it. And I really didn't want to be risking my life over a plan that didn't actually manage to come together.

Marguerite continued to stare at me, her pretty features a still pond, vacant of expression, but her eyes burned. I thought over my horoscope from that morning and couldn't help but wonder if it had been referring to her.

Good morning, Sagittarius.
The stars have spoken about your day!
Your fate balances on a knife's edge today, your plans lost in the roiling sea of destiny which is too murky to fully enlighten. But take heart, for success is not impossible and if you can find it in you to trust in an unlikely ally, then many truths may be revealed to you.

Marguerite Helebor was nothing if not an unlikely ally.

Nine minutes past.

I swallowed a lump in my throat as several students dared to start up whispered conversations, Professor Highspell striding into the open space at the centre of the room and glaring out at the perpetrators as she handed out a round of detentions and they all hissed their disapproval.

My heart began to sink as my gaze dared stray to the clock again, the seconds ticking by far too quickly, our carefully laid trap about to go off with only our abhorrent Cardinal Magic teacher to take the strike.

Not that I would feel bad watching Honey Highspell get knocked down a peg or two. But nothing that happened to her would be live broadcasted across the kingdom, it wouldn't become a beacon showing solidarity with all the others out there who were facing this persecution and were unable to fight back like striking Lionel Acrux would.

I fought the urge to glance at Gary again, not wanting anyone to notice my interactions today. I couldn't give anyone a reason to look at me for this. We'd covered our tracks, our magical signatures removed from what we'd done and all of us retaining strong alibies. This could work. It *would* work. Assuming the man who now called himself king-

Relief splintered through me, quickly followed by the urge to vomit with nerves as the doors swung open and Lionel Acrux strode into The Orb, flanked by a camera crew and Principal Nova. A camera-ready smile sat on his face as he looked out at his subjects and we all dropped from our chairs, falling to our knees as we bowed for him.

Bile rolled up the back of my throat as I lowered my head among the rest of my kind, every student in the academy showing - or at the very least feigning - subservience to that ungodly piece of shit as he strolled in like he owned the fucking place.

"Rise," Lionel cooed, beckoning with two fingers like a puppet master tugging on our strings, and everyone in the room pushed themselves up from the floor, returning to their seats.

I watched in disgusted fascination as Lionel paused there, smiling serenely, hardly even seeming to breathe while the camera crews circled him, and he waited for them to get into position before he went on. Everything about him was so fucking fake, the smiles, the charm, the promises to protect our kingdom from Orders he didn't like while making up lies about us. It was bullshit. And we planned on reminding the world that not all of us bought into it.

"Education," Lionel began, pressing a fist to his heart as he gazed around the room. "Is the epitome of the modern world. The greatest legacy any Fae can leave behind, and the one thing all those gifted with true and willing hearts will always find waiting for them. I myself, am a true believer in education, the revelation of facts and the adjustment of the world to best benefit those facts."

I stiffened at his words, the contempt lying beneath them as he addressed the supposed higher Orders on the other side of the room, his gaze refusing to lift towards those of us segregated at the back.

I curled my fingers into fists in my lap, hiding the small tremor running through me as I dared another glance at the clock.

Thirty seconds to go.

"As a true believer in the rise of the greatest to the top, I have come here today to offer up a grant to this most prestigious academy, one which will be used to supply a-"

A series of bangs exploded all around the central part of the room where the false king stood, both from the ground and the ceiling, balloons filled with glue and Pegasus glitter erupting as they were revealed from within the concealment spells that had been hiding them.

Lionel threw an arm up to shield himself, but he was too late, the thick white glue splattering him from head to foot, the iridescent glitter sparkling in the lights as he bellowed a furious roar.

A screen at the back of the room started playing that sex tape of him fucking a Pegasus girl in her shifted form, the sound of him groaning in pleasure while she whinnied, bouncing back and forth on a loop while everyone in the room cried out in surprise. Another video cut in of Lionel talking to the press outside the Court of Solaria, his words all edited together from his speeches over the years to create a song. The beat was damn good too, and I hoped this song did its job to remind everyone that this was a rebellion not an insurgence, and we weren't going to just take Lionel's shit.

I sang along in my head, fighting a smile or any kind of expression that could admit guilt and praising Gary for his remix skills and the DJ software his Mom had bought him last Christmas. Each word was trimmed from a different speech, but together, Gary had woven it to the rhythm, so it flowed into one seamlessly.

"I'm not here to save you,
No, I'm here to break you.

I'm just a lizard who wants it allll.

I've lied and spewed a load of shit,
I can't believe anyone buys it.
It's time to rise and make a staaand."

The video cut in intermittently with old clips of Hail Vega with the Councillors, smiling and laughing alongside Lionel's brother Radcliff. There were clips of the Vega twins too, hugging each other, their love for one another clear in their eyes.

Bernice and I had spent a lot of time gathering all the videos, and it had been her idea to include ones of our allies. Gary had done a beautiful job of making a graphic of a Phoenix bird fly around and leave a blazing trail behind it with the words 'join the rebellion!' in the flames.

"I'm lame and my friends all knew it.
Don't swallow my Orderist bullshit.
The Vega twins will return before too lonnng."

Videos of the Heirs were shown, all four of them standing united, the people cheering them, and the Vegas waving to an adoring crowd. The blazing graphic of the Phoenix burned through it all, giving way to a shining symbol of the bird with outstretched wings, the words *Long Live the Vega Queens* blazing beneath it.

Laughter cut through the air, but then another bang made people scream as the song came to an end, some of them racing for the doors in a frantic bid for freedom. The final balloon exploded right in front of the motherfucker, and Lionel threw an air shield up before him just like we'd expected.

The blood red paint inside the balloon hit his shield, the magic woven into it making it form words against the shell of hardened air.

All hail the king of bestiality who's been fucking so-called lesser Orders in the ass since long before his reign began.

"Arrest them!" Lionel bellowed from within his shield, trying to banish it and the words now emblazoned across it. But he found new air magic taking its place, the cast a mimic of his own which Bernice had designed herself. The magic had been triggered by him using his own power, and nothing in it would reveal the Fae who had cast the original spell but he couldn't banish it either, leaving those words hanging there before him while countless cameras caught every moment.

Mildred stepped forward with a furious cry, her beady eyes scouring the Fae at the back of the room as she hunted for prey amongst us, and more students leapt to their feet and ran.

I held my ground for a few more seconds, my excitement contained in my chest as I waited just long enough for the crowd to break in its entirety. And as a Dragon's roar rattled the ceiling, I got my wish.

Fae of all Orders sprang to their feet, carnage unfolding as everyone turned and fled, the cameras still rolling and every second of this latest humiliation and rebellion broadcasted live to the entire kingdom.

I finally gave in to the swell of the crowd, shoving to my feet and turning to escape with everyone else.

Adrenaline broke through my body like a dam, a wild laugh barely stifled in my throat as I sprinted towards Bernice, snatching her hand in mine, and running with her.

A gleeful moo parted my lips as we sprinted for the door, the stampede awakening the beast in me as we ran.

We didn't dare so much as look at one another as we raced from The Orb, refusing to give away the slightest indication of our involvement until we were far from here and alone. Then I was going to steal that kiss from her. Fuck the consequences. We could die for taking part in that stunt. We'd covered ourselves as best we could, but we could still die for it. There were no guarantees, and putting off tomorrow because I was afraid of today made no fucking sense to me anymore.

We sprinted down the path, my feet tripping over themselves as a pair of K.U.N.T.s stepped into our path, Kylie Major smiling cruelly as she raised her hands in warning.

"Why are you running?" she demanded, and the group of students stumbled and faltered, unsure what to do in the face of the two servants of the crown.

"Who said that?" someone called, and I had to fight a laugh as Kylie's face turned purple with rage. Even now, many of us still acted like she didn't exist.

"Because there were bombs going off in there!" a girl near the front of the group wailed dramatically, clutching onto her friend who started sobbing too.

Two assholes weren't exactly enough to stop the swarm of Fae trying to head down this path, but we all knew better than to attack a K.U.N.T.

I tugged on Bernice's hand as some more students began begging to get by, turning us towards Jupiter Hall where more of the spooked Fae were sprinting away from The Orb.

Kylie yelled a command for us to stop but we'd started a tide of movement, and I let the rest of the students sweep us along with them as we ran from her too. We just needed to lay low, to get out of sight and keep away until the false king had gone, and his minions stopped asking questions.

There would be an investigation, no doubt, but I didn't plan on being anywhere near it.

Bernice gave me a fearful look, but I only smiled in return.

We'd done it. Cast a blow against the tyrant who had taken our freedoms and civil liberties from us. It may not have been the end of him, but it was something, a sign to all the others out there who were being forced into oppression because of Lionel Acrux that we hadn't forgotten them. That our time would come.

I dragged Bernice off the main path, heading for a side door which led into the enormous gothic building that made up Jupiter Hall.

We ducked inside and sprinted along the bottom floor, aiming for one of the rear exits and escape beyond.

But just as we turned a corner and I spied one of the doors at the far end of the long corridor, a bang sounded behind us and Lionel Acrux's furious snarls filled the space.

"I cannot apologise enough, my King," Principal Nova was saying and my heart free fell into my ass as I realised they were heading right for us. A tyrant on a rampage about to come face to face with two lowly Minotaurs. I didn't like the sound of that one bit.

Pounding footsteps drew closer and I hurled a silencing bubble over us as I raced for the closest door, my heart pounding in alarm as I found it locked.

More footsteps closed in on us and I glanced across the long hall towards Nova's office, the only other door close enough for us to reach before they turned that corner, and undoubtably their motherfucking destination.

"Shit," I hissed as I dragged Bernice towards it, left with no option but to hope for an open window inside so we could escape.

"You will bring me the Fae responsible for this act," Lionel snarled, his voice sending fear tumbling down my spine as I yanked the door open, and we spilled into Nova's large office.

I sprinted for the window, but my heart plunged with despair as I spied the bars over it, no doubt put there to stop any little assholes from gaining access from outside and trying to change their grades, but that left us up shit creak without a fucking paddle.

"Here," Bernice hissed as those footsteps closed in on the door outside and I whirled towards her as she pulled open a closet, the space inside barely big enough for one of us, let alone two. It was also the only viable hiding place in the entire room.

"Fuck," I bit out as I gave in and ran to her, pushing her into the dim space between some of Nova's coats and cloaks and forcing myself in right behind her.

I tugged the door shut half a breath before the door to the room opened behind us and I held my breath, despite the silencing bubble protecting us as those footsteps thumped into the room.

"Search it," Lionel barked. "I won't be taken unawares for a second time today."

"Yes, my King," Mildred's ragged voice came in reply.

I pushed Bernice behind me as I began fumbling with a concealment spell, shadows growing around us, more coats seeming to appear to hide us from sight.

Fear made me cast slower than I needed to, and my heart raced to an uneven beat as I heard those footsteps thumping closer still, our deaths waiting just beyond that door, a cruel and bloody end which my stupidity had brought on not only me but Bernice as well. We wouldn't be able to talk our way out of this. We likely wouldn't have a chance to plead our innocence at all.

As someone gripped the knob of the closet door from the other side, I said a silent goodbye to my family, hoping they knew how much I loved them and understood why I'd had to fight back against the man who would now be my end, even if it was only in that one, small way.

The door was drawn wide, and I didn't so much as summon my power, knowing it was hopeless anyway, that my fate was sealed.

But as I blinked into the startled face of the girl who had come to check our hiding place, I didn't find a moustache or undercut jaw, no humungous, Faeroid-addicted warrior of the Dragon Guild. Instead, the pretty redhead blinked at me in utter shock, her face paling as her eyes flicked to Bernice where she peered around me, taking in everything in a split second.

Over Marguerite's shoulder, I could see Lionel standing with his back to me in the centre of the room, the scent of smoke a toxic tang in the air as it coiled beneath my nose.

Marguerite's shock lasted no more than a blink, her face returning to that unbreakable mask as she made a show of ruffling some of the coats beside me then drew back.

"All clear," she said blandly before swinging the door closed on us once more, saving my fucking ass for the second time and risking her own life with that treasonous lie.

Bernice gripped my arm tightly, her shock as clear as my own while we held the silence and waited.

"All clear behind the curtains and beneath the desk too, Your Highness," Mildred added gruffly.

"Good. Then be gone. I need a private word with my head of staff here at the academy," Lionel snarled.

The sound of the K.U.N.T.s leaving was followed by the sharp snap of the door, and I had to fight against the trembling of my own limbs as I felt a silencing bubble slide over us, Lionel's magic encompassing the room while Nova remained quiet.

"What was it I said that I required of you the last time I was here?" Lionel asked, his voice a deadly purr, and despite my better judgement, I leaned forward, pressing my eye to the small crack running along the edge of the door so I could look out.

The false king dropped into the chair behind the wide mahogany desk, a wind billowing around him which sent the carefully stacked paperwork on the surface flying to all corners of the room.

"I was to enforce your rule among the students, take precautions against the lesser Orders, and bring pride to your legacy as I nurtured the students within the new regime and prepared them for the new, greater world you are building for them to reside in," Nova replied almost robotically, and I angled my head to look at her where she stood before him, her head bowed.

"So why," Lionel snarled. "If my commands were so abundantly clear, have I found myself the butt of some joke, some...*prank,* set to undermine all I had come here to achieve?"

Nova began to apologise but Lionel released a Dragon's growl, shoving to his feet suddenly, his domineering presence clouding the entire room.

I took Bernice's hand in mine as his gaze turned murderous, his wrath a potent thing.

He raised a hand, and for a moment I thought he might blast our principal out of existence entirely, burning her to ash for not stopping our attack before it could begin. But instead of striking at her, he prowled around the desk and gripped her upper arms as he made her look into his eyes.

"You will hunt for the rebels hiding within this school," he commanded and the Coercion he laced his tone with was beyond thick, the power in it rough and brutal, undeniable. I almost succumbed to the desire to follow that command myself, and I wasn't even the one he had aimed the order at.

"Holy shit," Bernice breathed, her voice concealed within my silencing bubble. "Is he using Dark Coercion?"

We knew the stories, had read the articles put out by Catalina Acrux about the power her abusive husband had wielded over her. But seeing it here and now, watching as Nova was forced to submit to him, her mind not even her own as she nodded, made me sick to my stomach.

"I will," she agreed.

"You will, what?" Lionel hissed, shaking her so hard that a few strands of the dark hair contained in her bun fell free.

"I will, my King." She bowed her head in submission and he nodded in satisfaction at last, releasing her as suddenly as he'd gripped her, his hands leaving a trail of sticky glue and glitter behind on her clothes.

"The next time I hear about any form of rebellion in this school of yours, I will set hell upon the very walls of this place and watch all those who defy me burn," he purred wickedly, running a finger along the line of her jaw while she stood before him, a vessel awaiting orders.

That certainly explained her very sudden and very firm stance on her allegiance to the king and he alone. She'd once shown more than a little interest in the Vegas. I'd been there when she'd hinted to Tory that she was excited to see what they would do with their power once they learned to control it. It all made sense now, why the shift, why the sudden adoration of a tyrant who wanted nothing more than to toy with the people of this kingdom and force them to conform.

"I'll hunt down the perpetrators and make sure they are punished," Nova swore, but Lionel just clucked his tongue.

"No. You'll hunt them down, then hand them to me. I will deal with this personally. Is that clear?"

"Yes, my King," she agreed instantly, and he nodded once before shoving her away from him and striding for the door.

The bang it made as he hurled it against the wall made a flinch shatter through every piece of my body, but I didn't dare move as Nova lingered there a moment longer.

Thankfully, she only waited another second, her hand fisting at her side, some emotion flashing though her eyes which I couldn't quite untangle as she looked my way, making me fear that she might open the closet. But she turned and left instead, her footsteps fading into the distance as we waited there, terrified, furious, and somehow victorious too.

I exchanged a look with Bernice before we slipped from the closet and quickly exited the office.

"So, Nova is corrupted, Marguerite is on our side and…we just got away with that?" Bernice breathed in disbelief as we ran for the door at the far end of the hall.

I nodded almost robotically, glancing over my shoulder just in case everything was about to fall to shit after all. But no one appeared there, no Dragon leapt out to devour us and no K.U.N.T.s showed up to haul us away.

We'd made it. But I had the feeling that this wasn't an end at all, because if Nova really was under Lionel's control, then this game had just gotten a whole lot more dangerous, and we were nowhere near safe yet.

Scorpio
Gemini
Virgo
Cancer
Leo
Sagittarius
Taurus
Capricorn
Aquarius
Libra
Pisces

GERALDINE

CHAPTER THIRTY TWO

"Gandering geese are heading east, gandering geese are heading east," I murmured, my lips as heavy as two cowbells perched upon my face.

"Gerry, you're rambling," my Maxy boy said gently. "Are you alright?"

A sizzle of healing magic ran from him into my cockles and I wailed, unable to open my eyes and face the woeful world beyond. He was carrying me somewhere away from my lady when she needed me most, but I'd heard Tory encourage him thus, so who was I to contradict the word of one of my queens?

"It cannot be," I groaned, throwing an arm over my eyes as I hung as limp as a lamprey in his arms. "Poor, sweet, merry Darcy trapped with those crudsome creatures. And her watchful, loyal, fangsome 'pire too."

"We'll figure this out," he promised me, trying to press his Siren gifts into me, but I flailed and thrashed like a rollicking seal.

"Do not dare sneak into my chest like a thief in the night to snaff away my woes. I shall feel them in their fullness and tumble into their paltry pits if I must!" I crowed.

My slippery salmon sighed, and I felt the air grow warmer as we moved inside some place I didn't care to see.

The sound of guards trying to stop him ascending into the upper levels of the beauteous castle made me waft an arm at them.

"He is my steed. Allow him passage," I ordered, and Max grumbled something I didn't catch as he headed yonder.

"You'll have to tell me the way. You've never invited me to your room before," he said, an edge of bitterness to his utterance.

"Oh, my dear, angelic anchovy, I forget sometimes what a delicate daisy you are."

I flung my arm from my face, opening my eyes at last and pointing him hither and tither until we arrived at the foot of my door.

"I'm not delicate," he growled in that gruffsome tone of his which sent Lady Petunia into a frenzy.

I slipped out of his arms and threw the door wide, stepping into my modest room which was mostly given over to my baked goods. A long wooden table stood against the wall, running the length of the space and my single bed stood beyond it, with simple white linen a-clinging to it. Bagels in their many forms filled most of the table, but there were pastries too, and other baked goods which were fit for queenly mouths.

"You know, it's kind of a dick move to deny me food when you've got this much of it." He did not enter my pantry-come-bedroom, leaning his shoulder against the door jamb and giving me a grouchy grouper of an expression.

"Oh pish-posh." I wafted a hand at his grumbles, moving to the little wicker basket I'd made up this very morn, covered over with a cloth that had a salmon stitched into the cotton. I had hand-sewn it myself, using a needle made from the finest silver I could conjure with my earth Element. I flapped the cloth open and offered him the basket with a flourish, unveiling the various croissants and pain au chocolats I had baked in the shape of all his favourite sea creatures.

His mouth fell open, slack-jawed like a hammerhead shark who'd lost its hammer. "Are they for me?"

"Well who else? The cod's kipper?" I walked forward and thrust them into his arms, his eyes getting a ravenous glint about them. It seemed my lovely lobster was afflicted by hanger, and I would not forget it henceforth.

"These are my favourite," he said, all subdued now like a tame sea lion as he plucked a pain au chocolat from the basket.

"Well of course they are. Do you think I have not noticed the way you chomp and champ at these two types of pastry? You are like a fladdywhack with a handrail." I laughed a little, but then I remembered my lady Darcy was a captive of the lame lizard and his shadow trollop. Then I remembered Angelica's resplendent form cut down by that ugly maggot Mildred and vengeance called my name like a wandering will-o'-the-wisp.

Oh, woe is me and I am woe.

I sobbed, letting my misery fill the air and casting the salty tears from my eyes into a cup upon my nightstand.

"Gerry..." Max said sadly, and he let the door swing closed as he moved into the room, placing down his precious pastries and choosing me instead. Oh what a choice to make, for I was not nearly as crumbly nor sweet as a pain au chocolat.

He lieth down upon the bed at my back and I rolled away from him, the two of us barely fitting on the mattress, but he made it so, pulling me back into those gargantuan muscles of his. He was truly, truly a marvellous specimen of Fae. As big as an oxen, and likely as virile too. Oh, great stars above, why did he have to be an Heir?

I sniffed and snuffed, wriggling back into his arms, and reaching behind me to clasp his neck.

"Grave fates befall us like we sit beneath a bountiful apple tree of dire destinies, each one tumbling down full of rot and worms, instead of the sweet nectar we crave. Are we doomed, Maxy boy? Can we escape this festering tree and find another where the apples grow plump and ripe, where the sun shines upon its leaves and bathes us in its heartening light?"

"I hope so," he said darkly. "It's hard to see it though. It's like the stars are angry with us."

"But whatever did we do to invoke their wrath?" I croaked like a thirsty frog without a pond. "Once upon a yester-year, I believed the stars were not bias in their happenings. But if they are not, then why would they bestow great fortune upon a loathsome lizard who seeks to terrorise Solaria and all its virtuous Fae?"

"I don't know," my sweet salamander sighed. "Maybe all the stars care about is power."

"But if that were so, then my ladies would surely be the object of their bounties," I said, the answer hidden as if it were stuck to the base of a barnacle on the hull of a boat.

"I can tell my dad we can't meet him for dinner today," Max suggested.

"Nay, I cannot lay here like a prone prune all afternoon and eve, I must rise and meet with the Councilman who sired you. But first, I must return to my lady's side and beg her forgiveness for abandoning her in her time of dire need. I have been a loathsome lout of a servant this day, and I must face the price of my ineptitude th instant." I sprang out of bed, casting a vine whip in my hand, ripping my shirt asunder and lashing my bare back.

"Gerry!" Max barked, jumping up and trying to get a hold of me but I was as spritely as a wayward leaf in a hurricane, dancing this way and that as I struck at my back, evading him.

He cast a gust of air, snatching me up in it and pinning my arms to my sides as he closed in on me, looking like a legendary warrior of Ragoon.

He caught my cheek in his palm, his eyes a whirling ocean storm and my back hit the wall as he captured me like a crab in a net. Oh to be his crustacean…

My Lady Petunia blossomed like a flower in June, and his eyes dipped to my huge bosoms which were straining within a dark green corset I had woven from the silk of a dewmoth.

"You cannot look at me thus and not expect to dive deep into my lady waters," I panted. "Avert your eyes or make true on the vows that shine within them like the star you are named after, Max Rigel."

"Is that code for 'please fuck me'?" He smirked, and gracious, that smile was a mountain which I wished to climb, to bury my flag in its peak and announce it as mine.

"I could not be clearer," I panted. "Take me to Davy Jones' Locker, and plunder my treasure chest with your sea cucumber."

He deftly unlaced my corset, my bustsome breasts springing free, and he lowered his mouth to claim one of my nipples between his luscious lips. I cried out like a fig on a fiddle, my hands pushing into that dark, short hair of his before raking down the line of his back. I could not put words to how this swain made me feel, for it was as if there were no words yet forged to put a name to such emotions.

I yanked his hair tight, forcing his mouth to part from my rose bud and he looked up at me with an offer in his eyes, an offer of all I could ever dream for my Lady Petunia to be presented with.

"Ravish me like a knight of the Esterburn army. Seize me like the Castle of Norington and plunge your weapon into my moat," I gasped.

Max picked up me up like I weighed no more than a buttercup, even though I was rumbunctious, all muscle and curves, and he tossed me onto the bed, tearing my knickers from my Lady Petunia. I lay bare for him and his eyes oozed carnality as he crawled over me, trying to pin me down as if I were a teaspoon on his tea tray. But I was the tea master in this game, and he had better learn it fast.

With a, "Hi-yah!" I swung a leg over his hip and forced him to roll beneath me, capturing his wrists and winding them around my waist. I fused them to the base of my own spine with ice, then froze his ankles to the bed too.

"Gerry," he gasped, fighting like a turtle in a tailspin.

I pushed his pants down and sank down upon his Long Sherman, silencing his complaints, his groans filling the air and mixing like a cocktail with my own, giving into the delights of my petunia. I wetted my hand with my water Element, then slapped him this way and that across his cheeks, making him growl like a gunderghoul.

I kissed him next, my tongue between his lips and he garbled some wordage I couldn't decipher. Yes, I knew just what pleased him best even when he didn't know it himself, but my Maxy boy enjoyed a slip and slap just as much as he enjoyed a whip and whap.

"By the stars, you drive me crazy. I love you, Gerry," he panted as I did a hip wiggle followed by a jangle jive.

"Love!" I cried, throwing my head back and riding him as if I had an urgent message to deliver and only a simple pony between my thighs. "True, I love thee in return, despite your Heirsome flaws, your roots grown from a mighty tree of anti-royalists, and your muckly lineage."

"Fuck all of that," he said seriously, looking up at me with all the sparkles of the crown jewels within his eyes. "I mean it, Gerry. We'll work all of that out. I want you. Only you. The other shit is just politics."

"Yes," I agreed. "And politics may have ruled my rivers once, but I have sprouted new springs from the earth. I tried to resist you, my dear dolphin, but alas, fate drives me to your waters time and again. Swim with me, Maxy boy."

I rocked my hips faster and his biceps bulged like two fine blowfish, his head tipping forward to watch as he thrust up beneath me and showed my petunia the full extent of his daring Daniel. He was the largest I had experienced, though I was yet to bestow that truth upon his ears, lest I let his head garner too much size. But my, my, he was the possessor of a sea beast between his thighs, and I welcomed it deep into my coral reef, rolling my neck and crying out for more, though perhaps even I could not take more than what he gave.

I crested a wave and fell with a warble, singing like a song thrush for him as he sent me into the garden of ecstasy. And as I looked down at him, dazed, through spangled eyes, I knew we were not done. Not even close. My quails a-quivering, my cockles a-cantering.

I gave myself to him, knowing it was selfish when the world was falling apart beyond these doors, but I was a weak, weak waif of a whelk right now, and all I wished for was a moment in my lover's arms before I had to face the day once more.

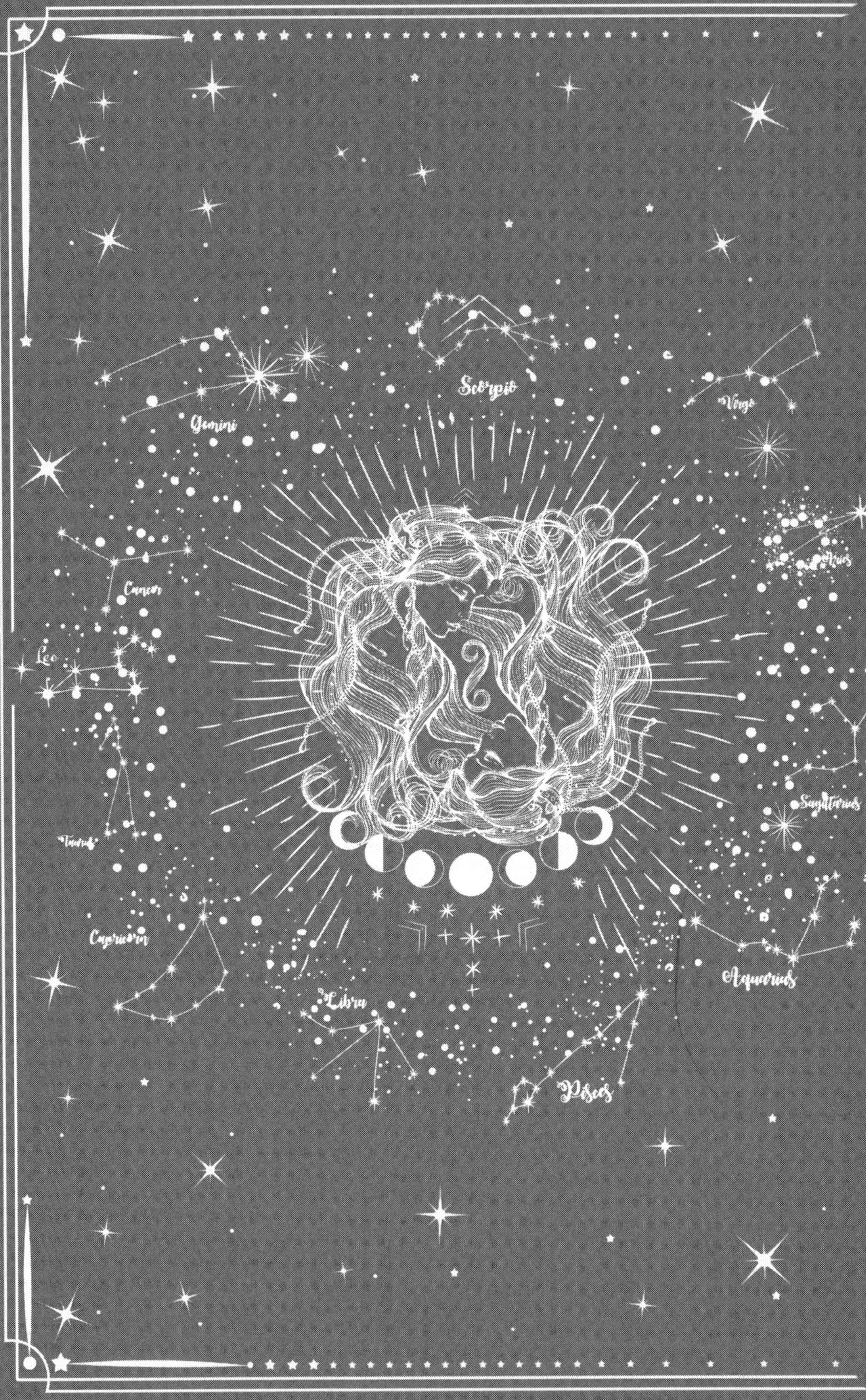
Scorpio
Gemini
Virgo
Cancer
Leo
Sagittarius
Capricorn
Libra
Aquarius
Pisces

DARCY

CHAPTER THIRTY THREE

Each time Orion was tortured, it took him longer and longer to come back to me, and it was breaking my heart. There was something in those awful weapons Lavinia was using to hurt him, some taint that was built of shadow and cruelty, and it was leaving a brand on his soul.

"Lance?" I tried to draw his attention to me as he sat against the wall, the wounds on his bare chest half healed from the brief moments Lavinia had let Horace heal Orion. She always made him stop while the bruises still bloomed, and the cuts were barely scabbed over, never allowing him full freedom from the pain she delivered. Horace didn't seem to care either way, only wanting to get away from me and Orion as soon as he could, trying to act like we didn't exist.

Now, Orion's eyes remained fixed on the cage bars, his expression empty.

"Talk to me," I urged, shifting closer and taking his hand, but his fingers didn't react to mine.

I was trying to stay strong through this, but my anger over him placing himself in this position with Lavinia always set the Shadow Beast stirring. Sometimes when that woman cut into his body, I lost control. The monster ripped out of my skin, and I was thrown into the pits of darkness in its mind, trapped in a vortex of wrath.

It seemed with every day that passed, my ability to keep the beast contained weakened, and I didn't know how much longer it would be until it possessed me entirely. That was a fear I didn't dare put a voice to. If Orion's sacrifice came to nothing because of my own inability to stop the Shadow Beast, I'd never forgive myself. That reality didn't bear thinking about. I had one task, and Orion was counting on me. I couldn't let him down.

I squeezed Orion's hand again, gaining no response. The pain of seeing him torn apart before my eyes was more than I could handle, and as much as I was trying to be brave, all I felt was a chasm splitting apart my mind, filled with vengeance and death. I was counting the marks left on my mate, promising them back to Lavinia tenfold with all the torment I could offer her, but it didn't make it any easier, because it didn't change anything here and now.

Orion never fought a single blow against him, facing each of them with a resilience that made me so goddamn proud. And if it was possible to love him even deeper, I did. I just wished with all my heart, on all the stars that ever were and ever would be, that this hadn't been the answer to breaking my curse. *Anything but him.*

"Lance?" I tried again, crawling into his lap, and cupping his cheek in my palm.

He blinked slowly, a storm of darkness twisting through his gaze as he finally focused on me, but he still didn't speak.

"Please come back to me," I whispered in desperation, tears rolling quietly down my cheeks. "I'm so sorry that this is our fate. It's all my fault. I should have stayed away from the rebels, I should have realised sooner what was happening to me. You shouldn't have to be paying the price of this curse. It isn't fair." I pressed my lips to his, tasting sorrow and salt between us. His mouth didn't move against mine, he didn't pull me closer, he wasn't there. He wasn't him.

"Lance," I begged, my voice shattering on the sharp rocks of terror. I couldn't lose him here in this cold room before a throne that was still claimed by a heartless king.

"I can help," a female voice made me whip around with a growl on my lips, and I found Stella Orion quietly closing the throne room door. She was in jeans and a black t-shirt, looking out of place in this grand room built for royalty.

"Stay away from us," I warned, rising to my feet, and hastily swiping the tears from my cheeks.

Stella ignored me, drifting closer, trying to look past me to Orion.

"It's the weapons she's using on him," she said in a voice dripping with emotion. "Every time she cuts him, the shadows get into his body. He's strong. It's a miracle he's lasted so long without succumbing to the lure of them. But I can draw them out."

I gripped the bars of the cage, my eyes locked on her, watching her as a lioness would watch its prey. I must have been at breaking point, because I couldn't help but latch onto the hope her words were offering me. But how could I trust this woman after all she'd done?

"Why would you help him?" I demanded. "You disowned him."

"He will always be my son. It doesn't matter what words have passed between us," she said in earnest, her eyes drifting over me. "Perhaps you will understand one day, if you have a child of your own." A sad smile lifted her lips as she closed in on me. "You know...I thought his relationship with you was some pathetic little rebellion against me."

"Not everything is about you, Stella," I said frostily. "I love your son more than you can even comprehend."

"I see that now. I've seen his silver rings."

"The rings don't change what we felt for each other before the stars offered them to us," I hissed. "The world decided to validate our love the second we were mated, but we loved each other long before that. The people who really care for us accepted that well before the stars had their say," I said passionately. "*You* are not one of those people."

Her mouth flattened into a sharp line as she approached me. She was taller than me, but I didn't feel any less powerful than her, even if she was looking down at me within a cage. Under normal circumstances, I was far stronger than her, and whether I had magic in my veins now or not, I would stand between her and her son always.

"I know why he loves you," she said, her lower lip quivering.

"You don't know anything about us," I refuted, but she went on as if I hadn't spoken.

"It's this...rebellion in you. He has it too. I can see why you make a perfect match."

My fingers locked harder around the bars as she stepped closer to the other side of them. I'd fight her like a damn mortal with fists and teeth alone if I had to.

"You don't know anything about me, and you don't know him anymore either," I said. "Your son is the most incredible Fae I have ever had the privilege to know, and he deserves happiness and peace. I vow on all I am that I *will* give him those things, and I will destroy anyone who takes them away from him. That includes you, Stella. I have a long list of enemies now, and your name sits close to the top of it."

"Forgive me," she sobbed, breaking apart and leaving me confounded as she lurched forward and wrapped her hands around mine on the bars. "I should have stuck by him when Lionel bound him to Darius. I should have been there more when Clara was taken from us. I should never have let things come this far. And I should have been a mother he could bring you home to."

I tried to pull my hands free of her, but she clung to me, desperation marring her beautiful features.

"There's nothing you can do that will ever earn my forgiveness," I said, yanking my hands away from her and stepping back. "To hurt him is to incite my wrath. You turned your back on him and left him alone in the world when he needed you the most. There is nothing that can undo that."

She lowered down to her knees, reaching through the bars past my legs to try and get to Orion.

"I can help him. Please. Bring him closer. Let me help him. I'll bring him back to you."

I stepped aside, looking to the man I loved with my heart cleaving in two. He wasn't present at all. There was a hardened iciness in his eyes that made me fear he might never come back to me. And the look of anguish on Stella's face had me wondering if she really did hold some love in her heart for him. But Orion had warned me how well his mother could lie…

"Baby boy, come to me," she tried, reaching as far as she could and grasping his leg.

He didn't stir and I struggled with the decision of what to do. I didn't want to trust Stella, but the blankness in Orion's eyes was frightening me, and I didn't know what other options I had. If there was even a small chance she could help him, didn't I have to take it?

I swallowed to try and shift the dryness from my throat, gazing at my Elysian Mate and feeling my will faltering. He was so deep in the clutches of the shadows, what more could she really do to him?

"Swear you won't hurt him," I hissed, looking straight at her as I made my choice.

"I swear." She offered me her hand to make a deal, but I knocked it aside. I had no access to my magic anyway, and I didn't trust the stars anymore.

When I'd first come to Solaria, I'd been so open to all the magic in the world, and I'd somehow had an unwavering belief that everything would work out for us. That the heavens weren't set against us, but it was impossible to believe that now after everything.

I dropped down to Orion's side, trying to drag him towards Stella, but the bulk of him made it nearly impossible.

I yanked harder on his arm and spoke to him in a plea, "You have to move."

He shifted vaguely forward, enough that she could reach his arm and relief scattered through my chest followed by a wave of apprehension. I really hoped I wasn't going to regret this.

Stella shut her eyes as she pressed her fingers to Orion's wrist, starting to mutter some dark incantation under her breath. I knelt close to him, anxiety burrowing into me as I let Stella do this, ready to shove her away if she gave me any reason to.

Orion groaned, wincing, and reaching for Stella like she held some answer to his suffering. She brushed her fingers over his temple as he leaned against the bars, her brow knitted in concentration, and I fought the instinct to get between them.

Darkness pooled against the edges of his skin, and she sapped it away into her own, her words intensifying as she wielded whatever dark magic this was. Slowly, Orion opened his eyes and I saw the man I loved in the depths of them once again, his silver rings almost seeming to glow for a moment. I lunged at him with a squeak of delight, knocking him sideways so his back hit the floor as I wrapped him in my arms and kissed the corner of his mouth. Then the dimple hiding in his cheek and the stubble on his jaw.

"You're back," I whispered, relief flooding me, and he carved his fingers through my hair as he held me close.

"I'll always come back to you, Blue," he promised, taking away the fear in my heart.

"The dark is deep," Stella panted, sitting back on her heels in exhaustion over that spell. "But I can keep it at bay. At least for a while."

I sat up, letting Orion sit too as we gazed out at his mother who had offered us this help, though it did nothing to change my feelings towards her. One good deed didn't erase countless bad ones.

"If you're waiting for a thank you, you will only get one from me," I said as Stella peered in at us like a stray cat in need of food. "Thank you for bringing this man into the world. He is the best thing you have ever done."

Stella swallowed hard, lips pursed and eyes watery as she rose to her feet and nodded again and again before she turned and rushed away across the room, hurrying out the door.

Orion turned me to face him, his mouth coming down hard on mine in a kiss that set my pulse racing and all thoughts scattering. He pulled me into his chest and the wild beat of his heart matched mine through the fabric of his flesh. We were one being in that moment, a creature of fury and hope that resisted the dark as if we were made of starlight.

A grinding of stone sounded behind us and we turned in an instant, finding a door opening up in the wall at our backs. Orion's fangs flashed as he shot to his feet in preparation of an attack, taking a sweeping look into the dark passage, his brow creasing as he listened for any signs of an approach.

A glimmering pair of silver wings caught my eye on the wall at the back of the passage and my lips parted as I got to my feet and pointed them out to Orion. Beside them was the mark of the Hydra, a deep purple flashing over it for a brief second before all went dark again.

"This is the passage I *saw* in Gabriel's vision," Orion said in realisation and a thrill darted through me. We'd looked for the thing since he'd told me my brother had *seen* it, but we'd had no luck finding it. "He showed me that I'd have three hours before anyone came back to the throne room."

"Can we use this passage to get to Gabriel?" I asked hopefully.

"No," he said with a frown. "This tunnel doesn't lead to him. He showed me that much. But Blue, this is going to lead us to some answer that will help us, I just know it."

I ran forward to dive into the passage, but Orion caught me by the waist and wheeled me around in his arms.

"Easy there, beastie," he said, a smirk in his voice. "Did no one ever tell you the tale of Beansprout Jacabee?"

"Erm, no. No one ever told me bedtime stories," I said, and he frowned at that.

"Well, my father told me hundreds."

"I want to know all of them," I decided. "Tell me about the beansprout thingy while we walk." I twisted away from him, running into the tunnel with a sense of hope that I'd long since lost.

Orion shot in front of me with a blur of Vampire speed, his huge form blocking my way.

A growl rumbled through his chest, sending a shiver of desire through me. "Whatever happened to you being obedient, Miss Vega? It could be dangerous in here."

I smiled, stepping closer and tiptoeing my fingers up his bare chest until I tapped him on the nose. "I think you're to blame for that, Professor. You taught me that the punishment for being bad, is so very, very…good." I ducked around him again, racing off into the dark on bare feet with his laughter following me. The sound lit me up inside and I held onto that feeling, not letting it slip away too soon.

He caught me again, this time pinning me to the wall face first with his hand pressed to the back of my neck. "You're asking to be spanked, Blue."

His other hand ran over the curve of my ass and my back arched like a cat at his touch. "No, I'm asking you to tell me about the bean man."

His hand clapped hard against my ass, and I gasped at the delicious pain, the way it sizzled through my skin and reminded me I was still here, still fighting for another day.

"Then ask nicely," he commanded, the pressure on the back of my neck increasing, and holy hell, I'd missed being held at his mercy.

I bit my lip, tasting a rare smile on my mouth and figuring I was going to enjoy this tiny moment of wildness. I let myself believe we were back at Zodiac Academy, playing the game of push and pull that always drove me into a beautiful kind of insanity.

"Please, sir," I said, my voice laced with lust, and he hmmed in approval of that.

His arm curled around my waist, and he tugged me upright, the two of us walking along into the dark together like this was a perfectly normal day and we were in a perfectly normal location.

"Shit," I cursed as I stumbled down a step, holding onto Orion's arm so I didn't tumble away into the gloom.

He held me tighter, a rumble of amusement leaving him. "I'll guide you. I can see just fine with my Vampire gifts," he said, his arm sliding up to rest over my shoulders and pull me closer. "If you'd rather, you can jump on my back like a little koala bear, and I'll run us there with my speed."

"But then there'll be no time for stories," I said, looking up at him, though the light of the throne room was long behind us now and I could hardly see anything at all.

"Alright, I'll tell you about Jacabee…"

We delved deeper into the tunnels, winding down into the depths of the palace while Orion told me a story which wasn't dissimilar to Jack and the Beanstalk, except when Jacobee made it up the beanstalk into the clouds and went sneaking into the giant's castle, he ended up skinned alive and eaten in gruesome detail.

"And that's why you should never go sneaking into unknown places," Orion finished sternly as I shuddered.

"That was horrible," I breathed. "Why would anyone tell children that story?"

"To try and scare them so they won't do reckless shit. Do you have any idea how reckless Fae kids are? I snuck off and went cliff diving with Clara when I was five years old. My dad fished us out of the water and grounded us for a week. If we ever have kids, I will never let them out of my sight."

A smile lifted my lips at the image of that. "You'd be a seriously protective daddy."

"I'd be the asshole parent, but I'm good with it," he said, only making my smile grow. "They can hate me so long as they keep breathing."

"You really think about that stuff?" I asked, trying to picture a future where any of that was possible now. It was all so out of reach, just pretty dreams stitched from our imagination.

"Only since you," he said quietly. "Is that what you want? Marriage, kids, some fairy-tale house? It doesn't have to look like that, I can paint our picture with whatever brush you choose, and make it look however you imagine."

I released a breath of longing. "I just want to be back with our family and friends, preferably with a jade green Dragon head mounted on the wall next to an ugly hat and boots made out of a shadow bitch."

He barked a laugh. "That's a future I'm banking on, beautiful."

Silence drew over us like a storm cloud, that future so unreachable in the face of everything.

"I can't watch her torture you much longer," I said, flashes of what she'd done to him playing through my mind and holding me hostage. Even if by some miracle we got out of here and the curse was broken, were we ever really going to be the same again?

"It's just blood."

"So you keep saying," I growled. "But it's the most precious blood in the world to me. And having to watch you suffer through her torture is just – just-" The Shadow Beast rose up inside me, a snarl pushing at the base of my throat, but Orion moved fast, his hand slamming down over my mouth as he yanked me back against his chest, holding me while I thrashed.

The Shadow Beast desperately wanted to come out, and my mind was spiralling down into a place where I would lose all control, the same place where I'd been during the battle. I'd kill without care. I'd seek out death like it was my sustenance.

"Remember who you are, Blue," Orion said, his biceps straining as he held me still. "Think of Tory, how she's waiting for you out there beyond these walls. Think of how much she loves you."

My thoughts fell on my twin and the Shadow Beast roared louder inside me, like it wanted her blood more than it wanted any other. The shift was going to take over, it was coming in so fast, so unavoidably.

"Your will is stronger than iron," he said firmly. "You can fight this. Do it for your sister, for your brother, for you, for *us*."

My eyes watered and stung, the pain of holding back the creature blinding me. But I had to stay here for Orion, I couldn't hurt him. And more than ever, I needed to prove I could control this curse that had its hooks in me.

Slowly, I managed to take hold of the Shadow Beast, forcing it deeper and keeping a grip on my mind. I melted back into Orion's arms, and he lowered his hand from my mouth, his fingers trailing to my collar bone and skimming across it, the shadows on my skin retreating from his touch and bringing me back to myself. Well, as much of myself as I could be with a giant, bloodthirsty monster living inside me.

"That's my girl," he exhaled, pressing a kiss to my hair. "You've got this."

"It's getting harder and harder to hold it back," I panted. "What if it takes my mind completely?"

"It won't," he insisted. "We have time. We just have to hold on for the remainder of my time with Lavinia."

"It hasn't even been a month yet," I said thickly.

"We can do this, Blue."

"For a grumpy ass professor who was sent to prison, power-shamed, and is now stuck here in hell, you sure have a lot of optimism these days," I said, a ghost of a taunt in my voice as I tried to seek out the light we'd found before. It was hard, but I was determined to have a moment with him that wasn't sullied by Lavinia, Lionel, or the shadows.

His grip on me eased and we kept walking, our hands finding each other and our fingers linking together.

"You are the only thing in this world that I'm wholeheartedly optimistic about, Darcy Vega, because I know I'll fight to death and beyond to keep you. And I'm starting to think you might do the same for me."

"Starting to think?" I said, a smile making my lips weightless. "There isn't an enemy in the kingdom I wouldn't face down for you."

"What about beyond the kingdom?" he teased.

"I don't know much about that. Most of the maps at the academy were only of Solaria. And the few world maps I saw seemed to have gaps in them where Europe is located in the mortal realm."

"The landscape keeps changing over in The Waning Lands. There's a violent war going on there between the Elementals. Each faction is prone to changing the terrain as new territories are seized to suit their needs. Some of it is underwater one month, while it's floating in the sky the next," he said, and my curiosity piqued.

"Tell me more," I urged.

"I don't know much more. Honestly, no one from outside kingdoms have been there in centuries. It's too dangerous."

"Holy shit. And what's beyond that kingdom?" I pressed.

"You're a curious little mouse today," he said.

"Or maybe a shrew," I said with a frown. "Darius used to call me that."

"A shrew?" he chuckled.

"I weirdly liked it," I said, trying to smile even though my heart weighed a ton. It felt far too soon to start having fond memories of him. It didn't seem real to me that someone with so much fire in their soul could be gone from the world. A part of me didn't believe it at all.

We delved deeper into the dark and the cold made my skin prickle as Orion guided me along the narrow passage. My mind turned to Gabriel, and even though I knew this tunnel didn't lead to him, I wished it did. I missed my brother so much and hated to think what he was enduring all alone.

A silvery light grew up ahead and I released Orion's hand, quickening my pace towards it, feeling him following close at my back. Ever the guard dog.

I rounded the next corner and found a beautiful silver door standing there, towering up high above me with the Vega Crest at its centre. I raised a hand, sensing ancient magic vibrating in the air I breathed and knowing with certainty that all I needed to do to open that door was touch it.

I pressed my fingers to the crest, tracing them over the Vega name, wondering how many times my father had done this very thing before. The doors clunked loudly, then began to swing inward, revealing an impossible view beyond.

It was the night sky, the stars twinkling within the swirling Milky Way galaxy. I could simply step into it if I wanted. The colours were dazzling, each planet and star hanging there in perfect detail as if it had been plucked from the heavens and shrunk down to fit into this room.

"By the stars," Orion breathed. "I thought this was just a legend."

"What is it?" I asked, whispering like the place required it and finding myself walking straight forward into its depths. The edge of the doorway made it seem as though I was about to step right into oblivion, but I carefully tested the floor and found it solid, like a liquid mirror at my feet.

"Amantium Caelum – The Lovers' Sky. It was a gift to a Vega queen of old. She announced to the kingdom that she would marry the Fae who crafted her the most beautiful magical gift. For years, Fae from all over Solaria brought every manner of gift to her door, but none of them were beautiful enough to impress her. One day, a young woman from Alestria came to the palace with a simple wooden box in her arms, and when she opened it for the queen, this is what came out. And that very night, they were mated by the stars."

My lips parted as I looked to him, drinking in the story of my ancestors. "Is it true?"

"Enough of it for this sky to exist," he said, and I walked deeper into the miniature universe, closing in on our solar system where the sun burned with real heat, warming my cheeks as I approached. The magic was captivating, so powerful it made the hairs along my arms stand on end and set my pulse drumming.

Orion followed and the doors shut behind him, leaving us in the glittering expanse of stars.

I moved closer to our planetary system, each of them small enough for me to hold if I wanted.

"Can I touch them?"

"Are you asking me permission?" Orion asked, a grin in his voice as I glanced over at him, biting my lip.

"No, sir." I reached out, brushing my fingers over Jupiter which was about the size of a tennis ball. It rolled into my palm, and I lifted it up to my eye level, admiring the intricacy of the magic. The storm that rolled around in its atmosphere was right there, swirling slowly as if this planet were as real as the one in the sky. I tried to place it back, and it floated smoothly from my hand into its rightful place.

I turned to Orion to ask him a question, finding him holding a glittering star in his hand, trying to place it among the Orion constellation.

"What are you doing?" I asked and he looked over at me like a naughty school kid who'd been caught getting up to no good.

"I'm moving the Vega star over here," he said. "It looks good here, don't you think?"

I laughed, jogging over to join him as he reached above his head again and tried to make the Vega star sit with Orion.

"Are you messing with age-old magic?" I asked sternly. "That's not very professorly of you."

"Well, it wasn't very professorly of me when I took a student to my bed either, was it?" he said. "Or when I had you over my desk, at the Fairy Fair, in the archives-"

"We don't talk about the archives," I jibed, and he nodded seriously.

"Great night, shit morning," he said matter of factly. "It all worked out in the end though, right?"

"Yeah, now we're Lavinia's prisoners and the whole world is doomed."

"Exactly. It's all coming together, beautiful," he said with fake enthusiasm, and I didn't let my smile fall, wanting to play this game of feigning safety as long as I could.

He let go of the star when he had it where he wanted it, but it shot back across the sky, settling itself in the Lyra constellation where it belonged.

Orion looked down at me, his eyes locking with mine as he smirked like a predator. "Oh well, I've got myself a Vega anyway." He hounded toward me, and I spun around, making him take chase as I quickened my pace across the room.

I headed past the sun and walked into the far-flung realms of the universe where I found a door hidden in the fabric of the sky, just visible from where I stood.

I reached out, trying to find a handle, but the door swung open at my touch like the first had. My breathing hitched as another room was revealed and I moved into a cavernous gothic chamber with arches and ornate stone pillars everywhere. But that wasn't what had stolen my breath, it was the treasures that lay all around me, mountainous piles of gold, intricate boxes overflowing with jewels, and right in front of me was an onyx throne, the polished black stone carved into an imposing seat with sharpened feathers rising from its arching back. It was all lit by everflames dancing in cages hanging from the vaulted ceiling and I could almost feel the touch of my ancestors who had cast them.

I walked towards the throne, Orion one step behind me, the two of us taking in the Royal Treasury with quiet awe.

"Darius would have loved this place," he said, my heart panging at his name.

"We never would have gotten him out of here," I agreed, scooping down to pick up a gold coin which had a Hydra engraved into its surface. The echo of my father's legacy hung around me and I rolled the coin between my fingers as I continued moving through the immense trove, feeling as though I was in a giant rabbit warren.

"No wonder Lionel wants to get in here," I said, passing the throne and heading deeper into the trove.

"This is your inheritance," Orion said firmly. "Let's hope the palace continues to keep him out."

"This seems like far too much gold for me and Tory to own," I said. "Think of all the good it could do."

"You'll be able to do that good when you're queens."

I breathed a humourless laugh. "You think that's still possible now?" I tossed the coin back among the nearest pile of gold, moving on before Orion could answer that. "How does gold even have value in this world? Can't earth Elementals make endless amounts of it?"

"Gold is particularly hard to craft. Only a very powerful earth Elemental can make it, and it will not hold the same value as this gold unless it's authenticated by the Bank of Solaria. There's a whole division of the FIB dedicated to rounding up and destroying counterfeit money too. Every aura has security magic imbued within it. It's an easy test to do yourself, I'll show you how." He picked up a coin, but I turned to him with a hollow look.

"I don't have magic anymore, Lance." Those words sliced at my heart, and I could have sworn the everflames above me flickered sadly.

His brow furrowed and he dropped the coin again, looking like he was going to convince me my magic would come back, but I didn't want to hear it. We didn't know what lay in my future, and there wasn't any point in speculating about it now.

I turned through one of the stone arches, discovering rows and rows of wooden cabinets filled with potions in stoppered bottles. At the end of the winding rows of cabinets, a burning egg stood in a gleaming silver frame. My fingers tingled from the memory of casting red and blue flames just like those, knowing them instinctively, as if they were a part of me. I guessed in a way, they were.

A large gold plaque stood at its base, and I read the words engraved into it with anticipation building in my chest.

The Untouchable Egg.

I lifted my head, reaching instinctively for the egg but Orion shot forward and caught my wrist in a vice-like grip, giving me a stern raised eyebrow.

"Blue," he growled. "Were you just about to touch The Untouchable Egg?"

"Of *course* not. That would be crazy," I said with a grin, lifting my other hand and reaching for it with that one instead.

He caught that wrist too, going all grumpy teacher on me. "This isn't a game. You don't know what could happen. It could be cursed."

"I'm already cursed. I can't be double cursed."

"By the moon, are you trying to give the stars ideas?" he hissed.

"Lance, it's Phoenix fire. I can definitely touch it. Move aside." I jerked my wrists back, but he didn't let go, gazing at me with his jaw ticking.

"You don't have your Phoenix anymore," he said, and I tried to ignore how much those words hurt.

"I know," I said tightly. "But I just feel like I can touch it. I'm sure I can."

"It could be a trap," he said in concern.

"Do you want me to pull the 'obey your queen' card, because I'm not above using it right now."

His frowny features lifted a little. "You know I get hard over you ordering me about."

"Well, you don't want to get a boner right here in front of The Untouchable Egg, do you?"

He pressed his tongue into his cheek as he tried to hide his amusement, releasing me, but not stepping aside.

"If you sense any kind of magic against your palm, pull your hand back fast. Go slowly."

"Got it. Tingly magic bad." I mock saluted him and he moved reluctantly out of my way, watching me like a hawk as if he was going to swoop in at any given moment and take me as far away from the egg as he could get.

"Slower," he said in a forceful tone, but my hand was itching to touch that fire, like it had been waiting for me forever.

There was a tug in my chest, driving me on and all I could see was that beautiful fire, the room fading around me. It reminded me of how I'd felt back in The Palace of Flames with my sister, while Queen Avalon trained us in the ways of Phoenix warriors. The shadows had been buried so deep by the power in that place, and my Order form had been so present with me the entire time.

Impossibly, I felt a single flame spark in my chest, like a burning feather left behind by my Phoenix when the Shadow Beast had devoured it. I basked in the heat of it, my breaths coming heavier as the power of my Order form trickled out across my limbs, just enough to offer me protection from the flames as my fingers sank into them.

They were warm and kissed my hand in greeting, wrapping around my fingers and pulling me closer. I lay my palm against the egg, its surface made of that beautiful metal which reminded me of the weapons we'd forged for our friends. I raised my other hand, picked the egg up from its stand and turned to Orion with a bright smile, finding him looking at me with an anxious crease between his eyes.

"Okay, you're holding The Untouchable Egg. Are you happy now?" he asked, his expression telling me he really wanted me to put it back.

"Very," I said lightly as I turned the egg in my hands to examine it. "What do you think is inside it?"

"Nothing good," he said darkly. "I don't think you should mess with ancient Phoenix artefa-"

I threw the egg on the floor, and it smashed into fifty pieces.

"Darcy!" he barked as a swirling, glittering coil of red and blue smoke twisted up from the burning pieces of the eggshell.

I noticed a glittering white crystal among the shattered egg and dropped down, picking it up and waving it at Orion in triumph. "See."

"Don't you 'see' me. You are looking for trouble today."

"We're prisoners to the Shadow Princess, I have to watch her torture you daily, I have no idea if everyone else I love is okay, and we're probably on a pre-destined path that will lead us to certain doom. What else can the stars really throw at us now?"

"Enough," he snarled, shooting forward, and clapping a hand over my mouth, his eyes two pits of wrath. "You are the most precious thing in this world to me. Stop tempting fate to come and steal you away. The stars have already proved they can make things worse, even when I believe we are at our limits of bad luck, they prove me wrong. So you will watch your words."

I peeled his hand away from my mouth, gazing resolutely back at him no matter how much this man made my heart flutter. "I'll do as I like."

"You're being stubborn just for the sake of defying me."

"No, I'm defying you because you're being an ass, and because I'm not yours to command."

"I'm not trying to command you. I'm trying to protect you. You are my mate."

"That doesn't make me your possession," I snapped.

He leered over me, and I was swallowed by the menacing existence of him, his power an aura I could feel wrapping around my lungs and squeezing tight. "Not a possession, no. But you *are* mine. You were mine before we met, and mine the minute we locked eyes. You are mine in this life, and every life we may experience from this point forward. You are mine in every reality you exist, and mine in every reality you don't. And I am yours in kind, in every way you can imagine. I will gladly be your possession, but I will also be your guardian, your keeper, your protector. And I will do whatever I can to turn you away from danger, because it is impossible for me not to."

"God damn you and your pretty words," I whispered, lost to him as always.

His mouth tilted in a smirk, and he reached out to trail his thumb along my jaw in a soft caress.

"Were they pretty enough to make you stop playing with ancient artefacts and pissing off the stars?"

I twirled the crystal between my fingers.

"I'll compromise. I'll stop pissing off the stars, but I'm not done with the artefacts." I lifted the crystal up before his eyes. "What is this?"

He frowned as he focused on it, intrigue colouring his expression. "That's a Heart of Memoriae crystal. It holds memories."

"How do I access them?" I asked excitedly.

"If they're for you, you can access them with blood, but-"

"Fang please." I lifted my thumb to his mouth, pushing it between his lips as his expression got angry again.

"Blue," he warned.

"Come on, there could be ancient Phoenix memories waiting for us in here," I urged, prodding at his canine, and making his fangs extend.

He relented, opening his mouth a little more and letting me slit my thumb open on his fang. I dropped my hand to rub a drop of blood over the crystal and I was stolen away in an instant, crashing into long lost memories of the past.

"All hail the first queen of the new kingdom of Solaria, Queen Elvia Vega!" a man bellowed, and I watched through the eyes of the queen in question, my hands curling over the heated ruby throne I sat upon.

A crowd cheered and my heart swelled with my victory. A land conquered, borders drawn and finally, I had my prize. This would be my legacy, and as my gaze locked with the Phoenix warrior, Santiago Antares, a man who had fought at my side through countless battles, I knew it was time to take him as my husband. He had proven himself worthy, and now that I could finally let my mind shift from war to the fruits of our labours, I found I craved him with a long-forgotten hunger I hadn't let myself indulge in many moons.

He smiled at me in that roguish, over-familiar way of his which was always pushing the boundaries of his position beneath his queen, but I would enjoy reminding him where he belonged.

The Palace of Flames was newly built and gleamed with the power of my kind, the Phoenixes in my court having imbued this place with the fire that lived within their flesh. I would offer a piece of myself to it too when the celebrations were done, but now, it was time to reap the rewards of our victory at long last.

The memory shifted and my mind fell into Elvia's once more as she stood under a waning moon, a flowing silver nightgown hugging her body.

I picked my way through the dark jungle where the air was thick and Faeflies danced among the trees. I walked barefoot up the hill where the trees thinned and allowed me to see right up to the vast heavens, the Milky Way stretching the length of the sky in a crystal fog of pink and blue. My heart was wild this night, and desperation had drawn me here to the peak of this hill where the single stem of a Nox flower stood. I had come here each night, waiting for the petals to open to collect the precious pollen from within. Once it flowered, it would only last until dawn and then not return for many years.

Its pollen held untold power, and when mixed with treckwit powder and elixir of dunebark, it created a potion that could temporarily make a Fae resistant to the Nymphs' ability to shut us off from our magic. I had thought our war was done when I laid claim to this new land, but it had been far from over. The Nymphs had risen against us to try and claim the kingdom from our grasp, and they had fought us with a bloody ferocity I had not predicted.

My Seers were blind to their movements, and though they held little of the weaponry and training we did, they made up for it in sheer numbers and their invisibility to us through divination. This pollen could help, but I knew in my heart it wasn't enough. No matter how many Nymphs we destroyed, more came in their place, claiming this land was theirs and theirs alone. I would not yield, would not try and strike peace, not when I had seen the brutality they offered us in battle. The Nymphs may have been a sister race to Fae, born of the same root many thousands of years ago, but I did not recognise them as equal.

The flower began to glow palest blue, and I gasped, hurrying forward, falling to my knees, and lifting the jar I'd brought to collect the pollen. The petals cracked open and more of that ethereal light spilled out, the moon seeming to peer this way to admire it too, and a smile broke across my face.

I raised the jar, ready to collect the precious dust within, but as I got closer, the petals began to fall, and the light began to fade.

"No," I gasped, reaching for the flower, but even my breath against it seemed to make it wither, the petals turning to vapour on the breeze.

It was gone in the next moment, no pollen, no light, no anything. I had heard of this possibility, the flower so delicate that even a breeze too warm or a night too cool could make it fade.

I let go of the jar and it thumped to the ground, rolling away from me as I let out a noise of anguish, looking up to the stars and wondering if they might answer my prayers.

"Please help us. Let us crush the enemy. Gift me this land and I shall forge it into the finest kingdom ever known," I pleaded, but the stars only glittered quietly, ever-silent.

I knelt there, delaying the inevitable return where I would find Santiago lying awake in hopes of my return, and I would have to voice another failure to him. Perhaps I was not the queen I'd thought I was, because every day that passed, it seemed I grew closer to losing my hold on all this power I had claimed for us. For the Phoenixes and our allies.

I pushed to my feet, resigned as I turned back to the jungle, when a light caught my attention above.

My lips parted in awe as a falling star came streaking across the sky, a tail of fire in its wake. It was racing through the sky right above me and without thought, I let my wings break free and took off to chase after it.

I flew fast above the jungle, my gaze never wavering from that beautiful burning being as it made its passage towards an inevitable impact.

My heart juddered at the direction it was taking, the star seeming on a collision course with my palace. Panic cleaved my heart in two and I put on a burst of speed, thinking of Santiago and the secret I held inside me. I had been waiting to tell him, knowing the time was all wrong, but when would it ever really be right? A Seer had seen *that I was with child, and if I could find a way to secure the throne, my baby boy would be a mighty ruler one day.*

I flew as fast as my wings would allow, pressing a hand to my throat to amplify my voice as I called out to my people, "Rise! Danger falls from above! Protect yourselves!"

The star crashed into the roof of the eastern tower, tearing through it, and disappearing into the jungle beyond before an echoing boom sounded as it hit the ground.

A shockwave slammed into me that had me squinting against the force of it, and I beat my wings harder to counter it.

Screams rose up from the palace as I flew over it, fire curling from the jungle below where a deep chasm lay in the ground, the fallen star gleaming within it, pulsing like it was a living heart.

I tucked my wings and plummeted out of the sky, the fire licking my skin as I landed in the flames and gazed up at the hulking shape of the fallen star before me.

A wave of unknown energy washed over me, running deep into my bones and I inhaled long and slow, almost moaning at the intensity of that power. It was too much, so tempting yet so very, very potent. I could hardly stand to be so close to it, yet I moved closer still, drawn to the magnitude of this divine being before me which had come to answer my prayers.

Everything blurred beyond the boundaries of my vision, and all I could see was the star that glittered like a million diamonds were buried in its surface. This power, it was the answer to everything. It could end the war, it could turn every endeavour to my favour. And in a moment of madness, I cast a sharp metal dagger in my hand and slit my palm open, moving forward and placing it against the star's surface.

I gasped as that power surged into me in a wave, seeking out my soul and feeling the weight of it.

"Vega," *it spoke inside my mind, knowing me like it had been there since the moment of my birth to this very moment now, watching me, perhaps even adoring me. Or maybe it wasn't love I felt, but pity.*

"Fae of flames and war," *it seemed to mock me with those words and that power slid deeper, climbing through my veins and splashing against my heart.*

It could wipe me from existence with a single whim, and I feared for the life growing inside me, wanting to pull back, but now that I was here, I couldn't move at all.

As my thoughts turned to my unborn child, the star's power shifted that way, circling around that tiny being and making me whimper in terror.

"Please, don't hurt us," I begged. "We revere you. This blood is an offering, to show you that I am your loyal servant. But I must beg of you one thing."

"All gifts have a price."

"I will pay whatever price you ask," I swore, and the star fell quiet, its light still pulsing with an energy that seemed to hum in every corner of my flesh.

"Then the choice will be this…" *That power swirled deeper within me, wrapping around my unborn child, and making me shudder in horror.* "Your first born or your first love. Offer me one, and I shall lend you the power to win your war."

I stilled, my heart shattering at the price, and I stood frozen in the face of it. That little life in me flickered like it knew it could be snuffed out at any moment, and tears tracked down my cheeks at the pain of the sacrifice that would be. Then my mind turned to Santiago, the man I loved to the depths of my being and beyond, his loyalty unfathomable. There would be other children, he would provide them, I knew that. And yet…I had seen *this one in the vision the Seer had offered me. I had* seen *him grow into a man and I had fallen in love with him there and then. My son was as real to me as Santiago was, so how could I ever make this choice?*

"Anything else," I growled. "Not them. Please don't take them."

"That is the price. There will be no other," *the star spoke as my tears dripped from my chin.* "Time runs thin. I will release my power if you cannot choose."

"Wait, just wait a minute," I croaked, desperation clawing at me. Why did it have to be this?

I thought on Santiago's words to me, his promises to win this war, his declaration that it was his one true cause in life. And I knew before I spoke the words that it had to be him, because he would make this choice if he stood here in my place.

"My husband," I forced the words past my lips and with a crack like thunder ripping the air apart, the deal was made.

I nearly fell to my knees from the terrible force of the power and my palm tingled painfully where it still lay against the star. The shining surface made me wince and I backed away, my eyes hurting and a ringing growing in my ears. I screamed as it intensified, begging to be spared, unsure if I had angered it somehow. But then the light faded away and I found a rough and unhewn gemstone laying in my palm that hummed with unimaginable power, so beautiful it left me speechless.

"Wield this, and you will win your war."

"Thank you," I breathed, and those words leaving my lips set the earth quaking and the sky singing.

No, not singing, that beautiful, haunting noise that hovered on the edges of my hearing was screaming, the stars above trying to defy what had been done, what this star had offered me going against all nature of its kind and mine. But the deal was done.

The vision shifted, and my mind reeled with all I had seen, the knowledge spinning violently in my head before I was plunged back into memories, these ones coming in a furious wave that set my pulse racing. First, I was Elvia again, flying into battle with burning wings and the Imperial Star buried in the hilt of a stunning sword. It whispered to her in her mind, telling her the power words she needed to wield it. With a word spoken to it, a blast slammed into an army of Nymphs beneath her, cutting through their ranks and carving them to pieces.

At night, the Imperial Star whispered more to her, telling her of dark magic, of powers lost, and powers undiscovered. Elvia taught all of it to her son who grew before my eyes in each passing vision, until one day he stood before a grave of ruby red and took his mother's sword into his grasp.

But still, the war waged on, and he used the Imperial Star to become an unimaginably powerful ruler. Despite his domination in the kingdom, he and his court were gaining enemies, the Dragons forming an army of their own and factions of Fae joining the Nymphs to try and destroy the Phoenix king.

Another generation passed, then another, each new ruler handed the Imperial Star to the next until finally it was passing into the hands of Avalon as she stood at her mother's deathbed.

"Keep the broken promise," her mother spoke, and I, as Avalon, curled my hands around the sword's hilt possessively, having waited far too long for this moment as I caressed the Imperial Star with my thumb. "It is time, Avalon."

"The war isn't won," I said firmly, and my mother pushed a Memoriae crystal into my hand too. It held all the knowledge of the star that the past kings and queens had acquired, each of them adding more to it every time they learned a new power word. Only a fool would give up this power. I would covet it always and ensure my descendants did too. It was part of what made us the greatest Order to ever live.

"Our kind are dying out, less and less Phoenixes are born each year," my mother rasped, the tide of death rushing in on her. "The Imperial Star is a curse, not a gift. It won't end until..." She died, her final breath rattling out of her chest, and I leaned down to kiss her cheek before turning away and leaving the servants to prepare her for burial.

I passed my cousin, Romina, in the corridor, nodding to her to let her know it was over and she sobbed, falling into the arms of her lover, Tomás. He was not a Phoenix, and she knew my feelings on the matter. There were few of our kind left now, and we needed to ensure our lineage remained strong. She had refused the marriage I had ordered her into with Vicente, and my mother hadn't had the backbone to force her to go through with it, but if she thought I would stand for this tryst with a Hydra now that I was queen, she was sorely mistaken.

I would give them one night more before announcements were made. I had better things to do right now, like sitting on my throne and commanding the Imperial Star to give me the world.

I was pulled out of the vision, having only a moment to sit in the confusion over what I'd seen. What was the broken promise? What were these memories not showing me? And what had her mother meant about the Imperial Star being a curse?

The vision changed once more and I *saw* the battle Queen Avalon waged with Lavinia, how she stole the shadows from the Nymphs using the Imperial Star and cast her enemy into a realm with all the shadows her kind needed to survive. It was brutal watching it again and I cringed at the sympathy I felt for Lavinia in that moment, witnessing Queen Avalon send her into oblivion and leaving her kind altered forevermore.

Then, my mind slipped into a memory belonging to Romina and my heart stuttered as I found myself running full pelt through a dark tunnel.

People were screaming, and terror consumed me as I raced along with the Phoenixes, our flames curling around us in the dark. More screams sounded behind me and I looked back, finding my cousins falling to their knees, the flesh melting from their bones before they crashed to the ground.

I didn't know what was happening, only that no other Orders were dying. A curse, it had to be a curse, but why?

Tomás kept hold of my hand, dragging me on at a furious speed.

"Don't shift," he tossed back at me, and I nodded in promise of that. Any Phoenix who we'd seen spread their wings, immediately fell to ruin. I would not let a single flame kiss my skin until we got out of these tunnels, maybe not even then.

"This way!" Queen Avalon called from up ahead and we followed her voice through the passages, turning this way and that until suddenly Tomás and I rounded into a dead end.

Avalon stood before us, her crown perched atop her head and her eyes bright with fire. She had taken the Imperial Star from the hilt of her sword and held it before her now with a manic look about her.

"A Seer has shown me our fate. Many Phoenixes will fall this day, and we will be forced to leave our dear palace behind. But one soul must remain bound here, for one day our kind will return to this place and when they do, the spirit of the watcher shall rouse and prepare them for what is coming. The rest of us will flee and make a future

further north while we wait for that time."

I shared a tense look with Tomás as more screams sounded out in the passage behind us.

"What have you done?" I demanded of this queen I had long ago learned to hate.

"Romina," my cousin and fiancé Vicente growled, stepping closer to Avalon's side. I was meant to marry him this month, but I had never heeded his or Avalon's warning to stay away from Tomás. I loved him, and no one would force me to marry another. Least of all a man who was blood-related to me and who had clearly been fucking Avalon for months. But no matter who she took to her bed, no seed grew in her. She could not produce the Phoenix heir she so craved, yet she would never give up trying.

I tightened my grip on Tomás's hand, stepping in front of him as Vicente raised his sword in his direction.

"Come here," Vicente barked. "We have little time to act."

"Do not dare speak to her that way," Tomás snarled, purple fire flashing in his eyes as he raised his own sword.

"Traitor," Vicente spat, looking to Avalon. "He raises a sword against a noble, Your Highness."

"Yes, I see that," she hissed, her eyes darting to Tomás and making me growl protectively.

"We are going, and you will not stop us," I said, pressing back into Tomás and making him retreat towards the only exit.

No other Fae had made it this far and though I was terrified of what lay out there in those tunnels, a worse fate was remaining here with these monsters.

Avalon raised a potion in her hand, the glass bottle holding a blackish liquid that glinted with magic.

"Grab her, Vicente."

Vicente came at me, and I drew my sword instead of using my gifts, lunging forward, and swinging at him before he could dare place his hands on me. I slit his arm open, and blood poured, making him swear as he backed up.

"You have been useless in this life, but perhaps you will be useful in the next." He darted toward me again, and I swung my sword with a yell of fury, the edge slicing across his chest this time. Flames burst to life across his skin in response and Avalon screamed, "No!" but it was already too late.

Vicente fell prey to whatever terrible magic was at play in these tunnels, his skin melting and his pitchy screams filling the air before he collapsed to the ground, just a pile of bones with his dagger clattering down at his side.

Avalon whirled on me, lifting the Imperial Star to her lips and speaking a single word against the stone which I couldn't catch. But in the next second, my limbs went rigid and the sword slipped from my fingers, my power immobilised by some other-worldly magic.

Tomás roared in anger and a blast of Hydra fire tore from his body, slamming into Avalon and knocking her from her feet. The Imperial Star was sent flying from her grip and tumbling over the ground, whispering angry words as it went. All Phoenixes shall be my adversaries from this day forth, and I shall twist their fates so they fail in all endeavours, their lives will be full of sorrow, and there will be no way out until the promise is kept. Either that, or their Order shall fall, and no more will ever walk this earth."

Tomás raised his sword, his lips peeled back as he rushed to behead the queen, but her wings burst from her shoulder blades, burning his arms and melting his sword in his grip. He cried out as he staggered away, and Avalon screamed as her skin began to melt.

She lifted the potion to her lips with a lament, swallowing it down in deep gulps before the curse consumed her entirely. It did though, her skin liquifying and the whites of her eyes burning bright before they were lost too and she turned to bones, her fire dying with her.

The Memoriae crystal hit the ground alongside her sword and the magic of the Imperial Star suddenly released me, sending me stumbling forward.

I ran to Tomás, healing the wounds on his arms and checking that he was alright.

"We must go," he urged. "We must get as far from here as we can and never return."

I nodded, kissing him fast then running to gather up the Imperial Star, the crystal and Avalon's sword. Then we turned and ran back into the dark tunnels, passing by the bones of the fallen Phoenixes.

As we rounded a corner, my gaze found my mother and father, clutching onto each other in an alcove as their wings burned bright at their backs. It was already too late even though I was screaming for them to cast away their Phoenixes. But the magic took them, and they fell to bones on the floor in a heap of treasure they had been carrying, their arms still holding one another in death.

A noise of anguish left me, and I could only keep moving because Tomás dragged me on, my vision blurred with tears as he led me away into the dark, and I placed my trust in him to get us out.

Somehow, we made it above ground, and we fled away into the jungle with only one thought in our minds. North. As far as we could go until we felt safe once more. And as we ran, the last of our people ran with us, falling into line behind me, the last Vega and Phoenix among them. With a weight in my chest, I realised that if that was true, I had just become their queen.

I was tossed out of the memory, finding Orion's hand firmly wrapped around my arm, urgency in his eyes.

"What did you see?" he asked, and I relayed it all to him, trying not to forget a single detail as he soaked it all in, and I blurted it in a stream of frantic words.

"Fuck," he breathed when I was done.

I lifted a hand to caress the spot where the Imperial Star had hung around my throat, anxiety tearing a line through my chest. "The Imperial Star cursed them. That's why all the Phoenixes died. And it's why Tory and I have failed time and again in this war. That old curse is still in place. We're fucked, Lance. Unless we can figure out what the broken promise is, we're never going to be free of the star's wrath."

I clawed a hand through my hair, trying to process all of this, my heart thrashing like a caged animal.

"This explains...everything," he said in shock, and I broke away from him, beginning to pace without thought as my mind worked over all we'd seen.

"Romina didn't know what the broken promise was either," I said, a frown knitting my brows together. "What the hell could it be?"

"I don't know," Orion sighed.

"Do you think the Imperial Star is still on the battlefield?" I asked, the sudden fear slicing a hole in my heart.

"If it is, then at least we know where to look for it," Orion said, though his expression was grim.

"And how will we do that when we're locked up here?" I said in exasperation. "We have to get a message to the others so they can retrieve it before someone else finds it. And we need to tell Tory to find out what the broken promise is so we can keep it."

Orion's silence told me he had no idea how to do that, and I was just as clueless.

"When I was up on that mountain after the battle, I saw a fallen star just like the one in those memories. I spoke with it, and saw it release its power into the world. If I'd known about all of this, I could have asked it for answers. Maybe it knew what the broken promise is."

"Why didn't you tell me this?" Orion shot in front of me with a blur of speed.

"It was the last thing on my mind after everything," I said, shrugging but he gripped my shoulders, his features intense.

"Do you have any idea how rare of an event that is, Blue? There are only a handful of Fae in the world who have seen it. Most of our kind would give anything to witness a Donum Magicae. I, myself, have studied it in countless books, but never have I had a true imagining of what it would be like to stand in the power of one of the celestial creators. What was it like?"

"It was…shiny," I murmured, my mind still distracted by the memories.

"Shiny," he deadpanned, his eyes narrowing, and I snorted, my shoulders dropping as I let go of the tension in my limbs.

"It was pretty cool, I guess."

"Pretty cool. You guess," he echoed flatly, and I broke a small laugh.

"I'll ask Vard to pluck the memory out of my head so you can watch it," I said, turning away from him towards a row of bookshelves and brushing my fingers over the ancient spines, wondering if any of them might hold the answer we sought.

"That's not funny," he growled as he followed.

"Gotta laugh to stop the tears coming," I said, my thoughts returning to all we'd seen. "Do you think Romina is my ancestor?"

"Yes. Queen Romina was the first queen to rule from The Palace of Souls. She built this place," he said, and my lips parted as I looked to him.

"What else do you know?"

He cocked his head. "So, you want my knowledge, but you won't describe the Donum Magicae to me."

"Alright, I'll try." I grinned. "Imagine a really, really, really shiny rock."

Orion gave me a hollow look.

"Didn't you ever go with Darius to melt down a fallen star for stardust and get a chance to see it sparkle its way out of existence?" I asked.

"Meteorites create stardust, not true fallen stars," he said.

"That's confusing," I pointed out. "Why isn't it called meteorite dust then?"

His attention slipped past me before he answered, and he shot forward, grabbing a diamond encrusted box off of the shelf.

"Now who's touching ancient artefacts?" I taunted.

His lips slanted up as he examined the circular box and the pair of weighing scales marked on its surface. "If you can't beat 'em…"

He popped the lid open and a miniscule, mechanical set of scales ascended on a little silver platform that resembled a miniature ballroom. A tiny girl made of wood stood on one side of the scales and she moved with delicate magic, leaping over to land in the other dish, then back and forth from one to the other, making the scales rock up and down as she danced. It was mesmerising and as music started to play within the box, I lost all focus on everything but that wooden girl.

A song curled up from its depths, the voice soft and feminine, trilling out a soothing lullaby.

"It's time to dance, to dice with chance, the scales they rise, and they fall now. Come to me, play with me, here in my lonely ballroom…"

The ground beneath me seemed to rise, and I rocked dizzily on my feet, reaching for the music box and that enchanting wooden dancer leaping this way and that. Orion was reaching for her too and our fingers grazed as we touched her, unable to resist her call. The moment we made contact, the world tipped and it was as though I was falling forward down a slippery hill, unable to stop as I went tumbling head over heels, losing sight of everything except the little wooden girl.

I hit a hard, silver floor at Orion's side in the tiny ballroom that lay within the music box. The walls were silver too, and the windows running along them were painted with an outdoor scene of a sunlit meadow.

I looked up in a daze, finding a towering set of scales above me, the girl now standing between the two scales, balancing there as she smiled creepily. She was five times bigger than us now, and as she jumped to the right, her feet hit the dish sitting above us, sending it plummeting down towards us with a groaning wail of moving metal.

Orion slammed into me, and we rolled across the floor, just avoiding the strike of the dish's base, and the dancer leapt into the other dish again with a laugh.

"Dance with me, play with me," she sang as the scales tipped once more.

I grabbed Orion's hand, the two of us jumping upright and running to the other side of the ballroom, the bottom of the left dish crashing down just where we'd been.

"You shouldn't have touched it," I said.

"Oh, you think?" Orion growled, holding firm to my hand as the dancer did a pirouette in the lowered dish. "I can't access my Order."

"Dance with me, play with me," the girl sung again, leaping up and springing overhead towards the other dish.

"We have to climb out," Orion said firmly as we ran for the opposite side of the room again and the floor juddered with the weight of the scales slamming down on it once more, making my heart stumble.

He started trying to climb the wall as I looked to the girl above, her song twisting through the air with a plea inside it. And I realised what she wanted.

"No, I think we have to do as she says. We have to play her game," I said thickly.

"Fuck that." Orion continued to try and climb out, and I looked around quickly as the girl leapt towards the other dish again, sending a wave of adrenaline into my veins. There were four strange circles on the floor, one within the other, and in the middle of the room was the smallest one of all. But it didn't mean anything to me.

"What's the game?" I called to the wooden girl and the largest ring around the edge of the room lit up in white. Her feet hit the dish, but it jarred to a halt as Orion and I readied to run out of the way.

The girl peered over the side of it, looking down at us with her painted face twisting in a smile. The music continued to play, sounding more eerie than beautiful now that I was trapped inside a tiny music box with a freaky enchanted matchstick bitch, and she opened her mouth, singing new words to the tune.

"When light is white, it's time to dance, but when it's blue, you best not move. For you shall be in peril. If you play, you'll make my day, and I'll release you with my prized possession."

"Okay, so…we just have to dance. Any chance you can dance?" I muttered to Orion.

"I've attended countless bullshit Acrux parties, I can unfortunately dance, but I'd rather fight." He looked up at the girl as if assessing his chances against her.

"No." I grabbed his hand. "We're not taking on the cursed ballerina and getting stuck in a music box forever. Let's just do what she says."

"Okay, but if your way doesn't work, we're trying my way," he said.

"Deal." I towed him over to the circle, realising those heading towards the centre all grew progressively thinner, leaving less space to dance on. The peril part of the game did not sound good, but we were in here now, so we didn't have a choice.

Orion pressed his hand to my lower back, taking hold of my hand and placing it on his shoulder while pulling the other into his grip.

"Follow my lead," he ordered, and I nodded, more than happy to do that because ballroom dancing was not my gift in life.

The music grew louder, announcing the start of the game, and Orion guided me around the circle of glowing white light in slow movements, giving me a chance to find the rhythm with him. I was just getting the hang of it when the light beneath us turned blue and Orion clutched me against him, the two of us becoming as still as statues as the music stopped.

The wooden girl cheered with a tinkling noise in her throat and a painted door at the end of the ballroom opened. "She can't see you, but she'll hear you if you move, so don't put one foot wrong or she'll feast well," she sang.

From the darkness beyond the doorway, I saw bones shifting. A Fae skull tumbled out to lay on the dancefloor and I held my breath, forcing myself not to move. Some creature was moving in there through the bones of long claimed victims, and I did not want to gain its attention.

Orion's fingers dug into me as he watched my expression, unable to turn his head and look that way himself.

An ivory white praying mantis appeared, stepping out into the ballroom, the bug no doubt small in reality but down here in this music box, it was a giant monster. Its eyes were punctured as if by a needle, proving it was blind, and I had to wonder which psychotic Fae had concocted this tiny, pocket-sized hell and who they had placed down here to die in it.

But that wasn't the end of the horror show, because our ring turned to grass beneath our feet, growing up and around us, the fronds reaching for us and tickling any exposed skin it could find. I clenched my jaw, remaining rigid even while the grass tormented us, trying to goad us into flinching.

The mantis came scuttling towards us, the sharp looking appendages either side of its mouth clacking together and its antennae sweeping around its body in hunt of us. But neither Orion nor I moved.

It went scuttling past us, searching the place but unable to find us, though I didn't know what would happen if it discovered us by chance. Maybe that was a part of it, those Libra scales representing how quickly our fate could come unbalanced.

After a minute, the wooden girl hummed a tune that lured the mantis back into its den and the doors shut behind it. The music started up again and the next ring lit up in white while the grass in the previous ring vanished. We hurried onto the new ring and Orion began guiding me around it, keeping me close.

"This is fucked up," he whispered.

"We've only got three more rings, including this one. We just have to make it to the middle and she'll let us go. That's gotta be the end of it," I said, convincing myself as much as I was him.

The light beneath us turned abruptly blue and the music shut off, the two of us holding the other tight and falling deathly still. The mantis came scurrying back out of the doors and the moment it began looking for us, air blew around the circle we were in, sending a barrage of it at our backs.

I worked hard not to move, Orion's muscular frame grounding me while the mantis hunted the ballroom for us, its pincers clicking across the floor and its mouth snapping. Somehow, we managed to remain in place, and the wooden girl lured the mantis back into its den once more.

I took a heavy breath, meeting Orion's gaze, determination passing between us.

"Just two more," I said.

"Yes, just two more rings of death. Perfect," he said dryly.

The music started up again and we moved into the next ring as it lit up in white.

Orion dropped his mouth close to my ear as we moved in slow circles, his body practically controlling mine as I mirrored his steps. "Of all the deaths we've faced, I would never have predicted we'd be threatened with a praying mantis in a music box."

"Or a singing matchstick," I looked up at the girl above as she twirled on top of the scales, coldness dripping through me.

"Life really is far more interesting now you're in it," he said with a ghost of a grin, but then the light turned blue beneath our feet and my heart turned to stone. We remained entirely still, and the door opened again, releasing the hungry praying mantis. It came scurrying along faster this time, blind eyes twitching and its slimy black tongue slicking the sharp edges of its mouth.

We are not gonna die in the jaws of a bug.

The floor turned to ice beneath us, the third Element to show up in the game and I swallowed a gasp as my feet slid backwards. Orion lost his footing entirely and his knee crashed against the floor as he fell, making the mantis let out a shrill noise as it came flying up behind him.

Its pincers wrapped around him, launching him across the ballroom towards its den, and moving so fast that Orion had no time to get to his feet before the mantis tossed him through the door and disappeared after him.

I ran to follow with a cry of terror, but the doors shut in my face and as I slammed into them, they sealed up tight, becoming nothing but a painting on a false wall.

"Let him go!" I shouted up at the wooden girl above.

"The door will only open again in the next round," she sang to me, and I looked back at the rings, the final one turning white.

I shuddered, hurrying over to it, knowing I had to play on if I was going to get through those doors. There was no way I was going to let him die at the hands of some insect.

The music started again, and I danced around the circle, making minimal effort and glaring up at the wooden girl with rage in my soul.

"Come on," I gritted out, anxiety clutching my heart.

The ring turned blue, and I fell still, though my legs were nearly trembling as I prepared to run. The doors flew open, and the mantis came stumbling out with Orion on its back, choking the life out of the thing as it screeched and flailed. Fire burst to life at my feet, and I jumped away from it, running forward and hefting an old arm bone into my grip from the mantis's graveyard, swinging it with a scream of fury.

"Get away from my mate, you creepy-crawly son of a bitch!" I cried.

I slammed the bone into the insect's face and it came crashing down to the floor where Orion took hold of its neck and pulling with all his strength. With a furious yank, he tore the bug's head clean from its body, tossing it away as greenish blood splattered the floor.

"No!" the wooden girl warbled, diving off of the scales above and coming to land right behind me.

I bared my teeth, rushing her with the arm bone raised and swinging it hard against her legs. They snapped in two and she went flying backwards, landing in the fire that was still burning in the central ring, her body dry as tinder and going up in flames in an instant.

She reached for me like I might come to her aid, and I stared icily at her as Orion moved to join me, sliding his arm over my shoulders and watching her burn with me.

"I do love a good bonfire," Orion purred, and a dark smile pulled at my mouth.

The matchstick girl cried out, a final song pouring from her before she was turned to a pile of soot and the music died along with her. The fire extinguished and magic whirled around us, making me lose sight of everything as Orion and I were thrown out of the music box, landing in a heap on the floor of the treasury. He had the tiniest smear of green blood from the praying mantis on his cheek and the arm bone in my grip was now fully sized. I tossed it away from me, looking to the music box in alarm as it began spinning on the floor, spitting out bones which became their normal size again as they landed in heaps of gold around us.

We scrambled upright, backing away from it, magic sending it into a frenzy until the last of the bones were ejected and the whole thing fell apart, pieces of metal and cogs shattering on the floor. Among it all was a beautiful opal, winking up at us from within the wreckage of the cursed music box.

"So that's what you were for. You were keeping this safe." Orion moved forward, picking it up and admiring it in his palm.

I moved forward to look down at the treasure, taking in the rivers of colour running through the gemstone.

"Is it a Guild Stone?" I asked hopefully.

"Feels like one," he said, running his thumb across it and the Guild Master mark on his arm suddenly flared to life, the beautiful sword shining along his forearm as it responded to finding this new stone. "Opal for Libra."

"Who do you think hid it in that creepy music box?" I asked.

"Some long dead Fae who didn't want anyone stealing his treasure," he guessed with a shrug, and I leaned up to wipe the gross mantis blood off his cheek.

His attention moved past me and he frowned, shooting forward and grabbing a book off the shelf at my back. I raised my brows at the beautiful cover which was woven with bronze feathers.

"Gabriel showed me this in a vision. I think it's important," he said excitedly, his eyes still bright from the fight we'd just had.

A Dragon's roar sounded somewhere far above us in the palace and we both stilled as the tremors of that noise reverberated through the walls.

"We need to get back," I said, picking up the Memoriae crystal I must have dropped when I went into the music box.

Orion placed the book in my hands along with the opal, then scooped me up and raced out of the treasury at speed.

It was hard to tell how long we'd spent down there, the time we'd been in the music box impossible to gauge, but had it really been three hours already? I hated the thought of returning to that cage.

The moment we made it through the wall, the secret passage started closing behind us and at the sound of footsteps coming this way, I tossed the book, the opal and the crystal back into the passage just before it shut tight.

The throne room doors flew open, and my heart lurched as Lionel strode in with Vard at his back and two big Dragon guards dragging Gabriel along behind them.

One of them was Mildred, her moustache twisted up at the corners and a violent shade of pink eyeshadow coating her eyelids. Lavinia floated in after them, looking almost translucent as she sailed along on her cloud of darkness. The dagger I'd found in the secret hatch in the throne was strapped to her hip, looking so bright between the shadows slithering around her body.

Lionel dropped onto the throne, ignoring us entirely as his butler Horace appeared, racing after them and kneeling before him to polish his shoes.

"Hurry up," Lionel bit at him.

Horace worked faster and faster, buffing those shoes like his life depended on it. And knowing Lionel, it probably did.

I realised I hadn't blinked, my gaze locked on my brother as he looked my way, his brow furrowing and lines of stress on his forehead. I ached to get to him, to kill every motherfucker around him and get him the hell out of here alongside my mate. But of course, there was no chance of that. So instead, we stared at one another with a thousand unspoken words passing between us.

I love you. I'm sorry. I hope you're alright.

The doors to the throne room were opened once more, this time held wide by two Nymphs in their shifted forms. Four of Lionel's Dragons came next, carrying a huge wooden chest inlaid with golden Elemental symbols.

"What's this?" Lionel demanded.

"This was in the Voldrakian carriage that arrived, sire," one of the men told him.

"Where are the Voldrakian royals? I requested their presence," Lionel barked, rising from his throne, and kicking Horace away from his feet.

"Perhaps this is an offering, sire?" Vard suggested, clearly trying to appease him.

Smoke spilled from Lionel's mouth, and he nodded stiffly, gesturing for the men to bring the chest to him. "Place it down. Let us see what fine gifts they wish to offer me."

Heavy gold clasps secured the lid of the chest and as the Dragons set it down on the flagstones, they worked to open each one. A snap sounded as the last catch was released, followed by a faint hissing sound, and I tensed as I noticed my brother stepping subtly behind Mildred. Orion and I backed up too.

The Dragons flipped the lid open and the biggest snake I'd ever seen surged out of it, its fang-filled mouth snapping down over the head of the closest man. He screamed, crashing to the floor, and using his water Element to cast a blade of ice in his hand, stabbing it into the snake's side. But it went right through the creature as if it were made of smoke and in the next second, the snake dissolved, turning to a thick purple vapour that surrounded the man and started liquefying his body against the floor. The other Dragons were in a frenzy trying to help him with magic, but nothing they did helped.

Lionel backed up, adding power to his air shield while the Shadow Princess drifted closer to watch the man die, curiosity lighting her eyes.

The vapour vanished and the only things left in its wake were blood and bone, all of it twisting and writhing under some power as it formed a single word across the flagstones.

FOE.

Lionel roared in anger, grabbing Vard by the throat, burning his skin as he fought to keep hold of his Order form and making the Seer yelp. "Why did you not *see* this?!"

Vard shook his head, his mouth opening and closing but no words came out.

Horace backed up behind the Seer, looking anywhere but at the mutilated body of the Dragon Shifter, acting as if it didn't exist and doing everything he could not draw Lionel's anger his way.

Gabriel glanced at me, his mouth lifting at the corner, and I smiled back. If the Voldrakians had decided not to remain allied with Solaria, was there a chance they'd go to war against Lionel?

"I-I'm sorry, my King," Vard stammered, and Lionel shoved him away with a snarl, rounding on Gabriel. "You *saw* this."

"Yes," Gabriel said, raising his chin, and Mildred looked back at him, her under-bite jaw dropping as she realised he'd used her as a shield.

Lionel's upper lip peeled back, and he raised a flaming fist.

"Stop!" I cried as Orion pressed closer to me anxiously, but Gabriel wasn't Lionel's target.

He swung around, slamming his fist into Vard's face, sending him flying to the floor with a yelp of pain.

Lavinia laughed, floating closer to Lionel. "Again, Daddy," she urged, and he stalked after Vard, slamming the shadow fist into him this time.

The beating went on and while all of Lionel's subjects were watching, I looked to Gabriel again. His eyes were glazed and I could tell he was lost to some vision, but I had no idea if he was *seeing* was something good or bad.

"What use are snivelling creatures like you to me?" Lionel spat. "I need a court full of loyal Fae who will do anything for their king. Who are useful to me beyond all doubt."

He stood upright, pushing a hand into his blonde hair, marking it with blood as a feral glimmer entered his eyes, like something had just occurred to him.

Gabriel blinked, focusing on me once more with horror washing over his features.

My stomach dropped and I mouthed, "What is it?" to him in desperation.

"Fear the Bonded men!" he blurted to me. "The night the Hydra bellows is coming, and fate has shifted! We must get word to the others, we must tell them that-"

Lionel silenced him with air magic, stealing all oxygen from his lungs as he sneered.

"Silence!" he boomed, turning his back on Vard who was twitching on the floor. "Mildred, return him to the Seer's chamber and have his lips sealed shut until I decide he is allowed to speak again."

"Of course, my King," Mildred said, bowing low.

"Gabriel!" I cried, grabbing the bars, and trying to will magic into my hands, but there was nothing I could do.

My brother was dragged away by Mildred, and Lionel didn't allow him to breathe again until he was beyond the door.

The prophecy my brother had given us once was spinning through my mind, the words turning over in my head.

Two Phoenixes, born of fire, rising from the ashes of the past. The wheel of fate is turning, and the Dragon is poised to strike. But blood of the deceiver may change the course of destiny. Beware the man with the painted smile who lingers close to your side. Turn the scorned. Free the enslaved. Fear the Bonded men. Many will fall for one to ascend. Suffer the curse. The hunter will pay the price. Do not repeat the mistakes of the past. Keep the broken promise. Mend the rift. All that hides in the shadows is not dark. Blood will out. Seal your fate. Choose your destiny.

I focused on the Bonded men, wondering who they could be and why Gabriel had been so terrified of them. Perhaps Tory had had more luck figuring some of the prophecy out, but at least parts of it were becoming clear now.

The first line had to refer to me and my sister, the second Lionel. Then the blood of the deceiver...that could be Darius. He was descended from the man who had deceived Lavinia at the battle against Avalon. So that added up. *Fucking stars.*

Then there was the eternal question of the man with the painted smile. I still had no idea on that one, but hoped Tor had figured it out.

Many will fall for one to ascend. Well, I guess that was kinda self-explanatory, though who that person was, I didn't know. It could just mean Lionel keeping his place as king after a bloody war. Though I hoped it meant another monarch could take his place.

Suffer the curse. Yup, think I had that one figured out. Thanks Shadow Beast.

The hunter will pay the price. Orion...shit. That had to be about him paying the price for my curse.

Mend the rift....I frowned. Could it be referring to the shadow rifts we closed? But then why wasn't it plural? Maybe it was meant more metaphorically...

I shook my head, thinking over the last lines but they were too vague for any new ideas to spark in me.

Orion and I exchanged a look of despair as we were left trapped in our cell, Gabriel's warning spinning out into the world without anyone to figure it out and work against whatever foul plans Lionel was concocting. I didn't know what to do. There had to be a way to use this prophecy to help us change fate, but if we couldn't even discover what it meant, I didn't see how we could.

Lionel directed Horace to clean up the guts of the man who had been killed, then marched from the room with Lavinia and his Dragons hurrying after him. Horace sighed, looking down at the blood with his head hanging low.

"Wish I'd never applied for this job," he muttered to himself. "Wash this, wash that. Polish my shoes, hand scrub my underwear...clean up all the bodies my queen has half eaten. And you know how many days off a year I get? None." He shook his head, clucking his tongue. "Shoulda listened to Jim. He said it'd be like this; said I'd regret it. And now look. Jim's off living his best life in Sunshine Bay and I'm here cleaning up entrails."

"Hey," Orion called to him, and Horace lifted his head, his eyes narrowing. "Any chance you hate Lionel as much as your job?"

"Don't you go talking to me, mate, getting me in trouble. I don't wanna be involved in anything. I just want an easy life," Horace said, not looking Orion directly in the eye. "The king's food was overcooked last week, and he incinerated Bob in the kitchen. I ain't getting incinerated for nobody."

"If you help us, we'll protect you from the king when we get out of here," I said, wondering if he might be able to get a message to our friends. But Horace shook his head, lifting a hand and casting a silencing bubble so he couldn't hear us anymore. As if turning a blind eye to us and all the horrors of this place somehow made him less responsible for it. But cruelty still happened whether you acknowledged it or not. Wasn't pretending it didn't exist just giving the monsters of this world license to carry on being monsters?

"Fucking coward," Orion muttered, turning his back on him, and resting against the bars.

We waited for Horace to finish cleaning up the remains of the dead Fae, and when he was gone, the two of us hurried to the back wall. I pressed my hands against it, willing it to open and the stone gave way at my touch. Orion took the book from inside and I sat beside him against the wall as the hidden door closed once more, leaning close to look at it in his lap.

"Do you think Gabriel will be okay?" I whispered, my mind still stuck on him and all he must have been going through.

"Gabriel is one of the strongest Fae I know. He's resilient. Like you." He brushed his fingers over my knee, and I relaxed a little, focusing on the book and hoping it had a gift for us which could change the trajectory of this war.

"Look at this…" His hand moved back to the book as he studied it, turning it over and running his fingers along the spine. I broke a smile at the fascination on his face and watched him as he continued his intricate examination of the book's binding.

"You're staring," he murmured, his mouth hooking up at the corner and revealing his dimple.

"It's hard not to stare when you look this cute," I said, and he glanced over at me with a dry look.

"Cute? Dogs are cute, like your little lap dog, Seth, but I'm-"

"Ohmagod," I gasped, cutting over him. "You just said Seth is cute."

His eyes widened in horror. "No," he hissed in warning like I was to blame for the words that had come out of his mouth, but I most definitely wasn't. "I meant it objectively. Of course I don't think the mutt is cute. But I suppose I can see, from afar, if I were someone entirely else, that that someone might find him marginally endearing when he isn't being aggravating. To me though, he is entirely aggravating at all times. And that will never change."

"Mmhmm," I hummed sarcastically, and his gaze narrowed.

He captured my chin in his grip and rubbed his thumb over my bottom lip. "Don't look at me as if you know better."

"I always know better." I smirked then took his thumb between my lips, biting down and tasting the salt of his skin.

He grunted, pushing the book aside as if it held none of his attention now, coming for me instead. But as tempting as that was, I didn't know how much longer we had before Lavinia came back and stole away our opportunity to read it. It might hold an answer about the broken promise, although I doubted a secret like that would be written down so simply, considering Romina hadn't known what it was either. Still, we probably should have been doing something more productive than this.

I released his thumb from my mouth, swerving a kiss from him and ducking low to grab the book from the floor.

"Forget the book. The answer to the broken promise isn't going to be handily detailed in there, or else some ancient Phoenix would have dealt with it long ago," he said, echoing my thoughts.

His fingers pushed into hair, gripping tight and pulling until I was sitting upright again, looking at the chaos in his eyes. He held me tight, moving in to kiss me again, but I brought the book up in front of my face to block him and he growled from behind it.

"You shouldn't play hide and seek with a Vampire, Blue," he warned. "You'll end up like Harriet Hidey-Hole."

"Who's that?" I laughed, peeking over the top of the book, but his expression said he was deadly serious.

"It's another children's story," he said, snatching the book and placing it behind him out of reach.

With his fingers still locked in my hair, I had no escape, and as he reared over me, pressing his chest to mine and forcing me to drop to the floor, I was pinned beneath him.

I curled my legs around him, the shadows shifting away from my body as my love for him made it harder for them to remain wherever he touched me. Between the solid weight of him and the firm ridge of his cock pressing against me, it would have been all too easy to submit. But we really did need to check out that book.

I stretched out one leg, my toes landing on the soft feathers of the cover, and I scooted it closer, reaching for it with my right hand.

Orion's mouth skated along my jaw and my breath caught at the light touch and the scrape of his beard. It was getting long now, and if we had been under any other circumstances, I would have liked the roguish look on him.

"Harriet Hidey-Hole liked to play hide and seek more than any other kid in her school," Orion told me the story as he continued to torment me with the lightest of kisses that set my skin burning. He yanked on my hair to pull my head sideways and expose my neck to him, making me release a curse that was wrapped in a moan.

With him, pain and pleasure were weapons he forged out of the sweetest kind of sins, and I was more than happy to let him use them against me. My pulse raced and I half forgot about the book beneath my foot as his kisses travelled to my collar bone and the graze of his fangs made my spine arch against the cold floor. He released my hair, slipping his hand beneath me into the hollow I'd created between my body and the tiles, curling his fingers against the base of my spine, and grinding the huge length of his cock over my clit through his sweatpants.

I moaned his name, wanting so much more than he was giving me, but he was taking his time like we had an eternity of it, when it was far more likely that the opposite was true.

"She would hide in trees and wooden chests; she'd hide in attics and barns and none of her friends could ever find her," Orion continued the story while I rolled my hips and tried to take what I needed from him, but he kept me in suspense. "She declared herself the best hide and seeker in the world, and dared everyone she met to play with her so she could prove it. No one ever found her, until one day, she bumped into a Vampire. *'I'm the best hide and seeker in the world,'* she said."

"Lance," I groaned in frustration, done with this story. I clawed my fingers down his back, grinding against him as he worked me into a frenzy.

"The Vampire told her she was wrong, and that *he* was in fact the best hide and seeker. She laughed at him and challenged him to a game. The Vampire agreed and said she could have ten full minutes to hide before he even began to look for her. So Harriet ran off, picking one of her favourite hiding places in the local barn where no one had ever found her. She climbed inside a haystack and sat quietly while she waited for the Vampire to come looking for her, certain she would never be found."

"I get it," I said impatiently. "The Vampire found her in her hidey hole."

"Yeah," he said darkly, dragging his fangs down over my breast and making me shiver as he ran the pad of his tongue over my nipple. "He was so high on the hunt that he ripped her to pieces."

"Fucking hell," I half laughed. "What's with your psycho kids' stories?"

"They're warnings. Ones you should heed." He sucked my nipple into his mouth, and it hardened to a tight bud as he teased it between his teeth. My fingers pushed into his hair, my head tipping back as he reached between us to push his pants down, but before he got there, the door of the throne room flew open.

Orion shot to his feet in a heartbeat, snarling like an animal as he used his body to conceal mine from view. I couldn't see who had arrived, and my thoughts were fully scrambled as I shoved myself up to my knees, the shadows spilling back out of my skin and wrapping around me tightly, covering every piece of me which had been on show.

I quickly grabbed the book, rising to my feet and moving close behind Orion before sliding it into the back of his sweatpants and pulling his shirt down over it. Then I stepped to his side, finding Horace there again, spinning a key on his finger while a couple of Nymphs stood behind him. "Time for your shower. Come on, chop-chop. I haven't got all day."

"The door isn't open," Orion deadpanned.

"Yeah, yeah, less of the attitude, mate," Horace sniped, walking forward and unlocking the door before directing us out of the cage. "You get a real treat today, seeing as the servant's quarters down 'ere have decided to shut themselves up as tight as a Duck Shifter's asshole. No one can get into the showers down there now. This place is haunted, I swear it." Horace turned and led us along while the two Nymphs moved to flank us.

"I've seen the ghosts in this place, Horace," I called to him, and his shoulders stiffened. "They're hungry, lonely souls and they want to feast on the traitors living in their queens' palace."

"Oh, and what queens would that be, eh?" he laughed, but there was a tremor in his voice that said he really was afraid of ghosts.

"Me and my sister," I said firmly. "This palace and its ghosts are loyal to us, and they don't take kindly to snivelling little creeps serving false kings between its walls. You'd better watch your back at night. One word from me, and they might come and find you while you sleep to peel the flesh from your bones."

"Shut your filthy mouth," he snapped over his shoulder, and Orion jerked forward like he was going to attack him, but I caught his arm, squeezing to stop him.

I didn't want him being punished for the sake of this worthless creature's death. Besides, if Horace died, he'd only be replaced, and that person could be far worse than this man who at least left us in peace most of the time.

He guided us through the opulent halls and into a guest chamber where extravagant murals of beautiful gardens and valleys filled with every kind of Order imaginable were painted in gleaming ink that almost looked as though it was still wet.

Horace gestured for us to step through a door, and we walked into a bathroom that was more of an indoor pool house than anything else. It had a tropical theme, the air thick with mist that rose in plumes from the green-blue pool in the middle of it, water rushing down over the branches of a huge tree that stood at the heart of it. Vines clung to the walls, and for a moment, I was transported back to the Palace of Flames, feeling like I was standing in the jungle once again where the air was thick and the heat pressing.

"Ten minutes," Horace barked, then slammed the door shut in our faces.

There were clean clothes left out for Orion, but as usual, there were none for me. Orion had insisted I wear his shirts plenty of times, but the shadows always cast anything I wore to ash after a while, so I refused them now. Besides, they always had green Dragons on them or slogans about how great Lionel was and I didn't want any of that shit touching me. Orion left his shirts off half the time for that very reason.

I waded out into the water and Orion stripped, hiding the book among the folds of his new clothes before stalking me into the water. It was deliciously warm, but the warmth was nothing to the heat I felt in my stomach as Orion hounded after me, naked, with the mist glistening against his bronzed skin.

I moved deeper into the pool until I was almost completely submerged, then slipped under the water and swam around behind him, rising once more. He spun to catch me, the water lapping around his waist, his abs tight, that dark dusting of hair running down below his navel and disappearing beneath the surface of the pool.

I bit my lip, admiring him and feeling the shadows retreating again, able to breathe a little easier as the pressure of them lifted from my chest. For a moment, it was like the Shadow Beast wasn't even here, though there was no touch of magic beneath my skin, and I felt terribly mortal standing in front of him. But at least I was still me.

He moved closer, curling a lock of my shadow-stained hair around his finger, and I looked down, finding it deepest blue once more. My pulse heightened at finding that old piece of me restored by the touch of him. Even if it was temporary.

"There you are," he said, shifting closer still. "The shadows try to hide you from me, but they forget that I'm a Vampire."

"And Vampires are the best at hide and seek," I said through a smile.

"So you were listening," he said.

"I'm a very attentive student." I smirked and he smirked back.

My nipples were still hard and water droplets were running down my naked flesh, his eyes watching the movements of each one, his thirst for me clear.

He moved close enough to make my breaths ragged, and a dagger of heat blazed through my core. He was the beginning and end of me, creation and ruin falling into harmony, and I didn't think a point in time would come when I would be done falling in love with him.

"Count to ten then, and come find me," I said.

His mouth twitched in amusement, and he nodded.

I lifted his hand, covering his eyes. "Don't cheat."

"I don't need to cheat," he said with a low chuckle in his throat that sent another wave of desire through me.

He started counting and I slipped under the water, swimming away across the pool and around the back of the large tree in the middle of it. I opened my eyes and squinted through the water, spotting a hole in the trunk which would allow me to swim into it.

I grinned, kicking hard and pulling myself through it before resurfacing within. I could stand up, the water lapping against my waist and my lips parting at the blue lights dotted here and there inside it, making the water reflect against the bark, rippling and dancing. It was fairly wide, big enough for a few people to stand here if they wanted to.

Orion suddenly surfaced beside me, and I gasped in surprise at how quickly he'd won, his grin saying 'told you so'. He came at me fast, pinning me to the wall and hooking my leg over his hip.

"Hm, this seems familiar..." He glanced around at the rippling light and my cheeks flushed with the memory of him taking me to the bottom of the Acrux pool.

"My memory's foggy, you'll have to remind me," I said breathlessly, and he looked down at me, his eyes shadowed and the devil lurking within them.

"There was a slit in your dress right here." He skimmed his fingers along my thigh the same way he had that night, and a burning trail of fire followed his touch. "And I wanted you as fiercely as I want you now." His mouth skated over mine, teasing me as I tried to lean into the kiss and remember a time when the only danger we'd faced together was being caught doing this.

His fingers slid further up my thigh, and I remembered the moment he'd stopped that night, knowing we couldn't go any further or else we'd change our relationship forever. I should have known then that there was no stopping this. We were two forces destined to unite, and nothing in this universe could have held us back from one another.

"I wanted to do this so fucking bad, Blue." His hand pushed between my legs, and he found me ready for him as his fingers slid into me. "You have no idea how many times I thought of having you like this."

"Did you get off over me?" I panted, clinging to his shoulders as he pumped his hand in a slow movement that sent a fire tumbling through my flesh. His fingers were so thick, driving into me and curling perfectly to caress that sensitive spot inside me. It was heaven and it had barely begun.

"Constantly," he half laughed, half growled then sank his tongue between my lips and kissed me with all the wild passion of the man who had kissed me in that pool. I remembered how forbidden this had been and drew him even closer, bathing in the knowledge that even if all else had fallen apart, we had ended up together when the world had told us we couldn't.

I was already coming undone from his touch, quivering in his arms, my moans turning desperate as he ground the heel of his palm against my clit and drove his fingers deeper inside me. I came hard, my pussy tightening as I gasped into his mouth, an earthquake shuddering down my spine.

"Good girl," he said gruffly, and pleasure skipped faster across my skin, my legs tingling as he hooked them up around his waist. He withdrew a little and fisted the thick length of his cock, teasing me as he drew his hand up and down it, holding me in suspense as he rubbed the tip of it against my sensitive clit.

I squirmed, lifting my hips and raking my nails down the back of his neck. "More," I insisted, and he pressed his tongue into his cheek, clearly enjoying having me at his mercy like this.

"You didn't say please," he said, dragging his cock down to my opening and grinding the tip there without entering me.

I bit my tongue, my stubbornness rising. If he wanted me to beg, then he was going to have to be firmer about it. "Make me."

His Adam's apple bobbed and he raised a hand, wrapping it around my throat and squeezing just tight enough to set my pulse pounding.

"Say it," he growled.

I was so turned on that I was already nodding, giving in to him, and he released my throat to allow me the chance to speak. "Please."

He thrust inside me in the next moment, the full length of him filling me to the brim and making me scream. He groaned in ecstasy, and I shivered in response, the feel of him skin-on-skin, the heat, the water lapping around us, and the masculine sounds falling from his lips driving me wild.

He fucked me deep and slow, our mouths coming together, and our bodies intertwined as we forgot the horrors awaiting us beyond this room and just sank into our love for one another. We kissed between breaths, uniting in a way that transcended all the destruction we'd faced between these walls. It was just us. Two souls who craved one another with all the calamity of a thousand falling stars.

We fucked until we were made new again and I forgot where I ended and he began. I fell apart for him once more, and his muscles tensed around me as he came too, my body gripping his in every way possible as we panted through the aftermath of our release in one another. His eyes burned their way directly to my soul and I didn't blink, not once, drowning in the galaxy of his gaze and the silver rings that branded him as mine.

I didn't want his body to part from me, knowing the moment he retreated, the shadows would return, like winter stealing away the summer. And as Horace started shouting at us to hurry up, I knew our sun was waning again and a frosted moon was rising once more.

After we were returned to our cage, I managed to sleep a little, leaning against Orion's shoulder. When I stirred, I found him with his nose deep in the feather-covered book we'd found in the treasury.

"Did you find anything?" I asked through a yawn, snuggling in closer to him, and his arm curled tighter around me.

He lowered the book to his knee, and I leaned in to see what was on the page.

"It's a history book about the war Queen Avalon waged against the Nymphs," he said, his eyes alight with new knowledge.

"What did you learn?"

"That it was a brutal war. There were nasty crimes on both sides, prisoners mutilated and tortured beyond recognition. This part describes how the Phoenixes would experiment on captured Nymphs to find their weaknesses." He frowned, pushing the book closer to me, and I took in the detailed sketch of a half-dissected Nymph who had a horrid look of pain on its face that said it was alive.

"That's fucked up," I whispered, turning the page, and finding a spell detailed there entitled *The Shadow Bind.*

A spell to bind the shadows within the subject to prevent further summoning.

My heart ticked faster as I imagined doing such a thing to Lavinia, and I read over the spell, falling still in surprise. "Wait a second… I know this cast; Queen Avalon taught it to me and Tory. It's a way to wield Phoenix fire to create an impenetrable barrier. This last bit is different though. I don't recognise it."

"That's dark magic," Orion said, his brows lowering as he placed a finger on the page, pointing to part of the instructions that said a 'blood chant' was needed. "That chant will only work using the blood of someone who chose to die," he said. I read over the chant listed beneath it with a frown.

"Do you think Horace would be game?" I looked up at him with a snigger, and he smirked.

"If I threaten to break every bone in his body before I kill him, I suppose he might go willingly," he mused.

I looked back down at the page, reading through the spell again.

"This spell could bind the shadows within Lavinia," Orion said in realisation. "She wouldn't be able to summon any more to her again. She would only be as powerful as the shadows locked within her. Maybe it would stop her rejuvenating. Maybe she'd be killable."

"But we don't have any of the things we need for it," I said, lifting my fingers and trying to coax Phoenix fire into them, sadness washing over me as nothing happened. "And I don't want anyone to have to die for this. We've lost too many people already."

I snapped the book shut, but as I shifted back onto my knees and met Orion's gaze, I didn't see the same decision in his eyes. I saw him thinking on it, like he was trying to work out a way this could be used.

"No," I said firmly. "No one else dies."

"Don't worry, beautiful. I'm only thinking of ways we might get one of our enemies to die willingly. Just as soon as the curse frees you and your powers and Order return," he said, and I relaxed, though a niggling feeling in my gut still made me uncomfortable about what this spell required to be fulfilled.

A sudden tug in my chest and a summons in my mind made my heart thump erratically. In the next second, my body had turned to smoke and I was tearing through the palace at high speed, away from Orion and towards the monster who owned me.

The Shadow Beast was scratching at the inside of my skin, pain spearing through me as it fought to get out and its unimaginable power seizing me. I fought to keep it at bay, fear flashing in my chest like oil catching light in a too-hot pan, but the Shadow Beast was already winning.

Fresh air surrounded me, and I materialised into the Shadow Beast as I landed at Lavinia's side on a dark hill out in the palace grounds, my four huge paws hitting the dirt and my claws digging into the earth. A roar spilled from my lips and Lavinia whooped, climbing up my shoulder and settling herself on my back, her fingers wrapping tightly in my fur and tugging. I felt a collar tighten around my throat which I hadn't been aware of before now and I was unable to do anything but follow her whims as the shadows guided me forward, down the steep bank towards a thick cluster of trees.

The scent of burning hung in the air and my skin prickled uneasily as we walked into the woods where the glow of a fire burned up ahead. I moved towards it as Lavinia kicked my sides to urge me on, scenting blood and embers on the wind.

"The king needs our assistance. Some of the Tiberian Rats escaped their cages," she whispered, leaning forward to speak in my ear. "He is burning all the ones he finds."

I shuddered in dread and she laughed, willing me on into the darkness between the trees. A spew of Dragon fire to my right made me flinch, and a squeal sounded as a rat fled from Lionel in its shifted form, the little furry white creature darting past us into the dark woodland with its tail smoking.

Pain dashed my heart as Lavinia forced me to take chase after it and I roared, trying to refuse her command but only finding the will of the shadows deepening. I was starting to lose the grip on my mind, and I held on as tight as I could, fearing what atrocities I'd commit if I let go of my consciousness now.

I gritted my teeth, battling the power that was trying to consume me, and managing to stay here.

"Yah!" Lavinia cried, striking me with a whip of shadow, and I growled as my skin split.

The little white rat ran fast, darting beneath logs and weaving left and right past the trees, using its small size to its advantage as I was forced to take a longer path.

"Catch it, cook it, kill it!" Lavinia cried, and another blast of Dragon fire behind us sent a wave of heat washing over me.

I prayed no rats had fallen in those flames, but Lionel's booming roar sounded a victory that made my heart wince.

The little white rat darted into my path again, squeaking in fear and leaping into a hollowed-out log to hide. I skidded to a halt, regaining some of my power over the Shadow Beast and starting to retreat, hoping I could at least give the rat time to run while I held Lavinia back.

Lavinia struck me again and I roared, whipping my head around and aiming for her leg. My teeth sank in deep, and she screamed, her shadow whip flying out and slicing across my cheek. I tried to drag her from my back, not letting go now as I tasted her vile blood on my tongue, but she struck me again and again before crying out a command. "Release me!"

The power in those words had my teeth loosening just long enough for her to get free and snap a muzzle of shadow around my jaws.

She dug her hands deeper into the fur at the back of my neck until she found skin and scratched it open with her nails, shadows pouring from her into me in a wave. The power was unimaginable, and suddenly she had control of me again, forcing me towards the log. My claws tore into it and the little rat squeaked in terror as I broke through the bark and exposed it.

I saw death. Tasted it on my tongue and felt like I was back on that battlefield again, tearing into my allies. Panic swept over me and a tiny spark of fire in my chest made my thoughts sharpen.

No.

I reared up, throwing Lavinia from my back, sending her flying away into the trees, and in the next heartbeat, I regained control on my body and shifted back to my Fae form. The muzzle was still latched tight around my mouth, and the shadows dancing across my skin slithered over the bloody wounds across my thigh and cheek, but I ignored the pain and dropped down to the log, grabbing the rat hiding within it.

It squeaked furiously, biting down on my finger and I cursed. "It's okay. I'm Darcy Vega. I'll protect you."

I held the rat up so it could see my face better and its little eyes widened in recognition. I started running, darting off into the trees and letting the shadows spill from my body so they clouded us in darkness.

A huge green Dragon swept overhead, and I tucked myself close to a tree to keep out of Lionel's sight.

"Get back here, beastie!" Lavinia crowed. "That fall broke my neck, you little witch. Maybe I'll break your dear lover's neck tonight and make you watch while the bones go pop, pop, crack."

I snarled at those words, taking off again and running through the trees, looking out for any more rats hiding in the undergrowth. There was nothing but embers out here, trees turned to ash and the ground hot beneath my feet. I kept moving, unsure where I was going, only that I would find a way to get this Fae to safety.

A violent tug in my chest made me stop in my tracks and I gasped, feeling the summons coming from Lavinia as it tore through me. I clenched my teeth, desperate to fight it, the Shadow Beast in me bellowing to answer its call.

"No," I hissed in refusal, forcing one foot to move forward, then the next.

My mind felt like it was being cleaved in two as I refused that all-powerful magic which bound me to Lavinia, and I was breathless from the small progress I'd made in moving away from her.

The rat squeaked, whiskers twitching and its little face nuzzling into my hand in encouragement for me to run. I hissed a stream of curses, continuing fight my way forward. The summoning spell snapped like a knife being torn free of my chest and I gasped, stumbling and falling into a flat-out run once more.

I made it to the edge of the woodland, spotting Lionel turning for the palace in the night sky, landing on the roof of one of the towers and roaring his victory to the sky.

"Dead, dead, dead, all the little rattys turned to dust," Lavinia sang somewhere that was far too close to me.

I sprinted on, breaking out of the trees, and pulling the shadows closer to me as I ran for the palace, having nowhere else to go. I couldn't get the rat beyond the wards, and the only place I could think to hide it was back in the throne room.

"Darcy Vega!" Lavinia hollered. "Come to me!"

The summons was easier to shake off this time, like the first tie I'd broken had been the deepest, and I was able to keep running through the pain of defying her.

I made it to a servants' entrance, pushing my way inside and running through the twisting hallways. I wasn't far from the throne room now, and I knew Lavinia was close on my heels, so I ran with every ounce of energy in my veins, clutching onto the rat and hating that I hadn't been able to save anyone else.

I made it to the throne room, shouldering the door open and sprinting bare foot towards the cage.

"Darcy," Orion gasped, already on his feet and looking panicked. "You're hurt."

I didn't answer, running to the edge of the cage and shoving the rat into Orion's hands. I willed my body to turn to smoke, somehow managing it and rematerializing within the bars. In the next breath, I was at the wall, opening the secret passage and grabbing the rat before tossing him inside, and it squeaked in surprise.

"You'll be safe in there," I promised it, sealing the passageway again as quickly as I could.

The moment the door was closed, Orion had his hands on me, looking at my wounds.

"It's nothing," I panted.

"You're muzzled like a dog and bleeding," he snapped, anguish flaring in his eyes. "That's not nothing, Blue!"

The doors flew open, shadows pouring out around Lavinia as she stalked towards us, venomous anger bleeding from her.

"Out," she barked, casting a whip of shadow that unlocked the door and wrenched it wide. It coiled around my throat next, dragging me out of the cage and sending me flying to the floor. More shadows wrapped around me, binding and binding until I was immobilised at her feet, but she didn't look at me as she passed by. Her eyes were on Orion.

"Get away from him!" I screamed, but I couldn't get free of the power she had me tethered in. My arms were lashed tight to my sides, and as she took hold of Orion and drew him away towards that awful room where I'd had to watch him suffer over and over, my screams grew to pitchy, desperate pleas.

The walls shuddered as if the palace could feel my pain, and the bricks themselves groaned as Lavinia dragged me after them into that nightmarish place to watch my mate bleed once more.

Scorpio
Gemini
Virgo
Cancer
Leo
Sagittarius
Capricorn
Aquarius
Libra
Pisces

ORION

CHAPTER THIRTY FOUR

My mind was hollow and dark, all good thoughts lost to a river of blackness that washed them away to an even blacker sea. I was a man adrift, searching for something I couldn't find in this colourless land of desolation.

If only I could find it, I knew I would see the sun again, it would break through the impenetrable clouds above and I'd remember what I was seeking at last.

I blinked, half here, half not here.

The shadows were calling, and they played with my soul, tossing it between them and taking bites out of it. If only I could remember why I should fight to reclaim it from these demons…

A hand was on my cheek and someone spoke a name, my name perhaps, though it didn't seem to fit me.

Orion was a hunter, but that couldn't be me. I was a fallen creature, destroyed by the dark. Hunters didn't die in the dark, they thrived in it. So, who were they talking to?

She moved into view, a beautiful girl with shadow-filled hair that moved as if caught in a wind. Her skin was deepest bronze, like the sun had left its warmth inside it, and my fingers twitched with the urge to touch her and find out if she could steal away this cold in me. I was made of ice, built of it vein by vein, a statue of frost coming to life, or perhaps it was the other way around. A man turning to stone.

"Lance Orion," the girl said in a tone full of fire. She was as warm as I'd hoped, her fingers brushing my temple next and sparking a small flame within the frozen wasteland of my chest.

"Come back to me," she commanded, her eyes full of tears she didn't let fall, and I could have sworn silver glinted out at me from within two pools of green. "You're stronger than the darkness she put in you. Come back and stay with me. This is where you're meant to be."

She leaned closer still, blinking so that those tears fell, and her eyes weren't green or silver or any colour at all. They were as black as the vast emptiness in me.

My eyes slipped closed, and I was lost once more, falling, falling, falling, on and on into an abyss that had no end. It was feasting on me, tearing great chunks off with its teeth and I had no mind to stop it. For what was there here except something I had forgotten to seek?

Lost… I was lost. And all the parts of me were scattering to a violent breeze. My name had been the first to go, but there was something more important than my name holding a few pieces of me together.

The girl.

Yes, that was it. The girl was important. She was the centre of the universe, a goddess who ruled me, and I gladly submitted to that rule. She was fury and light and a taste so sweet I would never forget it.

"Blue," I whispered, or maybe I only said it in my mind. I remembered now. It was her I sought, always her. We had promised never to part, and I couldn't break that promise. Even if I did turn to stone, I would find a way to walk, to follow her wherever she may go.

"Yes," she croaked, somewhere close and far away.

I felt her crawling into my lap, and my heavy eyelids found a way to open once more. She curled against me, kissing me softly, her tears making my heart heavy.

"Don't cry," I breathed, her pain the worst kind of curse to bear. "Don't shed tears for a man made of stone."

"You're not made of stone," she said, kissing me again. "You have a beating heart, and it loves me, remember?" She lifted my palm, pressing it to my chest, and sure enough, I found a heart there, beating slow but hard.

"Of course it loves you," I said. "How could it not?"

"If you love me then you'll snap out of this. You'll fight the shadows off," she demanded.

I nodded, because there was no option but to fight. I would always do so for her. But then my chin hit my chest and my eyes fell closed, the darkness rolling in once more.

It was deeper now, thicker, tainted by the memories of what had placed these shadows here. Weapons designed to drive them deep under my flesh, blades that cut through sinew and muscle, all those sharp edges wet with my blood.

Failure closed in on me, though I couldn't remember the rhyme or reason for it. I'd made a promise once, and this was where it had come to die, cast to ruin in this prison of my own destruction.

I knew I was letting her down, but then again, I couldn't quite remember who 'she' was. The cracks were forming, splintering through me like a lightning bolt had struck me in the centre. I'd fracture first, then I'd fall, all the pieces lost and impossible to put back together. If only I could find her one more time before I was lost forever…

A hand, warm and familiar, latched tightly around mine. It was pulling on something deep within me, yanking on those shadows which danced around inside me like gremlins. Magic was passing between this person and I, dragging out that darkness, siphoning it from me as a low chant brushed my ears.

It took and took, all the shards of my shattered self somehow finding their way back together, and my first coherent thought was of her. The girl I was here for. But beyond her and all the love I held in my being for that creature of fire and light, there was a cold, bitter reality awaiting me. A world where a curse gripped my mate, where I had made a vow with a monster, and where my best friend lay dead. It was an unbearable world in so many ways, but so long as she remained in it, it was where I would stay too.

I found her in my arms, her face buried against my neck and her sweet strawberry scent making it easier for my lungs to work.

I pulled my hand from the grip of the woman who had brought me back to her, ignoring Stella and hugging Darcy tight.

"I'm sorry," I whispered. "I won't leave again."

"You said that last time," she croaked.

"I'll do better."

"It's not your fault," she said. "I wish I could protect you."

Darcy clung to me like she was afraid I'd vanish again, and guilt split my heart open.

I looked to Stella, finding her hurriedly wiping tears from under her eyes as she sat just beyond the cage.

"Why?" I murmured, not understanding why she kept trying to offer me anything. Out of guilt perhaps. But not love. She wasn't capable of an emotion that pure.

"Because you are my son," she said thickly, then she rose to her feet and walked away, leaving us here alone, tangled in each other's arms.

Darcy peeked up at me through reddened eyes and I kissed her forehead, my love for her blazing through me. How had the shadows almost stolen her from me?

What would have become of me if Stella hadn't brought me back from the dark once again? Would I really forget my mate? Would I be lost within this body, my soul taken by the shadows and turned to dust?

If the shadows consumed the parts of me that made me who I was, then I would never return to her in this life or the next. I'd have no soul that could pass beyond the Veil. I'd be nothing, no one. Lost.

I held Darcy tighter, the terror of that reality more horrifying than any death that could be bestowed on me. Was this going to ultimately be the price for breaking Darcy's curse?

Lavinia was still working within the boundaries of our deal, so it wasn't like she would die so long as I remained breathing when the three moon cycles were up. But my soul…I'd never bargained for my soul.

I didn't voice any of this to Darcy, knowing it would only scare her, but it did put me in a predicament. I needed Stella to keep coming to me after Lavinia's torture, because if she didn't, I was fucked. I'd barely come back this time even with her help, and if another few hours had passed, perhaps I would have succumbed to the dark, my soul ravaged beyond repair.

I breathed in the scent of my girl, holding her and praying to the stars that they'd let us get through this intact.

A scratching noise came beyond the wall at my back and Darcy shifted out of my lap while I scooted aside to let her open the secret door. The wall parted at her touch and the white rat she'd rescued peered out at us as it sat up on its hind legs. It had two tiny magic blocking cuffs on its wrists, the things enchanted to shift to whatever size a Fae took in their Order form.

"Hello," Darcy whispered. "Are you alright?"

The rat nodded, then scurried back a little and shifted into his Fae form. A slim, incredibly pale man sat before us with a shock of white hair spilling into his bright eyes, and I recognised him as one of Gabriel's friends from Aurora Academy. The last time we'd seen him, he'd been working underground at the Library of the Lost.

"Eugene," Darcy gasped.

"H-hi," he stammered, pulling his knees to his chest in some attempt to cover his nudity. "Thank you for what you did."

He gazed at Darcy with a gleam in his eyes.

"It's nothing," she said. "I'm just sorry I couldn't help any of the others. Were they your friends?"

"I didn't know them," he said sadly, hanging his head. "I was caught last week meeting with some Sphinxes in Tucana to collect some rare books from them for the library. An FIB unit rounded us all up and brought us here. I was forced to shift into my Rat form and put in a tiny cage alongside all the other Rats down in Vard's awful, awful laboratory. They kept us injected with some serum that made us unable to shift back to our Fae form."

"How did you get out?" I asked.

"There was a big kafuffle down there earlier tonight; a Pegasus got free, and when he shifted, he kicked our cages and a bunch of them broke open. We got out through the pipes, but then, then…" He swallowed thickly. "Lionel came after us."

"Did you manage to see what Vard is doing down there?" I asked.

"He…" Eugene blanched, somehow turning even paler as he glanced around the empty throne room beyond us then lowered his voice as he went on. "We weren't kept close enough to see much. But I heard the screams, so many screams. He's experimenting on the Fae who are being kept down there."

"Experimenting how?" I asked, my gut twisting at the thought of our people enduring Vard's fucked up experiments somewhere close by.

"I may not have been able to see much, but I paid attention to them talking, listening to every word, every scream." Eugene swallowed thickly but went on. "He has been doing multiple experiments on Order shifting – both extracting the essence of a Fae's inherent Order form and then transplanting that intrinsic part of their being into another."

"You mean he's trying to change people's Orders?" Darcy asked, her face crumpled with horror at the idea. "But how can he do that? How could he possibly take something so vital from someone and shift it from body to body like it's nothing more than an interchangeable kidney?"

"There is a magical well deep within the chest of all Fae which resides right beside our hearts," I murmured, old biology lessons playing through my mind as I thought back on them. "You can feel it sometimes; when your Order form is dormant within you, and when you sense it awakening and yearning to get free."

"You mean the urge to shift?" she breathed, and I nodded.

"That chamber exists inside each of us, but it isn't some organ that can simply be transplanted, its woven into the very fabric of our beings. It's a vital part of us, linked to our souls themselves, and when we die, it fades away as our Order form goes with us, following us beyond the Veil."

"Which is why Vard cuts it out of Fae while they are still living," Eugene said darkly. "While their Order form is held within that chamber with the use of Order suppressant and their Fae bodies are bound to the table he dissects them on. So far as I have heard, no one has survived more than a few minutes with their Order form removed, nor after having a foreign Order form inserted into them. But he is voracious in his determination to make it work. He won't stop. And the false king has visited to inspect his progress enough times to let me know that he's keen for the experiments to succeed too."

I shuddered at the thought of that. "No doubt he plans to force all Fae to become the Orders he's deemed most worthy in his plans to eradicate those he's named lesser," I growled, and Darcy gripped my hand tightly in defiance of that.

"He also seems keen to see if Fae can survive without any Order form at all, and I fear…" Eugene shook his head, his arms curling tighter around his knees like he was trying to hide himself from the truth.

"What is it?" Darcy urged kindly, prompting him to go on.

"I fear that he plans to do that to the lessers. If he can find a way for us to survive the procedure, then he can simply cut our Order forms out of our bodies, remove them entirely and end the problem he has perceived with those of us he doesn't favour."

"That's…surely he can't be planning something so awful?" Darcy gasped, though the dark look I exchanged with her let me know that she knew that Lionel would do just that if he could, tyrannical son of a bitch that he was.

"You said Vard was doing multiple experiments?" I asked, my gaze fixed on Eugene's pale face and he nodded slowly.

"It was hard to glean precisely what the other work he was doing entailed, but… there were such screams coming from those subjects. Screams that went far beyond terror and agony and became something *else*."

"Was he torturing them?" Darcy asked but Eugene shook his head.

"I heard him saying that he was making them into something more than they were. There was talk of genetic engineering and using the DNA from creatures of the wilds to help create new soldiers for his army. Whatever he was doing to those Fae, I don't think they are themselves anymore. I think he was taking the essence of who they'd once been and stretching them into some new and awful mould. They were begging for death before their cries turned to roars…I think he was having more success with whatever he was doing to them too."

"By the stars," I breathed, scoring a hand over my face as I took in the atrocities that Lionel was participating in already. What fresh hell might he accomplish if he won this war and managed to maintain his rule over Solaria indefinitely? The thought alone was enough to make bile rise in my throat.

"We'll get you out of here," Darcy promised. "Maybe you could escape through the pipes again when it's safe to try."

Eugene shook his head. "Lavinia was taunting us all in the woods before you got there. She said the pipes are full of shadow now, that there's no way back in and no way out."

"We'll find a way. And we'll keep you hidden until then," Darcy swore.

"Thank you," Eugene squeaked. "And I hope you don't mind, but I made a little nest out of your things." He pointed to the book, the Guild Stone, and a few strips of an old 'Long Live Lionel Acrux' t-shirt I'd had half whipped off of me by Lavinia which must have ended up in there somehow. "I'll keep your treasures nice and safe. You can count on me."

He shifted back into a rat and jumped on top of the items, sitting there vigilantly, and I glanced at Darcy as she slid the door shut.

"How did you get him away from Lionel and Lavinia?" I asked.

"I fought off Lavinia's summons," she revealed, and my heart ticked faster.

"You did?" I asked hopefully, taking her hand, and pulling her closer.

She smiled as she nodded. "And I think I can do it again."

"You will do it again. And again, and again, and a-fucking-gain." I kissed her hard and she laughed, the sound so damn rare these days that it almost hurt to hear it. "Now we just need your Phoenix to wake the fuck up." I pressed my face against her chest. "Get out here, you little shit."

"Why don't you try one of your motivational quotes of the day on it?" Darcy teased.

"You're a useless bird that couldn't light a match, let alone start a forest fire," I growled, jabbing her in the side, and she laughed again. "Your Phoenix is almost as stubborn a student as you were."

"Hey, I was a delight to teach," she said with a grin.

"You were a delight to punish," I corrected darkly, and she bit down on her full bottom lip.

"A delight's still a delight," she said airily, and I laughed, dragging her down into my lap and nipping at her throat.

"Bite me like you mean it," she encouraged breathily.

"Only because I want to taste that fire in you," I said against her skin before releasing my fangs and sinking them into her. And there it was, her power deep and hidden away but still burning.

My queen's fight wasn't over yet.

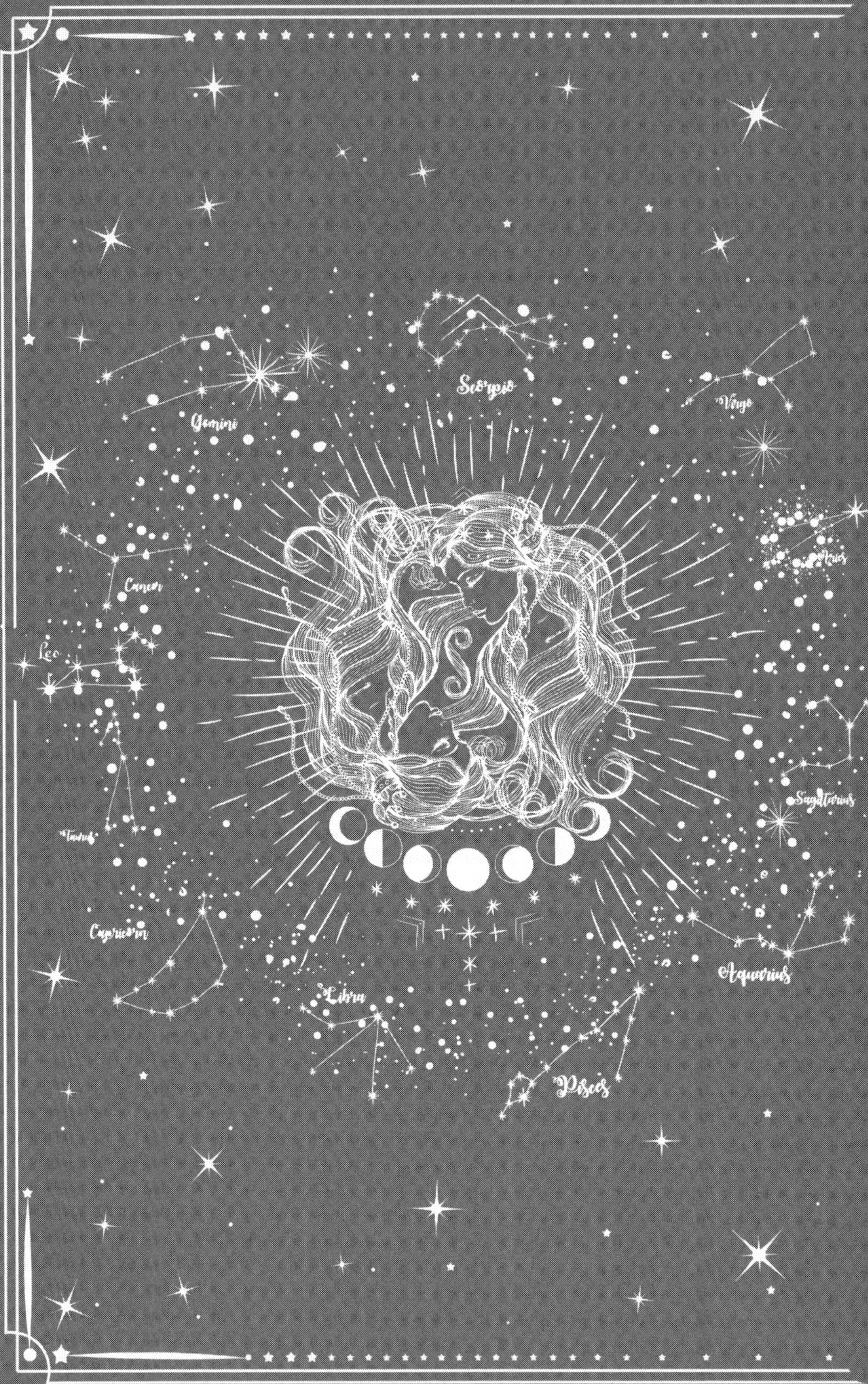
Scorpio
Virgo
Gemini
Aries
Leo
Sagittarius
Taurus
Capricorn
Aquarius
Libra
Pisces

TORY

CHAPTER THIRTY FIVE

Knowing that Darcy was being held in The Palace of Souls was a special kind of torture designed entirely to destroy me through fear alone. I'd lived that horror, had endured Lionel's cruelty and depravity first hand for months. He'd stripped away the things that made me myself, coated me in an armour forged of lies, terror, and false devotion.

I'd survived it. But barely. And now I had to force myself to remain here, doing absolutely nothing for days on end while we waited for the day of the fucking Hydrids meteor shower.

It was killing me. Causing actual agony within my soul, knowing that three of the people I cared most about in this miserable world were stuck with those monsters. And to make it worse, I had to force myself not to plan any kind of rescue attempt or attack on them in any kind of detail for fear of that decision being *seen.*

I tossed the blankets off of myself and got out of bed. Dawn was glimmering on the distant horizon, but the world was mostly dark and restful.

I needed to do something. And seeing as that something couldn't be the thing that had kept me tossing and turning all night, I was going to pour my restless energy into another task that could help us.

I strode into the closet and reached for a pair of leggings, hesitating as I noticed the latest ridiculously over-the-top gown Geraldine had acquired for me. From what she'd told me, there were some seriously gifted earth Elementals who had been dedicating their spare time to creating gowns for the true queens, and as I stared at the black dress which seemed to be sewn from an image of the night sky itself, I couldn't help but reach out to run my fingers over the fabric.

I didn't give much of a shit about pomp and festivity, of looking the part of a queen and playing at the politics involved in winning public affection, but I did understand the need for it. I could understand the power of symbolism clearly enough, and where I was going, that was likely to be exactly what I needed.

As I moved my hand over the fabric, I watched the way the tiny silver gems sewn into it caught the faint light as if they really were stars glimmering through a midnight of solace.

It was bullshit, but it was powerful bullshit.

With a sigh, I stripped out of the oversized shirt I'd been sleeping in and changed into the gown. The black fabric was as soft as silk, clinging to my torso while leaving my back bare for my wings. There were slits up either side of the floor length skirt, making it easy to move in, as well as comfortable. I ran my hands over the sides of it, my lips lifting as I found several hidden pockets before realising the way that it had been cinched in at my waist left a perfect space for me to hang my sword scabbard without it bunching the material and ruining the look of the gown. This wasn't just some fluff piece for public appearances; it was a dress made specifically for a warrior queen, and if I really was going to consider donning a crown at the end of all of this, then I was damn certain that was the only kind of queen I would consider becoming.

I strapped my scabbard into place, taking a pouch of stardust from the stash I kept close at all times, dropping it into one of the concealed pockets, followed by a wicked little dagger that I'd grown fond of, then I pulled on a pair of boots.

I stopped before the mirror and used a mixture of water and air magic to wash and style my hair so that it fell in an inky waterfall of loose curls, then forced myself to paint my face. This meeting mattered, which meant my recent lack of personal care had to be shoved aside. I wasn't dressing myself for vanity or any kind of self-healing – this was war. And it was time I stepped up and started playing my part in it.

With my eyes lined in kohl and my lips deepest red, I almost looked like my old self again, just a girl in a pretty dress…with a sword and a scowl sharp enough to cut flesh and bone.

"You lied to me," I said to my own reflection, though the words were intended for him. "You promised you'd stay."

Nothing.

Endless, hopeless, nothing. Even the ruby pendant which hung from my throat remained cool against my skin, like he was further away than ever today. I didn't know if that was a good thing or a bad one, but it didn't help with the desperate loneliness which was working to swallow me whole.

I blinked at my reflection just to prove to myself that I was still alive, despite the unnatural stillness that had fallen over me.

I was going to break soon. My walls were growing weaker and weaker, so tenuous that I knew I couldn't maintain them much longer. But not today. Not now.

I turned for the door but paused as I spotted a glimmering tiara peeking out from amongst the heap of Darius's treasure beside it. I plucked it from the pile and turned it over in my hands.

"You also swore you'd never see me as your queen," I murmured to the man who wasn't here. "So I'm willing to bet that this will make you all kinds of pissed."

I placed the glittering silver and blue tiara on my head and smirked in that obnoxious way which had never once failed to get a rise out of him as I felt a prickle of something stirring in the air, the ghost of a memory trailing down my spine like fingertips.

It wasn't real. But oh, how I wished it was.

I closed my eyes as I tried to summon him closer, tried to believe he was really there with me for just a few seconds. But even as I attempted it, the imagined sensation faded away, the wind as still as it had been the entire time, and my heart just as irrevocably fractured as it had been since I'd found his body on that hilltop.

I snatched the Book of Ether into my grasp and strode from the room without another moment spent lingering in the company of no one, taking the steps two at a time and barely even acknowledging the guards who had been posted at the foot of the stairs leading to my chambers.

They scrambled to bow at my unexpected appearance, but I simply told them not to tell anyone that they'd seen me until they came looking. I may have disliked the way people bowed and scraped for me now, but I had learned one vitally useful piece of information about the Fae who did; they would not disobey an order from one of their queens. Which meant that I was safe from discovery unless Geraldine decided on a four AM check in.

Thinking about that made me realise it wasn't at all unlikely, and I hurried my pace as I jogged down the next set of stairs and out of the doors, crossing the drawbridge and repeating my orders to anyone who noticed me.

The moment I was clear of the palace, I shifted, keeping my flames extinguished and simply drawing my bronze wings from my spine so that I could cover the distance I needed to more swiftly.

I beat my wings hard, speeding across the island terrain and spotting the jail within a few minutes before hurtling from the sky and landing heavily right in front of the guards on duty there.

All five of them had weapons drawn and magic igniting in their hands in a heartbeat, a fireball crashing into my air shield as I managed to throw it up with less than a second to spare.

"Probably should have announced myself," I said in apology as they recognised me and the man who had thrown the fire dropped to the floor with a wail of horror.

"Forgive me, my Queen!" he begged. "Sever my useless head from my neck. Remove my entrails and use them to spell out a curse upon my entire family. Take my eyes and feed them to any rodent you so desire. Chop up my-"

"Ew. Dude, stop," I said, wrinkling my nose at those suggestions. "You did good. You were protecting the realm and all that jazz. I just need to have a word with the prisoner, though, so no harm done. But can I grab the keys to his cell?"

The man gaped at me, then began sobbing about my magnanimous nature and the kindness my forgiveness had bestowed upon his family.

I tried to block him out as I held out a hand for the keys, but it was made harder as he crawled across the ground on his belly like a worm and started trying to kiss my boots.

"Stars take me now," I groaned as my discomfort grew and one of the other guards finally managed to snap themselves out of their shocked state and hand me the keys.

I nodded in thanks and hurried away from the weeping guard, pretending not to notice as he started licking the grass where I'd been standing while claiming it was blessed by the press of my boots.

"No wonder you were such an arrogant ass, if Fae treated you like that your whole life," I muttered to Darius, but once again, there was no kind of response.

I moved through the squat jail building which housed the huge night iron cage where Miguel was still being held, finding him sitting up in his bed, his posture stiff as he no doubt tried to figure out what all the crying was about.

"Have you thought about what I said to you?" I asked him, cutting past any niceties and bullshit. "Would your people consider an alliance?"

"Perhaps," Miguel said slowly, rising to his feet as he took me in in all my royal grandness. His eyes widened a little as if he was just now seeing me for what I could be, and I raised my chin.

"But it's all about trust, right? Our kind and yours have been at war for so long that it's hard for you to imagine the Fae not turning on you. While in turn, it will no doubt be hard for the Fae to trust that none of you will shift and try to stab us through the heart with your probey fingers."

Miguel snorted humourlessly, nodding. "It is hard to imagine any future where both kinds could fully cast aside those fears and prejudices."

"Yet you told me there are some Fae living among you who had accepted exactly that," I pressed.

"There are a few." He nodded thoughtfully. "But their entrance into our communities were mostly through a mixture of desperate circumstances. They are the kinds of Fae who found themselves needing escape from their previous lives enough to risk a little trust. Besides, convincing one or two through acts of continual humanity and kindness is different to convincing an entire Fae race through words alone."

"If you fought with us in the war, I'd say that would be action enough to prove your intentions to a lot of them," I countered.

"Perhaps. But others would still just think we were only doing so to meet our own ends, expecting us to turn on you once it was done."

I nodded, understanding that fear.

"Do you wish to remain hidden forever then? Ignoring the pain of the world beyond your little secret sanctuary?" I asked, and Miguel bristled.

"I was dragged from that sanctuary years ago by people who claimed to be my own kind. They trapped my soul and used my power to their own ends, then killed my child, my sweet Diego, without ever once allowing me to love him as I should have. It is hard to ignore such strikes against me."

"Personally, yes. But I'm not looking for one Nymph to come fight on our side. I'll level with you: we need more allies. We need more Fae to rebel against Lionel and Lavinia's tyranny, but we need more than that. I won't fight in another losing battle again. I won't watch the Fae who have placed their hope and trust in me and my sister be slaughtered because we hoped for the best. We need as much strength as we can acquire. We need allies. Or at the very least, I need help with this." I held out the Book of Ether for him to look at, and Miguel's eyes darkened as he took in the carvings on the cover.

"You still wish to find someone who can govern you in the old ways?" he asked, stepping closer. "You do understand the dangers of such power, don't you?"

"I wish for all kinds of dangerous things, all kinds of regularly," I replied with a shrug, withdrawing the book and holding up the key to his cell instead. "I'm thinking we could take part in a trust exercise," I said, shaking the key in temptation and watching as his eyes tracked the movement.

"What kind of exercise?" Miguel asked cautiously.

"I'll let you out of your cage, and you'll take me to this secret village or whatever the fuck it is. You can toss the stardust and I'll even close my eyes, if that helps – point being that I'll have no fucking idea where you've taken me, so I won't be able to give up your secret."

"Once you have travelled there by stardust and seen it for yourself, you would be able to do so again. It wouldn't matter whether you knew where it was on a map or not."

I sighed, trying to figure out how I could alleviate his concerns on that before offering him my hand.

"I'll swear on the stars not to do that," I said, though if he knew of my contempt for the glittery assholes in the sky above, he might have realised how thinly I would hold to any word made in their honour. But that didn't matter because I had no plans to break this promise. I wasn't going to lead a genocide into the heart of a peaceful settlement. No part of me would ever be capable of that.

Miguel reached for my hand, and I gave him the vow he wanted, a clap of magic passing between us as the deal was struck.

"So, if I am trusting you with the fate of my people, what exactly are you trusting me with?" he asked curiously as I released him.

"Simple. You get me, all alone in a village full of Nymphs. I'd say that's pretty damn trusting considering the power you're capable of wielding over my magic. I might be one powerful bitch, but I doubt I could fight my way free of an entire village if you all turned your rattles on me at once. So you'll have a Solarian princess at your mercy for the entirety of our little excursion without a single other soul around to protect me. I'd say that if I return from a place like that without having had anyone attempt to stab their little probes through my heart, then we will be making some big steps towards trust between our peoples."

"Our probes aren't little," Miguel muttered like a dude who had just had his manhood insulted, and a I grinned at him in challenge.

"Maybe you can prove that on the battlefield beside me one day."

Miguel grinned at that visual too, and I already knew his answer before he nodded. "Okay then, Roxanya Vega, I think we have a deal."

Those words were all I needed to move into action, and I quickly unlocked his cage, letting the door swing wide as I gestured for him to leave the confines of it, a free man, no longer a prisoner of war or anything of the like. The ex-Councillors were going to throw a fit when they realised that. Oh well.

The two of us headed outside, finding the guards still there, all of them gaping in alarm at the sight of the Nymph walking mere inches from their princess.

"Miguel is no longer being held captive," I told them firmly. "So there is no need for you to guard an empty cell. Go...eat some bagels or whatever. And when Geraldine starts freaking out over my little adventure, tell her I'll be back in time for dinner."

I took the pouch of stardust from my pocket and tossed it to Miguel without waiting for them to reply, turning my own magic on the wards which protected the island from the use of stardust, before cracking them open just enough to let us through. Miguel didn't hesitate as he drew a pinch of the glimmering substance out and tossed it over our heads, then we were whipped away from the shocked guards so fast that I didn't even see them disappear.

The stars spat us out in the heart of a forest, the trees dense and the canopy thick above, blotting out all signs of the sky.

I raised a hand to cast a Faelight, but Miguel caught my wrist with a shake of his head.

"If they realise a Fae is close, then they will hide so absolutely that we may never find them at all," he warned. "You'll need to follow me until we reach the High Nymph's seat."

"Is that like a Nymph queen?" I asked as I gave in and released the magic I'd been drawing on without casting a single thing.

"Our leaders are more like shamans than monarchs," he replied. "The wisest of our kind, rose to their positions by proving themselves worthiest of the role. I was once counted among them too. But that was a long, long time ago."

"Before you were forced to leave?" I questioned, and he nodded solemnly. "Have you been back here since then?"

"No."

Miguel raised his hands and began moving them in an unfamiliar pattern, his fingers shifting as he did so, becoming the probes of his kind. I forced myself to remain where I was, not retreating from the things which could oh-so-easily pierce my heart and rip my magic and life right out of me. Instead, I watched as he began to pluck at the air as if playing it like a musical instrument, a hum building around us as a soft mist began to grow from nothing at all, the colour of it paling as he played on until it was finally bright enough to give off a silver glow.

"This is how my kind lights the way," he said, a soft reverence to his voice which made me think that the shadows he'd just called on were entirely different to those Lavinia had claimed for her own.

Miguel's hands shifted back into normal fingers, and I gave myself a mental high five for neither flinching nor recoiling throughout that entire process.

The pale mist hung in the air above us, illuminating an almost invisible track through the trees, and I fell into step with Miguel as he began to follow it.

"Do you have family here?" I asked softly, and Miguel sighed, nodding slowly.

"I had a wife and three daughters," he admitted. "My children were so small when I was taken from here, I don't suppose I will even recognise them now." His voice was a hopeless, broken thing, and I realised that he had lost as much to this war as any of us. "I never loved anyone aside from my Octania," he added. "But I don't expect her to have waited for me. They will have known, even if they understood that I was unwilling, they would have known where I was and what I had become. She will have found out that I was married to another, that I fathered a child who wasn't hers..."

"Fuck," I said, because really, what else was there to say to that? He'd had his entire life stolen from him, had been forced to marry someone he hadn't wanted, had been enslaved to the point of fathering a child with her. I knew the shadows had taken him captive, but I was only just realising how deeply they must have delved into him to have stripped away an entire life and left him pliant to the whims of those monsters who had chained him.

"The willow," he said suddenly, and I had no idea why he was pointing out a random tree until I turned my gaze in the direction he'd indicated and saw it for myself.

The tree was enormous, its fronds a delicate, impossibly thick shield which hid its trunk from view altogether. Glowing blue and green Faeflies drifted lazily around it, and the scent of pine and snow brushed against my senses as I felt myself fall prey to its spell of beauty.

We moved towards it on silent feet, the trees shifting in a breeze I couldn't feel as if they were turning to watch our progress, and the hairs along the back of my neck stood on end.

The rustling grew and the fronds of the willow suddenly parted, a pale grey light blinding me as it was revealed within.

I lifted a hand to shield my eyes, squinting between my fingers as I continued to move across the fallen leaves, the soft crunch of my footfalls the only confirmation that I was still moving at all as I lost all sense of myself, only able to focus on that light.

"You must give in to the call of it," Miguel said from somewhere both far away and close at once.

"The call of what?" I breathed, but he didn't need to answer, the tug on my soul making it clear what he meant.

It was a similar sensation to when I had soul-walked to locate Darcy, this otherness to it, like all of me and none of me was in motion. But this time, I didn't leave the confines of my flesh, there was no rush of adrenaline followed by an escape of the purest kind, my connection to my body remained, my legs moving to the call of power, and as much as it should have terrified me, I simply gave in.

The grey light brightened and brightened as we moved into it until we were consumed entirely, devoured by it and taken somewhere at once away from where we'd been and yet somehow it appeared as though it had been in plain sight at the same time, hidden from us until now.

I blinked through the fingers of my still outstretched hand as I settled back into my body again, a hush falling all around us, though I could feel many eyes turned our way.

I dropped my hand and swallowed a lump in my throat as I looked at the crowd that had gathered, at least fifty Nymphs both in humanoid and shifted form, their attention fully on us, some with weapons in hand while others pointed their gnarly probes at our hearts. They wore simple clothing, their cloaks and shawls all in neutral colours and designed to keep the cold out.

"I guess they weren't expecting us then," I hissed to Miguel who took a step forward to place himself between me and the Nymphs who were starting to focus their attention my way, a few soft rattles breaking the silence as they tasted the strength of my power.

Oh yeah, this was a great idea, I just got myself all dressed up like a tasty Nymph party snack, then snuck off in the middle of the night without telling anyone where I was going on the word of a man whose mother-in-law knitted herself into a fucking hat. What the hell had I been thinking? I was like…seventy-six percent dead. Fact.

"Miguel?" a woman at the rear of the crowd asked in astonishment.

Suddenly, the weight of all those stares were turning from me to him, murmurs breaking out as they recognised him and got over the shock of our appearance.

"I have so much to tell all of you about the last twenty years," Miguel said, opening his hands before him in a gesture of peace. "So many, many things that la Princesa de las Sombras has been doing in her bid for dominion over the shadows. Of the things I was forced to do as her prisoner." His voice broke with what was undoubtedly shame.

I stepped to his side, placing a hand on his shoulder in solidarity.

"Don't blame him for the hell he endured while he was gone from this place," I said firmly, knowing all too well what it felt like to be forced under the control of someone you hated. And I'd endured a far shorter span of it than he had. "He's free again now. And he has used that freedom to try and fight back, as well as to find me and bring me here. Do you know who I am?"

"You're a Savage Princess," an elderly woman muttered, spitting in the dirt by her feet, and I fought the urge to scowl at her. "Your father hunted our kind without mercy during his reign. And his father before that."

"And many of your kind have hunted Fae, butchering them for their power without discriminating between man, woman, or child," I replied evenly. "Yet Miguel swore to me that you here are not like those monsters. And I was hoping you might do me the courtesy of not judging me by my father's reputation any more than I have judged your entire race by the actions of those corrupted by the shadows."

More murmuring broke out in the crowd, and I waited, eyeing them cautiously without calling on my own magic. I didn't need to be a Siren to tell they were filled with fear by my arrival in their sanctuary.

"Look, I didn't come here to cause trouble. Miguel told me that we have an enemy in common, and after some convincing, I found that I believe him. And I think you all know what they say about the enemy of my enemy?" The corner of my lips twitched at the thought of heading into battle with a Nymph army of our own, seeing the looking on Lionel and Lavinia's faces when they found out that they weren't the only ones with tricks up their sleeves.

"Why should we trust a single thing that comes out of the mouth of a Fae?" a large man growled, his lips peeling back in distaste.

"I'm showing you a level of trust by coming here, aren't I? Alone, vulnerable. Some might think that would earn me a little respect, if nothing else."

"Respect?" the man scoffed, and I gave him a shrug.

"Well, if not that, then at least it has offered me this audience with all of you."

"An audience with a girl playing queen, how very thrilling," a woman drawled, and I barked a laugh as she continued. "Lionel Acrux has made an alliance with some of our kind and offered them more than the Savage King ever did. And there are more than a few of us here who want to see how that plays out."

"I am playing," I agreed with her. "I'm playing a game of cat and mouse with the biggest, scaliest cat you've ever seen. He's one mean son of a bitch who likes to hunt those smaller than him for fun and watch them scream before he devours them whole. For now, the false king has allied himself with some of your kind, but he is already in the process of eradicating certain Orders of Fae who he deems as *lesser-*" I sneered at that word in contempt, "-so do you really believe he will keep an entirely different species at his side for long? Lionel hates anything and anyone who does not conform to his idea of powerful perfection. He covets Fae that fit that ideal and is planning to create an entire kingdom who follows in that line of thought too. He's using Lavinia and her hold on both the shadows and your people to help him get what he wants."

"The only reason those Nymphs even follow Lavinia is because they allowed themselves to become corrupted by her darkness in the shadows, and you well know it, Paula," Miguel chastised. "And those are the ones who follow willingly. You know me. All of you know how much I love our people here, how devoted I am to all of you and to our community. And yet, for the past twenty years I have been missing from your lives. Please don't tell me that you truly believed I turned my back on the people I loved and had dedicated my life to for the sake of Drusilla." He spat her name, and a few more murmurs broke out, faces creasing with doubt. "I was captured by her and her foul brother all those years ago. I was taken far from here and spent months locked up and at their mercy while they pierced my skin and forced la Princesa de las Sombras' power inside of me. I fought it. I fought for all of you here, and for my family most of all, but her power was unimaginable, and the agony I endured…"

He trailed off, and I reached out to clasp his arm, knowing all too well what that kind of suffering was like.

"I am ashamed," Miguel said in a small voice. "Ashamed that I was broken in the end. They flooded me with the darkness of her shadows and left me drunk on them, lost within the confines of my own mind, my body little more than a pawn to their desires. I was forced to denounce my marriage and unite my blood to Drusilla's in her place, all because I am a powerful Nymph and she wanted to use that power to her advantage." His voice cracked, but he went on, the rapt silence of the listening Nymphs making me wonder if we might really be getting through to them at last. "I was used to father a child. A boy who I couldn't even show a hint of love to, thanks to the control they had over me. A boy who sacrificed himself to save the sister of the woman who now stands before you. A boy who, despite being raised under their monstrous desires and being tempted by Lavinia's shadows for his entire life, managed to break free and see the world for what it was. He chose his own path and pledged his loyalty to the Vegas because he could see that they would fight for a better world."

"Diego will be remembered when this war is over," I promised him. "For so many things, but maybe most importantly of all for showing us that the Nymphs don't have to be our enemies. That you shouldn't all just be painted with the same brush because of the brutality some of your kind have enacted against ours. I know the power you all hold is terrifying to Fae, for valid reasons. But I'm a Phoenix who can level a village with a blast of fire which burns hot enough to melt stone. My husband was a Dragon large enough to swallow men whole, Vampires hunt other Fae as part of everyday society, and the list goes on and on. The point is that all of us are monsters in our own rights, and I don't think any of us would choose to be anything else. And so long as we control the power we were born with, then why should we? If we can live in peace and harmony, then isn't that for the best?"

Silence hung heavily as they considered our words, one man calling out to Miguel in question.

"If you were lost to the power of Lavinia's shadows, then why didn't you give our location up?" he demanded of Miguel.

"That was the single secret I managed to keep all these years," he admitted, his throat bobbing with the truth of those words. "I was forced to endure many brands of torture for that answer, the shadows driving deep into my mind in search of it, but I would never relinquish it. I would have died first. And when they realised that, they decided to keep me as their pet, use my power and continue the hunt for your location without my assistance. Though they mostly abandoned it once the Shadow Princess broke free of her prison and returned to this realm, in favour of serving her."

"Lionel and Lavinia won't stop," I said in a low tone, looking at the people gathered before me and meeting their eyes one at a time. "They won't ever be satisfied. They will just take and take and take, their hunger for power a scourge which will only end with their deaths. Which is why my sister and I intend to fight them. It is why we are raising an army and circling them like sharks in the water. Every day, more rebels emerge from the dark and announce their allegiance to us, but we need more. We need you. So I'm asking you to come to our aid when we call for you. To join us on the battlefield and see an end to their hateful rule. In return, I swear to stop the hunting of your kind. You'll be held to no differing law than any Fae. You'll be free to set up homes in any part of the kingdom you desire, and your rights will be protected by the crown."

"And what if you don't end up taking the throne?" a woman demanded.

I gave her a rueful grin and shrugged. "Then I swear that the Heirs will hold to this deal too. I can get that in writing for you, if you doubt my word on their behalf."

The Nymphs all broke out into discussion then, some of them seeming convinced while others voiced their doubts loudly and firmly.

"Come, they need time to think on this. You can rest and eat this way," a woman said, stepping from the crowd and reaching a hand towards us in offering.

"We can't linger here too long," I told her, taking a step closer all the same and falling into step between her and Miguel, who gave me a reassuring look despite the arguments that had erupted following my request.

It was impossible to tell if that had gone well or not, and I found myself wondering if I should have brought the Heirs here with me. At least they knew how to play this game of politics. They'd have known all the right things to say and how to spin every angry outburst to their advantage. I was just going to have to hope that brutal honesty would win these people over instead.

A strangled cry escaped Miguel as we moved through the crowd and he fell still, causing me to turn and look at the four women who had caught his attention. I could tell from the look of them that the younger three were sisters, their similarities to their mother clear enough too.

A lump caught in my throat as I looked between them and Miguel, understanding who they were, what they were to him. The life he'd had stolen from him. The sisters Diego had never even known he had.

"Go," I urged as Miguel remained frozen at my side, though I was sure it wasn't me he lingered for. "Don't let fear keep them from you for a moment longer than you've already lost with them," I insisted, giving him a small but firm shove in their direction.

Miguel tore his eyes from them for a single moment, nervously pushing his fingers into his dark hair in an attempt to flatten it, the motion reminding me of the way Diego had often tugged at his hat.

"You need me to-"

"I don't need you for anything anymore," I swore to him. "I'm fine right here with…" I glanced at the woman who had been leading us in the direction of food and she helpfully supplied me with her name.

"Uma."

"Yep. Me and Uma are good. Go speak to your family, dude. I'm a big girl. I don't need you to hold my hand the entire time I'm here."

Miguel took my arm and gave it a firm squeeze in thanks before turning and striding away from me. My gaze remained pinned to his back, watching as the four women who were his family stilled at his approach before breaking, the eldest of the daughters running for him with a choked sob, her arms wide. The others followed and within moments, all of them were clinging to him as he sank to his knees between them, murmuring praise to fate for finally shining on him and reuniting them at last. His wife fell on him with sobs, kissing him between prayers to the shadows and swearing she had known he would one day return to them.

A splash of warm water hit my cheek as I blinked, and I raised my fingers to it in surprise, a tear finding its way free of the hardened steel I had placed around my heart from witnessing his reunion with the deepest desire of his soul.

The pain inside me blossomed, throbbing like some immortal wound, set to bleed me dry from the inside out. My breath caught, and there was a ringing in my ears which I was pretty certain was drowning out the sound of Uma's voice as she encouraged me to follow her again.

I turned abruptly from the sight of Miguel and his family, a flash of fire burning through my blood as I raised my chin and held the heavy Book of Ether out to show the girl who was waiting for me.

"I need to speak to someone who might know more about this," I said to her, my voice a cold, unfeeling thing as I reined my emotions back in, stomping down on the ones that cut me deepest while burning through those which forced me to feel the loss of him so sharply.

I couldn't fall apart. Not here. Not in front of these people who needed to see nothing but an unbreakable monarch when they looked at me.

Uma looked at the book I held, then glanced behind her as if checking that no one else was watching us, her dark hair tumbling over her shoulder at the movement.

"That kind of magic is older than time itself," she breathed, taking a step closer to me. "It is death to most who try to wield it."

"I'm not like most people," I replied dismissively. "And I need to know more about this."

Uma hesitated, her gaze sweeping over me in an assessing way, and I narrowed my eyes at the judgement she was casting before she shrugged.

"Come then, I'll take you to the oracles, but don't say you weren't warned."

Uma turned off the main path and into the darkness between the trees, not bothering to look back over her shoulder and check that I was still with her. She followed some route I had to assume she knew by heart, because there were no markers in place to suggest that anything lay out there at all.

I resisted the urge to cast a Faelight, instead bolstering the air shield I had in place around my skin in case of surprise attacks and striding out into the darkness behind her.

Our footsteps were the only sound to break the night, the soft rustle of leaves shifting beneath our feet a repetitive accompaniment to our journey.

The lights of the village were soon left behind, stolen by the dense trees until we were deep in the darkness of the forest, with nothing at all to suggest that there was anything out here besides more trees.

Magic built in my fingertips as we walked on, and I flexed my wings, the feathers rustling softly as I wondered if Uma might be stupid enough to try and attack me. I doubted there could have been time to put together much of a trap since I'd arrived, but it was possible there were others waiting out here in the dark for me. Then again, she hadn't been taking me this way until I'd shown her the book, so unless she'd been planning on turning off of the main path anyway, it was unlikely that this was an ambush.

My boot thumped against a lump of stone hidden within the leaves, and the ground grew firmer beneath us just as the scent of damp began to taint the air.

"Be careful here," Uma said, beckoning me closer as I squinted to make her out in the almost non-existent light.

I moved towards her and stepped up onto a rocky shelf, a thicker patch of darkness ahead indicating a huge rockface barring the way on.

"There's a passage there," Uma pointed out and I could just about see a thicker slither of darkness marking the point she was showing me. "Follow it to the end and knock once. If they wish to speak with you, you'll be summoned inside."

"And if they don't?" I asked, turning to look at Uma, who was already backing away.

"It's been almost a year since they last deigned to speak with anyone, so don't be too surprised." She shrugged.

"A year? Then why are you leaving if you expect me to be turned away?" I asked.

"Can't the great Phoenix princess find her way in the dark alone?" she taunted, and despite the flicker of irritation her words sparked in me, I had to admit it made me like her a little more to know she wasn't too intimidated by me to speak them.

"Fine, go," I said dismissively, my attention moving to that narrow passage in the cliff face. "I won't be accepting a 'no' from them anyway."

Uma snorted like she didn't believe I would be able to force anything at all from these so-called oracles, but she was vastly underestimating the power of the promise that was cut into my flesh if she thought I would let them turn me away now.

I headed forward with confident strides, moving into the stone passage and shivering a little as a sensation like passing through cold water tumbled across my flesh.

Whatever kind of power had caused it wasn't like any I knew, and the knowledge that I truly could be walking towards something more powerful than me sank into my bones as I walked on.

The stone walls rose up high on either side of me along the trail, the night sky still visible far above, my boots crunching on gravel and twigs as I went. I tucked my wings in close to my spine to stop them from brushing against the walls. It would have been easier to shift, but I found some comfort in the presence of my Phoenix, so I kept it close.

The passage descended slightly, curving away from the forest entrance and making the dark press even closer, though as I glanced up, I spotted a few stars glimmering in the sky, always watching.

My bitterness was rewarded as the passageway tightened ahead of me, a roof forming in the rocks, a tunnel of deepest darkness the only way on. I steeled myself and kept my stride steady as I continued, lifting a hand to feel for anything before me as I headed into the cave.

After a few minutes of descending into the dark, all the while knowing that there was only one way out of here and that I could quite easily be backing myself into a corner, I came to a door.

It was almost impossible to see the thick wood blocking the way on, but the faint glimmer of pale shadows illuminated just enough for me to understand what it was.

I drew in a calming breath, summoning magic into my hands in preparation of anything which might come my way, then expelled it and knocked solidly on the door. Not once, like Uma had instructed, but three sharp strikes against the wood with my fist.

A pause followed where my heart raced and palms grew slick before the door ahead of me swung open and I was blinded by the light of a fire pouring from the space beyond it.

I looked down at my feet to shield my eyes, the things I had thought were twigs revealing themselves as a mixture of small bones, each marked with blackened runes and tossed haphazardly out onto the path.

I fought off the desire to recoil from the grisly sight and blinked as my eyes adjusted, holding my shield tight to my skin, just in case, while someone tutted impatiently.

"In or out. The fire will gutter if you linger with the wind at your back," a woman hissed, and I stepped into the space, tucking my wings in tight to make it through, the door slamming again behind me while I looked around in search of the owner of that voice.

The chamber I found myself in was large, a fading fire in a hearth on the far side of a hexagonal table. A collection of well-burned white candles were gathered in its centre, old and new wax merging and sticking to the dark wood.

There were sprigs of herbs hanging from the beams which supported the stone ceiling, the tips of them brushing the tops of my wings. Wooden shelves lining the walls were stacked high with jars and bottles, the labels marking their contents dim and faded beyond the point where I could easily read any of them.

The woman cursed, and I flinched as I spotted her bending over the fire, prodding it with a poker as she tried to reignite the flames which had been blown out with my arrival. I swore she hadn't been there a moment ago. There had been no one here. And yet there was no way she could have made it across the room from the single dim corridor which led out of here to my right without me seeing her.

"How did you-"

"Hush your nonsense and help me save this fire," she grumbled, tugging her cloak closer around her while remaining stooped over the hearth, meaning I couldn't see anything of her aside from the blood-red hair hanging down her back. "I spend half my cursed life trying to coax heat from this blasted thing."

"Here," I offered, stepping closer, a flame of red and blue igniting in my palm. "This won't ever go out if you don't wish it to."

The woman shifted aside, and I tossed the glimmering Phoenix flame onto the measly pile of sticks in the fireplace, resisting the urge to look smug as I solved her problem so simply.

"Hark at this one, gifting out magical flames as if they were ten a penny," another voice came from directly behind me, and I couldn't help but flinch as I whirled around, finding a woman there standing so close to me that adrenaline shot through my veins and magic instantly leapt to my palms.

Two daggers, one of wood, the other ice, formed in my fists, but if the woman noticed them, she didn't seem to care. Instead, she leaned into me, a curtain of ice-white hair falling forward to shadow her features, her warm brown skin swiftly hidden within the strands as she dropped her nose to my throat and inhaled deeply.

"What the fuck are you doing?" I demanded, jerking backwards to put some distance between us and knocking into a third body, a cry of fright falling from my lungs before I could stop it.

Where the fuck had they all come from?

I whirled on the newcomer, my eyes widening in horror as I took in the carefully formed stiches which sealed the lips of her deep red mouth permanently shut. She was beautiful aside from that disfigurement, her eyes a wild and stunning shade of gold set into a face so perfect that my breath caught at the sight of her. Her skin was a deep brown, her hair a bounty of curls which seemed to highlight the perfection of her cheekbones, but it was impossible to fully appreciate that with the stitches sealing her lips.

"What happened to you?" I gasped in horror, and the first woman chuckled as she moved around the table to join us too.

"Give the child some space, Loqui," she chided, gripping the other woman by the arm, and tugging her back a step so that I could breathe freely.

"Her mouth," I said, unable to tear my eyes from those horrific stitches. "What happened to her mouth?"

"There is a price to the power we own," the first woman chuckled, and as I looked to her, I stumbled back a step, a scream lodging in my throat, though I refused to let it out.

She was just as stunning as Loqui, though her features were vastly different. Her skin was so pale it was almost alabaster within the curtain of red hair, a dusting of freckles gracing a perfect nose and pale pink lips curving up into a smile as she sensed my full attention falling on her. I knew she had sensed it rather than seen, because her eyes, oh hell, her eyes had been sewn shut, just like Loqui's lips.

"This was a price you *chose* to pay?" I asked, the shock clear in my voice as the woman breathed another laugh.

"It was little in the grand scheme of what we gained. I am Vidi. It means 'to see'." She laughed again, her voice so much older than the beautiful body housing it somehow, filled with knowledge and wisdom beyond the years of the woman who looked to be little more than thirty.

"And I'm Audire," the third woman – the sniffer – said as she circled me to stand beside the others. She grinned broadly as I hunted the utter perfection of her face, the warm brown skin, eyes so dark they were almost black, and that hair a stunning contrast with its icy white tone. I hunted her for any signs of stiches and almost relaxed before she lifted her hair to expose the place where her ears should have been, two jagged scars remaining instead from where they had been severed.

"The aesthetic is just her choice in dramatics," Vidi said dismissively as I tried not to recoil. "Her eardrums were punctured to remove the sense of hearing, but she wanted scars to match her sisters'."

Audire looked to Vidi's mouth as she spoke, and I guessed she was able to read the words which came from them because her lips peeled back and she hissed like a cornered alley cat.

"Why?" I breathed, because I had all kinds of questions, but as I stared between these three beautiful, disfigured women, it was impossible to think of any aside from that one.

Vidi placed a hand on her heart dramatically, and my eyes moved over the cloaks they all wore like some medieval coven of witches, though I suspected they were something far more dangerous than that.

"See no evil," she breathed, a reverence to her tone as she indicated herself before reaching across and touching Audire's heart next. "Hear no evil." She moved her hand to touch Loqui's heart, but I found myself finishing the words for her as I came to a sick kind of understanding.

"Speak no evil?" I breathed, and they all nodded in eerie synchronicity. "So the aim is to avoid evil?" I guessed, and they all laughed that time, though the noise which came from Loqui was stifled by her sealed lips.

"The aim is to stifle how much any one of us can use," Audire contradicted, her words clear despite her inability to hear them. "To save us from consumption by the forces we taste."

I nodded, forcing myself to take their explanation and accept it, ignoring the urge to keep staring at the lengths they'd chosen to go to in aid of whatever power it was they commanded. Hadn't I sworn that I would do whatever it took to claim such power too? I wasn't going to blink at the first sign of just how steep that cost might be.

"I came here looking for help," I said, holding the Book of Ether out before me. Loqui elbowed Vidi aside, snatching it from me, then dropping it onto the table just as fast.

"What is it?" Vidi demanded as Audire gasped, hurrying towards the table and whipping open the first page of the book.

"Something old," Audire muttered, flicking the pages one at a time, hissing and murmuring as she did so while Loqui pressed her hands flat to the table and leaned in so close that she was in danger of getting a papercut to her nose. "Even older than you, dear sister."

Loqui laughed at that, the noise stifled by the stitches closing her mouth, and Vidi snarled, revealing gleaming, sharp teeth as she stalked towards them and shoved them aside. She ran a hand down the centre of the book, and I winced at the rough treatment they were giving the ancient pages, imagining Orion's face if he could see them.

"Sit, sit, sit," Audire barked at me, though her gaze never left the book as she waved me towards a chair on the other side of the table to them, beside the fire.

I nodded, moving towards the spot she'd indicated, wincing as my wings knocked against some of the herbs hanging from the ceiling and dislodging something which rolled over my shoulder and fell to the floor before I realised it was a huge, dead spider and recoiled.

"Put those things away before you take our entire house down," Vidi grouched at me, but before I could shift, Loqui was in my face, plucking a bronze feather from one of my wings and giving me a gruesome smile through the stitches in her face.

I fought the urge to recoil, my wings fading out of existence as Loqui moved away from me as suddenly as she'd appeared, grabbing several more items from around the room and shoving them into the pockets of her cloak.

I dropped into my seat and fought a flinch as I found Audire right beside me, somehow having circled the entire table in the time it took me to lower into the wooden chair, and she leaned in to inhale my scent again.

"Royalty," she spat, a wad of saliva landing in a heavy stone scrying bowl which she was holding before she set it down on the table with a thump so hard the whole thing rattled.

"Blood of the chosen," Vidi agreed, appearing on my other side and taking hold of my chin as she forced my head back, seeming to inspect me despite her eyes being sewn shut. "A burning flame in the dark. But she is one of twin flames; where is the other?"

I batted her hand off of me, her sharp nails scratching my skin. "Enough with the touchy-feely shit," I snapped. "I'm not a hugger, and I'm definitely not here for a makeover, so keep your hands to yourselves, okay?"

Vidi straight up cackled, tossing me a small velvet pouch, and I caught it on instinct, feeling several hard lumps inside the fabric as I closed my fist around it.

"Cast them," Audire demanded, inching back out of my breathing space when I shot her a scowl.

I tugged the string securing the pouch open and emptied five ice-white, tiny skulls into my palm.

"Wonderful," I deadpanned, wrinkling my nose at the little handful of death I now held, and Loqui gave me that devil's grin again, her stitches pulling tight.

"Animals have links to true magic which are less burdened than our own," Vidi said as Loqui reached out to stroke her finger over the head of what looked like a bird's skull, a series of tiny runes carved into the bone in blood red. "A sparrow for air, viper for earth, an eel for water, and a salamander for fire."

"What's the fifth one for?" I asked, shifting the skulls in my palm and looking into the empty eye sockets of an almost demonic-looking skull, though as it was barely bigger than any of the others, I knew it had to be some other small creature too.

"A bat for ether, because they are of air and earth, fire and water combined, and none of them at all. Something other," Audire hissed, her eyes on my mouth, reading my words as I spoke them.

The skulls seemed to warm in my palm at the sound of that word, like the ether awoke something in them.

Loqui grabbed a handful of dried thyme from a hook close to the fire, then plunged the end of the sprigs into the flames. She waited a moment until they were smouldering, the fire taking hold of them quickly, then she pulled them out again, stubbing them out on the table before me and scrawling a pentagram into place, surrounding the scrying bowl with the ashes. She tossed the last of the charred herbs into the fire and the pungent scent of them filled the space quickly as a haze of smoke drifted through the room.

"Place your mind upon the questions you most desperately desire answering, then cast the bones into the bowl," Vidi encouraged, the three of them backing up just enough to let me breathe.

There were so many questions I had, so many things I should have been asking before I even took part in whatever the hell this was, but I'd already come this far, and I wasn't going to turn back now.

I drew in a deep breath, focusing my mind on all the problems surrounding us, on Lionel and Lavinia, the armies they commanded and the struggles we were facing in trying to raise our own forces again so that we could meet them on the battlefield once more. I thought of my sister, my brother, and Orion trapped in The Palace of Souls and the single hope that we were placing upon a vision to save them. There were so many things I needed answers for, help with, but as I closed my fist around the skulls, Loqui leaned in to speak in my ear.

"What does your heart bleed for, Princess of the Flames?"

I raised my fist to throw the bones, my heart splintering at her words, the golden eyes of a dragon scorching through my soul as they tore my breath from my lungs, seeing me the way no one else had ever seen me, knowing my heart inside and out, owning me, claiming me, ruining me.

The skulls hit the edge of the scrying bowl and scattered inside it, tumbling over each other and rattling against the stone while my heart raced at the feeling of his hands on my skin, his breath against my lips, the powerful thump of his heartbeat seeming to pulse against my palm as if my hand were laying over it.

The three Nymphs lunged forward, Loqui and Audire staring down into the bowl while Vidi thrust her hand into it, her fingers tapping against the skulls one at a time, checking their positions while not moving them at all.

Loqui took a vial of white liquid from the pocket of her cloak and poured it into the bowl before I got to take a look at the way the bones had fallen, and they were submerged within it as she poured the contents.

Next, she took a sprig of hemlock and threw it into the mixture while Audire murmured something about death calling for death.

Vidi snatched my hand into her grip, a knife appearing against my fingertip and a hiss of irritation escaping her as the blade met with my shield. I didn't need her to bare her sharp teeth at me to know what she wanted, and I dropped the shield, too far down this path to turn back now, my need for answers all-consuming.

The blade pierced my skin and several drops of blood splashed into the milky water, swirling through it and tainting the colour while Vidi shoved my hand away from her again.

Loqui took the bronze feather she'd plucked from my wing and scored her thumbnail down the length of it, a growl building in her throat before a purple flame blossomed beneath her nail and the feather caught light. She tossed that into the bowl too, and I didn't even bother to protest as Audire cut off a lock of my hair and threw it into the mix too.

The two Nymphs who could use their mouths began speaking in unison, their words ancient and unknown, thrumming with power that set the fine hairs along my arms on end and made a shiver track down my spine.

They stopped abruptly and Loqui leaned in, her luscious curls falling forward to mask her face as she held out a single finger and tapped the very centre of the liquid in the scrying bowl.

"Look," Audire commanded as the three of them drew back.

I pushed myself to my feet on trembling legs as I leaned in to get a look at the image which was beginning to appear inside the bowl.

"Darius?" I breathed, something inside me wrenching free as a sob caught in my chest and I looked at that all-too-perfect face of his staring back at me from the depths of the scrying bowl.

His expression was hard, the image not drawing any memory that I could place, making me wonder if this was real, a view of him beyond the Veil, wherever that might be.

His deep brown eyes met mine and a thunderbolt speared its way through me, my tears falling free at last, splashing down into the water and making the image of him ripple and twist.

"You promised you'd stay," I hissed at him, swiping at my cheeks in an effort to banish the tears which were ruining my view of him.

"You promised you'd find me," he replied, a dark and taunting grin on his lips which looked nothing like the smiles I remembered. "Tick tock, Roxy."

"Wait," I gasped as the ripples continued to spread across the bowl, the image shattering even though I'd barely gotten a look at him at all. "Do it again," I demanded. "Bring him back."

"Bring back the dead?" Audire chuckled, getting to her feet and taking the scrying bowl from the table. "Not possible, Princess of the Flames."

"You could follow him into death if you require your reunion so dearly," Vidi suggested, swiping a hand over the pentagram that had been drawn onto the table and smearing the edges of it.

A breath of fresh air tumbled through the room as the lines of that shape were broken, and I felt the power they'd been wielding fade with it.

"I can't follow him into death," I snarled. "I'm needed here. *He's* needed here."

"Pity," Audire sighed, and I couldn't tell if she was referring to him being dead or my unwillingness to follow him beyond the Veil.

"I want to learn more about the magic in that book," I said firmly. "I want to learn more about the things you just did."

"It won't bring him back," Vidi said, amusement colouring her words. "Not even one of the most powerful Fae in Solaria can do that. There is no doing what you want done. The stars have chosen his fate."

"It won't be undone," Audire agreed.

"Fuck the stars," I growled, and the three of them recoiled like hissing snakes.

Loqui tossed a handful of sage into the fire and Vidi poured some salt from a glass shaker into her palm, swiping it over her tongue while Audire simply began begging the sky for forgiveness as they all worked to clear their home of my curse upon the celestial beings.

I swore and shoved to my feet, reaching for the book and grabbing it just as Loqui slammed her hand down on the pitch-black cover to halt me.

Her sewn-shut lips curved into a wicked grin, and she pressed a single finger to them, urging me to remain silent while her eyes seemed to swirl with unnatural darkness.

"Such things are not within the bounty of any gifts known to Nymph or Fae. You would be better served turning your grief upon your enemies than you would wasting your time with us," Audire spat, but despite her words, she didn't look angry, her gaze wild as she shoved the heavy table aside and I was forced to release my grip on the Book of Ether as I stumbled back out of its way.

"Beauty is the curse of the stars themselves," Vidi sighed, shrugging her cloak from her shoulders, revealing a lithe, naked body beneath. She was a stunning creature, even with the stitches securing her eyelids, every curve of her porcelain flesh seeming designed for seduction and temptation.

I opened my mouth to question what the fuck she was doing, but Loqui shook her head in a silent reminder, offering Vidi a wicked-looking stone dagger, its sharp blade etched with runes.

Vidi accepted it, rolling her shoulders back and smiling as she held the dagger to her own wrist.

I flinched as she swept it towards her arm, but before I could see what she'd done with it, Audire's hands fell over my eyes, her body pressing flush to my back and her nose burying itself against my neck as she inhaled deeply.

"Say nothing, see nothing..." she breathed in my ear, the words so soft I almost didn't catch them at all.

Something hot and wet sprayed across the lower part of my face beneath the hold of Audire's hands which shielded my eyes, and I flinched back against her, my heart thrashing wildly as the sound of stone scraping against stone filled the room.

Audire shifted her thumbs against my eyelids, brushing them closed in a clear demand just as a hellish scream tore through the space surrounding me and every muscle in my body locked with fright.

Audire shifted her hands from my eyes to my ears, the weight of her soft palms pressing against them, somehow blocking out all sound so that I was lost in a void of sensation.

"Hear nothing."

I couldn't even tell how I had understood those words at all, the knowledge of them seeming to have built within my mind rather than me actually hearing anything.

I staggered as the flagstones beneath me shifted, but Audire held me close, the warmth of her body pressed to my back one of the only things I was certain of in this world as I started to lose my bearings on my place in it.

The urge to open my eyes consumed me, but I fought it, even as a drop of what I had to assume was Vidi's blood rolled down my face and across my lips.

I jolted in surprise as a mouth was pressed to mine, the lips full and seductive despite the ridges of cotton which I could feel sewn through them, letting me know that it was Loqui stealing a kiss from me.

Something lodged deep in my chest began to cleave apart as the two Nymphs pressed closer to me, trapping me between them while it was unlocked, and my lips parted on an inhale as Loqui kissed me harder.

Fingers took hold of my right hand, turning my palm over before trailing across the lightning and sun steel scar which lay there, studying each ridge and facet before the fingers were replaced by a tongue.

I recoiled against Audire, whose nose grazed across the side of my throat, a vibration in her chest making me think she was laughing, though I couldn't hear anything to confirm that.

Vidi rolled her tongue over my scar, tasting the oath I'd made within it before starting an ascent up the inside of my forearm, my nerves lighting at the indecent touch, a dark and beckoning desire awakening in me.

It wasn't like any lust I had ever felt before, not the all-consuming heat I had burned through with Darius.

No. This wasn't sex, nor anything like it, despite the way they were all pressed against me, their mouths on my skin, my heart racing. It wasn't a physical act at all. They were calling to something locked deep within my soul, urging it up and out of me, coaxing a flame which I hadn't even realised was burning to life.

I tipped my head back against Audire's shoulder, something I guessed was a moan rolling through my chest as Loqui's sewn lips moved from my mouth to my throat, her fingers teasing the fabric of my dress open so that the chilled air rose gooseflesh across my body.

A rumble moved through the ground at my feet, the echo of it passing through my soul and rattling it to its core, molten eyes looking back at me from within the confines of my own mind.

He seemed so real, like he was right there before me, waiting for me to do something, change something, take *something.*

Vidi's tongue moved back down my arm as she remained on her knees beside us, her fingers taking possession of my scarred hand and turning it so that my own fingers were pressed to the heated skin of my thigh through the slit in the side of my dress. Her hand interlaced with mine as she began to guide it up that silken skin, fire igniting everywhere inside me as I was lost to the memory of Darius, the countless words he'd spoken to me, declarations he'd made tumbling through my mind and drowning me in the loss of him.

Audire's fingers shifted through my hair, massaging my scalp while she kept her palms pressed down over my ears, making me arch between the press of her body and Loqui's as something rich and potent spilled through my veins.

"The cost of honing ether is higher than you can imagine." That voice ricocheted within me, and I was struck with the knowledge that it came from not one, but all of them somehow.

"If the cost of this is my soul, then I'd gladly pay the price," I thought back at them, the pure truth of those words burning through me even hotter than the flame they were kindling.

All three of them laughed at those words, their amusement slipping through me without me needing to hear it.

"So easy to promise the world when you don't hold it in your grasp."

"Is that the price?" I asked, distantly aware of Loqui's fingers moving over the skin above my thrashing heart as she painted a symbol there.

I knew what it was, whether through the feeling of her touch or just the power it held. A pentagram. And though I knew I probably should have been fighting this, running or screaming or something of the kind, I made no move to try and escape them. I didn't have much hope beyond the power of these three witches, and if they wanted to toy with me before giving me what I needed, then I wasn't going to fight them.

"We told you: there is no returning from death."

"I don't accept that."

More amusement twisted from them into me, Vidi's hand guiding mine higher, drawing my fingers closer to my core while the vision of Darius consumed me. Memories of the two of us together in heat and passion and hatred all merged. I couldn't just recall them; I could feel them. The heat of his skin against mine, the power of his body claiming me, each thrust, each lick of that sinful tongue, every kiss and conquest and burst of pleasure he had ever given me.

"We can give you this," they offered. *"A memory dipped in reality. You can partake in it for as long as you like, feel every piece of it, relive each sordid, beautiful memory as if they were taking place in the now."*

I trembled, the feeling of him so fucking real, the weight of his impenetrable stare consuming me, the nearness of him so close to truth. I knew they were holding back, that they really could offer me a trip right into those memories. I could immerse myself inside them, let myself believe that they were real all over again. But I would lose myself in them if I did that, I could feel the weight of that truth pressing in on me. If I accepted this gift from them, I would be trapped in those memories until my true body wasted away right here in this cave in the middle of nowhere, my magic no doubt a gift they'd claim as I took my final breaths.

It would be a beautiful death, lost in the arms of the man I loved. But not a real one.

"I'm needed here," I told them firmly, trying to claw my mind away from that deepest of temptations even as I felt the tears rushing down my cheeks, my grief breaking free of its walls at last.

Audire tugged me closer to her, tasting my tears where they coated my skin, an echo of pain travelling from me into the three Nymphs, making them all suck in shuddering breaths.

"Show us this," Vidi purred, her thumb tracing the scar on my palm even as she guided my hand around the curve of my thigh, moving closer to my core inch by inch.

I gave in to her request, so broken by my grief that I wasn't even certain I would be able to deny them anything anymore.

I was back on that hilltop, Darius still and cold beneath me, his blood mixing with mine as I slit my hand open on the blade which had stolen him from me, cursing the stars themselves with all the power I possessed and more.

The three Nymphs gasped at the weight of the magic I'd called on, whispers breaking out between them in a language I couldn't understand as I leaned back against Audire, unable to summon the energy to even move anymore.

"Ruiner of Destiny," they whispered, and I inhaled sharply, my magic sparking within me as they called on that new and untested flame inside of me, beckoning it closer once more.

Loqui's fingers sketched the image of a pentagram over my heart again, a sigh escaping her which I could feel in the depths of my soul.

"We can't give you what you seek," they said, and though I had already realised that, it still cut me open. "*The deepest desire of your heart is not one any can grant."*

"Then what can you give me?" I demanded, refusing to just leave here with nothing more than I had held when I arrived.

"A path," they whispered, Audire's lips skimming across the side of my neck and making a shiver dance through me. "*One you can tread in search of your answers."*

"What do you want for it?" I asked, my heart lifting with hope even as I tried to hide my desperation from them, because I knew I would agree to whatever they wanted from me now. I couldn't turn back. Even if they could only offer the slimmest sliver of hope, I would take it and give them whatever they wanted in exchange.

They began murmuring to one another again, Loqui's hands skimming the neckline of my dress, teasing it open further, my breasts almost spilling free of it while Vidi's hand and mine were just a breath from the apex of my thighs, the memories of Darius that they had offered me still heating my skin.

"Virgin blood is the most powerful for our kind of magic," they breathed, their voices inside my skull a whisper of seduction as I saw him there again, sitting on my father's throne, spilling his heart out to me while I refused to hear the words and instead dropped to my knees before him. *"We want a taste of what you've had, what we can never truly claim for our own."*

I swallowed a lump in my throat as I processed that, my skin flushed with heat as they continued to caress me, presenting me with image after image from my own memories of flesh claiming flesh. Tattoos slicked with sweat and a wicked grin designed purely to ruin me.

"That's it?" I asked, uncertain of what exactly they meant by that, but knowing I was willing to give it to them.

"One night to taste what you have tasted, to linger in your lust," they purred, and the movements of their hands on my skin began to merge with the memories of his, his callouses rough against my softness, the bite of his stubble a sinful scratch I could never get enough of. *"Then we will give you a path to take. One wicked and steeped in sin. One which might lead you to the answers you seek or which may end in your own departure from this world. Hope. Though only the briefest flicker of it, at that. Do we have a deal?"*

Their words were heavy with warning and uncertainty, nothing at all to say they even believed that what I sought was possible, but it didn't matter, because I didn't need anything other than a path to follow, so if that was what they were offering me, then I was going to take it with both hands.

"Done," I said out loud, magic wrapping around that word and binding me to it so sharply that a cry escaped me.

Loqui's stitched lips pressed to mine to silence me once more, but it didn't seem like they were concerned with me keeping to their oaths anymore as Audire slipped her hands from my ears and she slowly rolled them down my spine.

I opened my eyes, looking between the three beautiful women who surrounded me for the briefest of moments, each of them having shed their cloaks at some point since my eyes had been closed, revealing the perfection of their nakedness and making my breath catch in my lungs.

They were creatures designed for lust, every inch of them endlessly different from each other while all wildly captivating in their own ways. The thought of them being virgins seemed absurd, the scent of sex seeming to cling to their flawless skin as I watched the way their hands moved over my body, teasing and plucking at my dress while not quite exposing me to them.

We weren't in the cave anymore, the chill of the air pressing in around us as we stood in a pentagram-shaped clearing within a ring of ancient, enormous trees. There was a stone altar beside us, stained with what was undoubtably blood, this place used for sacrifice far more often than what they had requested of me.

My gaze fell on Vidi, still kneeling beside us, as her tongue traced a line up the side of my thigh, her eyes full of heat and lust as she looked up at me, pressing my own hand closer to my core even as I spotted the freely bleeding wound on her wrist.

She was smeared in bright red blood, not the blackish, tainted blood of the Nymphs Lavinia controlled, but blood as red as any Fae's, like proof itself of her taint on the shadows.

My breaths became shallow as I watched her moving her mouth over my skin, the blood staining her flesh both horrifying and transfixing, like the sacrifice she had made for her power was an intoxication of its own.

"Roxy." The deep growl of his voice had me frozen for three eternal seconds before I snapped my head up and found him there, his shirt already off, those tattoos I loved so much peering back at me like the deepest temptation.

I understood then why the three Nymphs had stopped shy of actually undressing me, of touching me any more than they had so far, Vidi's fingers stroking the skin between my thighs without attempting to shift those final few inches to my core. They were virgins and would remain as such throughout this night, but they intended to see me destroyed in every way my memories could conjure before the sun rose to sate their own repressed desires.

I looked at Darius, the edges of his skin shining with a faint, golden light, proving him to be nothing more than a memory, and I did remember this. We hadn't been in a forest clearing, surrounded by three entities of unthinkable power. We'd been in our room at The Burrows, my core still aching after a night spent in his arms, yet his desire never faded one bit, his need for me never sated in the least.

"You're wearing far too many clothes," he teased, the look he gave me peeling me apart from the inside out.

Grief threatened to consume me, the memory too real, too much to bear, but Audire ran her teeth along the shell of my ear and whispered to me. "Give yourself to it completely. Forget the here and now and let it take you to then. To him. Bring us with you."

Her fingers curled into the thin straps which secured the back of my dress, her knuckles skimming over that deliciously sensitive spot where my wings would emerge if I shifted, and I moaned softly as I let myself do as she'd commanded.

This was the price they sought. And I wasn't going to flinch from it, even if I feared the pain I would be left in when the sun finally rose.

I dropped my hands to my waist, unbuckling my sword belt as I stared at the vision of Darius, his eyes full of heated promises as he unbuckled his own belt, mirroring me.

I let the sword fall to the floor, drawing my hand higher beneath my skirt alongside Vidi's, a soft moan escaping me as my fingertips brushed against the wetness soaking my panties.

The three Nymphs moaned too, their hands moving both across my body and their own flesh, seeking out that need in themselves as I began to touch myself, just like I had that day in The Burrows, teasing him, tempting him.

Darius growled softly, the sound raising the hairs along the back of my neck, and I pushed the fabric of my panties aside, two fingers sliding into my slick heat and causing me to moan again.

Vidi's hand remained on mine, though she was careful not to touch me aside from the back of my hand as she guided my movements, her blood dripping down my thigh from the still-bleeding wound on her wrist.

Darius's heated gaze roamed over me as I fucked my own hand for him, my teeth sinking into my bottom lip as my release closed in on me from nothing but the weight of his stare.

I slipped the strap of my dress from my shoulder, exposing my breast and hardened nipple, my free hand seeking it out and tugging while Loqui's fingers slid down my side, caressing my skin.

"Come for me, Roxanya," Darius growled. "Come for me so prettily, the way you always do."

"I still fucking hate you half the time, you know that, right?" I panted, my words the ones I'd spoken to him all those months ago, and he grinned in that very same way he had then too, pushing his pants down and taking his huge cock into his fist.

My eyes became riveted to that spot and the motion of his fist, the women surrounding me fading away as I fell deeper into the memory, a cry of ecstasy breaking from me as I did exactly what he'd told me to do, no matter how much it infuriated me.

Darius gave me that cocky grin, beckoning me to him like he expected me to refuse. But I didn't.

I strode across a blanket of dried leaves and twigs, my dress slipping from my body as I shrugged it off and let it fall from me entirely, my memory providing a different floor and a bed where I vaguely knew there was nothing but that stone table.

I was distantly aware of the Nymphs trailing me as I moved, their hands caressing my skin, their magic linking them into my memories and their power stoking my lust beyond all measure. But I was used to feeling lust with that intensity in the presence of the man I loved. The passion that had blazed between us was unrivalled by any other in this realm and all realms. None burned with the intensity which had consumed us, and none could surpass the need I felt for him in all forms.

The Nymphs traced their fingers over my skin, painting runes against my flesh in Vidi's blood, the darkness surrounding us intensifying to the point where I could hardly even recall the trees, let alone notice the frigid air which tried to bite at my exposed skin.

I gave myself to the heat roaring between Darius Acrux and the Vega princess who he was forbidden to love. Gave myself to the ties I had made between him and myself in life and in death, through marriage and the destruction of our Star bond, through hate, betrayal, vengeance and violence. I was his and he was mine. And as the ghost of him wrapped his hand around my wrist and tugged me closer, I gave up any attempt to remember that this was just a memory playing out in my mind.

I didn't care that it wasn't real because as soon as I gave myself to it completely, it *was* real. His tongue was sinking between my lips, his hands grasping the curve of my ass and yanking me into his lap, his cock sinking into my wetness so fucking perfectly.

My heart trembled in my chest as the feeling of his skin against mine consumed me entirely. I had missed this, missed him so incredibly, and somehow, for this stolen moment in time, he was here, the shattered pieces of me gluing themselves back together, tears of pure joy rolling down my cheeks.

"It's you," I murmured, my fingers tracing the length of his jaw, savouring the bite of his stubble as I devoured the sight of him and drank it all in. "Only you."

He gave me a smile which cast my heart to ashes, his fingers roaming over the tattoo on my thigh which echoed that sentiment and my gaze dipping to the one which wound around his hip.

There is only her.

I should have known I was his that first moment I saw him, lounging on that red couch, draped in arrogance while he stole the air from every inch of the room. I should have known it when he was taunting and tormenting me, should have known when his eyes trailed me everywhere I went, and when I dreamt of him despite myself night after night. I'd been so fucking blind and so fucking stubborn, but I had been his throughout it all.

"By the stars, I love you," Darius groaned, his big hands squeezing my ass as he drew me down onto him more firmly, savouring the connection of our bodies while we both panted through the moment of resistance.

"I love you," I replied, my fingers moving over his pec, skimming the ink which stained his bronze skin until I could feel the thundering of his heart beneath them. It was a lie, a beautiful, tempting, lie. But I didn't care. There was only him.

I gave in to the need in my flesh, moaning his name as I gripped his shoulders and began to ride him, tipping my head back as I languished in the impossibly full feeling of taking him inside me. He was huge in every aspect, this immovable, unbreakable being who was bound to me in so many ways.

Darius growled against my skin as he drove his hips up into me with force, fucking me hard and deep, driving himself in to the base so that my breath was stolen by the force of his claiming and my nails broke his skin where I clung to him.

I met his passion with my own, rocking my hips and placing a hand between us, rolling my fingers over my clit while he sucked on my nipple hard enough to make me gasp.

I cried out as I drew close to the edge, but he snatched my wrists into his grasp, halting my fingers on my clit and moving them to the base of my spine where he pinned them in place with one of his huge hands.

"When you come this time, it will be entirely for me," he growled, that bossy tone enough to make me want to punch him. But I forgot the impulse as he thrust his hips up into me again, making my tits bounce while the oracles still stroked and caressed me distantly, drinking in every moment of this as they *saw* him too, *saw* both of us, felt what we were feeling.

It should have been putting me off, but I was lost to him the way I always had been, my need for him far greater than any shyness or embarrassment I might have felt at the thought of us being watched like this.

Darius moved his free hand to my clit, taking over from what I'd been doing as he lifted his hips in a destructive, ruinous movement which had me forgetting my damn name as he slammed into some insatiable spot inside of me.

"Please," I begged, needing him to finish me while he just toyed with me instead, his thumb making my clit sing, then stopping right as I was about to combust.

Over and over again he edged me until I was pleading, cursing, begging and he was grinning through our kisses, loving his ownership over me before finally giving in.

He slammed into me with a Dragon's roar, coming inside of me while completing his conquest of my body with that triumphant thrust and the destructive pressure of his thumb.

I came so hard I almost blacked out, my head rolling back and a cry of purest bliss escaping me while my body was engulfed in the kind of ecstasy only this damnation of mine could deliver.

He rolled us over, laying me on my back, and I blinked up at him as I panted there, my heart leaping in horror as he faded away and the frozen stone of the table beneath me replaced the illusion of our old bed.

"Wait," I gasped, the moans of the Nymphs surrounding me as that memory captivated them too, their hands moving over my skin as they painted more runes onto my body which I couldn't read or decipher.

"More," Vidi snarled, and I glanced towards her pale form, her sharp teeth flashing at the demand while Loqui moaned in frustration from behind her sewn-shut lips.

"More," Audire agreed, baring her teeth too, her hands moving up my thighs as she seemed to draw the feeling of pleasure right out of my sated flesh and into hers.

My lips parted on some reply, but whatever it had been died instantly as Darius strode towards me through the trees, his eyes full of something which bit into me so deeply it hurt.

It wasn't real, but...it was. Fuck, it was real. I didn't care if it was a memory, didn't care if I was trading this look at him for some tiny glint of hope, didn't care if they were seeing and experiencing all of it with me because he was here and he was mine, and if it only lasted one night, then I'd still take it.

"Is it totally conceited of me to hope you might be waiting for me?" he asked, hesitation, hope and need in his dark eyes.

"Yeah," I agreed on a breath as I drank in the sight of him standing before me in a half unbuttoned black shirt and smart trousers. The shitty sweatpants and shirt I'd been wearing that night seeming to materialise on my body as I pushed to my feet so that I could relive it just as it had been, that moment of perfect clarity when we had finally been able to just become...us. "But I think I've always been waiting for you, so maybe you're right."

"Even when you hated me?" His voice was a dark purr which set every piece of my flesh buzzing with need.

I could see what this was now, how this night would play out, me and him over and over and over again until I was aching, fractured, and broken for him even more than I had been. This was torture of the sweetest kind, and I was a glutton for punishment because I was all in. I could never say no to him anyway. Not in any way that lasted.

So the night passed with me in his arms, his body possessing mine, my heart racing to a pace that only he had ever been able to set it to as I fell apart for him time and again.

The Nymphs drank it all in, crying out in pleasure with me, their magic sharpening the memories so much that I really was reliving them. Every pleasure filled moment, every thrust of his hips, every kiss, every 'I love you'. All of it.

Until I passed beyond the point of taking any more of it, my body wrung out, used, and destroyed from so much pleasure. Darkness invaded my mind and stole me away, though I knew that even as I was lost to the memories, I continued to play them out with him. More and more and more. Past the sunrise and through the next day and night too, endlessly his, my energy torn from me, my body and flesh exposed until finally, with the second sunrise, I was left lying on the stone table in the heart of the pentagram. My naked body was stained with Vidi's blood, countless runes painted on every inch of my exhausted flesh, overlapping each other beyond the point of recognition.

My heart was still racing as I woke, blinking up at the light filtering down to me through the trees overhead, tiny dust motes swirling through it, highlighting small parts of my body.

I was panting, an ache between my thighs speaking of all I'd done in those endless hours and tears dry on my cheeks, my eyes puffy and aching from spilling so many.

He was gone. Only the ghost of his touch lingered on my body, love bites and scratches marking my skin like it truly had been real.

The oracles were long gone, sated from their ride through my nights of lust with Darius Acrux, having taken more than my bargain with them had initially agreed to. Though as I pushed myself to sit up, I found a scroll sitting on top of the Book of Ether beside me and decided I didn't care about the extra time they'd added onto our deal.

I unfurled it carefully, my heart hurting with the loss of him all over again while I tried not to give too much thought to the hedonistic memory orgy I'd taken part in last night. I'd sworn that I would do whatever it took, and if that meant fucking the ghost of him in my memories until I passed out, then it didn't seem like the worst thing that could have been asked of me.

The message they'd left me was simple, though the path they were directing me towards was likely anything but.

In the heart of the Damned Forest, beyond the Waters of Depth and Purity, lies the Ever-Changing Winds of Sky and Spirit. The Endless Drop will take you through the Fires of the Abyss and beyond them, where the ether lies thickest, your answers await.

I read over the words twice, not knowing what they meant but feeling that tiny ray of hope shining brighter at them all the same.

From the ache in my stomach, I knew I'd been gone longer than I'd meant to be. This dawn the second that had passed since I'd arrived here, the rapture I'd encountered in this clearing taking more than its toll on my flesh.

I needed to return to the island and explain myself. But as I pulled my ruined dress onto my aching body and wondered how the fuck I was supposed to explain this, I couldn't help but smile just a little. Because we were going to rescue Darcy and the others from The Palace of Souls, we were going to kill that Dragon motherfucker, and once we did all of that, I was going to find the place known as the Damned Forest and keep my promise to the heartless stars once and for all.

Scorpio
Gemini
Virgo
Cancer
Leo
Sagittarius
Capricorn
Aquarius
Libra
Pisces

CALEB

CHAPTER THIRTY SIX

"We shall not rest! We shall not slumber! We shall not stop until our lady is returned to us!" Geraldine bellowed, thumping her breastplate and inciting a roar of agreement from the gathered rebels who raised their swords and sent crackling blasts of magic towards the sky as they hyped themselves up for a fight.

"Forgive me," the former prison guard pleaded from his knees beside Geraldine, his eyes puffy from all the tears he'd shed. The other rebels who had been guarding the jail when Tory had shown up and released Miguel were in similar states of distress and had been for the thirty-odd hours since she'd gone missing with him.

"Geraldine," I barked, shoving my way between the gathered crowd of around fifty Fae and making my way towards her. I used my gifted strength to force them to move when they resisted and shot between the last of them before coming to a halt mere inches from her.

"I thought we decided to trust Tory and give her a bit more time?" I snarled, the small army at my back seeming like anything but that.

"Oh, my sweet winter child," Geraldine gasped, looking towards the rising sun and clutching her hand over her heart. "She is lost to the darkness of her grief, tempted by the night and now plunged into danger. She swore that she would return that very eve for her supper – so how can I linger knowing that she is lost out there in the world, after an entire night more has passed while she is at the mercy of that dastardly Nymph and who knows what else?"

"The princess chose to abandon the safety of our stronghold," Tiberius said as he pushed his way through the crowd, my mom and Seth's allowing him to forge a path between the clamouring rebels. "We cannot send much needed soldiers out in search of her on some fool's mission. We have no idea where she has gone and no reason to believe she is even-"

"Hush your mouth, you sallywhacker!" Geraldine shouted, pointing a finger at Tiberius, and striding towards him with vines rising from the ground at her back, the challenge in her gaze clear as day.

"You don't seriously mean to fight me over this?" Tiberius scoffed.

Geraldine slapped him with a vine that had snuck up over his shoulder while he was too busy puffing his chest up to notice, and his head wheeled to the side as a large, oval welt instantly appeared on his cheek.

I caught the tiny sound of amusement that escaped my mom as Tiberius roared furiously, metallic green scales erupting across his flesh and coating his arms and neck beneath the cuffs of his grey shirt.

He advanced on Geraldine with a cyclone building around his fists, and the rebels scrambled back as a fight looked about to break out.

"Dad! What the fuck?" Max yelled as he and Seth finally caught up to me, Seth running in his Wolf form with Max on his back.

"Stay out of this, son," Tiberius demanded, and Geraldine howled like a banshee as her vines sped forward like a hoard of vipers.

I shot aside, leaving them to it and shaking my head as I came to stand beside the other Heirs.

"She's determined to go after Tory," I muttered, but Max wasn't listening to me.

He jumped from Seth's back and ran towards the fight between his dad and his girlfriend, a stray vine slapping his ass hard enough to make his knees buckle as he yelled at them to stop again.

Seth shifted beside me, and I looked to him, my eyes falling down his body instantly, tracing the defined curves of his abs before dropping to his cock. Flashes of memory spun through me of the two of us alone, mouths meeting, hands wandering, passion burning-

"My eyes are up here," Seth teased, but there was an edge to his voice as I snapped my gaze back up to meet his, a moment of silence passing between us which held a question neither of us voiced.

"You great, gallumping sea whale," Geraldine hollered as she was hurled through the air over our heads, and I looked up to watch her go soaring by with interest, the sharp points of her breastplate glinting in the sunlight as if she had diamond nips. "You shall rue the day you took on a Grus!"

Tiberius folded his arms as he watched his magic toss her away, the smug smile on his face the last thing I saw before the ground beneath his feet disappeared and he plunged down into an enormous pit.

My mom threw Antonia over her shoulder and shot her out of the way before they ended up falling in too, and the gathered rebels all ran in different directions to try and avoid the magic as it was thrown back and forth.

The crowd ran in every direction, not knowing where best to go to escape any wayward magic which was blasted from the fight, and a huge, muscular Bear Shifter smacked into Seth as he was almost knocked from his feet by the rioting.

"Sorry, man," the guy breathed, backing up a step and offering a peace sign which instantly froze my blood in my veins.

"It's fine," Seth replied dismissively, the peace sign he gave him in return making a stone drop into my gut as I fought against any outward reaction.

I narrowed my eyes on the Bear Shifter and his puffed-up chest, noting the shitty pornographic tattoo on his right bicep and scowling at it as I considered shooting after him and showing him what a real predator looked like.

I felt Seth's gaze on me as I scowled at his latest conquest, and I wrenched my eyes away, my face a careful mask.

Max had dropped Seth's clothes when he'd run off, and I grabbed them in a blur of speed, dropping to my knees in front of Seth and holding his sweatpants out for him to step into.

He blinked down at me in surprise as I tapped his calf to get his attention, heat rising in my blood as I worked not to look at his dick again from my new and much closer position.

Seth stepped into his pants obediently and I stood, my knuckles grazing the backs of his legs as I gently pulled them up for him, our eyes meeting once more as I drew them over the hard muscles of his ass.

I hesitated there, meaning to step back but finding the task impossible as the heat of his skin reeled me in like a fish on a damn line. I gave in to that sensation instead of drawing away from it as I inhaled a lungful of air laced with his breath.

I slid my fingers around his waistband, tracing my way from his spine to his hips, following the curve of the fabric along his sides then across his lower abs all the way to the line of hair beneath his navel. My fangs snapped out as I hovered there, too close to him for propriety and yet too far to take what I was really aching for.

Seth made no move to touch me in return, his eyes two hard chips of ice as he looked at me, reminding me that I was crossing a line, that there were other Fae here and that we didn't do this. But my unspoken want for him was starting to blur the lines which I once hadn't even had to look for, and it was getting harder to resist finding these kinds of excuses.

"Did you run last night?" I asked him, and he nodded, a flick of his fingers stabilising the ground beneath our feet as it started to tremble beneath the force of Tiberius's power as he worked to dig himself out of the grave Geraldine had dug for him.

"Are you thirsty?" Seth asked slowly and I took my turn to nod, my fingers still skimming beneath the line of his waistband. "Well, stop dancing around the point then," he snapped, and I flinched the smallest amount because his words had cut a bit too close to the truth that I couldn't admit to him.

I covered my reaction to his accusation by yanking him towards me and sinking my teeth into his throat. I barely even heard Geraldine yodelling a battle cry as I was stolen away on the tide of his moonlit power, a groan escaping me as the decadent taste of him rolled over my tongue.

My fingers flexed, pushing a bit lower beneath the fabric of his pants, hidden between our closeness, and he growled at me as he took hold of the back of my neck and fisted his hand in my curls, cementing our bodies together.

"Fucking…stars…balls," he panted in my ear, his chest heaving against mine while I took my fill of him, my cock stirring at his nearness, my mind on the feeling of his mouth wrapped around me as I pushed my hand a little lower.

I was supposed to be forgetting about that, supposed to be okay with my place as another notch in his belt, but every time I got close to him like this, it was all too easy to forget that. All too easy to let myself think of other things I wanted to try with him. All too easy to indulge in the idea that he might think of me differently to the others he took to his bed.

"Take that, you cantankerous cretin!" Geraldine's voice was accompanied by something splashing against my cheek and I forced myself to pull back, releasing Seth as I looked around to find Tiberius coated in mud from head to foot. Geraldine was eighty percent trapped in a block of ice, just her head, arm, and one pointed metal boob poking out the top of it.

"Oh, Cally," my mom's voice made me flinch away from Seth, snatching my hand out of his waistband so that the elastic snapped against his taut abs, making him curse. "You always were a messy eater."

"Gah, stop it." I tried to bat her off as she licked her thumb and made a move to swipe at the corner of my mouth where I was guessing some of Seth's blood was showing on my skin.

"What have I told you about letting your chums feed on your magic in public, Seth Capella?" Antonia barked, clipping him around the ear like he was a naughty pup and making him snarl as he tried to escape her too. "Do you want the whole world to see pictures of you submitting for an Altair? Do you want them to think you let him push you down beneath him and have his way with you day and night, at his each and every whim, plunging his huge-"

"Mom, what the fuck?" Seth cried but she continued regardless, managing to clip him round the ear again.

"-teeth into you whenever the urge arises?"

"Ugh, you make it sound so weird," Seth howled while I tried to shoot away from my own mother, but she just shot right into my path and managed to get me with her licky thumb, stealing the drop of blood from the corner of my mouth.

She promptly sucked the blood off, and I snarled at her furiously as her eyes lit at the taste of his blood.

"Mom," I snapped angrily. "He's *my* Source. You can't just go around drinking his fucking blood, or I'll-"

"You're his what?" Antonia cried, her fury cutting my words in two, and Seth shot me a look which said he had half a mind to beat the shit out of me. "Since when in the history of the stars themselves has a Capella *ever* been the Source of a Vampire? Oh heavens, I can see the headlines now. 'Seth Capella, on his knees for an Altair.' Think of the polls. The whole world is going to think you've bowed for him, and then they'll question everything about the balance of power – as if Darius's death hadn't already thrown enough of a rotten egg into the mix."

"Mom, for fuck's sake, stop it," Seth barked. "You're making it into a much bigger deal than it-"

"You will relinquish your claim on him this instant." Antonia whirled on me, her eyes flashing silver with her Wolf and a finger pointed straight in my face.

I bared my fangs at her in reply, every muscle in my body going rigid in a clear refusal of that demand.

"No," I snarled. "I won't. He's mine."

"I don't see what the big deal is, Toni," Mom said, baring her own fangs at Seth's mother. "Maybe I should think about claiming you or Tiberius as my own on-tap blood supply too."

Antonia snarled ferociously as her attention whipped from me to my mom, but before the chaos could descend any further, a crack seemed to tear through the air itself. The wards surrounding us were wrenched open by some incredible power, and a flash of light had us all spinning to look as Tory and Miguel appeared from thin air, stardust twinkling around them for a moment before vanishing.

Tory lifted a hand and the wards sealed themselves up again, a dome of pure power glittering high above our heads for a brief moment before it cleared and became invisible once more.

My lips parted as I took in the sight of her skin covered in smears of blood, her beautiful black dress torn and filthy, and a haunted look in her eyes as she sagged against Miguel for support.

"What happened?" I demanded, shooting forward, and snatching her from him, hoisting her into my arms where she expelled a breath and let herself slump against me.

"I'm fine," she muttered. "Just exhausted and tapped out. Miguel is still one of the good guys."

Geraldine was wailing from her giant ice cube, and everyone else seemed torn between surrounding Miguel and getting closer to Tory for an explanation.

"Where the fuck did you go?" Max half yelled as he stomped towards us. "Gerry has been having kittens. We didn't know if you were dead or kidnapped or-"

"Watch out, Max, or people might start to think you care about a Vega," Tory taunted, and I was glad to see that she was still very much herself despite the state of her.

She shifted in my arms again and I realised she was pushing the Book of Ether between her side and my chest, using the material of the gown she was wearing to try and hide it. No doubt she didn't want any of our parents asking questions about it, and I gave her a slight squeeze in understanding.

"Does Miguel need locking up?" I asked, drawing her nearer in my arms to help hide the book as everyone closed in around us and the sound of shattering ice signalled Geraldine breaking free of her prison.

"No," Tory said firmly. "He's on our side. Maybe get him a bagel or something, Geraldine?"

"But, my lady," Geraldine protested, looking at a total loss as her bottom lip wobbled.

"I'm fine, I promise." Tory tried to wave her off. "I just want to get near a fire and have a bath, then I'll fill you all in. Focus on what we need for tomorrow, okay? The Hydrids meteor shower is almost here, and we need to be ready to move, for Darcy's sake."

"I'll take you to your room," I said, glancing between the others for the briefest of moments, making sure Seth and Max understood that I needed to get her out of here before shooting off and leaving them all behind.

The world passed us in a blur, and I raced over the drawbridge and up the sets of stairs to the extravagant rooms Geraldine had created for the Vegas, turning to the right into Tory's.

I tossed her down on the bed, making her bounce as she rolled over, the word asshole carrying back to me in a muffled voice as she faceplanted the pillows.

Fire blossomed in my palm and I filled her fireplace with it before dropping down on the bed beside her with more flames licking their way across my hands and forearms.

Tory kicked her boots off, leaving the Book of Ether in the space dividing us as she sighed at the warmth of the flames and unbuckled her sword too, tossing it on the carpet.

"What's with the bloodstains?" I asked, pointing to her arm where it looked like someone had been doodling all over her in gory ink. The marks were hard to make out, so many of them drawn on top of others but I recognised a couple of runes drawn in the freshest of the blood.

"Oh, you know. I went to some creepy cave and met these three witches who practice dark magic-"

"No such thing as witches, Tor." I gave her a nudge and she rolled her eyes at me.

"Well, they were Nymph witches who called themselves oracles. And they looked like goddesses given flesh. I swear to fuck, I almost wish I was gay for the sake of those women alone."

"Almost?" I teased.

"Well, I have a pathetically prevalent obsession with cock, but aside from that..."

I choked out a laugh and she gave me a grin, but it died somewhere along the way, her eyes glazing as they moved to something else that had happened.

"Tell me," I urged, and she blew out a breath.

"It was...honestly, Caleb, it was all kinds of fucked up, and I'll admit that I pretty much just gave in to the call of their magic and promised them the world if they would only help me find my way back to him."

I didn't need to ask who she meant, my own heart aching as I reached out and took her hand in my flame-wreathed fingers, giving her a gentle squeeze which she returned before withdrawing her hand from mine.

"You can't come back looking like that-" I waved a hand at the bloodstains and filthy dress "-and not explain it properly."

"Fine." Tory turned to look up at the ceiling, expelled a harsh breath, and said, "I may have spent an entire day and night engaging in what could objectively be called a memory orgy where the three of them all lived through a hell of a lot of mine and Darius's sex life by bringing my memories to life and watching me fuck him repeatedly until I blacked out."

"What the fuck?" I spluttered, and she groaned, throwing an arm over her eyes so she didn't have to look at me.

"I dunno, dude. It was...so real. He was there, he was touching me and kissing me, and I could feel all of it. But he wasn't there at the same time. The places I could see didn't actually exist around us, and I honestly don't know if I was just laying on a stone table masturbating the entire time while the three of them all pawed at me and got their kicks from the show."

"Wow," I said, not entirely sure what the hell I was supposed to say to that because it sounded seriously fucked up, as well as at least a bit hot, and if the ache in her voice was anything to go by, it had only really served to sharpen her grief. "If they were so beautiful, then why don't they just get their own kicks instead of wanting to watch you and Darius go at it all night long?"

"Well, they were all virgins to aid with their dark magic shit - which doesn't exactly bode well for me if that is integral to using it fully, by the way - and they'd also made a few interesting choices like sewing their eyes and lips closed to keep a certain level of evil from fully corrupting them - not that I'm convinced it had helped. But either way, I'm not sure all that many Fae would be brave enough to fuck them, even if the virginity barrier wasn't there-"

"Aside from you, who effectively fucked all three of them," I pointed out, and she scowled at me.

"It wasn't like that. Well, I guess it was but… It was…me and him." She sighed, the pain of his loss pressing down on her. "Me and him with a trio of witnesses," she added with an amused snort.

"Witnesses who were getting off on it," I pointed out.

"Yeah," she agreed with a shrug, like that was the least of it.

"So what did this orgy get you? A night with him?"

"Yeah…" She trailed off, glancing towards the door before taking a rolled piece of parchment from inside the front page of the Book of Ether and holding it out to me.

I extinguished the flames on my hands, taking it and opening the scroll, frowning at the cryptic message while trying to gain some understanding of what it meant but coming up blank.

"Do you know where the Damned Forest is by any chance?" Tory asked me and I shook my head.

"Never heard of it. What's there?"

"Answers. Maybe. The only chance they thought I might have of finding a way to him without passing beyond the Veil myself."

I frowned at the words again, but they meant nothing to me. "If that's some place in Solaria, then it isn't on any map I've ever studied. And believe me, I've studied way too many of them," I said, handing her the note back, and she sighed as she tucked it into the book again.

"Figures. But I'm going to work it out. I have to."

I nodded, understanding that just as I understood how dangerous this magic she was messing with might be. But it was Darius. I would go to the ends of the earth with her to bring him back if that was what it took, no price would be too steep.

"I need to wash this Nymph blood off," Tory groaned, brushing a hand over the stains on her arm.

"Did they kill someone for all that blood?" I half teased, half questioned seriously.

"No. Vidi, the one who had sewn her eyes shut, slit her wrist for it. I think ether requires a sacrifice and an anchor to work fully. She was using the tie of her blood to my skin to draw the memories from me and make them as tangible as they were. She made him real."

Tory swallowed thickly, and I didn't need to ask how being with him like that had left her feeling. It must have been like stepping into the past without having any chance to change the future she knew he was going to face.

"I'm sorry," I said, knowing it didn't do anything to help her, but she gave me a wry smile all the same.

"I understood what it was when I agreed to it. And it wasn't something I could have refused, no matter how badly I knew it was going to hurt when it was over."

Tory stood and moved to the huge bathtub beside the window, casting hot water into it with a mixture of water and fire magic, her power already replenishing from the flames in the room.

I picked up the Book of Ether as she stripped off, not looking her way as I started leafing through it, despite having done so multiple times before. I kept finding new notes or incantations every time I looked at it, like the book had been judging me every time I gave it my attention and was willing to release a little more of its knowledge on each visit. I knew that made no sense, but I didn't know how else to explain it.

"It says here that soul walking can be used to find your heart's desire, but the description doesn't seem entirely like what you did when you located Darcy and Orion," I said thoughtfully, reading over the use of various crystals to locate things like riches or lost treasure. "It's not as simple as finding someone you share blood with, but I think it can be done."

"What's the cost?" Tory asked, her back to me as she climbed into the bath and sank down into the hot water.

I skimmed the page and winced. "Err, there's heavy indication that an infant animal could be used in a sacrificial-"

"Ew. No. Give me a green Dragon asshole to bleed out in payment and I'll be all over it, but I'm not murdering a baby bunny. What else?"

"It's a little unclear, but there is a notation here which says 'one month.' Do you think that's a month off of your life or a month of servitude to some goat beast, or-"

"A goat beast?" Tory asked, turning her head and arching an eyebrow at me over the rim of the tub. "What would I have to do for the goat beast? Feed it shoes and take it on walks up mountain trails?"

"Probably. Hang on, I think there's more to this anyway…"

I trailed off as I read more from the book, turning the pages and cross-referencing with indexes and other chapters. Honestly, the entire thing seemed to have been written with the sole intention of confusing the reader, not a single spell or divine rite laid out clearly.

The door banged open, and Geraldine shrieked like a new-born velociraptor as she flung herself over the threshold, tears streaming down her cheeks as she raced towards Tory with her arms outstretched.

"Well, isn't this cosy?" Seth commented as he and Max followed her into the room, closing the door again behind them while Geraldine half submerged herself in her efforts to hug a rather wet Vega. "All snuggled up in bed while Tory gets naked."

"She was covered in blood," I replied, my eyes still on the book as I beckoned him closer. "She needed to wash it off, don't you think?"

"I'm surprised your tongue didn't manage to get all of it without the need for the tub," Seth sniped, his tone making me look up at him with a frown.

Max rolled his eyes at the two of us and headed into the en suite, muttering something about a public shit being less uncomfortable than this as he went.

"Nymph blood doesn't really do it for me," I deadpanned, wondering why Seth was being so fucking pissy. Was he considering what his mom had said about not being my Source? Was he really thinking about breaking off our bond like that for the sake of appearances?

My heart began to thrash unevenly as I considered it, and I dropped the book onto Tory's pillow as I looked at him more closely.

"No? What does do it for you then, Cal? Because I'm finding it pretty damn hard to tell these days," Seth practically growled at me as he held his ground by the door, and I shot towards him, meaning to meet that challenge in his eyes but falling still a mere breath from him instead, my hand snapping out to grip his throat. I didn't squeeze though, my fingers brushing over his Adam's apple softly instead, grazing his skin until I found the still unhealed bite wound, then lifting my eyes to his.

"If you plan on doing what your mom told you to, then just say it," I challenged, my voice a rough whisper which I doubted the others could hear over Geraldine's loud recounting of how worried she had been about Tory while she took on the job of washing her hair for her.

Seth's lips parted on the words, the rejection shining in his eyes just like that fucking peace sign, waiting to taunt me tirelessly, but he didn't speak them.

Something shifted and hardened in his eyes, his gaze sharpening as the Alpha in him rose its head and he bared his teeth at me again.

"No one else can handle you the way I can, pretty boy," he taunted instead, knocking my hand from his throat before grabbing me by the front of my shirt and whirling me around so my back slammed into the door with a solid bang.

He was in my face instantly, speaking so close to me that I could taste every word as they passed his lips.

"The next time you come looking for a drink from your Source, I'm going to make sure you remember that. I'll pin you beneath me and remind you who the most powerful Werewolf in Solaria is, and you'll be offering me *your* throat in submission to prove that you haven't forgotten."

My heart thrashed at his words, blood thundering through my body at an impossible pace and my breath catching in my lungs as he shoved himself away from me and left me panting for him against the fucking door like some pathetic fan girl.

Seth stalked across the room, scooping a half empty bottle of tequila out of Tory's things and taking a long swig from it, his back to me in a clear insult which I knew I should have been calling him out on.

But I couldn't find it in me to do it. He hadn't rejected my claim on him. He was still my Source. And the promise he'd just given me made me ache for the hunt despite the fresh supply of magic I still had tearing through my veins from biting him less than half an hour ago.

Geraldine had bundled Tory out of the bath and wrapped her in a black silk gown, despite the half assed protests she was getting over all the fussing.

But as Tory let herself be guided into a chair and Geraldine bellowed a command for someone to bring a fresh platter of bagels, I could tell that she didn't mind the attention nearly as much as she claimed.

The sound of the toilet flushing reached us, and Max returned to the room, a scowl passing over his face as he looked from me to Seth. I tightened my mental shields, not wanting him to see the messed-up shit I was dealing with at the moment. Max had his own pain to contend with, his relationship with Geraldine too, and I knew he was drowning in the constant flood of fear and grief the rebels were emitting at all times as well. He didn't need my bullshit piling on top of that, and I refused to place the burden of it on him.

"Are you going to tell us where the fuck you've been then, little Vega?" Max asked, dropping down onto Tory's bed and lacing his hands behind his head.

"I'll tell you," Tory agreed as Geraldine began brushing her hair, murmuring about wildebugs and snaggletooths living in it soon if she didn't get all the snarly-gnarlies out. "But we're going to need to focus on our plan to rescue Darcy, Orion, and Gabriel before we can do anything about it. The Hydra is still set to bellow at The Palace of Souls tomorrow, right?"

"As clearly as a moonday maw, my lady," Geraldine agreed, and Tory visibly relaxed.

"Good. Because I am more than ready to get my fucking twin back."

Scorpio
Gemini
Virgo
Cancer
Leo
Sagittarius
Taurus
Capricorn
Aquarius
Libra
Pisces

LIONEL

CHAPTER THIRTY SEVEN

I pulled on my favourite blood-red smoking jacket and admired myself in the gilded mirror in the rooms I'd claimed for myself.

I was still having trouble accessing Hail Vega's old chambers, the grandest in the palace, and worse than that, I still could not get even close to the treasury. It was as if the corridors shifted and changed every time I delved into the deeper regions of the palace, though it was surely just some spell set to confuse me. Whatever pathetic magic had been placed here to try and keep me out would dissolve in the face of my might eventually though, I was certain of it.

Lavinia had travelled north to visit her army of Nymphs this evening, and I was finally free of her at last. If only for one night. But I would certainly be making the most of it.

I had summoned Francesca Sky to me, the FIB agent a beautiful specimen who had often crossed my mind since our last meeting. It was time I got a taste of sweet, warm flesh again. And hers was a delicacy I would spend many hours enjoying.

She was most willing. Her answer to my summons having come swiftly, as I had predicted. I had seen the way she flushed in my company, how she admired my great size and looked up at me through those thick lashes with want. I was the most desired man in the kingdom now, I supposed. The Dragon King. The greatest Fae to ever live.

I slipped a belt through the loops of my trousers, fastening it tight and running my thumb over the golden clasp shaped like a Dragon's scale, feeling the little touch of magic it gave me. I had laid naked upon my newly acquired gold offered up from the Dragon Guild all afternoon, recharging my power and writhing in my trove. Though I had been sorely reminded of the treasure that had been stolen from me, some of the most valuable pieces of history among my trove now vanished into the rebels' grasp.

I growled, smoke pooling between my lips and heat rising in my chest like a furnace. *No, I must not dwell on that tonight.*

I would soon find my way into the palace treasury and lay claim to all the priceless jewels that were hidden within. *Mine. All mine.*

A nervous knock came at the door which I was growing far too accustomed to.

"Enter, Vard," I growled, the Cyclops irking me as always. He had been working on Gabriel Nox's mind day after day now and had produced little of substance, telling me all he could see in the Seer's head were visions of a giant nest shaped like a falcon and fine sticks inlaid with gemstones. I had no idea what trickery was at play, but there was something the Seer was doing to evade being broken again. But Gabriel would *see* the rebels make a mistake soon enough, and then Vard would pull the vision from his head and I would march out to obliterate them that very same day.

The next time I met with the rebels, I would not leave a single one of them to breathe another breath. I would eradicate them, every man, woman, and child, burned to ash so that they could never rise against me again.

"Sire, I have made some progress today with my experiments. I thought you might like to come and see?" Vard asked hopefully, like a mutt looking for scraps.

I pushed a hand through my golden hair, styling it just so and taking a moment to admire myself longer in the mirror, letting him wait on my answer.

"If you waste my time again, I will be most displeased."

"I promise you will want to see this," he said eagerly. "Come, sire. I will bring a smile to your face this day yet."

I turned, letting him lead me from the room and down into the belly of the palace where I allowed him to conduct his experiments. I followed him into a brick walled room where a woman was strapped down on a metal bed in the middle of it, the sound of rebels crying and begging from nearby cages irritating me. I cast a silencing bubble over them so that I didn't have to listen to their unFae whimpering and followed Vard over to the woman.

Her eyes were glassy, though she was still with us, her fingers twitching a little to let me know as much. She was young, pretty perhaps, if it weren't for the tubes sticking out of her flesh, feeding some glowing blue potion beneath her skin.

"Look," Vard said, picking up a little wooden tongue depressor and using it to peel the woman's upper lip back.

Vampire fangs were revealed, and I looked from them to Vard blankly. "And?"

"And she is a Harpy by birth," he said with a twisted smile, making the scar across the side of his face crease.

"Has she shown interest in feeding?" I asked, my curiosity piqued at last.

"A little," he said. "These trials have been far more successful than my Emergence trials. I spent many years trying to switch the orders of children before their Orders awoke. That seemed most logical, you see? But I had little success with it, though I learned much about the inner workings of the Orders and how to contain them once they are removed. Each Order is different, some trickier to sustain than others when they are cut from a subject. And I believe children can be useful to this area of science yet."

I nodded, my curiosity deepening. "And does the essence of these Orders die once the subject dies?"

"Some do, others live on," he breathed excitedly, leading me over to a metal cabinet which had frost clinging to its exterior. He opened it with a wave of his hand and a flash of magic, tugging the doors wide and showing me the rows of large glass jars inside. Light glowed inside them, flickering, pulsing, each moving to its own particular rhythm. I read the labels on them all with intrigue. Manticore, Cerberus, Werewolf, Medusa, Vampire, Centaur.

"My babies are waiting for a new home," Vard said, snapping the doors shut with a gleeful smile. "Your cousin Benjamin has been quite helpful with this project. Perhaps you would permit him back into your court?" he asked sweetly, clearly put up to this by my uncouth cousin, and I bristled.

"Benjamin may assist you, but I will not risk bringing him into my court. He is a gambler and a liability. No Dragon worth their salt should gamble away their trove, it's despicable," I spat.

"Of course, sire," Vard said, bowing his head and leading me back to the girl strapped down on the table. "Now let me see if I can get our friend to feed."

The newly made Vampire gnashed her teeth, thrashing wildly, her empty eyes filling with a murderous want. But that hungry, riotous need in her suddenly turned into a fit, her body starting to jerk, her eyes rolling into the back of her head.

"No, no, no. Hang on." Vard pressed healing magic into her skin, but blood was dripping from the woman's mouth, her ears, her eyes, the thrashing of her body only gaining in intensity before she fell all too still, eyes wide and death stealing her away.

I clucked my tongue in annoyance.

"What did I tell you about wasting my time?" I snarled, and Vard winced from my tone, lifting the wooden tongue depressor and shrinking behind it as if it could save him from my ire.

I caught him by the throat, fire blazing in my palm, and his scream echoed around the room as I felt his skin sizzling beneath my heated grip. I released him before I burned my way too deep, and he staggered to the ground, holding his neck with a whimper.

I turned my back on him, leaving him there to heal himself and striding for the exit, but his calls made me pause on the threshold as he dared cry out for me again.

"Sire! There is another subject you should see – the other experiment I have been working on!"

Curiosity rose in me unwanted, but I couldn't resist the urge to turn back fully, my gaze moving over the pathetic creature who called himself my Royal Seer. The only reason I still kept him in my court was because of the few exceptionally useful visions he had managed to conjure during his time of service to me. He may have been a pitiful waif of a Fae, but occasionally, he proved his worth. I would not have found the rebels' hideout without him, and I could not forget that.

"Show me," I growled, and he nodded quickly, scrambling to his feet and beckoning me after him.

He hurried across the room towards the next chamber, guiding me past the corridor which led to the cells holding the Fae destined to become his next test subjects, their cries for mercy stirring my blood as I ignored them.

Vard strode into a dim corridor where thick metal bars marked the front of huge cells, the test subjects within those on our left recoiling from us while we passed two empty cages on our right before Vard finally fell still.

He reached out for a clipboard hanging from the bars and I drew closer to him, peering into the cell, seeing only shifting darkness within.

He offered me the clipboard and I snatched it from him, my eyes roaming over the information there detailing the subject's name as Will Oli, his Order form a Vampire and his Element fire. Beneath it was the name of a monster which I knew lurked in the bowels of this world; Obscuro, a beast of twisting darkness with rows of sharpened teeth that could skin a Fae in minutes.

"These are the genetic mutations you've been working on?" I asked curiously, and Vard smiled toothily at me, the movement stretching his scar and making him seem even uglier than usual.

"I call him, the Oliwill," he breathed, his excitement palpable.

I stepped closer to the bars as I spotted movement within the cage, the darkness seeming to shift in the rear corner.

I walked all the way up to the bars, squinting to see better before flicking my fingers and casting a Faelight into existence.

A shriek erupted from the cage at the illumination of the bright light, my heart leaping as a creature of smoke and flame shot towards me with the speed of a Vampire, death flashing before my eyes as I caught sight of a feral face hidden within the thick smoke.

I stumbled back, my feet tripping over themselves, and Vard snatched my arm into his grip to keep me from falling as the thing in the cage wailed with hunger, lashing its near formless body against the bars.

"He's hungry," Vard purred, watching the thing he had created with wicked delight, and I found myself staring as I straightened, taking in this creature of chaos.

"What does it eat?" I asked in a low tone, cocking my head to one side as I surveyed the beast, its body humanoid, but ghostly too where the smoke parted to reveal its lengthened limbs.

Vard's smile widened and he lifted his hand, casting magic towards the rear wall of the cell. It parted at his command, a prisoner revealed in the chamber there, her face written with terror as the Oliwill snapped its attention to her.

She barely managed to scream as it shot for her, blood spraying across the walls in a wide arc as the Oliwill made a feast of her in seconds, flesh and bone shredding within its wide, tooth-filled jaw.

"You have control of this creature?" I demanded, as a vision spread before my eyes, of me wielding this thing at my will, setting it on those who disobeyed me, using it to tighten my hold on this rebellious kingdom.

"I used collars in my previous experiments, but I am designing new methods to control them, ones which are hardwired into their minds and cannot be broken by outside forces. Though as of yet, I haven't perfected that," Vard admitted in a small voice. "And…"

"Spit it out," I snarled, making him flinch as I allowed my Faelight to dim, leaving the Oliwill to its meal of rebel flesh.

"Only around one in fifty survive the modification, and even then, they don't live for long."

"How long do they manage?" I demanded and he flinched.

"The Oliwill is the first of this batch to make it beyond a day. The records of the processes I used when I first developed these methods were all destroyed when the Celestial Council voted against me continuing with these experiments," he sighed, casting his eyes to the floor, and I didn't miss the tone of accusation there.

"As you know well, I voted for those experiments to continue. And without me taking the throne, you wouldn't have ever been granted the permission required to restart them," I growled, and he cowered like the snivelling cockroach he was.

"Of course, sire. I didn't mean any disrespect. I only meant to explain why I am struggling to recreate such viable subjects. Oliwill is doing better than the others, but even he is showing signs of deterioration. At the current rate, he will be dead before dawn…"

I cursed as I looked from Vard to the cage containing the gruesome creature, my need for more power consuming me as it always had. I would never get enough, never reach the epitome of all I craved.

"Keep working on it then," I commanded.

"I shall, of course. I had great success in the past with such mutations, but it is proving difficult to recreate without my original notes to go on." He sighed again. "However, I have a woman I am prepping. Mary Brown. She is responding well to the initial stages of the trial. Perhaps she will respond as well as my dear Ian did."

"Good. Only bother me again if you make a success of it next time." I turned and strode away from Vard as he simpered in my wake, slamming the door shut behind me.

When I made it back upstairs, I walked to the lounge I had asked Horace to prepare for my date and found him waiting with a fine bottle of whiskey and my favourite cigars. I relaxed, the tension rolling out of my body at finding him living up to my expectations for once. His minor mistakes were becoming fewer, but I still missed the perfection Jenkins had brought to this role. *Lavinia just had to go and fucking eat him, didn't she?*

I clipped the cigar and lit it with a flame cast upon my index finger, wafting Horace away to pour me a glass of whiskey and dropping into the large wingback chair by the fire. Yes, this was good. I could breathe again now that Lavinia was no longer in the palace, and when Horace passed me my whiskey in a golden chalice, I thought on how I might regain control over Lavinia, taking a long sip of the fine drink. I really had to get a hold on her before she demanded an heir from me again.

I shuddered at the thought of her taking me to bed, of getting me to give her some monstrous child again. I had to try and avoid that fate at all costs.

I had a host of diviners reading the fates for me regularly in every manner they could, and I received daily Horoscopes from the Horometer at Zodiac Academy too.

Just this morning, I had been offered a grand forecast from the stars.

I took out my Atlas, reading over it again and enjoying another sip of the fine whiskey.

Good morning, Aries.
The stars have spoken about your day!
Power blossoms in your life like a spring flower reaching towards a bright blue sky. The day ahead is set to be a bountiful one indeed, but the turbulent nature of your ruling planet, Mars, may bring lows along with the highs. Ride the highs while they last and reflect on the lows. Your need for sexual connection is finally coming to fruition as the alignment of Venus in your chart predicts a fiery experience in your near future.

I smiled, putting my Atlas away and thinking on my highs, anticipating many more to come.

The academy was well under my control now, many of my Nebula Taskforce placed within its ranks, and I had Dark Coerced anyone who had opposed my reign. I had big plans for the academy, a place to train the higher Orders and recruit them to my army. I would have the curriculum overhauled, and all lessons would focus on creating warriors out of my allies. I had dreams of an army which could one day crush all others. With the lesser Orders eradicated, the pure lines would live on, generation after generation, making Solaria the greatest power on earth.

I could be the king of the entire world one day, but there was one thing I needed to ensure that. Time. And I could secure it as soon as I found the Imperial Star. If the legends were true, it could grant me immortality and I would remain here forever, conquering the realm piece by piece.

My cock stirred at the mere idea of it, and I took a toke on my cigar, rolling it between my teeth and settling back into my seat. Things were not perfect, but problems could always be solved. I just needed to think on how to handle Lavinia, and once she was subdued, I would kill Gwendalina Vega. Perhaps I could even find a way to use her to lure her sister to me, then kill them both in a bloodbath of my own design. It had worked once before, after all.

A woman stepped through the open door and my eyebrows arched at Stella Orion in a tight navy dress and high heels. She looked ravishing, yet her expression did not speak of her delight at seeing me like I expected.

"Good evening, Your Highness," she said respectfully, bowing her head for a moment before glancing at Horace. "I thought we could have a word…alone?"

"Of course." I wafted my hand at Horace, and he scarpered from the room, shutting the door behind him as he went.

Stella remained across the room, folding her arms as she inspected my outfit, and her eyes brightened a little. "Were you expecting me?"

"No," I said simply. "I have company arriving soon."

"What kind of company?"

"The female kind," I admitted.

I didn't care to lie to her. What did she expect? I was the king now, and my needs were as infinite as the sky.

Her eyes rippled with some weak emotion which I wasn't going to bother to decipher, and she folded her arms.

"Why did you bring me to the palace?" she asked.

"You know why. I enjoy you very much, Stella. But I cannot escape the wants of other women. I am the most desired Fae in Solaria. And as king, I shall be pleasured by the beauties of this land as is only right for a man of my status."

Her throat bobbed as she nodded, seeming to accept that.

"How is the new rift coming along?" I asked, flicking a silencing bubble around us to keep our secret between us.

"Slowly, as you asked," Stella said. "But sooner or later, Lavinia will figure out that I am stalling on it, and what will happen then?"

"I'm working on it," I assured her. "Just buy me a little more time. Now off you go." I jerked my chin at the door. "Who knows, perhaps I'll have my fill of my company early, then come seek you out in your bed tonight too." I smiled seductively, and her lips twitched as if she was going to object, then she bowed her head and left me there.

I chuckled to myself, puffing on my cigar again. She was learning her place in this world, and it was at my beck and call. I liked the way it sparked a fire in her, and I'd enjoy extinguishing that fire just as much. She was my plaything now, and she liked it too. She would admit that to herself eventually.

I flicked the ash of my cigar in the ashtray, gazing into the fire in the hearth, thinking on my issues. I had always been a master problem solver, and I had made it through greater challenges than these.

There was an answer just out of my reach, my diviners had spoken of it many times this past week. The stars were turning in my favour again, shining down on their favourite Fae and blessing me with their light. Indeed, the answer was coming, I only needed to be patient.

Scorpio
Gemini
Virgo
Cancer
Aries
Leo
Sagittarius
Taurus
Capricorn
Aquarius
Libra
Pisces

FRANCESCA

CHAPTER THIRTY EIGHT

My hazel hair was pinned back with a silver clip which hid a tourmaline crystal, the magic of which I was going to need tonight if I was ever going to pull this off. I brushed my fingers over the colourful stone, casting a concealment spell to divert anyone's attention from it.

My heart was galloping like a Pegasus about to take off into the sky, and I took a moment to relax as I sat in my car not far from the gates of The Palace of Souls, just out of sight of the guards. Mom's voice rang in my head, her words always knowing how to calm me.

"Francesca, you are only as strong as you feel you are. Power is nothing without confidence."

She'd taught me how to claim my place in the world, and I'd followed in her footsteps in the end, taking up a position in the FIB. I'd never known my father, and it had never occurred to me to go looking for him either. My mom hadn't planned on having children, but later in life, she had fallen pregnant with me by chance while she was out training on the Isles of Kahinti. There was an entire town there built with the sole purpose of FIB agents partaking in simulation exercises.

FIB units from all over Solaria went there every year, and my mom had had a brief fling with one of the officers. She'd told him about me, but he'd decided he didn't want anything to do with me, and I'd taken up the same opinion when I was old enough to care.

So Mom had been my person, but a few years ago, I'd had to watch her fade away from me, piece by piece. She'd had a good, long life, and she hadn't been afraid of stepping beyond the Veil. In fact, she'd been excited to see long lost friends and family again, but her single regret was leaving me here alone. I'd tried to ease her worries; I had lots of friends among my colleagues and outside of them too. But I was pretty sure she was angling at something else, because towards the end, she'd kept asking about one man. The man who I'd seen a future with once. The man who was the reason I was sitting outside this palace now, about to do the unthinkable for.

I'd coped with Mom's loss in the end, though it changed me, as all death does. I'd seen agents die long before their time in the line of duty, leaving young families behind to try and handle life without them. That was the kind of death that seemed devastatingly unfair, though others would say that as long as they had died fighting for a better world, then their death was not in vain.

Mom had known that too, and she had instilled in me a moral compass which was spinning now, driving me to do the right thing even when it terrified me. But of course, it wasn't really my morals that had me sitting here in a fitted red dress with a slit up one leg and gold jewellery draped around my throat and wrists. It was him. Forever him.

I flipped the sun visor down and checked my makeup in the mirror on the back of it, my eyes smoky, my lips the colour of blood. Lance Orion may have been mated to another woman, but I had loved him first, and I wasn't going to let that love turn to bitterness. It may have been unrequited, but that didn't make it invalid. Though that didn't make it hurt any less.

I vividly recalled the moment when I'd been summoned into work after his arrest, my friend tipping me off on the whole thing. And I'd actually laughed, certain there was a mistake, that I'd turn up at the precinct to find Lance telling me the truth, then I'd use my Cyclops gifts to clear his name. But it hadn't turned out that way. When I'd seen him, he'd looked desperate, broken, terrified. He'd turned me away, and I wasn't sure if that was the moment my heart had shattered or if it was the moment when he'd pleaded guilty and been sent to prison.

I knew him. And I knew that what he'd spoken on the stand had been a lie the moment it left his lips. He sacrificed himself for a Vega princess, a girl who he had spent months agonising over because of her threat to the Celestial Heirs, and in particular, Darius Acrux.

None of it had made any sense until I'd been delivered the final piece of the puzzle in the form of one of the worst nights of my life. Finding him under the stars, newly mated to Darcy Vega, watching him kiss her like she was the lifeblood of his soul, like he could no longer see anyone or anything else. Yes, my heart had broken the moment his illegal affair had come to light, but it had been crushed and set on fire the night he had been mated to her.

I guessed I'd foolishly held onto some quiet hope that she and him wouldn't last, that he would one day come back to me and we'd pick up where we left off. But no one could defy silver rings.

I'd convinced myself the two of us were meant to be, but the stars had had other plans the whole time.

Wasted. All those years loving him, trying to pretend what he and I had was just sex, telling my friends that was all I wanted from him, and that it suited me just fine. But deep down, for years, I'd harboured that love for him and had been too much of a coward to admit it. Now all that silent suffering seemed so fucking pointless.

Why did I let the years tick by? Why didn't I Fae up and confess the truth to him? Or better yet, why didn't I cut things off and give my heart time to get over him?

As my mom would say, *"Regret is the enemy of the future."*

I couldn't move forward if I kept looking back, and yes, I'd had a little time to heal now, but honestly…it was like my heart wasn't capable of letting him go. So here I was, about to risk my life for him. A fool? Maybe. But I valued him far beyond my own selfish desire to be loved by him. We were friends, Nebula Allies to be precise, and nothing would change that. I would be here for him whether my heart pined for him or not. And as his Nebula Ally, I was here for his Elysian Mate too.

The moment my captain got wind that Lance Orion and Darcy Vega were being held by the king, I'd put my plans into place. The FIB were firmly under the thumb of Lionel Acrux now, and he had planted several of the Kings United Nebula Taskforce among my ranks to ensure we followed through on the new laws.

At first, I'd thought to run, to seek out the rebels and join their ranks, but then I realised that I was in the perfect position to spy on what the king was up to. I'd had to round up 'lesser' Fae and send them to the Nebular Inquisition Centres, but that meant I'd seen inside those camps, I'd seen what the king was doing, and my memories would become a weapon the moment I managed to hand them to the rebels. They could expose Lionel's regime and open the eyes of the civilians who believed the bullshit the false king fed to them about protecting them from traitors and insurgents.

I rolled the plain silver ring on my thumb, a gift from my mother who had also been of the Cyclops Order. The ring was a memory loop, something that could only be created by Cyclopses, and was now home to any memory I wished to store within it. It was the truth as brutally as I could present it, the things I had seen so chilling that I pitied the Fae who had to watch it. But Lionel could not get away with his plans to cull the 'lesser' Orders, taking everything they owned, then handing it out to his Dragon friends and anyone he deemed worthy. He was a monster. And I was about to walk into his lair and cast my first stone against him.

I placed a firm barrier over my mind, then stepped out of the car, locking it and slipping the key into my purse which hung from a chain over my shoulder. I walked around to the gates on high heels, a couple of Dragon cronies eyeing me in my skimpy outfit before letting me pass.

My heart was beating faster, but I called on my training and worked to convince myself that this was just another drill, pretending I was going through the motions to pass my latest evaluation. It was easier to think of it like that, a trick I'd picked up from my captain.

By the time I'd climbed the steps up to the imperial entranceway to the palace, I was calm, composed, and ready to face the Dragon King.

I was let inside by a servant, and I followed her along the winding corridors, the scent of smoke hanging heavily in the air. I was led into a grand lounge with low lighting where Lionel Acrux was manspreading in a huge wingback chair by a blazing fireplace, puffing on a cigar. He wore a dark, blood-red smoking jacket, and his eyes glinted jade green for a moment as his gaze fell on me.

The servant bowed and hurried away, leaving me there like a meal for the beast, and my confidence faltered for a moment. *Fake it 'til you make it.*

I raised my chin, not letting him see a fraction of fear in me. I was a predator just like he was, and I wasn't going to let him turn me into prey.

"Good evening, my King." I bowed my head respectfully and when I looked back up, his head was cocked to one side.

"I am glad you responded so quickly to my invitation, Francesca," he said, smoke streaming between his teeth as he exhaled. "Though I have to say, after our last meeting, I am surprised you did not reach out sooner."

"I would never be so brazen to assume you wanted me here, Your Highness. Besides, I am always so busy with work," I said apologetically, falling into the act I'd been practising for days in front of the mirror, preparing myself for this interaction. He had to believe I was here for him and only him, wholeheartedly trusting that I wanted him, and that no other cause had brought me to his door.

"You could not take a night off for your king?" he asked, a lilt of charisma in his voice.

"I was only trying to please my king by doing my duties in the FIB," I said, and he released a rumbling laugh.

"Hm, you are a well-bred creature indeed, Francesca. Duty above pleasure, that is the way of powerful Fae such as you and I. But we must indulge ourselves occasionally, no?"

"This is quite the indulgence," I said, biting my lip a little as I moved deeper into the room and brushed my fingers over the back of the green armchair that sat opposite him. It was far smaller in size, the seat much lower than his, and I had to wonder if that was intentional.

Had his wife sat here across from him? Had she ever loved him? Or had she always feared this terrible man? I couldn't help but pity her for the life she'd been forced to lead in his shadow, the article which had been published about her marriage to him filling my thoughts for a moment. He had trapped her mind with Dark Coercion, had made her bend to his will in everything, even making her play whore with his friends for political advantage. And yet the woman I'd seen in the photos accompanying that article on her marriage to Hamish Grus only filled me with admiration. If she had endured a lifetime in the company of this monster without breaking, then I could certainly hope to survive a single night.

My gaze slipped to Lionel's shadow hand which was as black as soot and smoky like it wasn't entirely solid, the sight of it making me wary, though a twinge of satisfaction filled me at the thought of the original having been destroyed by a Vega.

Lionel stubbed his cigar in the gold ash tray on a table beside him, pushing to his feet and dominating the space with his enormous size. He moved toward me, and I dropped my eyes subserviently as he approached, stepping right into my personal space so the scent of cigar smoke and danger wafted into my lungs.

Keep breathing, Francesca.

"You are lucky," he said with a chuckle. "I do not bring many women to the palace."

"What of your queen?" I asked, my skin prickling at the thought of the shadow queen lurking in this cavernous place. Was she close? Could she see us now? I found I feared her even more than the monster now standing before me. The press spun stories about her, touting her as this mystical goddess who had come from the shadow realm to offer all of her love and power to Lionel, but I saw the truth. She wasn't Fae. She wasn't even Nymph. She was a weapon more powerful than anything I had encountered during my time in the FIB. I'd faced plenty of monsters, but she was something wholly else. An entity that defied nature and offered Lionel untold power.

"She is preoccupied," he purred, leaning closer and caressing the gold necklace around my throat, a perfectly intricate little chain that a Dragon would certainly be captivated by. "And I am the king. I do as I please."

"What is it you would like, my King?" I glanced up at him through my lashes. He would have been attractive if he wasn't so awful, but it wasn't impossible to pretend if I imagined him as anyone else but the man he was.

"Is it me?" I pressed. "Am I what you want?"

He nodded, and I leaned into him, placing my hand on his powerful chest, the sturdy thump of his heart sitting right beneath my palm, though I could sense an air shield against his skin too. He wasn't taking chances. He would have been a fool to.

"Yes, and you want me in return, do you not?"

"I do," I said huskily. "I wish to please my king more than anything."

I knew how far down this road I might have to go, and I'd made my peace with that. It was the price I'd pay to get an opportunity to reach Lance, but I had a plan to distract the false king yet that might buy me time.

I leaned up, looping my arms around Lionel's neck and touching my mouth to his in an offering. He gripped my back, yanking me closer and sinking his tongue between my lips, fire and brimstone washing over my senses.

I pressed my finger to my left palm, casting the emergency response spell that linked directly to my FIB partner. I'd had to entrust her with this plan. She was a good friend and despised Lionel as deeply as I did, but it had taken some convincing to get her to help me out tonight. I hated to put her at risk, but the plan was solid, and Lionel shouldn't suspect her so long as things went smoothly.

Lionel's kiss became hungrier and I tried to ignore the crawling sensation in my skin as I let the monster have me.

Come on, Lyla, hurry up.

A knock came at the door but Lionel ignored it, his hand sliding down to squeeze my ass.

"My King?" a woman squeaked. "Apologies, but there is an urgent matter."

Take the bait, asshole.

Lionel sighed as our lips broke apart, his frustration clear. "Forgive me." He turned, striding over to the door in anger and wrenching it open. "This had better be important."

"The northern wards were breached," the woman stammered.

Lionel stiffened, then glanced back at me. "Wait here, Francesca. I will return shortly."

I nodded and he slammed the doors between us, a lock clicking before the heavy pounding of his footfalls headed away from me.

I took a steadying breath, wiping my mouth a little to try and get the taste of him off of my lips. I counted to sixty before I moved to the door, pressing my ear to it, and listening for any sound of anyone out there. The faint shuffling of feet made me certain he had stationed someone there, and I shut my eyes, drawing on my gifts and reaching for the mind of the guard. Their mental shields were poor and my power was great. I snagged them under my control in moments and urged them to open the door.

Lionel's butler was dumb-looking with a shock of red hair and teeth too big for his mouth, his glazed eyes falling on me as I kept him trapped within my thrall.

"Take me to Lance Orion," I commanded, pressing my will into his mind, and he nodded vaguely, leading me off down the corridor while I worked to maintain the connection, binding him to my will, making sure he wouldn't remember any of this once it was done too.

My pulse came quicker with every turn we took, passing under gleaming chandeliers and through magnificent arches. The Palace of Souls held a beauty like no other, gothic and intimidating in some places, yet quaint and inviting in others.

Eventually, I was led into the throne room where the huge Hydra throne stood with its many heads and hollowed seat at its heart. The prize this kingdom had been struggling over ever since the Savage King fell.

I gasped as my eyes landed on a cage of night iron beyond it, bolted against the wall where two Fae sat close together within the bars. I ran forward, leaving the butler immobilised by the door as love and pain rose together in my chest at the sight of Lance Orion.

"Francesca?" he gasped in shock, rising to his feet and wincing at the half-healed wounds on his bare chest.

Darcy leapt to her feet too, and I took in the girl who had claimed the heart of the man I loved, finding her nothing like the one I remembered. Her eyes were inky black, no sign of a silver ring within them, and shadows clung to her body, her black hair shifting eerily in the way Lavinia's did. I didn't know what I was witnessing and had no time to ask as I pulled Orion into an embrace through the bars.

He slid one arm around me, drawing me close, and my carefully constructed mask started to come apart.

"What have they done to you?" I breathed, not wanting to know but needing to just the same.

"It doesn't matter. What are you doing here? What's going on?" he demanded, releasing me and stepping back.

Darcy moved closer and I looked to her, feeling so many things towards this girl. I had envied her night after night the moment I saw her mated to Lance, but it had become more than that. I'd seen what she and her sister had done in this war, and I idolised them in a way I never could have predicted. My loyalty had always been firmly with the Celestial Council and the Heirs, but I couldn't deny the Vegas' power anymore. She had to get free of here alongside Lance, and they had to return to the rebels to fight.

I cast a silencing bubble around us all, then gripped the bars, using my air Element to bend two of the bars apart.

"Quickly," I urged, reaching for the clip in my hair and pulling it free. I twisted the small tourmaline crystal out of the clip and gripped Orion's forearm, running it up and down.

"What is that?" Darcy asked.

"Francesca," Orion hissed before I could answer. "I can't leave here."

"Nonsense," I said dismissively. "I have a plan. I have a small amount of stardust. We just need to get beyond the wards, and it'll be fine."

I ran the crystal up his other forearm, and the crystal glowed yellow in my palm. "Ah, here. They've put a tracking spell on you," I said, pressing my thumb to the spot and shutting my eyes as I cast the spell which would break the invisible tracking mark placed on him.

"Shit," he growled, but I smiled as I felt the spell break, reaching for Darcy in an offering.

She moved forward hesitantly, and I took her arm, not giving her time to refuse as I ran the crystal up and down, finding the spell on her too.

"Fran, you have to go," Darcy said urgently. "It's not safe for you here. We can't leave."

"What do you mean you can't leave?" I scoffed, breaking the spell on her and backing up. "Come on. *Move*."

Darcy and Lance shared a hopeless look, then Darcy rushed toward me, squeezing my hand. "Listen, Gabriel is being held here in the Royal Seer's chamber." She started listing off directions hurriedly, but I wasn't listening, looking to Lance in frustration.

"We have to move!" I commanded, hating the way he was still standing there with no urgency to run. I was breaking them out, didn't they get it? This was their chance to escape. There might not be another.

"I can't," he said, shaking his head, and my heart started to splinter. The crystal crumbled to dust in my palm, the last of its power used up, and I pulled my hand out of Darcy's, moving toward him and cupping his cheek, so many years of loving him pouring out in my chest.

"Please. I came to get you out. I can't leave you here. Why won't you move?"

"Darcy is cursed. I am the answer to that curse, and I must remain here until my debt is paid," he said thickly. "Please, Francesca, you need to get out of here. It's not safe here."

"What have you done?" I whispered in horror, panic welling in me. What did he mean he had to stay here? That he had a debt to pay? And what curse?

"Please go," Darcy begged, but I couldn't turn my eyes from the man before me, seeing that he was really refusing to leave. And I suddenly had the most desperate fear that I might never see him again if I turned away from him now.

"Did you ever love me?" I asked quietly, the words choked and making me feel weak and foolish. The question had haunted me ever since I'd learned of him and Darcy Vega. Had I always been just a distraction, or had there ever been a time when he'd considered a future with me? A time when I'd made his heart beat with the furious passion he always garnered from mine?

"Francesca, please," he rasped. "You must go."

I moved closer to him still, refusing to leave and releasing a wave of healing magic into his body to steal away those awful wounds on his chest. Was she worth all this pain? Even a mate offered from the stars wasn't worth suffering like this for, was it?

Though as I thought of my own unrequited love for him, I knew I would take any pain and more for him. It was my bane, an anchor hanging my neck which I'd never found a way free of. I couldn't even pinpoint the exact moment when I'd fallen for him, maybe it was in the space between our kisses, or the nights curled up on his couch watching Pitball, drinking beer. Just being with him had always felt like the right place to be. But those days were gone, never to return, and I hadn't even had a chance to say goodbye.

"Answer me," I begged. "Tell me if you ever looked at me and saw a life at my side, a wedding, children. Was it ever me? Even for a fraction of a moment?"

His throat bobbed and his brows drew tightly together, guilt marring his features before he voiced the word that fell like an axe against my neck. "No."

I nodded mutely, knowing I should be moving, running, trying to get back to that room before Lionel could discover me missing.

"I love you as a friend," he said hurriedly, like he sensed the agony he'd caused me with that one word. "You've always meant so much to me. But I just never…it was never more than that. I'm sorry."

I nodded again. All the years I'd spent yearning for this man really had been wasted. I had tortured myself over him, I had convinced myself that there was hope when there had always been none. And I could have saved myself so many nights of longing if only I'd asked him this question sooner.

The tears stung my eyes but didn't fall. I kept them back in the face of everything, shifting my mind onto what mattered.

"We can figure out the curse together. There may be another answer. I'll take the two of you somewhere safe," I said firmly.

"There's time to get to Gabriel," Darcy implored, gripping my arm and pulling me around to face her so that I stumbled a step away from Lance. "Go to him," she insisted. "Get him out. He can leave here, but we can't."

"I will never leave Lance behind," I growled.

"You will do as I command," Darcy barked and I flinched, the power in her words making something wholly Fae within me quake. I saw the Savage King in her eyes and felt his authority ringing through the air, but that authority belonged to her now, this princess whose bloodline once owned the intimidating throne at my back.

The throne room door was flung open with a resounding boom that made me whip around in terror, my hands raising defensively as Lionel Acrux came barrelling towards me, his features twisted into a sneer.

"You dare betray your king?!" he bellowed, air magic blasting at me, and I cast my own air back with a cry of alarm.

His power outmatched mine tenfold and it crashed through mine, snatching me up and throwing me at his feet against the stone floor, a crack sounding as my arm broke beneath me and agony tore through the limb.

His hand latched in my hair, and I looked up at him as pain splintered through me, my two eyes sliding together into one and the full force of my Cyclops gifts slamming against his mental shields. He roared in anger, his teeth bared as he worked to keep his shields in place, and I lost my grip on the butler as I focused all of my effort on breaking into the king's head.

He had a wall of steel surrounding his mind, but my power was a spear of pure, diamond-tipped titanium. With a cry of effort, my gifts flared from me and I punctured his shields, stealing into his mind.

My breath was torn from my lungs as I found myself falling through the black pit of selfish cruelty which tainted the inside of Lionel Acrux's head, his thoughts a pit of thorny vines tearing into me as I was tangled within them, flashes of memory spilling into every part of my being.

I took it all in, from the glimpses of him raising his fists against his family to the torture he had inflicted upon all who had stood against him.

My mind spun with so much cruelty and the unending desire for power which ruled this dark creature, impossible to sate and endlessly hungry for more. I almost lost myself in the tangle of that darkness, but I was no newly shifted fledgling cast adrift in the mind of a more powerful Fae, and I knew well how to wield my gifts even in the dark.

Secrets. The word was a demand which echoed from me endlessly, the world outside of us fading to nothing as I latched onto his mind, whips of my Cyclops power lashing against his defences as I threw all I had into this attack, knowing it was all I could do, the only chance I had against one so powerful as him.

Distantly, I heard Orion fighting to reach me, his yells for Lionel to release me cutting the air in two, but a blast of water magic from the butler silenced his plight.

"Stay back," he crowed, the sounds of a struggle coming in answer, but I was too deep into my gifts to be able to tell what was happening.

Lionel bucked and thrashed against the talons I was sinking into his mind, but I only dug them in deeper, that command resounding from me again as I gave everything I had to this one chance, his body immobilised while I trapped him in his mind.

Secrets!

I bellowed the demand through his skull, and with a resounding crack, my power carved through his remaining resistance and everything I was hunting for spilled from the false king into me. Thoughts and memories poured from him in an endless torrent, his mind crumbling to my demand, and more knowledge than I could easily dissect filling me at once.

I didn't attempt to make full sense of any of it, simply channelling every single conniving, deviant, hidden moment from his past into the ring on my finger, recording all of it.

I recognised the image of Lionel's dead brother Radcliff, his eyes wild with fear as he lay in his bed, woken in the night and attacked in the most unFae way imaginable as Lionel pinned him in place, a glass pressed to his chest containing a norian wasp. Murder. UnFae and disgusting. It was no accident, no divine intervention which had placed Lionel into his brother's position on the Celestial Council, just the cowardly actions of a jealous man with his eyes set on the greatness he was too inferior to claim for himself in any other way.

More and more of Lionel's secrets sped through me, whispers into the ear of the Savage King, Dark Coercion flowing into the mind of our monarch and turning him into a puppet of wrath and violence, unable to see the traitor who hungered for his throne. It was shocking, this revelation rattling me to my core, but it all made so much sense too.

There was far too much for me to decipher with the speed at which it passed me, but I took it all greedily, stealing every memory I could take, all the terrible, cowardly secrets this so-called king had used to place his unworthy ass upon the throne.

Blinding pain cut through my side and I screamed as my connection to Lionel's mind was severed by the unexpected attack, stumbling back, and clutching the dagger of ice which the fucking butler had plunged into my side.

My Order form fell from my grasp as I shifted back, and I barely managed to rip the dagger from my body before Lionel was upon me, Lance's pleas for mercy ringing in my ears.

Lionel punched me so hard that I was thrown to the ground, my head cracking against the stone floor and unforgiving stars bursting before my eyes, pain carving through my skull and everything spiralling.

The king's foot slammed down on my back next, and he crushed me beneath him, grinding his heel into the bone until a snap sounded that sent fire raining through my flesh and a scream pitching from my lungs. He stood back, and I tried to crawl away from him, dragging myself across the floor with a gust of air while he prowled after me.

I twisted towards Lance, finding him and Darcy frozen up to their waists in ice so that they couldn't make any move towards me out of their cage. I subtly slid the ring from my finger, wrapping it in a knot of air and casting an illusion across it to hide it on the tiled floor before sending it skittering away into their cage, hope riding on that precious piece of my mother's jewellery.

I reached for Lance, his eyes locking with mine, and I used the last of my energy to offer him the best memories of us I had. He let them all in, every one of the beautiful moments we'd shared, every day at Zodiac Academy together. And he saw my truth then, seeing himself through my eyes and how he had made my heart pound and love fill me up to the brim until I had barely been able to contain it in my flesh. He may not have loved me as I'd hoped, but he had loved me all the same. His smiles in those memories reminded me of that, his laughs, his light, all the good we'd shared long before darkness had crept into his life and blotted out the brightness in him. And I realised we'd possessed something far more valuable than what I'd been trying to gain from him all along. He was my friend, and I was his. And there was no truer love in my life than that.

"No one defies the Dragon King," Lionel hissed, then fire blazed, surrounding my head and swallowing up my vision of Lance as I screamed and fucking screamed.

Starlight flickered at the edges of my vision and the pain roared along with those flames which burned through flesh and bone, until suddenly I was set free of my body, set free of my chains and every regret I had ever had over Lance Orion. Because my fate was set. My life was over. And there was no chance left for me to change a single decision or path I'd taken.

That was the way of life, the past was sand turned to glass, never to be undone. And all I could do now was make peace with my end.

Scorpio
Gemini
Virgo
Cancer
Leo
Sagittarius
Taurus
Capricorn
Aquarius
Libra
Pisces

ORION

CHAPTER THIRTY NINE

"No!" I shouted so loud it burned my lungs, panic exploding through my body as Francesca's life was lost to Lionel's fire.

She was gone, already fallen still, her soul departed from this world. But I didn't stop fighting to get free of the ice Horace had trapped me in, still trying to refuse the truth that was painted starkly before my eyes. I managed to use a burst of Vampire strength to break it apart, but Lionel's gaze shifted to me, and I collided with the bars Francesca had bent open as he snapped them back into shape.

"Monster," I spat at him, clawing my hands over my head, trying to tear out the image of what I'd just witnessed.

Darcy reached for me, but the ice was still holding her legs down, and I shattered it around her with a sharp kick, yanking her out of it and pulling her against me. She held me tight as anger and grief wove themselves deep into my heart, nestling there alongside all the other losses I'd faced.

"I'm sorry," Darcy breathed. "I'm so sorry."

It wasn't her fault, none of this was. It was the fault of the fucking asshole king and his bitch queen.

I turned to Lionel as I clutched Blue protectively against my chest, pointing a finger at him as he shed his jacket and tossed it onto the throne, heat radiating from his body so furiously that it made the air shimmer around him.

"Your death is coming, I swear that to you. It will be so bloody and terrible that it will be imprinted on the minds of all who are there to witness it forevermore. And I pray, I fucking *pray*, I am one of them." My voice echoed with a hint of power which I hoped to the stars meant they were laced in prophecy.

Lionel wetted his lips, striding forward, his pupils turning to Dragon slits and smoke spewing from his nostrils.

"Lavinia is not here. Perhaps I shall make a massacre in this room tonight."

Horace shuddered, backing up like he feared Lionel's rage might spill in his direction, and I threw a murderous glare his way for his part in Francesca's death. I would not forget that.

"Get away from us," Darcy snarled, trying to fight her way free of my arms, but I held on tight, fearing he might come for her next.

"Daaaaddy," Lavinia's ethereal voice floated from the doorway, and Lionel stilled before turning reluctantly towards her.

I hated to be relieved at her presence, but it was impossible not to be. That horrid creature was the only thing stopping Lionel from killing Darcy and I, and so long as she was here, he couldn't touch us.

"Yes, my Queen?" Lionel muttered, his chest rising and falling as he caught his breath. "You are back earlier than I expected."

Lavinia swept forward on a gust of shadow, hovering before him and peering down at Francesca's body as the flames crackled out of existence around her blackened skull.

Bile rose in my throat, and the loss of my Nebula Ally stamped permanent damage into my heart. *Why did she have to come here?*

Guilt swept over me at the realisation that she had done this for me, and I didn't know what to do with all those final memories she'd gifted me, the truth of her love for me clear as day. How had I never seen it before? Was I so fucking blind?

"Who's that?" Lavinia sniped, hurrying over to Francesca's body and leaning down at an unnatural angle, sniffing deeply.

"A traitor, that's all," Lionel said quickly. "She is dead now. I will have Horace deal with her body."

He snapped his fingers at his butler and the man rushed forward to do as he was bid.

"Yes, sire," Horace said tightly, glancing at Lavinia with fear in his eyes, then back to the corpse.

Lavinia blocked his path forward, smiling creepily.

"She's still warm," she whispered. "No need to waste the flesh."

She dove on Francesca's body, biting and tearing into her skin with savagery, making me roar in anguish.

Horace let out a noise of horror, stumbling away and looking at the wall, fixing his gaze there and pretending nothing was happening.

"Get away from her," I demanded, but Lavinia started wrapping Francesca up in a web of shadow, binding her body until I could no longer see my friend within it.

Even Lionel looked disgusted by the display, and Darcy gripped my arm so tightly that her nails dug deep into my arm.

Lavinia left Francesca's body there on the floor as she dropped onto all fours and scuttled her way over to Lionel, raising herself up again and sniffing all the way along the length of his body, lingering by his mouth. She screeched like a banshee, and Lionel grabbed her throat with a fistful of flames, trying to get her under control before she attacked. But Lavinia was stronger, huge whips of shadow spilling from her and yanking him away. She threw him to the floor and his own shadow hand lifted, punching himself in the face.

"Ah!" he cried, lifting his Fae hand and casting an air shield to hold her back, but her dark power tore through it in moments, latching onto him and dragging him back across the floor towards her. Horace stared after his king in shock, looking lost as to whether he should try and help.

"You fucked that whore!" Lavinia screamed. "You betrayed the sanctity of our marriage!"

"No – wait – please!" Lionel cried, trying to get a hold of his power to stop her, but his shadow hand twisted the fingers of his Fae hand, breaking them all. He wailed again, his shadow hand slamming into his face with a bone-crunching blow, and my breathing stalled as I watched, basking in his pain.

"Horace!" Lionel barked, and his butler stumbled towards him, raising his hands with wide eyes. Before he could do anything more than clumsily splash water on the floor and almost fall over it onto his ass, Lavinia caught him in a net of shadow.

"Stars, have mercy!" Horace broke down immediately, sobbing like a child, and Lavinia threw him out of the throne room, sending him tumbling away along the corridor out of sight.

She turned her attention back to Lionel, a twisted look of rage on her face. "How dare you insult me like this?"

"Wait," Lionel begged. "Just listen to me for a mo-"

Lavinia sent Lionel flying into a wall and flames burst from his broken fingers as he tried to fight. A wave of shadow snuffed them out and then snaked up his body, tearing his shirt open and slashing a great gouge across his chest.

"Ahhh!" he screamed.

"Kill him," Darcy growled under her breath, hope lacing those words.

"Yes, fucking kill him, you psycho," I urged.

Lavinia closed in on her prey, lifting Lionel up on a swirl of shadow. She raked her blackened, sharp nails down his stomach, spilling blood and making him cry out once more. His shadow hand grasped between his own legs, squeezing and squeezing while his eyes rolled back into his head and his mouth opened in a pitchy wail.

More shadows poured from Lavinia, diving down into his throat and making his body spasm and jerk beneath her tremendous power.

"You are *my* king," she spat. "*My* Acrux king. And you will not touch any other woman but your queen. I have waited long enough for you to give me my promised heir. The last was stolen from us, but this one shall be the mightiest creature I can bring into this world. It shall be our legacy."

She threw him to the floor and his head cracked against it with a thwack that made my heart jolt hopefully.

"End the motherfucker. Come on," I hissed.

Lavinia floated from the room, humming an eerie, joyful tune as she dragged Lionel after her across the floor, the cuts on his chest leaving a trail of blood across the tiles as he went, his shadow hand locked tight around his other wrist at the base of his spine, immobilising him.

Lionel's eyes fell on Darcy and I, a look of utter shame falling over him as he found us watching his downfall with rapt attention.

"Look away," he commanded in a ferocious growl.

I didn't and Darcy didn't either, staring at his shame and drinking it all in.

"We see you, Lionel Acrux," Blue said icily. "We see your weakness."

Francesca's body was dragged along by shadow binds too, and Lavinia stole them away through the cavernous doorway.

Lionel's screams carried off into the palace, and Horace came scurrying back into the room with his eyes bugging out of his head. He cleared his throat, then used a blast of water magic to clean up the blood before hurrying off again and shutting the doors, muttering, "Oh my stars. Oh my fucking stars. Wait 'til Jim hears about this."

"Lionel's not the power in this place anymore," Darcy said, and I looked at her, finding so much strength in her eyes that it helped ground me in the wake of everything that had happened.

I backed up, sinking down against the wall, and cupping my head in my hands. "By the sun, Francesca, why did you have to come here?"

Darcy knelt at my side, laying a hand on my shoulder. "She loved you."

"I know," I whispered, guilt drowning me. "I never realised. Was I a fucking idiot?"

I glanced up at Blue and found a heavy sadness in her eyes. "Sometimes feelings are only obvious to the people experiencing them. You couldn't have known if she didn't want you to know."

I nodded, releasing a long breath, and Darcy moved forward, wrapping her arms tightly around me. I leaned into her, closing my eyes and just sitting in the pain of losing my friend. Why did everyone around me keep dying?

"I'm the reason she came here," I said, horrified by the cards that had been dealt tonight.

"She didn't know you couldn't leave," Darcy said, and though I knew that was true, it didn't make me feel any less shitty about what had happened. All the memories she'd offered me in death kept cycling through my head, and I swiped a hand down my face in despair. I didn't want to see myself like that, through the eyes of a friend

I thought I knew. But I hadn't known her, because she'd kept this secret all those years. I would never have slept with her if I'd known. I wouldn't have tortured her like that.

"I feel like such an asshole," I said, and Darcy pushed her fingers into my hair, stroking soothingly.

"You didn't know," she repeated, but now I knew...now I fucking knew.

I turned my arm over, examining the place where the tracking spell had been hidden. Some fucking asshole must have cast them on us while we were sleeping. My bet was on that snake, Horace.

A clink sounded as my foot shifted, and I looked down beyond my foot, spotting a simple silver ring there. I leaned forward, a sense of urgency filling me as I picked it up, rolling it between my fingers, and Darcy sat back to look at it too.

"What is that?" she asked.

"It must be Francesca's," I said on a breath, glancing up at the open door to make sure no one was spying on us.

"Maybe she meant for you to have it," Darcy breathed, and I nodded, turning the silver band over and feeling a weight of power humming within it. It was familiar, like the scent of a time long lost, days at Zodiac Academy working on assignments together in the library and joking together in The Orb. It was her.

"I know what this is," I said quietly. "It's a memory loop. Cyclopses use them to record what they see, and the memories locked within it can then be played for others to view."

"Like a window into her mind?" Darcy asked curiously and I nodded.

"Or a window into the mind of anyone she used her gifts to see into."

"How does it work?" Darcy asked.

In answer, I slipped it onto my pinky finger, the slim silver band only reaching the first knuckle before it lodged there. I took Darcy's hand in mine, bringing her along with me as I drew in a breath and delved into the power locked inside that ring.

At first there was nothing but darkness, then a room seemed to open up around us, the walls pale blue and lined with doors. Each of the doors had a date embossed into the wood and as I cracked open the closest one, I spied the memories within.

"Is that an FIB raid?" Darcy asked as we peered through Francesca's eyes while she ran beneath a half moon, ten other agents all in their official uniforms running in formation around her. I only nodded in answer to Darcy's question as we watched the raid play out, the family of Sphinxes wrenched from sleep as the FIB agents stormed their home.

I had to fight the urge to turn away as I saw agents brutalising the man who I assumed owned the home, five of them laying into him while he screamed in pain beneath the blows of their boots. Francesca's feelings of horror laced the memory, and we watched as she turned from the room, heading further into the house as the agents began hunting for more family members. She took the stairs two at a time, casting her awareness out from her body with her Cyclops gifts until she sensed a cluster of minds hiding in the attic above.

Francesca broke into a run, her heart thundering as she sent a wave of mental images to her partner Lyla, the agreed signal making Lyla call out to the other agents to follow her into the lower level of the house, keeping them away a little longer.

Francesca burst through a hidden door which led into the eves of the house, hiding the sound within a silencing bubble before ripping apart the concealment spells which had been cast to hide the old woman and four kids hiding there. The frail lady stepped forward, water magic coiling around her gnarled fists as she placed herself between the children and death, but Francesca raised her hands in a gesture of peace.

"You need to run," she hissed, opening her fist to reveal a tiny pouch of stardust, just enough to transport them far from here. "Right now." She tossed the old lady the bag of stardust, her Cyclops gifts working to wipe the memory of her face from the woman and children, just before the woman threw the stardust over their heads and they were whipped away into the safety of the stars.

Francesca let out a shaky breath, her mental gifts reaching out around her to make certain that none of the other agents had detected anything amiss, before returning to the raid as if nothing had happened. But it had. She'd saved those Sphinxes, and as Darcy and I glimpsed the memories locked behind more of the doors, we found further evidence of her rebellion against the crown.

Sometimes she had only been able to bear witness to the atrocities taking place, other times she managed to free some of the terrified Fae the FIB had been hunting. Her memories showed the insides of the Nebular Inquisition Centres and the disgusting living conditions there, alongside the barbarities taking place. She had even gone so far as to log memories of herself reading secret documents which detailed the upcoming plans of the king and where he was aiming his wrath next.

I marvelled at the risks she'd taken, her braveness overwhelming me until we reached the door holding tonight's date.

Almost a month had passed since my deal had been made with Lavinia. Time had become so fluid here, the days merging into one another, my time spent lost between the agony of my torture and the numbness of the shadows she threaded into my veins. Such a long time, and yet not even a third of what I owed her had passed.

My heart raced as we watched Francesca preparing herself to come to The Palace of Souls, the lengths she had gone to in a bid to try and free me from this place. It hurt to see how broken she had felt over my plight, how much she had been willing to risk as well as the understanding of what it had cost her in the end, all the while knowing I was unable to cast my bonds aside and escape.

The moment when she managed to breech the walls of Lionel's mind had a gasp parting my lips, his truth spilling out all around us as she carved his most shameful secrets from his head, the years of cunning plots and underhand tactics utterly overwhelming. He had dreamed of the throne for such a long time, manipulating and scheming to steal it for his own, and it destroyed a piece of me to know how well he had managed to execute those plans.

As the memories faded and we drew ourselves out of them, I couldn't help but feel overwhelmed by all of it, by my grief over losing the friend I had known since I was a kid, and my guilt for never realising what she'd felt for me.

"She didn't die for nothing," Darcy murmured softly, her hand curling around mine where I still wore the ring that contained so much evidence, the precious legacy of a woman who had deserved so much better than she'd received. "The memories she gathered and the truth she uncovered can be unleashed as a weapon against him, Lance. She could change everything in this war if we can get these memories out to the public."

I nodded vaguely, feeling that dark numbness washing over me again. Stella's magic may have driven the shadows out last time, but Lavinia had tortured me again since, and they were starting to play havoc with my soul. I fell a little deeper into them, not letting them take me away entirely, but finding a place where the sharpness of my grief was dulled.

I turned, taking Darcy's wrist and guiding her hand to the wall where that faint mark of the Hydra was, and the stone door rolled open. Eugene squeaked in greeting, hurrying forward and brushing his little face against my hand. I held out the ring and leaned down close to him, whispering, "Keep it safe with everything else."

Darcy took the piece of bread we'd saved him from our last meal, holding it out for him and he fell on it ravenously, eating every bite, then squeaking again and carrying the ring into the gloom beyond the passage door. He lay on a nest containing the Memoriae crystal, the opal Guild Stone and the feather- bound book, protecting them all.

A tiny little Tiberian Rat for a guard didn't seem like much, but Eugene was powerful, and we'd find a way to get him out of here yet. Maybe then he could reach Tory and the rebels. It was a lot to hope for, but at least it was something outside of blood and torture to focus on while we were stuck here day after day.

The first month with Lavinia had almost passed. We were a third of our way through this nightmare, so I held tighter than ever to that glimmer of a possible future with Blue. And I wouldn't be letting go.

Scorpio
Gemini
Virgo
Aries
Cancer
Leo
Sagittarius
Taurus
Capricorn
Aquarius
Libra
Pisces

LAVINIA

CHAPTER FORTY

I left Lionel sated and recovering in our bed, his eyes staring unseeingly at the ceiling as he panted and twitched, the echoes of the pleasure I'd delivered him lingering even after our flesh had parted.

"I will have a new heir for you by dawn," I purred, running a finger down the valley between my exposed breasts as I remembered the bite of his touch as he had thrown me down beneath him.

Such a powerful beast, my husband. And such a beast he had wed when he joined himself to me.

I bit my lip as I thought back on the lust-filled shriek that had escaped him as I took control, the desire and wariness which had melded in his gaze when he was forced to look upon my power and remember who the true might in our relationship was. It scared him, and yet it thrilled him too. I could tell. As he fisted the sheets and called my name in a beg for his release, I had heard it, the need for me. Even if he was a creature not prone to accepting his own vulnerability, he was forced to explore it with me, forced to look inside himself and face the weaknesses he found there. But I didn't mind his vanity or the need he had to cling to his supposed dominion over me. No, I didn't mind pretending for him, so long as I got what I needed from him.

And with the sticky evidence of our joining glistening between my thighs, I knew I had it. The Dragon seed. My shadows were already drawing it deeper inside of me, pulling it up into the void where my womb had once been and fusing that seed to a seed of my own, creating a tendril of shadow and power beyond anything that had been seen in this realm in all the years I had haunted the earth.

I fed myself into that seed, a tiny life forming inside of me even as I stared down at my Dragon, tangled in the sheets and covered in perspiration from our union.

He wasn't thinking about that pretty little nothing now, was he? Wasn't distracted by the idea of sinking his little cock into her pathetically willing body. No. He had been reminded what a true match for him was capable of, and I could tell by the way he had fallen into silence that the only memories on his mind now were the things I had just done to him. My pretty little Dragon.

I moved to sit beside him, and he stilled, his eyes shifting to me as a tug on his shadow hand had him caressing my cheek lovingly, the way I had seen my pet do to his blue-haired princess.

"I can feel it inside me," I breathed, parting my thighs as he glanced down, letting him see everything while my belly began to swell with new life.

"Will this one be Dragon-born like you promised?" he hissed, some of his grit coming back to him as he caught his breath.

"This one will be so much stronger than the last," I swore to him. "A Dragon child with a heart of shadow. An heir both of us will be proud to call our son."

A flicker of something passed through his gaze, and I pouted.

"Are you thinking of the one you killed? Do you miss your poor, dead boy?" I asked curiously, and his lip curled back as he wrenched control of the shadow hand away from me, wrapping it around my throat and squeezing until my breath was cut off. I grinned at the game, enjoying the pressure of his fist around my neck and the threat of violence which danced in his eyes.

"Darius was a failure in the end, but his potential was there in spades. He was a perfect specimen. A worthy Heir. Or at least he would have been had that Vega whore stayed out of his fucking bed. I often think of what he could have been and regret not doing more to shape him into such. But no, I do not mourn him, nor regret what I did. He was tainted in the end. A failure. So do not think I won't destroy the thing growing inside of you in a similar fashion if it disappoints me too."

I smiled at him through the pain of his hold on me, my hand moving to his spent and flaccid cock as I tried to stir some reaction from it.

"Do you want to go again?" I purred, forcing the shadow fingers to relax enough for me to speak, before letting him crush my throat in his hand again while wondering if I might find release this time if we did.

"I am not some performing dog," he snapped. "My cock won't be ready to function again until at least tomorrow, as you well know."

I pouted and his eyes flashed with fury as my disappointment in his performance blazed clearly across my features.

"Then I suppose I should focus on giving you the Heir you so desperately desire," I said, blinking at the shadow hand and grinning as it flew from my neck and slapped him across his own face.

Lionel roared furiously, but I was already gone, twisting away into shadow before floating beneath the door and heading towards the north tower. I shifted back into my corporeal form and took hold of the closest wall, scuttling up the side of it, shadows peeling away from my skin behind me as I began to crawl my way to the highest floor.

My belly swelled larger with every passing moment, the life inside of me growing fast, a claw scraping against my insides in ecstasy-laced agony.

I moved faster, scuttling over the ceiling as it spiralled up and up above the stairs, until I finally reached the door to the chambers I'd claimed for my own in this highest point of the palace.

I became nothing but shadow once more, slipping beneath the door and emerging in the round chamber beyond it, finding my nest of harmony awaiting me inside.

I had been building it for months now, knowing I would need the power of it to gift this shadow child the power its sibling had been denied. This child would not be as easily ended as its brother. It would be born in blood and ruin and unthinkable power.

The nest had been built with the bones of my enemies, dark artefacts set amongst them, carved with ancient runes and cloaked in the darkest of my shadows.

Four Fae heads stood on spikes, each looking inward to witness this birth, the souls of the dead trapped within them, unable to move from their positions while forced to watch every moment of this. They screamed as I fell to my knees in the middle of the room, my hip cracking as the child within me kicked so hard it broke bone. Their torment and desperate pleas for release into the world set calmness washing through me as I fixed the damage to my body and moved to squat between the rotting heads.

The shadow child fought to break free of my womb, but I refused the urge to push, cursing as I reached for a sliver of malachite, the green and black stone glowing with the essence of darkness I had forced inside it in preparation of this. The crystal was used for manifestation, change, and empowerment, all the things this child of mine would need before it broke into this world.

I tipped my head back and began chanting to the shadows, drawing them to me even as the life within me fought and writhed for freedom, coating my arms and hands in their power, pushing as much of it as I could into the shard of crystal.

When my fingers burned with the power I was wielding, I turned the sharpened point in my hand and plunged it into my stomach, breaking through the wall of flesh, blood, and shadows while driving it into the creature I was still growing.

The babe roared, and the heads witnessing its creation screamed at the sound of nightmares erupting from the opening between my thighs.

I met the horror-filled gaze of the closest head, the Fae who had wielded fire in his living form and now remained trapped inside a decaying skull.

He would be the first.

I smiled at him, a wicked, sinful thing which saw my teeth growing to sharpened points in anticipation of this next part. For he would not be finding release beyond the Veil. No, he would be joining with the new life inside of me, becoming a part of him and lending his Element to him while no doubt screaming forever more from his place trapped inside my darling child.

There were three more heads for me to devour once I was done with his and countless shards of darkness to pierce my skin and my babe's too.

The night would be long and filled with endless pain for every one of us trapped inside this chamber. But with the dawn, I would birth the strongest creature this world had ever known, and all would bow at his feet when he turned his hunger upon them.

Scorpio
Gemini
Virgo
Cancer
Leo
Taurus
Sagittarius
Capricorn
Aquarius
Libra
Pisces

GERALDINE

CHAPTER FORTY ONE

'Twas a gobblesome gooseberry of an eve as the setting sun shone bleakly through the misty clouds, a chill to this air which burned its way right down to my britches, sweet Petunia, and beyond.

"What a day for a king to fall," I said solemnly, a wild look in my eye as I gazed between this roguish crowd of rapscallions, all primed and eager for the fight. I had discussed the options long and tirelessly, my queen and this band of hapsom heathens were the selection we had concluded upon. This was not the moment to take an army into battle. No, we could not risk such with cheeky Gabe, dear Darcy, and her Orry man in the path of violence. So only I, my queen, the three mostly irrelevant Heirs to nothing, sweet, heartbroken, wingless Xavier, and the devilish Storm Dragon and his family of heathens were present. We had to be both swift and subtle, a small band of merry Fae on our way to topple a tyranny. What fun. "Are we all firm and flanly on the plan?"

"We just need to confirm who's going after what," Seth replied, a doggish excitement in his eyes which I knew all too well myself.

"Much pondering has gone into this," I agreed with a solemn nod.

"When?" Max demanded, my poor, floatsome sea trout still believing that he should be privy to all war councils despite his low position on the outskirts of the royal court.

"Bend the knee, dear salamander, and perhaps you will be invited to the next meet of highest security personnel," I said with a shrug, and Tory pressed her lips together to hide her amusement at his glower.

"Who the hell was in this meeting then if it was only made up of A.S.S. members?" Maxy boy demanded.

"I, of course, chaired the function; Tory, presiding as the only queen currently in residence. Then dastardly Dante, luscious Leon, and the rest of their closest famiglia-"

"Wait, when did the Dragon and co bend the fucking knee?" Seth huffed, and I sighed heavily, pinching the bridge of my nose.

"We were hardly going to bow to lame Lionel, were we doggy dude?" Leon said with a chuckle.

"Lionel Acrux forced me to bow to him once through trickery and blackmail," Dante said, his Faetalian accent as decadently delicious as always while his electricity made the air crackle in quite the scandalous way. "I figured it was time I got to choose my own monarchs."

"And did you simply forget that the three of us are still standing between the Vegas and the throne, even if Lionel dies today?" Max growled, indicating himself, Caleb, and Seth, and I had to admit he got my waters flowing when he went all feral like that, but we had no time for his kaboodle right now.

"We discussed it briefly," Leon said with a shrug. "And we decided to bet on the savage horses. You guys just seem kinda flappy since the other one died. Didn't seem like the right choice. No offence."

"His name was Darius," Caleb snarled, and tension radiated through the room, but I wouldn't be having that.

"Enough!" I barked, my Cerberus form punching though on the word, making many of them flinch in their flans. "We are here to discuss our plan for the final time, not dally on the narry winkle. Let us confirm the actions."

"I received a message this morning," Dante interrupted. "From the woman who Lionel tried to force me to procreate Storm Dragons with."

"How did such a message make its way yonder?" I gasped, my mind an instant flood of hatches which needed the aid of a baton as I wondered where the leak had sprung. We could not afford any mishaps such as someone telling the enemy where we wandered.

"Calm down, bella, it's nothing to worry about. This message came via mia famiglia who are still on the mainland, hiding from the eyes of the false king. Juniper managed to send word to my cousin Fabrizio, and he got a message to Rosalie via one of her omegas. There's no leaks in your security."

"Well, thank Fanny for that." I sank down into my chair and fanned my face as I tried to recover from the pointless bout of panic which had almost taken hold of me.

"What did Juniper have to say for herself?" Tory asked, leaning her forearms on the table and looking to Dante for the answer we were all on tenterhooks over.

"That the three boys she gave birth to just Emerged in their Order forms," Dante replied, his eyes dark.

"And let's just say... they weren't little Dragon babies," Leon snorted, before schooling his expression at a look from Dante.

"No. They aren't," he continued. "And when Lionel finds out, Juniper believes that he will have them put to death. She is asking me for help before that can happen. She wants to get them out of there, and she's offering to give us every drop of information she has on Lionel and the Dragon Guild if we will help her."

"How does this tie into the plan for today?" Tory asked.

"She said that she's been called to The Palace of Souls today with the three little butt-sniffers," Leon said. "So we figured we could snag them out of there before lighting the place up."

Tory nodded thoughtfully while the three supposed Heirs all broke into discussion at once, suggestions flying nerry and narry from their flappy traps.

"Will you be able to strike at Lionel while rescuing them?" my queen asked, cutting over their nabble grabble. "Can you break his shields with your lightning and end him while the rest of us go after Darcy, Gabriel, and Orion?"

"I wanted to be the one to strike at my father," Xavier said suddenly, breaking his silence and making us all look at him. "You said you would consider that request."

"And I did," Tory replied. "Just like I considered the fact that I would love nothing more than to rip his fucking head from his shoulders myself, then watch his eyeballs melt beneath the power of my Phoenix Fire. But Geraldine thought-"

"And I am most egregiously sorry, dear brother," I said, reaching across the table towards him despite his furious expression as I tried to explain myself. "It is just that as we know, they have Gabriel, they also have that abominable Vard. Any plan made too firmly, particularly by those of you they will be turning their eyes towards in expectation to kill the monstrous monarch, are the most likely to be *seen*."

Xavier snorted in that horsey way of his but nodded finally. "I guess the point is that he dies. It doesn't really matter who ends him."

I nodded sympathetically, growing a little bushel of carrots beneath my hand, and leaving them on the table for him in offering.

Xavier frowned at them like he knew I was just trying to placate him with the treat, but he snatched them up and started angrily munching all the same.

"Gabriel will be looking our way," Dante agreed. "But if the prediction he sent us comes true, then that won't be enough to save Lionel from death. He will be distracted by our presence though, and hopefully be unable to *see* the rest of you as you go after Orion and Darcy."

"When I soul walked to locate Darcy, I saw the two of them locked in a cage in the throne room," Tory said, though she had told us before and I had often wept upon my pillow as I thought on such a travesty. "So our best guess is that they're still there. Gabriel is most likely in the Royal Seer's Chamber. If either of them aren't in those places, then I'd bet they'll be locked in the north tower – that's where Lionel liked to keep me when I was under his control."

"Two groups then?" Caleb suggested. "One goes for Orion and Darcy, the other for Gabriel."

"Maxy boy?" I asked, and that scoundrel of a sea lion looked my way with a frown on his brow. "If I were in mortal peril, would you risk all to save me, throw yourself between me and death, give up everything just to see me survive?"

"Of course I would, Gerry," he said, his eyes softening like the wet kipper I had suspected he was.

"Thank you for admitting that most crippling weakness," I replied. "As such, I shall be in a differing group to you, ensuring that the mission is put before anything else and nothing is risked on account of my worthless existence."

"Wait just a second-" Max tried to interrupt, but I cast a silencing bubble around him so subtle that he didn't even notice, his nonsensical tirade trapped within, allowing the rest of us to finalise the plan.

"We'll use the royal tunnels to gain access to the palace," Tory said, handing out the rings she had crafted for each member of our little crew of chaos so that we could make use of said passages.

Max realised he was trapped in the silencing bubble and began fighting my magic off, but I tightened my grip on it as my queen continued, coating it in ice so that we didn't have to look at his furious face.

"Once we get inside, me, Xavier, and Max will go for the throne room in search of Darcy and Orion. Geraldine, Caleb, and Seth will go after Gabriel," Tory decided, and a quiver of anticipation warbled through me as we set our path at last.

"So you're just telling us what to do now, are you?" Seth demanded with a growl while Max began hammering on the silencing/ice bubble, and I pressed more power into containing him so that we could wrap up these shenanigans and get going.

"You could have attended the meeting where these things were discussed had you bent the knee," I said, rolling my eyes at the irksome pup.

Seth looked about ready to pop his long sherman, but Caleb rested a hand over his and shook his head.

"The plan seems solid to me, and the longer we wait, the more time there is for Lionel to *see* these decisions. Let's just go with it," he urged, and Seth narrowed his eyes.

"Oh sure, let's just go with Tory's plan. She's so pretty and has such perfect hair and has magical tits that can-"

"Dude, are you in love with your dead best friend's widow?" Leon hissed in a whisper so loud even the clams in the distant sea could surely hear him. "'Cause that's fucked up."

"No," Seth blurted, looking horrified while Tory wrinkled her queenly nose at the suggestion.

"Can we just all agree to the plan and get moving?" Tory asked, pushing to her feet, and I darn near knocked my chair over in my haste to rise with her.

"I'm down with it," Caleb said, and Seth agreed after a firm nudge from him to confirm it.

The others fell into line too, and everyone filed from the room, heading outside so that we could stardust our way to The Palace of Souls and the grand destiny which awaited us there.

The sound of shattering ice filled the room just as I stepped over the threshold, and I glanced back to find a rather dishevelled and crabby looking crustacean scowling at me as he finally burst free of my power.

"What the fuck, Gerry?" Max demanded, realising that everyone else was already gone.

"Chop, chop, Maxy boy," I called as I headed away from him and his nonsense. "Or you'll be left behind."

Scorpio
Virgo
Gemini
Cancer
Leo
Sagittarius
Taurus
Capricorn
Aquarius
Libra
Pisces

MILDRED

CHAPTER FORTY TWO

Today would be a grand occasion. All of Solaria would hear of it and tremble at the thought of what such important and bountiful news meant for one and all. Especially me. Me above every other.

Just as they had in every moment since our mighty and fearsome overlord had taken his rightful place on the throne. Once more, the might of the Dragons would be celebrated beyond all else. And I, as the most pure-blooded female of my generation, would be the one to take a central role in all of this. I would be a paragon for all who should come after me, a perfect example of what a Dragon should be. Virile, sturdy, and with a fine coating of hair upon my breasticles and upper lip to prove the power that lived in my lineage. Just as my mother had always told me, *'A sprouting hair upon bust or chin, proved there was a true Dragon within.'*

I would more than willingly sacrifice my mind, soul, and body to the greatness of our king, and I couldn't wait to offer him whatever pleasure he asked of me in my devotion to him. He could take me, use me, ruin me, and I would always be willing to bend to whatever his needs required.

I looked into the mirror and smoothed out the voluptuous folds of my virginal white dress, taking a moment to comb my moustache. My fingers twitched with need as I finally gave in to my favoured vice, sliding the small dressing table drawer open and revealing the premium Faeroids I had awaiting me inside.

I licked my lips and took a syringe from the little bag I kept ready for my twice-daily doses and tried to calm my breathing as I drew up my evening taste. I plunged the needle into my thigh with a low groan, my eyes rolling back in my head as I slowly depressed the plunger, languishing in the feeling of the drug as it sank into my system.

I rolled my broad shoulders back and smiled, exposing the lower row of my fearsome jaw. Yes, I was quite the beast inside and out, and the world would see it clearer than ever today as I walked among my brethren to fulfil my destiny.

Never had even a Dragon queen looked so like her Order form while in her Fae body. I was exquisite. And before the eyes of the entire Dragon Guild, I would give myself to King Acrux in every way he wished, letting him plunder every region of my being as I became so much more than I already was.

I tossed the spent needle in the trash and stepped from the chamber which I had used to get myself ready, gifted to me by my dear uncle Lionel for use when I was at court like this, then headed out into the grand corridor with a spring in my step.

"Well, if it isn't the she-beast herself," a snivelling voice drawled, and I narrowed my eyes to look upon the loathsome Cyclops, Vard. Enduring the company of any Order barring Dragons was always hard to bear, and this cretin of a creature was particularly unpleasant.

"Move aside, I have somewhere to be. Somewhere that does not require the attendance of a Cyclops," I sneered the word, shoulder-checking him as I passed and knocking him into the wall.

He cursed as he almost fell to the floor, scrambling to right himself while I marched proudly on towards my destiny. The stars had laid it out for me, the bounty of the Dragon King himself spread before me as I readied myself to open for him and welcome him deep inside me. I was and always had been his creature, the closest thing to a Dragon queen this land knew. And I was more than willing to take up my position and vessel for his bounty, just as soon as he was ready to drive it into me with the force of his might.

This celebration was exclusive to our kind, the Dragon Guild gathering in tight rank to witness him coming inside of me all at once.

I was floating on a cloud of supremacy, and I wouldn't linger for the words of a squalling Cyclops who was on the out and uninvited.

"You know, I have been working on a creature not unlike yourself. Half Turnian Hog, half lizard, though Fae at its core," Vard hissed as he hurried to walk with me, his lank hair clinging to his cheeks.

"If I were to care for the words of a lowly thing such as you, then I might take the time to roast you in Dragon fire and see how you like the taste of your own face melting. But I have far more important business to attend to than whatever it is you wish to jabber at me about," I clipped.

I turned from him and his repugnant features, heading down a long corridor as I took a roundabout route through the palace, avoiding the south wing which had somehow sealed itself from use. I had offered to blast a hole into the area for my king, but he had refused me, claiming it would not work. It was confounding, but I had to assume that it was just some old Vega trick at play. Their cunning schemes knew no bounds, but my king would no doubt destroy all lingering embers of those unworthy flames soon enough anyway.

"I *saw* something in the mind of the so-called 'greatest Seer of our time' about you," Vard hissed, his stumpy legs somehow maintaining pace with my wide and imposing stride despite my attempts to shrug him off. "Something in his memories, the morning of your wedding. Or should I say, the morning when you inexplicably ended up hog-tied in a closet and the man set to marry you escaped the fate of horrors lurking between your scaley thighs."

I whirled on him, a cloud of Dragon smoke spilling between my lips and sliding up his mismatched nostrils as I fisted a hand in his shirt and threw him against the wall. I snarled in his face, lifting him until his toes no longer touched the floor and he was eye to eye with me.

"Spit it out," I growled, and he smirked at me as he shifted, his ruined eye merging with the other to reveal the damaged Cyclops eye in the centre of his face. Ugly little thing he was. All sinewy and no meat on his bones. A single bite in my shifted form would see him swallowed right down into my belly. Though I didn't like to think of the indigestion I would endure if I gave in to that urge.

"I can show you," he offered, the greasy feeling of his mind trying to permeate mine sliding over me.

I had a will of iron and mental shields more impenetrable than my closely guarded vagina – destined only for the use of a Dragon of purest blood and honour. None had tried to breech either thus far, but I was ready if they did. And always wary. For a vagina such as mine was a high prize to claim indeed. No doubt my snookums had dreamed of it day and night before his demise. *Ah, snookums…if only you had possessed a modicum of loyalty in that decadent skull of yours, you and I could have had something truly magical. But the Vega whore beguiled you clean out of your senses, and it was not to be.*

"It'll only take a moment," Vard purred, and by the love of the stars, I felt my will wavering.

That entire day was a black hole of nothing to me, a wide expanse I had thought over time and again in search of answers. It haunted me, the missing time, the need to know precisely what had happened to land me in that closet instead of my marital bed.

"Show me," I hissed, my mental shields slipping just enough for him to slither in like the worm he was.

I saw my own face as I answered a knock at the door to the chamber I'd been gifted to use for a bridal suite. My eyes widened, then fell slack as I was struck with a blast of air magic to the chest, feet whirling over my head as my wedding dress ballooned around me.

Gabriel Nox strode into the room, his chest bare and black wings tucked tight to allow him through the doorway as he grinned like a fiend.

I threw fire at him, a roar escaping me as I emerged from the voluminous dress like a baby bursting from the womb. But he had already *seen* my strike before I'd even thrown it, his laughter ringing out as he smothered my flames with more earth magic. A wad of dirt smacked me in the face as I leapt for him again, vines snaking around my arms and immobilising them.

Humiliation tore through me as I was forced to watch my own failure at the hands of that plumped up, half plucked pigeon, and I bristled, trying to pull away from the memory.

But Vard kept hold of my mind, the hooked tentacles of his power burrowing deep as he feasted on my memories, stealing my magic while trapping me in the hell of watching this horror play out.

Gabriel hoisted me into the air with a single vine noosed around my ankle, kicking the door shut behind him as he moved closer to me and I spun in a slow circle, my dress falling around my face. Stuck in the memory that belonged to Gabriel, I could feel his emotions as I watched the show unfold, his dark amusement and smugness, his contempt for me despite my clear superiority over his half shifting kind.

His hands brushed my spine, and the zipper was released, the wedding dress falling like confetti and leaving me still spinning slowly, suspended by the vine, my bloomers on full display.

"When my snookums hears of this, he will castrate you! You dare to lay your hands upon his bride?" I roared.

Gabriel barked a laugh. "Darius is more likely to kiss me than kill me for saving him from these nuptials," he taunted. "Believe me – I've *seen* all the ways this future plays out and there isn't a single one of them that includes him being upset over me saving him from the hell of a union with you. But it's okay; I plan on making him suffer for a while before giving the game up. He deserves it for the shit he put my sister through, after all."

My mouth parted on what no doubt would have been a torrent of perfectly tuned abuse, but he spoke over me as if he didn't even recognise my superiority as a pure-blooded Dragon.

"Break any protection spells you have in place to stop Fae from impersonating you," he boomed, his voice thick with a Coercion so potent that in my dishonoured and dishevelled state, he managed to puncture my mental barriers and force his will into me.

I gasped as I watched myself do just that, allowing him the opportunity to disguise himself as me.

"No!" I wailed in the here and now, watching in horror as he shifted into me – taking my bridal gown from the floor and exchanging his jeans for it, taking his sweet time to apply my specially chosen puce-brown lipstick to his own lips and smacking them against his teeth before turning back to me with a grin.

"Don't worry – I'll let him enjoy his wedding before breaking the news to him," he said, my own voice taking the place of his as he moved towards me again, his eyes alight with menace. *"Now open wide and swallow down this memory potion like a good hag."*

His compulsion struck me again, and I roared as I was forced to watch him pour the potion between the lips which had been destined to kiss my snookums at the altar. This was the twist of fate that had stolen Darius from me and delivered him into the conniving arms of the Vega whore. I would kill her for his death. For corrupting him beyond all point of reason and forcing my king to deal with him as a traitor instead of a son.

My eyes burned as I watched the bridal me turn vacant eyes on the room, forgetting all that had transpired while Gabriel let me fall to the ground, hogtied me, and gave me a kick to roll me into that star-damned closet.

The memory fell away, but Vard's mind stayed locked with my own as I found myself staring at the wall where he had been pinned, nothing in my fist any longer and no sign of him anywhere close by.

"The other Dragons all enjoyed this little memory when I shared it at the Guild dinner for entertainment last night." His voice rattled through my skull as his slithering presence clung to me even while his physical form scuttled off to a safe distance. "Just in case you're wondering why they're all laughing so much today."

He released me from his hold, and I whipped around, a bellow escaping me before I slammed my fist into the wall hard enough to break knuckles.

If I didn't have a very important role to fulfil for my king, I would have hounded after him and roasted him alive. But as it was, the vermin's luck held true, and I was forced to turn and march away towards the grand occasion awaiting me.

One of these days I'd catch that snivelling rat though, and I'd do him the honour of finding out just how few pieces he needed to be in before I could swallow him whole.

Scorpio
Gemini
Virgo
Cancer
Leo
Taurus
Sagittarius
Capricorn
Aquarius
Libra
Pisces

Seth

CHAPTER FORTY THREE

I tumbled through a sea of stardust, floating past fluffy, colourful nebulas that were bigger than my mind could ever really comprehend. Then my feet hit the ground back in a misty woodland where the moonlight cut through the trees in angular shafts.

I flexed my fingers where my Phoenix fire gauntlets were wrapped around them, the clink of metal and heat of the flames within them sparking a thirst in me for a fight.

Caleb twirled his twin blades in his grip before sheathing them, one on each hip, and pushing his fingers through his gold curls, looking like a movie star ready for his close up. Just beyond him, Max brushed his hand over the metal bow strapped to his back then folded his arms, the blueish tint of his scales rippling across them and an arrogant slant to his lips that could have melted panties from fifty feet away. I turned my face to the wind, letting it tousle my half-braided hair as I glowered into the distance, ready to take on the damn world and win.

"Are you all quite done posturing like a bunch of peacocks at a tea party?" Geraldine snapped, looking between us Heirs with narrowed eyes.

Xavier and Tory shared a smirk at our expense, and I scoffed.

"It's not our fault we're naturally radiant," I said.

"Naturally arrogant, you mean," Tory corrected, arching a brow at me. She was wearing leather pants, plus a scowl deep enough to cause real bodily damage, and was looking all kinds of badass herself – she just needed to work on her signature pose and she'd be good to go. I could see it now on the front of a magazine. Bitchy Flame Eyes in beast mode.

"That too," I agreed with a sideways grin, and she almost cracked one in response.

Oh shit, Xavier needed a team name too. I looked him over, from his athletic frame to the doom clouding his once-bright eyes, to the dark, floppy hair which glimmered with purple glitter and I instantly had my answer. Twinkle Stud.

"You are still posing like the last daisy in the meadow before a merciless winter, you heinous hound." Geraldine darted forward, clapping me around the ear, and I yelped like a scolded pup before barking at her. She barked right back, and I straightened up to my full height, ready for a brawl, but Caleb pulled me back by the shoulder.

"Enough, we need to go," he said firmly, and I fell under the spell of that deliciously dominant voice he kept using with me lately. Or maybe it was just that my cock was paying more attention to it these days. I'd have butted chests with him and gone Alpha Wolf on him in the past, but now…fuck, I always thought I was an unwavering Dom in the bedroom, but when it came to him, I could play Sub sometimes. Though the idea of having Cal beneath me, showing him exactly how much fun two guys could have together was seriously appealing too.

Oh my stars…I'm a switch.

"But she's doing that thing again with her words," I grumbled.

"I love that thing," Max said, grinning as he stepped forward.

He leaned in to kiss Geraldine, but she ducked away from him, twirling wildly to keep out of his hold. She was the only one of us who'd decided to wear full armour for this mission, and the sharp points of the metal encasing her tits nearly took out Xavier's eye as she continued to spin and prance away. She whipped out her flail and pointed it at Max.

"Do not distract me, you cad of a codfish. We have a duty to our dear, sweet Queen Darcy, her noble brother, and her fine fellow Orry man. We cannot dither and dother here any longer. Come – yonder!" She turned, marching off into the thick woodland, and Tory took to her side as we followed.

Xavier had a taut look on his face, and I drifted to the back of the group to join him, sensing he was all up in his feels and in need of a little Seth snug. I slipped my arm around his shoulders, but he shrugged me off, making me whine at the rejection.

"Don't," he muttered.

"But you're sad or angry, or maybe both. Hang on, I'll ask Max." I opened my mouth to call out to my friend, but Xavier elbowed me in the ribs, and I cursed.

"Lionel is going to be so close to us today," he said darkly. "How am I supposed to just keep away? I want to kill him, Seth. I want to make him pay for taking my mom and Darius from this world." His hands trembled and vines curled around them, his earth Element spilling from him in his rage.

I nodded seriously, my heart sinking for him. "Dante will fry the motherfucker good. He'll cook him up like crispy tofu, and we can get a Cyclops to pull his memories out later so we can watch it all in slow-mo on repeat with a bag of popcorn in our laps. But before that, we have to save our friends so we don't lose anyone else."

He looked to me, the anger in his eyes melting like hot candle wax and shifting to determination instead. "You're right. We have to get them out."

"That's the spirit, Twinkle Stud."

"What did you just call me?"

I just smiled, knowing he'd heard and that he definitely loved it. *You're welcome, Twinkle Stud.*

We followed the others up to an ancient tree standing at the heart of a clearing, the bark knotted and gnarled, huge roots spreading out beneath it. There was a symbol etched into the bark of the tree in the shape of a Hydra, the little fella looking pleased to see us in the moonlight.

Tory moved forward, placing her hand against the symbol to open a secret door, and adrenaline buzzed through my veins. The dark tunnel beckoned us, and I could have sworn I heard a war drum starting up deep underground, urging us on. Or maybe it was just the frantic pounding of my heart.

I glanced up at the sky between the thick trees one last time, a meteor choosing that exact moment to speed by, heralding the event which had drawn us here. The Hydrids meteor shower grew in intensity in the heavens above, and my lips parted in awe at the beauty of the meteors streaking across the sky in blazes of celestial light.

We descended into the passage, casting Faelights to see by, and following Tory's lead into the depths of the Savage King's secret tunnels.

When we met a fork in the path, Tory turned to us, her sword in her grip and her eyes glinting with Phoenix fire. "We go left here, and you guys go right. Come back here as soon as you have Gabriel. Remember not to plan any of our enemy's deaths, no matter how goddamn tempting it is. We can't let them use Gabriel to *see* us coming."

"Of course, my lady. I shall not think about how I wish to impale that terrible toad of a Dragoon Mildred on the pointiest stick I can conjure." She whacked herself over the head hard. "Drat, there I go thinking of it. Well, it is gone now, I assure you I have no plans to make it come to fruition. Not this day, at least. But one day, I shall avenge my dear Angelica. Alas, it is not this day."

"Be careful," Max said to us, his gaze lingering on Geraldine.

"We shall be the most careful of caterpillars, crawling in lame Lionel's back doors and claiming our valiant friends from his clutches," Geraldine said with a firm nod.

"Good luck," Caleb said, and every one of us took a quiet moment to stand in that goodbye, knowing deep down that there was a chance some of us might not make it out tonight. But we weren't going to put a voice to any of those fears in case the stars listened in and decided to play havoc with our souls.

Max, Xavier, and Tory headed off into the dark tunnel to the left while Geraldine, Caleb and I went right, a whimper in my throat as I looked over my shoulder and silently wished them the best of fortunes.

We quickened our pace through the passage, and I inhaled the damp air, moving closer to Caleb and jolting as our hands brushed. His little finger curled around mine for the briefest of eternities, and I forgot how to draw air into my lungs, but then our hands parted again and I wasn't sure it had even happened.

The Faelight hovering above Geraldine didn't cast much of a glow back here, and as I glanced over to try and examine Caleb's expression, I found him already looking at me. His features were heavily shadowed, and I wasn't sure what to think as our eyes met and my heart rioted. I used to touch him so liberally, never thinking anything of wrapping my arms around him, nuzzling his face and neck. That was me. It was the way I was with all my friends. But now, every time my skin made contact with his, it felt forbidden. Like I was crossing some line, but I didn't know what the line represented.

Everything had changed now, and somehow, I still had no idea where I stood. I was living in a torturous paradox, where on the one hand, I couldn't bear the emotional pain it caused me after we'd pushed the boundaries of our relationship into friends with benefits, but on the other, I wanted Caleb to use me in any way he saw fit and feast on the scraps of his attention whenever he tossed them my way.

I had never experienced anything so hot as watching Caleb Altair fall to ruin for me, and I had never come so hard as I had with his hand wrapped tight around my cock. I was an addict for him now, and there was no hope for me. If he came to me again, I wouldn't say no. I should have had more pride, should have protected my heart with dignity and shielded myself from the inevitable destruction that was coming my way because of this. But I was a willing sacrifice, walking into the shrine of unrequited love and handing him a knife so he could cut out the pounding muscle in my chest and devour it whole. I could think of no better end for my heart than one delivered by him anyway.

"Avast," Geraldine hissed, and I almost crashed into her as she came to a sudden halt. "We have reached the innards of the palace. A doorway layeth here, I sense it in my brandycocks." She ran her hands over the wall ahead of her and a grinding of stone sounded as it started to slide open.

I tensed, ready for an attack, while Geraldine raised her flail and Caleb took a dagger into his grip. Silence washed over us from an empty hallway beyond the hidden door, a navy carpet running the length of it and giant silver mirrors hanging on the walls.

Geraldine stepped out into the palace, and we followed, keeping close together while I lifted a hand to cast a silencing bubble around us along with an air shield.

"Jiminy crockpot," Geraldine breathed in awe. "My eyes are not worthy of the beauty housed in these halls. I will scrub them with seaweed and salt upon my return to our safe haven."

"Which way to the Seer's chamber?" I asked.

"Yonder!" she cried, taking off at a gallop, and Caleb and I shot after her.

She was damn fast, moving like an alley cat with a feral dog on its tail, sprinting out into the next corridor before hanging right and leading us through a maze of luxurious lounges and tea rooms, then skidding to a halt in front of a grand wooden door, cupping her ear against it.

We gathered close at her back, and Geraldine caught a fistful of Caleb's shirt, yanking him nose to nose with her.

"Put those bat ears to good use and use your auditory aptitude to gauge the danger awaiting us beyond this door, good fellow," she commanded, grabbing onto his ear and yanking on it to get it closer to the door.

"Argh. Stop that." Caleb knocked her away, rubbing his ear, then moving nearer to listen anyway.

Geraldine leaned close, pressing her ear to Caleb's other ear which wasn't against the door.

"Perhaps I can use you as an ear trumpet," she whispered to herself, and I sniggered.

"It's clear," Caleb announced, stepping back and opening the door, nudging Geraldine away from him as he did so.

My heart jumped into my throat so hard it nearly knocked some teeth out as we came face to face with Stella beyond the door, her eyes widening in alarm.

"For the true queens!" Geraldine cried, leaping forward with her flail held high, swinging it toward Stella's head without a moment's hesitation.

Stella cried out, but her voice didn't reach us, revealing that a silencing bubble surrounded her and in the next second, she shot backwards several feet with her Vampire speed, avoiding the brutal swing of Geraldine's flail.

Caleb moved in a blur, rushing to catch her before she could disappear with a burst of her Vampire speed. But Stella didn't even try to run, letting Caleb take her arm and raising her other hand in surrender.

I extended my silencing bubble over her, and she let hers pop so we could hear her.

Geraldine lunged forward again, swinging the flail like a woman possessed, rolling her hips as she went.

"Wait," Stella gasped, her fangs winking at me from her mouth. "I can help you."

Caleb threw an arm up to block Geraldine's strike, the chain of the flail snapping around it, spinning around tight, and he growled through the pain.

"By the moon, Cal, are you alright?" I lurched forward, unwinding the flail from his arm, and healing away the marks.

"How dare you?" Geraldine cried, holding a hand to her chest in shock at what Caleb had done. "My flail was destined to crush the skull of this wench! She is a callous cockroach, a hag of a hornet, a-"

"Cunt of a caterpillar?" I offered.

"Precisely!" she cried. "And I shall smite her down this day in the name of her brave and fearless son, who has taught us that even a shamed creature such as he can rise back through society under the name of love, virtue, and honour!"

"She helped us before," Caleb said and I guessed he had a point, though Geraldine also made good points. I was inclined to end Stella for her treatment of Orion alone. He was my moon friend after all, and what kind of moon friend would I be if I didn't kill his treacherous, black-hearted mother now that the opportunity had presented itself?

"I dunno, Cal. I think her face would suit her better if she wore it on the back of her skull," I said darkly, stepping up to Geraldine's side. "I'd like to have the honour though."

Caleb's throat bobbed as he took in my words, and Stella looked to me in horror.

"I can help you," she said quickly. "Tell me what you need."

"We're here to rescue our friends, of course," I said.

"Hound, shut your flapper trap this instant," Geraldine snapped. "Do not divulge our plans to this crustacean of a crout."

"It's fiiine. She'll be dead in a sec anyway." I slowly circled Stella, a Wolf hungering for a kill, and she twisted her head to watch me go, her eyes glittering fearfully.

I loved the power this game fed to me, and I could feel Caleb being tempted into playing along. He wanted to see me do it. He'd enjoy every second. Because we may have lived in a civilised society, but we were animals at our core. And the promise of death had all of our inner natures coming to the surface.

Caleb flashed his fangs at me in a warning to keep back, and I smiled demonically. *Maybe I will, maybe I won't.*

"She might be useful like last time," Caleb said, like he was trying to talk me down, but I just licked my lips.

"We don't need help this time," I said. "We have a plan. What can she really offer us?"

"The whelp has a point," Geraldine agreed. "Let us cast this wench from the world before we are found dithering here like a pot of begonias upon a doormat."

"Listen to me," Stella growled. "You can take the others, but my son cannot leave here. He has-"

"Silence crone!" Geraldine threw out a hand, casting a wedge of soil into Stella's mouth and making her choke and splutter.

I gnashed my teeth by Stella's ear, and she flinched away from me so forcefully that she almost fell over, only remaining standing because of Caleb's grip on her. I laughed and Geraldine sucked in both of her lips to hold back her own laugh, recomposing herself quickly.

"We must do the honourable thing by our dear professor," Geraldine said, puffing out her chest. "We must put his mother to death."

"Look, no one is more bloodthirsty for her death than I am," Caleb said, his fangs out and proving he meant every word of that. "But she was useful when we went to Acrux Manor before. She might be a despicable mother to Orion, but something tells me she's got cold feet on her evil bitch business."

"I dunno, Cal," I said doubtfully. "She's probably just stalling to give Lionel time to come find her."

Stella scraped the last of the soil off of her tongue, hissing angrily and glaring between us.

"Listen to me, Lance has taken on the burden of breaking Darcy Vega's curse," she said, a tremor in her tone, like she really gave a damn about her son. "He's made a deal with the Shadow Princess. You cannot take him from this place."

"And why would we believe you?" I snarled. "You just want to keep your son here so you can try and corrupt him again. But we corrupted him first. He's *ours*. You can't have him."

Her lower lip trembled. "Yes, I know I lost him a long time ago, but I'm trying to protect him now. He made a Death bond with her."

"A Death bond?" Geraldine gasped, throwing a hand to her heart. "No, it cannot be. Not my lady's sourplum. Not her dear Orry man."

"She's lying," I barked, and Stella flinched again. "Give her to me, Cal. I'll make her tell us the truth."

"We're wasting too much time," Caleb said, his brows drawn tight.

He raised his hand, slapping his palm to Stella's forehead and casting a sleep spell on her before she could stop him. She collapsed in a heap at his feet, and Geraldine shrieked.

"I do not wish to flail her face in while she slumbers! I wish to fight her like Fae, like the glorious Gadrivelle in the war of seven soothsayers! Rouse her this instant," Geraldine commanded, lifting her flail threateningly.

"No," Caleb said, drooping down with a surge of speed and picking Stella up. He vanished in the next second and returned empty-handed from the direction we'd come from before we could do more than whirl around to search for him.

"Where is she?" I demanded.

"Sleeping in a chair somewhere far away from us. We're leaving her alive, her death belongs to Orion. Besides, we're not killing a woman who surrendered to us," Caleb said, a ring of authority in his voice.

"But she's awful," I pushed, my hackles rising as I lunged at him, my chest slamming against his. "You had no right to make that decision. You're not in charge of us."

Caleb bared his fangs at me, his eyes sparking with a challenge, and heat coursed through my veins. He wanted a fight? I'd give him a fucking fight.

"We have a plan, and we have to stick to it. If we kill her, Vard could *see* it, then how long do you think we have until we're found, huh?"

"You don't just get to make the call. You're an Heir, not a king," I hissed, butting my forehead against his and growling deep in my throat. My instincts were making me feel entirely Wolf, and Caleb rose to meet the beast in me with a beast of his own.

"You're looking to get put in your place, pup," he warned.

"And where's my place? Because last I checked, it was at your side, not beneath you."

"That's not how I remember it," he said, a smirk tilting his lips, mocking me right fucking there in the open with what we'd done in secret.

It struck me like a bolt of lightning to my chest and I howled in rage, rearing back and slamming my fist into his face. He stumbled away with a curse, but as I went for him again, he moved with his Vampire speed, coming up behind me and locking his muscular forearm around my neck, yanking me back against him.

"Submit like a good pup," he growled in my ear and my cock liked that a lot, but my Wolf didn't.

I threw my elbow back hard enough to wind him, and he shot away again as I turned to get hold of him.

"IMBECILES!" Geraldine crowed, diving between us and slapping a hand to each of our foreheads as Caleb came at me from the front. She looked from me to him with her teeth bared and eyes wild. "You two have danced the four-legged mongo long enough! It is as clear as a summer's day on a Tuesday morn that each of you are twitterpated with the other like bucktoothed rabbits gazing into the lambent glow of a thousand Faeflies. My eyes may be open, but if they were welded shut with the solder of sun steel, I would still perceive it as plainly as an unbuttered bagel. Seth Capella, you resemble a bloated cagafrog when you gaze upon this toothsome behemoth before you, and Caleb Altair, it appears as though your jaw might fall from the corners of your face and shatter against the flagstones every time you glance yonder at your merry mutt. So stop this unendurable foxtrot and lay your truths upon the chantry of each other's fervour this instant!"

We both looked at Geraldine in dumbfounded confusion, and my mind ticked over the crazy words she'd just spewed at us. My brain was stuck on the four-legged mongo, and I couldn't figure out what the hell she was on about. I glanced at Caleb, wondering if he was any closer to understanding her than I was, but he shook his head to confirm he was clueless too.

"Um, what?" I balked.

Geraldine threw her head back in frustration, tossing a hand to her forehead. "I couldn't be any clearer if I knitted you both a jotsom scarf and threw you into the river of Meul. Alas, I cannot wade a single step more in this quag, it is time to we focus our attentions on our beloved Gabriel and return to our friends with him in tow post-haste. If Stella's ramblings had any trueness to them, then we must quicken our strides and see what can be done about Darcy's Orry man. But the sands of time are already slipping through our fingers, chaps, so we must seize the hour and forge onward."

She took off at a furious pace, and I shared a glance with Caleb that said we were going to drop this argument for now. Geraldine was right; we had to get a move on, but I had every intention of finishing that fight with him later.

We jogged after her, following her down a hall where gleaming swords were mounted on the walls, then she stopped abruptly in front of an engraved wooden door and pointed at it dramatically with her flail.

"The Royal Seer's Chamber," she breathed ominously, and I drew our silencing bubble in tighter around us. "What misery shall we find our Gabriel in? What lays yonder may never be unseen."

I moved to open the door, but Geraldine karate chopped my hand away from the handle with a 'yah!'.

"Ow," I cursed, narrowing my eyes at her. "Was that really necessary?"

"Your unworthy paws cannot handle the intricacies of opening such a door." Geraldine moved forward, raising a hand in a theatrical movement then slamming it down on the handle and opening the door like a normal fucking door.

"How was that intricate?" I asked in frustration, but Geraldine was already gone, marching into the room with her flail raised high.

I followed her inside with Caleb, taking in the beautiful room where portraits of long-dead Fae stared down at us from the walls, my eyes falling on the glass throne at the centre of the chamber. It was stunning, a work of art in itself, with silver gemstones inlaid all over it, mapping out the constellations. At the far end of the chamber, a portrait of Merissa Vega hung, her face tilted towards a night sky, the beauty of her so similar to that of her daughters.

My heart sank like a stone in a well. The room was empty, nothing but chains around the chair to even suggest Gabriel had been here.

"Blaggerflooks," Geraldine cursed, running over to the chair and dropping down to run her hands over the seat. "It's as cold as a winter's eve. Not an echo of the warmth of his dandy buttocks remains. He has been gone some time. Or perhaps he was never here at all."

"Let's head to the tower," Caleb said decisively.

"Yeah, I'll lead the way," I said, throwing him a look that said 'stop being a bossy asshole'.

"How about I carry you both and speed this shit up," Caleb suggested, eyes glittering.

"I can walk just fine," I said stubbornly.

"Nonsense you nincompoop." Geraldine slapped me around the back of the head. "We shall ride upon our fangly steed and quicken this escapade up a notch. Let us head thither at once!" She leapt onto Caleb's back, wrapping herself around him and Caleb opened his arms for me.

"Hey, how come I have to ride in your arms like a baby? I'll go on your back. Get down Geraldine." I moved forward, grabbing her leg, but she kicked out like a new-born foal, her boot slamming into my dick.

"*Motherfucker.*" I crumpled with a howl of pain, and Caleb took the opportunity to scoop me up in his arms and shoot off into the palace. I wasn't being held like a baby at all – I was a motherfucking purse hanging limp beneath a grandma's arm.

"Left, right, left," Geraldine called the directions to him, tugging on his ears to drive him like a racehorse while I craned my neck to scowl up at them.

"Stop that," Caleb hissed, but Geraldine ignored him, steering his head this way and that, and he couldn't do anything about it while his arms were wrapped tight around me.

We soon entered the tower and started circling up the dark spiral stairway so fast that my head spun.

"Avast!" Geraldine roared the order to stop, and Caleb came skidding to a halt at the top of the tower, right before a door. We were on a dark landing with black brick walls and a worn wooden floor. The single window high above us let in little of the moonlight, and I didn't think it was worth casting a Faelight in case it drew attention.

I pushed out of Caleb's arms and Geraldine jumped down, rushing forward to feel out the area for defensive spells.

"Drat, there's a security ward here. I shall try to disable it. Come, Caleb, lend me your power." She snatched his hand into her grip, and I pursed my lips at them as he offered her power and the two of them got on with their little job together.

"Fine, I'll just stand here like an unwanted almond," I said loudly, but they ignored me. "No one likes an almond."

They kept their backs to me, and I growled, moving further along the wall that blocked our way into the room, brushing my fingers over it with the hand that held the ring Tory had gifted me, hoping there might be a secret passage which would let us in so I could save the day.

"Even almonds don't like almonds. They're the eggplant of the nut world," I muttered. "Actually, I don't think they're even a true nut. I'm pretty sure they're a seed posing as a nut. Fucking undercover little seedling bastards."

I left them with their own silencing bubble as I moved further away, casting one around myself and continuing to delve deeper along the shadowy passage.

A grumbling of stone made me pause and I whipped around, hoping to find a doorway opening in the wall, but instead just one single brick slid aside, giving me a view into the room beyond. I shuffled in close to the wall, peering through it, looking for Gabriel, Orion, and Darcy with hope nearly making my heart burst.

It was dark in there, and there was a smell like ash and death that made my instincts prickle with warning. My throat thickened and I squinted harder to see through the gloom, lifting a hand to cast an enhancing spell over my eyes. The room became clearer, and I froze at what I saw in there. Lavinia was writhing in a nest of shadows, chewing on a severed head that had such life in its eyes that I could have sworn it was somehow aware of what was happening to it.

Nausea gripped me as Lavinia suddenly rolled onto her back, spreading her legs wide and revealing a gaping black hole where her vagina should have been.

I screamed, the sound trapped within my own silencing bubble and slamming back into my ears triple-fold. A thing; a horrid, massive, thing was crawling out of that hole, shadow and blackish blood everywhere as that monstrous demon creature dragged its way out of her body and into this world.

"No, no, no, no, no, no," I said in horror, backing up, wanting to claw my eyes from my face to try and unsee what I'd seen. But there was no unseeing it, no unseeing it at all. "You're not Darcy. Not Darcy at all."

Lavinia bent over backwards like she was made of rubber, her legs spread wide and some awful chant leaving her lips as she birthed a monster. The power in that room was unimaginable, the pressure of it making my ears pop and the magic in my veins sizzle. It was too much. We couldn't fight it, couldn't go near it without falling prey to those terrible shadows seeping out of her nest. They were drifting this way, coiling out like tentacles coming to take hold of me and drag me into a pit of desolation. Or worse, Lavinia's vagina.

I forced my mind to click into gear and jerked backwards, taking my hand from the wall so the brick slid into place again. My heart was beating furiously and all I knew was that we had to go. Run as far as we fucking could from this room and never, ever, ever look back.

I sprinted to the others, panting as I merged my silencing bubble with theirs.

"I saw through the wall," I blurted, and they turned to me.

"By the stars, are you alright?" Caleb asked, moving closer in concern. "You look seriously pale."

"Yeah good, great, dandy. But let's go. I saw some stuff. Some really not good stuff. Gabriel's not here. No one's here. Well, someone's here. But it's not our friends. We need to just...just go. Because I've seen something and, and...and..."

"Goodness, he's as shaken as a twoddle stick," Geraldine murmured to Caleb.

"What did you see?" Caleb pressed, but I shook my head, vowing upon every drop of love I possessed in my heart for him that I wouldn't subject him to knowing what I'd seen. I'd tell them all about that freaky shadow baby when I could, but now was not that time.

"We just need to go. Please, trust me." I swallowed the lump in my throat and Caleb frowned, nodding his agreement.

"Okay, let's head back downstairs and find the others," he said. "Maybe they've had more luck than us."

Geraldine jumped on his back and I let Caleb lift me into his arms, curling into him and pressing my face into his shirt, trying to process what I'd seen. I didn't think a day would ever pass now when I wouldn't think of it. I was changed, altered forevermore.

Stars save me from the unholy demon vag.

We made it down to the ground floor and Caleb came to a jolting halt that nearly sent me flying from his grip like I was in a car crash. Thankfully, his arm remained latched around me like a seatbelt, tugging me back tight against his side. I frowned at the corridor ahead of us where heavy footsteps were pounding this way, but Caleb was already moving back in the direction we'd come.

"Fuck, there's Nymphs everywhere," he cursed, clearly picking up on them with his Vampire hearing. He darted into a closet before the Nymphs made it this way, and our silencing bubble closed in around the three of us.

"By thunder, we can't stay here," Geraldine whispered.

"Well, we can't go out there, there's too many of them. Look." Caleb pointed at the keyhole and I wriggled out of his arms, lowering down to peek through it and spotting the lines and lines of Nymphs heading past the door and into an open lounge across the hall. Yup. That was death's door right there, and death was standing outside it, twirling a finger on his key and whistling for us to come running.

Some of the Nymphs were in shifted form, while others were in their Fae-like form, sipping tea like it was going extinct and clearly in no rush to move on.

"Kaboodles," Geraldine cursed. "We'd best wait here until they move on. Even with my flail, your daggers, and the mutt's claws, we would cause too much of a stir if we attacked them, and we mustn't alert the dastardly Dragoon to our presence before our dear Dante has had a chance to rain down a death storm upon his noggin."

I sighed, dropping down on my ass with a huff and burying my face against my knees, finding only a demon vagina staring back at me in the gloom. I shuddered, but as Caleb dropped down beside me, his hand found mine in the dark and warmth spread up my arm and deep into my heart.

Alright, maybe hiding here in a closet wasn't so bad. I just hoped Max, Tory, and Xavier were having more luck than we were.

Scorpio
Gemini
Virgo
Cancer
Leo
Sagittarius
Taurus
Capricorn
Aquarius
Libra
Pisces

TORY

CHAPTER FORTY FOUR

I pushed open a hidden door which let us out into a corridor not too far from the kitchens, my gaze flicking between Max and Xavier as they stepped out to stand beside me.

"All good?" I asked Max, our silencing bubble hiding my voice.

"I can't feel anyone close by," he confirmed as I straightened the tapestry we'd had to slip out from behind, my eyes moving over the green Dragon stitched into it. "But there is something…"

I looked to him as he pushed into his gifts, a frown furrowing his brow.

"What is it?" Xavier asked, a note of caution to his voice, and I knew the prospect of us coming face to face with Lionel had to be eating at him. He'd suffered beneath the tyranny of that asshole for far too long and had lost too much at his hands for this not to be unnerving for him.

"It's like a mass of pain and fear…" Max turned and started walking away from us, moving in the opposite direction to the throne room.

"Hey," I hissed. "You're going the wrong way. Darcy and Orion are being held back there."

I jerked my chin down the corridor that led towards the throne room, but Max ignored me, upping his pace as he headed towards a window further along the wide hallway.

I exchanged a look with Xavier then hurried after him, jogging until I made it to the window where a view of the foggy grounds gave way to a glimpse of the distant amphitheatre illuminated in the pale moonlight.

"Shit," Max murmured, his eyes fixed on that place of war and ruin.

"Show me," I demanded, snatching his hand into my grip and Max only hesitated for a moment before pushing what he was feeling into me.

Flashes of memory danced behind my eyelids, people screaming, cold stone floors, iron bars, torture.

"Fuck," I hissed, yanking my hand away again while Xavier snorted horsily.

"What is it?" he demanded.

"Prisoners," I answered.

Max remained standing there, lost to the swell of misery and fear that was pulsing from the amphitheatre.

"We need to warn Dante before he casts his lightning at that place," Max said in a low growl, his eyes flashing with concern for the people who would be right in the firing line if Dante unleashed his power in the way we'd planned.

"On it," I said, taking my Atlas from my pocket and calling Leon, who should still be in his Fae form if they'd stuck to their plans.

The call connected on the third ring. "Heyyy," Leon crooned, and I expelled a relieved breath before launching into an explanation about the trapped prisoners, but I was cut off as he continued speaking. "I know, I know, it's easy to be shy when you're calling a living legend, but don't worry, even I get intimidated by me sometimes – it's a Charisma thing. So just take a breath, relax, and remember that I am far too busy to waste my time checking voicemail boxes, and as such, this isn't one. P.S. If you're trying to contact my merch shop call 5318008-535173. We're now taking pre-orders for next year's tiny snakes in tiny hats calendar. Byeeee."

The call cut off and I blinked at my Atlas for several seconds before cursing and dialling Dante instead, hoping that by some miracle the Storm Dragon wasn't in the air yet and we still had time to stop this.

"Heyyy," Leon's voice answered after the fourth ring, and relief tumbled through me.

"Leon, you have to get Dante to-"

"What do you call a more impressive Fae than a Storm Dragon?"

"What?" I demanded, but Leon just kept talking.

"Leon Night!"

"Leon, I don't have time for-"

"Fan mail can be redirected through my PO box – please stop harassing my pals to try and get hold of me. Ciao."

The call cut off without an option for voicemail and I cursed that fucking Lion Shifter and his nonsense as I spotted a darkening cloud on the horizon, lightning flashing in its heart.

"I can't get hold of them," I breathed, the approach of that cloud like a death toll sounding the end for the rebels trapped in the amphitheatre. "You two are going to have to go and get the prisoners out."

"We aren't leaving you here," Xavier protested, stomping his foot, but I just shook my head, moving back towards the tapestry and yanking it aside so they could head back down into the tunnels.

"You know I can't leave here without Darcy and Orion. And I know you aren't going to let all of those people out there die for the sake of staying with me. We can't all be in two places at once, and I'm not walking out of this palace without my twin. I'll die here before I abandon her. So you need to go, and you need to go now. There's no point in trying to argue with me over this," I said firmly, opening the door with a press of my hand.

Xavier seemed inclined to protest, but Max caught his arm, shaking his head.

"She's not going to change her mind, man. And those people out there need us. I trust her, don't you?"

Xavier didn't look like he trusted me one bit, and to be fair, I wouldn't have either. I was beyond the point of limiting myself in what I would do to protect the people I loved, and I knew that I was likely to stain my soul in all kinds of sin in my effort to release my sister tonight.

"Tory," Xavier began, but I cut him off by throwing my arms around him.

"I love you for wanting to stay," I breathed, crushing him in my hold. "But I need you to accept this and go."

I pushed him back and he gave me a heart-wrenching look before nodding and following Max into the passageway.

"Stay safe, little Vega," Max growled, his gifts slamming into me as he offered me courage and determination. I accepted the feelings with a grim smile.

"If you see Lionel, cut his head off for me," I replied darkly, letting the stone door close between us and replacing the tapestry as I was left alone in this place which should have been my home.

I drew my sword and broke into a run, my steps hidden within my silencing bubble and Phoenix fire building in my veins.

I'd spent enough time in this place to know all of the shortcuts and quiet corridors, and I sprinted down a long hallway without another moment's hesitation.

A door to my left burst open and my heart leapt in panic before I realised no one was there, my sword lowering as I took in the route the palace was offering me, the faint, glimmering silver footprints on the floor.

I may have scorned the stars, but this place, the legacy my parents had left here for me, was different.

I turned from my intended path, darting through the doors before they swung shut behind me, the sound of several male voices echoing in the corridor I'd just escaped a moment later.

Another door swung silently open ahead of me and I sprinted for it, following those silver footprints and trusting them to keep me safe as I began a slightly longer route to my destination.

It took me hardly any time to reach the entrance to the throne room though, and I didn't meet a single soul along the way, thanks to the help of the palace itself, my feet falling still as I closed in on the heavy doors which barred my way.

I skimmed my fingers across the carved wood, testing the entrance for magical detection spells and locks, discovering several of each, the magic carefully crafted and difficult to find. But I hadn't been wasting my time while waiting for this opportunity to come around and I doubted there was a spell like this left in the world which I was incapable of disarming now.

The lock clicked faintly as I disabled it and I shoved the door wide, letting it bang against the wall as I took in the towering room beyond. I threw my silencing bubble out, encasing the entire throne room in it and whirling towards the shocked looking Fae who had been standing to the side of the room.

A tall guard gasped in alarm as he took me in, choking on smoke as it rose in his lips, revealing him as a Dragon. A shield of air magic flew up around him, and I shattered it with a missile of blue and red wings.

I was sprinting for him before the smoke even dispersed, and he threw an arm up to cast at me again, just in time for my sword to cut through flesh and bone, severing the limb and spraying me in a glorious arc of red blood.

His scream cut off sharply as my sword slit his throat open, and I sidestepped his corpse as it tumbled to the floor with a sickening thump.

I didn't spare him another look as I turned for the cage on the far side of the huge Hydra throne, my heart racing and aching as I spotted my sister there, shadows clinging to her where she stood beside Orion, gripping the bars which held them, their eyes wide in surprise.

"Tory," Darcy choked out, and it was like I hadn't been able to breathe until that moment, like my heart had been frozen for weeks and weeks since the last time our gazes had locked and our souls had been in the same place.

I ran to her, sheathing my sword and throwing my arms around her through the bars of the cage, a sob of relief tumbling from me as I crushed her in my hold.

"Thank fuck I found you," I exhaled, the bars cutting into me as I refused to allow so much as an inch of space to remain between us. "We need to go."

I forced myself to release her and moved my attention to the lock on the cage door, my eyes flicking to Orion as our grief over Darius passed between us and my heart twisted in agony for a moment.

"I missed you too, asshole," I said, pushing my power into the lock, the damn thing twice as powerfully protected as the door had been.

An enormous sound made all of us flinch as the Hydra throne at my back began to bellow and I whirled around in fright, whipping a dagger into my palm as I stared at the thing, the magic invoked by the meteor shower making the walls themselves rattle. I raised my eyes to the windows set in the roof high above us, my breath catching at the sight of the meteors tearing through the ever-darkening sky, signalling the arrival of the prophesised moment Gabriel had foreseen.

"Gabriel sent me a prophecy on the battlefield," I explained as I turned back to the cage. "The Hydra bellowing in a spiteful palace – Dante is going to take the opportunity Gabriel offered us to kill the fucking king while I came here for you."

"He *saw* Lionel die?" Orion gasped.

"Let's hope so."

I gripped the lock again, summoning my magic as the noise from the throne fell away again, the magic of it making my skin prickle with awareness, and I could have sworn the air itself stirred with the presence of our parents, as though they were watching this moment, urging me on.

Darcy's hand fell over my wrist and she squeezed tightly, taking my hand from the lock and forcing me to look at her.

"Tory, you have to leave us here," she said, her eyes full of pain and heartbreak. "Lance made a Death bond with Lavinia to break the curse on me. He can't leave for two more months, when their deal will end, and I can't be trusted among the rebels until then either-"

I blinked at her in confusion, the words tangling in my mind before finally aligning into a horrifying truth.

"You fucking idiot," I barked at Orion as those words sank in, my fist snapping out and punching him straight in the balls.

Orion doubled over with a curse, stumbling away from the bars and wheezing out a breathy, "Why?" but I just glared at him.

"What is it with the self-sacrificing bullshit you men keep throwing at us? We're fucking princesses born to the most powerful bloodline in the whole of Solaria, the first Phoenixes born in a thousand years, and we claimed all four motherfucking Elements just to put the icing on the cake. We aren't damsels in distress, we didn't ask you to do any of this shit, and I'm so fucking sick of having to clean up the mess your knight-in-shining-armour routines keep causing!" I yelled, punching the bars which separated us and letting him know with a glare that if he'd been standing closer to them then that it would have been aimed at his balls again.

"Shit, Tor, I've missed you so much," Darcy said, a half laugh, half sob escaping her as she shifted her grip on my wrist to my fingers and squeezed them tight.

"Don't say that," I snapped, yanking my hand out of hers and returning my attention to the lock.

"Why not?" she frowned.

"Because you might be saying you missed me, but what you're really saying is goodbye, and you can stick it up your ass, Darcy. So Orion made a Death bond – sounds like he's stuck here, but you're not, are you?"

Darcy sucked in a sharp breath, moving towards Orion in what I knew was a refusal to leave him, but I ignored her. My concentration was too scattered by their world-altering announcement to break the magical lock, so I simply brought Phoenix fire to my fingertips and melted the whole thing, tossing the glob of molten metal aside and yanking the door wide so that she could get out.

"I'm not coming with you, Tory," Darcy said fiercely, but I could tell with one look at her that she was tapped out, her magic and Phoenix both out of her reach, and that meant she couldn't do shit to stop me taking her. I'd been too broken without her, and I wasn't going to leave her in the hands of Lavinia and Lionel to do what they pleased. It was a miracle she was still breathing at all.

I looked to Orion, knowing without asking that he'd agree with me on this, and he nodded.

"Blue, listen to her. You need to get out of here. It's only two more months. I can take it. I will gladly take it in payment for your freedom from the-"

Darcy slapped him so hard that his head wheeled to one side, and I arched a brow at her as she snarled at him, like full-on snarled as she stalked right into his personal space.

"Tory was right about the self-sacrificing shit, Lance," she hissed. "If you can enter a Death bond to save me, then I can sure as hell stay here in this cage with you if I choose to do so. The two of you can't make that choice for me. You need me here."

"Tory needs you with her," he growled back, the low blow like a punch to my heart as she turned to me with pain in her eyes, knowing the truth of those words even if I was trying to mask how much I was hurting right now. I did need her. I needed her like I needed air in my lungs, and I was breaking more and more every day that I was forced to remain without her. She was my rock, my sanity, the one thing I had always and would always fight to the death and beyond for, and without her, I was nothing but a ruinous shell of the girl she loved in return.

"Tor..." Darcy shook her head hopelessly, and I swallowed thickly, a small, pathetic little girl inside me wanting to beg her not to turn her back on me now when I had come so far for her, when I had already lost so much. I didn't know how I'd cope with it if I left this place without her. I couldn't even fathom the possibility of that happening or what would happen to the last dregs of my soul which were only clinging together because of my love for her.

A roar from somewhere beyond the palace walls had me turning away, taking the coward's way out as I snapped my gaze from hers, not wanting to have to watch her make the choice I would never make. I would never leave her on her own. But the fear building in my chest was telling me that she was about to abandon me to the dark all over again. She was going to choose him over me.

"We need to give her what we found," Orion said urgently, moving to the back of the cage where the bars had been welded to the wall of the throne room itself, and Darcy moved after to him to open a secret door in the wall.

I blinked in surprise as a little white Rat poked his nose out of the opening, a tiny nest revealing itself beyond him with something glittering inside it.

"This is Eugene Dipper, and we found another Guild Stone. We also found this book on Queen Avalon's reign, and there's a Memoriae crystal full of Phoenix memories here too," Orion said.

"Shit, you have been busy," I said in surprise.

"There's also a ring full of Francesca Sky's memories," Orion added, his voice tightening a little on those last words as he wrapped the items in a wad of navy-blue fabric with tiny jade green dragons embroidered all over it.

"You need to get them out of here," Darcy said seriously. "Fran's memories need to be shown to the press, and you need to see all this stuff about Phoenixes, Tor. It's important."

I accepted the small package automatically, my gaze moving back to my other half as I slipped them into my pocket.

"Don't forget Eugene," she said, lifting the rat from the hole in the wall and passing him to me.

The large rodent leapt from her palms, landing on my shoulder and nuzzling my cheek in greeting before scurrying across my collar bone and shifting the fabric of my shirt aside as he attempted to nestle down towards my tits.

"Ew, stop that," I snapped, grabbing the Rat Shifter by his tail and holding him up before my face where he squeaked angrily as he spun in a slow circle. "I'm assuming you don't want me to burn all of that pretty white hair off and turn you into a Naked Mole Rat Shifter, so I suggest you sit in my pocket like a good Rat and don't try to bury yourself in my damn cleavage again."

Eugene squeaked in a way I could have sworn was apologetic, and I rolled my eyes, dropping him into my pocket before giving my attention back to Orion and my sister.

"We can't linger here," I said firmly, refusing to accept the answer shining in my twin's eyes. The Hydra had already bellowed, the wheels of fate were turning, and I didn't want to tempt it again. "Caleb, Seth, and Geraldine are busting Gabriel out, and Dante is about to strike at Lionel. Like I said, at the end of the battle, before he was taken, Gabriel sent me a prophecy. He said that the king can fall today. We're going to end all of this, but we can't stay here, it's not safe. But if Lionel really does fall, then we can go after Lavinia next, we can kill her and end the Death bond, we'll come back again."

I gave Orion an apologetic look as I grabbed Darcy's arm, yanking her towards the cage door, but she dug her heels in.

"Tory, I can't!" she yelled when it became clear that I was going to ignore her attempts to shake me off.

"Go with her, Blue," Orion growled, backing me up, and for once I was okay with the self-sacrificing because right now, she needed to realise that she couldn't stay here. "You know Lavinia won't let anything happen to me while our deal is in place. It's only two more months and then-"

"Then what?" she spat, ripping her arm from my grasp and whirling on him. "She's not just going to shake your hand and let you walk out of here, is she? She could have Lionel cage you instead and she wouldn't be breaking her part of the deal so long as she lets you go first. Then how long do you think he'll keep you alive without Lavinia stopping him?"

"I can figure out a plan by then, but it's no better if you're here to face her when that time comes, is it?" he shot back.

"We have to go," I insisted, closing in on them again, but Darcy whipped towards me, the defiance in her gaze making it clear she had no plans to come with me, and something cracked inside me as I took in that choice, that rejection. I got it, she loved him. But I had never put any love of mine above my love of her and never would have either. It broke something in me as I took in the decision she'd made, the last piece of the girl I'd been shattering as I found myself utterly alone in the world with no one to hold on to at all. I swallowed against that pain, and I knew she could see it as tears welled in her eyes, but she wasn't going to change her mind either. She'd picked, and it wasn't me she chose.

"You found the star," Darcy gasped, her eyes falling to the necklace I'd been wearing since finding it on the battlefield. My own ruby pendant hung beside it, warming as if trying to soothe the ache splintering through me as I fought to stay upright beneath the weight of the hopelessness I felt pushing in on me.

"Yeah," I grunted, knowing it was important but not really giving a shit about it in that moment. "I've been keeping it safe for you. When we get out of here you can-"

"Just stop, Tor, and listen to me. You need to keep the broken promise. I still don't know what that means, but it's to do with the Imperial Star – it was a gift bought with death, and there's some price that should have been paid for it a long time ago. I can't explain all of it now, but it's a curse, Tory. Look at the memories in the crystal and maybe you can figure out more of it, but it's important. Our bloodline is cursed, and I'm afraid that we won't ever be able to win this war unless that curse is broken-"

"What are you talking about?" I asked, my mind cracking with whiplash as I tried to follow what she was saying at a hundred miles a minute. "Are you saying everything that has happened to us is somehow because of this thing?" I pointed at the Imperial Star, and she nodded fearfully as she looked at it too.

"Yes. Our ancestor made a deal with a fallen star to claim it – but she broke some part of the deal she'd made, some promise that she had to keep and never did, but the memories didn't show me what. The legacy of its power descended through the generations, and with each new owner who didn't keep the promise, I think the curse deepened, making sure all Vega lives were steeped in sorrow. I don't know what the promise is, but you have to figure it out, Tor. You have to fix it so we can end the cycle and be free of this plague," the desperation in Darcy's words had me nodding my agreement, the oath leaving my lips without hesitation because I would do anything for her, always. Even if it did sound insane.

"You can help me do that when we get out of here, Darcy. Please, just come with me now. We'll find a way to break the bond Orion got himself into and come back for him," I swore but she was shaking her head and I'd already seen that decision in her eyes, already knew she wasn't planning on coming with me even after all we'd risked in coming here to rescue her.

"Just go, Blue," Orion demanded, moving up behind her, but still she was resisting.

My heart thrashed with the thought of leaving this place without her, rebelling against the idea of being parted from my other half so soon. I couldn't leave her here. I wouldn't.

"I'm dangerous," she breathed. "The beast inside of me is volatile, and I can't always control it. I'm no good to you or the rebels, I'd just be putting you in danger."

"Fuck danger," I snarled, closing in on her. "All I want is you."

I looked to Orion desperately, realising that she wasn't going to see sense on this as she continued to refuse, and he gave me a slight nod of agreement, both us knowing that we couldn't accept that answer.

She would hate us for it, but that was okay. I could take her hatred so long as she was safe and as far away from Lionel and Lavinia as I could manage.

"You need to leave, Tory," Darcy began again, but as her lips parted on more words which I knew I didn't want to hear, Orion snapped his hand out and struck her in the temple.

He caught her as she sagged to the floor, her eyes widening at the betrayal as she passed out. A choked sob escaped me as I dropped down to my knees, brushing the shadowy strands of her hair from her face.

"I'll keep her safe," I swore to him, my hand grasping his and squeezing tightly as I felt the pain it had caused him to do that to her. But he'd had no choice. I had no choice.

"I'll hold you to that," Orion snarled, his dark eyes meeting mine with nothing short of a threat in them, and I threw my arms around his neck, Darcy pinned awkwardly between us.

"I'm sorry," I breathed, hating myself for abandoning him here, and the thick muscles of his own arms banded tightly around me in return.

"Don't be," he growled. "Never be sorry for protecting her. That's something the two of us will always put above everything else."

I nodded, a rogue tear splashing against his neck as I fought the repulsion inside of me at the thought of leaving him here, but there were no other options and time was running out.

I released him, reaching for my twin as I gathered my magic to transport her out of here. But before I could cradle her in the air I'd conjured, her body began to fall apart between us, clouds of shadow pouring from her and then growing and growing, forcing us back as the shift took her.

"Run!" Orion roared at me, but it was already too late, my eyes widening in horror as the enormous Shadow Beast that lurked within my sister's flesh took complete control of her. Coils of darkness rushed out of her skin, slamming into Orion and tethering him against the back wall of the cage. He cried out at me again to flee, but I wasn't going anywhere without my twin.

Darcy rose before me as a giant creature of dark fur, bearing drool-coated fangs at me and lunging forward with my death flashing in her eyes.

My sister was lost, and a monster had taken her place.

Scorpio
Virgo
Gemini
Cancer
Leo
Sagittarius
Taurus
Capricorn
Aquarius
Libra
Pisces

XAVIER

CHAPTER FORTY FIVE

"This way," Max said, and I kept close to his back, drinking in the feeling of courage he was letting spill from his skin into the air. It clad my heart in iron and drowned away all my fears, but I knew I'd be walking this path whether I felt brave or not.

"What can you feel now?" I asked, turning a corner and hurrying past large windows with heavy white curtains hanging closed over them.

"Fear," he murmured, and I noticed his scales were climbing his neck, rushing over his dark skin and making it shine blue. "Desperation."

"How many do you think there are?"

"Enough that it'll be a challenge to get them out. But if we're fast and the stars are with us…" He let the end of that sentence hang in the air. When were the stars ever with us lately?

We were banking on the line of a prophecy that we could have interpreted wrong, but we'd been reading the cards too and making sure the stars were giving us good omens. It seemed like things might just work out, but then again, our astrology supplies were still limited, and the only horoscopes we were able to receive were forged by Washer. I shuddered as I thought of the one he'd sent me this morning.

Twinkle, twinkle, weenie Fae, the stars have spoken about your day!
Sagittarius, you are amping up for a long, smooth shaft of destiny to plunder you from behind. You won't see it coming, but if you pay attention, you may feel it tickle you before it drives in deep and sends you into a whirlpool of calamity.
Hold on to the fiery spirit of Mars, for it will gild your rocket in flames, ready to shoot its load into the sky and save you from the swinging sword of fate.

Someone needed to take that responsibility away from him, and fast. I didn't need to start my morning with that disconcerting shit, but Tyler thought they were hilarious and always read them out to me even when I tried to escape them.

Max slowed as he approached a door with a delicate glass window set into the wood in the shape of two wings. He tentatively peered through it, then took hold of the handle and opened the door, extending our silencing bubble around the hinges just in case they creaked.

The night air wafted in, and we hurried out into its grip, rushing down a path that led away across the grounds. I cantered along at Max's side, tossing looks at him for direction and finding his forehead creased in concentration. Or maybe it was in discomfort. I couldn't imagine what it was like to feel what others were feeling around you, especially when those emotions were bad. He must have been suffering back on the Island of R.U.M.P, surrounded by rebels who were in the midst of mourning for those lost in battle, every fear broadcasted to him at all hours of the day and night.

How could he stand it? I'd seen him going between the people, offering them comfort, and taking away some of their pain, but wasn't he having to take their burdens on himself in those acts of kindness too? It sounded like hell.

The amphitheatre loomed out of the darkness, framed by the meteor shower in the sky, the beautiful streaks of light tumbling across the dark canvas above.

Something about the sight of those celestial rocks spilling through the heavens in a display of burning light gave me hope, and I held on to it with all my might. Between that and the confidence Max was feeding me, I didn't falter at all as we closed in on the ominous building where so much death had been delivered.

It was hard to believe one of my best memories lived within these dark grounds, far out in the gardens where me, the Heirs, and the Vegas had found a moment of peace in a snowball fight. That day seemed so unreal now, like it was just a sweet dream I'd woken up from and wished I could return to. Would we ever claim moments like that again? Or was the future a dark, desolate thing where nothing good could ever bloom?

Max hugged the curved wall of the amphitheatre, following it around as we hunted for a way in. I let my hand trail across the brickwork, my ears pricked and listening for any sound of movement within the amphitheatre or beyond, but all was eerily quiet.

"Here," Max hissed, ducking through a doorway, and I trotted after him down a few stone steps into a dark passage. A cold wind rattled along it, making a groaning sound that set the hairs rising along the back of my neck.

We remained in the dark, not casting Faelights in case we drew attention to ourselves, and I was glad of my fondness for carrots, because they were definitely helping me see through the gloom now. Or at least, that was what my mom used to tell me. At the thought of her, my heart wrenched in two and Max glanced back at me, feeling my pain.

"You okay, man?"

"I'm good," I bit out, working to block him out with a mental shield, but I'd missed a helluva lot of school lessons since having to leave Zodiac, and now that Orion wasn't around, I knew I was really starting to fall behind in some basic skills. Whenever I practised magic, I focused on harnessing my Elements and wielding spells that could help me in battle. I was starting to neglect simple spells like these shields, but I moved it swiftly to the top of my list because if I was ever caught by the enemy, my mental barriers needed to be unbreakable.

A booming roar which sent me tumbling back into childhood memories of dread at my father's arrival had me falling entirely still, my head craning back as if I might be able to see through the roof above my head into the amphitheatre above.

"He's up there," I breathed, the knowledge that I was so close to the monster who had stolen everything good in my life from me sticking my feet to that spot. I found myself equally desperate to turn and flee while the desire to race up there and rip his head from his shoulders almost consumed every piece of my grieving soul.

"Breathe," Max commanded, his hand landing on my shoulder, the gifts of his Order sinking into my skin like hot oil, soothing the sharpness of my own emotions and allowing me a moment of clarity. "We knew he was up there somewhere. And we also know that with a bit of luck, he's going to be burned alive within a bolt of lightning before the night is done."

I nodded firmly, reigning in that need for vengeance and trying to remember why we were here, the trapped rebels who would die without us to free them.

"You ready to move?" Max asked, his connection to my calmer emotions clearly telling him the answer to that, but before I could reply, my father's voice called out from somewhere in the amphitheatre above as he began to give what sounded like some speech.

We exchanged a look, and Max quickly cast an amplifying spell so that we could hear his words. I fought a flinch as Lionel's voice suddenly sounded right beside us.

"-a great honour for each and every one of you," he exclaimed. "My most loyal subjects, joined with me in ways far superior to all others, just as our great and noble Order is superior too. As esteemed members of the Dragon Guild, I could think of no finer Fae to join me here today to receive this coveted accolade and bear witness to me once again strengthening the iron fist I hold upon my crown."

"By the stars, your dad is an asshole," Max muttered, dispersing the magic that allowed us to listen to Lionel's words, leaving only the distant rumble of his voice for us to hear as we crept on into the depths of this place.

"Tell me about it," I replied in agreement.

"The prisoners are close," Max said, leading me down a narrow passage where fire burned in sconces on the walls. "There's a silencing bubble here," he added in realisation, pausing as he raised a hand and moved his fingers in an intricate pattern. The magic dissolved under his touch and the sound of people groaning and sobbing reached us from up ahead.

I lurched froward, ready to dive in there and break our people out, but Max's hand slammed against my chest to hold me back.

"Wait," he said. "There's Order suppressant gas down there."

"How can you tell?" I asked, but it was obvious in the next second as I lost my grip on my Order, the feel of it like a sleeping creature in my chest which I couldn't rouse.

"Because your wings are gone," he said with a lilt of teasing in his tone.

"Hilarious," I growled.

"Too soon?" he asked, nudging me, and I noticed his scales receding all over his skin as his Siren was shut down too.

"Way too soon," I hissed, taking the silver Pegasus horn from my pocket that had been a gift from the twins and gripping it like a dagger. "Come on, let's free them and get the fuck out of here."

We jogged forward, turning the corner and finding ourselves in a dungeon full of barred cells, the rebels within them wearing magic blocking cuffs and looking half starved.

My breaths started coming heavier, my thoughts turning to Mom, Darius, and Hamish. I couldn't get enough air into my lungs, and I could only breathe faster as my focus narrowed to the prisoners in front of me and all the fucking injustice Lionel Acrux had caused for them all.

A roar left me that was worthy of the Dragon I'd been born to become, my horn slamming into the closest lock on one of the dingy metal cages, sending the rebels inside flinching back in surprise. I felt Max widening our silencing bubble around them all, leaving me free to cause as much noise as I wanted.

I swung around, slamming my horn into the lock on the cage at my back next, red and blue fire tearing along the length of it.

Blood pounded in my ears and the grief I'd been harbouring poured out of me in my movements. The rebels cheered, but it was just a din I was hardly aware of as I continued to cut through locks with furious strikes of my metal horn. I pictured Lionel's face with every blow, wishing I could have a chance to cleave his head apart.

Then the good memories spilled in, and they were somehow more painful than the simple, excruciating thought of death.

I flew beside my mom, my wings wide and glitter tumbling down my back, sparkling under the moonlight as we soared above Acrux Manor and stole a moment of freedom in the sky. Mom was in her silver Dragon form, swooping overhead, her lips lifted in a beast's smile as her eyes remained stitched to me. I neighed my joy, kicking my legs and flying up and over her back, spiralling around her, my wingtips brushing against her scales. She released a warm breath from her mouth and I flew through it, feeling the watchful gaze of the girl who had offered us this moment.

I glanced back toward the manor to where Tory stood, wondering if she would ever truly understand how grateful I was to have my mom back after so many years of missing her, sometimes blaming myself for her withdrawal, other times wondering if I'd imagined a different mother when I was young.

We had been prisoners of this house and the man who ruled it for so long, and all that time we could have had each other, but Father had ensured that was robbed of us too. Isolating us. There was true power in making someone feel as though they were alone in the world, and after Darius had gone to Zodiac Academy, I had felt that on a terrifyingly real level, unable to see a future where I would know joy or companionship again. But now Mom was back, it felt like there were new possibilities awakening alongside her, a chance for something good.

I thought of my time in The Burrows, my mind locking on one memory in particular.

I was heading along one of the passages after a night with Sofia and Tyler, my chest feeling so full of love and light that my skin kept glowing. I tried to hide it for a while, then remembered I didn't have to hide anything anymore. I was free, and no one here would judge me for being exactly who I was.

I let myself glow with the starlight that seemed to live in my skin because of my Pegasus, and I admired the way my hands gleamed. I'd spent so long fighting the instincts of my Order when I was stuck back at Acrux Manor, and this was the first time I'd ever experienced this part of it. I felt another shackle of my past releasing me, surprised to find that there were still tethers on my soul, but I guessed shaking off a lifetime of suppression was never going to be easy.

"Hey, Xavier," Darius's voice made me turn and I found him jogging to catch me. We were alone in the corridor, just the two of us, and I smiled at my older brother, though my cheeks flushed hot at the thought of him seeing me like this, shining like a freaking star in the middle of the corridor.

I opened my mouth to explain, but his hand came down on my arm before I could, lifting it up to examine my skin with a grin on his lips.

"You're happy," he said in realisation, and I could feel his relief dripping into those words.

"Things are good. Impossibly," I said, and he nodded, that smile only widening as he continued to study my shining skin. "What do you think?"

For some reason, I felt a knot rising in my chest, suddenly fearing him making a joke about my glow. Darius was always supportive, but we often ribbed on each other. But when it came to this, I needed it to not become the butt of some joke.

He released my arm, his dark eyes flicking up to meet mine and his smile dropping away to become something fiery and intense. "I think happiness suits you, Xavier. And I think that if Sofia and Tyler make you this happy, then you should hold onto them as tight as you can."

"I held on tight to you, but clearly not tight enough," I snarled through my teeth as I came back to reality, slamming the horn into another lock as more and more rebels ran out around me. "You were one of the things that made me glow. But now you're gone, and you took all of my light with you."

I cut through the final lock and sagged against the iron bars, the horn dropping from my fingers and clattering to the stone floor. I braced my arm against the metal and buried my face in it, hating the world, but most of all, hating Lionel.

Worried murmurs broke out around me, and a hand pressed to my back as Max made it to me. He didn't have his Siren powers, but his aura still helped calm some of my erratic breathing.

"Xavier," he said gently. "You did good. We can finish this together, but I need you, okay?"

I swallowed back the razor that seemed to be buried in my throat, forcing down my bitter, desolate emotions with it. I had to keep my head. Max was right. This wasn't done yet, and we needed to get the rebels out of here before Dante's lightning strike. It could come at any second. We had to move.

I sucked in a breath and shoved away from the cage, finding Max holding my horn out for me and I nodded to him in thanks as I took it. The rebels were getting riled up, and as I focused on what they were saying, I realised we had a problem. Max had cut the magic blocking cuffs off of their hands, and some of them clearly had enough magic to cast, flexing their fingers as vengeance danced in their eyes.

"The king is up in the amphitheatre, I heard his servant talking about the event this afternoon," one woman called out.

A man stamped his foot, a moo rising in his throat. "We must go up there and see to his end!"

"No," Max barked, his fierce tone making everyone falter and look to him. But with his Siren disabled by the suppressant gas, he couldn't use his gifts to calm them, and his authoritative tone was the only weapon remaining in his arsenal. I just hoped it would be enough. "We have to leave, we must-"

"We cannot leave!" another woman cried. "We need to destroy him. There are enough of us here. I, for one, will act unFae and join forces to end the monster who has caged us. Who's with me?"

A cry of ascent went up, and I shared a look of horror with Max. Before we could stop them, the rebels charged out of the dungeon in the direction of the arena.

"Wait!" I shouted as they disappeared into another passage.

"Fuck," Max cursed, and we took off running after them up a series of steps.

The Minotaurs among them were mooing wildly, a stampede breaking out and driving the rebels on faster and faster somewhere ahead of us.

"I'll try and get ahead of them," Max said, lifting himself up on a gust of air and rushing forward on a furious breeze to try and catch up with them.

A boom of thunder sounded in the sky somewhere high above and sent dread down my spine. Dante was here.

I turned the next corner, finding Max trying to cut his way through a wall of vines someone had cast in his path, and I ran forward to help, hacking through them with my horn.

We broke through the barrier, and I found the rebels had made it to a set of doors at the end of the corridor.

Battle cries left them as they raced out onto a bed of sand, and my heart warred in my chest as Max and I were forced to keep going, to try and stop them before it was too late. But as I made it to the doorway, I found a host of around two hundred Dragons standing all around Lionel in the sand, all in their Fae forms wearing the cloaks of the Dragon Guild like some fucking cult gathering around their deity.

The sky had fallen fitfully dark overhead, the sight of the meteor shower blotted out by the enormous storm cloud rolling in, a flash of lightning illuminating the heart of it where I spotted the silhouette of a Storm Dragon for a fraction of a moment.

My father's eyes widened in surprise at the rebels charging his way, and time seemed to slow as all two hundred of the Dragons surrounding him turned to protect him. They wore dark blue robes where Lionel wore green, and each of them had the sleeve of their right arms rolled up, revealing a red Aries mark branded onto their skin. Lionel's forearm was covered in all twelve star sign symbols, marked there in thick, dark red lines, connecting him to every Dragon that stood between us and him.

Horror pooled into my gut as I took in what he'd done, what he'd just placed between himself and the world like a wall of pure muscle and power. He'd Guardian bonded himself to them. Every last one.

I staggered to a halt, Max stopping beside me and grabbing an arrow from the quiver at his back, nocking it onto his bow and taking aim at Lionel, his lip peeling in a snarl.

He let the arrow fly, Phoenix fire igniting along it, ready to tear through any shield Lionel had in place before he spotted us. It carved through the air, then through shield after shield on course for destruction, but a large Dragon with dark hair and even darker eyes launched himself into the path of it at the last second, the bond he was now a slave to driving him to sacrifice himself before allowing any harm to come to his king.

The arrow drove deep into his chest before he fell dead at Lionel's feet, a look of pure rapture marking his features, which was more terrifying than the bloodshed.

Lionel's eyes snapped onto us just as the rebels collided with the army of Bonded Dragons, and the roar of battle filled the air as my view of him was stolen.

I raised my horn, forgetting everything except my hunger for my father's death as the call of war sung to me.

"Run!" Gabriel Nox's voice daggered through my skull, and the ferocity of his tone managed to turn my gaze to him where he was held up in the stands, bound in chains on his knees next to Vard. "Fear the Bonded men! You cannot win! Death is coming! The prophecy has changed!"

Vard slammed a hand over his mouth and started dragging him through a door at their back just as Lionel opened his mouth and bellowed a command, "Burn every last one of them!"

Scorpio
Gemini
Virgo
Aries
Cancer
Leo
Sagittarius
Taurus
Capricorn
Aquarius
Libra
Pisces

DANTE

CHAPTER FORTY SIX

I was already in a free dive, my eyes locked on Gabriel who was being dragged through a doorway by Vard, electricity crackling all over my body. I'd gotten a little overexcited flying here and had accidentally zapped Leon in the ass and fried all of our Atlases. So we were on our own now, but so long as everyone stuck to the plan, it didn't matter.

Leon held on tight while I kept my storm powers from hurting him again, housing it all in my body, ready to explode from me the second I could. But I had to reach Gabriel, Juniper and the kids first.

I let my storm fly free, sending it towards the wards doming the palace. A vicious lightning strike daggered out from my jaws and thunder cut through the air just as it impacted and took out the magic, the power of the wards sizzling out of existence and drawing every eye below us right to me.

I swooped low as fast as I could, my focus consumed by Gabriel.

We're coming, Falco.

"Gabe!" Leon bellowed, leaping from my back the moment we closed in on the stands, a fist full of flames slamming into Vard's single eye.

Vard's head snapped back and he hit the wall, but the asshole fought back, *seeing* Leon's next punch coming and blasting fire back at him in a swirling vortex. Leon fought to get hold of the Seer's flames, the two of them locked in a brawl of power.

My talons dug into the stone seats as I landed awkwardly, lumps of masonry tumbling away beneath me as I fought to hold myself in place and grunted a command at Gabriel to get up. He scrambled to his feet, eyes wide and full of prophecies, halting him in his tracks before he made it to me. I clambered higher up the stone seats to get closer to him, extending my wing in desperation.

Get on, Falco.

Down in the arena, the rebels were colliding with the Dragons, and sweeping waves of fire slammed into them, consuming our people in the flames. The screams tangled with the air, but I couldn't look to see what was happening, my task set on the man before me.

Dalle stelle, this was fast falling apart. But Gabriel was right there, and I wasn't leaving without him.

Fire burst over my wing and I yanked it back as Mildred Canopus came running up the steps, her teeth bared and fists swinging. The fire surrounded Gabriel in a ring, cutting me off from him, and I roared my fury, turning to her, ready to end this brutta cagna.

She leapt into the air the same moment I sent a bolt of lightning at her from my jaws, the oafish girl shifting and tearing out of her clothes, giving me a view of a very hairy, very naked Mildred before her Dragon took over and she released a furious blast of hellfire from her jaws.

I was forced to move, taking off into the sky and blasting lightning back at her, making her yowl as some of it hit her brown scales and crackled over her body.

"You have to go!" Gabriel cried from within that ring of fire, my gaze locking on him below me as I swung the sharpened spikes on my tail into Mildred's face. "There's no hope for me this day!"

I roared in answer to that, refusing those words, and Leon denied them too, getting hold of Vard and slamming him against the wall by the throat. The Cyclops was done for. Leon would kill him in the next second, then take hold of those flames around Gabriel and we would get him out of here. I could see the possibility of that fate unfolding, but then more Dragon Shifters came running up the stone steps, and my heart floundered.

Mildred snapped at my tail, forcing me to fly higher, and I roared in fury, sending another blast of lightning over my back towards her.

She dove to avoid it, sweeping over the crowd of rebels below as she went and unleashing a blast of fire that killed several in their tracks. I found the rest of my family rushing into the fight, cutting down Dragons as they tried to get to Lionel, Rosalie howling in command to her Wolf pack, but he was standing within a shield of endless Fae, all willing to die for him.

I snarled in anger, wanting to blast the amphitheatre to dust, but I had to hold on until I could get everyone I loved out of here.

Leon was forced to fight the Dragons coming his way, and Vard took the opportunity to seize Gabriel, yanking him through a door and disappearing from sight. I roared in anguish, turning back for them, but Mildred flew up to block my path once more.

I lunged forward, aiming for her neck as my wings beat harder, thunder booming above and rain crashing down over my scales as my storm tumbled out of me. I collided with her, my teeth tearing into her side and my talons raking down her belly. She kicked me back before I could do enough damage to end this, but I released a blast of lightning aimed to kill.

Mildred roared as it impacted with her chest and she went tumbling out of the sky, crashing onto the stone seats below and shattering them beneath her weight. She continued to twitch, and I cursed internally that I hadn't killed her, but I couldn't send a full blast of lightning down there or it would fry everyone else in the amphitheatre. With the rebels involved now, that was no longer an option.

A cry drew my gaze beyond Mildred, and I spotted Juniper running up the steps with her three children in front of her, waving her arms at me in desperation.

I tucked my wings, aiming for her and swooping low to pick them up. One of the kids screamed in alarm as he spotted me coming, and all three lost control of their Order forms, shifting into a trio of squat little Griffins who looked about ready to bolt.

Lionel cried out furiously as his attention fell on us, and I snarled a warning to Juniper as he sent a blast of Dragon Fire spiralling towards us. Juniper cried out in panic, a shield of air exploding around her and the three boys, the power of it only just managing to hold beneath the weight of Lionel's flames. The movement forced the sleeve of her cloak to shift back and relief tumbled through me as I spotted the bare skin of her arm, confirming to me that she hadn't taken part in the Guardian bond ceremony and was still free from Lionel's control.

A swarm of rebels all threw their power at Lionel at once in an unFae attack, and he was forced to turn his attention to them just as I managed to land beside Juniper.

"Thank you," she breathed, her hand brushing against my snout.

Her tear-filled gaze met mine, and I nodded once, lowering my wing to them on the steps. She managed to convince two of the three kids to shift back into their Fae forms, hoisting the smallest into her arms when it became clear he was too rattled to move, and he buried his eagle's head against her neck while tucking his wings close to his spine. All four of them clambered onto my back, settling themselves there, and the thrashing of my heart calmed a little at the knowledge that they were safe.

I took off as fire came at me from all directions, flying fast for Leon where he was cornered against the wall by three unFae stronzos, their dark blue capes billowing around them as they fought him.

I knocked the Dragon Shifters down the stone steps with my talons, my claws gouging deep into shoulders and necks, causing as much damage as I could before I gently grabbed Leon.

He clung on tight to my foot as I banked hard and flew up towards the dark sky, giving him time to climb my leg and get onto my back.

"Vard took Gabe," Leon said in anguish, and I grunted mournfully in acknowledgement.

It wasn't over yet though. There was still time to finish the false king.

I turned my gaze onto the blonde bastardo below us in his ring of safety, and he turned his gaze to me, a smirk lifting his lips.

His mouth opened in an order I couldn't hear, but in the next seconds, four of his Dragon Guild members shifted and came tearing towards me from below, fire pouring from their teeth-filled mouths.

"Go!" Leon cried.

I bellowed in frustration, turning and taking off into the clouds, sending a stream of lightning falling from my tail to slam into them. But their roars kept following us, and the children on my back screamed in panic as the huge beasts gained on us.

I knew this day was done. In all honesty, I'd known it the moment Gabriel had spoken his truth. He had already *seen* how this would play out. Fate had changed, our one chance was lost. And now all we could do was retreat with as many of the people we loved as we could. So with them in mind, I drew storm clouds around me and worked to lose my pursuers in the mist, defeat making my heart weigh a ton.

We'll come back for you, Falco. A morte e ritorno.

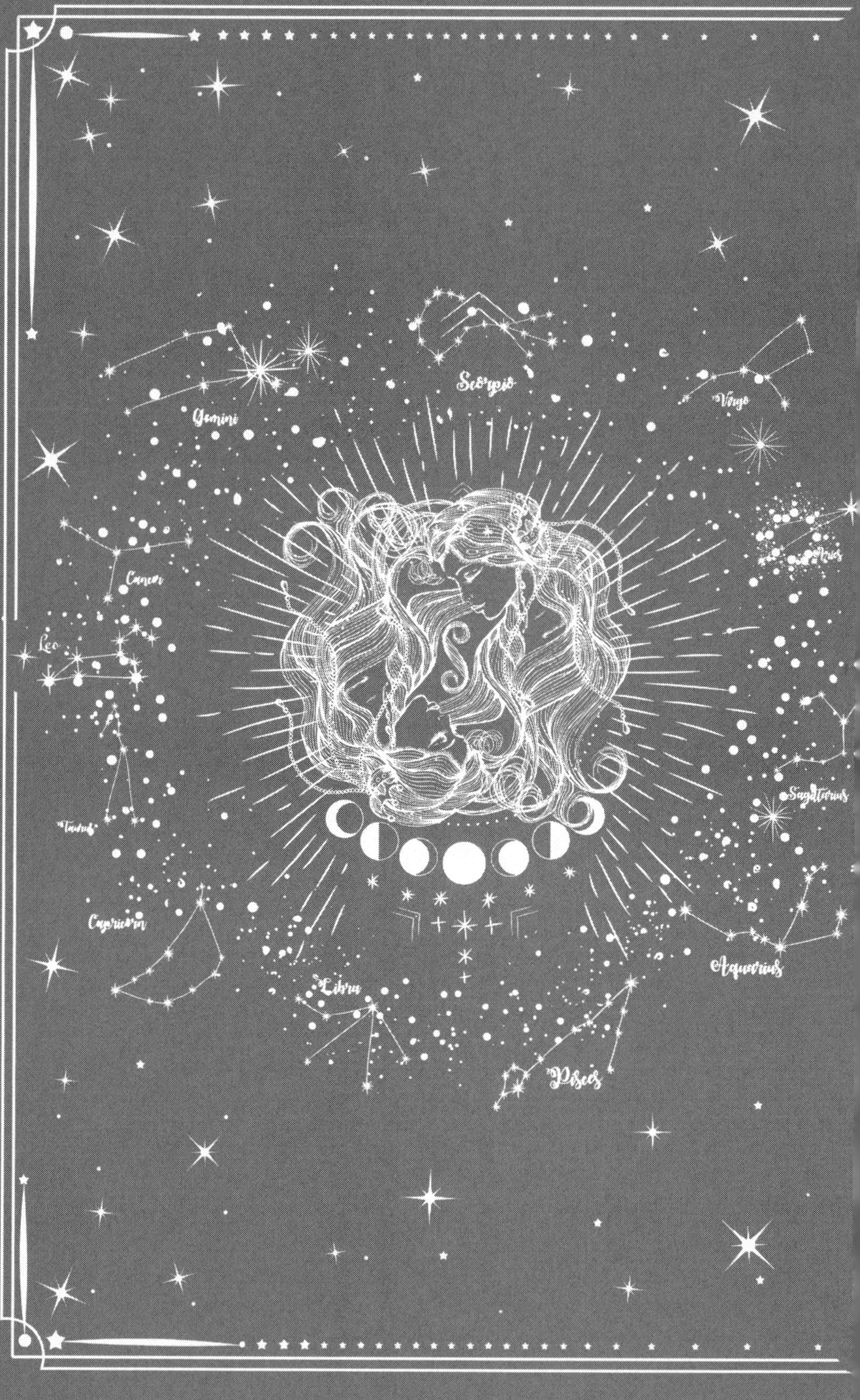

Scorpio
Gemini
Virgo
Cancer
Aries
Leo
Sagittarius
Taurus
Capricorn
Aquarius
Libra
Pisces

TORY

CHAPTER FORTY SEVEN

Darcy swiped at me with an enormous paw, her claws slamming into my air shield so hard that I was forced to absorb the blow and let her move me rather than shatter it. I was flung across the room, the air I was wielding wrapping me in a vortex of my own design and setting me on my feet behind the throne.

"Darcy," I barked, like I was scolding a naughty pet. "You know me, you hairy asshole."

Darcy roared, whirling on me and charging again, forcing me to retreat around the throne, keeping the enormous stone-built chair between us.

"I don't think insulting her is helping," Orion called unhelpfully from his position in the cage where he was still chained to the wall by the shadows, and I flipped him off as I darted away from my beast-sister's attack.

I lifted myself on a gust of air, rising above Darcy as she launched herself at me again, swiping her lethally sharp claws like a cat trying to bat a fluffy little toy – a cat set on murder, its tasty reward for catching me.

I was forced to shoot away from her again, hurling myself across the space with my air magic to gain some room.

I threw earth magic towards her as I landed behind her, vines growing with incredible speed all around her, binding her tightly while she roared in fury and snapped her jaws in an attempt to bite them off.

"Look at me," I demanded, running into her line of sight, my heart pounding as something in the wild creature's gaze shifted. I could have sworn my other half was looking back at me from within those beastly eyes.

But the moment I relaxed my guard, the beast fell apart, becoming nothing but shadow and causing my vines to slacken and fall to the stone floor uselessly as she escaped them.

I cursed as the smoke swept towards me, throwing a hand up and casting air at it to blow her away from me.

The shadows roiled furiously as they fought my air magic, and I grunted with the effort of holding them off, planting my feet and pushing more energy into keeping her dark power at bay.

"Tory, behind you!" Orion shouted and I looked over my shoulder a heartbeat too late as a tendril of shadow shot towards me.

The power of the strike was far greater than it should have been, my shield cracking from the impact and my knees buckling, sending me staggering forward while I focused on maintaining it.

Another strike hit me from the front, then the side, above, below, lashes of shadows whipping at me with tremendous force from all around while working to find a weakness in my defences.

I gritted my teeth as I threw all of my power into the shield, the bubble of air magic starting to glow red and gold as my fire poured into it too, the roars of the invisible Shadow Beast echoing off of the walls.

"Here!" Orion yelled from the other side of the throne room, banging an empty food bowl against the bars to try and draw her attention away. "Come for me!"

The Shadow Beast threw ribbons of darkness at him too, and my heart leapt into my throat as I saw certain death spearing for him. He had no magic, no way of moving, and no chance at all against the savagery of that blow.

"Stop!" I roared, my own shield falling away to nothing as I threw everything I had across the room towards that piercing slice of darkness.

My shield blinked into position around Orion less than a second before the shadows collided with it, the force of the blow resounding through me to my core as I held her off. I couldn't let her hurt him. Couldn't let her face the fate that I'd been dealt with Darius stolen from me. I wouldn't allow her to lose the man destined to be hers after all they'd survived to get to this point.

The Shadow Beast materialised in front of me, and my heart stalled as I stared up at it. It was twice as large as a Werewolf, its black fur thick and ears pointed, its face resembling a bear's.

"Darcy," I spoke calmly, my arms wide before me. "You can control this. I know you can. You've always been the strong one, the one who could deal with anything in your own calm and indestructible way. I know you can-"

She came at me so fast that I acted on instinct alone, drawing my sword with a rattling rasp of metal, swinging it high to catch the sharp curves of her claws a bare moment before she could chop my fucking head off with them.

"Fuck you," I snapped, the sound of those razor-sharp claws grinding down the length of my blade, setting my teeth on edge.

Darcy bellowed and swiped at me again, forcing me to leap over her other paw before kicking the back of it and striking her hard enough to sting.

"Stop it," I snarled, wrenching my blade aside and knocking her hooked claws from it before whirling away from the snap of her jaws. "This is like the time I borrowed that little black dress you'd been planning to wear to the school dance and got it all oily down at the bike shop. You tried to bite my head off then too – though not as literally. Do I need to sneak you into the movies to see an overrated chick flick this time too? Or-"

She came at me so fast that I was almost cut to ribbons by her claws before I dove aside, tumbling into a roll before straightening again with my sword raised defensively. I wouldn't strike her. Not once. But I wasn't inclined to let her eat me alive either.

"She's lost to it, Tory," Orion called from the cage, but I ignored him. This was between me and her. No matter how far either of us had ever fallen before, there had never once been a time when the other couldn't drag us back to ourselves.

She was it for me and I was for it for her. That one, immovable thing. That tether to the here and now.

Darcy spun to face me once more, her teeth bared as she prowled towards me, nothing but a need for carnage shining in the shadowy depths of those soulless eyes. But she was there. I knew it. And she would never hurt me.

I swallowed thickly and lowered my sword, sheathing it while I held eye contact with her and raising my chin as I moved my hand away from the hilt.

Not a scrap of magic shone around me or blossomed in my blood, ready to be put to use.

There was nothing at all between us but the truth of who we were. Gemini twins. One and the same.

The Shadow Beast stepped closer, padding towards me so slowly that I could count the thrashing beats of my heart between each step.

"Just you and me, Darcy," I said in offering, taking my own step closer as my pulse began to slow, our gazes locked.

Orion was shouting out in warning to me, but I ignored him. She was in there and she would never hurt me. She was in there and she would come back to me.

Darcy paused mere inches from me, the heat of her breath washing over my face as her lips curled back in a snarl that revealed every sharp tooth in that terrifying mouth.

For a brief, all too foolish second, I wondered if it was an attempt at a smile. But in the next blink, she was on me, a scream tearing from my throat as I was thrown to the ground, claws slashing across my chest and cutting into my neck followed by the hot splatter of my blood across the flagstones.

I tried to fight back, my hands sinking into soft fur as I kicked and struggled beneath her enormous weight, those claws cutting so deep that I was almost blinded by the pain of it.

Power surged through my blood, and I called on it to save me, my Phoenix singing mournfully as its power blossomed in my core, but the piercing cut of her teeth ripping into my shoulder silenced all of it.

The shadows were driven into me and I screamed, lashes of that darkness I had worked so hard to banish from my memory delving deep into my chest and latching onto the essence of my magic.

My power tore its way out of me and the Shadow Beast devoured it. Earth, fire, air, water, all of it shredding its way from my soul and into the jaws of that terrible beast which had taken control of my sister so completely.

I was a fucking idiot for thinking she would be able to fight it. Now that I felt the raw power of the thing, I knew there was no stopping something so immeasurable. I could sense Lavinia's control, the unending power of the shadows feeding this curse and making it unstoppable.

My Phoenix cried out as that was stolen from me too, shadows carving their way through each and every part of me. All of it was ripped away like it had never even been.

The weight of that terrible power sucked everything from me, and I stopped fighting back, my vision blurring through either the loss of my magic or of so much blood.

My fingers scrambled dumbly for my pocket and the sharp tigers eye crystal I had there, its colour a mixture of brown stripes, and the power I'd imbued it with before setting out on this mission humming inside it. My own magic coiled around the power of the crystal, accentuating its innate gifts of protection, power, and determination so that I could draw on them now, the laguz rune etched into its side, for life energy.

I had already come close enough to death to know that I didn't like the scent of it, and despite the love I knew awaited me beyond the Veil, I wasn't going to relinquish my hold on life any time soon. Darcy needed me, so this was where I would stay.

Orion was shouting at Darcy to stop, to remember herself before it was too late, but I was almost certain it was already far too late for any of this to be undone.

My fingers finally located the sharp little crystal, and I summoned the last of my strength before driving it into my side, piercing the skin and pushing it into the wound with a grunt of pain, the magic within it practically burning as it met with my blood, joining its own power to mine.

"Vivere," I choked out, the ether stirring the air around me as I called on it in this last, desperate plea for my pathetic life. There was a cost to wielding it, and I gave it what it wanted, surrendering memories of heartache from my childhood for the magic to feast on. But it wasn't death I was fighting against. It was what my end would mean for the girl trapped inside the creature who was trying to claim it. She couldn't bear that weight. I wouldn't allow it.

My vision blurred again, and I wasn't sure if I'd done enough to save my sorry soul as my limbs fell limp, my head turning towards the throne where my father had once sat and commanded such horrors, all because of Lionel Acrux.

Horror sliced through me, my numb fingers finding the strength to reach for my throat while the Shadow Beast's teeth drove deeper into my shoulder, seeking out the very last of my magic to devour.

The ruby necklace Darius had given me was still warm against my skin like always. The sensation of his callused hand pressing over mine almost overwhelmed me as I gripped the blood red stone, the feeling of his eyes on me, of him waiting for me just a few steps away enough to make a sob catch in my throat.

I could have sworn the warmth of Dragon fire seeped into my veins from the ruby pendant, like Darius was trying to lend me his strength too. But it was no good. I had nothing left. And as the Shadow Beast crushed my flesh in its powerful jaws, a padded foot pressing down on my chest, claws sinking deeper into my skin, I lost my grip on the world, my sister, and everything else, then I fell away into the void.

Scorpio
Gemini
Virgo
Cancer
Leo
Sagittarius
Taurus
Capricorn
Aquarius
Libra
Pisces

ORION

CHAPTER FORTY EIGHT

I yanked against the shadow restraints holding me back with all the force I could muster, using every ounce of Vampire strength I had to get to Tory.

"Blue!" I bellowed, my voice ripping out of my lungs and echoing around the entire throne room. But she was gone, no glimmer of her in that rabid beast which was tearing into her twin's flesh.

She would be destroyed by this, she'd never come back from it if she killed her other half, and beyond that, Tory had become like kin to me. I couldn't see her die. I'd sworn to Darius that I'd protect her and wherever my friend was now, I knew he could *see* his moment, that he was roaring my name in the sky and demanding I save her.

But I couldn't get free of the fucking shadows. Each bind I snapped through was only replaced by another, hauling me back whenever I gained a single step.

The Shadow Beast tossed Tory toward me like a broken doll, and she lay limp and bloody just beyond the cage. So close and yet so fucking far. Her face was pale, lifeless, and I had the most dreadful fear that the beast had killed her.

That bear-like creature stalked close, muzzle bloody and a hunger in its eyes for more death. And its gaze was set on me.

"Darcy Vega, fight your way back to us!" I commanded, but those eyes were pitch black and held no sign of my mate in them. All I could see was Lavinia's influence, a cold, wicked thing that held no love for anything in this world. Least of all us.

The Shadow Beast roared, leaping forward and tearing the cage to ribbons as it came for me. The shadows yanked me back against the wall, a fresh kill ready and waiting.

My eyes fell on Tory again, the blood rushing from her wounds and life steadily pouring out of her.

No. I won't let this happen. I refuse this fate.

Panic welled, followed by a fury so acidic that it burst from my chest in the form of a roar, my fangs extending and my blood pounding with some foreign feeling I'd never experienced. My Order was more present than it had ever been, my mind on overdrive, my vision heightened so much that I could physically see the pulse points on the Shadow Beast and Tory. Red curtained my vision and the animal in me called out for its brother, my sanguis frater.

With a feeling like being jerked awake, my vision suddenly doubled, and I could somehow see a whole different location. I felt my mind merging with another, and knew without having to ask that it was my coven brother I was connected to through this impossible magic.

I was in a dark corridor, hurrying along with the speed of my Order, carrying someone on my back while Seth was tucked under my arm. As I turned to look over my shoulder, I took in lines of Nymphs all rushing away in the opposite direction, calling out to Lionel in a promise to come to his aid. I shot towards a tapestry, pulling it aside and opening a hidden door in the wall, placing them down once we were within the safety of the Savage King's passages.

"Caleb?!" I blurted, speaking it aloud but it echoed into his head, and I could feel the moment he jolted back a step in surprise.

"Orion?" he gasped. "What am I seeing? Is that Tory?"

"Get to the throne room – now!" I bellowed, not questioning this any further as Caleb shot off in a blur of speed.

The tunnels shot past him, followed by the extravagant hallways of The Palace of Souls, turn after turn, all of it leading him closer to me, my fangs prickling with bloodlust as he drew closer, the desire to fight at his side consuming me.

I saw the moment he reached the throne room, viewing myself through his eyes while watching him arrive at the same moment, and somehow my mind was capable of keeping up with those two realities. The Shadow Beast bent the twisted bars of the cage further apart to get closer to me and its paw slashed across my chest, claws tearing into my skin. Pain burst through me and the connection between Caleb and I snapped, our minds wrenching apart.

Caleb raced forward, launching himself onto the Shadow Beast's back and yanking its fur hard enough to make it yelp and turn away from me.

"Free me!" I shouted as the Shadow Beast tried to unseat him and he worked to keep hold of it.

He swung down around its throat, using his Vampire strength to flip the beast off of its feet and slam it down onto its side, casting a dome of earth over it to keep it there. But it wouldn't last long.

He shot towards me in a blur, unsheathing one of his flaming daggers and severing the shadows binding me in a furious action that had me free in moments.

I staggered into his arms, my blood soaking between us as I shoved him towards Tory.

"Get her out of here," I growled, our coven bond buzzing keenly and begging us to stay together, hunt together. But that wasn't our fate today.

"Fucking hell," he cursed as he lurched towards the girl who was bleeding out on the floor, the savage wounds carved into her body and the sallow tone of her skin. Only the faintly flickering pulse at her throat confirmed to me that she was alive, and I had no fucking idea how that was even the case.

Caleb scooped her into his arms and released healing magic into her body, his brow pinching in concentration as he fought to work on the shadow wounds.

"Run, Caleb," I urged. "Please, you can't stay. And I won't leave Darcy." I looked to the dome of earth surrounding my mate as is shuddered and cracked, her power almost breaking through it already.

"I'm not leaving you," he said anxiously, a stubborn refusal rising in his gaze even as he fought to heal the wounds on the girl in his arms. "You're my sanguis frater. I can't walk away from you now that I've found you."

"I made a Death bond with Lavinia, Caleb," I revealed in a low voice and he immediately shook his head, trying to defy the honesty he could see in my eyes. But then our bond sang like a tune in my mind, an understanding passing between us, like for just a moment, we could see the world through each other's eyes.

"No," he begged, like he could make it not true by pure will alone, but he was giving in, because he had felt the reality of my situation and there was no refuting it.

"I'm sorry. You have to go," I urged. "Get Tory out of here, and don't wake her up until you're away from the palace. Trust me."

Caleb rose to his feet, Tory's wounds healed enough to at least staunch the bleeding. He gazed at me in confliction, but finally relented. "Alright. I trust you, brother."

He held Tory against him with one arm, reaching out and taking hold of the magic cuff on my right wrist, focusing on the metal and forcing the lock to melt. It dropped to the floor with a clatter before the heated metal could burn me and he quickly released the other, grabbing my hand and sending a flow of healing magic into my body in a wave.

Our eyes locked, an unspoken promise between us that we'd find each other again soon. We didn't need to say anything. No goodbyes. Because whether in this life or the next, we would always find each other now.

He was gone in a flash of speed, my last hope to save Darcy from this place speeding away with him and in the same moment, the Shadow Beast tore through the dome of earth which had been caging it and came charging toward me.

I raised my hands, the rush of magic in them making me heady from how rarely I'd been allowed to wield it. Just as the Shadow Beast lunged, I threw myself skyward with a blast of air magic, avoiding another vicious swipe of its claws. I turned my gaze to the door, sealing it shut with ice around the handles, holding it with a fierce magic, my decision solidifying with it.

I'd remain here until Blue came back to me. However long it took.

Scorpio
Gemini
Virgo
Cancer
Leo
Sagittarius
Capricorn
Aquarius
Libra
Pisces

CALEB

CHAPTER FORTY NINE

Healing magic tumbled from me into Tory's bleeding body as I cradled her close to my chest, her head lolling against my shoulder while I shot down the corridors of The Palace of Souls so fast that we were little more than a blur to anyone who might have looked our way.

I considered how terribly wrong everything had gone and failure and panic threatened to overwhelm me. Darcy and Orion were still trapped in this hell, we hadn't been able to find Gabriel anywhere and if the screams echoing across the palace grounds were anything to go by, then something incredibly fucked up was taking place in the amphitheatre too.

I shot towards a painting which I knew concealed one of the entrances to the secret passages, and I didn't even have to use the ring Tory had given me to open it, her blood working before I could make it to the door thanks to so much of it staining her body and clothes.

The wounds the Shadow Beast had given her wouldn't heal properly, the venom in them fighting my magic no matter how much of it I pressed into her, and the pallor of her skin was turning a sickly shade.

I wasn't letting myself think about how slow her heartbeat had gotten, the too-quiet thump of it registering in my ears far too infrequently.

Fuck. How had this gone so epically wrong? What had changed to make the fate Gabriel had *seen* for this night change?

None of that mattered right now though, none of it made the slightest bit of difference aside from the fate of this girl in my arms.

Once, me and the other Heirs might have seen her death as a blessing in disguise, but now, it was hard to think of many worse fates for ourselves, or Solaria as a whole, than to see one of the Vegas die while Lionel Acrux reigned.

I tore along the dark passageways, my enhanced eyesight all I needed to guide me down steps and through narrow turns until I was skidding to a halt between the others.

"Oh, holy raisin bran on a Wednesday morn!" Geraldine cried as she took in the wounds on Tory's shoulder and chest, the taint of the shadows clinging to them even as her blood pulsed from her.

"What the fuck happened?" Seth asked in alarm, grabbing her wrist and pushing healing magic into her body.

The wounds tried to close for a moment, but they just peeled open again the moment he released his hold on her.

"It's the Shadow Beast venom," I said, looking between my bloodstained, battered friends. "Darcy was lost to it entirely and Orion has made a Death bond with Lavinia so he can't leave here. We can't do anything for them right now and Tory won't stop bleeding-"

"Pull back her tunic and let me at thine snarvy coils of doom," Geraldine demanded and when the two of us gave her a blank look she simply knocked Seth aside and ripped Tory's shirt open to fully reveal the wound. "These tunnels are too darn narrow for my regal form," she cursed then half shifted her face so that her jaw turned canine, lines of drool hanging from those poisonous, lethal teeth of her Cerberus.

Geraldine conjured a gingko leaf into her palm, catching the drool on it and crushing it in her fist. She shifted back as she finished making the poultice, then stuffed the slimy green mixture into the bite wounds on Tory's shoulder.

Tory arched in my arms, a noise of pain escaping her, and I hurriedly cast a sleeping spell on her, cursing myself for doing it while knowing it was our only choice. She wouldn't willingly leave here without Darcy, but right now, saving her sister wasn't an option.

"That'll stem the dastardly venom," Geraldine said firmly. "But we must hurry. We need to acquire the healing antivenom of a Basilisk post haste!"

I grunted as she leapt onto my back, slapping my ass like I was a reluctant mare awaiting a gallop.

"Start running," I said to Seth, my heart twisting at the thought of leaving him down here even if it would only be for a moment. "I'll be right back for you."

Seth nodded, turning away and breaking into a sprint as he headed on down the tunnel. I shot past him in a blur of motion before he'd taken more than a few steps.

Geraldine damn near strangled me as she hooked an arm around my neck to support herself, but within a matter of seconds, we made it to the farthest reach of the passages, and she jumped back down again.

I turned to her, passing an unconscious Tory into her care and Geraldine began some kind of keening song as she held Tory close.

I shot away again without another word, finding Seth quickly and hoisting him onto my back before speeding back to re-join the others.

"Where are Max and Xavier?" I demanded, looking around fearfully as I failed to spot them anywhere.

"Leave them a message," Geraldine demanded, her grip on Tory unwavering, though pain flashed through her eyes which told me her heart was wrenching at the thought of us abandoning them here. "We have no time to spare on lollygagging. The queen needs care immediately."

One look at Tory's pale face and bloodstained skin made that clear enough without me being able to hear the ever-weakening beat of her pulse. I still balked at the idea of leaving without the others though, and Seth's lips peeled back in a snarl at the idea of us abandoning them here too.

"You go," I told Geraldine as I glanced back down the passageway, using my gifted hearing to listen for any sign of my brothers. "Save her and we'll save them."

"Or die trying," Seth added grimly, though there was no hesitation in him as he accepted that possibility.

Geraldine looked ready to argue but she raised her chin instead. "You are a pair of stalwart and brave souls. Return my slippery salmon to my arms and I shall be forever in your debt."

I nodded to her and pressed my hand to the wall, the ring Tory had forged for me opening the secret door hidden there.

Geraldine exited the passageways into the crisp night air with Tory clamped tight in her arms and they were gone in a flash of stardust the moment they stepped beyond the wards.

I exchanged a look with Seth as the rumbling of stone sounded the door closing once again and jerked my chin at him in a demand for him to hop on.

"What's one more fight?" I teased, the distant boom of thunder making the walls around us rattle with a promise of death.

"I always did like you bloodstained and violent," he replied, climbing onto my back while his words made my heart leap.

"Ditto," I replied, and we shot away towards death together for what felt like the hundredth time.

Scorpio
Gemini
Virgo
Cancer
Leo
Sagittarius
Capricorn
Aquarius
Libra
Pisces

XAVIER

CHAPTER FIFTY

I had a rough shield of metal cast against my arm as Dragon fire rained down on me, and I lifted it skyward to remain safe beneath it, freezing my shield with ice so the fire stuttered out against it.

The Dragon asshole I was fighting was tall, muscular, with a thick grey beard and mean eyes. I knew him well. Lionel's friend, Cyril. Or Uncle Cyril, as I'd been encouraged to call him. My father had tried to tighten the bonds of the Dragons by making it seem like we were all closer family than we really were, commanding Darius and I refer to his friends as aunts, uncles, brothers and sisters, as if we were some sort of incestual Dragon cult. Which in a way, I guessed we were.

I'd always hated Cyril and his creepy aura, the way he acted as if he was better than everyone else. He was involved in running the Nebular Inquisition Centres now, and I had no doubt that he was responsible for countless atrocities in this war.

"You are a stain on your father's name, you should be ashamed of yourself, you little runt," he spat at me, fire blasting from his hands again, and I sent my own fire back at him. "He should have drowned you at birth."

Max was just beyond us, standing on a pillar of air and firing his Phoenix arrows at anyone who got too close, working to move nearer and nearer to Lionel as he went. I prayed he would get a chance to finish him, but the odds here were stacked firmly against us. The Oscura Wolves had joined the fight, but there still weren't enough of us, and I could see the way this battle was turning. If the rebels didn't make a run for it soon, they were going to fall.

My fire curled around Cyril's head, blinding him and I ran forward as he worked to take hold of the flames, yanking my metal horn free of my pocket, my hand shaking around it. I hesitated, rage twisting through my chest, but I held back for a fraction of a moment, unsure if I could really do this. But then I thought of all the Fae who had suffered at the hands of men like Cyril, the monsters who made up my so-called family were a plague on this earth. And before he could escape my flames, I made the decision, plunging the horn into his chest, a shout of effort leaving me and my arm jarring as I cut right through bone.

I was surprised at how good it felt, how a twisted kind of justice filled me up and set my heart thumping with his oncoming death.

He spluttered, blood splashing over me from his lips as the fire died out and he was left looking at me eye to eye.

"I'm no runt," I snarled, turning the horn as he tried to get hold of his Element, but death was coming in all too fast now. I'd sat across so many dinner tables from this man, listening to him harp on about the 'higher Orders' and the need for more laws to 'control the numbers of the lessers'. He wanted inter-Order marriages banned, and even spouted bullshit about finding ways to stop Orders like mine from breeding at all.

He was a monstrous nothing, and I found a twisted pleasure in watching the life fade from his eyes. I'd been pushed to the edge, had my family stolen from me and now I was offering some vengeance in payment for that. This might not have been the Fae who'd killed them, but he was certainly one who'd tormented them. Darius had hated him as deeply as I had, and Mom had been forced to pretend she liked him when inside she'd probably been screaming.

"This is for them," I hissed, all the poison of grief gushing out of me into this foul Fae. "And you won't be the last."

I yanked my metal horn from his chest, setting fire to his body and taking a moment to watch him fall to nothing in my flames.

I turned my back on him in a final insult, adrenaline making me dizzy as I ran to take on another enemy with the taste of blood on my lips. I didn't know this side of me, but I didn't want to harness it either. I was on a path of destructive revenge at last, finding an outlet for all this pain which had been consuming me day after day.

I sought out Dante in the sky, but nothing but flashes of lightning far up in the clouds signified his movements now, and as I searched for Gabriel, I saw no sign of him either.

Gabriel's family were retreating from the fight as the Dragons decimated our numbers, the Oscura Wolves baying wildly as Rosalie led the retreat, only a few rebels still standing and a whole host of Dragons killing anyone who even looked in Lionel's direction.

My father's gaze locked with mine and a sneer lifted my lips as he saw me, truly saw me as I stood above Cyril's burning body.

I was moving before I could even think about the consequences, leaping over dead bodies and raising my horn while keeping my shield high. I needed to kill him, to slice his worthless head from his shoulders and hear the satisfying thump of it hitting the ground. For Mom, for Hamish, for Darius.

A bellow of determination left my lips as Lionel boomed an order for his Bonded Dragons to turn their attention to me. I felt no fear as I ran on, every muscle in my body working to bring me closer to the man who had stolen so much from me.

I knew this would equal my end, but it didn't matter if I took him down with me. If it bought my friends peace, and made sure Tyler and Sofia were safe once and for all. They had each other. They would mourn me, but they were together. I wasn't leaving them alone.

As fire and death was cast my way, I urged the ground to rise at my sides, blocking their blasts of magic with earth and keeping my feet. The sand was quaking with the Dragons' combined power as they tried to tear the world apart to defend their false king. The man they were now bonded to and would do anything to protect. But I had three Elements and a whole lifetime of hatred burning through my core, and somehow between the ground rising around me and the shield I held above my head, I managed to avoid the strikes aimed my way.

Lionel raised his hands and added his magic to the fight, the ground turning to lava at my feet and red-hot magma spewing up from miniature volcanos that burst from the sand either side of me. Deep down, I knew it was unlikely I'd be able to make it to him, but I kept running all the same, placing my faith in the stars and praying they'd grant me one infinitesimal chance to end him.

I was almost at the edge of his air shield when fire burst out around Lionel, and I lost sight of him among the flames. Everywhere I looked the fire was raging, my boots were melting against the sand as it continued to liquify under the intensity of it all. The heat was overwhelming, sucking away all oxygen with it and even my shield began to soften as fire curled down from above.

I was in a melting pot, about to be cooked alive and for what? I hadn't gotten close, hadn't landed a single wound on my father, and now I would die in this furnace with nothing to show for it, and the only comfort I had was that Darius and Mom would be there to welcome me beyond the Veil.

I wasn't ready to die. I'd tasted such a small slice of freedom and I craved so much more than I'd been offered. My life had been small, insignificant maybe, but it had been mine. And I'd only just reclaimed it.

The heat blazed at my back and my clothes set alight, my adrenaline high but not enough to steal away the pain that was driving into me now.

I sought out the stars above me on instinct, but all I could see was fire, so bright and hungry it seemed it would burn on forever.

A shadow descended from above and a hand reached for mine, taking it and squeezing tight. It was familiar and pulled me close, my heart cracking as I waited for the pain to stop and my soul to be led into the beyond. It had to be him, his large hand locked around mine, the way he drew me closer with force so very like Darius.

"I'm sorry I failed," I spoke to him, wrapping my arms around his neck, the sensation of flying taking over me as I left my body behind in that burning pit.

He held me tighter, and I buried my face against his shoulder, hating myself for this failure and wishing I could rewrite the fate this night had offered. But at least I was with my brother again. At least my mom would be here now, and I could spend eternity with their souls. We were free, even if we were lost.

I was suddenly thrown onto my ass and doused in freezing water, the flames clinging to my clothes hissing as they went out.

"*Xavier*," Max gasped, kneeling over me, and pressing his hands to my chest which was now bare as the scraps of my shirt turned to ash in his water.

Healing magic washed into me, and I blinked in shock at my saviour, realising it hadn't been Darius holding me at all. It had been Max, coated in armour built of ice with a whirlwind of air magic surrounding me. He'd leapt into those flames to save me, risked everything just to pull me from them.

"I flew us to the edge of the palace, but we need to get to the Savage King's passages. All the rebels are dead. Dante and the Oscuras are on the run, but the Dragons were keen on their heels. Can you move?"

Grief filled me over so much death and a ragged breath left me as I processed that. All the rebels we'd tried to save had fallen. We'd failed them.

"I can move," I said, then lunged up, wrapping my arms around him. "Thank you."

"Save it for if we actually get out of here," he said firmly, pushing me off of him and yanking me to my feet. My pants were half burned off, but scraps of denim still clung to crotch and thighs, though a wind around my ass cheeks said the back of them hadn't fared too well, so that was great.

I glanced back at the amphitheatre, spotting lines of the Oscura Wolves spilling out of it with a lilac-haired girl shooting ahead to lead the retreat, racing for the edge of the wards where they would no doubt stardust to safety.

I guessed we were all on our own now, and as I spotted a group of Dragons charging towards us across the frost sprinkled ground I knew we were almost out of time too.

I wrenched open the closest door and ran into the palace, the sound of Dragon roars heading our way at an alarming pace.

Max and I sprinted along the pristine corridor, our hands tracing the walls as we searched for a way into the passages.

No secret door opened, and my heart rioted as we ran on, moving faster and faster through the palace.

I shoved through a carved wooden door and Max darted after me into the enormous dining room where a table ran the entire length of it with enough seats for over a hundred people. It was laid out with golden plates and cutlery, a feast ready and waiting on the table for the Dragons.

At the far end of it was a golden throne with a red velvet backing and two dragon heads for arms, like a cheap mockery of the real Solarian throne that had belonged to Hail Vega. But that wasn't what stole my attention most. Beyond it, mounted on the wall as a sick trophy were my wings, the two of them glittering lilac with a rainbow sheen to them like oil imbued in the feathers. My heart lifted and I found myself moving towards them instinctively.

"Come on, keep looking for an entrance to the passages," Max called, not noticing what I'd seen as he hunted the walls for a way out.

I grabbed a chair from the table, carrying it to the wall and climbing onto it, my fingers just grazing the tips of the feathers.

"Help me," I called to Max. "I need your air magic."

"What?" Max snapped around, looking over at me and he stilled as his gaze fell on my wings.

"Please," I urged, knowing this was small in the face of all the chaos of tonight, but it meant everything to me.

He ran over to me, the decision brightening his eyes as he raised his hands and used his gifts to lift them from the hooks they were hung on, folding them carefully and placing them in my arms, their heavy weight making me grunt.

I jumped down from the chair, holding onto them tight and thanking him on my next breath.

Lionel's roar rattled the whole palace, reminding us that we weren't out of danger yet and the sound was so close it set my heart hammering. They were just beyond that door, the heavy footfalls of his Bonded Dragons about to corner us, and with them acting unFae, we stood no chance at all.

"Keep looking for a way out," Max commanded, and I nodded.

A thick layer of ice built around Max's hands, the temperature plummeting as he flexed his fingers, building up the magic there and summoning the wrath of winter into his palms.

I ran to the nearest wall, brushing my hands over it and seeking out an exit, not even bothering to ask the stars for help.

Our escape was down to us, and I'd already survived one death tonight, so I didn't plan on falling prey to another.

Scorpio
Gemini
Virgo
Cancer
Leo
Sagittarius
Capricorn
Aquarius
Libra
Pisces

MAX

CHAPTER FIFTY ONE

Ice crackled from my fingertips, racing across the floor, crawling up the brickwork and over the heavy wooden door which led into this room. I willed it to grow and thicken, creating an impenetrable barrier between us and the Dragons who were making their way closer with every step. I anchored the ice into the mortar of the bricks themselves and kept pouring my magic into it, feeling my way along the corridor beyond as I coated the walls, floor, and ceiling in a sheen of deadly frost.

My magic was aching for this release, the pain and horror that had flooded me with the annihilation of the rebels having bolstered my reserves to their maximum level.

I was one of the most powerful Fae in all of Solaria. So let the Dragons come at me if they thought they could take me.

My skin prickled as I tried to call on my Order form, coaxing it from the depths of my bones and feeling it stir as the suppressant began to fade from my skin, but it wasn't enough to release it just yet.

The moment I'd realised the suppressant was in the air, I'd started creating my own oxygen, sealing a mask of magic around my face so I didn't inhale another drop of it. I'd only drawn in a breath or two of the suppressant, and at that diluted level, I knew it wouldn't be able to keep its hold on me for much longer.

I felt the vibrations of the Dragons' footsteps as they pounded down the corridor across the sheen of ice I'd cast beneath them. I doubted they even noticed it in their rush to catch up to us and I let my power build as I counted them across it.

Sixteen. Shit odds, but then again, none of them were me.

My fingers began to tremble as more and more power crested in them, aching for the rush of release, crystals of ice forming across my skin and raising goosebumps in their wake. My breath rose in a fog before me, my power changing the environment itself in its desperate need for an outlet.

I closed my eyes, focusing on those sixteen pairs of feet as they thumped over my magic, the temperature still dropping around them as they closed in on us.

"I think there might be something here," Xavier said from behind me, but I didn't turn to look.

"Tell me when there is, not when there might be," I grunted, the effort of holding back making my entire body shake.

A wave of fire blasted the ice on the other side of the door, the power of the strike echoing through me as they rattled and held.

I took that as my signal and unleashed hell.

My magic ripped from me in a brutal wave that had me buckling forward, the ice lining the corridor outside exploding with a sound like shattering glass as razor sharp spears shot from every wall, the floor and ceiling at once.

The Dragons were impaled, limbs severed, and organs punctured, and their screams filled the space beyond the door, my power booming through the entire palace.

Their pain hit me like an anvil to the skull, the raw agony filling me up and recharging my magic as I sucked it in like a whirlpool hungering for fresh souls.

Xavier cursed loudly, the awe in his voice barely touching me. I fought off the sensation of my own body being torn apart, their agony so potent I could taste it.

A groan passed my lips as I summoned my power again, forcing their emotions to one side from my own while still absorbing everything I could, ready to hurl it at them for a second time.

Navy blue scales erupted across my body and the weight of all that emotion finally tore through the Order suppressant's hold on me. I grinned wickedly as I straightened, my mind shooting outwards and latching onto every single one of the remaining Dragons.

The sheer agony they were experiencing gave me my in, my own determination shattering their mental shields just as my ice had shattered their bodies.

There were eleven of them still breathing, their minds falling to my will as I invoked the full power of my Siren form and I parted my lips on a song which I had never dared to utter before.

This wasn't the lure I released once a month, it was no source of secrets or discovery, but a brutal, merciless Dread Song which was designed solely to rip the sanity from the minds of any who heard it.

I threw a hand at Xavier, sensing his mental shields at my back, the walls around his mind crumbling even though I wasn't aiming any of my gifts at him intentionally. A silencing bubble wrapped itself around him so tightly that not even a breath of fresh air could pass through it, sealing him away from this most terrible gift of my kind.

The Dragons beyond the door screamed with pain far more potent than the agony of their minds as my song carved its way into them, forcing them to relive all the worst moments of their lives and bringing every nightmare they had ever experienced to life within the confines of their heads.

They were trapped there, their terror fuelling my power until I was brimming with magic, overwhelmed by the force of all I was stealing from them, their minds quaking and trembling in my grasp.

A brush of magic against my arm made me peel my eyes open to look at Xavier where he was gesturing to a hidden cabinet filled with priceless liquor, no passageway in sight.

"There's nothing here," he mouthed from within his silencing bubble, and I nodded my understanding. We'd hit a dead end, which meant our only way out was through our enemies.

I looked towards the door again, the song rolling from the depths of my chest as it blasted through the minds of the immobilised Dragons beyond it. I could feel more of them heading closer through the palace now too. Too many even for the glut of magic which was roiling inside of me to deal with.

I couldn't stop my song to speak, and Xavier wouldn't have been able to hear me within his silencing bubble anyway, so I beckoned for him to follow me before blasting the doors apart with a shot of tornado worthy air.

Ice and wood splintered, the lumps of it crashing into the broken, bleeding bodies of the Dragons beyond the door and adding even more pain to all they were feeling.

The Dragons stared at me with wild, terrified eyes while they clawed at their wounds, some of them starting to bleed from the nose, ears, and eyes as my Dread Song cut their minds to shreds.

Xavier muttered something at my back as I stepped into the carnage, my hand sweeping out and directing the bloody ice aside as if it were nothing, leaving limp and bleeding bodies sprawled across the floor.

A Dragon to my right tried to reach his hand towards me, a desperate plea filling his eyes as they met with mine. But I could see what he was reliving, the horrors he had committed now turned on himself in his own head, and I didn't feel an ounce of pity for him as I sang even louder and watched the capillaries burst in the whites of his eyes. Blood began to stream down his cheeks, and he toppled over, convulsing and thrashing against shadowy demons which no one but he could see.

I stepped over him, glancing back to look at Xavier who was carrying his huge, Pegasus wings with care, their weight unbalancing him, but there was no question that he was keeping hold of them no matter the cost.

A bang sounded to our left and I whirled towards it as a door flew open there, but there was nothing and no one in the space beyond it.

I wasn't sure if it was intuition or insanity to follow the newly opened path, but I leapt towards it, feeling the other Dragons drawing closer, their roars of fury echoing throughout the palace halls.

Xavier broke into a run with me, my chest aching as the Dragons trapped within my song all began to topple like the others, their minds cleaving and breaking, locked within their own nightmares forevermore. No magic could fix what I had broken in them, and they would suffer their own vile terrors until someone saw fit to put them out of their misery with death.

We sprinted through the door, finding no one beyond it even as we headed into the huge ballroom, the one I'd heard had been locked to Lionel since he had taken ownership of the palace but had apparently opened itself to aid us.

The roar of the Dragons drew closer, but the moment we crossed the threshold, the door at our backs slammed shut once more, the sound of a lock echoing around us and making my breath catch.

My Dread Song faltered then fell away entirely and the last of the minds I'd been holding with it shattered. I grabbed one of Xavier's wings from him, releasing him from the silencing bubble too.

"We need to get out of here!" he cried.

We tore across the enormous ballroom, the stunning paintings of every Order form imaginable which decorated the walls all seeming to turn their heads and watch as we ran for our lives.

"I will mount your heads on spikes at my gates when I finish ripping you apart, traitors!" Lionel's voice boomed through the air, a spell making it resound across the entire palace and beyond.

We made it to the far side of the ballroom to a huge set of double doors which flung themselves open for us, silvery footprints appearing in the middle of the parquet floor ahead and turning down a small passageway that I wouldn't have otherwise noticed.

A narrow staircase appeared before us, circling down out of sight and almost impossible to navigate while holding the precious Pegasus wings.

The sound of shattering glass reached us from the ballroom and a Dragon's roar came straight after it as they began to rip the palace apart in their hunt for us.

"Follow my lead," Xavier commanded, elbowing me aside and throwing one of his beautiful wings down onto the steps ahead of him before leaping onto it and pushing himself off.

He began to slide, and the iridescent sheen which sparkled across the rainbow feathers seemed to light the stairwell. He picked up pace quickly and disappeared with a whinny of either fright or excitement.

I didn't have time to waste on questioning his logic, tossing the wing I'd been carrying down too and leaping onto it and starting to slide.

I cast air at our backs to make us move faster, the spiralling staircase whipping by so quickly that we could have given a Vampire a run for their money as we sped away into the bowels of the palace, and a whoop escaped me despite the terrifying reality of our situation.

I skidded off the bottom step, clinging to the bony ridge of Xavier's severed wing with blanched knuckles and my heart thundering with adrenaline as I spun out.

Xavier was already on his feet, whinnying at me encouragingly and pointing out more silver footprints leading away into the dark, taking off after them with his wing held awkwardly in his arms once more.

I scooped up the other wing and raced after him, hoping we weren't complete fools to be following some random footprints to fuck knew where, but it was pretty much the only option we had left to us at this point, so I was all in with it.

The sound of stone grinding trembled around the dim passageway and Xavier called out in triumph as he spilled through the darkened entrance to the hidden tunnels beneath the palace.

"Your hearts are pure and bound in steel. You'll find safe passage here," an ethereal, feminine voice whispered the moment I crossed the threshold, and a shiver trailed right down to my core. The ghost of whoever the hell had been helping us vanished once more and the entrance closed at our backs.

Xavier tossed a Faelight out ahead of us and I almost yelled in fright as a blur of motion shot our way. But before I could even summon my magic, Caleb skidded to a halt before us, Seth leaping from his back and hurling his arms around me.

"We saw the amphitheatre collapse," he choked out, crushing me in his embrace. "And we thought, for a moment we thought that maybe-"

He was cut off by Caleb throwing his arms around us too, pulling Xavier into the Heir sandwich and cursing in relief as their love and fear washed over me.

"I love you assholes too," I choked out. "But we need to get the fuck out of this place."

"Agreed." Caleb released us and threw his hands out before him, casting a sled out of wood and vines, along with a harness which he strapped around his own chest, ready to drag us all away. "Come on, we aren't splitting up again tonight."

The rest of us agreed to that happily enough and Seth and Xavier loaded the battered Pegasus wings onto the sled before the three of us leapt on too.

Caleb broke into a sprint with his gifts, and I cried out, clinging to the edge of the sled for dear life, the fucking thing swinging around corners with enough violence to risk caving our heads in on the walls with every turn.

He didn't slow though, the roaring Dragons giving us every bit of motivation we needed to get the fuck out of here as quickly as we could.

Suddenly, we were bursting from the far end of the passageway and into the frostbitten air beyond the outer edges of the magical shields which had been keeping us from stardusting away.

Seth hurled stardust over our heads, and we were whipped into the embrace of the heavens, escaping the clutches of the false king once more, and the weight of our utter failure crushed us as we went.

Scorpio
Gemini
Virgo
Cancer
Aries
Leo
Sagittarius
Taurus
Capricorn
Aquarius
Libra
Pisces

DARCY

CHAPTER FIFTY TWO

Darkness was everywhere, pushing me down under a river of shadows that tried to snuff out who I was at my roots. But I was fighting to stay here, refusing to give up, because the moment I did, I'd never come back. This was the end of me, the Shadow Beast would take over and the fragments of my soul would be devoured by its power.

Every time I clawed my way back to the surface, the Shadow Beast's will slammed against mine, forcing me back down. Or maybe it was Lavinia's will, or the power of the curse. I didn't know anymore. All I knew was that with every inch of power I gained against the Shadow Beast, it claimed triple back.

I couldn't fight my way out. I couldn't even see a path that might lead me back to myself anymore.

Blood hung heavily under my nose, and I was lost once more, chasing a dark haired man who flew above me in the air, calling out to me with words I couldn't comprehend.

I hungered to kill him like it was written into the fabric of my skin. He would die in my jaws and this rage in me would be sated. It was eternal, this torment. And the only thing that could settle it was death.

My mind hooked onto the bloodstained girl who had laid beneath me just moments ago, and something cracked in my head, allowing me to see clearly again for a single second.

Tory.

I roared at the Shadow Beast in my mind, refusing to back down as I held onto that sliver of control. This monster had turned my own body against my sister, and I was going to force it to bow down to my might, because I was not submitting. I was not going to forget who I was again. I was not giving up.

I fought tooth and claw to regain control, my eyes falling on Orion where he stood above me on a gust of air, begging me to come back to him.

I'm here.

But I couldn't get to him, no matter how hard I tried to escape the Shadow Beast, it wouldn't relinquish me.

"Calm, little beastie," Lavinia's voice circled in my head. *"Rest."*

The Shadow Beast's grip on me shattered in a wave and I gasped as the shift flooded over me, my knees hitting the floor as I returned to my Fae form, my mouth wet with Tory's blood and horror racing through me at what had happened.

The shadows coiled thickly around me, hugging my body even as I tried to banish them, their touch weakening me to the point of dizziness. If there was any magic left in me now, it was down to dying embers, and I certainly felt none of it present.

"I've got you, Blue." Orion was there in the next heartbeat, pulling me close even as I tried to push him away.

"I hurt her," I said, pain driving a stake into my heart. I was shaking, panic blinding me, consuming, devouring, swallowing as I became fully myself again.

"I hurt her," I repeated, her blood in my mouth, my hands, everywhere. It was everywhere. I was frozen in shock, terror binding my limbs as I thought of the terrible, impossible possibility that she was gone. That I had ripped her out of this world, and nothing could ever undo it. If that was true, I would never recover. I couldn't live without my twin, I wouldn't.

Orion caught my head between his hands, and I stared at him, unable to blink, to do anything at all but tremble in the wake of what I'd done. My twin. My fierce, remarkable sister who had been my heroine more times than I could count. She was passion and resilience and fire set alight. She was my burning beacon, and I may have just doused her flames forever.

"She's alive," Orion spoke slowly and deliberately to me, forcing me to hear those words. "Caleb took her. He'll heal her, I promise you, Blue."

"I hurt her," I breathed again, my mind stuck on that single reality. The memories were flooding in, of me holding her down, my claws breaking her skin, my bite deep and venom rushing from me into her.

"It's not you, how many times must I tell you that?" He shook me a little and I drank in the honesty in his eyes.

"If I was stronger, I could have held it off. I've fought it off in the past. Why not this time?" I croaked, finding new words to speak, but they were weaponised, cutting me open as I faced this awful reality. That I was responsible for nearly killing Tory, and all I had now was the hope that Caleb would save her. But what if he couldn't?

"This is a shadow curse," Orion growled. "And I'm starting to think the entirety of the shadows drives this power. I thought your Phoenix could burn it out, but maybe the curse can't be destroyed by will alone. Maybe it can only be broken by the terms set out upon it. You can fight with all the power of the stars in your veins, and still, it won't be enough. I think perhaps there is only one answer to this, and it is me fulfilling Lavinia's deal."

"What if this is all a game?" I whispered my most desperate fear. "What if Lavinia knows that the curse will consume me before three moon cycles are up? That doesn't break her deal. It doesn't break the terms."

He took my hands, drawing me closer, his eyes the most vivid I had ever seen them, like the night sky lay right there within his irises. "I will break this curse, come what fucking may. Do you hear me, Blue? It is a truth as certain as the sky is above us and the ground is below."

I opened my mouth to answer that, to echo my constant fury over him offering himself up to this curse and hating that he had to go through hell for me to break it. But then a tug in my chest told me Lavinia was summoning me and my body turned to smoke before I could even try to resist.

Orion cursed, shoving to his feet and as Lavinia yanked on the tether of my soul, I was forced to answer her call, flying through the air towards a vent in the wall.

"Darcy!" Orion called after me, casting away the ice that covered the doors before I could slip away through the vent, I willed the Shadow Beast to take the path through doors instead. I rushed that way and Orion shot alongside me with his Vampire speed, following the dark fog I was lost to as I flew through corridors left and right.

I arrived before Lavinia and she forced the shift over me, a roar tearing from my lips that made the chandelier above tremble as the Shadow Beast took control once more.

I still had my mind, but for how long?

Lionel didn't flinch, standing before us in the huge hall with thirty or more Dragon Shifters surrounding him in their Fae forms, dark blue robes hanging from their shoulders.

Orion came to a halt at my side, pressing his hand against my shoulder, his fingers knotting in my fur, and I kept hold of my mind, focusing on his presence as the rage in me simmered down.

"You did not consult me about this!" Lavinia screeched at Lionel, stepping closer to me.

The shadows danced in her hands threateningly and I realised that this was some kind of standoff. That the Dragons weren't simply standing close to Lionel, but that they were surrounding him protectively, a few growls carrying from the open door at his back letting me know that there were even more of them close by.

Was this it? The moment when Lionel and Lavinia's unholy alliance fell apart? Had she summoned me here to fight for her?

I worked to keep my head, though if she wanted me to attack Lionel, I couldn't see me objecting to that. I'd savour the opportunity. Though the Shadow Beast didn't try to take hold of me fully regardless.

"I am the king," Lionel said calmly. "I do not need to consult anyone on my plans, nor do I see why you would have any reason to object to them."

Lavinia gnashed her teeth together near one of Lionel's Dragon guards and he raised his chin, a flicker of fear in his eyes, but he didn't back down.

It was then that I noticed the Aries mark branded on Lionel's guard's left arm near the crook of his elbow. My eyes flashed to the next Dragon then the next, realising what Lionel had done with a sinking, ominous sensation in my chest. *No.*

My eyes moved to Lionel's arm last, and he turned it outward as if welcoming the inspection, the corners of his lips twitching up as Lavinia and I stared at the line of star signs which were now branded all the way up his inner forearm. All twelve symbols, some seeming thicker and darker than others, implying more souls with that star sign had been bonded to him. Holy shit, how many Dragons had he made into his Guardians? How many of them were now set to throw themselves between him and death when it came calling his name?

Orion's fingers tightened on my fur as he noticed it too and I felt the keen rush of his magic tingling against my side, reminding me that he was free of his cuffs.

"I have ensured that I am safe from all enemies," Lionel said smugly. "I cannot be touched."

Lavinia flicked her finger and Lionel's shadow hand lifted, latching tight around his own throat. At once, several Dragons ran to his aid, their combined strength dragging the shadow hand back from his neck and freeing him from Lavinia's control.

She shrieked like an alley cat, raising up on a plinth of shadow and wailing furiously.

"You dare do this on the night when I have worked so tirelessly to birth you a worthy heir!?" she demanded.

I shifted my paws, looking to Orion, finding him baring his fangs at that news. Could this night get any worse?

"Then where is this heir?" Lionel demanded. "Bring him to me at once, my Queen, if you have fulfilled the promise you made." I could have sworn there was a touch of mocking to the title he gave her, but it was hard to be certain.

Lavinia released a high-pitched noise that made me flatten my ears and growl in discomfort. A thump sounded in the room above us, the ceiling trembling from the weight of whatever had just landed on it.

Lionel frowned, peering up at the ceiling as heavy footfalls travelled overhead.

"He has likely found some bodies to devour in the wake of your little party," Lavinia said bitterly, and I prayed those bodies didn't belong to anyone I loved.

"Party?" Lionel spat. "An entire wing of the palace has nearly been obliterated, I have lost around thirty Dragons, and the amphitheatre lays in ruins. I may have emerged victorious this night, but the rebels will pay for their insolence in trying to assassinate the King of Solaria."

"I do love when you get bloodthirsty, Daddy," Lavinia crooned, her voice becoming honey sweet as though she hadn't seemed set on death a moment before.

My hackles rose as Lionel's new Guardians sized me up and Mildred stalked forward to the front of the line, raising her hairy chin and assessing me through beady eyes.

The thumping sound carried down the stairway beyond the room and I turned to look that way as everyone's gaze fell on the door. It swung slowly open, revealing no one beyond it, but my senses told me to beware.

A grotesque creature arrived, scuttling across the ceiling, its features sharp among the shadow it was clearly made of. It was as big as a Dragon Shifter, its hulking form falling from the ceiling and landing with a thump at Lavinia's side.

I fought the urge to recoil as the shadows sank into the thing's skin, a man slowly appearing from the darkness, his face a picture of handsome cruelty. A demonic smile curved his lips and a sinister emptiness stirred in his gaze. He was naked, his powerful body marked with scars of shadow which seemed to pulse like living veins against his tanned skin.

"Hello, Father," he purred, his voice a wicked seduction.

Every muscle in my body locking tight, knowing on some soul deep level that an apex predator had just appeared among us, his appetite for blood insatiable.

The Dragons all shifted protectively in front of Lionel, closing ranks, their eyes taking in this new, monstrous arrival and a low growl rolled from my throat.

"I named him Tharix," Lavinia cooed, reaching up to brush her fingertips along his jaw and as I looked between them, I could see similarities, the slant of his cheekbones were just the same as hers, and the cruel curve of her lips mirrored in his. Though how the hell she'd birthed this fully grown man a matter of hours ago was beyond me. "It means prince in the language of old. Isn't he perfect? Come closer, Daddy, say hello to your son."

Lionel lifted his head, eyeing the monster with caution, but with a hint of intrigue too. "He does appear to be a powerful specimen," he observed, his eyes roaming over every inch of Tharix's body with approval and I noted some similarities between them too, this impossible union of their DNA, all packaged up and ready to fight for them.

"But is he Dragon born?" Lionel added sceptically.

"He is of his father's seed," Lavinia replied proudly. "He is just as pure blooded as you, my King, and he is gifted with all four Elements. Though I will admit he is blessed with the gift of the shadows too."

This dire reality closed in, the immensity of their offspring's power unthinkable.

"Show me," Lionel demanded and Lavinia gave Tharix a curt nod, ushering Orion and I back to make room for him.

Tharix remained entirely still as we retreated, the Dragon Guardians all tensing as they remained in place surrounding Lionel, ready for an attack, but none came.

Instead, Tharix leapt forward with a feline pounce that became a shift so abruptly my heart leapt at the change.

A Dragon form burst from his body just as Lavinia had promised, its scales a matt obsidian which seemed to suck all of the light from the room into them, making it near impossible to define any details beyond his immense size and poised wings.

The Guardians closed ranks around Lionel, magic glimmering in the air as they threw shields into place.

"Oh my," Mildred gasped, fanning herself as if she was flustered.

Tharix reared back, showing off the full size of him, my heart plummeting as I realised he was at least as large as Lionel in his shifted form, perhaps even as big as Darius had been. The roar which echoed from him was a thing of nightmares, screams breaking out in reply to it from all around the palace as servants and guards were terrorised by the mere noise which spilled from him. And that was nothing compared to the shadows pouring from that deadly jaw, coiling from his mouth in hungry strikes which I had no doubt would peel the skin from the bones of any Fae unlucky enough to find themselves within range of them.

"That will do, sweet pea," Lavinia purred, shooting closer to the enormous beast and trailing a hand along his flank.

Tharix complied instantly, shifting back into his Fae form, that wicked smirk in place once more and now that I knew what lurked inside of him, I could recognise the darkness which peered out of his eyes. A nightmare given flesh.

"Magnificent," Lionel breathed, stepping forward, causing his Guardians to scatter to make room for him. "Will he do as I say?"

"He is entirely obedient to your whims, my King," Lavinia promised. "Try it out."

"Break three of the Vampire's ribs," Lionel commanded, and I roared in answer to that as Tharix closed in on Orion and my faithful mate didn't so much as concede a step.

"Don't fight when he breaks your ribs, pet," Lavinia commanded lightly as Orion tensed in preparation to attack the monster closing in on him. "This will count as part of my torture."

Orion snarled and I swung around to protect him, placing my body between his and Tharix.

The horrible creature lowered to the floor in a crouch, scuttling beneath me and leaping to his feet at my back so fast that I could do little more than twist around, snapping my jaws at him. Lavinia cast a leash around my throat before I could pounce, yanking me back.

Orion gazed at the horrid new Heir as it approached him, Tharix casually prowling into his personal space before reaching out and gripping my mate's sides, his dark eyes alight with excitement.

I thrashed, trying to get to Lance, and Lavinia laughed like we were playing some game, pulling me back once more as Tharix squeezed and Orion's ribs broke with a snap, snap, snap.

Orion hissed in pain, his fangs bared, and the moment Tharix released him, he cast a blade of ice in his hand and slammed it into the monster's temple with a roar of defiance.

Tharix crumpled to the floor with a thwack, blackish blood pouring from the wound. Lavinia screamed in rage, but Orion had obeyed her order to let Tharix break his ribs, she had said nothing to hold him back after it was done.

"Who released you from your cuffs?!" Lavinia screamed. "Come here this instant and do not cast a single spell more or I will cut off your pretty little Vega's fingers and toes tonight."

Orion stalked over to her, darkness in his eyes while glaring defiantly at Lavinia.

I flinched in alarm as Tharix twitched then began to move, death somehow having spared him as he slowly recovered, pulling the ice blade from his temple with a jolt before tossing it to the floor and returning to his feet.

The Dragons shared disconcerted glances, but Mildred clapped excitedly.

"Oh, he's perfect, isn't he Uncle Lionel?" Mildred cooed. "What a big strapping son you have. He is quite the catch too." She fluttered her lashes at Tharix who seemed unaware of her existence, his gaze falling on Lionel like a feral dog hoping for a bone.

"He hasn't gained my full approval yet," Lionel said, eyeing the creature carefully before his gaze moved to Lavinia. "But well done, my Queen. I look forward to seeing his capabilities in battle."

"You will enjoy his barbarity, my King. He has quite the thirst for blood." She smiled widely, her eyes roaming over the Dragons around Lionel before she bowed her head in submission. "I will bid you goodnight. I must find my pet some new magic blocking cuffs before I punish him for hurting my poor baby."

"I'll come to your chamber once you are done with that," Lionel said, his gaze roaming over her appreciatively, and I fought the urge to gag as their weird ass relationship turned on a dime once more.

Lavinia preened beneath his attention and she pushed her fingers into Orion's hair absentmindedly, then yanked the leash around my neck tight, making me snap my teeth in fury.

I was forced to follow her out of the room, leaving Lionel and his beastly new Guardians behind while Tharix followed at my heels, his eyes two pits of nothing, no soul within them at all.

"Heal yourself, pet," Lavinia whispered to Orion, and he raised a hand to do so, fusing his ribs back together, but when he dropped his hand, Lavinia caught it, threading her fingers between his and making me bristle.

We were taken back to the throne room, and the gates of hell seemed to close at our backs. This night was draped in despair, and I couldn't escape the clutches of it.

I thought of Tory and tipped my head back, a saddened howl rising from my throat and colouring the air as black as this forsaken evening. My twin needed me, and I couldn't reach her. We were a single entity torn in two and cast to opposite sides of an uncrossable river. I had to return to her, some way, somehow. Because without her, fate couldn't change. I knew that from the depths of my being.

But until I could cut the Shadow Beast out of me and slay it once and for all, I couldn't be close to her. Not now that I was one of her greatest threats.

Scorpio
Gemini
Virgo
Aries
Cancer
Leo
Taurus
Sagittarius
Capricorn
Aquarius
Libra
Pisces

TORY

CHAPTER FIFTY THREE

The circular table that we had taken to using for these so-called war councils was full of noise, a clamouring train of voices that wouldn't cease and only seemed to grow louder while my head pounded from the force of it.

Or maybe that was the aftereffects of the venom my sister had tried to kill me with last night.

My side burned with pain where the tigers eye crystal still sat within my skin, no one having noticed it during their efforts to steal me away from my other half and go running from Lionel Acrux yet again.

I didn't remove it though. Despite the burn it caused, I could feel the power of it pulsing through my veins, imbuing them with strength even as my own body rebelled with an ache for rest.

But there wasn't going to be any rest for me. Not since I had awoken to find myself back here, my wounds healed with Basilisk anti-venom, countless hours having passed while they mended me and kept me subdued throughout, too afraid of my rage to wake me before it was done.

A pile of food sat before me on the table, untouched and ignored while Geraldine constantly shot me concerned looks over it.

I ignored her too.

I was too furious with all of them to do anything at all other than sit here in silence and take in the facts of everything that had gone so horribly wrong once again.

The only pale light of good that had come from our ordeal was the fact that Xavier had managed to reclaim his wings. Sofia and Tyler were with him now, the best healers the rebels had to offer trying to figure out whether or not they could be reattached, and I hoped to hell and back that they would find a way.

The Heirs and their parents were arguing so loudly that my head was spinning with it, Geraldine's wails of adamant outrage cutting through the domineering bullshit like a knife as they all fought over the next moves we should make and dissected every problem we now faced.

A huge group of rebel prisoners had died last night, when one of the queens they'd sworn to follow showed up and failed them. Gabriel's prophecy had turned to hell on earth. I had to assume that either Lionel had managed to rip the warning my brother had sent me on that battlefield from his mind and twisted it against or us, or the stars had all colluded to fuck with our fates once more.

If what Darcy had claimed was true, then the latter was just as likely as the former. Because our bloodline was cursed. And the promise I needed to keep to end that curse was a mystery.

As they all continued to argue back and forth, discussing possible strikes or ways to rally our forces, I knew that none of it was what we needed. This army was decimated and on the run, fast losing any hope they'd been clinging to and now cast adrift with a bunch of squabbling Fae, waiting for us to produce some fucking miracle which none of us could find.

Geraldine was pushing for us to make a strike, something big which would help to not only turn the narrative of this war in our favour, but also draw more rebels to fight for us. We'd been sending groups out to destroy the Nebular Inquisition Centres and release the Fae being held there, but we needed to do something bigger. She had the idea to attack the Court of Solaria, take out Max's evil stepmother and the newly formed court which Lionel had given to her to preside over, and maybe plot to take out some other important members of his regime too.

It sounded like a solid idea to me, but I just couldn't focus on the war as a whole right now. My mind was too tangled in my own personal priorities, and I couldn't summon the energy required to engage in the constant arguments taking place in this room.

Something shifted in my pocket, and I flinched before remembering the Tiberian Rat who Darcy had given me to save. One lone survivor amid the carnage we'd escaped.

I drew him out and placed him on the table alongside the other things they'd given me.

"Darcy wanted us to have these," I said, shoving to my feet and leaving the items there, the little Rat quivering among them. I knew they were important, but none of them would offer up any of the solutions I needed, and I just didn't have it in me to sit at that fucking table for one more minute.

I turned and strode for the door, ignoring the calls from behind me as the others protested me leaving, but there was nothing for me within those walls. I needed to do something, not sit around and fucking talk about how much we'd failed again.

I ripped the door open and came face to face with Dante Oscura, his powerful body crackling with lightning as he stood shirtless and bloodstained from battle before me, his eyes darkening as they met mine.

"I don't see my brother with you," I growled in a low voice, my back tingling where my wings lay dormant, as if they were hungering to escape the confines of my flesh.

Rosalie snarled low and rough behind him, she and Leon stepping closer to flank him while I stood my ground before them. Just little old me against a pack of hellhounds.

"And I'm failing to see your sister, piccolo regina," Dante replied darkly, electricity sparking against his skin.

"That's enough," Tiberius Rigel boomed from behind me, but I didn't turn to look his way, my ache for an outlet to this fury pushing me into recklessness.

"I didn't ask the opinion of a man who stayed home with the children while the rest of us went to war," I sneered, my eyes still on Dante but my words for the ex-Councillors who seemed so adamant to believe they had a say in this war which they were yet to play any real role in.

"You know full well that you concocted that hair-brained scheme without our knowledge or approval," Tiberius seethed. "Likely because even in your arrogance, some part of you understood that an army of entitled youngsters playing dress up would never succeed in toppling the Dragon King and-"

I whirled to face Tiberius, but Max had gotten there first, his chest slamming into his father's as I found the two of them on their feet, facing off against each other.

"The so-called youngsters in this room have fought and bled for this war," Max snarled. “We’ve seen death and mayhem unlike anything you’ve ever experienced in your cushy office jobs. We’ve fought alongside friend and foe alike and lost more than just those we loved along the way. We’ve sacrificed our souls to this cause, pieces of us fracturing and breaking off with every heinous act we are forced to commit in the name of fighting against Lionel’s tyranny and oppression. Meanwhile, the three of you spent years sitting across tables from him, turning a blind eye to any signs of what he was up to behind closed doors. He didn’t just seize this opportunity when the Shadow Princess crossed over into our realm – he’s been plotting this for years. He was Dark Coercing your fucking king, the man you were all sworn to serve and protect at all costs, and you didn’t even see it. So don’t try to talk down to Roxanya Vega now that she is standing there before you, bloodied and broken from everything that has been stolen from her thanks to all of those failures. You should be on your knees begging her forgiveness.”

Antonia Capella sucked in a sharp breath at the suggestion of them kneeling before me, even if Max hadn’t meant it in the sense of them bowing. I glanced from her to Melinda Altair, expecting the same outrage there but finding something far softer instead, her eyes bright with regret.

“We know we failed all of you when it comes to Lionel,” Melinda said softly, her gaze meeting mine and my heart wrenching painfully as I was forced to endure these words. “We should have seen it sooner, should have…” She shook her head, sighing. “Regrets and what-ifs do us no favours now. But I can assure you that I have spent many nights awake in my bed, pondering more moments than you can comprehend, wondering if I missed the signs, realising when I was manipulated, and hating myself for my failures when it came to that lying piece of shit. At first, I think I gave him too much leeway because I assumed he was grieving the death of his older brother, and my love for Radcliff made me want to…I don’t even know. I suppose I just wanted to believe in the power of the Fire Heir and then Councillor because without him, the balance required to sustain our kingdom would have been lost.”

“Our four families have been matched in power for generations,” Antonia agreed. “Second only to the house of Vega. And after your parents died and we believed you and your sister had been killed with them, we had to focus on ruling, on figuring out how to lead without a monarch to instruct us. And believe me, we made a lot of changes which were better for our people than the iron fist of the Savage King had ever-”

“Except it wasn’t the Savage King who commanded such hatred or committed such atrocities, was it?” I sneered.

“No,” Tiberius said on a breath, his shoulders slumping as the tension between him and his son dulled, and he sank back down into his chair. “And I wish to the heavens and beyond that we’d seen that sooner.”

Caleb drummed his fingers on the table, looking from the shame-faced ex-Councillors to me, arching a brow as if asking ‘what now?’

There was an ache in my chest where Darcy’s rejection had carved a piece from my heart. I may have been able to understand her reasons for staying while I was dragged back here, but it didn’t make it hurt any less. She was my other half, but I wasn’t even certain that I was half a girl at all without her now.

“We need a bigger army,” Seth said in a low voice, his eyes moving to the map lying in the centre of the table, Solaria sprawled out before us, taunting us as if it held all the answers but refused to share them.

“Maybe some weapons too,” Caleb agreed, but as the noise started up again, I turned from the room. Nothing they schemed for in there was going to make any kind of immediate difference, and I was done sitting around tables and fucking talking. I was going to act, and I didn’t give a shit what anyone else thought about it.

Dante and his family were still barring my way out, but I didn’t slow, shoulder-checking the enormous Dragon Shifter and giving myself a dead arm in the process. But I moved him, slipping between him and his cousin while Rosalie bared her teeth at me in warning.

I exited the room, ignoring Geraldine as she tried to call me back and heading up the two flights of stairs to my room.

Footsteps sounded softly at my back, but I ignored them, climbing steadily and leaving the door wide behind me as I moved into the luxurious space.

My clothes were ruined and filthy, my own blood staining them more than any enemy's, and I stripped out of them without care. I used my water magic to draw the blood from my skin, my clothes, and my sword, directing it into a glass decanter sitting on my desk, then I cleaned myself with a rush of ice-cold water and used air to dry off again.

I grabbed an oversized shirt from the closet and tugged it on, the black material swamping me and making me think of Darius even though the item had never belonged to him. Nothing of his, barring his treasure, remained to me now. That, the ink on my thigh, and the necklace which seemed to pulse with the presence of him from time to time.

I scratched at the throbbing wound where the tigers eye crystal was still embedded in my side as it burned with that dark magic once more, the taint of it sinking into my body and making me shiver.

I had only brought it as a last resort, my studies on the magic it called on making me more than wary of it, but now that I'd been forced to use it and had survived, I had no inclination to draw it out. That thing had helped me cling on to my miserable excuse for a life when fate had tried to steal me away from it, and I wasn't done wreaking havoc here yet.

The crystal was imbued with a form of necromancy which made me shudder to think on, but it basically laced my skin with the power of a long-dead soul, anchoring me on this side of the Veil. It wasn't immortality, but it was as close as I could get. There was a cost of course, but childhood memories weren't things I cherished. Reliving some of the worst things Darcy and I had endured for the benefit of the soul I had coaxed into being my anchor was an acceptable price for this power.

I'd felt it in the dark before waking up in this place, Basilisk antivenom sliding through my veins and healing my wounds. Death had come calling for me in the moments before we'd made it back here, and I would have gone with it had the crystal not secured me to this plane. I'd felt the tug, seen the shimmering light of the Veil and even felt an urge to accept that call. Darius would have been waiting for me there, beyond the shroud of light. He'd have been there, and I could have reunited with him, far from all the rot and ruin and agony of this life I clung to.

But that wasn't the path I was going to tread. I wasn't going to let the stars shepherd me to my damnation so easily

"Dante loves Gabriel like a brother too, you know," Rosalie Oscura said as she padded into my room without any inclination to ask permission, nor give an explanation for how she'd made it past the guards standing at the foot of the stairs. "He would have gladly given his life if that was what it took to rescue him from the clutches of that pezzo di merda, Lionel Acrux."

"Everyone who fought last night was willing to lose their lives," I grunted, taking the Book of Ether from the shelf where Geraldine had placed it when tidying, dropping onto my bed with the intention of reading it and finding some answers of my own.

"Well, you're certainly arrogant enough to be a queen," Rosalie commented lightly, ignoring my dismissive tone, slinking closer. She prowled like the Wolf she was, dark eyes shimmering with moonlight as the predator in her moved closer to the edges of her skin. I doubted she ever strayed far from the animal in her.

"Did you want anything in particular?" I asked, flicking the pages over one by one, seeking something, anything. I didn't even know what aside from the fact that I was done waiting here for something to happen.

I'd been hanging on for Darcy, but she'd made her choice and it wasn't me. It hurt. Hurt so fucking bad I could hardly breathe, but there it was. I wasn't about to throw myself a pity party over the fact, despite how tempting the idea of that was. So now I was going to be selfish too. The winter solstice was almost upon us, and I was done waiting to fulfil the promise I'd made.

"I don't suppose you know much about Moon Wolves," Rosalie said, her Faetalian accent colouring her words as she perused my room, trailing her fingers over Darius's treasure and making some feral part of me want to bare my teeth at her.

She gave me a knowing grin and released the gold coin she'd picked up before moving to my bookshelf instead.

"I know that *you're* a Moon Wolf, if that's what you're referring to," I said, watching her as she plucked the ancient book on earth magic from the shelf and let it fall open to a random page in her hands. "Seth was bitching about it relentlessly the other night after he drank too much of my tequila. He seems to think the moon should have favoured him too."

Rosalie snorted, her hand raising as she used her earth magic to cast a pale stone moon into her palm, every crater and ridge on its surface looking eerily accurate as she set it spinning in her hand, then cast a levitation spell on it so it drifted towards the ceiling.

"That pup spends too much time thinking about the things he can't have, when he should be claiming the things he can," she said, rolling her eyes.

"If he heard you call him a pup, he'd probably challenge you to another fight – I heard the last one was turning nasty," I said blandly but Rosalie just grinned.

"That was fun. Especially the part when he started crying because he thought he'd killed me."

I couldn't help the bark of laughter that escaped me at the wickedness in her dark eyes, and I found myself more curious about this little visit than I had been. I hadn't had the opportunity to spend all that much time with Rosalie Oscura before now, but I got the feeling she was precisely my kind of girl, especially when it came to making bad choices for all the best reasons.

"If you hadn't tricked him, he'd have won, I suppose," I said, and that steely wildness flashed in her eyes again.

"He's the only Wolf I've ever met who might stand a chance – but I think I'd have a good shot at winning if it really came down to it," she replied cockily and I eyed the tattoo crawling up the side of her neck, the rose vines echoing her name, yet I got the feeling there was more to them than simply that.

"Why's that?" I asked curiously.

"Because I fight dirty," she replied with a feral grin. "And for all his Alpha bullshit, Seth Capella is a clean-cut rich boy when you get to the bones of him. All the Heirs are - even Darius was, beneath that rough, inked exterior of his."

My heart hurt at his name, but I didn't let that stop me from thinking of him, refusing to balk from the pain of his memory and risk losing him altogether. "Oh, I know. I gave him shit for it relentlessly."

"Woman after my own heart," Rosalie purred, moving to sit beside me on the bed, her knee brushing my thigh as she crossed her legs and placed the book in her lap. "Though I think I'll stick to the real villains over the broken hero types, if it's all the same to you."

"Why fight in the war if you don't care for heroics?" I asked.

"I'll never say no to a fight. Besides, my grudge with Lionel Acrux was personal long before he gave me the additional reason to kill him of being a tyrannical stronzo with a small cock complex."

"Personal how?" I asked curiously and she pursed her lips, seeming like she didn't want to answer for a moment before deciding she would.

"A few years ago, I tried to steal something from Lionel's manor with Leon Night and his brother Roary," she admitted, her jaw tightening as she spoke that last name, her emotions shutting down in a way so similar to my own natural defences that I recognised it instantly. "It...went to shit. The Dragon stronzo discovered us before we could escape. Roary saved me, but by doing so he cast his own fate and he was captured. He's been in Darkmore Penitentiary ever since."

"Rosalie," I breathed, reaching for her sympathetically, knowing how much

Darcy had suffered while Orion had been trapped in that place for a few months, let alone a few years. And despite how hard she was trying to hide it, I could tell that this leader of Wolves loved the man who had been taken from her. "Were the two of you together?"

Rosalie snorted dismissively, leaning into my touch then withdrawing again as she shook her head.

"Roary is ten years older than me. He thinks I'm just some dumb pup, so no, we were never…anything. Or at least, I was never anything to him."

"If I'm ever in a position to free him," I began, because surely if Darcy and I took the throne we would have the power to release people from prison, but Rosalie shook her head sadly.

"He made a Death bond with Lionel Acrux. One that cannot be broken. The only way he could get around it would be by breaking out," she said bitterly, flicking a page in her book as if searching for something to do with her hands. "Or if someone breaks him out…"

"Has anyone ever managed that before?" I asked, my brows arching at the thought of all the security they had containing that place.

"No," Rosalie laughed hollowly. "It's buried deep beneath the earth and surrounded by all kinds of magical, physical and even living barriers to escape. No one has even come close. To attempt escape from that hell is to welcome death."

"So why do I feel like you're planning on breaking him out of there?" I asked, wondering if she was insane and she leaned closer conspiratorially.

"Because maybe I am."

Before I could reply to that, Rosalie pushed the Book of Earth into my lap on top of the Book of Ether, her finger pressing down on a spell I hadn't paid much attention to before now.

"Moon Wolves are gifted foresight and intuition not governed by the stars because the moon herself is a celestial being all of her own variety," Rosalie told me, continuing with what she'd begun talking about at the start of this conversation. "There are many other gifts I am rumoured to have, some of which I've proven true or false, others I may yet discover, it's hard to say. But I can always tell when two souls are destined to be with one another. Or sometimes even more than two."

"What do you-"

"I have never felt anything like the connection I felt between you and Darius Acrux," she breathed, shifting closer to me so that all I could see was the beauty of her features, the full lips which seemed designed entirely for seduction and the cunning glint in her brown eyes letting me know that nothing ever got past her. "The power of your love and hatred burned hotter than the sun itself, the constant tug and pull, a war unending and a passion unyielding. You were two stars always set to collide and cast the world on fire because fuck the consequences."

"Why are you telling me this now?" I asked, my voice weak as the loss of him surrounded me, the memory of that love we'd felt echoing in all the empty places of my soul and making them ache with longing. The ruby necklace I wore seemed to heat at her words too, the echo of his hand slipping through my hair, a memory that was somehow tangible like his ghost was leaning in to listen.

"Because that fire hasn't gone out yet," Rosalie breathed, taking a lock of my ebony hair and winding it around her finger until it pulled tight, like she'd known I'd imagined his touch there too. "I feel a chord of it straining to remain in place. And I think it's time you tugged on it."

She gave my hair a little pull, the corner of her lips twitching with amusement as I sucked in a sharp breath. In the next moment she was on her feet, backing away towards the door.

"That's it?" I asked, frowning in confusion as she began to leave.

"Segui il fuoco," she replied as if I had a clue what the fuck that meant. "I'm horny and my pack have been begging to fuck me for a full week now. I usually prefer the efforts of a real Alpha, but they're in desperately short supply around here. I'd ask you to take a tumble with me, but your heart will always be with him, and I don't want any part of anyone else's love story."

I arched a brow at that suggestion, wondering if I might have taken her up on the offer if Darius hadn't already ruined me for every other Fae.

"I thought the army was crawling with Alphas?" I asked because I'd noticed plenty of posturing bullshit going on in the barracks and training rings whenever I'd gone near them.

"Plenty of Betas like to think they're all Alpha, amica, but it's a sad reality that far too many of them fall flat when put to the test." Rosalie sighed in disappointment.

"So, you'll just have a pack orgy and hope for the best?" I teased and she grinned.

"I can always get myself off if I have to – but Jessibel has been dying to get between my thighs and Andre has been sending me dick pics for two weeks straight. So, I might as well let them shoot their shot. Who knows, maybe I'll like it."

"Enjoy," I called as she left, sauntering off like she ruled the damn world and hell, if I didn't know better, then maybe I'd believe that she did.

I looked down at the book in my hands, frowning at the spell she'd pointed out to me and snapping my head back up as I called after her, but all I got in reply was a distant laugh from her as she shouted, "You're welcome!"

I stared at the page, wondering how the fuck I'd managed to miss something so fucking obvious as I read over the title there.

To raise the trees of the damned.

My brows lifted in surprise as I read the words beneath it, the damned trees which could be grown like a living curse, the heart of their victims bound to it, their entire family line tied to its existence.

Once the blood of the intended is added to the seed, the essence of the caster's soul must be leashed to its roots. The light of the moon helps raise the shadows to assist in the growth of the sapling, and the longer the bone chant continues, the larger and more powerful the tree itself shall grow.

I looked over gruesome pictures of bloodletting and sacrifices of small children, but so far as I could tell, the growth of the tree simply required the blood from a member of the family you wished to curse. Not every drop, just enough to infuse the seed.

The harvesting of the seed was a shit show of horrors which I had absolutely no interest in, especially as the only motherfucker who I would like to curse went by the name of Lionel Acrux, and I had no intention of dragging Xavier into the punishments which were fit for that son of a bitch.

But the bit that mattered lay at the foot of the page – the directions to the Damned Forest where all of the cursed trees grew, their roots rotting the soil beneath them and their leaves filling the air below their canopies with toxic pollen that destroyed all life.

To reach the Damned Forest you must drink a dose of wolfsbane mixed with larkspur from a chalice scrawled with the runes halgalaz and raido, and carve the name of your deepest desire into your flesh, then follow the ache of your heart before it gives out on life itself.

So all I had to do was poison myself in a cup marked with the runes linked to trials and travel, cut my flesh open and hope the wind whispered the fucking answers to me. At least it didn't sound utterly insane or anything.

Fuck.

But I already knew that I would do it, my fate sealed the moment I'd laid eyes upon that book. No. My fate was sealed well before that. With the blade which stole the man I loved from this world and left me here alone to suffer through his loss.

I strode across the room and began to gather a pack together, the Book of Ether watching me silently from the bed as I thought over everything I'd learned from those books since we'd taken them for our own.

I had a plan. A plan which I could admit had holes in it and may well have been suicide, but I was hoping it just might work anyway. I'd been holding off on trying it, hoping to find something else in those ancient pages to help me, but I was done. Done waiting, done giving my all to everyone else, and done hungering for the impossible while my curse upon the stars went unanswered.

The winter solstice was almost upon us, the longest night of the year holding its own power which would aid me as the space between realms became thinner. I'd been studying relentlessly, learning all I could of the magic predating the stars' involvement, and I knew how dangerous what I was planning could be. But I'd given all I could to this fight as I was, and if I didn't give myself to my oath now, then I knew I would fall to ruin before I ever did so.

Sacrifice, blood, pain. I didn't care. I'd offer it all willingly and throw myself upon the pyre of my own destruction if it wasn't enough, because the world wasn't the place it needed it to be without him.

So if this was what it took to right that wrong, then I'd do it. Darcy had abandoned me, we were losing the war and there was little else left to me beyond this desperate, foolish hope. And it looked like I was going to give it all up for that chance, because without it, I was already lost anyway.

Scorpio
Gemini
Virgo
Cancer
Leo
Sagittarius
Taurus
Capricorn
Aquarius
Libra
Pisces

SETH

CHAPTER FIFTY FOUR

The war council droned on hour after hour. I'd given my opinion fifty times, but no one was listening because everyone was arguing, so now I sat with my face in my hands at the table, healing away a headache that was gnawing deep into my brain.

"The Court of Solaria could still be accessed by our magical signatures," Melinda was saying. "There's a chance Lionel won't have thought to remove our access."

"Prairie dogs on a gormless morn," Geraldine lamented, slapping a hand against her forehead. "Of course he will have thought of such a thing. He is a devious Dragoon, and we must not underestimate him. Nay, I say we attack with the full force of our army, strike like a thunderbolt and destroy his court in one, mighty buttock of a hit."

"That's suicide," my mom scoffed. "Do you have any idea how many protective spells and wards we'll have to break through before we can even reach anyone inside?"

"We have a legendary Vega Phoenix on our side. She can break through any wards," Geraldine laughed riotously, smashing her fist down on the table.

"You mean the same Vega Phoenix who returned on the brink of death from a fight that you decided to keep us out of?" Tiberius growled.

Geraldine opened her mouth to respond, but I shoved to my feet. "Shut up!" I barked, making everyone in the room flinch around to look at me, but I didn't have anything more to say than that. I just wanted them to shut the hell up. All this fighting was getting us nowhere. But when they realised, I had nothing to add, they went back to squabbling and I growled in frustration. Geraldine announced another brazen plan to attack the Court of Solaria, that involved a hell of a lot of flammable Faesine and a dangerous amount of fire, and my mom started lecturing her on her recklessness.

My gaze fell on the little white Tiberian Rat sitting on the table, quivering as he lay his body protectively over the items Tory had been given by Darcy and Orion. I moved over to them, reaching for the Rat, but he squeaked, raising a tiny front paw to try and fend me off.

"It's okay, little guy," I said, and he relented, letting me lift him gently into my hand. "I need you to shift and tell everyone what this stuff is, can you do that?"

He nodded and I set him down on a seat where he shifted into a pale skinned man with a shock of white hair. I flicked a finger and wove some pants for him out of leaves and he gave me a grateful smile.

He cleared his throat lightly, trying to get everyone's attention, but no one in the room had even noticed he was there.

"Hey! The Rat man has something to say," I snapped, and they all looked to me again, but I pointed at the guy on the chair.

"Um, hello, hi," he stammered, giving them an awkward wave and Tiberius placed his hands on his hips impatiently. "I'm Eugene Dipper. And I've been sent by Queen Darcy to, um, give you these items." He reached for the crystal first. "This is a Memoriae crystal. I think it has something to do with Phoenixes, um, maybe? And this feathery book, well that's also to do with Phoenixes, I think. Then there's – oh that's just a scrap of underpants – but this, yes, this is a ring. A special ring. Also with some memories, I think. Um, memories that can help maybe. And stuff that should be printed in the press."

Geraldine came bounding over, snatching up the book, the crystal and finally the opal with a screech like a dolphin. "This is a Guild Stone!" she cried, holding the opal up to the light. "Our great and magnanimous Darcy has seized another! I shall put it with the rest of the stones at once and protect them with my worthless life."

"It's not worthless," Max snapped, but she ignored him, pushing the items down into her cleavage, even the damn book.

"What's a Guild Stone?" Melinda asked.

"Hang on a moment, let me see those things," Tiberius hurried toward Geraldine, reaching for her tits, and she arched a brow at him before he jerked his hand back again.

"I command you to show me them," he boomed.

"Who are you to command a lady of the royal court? I do not answer to a silk smothered moth and never shall," Geraldine said, then pointed to the ring left on the table. "Seth Capella, I command you with the task of presenting our noble Tyler Corbin with that ring, can you manage such an important mission?"

"You mean, just take this ring to Tyler?" I asked dryly.

"You're right," she sighed. "It is far too much for your simple mind to handle." She reached for the ring and I slapped her palm away with a growl, picking it up and pocketing it.

"I can handle it. And my mind is very complex by the way."

She tittered at that and I glowered at her.

"We should look at those items first. Let me see that ring, pup," my mom said, moving closer to me, but Geraldine blocked her path, stretching her arms wide on either side of her.

"Nay! We have it in hand," she insisted.

"It's not in hand. None of this is in hand," Tiberius huffed.

The arguing instantly broke out again, drawing their attention away from me and the ring and I sighed, giving Eugene an apologetic look.

"We'll make sure all of these items are protected," I said. "Why don't you go get yourself some food. Find Washer, he'll assign you a room and fetch you some clothes too."

"O-okay," he said, getting up, but pausing before he left. "These things are very precious, Seth Capella. I know I didn't explain it that well, but...Darcy risked her life to save me, and I promised I would protect these items and get them into the hands of the rebels. You will make sure they're properly looked at, won't you?"

"Yeah, I promise, man." I said, patting his shoulder and he relaxed, his duties done as I dismissed him, and he headed out of the room.

I was drained as fuck, exhausted to my bones, no matter how many energy boosting spells I'd cast on myself. I'd had hardly any rest last night, watching over Tory and fearing she wouldn't pull through. But I didn't even want to sleep now, I just needed to think about something that wasn't the miserable realities we were constantly handed.

I leaned forward, resting my forehead to the cool wood of the table, trying to shut out the world and find a place in my mind that wasn't full of turmoil.

I heard someone take a seat at my side, extracting themselves from the heated debate going on between Geraldine and the ex-Councillors.

"You good, man?" Max asked, resting a hand on my shoulder in an offering to siphon away some of my stress.

"Sorta." I let my walls down and sighed as his Siren gifts washed into me.

Max flicked a silencing bubble around the argument and quiet fell over me at long last. A horrid image of Lavinia's nest slipped into my mind, and I jerked away from my hands, my chair flying backwards and my arms wheeling either side of me. Before I could cast air to catch myself, Max grabbed the back of the chair and slammed it back down onto all four legs, observing me with a frown.

"What the fuck was that?" he asked in a low tone. "I felt terror, revulsion, horror. What's happened?"

I swallowed thickly then leaned into him with a whimper, nuzzling his collar bone, and he drew me in for a hug.

"Seth?" he pressed.

"There was a demon vagina," I whispered into his shirt, the clean, familiar scent of him settling my rampant heartbeat.

"What did you just say?" he asked, trying to push me back so he could hear me better, but I burrowed in deeper, clinging to him like a new-born pup.

He continued to soothe me with his Siren gifts, and I shut my eyes again, holding tight to one of my favourite people in the world and letting him comfort me.

"Did you say the word vagina?" Max pressed in confusion.

Fuck, I had to tell them about the monster baby. It was important news. Big, scary shadow news. But every time I tried to let the words out, I saw that gaping black hole between Lavinia's thighs and watched her devour a Fae head right into it while something inside her…munched down.

"Max," I croaked. "I don't think I'll ever be the same again."

"Tell me what's got you like this," he asked gently, trying to prise me off of him so he could talk to me better.

I crawled fully into his arms, my bulk making him grunt as I slammed down onto his lap and hugged him tight enough to choke him. Just a friendly little choking.

"Seth," he rasped, his Siren gifts running into me deeper and making me relax.

I sagged against him, closing my eyes, and wondering if it would be the worst thing in the world to take a nap here. Leon Night was doing just that across the table, his head resting on his arm and a deep purr coming from his body with every breath he took. He looked so cosy. And I wanted to be cosy. Cosy and safe and free of demon vaginas forever.

Max shoved me back and my ass hit the seat of my own chair, making me yip like a scolded puppy.

"Talk," Max encouraged, and I sighed, giving in. I had to tell everyone about the monster baby if nothing else.

Max cast away the silencing bubble and Geraldine's voice filled the air mid-sentence.

"-cannot demand any such thing of the true queens' rebel army. It is their birth right to rule! And you cannot tramp into our marshes and assert yourselves as leaders when you have not even fought alongside us. You were not there when The Burrows were breached, you did not face what we have faced as a united front."

"But we would have, had we been present," Tiberius said in exasperation. "It's neither here nor there whether we fought in that battle. We're here now and we're asserting ourselves as leaders. We are the rightful rulers of Solaria, and have been for years."

"The Vegas have no experience in war," my mom added.

"Oh, and you do, madam?" Geraldine scoffed, flapping her hands dismissively. "The Vega Queens have fought arm to arm with their people, which is far more than can be said about any one of you!"

"I have been well versed in the ways of war," Mom said in a growl. "You forget

I served through the reign of the Savage King. I have seen far more bloodshed than you will ever know, and I have fought against insurgents countless times. And let's not forget our years of training. The Vegas have had hardly any formal education, how can you expect them to lead this army to victory when they haven't been taught advanced spells?"

"Oh-ho, but they have, Councillor Crumberry," Geraldine said with a smug look and Caleb glanced my way, a smile twitching his lips and mine twitched back. I couldn't exactly go against Geraldine's side of this argument. I once would have stood firmly on the side of my mom and the other ex-Councillors in this, but now I was a cat up on a fence, looking down at the bickering neighbours on either side, unsure which way I wanted to jump. Sure, I still wanted my seat on the Council, but I couldn't deny how much I admired the Vegas for all they'd done in this war.

From the sounds of how things had gone in that battle before Darcy had beasted out and Lionel had gained the upper hand, they had been a destructive force of nature tearing through their enemies. I didn't wanna proclaim that if me and the other Heirs had been there, we might have won. But like, yeah, I would have smashed some people up for sure. I hated that I hadn't been able to fight alongside the rebels when it counted most, that I hadn't been there for Darius when…when…

A whimper left me and Max stole some of my pain away, a heavy sigh leaving him that spoke of our shared grief.

"They had a sneakstick up their sleeves," Geraldine said haughtily.

"What was that then?" Melinda asked, folding her arms.

"Professor Lance Azriel Orion," Geraldine thrust her chin into the air. "He taught them as much as he could during our Burrow time. They have learned far more than you can comprehend in your cabooses."

"He's just one teacher," Tiberius said dismissively.

"Nay, they had the valiant Gabriel Nox and the lechsome yet loyal Brian Washer!" Geraldine crowed, kicking a chair aside and sending it smacking into Leon's leg, but he didn't stir from sleep at all. "Besides, Lance Orion is not *just* anything, you cantankerous crout! Unless you count that he is just and true. But let me tell you a-something of my Libra fangdangler. His moods may be as dark as a stormy day when he blesses us with his wise and boundless knowledge, but he is the greatest professor I have ever had the privilege of knowing, so I will be damned if I will stand by and let you besmirch his name, and blacken it like it is drenched in tar. Nary a day goes by that I, nor any one of your burly Heirs, do not cast spells taught to us by the man who's named after the prominent constellation which rests upon the celestial equator in the sky. The Hunter, Orion. Yes, he may be ravishing and virile-"

"What's that got to do with anything?" Max called to her, but she barrelled on without paying him any attention.

"And yes, his buttocks are firm enough to draw a wandering eye or two from every direction-"

"Gerry," Max barked.

"But I learned to sequester Lady Petunia's throbbings in class in favour of listening to his teachings, as all of us would agree was a challenge." She looked to Caleb, Max and me for us to confirm that, and I nodded several times in agreement before Max kicked my ankle and I started shaking my head instead.

Tiberius pinched the bridge of his nose. "We've gotten side-tracked. We must focus on our next moves, and frankly Geraldine, I am not going to waste another breath debating the merits and faults of the Vegas. They are not currently present. And as such, we must continue without them."

"I have something to say," I said, and everyone's attention turned to me.

Dante kicked off of the back wall where he'd been lurking like a menacing creature of darkness, his fingers flexing and drawing my gaze to the chunky gold rings on each of them. Our Faetalian Dragon friend was looking particularly gangsterish today, and that air of danger about him spoke of what he was capable of.

"What is it, amico?" he asked, his tone commanding the air.

"I saw…something," I said, pushing to my feet.

"Well bravo, young whippersnapper. Your vivacious description doth bring a tear to my eye," Geraldine said dryly.

"Give him a second," Max urged, and Geraldine nodded patiently, turning her focus back to me.

"Go on then, my chum," she encouraged.

I cleared my throat, eyes closing for a second and I winced as I found myself staring down the barrel of a loaded vagina. My eyes flew open again and I quickly slapped on a fake look of carelessness, sensing Caleb watching me closely.

"Lavinia has given Lionel an Heir. It's a monster. It's not Fae." I fought a shudder, my hand tightening into a fist at my side. "I think it's powerful, but I have no idea what it's really capable of. I only saw it for a second."

"In the north tower?" Caleb asked in a low voice, and I nodded briefly.

"By the stars," Melinda breathed, tugging on a silver necklace around her throat.

"Thank you, Seth." Tiberius inclined his head to me. "Is there anything else?"

"It…um…no," I decided, pushing away the sense of standing before that terrible muff.

It wasn't even like a vagina really. Vaginas were great. It was like…the anti-vagina.

I fell back into my seat and the discussion pressed on, soon escalating into an argument once again.

By the time it was done, I'd cast three wakefulness spells and eaten my way through four doughnuts that Geraldine had produced from the stars' knew where. There were a few extra nice looking ones which she was keeping aside for Tory that kept winking at me too, and I fully planned on playing my little snack hunt game with those later when she tried to snaffle them away.

Caleb looked tense as the Councillors trailed out of the room and Dante zapped Leon in the ass with a bolt of electricity to wake him up.

"Noooo. You had doughnuts?" Leon lamented, his eyes locking on the piece left in Dante's hand.

"You could have had them too if you'd been awake, Leone." Dante grinned, and Leon lunged for the piece he held.

"Give me that," he growled, and Dante relinquished it to him, laughing at the Lion Shifter as he scoffed it down like it was the only piece of doughnut left on earth.

Geraldine snuffled the extra fancy Vega doughnuts onto a shiny platter with its own motherfucking cloche before he could spot them, but I saw. I knew. And I'd soon be hunting that down in Tory's room when she hid it for me to find.

They waved goodbye and headed out of the room, and I pushed to my feet as Max drifted over to Geraldine. I was left alone in front of Caleb, opening my mouth to speak, but he got there before me.

"I'll see you in a bit," he said, then shot out of the room with a blur of Vampire speed, leaving my long hair fluttering in the breeze he left behind.

Geraldine kissed Max, clawing at his arms and mumbling something about him being a felon of a fish who she needed to raid her sea cave while she was all riled up.

"See you later then," I called to Max, but he didn't answer, all caught up in Geraldine's canoodling. "See you later!" I called louder.

Nothing.

I huffed, walking out the door, unsure where to go. I thought of heading off to find Tyler to give him the ring, but I knew he was with Xavier right now, and Twinkle Stud needed him while he was going through attempts to have his wings reattached. I seriously hoped they figured it out, and I decided the ring could wait until morning.

Right now, I wanted company. Needed it really. And there was only one person I desired the company of right now. Despite knowing I should give him space and respect the solitary needs of Caleb's Order, I found my feet tracking the path to our secret hideaway on our very own corner of the island, wondering if he'd headed there too. Hoping he had. And that he wouldn't turn me away.

As I closed in on the treehouse Caleb had cast up in the oak tree at the edge of the isle, I slowed my pace, spotting him sitting on the porch I'd added to the side of the structure.

His hair was wet from a shower and a mug of black coffee sat in his hand. The steam swirled up and was lost to the wind, and Caleb just stared unblinkingly at the horizon like his mind was elsewhere. He resembled a painting, the sharp slant of his cheekbones like an artist's brush strokes and the harsh grip of his fingers around his mug making the muscles in his arms swell. There was a paradox to his expression, a frown on his brow yet his lips tilted up ever-so-slightly, like whatever he was thinking about caused him both immeasurable pain and infinite pleasure.

I didn't move a muscle, knowing his hearing would pick up my approach soon enough and I'd break this enchanted moment forever, losing it like sand between my fingers.

I committed it to memory, truly committed it with the power of magic, painting it into the fabric of my mind and keeping it always. I wanted to remember him like this, distracted, not trying to be anything aside from exactly what he was. This beautiful creature with a heart made of iron and soul tarred with sin.

I'd have paid any price to glimpse inside his mind in that moment, but my best friend remained a mystery. Something that was seeming far more common lately than I liked. There was a time when I could have read his thoughts before he spoke them, the two of us always so strangely in sync, but those days were growing fewer and I feared what that meant for us long term. Were we ever going to be on the same page again, or were we destined to live in different chapters of the same book? Maybe one day we'd be torn apart into stories of our own, written in different languages.

"Are you going to join me or just stand there until the grass grows high enough to swallow you?' he called, lifting his head, and turning to me with a wry look that said I'd been busted from the moment I arrived.

I took an immediate interest in the grass he'd mentioned, dropping down to a crouch and patting at it to try and cover for why I'd been standing there like a lost lemon. Fuck, what now?

"I lost something out here," I said, not bothering to raise my voice, sure his Vampire ears would pick it up.

"Oh yeah?" he called. "What's that?"

My heart. To you.

"My…" *Think, dammit!* "Moon nuts."

Yep, that was what I went with. A solid cover.

"Your what?" he called.

"My moon nuts," I barked, rising to my feet and walking over to the tree trunk, brushing my fingers over it, the new magic I'd added not allowing anyone access in here but me, Cal and Max. Although neither of us had actually told Max about this place, even though he was definitely sleeping in a muddy crag of a room in the new palace. For some reason, we just vigilantly kept this treehouse secret and returned here late each night like we were hiding it from everyone.

Caleb was always here when I arrived, and I'd wordlessly curl into his arms and fall asleep. That was it. I knew he was doing it because of my Order needs, but the reason I kept coming back was because my sad, pathetic little heart begged me to do it. And I always gave in to that lump of muscle, letting it guide me to my doom and beyond.

The relief I felt every time I slid into bed with him was euphoric, like all day long tension was building in my muscles to the point of pain, and it only released the moment I lay down with him. It was like drinking sweet tasting poison night after night, knowing it would one day melt my insides, but in the meantime, I was addicted to its flavour.

Vines crept down from above, coiling around the tree trunk and binding tight together to form a ladder, and I climbed up to the porch, dropping down on the mossy swing seat and pushing my fingers into Caleb's hair to dry it with my air magic. It was something I did on instinct, an act I'd committed countless times for him before, but as he looked to me now, it felt like I shouldn't have done it.

I was crossing that barrier again, my intentions not pure anymore. I wanted him. Fuck, I had to play it off, keep my cool and harden the fortress I'd built around my emotions before he saw the truth. I'd always been touchy feely with the other Heirs, it was my nature, but now every touch I offered Caleb felt like a secret we weren't allowed to put a voice to.

He never told me to stop, but at the same time, he never told me to keep going. Not unless he needed an outlet, a moment of weakness and the press of a heated body against him. But he had Tory for that now. He hadn't initiated anything like that with me for long enough that I was pretty sure we were never going back there. Was he falling for her again? Had he ever really gotten over her?

"Thanks," he murmured as I dropped my hand, giving him a casual smile that said it was nothing. Only touching him like that was always something these days.

"That coffee smells good," I commented just to say anything, and in a flash of speed that had my head spinning, he vanished inside and returned a beat later, placing my own coffee into my hands while not having spilled a drop from either mug.

I took a sip of the milky, sugary concoction that was made perfectly to my liking and swallowed down the caffeine greedily. The war council had gone on long enough to leave my head pounding and tiredness wracking my bones, and the zing the coffee gifted me helped perk me up again.

"I didn't get a chance to tell you before, and I didn't want to bring it up in the war council, because I'm pretty sure our parents would have lost their shit – especially my mom – but something happened back at the palace between Orion and I," Caleb said.

"What do you mean?" I asked.

"Our minds sort of connected," he said with a frown. "I heard his voice in my head, and I could see through his eyes."

"Fuck," I breathed. "Like he could hear your thoughts?"

"Yeah, I guess," he said, and I scowled, envious of that, though that probably wasn't my top priority of things to take away from this news.

"Can you do it again?" I asked.

"I've been trying," he sighed. "I can't figure out how to make it happen."

"Can you try on me? Or is it a coven thing?" I asked, disguising the envy in my voice.

How comes everyone around here kept get fancy bonds and shiny marks? I never got any, and I'd been to the moon. Not even she had given me a little ring in the eye or a moon mate crescent behind my ear. *Oh, to be a moon mate. A Wolf could dream.*

"It's a coven thing, I think," he said, and I nodded, glancing out to the sea where the sun was beginning to sink. Another day gone. Another battle lost. Was this floating rock containing the last remnants of a dying faction of rebels? If we were all wiped out, would Lionel's reign stretch on and on, or would others rise against him one day?

I didn't like the idea that we were the only ones fighting, not when failure kept knocking at our door.

"We should get some rest," Caleb said, and my gaze flicked back to him, finding him looking at me intently, his navy eyes seeming to peer right through into the cavity of my chest where my heart was chanting his name. I mentally clapped a hand over its traitorous little mouth, but it was giving me away anyway, pounding frantically and surely noticeable to him. His knee knocked against mine, his fingers brushing my leg as he dropped his hand between us, and the want I felt for him intensified.

He seemed closer than before, the distance between our mouths withering, and I wasn't sure if it was me leaning in or him. Probably me.

My hopeless longing for him always made me weak, and if there was any chance of feeling the roughness of his mouth against mine again, I'd seize it here and now, leaving my agonising questions at the door and walking willingly into my ruin.

"Coooweeeee! Who resides in this barky abode?" Washer's voice made me straighten like he'd shoved a hot poker up my ass, and I slammed up my mental walls before his Siren powers could even get close to touching me.

Caleb was suddenly sitting on the far end of the swing seat, pushing a hand into his hair and looking like he'd never even been within an inch of me, but I could still feel the lingering heat of his breath on my lips. My imagination was fucking wild, but that had been real…hadn't it?

"Sorry to ding on your dangler," Washer cried, starting to do some lunges on the grass below the treehouse. He was in some skin-tight yoga pants that he'd gotten from the stars only knew where, and his chest was bare, the light blue scales of his Order form hugging his sun baked flesh. "Some of the rebels are gathering down on the north beach for a little celestial wangle. It's going to be a full moon tonight, and as it's December it'll be a cold moon! And better than all that, Venus is going into retrograde. That sexy, sultry mistress of a planet will be thrusting some of her sauce deep into our crevices, and while everyone is feeling a little blue, it should go some way to getting our spirits nice and limber again, all supple and warm inside us. How's that sound, boys?"

"I dunno…you made something kinda awesome sound gross." I grimaced.

I hadn't even realised it was going to be a full moon tonight. With everything going on, I'd lost track of her cycle, it was no wonder I was feeling extra drawn to Caleb today, my instincts were heightened as fuck.

"Don't be a silly sausage, Capella. We must keep pumping on and use the advantages the heavens offer us. Tonight, we can delve into the crannies of our minds and find the answers that will help us win this war," Washer said. "Venus in retrograde is also the perfect time to reflect on the loves of the past, the mistakes we've made in relationships, and it is a chance for rebirth. A time to start anew in matters of the heart. As an added bonus, we'll all feel a little bit horny." He laughed loudly, lunging deeper and making his pants tighten even more around his crotch so that we could see the clear outline of his cock and balls.

"By the stars." Caleb shoved to his feet and looked down at me. "Get drunk with me."

I was already nodding, excitement bubbling in my chest because fuck, after everything all I wanted to do was dive into oblivion and forget all of our problems.

"Yes, yes, yes." I leapt forward, licking his cheek and barking.

He scruffed my hair, smirking at me. "Good boy," he teased and either Venus was already toying with me, or I was just way too hot for my best friend, because my cock did a happy dance in my pants.

"Carry me." I jumped onto his back, and he hitched my legs around his waist before jumping straight over the balcony railing.

We whooshed towards the ground, and I threw out my palm, casting air beneath Caleb's feet so he sailed over Washer's head, and he whooped in exhilaration as we left our pruney professor behind.

We travelled fast across the island, tearing over the heads of a group of rebels battling in the training arena, then wheeling past the huge falcon-shaped nest Leon and his family were building which helped distract Gabriel from *seeing* anything except that fancy pile of twigs. I mean, twigs was severely underselling it. It was a nest to rule all other nests and I guessed that kind of shit was basically porn for a Harpy, so good for him.

My gut yanked and my mind snapped back to the moment when I'd seen Lavinia in her horrible shadow nest, birthing that hideous shadow spawn into the world while munching down on some poor fucker's head.

I clung to Caleb a little tighter, trying to fight off the memories, but they just kept coming for me like that demon vagina had. It had wanted to suck me into it and never let me go. It was like it had marked me for its next meal, that gaping muff thinking of me now, wanting to swallow me up into nothingness.

No, no, no, I can't die like that in the clutches of a monster vag.

"Seth, you're choking me," Caleb gritted out and I realised my arm was locked tight around his neck.

I loosened it, fixing my mind on the alcohol we were heading towards, wondering how much I was going to have to drink to forget about Lavinia's horror hole.

We arrived on the beach where the party was already underway, and I jumped down, jogging across the sand and grabbing a bottle of rum out of an apple crate someone had left there. Probably the same someone who shouted 'hey!' as I walked away with his rum, but such is life.

I spotted Geraldine out in the water, naked and facing the horizon, doing some sort of strange dance that a bunch of rebels, including Justin Masters, were doing with her.

"Max won't like that," I pointed to her with the bottle of rum as I returned to Caleb.

"Doesn't look like he's here yet." Caleb looked around and I flicked the cap off the rum, wondering where Max had gotten to – the last I'd seen of him it had looked like he and Geraldine were getting hot and heavy, but here she was, naked as the dawn while he was nowhere to be seen.

I took a long, long swig from my stolen booze, silently begging it to calm the whirlwind of pining/demon vag/grief which was clogging up my mind. It burned like a motherfucker, and I was halfway through the bottle when Caleb turned back and snatched it from me.

"Slow down, asshole," he said, taking a sip himself and my head swum already.

"Hey, Hadley!" Caleb called, spotting his brother sitting by a fire, playing with the flames, and creating different shapes out of them with his magic. My little brother Grayson and sister Athena sat opposite him.

Caleb's brother shoved to his feet, stalking away from the fire towards us, swiping a dark lock of hair out of his eyes, looking as pissy as if he had a pitchfork shoved up his ass as he joined us.

"What's up with you?" Caleb asked.

"Athena's being a bitch. Again. Nothing new," he said.

"Watch your tongue or I'll rip it out," I growled, squaring up to him.

Hadley huffed a breath, looking like he was really considering taking me on, and as much as I didn't want to beat the living shit out of Cal's little brother, I was more than willing to if he didn't stop being an asshole to my sister.

"Fine," Hadley said dryly. "Athena is being a female dog."

"That's better." I walked forward to pet his head, but he knocked my hand away with a growl. Angry little Vampire, he was. He didn't hold Caleb's relaxed demeanour; he was always tense like he was about to bite. "Play nice, or you won't be allowed to play with her at all."

Hadley rolled his eyes at me, but said nothing more, and I swept past him, leaving him with Caleb and breaking into a bound as I headed towards my brother and sister. I collided with them, knocking them both off the log they'd been sitting on and locking them against my chest.

"Argh, Seth," Athena growled, trying to wriggle free, but Grayson barked a laugh and nuzzled into me. I swear Athena had the least Wolfy nature in my family, you had to force cuddles on her half the time, but she always got squishy in the end. She fought her need for snuggles, but everyone needed snuggles.

I nuzzled both of their heads, holding them down and reminding them that I was their big brother and Alpha, so if I wanted a hug, I was getting one.

When I finally let go, Athena pouted, looking around as if she was worried I'd damaged her precious reputation.

"What's up, pup?" I knocked my knuckles against her cheek, and she batted my hand away.

"She's pissed at Hadley," Grayson filled me in. "Because she luuuurves him."

"Shut up." Athena threw a fist, slamming it into her twin's arm with a growl. "I don't love him, I despise him. He's like a flea that won't die."

"Athena," I snapped. "Don't talk like that. You don't want Hadley to die."

She pursed her lips. "Maybe I do."

"What's happened?" I asked in concern, shifting towards her.

Grayson whimpered, trying to nuzzle Athena, but she pushed him away, eyes firmly on the fire instead of either of us.

"Hadley found the postcard Athena got from her friend Levi," Grayson whispered to me as if Athena couldn't hear him. My heart clenched as I remembered the guy Athena had gone to high school with. They had been best friends for years, but then Levi had been killed in a hit and run on a family visit to Alestria, and Athena had never gotten over it. He'd sent Athena a postcard the day before he'd died, telling her about his visit but worse than that, he'd revealed his feelings for her in that message. And she had never gotten closure on the whole situation because he'd been fucking killed before she could even see him again.

"Shut up, Gray," she growled, but he kept going, lowering his voice more and shifting closer to me like that would make any difference.

"Hadley took a picture and put it all over FaeBook, calling out Athena's 'mystery lover' to come forward because Levi never even signed his name. But Hadley doesn't know he died, and Athena won't tell him," he whispered.

"Who died?" Hadley shot back to us in a blur, looking down at Athena whose jaw was grinding like she was turning her teeth to dust.

"No one. Get fucked," she snapped at him, rising to her feet. He was taller than her, but she looked just as fierce as she rolled her shoulders back and prepared for a fight.

"What is your problem?" he hissed. "Can't stand that I outed your secret little relationship? Who cares anyway? What's he got to hide? Is he a false king supporter?" Hadley sneered.

Athena threw out a hand, a blast of air magic tearing from her and hurling Hadley down into the fire.

He cursed, wrangling the Element with his gifts and shoving to his feet, gathering all of the flames into a ball and launching them at her. She leapt sideways to avoid it, but it singed off the tips of her hair and she gasped, patting the strands before they caught light.

"Why can't you just stay out of my life, parasite?" she barked.

"It's a small island, love, where am I meant to go?" Hadley tossed at her.

She bared her teeth, the Wolf in her rising and I wondered if this was going to descend into an all-out fight.

"How about into the sea? Take a long fucking swim to the bottom of the ocean and see if you can hold your breath for an hour," Athena said coldly.

Hadley released a harsh breath through his nose, though I caught sight of a wound in his eyes before he shut the world out again, his face an icy mask of hatred. He walked right up to her, hitting an air shield a couple of inches from her body as she glared out at him in defiance.

"Why don't you run along and find your lover boy?" he sneered. "Are you going to tell him about how you spread your legs for me the other night and moaned my name like it was your favourite star in the sky?"

Athena's face paled and I shot to my feet with a snarl.

"You promised you wouldn't tell," Athena whispered in horror, looking at him in betrayal and Hadley's jaw ticked.

"Who are you more ashamed more of? Me or your secret boyfriend?" he asked nastily. "Because maybe it should be *us* who are ashamed of our weakness for *you*."

"That's enough," I snapped, walking towards them but Athena shook her head at me, then turned and ran away into the crowd on the beach.

I caught the hood of Hadley's sweater in my fist before he could shoot off into the distance too, and he growled as he looked to me. "*What?*"

"Firstly, you talk to her like that again and I'll rip your balls off and make you swallow them one by one. Secondly, she doesn't have a secret boyfriend. That postcard is from a boy who died years ago. He was her best friend in high school, and that's all I'm gonna say on the matter because it's not my place to enlighten you. But if Athena ever forgives you for this mess, then maybe she'll tell you. I'm guessing not though. And if you don't apologise to her by dawn, I'll do the ball thing. Then I might break your legs too. And I might rip your ears off and feed them to a hungry dolphin. There's a lot of pieces of you, Hadley, and a lot of dolphins out there." I angled his head to the sea then clapped him hard on his back, sending him stumbling on his way after my sister.

He looked over his shoulder at me though, shock rooted in his features.

"He's dead?" he rasped.

"Yeah," I confirmed. "And she never got to say goodbye. So, who's the bitch now?"

"Fuck." He clawed his fingers through his hair then shot away from us in a blur, calling my sister's name. I wondered if he'd actually find her, considering she was seriously good at hiding when she wanted to. But then again, Hadley was a Vampire with an obvious taste for her blood, so he probably had a half decent chance.

I turned to Grayson who was swigging a beer, looking up at me from the log. He wasn't one for drama, more of a go-with-the-flow kinda guy. "Those two really just need to talk to each other."

"I dunno, man, Athena doesn't let go of shit easily," I said. "Sorry isn't gonna cut it."

"Yeah…" Grayson got up and looked over my shoulder, drawing my attention to Max as he came running down the beach. I turned to watch him go, powering along in a fitted black shirt and jeans, his brow furrowed, and his eyes set on the naked Geraldine out in the water.

"Gerry!" he shouted but if she heard him, she didn't show any signs, continuing to bob and jump in the water, her arms raised above her head as the A.S.S. members around her all mimicked her movements. "Put a bikini on at least!"

She glanced over her shoulder, her crimson hair plastered to her back and her eyes sharpening on him as he started wading out towards her fully clothed. "Then how shall my sweet flowers absorb the erotic power of Venus while she moves into her glorious retrograde, you silly seabass?"

Geraldine leapt into the air, doing a one-eighty spin and landing in front of him, huge tits bouncing and almost hitting him in the face as he made it to her.

Justin stood close by, his lips parted as his gaze watched the bobbing of Geraldine's breasts on the water and Max lunged at him with a ferocious snarl and a wave of water riding at his back, taking him down under the waves and disappearing into what was likely a watery end to Justin.

I chuckled as Geraldine shook her head and returned to her dance.

Justin's head shot above the water only to be yanked down again, his scream cutting off as Max stole him away into the depths of the sea.

Man, I loved that guy.

Caleb's hand landed on my back, and I jolted at his touch, knowing it was him before I even looked sideways, finding him tipping more rum down his throat. I snatched the bottle from his grip, splashing rum over his face and making him curse before my lips closed around the neck and I finished off the drink.

My thoughts were on the seriously fuzzy spectrum, and I smiled stupidly at him, letting the bottle slip from my fingers, my eyes catching on the moon rising just beyond his head, haloing him in its silver light.

"Stay right there," I whispered, taking my new Atlas from my pocket. I reached out, mussing up his hair a bit and arranging a golden curl just so, letting it fall into his eyes.

"What are you doing?" he asked through a smirk.

"Shh, let me work my process," I breathed. "Hold that smirk."

I touched the corner of his lips, his eyes lighting as I pulled it down a little, giving him just enough intensity about him, but also a look of pure sex appeal. I'd posed him for photos before for magazines, so it wasn't like this was any different. Except this photo might just be for me.

I lifted the Atlas, swiping onto the camera and reaching out again, holding his chin and shoving his head just an inch to the left, angled down ever so slightly, his eyes shadowing and the light behind him deepening.

"Perfect," I said, snapping the shot and grinning at the result as I showed it to him.

"You have an eye for that," he said, plucking the Atlas from my hand and tapping on FaeBook.

"No wait," I complained, wanting to keep that picture for myself, but he was already uploading it.

He slid his arm over my shoulders, pulling me close and snapping a photo of us and I flashed a Wolfy smile at the last second, so I wasn't pouting in the picture. He added it to the post and started typing something out, moving away from me so I couldn't see.

"What are you doing, Cal? Declaring your undying love for me?" I asked jokingly, a small part of me whimpering inside as I cut myself on my own words.

He snorted. "In your dreams," he said.

"My dreams are saved for more interesting scenarios," I said lightly, acting as if I gave no shits. When I really gave so many shits.

He finished posting and tossed me my Atlas, and I caught it out of the air. Caleb shot behind me in the next second, flicking a silencing bubble around us and speaking in a low voice close to my ear. "Like fucking one of your best friends?"

My throat tightened, threading itself into a knot, and I turned to him with a growl. He stalked around me, coming eye to eye with me with some dark emotion flaring in his gaze.

"If we fucked, you'd fall in love with me," I laughed, playing the best faking game I knew. "I know how to keep it meaningless."

Why was I saying that? In some pathetic attempt to reassure him he could have me and I wouldn't make it weird for him? By the stars, I was pitiful. But the rum was saying yes, and Venus was saying double yes, and my cock was in the infinity yes region, so here I was, promising I wouldn't fall in love with a man I had already fallen for some time around the moment he'd bought me a ticket to the moon, and I was hopeless to stop it.

"I'm well aware of that," he said icily, and I wasn't sure exactly why I was pissing him off, but it always seemed to go this way whenever we hooked up. Then again, maybe it was just because Tory wasn't here, and he wanted something fast and easy while she was out of sight. Seemed like a dick move, but then again Venus was at work tonight and it wasn't that simple to resist celestial urges.

"You don't get attached, do you Seth?" he pushed. "I'm just one in a long line of conquests, but the difference is, I'm not a simpering Beta or Omega, I'm an Alpha."

I reached out, taking his throat in my hold, and I was sure to anyone around us it would have looked like we were in the middle of a fight. But it was deeper than that, a struggle of wills, and all the raging sexual dominance between us clashing in the air.

"You don't know the first thing about how to please a man. You may have had plenty of girls in your bed and even made them come on command, but you're a virgin at this, and that makes me top dog in the situation. So if you wanna learn, then I'll teach you, Cal, but you'll have to give yourself over to me, and I just don't think you have the balls to do it."

I shoved him away from me, prowling past him and popping our silencing bubble, leaving him behind and not looking back but I made sure to toss a peace sign at the first guy I spotted just in case he was watching me go. The guy in question turned out to be a Nemean Lion Shifter who was in the middle of demonstrating the way he was able to lick his own ass, so that was just great.

My blood was running hot, and Venus's influence was intensifying as the night grew thicker.

I looked at my Atlas, checking out the post he'd dropped on FaeBook, the photo of us together taking dominance over the post as he called upon each of our fangirl followings.

Seth Capella: *Calling all my Moonbitches and Caleb's Calgals. Who's looking hotter tonight? #jointhehotsideofthewar #lameLioneldoesnthavethesecheekbones*

There'd been all kinds of magazine polls done on this very thing in the past for all four of us, but the answer always changed depending on where it was printed. Elemental Weekly had subscribers made up of all our fandoms, and Max's Maximinions had come out in force for the last poll I could remember. But the month before that Darius's Darihussies had smashed the rest of us off the chart. Caleb and I had been neck and neck one month, only to have him steal it from me last minute. I'd won two months in a row last year though, and did I ever let them forget that? Not ever.

My ego drew my eyes to the comments on the FaeBook post, and I mentally counted up who was winning so far.

Kathleen Goodwin: Well bend me over and call me a bridge between two towers – there's no way I'm picking! #ridemyhighway #Idontmindifyouhighfive #twowaystreet #bridgebros #twoHeirsinmythoroughfare #theresnotollonthisbridge

Sophie Ruddock: I WOULD CEASE TO EXIST IF I STOOD THAT CLOSE TO CALEB ALTAIR #hottestHeir #fang-girling #hecanAl-tearmeintwoanytime

Melanie Sivulovic: Sethhhhhhh ahhhhhhhh please please please reply to my comment!!!!! And OH MY STARS of course it's you. You're so hot. I'm crying. Ahhhhh! #Heirwiththebesthair #AlphaofAlphas #ifIhadtokillsomeonetokissyouIwoulddoitnoquestionsasked

Robyn Johnson: No one will ever compare to Darius. I bet even his corpse is hot #Iwouldbonehisbones #stiffforthestiff

Mandi Atkinson: THAT'S NOT FUNNY! DON'T YOU DAAAARE SPEAK ABOUT HIM LIKE THAT!! I WILL MEDUSA HAIR THE FUCK OUTTA YOU! COME FIND ME AT 112 SOLIUM DRIVE, I DARE YOU!!

Eve McGaughey: Darius's ghost actually visited me. I haven't told anyone about it yet because he told me not to tell. It was a wild experience. He came into my bed in the middle of the night and plunged his giant Dragon meat into my Fae flan #Igotghosted #deadmendoitbest #hecamebackandhecamehard

Ashley Mathews: I run a kink store called Kinky Farm and business is BOOMING after we introduced a new range of Pegasex dolls which include a blow-up Caleb Altair! We're always selling out of Calegasus glitter lube too! It's wonderful what he's done for the kink community #Orderformsexisnothingtobeashamedof #Pegasexdollsnowonsale #allCalegasusproductscomewithaCalebAltairspicyartprint

Nat Lenny: OMS!! Seth you look SO good. Can't believe you're taking time to speak to us lowly ants when you're all busy fighting in a whole ass war! #youresobrave #Iwillbeyourally #wecanjoinforcesanytime

Lucy Burfoot: I'm a #mareforAltair and I don't care! #whipmeandwatchmeneighneigh #getyourspangledangleinmywangle #hotforthetrot

Hannah Maye: I'd let you gobble me up if you found me wandering in the woods Seth #bigbadwolf #littleredridingwhore

The comments went on and on, and I tucked my Atlas away as I made it down to the water's edge, feeling marginally better for the attention. I pulled off my shirt to go and join Geraldine in her wild dance, wanting to hear more about this erotic nipple juice she'd mentioned. But before I stepped into the foamy tide, Justin flopped out of the water, dragging himself up the beach while fifty starfishes clung to his body, leaving bloody welts across his skin.

"They're eating me!" he wailed as Max walked out of the water behind him like a hot, mystical merman with an evil vendetta, his Siren powers spilling from him, and my stomach growled with hunger as the magic he was pushing into the starfishes hit me.

"Get him, Max," I encouraged, and he shot me a feral look before grabbing Justin by the ankles and hurling him back out into the waves. Max dove after him like some sort of killer whale hunting a squishy little seal, and I didn't like Justin Sealington's chances.

I waded out to join Geraldine, stripping off my clothes and tossing them back on the beach with my air magic as I went. I was soon in the row of Asses where I could just let my inner crazy come out, dancing in time with them as we gazed up at the sky where Venus winked at us.

"Wait for me, Venuslings!" Washer cried, running out to join the parade and he slapped my ass the moment he got close.

I sent him flying away from me with a snarl and a blast of air magic, but continued my dance, letting the rum take the reins and feeling my cock tingle from Venus's power. My nipples started tingling too, and holy shit, Geraldine was right. There really was something to this naked ocean rumba.

"Grant us your amorous gifts, milady Venus, and let them lead us to clarity by dawn that shall help us see the way forward in this war!" Geraldine crowed, her arms flying back and forth above her. "We shall romp beneath the moonlit sky and let you guide us to the crystal clear waters of the mind that only a good rollicking can provide!"

"Come onto me Venus!" Washer yelled, rubbing his bare chest, and tweaking his own nipples.

My nose wrinkled and I started to get the ick as he began thrusting to a beat entirely within his own head, the wet slap of his dick hitting the waves carving its way into my brain until it was all I could hear.

Nah, I'm out.

My dick was powerful enough without being charged by the power of Venus.

I turned back to the beach, my eyes automatically seeking out Caleb, but I couldn't find him among the masses. My gaze fell on Leon's friend Carson where he was sitting with a tattoo kit laid out beside him on a log, a Faelight hovering over the arm of a guy he was inking up. My mind snapped onto exactly what I wanted to do, and I strode towards the long-haired dude with his Disney tattoos and growly looking face, shoving the Fae he was working on onto the floor.

"My turn," I demanded, my words a tiny bit slurry but Carson definitely hadn't noticed as he looked up at me coolly.

"Hey!" the guy on the floor shouted and I looked down at him, snarling deep in the back of my threat.

"Problem?" I hissed and he realised who I was, his face paling as he shook his head and scampered away with the half-finished tattoo of Venus on his arm.

"I want a tattoo," I told Carson.

"No shit," he said. "But the shop's closed. You just lost me a good customer, asshole."

"His tattoo idea was as boring as a banana on a bridge. Anyone can get Venus marked on them, it doesn't make them any hotter," I said.

"It's not about what he wanted, it's about where he was getting it. Do you know how much pain a wrist tattoo causes?" he growled, and I frowned at that odd comment.

"So you like to tattoo in places that hurt?" I asked.

"Yeah, but judging by a prissy guy like you, I'm betting you want a tattoo of the stars on your chest, just like every other preppy asshole and his grandma like to get. Or maybe your mommy's star sign?"

"I'm not a preppy asshole." I grabbed the collar of his shirt in my fist and his eyebrows raised in surprise. "I want a tattoo between my shoulder blades, right over my spine. That painful enough for you?"

A slow, psychotic sort of smile spread across his lips, and I sensed this guy was hiding some serious danger beneath those Disney tats.

"Tell you what, Heir," he purred, eyes dark and deadly as he took hold of my hand where it gripped his shirt. "I'll do your tattoo, but I get to break a bone in your hand any time I feel like it. And you can only heal it when I'm finished inking you."

My lips parted in surprise, and he released a breath of amusement, knocking my fist off his shirt.

"That's what I thought." He stepped past me, but I slammed a palm to his chest to halt him, my decision made.

"Deal," I said firmly. Who needed fingers anyway? I wasn't about to start playing the flute. Unless... No. If I took up the flute tonight my power of seduction would be too great, I'd end up fluting every fucker on this beach straight into my bedroom like the Pied Pooper. I mean the Party Pipper. No, that wasn't it either... Well, anyway, I couldn't take the risk. No fluting for me tonight, not with the cold moon and Venus at work and not while my hair was looking so fucking good, the risks were too high.

"Well, you're either a stupid fucker, or you're less prissy than your ex-Councillor mommy. Come on then. We'll need proper light for this." He scooped up his tattoo kit and led me up the beach.

I followed him, wondering if I might regret this, but knowing the pain was worth it if it turned out how I imagined. So a few broken fingers seemed like a fair price to pay to the violent tattoo man.

Scorpio
Gemini
Virgo
Cancer
Leo
Taurus
Sagittarius
Capricorn
Aquarius
Libra
Pisces

GERALDINE

CHAPTER FIFTY FIVE

I threw my head back, my eyes locked on the bright and glimmering planet in the sky as I rolled my hips and sang to Venus where it hung above the full moon which was arcing across the heavens.

I could feel every ember of their combined power rolling into me, my core slickening at the heady weight of it as the two celestial beings worked me up into a certifiable frenzy.

Justin's occasional screams made my wick flicker too, and I bit down on my bottom lip while I watched a glimmering herd of Pegasuses soar across the night sky.

I strode further out and a pulse thumped through the sea itself, my eyes set on a glistening rock catching the iridescent light of the moon upon it.

I was a slave to the urges of my sweet Lady Petunia, my hands roaming wildly as the night fever took me in its grasp and the needs of my flesh blotted out all else.

We needed this, all of us needed it after more defeat at the hands of that dastardly Dragoon, but I wasn't going to allow our failure to darken my light. Oh no. The quests most sorely fulfilled were always those most worthy of song. And I held faith that we were yet to sing our victory to the very moon which rose over us now.

She waited for us and offered up this night of wanton abandon because she understood our need for such free revelry and release after so much loss.

It was a commiseration in group form, our grief and fear and sorrow combining beneath the light of the cold moon and stars as we were offered this brief respite from all of it, a way to process and move on before the woes of tomorrow rose their ugly snouts once more.

My feet made it to the rock and a wily smile took root on my face as I caressed the smooth stone, worthy of the most sinful of seabasses.

Only the cream of the Siren crop would dare mount such a rock on a night cast in moonlight and shadow so potent. Only him…and his lady true.

I called on my magic as I perched myself upon the rock, positioning the long tendrils of my hair to cover my bountiful bosoms and crossing my legs just so. Like I was a dandy girl, untouched and sanctimonious, simply awaiting a rapscallion to come plunder my sea cave.

I brushed a hand up the full curve of my thigh and an illusion spilled over me, a rainbow of Siren worthy scales appearing over my skin and glittering in the moonlight as I reclined upon my rock.

"Oh coowee," I called, cupping a hand around my mouth to steal the attention of my salacious swordfish and drawing his eyes to my offering.

Maxy boy kept one hand on dear Justin's head as he held him beneath the waves, his thrashing limbs bobbing up and down as the water crashed over him and he pointlessly floundered.

But I had little attention for the struggles of a drowning dragonfly, my seductive gaze fixed on the tempting trout I wished to catch with my net.

"I find myself in need of your masculine prowess, you scoundrel of a seahorse," I purred, my voice almost lost to the waves, but the darkening look in my Maxy boy's eyes made it clear he had heard me.

Our gazes locked and he prowled towards me, forgetting Justin and leaving him to bob on the surface like a lost cork, coughing and spluttering as he fought for the sweet taste of air once more.

I repositioned myself as Max drew closer, biting down on my bottom lip and parting my thighs to reveal my lavish garden to him.

"Do you recall the night we first transgressed like this?" I asked, watching the way his navy-blue scales rippled over his tightening abs where his shirt had been ripped asunder in his brawl, that dark skin of his begging for the touch of my tongue with every step he took closer to me.

"You know it drives me feral when you reveal your body to the entire world, Gerry," Max snarled, the lust in his expression tainted with a rage I wanted to feel right down to the cornels of my cockles.

"And you know mighty well that I must offer the fullness of my flesh to the sky when it commands it of me," I replied firmly, unyielding as always.

Max's jaw ticked as he fell still at the foot of my flawless rock, the sound of the Oscura wolfpack coupling like the animals they were filling the air for a moment as Venus seemed to beg us to join them in their rumpus revelry.

"I think you get off on riling me," Max growled, his eyes moving from my naked body to the water behind him and the beach beyond that, countless Fae out dancing and canoodling beneath the stars, all of them fully able to see us where we perched out here at sea.

"And I think you're a barrel headed barracuda who can't see the sand for the beach sometimes," I huffed, slowly trailing a hand down my side as I worked to lure him just the way his kind lured so many others.

"What does that mean?" he demanded, taking a single step closer to me, his powerful body rippling with a potent energy that made a wanton moan rise in my throat. I knew what I needed of him this night, and better yet, I knew what that jealous beast in his chest required too.

"That you wiffle and waffle over the display of my curvaceous form because you fear some other villainous cad might come claim what you seek to brand as your own."

"And why wouldn't I think that?" he demanded, his anger ruling his lust, the force of it spanking me in a tantalising way as he allowed his gifts free reign and tried to rile me too. "Every fucker and his pot plant looks at us and thinks we make no sense. Every prick in your Ass Club laugh behind my back and whisper about you using me before finding someone better suited. They look at me and see a passing phase, a sweet distraction, but not a threat. They don't see me and you as long term because you're a royalist and I'm an Heir. And they circle you like fucking vultures, hoping to swoop in the second you decide to discard me."

I sighed at his waffling outburst, my fingers rolling down my side once more, banishing the illusion of scales there and leaving me just as I was; a wild beast with a canine heart which thumped solely for the heart of this kipper. No matter how unsuited we may seem to have been.

"Then perhaps instead of pouting about it, and drowning silly dragonflies, you should show them that that isn't so," I challenged, my waters tingling in the most delicious way as I pushed myself up onto my elbows and gave him a taunting look. "Right here on this beach, before the entire world. Why don't you show them how thoroughly you've claimed my wanton heart and how deeply you've taken root in my loyal soul? They don't need to see the flappings of a jellyfish all a-bother with his jealousy. They need to see a shark claiming the blood that's his by brute force and masculine wiles alone."

"Are you…asking me to fuck you out here in the open where everyone can see us?" Max asked and by golly, if the moon had been just a touch brighter, I could have sworn his blush would have been reflected in the waves themselves.

"Good gander, do not be so crass," I gasped and he relaxed a touch before my wicked grin gave the game up and I moved onto my hands and knees before him, presenting myself in all my glory as I looked back over my shoulder. "I am merely suggesting you release that slippery salmon which is trying to burst your zipper asunder and take me like a garden in full bloom upon this most mermish of rocks, showing the entire world how my Siren side-piece can make this Cerberus howl."

Max gaped at me for several seconds and I arched my spine, knowing that Venus approved as I felt the brush of her light on my skin before I let my mental barriers fall and allowed him a glimpse at all of me with his Siren gifts.

I let him see himself as I saw him, a powerful, wonderful sea beast, come to plunder my rock pools and harvest the pearls from my oyster. I let him feel the power of my love for him and the ache my heart held without him close. I gave him my want, my need and my heart and he groaned as he let the purity of his love and desire for me spill from him too, until I could feel it more deeply than I could feel anything other.

He stalked me like the beast I knew him to be, and I moaned freely as his hands rounded my bumtous bottom. Max cursed like the blaggard he was, unbuttoning his fly and shoving his pants down as he finally gave in to this and his velvet shaft pressed to Petunia in a kiss of greeting.

"Yes," I sighed, arching back into him and he growled my name as he sank in deep, the feeling of him plundering me just as wholesome as I had known it would be.

"This is insanity," Max swore as he began to move in me, his lust and mine tangling in the air with our love for one another and I could feel that combined emotion spilling out from him as he lost control, taking me deep and rough like the feral creature he was.

Countless eyes turned our way as his power lashed from him, moans spilling from the lips of those who felt it and the writhing bodies on the beach growing in number as more and more Fae fell to the power of the Siren who rode me so skilfully, finding their own partners and joining us in our union.

"Oh, great galloping narwhals!" I cried as he took me deep and hard, owning, claiming, marking me before one and all as we made certain that everyone knew that I was his and he was mine.

Venus purred her enthusiasm through my veins as I fell apart for him with a warble of delight and he pumped faster and deeper as he gave in, forgetting the Fae watching us, forgetting his doubts and insecurities, and remembering us. Only us. Beneath the light of the moon, as one. Now and evermore.

Scorpio
Gemini
Virgo
Cancer
Leo
Sagittarius
Taurus
Capricorn
Aquarius
Libra
Pisces

CALEB

CHAPTER FIFTY SIX

I'd moved well away from the crowded beach, stalking along the coastline into the night where I might seek some semblance of peace and quiet.

I hurled a stone towards the sea with all my gifted strength, watching as it skipped the waves twelve times before sinking out of sight into the depths of the ocean.

The moon was watching me, mocking me, playing Seth's taunt on repeat over and over while I scowled at nothing and everything.

Who the hell was he to call me a fucking virgin? And why, if there was as little truth to his words as I was trying to convince myself, were they making me so fucking angry?

"Oh no!" a male voice drew my attention and I glanced up to find a herd of Pegasuses cantering down onto the beach, some in shifted form, some just butt naked and smeared with glitter as they ran in their Fae bodies. "Caleb Altair has found us! He's horny for the horn!"

I narrowed my gaze as laughter and whinnies spilled through the air, a couple of the herd eyeing me like they were hoping there might be some truth to that rumour while others shifted from hoof to hoof, looking ready to run.

"Fuck off," I snapped, striding towards them, and letting them see my fangs. The laughter stuttered out and a few released nervous whinnies. "And give me that." I snatched a bottle of gin from the closest guy, daring him to refuse me with a single look, but he just raised his hands in surrender.

"It was just a joke, dude," said the guy who had started this shit as I closed in on him. "But, er…" He glanced at some of the herd surrounding him and raised his chin as he made himself stand his ground, apparently the Dom in this herd. "In all honesty, there are a few of us who wouldn't mind one bit if you like a bit of glitter when getting off. And if you did…or *do,* then you could totally join us for a-"

"I have no interest in washing glitter off my cock for the next fortnight, so that'll be a no," I growled, shoulder checking him as I passed him by, reminding him without words that he was damn lucky I wasn't in the mood for a fight.

"If you change your mind, we'll be down by the cove," a girl called hopefully, and I turned my attention to her briefly. She was hot. Shit hot in fact, her lips full and seductive, her tits round and her dark nipples firming as she ran a hand down her chest to toy with them in what should have been a seriously tempting offer. Especially as one of her friends moved closer and began to touch her too.

But I felt no inclination to change my mind, despite how much easier I knew it would be to forget about this pointless infatuation with Seth and use them to help me get over it. They weren't what I wanted. But he only wanted me when it suited him. So the whole situation was fucked.

I shook my head in denial, turning away as they started making out with each other. I strode off through the sand, the tug of both Venus and the moon hard to ignore as the celestial beings made my cock throb with a pointless need.

I broke into a sprint, only stumbling a little as I raced around the island at my fastest speed, the world blurring then spinning as the alcohol I'd consumed did a fucking number on me.

A tree root leapt out of nowhere and I cursed as I fell sprawling into the dirt, rolling several times before crashing into a tree and cracking at least a few ribs.

"Ow," I wheezed, staring up at the sky above me, a low hanging cloud seeming to watch me, its form shifting the longer I looked until I was almost certain I could see a pair of outstretched wings, a roaring mouth. "Trust you to turn up just in time to see me fall on my ass," I grunted at Darius. Or the cloud. Whatever.

I pressed a hand to my side, frowning in concentration as I healed myself, letting the magic go a little further than my ribs to lessen the effects of the alcohol too and admitting to myself that I was probably a bit too drunk.

I pushed myself upright, shoving a hand through my blonde curls to dislodge the dead leaves and twigs that had gathered in them, then using my earth magic to remove the dirt from my clothes. The bottle of gin was gone, lost to the wind or the sky...or probably just rolled into a bush.

I was a fucking idiot who was now wandering around in the depths of the woods with a semi thanks to motherfucking Venus and the moon playing with my libido. My mind snagged on my best friend and the word virgin echoed through my skull on repeat.

Fuck him.

I forced my mind away from him and turned towards the heart of the island, trying to think of something else to give my attention to. Our attack on the palace had well and truly gone to shit, and I hadn't wanted to even think about it since leaving the war council, but I knew I was being a terrible friend by running around out here getting drunk while Tory sat alone in her room, heartbroken all over again.

I focused on her, shoving out the memory of Seth's mouth on mine and breaking into a run again. Venus wasn't having her way with me tonight. In fact, I was pretty much decided that she wasn't going to be having her way with me ever again. At least not so far as Seth Capella was concerned.

This whole thing with him was dumb and reckless and only served to crush me every time I caught him trading peace signs with random Wolves here, there and everywhere.

Maybe I should just go fuck around with that Pegasus herd. Make us even.

But I didn't falter from my path despite that completely rational thought, heading straight towards R.U.M.P. Castle in the middle of the island instead.

I sped across the drawbridge then halted, a spike of fear jolting through me as I heard a scream coming from the rooms Geraldine had created for the families of the Heirs.

"Mom?" I gasped, shooting that way so fast that I was hardly aware of anything around me until I was smashing the door to her and dad's private chamber apart with a blast of fire magic and came skidding to a halt in the middle of the room.

My mom screamed again and this time it really was laced with horror instead of the last one which I'd clearly not noticed had come from lust.

My mouth fell open in dread as I took in the mortifying sight of her and my dad half covered in blood from where they'd apparently been pouring a cup of it over their naked bodies, mid-way through fucking in some kind of sex swing at Vampire speed.

"Stars save me," I gagged, turning and shooting from the room while fighting the urge to scream myself. Their angry shouts followed me down the hall and I shuddered.

Dad was yelling at me to fix the fucking door, but no. Fuck no. I wasn't going near that room ever again. And I doubted I'd ever be going near my parents again either. They weren't supposed to have sex. They'd done it only the number of times it had taken to conceive me and my siblings, and they'd hated every moment of it. That was the lie I liked to tell myself and the one I doubted I'd ever be able to convince myself of again now that I'd fully witnessed them in their Vampire kink finest. *Fuck my life.*

Fucking Venus. Fucking moon.

I sped up the stairs, smacking into the banister and nearly sending myself flying right over the top of it before catching myself and racing on up. Yeah, I was still a bit drunk.

I barely paused for the guards who stood watch at the foot of the stairs to the royal chambers, just lingering long enough to let them see my face and confirm I had permission to pass. It still rankled a bit to have to go through that bullshit, but I'd accepted the rebels were predominantly royalists, and in our current situation, it seemed like the least of our problems.

I didn't bother knocking, knowing Tory likely wouldn't answer me regardless.

"I get it, you're feeling like shit and all kinds of miserable, but I need to help me bleach my eyes and to listen to me vent for about an hour solid on all the reasons why parents should be banned from having sex, so if we can just focus on the me issues for a bit then..." I trailed off, looking around the empty room in confusion before checking the en suite and closet to be sure she really wasn't here.

Where the fuck was she then?

I moved to the bed as I spotted a note on it, the paper folded over and the words 'hey asshole' written in Tory's no nonsense script at the top of it.

I flipped it open, my frown deepening as I read the message inside.

I've reached my limit with this shit, so I've gone to take my destiny back from the stars. Gerry, I love you – lead the rebels against the Court of Solaria like you suggested. Make that scaley bastard pay. The rest of you, try not to cry too much if I don't make it back, I was a mean bitch anyway. x

"Shit." I dropped the note and sank down onto her bed, reaching for her nightstand drawer where I knew she kept her tequila supply. This was bad. Geraldine was going to lose her fucking mind. The rebels might just lose their entire reason to keep fighting, especially if we couldn't figure out some way to get Darcy back here. How long was Tory going to be gone for? What the fuck were we supposed to do now?

It didn't escape my notice that I was now freaking out over a missing Vega, but at this point our fates had all become so tangled that the question of the eventual leadership of Solaria had barely been on my mind at all recently. All that really mattered right now was that our kingdom wasn't ruled by Lionel or his shadow bitch. The rest would all come after we assured that was the case – it didn't even matter right now.

My thoughts slipped onto Orion, and I ached for my coven brother with a new brand of longing. I couldn't figure out how to reform that mind connection with him no matter how hard I tried, and it just...fucking sucked.

My knuckles bumped against the edge of a box instead of the bottle of liquor I'd been hunting for, and I turned my eyes to the drawer I was rummaging through, my brows arching as I found a sparkly new vibrator sitting in it with a clear plastic window revealing the golden scaley sex toy within. I almost laughed as I lifted the box out of the drawer, the unlicenced 'Big D' merchandise printed with an old photo of Darius doing one of his best smoulders. I read the product info and bit back a smile.

Comes with one ultra-thick Big D Fae cock in russet red – complete with expanda-

pound technology and mega-vibe deep penetration – reach spots you never knew you had as the Fire Heir sets your body alight.

Or for the truly enamoured, go XL with the Glitzy Dragon shifted D – this mega sized vibrator is anatomically perfected with the shape, scales and golden glow of the Fire Heir's shifted form. Shaped out of glittering glass, this internally heated pound machine will have you screaming like you're being torn open right there in the bedroom – and maybe you will be. Also includes smoking hot Big D lube, for that slick grind you know he can find!

"Wow," I muttered, wondering why the fuck Tory would have bought this thing, then wondering if she actually had any interest in fucking his shifted mega-cock, then shuddering at the thought and realising I absolutely didn't want to know and hoped they hadn't…I mean each to their own, but a shifted Darius weighed around fifteen tons and I didn't wanna know how much of that was his cock. Surely they hadn't…

I turned the large box over and read the back of it with a mixture of amusement and irritation over the unofficial merch. Darius likely would have just found it hilarious, and I would have had to set my own lawyers on the case of ceasing the sale of it, alongside the rest of the range which were listed on the back of the box.

I lifted it into the light to see the thumbnail images of similar sets which were available for Seth, Max and me. Max's set included a vibrator which squirted and self-lubricated as well as a scaley blue option which played Siren songs while pulsing in eighteen different patterns. Seth's included a self-choking leash which would magically tighten around the user's throat, releasing upon…well, release. The shifted version of his looked all kinds of hairy with a giant lipstick poking out of it and apparently howled when the user climaxed. The lube in his set came with a Wolf tongue-shaped dispenser which was a nice touch.

I almost didn't want to read my own set's contents, but it was kinda like looking at a car crash and I couldn't quite convince myself to look away now.

Let yourself indulge in the Terra Heir collection. The XL vibrator comes complete with ultra-speed Vampire pulsation technology and deep pounding impact. Also includes a set of real biting vampire teeth, laced with a hint of duneberry oil to make your pleasure echo on. And if you're ready to get really wild with Big C's fetishes, this set includes a Pegasus horn double-glitz, XXL dildo and rainbow horn butt plug as well as glitter-dumping lube. And for an added bonus – we've thrown in a set of vine restraints grown organically by our local earth wielders, right here at Kinky Farm.

"For fuck's sake," I growled, trying not to imagine a load of random Fae getting themselves off while thinking about me and simultaneously ramming a Pegasus horn dildo where the sun didn't shine.

I turned the box over and found a note taped to the side of it which hadn't been opened yet, Tory's name scrawled across the front of it, making me wonder if she even knew this thing was here – but who could have gotten into her room to leave it for her? I seriously doubted Geraldine would have bought her this.

Curiosity got the better of me and I tugged the note open, deciding I'd blame Venus for it if Tory was pissed about it when she came back.

My dear queen,

Self-care in times of grief are of upmost importance, so I got you this gift to help ride you through this storm. A little pleasure can run oh so deep when your crannies are crammed with hurt, and I hope this teeny weeny bit of relief can help you through the dark and lonely nights.

Please don't hesitate to come dump on me whenever you need it. I will be waiting to plunder your innermost recesses whenever you want me to.

Your loyal servant,

Brian Washer

I should have fucking known.

A bang sounded beyond the door, and I tossed the Darius sex toy set out of my hands as if it had burned me, the box thumping to the floor face down just as the door was flung open and Rosalie Oscura half threw Seth into the room.

"Here's what you were looking for, cucciolo sciocco," she growled, flicking her ebony hair back over one shoulder as Seth stumbled against the wall and scowled at her. He was shirtless, his half-shaved hair dishevelled and trailing over his face in a way that made me want to brush it back so I could see the warmth of his brown eyes better.

"I should challenge you for that shit," he snarled, barely even seeming to notice me. "I should come for you and take your pack and make them mine, and then they'd have to listen to all of my wonderful advice and wouldn't be held back by your wily ways."

Rosalie growled, her eyes flashing silver as she stalked towards him, and I shot to my feet, getting in her way.

"What's going on?" I demanded.

She fell still, that hunter's gaze sweeping over me like she might just go for my throat instead, before she relaxed and shrugged, the picture of innocence all wrapped up in sin. That girl was trouble with a capital T, and I was beginning to think that neither Seth nor I had the first clue on how to handle her, let alone figure out her next moves.

"Your boy decided to invite himself to the orgy my pack is indulging in down on the beach," she said, curling a finger around a lock of ebony hair as she leaned back against the door frame.

"He...what?" I asked, my throat tightening on the word as something sharp twisted in my chest.

"They needed me," Seth snapped behind me, but I couldn't bear to look at him, my teeth grinding as I fought to hide my feelings even as they were crushed in his fist and scattered across the room on a wind as savage as he was. "I can't help it if Venus demanded my involvement."

Rosalie tutted loudly. "They would have welcomed your involvement, stronzo, but you weren't offering them your cock, were you?"

"What the fuck was he offering them then?" I demanded, my words practically a shout even as I tried to contain myself.

"Advice," Rosalie sneered, her narrowed eyes flicking over my shoulder towards Seth who huffed loudly.

"They needed it," he barked. "They were thrusting out of rhythm, and I only saw one guy who was touching more than one other person – you can't call it an orgy if it's just a bunch of couples fucking in a line. You need a level of crossover that they weren't achieving. I wanted to see a cock in the ass of a guy whose cock was eight inches deep in a third guy whose mouth was on a girl while she took it in both holes, while another two girls finger fucked each other and played with some side balls. It was a shambles!"

Rosalie gave me a flat look which seemed to say that this was my problem, and I finally turned to look over my shoulder at Seth.

"So you...weren't joining in with them? You were just trying to direct them?" I asked, piecing his words together.

"Yeah, I was trying to be an orgy conductor, I waved a stick and everything to make it easier for them to follow my orders. And they might have gotten somewhere if they hadn't all started bitching and crying, then calling their Alpha over to help them. *I* was helping them, Cal! They needed me! Their Alpha wasn't even joining in! They said she'd already gotten what she wanted from them, but what true Alpha doesn't stay balls deep until the final orgasm rolls through the group, Caleb? The Alpha should be the first and last to come with countless more orgasms in between, not just some starter to the feast who ducks out after six measly orgasms!"

Rosalie blew a breath out of her nose and gave me a pointed look.

"He told my pack that the reason I wasn't joining in was because they weren't performing to the necessary level," she deadpanned. "I don't need the headache of trying to console my entire pack while they all go ultra-sub for me in some pointless attempt to get me off, but that's what he's given me – I'll be dealing with the fallout from this for months."

"And you're only interested in Alphas," I muttered, remembering that about her as the memory of me and Seth both owning her body at once ignited in my mind, and she flashed me a grin like she was remembering that too.

"So, is that why you brought me here and healed away my damn booze?" Seth demanded suddenly. "Because you want him and me again? Is that what you want too, Cal? To change it up? Bring a girl back into the mix?"

"Fuck no," Rosalie said before I could utter a single word. "I had my fun with you boys, but non sono il terzo incomodo. Some new rebels arrived today from the mainland and there was a Manticore among them looking to fight the entire world. I'm planning to go see if he fucks as well as he fights. I just needed to hand off this stronzo before I go hunting." She pushed off the doorjamb, offering us both a wicked smile as she went. "Divertiti."

Rosalie shut the door behind her, leaving me and Seth hanging in the awkward silence remaining in her wake. I cleared my throat, moving away from him and pushing my fingers through my hair as I tried to get my thoughts back in order.

For a moment there I'd been about to lose my mind over the idea of him fucking her pack. I'd been ready to rip the world apart and damn the consequences over a betrayal which I had no right to feel. He wasn't mine and I wasn't his. This whole thing was just…messed up.

"Should have known you'd be here," Seth muttered behind me. "Is she cleaning herself up or just hiding under the covers?"

"What are you talking about?" I frowned.

Seth stalked across the room to the crumpled bed and whipped the covers off with an "Ah-ha!" before staring blankly down at the empty sheets.

"Where is she then?"

"Who?" I asked.

"Tory, obviously," he growled. "Is she moisturising her perfect tits or lubricating her vag or doing something equally feminine somewhere?"

"She's gone," I said, wondering why he kept going on about her tits so much recently. "I dunno when she'll be back."

I found the note she'd left for us and held it out for him, and he snatched it from me, his eyes tracking over the words while his frown deepened.

"She can't just take off," he snarled, crumpling the note in his fist, and tossing it aside.

"Who can stop her?" I asked and he looked at me as that loaded question hung between us, because there was a time when it would have been clear that any one of us could have stopped her if we'd wanted to, but now…

Seth's eyes narrowed and he shook his head suddenly. "I need to go," he muttered, stalking past me, his shoulder slamming into mine as he went, knocking me aside and sending a spike of pain through my arm.

I whirled around, a snarl rising in my throat automatically, but it stuck there as I spotted the dark lines of the new tattoo shining on his skin, the intricately beautiful design sitting perfectly between his shoulder blades just like we'd discussed all those weeks ago. It was a crescent moon with a wolf perched upon the curve at its base while a bat hung from the curve above, their faces angled towards one another, but they were just out of reach. Within the moon was a clock with no hands, only a ring of numbers and shattered cogs spilling from beneath it in a beautiful pattern.

"You got the tattoo," I said dumbly, because he obviously knew that already, but he stilled at my words, glancing over his shoulder at me with one hand on the doorknob.

"Yeah," he grunted.

"You added stuff to it," I said.

"Yeah."

"What does it mean?"

He shrugged, lips locked tight and secrets in his eyes.

I shot towards him, coming to a halt right behind him, so close that the scent of him engulfed me, making my lungs expand and that knot in my heart loosen just a little as I reached out to trace the lines of ink.

Seth's skin peppered with goosebumps at my touch, his shoulders rolling back, the muscles tightening and seeming more defined as he exhaled slowly.

"It's beautiful," I murmured, my pulse thumping erratically as I continued to trace the pattern, unable to stop myself from stealing the excuse to touch him.

"Stop," Seth growled, the threat in his tone forcing me to still, but my fingers remained against his skin.

"Why?" I dared ask, using the excuse of the alcohol I'd consumed tonight, even though I knew I'd healed myself of most of its effects. I started to move my hand again, but Seth whirled on me, snatching my wrist into his grasp and knocking me back against the wall, pinning me there with a feral snarl.

"I said stop."

I raised my chin, eye to eye with him, his lupine gaze whirling with silver and brown, the fury in him intoxicating even if I knew it should be terrifying. "And I asked why."

His fingers flexed where he still held my wrist, his jaw ticking and a noise somewhere between a whine and growl rising in his throat.

"You were an asshole tonight," I said, my muscles flexing at the memory of his words to me, the way they'd been burning their way through my skull incessantly since he'd spat them.

"I'm an asshole every night, Cal, you just like to forget that when it suits you or when it isn't aimed your way," he deflected.

"Does the mixture of the moon and Venus make you think you're some kind of sex guru then?" I bit out. "Because you seemed all too keen to tell me how much better you think you can fuck than me, and then you went on to try and convince others of the same thing. Were you going to join in with Rosalie's pack once you got done telling them how to fuck too?"

"What if I was?" He shrugged, pushing away from me and turning his back, prowling across the room like an animal, the light from the flickering fire making shadows dance across his new tattoo. My mouth dried out as I watched him walk away from me, the insult and arrogance making the monster in me raise its head.

"You didn't seem up for the challenge I gave you, so why not get my kicks elsewhere?" he added.

My blood pumped hot and furious through my veins, the implication in his question making me want to both punch him and prove him wrong. I shot towards him with a snarl, my fangs snapping out with the desire to remind him of exactly who he was baiting.

But instead of colliding with the firm plane of his body, I crashed into an air shield, the force of my impact with it breaking my fucking nose as I hit it at full speed and stumbled back.

A vine snapped around my ankle and threw me off my feet, and I cursed as I fell sprawling onto the bed, my own blood pissing down my face.

I healed my nose with a flash of magic, but Seth wasn't done with his little power display, and he snarled like a beast as he pounced on me. He caught my wrists in his hands, pinning them above my head as he straddled me, his hips grinding down against mine as he used his weight to hold me in place beneath him.

"You look good down there, Caleb," he taunted. "Wanna know how good it can feel subbing for me too?"

I bared my fangs at him as I tried to buck him off of me, my heart galloping in my chest. I was caught between fury and the thrill of this game which I knew neither of us would willingly lose.

"I think subbing suits *you* better," I hissed, yanking on my arms but finding them held in place with vines as well as his hands so I couldn't release myself. "You practically melted for me when I called you a good pup."

Seth scoffed darkly, his eyes flashing. "Nah, I just let you think that. I wanted you to feel good about yourself as the big, bad Vampire, but really, when it comes down to it, you're just a scared little boy, aren't you, Caleb? You thought you'd play with the Wolf and see if you liked it, but now you're in over your head, wondering if it's safer to go crawling back to your ex and her tits and-"

"Why the fuck are you so obsessed with Tory's tits?" I demanded, and he growled at me.

"Because I don't take kindly to being used as a distraction," he replied harshly, his abs rippling as he pushed his weight down on me harder, keeping me beneath him. "And that's what I am to you, isn't it? A little experiment with something new. One that gets you off because of the novelty of something different after years of doing the same vanilla bullshit. But deep down you are vanilla, Caleb, and I'm a fucking rainbow sundae which you can't handle aside from the odd lick."

"I can handle more than you can, asshole," I snarled, jerking on the vines he'd used to restrain me and snapping them with a surge of my gifted strength.

I flipped us over, knocking Seth beneath me on the bed and rearing forward, my eyes moving to his neck. But before I could lunge, he rolled us again, his hand gripping my throat and forcing my head back before his lips captured mine in a brutal, punishing kiss.

I opened for him, my spine arching against the mattress as his tongue sank into my mouth and my heart flipped over in my chest, rage shifting to lust in an instant, my mind scrambling with the change.

"Prove it," he growled against my mouth, his teeth sinking into my bottom lip and making me groan as I flexed my hips beneath him.

The words he'd tossed at me on the beach were echoing through my head. He'd taunted me over the thing that had been haunting me since I'd first realised how much I wanted him. Reminded me that he knew just as well as I did that I didn't know what I was doing when it came to me and him. I hadn't fucked a guy before and my fear over that and how many others he had to compare me with had been holding me back for weeks. But he'd also challenged me to let him teach me. He'd told me he would, and with the weight of his body crushing mine to the bed and the throbbing of my cock as I ground myself against him, I knew I wanted that more than ever.

My heart rioted with anticipation and exhilaration, but as the clouds shifted beyond the window, moonlight flooded over us, kissed with the glow of Venus's power where the planet hung in the sky high above the moon itself. I felt the desire they commanded swelling within me, my need for him surpassing my fears and insecurities as I just let myself feel that desperate plea of my body.

Fuck, I wanted this. I was so sick of trying to imagine it, of fucking my own hand while thinking about it, of watching him when he didn't know I was watching him and aching for the right words to say to ask him for this. But I realised that I didn't need words. He'd made it clear what I would have to do to seize this piece of him, and no matter how fleeting the importance of this was to him, I knew I wanted it anyway.

I broke our kiss, wrenching my head back and glaring into his eyes, the taste of him mixing with the blood which had spilled over my mouth as I licked my lips. Then as his eyes turned wary and his hold on me threatened to slacken, I steeled myself and lifted my chin.

My head fell back against the pillows, my gaze breaking from his as I focused on the headboard instead, his sharp inhale the only confirmation that he knew what I was doing, what I was offering as I bared my throat to him in submission, just like he'd told me I would.

I swallowed thickly as he remained unmoving on top of me, the weight of his stare feeling like an unholy judgement taking place over my flesh while he assessed the offer I was making.

Never in my life had I submitted like this. Not to anyone in any way. No one but him.

The brush of his mouth against my throat was a thrill and a sin, wicked pleasure coursing through me as his stubble raked against my own, his lips touching that most vulnerable, sensitive spot.

A tremor burned through my flesh at the feel of his mouth against my skin, at the knowledge of how easily he could tear my throat out if he willed it. I was his in that moment, utterly, undeniably, his.

Seth moved suddenly, the Wolf in him taking over and the sharpness of his teeth sinking into my skin stole a gasp from my lungs as I arched beneath him.

He growled as he bit me, the Wolf in him taking control while the Vampire in me riled against such an impossibility. No one had ever bitten me like this. Not once. Hell, no had ever bitten me at all aside from Orion, and this couldn't have been further from that reality if it tried.

I cursed as I ground my hips upward, my cock throbbing with need as I rubbed my crotch against his, feeling his own erection straining through his jeans as he ground down onto me too.

Seth released my wrist, his hand moving down the front of my shirt, flicking the buttons open so easily that it was as if they'd never been there at all, his fingers pushing between the fabric as he explored my body, his teeth sinking deeper into my neck.

"Fuck," I hissed, my cock throbbing with desperation, my hips bucking against his, the need in me making me pant for him as he took complete control of me.

Seth unzipped my fly, his hand fisting my cock while a low growl escaped him, the vibration of it echoing through my entire being. He moved his hand in a perfect motion, his thumb smearing the precum from my tip all over the head of my cock as he took possession of me.

"Wait," I panted, but he ignored me, pumping harder, his tongue lapping against my throat as that growl rumbled through him again.

I was so turned on that I was nothing but putty in his hands, falling prey to his desires entirely. As he bit down even harder, the command there was undeniable and my entire body arched from the bed as I came for him, my seed spilling in the space between us as he stroked me through every bliss filled moment.

Seth withdrew his teeth from my neck, rearing back and giving me a predatory grin, his teeth still stained with my blood as I panted beneath him.

"Good boy," he purred, mocking me with that fucking smile, his fingers gathering my cum onto them before he pushed them into his mouth and sucked them clean. "But don't go thinking I'm done with you yet. You wanna learn from the big, bad, Wolf? Then I'm going to make sure you get a really thorough lesson."

"Seth," I growled, a warning in my tone, but his eyes were dark, hard, like he was here and wasn't all at once.

"You want to learn this lesson or not, pretty boy?" he taunted, his hand moving to fist my hair. He yanked my head back, his eyes flashing with menace as he took in the bite he'd left on my throat.

I blinked at him, wondering what madness had taken hold of both of us as the man who was my best friend and deepest desire looked down at me like I was both of those things, and yet somehow nothing at all to him. He seemed angry with me even as the lust between us coated the air so thickly that I could taste it.

"You look like you want to hurt me," I said in a rough voice, and he cocked his head to one side, half a shrug shifting one powerful shoulder. "Are you gonna tell me why you're so pissed at me or are you just looking to hate fuck it out of your system?"

Something shattered in the dark aura he was giving off, a flicker of pain breaking through his gaze like the first light of dawn before it shuttered again so quickly that it was impossible to tell if I'd just imagined it entirely.

"I could never hate you, Cal," he muttered, moving backwards as if he was going to leave but I caught his wrist to stop him, though the look on his face told me plainly enough that he wasn't going to tell me what was wrong with him.

"I'm angry too," I said, jerking my head to one side and forcing him to release his hold on my hair. "Angry at the whole fucking world. For Lionel, our fate, for our terrible fucking luck. For Darius. For everything. But I don't feel like that when I'm with you. You make me forget, even if it's only for a little while."

"You make me forget too," he said, shadows passing behind his eyes as we shared that pain.

I pushed up onto my elbows, moving so close that I was inhaling his air, our mouths brushing without quite closing the fullness of the distance which parted us.

"Good," I spoke against his lips, and he released a low groan, his gaze burning into mine like he was hunting for the deepest parts of me, looking to claim them for his own.

I kissed him. It wasn't the brutal claiming kisses that we'd shared so far, more like a question and a plea, my soul laid bare in offering to him and his rising up to brush against it.

The moonlight spilled in from the window, and I groaned as our kiss deepened, my hand pushing into his hair, scraping over the shaved side of it before tangling in the longer length beyond. He was so powerful, this dominant, wild creature, set loose from a dream and come to rip me away from the reality I'd once known. I hadn't ever felt lust like this, the intensity of it stealing my breath and the need for more overwhelming me.

I pushed forward and he let me move him so he was kneeling over me, giving me access to the rest of him as I began to kiss my way along his jaw and down the side of his throat.

Seth pushed my shirt from my shoulders, and I helped him, rolling my arms back as the fabric slipped from my body. He cursed as he watched me kissing my way down his powerful body, licking the lines of his chest and abs until I took his cock in my hand and began to pump it for him.

I hesitated as he knelt up, making it easier for me to continue the descent of my mouth, his cock glistening with precum as I dropped my eyes to it. The words he'd spat at me earlier rose up in my head, tangling with the doubts and fears I'd been battling whenever I'd thought of doing this to him.

But as I raised my gaze to meet his, Seth gripped the side of my face in his hand, a growl of desire rolling through him which had my cock throbbing with a need for more already.

"Show me how you like it," I said, the words sticking in my throat as I forced them out, my skin burning with what I refused to admit was embarrassment, or fear of fucking this whole thing up, as the warm brown of his eyes turned to magma and the smile he offered me turned feral.

"I got you," he swore, his hips shifting as he looked down at me, the need in his expression bolstering my confidence as I dropped my gaze to his cock once more.

It wasn't like I'd never used my mouth on anyone before. I could do things with my tongue which had girls screaming within seconds. And yeah, this was different, but maybe it wasn't so different that I couldn't use any of those moves on him. Because the idea of Seth Capella panting my name in ecstasy had my blood pumping so fast that my hesitations were melting away and my need for him was overwhelming each and every doubt.

I leaned down and brought his cock to my lips, my tongue tracing a circle around his glistening tip as I tasted him and the curse which slid from his throat in reply urged me on.

I licked him again, then sucked the head of his cock into my mouth and circled him with my tongue.

"Fuck," Seth panted, his hand pushing into my hair and tightening in my curls. "More." He pushed his hips forward slowly and I groaned my approval around his shaft as I took him deeper, relaxing my throat as I worked to take as much of him into my mouth as I could.

The taste of him was making my entire body buzz with electricity, the noises he was making sending me into a frenzy of need as I drew back then took him in again.

Fuck, he was big. My fist pumped the base of his cock in time with the movements of my mouth as I sucked and licked at him for a few moments and Seth swore as he tried to hold himself back.

I took him into my mouth again and again, my head bobbing as I got used to the feel of it, my tongue exploring the head of his cock every time I drew back.

Seth began to tremble as I toyed with him, his hand fisted so tightly in my hair that it was dancing the line of pain.

"Shit, Caleb, I can't keep holding back," he panted, hips flexing with the need to take more from me, the urge to go faster, harder.

My fangs prickled at the sound of his desire, and I grazed the sharpening tips up the length of him before pulling away entirely.

"Then stop holding back," I commanded, licking his tip while holding his gaze, the moonlight illuminating his powerful body where he knelt over me and my cock stiffening at the sight of him, aching for more already.

Seth growled his agreement to that and with a thrust of his hips, his cock drove into my mouth, right to the back of my throat until it felt like I might choke on him, my eyes burning from the sensation. He drew himself out halfway then pumped himself into me again, growling with pleasure as I rolled my tongue up his length despite the brutality of his claiming.

He gripped my hair in both fists and drove me onto him as he fucked my mouth and something in me ruptured as the feeling of owning his pleasure like that turned me on so much that I could hardly take it.

I shifted beneath him, one hand gripping the firm muscle of his ass as I urged him on, the other fisting my own cock to gain some relief from the torture of my need for him.

Seth dragged his hips back and I called on my gifts, flicking my tongue against him so fast that he cursed again, my name breaking from his lips before he thrust right to the back of my throat once more.

That was all the encouragement I needed and as he pulled back I did it again, my tongue flicking and twisting around him as I sucked on his cock, urging him to give in to me and groaning my own pleasure as he exploded into my mouth with an echoing howl that marked his release.

I swallowed greedily, the taste of him intoxicating as I took every drop, pumping my own cock harder as I felt a second release coming for me, my body aching with need for it.

"Stop," Seth panted as he shifted back, his hand gripping my bicep as he forced me to release my hold on my cock. "I'm the only one making you come tonight. So keep your fucking hands to yourself or on me."

The Alpha ring to his tone had my fangs snapping out fully and I lunged for him, throwing him down onto the bed beneath me and sinking my teeth into the pulsing vein in his neck. Moonlight and earth washed over my tongue as I drank deeply, grinding my hips down against him so that I could feel the heat of his flesh against the throbbing head of my cock. I needed more. Fuck, I didn't think I would ever get enough of him at this point, and I wasn't sure I ever wanted to either.

"By the stars, where is the lube when we fucking need it?" Seth hissed.

I forced my teeth from his throat and looked down at him in surprise, my body aching for what he was suggesting more than I could put words to.

"There's some here," I said, my eyes flicking from him to the box of unlicenced sex toys I'd found earlier where it still sat on the floor.

"How would you know that?" Seth growled, his Wolf rising in his expression.

"Because I found this earlier." I leaned down and grabbed the heavy box from the floor, ripping it open as Seth coughed out a surprised laugh.

An enormous, golden Dragon dick dildo fell out and smacked him on the chest, making me laugh too before I tossed it aside and gave the box a shake to empty the rest of the contents onto the bed beside us.

I glanced at the bottle of lube without really looking at any of the other things lying around it, my mouth drying out at the thought of what we might do with it.

"Oooh, blind bag!" Seth cooed, snatching a sealed silver bag from under the vibrator which had been modelled with Darius in mind.

I knocked the vibrator off of the bed too, while Seth ripped the bag open with his teeth. His expression went from excited pup to insatiable Alpha as he took a golden butt plug out of the bag and held it out, rolling it between his fingers.

"How vanilla are you feeling, Altair?" he purred, running his tongue along the side of the sex toy and making my heart thrash in my chest.

"You tell me," I said, anticipation building within me as I watched him suck the entire plug into his mouth before releasing it again.

Seth didn't answer me, his mouth rearing up to claim mine before any fears or doubts could rise within me and ruin this. He shifted beneath me as he shoved his jeans off fully and I followed his lead as I pushed my pants the rest of the way off too before dropping back over him to reclaim that kiss.

I kissed him hard and deep, my fingers roaming from the curve of his knee all the way up his side, as the expanse of bared skin made my blood pulse with a need unlike any I had ever experienced with anyone else. I wanted to own him with that kiss and force him to submit to my claim on his soul. But of course, he wouldn't ever just let something be that easy.

Seth pushed me back until I was forced to stand, getting to his feet with me and hounding me back towards the wall, his mouth on mine the entire time as we kissed with a desperate, endless need that just couldn't be sated.

My spine hit the cold bricks and a couple of the flowers adorning the ceiling were knocked loose, falling around us as Seth ran the warm metal plug up the back of my thigh. I growled my approval as his other hand gripped my ass, his fingers slick with lube which I hadn't even seen him opening.

He kissed me harder as his fingers pushed between my cheeks, my muscles tensing then relaxing as I forced myself to give in to him, to follow his lead as he began to massage the lube into my skin.

He pushed a finger into me, then a second, grinning against my mouth as I panted through the unfamiliar feeling, a deep growl rolling through my chest as he massaged my inner walls.

"I'm gonna have so much fun teaching you all the things you've been missing out on, Cal," he taunted, his fingers driving deeper and stealing the breath from my lungs so that I had no hope of replying.

I reached for my cock as the ache in it grew to the point of desperate need, but Seth flattened himself against me, refusing me with a warning snarl which was accompanied by the metal plug reaching my ass.

Seth removed his fingers and I cursed at the empty feeling left by them. He kissed me then, tongue undulating with mine, our pulses falling into a blissful rhythm, and I moaned into his mouth as he slid the lube coated plug into my ass.

The toy stretched and filled me, the urge to tug it out again rising up fast before he drove it in a little more and a gasp tore my mouth from his.

"Fucking hell," I breathed at the exquisite fullness of it, my mind blanking for several seconds as I just leaned against the wall and let myself adjust to it.

Seth moved away from me as I stood there, panting and fucking aching for release with my cock a rigid beacon of my needs.

He dropped back onto the bed, squirting more lube onto his hand and letting me watch as he slicked his solid cock with it before coating his ass with it too.

"Come on then, Caleb. I dare you," he teased, reading the uncertainty in my face while he taunted me with his confidence.

I raised my chin at that look in his eyes, the knowing one which said he was in his element here and I was at his mercy. Because fuck that. He may have had plenty of guys before me, but he had never had *me.*

I shot towards him so fast that he couldn't even blink before I was on top of him, my weight driving him down onto the mattress and my mouth claiming his once more.

I hooked his powerful thigh over my arm and drove my hips forward, my cock sliding through the lube which coated him before I helped myself to more of it and covered every inch of me in it. This might have been my first time with a man, but it wasn't my first time doing anal, and if Seth thought he was going to be coaching me through every second of this then he had another thing coming.

I pushed his leg further up my arm, kissing him deeper as I angled his hips just right and the tip of my cock finally nudged against his opening.

Seth grinned against my lips like he knew just how this would go and I growled my defiance of that, thrusting forward and sinking deep with a masculine moan which said that he was entirely mine.

"Shit," Seth hissed as I began to fuck him, knowing how he liked it from all the countless stories he'd told me over the years. He wasn't some soft petal who wanted to be taken sweetly. He was all Alpha and he liked to fuck hard and fast.

I drew back and thrust into him even deeper, the perfect tightness of his ass making my damn head spin as his body hugged my cock with mind blowing intensity.

I pinned him beneath me, driving myself in and out of him, but he didn't just lie back and take it, his hips rising up to meet mine, his fingers biting into my ass as he urged me deeper.

"By the stars, you're so fucking big," he cursed, head tipping back with a howl as I pounded into him, taking and giving and losing myself entirely as the power of Venus and the moon collided, stoking the fire of this desire between us to new and unstoppable heights.

Seth rolled us so suddenly that I just blinked up at him as I found him straddling me, his hand wrapping around the girth of his shaft as he began to ride me, pushing down on my cock as he took control of the movements and fucked me even harder.

My breath caught as the new position drove the plug further inside me, pleasure radiating from the full feeling of it and making me pant his name.

I reached for him, staring up at him as I drove my hips up to meet every thrust, watching the way he pumped his own cock for me with a feral need which had me so close to finishing that I had to bite down on my tongue to hold back.

I didn't want this to stop, never wanted to untangle my body from his, or to feel anything other than that perfect tightness of his ass gripping my dick.

I needed more, all of him, and I snatched his hand into my grip before sinking my teeth into his wrist.

Seth howled again as I began to feed, and I wrapped my free hand around his hip as I helped guide his movements over me.

My body was shaking with pleasure, the need for release making my eyes roll back in my skull as I pounded into him again and again until finally, I was coming so hard that my entire being trembled with it. The hot splash of his seed spilled over my chest as he fell apart in time with me and the way he gasped my name had me undone.

I yanked my fangs from his wrist and captured his mouth in a kiss as he collapsed on top of me, the two of us coated in sweat and panting heavily through the aftermath of our worlds shattering apart beyond repair.

I pulled out of him, and he rolled onto the bed beside me, the two of us staring up at the ceiling as we let our thrashing hearts calm down in the wake of that mind blowing sex.

The silence stretched as we lay there, shifting from comfortable to tense without either of us moving a damn muscle.

"Right," Seth began but I cut him off.

"Can we just…not," I said, my eyes flicking to him beside me then away again. "You don't have to throw me the peace sign and walk out on me."

"I wasn't going to," he replied, and I turned to him with a frown as his eyes roamed over my expression and he cleared his throat. "I mean, the peace sign is just for blow jobs, and we fully fucked, so I'd have to add the okay sign too – you know because it makes a hole with your finger and thumb so-"

"Seth?" I sighed, ignoring the tightening in my chest at his flippant bullshit and rolling onto my side to face him.

"Yeah?" he asked, his eyes softening, like he felt bad or something, like he could see all the words warring to get out of my chest and pitied me for them.

I blew out a breath then gave him a push, so he was forced to roll away from me. "Let's just go to sleep, yeah?"

Seth didn't say anything for several seconds, his powerful body tense as he lay with his back to me, and I stared at the new tattoo decorating his skin. I reached out to brush my fingers over the ink and he released a long breath, relaxing into the pillows at last and letting me shift closer to him.

I pulled the covers up over us and let my eyes fall closed as I wound my arm around him and made him into my little spoon.

I could have sworn I heard Venus and the moon chuckling as I drifted off with Seth held tight against me, and a small smile pulled at the corner of my lips in reply.

Scorpio
Virgo
Gemini
Cancer
Leo
Sagittarius
Taurus
Capricorn
Aquarius
Libra
Pisces

SETH

CHAPTER FIFTY SEVEN

Wide. Awake. That was me.

Sleeping was the game, losing was my name.

I barely even blinked as I stared out the window at the cold moon dancing with Venus in the sky.

I'd fucked that moon, that beautiful, mystical moon with all her charm and wiles. But nothing. NOTHHIIIINNNNNGGG. Could match the way it had felt to fuck Caleb Altair. Moon craters be damned, I had experienced something transcendent, but hell did it feel temporary.

Cal was sleeping, or maybe he was pretending to sleep like I was, but I didn't dare ask, laying there and replaying it all in my mind again and again as the night closed in on dawn.

While the night was still here, it felt like I was lost to an enchantment that was bringing my wildest dreams to life, but I knew the cresting sun over the horizon would break the spell. Caleb would wake up, no longer drawn to me by Venus, and there would be nothing but stark truths to face in the morning light. Why was everything so much easier in the dark? Sex, secrets, snacks. All three were best indulged in at midnight. But the dawn always came, and I couldn't hold it off now even with all the will in my heart.

I lay there like that, languishing in the weight of his arm curled tight around me, afraid to break the spell of that moment until I could no longer see Venus or the moon playing together, the stars glittering faintly as the sky paled, stealing them away, giggling at me as they vanished.

I shifted a little, wondering if it might be best to slip away before Caleb woke up. Then, when I saw him next, I could just go on acting like nothing had changed. But fuck, everything *had* changed. It would be a bitch move, but I just didn't know how to deal with the serious conversations that needed to be had. I could see where the lines were drawn. Was I supposed to pour my heart out now and tell him that I'd been in love with him for fuck knew how long? Or would that send him running for the hills?

Maybe I should play it cool, keep hooking up with him here and there, never playing with fire too long and avoid being burned too deep. *Or*, I could hook up with him as much as I possible and embrace the inferno that was going to engulf me when reality came crashing in.

The problem with all those options was that none of them ended in a happily ever after. I had to pick a fate that would inevitably lead to my heart being obliterated, and yeah Caleb was worth the heartache, but by the stars, why couldn't there be an option D where this all worked out?

Haha...option D.

Caleb's arms tightened around me, drawing me harder against the firm planes of his body and I relented, snuggling back into him as the Wolf inside me wagged its tail contentedly. This here, was the reason I'd inked a clock on my back with no hands. I wanted time to stop whenever I was with him like this, no tick, tick, tick of the unavoidable passage of time that would lead to us parting.

What if you tell him you love him, and he says he loves you back?

A rogue voice spoke in the back of my head that sounded an awful lot like Darcy.

Dammit, I missed my little Phoen Dream. But the tiny version of her in my head was full of shit. Caleb was exploring his new urges in a safe space, AKA, me. And maybe there was *something* there between us, but from his side, I couldn't see it being love. Not ever if I was totally honest with myself. I was his bro. And beyond that, we were both duty bound regardless of how we felt about one another.

One day, if we took our parents' seats on the Council, we would have to provide Heirs of our own that upheld the long lineage of balanced power. We had to provide separate Heirs from separate partners who would keep our bloodlines going. And they had to be raised independently, their opinions their own and their bond with the other Heirs of their generation one of mutual love and respect, while they maintained their own independence from one another as representatives of individual houses.

Hundreds of years ago there had been tens of bloodlines with power equal to ours, but through inter marrying – and more than a few of the families being annihilated by their rivals – most of the powerful families had been lost. By the time our ancestors realised that our tendency to cross marry between our families was slowly carving down the number of bloodlines left with our level of power, it was too late to stop the decline in numbers. Laws had been put in place to prevent marriage between the most powerful bloodlines left in Solaria, but it had come too late. There had only been eight viable bloodlines remaining at that point, and then there'd been a war which saw the other four wiped out.

Luckily for us, the Capellas, Altairs, Rigels and Acruxes had been on the winning side of that war, but unluckily for me there was no way in hell that we would ever be able to be together like that. The rules were clear, the laws set down so firmly that there was no way around them and our responsibility to our kingdom was unavoidable. Fuck, I had never in my life wished to be rid of my title and the power I owned, but for him, I almost wished I could give it all up.

My mind was working on overdrive now for solutions while tiny-brain-Darcy cheered me on. And I was lost to the thrill of even thinking about a future where Caleb loved me enough to try and stay with me.

I supposed we could give up our position as Heirs to a sibling, but we were in the midst of war and Hadley, Athena and Grayson hadn't had nearly enough training to take up those roles. Xavier might be able to play catch up if he could be convinced into the Fire Lord position – and frankly, he probably wouldn't be getting a choice about it in the end.

But for Cal and I to give up our positions during this time of kingdom-wide conflict after we'd already lost Darius? That would be selfish as fuck, and more than that, it could shake the foundations of everything we'd built our entire lives, gaining favour with the people and preparing to rule. We were going to have to call on those very people soon, rallying them to our army publicly. We were only biding our time until we made that call official. Waiting until we'd gained a real foothold in the kingdom so that we had somewhere to summon them to. There were thousands of Solarians who supported us, who had been fully invested in our rise to power for years, and who would no doubt come to our aid if we could offer them protection from Lionel's tyranny once they'd been rallied.

No, abdication wasn't an option. And I would never ask it of Caleb anyway, even if I was somehow lucky enough for him to want me as fiercely as I wanted him.

We were a guaranteed train wreck, but right now we were still sailing along the track. So let the clocks stop ticking.

Caleb stirred and released a low hum in his chest, a sound that made me feel so safe, I never wanted it to end. The sun wasn't here yet, we still had a few more moments of dark. Maybe only a minute more, and it really felt like the apocalypse was coming the second the dawn came.

"Morning," Caleb said gruffly, his lips brushing the back of my neck as he shifted my hair aside.

The touch of his mouth set off fireworks in my chest, and I mentally danced under their raining sparks of light.

"Do you remember who you're in bed with?" I asked, a teasing lilt to my voice and his hands slid up to my pecs, cupping them and squeezing.

"Bessy, isn't it?" I could feel his smirk against my skin as he kissed me again and it sparked a smile of my own.

"That's my sister, you cad," I gasped, faking insult as he chuckled and ran his hand down over my abs, then lower still until he was squeezing my already hard cock.

"Cal," I said breathlessly, the light creeping higher in the sky like a loaded gun about to point directly between my eyes.

He ground into my ass from behind, showing me how turned on he was already, and that last night hadn't just been a dream stacked on a rainbow.

He leaned forward, his fangs scraping my ear and making me shiver against him, his fist beginning to roll smoothly up and down my length in slow, languid strokes.

"Any regrets?" I asked him roughly, reaching back to fist my fingers in his curls, and he nipped at the swell of my bicep as he drew me onto my back.

"I do have one," he murmured.

"Oh yeah?" I asked, tone casual, heart hammering painfully.

"I left the butt plug in," he snorted, and I burst out laughing.

"Dude." I shoved him off me, rolling him onto his front and reaching down to take it out for him, tossing it away between the sheets.

He remained lying on his front, one muscular arm curled up around his head while he peeked at me sideways. I dragged the covers down his bare body, admiring all that hard, silken skin. He was paler than me, skin like sun drenched moonlight whatever the fuck that meant. But it was true.

I rolled my fingers down his spine, over his broad shoulders and he watched me admiring him, navy eyes pinned on my expression. I'd seen his body infinite times, but never like this, fully relaxed, post sex, in a setting where I could just admire him.

My hand reached the base of his spine and I ran my palm over the firm muscles of his ass, kneading my fingers into his skin as I went, my eyes darting up to see his reaction.

"We're a bad idea," I voiced part of my fears, feeling the rising sun gilding my back in gold.

"The worst," he agreed, and a sharp lump rose in my throat. "Now get over here and kiss me, Capella."

I pressed my tongue into my cheek then leapt onto his back, making him wheeze a breath as I didn't even try to save him from the impact of my weight. Then I pushed his legs wider with my knees and reared over him, my cock pressing between his ass cheeks and making his shoulders stiffen.

I caught his hair in my grip, yanking his head around to steal a kiss from his mouth and grinding down on him. "Do you wanna find out what it's like to be a bottom, Cal?"

He tried to push to his knees, but I pressed my weight down to keep him in beneath me, and he snarled, fangs bared as I kissed him lightly with a taunting grin.

I drew back a little to see his expression and whether he might be tempted, the sunlight spilling between us and making me lose my grip on his hair. He looked celestial, like some otherworldly creature created by the stars, his curls turning to liquid gold in the light, and his eyes softening to two pools of the most intense blue I'd ever seen.

The words came to my lips unbidden, and I bit them back, the I love yous champing at my tongue and demanding I give them away. But what would he say? He'd probably run. It would be too much on top of everything else, and it would break this fragile thing we had between us. Despite that, I still wanted to release this truth in me. It was like a caged bird that had never spread its wings and was doomed to gaze at a sky it could never truly touch.

Say it.

No tiny Darcy – it'll ruin everything!

But the words were coming, my lips were parting, tongue shifting into that position for the L part of the sentence, while the back of my throat tightened on the I.

"Seth?" Cal frowned like he could sense some impending truth headed his way.

I was a car skidding on ice, and he was a gambolling fawn who'd stumbled into the road, about to be hit by a speeding ton of metal. I couldn't stop it. It was happening. I was no longer in control of it-

The door flew open, and I looked around in alarm, the car crash occurring in my body instead as my heart collided with my throat.

The worst possible people to ever walk into this room strode in, and I gaped in horror at my mom and Caleb's.

"Tory Vega, we really must-" Mom started, then her jaw fell slack and Melinda let out a shrill cry as she spotted her son pinned beneath me.

"Get out!" I shouted and Caleb reared back, throwing me off of him so I hit the bed at his side, before grabbing the comforter and dragging it over us.

But they didn't get out, oh no, they moved closer, eyes wide and stern expressions knitting their eyebrows together.

"Seth Capella," Mom snapped, clutching the collar of her blue shirt.

"What in Solaria do you think you're doing?" Melinda whispered shouted at Caleb.

Caleb sat up in bed and clutched the comforter tight to his abs, holding it high enough to hide his boner. Mine was sinking like it was a boat that had struck rocks, heading to the bottom of the ocean never to return.

"Do you have any idea of the scandal this could cause?" Mom barked, an Alpha ring in her voice that made me wince. "How many people know about this? Is Tory here too? Have the three of you been at it together or-"

"Tory isn't here," I snapped. "And no one says 'at it' - gah."

"No one knows," Caleb answered quickly, and I nodded in agreement to that, but Mom's eyes narrowed on me and she pointed right at my face.

"Don't you lie to me, pup. You can't keep your mouth shut about anything. Or is this the first time this has happened? Have you not had a chance to go blabbering about it yet? Oh stars, please tell me this is the first time."

"Yes," Melinda said hopefully. "Venus and the moon led you to each other's beds, right? That's okay. It happens to the best of us. Remember that time there was a Lunar Eclipse when we were studying at Zodiac Academy, and you, me, Tiberius and Radcliff let Hail Vega dom all of us?"

"Oh yes," my mom chuckled. "That was a fun night."

My jaw fell slack as she let that bomb drop on our heads and blow up in our faces.

"You fucked Tory and Darcy's Dad?" I breathed.

"And each other?" Caleb gasped, which actually might have been more of the shock here.

Melinda quickly cast a silencing bubble around us all, and swung the door shut with a vine cast from her hand. She sat on the end of the bed, and I shrank away into the pillows as my mom decided to sit right next to her too. On the bed. Right on the very mattress Cal and I had fucked on.

Oh my stars, this is not happening.

"We all have urges," Melinda said in understanding, looking between the two of us with a doting smile, like this wasn't weird as fuck. "And there is something wildly alluring about doing the deed with the other Heirs, what with it being so taboo, so scandalous-"

"Doing it?" Caleb blanched while I just begged the bed to swallow me whole.

"There's nothing strange about feeling a pull to the kind of power only our four families and the Vegas wield – nothing at all. So long as it's simply casual orgasms and kept private then it's fine," Melinda said soothingly, patting Caleb's hand but he snatched it away like he was remembering the fact that it had been wrapped around my cock thirty seconds ago.

"My Seth can never control the whims of his winky," Mom laughed, and heat flooded my cheeks.

I couldn't look at Caleb. Possibly ever again.

Why did she have to say winky?

"So tell me, was it just last night?" Mom pushed, looking me right in the eye and stars help me, I couldn't fight the divine force at work behind her gaze, and I started shaking my head.

"*Seth,*" Caleb snapped, punching me in the arm.

"I'm sorry," I breathed, unable to tear my gaze from my mother's concerned face as she turned to Melinda.

"This is not good," Mom whispered to her like we were no longer a part of the conversation. "It was one thing when Caleb was fooling around with Tory – everyone knew then that she would never take the crown and that it wasn't serious. But times are different now. We can't allow the world to see you as party boys anymore, dipping your dongles in whatever honeypot catches your eye."

"Kill me," I breathed. "Please, just kill me and let it be done."

"Antonia is right, Cally," Melinda agreed. "The kingdom needs to take you boys seriously now more than ever. They need to see you as unbreakable pillars of strength, they need to be assured that you care about propriety and our laws. Even a dalliance with one another will look bad now – everyone likes getting their wick wet, but the two of you are the future leaders of your bloodlines. You know the law. There's no future in it, and it will only look bad if it comes out that you've been spending your time between battles doing the sideways salamander, okay Cally?"

"Please don't call me Cally right now," Caleb said, burying his face in his hands and Melinda breathed a laugh.

"After what you burst in on me and your father doing last night I would have thought you'd be a bit less precious about your own sex life," she said and I almost asked the question before realising I didn't want to know.

"We already have one scandal to deal with after last night's antics, though I think Tiberius is already spinning the tale to cover the damage," my mom said thoughtfully.

"What antics?" I asked, instantly regretting it because it only dragged this conversation on for longer.

"Oh Max bent that Grus girl over a rock and gave her a jolly good rodgering in front of the entire rebel camp last night," Mom explained. "The footage is all over social media of course, but she is a very vocal advocate of the Vegas and was on all fours in front of an Heir so…the story was easily spun to look good for him – at least as good as a public romping can look of course."

"By the stars," Caleb groaned between his fingers and I could already imagine Geraldine reading that article and retaliating tenfold. Poor Max. But also, poor me and my poor boner because it was well and truly dead.

"Right, we need to do some damage control. Firstly, who knows? We need a list of names." Melinda went into politician mode, and I was pretty sure my dick deflated so far that it crawled up inside me never to return.

"Seth," Mom growled. "Start talking."

"No one knows," I lied, feeling Caleb's eyes on me now like he was wondering if I really had told anyone.

"*Pup*," Mom pushed, a warning in her voice. "I'm going to count down from three, and if I get to zero and you haven't told me, then I'm going to ban you from running with my pack for a week and I'll tell that strapping Oscura Dragon to refuse to let you run with the Oscura pack too."

"Mom!" I cried. "That's not fair, I don't have any other Wolves to run with."

"Well you should have thought of that before you boinked your friend," Mom said sternly.

"Don't say boink," I begged.

"Three," she started. "Two."

I pressed my lips together, refusing to give that answer.

"One," Mom growled, arching a brow at me. "Oh, you are being a naughty little pup. You will give me that list even if I have to get a Cyclops to pull it out of your head."

"There's no list," I pressed, but I wasn't sure if anyone in the room believed me.

Melinda spotted something on the floor and shot over to pick it up. If I'd thought this morning couldn't get any more mortifying, it somehow did as she picked up the XL Darius Dragon vibrator and looked to my mom in shock.

"Oh stars, this is because they're mourning their friend." She looked to us in sympathy. "Did you all used to romp together at King's Hollow? Are you trying to rekindle some of the magic?"

"No!" I cried, but Melinda didn't seem convinced, laying the huge, scaly, golden dildo on the end of the bed like it was some kind of sacred offering to us.

"Right," Mom said firmly. "You two need to get up, get dressed and part ways. No more of this. Imagine the scandal. We can't have this getting out. People are already shaken by the new power in Solaria, we can't have them thinking there's any threat to the bloodlines. If you two need comfort sex, then find it elsewhere."

"It's not comfort sex," I blurted, refusing to let her dismiss this, even as embarrassment nearly choked all words away from me. I felt Caleb's eyes on me as my mom's brows lowered and a dangerous glint of fear winked at me from her irises.

"Then what is it?" she hissed.

I opened and closed my mouth, a dumbass fish dragged from the water and dying on dry land. I couldn't speak. This wasn't how it was supposed to go. It wasn't supposed to end yet.

"It's nothing," Caleb cut in. "We were just fucking around."

"Yeah," I rasped as his words gutted me, slicing through the muscle of my heart and carving it up on a silver platter complete with a sprig of coriander as a garnish. "Nothing."

That word echoed on inside my skull and both my mom and Melinda looked seriously relieved.

"Well then, that makes this easier," Mom said, wiping a metaphorical bead of sweat from her brow and breaking a laugh. She patted my leg through the comforter and I cringed, shrivelling inside. "We all have our fun when we're young, and it's natural to want to try out different things. After being with less powerful Fae for so long, it can be thrilling to have a bit of nookie with another Alpha on your level. But we must be careful. There are other Alphas out there, ones almost as powerful as you, so you don't need to seek this from each other. Especially now while your public image is so important. Okay, pup?"

"Whatever. And I'm not a pup," I muttered, though I felt like one right then.

"Okay, Cally?" Melinda asked Caleb.

"Yeah," Caleb murmured.

"Hey, why don't you go have a romp with Jerry Bodkin's boy?" Melinda suggested to Caleb excitedly. "He's had his eye on you for weeks."

"Oh that sounds lovely," my mom encouraged, turning to me. "And you could have a threeway with Mr Berrick's son, Timothy, and his friend, oh what's his name again, Melinda?" She snapped her fingers as I gaped at them in horror of their efforts to set us up with their friends' kids.

"Egbert?" Melinda said.

"That's the one!" Mom smiled.

"No," I growled. "I don't care who Egbert and Timothy are, and I don't want anything to do with them."

Mom tutted like I was being unreasonable. "Well, if you want something a bit more taboo, Mr Berrick himself is single and quite the looker too. Do you like a bit of an age gap, pup? You always did say Professor Orion was – oh what was the word – dashing?"

"I didn't call him dashing," I balked. "Who the fuck uses that word?"

"I'm sure it was that – or maybe you said he was debonair," Mom continued while I willed the pillows to grow mouths and swallow me whole.

"Debonair?" I breathed, shaking my head in refusal. "That word's never left my mouth, ever."

"So where is Tory if she didn't take part in this rumpus? We need to speak to her," Melinda questioned, looking around the room as if she wouldn't have been at all surprised to find Tory had been involved in this somehow after all.

"Gone," Cal said darkly. "She left Geraldine in charge."

"Gone where?" Melinda frowned.

"She has something she needs to do. She didn't explain more than that in the note she left. I don't know how long for so your conversation with her will have to wait."

"That girl," Mom scoffed. "She can't just wander off here, there and everywhere whenever she feels like it, then place people in charge as if it's her right to do so. We are the Councillors, and it's about time everyone remembered that."

Caleb muttered something that sounded a whole lot like *ex*, but our moms either didn't hear him or ignored it.

"Good luck convincing the rebels of that," I said, and Mom clucked her tongue at me.

"You should be out there winning their favour, pup. You were always so good at that. Come find me later and we'll do some moral boosting around the island, how about that?"

I shrugged, non-comital.

"Well, we'll leave you to get dressed," Melinda said brightly.

"Gosh what's your father going to say about all this?" Mom asked with a chuckle.

"Don't tell Dad," I begged, but she waved me off like I was joking, heading out of the room with Melinda and the door swung shut behind them. I was almost certain I heard the name Hail Vega and the words 'tied us up' but I shut my ears against listening to another fucking word of that before I was mentally scarred for life.

Silence fell over us and neither us moved as we sat in the fallout of that nuclear bomb, not looking at each other.

"Well then," I said at last, shoving out of bed and grabbing my boxers from the floor, pulling them on. "I'm going to go shower in boiling hot water and see if my dick will ever come out of hiding."

"Me too," Cal muttered, and I glanced back at him, finding him standing and fully dressed, having used his Vampire speed to do so. "Like, not with you. In a separate shower. Somewhere…else."

I nodded stiffly and his mouth twitched like he wanted to say something more, but then he was gone, speeding out the door and leaving me there with the scent of him still plastered to my skin.

A horrid certainty washed over me that we were never going to hook up again, and I stood in the despairing light of the sunrise which devoured the last of that perfect night.

Time didn't stop, it never did.

Scorpio
Gemini
Virgo
Cancer
Leo
Taurus
Sagittarius
Capricorn
Aquarius
Libra
Pisces

XAVIER

CHAPTER FIFTY EIGHT

I was standing in my Order form in a glass tank just big enough to surround me, with my head poking out of a hole at one end of it. The tank was full of a light pink potion that had expanded overnight into a squishy solution that resembled marshmallow. I felt like I was floating in a cloud, my skin buzzing where the potion soaked into it. Supposedly, this was meant to help the healing process when it was time to reattach my wings, but after the first few failed attempts using different methods, my hope was beginning to fade.

My wings hung in a harness from the ceiling, a magical wind making them rise and fall in a flapping motion, the bony, severed edge of them covered in the same gloopy stuff I was bathing in. The room was fairly large, with a few worktables set around in the corners, the place part of the plain wooden building made for the healers to use.

Tyler and Sofia were sleeping on the floor in a bed of mossy blankets, naked after a night in the thrall of Venus and the cold moon. They'd wanted to break me out of here to join them, and I'd been seriously tempted too, but I hadn't fucked either of them since the time I'd failed to finish. I liked to watch them together, that was it, seeing their passion for one another giving me relief in a different sort of way.

I wasn't going to be their disappointing Dom, and until I was sure I had my head straight enough to fuck them right, I wasn't going to be tempted their way again. I needed them like the earth needed to turn, but I also needed to be a good enough stallion, worthy of leading our herd. And I hadn't felt like that since the battle. It wasn't just losing my wings, or even Darius or my mom, I'd lost something else out there on that field of destruction. Something intrinsic which had abandoned me, leaving me worthless without it. My confidence perhaps, or something deeper. A piece of me that couldn't be reforged.

"Ah, good morning, Mr Acrux." The healer, Iris Ganderfield, stepped into the room, her auburn hair unbrushed and a couple of leaves sticking out of it. One of her tits had escaped the confines of her tank top, revealing a shiny nipple tassel with a scorpion tail on it, the welts around her tit showing how many times it had stung her.

I cleared my horsey throat, my eyes darting to the thing then to anywhere else.

"Oh by the moon!" Iris cried, waking Tyler and Sofia up before she wheeled around to cover herself and yanked the thing off, tossing it in a trash can.

Iris turned back to me, her cheeks flushed red. "Sorry about that, things got a little wild last night. Shall we get started?"

I nodded and Tyler and Sofia slipped out of the room to get dressed while Iris used her water magic to rinse away the potion covering me, leaving my skin tingling all over. When she was done and the potion had swirled away down the drain by my hooves, she opened a door in the front of the tank and I trotted out, looking to her expectantly.

"Okay, like we did before, Mr Acrux. I'm going to cut into your shoulder blades and attempt to reattach the wings. I'll keep the area numb, so you won't feel it."

I snorted in agreement, and she moved onto a stepladder to one side of me while lowering the wings with a levitation spell. "Here we are now, relax please."

I did as she said, her fingers trailing over my shoulder blades, numbing the whole area before she got to work.

I shut my eyes, thinking of the sky, picturing myself soaring through the clouds again. I ached for it with all my being, and I focused on the Pegasus constellation, naming the stars within it and making a wish on each one of them to grant this reality to me.

By the time Iris was done, Tyler and Sofia had returned, fully dressed and looking hopeful.

Sofia moved to brush her hand up and down my nose. "Looking good," she said encouragingly.

"They're a bit singed," Tyler murmured, and I stamped my foot in annoyance. "But the dead feathers will fall out and you'll grow new ones," he added with a grin, slapping me on the shoulder.

"Okay, I'm going to lift the numbness spell now, Mr Acrux," Iris said. "Tell me if you can feel your wings."

I held my breath and sensed Sofia doing the same, her eyes unblinking as she fixed them on my feathers, and my heart squeezed at seeing how much she wanted this for me. I nuzzled her face, telling her with my gaze that it was okay if it didn't work. That we had to be prepared. But she released a horsey snort that said she wasn't allowing me to think negatively right now. So I did as my beautiful Sub willed and tugged on the final ribbons of hope in my chest, my attention moving to my shoulder blades where my wings were now fused back to the bone, still supported by the harness that hung from the ceiling.

"Easy now, how's that?" Iris asked as she withdrew her magic from me, the numbness evaporating.

My heart galloped as I flexed my shoulders, feeling for my wings and they moved in response, sensation starting to flow down the length of them. It was slow, and they felt seriously heavy as I tried to move them again, but they were really there.

I neighed with the thrill of reuniting with them, bobbing my head excitedly and Sofia squealed, throwing her arms around my neck while Tyler let out a whoop of joy.

"If the procedure has been successful, full sensation should return within the hour. If you want to quicken it up, I suggest you head outside and start practising your wing movements. Flight will be precarious at first, so your Subs are best to go with you, and ideally you should place an air Elemental on the ground ready to catch you if they fail."

I whinnied, letting myself believe this had actually worked at last and rearing up in elation.

"Do not shift back into your Fae form until you've had a successful flight today, Mr Acrux," Iris warned. "You must make sure they are fully reanimated first, or you could risk tearing them straight off again when you shift."

I snorted my agreement of that, folding my wings carefully against my back and trotting towards the door. Sofia ran to open it, and I cantered out of the building with her and Tyler on either side of me, desperate to flex my wings and ready myself for flight.

I galloped to the top of the hill ahead of me, stretching my wings wide, the weight of them easing as my muscles grew accustomed to them again and sensation returned even more.

"Well dingle my dongle." Washer sprang up from a patch of long grass to my left in a tiny Speedo with three very naked, very satisfised looking Fae left cuddling each other in the fronds. "Your mighty wings have been restored!"

"He needs some time to prepare for a flight," Tyler said in a tone that clearly meant fuck off.

"Well say no more, my boy," Washer said, moving in front of me, not getting the message. "Follow my arm movements with your wings, young Xavier. I am an expert in the bendings of the body. A little flexing and jangling should get them in ship shape order."

He began squatting, stretching his arms either side of him and flapping them like a bird with every squat he did. "Hup, then down. Hup, then down."

He was drawing the attention of a bunch of rebels at the bottom of the hill and a crowd began to form as they noticed my wings were back in place.

"Go on, Xavier!" a young girl called to me, her eyes bright as her mom swept her into her arms so she could see better.

A cheer went up and my cheeks warmed at the attention, my gaze moving back to Washer. Well, it didn't look like they were going anywhere. So…fuck it.

I started flapping my wings, mimicking Washer's movements and Sofia and Tyler gave in, joining him in the grass, doing the squats and wing flaps, sharing stupid grins.

I whinnied a laugh at them, glitter tumbling from my mane and my wings flashing in the sunlight.

An oooh broke out from the crowd, their cheers growing louder, more and more people showing up to join in. This was not how I'd planned for this to go. If my wings failed me when I took off, I was gonna go tail over tit down that hill and they'd all be there to watch. And considering my track record, that was the far more likely scenario here than me soaring majestically overhead into the sky.

Tyler whipped out his Atlas, aiming it at me and starting to record. "Today, Xavier Acrux has had his wings restored after they were viciously torn from his back by his cruel father, the asshole king. Lame Lionel displayed them on his wall like a trophy and Xavier seized them back in a daring act. Prepare for your mind to be blown, because I'll be sharing his memories from that wild night in the next article of The Daily Solaria. Long live the Vega Queens!" He shot me a thumbs up and I dragged my front hoof across the grass, readying to take off, adrenaline thumping through me.

"I've got you if you fall, bro!" Seth Capella pushed his way to the front of the crowd, and I spotted Max and Geraldine muscling their way through too.

"Oh my dear, Pego-brother!" Geraldine squealed. "Fly to the clouds and into the yonder. Leave a merry trail of colour in the sky and neigh so loud it stirs your ancestors beyond the Veil." She wiped a tear from her eye, and I lifted my chin, my chest expanding at all the encouragement.

"You can do it," Sofia whispered, moving forward to kiss my nose. "I believe in you." She smiled then stepped aside and nerves warred inside me as I prepared to try.

Please, please, please don't let me make an ass of myself.

The ex-Councillors appeared among the masses and Caleb too, plus Athena, Hadley and Grayson. If this was about to go tits up, then nearly everyone I knew was going to be here to witness it. The stars were probably giggling their shiny asses off, setting me up to make an idiot of myself again. But I couldn't back down now.

Antonia Capella began howling and the noise was echoed by her pack, Seth baying loudly and all manner of noise carried up from the crowd, roars, snorts, grunts and cheers clamouring together.

"Yah!" Washer cried, slapping me on the rump and I whinnied in alarm, taking off at speed down the hill.

Fuck, fuck, fuck a duck.

Don't mess this up.

Don't fall down.

Don't embarrass yourself.

Come on, this is your moment.

I flapped my wings, the feel of them responding drawing a furious, delighted neigh from my throat. The wind swept under them, offering to scoop me up into its embrace and fear dashed my heart, but I wouldn't let it have me. I placed my fate in the hands of whatever star was watching over me this morning and let them have me, kicking off the ground and angling my face towards the distant heat of the winter sun.

My stomach free fell, but I didn't. My wings flapped and I climbed, impossibly climbed, my hooves kicking, my tail swishing, my body rising and rising.

My wings flexed once more, fully responding to my will and I neighed wildly, happiness pouring through me like purest sunlight. I made it to the clouds then tucked my wings and spun, letting myself plummet towards the earth where the crowd was hollering, and Tyler was recording my every move.

Seth raised his hands, ready to catch me with air, but my wings snapped out and I caught myself, my hooves just grazing over the heads of the crowd and their whoops lighting me up inside.

I began to glow, all of me, head to foot sparkling like I was made of freaking starlight, and Sofia raced down the hill, stripping off her clothes as she went, tears of delight splashing down her cheeks before she shifted and took off, racing to meet me in the sky.

Tyler jumped up and down and Washer tugged him into a hug, plastering Tyler's face to his waxed chest for a second before releasing him and Tyler stumbled, falling onto his ass in his haste to escape.

I whinnied a laugh, tucking my wings and wheeling over and under Sofia, riding the wind while she chased me in circles.

Tyler tossed his phone down, stripping out of his own clothes and leaping forward, shifting into his beautiful silver stallion form, and flying up to meet us. Our noses touched and the three of us flew for the clouds above, my heart feeling ten times its normal size as I got to fly again.

We danced this way and that, spiralling and free diving, leaving trails of glitter behind us and creating a display of light and colour for the onlookers below. As I rose towards a swathe of fluffy clouds and streamed through them, my magic began to recharge and I whinnied in sheer joy, that noise echoing out through the sky around me.

The clouds shifted and the heavy beating of huge wings sounded, making me turn towards it instinctively, my ears twitching with the familiarity of that noise. My heart lurched and a glint of gold made me fly that way, seeking out my brother in the clouds, breathing in the scent of smoke on the air, certain he was here. Maybe not in any corporeal way, but the ghost of him was present, I could sense him everywhere.

I released a neigh, calling out to him, and I could have sworn a Dragon's roar sounded somewhere far, far away, in another realm I could never reach until my day of reckoning came upon me. But as painful as it was to feel him again, it made me happy too, sharing in this moment with him.

When I finally landed, breathless and full of warmth, I found Athena and Grayson running towards me, their arms wrapping around my neck.

"I'm so happy for you, dude," Grayson said, nuzzling my shoulder.

Athena stepped back, patting the soft space between my eyes and smiling widely at me. Hadley shot to her side and she glanced at him, some secret passing between them that didn't seem like any kind of secret at all, especially as their hands grazed and their fingers didn't part.

"Look at you," Hadley said with a slanted grin. "The Dom of all Doms."

Melinda Altair slipped past him with Antonia and Tiberius close on her heels, Caleb's mother looking close to tears as she stroked her fingers over my nose. "Your mom would be so proud of you."

My throat closed up and a little whinny left me as she moved in to embrace me, laying a kiss by my ear. "We're all here for you, Xavier. Every Altair is your family now. Okay? If you ever need anything, you only have to ask." She stepped back, and I found Antonia gazing at me with a tinge of sadness in her otherwise proud gaze.

"Catalina and Darius are watching you now, I know it," she said, and I released a soft noise of sadness, sensing she was right. I could still feel Darius somewhere close, eyes bright and his smile set on me, and my mother's presence joined him too, just for a moment, the touch of her hand grazing my cheek. But they weren't really here. Not in the way I needed them to be.

The crowd started moving forward, congratulating me one at a time, some of them touching my wings and murmuring prayers to the stars like I was some sort of gifted creature whose wings could bless them now. And as weird as that was, I let the rebels take some hope from me, my own reserves overflowing for once. Because maybe they were right. Fate was throwing me a bone, now I just needed to convince the stars to give me the whole skeleton.

Tyler and Sofia appeared beside me in their Fae form, pulling on their clothes and Sofia held out some sweatpants for me in offering.

"Do you feel ready to try and shift?" she asked, and I hesitated before bobbing my head.

I focused on the shift, letting it run over me all at once, my heart hammering uncertainly. It was natural though, and as I let my Order fall away, my wings easily went with it.

I released a breath of relief as another cheer rose from the crowd, a man in the back crying, "Golly! Look at that dazzling dongle!" as he spotted my dick piercings, and I took the sweatpants from Sofia's hand and tugged them on.

The crowd began to disperse, but Seth ran over to join us, a touch of darkness under his eyes telling me he didn't get much sleep.

"Hey," he said as he arrived, placing a hand on my shoulder before taking hold of Tyler's shoulder too and nodding to Sofia. "I need to talk to you all in private. I have a secret in my pocket you all need to see."

"Ew, are you hitting on us?" Sofia wrinkled her nose.

"Stars, no," Seth balked. "I'm in love with-" he half choked on those words. "The moon."

Well, that checked out.

"Come on." He jerked his chin in the direction of R.U.M.P. Castle. "Get moving."

He wouldn't answer a single question about whatever secret was hidden in his pocket as we walked to the castle, despite me casting a silencing bubble and assuring him no one would overhear us.

"This is top secret," he kept saying. "Very important. The most important task ever, some might say."

We finally made it to our room, and I used my magical signature to open the door, leading the others inside.

"So what is it, dude?" Tyler asked Seth, but the Wolf went running across the room, yanking the curtains shut and turning the lights down until they were almost off entirely.

"What are you doing?" Sofia asked in confusion as Seth went running back past her to the door, checking it was locked three times before binding it shut with vines, along with a wall of air.

"I think he's being dramatic," I said with a horsey snort of amusement.

Seth sprang up onto the bed, pushing a hand into his pocket and beckoning us closer.

"Are we absolutely, one hundred percent sure he isn't about to get his dick out?" Sofia whispered to me.

"With Seth, we can never be a hundred percent sure," I admitted. "But I'm like eighty percent convinced."

Seth took his hand from his pocket, his fist tight around something and he cast a Faelight above us, turning the colour of it purple so an eerie glow filled the room.

"Xavier Acrux, Tyler Corbin and Sofia Cygnus," Seth said mysteriously, waving his free hand above his fist like he was about to do a magic trick. "I'm about to set you a task that could change the fate of this war. It's the most important thing you'll ever do. In fact, once it's done, you may never truly feel satisfied by anything in life again. Even each other."

"Dude," Tyler laughed, and Seth reached down, pinching his cheeks so Tyler's lips pursed out awkwardly.

"I'm not your dude. I'm the master of fate, the weaver of destiny," he breathed. "What's about to happen in this room will go down in history forever."

"He's definitely about to get his dick out," Sofia whispered, and another snort escaped me.

"Silence, mare!" Seth crowed, releasing Tyler, and pointing a finger at Sofia. "Don't cheapen this moment with your dick mutterings."

My amusement broke into an all-out neigh of a laugh and Seth flicked his hand, bringing a bagel to him on a gust of air from the basket Geraldine had left for us this morning. He slapped me with it, and I opened my mouth to berate him, but he shoved the bagel into it to silence me. Damn, that bagel tasted buttery. Oooh, and had she added some grated carrot?

"You're all not taking this seriously enough. I want your most serious faces on or I'm not going to show you what's been hiding in my pants waiting for you."

Sofia shot me a look that told me she was still convinced Seth was about to get his cock out in some weird prank, but I shook my head. He wasn't gonna come in here and expose himself to his dead best friend's little brother…right?

I swallowed a piece of the bagel and took the rest of it from my mouth as Seth eyed our expressions.

"Seriouser," Seth demanded, twirling a finger so more bagels came flying at us, bouncing off our heads as we fought to fix darker and darker expressions on our faces. I was playing along out of sheer curiosity at this point, and I was pretty sure the others were too.

"Okay, that'll do," Seth said at last, then held his fist closer to us. "Behold…a gift from Darion."

"Who's Darion?" I breathed and Seth stood upright, jerking his fist away from us again with a huff.

"By the moon, you don't even know anything, do you? Darion. As in Darcy and Orion. Dar-ion. It's their couple name. Like you guys would be…Xavylia. And Tory and Darius are Torius-" His expression grew tight and he barrelled on. "Geraldine and Max are Maxaldine. And well, obviously we're not a couple and never would be or anything, but just for shits and giggles as we're the only ones left out, Caleb and I would be Saleb. Everyone caught up now?" he asked in frustration, and we nodded as one.

He thrust out his fist, his face becoming tense again and a brooding look falling over him.

"Are you pouting?" Sofia teased and Seth jerked his fist back once more, making Tyler groan impatiently.

"I'm not pouting. I'm just intense and interesting, Sofia," Seth said. "I'm making the moment more mystical."

"Can we just see what you've got, man?" I pressed.

"You're ruining the magic of it all," Seth complained. "Don't interrupt me this time."

We fell quiet in agreement, all of us clearly wanting this to be over so we could just see whatever the hell it was he was hiding.

"I present to you, the most enchanting, world altering thing you've ever seen," Seth began.

Oh shit, maybe he *was* going to get his dick out.

"Behold! The Ring of Doom." He opened his hand, revealing a plain circle of silver metal in the centre of his palm, looking unassuming and altogether uninteresting.

"That's it?" I frowned and Sofia reached out to prod it, but it didn't do anything at her touch.

Seth snatched it away again, shaking his head. "You don't understand the magnitude of this. I put it on this morning while I was in the shower, and you have no idea – no ideeea – what's in it."

"That's because you haven't told us," Tyler said with a snigger.

"You!" Seth rounded on him, pointing a finger right in Tyler's face. "You will be known from this day forward as the Herald of the Truth. You're gonna need robes, and a staff and some sort of fancy hat. It's probably best you grow a beard and make sure that beard is grey and long enough to tuck into your belt. And you'll tell the whole world about the brave and handsome Werewolf who brought you this ring, half dead from crawling his way across the land on broken legs with only one arm-"

"I thought I was the Herald of the Truth, so why would I lie?" Tyler folded his arms.

"We can work out the details later." Seth waved a hand. "Here." He took hold of Tyler's hand, jumping down from the bed and pushing the ring into it. "Put it on. It's a memory loop belonging to Francesca Sky."

"Orion's FIB girlfriend?" I asked, vaguely remembering her.

"She wasn't his girlfriend, Xavier. She was his BFF BJ buddy." He flashed me a peace sign like that meant anything then carried on. "Anyway, sadly, she died. Lionel murdered her real bad, but she got all these memories while she was in the FIB." His face fell. "It's awful. Fucking blood chilling, actually. But the world needs to see it. She got into Lionel's head and saw so much of what he's been planning all these years. She saw all the things he wants to hide from the world, and it's right *here*."

My jaw dropped, realising Seth hadn't been kidding at all. This *was* serious. Something that could really change the whole fate of the war.

"Oh my stars," Tyler exhaled, turning the ring over in his hand.

Seth cupped his cheek, making him look at him. "Get it all out there. Let the world see who he really is, Tyler."

Tyler nodded, his eyes gleaming and a hopeful smile lifting his lips. "I'm on it. I'll get the memories uploaded to my Atlas straight away."

Seth gathered us all into a group hug and a whinny left me that was full of rebellion, the sound echoed by my Subs while the Wolf howled.

As we fell quiet, Seth grinned demonically from ear to ear, looking between us all. "Let's shove this grenade up the false king's ass and pull the pin."

Terrifying evidence comes to light after heroic FIB Agent is brutally murdered by Lionel Acrux.

The days of speculation are over. The truth will out, and that time has come. The Daily Solaria recently came into possession of a memory loop belonging to the talented FIB agent Francesca Sky after she was killed by the false king. A picture of daring and courage like no other is being painted of Sky after memories were uncovered in a ring she used to store them, wielding the abilities of her Cyclops Order during her time in servitude to the king.

Not only did Sky save over seventy-eight Fae from being sent to the Nebular Inquisition Centres, she was able to uncover the secrets hidden beyond the walls of said centres. And it is not for the faint of heart – click here to watch the memories of the centres Sky visited during the king's reign.

Beyond this, shocking revelations have come to light within memories stolen from the king himself. In Sky's final moments, she used her Cyclops gifts to break into his mind and seek out the truth for all to see...

The depths of Lionel Acrux's plotting has known no bounds for many years, and the truth I am about to reveal to you will rewrite history itself.

In chilling moments seen through Lionel Acrux's eyes, countless memories can be watched here *of him using an outlawed magic called Dark Coercion upon the Savage King himself, Hail Vega. It seems, the Savage King was not savage at all, but a victim of Lionel Acrux's manipulation, abusing dark magic to bind people to his will. Hail Vega was not the first victim of the false king, and he was by no means the last either. The memories contained in Lionel's mind have unlocked new truths that will rattle the foundations of his reign.*

It has become clear that Lionel was responsible for his older brother Radcliff's death, an Heir who was destined for greatness and was stolen away in a callous act of unFae cowardice. In a harrowing memory seen here, *Lionel trapped a norian wasp against Radcliff's chest during his sleep, and held it there, restraining his brother with air magic until he succumbed to the lethal effects of its sting.*

It was Lionel's first murder, but not his last. More of his brutality can be viewed here, *and a list of his victims can be found* here, *with deepest condolences going to the families of his victims – we hope that at least some peace can be found in knowing the truth. Please be advised that some of these memories are difficult to watch, and have remained uncensored to ensure nothing of the truth is left unexposed.*

It must be mentioned, that the memory loop was able to come into our possession thanks to two brave souls who are currently prisoners of the false king himself. Memories from Sky show both Darcy Vega and her Elysian Mate Lance Orion, trapped in a cage of night iron in the throne room at the Palace of Souls, the haunted look in their eyes telling of what they have suffered through during their incarceration. We pray to the stars that they remain safe, and will soon find a way free of the false king's captivity.

With thousands of memories to work through, the team at The Daily Solaria will likely discover more secrets yet. And you will of course be the first to know about them. We apologise for any distress this article may cause, but it is our duty to expose the truth, and we will not rest until we see the false king fall.

It's time to rise, Solaria. For the good of our kingdom.

Long Live the Vega Queens.
-Tyler Corbin

Scorpio
Gemini
Virgo
Cancer
Aries
Leo
Sagittarius
Taurus
Capricorn
Aquarius
Libra
Pisces

LIONEL

CHAPTER FIFTY NINE

"How bad is it, Vard?" I growled, standing in front of the red doors which would lead me to the balcony overlooking the crowd outside the Court of Solaria. The room I was in was huge, large enough to accommodate my Dragon form at least three times over, and there were grand paintings on the walls depicting my succession to greatness. Floorboards ran the length of the space and opulent white couches sat around it, along with golden statues of my kind that I had brought here.

"Um," Vard hesitated, moving to straighten my tie, and I slapped his hands away, grabbing his shirt in my fist then yanking him closer as smoke seeped between my bared teeth.

"How. Bad. Is. It?" I snarled.

"Do you want me to sugar coat it?" he stammered, his good eye wild with terror.

"No. I do not want you to sugar coat it, you fool. I want the truth. The cold, hard, fucking truth. And if you do not give it to me in the next three seconds, I will dismember you and feed you to Lavinia."

"A-alright, sire," he gave in, dropping to his knees and bowing his head in submission. "The kingdom is in uproar, Your Highness. The people are losing faith in you. They want answers. They cannot easily deny the truth that has been presented to them among Francesca Sky's memories."

A growl rolled through my chest, and I contained the urge to break some bones in my snivelling Seer's body. At least until I returned to the palace later tonight.

That bitch had caused me more trouble than I had ever imagined possible, and the Vega girl I kept caged had secured this fate. She must have gotten that memory loop out of my palace during the attack, handing it to her disgusting allies.

I seethed, rage blossoming through me like a cold, dark winter that would never end.

But I pushed a hand over my hair and fixed my features into concern, the face of a man who would not be so easily accused of murder.

"Open the doors," I commanded and Vard scrambled that way, pulling them wide for me.

I raised my chin, walking out onto the balcony and a tumult of angry shouts slammed against me. The crowd was lit by Faelights and the press were there, angling their cameras at me, waiting to capture every moment of this.

I raised my hands, asking for silence and the crowd simmered down. My heart was thundering out a shaky beat in my chest, but I didn't let it show on my face. I had to be solemn, I had to regain their trust, or my reign could come under threat.

"Friends," I called, amplifying my voice with a flash of magic, a round of boos coming in response and unsettling me. I moved forward, curling my hands over the railing and keeping my perfectly crafted mask in face. "Listen. Do you not owe your humble king a moment to speak in response to the despicable lies being spread about me?"

People frowned, sharing looks and the press lapped it up, one of the cameramen even licking his lips as I felt that lens zoom in on me.

"Yes, we must let our king explain," Gus Vulpecula moved to the front of the cordoned off area where many of my Dragons were positioned to hold the crowd back. "He will quell our fears! Let him speak!"

"Yes, let him speak!" someone else called, and the murmurs hushed down again.

I wetted my mouth and prepared to give them the speech I had been preparing from the moment I'd found about what that fucking filthy Pegasus had printed about me in The Daily Solaria. This was a hiccup, nothing more. I could handle it. I *would* handle it.

Sweat began to collect on my brow and I tried to loosen the tie at my throat a little, the quiet pressing in on me as they waited for me to speak.

"The rebels have been plotting this for some time. Francesca Sky was among them, and yes, it was I who killed her when I discovered her treachery. To protect our kingdom."

"Murderer!" someone yelled, and fire burned the back of my throat, but I simply hung my head in sadness before going on, acting as if this burden weighed heavily on my back. It did of course, but not for the reasons they all believed.

"Francesca Sky was an immensely powerful Cyclops, able to forge memories and feed them to her rebel accomplices. She has painted me out to be a savage villain to try and sway my kingdom against me. But she went too far, you see? For it is preposterous when you truly examine it. So many memories, from me ruthlessly killing my own beloved brother, to me somehow being responsible for all the atrocities Hail Vega committed during his reign. She has concocted this fantasy and tried to make you all swallow it. But what Fae in this realm could be capable of so many abominations?" I scoffed and some of the faces in the crowd softened, their rage turning to thoughtfulness as they listened to me. Sheep, the lot of them. Easily led to slaughter, and I would do so now, a butcher wearing a smile and promising them green pastures in my company. "Am I to be responsible for every crime in history? Am I to be blamed for levelling entire cities by wielding the Savage King as my puppet somehow?"

"We saw it. You used Dark Coercion on Hail Vega!" some little fucking whore shouted up at me, pointing an accusing finger.

I held a hand to my heart in shock. "How could one Fae control a man such as him? He was the most powerful Fae of his time. And I served him dutifully, year after year. I did what I could to stop his tyranny, I tried to curb his rages, but what was I to do? If I wanted to take his throne, I could have challenged him. Surely that would have been a far simpler way to seize power instead of trying to control his mind or some nonsense." I shook my head.

"You would have lost that fight, that's why you used forbidden magic to control him!" a man bellowed, and I narrowed my eyes at him.

"So which is it? Am I so powerful that I had the Savage King under my control or not powerful enough to have challenged him? Surely if I were capable of manipulating him as such then I would have to be deemed the more powerful of us anyway, and if that was so then why didn't I enter into that challenge?" My words spun circles around their doubts, binding them up in their own confusion. Some might think that I was more powerful than Hail Vega for manipulating him the way I had, and I might even agree with that, but it wasn't the narrative they needed, so it wasn't the one they would get. For now.

"What about the Nebular Inquisition Centres?" another man cried. "My sister has been taken to one, and I haven't heard from her since. You're murdering Fae in those centres. If you have nothing to hide, then let us see inside them."

A cheer of ascent went up and I nodded, having been prepared for this.

"I, of course, will allow the public to visit the centres. There are two in this very city which I will open the doors to tomorrow, and you will see that they are simple interrogation centres. Designed to find and stop terrorists from rising up among us and hurting our people."

I had several of my most loyal court members working on it now, Linda Rigel heading up the division to ensure the centres were fit for inspection. There would be no trace of cruelty, no single drop of blood to be viewed within them when those doors were opened tomorrow. And I had made sure a new segment of Sphinxes and Minotaurs had been rounded up to be sent to them, none of them ever having stepped into a centre before. They would be treated well, and their stories would be released to the press immediately, proving the rebels' wrong in their findings. It was a pain, but it was necessary. Sometimes the people didn't know what was best for them; it was the burden of the masses to remain ignorant, and the burden of the powerful to keep them so for their own good.

I would have to tirelessly re-establish my image now, and those fucking rebels were to blame. When I found their new stronghold, I would make sure every one of them was cut to pieces slowly, feeling every ounce of pain this world could offer them before I snuffed out their worthless lives.

Music started up somewhere in the crowd and a cold lick of dread dragged up the length of my spine as I recognised the fucking song that had been played in The Orb at Zodiac Academy, my own voice taunting me as my words were twisted into a rebellious provocation.

"Turn that off!" I barked, losing it for a moment and the crowd looked between themselves for the perpetrator, but none was produced.

I hunted for the source and my Dragons pushed into the masses to try and find it too, but then I noticed it was coming from the ground itself, the music rumbling beneath the street and growing louder by the second.

I had wards in place all around the Court, but I suddenly realised I had not thought to cover the sewers.

Mildred Canopus stepped on top of a manhole cover and went shooting into the air as the whole thing was propelled skyward by a blast from below, a scream of pure terror leaving her as a spray of shit flew up after her. Another drain exploded and more faeces was flung into the air, the crowd scattering in an instant as screams went up and chaos ensued. The music boomed out of the sewers and I turned to flee inside, my Dragon Guardians shifting everywhere in a bid to protect me from the showers of shit.

But before I could make it inside, a Griffin shot out of one of the drains with a lilac haired girl on its back who had a bird-like mask on her face, the rebel angling a hand towards me and air magic sending every spurt of shit my way in a spinning vortex.

I cast an air shield behind me, running inside and knocking into Vard, the useless Seer not even *seeing* me coming as the two of us went flying to the ground. A guttering feeling spread through my chest, and I gasped in terror as access to my magic was locked down.

"What's happening?!" I bellowed and Vard winced as spittle flew from my mouth.

"I asked the FIB to set off anti-magic spells to keep you safe from the rebels," he blurted.

In the next second, shit was raining down on us, splattering me all over and slapping into Vard's ugly face beneath me. I roared in fury, staggering to my feet, but the blast of it only increased, sending me tumbling head over heels through the room, flipping upside down over a couch and slamming into a wall.

Mildred's huge Dragon form flew up to block the blast, taking it all to her chest and face as she spread her wings to rescue me, but the damage was done.

I cried out as the Griffin shit mixed into the sewage got in my eyes, burning so deep that I screamed in agony.

I wiped the shit from my eyes, squinting to find two of my Dragon Guardians running into the room to protect me, flanking me, and raising their hands.

"You can't access your fucking magic in here," I barked, and they took that as a command to shift, the two of them exploding into their huge Dragon forms and squeezing me between them. And not just anywhere between them, oh no, right between their fucking bare assholes, one on either side of my face as their tails swept through the space above me.

"MOVE THIS INSTANT!" I bellowed, my voice muffled by the press of their scaly backsides, and they both reacted so quickly that I was sent flying down into a pile of shit again.

"My King!" Vard wailed, trying to escape the never-ending blast of faeces, slipping and sliding in the filth as he tried to get to me.

I skidded along on my knees, crawling my way out of the room as curses poured from my tongue and the stench made it unbearable to breathe.

"Find who did this!" I yelled. "Bring them to me at once!"

When I was out of range of the shit blast zone, I shoved to my feet and stalked away into the depths of the Court, hunting for a shower. I would have to wait here until my Guardians dealt with the mayhem outside, and until that lilac haired girl was brought to me to be devoured bite by bite, I would never fucking rest.

Scorpio
Gemini
Virgo
Cancer
Aries
Leo
Sagittarius
Taurus
Capricorn
Aquarius
Libra
Pisces

ORION

CHAPTER SIXTY

A new night iron cage had been brought to the throne room since the last one had been destroyed, and I had some shiny new magic cuffs on my wrists too. Joy.

Darcy was pacing like a caged tigress, back and forth before the bars, her fingers occasionally brushing them, and her eyes glazed as she thought on whatever was circling in her mind.

"Tory will be okay," I assured her, certain it was her twin's fate that held her attention.

She nodded slightly but said nothing, continuing her pacing. It wasn't natural for us to be held like this, and I had to think even my time in Darkmore had allowed me more freedom. Though at least I had access to my Order now, and I didn't have to wait for short stints in the Order yard to access it. I certainly didn't miss the constant gang collisions from varying criminal motherfuckers and having to fight for even an inch of extra space in the shared showers. And at least I had my mate here.

Ah fuck, am I really trying to look on the bright side? There is no star damned bright side. There's just a shit fate or an even shitter one.

"Blue," I tried to get her attention, but she ignored me, rage lining her features. "Blue…" I tried again more firmly, but she only seemed to get angrier.

She whirled on me suddenly and I kicked away from the back wall where I was standing, opening my arms to pull her closer, but instead she punched me square in the chest. My eyebrows arched in surprise at the impact of that ferocious little attack and she cursed, shaking out her hand and pointing at me with her other one.

"*You.*"

"Me?" I questioned calmly despite her rising rage.

"You knocked me out with some Vampire ninja move when Tory was here," she accused. "You were going to let her take me."

"I was, yeah," I said simply.

"You are such a hypocrite," she snapped. "You would never leave me if this was the other way around."

"Guilty," I agreed.

She snarled, coming at me again and I let her use me as a punching bag as she lost her shit. It was pretty fucking cute actually, even when she landed bruising hits that showed how damn wild she could be.

She was red in the face when she was finished, and I arched a brow at her. "Are you done?"

"You know what, Lance?"

"What, beautiful?" I asked.

"Sometimes you're an asshole."

"Don't sell me short, I'm an asshole all the time."

She growled, eyes flashing with ire as she didn't get the rise out of me she so clearly wanted. But I was well versed in people hurling shit at me. I was a teacher after all.

"Why are you so calm?" she spat.

"Why are you so angry?" I countered.

"Because life is a bag of crap," she hissed. "And you're standing there like – like you're not even bothered about anything."

"Trust me, I am bothered about several things, but getting in a blind rage about them isn't productive."

"Well colour me unproductive then," she muttered, returning to her pacing and my mouth twitched up at the corner.

Stella had returned to me again in the night, drawing back the darkness Lavinia had left in me. She'd even given me some vile tasting potion to help keep a barrier between me and them the next time Lavinia stole me away to her torture chamber. I wasn't sure what to think of it all, but I certainly wasn't above accepting her help. I would take what little I could get from her, and she could let it assuage her guilt over me, or not. I didn't really care either way. It certainly wasn't going to equal my forgiveness.

I lifted my gaze to the bars above me, pulling my shirt off which was an extra fun little piece of Lionel Acrux merchandise today, the word K.U.N.T. spread across the middle of it above a metallic green Dragon.

I jumped up, catching hold of the bars and starting to do pull ups. There was little else to do in here but workout sometimes, and trying to beat my personal best of five hundred gave me something to focus on. When I hit a hundred, Darcy's gaze flicked my way then she cursed and looked elsewhere, continuing her pacing.

Her eyes slipped my way a few more times, and alright, maybe I was trying to get her attention now as I reached three hundred, sweat slicking my skin and my muscles tight.

She bit her lip, keeping her gaze firmly elsewhere again and as I reached four-ninety, I started counting down the final ten, my arms and shoulders burning. Darcy paused to watch me smash my goal by another ten and I hit the floor with a heavy breath, picking up the K.U.N.T. shirt and wiping my face with it. When I pulled it away, I found Blue standing still, her eyes flicking up from my abs.

"Can I help you, beautiful?" I asked through a smirk, and she rolled her eyes at me, turning away.

She fell into her own workout routine, which was all bending and stretching, the shadows barely concealing her nakedness as she ignored me completely. I watched with rapt attention as she did the downward dog and I cocked my head to one side, my gaze riveted to her ass, my cock twitching happily.

When she was back on her feet, swiping up one of the water bottles we'd been given this morning, she raised a brow at me.

"Can I help you, beautiful?" she parroted me, and I pressed my tongue into my cheek.

"You can, actually." I beckoned her closer, but she just tossed her hair and placed her bottle down before kicking up into a handstand.

I moved behind her and she rested her feet on my chest before kicking hard to flip herself back upright. I prowled forward before she could escape this time, capturing her waist and yanking her flush against me, my pulse rising. The shadows receded from her body and I smiled at the feel of her warm skin against mine, so perfectly soft.

"How about you lie down and spread those pretty thighs for me like a good girl and I'll use my tongue to make you like me again," I offered.

"How about get fucked," she said airily, and I growled, my hold on her tightening.

"How about you watch your mouth, or I'll stop playing nice."

"Maybe I don't want you to play nice," she said, eyes sparkling furiously. "Maybe I'm sick of you being nice with your overprotective bullshit."

"Someone really pissed in your cereal today, didn't they?" I growled.

"The stars have been pissing in my cereal since I showed up in Solaria. I used to think it was all magic and rainbows here, but it's not, is it? Tory was right all along. It's bullshit."

"So, what are you gonna do? Go back to the mortal realm?" I asked dryly.

"Maybe I will," she said, looking for that reaction in me and she was getting it now, though she was also getting me hot as hell.

"You're being a brat," I warned.

"So, what are you gonna do about it?" she demanded, and I flipped her around, shoving her forward so she was forced to grab the bars to stop herself falling to her knees. The moment she was bent over in front of me, I spanked her hard enough for the clap to echo around the whole throne room.

"Ah," she gasped, all lust and want tangled with that sound. I needed an outlet. She was pissing me off and I was clearly doing the same to her, so if this was what she wanted, I was more than willing to play her game.

I pressed up against her ass, letting her feel the full swell of my cock and riding my hand along the length of her spine. "Look what you do to me. You drive me crazy." I gripped her hips in a bruising hold then dragged my hands up over the nip of her waist and higher still, sliding beneath her and squeezing her breasts roughly.

She ground back into me with a heady moan, panting, "Fuck you."

I tugged her nipples hard, grinding them between my finger and thumb of both hands.

"You sure you can handle this, little mortal?" I taunted, aiming to rile her and she tried to stand up, but I moved my hands fast, one locking in her hair, the other forcing her to stay down as I splayed it over her back.

"I'm not a mortal," she snarled.

"Are you sure? You look like an angry little mortal to me."

"Asshole." She twisted sharply, trying to get free but I yanked on her hair and held her down, laughing cruelly.

"What did I say about watching that filthy mouth of yours?" I spanked the side of her ass cheek hard enough to make her spine arch and a string of curses fall from her lips, only causing me to spank her again. "Manners, Blue."

"I hate you," she hissed, that fire in her only burning hotter. She was a wild thing today.

"Are you sure?" I asked, slowly sliding my fingers between her legs. "Because I'd bet you fifty auras you're soaked for me, beautiful."

"I'm dryer than your humour," she said.

"Liar." I slid my fingers over her wet pussy, grinning at my victory. "You owe me fifty auras. Though I'll take payment in other forms seeing as you're fresh out of cash. Why don't you get on your knees and open those silky lips for me?"

"I hear mortals give shit blowjobs. You might get your dick bitten off," she said, and I broke a laugh, spanking her again, making her cry out in pleasure and pain.

"I'll take the risk."

"Pass," she said lightly. Fuck, she was being difficult.

I ran my fingers over her clit, slicking it with her arousal and she gasped, her back softening and her thighs parting wider.

"That's it. Stay still," I ordered, letting go of her hair and reaching for my pants to push them down, but she took the opportunity to stand upright and run away from me, the shadows rushing over her skin once more.

I folded my arms, my jaw grinding as she continued with her defiance. "I can catch you in the blink of an eye," I reminded her and she decided that was the perfect opportunity to flip me off.

My gaze narrowed. "You're asking for trouble."

"And yet here I am, perfectly free from trouble." She shrugged. "Maybe you've lost your touch at this. Or are you afraid you'll hurt the fragile little mortal?" There was bitterness in her tone, but a challenge there too, a determination for me to prove she could handle anything as the Fae she was.

I shot forward, decision made, trouble impending. I picked her up, flipping her upside down and making her squeak in alarm. I threaded her legs through the cage, bending them over the horizontal bar near the top of the cage so she hung from it before me, her mouth lined up perfectly with my cock.

I pushed my pants down, freeing my throbbing length and pushing it between her lips. She didn't resist me, holding onto me for support and sucking the length of me, making me growl in pleasure.

I forced her knees wider, gripping her ass in both hands and dropping my mouth against her pussy, lapping at her clit and making her moan around my cock. I thrust between her lips, playing her at her own game and letting her find out for herself if she could take it, while feasting on her in turn.

Her nails dug into my ass and I growled, high on this girl and her feral nature. We were full of pent-up energy and a hundred reasons to hate the world, but here between us we found an answer as always.

She took the length of me into her throat once more, her tongue running all over my shaft and driving me crazy as I thrust deeper. Her lips were velvet soft and perfectly designed to destroy me, but I wasn't giving in to her power yet.

She choked on my cock and I drew my hips back, but she clawed her nails into my skin, forcing me closer again, proving she could take it. I was more than happy for her to prove her point and as the tip of my cock slid against the back of her throat and she sucked, I nearly exploded there and then. I only held on by sheer force of will and I lapped my tongue over her clit, faster and faster until I was using my Vampire speed to bring her to ruin.

She moaned, her throat vibrating around the tip of my dick and I growled against her pussy, ecstasy calling my name and begging me to dive into it. She was going to fall first though. My tongue slid over her clit once more lightning fast and she came beautifully, her thighs tightening around my ears and holding me there as I prolonged her pleasure with long, slow strokes of my tongue.

Darcy lifted a hand, caressing my balls and I all but lost my mind as I fucked her mouth, drawing all of my focus. Two more pumps had me finishing with a roar of pleasure and she moaned, her throat gripping the head of my cock.

I stilled inside her and she swallowed me down, her lips tight around me and her hand squeezing and massaging my balls, making me fucking dizzy.

When I was totally spent, I slid out of her mouth and hooked her legs off the bars, catching her by her ankle before she cracked her head on the floor and swinging her up into my arms.

Her lips were red, her hair fucking everywhere and her eyes watery as hell. She pulled my pants up with her free hand, looking seriously pleased with herself and I reckoned we'd just put our issues to bed.

"Perfect." I crushed my lips to hers and she melted into me, her arms winding around my neck.

She nuzzled against me like a cat, and I grinned stupidly at her, nuzzling her back as if I was one of the cuddlier Orders. Only ever for her. And alright, maybe Darius in the past.

"Happy?" I asked.

"Happy," she said through a cute smile, and her eyes flashed green as she gazed up at me, her silver rings shining bright around them, a mark of her bond to me.

"Darcy," I gasped, but then they became dark again and she frowned as my face fell.

"What is it?"

"Your eyes." I brushed my thumb over her jaw, kissing her softly. "They were yours again. Just for a second, but your rings were there."

"Really?" she asked, all hope and light about her at last, like I'd tamed the savagery in her. At least for now.

"Really."

She slipped out of my arms, the shadows washing over her skin again and wrapping around her body like a gown woven from shade. She moved to the edge of the cage, examining her eyes in the reflection of the bars, trying to see for herself and my heart stammered as I feared she would be disappointed.

My head snapped up as I heard the approach of heavy footfalls and I shot closer to Darcy, gazing at the door.

Darcy stood straighter, her instincts alerted by my reaction and the two of us tensed like guard dogs waiting for a thief to break into their home.

Of all the Fae I'd feared walking through that door, my mother was the least of them and I scowled as Stella scurried into the room, casting a glance over her shoulder as she moved towards us.

"What do you want?" I barked, hearing Darcy's heart leap.

She scowled out at my mother who was approaching us within a silencing bubble, and I gripped the bars, my hackles prickling as danger trickled closer.

"I'm sorry, Lance," Stella croaked, looking defeated as she stood there before us in a jet black robe that hung down to her bare feet. She angled her raised hand towards Darcy, and a powerful wave of slumber crashed into her before I could do anything to stop it. Darcy grabbed the bars of the cage to try and keep herself upright and I held onto her with a curse, her limbs going limp as she sagged in my arms.

"Stop! What are you doing?" I demanded of Stella frantically, but then my knees buckled too, that same spell falling over me and the two of us clung tight to each other before we hit the floor in a tangle of limbs.

I was half aware of Stella approaching, her shadow falling over us as she opened the cage door.

Panic cascaded over me.

I tried to rise, tried to fight. But the spell was stealing me away into the abyss, and I couldn't do anything at all as she leaned over us, taking hold of Darcy's arm in a possessive grip and whispering, "I never wanted it to come to this."

Scorpio
Gemini
Virgo
Aries
Cancer
Leo
Sagittarius
Taurus
Capricorn
Aquarius
Libra
Pisces

TORY

CHAPTER SIXTY ONE

I knelt on the edge of the cliff where Darius's coffin had been laid to rest, looking out over the world with the Dragon tree guarding him like an immortal being set to watch him for all of time.

I'd broken when I arrived here, like I knew I would, like I had to allow myself to if I wanted any hope of summoning the strength to see the rest of this through.

I wasn't sure exactly how long it had been since I'd arrived, but the sun had set and risen again, and the sky was now streaked with pink and orange as it began another descent.

I took the pack I'd brought with me from the floor where I'd left it, carefully laying out the things I was going to need if I wanted to do this.

To reach the Damned Forest you must drink a dose of wolfsbane mixed with larkspur from a chalice scrawled with the runes halgalaz and raido and carve the name of your deepest desire into your flesh, then follow the ache of your heart before it gives out on life itself.

I hadn't dressed the part of a warrior queen before setting out to do this, instead opting for black jeans and a red crop top which was open at the back for my wings. I'd thrown a leather jacket on too because it was December now and even if my fire kept me warm, I didn't want to tempt the elements to try and freeze me. Darius had fallen for everything about me that wasn't royal long before he'd come to accept my bloodline anyway. For him, I was Roxy. The girl who fought back, the one who brought him to his knees and had forced him to challenge the stars themselves once before already. We'd won that time. So I liked our odds now too.

I brushed my fingers against the ruby pendant I still wore, but for once the gemstone was almost cool to my touch, no lingering sense of him clinging to it all. A feeling of unease rolled down my spine and for a moment I thought I heard his voice caught on the wind, warning me not to risk this, not for him.

I cast a sidelong look at his body in the frozen coffin, narrowing my eyes at his still face and shaking my head.

"Nice try, asshole," I muttered. "But danger never once stopped you."

I set the silver chalice I'd taken from his treasure hoard on a flat rock before me, placing a half empty bottle of tequila next to it, followed by the delicate purple flower of the wolfsbane plant. It was a beautiful flower, so innocent looking for something deemed the queen of poisons.

The roots were the most poisonous of all, and I'd considered that when selecting the plant to bring with me, but the book hadn't called for roots specifically, so I intended to make my potion with the much more appetising looking petals.

Next, I drew the larkspur from my pack, the white petals I'd selected seeming so harmless too, death disguised in beauty. I had to admit I liked their style.

I took a dagger from my belt and slit the tip of my finger open, then took the chalice into my hand. The instructions hadn't called for blood specifically, but I'd read enough in the Book of Ether to understand how powerful blood magic could be, and I was going to take any bit of help I could in making sure this worked.

I concentrated as I drew the first rune onto the side of the chalice, halgalaz looking like a capital H with the central stroke dropping down at a diagonal on the right side. The moment my bloodied finger met with the silver of the cup, I felt the power of that age old rune rumbling through me, rattling some ancient power which resided in my core as if trying to wake it up.

Halgalaz for trials, tests and the wrath of nature. No doubt I would be put to the test wherever this incantation led me, but I was ready for it. Ready to make good on my promise to the stars. And as if the blood in my veins agreed, the lightning-marred scar on my palm seemed to tingle like it was waking up.

I was panting by the time I completed the rune, my hand trembling where I held the chalice still and my vision shaky, but I simply turned the chalice around and began to paint the second rune into place.

Raido for travel and relocation. The rune resembled a capital R with sharp points, and the effort it took me to scrawl it onto the cold metal was almost enough to make me black out. I'd been using runes a lot recently, casting them to try and catch a glimpse into my future that wasn't so wholly reliant on the power of the stars, and marking them as wards against evil around my friends' rooms. But I had never felt the magic I felt stirring in them now. I'd never come so close to shattering beneath the force of them either.

I set the chalice back down on the rock, busying my trembling hands by snatching the tequila into my grasp and unscrewing the lid.

I took a long swig, letting the burn roll through me and settle in my gut as I caught my breath.

"Here's to us, husband," I toasted him, clinking the bottle against the coffin beside me, feeling nothing in reply to my sentiment before taking another swig then pouring a healthy measure into the chalice.

The incantation had called for a dose of wolfsbane mixed with larkspur, but there had been no mention of the liquid it preferred for brewing it. Water was the obvious choice. But tequila had always been my comfort spirit.

I shredded petals from the two flowers, dropping them into my drink and stirring the deadly concoction with a finger. Either of those plants could be deadly. The combination of both even more likely to rip me beyond the Veil if they got any say in it.

The tigers eye crystal which was still humming beneath my skin reassured me that that wouldn't happen, the starving soul I'd lashed to it still clawing through my most painful memories at its leisure in payment for the tether it was offering me to this realm. It wasn't a ghost as such, more a cursed spirit, unworthy of crossing over for reasons unknown. The spells I'd used to locate it had warned against me trying to find out what it had done to earn such a fate. I didn't care anyway. It didn't matter what manner of heinous creature it had been in life, all that mattered was that it continued to hold my soul within my body, then gave me a chord to pull on if I was unlucky enough to sink towards death once more.

And as I stared into the chalice of poison I was about to drink, I had to accept that that seemed all too likely.

"Fuck it." I lifted the chalice and gulped down the contents, the petals sliding down my throat on a river of booze, ready to kill me if they got the chance.

I picked up the dagger, well aware that I was already on the clock as the toxins contained in the plants began to work their way into my system. Larkspur would be the one to fuck me over fastest if it got its claws into me, the paralysis it could cause likely to stop me from continuing down this path if it set in too quickly. But I was hopeful that it wouldn't do that.

The wolfsbane would be the motherfucker which was already beginning to make my heart tremble in my chest, my tongue tingling as it got to work on me. Larkspur would stop me moving, then the wolfsbane would make my heart give out like a power couple working together.

I didn't have long.

I placed my left forearm across my lap and gritted my teeth as I began the last part of this spell, carving the name of my deepest desire into my flesh.

I sucked in a sharp breath as the dagger slit through my skin, the pain sharpening my thoughts as the tequila tried to offer me a way out with a little dizziness. It hurt like a bitch, but I told myself it could have been worse as I continued to carve his name into my skin. He could have had a longer name, like Bartholomew or Constantine. God, he would have been utterly unbearable if he'd been named Constantine. I could practically taste the elevated rich boy snobbery even now. I'd bet he would have insisted on everyone full-naming him too. Though to be fair, Constantine didn't exactly lend itself to a nickname. I'd have gone with Conny though, purely because I knew it would have driven him insane.

"Lucky for you, you were a Darius," I gritted out between my teeth as I finished carving the bloody S into my arm and damn near dropped the knife as my muscles trembled with weakness.

My pulse echoed in my ears, a slow blink curtaining my vision as the poison got to work on me, and I cursed as I fought to keep my focus on what I had to do.

Follow the ache of my heart before it gave out on life itself. Simple enough.

I pushed myself to my feet, my fingers locking around the strap of my pack then releasing again as my strength faltered. I needed the books and supplies in that pack. Needed them and yet…

My fingers fumbled with the strap again, my pulse weakening as I staggered where I stood. I blinked at the bag, the dizziness I was experiencing going far beyond a few shots of tequila. In hindsight, the booze probably hadn't been the best choice. Now my body was fighting a battle on three sides. Shit.

I dropped to my knees - not entirely intentionally - and pushed my fingers into the side pocket of the pack. My tongue began to feel leaden in my mouth and I drew in a shaky breath. Well, being poisoned officially sucked. But I was sure it would work out okay. Like sixty-five percent anyway.

The velvet pouch I'd been hunting for brushed my fingers and I tugged it from the pocket, shoving myself to my feet and managing to loop the pack over my arm.

I could feel the tug in my heart, my gaze lifting to the eastern horizon where something in my gut told me my destiny was waiting.

The urge to shift pressed in on me, some innate part of myself telling me I needed to fly, but I forced the impulse aside. Flying would take too long. That much I was certain of. But stardust…

In all fairness, I knew I shouldn't have even been considering stardusting to some unknown location. I understood the risks involved in trying to travel to a place that I had neither visited nor knew the location of on a map. I could become lost in the in-between, no destination in mind to draw me free of the grip of the stars themselves.

But that was a risk I was going to have to take. I had a plan for making sure I didn't end up colliding with anything on the other side too. So I closed my eyes as I focused on that tug in my heart. The call of my one true love… Ah shit, being poisoned was making me go all romantic.

I stumbled a step then righted myself again, my vision blurring then clearing. The stardust seemed to weigh me down impossibly, the little bag like a lead weight in my palm, but I refused to let it go.

My slowing heart was pulling me towards him. He was waiting for me to act.

The ruby pendant I wore heated against my skin, the warmth of it burning through me as that sense of him appeared at last, a brush of lips against mine, a silent plea for me to hurry.

I threw the stardust, focusing entirely on that tug in my chest with one minor discrepancy as I commanded the stars to release me into the sky far above my intended landing place.

The world lurched out of existence around me, the whispering of the stars impossibly loud against my ears as they watched me pass through them, and I couldn't help but flip them off as I went.

Their fury and outrage hissed all around me and they flung me from their embrace, gaining the last laugh as I found myself far higher than I'd intended to be, my arms cartwheeling as I began tumbling through the sky miles above an endless forest of blackened trees, my pack wheeling away beneath me.

A scream ripped from my throat, the ruinous landscape that surrounded this place seeming to mock me as I tumbled towards death at an alarming pace, the wind whipping around me violently, working to rid my mind of the fog closing in on it.

My Phoenix was groggy to respond to my call for help, so I threw my hands out before me instead, air magic spiralling from my palms, catching me in an invisible net just as I reached the tips of the tallest trees.

I stared at the blackened leaves, the bone white branches beneath looking so unreal that I had to blink to be certain I wasn't hallucinating. A sense of dread seemed to hum from this place, the Damned Forest a sea of blight beneath me.

I reached towards one of the blackened leaves just as a pulse of pain echoed through my body and a scream erupted from my lungs as I lost control of my magic and plummeted from the sky.

Branches slapped against my skin, my limbs striking the thick foliage and the rock-hard branches beneath until I felt like I was being beaten within an inch of my life.

The fog in my mind was too thick and the panic of my fall too intense for me to be able to summon my power to save me.

Terror tumbled through me, the ground speeding ever closer.

A blast of power sprang from me at the last second, earth magic erupting from my palms just in time to soften the earth, but I still collided with it far too hard. My arm snapped with a thunderclap of a crack as I landed on it, and a scream of agony escaped me, the tigers eye lodged in my side flaring with power as death beckoned me close once more.

"Fuck!" I screamed, my pulse swerving unevenly.

My heart faltered beneath the power of the poison, and I rolled onto my side, throwing up on the ground until my stomach cramped with emptiness, and I was left panting over a pool of my own vomit.

My fingers fumbled against my jacket pocket as the too-slow thump of my heartbeat ricocheted throughout my skull, my left arm hanging limp at my side, the letters of Darius's name bleeding onto the dirt beside me.

He was laughing. That asshole was watching me from somewhere and laughing his damn ass off as I came far too close to faceplanting my own vomit.

My fingers spasmed instead of taking hold of the little vial which Rosalie Oscura had left on my bed when she'd left my room last night. There was a label on that vial. A deal on it which I knew I could easily come to regret one day, but one which I'd agreed to by accepting the gift anyway.

One dose of Basilisk anti-venom in exchange for the true queens turning a blind eye in Alestria from time to time once we win this war xoxo

Yeah, if I made it out of this war alive and somehow ended up with my ass planted on a throne, then there was going to be all kinds of shit taking place in our kingdom courtesy of the Oscura Clan which I would be obligated to ignore. But if that was the price of this help, and more than that; their help in fighting this war, then it was one I was willing to pay. No doubt we could come to an understanding and draw at least a few lines in the sand. Hopefully.

I cursed as I managed to tug the vial from my pocket only to promptly drop it on the ground, the clear liquid inside the glass winking at me as it rolled just out of reach.

My body was giving up on responding to my commands, the paralysis of the larkspur working to immobilise me so I couldn't move, while I was left to feel every agonising moment of my death.

No. Fuck no. I hadn't come this far to die here in this forest. I hadn't done all of this only to fall at the first real hurdle.

I rolled onto my front, a cry parting my lips which I followed up with a string of curses as I began to shuffle myself towards the vial across the dirt with what little control I had of my body.

My arms had given up entirely, though that made no difference to the utter agony coursing through my broken arm as I dragged it through the dirt, my gaze locked on that little bottle. I just about had control over my right foot and my abs. Perfect.

I inched towards the vial of Basilisk anti-venom, the irregular, slow thump of my heartbeats resounding through every inch of me as my vision swam and I blinked furiously to clear it.

Just a little more. A few inches.

My neck gave up before I made it, my face smacking into the dirt and my mouth filling with soil which I spat out furiously.

Not like this. I wasn't going to die here in the middle of fucking nowhere with nothing to show for all I'd sworn to do to the stars. I had vengeance to dole out and a promise to keep to the man I loved. I refused the fate which was calling my name and dug my toes into the dirt as I shoved myself forward a little more.

The tigers eye in my side was burning so hot that the pain of it almost surpassed that in my arm, the spirit I'd tethered to it shrieking as my death loomed. It wasn't immortality. It held no real sway over life and death. It was merely a foot wedged in the door, holding it open just enough for me to slip back through if I were forced onto the other side for a moment. But the door was pressing down on that foot now, the soul wailing in fright as the pressure increased beyond the point of what it could refuse. It was going to break, going to fail.

My eyes fell shut without my permission and I was lost in the void of space between my too slow heartbeats. Seconds passed while I hung there, dragging on and on until that thump reminded me that I wasn't quite done yet. And the tingling in my palm seeming to urge me back towards my goal.

I dug my toes into the dirt, then shifted forward another inch and the cool glass of the vial butted against my lips at last.

I didn't think, didn't hesitate, just snatched that bastard into my teeth and bit down on the glass hard enough to shatter it.

The anti-venom burst over my tongue in a wave, shards of glass cutting my lips and tongue as I spat them out again.

I wondered if I'd been too late as the fire in that crystal burned hotter, my side an inferno which was working to consume me.

The soul bound to it screamed as it was suddenly yanked through that door, and I caught a glimpse of golden eyes peering at me from the darkness within the rift there before it snapped shut in my face and I was hurled away, returned to the agony of my body and flung onto my back.

The anti-venom cut through the poison which had been killing me, and I sucked down deep breaths as I quickly regained the use of my body, all of the symptoms fading fast. *Thank you, Rosalie.*

I gripped my broken arm in my good hand, gritting my teeth through the pain as I healed it, green light spilling out around me, first setting the bone then healing the carved flesh which had spelled out Darius's name. I was glad of that – I might have gotten a tattoo to express my love for him, but I didn't need some grisly scar to accompany it, branding myself as his possession.

The tigers eye thumped into the dirt beside me as I healed myself, my body pushing the now useless crystal from my skin, and I released a heavy sigh, finding myself without pain for the first time in days.

"Smashed it," I muttered to myself, wondering why the fuck anyone had ever thought coming to this place was a good idea. But as I pushed myself upright, it quickly became clear that over the years, long ago, plenty of Fae had found a way.

I brushed the dirt from my clothes as I stood, craning my neck to look up at the enormous trees which made up the Damned Forest. The trees themselves were monstrous things, their eerily white bark a stark contrast to the pitch black of their leaves. Sap had spilled down the trunks of a few of them, the colour equally dark, looking like trails of blood or perhaps tears which tracked their way down the wood.

No leaves had fallen to litter the floor and the soil I was standing on was barren, blank, not so much as a weed breaking free of it. They didn't even seem alive, and no birds moved in their boughs. This place was something beyond the labels of life and death, something wicked and malignant.

Silence.

Endless, hopeless, silence surrounded me in every direction.

The quiet here was perpetual, beyond that stillness which overcame a forest when a predator drew near, beyond the haunting nothingness that appeared in the blackest of nights. This was a hush so profound it made me question my own senses, though I didn't dare make another sound of my own to break it and test them.

I looked around, the darkness pressing in between the trunks of the trees as the sun continued its descent somewhere far away from here, in another time and place, the longest night about to set in. I couldn't imagine how such a place could even exist in Solaria, how it could just be here, undisturbed and unchanging for…millennia if I had to guess. There was such history to this forest that I couldn't imagine there had ever even been a time when it wasn't here.

I turned in a slow circle, uncertain of how I was supposed to find the Waters of Depth and Purity or any of the rest of it.

I closed my eyes, raising my hands as I called on my water magic, reaching out into the world around me as I hunted for a source of water, searching between those lifeless trees for any sign of a direction to take.

There was nothing.

But I wasn't some fool who had come here unprepared.

I abandoned my hunt for a source of water, instead looking around for my pack and spotting it between two towering trunks further into the trees.

I headed for it, hoping the protection spells I'd cast on it had been strong enough to keep everything inside it safe throughout its fall. I flipped it open and checked inside, sighing in relief before tugging the Book of Earth from its place among the other tomes.

I grabbed a handful of rune-carved bones from a side pocket too, then used the toe of my boot to scrawl a pentagram into the dirt.

I dropped the book into my lap as I finished, raising my hand above it and letting my mind fall blank, waiting for the ink and parchment to surrender its will to me.

The book obliged, the heavy power it contained shifting as I connected my magic to it and silently asked it to open for me.

Pages flicked past quickly, my eyes widening as I watched them go, my magic directing them to give me what I needed to find my way on from this place.

It fell open on a page titled *To build a Bridge to the Beyond.* I scanned the words, wondering if what it was suggesting might work before pouring the little bag of bones out into my fist. I shook them, letting my power coil around them before dumping them on the book and watching how they fell.

I'd been reading up on this, studying it tirelessly, making sure I could interpret them with as little difficulty as possible, but it turned out I didn't need some superior understanding of the possible meanings the runes could hold. The runes didn't fall where I'd directed, all but one of them tumbling from the book to land on the ground beside me, despite how carefully I'd cast them to land upon its pages.

I leaned in to look at the one which had remained alone. Dagaz, its shape like a pair of triangles joined at one corner, was lying directly on top of one word. *Beware.*

My skin prickled, the rune's meaning of awareness resounding within me as I began to get the feeling that I wasn't alone within these trees at all.

I scanned the instructions on creating a bridge once more, the use of ether combining with earth magic to turn a tree into a powerful walkway between destinations. It suggested selecting a tree with a lot of innate power like oak or ash, but as my only options were the damned trees surrounding me, I'd be going with one of them and hoping for the best.

I stood abruptly, placing my things back in my pack and surreptitiously glancing around. Nothing. But that did little to ease the feeling in my gut that something was lurking close by, something hungry and desperately alone.

I lifted my chin and stalked towards the closest of the damned trees, fire flaring at my fingertip and scoring a slice straight through the bark as I began the spell required to create a bridge.

A howling cry broke from the trunk, and I flinched, spinning around to see a flash of movement at my back…or had I?

I peered at the trunk I could have sworn someone had just leapt behind and drew my sword.

My steps were silent as I advanced on it, the white bark near glistening before me, my gleaming sword somehow seeming vulgar in this place of serene, terrifying beauty, but I didn't sheathe it.

I leapt around the tree, my sword raised as a cry escaped me, but my blade met nothing but ice white bark and I half decapitated a low hanging branch instead of finding some assailant waiting for me.

That tree wailed too, the sound like a beacon of dread, a death cry from a thing built of nothing but rot and hatred.

I glanced around once more then sheathed my sword, hurrying to cast the magic I needed to create that bridge, wanting to get the fuck out of this place. Fire reignited on my fingertip and I burned another mark into the trunk, my chest hollowing out as I roused my power and concentrated on with what the Book of Earth had instructed.

But as I steeled myself to drop into the abyss of ether which I could feel coiling within me, a soft voice caught my ear and I fell utterly still instead, listening.

It was a child. And she was singing.

I turned to my left, frowning as I found the light there darker than in the rest of the forest, a tumbling layer of fog appearing across the dirt at the foot of those towering, cursed trees.

The song was a summons, a lonely, harrowing tune which I knew I should recoil from, but as I began to back up, a tendril of that fog curled its way around me, and I breathed it in.

The song stuttered out, an endless silence stretching throughout the trees until a piercing scream cleaved the night apart and set my heart racing with fear.

The next thing I knew, I was running, sprinting through the mist into the shadows between the trees, nothing on my mind beyond the safety of that child, and the eternal darkness set to swallow me whole.

She was in there somewhere, that little girl was screaming out for me to help her, and she was so familiar, so painfully afraid that I had no choice but to run for her. Away from my purpose in coming here, away from all I'd brought with me, and away from the ruby pendant which had tumbled from my throat.

Scorpio
Gemini
Virgo
Cancer
Leo
Taurus
Sagittarius
Capricorn
Libra
Aquarius
Pisces

ORION

CHAPTER SIXTY TWO

The clink of chains and a bite of cold metal brought my awareness into keen focus, the sleep spell tugged from my mind violently enough to make me snarl.

My eyes snapped open, and I found Stella walking away from me in a stone chamber I didn't recognise, nothing but a huge, cylindrical glass tank of blood standing in the centre of the darkened room. The tank stood in an intricate silver base which formed two bird-like talons that grasped the sides of it, a tarnish to it that made me think it had to be old.

I was chained to an upright metal rack, my arms yanked tight above me, and my ankles tethered too.

My pulse thumped a dark tune in my ears and I glanced to my right, finding Darcy there on a rack of her own, her head hanging forward as she remained asleep, her hair inky and swirling about her as the shadows hugged her body, slithering like a python around her form.

I yanked at the chains holding me in place, sensing I still had access to my Order form, but they were made of sun steel, and I couldn't break through them despite my strength.

"What is this?" I rasped at Stella, my heart starting a war in my chest, battle cries spilling through the centre of my being.

My mother moved towards Darcy and panic sharpened inside me, a bane of terror binding my limbs.

"Get the fuck away from her," I snapped, the animal in me rising as my pulse drummed even louder inside my head. I couldn't control anything in this situation, I couldn't protect my mate, and it was driving me mad with fear for her already.

Stella lifted a hand in the direction of a table where a steaming cauldron lay beside a range of bottles and a curved silver dagger shaped like a Vampire fang. She cast air, and the blade shot into her grip, her fingers winding tightly around it. There was something about that blade which called to my Order, my fangs prickling and my instincts flaring.

"Don't touch her!" I roared, terror making it impossible to breathe as that bitch raised a weapon toward Blue. "You stay the fuck away from her or I'll make you pay. I'll rip every organ from your worthless body and keep you alive until I claim the last one."

“Royal blood is so very powerful,” Stella whispered, ignoring me entirely and carving a long slit down Darcy’s forearm where it was bound in place above her.

“No!” I yelled, jerking harder against my restraints.

Stella lifted another hand, summoning a vial to her from the table and capturing every drop of Darcy’s blood inside it before turning towards the tank. My girl didn’t stir, and I spat insults at Stella who continued to act as if she couldn’t hear me.

My mother cast air beneath her feet, rising up to look down into the huge vessel of blood, pouring the contents of the vial into its depths, and the blood sizzled and hissed with some unknown magic. The air grew somehow colder, my breath rising before me in a cloud of vapour as that magic took root in this chamber. It was dark, forbidden, and cut to the root of me and my Order. It was an ancient, intangible power that seemed to whisper death through the heart of me.

“It’s taken me such a long time to gather this blood, Lance,” my mother said solemnly. “I would have done this sooner if I could have.”

Stella let the black robe slip from her body, her naked back to me before she lowered herself slowly into the tank with her magic, making the deep, red liquid swirl within the glass container.

“The blood of a hundred sinning Fae,” she purred, her fangs glinting before she was submerged completely.

“Blue,” I called to Darcy, my muscles straining as I tried harder to get free. “Wake up!”

She didn’t rouse, still captured in Stella’s magic, and I cursed, thrashing against the chains to no avail.

Stella eventually emerged from the blood, rising out of it with her head tipped back, a groan of delight leaving her as she swallowed a mouthful of it, crimson pouring down every inch of her body and dripping from her feet as she hung suspended above it by her air magic.

She lowered herself down to the floor, drenched in the blood of a hundred Fae as she fixed her gaze on me. Magic crackled around her in the air and my heart beat with a fury that would surely equal its end.

My mother raised a hand, flicking a finger at the table, picking up a vial with her air Element and sinking it into the potion. She filled it to the brim before carrying it towards me on a breeze, the liquid deepest magenta and glittering with whatever power was imbued within it.

Stella shot towards me in a blur, her other hand rising to clasp my chin and force my head back.

“Drink,” she commanded, and I locked my lips tight together, trying to keep this from happening through sheer force of will. But without my magic or freedom from these chains, I had no chance of stopping her.

She peeled my jaws apart with her gifted strength, the potion tipping directly into my mouth and making me choke as I tried to stop myself from swallowing. But Stella snapped my mouth shut and pinched my nose, making my reflexes kick in so I had to swallow. It burned along my insides and left an acrid taste on my tongue like decay and certain death.

“Fuck. You,” I panted as she released me.

She gazed at me woefully through the blood staining her face. “It’s the only way.”

“The only way for what?” I demanded.

She cast the vial away from us and let it smash against the wall before shifting closer to me.

“Long ago, our kind ruled the world,” she breathed. “Blood holds untold power, Lance. But these powers cannot be fully unlocked unless we embrace the Vampire ways of our ancestors.”

“Get your filthy fucking hand off of me,” I hissed, but a sudden rush of hunger hit me, and I jolted as the power of the potion kicked in, the burning in my throat building and building. My thoughts began to scatter, and my eyes sharpened, seeing one thing before me and one thing only. Blood.

"Here, baby." Stella raised her wrist, offering it to my mouth and my fangs snapped out.

Some voice in the back of my head told me not to do it, but the potion had hollowed out my insides and I was so very, very hungry. The scent of blood drove me to insanity, and I lost what little restraint I had left to the magic in that concoction, rearing forward and sinking my fangs into her wrist.

"Yes," she gasped, reaching up to clasp the back of my neck while her blood rushed into my mouth, and I swallowed greedily.

I could taste the blood on her skin too like it was somehow a part of her now, and I tasted my mate's blood among it all, that heady mixture of sunshine and fire rolling through me.

I could feel myself reaching the point of fullness, my magic reserves swelling and giving me an unwanted high. But as I tried to retract my fangs, I couldn't do so, forced to keep feeding while Stella took my other arm in her grip and suddenly drove her own fangs into my wrist.

No!

I roared inside my head, trying to stop, knowing what this would lead to. It went against everything the Vampire Code taught me, and more than that, I had done it before. Bound myself to Caleb Altair and formed a coven with him, a coven Stella was now on the path to binding herself to as well.

I desperately tried to pull free of her skin, but I kept feeding despite my own internal demands, and Stella drank from me in turn. We were forming a circle, exchanging something vital between us, and with it, I could feel her magic flowing into me, and mine flowing right back into her.

Power built between us like a living, writhing creature that howled and begged for more. I couldn't stop. Couldn't break away as this wicked fate fell upon me like a dagger in my soul.

The bond was forming, my rivalry with her lessening, slipping away further and further until I was free of it entirely. But it didn't make me love her, no power on earth could do that. If it was her intention to try and form some connection with me, then fuck her. I would never embrace her as I had Caleb.

The magic echoed in my chest with a finality that promised it could never be broken, and Stella tugged her wrist away from my mouth, releasing me from her fangs in the same moment.

"Why?" I begged of her. "You had no right," I gritted out as she smiled at me sadly.

"I love you so much," she said, her eyes watery. "Trust me, baby, it's for your own good."

She pressed a palm to the bare skin over my heart, marking a bloody handprint there and feeling the furious pounding of the muscle beneath my ribs.

"Nothing you've ever done has been for my own good," I said heavily, my mind sifting through every sin she had committed against me and the people I loved.

"Wake," she commanded, turning to Darcy, and retracting the sleep spell from her at last.

"Lance?" Darcy gasped, looking for me, her eyes widening as she took in the bloody, naked form of my mother, then she turned to me and faced whatever heartbreak she could see in my eyes. "What has she done to you?"

"Coven bonded us," I spat.

"What?" Darcy's expression twisted in horror, vengeance shifting across her features as her gaze moved to my mother.

Stella retreated, moving towards my mate and I was glad this coven connection didn't have any effect on how fiercely I wished to protect Darcy against my mother's advance.

"Move. Back," I commanded, but Stella continued to gaze up at Darcy, sucking a line of blood from her own lips.

"A lover's promise made in solemn silence," my mother murmured to herself like she was reciting some instructions, then she cast a silencing bubble around herself and Darcy so I couldn't hear her next words, a curse leaving me in anger.

Darcy's eyes widened and her gaze flicked my way, some knowledge flashing in her expression that sent a wave of terror through me. What the fuck was Stella saying to her?

"Don't listen to her," I called. "She's a liar, a fucking manipulator. Anything that comes out of her mouth is dirt."

Stella gripped Darcy's face, forcing her to look back at her, her mouth moving but an illusion fluttering over it kept me from reading the movements of her lips.

I snarled again, tugging forcefully on the chains holding me down and swear words spewed from my tongue, all aimed at the bitch who had brought me into this world.

Stella dropped the silencing bubble at last and suddenly released Darcy from her chains.

"What did she say to you?" I cried, but Darcy didn't look at me, her lips pressed tight together and a decision weighting her gaze.

My girl nodded to Stella and my mother smiled, her shoulders dropping in relief as they seemed to make some agreement between them.

"Stop," I begged, dread racing through me as Stella drew Darcy towards the tank of blood. "Don't do anything she says, Blue. Whatever she's promised you, she's lying."

Darcy glanced back at me, a burning fear shining in her eyes before Stella raised her skyward with air magic and starting lowering her into the pool of blood.

"I love you," Darcy breathed, and I shook my head in refusal of this situation as she sank into the murky depths of darkest red.

"Blue!"

Stella shot up into the air, releasing a noise of satisfaction and using her earth Element to cast a silver lid over the tank, fusing it shut.

"No!" I cried, my pulse hammering, panic spewing.

There was nothing I could do. I couldn't get free. Couldn't get to my Elysian Mate as she drowned in that vessel of death.

"I'll do anything, Stella – anything you want! Just let her go, don't hurt her. Please don't hurt her."

Stella moved to stand on top of the sealed tank as Darcy made it to the edge of the glass, her hands pressing to it and her eyes sparking with alarm. She started bashing her fist against the glass and my mind snapped, sinking into a dark place where only barbarity existed.

The Death bond began to rise, my heart ricocheting off the walls of my chest, thump, thump, thumping its way towards annihilation. Her death equalled mine because of the deal I'd made with Lavinia, and Darcy was closing in on it, her fists bashing harder against the glass and shadows spilling from her skin, driving against the tank too. But it didn't even crack. She was locked in there and Stella's expression told me she was not going to let her out.

I thrashed with all the power in my body, veins straining along the lines of my muscles, the metal not giving even a little.

"Death will release you," my mother whispered, eyes on me, full of love and I bellowed in anguish.

My Elysian Mate bond was far stronger than any coven. It was built from the magic of the heavens, woven from starlight and the unending, destructive power of love. I would kill Stella for this. I would crush her soul in my fist and turn it to dust before it could slip away beyond the Veil. She would not pass on. I would not allow it.

Stella swept towards me on a gust of air, slicing her palm open and slamming it against my right hand with ancient words streaming from her lips.

"Matrem consanguinitate religatam et ultra. Filii mei vinculis mortis suscipio," she whispered.

Magic crashed against me, binding with the terror of losing my mate and setting the Death bond working faster. It was burning through my flesh, tearing a line from my soul right to that place where my palm connected with my mother's.

"I am his blood, his kin, his coven!" She tipped her head back, the words pouring from her into the air and tainting the chamber with an almighty power. "Eius vinculum meum est!"

A sound like thunder tore through the air and all at once, the room went dark. I was certain death had come for me as Stella's brutal magic took me hostage, and I called out for Blue in my final moments on this plane, but no reply came.

"Ab ipso peto nunc et semper – his bond is *mine*," Stella panted, and a flash of red light exploded between our palms, throwing her away from me as power poured from my body into hers.

It was so forceful that it shattered the glass tank and Darcy was washed out of it on a tide of blood. She coughed and spluttered, pushing to her hands and knees and a desperate relief ran over me at finding her alive.

Stella caught herself with air magic before she could hit the floor, rising above me as her entire body began to glow with the crimson light of the Death bond. But it was no longer tied to me, that almighty, wicked power impossibly absent from my body. And somehow, in my bones, I knew that Stella had taken it from me and bound it to herself instead, but I couldn't fathom why she'd do such a thing.

She lifted a hand, tears running down her cheeks and carving lines through the blood staining her face. She flicked her fingers and brought the fang-like dagger flying towards her across the room, catching it in her grip.

"Why?" I gasped as she angled it towards her own heart.

"Because I am your mother. And I love you more than life itself," she exhaled then drove the dagger into her chest, a scream leaving her as she used the strength of her Order to carve her heart from the cavity of her ribs and yanked it out of her own body, skewered on the blade as she held it before her.

A single moment of life remained in her eyes, and she offered that moment to me, her fingers flicking so the chains released me from the rack, and I fell to the floor.

In the next second, she was dead, collapsing in the pool of blood, her body broken and the bloody knife sitting upright beside her where it was sunk deep into a still-twitching heart.

Darcy scrambled to my side, wrapping her arms around me and I knelt there in shock, unsure what to think, what to do. My heart hurt in a way I would never have expected from witnessing my mother's demise, and I didn't know if it was the coven bond she'd forced on me or some long lost love for her stirring in my bones. Deep down, I knew coven bonds couldn't forge feelings as powerful as these, and I hated the way my emotions fragmented and confusion rattled my mind. I felt the collar of shadow dissolve around my throat, liberating me from the Shadow Princess's control once and for all. My mother's sacrifice had freed me.

"I'm sorry," Darcy said. "I had to. She said the Death bond had to be heightened for the spell to work, on the verges of killing you. She promised she'd save you, and that it was best you truly feared you were going to lose me. I just had to take the chance because as much as I hate her, I've seen her love for you over these past weeks, Lance, and I trusted the depths of it in the end. She said we'll have a chance to run tonight because Lionel is at the Court of Solaria with his Dragon Guild."

I managed to look at her, a lump in my throat burning deep, but the words on my lips fizzled out of existence as I found her silver rings glinting at me from green, green eyes.

"Darcy," I gasped, looking down at her body, no sign of the shadows clinging to her at all. She was naked, drenched in blood, but wholly Fae.

But then she screamed a horrible fucking scream, clutching her chest and crumpling beneath me. The shadows rushed out of her skin, snaring her limbs and she arched against the bloodied floor, not seeming to see me at all as some terrible pain took hold of her.

Her screams were all I could hear, her agony the only thing in existence. And I was helpless to stop it.

Scorpio
Gemini
Virgo
Aries
Cancer
Leo
Sagittarius
Taurus
Capricorn
Aquarius
Libra
Pisces

TORY

CHAPTER SIXTY THREE

The fog rose all around me as I ran on, any lingering sign of the setting sun far above the canopy of black leaves stripped away until I was left in nothing but a sea of those bone white trunks with tendrils of grey coiling around me.

The longest night was upon me, and the winter solstice was in full effect.

I panted through the exertion of my run, uncertain how long I'd been chasing those screams, but finding myself exhausted by my desperate hunt.

I leapt between two of the cursed trunks and skidded to a halt on the soft earth as I found a stone hut there, its walls squat and grey, the mist curling from its chimney in an eerie imitation of smoke.

The wooden door stood wide, the girl's screams coming from within.

My breath caught in my throat and I drew my sword, stalking to the threshold. Fear made my bones quake as I closed in on the darkness within that building, something soul deep telling me that I wouldn't like what I found in there.

But the girl was crying now, her sobs radiating through me with a gravity that was inexplicable, like her pain was my own, like she was shattered and ruined beyond repair and there was nothing left in this world which could free her from her suffering.

Phoenix fire lit along the length of my blade, and I rolled my shoulders back as I fought the urge to shift, knowing there wouldn't be room for my wings inside that tiny building.

"Closer," the mist seemed to whisper. *"Help her."*

Its encouragement did nothing to bolster my confidence, and I swallowed against the knowledge that this was a very well laid trap. One put in place to lure any Fae foolish enough to set foot in this forest of curses and evil. But that didn't mean the girl wasn't real. I could feel her pain. I couldn't leave her to this fate.

I swung my sword out as I reached the door, the brittle wood bursting alight with little more than a thought from me, red and blue flames devouring it, making sure no one could lock me inside once I stepped over that threshold.

The space within the hut was dim, but I solved that flaw with a flick of my fingers, throwing flames out to each corner, revealing all the secrets the shadows might have been holding. But there were none. Only a sobbing girl with ebony hair sitting in the middle of the room, her face buried against her knees.

"What's wrong?" I asked her, the hairs along my arms standing on end as the wrongness within that hut pressed in on me.

I slipped into the room, my gaze skimming the bare walls surrounding us again just in case I'd missed something.

"I'm all alone," she sobbed, a shiver going through her small frame. "All alone and it's all my fault."

"Why is it your fault?" I asked softly, dropping to one knee before her while keeping my sword in hand.

"Because I wasn't enough. I couldn't give them enough, couldn't keep them safe. They all left me because I'm toxic, poison, the last choice."

I swallowed the lump which rose in my throat at her words, the heartfelt depth of them resounding with some long-hidden part of me. How many times had I felt that way when I was a child? When no one ever wanted to keep us? When I knew that I was the reason Darcy had never been wanted either?

"You have no one at all?" I murmured, reaching for her arm, the touch of her frost-cold skin making a chill run into me too.

"I had a sister," she breathed. "But in the end, she didn't pick me either. Because she knows, she sees it."

"Sees what?" I urged, cocking my head to try and see her face but she kept it buried against her knees, that ebony hair a curtain which spilled down over her too slim frame.

"How empty I am inside. How worthless."

The girl lifted her head, and I stifled a scream as I lurched away from her, finding myself staring into my own face minus around ten years. Except instead of the stubborn, wilful child I'd often seen in the mirror, this version of my former self showed the gaps in her soul on the outside. The scars that had been left with every rejection she'd suffered marred her face, jagged lines cutting to the bone like everything covering them had been a mask.

"No one will ever truly choose me," she hissed. "They can see my broken edges. They can taste my easy lies. They know me when they look at me, no matter how hard I try to hide the truth."

"What truth?" I demanded, my hand trembling where I gripped my sword, this fractured piece of me wounding me with every word flung my way.

"That I'm not worthy of the faith they wish to put in me. That I'm a selfish, stubborn creature who cannot and will not ever put the needs of others above her own. I stopped anyone from choosing my sister until my sister was forced to stop choosing me. She had to, to be free."

"Free?" I breathed, my back hitting the wall as I just stared at this girl who was me and who wasn't me at all. "You think I'm a tether on her?"

I knew that she did because I'd always known it myself. Darcy was the one everyone was drawn to, she was the one who could summon strength and courage so easily while I was too jaded by life, too caught up in fighting the world off to ever truly let anyone breach my walls.

"Aren't you?" the girl demanded, her eyes full of pity and reproach.

I opened my mouth to deny it, but how could I? I'd been a burden on her for our entire lives, I'd made it harder for her to make friends, meet boyfriends. My lack of trust in the world had forced her to hold herself back too. And when we'd come here, to the land which was always intended to be ours, I'd kept holding her back, shielding her from the world whenever I could and fighting it off whenever I had to. Would she have suffered half the things the Heirs had put her through without me there antagonising them at every turn? Or would she have found a way to peace so much sooner?

"She made her choice," crowed the scarred girl who I didn't want to admit was me, getting to her feet and padding towards me, the thin nightgown she wore revealing more scars on her arms and legs. They were violent, vulgar, the truth of me. "And it wasn't you, was it?"

A lump of iron lodged in my throat as I fought the pain those words caused me, fought the memories of Darcy rejecting me in that throne room after all I'd risked to reunite us. I'd spent the weeks since the battle fighting to get back to her, desperate to save her, only to find out she didn't need or want me to rescue her. She'd made her own choice, was treading her own path. And despite its brutality, she had chosen to stick to it rather than come back to me.

"Would you carve the silver from her eyes?" the scarred me purred, and I could feel the emotions she was trying to lure from me, the jealousy she was trying to stoke. "Would you slip a knife between her mate's ribs in the dark?"

"Of course I wouldn't," I hissed, my grip on my sword tightening as she stepped closer still.

"You didn't let yourself notice it before, did you? When you had your own mated male to distract you, you tried so hard to ignore it, but it was always there, wasn't it? That choice she'd made. She lied and lied to you, left you all alone for months on end and watched you shatter rather than give up her truth. She chose him then too. And you were left to rot in the reality of what you are, what you always have been."

"And what's that?" I whispered, a tear rolling down my cheek as her words cut me open, cut me where the scars which marked her own skin lay and worked their way beneath my bones.

"A burden. Unwanted. Selfish. Alone."

I almost crumpled at that assessment of what I was, of *who* I was at the heart of myself, but as I felt the fog curling around my legs, the fires I'd lit dying down around me, a voice echoed through my mind. A soul connected to mine through love and death and grief and hope. My other half. My reason for fighting as hard as I did.

"It's you and me, Tor. No matter what, wherever we are."

The oath she'd made to me when I truly had been the age the thing wearing my face was pretending to be. The promise that she didn't want anyone or anything else more than she needed me. Soul-deep, unbreakable, the foundations of us both. And I wasn't going to let this creature of lies twist my own insecurities into my downfall.

"There's a problem with the tactics you're trying to use on me," I growled as I pushed all of that despair, self-loathing, and heartache away from me, stoking the fire inside myself with all the anger I'd been bearing for so fucking long that I was ready to combust with it.

"Oh?" the girl asked, tilting her head like she doubted me, but her tricks weren't going to work anymore. They were nothing, insubstantial, the petulant insecurities of a child, but they weren't even close to the truth of the woman I'd become.

"You're assuming I'd rather die here, sacrifice myself in her name, free her from the burden of my weight around her neck."

"Won't you?" she cooed, something unholy flickering through her eyes as her bare feet padded closer. "Won't you lie down here and set her free? Or will your selfishness keep growing and growing until it consumes both of you? Will you curse her even further than she has already been cursed?"

"My love for her *is* selfish," I snarled in agreement. "And I'm no hero. Perhaps if I was, I *would* sacrifice myself here and now, lay down my life in the hopes that it might buy her the freedom you claim it would. That it might leave her free to rule without me, to love without me, to just fucking *be* without me. But my death would be the destruction of the beauty in her soul. My end would be the ruin of all the light in her world. So no, I won't sacrifice myself so that the world can have more of her. I'd rather sacrifice the world itself, just so that I can be there to make sure I see her when she rises up to claim it. By her side, where I belong. Two halves of one fucking whole. And if you don't know that much about me, then you aren't me at all."

The girl screamed again as I swung my sword at her, the blade carving through her neck with an impact that made my bones rattle as her blood coated me.

But I knew it wasn't as simple as that, her scream echoing on and on, bouncing through the silent forest like a summons for every branch and bow within the cursed forest to turn their attention on me, to aim their darkness my way and cage me so this scarred girl could destroy me.

I didn't wait to find out if the blow had been enough to kill her, I just turned and fled, heart thundering, muscles quaking. Phoenix fire erupted wherever my feet fell, the entire world bursting into flames at my back, and I let it all burn.

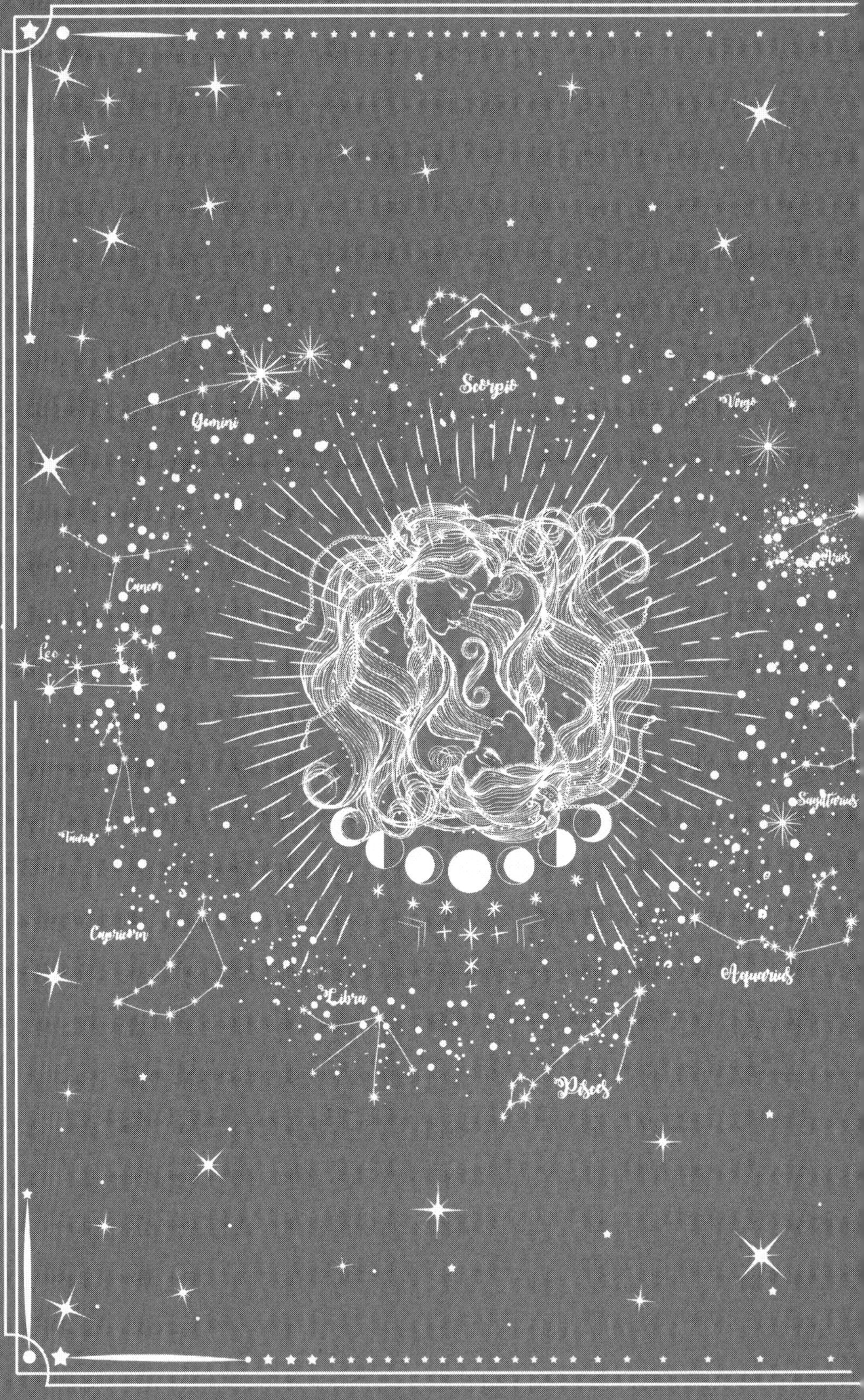
Scorpio
Gemini
Virgo
Cancer
Leo
Taurus
Sagittarius
Capricorn
Aquarius
Libra
Pisces

DARCY

CHAPTER SIXTY FOUR

The shadows were thick, twisting around my skull in a vortex, the Shadow Beast roaring deafeningly loud inside my head.

I clutched my ears, trying to drown it out, knowing I was screaming but unable to hear my own voice over the noise of the beast. Something was tearing down the middle of me, magic cleaving me apart and driving an axe into the centre of my being.

It was going to kill me. I was sure of it. There was no way I could survive a pain this deep. It was entrenched in everything I was and everything I could ever be. And I could have sworn the Shadow Beast felt it too.

There were whispers in my head, the shadows frantic, rushing through me like ghosts darting into the space between my soul and my physical being. They were biting, clawing, trying to find a way out of this body because it was about to be ripped in two.

And all I could think of was Tory and how I'd never get to say goodbye. How I desperately missed the fire in her eyes and the way every atom that made her was an answering call to the atoms that made me. We weren't meant to be torn apart; it was unnatural. And I was so fucking terrified that I couldn't claw my way out of this darkness and find my way back to her, letting her down and leaving her here on this forsaken earth alone. We weren't made to exist apart, we couldn't, and it was my duty to return to her as well as my most desperate, heartfelt desire.

I heard my screams at last, the Shadow Beast's roars sounding suddenly separate, booming around the room.

I was thrown violently backwards against the wall as a thick, blackish smoke poured from my chest and I gasped, my eyes flying wide as I fell prey to this excruciating torture.

Orion was before me, calling my name, his magic restraining cuffs broken at his feet and a Faelight hovering above us to light the dark chamber.

He tried to get to me, but the power pouring from my skin was like a raging hurricane blasting through the room, and it knocked him back time and again.

The howling noise grew to a crescendo and I could have sworn my soul was being severed clean from my body as a violent sucking feeling dragged at my chest. The shadows sped from me in a tornado of black, and where it landed the Shadow Beast began to form.

I couldn't move, pinned there against the stone wall as the Shadow Beast somehow materialised without me, my skin still my own, while it stood solidly before us as its own, snarling being.

Every last scrap of the shadows left my body and I hit the floor, collapsing there in a heap, looking up at the monster who was no longer one with me, at a loss to what was happening.

The Shadow Beast seemed momentarily dazed, sniffing the air and gaining its bearings as I pushed myself to my knees and Orion shot towards me, looking me over in concern.

"Her blood was my blood," he said in explanation. "She paid the price of your curse in her death. You're free."

Before I could have a second to register that, the Shadow Beast collided with us, throwing Orion away from me. He tumbled over the floor, swearing as he hurried to cast air magic, but the Shadow Beast slammed into me before he could. It swung a paw for my head, and I ducked low, its claws slashing and tearing through the wall at my back instead.

We went flying through the bricks into another dark chamber and I scrambled away from the monster, darting beneath a wooden table to hide. I was naked, bruised, covered in blood and dust too, probably looking like some sort of wild creature who'd just crawled out of the depths of hell. My body ached from the impact with that wall, but I'd miraculously avoided anything life threatening as I did a mental scan of my injuries.

The Shadow Beast prowled away from me, sniffing the air and I lifted my fingers, trying to bring magic to them, but the well in my chest was just as empty as before.

Panic stole over me as I considered what that meant. Had my magic and Order been stolen forever, even though I was free of it? I flexed my hands, feeling stronger than I had in weeks, and that meant I could fight, even if only with my damn fists.

Orion appeared, silhouetted in the hole in the wall as his Faelight trailed after him, his expression stricken with worry.

"Blue?" he hissed.

His Faelight offered me a better view of the room and I peeked out from my hiding place. The long chamber was an armoury, rows of shields and weapons stretched the length of it, hung on racks on the walls between beautiful coats of arms and suits of armour. The Shadow Beast was at the far end of it, sniffing the air and searching for me.

"I'm here," I whispered, waving to catch Orion's attention and relief washed over his features.

"Stay there." He shot past me in a blur of speed and The Shadow Beast roared, wheeling around to intercept him. My teeth clenched together in refusal of his words.

"That's *my* goddamn kill," I growled as Orion worked to capture the Shadow Beast in a sphere of air at the far end of the room.

I slipped out from under the table, and I stole the time Orion was buying me to grab a breastplate with two gleaming silver Harpy wings across it, pulling it on along with a pair of training shorts and some boots.

Then there were weapons, beautiful, shining weapons all hanging on the wall in front of me. My gaze locked immediately on a gleaming white sword with the Aquila constellation running the length of the blade, which I could have sworn was linked to the Harpy Order.

My hand closed around the hilt, and I felt certain this had once belonged to my mother. There was an expectant energy in it like it had been waiting for me for a long, long time and emotion burned hot in my chest. It was like she was just behind me, a hand braced on my shoulder and her love winding around my heart.

My gaze turned to the Shadow Beast which Orion was working to contain, my pulse slowing to a steady thump as destiny whispered my name.

"Move aside," I called to Orion, and he looked back at me over his shoulder, his brows lifting in surprise as he found me ready for battle. "This is my fight."

"We can do it together," he said firmly.

"No," I demanded.

"You have no magic," he said, protectiveness sparking in his eyes, but I wasn't backing down on this.

The Shadow Beast and I had unfinished business, and I was going to make it pay for the suffering it had caused me and my mate, for stealing Geraldine from this world, for killing so many rebels.

"I don't need magic, I have fury and my mother's sword." I hounded forward, raising my sword to point at the beast within the shell of air magic Orion had forged, its huge claws tearing against the barrier as it fought to break through.

I felt terribly mortal, and the fact was, I may never feel another drop of magic blazing through my blood again. This creature had taken that from me, and I didn't care that I would be risking my life for revenge. I needed to do this, to kill this beast which had stolen the crucial part of me which made me Fae. My Order, my power. But it hadn't stolen my ability to fight. And while I still drew breath into my lungs, I would do so with every ounce of energy I possessed.

"I can't let you do this," Orion said as I moved to his side.

"I'm not asking," I said darkly. "I'm ordering you to."

Our gazes locked and a heavy hum of energy passed between us, his desire to protect me clashing with his want to obey his queen. His features were strained from the effort it was taking to hold the Shadow Beast back, and I knew it was going to break through his shield at any moment.

"Do you believe in me, Lance Orion?" I asked and his throat rose and fell.

"My belief in you is without bounds," he said heavily. "But-"

"Then why would you steal away my chance to fight the creature who has tormented me, stolen my will and forced you to bleed and bleed for my curse?" I hissed. "Would you truly deny me this kill?"

He opened and closed his mouth, fear and love chasing each other in his eyes, but then he relented, bowing his head to me.

"Of course not, my Queen." He stepped back and I nodded to him, encouraging him to dispel his air shield.

I lifted my newly claimed sword, muscle memory igniting in me as I stood as a warrior before the shadow who had enslaved me, ready to meet it head on.

Orion released the shield of air, and a cry of purest fury left my lips as I charged forward, sword high, ready to carve the Shadow Beast's head from its neck. I may have been a shell of a Fae, and this might well have been the last fight I ever fought in this world of twisted fates, heartless stars and extraordinary magic, but I'd fight it well. I'd do my twin proud, and I'd try my very best to provide some justice for those who had fallen prey to this monster.

I sprang onto a table full of deadly blades, sprinting across them as the Shadow Beast leapt to meet me. A battle cry fuelled with all the grief in my heart poured from lungs, and I jumped off the end of the table, the white sword glinting with power as I swung it towards my target. But the Shadow Beast veered sideways to avoid the worst of the blow, the blade's edge tearing down its shoulder instead of piercing its heart, spilling blackish blood.

It howled in agony as I landed beside it, and the animal threw out a paw which slammed into my gut and knocked me flying into a suit of armour. It came crashing down and I rolled away from the heavy metal, shoving to my feet and running to engage the beast once more.

Its bear-like jaw peeled back in a snarl as the Shadow Beast lunged, gnashing those deadly teeth while I swung my sword in an equally deadly arc, carving a deep cut into its muzzle and forcing it to retreat.

I pressed my advantage, but the Shadow Beast turned to smoke before my eyes, my sword slashing through the heart of that dark vapour and making a curse of frustration leave me.

I kept my gaze on the hellish shadow as it whirled around, trying to get behind me and I kept my sword high, ready to attack the moment it rematerialized.

"Come on," I encouraged. "Stop hiding and fight me!"

The shadow surged forward, latching onto my ankles and dragging me across the floor at high speed before swinging me towards the wall. I smashed into it and my grip on my sword loosened as my knees impacted with the floor, the wind knocked out of me.

I tightened my hold on the hilt of my blade, but the shadow threw me into the air towards the high, arching ceiling and I cried out, forced to let go of my weapon as I reached out wildly to catch hold of something. My hands wrapped around a large wooden chandelier hanging from the roof and I held onto it with all my strength as the light swung violently above the chamber.

The Shadow Beast returned to its animal form, leaping from the floor and snapping at my ankles. I gasped, hooking my leg over the circular wooden base of the chandelier, and holding on tighter, my stomach flipping over as I swung above certain death.

A scuttling noise caught my ear and dread pounded through me as I turned to look in the direction it had come from, my gaze settling on the monstrous form of Tharix as he crawled upside down along the ceiling, coming right for me, a wicked smile on his handsome face. The whites of his eyes were showing and his black pupils were locked on me, tongue slicking out over his lips as he closed in on me.

Fear twisted through my chest, and I gazed from one fatality to another, trying to figure out which one was likely to reach me first.

Orion appeared on a magical gust of air, a cutlass in his grip as he swung it into Tharix's stomach and drove it forcefully through him into the ceiling.

Tharix shrieked like a banshee, swiping at Orion who ducked the blow before soaring higher and stabbing at Lavinia's son with blades of ice, over and over, everywhere he could land a strike.

Black blood spilled down over Orion and shadows poured out of Tharix from every hole punctured in him, the coils of darkness wrapping tight around my mate and reeling him in like a spider preying upon a fly.

Orion cast ice shards out from his skin, severing clean through the shadows holding him and wheeling away from Tharix before Lionel's new son could take a bite out of him.

The Shadow Beast caught my boot in its grip, and I screamed as I was ripped from the chandelier, tumbling through the air before hanging upside down from the monster's jaws. My foot slipped out of my boot, and I hit the floor, scrambling underneath its furry belly and hurriedly searching for a weapon. The white sword was just beyond the beast and I dove for it, my knees crashing clumsily against the stone floor as I took the blade into my grip.

The Shadow Beast swung around before I could drive the vicious sword into its stomach and I leapt to my feet, forced to run as it snapped at my heels and I had no room to counter the attack. I needed to get some space between us, but I could feel its hot breath on my neck and knew one single stumble would see me dead.

I couldn't turn to look for Orion, all I could do was run and hope he found a way to kill Tharix while I found enough strength in me to slaughter my own opponent.

The palace walls were rumbling, and the stones beneath my feet were humming like the building was coming to life. The ghosts of this royal place were roused, long lost magic stirring in the walls and crying out for vengeance.

I would damn well live up to the reputation of the Vega name today, and prove why I was a queen of fire and ruler of death. The shadows had haunted me too long, kept me subdued when I should have been rising like the Phoenix I was. I may have been deep in the ashes now with no magic or Order to claim, but the embers were catching in my soul, and it didn't matter if I was practically mortal, because I was still a Vega Queen, and I wasn't even close to finished yet.

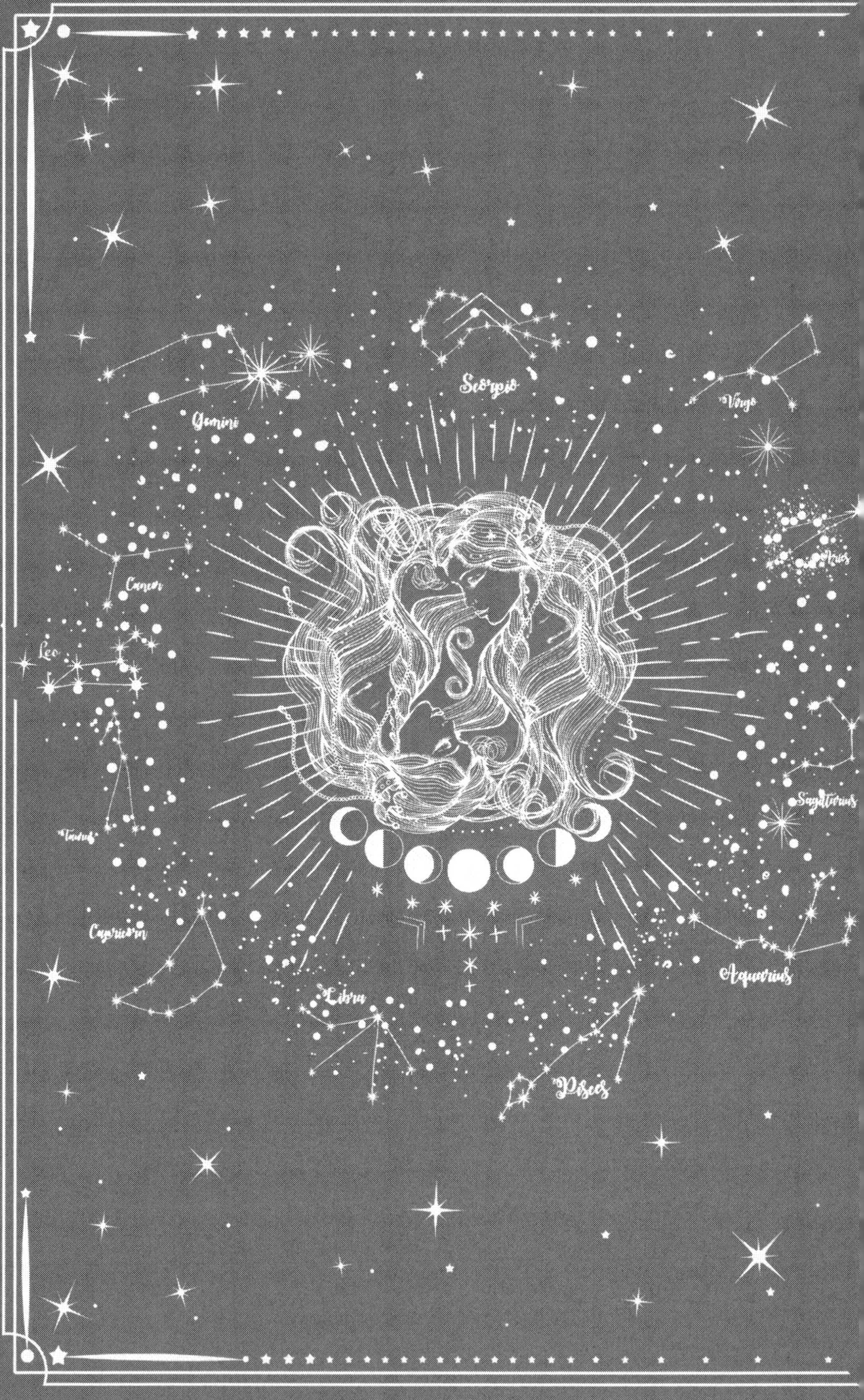
Scorpio
Virgo
Gemini
Cancer
Leo
Taurus
Sagittarius
Capricorn
Aquarius
Libra
Pisces

TORY

CHAPTER SIXTY FIVE

My legs burned from running through the trees, my heart thrashing wildly as I raced away from that girl and that hut, the fading version of myself who I'd both feared and hated in the deepest recesses of my mind for so long. I'd faced the worst of myself and emerged from the despair it had tried to drown me with, and I felt lighter for it. Like looking into the face of the truth I'd feared for so long had set me free from some of it.

I could see the lies mixed in with those fears, the ones I'd convinced myself of for so long that it had been hard to see through them. But observing them from the outside made it easier to do so somehow. And though I certainly wouldn't have said I was cured of my insecurities and the reasons I had for being the way I was, I could forgive myself for some of it. I could see how certain parts of what I'd blamed myself for had never really been my fault in the first place.

I'd felt distant from the mortals who surrounded us for my entire childhood, always secretly hoping for a love that might surpass my difficulties and see beyond them. But we never would have fit in that place, even if I'd worked harder to play nice, had smiled more or tried to make friends with people who didn't understand me. Because our home was here, in Solaria. And that was where I'd found my place at last, with Darcy right there beside me.

I needed to find my pack, needed to finish the work on creating that bridge, then hope to hell that I could figure out where the Waters of Depth and Purity were.

The darkness pressed close beneath the trees, but the eerie, bone white colour of their trunks made it possible for me to see a path between them.

I didn't want to risk a light. Not with that thing still out there, the knowledge that it was hunting me rooted in my soul.

A glint of red in the dark caught my eye and a choked sob escaped me as I hurled myself towards it, snatching the ruby pendant from the ground and feeling the heat of it radiating into my skin.

I hurried to fasten it around my throat once more, the weight of it a relief which hit me soul deep.

The wind stirred around me, fingers ghosting along my arm, and I closed my eyes as I tried to lean into that fictitious feeling of him.

But the touch didn't seem like those I'd imagined before, it was more of a tug than a caress, an urgency filling me as the sense of him increased and I could have sworn I heard his voice hissing, "*Run.*"

My eyes snapped open, and I spun around, whipping my sword from my sheath once more. The young version of me stood between two of the towering trunks, a new scar ringing her throat where my blade had sliced into it, blood trickling down to stain her white nightgown.

"You killed him," she snarled, her words like a bullet to my gut. "You were the reason he fought in that battle. You were the reason he was so desperate to defeat his father. He'd been planning to challenge him long before you came and uprooted his entire life. He'd been waiting until he was ready to win. You made him strike too soon. You. Killed. Him."

Her words seared the skin from my bones and made me bleed out at her feet, those cutting, ruinous accusations which I'd never let myself look at in the light of day. But the whispers of them had chased each other in circles during the night, keeping me up hour after hour, reminding me of all the pain I'd caused him when I'd refused to love him beneath the stars, hissing at me that I should have seen what Lionel had been doing to him long before I had. I should have seen and been the lifeline he'd so desperately needed. But instead, I'd become the weight which hung from his shoulders and dragged him beneath the surface. I'd added to his pain and his burdens, and I'd given him even more to hurt over in the short time he'd been gifted in this life.

Despair reared its ugly head as she took a step closer to me, and I didn't know if it was her power or my truth which was working to destroy me, but it didn't matter.

Despair may have been a tempting escape, an easy cop out to my situation, but I had never been the kind to linger in my sorrow.

"I didn't kill him," I said in a low voice, raising my sword as I steeled myself to face her. "But I will keep my promise to avenge him."

No, sorrow and despair weren't the path I'd been born to tread. But vengeance? Wrath? Anger? Violence? I could marry myself to those emotions just fine.

The girl's eyes widened as I charged her down, her arms widening as if she might be readying to hurl some terrible power at me, but she didn't. She did nothing at all to stop me, my blade piercing her heart of fear and nightmares, and a crack resounding throughout the entire forest as her body split and sundered.

I jerked my blade back, watching as those scars on her skin began to glow with an inner light, the corners of her lips lifting as her familiar green eyes met my own.

I threw a hand up to shield my face as she exploded into that light, golden flames arcing from her before splitting apart and dispersing, fading into nothing in the face of my fury and leaving me alone in the silence of the forest once more.

I was panting, trembling, aching all over and I knew I was nowhere near done with this place. Yet as I cast a Faelight above my head and turned back to hunt for my pack, I found the strength to keep going in the promise carved into my palm.

My feet seemed to know their own route and within moments I spotted my pack, sheathing my sword once more as I hefted it onto my back and turned my attention to the huge trunk I'd begun to cast the bridge magic on.

I expelled a heavy breath, the anger that girl had awoke in me rising as I closed my fist around the scar which bound me to my promise.

"I'm coming," I told him, knowing he was close, haunting my steps as I strode to the trunk and allowed my fire to ignite on my fingertip once more.

I didn't have to concentrate anywhere near as hard as I had when I'd started this, the movements coming easily as I burned the Elemental symbol for water into the bark of the tree, its screams doing nothing to slow me. Next, I scrawled the truth of my heart into the wood. The flame and the Dragon. All I needed in this world and any other.

A rumble started up in the ground beneath my feet as I slit the scar on my palm open with my dagger, blood trickling between my fingers while I sank into that well of old magic hidden within the world.

I could feel it stirring in the air around me, humming in the centre of the damned trees themselves and purring as it brushed against the potency of my rage.

The power of ether crested like a wave around me as I summoned it to do my bidding, offering up the blood of my vow to it until I felt it lifting me from my feet, the swell of that wave ready to break over the earth all around me.

I slammed my bloody palm against the bone white trunk of the still screaming tree and the power which erupted from me sent a shockwave tumbling out into the forest as the tree was ripped from the ground.

Roots tore their way out of the dirt beneath me, soil cascading all around as the enormous tree screamed louder, its fate already sealed, and a groan loud enough to be heard for miles filled the air before the echoing boom of it crashing to the forest floor consumed all else.

The tree's screams cut off sharply and I threw my arms up to shield my face as I felt the curse which had been bound to it shattering, the ether vibrating with the power of its end. And I wondered if somewhere out in the world beyond this place of doom and damnation, the ancestors of the Fae who that curse had been intended for might suddenly find their luck changing.

The power I'd summoned fell away and I dropped from the air, almost slipping on the smooth bark of the fallen tree trunk as I landed on it, my Bridge to the Beyond stretching out ahead of me.

Magic crackled in the air surrounding it, the forest blurring either side of it, like it no longer led between those trees, but had carved a passage through the fabric of the world itself. This had been the ancient form of travelling by magic before stardust had been cultivated to fulfil this purpose. It was unstable and short-lived, but so long as I could cross before the magic faltered, it would deliver me to the destination I desired.

I started walking without hesitation, a little magic healing the cut on my palm and a flame igniting at my side to recharge the power I'd burned through.

I kept my gaze fixed ahead as voices tried to lure me from either side of the bridge, remembering the warnings in the Book of Earth as I refused to look their way. If I was tempted left or right, then I would fall prey to the things that lurked between realms, and no part of me would remain to be found ever again.

One foot in front of the other, I continued, the hazy white light either side of me flickering in my peripheral vision, but I didn't look at it. Not once.

There was a presence at my back, footsteps hounding my own. But I didn't turn. Because I knew who was stalking me into the dark, and I had always enjoyed his brand of violence best.

Scorpio
Gemini
Virgo
Cancer
Leo
Sagittarius
Capricorn
Aquarius
Libra
Pisces

ORION

CHAPTER SIXTY SIX

Tharix healed far too fucking quickly for my liking, and now he was chasing me around the ceiling of the armoury while I balanced on a gust of air and threw ice blades at him with the full ferocity of my Vampire strength.

With every blow I landed, Tharix jerked back from the impact, pausing only long enough for him to tug out my weapon and heal himself, shadow coiling around his body and feeding him the power he needed to rejuvenate. He was a ruthless opponent, gifted with all four Elements as well as the shadows too, and it was taking everything I had to block his attacks.

I tried to catch sight of Darcy below, the Shadow Beast's roars carrying back to me from the far end of the room, making the walls tremble. The odd battle cry coming from her assured me she was still breathing at least.

"Come on, beautiful. Kill that motherfucker," I said under my breath. Maybe I was a fucking fool to step aside and let her claim that fight when she had no magic to wield, but if there was one thing I'd learned about that girl, it was that she could do anything she put her mind to. And I wasn't going to stand in the way when I could see how much she needed this kill. It was Fae instinct to cut down your enemies, and I trusted her ability to do so.

I cast a spear of ice in my palm as Tharix scuttled across the ceiling upside-down, moving almost as fast as I could with my Order gifts. His face didn't match the horrid, callous aura his body gave off, his features too handsome to belong to a monster born of the two most heinous Fae in existence.

I waited in place, using myself as bait and taking a steadying breath as I waited for the perfect moment.

"Over here, you brainless fuckwit," I encouraged, my arm held back behind me ready to launch the spear directly between Tharix's eyes.

The high of the fight had my blood pumping and adrenaline coursing through my veins. Being able to unleash the full magnitude of my power once more was sending me into a bloodthirsty fever, and I hungered for the death of my enemies with a voraciousness I hadn't felt in a long time. I was free, Darcy's curse broken, and Lavinia's Death bond lost to the demise of Stella. We weren't exactly out of the shit pit yet, but we were halfway up the walls and reaching for the sky.

Tharix screeched as he closed in on me, barely a thought behind his eyes except a need for my death, but I'd be damned if I was going out of this world on the day my mate and I had been liberated from our chains.

I launched the spear with a shout of effort, the deadly weapon carving through the air with such power that it practically sang as it went.

It slammed dead centre between Tharix's eyes and his shrieks were cut off, his grip on the ceiling falling slack and his muscular body tumbling down to slam into the flagstones below. He may have been gifted with the four Elements, but he'd had no training in harnessing them yet, and clearly his parents hadn't taught him how to catch himself with air.

My mouth twitched up at the corner as I released the air from beneath my feet, dropping at speed and landing on his chest with a thud that made his body jerk beneath me. I left the spear lodged in his skull, raising a hand and using air to hook a double-headed axe off a rack on the wall, summoning it into my fist. It was heavy and cold in my palm, a perfectly lethal piece of weaponry that would be fit for parting Tharix's head from his shoulders.

I stepped off of him, moving to angle myself to the side of his neck, raising the axe above my head with a twisted satisfaction before bringing it down with all the power of a god brimming in my veins.

But before the blade's edge could cleave into his skin, Tharix's hand shot out and powerful vines grew from him palms, capturing the handle just above my hands, a hair's breadth before I could finish him.

I gritted my teeth, shoving my weight down to try and break through his hold, but he started pushing back, his power unimaginable and more vines latching around me, trying to tear me away from him. My biceps trembled with the effort of forcing the axe down and his own arm shook with equal effort, keeping me at bay with both his magic and his incredible strength. His eyes were still closed, the spear still firmly lodged in his head, but somehow, he acted as if he could see me regardless.

His other arm came up, fingers flexing and shadows burst from him, slamming into me and crashing into the air shield mere inches from my skin. I was forced back from the impact, losing my grip on the axe and Tharix tossed the weapon away across the room where it clanged along the floor somewhere out of sight.

I spat a curse, ripping myself free of the vines wound around my arms, then turning tail and shooting towards the nearest weapon rack. I grabbed weapon after weapon, hurling them at Tharix as he started to rise, reaching for the spear in his fucking face. Whips of shadow and blasts of Elemental magic knocked my weapons away one after the other, and I increased my speed, throwing two, three, five at once, forcing him to work harder to parry my blows.

But the asshole managed it, regaining his feet and yanking the ice spear from his skull without care. Blackish blood poured down his face for a second before the shadows rushed into that hole and healed it for him.

His dark eyes locked on me, and he started striding towards me, slow and steady, psycho killer style.

I stood my ground, using my air magic to grab hold of every weapon hanging along the walls so that they floated above us, the sharp points angled towards my enemy.

I smirked as he stopped walking, taking in the tens of weapons that hung around us in the air with curiosity. Then I sent them flying, blasting all of my power behind them so they plunged toward him with terrifying speed, coming at him from every angle. He sent whips of shadow out in all directions, knocking away as many as he could manage, but it wasn't enough. It was never going to be enough.

My heart lifted with my victory, but Tharix turned to smoke and the weapons slammed into the space where he'd just been standing, clattering loudly against the floor, and bouncing away in every direction.

"Fuck," I spat, turning as the Shadow Beast roared to my left.

Darcy was climbing the racks to escape its powerful jaws, the creature snapping its teeth. She jumped off of the rack, grabbing a dagger as she went and driving it down into the Shadow Beast's back as her feet hit its shoulders, a scream of defiance leaving her.

The creature roared and I definitely got an inappropriate semi over my girl's display. The Shadow Beast reared up, throwing her off of it before she could kill it, and the dagger remained deep in its back while she went rolling across the floor.

I lost sight of her as a cloud of shadow slammed into me and drove against my air shield, trying to find a way through as it backed me up against the wall. I blasted the shadowy form of Tharix away from me with a torrent of air and he shifted back into his corporeal form before I could find an air vent to stuff him into. His feet hit a wooden table across the room, and I gave up wasting my power on trying to blast him away.

I cast the nearest sword into my grip and swung it in my hand, a ring sounding through the jet black metal. I noticed the Hydra constellation etched onto its surface, and as I grazed my thumb over it, purple fire burst out along the blade. My lips parted in surprise before curling up into a sinister smile.

Holy fuck, looks like I just got hold of the Savage King's blade.

I tipped Hail Vega a mental salute as I faced my enemy within the old king's armoury, raising his weapon and feeling the walls shiver around me. I wondered if he was looking this way from beyond the Veil, and my chest swelled at the thought.

"You'd better be watching, sir. Because this fight is for the Vegas."

Scorpio
Gemini
Virgo
Cancer
Aries
Leo
Taurus
Sagittarius
Capricorn
Aquarius
Libra
Pisces

TORY

CHAPTER SIXTY SEVEN

The world had bent and shifted around me as I passed through a ripple in the world on that bridge, nothing and nobody existing beyond it while I was crossing, balanced on the thick, bone white trunk.

It was a little like travelling via stardust, but instead of those glimmering eyes watching me pass them by, all I felt beyond the edges of the bridge was an endless drop into a lightless void filled with creatures of malice and greed.

If I slipped, I knew I wouldn't ever return here. That dark would consume me, bit by bit.

By the time the end the of the bridge became visible ahead of me, I was more than ready to step from it, and I leapt down from the trunk onto grey sand with a sigh of relief.

I was still in the Damned Forest, the white trees all around me in every direction but one.

Directly ahead, an expanse lay before me, a body of water so still that it seemed more like glass, reflecting the sky above so perfectly that stepping into it would have been like sinking into the heavens themselves.

I strode towards it, my chin held high and that otherworldly sense of him still close.

This was going to work. Whatever it took, I was going to claim the answers I hunted here and keep my oath to him and the stars.

I paused at the edge of the water, looking out over the endless expanse of it to the horizon where it faded from sight. How was I supposed to pass beyond something so immense? I would have called it an ocean if it hadn't been so perfectly still.

I took the Book of Water from my pack, opening it and turning the pages as I hunted for a passage I half remembered about crossing a great sea. I'd dismissed the magic there as irrelevant, but perhaps there had been more to it, something which could help me.

I flicked through page after page until a phantom hand seemed to reach out and flip the book open to a specific one, my heart damn near leaping from my chest and a curse spilling from my lips.

To pass across a great sea, you must simply pay the ferryman.

Well, that sounded a whole lot like travelling into the realm of death, and if I'd been here for any other reason, then I probably would have run screaming for the fucking hills before attempting it, but I was beyond the point of return. I hadn't come all this way to leave without fulfilling my vow, and I refused to back down even now.

My gaze roamed over the image accompanying the vague instruction, a crying girl throwing a gold coin into a river while calling for the ferryman to aid her.

That seemed…suspiciously easy.

I returned the Book of Water to my pack and took the small coin purse from the bottom of it, taking three ancient, golden auras from it and holding them tight in my fist. I'd borrowed them from Darius's treasure, my research on the five books I'd stolen from the Library of the Lost having prepared me for the use of both gold and gemstones. So I'd thought to bring some of each just in case.

I moved closer to the water's edge but made sure not to so much as nudge that iridescent pane of liquid with the toe of my boot.

I raised my fist above the water and pushed my power into the magic of the world, calling out across the silence and hoping this wasn't an act of insanity.

"I need passage from the ferryman!" The three coins I dropped into the water splashed loudly, the ripples they cast spreading out across the surface in an unholy arc, like a signal designed to tell every beast and monster within that water precisely where I was.

Nothing but that creeping silence greeted me for several long minutes, but then I heard it.

A faint splashing sound caught my attention and I looked to my right, finding a figure shrouded in darkness guiding a raft along the water's edge towards me.

The flame at my side burned hotter, my power swelling within me as the heat of it warmed me through and helped give me the courage to hold my ground while the raft drew closer to me.

It bumped against the sand before me, and I tried not to flinch as the figure standing on it lowered their hood.

My father stood there, his gaze expressionless and hard, the mask of the Savage King firmly lining his features and nothing but contempt oozing from him as he waited for me to board his vessel.

"What is this?" I hissed, holding my ground as I stared at the creature who I knew couldn't really be a relative of mine.

"Your chance to cross," Hail replied gravely, waving a hand at the small space beside him on the raft. "If you can face the cost of passage."

A glint of gold caught my attention and I glanced down, spotting the three coins from Darius's trove still sitting there, ignored and unwanted by this thing wearing my father's flesh.

He didn't wait for me to think on it, his pole sinking into the water as he pushed off, floating away from the edge, and leaving me on the bank, a certainty filling me that this was my only chance at making it across that water. I could try to fly, but I doubted it would work, the magic here more than able to make that journey endless if I didn't fulfil its requirements for passage.

"Fuck my life," I muttered.

I backed up, still unwilling to touch so much as a drop of that water and taking a running jump from the bank instead. I landed heavily, the raft bobbing wildly, but Hail barely even looked at me, simply pushing us further out into the water with his pole.

"Why are you wearing my father's face?" I ground out as the creepy as fuck fog began to rise in the trees behind us, tendrils of it crawling over the surface of the water.

"I am wearing the face of your enemy," he replied simply, his voice a cruel and aloof thing.

"Well, I'm sorry to burst your bubble, but my father isn't my enemy. Lionel Acrux tops that miserably long list," I told him, folding my arms against the chill.

The fog continued to build around us, slowly working to hide us from view. Nothing but the soft splash of the ferryman's pole sounded while a pause just long enough to venture into uncomfortable stretched between us.

"Lionel Acrux did not make me into the monster your kingdom feared above all others," Hail purred softly. "He only aimed my nature at those he desired to see wounded."

"What's that supposed to mean?" I bit out.

Instead of answering, the ferryman waved a hand before me and as I looked down into the water where he'd indicated, I saw what I had to assume was a memory from the past.

My father was in his shifted form, the many headed Hydra resembling a Dragon with its black scales and reptilian body, though the fire which burst from one of its mouths was a toxic looking purple instead of red.

I forced myself to watch as Hail raced towards a small army of Fae, around a hundred of them pouring from the edge of their village to fight him, their screams filling the air as he cut through them without hesitation. Their cries for mercy haunted me as I watched him burning those who ran, ripping bodies in two, bellowing his fury at the world then turning towards the village at a terrifying pace which promised more carnage.

My lips parted on a plea for the memory to stop, but it fell away anyway and changed to a new vision. Instead of seeing my father cutting through countless Fae like it was little more than a game to him, I saw myself in the battle. I was in my shifted form, my enemies turning and fleeing as Phoenix fire raged from me, wings of red and blue tearing from my outstretched fist and hunting them down as they ran.

"It wasn't like that," I hissed as I watched myself cutting through Nymphs and Fae, a snarl on my lips and bloodlust lighting my eyes.

"Do you deny the truth of your nature?" the ferryman asked mildly. "Can't you face what you are at your core?"

"That isn't me," I denied. "I never wanted to do any of that. I had no choice. I had to protect the people who-"

I was cut off as the vision in the water became my father again, his face set with self-loathing as he carved a hand through his dark hair, pacing before my mother.

"I had no choice," he said, a near pleading tone to his voice while Merissa looked at him like she didn't know him at all. "They were threatening our kingdom. They were going to hurt the people I have sworn to protect. They were planning to hurt *you.*"

I tore my gaze from the water and scowled at the ferryman.

"Lionel Acrux made him believe those lies," I said.

"What's your excuse then?" he asked.

I flinched at the implication in his words, shaking my head in a refusal of them as more moments from the battle played out in that water. I was blood-soaked, furious, vicious, unstoppable.

A monster.

I'd never seen it before but there it was. The thing which was such an intrinsic part of me, and it was capable of so much destruction, so much pain and death…

"What is selfless and selfish. Kind and cruel. Endless and fickle. Priceless and without cost. The harbinger of war and the one thing which can end it just as surely?" the ferryman asked, his words a taunt as the riddle washed over me and I just shook my head, having no idea what he meant. "What is excuse and reason. Validation and violence. Need and demand?"

"I don't know," I replied, and his laughter was cruel and cold.

"Yes, you do."

Scorpio
Gemini
Virgo
Cancer
Aries
Leo
Sagittarius
Taurus
Capricorn
Libra
Aquarius
Pisces

DARCY

CHAPTER SIXTY EIGHT

On a scale of one to totally fucked, I was sitting at an eight point five. I was under a table; the Shadow Beast sniffing the air as it stalked me while I caught my breath and held tight to the white sword that had been sent flying under here during our fight.

I could hear Orion still in the throes of battle with Tharix, and I sent him some good thoughts while focusing on what the hell my next move was.

Without my magic, I was relying solely on my physical strength, and I knew I couldn't go on like this forever. The wound Stella had cut into my arm was stinging, though the blood had stopped flowing, but now I had a collection of bruises and cuts to add to it, including a slit across my forehead and a deep scrape over my shin from one of the beast's claws.

I'd lost my other boot, so I was now shoeless too, and my breast plate was badly dented, pressing in on my chest a little too tightly. Not to mention the blood which was dried and caked against every inch of skin from the nice little bath Stella had given me.

All in all, I wasn't in the best shape, but I wasn't in the worst shape either. I just needed a plan to finish this before I made an error that let the Shadow Beast get its venomous teeth in me.

The beast dropped its head, sniffing deeply, too close to me for it not to pick up on the scent of blood I was trailing everywhere I went. It roared keenly, lunging at the table and flipping it into the air, unveiling me beneath it.

The monster aimed a swipe at me and I brought my sword up with a yell of effort, slashing at its huge paw. The Shadow Beast howled in pain, stumbling back and limping, blood leaking from the deep wound I'd sliced into the pad of its foot.

I gained my feet, pressing my advantage and lunging to strike its exposed throat, my pulse raising and hope fluttering through me. My blade slammed against it, then bounced off with a judder that ran right down the length of it.

"What the fuck?" I breathed, stumbling back a step, then remembering the collar of shadow that was in place around its neck.

The Shadow Beast lunged forward, teeth snapping, and I ducked, narrowly avoiding a fatal bite. I was forced to run between its front paws, then I jumped, catching its fur in my fists and climbing up and over its shoulder. The Shadow Beast swung around, baying in anger as it tried to shake me off, but I clung on tight, clambering higher until I was sat astride its back.

I hefted my mother's sword over my head, but the Shadow Beast started running the length of the armoury with a furious howl tearing from its lips that set the hairs raising along the back of my neck. It was moving so fast, I was forced to hold on or be sent flying off of it, so I tucked myself in tight, gripping my sword and waiting for my next chance for a kill.

We crashed through the back wall and I ducked behind the beast's head, flattening myself to its body with a gasp, holding on for dear life as it tore through another room I couldn't focus on before slamming into another wall, dust and debris tumbling over me. I somehow avoided the falling bricks that were cascading everywhere, clinging on even tighter as the Shadow Beast found itself in a stairwell and began running up the steps at speed.

We made it into a wide corridor where candelabras hung above us, and the Shadow Beast slowed its pace a little, giving me a chance to act. I sat up fast, lifting my sword and driving it brutally into the fleshy bit between its shoulder blades. The Shadow Beast yelped in agony, stumbling forward and crashing to the white carpet beneath us.

I jumped off of its back before I was crushed when it rolled, landing between its paws as blackish blood oozed out all around it.

I drove the sword into its chest in a vicious strike that made the Shadow Beast scream and from that wound spilled light. A glorious, blazing blue light that forced me to raise a hand to shield my eyes. Confusion raced through my head, and I moved forward, ready to finish the Beast once and for all, but as that light caressed my skin, I gasped. The touch of it was so familiar that it made me hurt inside, a noise of pain falling from my lips as I reached for it in desperation. Magic. And not just any magic. It was *mine*.

My fingers slipped deeper into the light, and it poured out of the Shadow Beast in a flood, slamming into my chest with such force that I was thrown to the floor at the monster's side. The light rushed all over my body like it was kissing me hello, then dove deep into my chest.

I sucked in air, my back arching against the floor as a moan of delight left me, the power of water spilling through my veins like a torrent of swirling rivers and roiling oceans living in me at once. Next, a green light flooded from the Shadow Beast and crashed into me, the power of earth thundering beneath my skin like an earthquake, rumbling its excitement at finding its way home.

Vines curled out along my arms, hugging my body and I all but sobbed at how good it was to feel it again. Then a deep, reddish glow poured from the Shadow Beast into me, and the warmth of my fire Element returned, heating me through to my core and promising I would never be cold again. No more frozen tiles draining the warmth from my bones, my fire would always be there to breathe heat into my skin like my very own sun living inside me.

Finally, the power of air came rushing towards me in a gleaming arc of white light, my blue hair flying around me in a storm before it slipped into me, and a laugh of purest joy burst free of my lungs. A hurricane of power twisted through me in a wild, glorious tempest that set my skin buzzing with energy. It was life itself, a storm in the summer and the freshest wind whipping through the highest peaks of the tallest trees.

I lay there with my Elements, bathing in the sensation of them washing together and finding a balance between them once more as all that power settled inside me where it belonged.

But there was one vital piece missing that made me ache, and as I turned to look for it, it came to me. A beautiful Phoenix bird flew from that gaping wound in the Shadow Beast's chest, wings of red and blue fire bursting from inside it and flying above me in a circle, a heart wrenching cry leaving its long beak.

Then it swept towards me, and I opened my arms wide to embrace it, the bird diving into the furthest regions of my chest and reuniting with my soul.

Tears of happiness slid down my cheeks as my Order fused back to the core of who I was, fire exploding out along my arms and laying claim to my skin at last. I twisted my fingers through their loving heat, my head falling back against the soft carpet as a sigh of sheer rapture left me.

I was me again. Whole, and unbreakable. And no shadow would ever find its way into my body from this day until my last.

As tempting as it was to buckle under the magnitude of what had been restored to me, I couldn't let myself linger there any longer, knowing Orion still faced Tharix. I had to move.

I got up and stepped towards the Shadow Beast to retrieve my mother's sword, picking it up and holding it tight as I examined the monster before me. It was still breathing, but only just.

I lifted the bloody sword higher, darkness coiling inside me as I looked down at this creature who had stolen away my will and forced me to kill time and again. It was easier to see it as separate from now that it no longer resided inside me. Orion had been right. I wasn't responsible for the terror caused by this animal. It had infected me with its cruelty, but it had never been my will behind the deaths it delivered, though I wasn't sure I'd ever really let go of the guilt. Or my rage over the injustice of the curse.

My upper lip peeled back, and I walked around to its head so it could see me, free from its binds, ready to make it pay for what it had done. It didn't try to rise, already too close to death, and acceptance glimmered in its pain-filled eyes.

I took a moment to press my hands into its fur, feeling for the collar around its throat, my fingers hooking around it. I pushed the fur aside, frowning at the dark and unwelcoming power it emitted, telling me exactly who had put it there.

"Lavinia," I spat her name, my frown deepening as I glanced at the beast's dark eyes and a thought crossed my mind that made me shudder inside. "Are you a prisoner too?"

I called on my Phoenix and felt it rise, a moan leaving my throat as I wielded that deeply innate power, red and blue flames dancing in my hand, filling me with the most riotous kind of joy. I pressed them against the collar, driving them deep and burning away the power which held it there. With a hissing noise, the collar broke under the intensity of my flames, and it hit the floor beneath the Shadow Beast, turning to ash.

The Shadow Beast whined, the sound so mournful that it tugged on my heart strings. It was grief, regret, and I shared in that exact same pain, knowing it far too well.

I moved cautiously around in front of it, finding its hellish black eyes changing until they were a beautiful burnt umber colour instead.

My lips parted and that ounce of pity I felt grew to a leaden weight inside me which I couldn't ignore. I made a decision, knowing I might regret it, but having to take this risk, because if this creature had been bound by Lavinia's power, then it was as innocent as I was in all of this. But then again, if it wasn't, I was about to make a grave mistake.

"I'd hope someone would take the risk if it was me," I whispered, reaching out and pressing my palm to the soft spot between the beast's captivating eyes, not letting myself back down on this. It was instinct, and I had to trust it.

I sent a flood of healing magic into the beast's body, not knowing if it was even capable of healing this way, but I found unknown magic inside the creature which was entirely alien to me, and somehow, I latched onto it, fuelling its ability to heal and letting it do the rest of the work. Shadow coiled out from its limbs, unlike any I'd seen before. It was pale grey and shimmered with an iridescent light which seemed to glow from within.

The Shadow Beast whimpered pathetically, but after a few moments, it let out a bark that made me stagger back and raise my hands defensively. A thump, thump, thump noise sounded, and I side-stepped cautiously to see where it was coming from, expecting an attack at any moment as the creature raised its head. Its fluffy tail was wagging, hitting the carpet like a dog happy to see its master.

"Holy shit," I exhaled.

The Shadow Beast rose to its feet, and I cast a firm air shield around me, ready to go back to war with it if I had to. But as it ran forward, grunting happily, it leaned down and licked the solid shield around me, making me stall in shock.

"Blue, get back," Orion barked, appearing behind me at the top of the stairwell that had been all but ripped apart by the monster which was now licking me.

"It's okay," I said quickly, achingly relieved to find my mate was alright.

He raised a black metal sword in his hand with purple fire licking along the edges of it. It looked like a sister to the white sword I'd claimed.

"What do you mean 'okay'?" he demanded, stepping froward with his eyes locked on the beast. The huge shadow creature sat down in front of us, wagging its tail more excitedly, its tongue hanging out the side of its mouth.

"It was a prisoner," I blurted. "Like I was. But I got my magic and Order back from it and-"

"You did?" he gasped, rushing toward me with hope blazing a trail through his eyes.

"Yes." I smiled widely, casting a flame in my palm as proof and loving how my magic reserves swelled in response.

"Thank the sun," he said, happiness lighting his features despite all the darkness that still surrounded us.

"Um, also, the Shadow Beast is free too and… I think it's coming with us," I added quickly.

"What?" Orion growled, his expression falling stern in an instant.

A shrill cry came from behind him, and he turned with a curse, raising his free hand and blocking the stairwell with a thick wall of ice, closing up every gap before turning back to me. "We need to move. My magic will hold it for a bit, but-"

Tharix broke through the ice and I raised my hand, casting a huge, impenetrable wall of Phoenix Fire across the width of the corridor to hold him back.

"I can take him," I growled determinedly. "Go to Gabriel and get him out."

"No, Blue. Tharix can't die. I think he's fed by his mother's power," Orion said gravely, taking hold of my wrist. "We need to get out of here. My magic is running low and it's only a matter of time before Lionel returns with the full force of his Dragon Guardians."

I released a sharp breath of frustration, looking into his eyes and seeing the truth in them. Tharix screeched beyond my wall of fire as he tried to get through it but failed, and I figured that would have to be good enough for now. We couldn't waste time trying to kill an unkillable thing.

"Come on then." I turned, running down the hall, but Orion slammed into me, scooping me into his arms and speeding away from the Shadow Beast through the palace as I tucked my mother's sword to my chest. I took a moment to create sheaths for each of our newly claimed swords with my earth Element, binding them around our waists. Hell, it felt good to cast magic again. It was like the roots of me had been restored and were flourishing inside me, expanding to fill all the empty spaces.

"How exactly did you retrieve your powers?" Orion asked in awe, glancing down at me as I gripped his arm for support.

"I nearly killed the Shadow Beast, cut its chest open and they all came rushing out with my Order."

His mouth twitched up at the corner and a wild delight filled his eyes. "Fuck, I wish I'd seen that."

"I'll give you the play by play when we get out of here," I said.

"Counting on it." He slammed to a halt, and I nearly got whiplash as I realised that we were outside the Royal Seer's Chamber.

I jumped from Orion's arms, blasting the door off its hinges with air magic, sending it flying across the room and hitting the wall. I ran to Gabriel who was slumped on the glass throne at its centre, unconscious and lined with cuts to his face. My heart tugged and vengeance stole through me at the motherfuckers who'd dared do this to my brother.

I woke him with a touch of magic to his temple, pouring healing magic into him too to wipe away his injuries.

Gabriel gasped awake, his eyes full of visions as Orion took hold of his chains, tearing them apart with his Order strength.

My brother reached up and clasped my cheek, a smile lifting his lips and knowledge filling his gaze. "You did it."

"I did it," I confirmed with a grin, pulling him to his feet. "And now we've gotta go."

My heart leapt as the Shadow Beast arrived, grunting in greeting and bounding over to us, but it didn't attack, only looking happy to find us once more, and I was pretty happy it had too.

"By the fucking stars," Gabriel breathed as Orion moved to break him out of his magic restraining cuffs.

"It's okay. He's on our side now. I think," I said. "Or maybe it's a girl. I don't really know."

"It's not coming with us," Orion muttered, and I arched a brow at him.

"It is," I said simply.

"It is not," he insisted. "And who's to say it won't turn on us all as soon as it gets hungry?"

"It's free now. It won't hurt us," I said firmly, hoping I was right about that, but I couldn't just leave it here to become Lavinia's prisoner again. At the very least, it was a weapon that could be wielded against us if we left it behind.

"Even if that were true, how are we supposed to smuggle a huge beast of death out of here discreetly?" Orion pushed.

At his words, the Shadow Beast turned to smoke, though now it was that pale grey colour instead of the dark, festering colour of rot it had been under Lavinia's command, and it moved to hover by my shoulder like it had understood him. I snorted and Orion gave me a dry look.

"No," he growled.

"Yes," I retorted, and Gabriel got up, stepping between us.

"This really isn't the time for marital bickering," he warned.

"It's not marital if we're not married," I pointed out.

"We will be married," Orion said in a growl.

"Says who?" I balked.

"Says me," he snapped. "I will wed you the moment this war is over."

"Oh you will, will you?" I narrowed my eyes at him. "We're already mated, why would we get married too?"

"Again," Gabriel cut in. "Really not the time. We need to go."

"Can you see the safest path out?" I asked my brother, and he took a moment to look into the future before nodding and gesturing for us to follow him.

"It's best we move without our Order gifts for now, there are guards outside the palace, but they'll move to new posts soon. We need to time this just so," Gabriel said mystically.

"Wait," I said, grabbing his arm before he could exit the chamber. "There were tracking spells cast on us before, what if you have one?"

"I doubt they'd bother putting one on me, they would be fully aware that I could *see* such a fate if I ever escaped. But I will make sure." Gabriel took a moment to investigate his future then came back to me with an encouraging smile. "Nothing."

"Good," I sighed, and he led the way out of the room.

I hurried down the corridor at his back with Orion beside me and he leaned low to speak in my ear. "You *will* marry me."

"You know, people usually ask someone if they want to marry them, not just command it," I whispered.

"You're already mated to me by the stars, what's there to ask?"
"Just because we're mated doesn't mean you get to skip a proposal." I shot him a sharp look. "So you'd better ask really, really nicely the next time you bring this up. And I am making no promises that I'll say yes."
"Or that I'll agree to it," Gabriel tossed back over his shoulder.
"And since when do I have to ask your permission?" Orion asked in shock.
"I second that question," I called to him.
"Since I'm your brother, it's my duty to look out for you," Gabriel replied, taking a sharp left down a short hallway and we hurried after him.
I scoffed, but Orion frowned, looking like he was taking his friend's words super seriously. Which was ridiculous because as much as I loved Gabriel, I sure as shit wasn't going to be waiting for his permission to marry Orion if I wanted to.
"Darius didn't ask your permission to marry Tory," Orion said.
"I know. And I'll be taking it up with him beyond the Veil, but as we're currently on two different planes, and I don't plan on dying anytime soon, he'll have to wait for the ass kicking I plan on presenting him with in the afterlife. You, however, don't get to escape me via death, so you'd better be nice as pie to me if you're determined to marry my sister." Gabriel darted right, then slowed, pressing his back to a wall as his eyes glazed with a vision.
Orion and I moved in protectively around him, swords lifted and magic crackling in our free hands.
"Love you." Orion shot me a wink and I melted for him as always.
"Love you back. Let's get home."
"Where is home these days?"
"Wherever our family is," I said with a tug in my chest, missing them all so damn much. We had to get out of here and find our way back to them.
"And who are we counting as that beyond us three, Tory, Xavier and Caleb?" he asked.
"Max, plus Sofia and Tyler. And don't act like you're not dying for a Seth snuggle," I said with a hint of a smirk around my lips.
"Actually, I think I'll go back to the cage," he deadpanned.
I shook my head at him, but then my thoughts turned to the girl missing from our family, my heart ripping open at the loss of Geraldine. There was no way the world would ever be the same without her in it.
"This way." Gabriel jolted back to alertness, rushing ahead of us once more.
I forced away my grief, focusing on what needed to be done now. We couldn't make a mistake, we had to get out of here. If we were caught by Lionel and his Dragon Guardians, there was no reason for Lavinia to hold back on him killing us anymore.
We crossed through a smoking room and slipped through a door into a vast hallway of imposing paintings of Dragons and a silver edged glass doors leading out to a wide stone balcony. Gabriel slowed to a halt in a pool of moonlight and I moved to his side, frowning up at him, finding his eyes glazed and a crease of concern on his brow.
"What is it?" I asked in a whisper as he came back to us.
"The way is clear, but…I have a terrible sense of something ominous in the air."
"Can we go fast now?" Orion shot to his side. "I'll run while you and Darcy fly."
"Yeah, it's time." Gabriel took his shirt off, tossing it aside and revealing the myriad of tattooed symbols he had all over his body. His black wings burst free of his back, and he turned to the balcony doors, pushing them wide. "Climb down here, we'll stay above you, Orio, and we'll make a straight shot for the woodland beyond the grounds. The moment we breach the wards, Lionel will return, but so long as we keep moving, we should be long gone before he can catch up to us. And I'll be able to use my Sight after that to evade him."
He flexed his wings and I breathed in the clean, crisp winter air as it whipped through my hair. Freedom was begging me to claim it, demanding I find a way back home, to my sister, my friends. I was on the path to them, a new fate unfolding at

last. For a second the weight of Stella's sacrifice hung in the air, and gratitude swept through me for what she'd done. She may have been a toxic woman who had followed a road of destruction and foul deeds, but in the end, she had chosen to offer her life for me and her son. And there was no denying the good in that.

With only the breast plate covering my upper half, my wings were able to stretch free and I called on them, a thrill buzzing through me in anticipation of feeling them again.

I all but moaned as they came to me, the bronze sheen of feathers rising at my back and my Phoenix singing inside me.

Orion's eyes lit up as he watched me. "That feel good, beautiful?"

"So good," I exhaled.

"Come on," Gabriel urged, hopping up to crouch on the curved stone railing of the balcony, his eyes moving across the ground like a bird of prey hunting for a kill. "We'll fly low. Let's use the cover of those trees to move." He pointed to a path that headed through a woodland toward the perimeter of the vast grounds.

I nodded, moving up behind him, hungering to fly once more, my wings beat at my back, ready to cast me into the sky.

A shadow crossed the moon and all three of our heads snapped in that direction. I threw an air shield around all of us and Orion grabbed my hand, his power merging with my own to strengthen it further.

Lavinia appeared, hanging above us, almost hidden against the dark sky that was woven between the stars.

She descended like an omen of certain death, huge lashes of shadows sweeping from her hands and striking the dome of power surrounding us with a terrible strength, making us stagger back as we fought to hold it in place.

Gabriel jumped back down onto the balcony with a curse, looking to the sky as Lavinia hovered above us, vexed and hostile, shadows coiling from her body and her face set in a snarl.

"What have you done?!" She pointed at Orion in livid accusation, and I let Phoenix fire spill out over my wings to draw her attention to me, making her screech in horror. "No!" she cried. "How is this possible?!"

"The curse is broken," I spat. "We're no longer bound to you."

"Where is my Beast?" she snarled. "Come to me. Rip these traitors apart."

The Shadow Beast hovered closer to me in its smoky form, but didn't answer her call. It was no longer her captive, and I would offer it a chance at true liberation this night. I was on the doorstep of escape, and I would be walking through the exit with my entourage in tow, so fucking help me.

"No one's coming to your aid, Lavinia!" I shouted, throwing more power into our shield while keeping my gaze firmly away from the thick vines Gabriel was summoning up from the ground beneath her, sneaking their way into the sky behind the shadow bitch.

Gabriel added razor sharp thorns along the length of the vines, weaving a net ready to capture her. All we needed was a chance, but as my mind turned to the Imperial Star and the curse that plagued my bloodline, I knew I was going to have to muster the strength of every Phoenix who had come before me to twist fate in our favour. But so be it.

Lavinia growled, the air shuddering with the guttural noise. "Are you sure about that, little Princess?" she hissed and at a movement of her head, Nymphs crept out of the woodland below, all of them having merged so well with the trees, we'd not seen them coming. There were tens of them, perhaps hundred more hiding out there in the dark, but even that new challenge didn't make me falter.

I'd risen from the belly of the palace, had bathed in the blood of a hundred Fae, battled a monster, and retrieved what had been lost to me. Now we were perched on the edge of salvation, and by the stars, the sun, and the moon, we would be leaving here together tonight.

Lavinia whipped our shield once again and Orion and I dug our heels in as the dome of air magic was forced back a foot.

A Nymph let out a horrid shriek, pointing to the net with its long probes and Gabriel threw it at Lavinia before she could turn to stop it. The net slammed over her, wrapping her up, binding tight and spilling blood as the thorns dug deep.

"Go!" I commanded and we ran for the edge of the balcony while Lavinia was fighting her way free of the net.

Gabriel glanced my way and I let my plan unfold in my head, his eyes glazing for a second before he *saw* what I wanted him to do, and he nodded his agreement. He lunged at Orion, grabbing hold of his right hand and carving his palm down it. Water magic ran between his fingers, and he used it to gather Stella's blood from Orion's palm, before trapping it in a red crystal of ice.

"What are you-" Orion started, but as Gabriel tossed me the blood crystal, he grabbed Orion and leapt from the edge of the balcony, wings snapping out and catching them on the breeze.

Orion shouted my name and fought to get free, the two of them heading out of sight beneath the trees where an army of Nymphs awaited them. But I couldn't let my mind snag on that fearful thought, knowing I had my own part to play in this escape, and trusting them to forge a path between our enemies.

I bound the crystal to my wrist with a pouch cast from leaves then sprang from the railing, racing into the sky towards Lavinia, my wings burning a blazing trail through the air at my back as I locked her in my sights. She was still thrashing within the net, trying to break free and I readied to attack, my pulse warring and vengeance purring my name.

Phoenix fire tore out of me, and I released a roar that was fuelled with all the anger and pain this witch had caused me and Orion.

Her shadows sliced through the net caging her, but she was still too distracted to notice the fireball of death coming her way. It collided with her in a shower of deadly sparks, knocking her from the sky and she screamed in terror, tumbling down towards the trees.

I dove, chasing after her and the Nymphs' rattles burst into my skull the lower I got, locking down my magic. But I didn't need magic when I had my Order and a plan to destroy Lavinia once and for all.

Lavinia's hands raised before she hit the trees, her features a picture of vengeance as she sent coils of shadow towards me, snapping around my wings and binding them tight.

I lost control, and a scream escaped me before I hit the tree canopy and tumbled to the ground below, landing in a patch of grass. Lavinia hadn't been so blessed, her body smouldering as it lay in a crater, her spine bent backwards over the burning husk of a log.

My Phoenix fire flared, burning through the shadows as they fought to hold my wings, but Lavinia's dark power turned to nothing under the intensity of the blaze.

The clash of battle in the distance told me Orion and Gabriel were facing fights of their own, but I couldn't turn my attention to them now. A fight for retribution was waiting for me, a chance opening up for me to avenge all of those who had fallen prey to Lavinia's malice.

I ran towards my enemy, Phoenix fire twisting from my fingers and crashing into her while she fought to get up, her shadows already healing the burns and broken bones I'd caused with my attack.

Shadows exploded out of her, slamming into my fire and working to keep it back, my Phoenix flames eating through her dark power just as ruthlessly.

I screamed my hate at her, all the injustice of what she had done to Orion tearing a fissure in the centre of my chest. I wanted her to pay, wanted her to hurt. And I'd take pleasure in watching her die. But I couldn't send her into death yet. First, I needed to cast the spell on her that I'd learned from the book we'd found in the treasury. If I managed to pull this off, she would no longer be able to call on the shadows to heal herself. And as I now had an ice crystal which held the blood of a willing sacrifice, I had exactly what

I needed for the spell to work.

Stella's death had freed us, and it was the answer to this shadow bitch's undoing too. For all the misgivings of Orion's mother, I had to be thankful to her for that.

I cast a dome of Phoenix fire over the crater, trapping Lavinia within it as she fought with all the power of her shadows to get out. I couldn't hold her forever, and the effort it took to keep her there made my head thump with pain.

I growled as I held on, raising my hands, and moving them in the intricate pattern taught to me by Queen Avalon, chanting the spell loud and clear for her to hear. "I bind the shadows within. I close the doors against your skin." I repeated the words in the old language and Lavinia shrieked, fighting harder to escape. "Umbras constringo intus. Pellem tuam claudo fores!"

The ground exploded, her power pouring out into it and the shadows uprooting all the trees around me. I was forced to fly, boughs slamming into the dirt while I darted left and right to avoid them, my concentration wavering and allowing Lavinia to rip through the earth and escape beneath my flames.

I cast my fire away with a huff of frustration, and Lavinia flew towards me with a shadow sword formed in her grip. I raced for the sky, higher and higher, the stars glittering as they watched, their intrigue in this fight threading through the atmosphere. And for once, I was more than happy to give them a show.

I felt Lavinia racing after me, closing in at my back and I snatched the white sword free of my sheath, raising it and turning to meet her. Her shadow blade slammed into mine with a noise like a bomb going off, and the impact reverberated through my body.

I gritted my teeth, my wings beating at my back as she pressed her sword hard against mine and my arm trembled with the effort of keeping her back. But as she got closer, her strength forced my sword near to my chest, the pressure of her blade intensifying. Her face lifted, triumph dancing her in her obsidian eyes, the shadows wriggling beneath her near transparent skin. But this wasn't the end for me.

I brought my feet up and kicked her square in the chest, retrieving an inch of space and beating my wings hard, flying towards the sky with tremendous speed. She was on my tail in a heartbeat, her legs nothing but shadow while her arms were outstretched and that sword in her grip was held ready to skewer me.

I sent Phoenix fire pouring out from my wings, down my back and tumbling over my bare feet. She screamed, forced to swerve this way and that as she tried to avoid the heat of my flames and I flipped over backwards in the sky, tucking my wings tight and falling towards her with my own sword held ready. The stars seemed to shine brighter, dazzling, and always watching.

My blade sliced right through Lavinia's back, flesh, bone and shadow torn apart beneath my mother's gleaming sword and Lavinia wailed, her whole body turning to black shadow.

I twisted around, my burning feathers carving an arc through the ghostly shadow of my enemy and Lavinia's screams sounded within that cloud. She shot away from me as far as she could go, that fog of darkness swallowed by the night until I couldn't see it at all.

I hunted for her, eyes whipping this way and that, my blade ready for any strike that might come at me. But there was no sign of her, and I realised the Shadow Beast had left me at some point too, no longer hovering at my back.

I adjusted my sword in my grip, the heavy rattles of the Nymphs still carrying up from below, the roars of Orion and Gabriel's fight reaching me.

"Lavinia!" I bellowed. "Fight me like Fae!"

She materialised out on a grassy bank before the palace, healed and whole once more. I set her in my sights, grit and determination fuelling my movements. I sheathed my sword in favour of my fire, flying towards her across the sky, aiming to meet her on the ground.

"The king is coming home!" she called to me with a joyous laugh. "Soon you'll be trapped like bees in a jar again, and I will let him bleed you out. And when he is done, I'll lock your souls in your bones so I can feast on you all for days to come."

Scorpio
Gemini
Virgo
Aries
Cancer
Leo
Sagittarius
Taurus
Capricorn
Aquarius
Libra
Pisces

TORY

CHAPTER SIXTY NINE

I was on my knees, bile rolling up my throat as my gaze remained locked to the visions of me in battle, the merciless creature which lived just beneath the surface of my skin and had torn through countless lives so easily.

I wasn't sure how long I'd been trapped there, staring at myself, tears burning down my cheeks as I watched the carnage I'd unleashed without flinching. Flashes of my father's terrible reign were interspersed with what I saw. I listened to his justifications, his excuses, the words he spoke echoing my own. But he had an excuse for what he'd done. Lionel had been the cause of his brutality. My actions had been entirely my own.

I couldn't remember why I'd ever come to this place, the truth of what I was at my core devouring me until I was nothing but a relic of the girl I'd been, kneeling there before my own truth and sobbing at the reality of what I was.

How could anyone believe that someone capable of such violence could be worthy of a crown? How could anyone believe that a monster made of a wicked fury like that could be deserving of love?

I choked on that word as it resounded through my mind, crippling me beneath the weight of it as I felt golden eyes resting upon me from somewhere beyond my own reality.

"Get up," the wind seemed to growl in a tone so familiar that my pulse thumped loudly at its command, though I remained kneeling where I was, watching my own destruction play out.

I was the thing that the people of this kingdom should fear, the true heir to the monarch they had all hailed as savage beyond reason. I was merciless, vengeful, furious. And those parts of me had only festered since that battle. Any softness I had once been able to lay claim to had been burned away by the flames which had coated my body that day. By the loss of…

I lifted my head as the ghost of a touch brushed my cheek, my limbs trembling in the wake of my own destruction there upon that ferry, at the foot of a creature who wore my father's face.

"Get up, Roxy," the wind snarled, and my chin lifted higher at that name. That fucking name.

I found the ferryman smiling down at me with nothing but malicious intent in his foul gaze while I broke at his feet.

"Few can face the horrors of their own self and stand by them," he purred in the doting voice of a father who I had never known. "Especially those guilty of the acts you have committed. What is unbreakable and yet so easily shattered, what is cunning and honest, brutal and vulnerable, pure and tainted?"

My eyes flicked to the water once more and for the briefest moment I saw something beyond my own form raging my way across the battlefield, merciless and ruinous. I saw a golden Dragon tearing across the sky, fire erupting from his jaws while light glinted from his metallic scales and set my heart pounding in my chest.

"What is greater than all fear?" I hissed at the ferryman as I met his gaze once more, the tears drying on my cheeks as I summoned the last of the strength in my limbs and sat back on my heels. "What is more powerful than selfishness and more brutal than hate?"

"You may only answer once," the ferryman purred and this time there was a crack in his voice, in the perfect visage of my father, a guttural growl tinging his words as if he could see the truth of me just as plainly as I was beginning to see it too and it wasn't such an easily destroyed thing after all.

"What will fight without end and destroy without mercy?" I demanded, rallying my strength as I pushed myself to my feet and faced the demon which haunted me.

"Look into the depths of the pool again," he crowed. "See the truth of what you are."

"I did look," I replied, my voice a brittle, ravaged sound as I thought over all I had seen of myself, of the savagery, the endless, formidable power and of how furiously I had turned that upon my enemies. "And I saw something which you had been hoping I'd forget."

"What is that?" the ferryman asked, the water beginning to churn beneath us, the ferry bucking precariously, making my gut swoop as I fought to keep my balance.

"The reason I became that creature." I pointed to the burning monster who raged across that battlefield without turning my head to look at her again. Because I had already looked, I had already seen, and I wasn't afraid anymore. "Love."

The ferryman hissed like a wildcat as I answered his riddles with that word, my skin erupting into flames as my wings tore from my back, shredding through my jacket and making my pack thump down on the raft as I let him behold the creature of nightmares that resided within my soul.

"Love makes a monster of me," I continued, stepping towards him, the print of my boots burning themselves onto the wood of the ferry which hissed and spluttered in useless protest. "I have tasted the depths of love born from the embers of hate and I have lived through every emotion between the two. I have sobbed and raged and begged and cursed the stars themselves, but none of that made the slightest bit of difference. So I let that love turn to vengeance, I let it fester and blaze inside of me, and I found a way to defy the stars themselves. You're standing in the way of that path, which means you must have been hoping to meet with this monster yourself."

"Love is pure," the ferryman denied, backing up a step as I advanced. "Love is sacrifice."

"I *have* sacrificed!" I shouted and the flames which lit my body blazed like a beacon for all to see. "I have given everything I was and everything I am to this fight. I have cried and raged and pleaded for the heavens to favour us just *once,* but they turned their games on us instead and took all I had to offer. I never promised to give them any of this. I never agreed to the price they chose, so let my love be unbreakable and brutal and cruel and endless, the harbinger of war and the summoner of violence. Let it be all those things and more because I am done sacrificing myself for the stars and their entertainment. I am done being a puppet in their games. They took from me too many times and now they will have to face the monster they made when they incited me because I. Have. Had. *Enough!"*

I stomped my foot down on the ferry with that final word, power erupting from me as the wooden raft bucked wildly beneath my feet and the ferryman screamed as he was thrown from it, the roiling water hissing and spitting as he plunged into it.

The world seemed to shudder as he disappeared beneath the waves, echoes of his demise radiating out from that place as if the entire balance of the Elements themselves had shifted with his defeat.

But as the raft was flung across the water and my wings flared to help me maintain my balance, I spotted an edge to that eternal pool, an end to the drifting and I fixed my eyes on it. I may have been a monster, but I had never claimed not to be.

The wind picked up as I closed in on that edge, the world itself seeming to plunge away into nothing beyond it, and the raft I was perched upon gaining speed as I raced towards it.

There was a pulse echoing through the air itself, a vibration in the world which had started with the ferryman's death and would only end when I finished with what I'd come here to do. Or when I died trying.

The ferry bucked and swayed beneath me, that edge racing closer with every heartbeat and as I shot over the precipice, I leapt into the sky, grabbing my pack as my wings flapped hard and caught in an updraft.

Coiling smoke hid the drop beneath me as the raft shot away into it, no sound marking its passage, nothing at all indicating it had even impacted with something at the bottom.

The wind twisted around me, spinning me on the spot and making my flames flare as it kissed its way through them, a greeting and introduction.

There were voices in that wind. Breathy pleas and heartfelt prayers. My chest ached as I heard them all, countless voices crying out to the stars to save them, while nothing but silence came in reply. I heard my voice, felt my chest ache with the sobs that had wrecked me when I found Darius on that battlefield, his body cold and empty, his soul gone and mine shredded right along with it.

For a moment I was paralysed there, caught in that memory, in the pain which had carved out a piece of me ever since. In some ways, I was still there, on that battlefield, holding his cold hand in mine and begging fate to change its mind.

I hadn't left him. Not for one moment. I hadn't released his hand even when I'd taken the dagger which had killed him and sliced my own flesh open with it. I hadn't let go. And as that scar tingled along my palm, and the scent of smoke and cedar seemed to billow around me and my own vow to him buzzed through the air, I knew I never would.

He was the destroyer of me. The ruination of the girl I'd been and the creator of the woman I had become. He was my one true love, without any help or hinderance from the stars. He was more than my Elysian Mate. He was more than my equal. He was my end. And I was ready to keep the vow I'd made to him all those weeks ago.

The Winds of Sky and Spirit continued to whisper to me, but I was beyond listening to them anymore.

I tilted my head to look down into the smoke coiling beneath me, looking towards the endless drop and knowing for a fact that I would not fall forever once I gave in to it. Because it may have been eternal for a soul who relied on the stars to grant their wishes. But I was a queen, come to make my own prayers a reality, and there was no power in this realm or the next which could deny me.

My Phoenix blinked out of existence in a flash of fire which arced into the sky, my wings fading and the heat dissipating as I plummeted out of the air and shot into the smoke which held whispers of my unfulfilled promises in its grasp.

Scorpio
Gemini
Virgo
Cancer
Leo
Sagittarius
Taurus
Capricorn
Aquarius
Libra
Pisces

GABRIEL

CHAPTER SEVENTY

I'd managed to cast a roughly hewn metal blade in my hand before the Nymphs had stolen away my magic, and I flew through the canopy above them, cutting down as many as I could. But the tide was unending, Lavinia's entire Nymph army spilling onto the grounds as she summoned them to her aid. Their tree-like forms turned grimacing faces my way, hatred seeping into their hell born eyes. The rattles of so many were weighing down on us, my magic impossible to reach as they worked to keep it subdued.

Orion shot between them with his Vampire speed, stabbing and gutting them, bringing them to their knees as he evaded the deadly stabs of their probes. His blows were feral, fuelled by the strength of his Order and the rancour in his heart.

A flash of The Sight dashed through my head, the black sword in his grip lighting with purple fire, and I knew at once that it had been Hail's weapon. I pushed deeper into The Sight and *saw* myself doing an accidental hand movement with that sword that sent Hydra fire bursting out in all directions in a deadly inferno.

I sensed a shift in the air as I hurried to catch Orion, flying after him through the trees and moving as fast as I could. It was almost as if another presence was with me, and a glimpse of the past stole through my mind of me splashing in the warm, summer waters of the lake on the palace grounds while Hail taught me to swim as a child.

"Go on, Gabriel!" he cheered.

Those words seemed to echo in the now instead of the past, giving me a flare of energy. That memory had been lost to me; the powerful blocks I'd had put on my mind when Ling Astrum had hidden me from the world may have been broken years ago, but there were lasting effects, gaps in my childhood I couldn't perceive. But in time, I hoped to uncover all the precious moments I'd lost.

"Orio!" I called, and he glanced up at me as he slowed to drive his sword between the shoulder blades of a Nymph.

It turned to ash before him and I landed at his side, catching my breath and bracing my hand on his shoulder. But lingering there for even that small measure of time allowed us to be surrounded in seconds, too many Nymphs to count stepping through the trees with rattles in their chests, closing in on us with probes raised and a thirst for death in their eyes.

"Give that to me." I snatched the sword from Orion's grip, and he bared his fangs, turning to our enemies, ready to rip their throats out with nothing but his teeth.

"Stay close," I warned and despite how near to us the Nymphs were getting, he knew to obey me, to trust in my visions. He'd learned that lesson long ago.

I may not have been able to *see* the Nymphs' movements, but I could *see* this fire and its potential. If only I could move the sword in just the right way, and ignite those flames.

"Noxy," Orion pressed urgently. "What's the plan? Because as much as I'm enjoying this playtime in the woods with you, I think we're about to be as fucked as Goldilocks when she broke into the three bears' house and got herself eaten for breakfast."

A Nymph ran at him with a magic-locking rattle rolling from its tongue, and Orion stooped low, grabbing its legs and flipping it onto its back with a cry of effort, the ground trembling as it hit the earth. A sharp and brutal kick to its head finished it, and Orion picked the corpse up, hurling the body at the line of Nymphs and knocking them back.

"Noxy!" he barked, putting on a spurt of Vampire speed to get behind me, and the sound of grunts and shrieks came as he fought to keep them at bay.

"Just a second." I swung the sword again, calling on the memory I'd *seen* once more, but it wouldn't come to me now.

"Hurry the fuck up." Orion sped around me in a circle, knocking away all the Nymphs who were trying to get to us, a line of tension on his brow.

I twisted the sword just so through the air and purple fire raced out of it in a spiral, making me grin in delight.

"I did it," I announced as Orion went soaring over my head, thrown from the arms of a towering Nymph with a sneering face. He hit a tree trunk to my right, slamming to the ground with a groan.

"That's great, Noxy," he spoke into the grass, shoving himself up and shooting back to me, a line of blood trickling from a cut in his hairline, but he was thankfully alright apart from that.

I swung the sword as our opponents rushed in once more, gazing out at them menacingly as I wielded my father's blade. Alright, so he wasn't my blood father. But I'd *seen* enough of our relationship to know he had loved me down to my roots, and I was inclined to feel the same way.

The purple fire exploded away from us in every direction, and I yanked Orion against my side to make sure not an ember of it touched him. The tornado of savage flames carved through our enemies like they were made of paper, turning the first rows of them to soot while the others ran for their lives, screeches of terror rising into the air all around us.

"Ha," I laughed, looking to Orion.

"Cutting it close, don't you think?" He plucked my makeshift earth sword from my sheath to arm himself, then his gaze turned to the sky. "Where is she?"

"You should keep this." I offered him the black sword, knowing it was far more likely to protect him than a roughly crafted blade was.

"No," he said firmly. "It's a family heirloom. All yours, Noxy."

There was no time to argue with him, so I nodded, looking to the future once again and finding a path for us.

"Let's get into the sky so we can see better." I moved behind him, hooking my arms beneath his and drawing him tight against my chest.

"Is this our Titanic moment?" he murmured, and I sniggered before kicking off the ground and carrying him high above the treeline.

My gaze fell on Darcy where she hovered above a sphere of red and blue Phoenix fire swirling on the hillside close to the palace, and I assumed the shadow bitch was contained within it.

"Damn," Orion breathed.

"Do not get a boner over my sister while I'm touching you," I warned.

"Too late," he muttered, and I cursed, flying us towards Darcy as fast as I could.

A roar caught my ear before I made it to her and I turned in the direction it had come from, a host of Dragons materialising beyond the golden gates. Some were still in their Fae forms, a regiment of Lionel's Bonded men in their navy robes, striding forward with intention, shouts of fury leaving them as they spotted the battle raging out this way.

"Capture them!" Lionel boomed as he shoved his way to the forefront of the mass of Guardians he'd bound to himself.

Those of them who hadn't yet shifted did so, taking off into the sky with Lionel's gigantic jade form among them, heading right this way.

"Fuck," I hissed, then turned my gaze to the clouds above and flew for them fast. "Darcy – move!" I called, and her head whipped around, fire daggering off of her skin and a wild fury burning in her gaze. She looked to the Dragons speeding this way, nodding to me and I shot towards the clouds for cover, leading the way for her to follow.

As soon as we got high enough, the Nymphs' power released us, and magic crackled back through my veins. I released Orion and he stepped out onto the air, using his newly restored Element to hold him in the sky.

My sister still hadn't appeared, and fear trickled through me at the sound of nearly two hundred Dragons bellowing below us.

Don't do anything stupid, Darcy.

"I'm going back for her," Orion growled, already descending and I nodded as I followed, steeling myself for what it would take to get us out of here now.

A huge set of jaws broke through the clouds beneath us, so wide, Orion was doomed before he could even try and get away. Sharp teeth slammed shut around him, blood pouring and a scream tearing from my throat, giving away my position as another set of jaws broke free of the clouds, green and gleaming. They must have scented us on the wind, and even as I blasted ice blades in my hand and sliced into the roof of Lionel Acrux's mouth, I was already lost, the jaws closing, teeth shredding through my skin-

I jarred out of the vision with a yell of horror leaving me, finding Orion gripping my arm, anxiety in his eyes.

"What is it?" he demanded.

I took a moment to assure myself that neither of us was dead, the pain and grief of that experience clinging to me as I reached out to clutch my friend's arm and hold tight to him, the thought of losing him too terrible to conceive. We were still in the woodland, our feet firmly planted on the ground. No doom had befallen us yet. But the Nymphs were regrouping, already turning back this way as the flames from the Hydra sword simmered out where they'd been licking the trees around us.

"The Dragons are coming," I rasped, a ripple of visions crossing my mind as I followed all the paths of fate, trying to seek out a way to survive this night. But if they showed up, there were too many to face, and we would certainly be killed. "Death awaits us if they arrive. Our only chance is to fight our way past the Nymphs then run before Lionel decides to come home."

"Then let's find Blue and get the fuck out of here," he said firmly, but a terrible roar filled the air and my stomach dropped as I wondered if my vision had come too late. That the Dragons were already here, and the iron bars of fate were closing in around us, setting us on a final path towards an imminent, gory end.

But as I turned to seek out the source of the sound, it wasn't Lionel I discovered there, but Tharix, the barbaric son Lavinia had sired for the false king.

He was running across the ground on all fours, his face fixing in a snarl and bloodlust gilding his black eyes as he closed in on us. He was a creature designed to rain death down upon this world, and I couldn't perceive a single one of his actions, the core of him built from shadow.

The Nymph rattles still filled the air, more of them returning already as the purple fire from Hail's sword extinguished against the charred tree trunks circling us.

"I'll get up above him," I decided, flexing my wings. "I'll strike at him from above with Hail's sword while you distract him on the ground. At least the fucker can't fly."

Tharix leapt into the air and a shift tore through his body that made me stagger back a step in shock, an enormous black Dragon shredding through his skin and taking off into the air on leathery wings that stole away the light of the moon.

"Oh yeah, by the way Noxy, Tharix can shift into a shadow Dragon," Orion deadpanned, then shot towards me, giving me a shove in the only direction that was open to us between the trunks.

I took off, flying at his side as the two of us used our Order speed to put as much distance as possible between us and the Dragon born of shadows who was already taking chase.

"Any chance you can do that fancy tornado fire thing again?" Orion called, zig-zagging through the trees.

"It needs time to recharge," I breathed as I *saw* that fact.

"Great. Got any more good news for me or is that all of it? I suppose my numbers didn't come up on the lottery this week either?" Orion asked dryly, the sound of Nymphs crashing through the trees somewhere to our left telling me precisely how fucked we were.

I glanced back at Tharix as he swept through the air above the canopy in hunt of us, flexing his wings and opening his lethal jaws, revealing a tornado of shadow swirling in his mouth. His deathly black eyes locked with mine and I shoved Orion as hard as I could, sending the two of us tumbling to the ground, narrowly missing the blast of shadows which poured from Tharix's jaws as we went rolling down a steep hill.

The woodland behind us was decimated by Tharix's immense power, bark, soil and debris flying everywhere in its wake.

"I hear the Veil is lovely this time of year," I said, leaping upright and pulling Orion with me, ignoring the echoing pain in my side as we kept sprinting away through the trees.

"Fuck you," Orion panted, then he yanked me to a halt so violently I almost got whiplash. He tugged me down into a huge, hollowed-out log and I ducked low, the two of us crouching side by side inside it.

"Nymphs," Orion growled. "Straight ahead. I'll listen and see if I can find a clear path."

The roar of Tharix above set my heart pounding and Orion cocked his head, focusing as he listened for the sound of their footsteps.

We were running short on time; Lionel and his Dragon army could arrive at any moment, and death seemed to keep creeping closer at our backs.

"Anything?" I hissed low, the sound of the Nymphs searching for us making the hairs on my arms prickle to attention.

He looked up at me through the gloom, and I felt the weight of that look, the answer I couldn't bear to accept. There was no way out. And my Sight was useless to help us.

"So...do we try to run through the Nymphs or take our chances in the sky with the Shadow Dragon?" I asked, keeping my tone light so I didn't unveil the terrible fear that was ricocheting through my body.

"If we can get high enough, we'll get our magic back," Orion suggested, and I nodded in agreement to that.

"I'll move us as fast as I can," I promised.

"You'd move faster without me," Orion said darkly as if he was about to construct a new plan where I left him behind.

"There's no future in which I leave you here," I spoke before he could dare voice that idea.

He sighed. "Alright, let's go take on the unkillable asshole," he said.

"Love you, Orio," I muttered.

"Likewise, Noxy," he answered, and we moved as one, rushing out of the log where fifty Nymphs shrieked as they spotted us. They tore towards us, their probes reaching, their beady eyes locked on their prize.

I grabbed Orion, my wings flapping hard, and I took off with all the speed of my Order burning through me. We moved fast, breaking through the canopy and Tharix roared as he spotted us, sweeping this way on wings as black as midnight.

I kept my gaze on a patch of cloud above, my wings beating furiously and my heart thundering out what could be its final beats.

I was desperate to feel the rush of my magic returning, begging to grasp it, but the air boomed behind me, and a roiling blast of shadows collided with my back as they were propelled from Tharix's lungs.

I cried out as my right wing snapped, but magic tingled in my fingers as we sailed higher, propelled onwards by the blast. I waved a hand, casting an illusion that I prayed would give us a chance if nothing else. The illusion tore away from our bodies, looking just like us as it shot across the sky while I cloaked the real Orion and I in shadow.

Tharix bellowed, falling for my bait and flying after my false cast. But the small lurch of victory I felt was swallowed as I lost momentum and began to fall, my magic locked down once more and my broken wing failing me in our moment of need.

Orion scrambled to cast air, retaining scraps of his power, and slowing our descent just enough as we clung to one another, pinwheeling down towards the waiting ground. But as we hit the treeline, his magic was stolen entirely, the Nymphs' cries of hunger below tempered by their deathly rattles.

Orion caught hold of a branch as we fell, holding onto me with his other hand, straining to haul me up onto it with his strength as a grunt of effort left him. He held me in place and the Nymphs below us screamed in anger, jumping up to try and reach us, their probed fingers grazing the branch we rested on.

I wasn't ready to die. Not when my family waited for me, and the thought of never seeing them again made my heart cleave open. I may have *seen* visions of my son growing up and of the life he would lead, of the day he met his perfect match, but I wanted to truly experience it. I wanted to be there when he was Awakened and cheer him on when he graduated. There were so many possibilities for his future, but there were moments of happiness he could claim if we could only find our way through the dark. And I had to be there for him.

I winced as I tried to move my broken wing, but it hung limply as a promise that I wasn't going to be flying again anytime soon.

The branch cracked loudly, and Orion and I shared a look, the knowledge of what was about to happen shattering between us like broken glass. At least if I had to die this day, then my best friend was here with me. But I wasn't giving up until the final door of fate closed firmly in my face.

The branch gave away and the two of us drew our swords as we fell, hitting the ground heavily between a circle of monsters.

The first Nymph grabbed me, and I swung my blade with a feral noise leaving my throat, my determination to see my family again ringing right down to my core.

I cast my first enemy to ash, hearing Orion colliding with another Nymph at my back, but I couldn't turn to look his way, and I prayed I hadn't already seen him for the last time.

The next Nymph made it to me, and I severed its probed hand from its wrist with a bellow of determination. It made a noise of anguish that sounded an awful lot like the word Gabe and I slammed my sword into its heart with a snarl.

"Don't. Call. Me. Gabe." I yanked the sword back out and it turned to ash before three more took its place.

I was surrounded in an instant and I was thrown down between them onto the mossy ground. One of them stamped down on my broken wing while another locked its sharp probes around my throat to choke away the cry of pain that pitched from my chest.

I severed its arm with a powerful strike of my blade, a thud sounding as the limb hit the ground and the Nymph reared back in agony. Another Nymph lunged at me, tearing the sword from my grip and tossing it away.

A yell of pain carried from Orio that echoed mine and I writhed madly, my muscles bunching as I tried to get up. But the biggest of the three reached for my chest, its probes slicing through my skin and making me bellow. My heart thundered as those probes dug deeper, hunting out my magic and my lifeforce.

I was dead, pinned down, and at their mercy. The sound of Orion being struck by an enemy of his own sent a wave of despair through me. It was over. Our fight lost.

I sought out the night sky between the ugly, horned heads of the Nymphs leaning over me, mourning my death before it had taken me, because I had so much I wanted to experience in this world. So much love to share with the people I adored. Life was this fleeting, precious thing and it had barely begun. *Let us have more.*

A furious roar cut through the air that made the ground tremble and my first thought went to Lionel, our fates sealed by his arrival. But then the Shadow Beast slammed into the three Nymphs above me, taking them to the ground and pinning them beneath its huge paws. It ripped their heads clean off, spraying black blood all over me before it leapt right over my head and snarled at the Nymphs coming our way, placing itself between us and them like an attack dog.

They hesitated, backing up in the face of the powerful creature, and I took hold of its fur, hauling myself to my feet, my right wing hanging awkwardly at my back and pain shuddering through me.

"Holy fuck," I breathed, and the Shadow Beast turned my way a little, grunting at me affectionately.

"Orio?" I turned to find him behind me, his lip split and his left leg pissing blood, but relief echoed through me at finding him alive. I moved to pick up Hail's sword as Orion limped my way with exhaustion in his eyes, taking in the Shadow Beast, his expression shifting to shock.

The Shadow Beast hounded forward, nuzzling my arm and grunting again like it wanted me to do something. It took me a second longer to realise it was urging me to climb onto its back, and as I was totally fucked regardless, I did, hauling myself up its side and swinging a leg over its shoulder blades.

Orion gazed at me astride the Shadow Beast, hesitation pouring from him, but at a forceful jerk of my head he shot forward and climbed up behind me. It wasn't like we could be picky about our allies right now, and this animal had just placed itself between us and certain death.

"Are you sure about this?" he asked.

"It saved our lives," I said with a shrug, knotting my fingers in the Shadow Beast's fur. "Get us to Darcy," I commanded it, hoping it would understand and it seemed to because it lunged forward, knocking Nymphs down like bowling pins then charging away through the trees.

Tharix roared in the sky, and I craned my neck, finding him no longer fooled by my illusion as he spotted us below. He turned to take chase, but the Shadow Beast was well ahead of him for now, moving furiously along on its mighty paws.

We were on borrowed time, and if we didn't get to Darcy and make our escape before the Dragons arrived, there was only one way this was going to go. And it would be a bloody, harrowing end.

Scorpio
Gemini
Virgo
Aries
Cancer
Leo
Sagittarius
Taurus
Capricorn
Aquarius
Libra
Pisces

TORY

CHAPTER SEVENTY ONE

The fall came to an abrupt end, the ground cracking beneath my feet as I landed. The smoke which I'd been plummeting through billowed out all around me as my arrival made it quake and race away, clearing some space for me to see.

Even the air here seemed to know why I had come.

The world around me was made up of nothing and everything at once. A barren wasteland everywhere I looked and yet life was sparking in my peripheral vision, like staring at it made it blink out of existence, but it could never truly be vanquished.

I knew what I was supposed to be facing here, and as if my thoughts alone conjured them, flames erupted before me, a doorway appearing in the heart of them, the view through it obscured in darkness.

The Fires of the Abyss.

The gateway between realms.

I stepped towards it, the weight of my pack growing as I closed in on the heat of the flames and for once, I didn't feel the power of the fire sinking into my skin and feeding my Phoenix. Those were no normal flames. And I had the feeling that even my Order gifts wouldn't be enough to grant me immunity from them.

I dropped my pack, pulling out the Book of Fire as if in a trance, my hands seeming to know what to do even before my mind had given thought to it.

I flicked through the pages and stopped on one, my finger pressing down on an image of a man whose body lay on a burning pyre, then my gaze shifted to the caption which went alongside it.

Only a sprit torn from its body may pass the burning gate, as was written by the stars themselves. But it has long been pondered that a spirit still tethered to its mortal flesh may slip by unnoticed on the back of another who faces their true passage.

I read the words over twice, wondering if I was going to need to summon a sacrifice to me somehow, some lowlife member of Lionel Acrux's army who I wouldn't mind killing in the name of what I needed. I wasn't sure what it said about me that I was willing to consider that, but I'd walked too far down this path to turn back now, and I didn't think there were many prices I wouldn't pay.

But as I read over the words again, I wondered if they were more of a clue as to the next part of my plan than instructions for this, and I removed the scraps of my leather jacket which were left after my wings had punched through it and tossed it aside.

I already knew how I might get through the burning gate after all.

My pulse picked up as those thoughts began to twist through my mind and I snapped the Book of Fire shut before returning it to my pack and taking the decanter of my enemies' blood from it instead.

I set it on the ground then took the bag of rock salt out next, followed by the five glass crystals I'd selected for this purpose.

I took a bound bunch of dried thyme from my bag and laid that down alongside the rest.

The burning gate flared like it knew what I was planning to do, the heat of the flames licking over my skin and making my flesh prickle from the intensity of it.

I picked up the bag of rock salt and began walking as I poured it, marking out a pentagram on the ground, the centre of which was big enough to contain my body. I murmured words in the ancient language of the runes, my finger painting out the symbols as I went, scoring the air with flames which fell to the ground, burning the runes into the rock on the pentagram's outer edge.

When that was done, I gathered the five crystals, taking them into my fist one at a time and pressing my power into each of them before placing them at the points of the pentagram. One filled with swirling blue water magic, the next green earth magic, then blazing fire and purest air. Last of all, I reached into that untold well of power at the depths of my soul and summoned the ether forth.

It rose up within me like a wave of pure energy, my breath halting and organs stilling for several achingly long moments as I channelled it into the crystal and placed it at the head of the pentagram. It glowed like the others, but the heart of it was deepest black, more like a void of light than any colour my eyes could detect.

My fingers shook a little as I positioned it and I willed them to still, knowing I would need far more power than that before this was done.

I had faced my fears, faced my truth and now I would have to face the price this magic asked of me.

The light which had pierced the smoke to find me at the bottom of this abyss flickered as I worked, a sound rattling through the world, a demand making the earth tremble, like the stars were screaming at me, raging at me as they perceived what I was doing.

"I cursed you," I snarled, throwing my hand up towards the sky, ether tumbling from me as I bared my scarred palm to them, making the sky quake at the power I unleashed. "I made you a promise. And it is time you saw it come to pass."

I moved into the centre of the pentagram, rallying my magic with every move I made, taking the bound thyme in my fist before cutting my arm open with the very dagger that had stolen the man I loved from this world.

My blood spilled hot and fast, ether dripping from me in every splash of red as I let it fall over the dried herbs. Thyme for communicating with the dead. A path cracking open and remaining so, for just long enough.

When the dried herbs were splattered with my blood, I threw the bunch from me, straight into the heart of that gate. The entrance roared in fury as I lashed my power around it and threw my will at it.

It wasn't intended to be a passageway, merely the heart of the flames in this world, a link to every flame in every Fae who possessed that Element. But I didn't care. I wasn't interested in the design the stars had laid out for it or for anything else, and as I tethered the gate to my will, I felt a crack shudder through the foundations of the earth itself.

"Surrender," I hissed, digging my heels into the dirt as the ether roiled within me, trying to become a leash on me instead of the gate.

I threw my hands out, Elemental magic blasting from me and erupting at the four points of the pentagram dedicated to them.

Fire sprang to life beside the fire crystal, a rotating ball of water next, then a swirling orb of air magic and a flourishing glade of green grass. Between the gate and me, only the crystal filled with ether remained, and as I dug into the depths of my power, summoning the heart of that most ancient magic, a girl of pure light broke from it.

I fell to my knees as the power needed to summon her ripped from me, panting as I stared up at the figure whose features were entirely obscured by that blinding light. She planted her feet before me as my connection to the gate tried to pull on me once again, and I bared my teeth in a grim smile as she drew a staff of golden energy and threw a tendril of dark ether straight at the flames.

I was knocked back onto my ass as the pull of the gate snapped suddenly, my grip on it becoming iron, my will its will and my lips pulled up as I realised what I'd achieved.

My breaths were ragged, and the cut on my arm throbbed painfully, but I wasn't done, and I couldn't spare a moment to rest.

I scrambled for the decanter of blood, looking at the deep red of the liquid as it swirled within the glass, remembering the way I'd siphoned it from myself after I'd woken in my room, the blood of my enemies which had covered my body now a weapon ready for me to wield.

I took the lid from the decanter and dipped two fingers into the blood, a deep breath filling my lungs. I positioned myself in the very centre of the pentagram and focused on the magic which began to rise to my call.

I painted runes onto my own skin while drawing the ether into myself, filling my body with it like I was a vessel for it and nothing more.

As the ether met with the runes I'd drawn onto myself, it grabbed hold of them, the power burning through them and making me grit my teeth as they branded my body one after another.

I cursed as the pain drove into me relentlessly, the magic burning all the way to my bones as it carved through my body, passing over me like flesh held little meaning to it and it was seeking the real prize of my soul.

The scream that erupted from me as I fell to the ground was un-fucking-ending, and didn't come close to aligning with the reality of the pain which ripped through me as my soul was set alight within that power.

Everything was ripped from me, my Phoenix crying out as my connection to it was lost, my hold on my power guttering as it was taken from my control, falling into the depths of the magic I'd begun to wield and no longer held in my grasp.

The spell was like a living being, its own wants and needs a terrible thing to behold as it looked upon the world with a hunger unmatched by any other. It wanted to use me to that end, to destroy, to obliterate, to devour.

My grip on myself flickered as its hunger almost consumed me, but as I was swept along on the tide of its catastrophic desires, a glimmer of my own needs called to me, the golden eyes of my damnation and the reason for all of this. The man I had chosen for myself, despite every reason I'd had to reject him, despite the stars pushing and pulling at us, despite the Veil which had closed between us. He was mine and I was his and I had come here to return him to my side.

With a flare of power that burst from the last recesses of my being, I ripped control of the ether back into my grasp and forced it to fall to my will.

"Open a path," I hissed, my fists clenching, blood squeezing between my fingers and my spine arching against the rock beneath me.

The universe rebelled at my demand, but I refused to back down, every beat of power I owned, every bit I could claim and steal from the world surrounding me, buckled and bent as I forced my will over it.

I had come here to see him, and I refused to let death have me before I did.

Everything surrounding me shuddered and heaved, the laws of nature themselves working to deny me this one request, but I only pushed more power into my command, only called on more of the ether and bound it to my will until a great, rending boom filled the air and the world around me shimmered like oil.

The power ebbed and flowed, releasing me from the agony of wielding it and allowing me to roll onto my front as I fought to stop the haunting ache in my soul.

I pushed to my feet, limbs trembling with exertion and my breaths coming in shallow pants as I took in the gap between realms which I'd forced into being, hanging there, contained within the gate of flames.

My feet stumbled over each other as I moved towards it, the rest of the world seeming to melt away until there was nothing but that tear in the fabric of the universe itself, that ethereal light blinding me from whatever lingered beyond it.

I didn't pause as I staggered closer, my heart thundering, proving to me and all who might hear it that I still lived. Even as I took that final step and walked into death itself.

Scorpio
Gemini
Virgo
Cancer
Leo
Sagittarius
Taurus
Capricorn
Aquarius
Libra
Pisces

DARCY

CHAPTER SEVENTY TWO

My arms shook with the power that was pouring out of me, feeding the sphere of Phoenix fire I had Lavinia trapped inside. Every direction was covered this time so she couldn't escape, and as she threw herself at the flames with screams of pain, I let the spell spill from my flesh into the air.

My burning wings beat at my back as I gazed down at my prey from above, the heat emanating from me making the air shimmer. The palace beyond me was lit up by my flames, its towering walls coloured in red and blue light.

"Adiuro te. Fores claudo. Adiuro te. Fores claudo," I chanted the words I'd memorised from the feather-bound book Orion and I had discovered, power snapping through the atmosphere and making Lavinia lament. "I bind you. I close the doors!"

I tugged the ice crystal from the pouch on my wrist which contained Stella's blood, adrenaline setting my pulse skipping.

The Nymphs were far enough away from me that their rattles couldn't reach me here to steal my magic, and I cast a gust of air in my hand, carrying the crystal upon it and guiding it along to hover above the sphere of Phoenix fire where I held Lavinia captive. I urged the flames to part, just enough to let the crystal through and dropped it down towards the shadow bitch, letting my fire melt it as it fell so the burning hot blood splashed over her.

"Ahhhh!" she cried in agony and a twisted pleasure ran through me from the sound. She had tortured Orion, and I was more than willing to return the favour, to watch my flames eat away at her body so slowly that she felt every bite.

Her hand shot out through the hole I'd made in the flames, and I willed the fire to close, her fingers flexing and shadows dancing in her palm, but my Order gifts snuffed them out and she yanked her hand back with a wail.

"Adiuro te. Fores claudo. Adiuro te. Fores claudo," I spoke faster, the power building around me, sending my blue hair dancing in the wind.

The magic tearing from my body was colossal, the atmosphere droning with the energy that swept out of me. I was containing almost the entirety of the shadows in that single sphere of fire, burning away her access to them, scraping them from her soul and casting them back into the shadow realm where she could never reach them again. It was a force like no other, the flames so hot they rivalled the molten core of the earth, melting the ground to a pit.

The spell suddenly locked in place, binding to the entirety of who she was. The wind fell still, and a weighted breath left my lungs, the entire universe seeming to hush in the face of this power.

"*No,*" she sobbed, and a rush of victory flooded through me.

She could no longer summon any shadow outside of those I'd trapped in her body. She was weakened so deeply that she should be killable. And killable creatures could burn.

The sound of Nymphs screaming in the distance echoed out of the woodland, their pain the pain of Lavinia. But there was another sound among their cries too, shrieks that almost sounded joyful, but I didn't know why.

I flew a little nearer to Lavinia, closing the fire around her and hearing the sweet sizzle of skin burning in my flames. She might not have been mortal, but the spell should have slowed her ability to heal, and certainly rejuvenate. Then the magic of my Phoenix would be enough to finish her, and I revelled in the opportunity.

A Dragon's roar sounded off in the distance and my spine prickled, but I didn't turn my gaze from Lavinia in my trap. Nothing would turn my focus from this task. Her death was mine; I'd declared it so and was making good on that vow at last. She would pay for what she'd done with every drop of pain I could wring from her flesh.

I was so close, I had her, and I wasn't letting go this time. Fire flared so hot from my skin that the grass was withering on the bank and my power was making the air ring like the tolling bells of destruction.

"Darcy!" Orion's voice broke through the dark cloud of vengeance in my head.

I turned to find the Shadow Beast bounding up the hill with Orion and Gabriel on its back, and my lips parted in surprise.

I gasped as Tharix came tearing along behind them in Dragon form, his jaws spread wide and shadows flourishing from his mouth. I raised a hand in defiance, protectiveness charging the fiery atoms in my blood as I created the form of a Phoenix bird from my flames, sending it away from me. It flew with a heartfelt cry leaving its beak, soaring over the Shadow Beast, and aiming for Tharix.

The bird collided with the shadows pouring from the dragon's mouth, guttering them before they could sweep down on Orion and Gabriel, and giving them a chance to get to me while I worked to keep Lavinia trapped inside my sphere of power.

Tharix bellowed to the sky, turning to evade the flames I sent chasing after him, keeping him at bay for as long as I could. But as he climbed into the sky, he wheeled over the tips of my fire and came for us once again.

Shadows poured from his mouth and I swore, willing flames out everywhere to stop them. I cast a shield of Phoenix fire above the Shadow Beast to keep Orion and Gabriel safe as the beast carried them to where I hovered in the air.

A line of shadow shot through the sky, and I shielded myself, realising too late that the attack wasn't meant for me. The plume of darkness crashed into the sphere of fire holding Lavinia and I turned my attention back to it in desperation, trying to hold it in place under Tharix's strike. But the shadows managed to carve a hole in my flames and Tharix swept down from above, scooping Lavinia's smouldering body out of it with his talons and taking off into the sky.

"No!" I screamed, sending my flames after them, giving all of my passion and hatred to the cast.

I extinguished every other fire burning around me, sending all my power into forming a giant Phoenix bird that was ready to rain death down on their heads, but Tharix was climbing ever higher, fleeing as fast as he could to save his heinous mother. He was getting away and my teeth bared, my wings stretching out as I climbed higher, planning to go after them myself.

"Darcy!" Gabriel cried, and I turned towards him with my heart in my throat. "We have to go. The fates are turning against us. None of us will survive this night if we don't leave this instant."

My soul cracked at that reality, and I glanced back in the direction Tharix had taken, his dark scales lost among the sky. My flaming Phoenix bird circled above, hunting for him, but finding no trail to follow.

I had to go after them, had to finish off the monster who had tortured my mate and forced me to watch.

"You go," I called to them, and Orion's eyes darkened in refusal of that.

Gabriel shook his head, telling me that he wasn't going to leave either, and the terrifying possibility of their deaths stared back at me. If I stayed, they would stay. And my brother's prediction would come true. I couldn't allow that, and as unbearable as it was to turn away from this fight, I knew I had to. There was a chance for escape here, and they needed that more than they needed avenging.

A shriek made my eyes whip to the trees, finding the Nymphs coming at us fast, though many of them were slowing in their battle charge and blinking heavily. I frowned in confusion as I realised shadows were lifting from their bodies, coiling up and away into nothing in the sky, a heavy spell seeming to snap and shatter.

Those very same Nymphs turned on their brethren, probes stabbing, yowls of purest hatred leaving them, and a brawl braking out that shook the hillside.

I landed in front of my brother, and the Shadow Beast roared excitedly, sprinting towards the palace.

"What's happening?" I glanced back at the Nymphs and Orion called out in answer.

"Whatever you did to Lavinia, it must have caused this," he said.

"Some of them were under her control unwillingly," I breathed in realisation, thinking of Diego and how he'd had to use his hat to fight the will of the shadows. "My spell must have broken her power over them." A phrase from the prophecy circled in my head and I wondered if this could be its meaning. *Free the enslaved.*

"The Dragons are here," Gabriel gasped, his grip tightening on my waist. "Go!"

A glimmer caught my eye, and I spotted the dagger Lavinia had taken possession of, laying in the smouldering pit where I'd had her trapped. I used a whip of air to bring it to my hand, my thumb brushing the crimson garnet gemstone in its hilt as I tucked it into my waistband, cutting a hole in my shorts so the blade stuck through.

"Get to the perimeter, turn the Shadow Beast around," Orion demanded.

"There's no time," I said decisively, a plan firmly in mind as the Shadow Beast charged towards the palace where two ornate silver doors stood.

They flew open for us without me having to cast a single drop of magic, and the moment we made it inside, they slammed shut behind us and locked tight.

We charged down the hallways and the shutters over the windows began whipping closed, blocking out the light and locking themselves down to keep our enemies at bay. The palace was groaning, the echo of doors, shutters and windows closing all around the entirety of the building, and the magic in this place fizzled deep into my veins.

Gabriel held onto me as I tugged on the Shadow Beast's fur to guide it through the halls, taking the quickest passage I could think of through the palace towards Lionel's bedchamber.

As we left the rattles of the Nymphs behind, I glanced back to find Gabriel and Orion healing the last of their injuries away and Gabriel's wing cracked as it snapped back into position, making my heart flinch as it did so. My brother offered me a flood of healing magic next, seeking out any injury that might lay on my skin, though I was too high on adrenaline to be sure if there were any at all. I thanked him, squeezing his hand, determination filling me at getting him and Orion out of here.

"You have a plan, right?" Orion called.

"She's got a good one," Gabriel replied, clearly *seeing* the path I was on.

A clamour of Dragon roars sounded beyond the building, setting my nerves on edge at how close they were already. We hurried up a silver carpeted stairway and as we reached the landing, a flash of green scales beyond the vast window ahead made me cast an air shield around us. I got it in place half a second before Lionel's sharp green talons slammed into the glass, sending jagged shards raining down everywhere, tearing the curtains to shreds and bouncing off of my shield.

The palace shutters slammed shut before he could get inside, and I threw out a hand, casting vines to keep them closed while Orion and Gabriel froze the rest of the shutters along the hall.

We veered around, taking the stairs onto another landing and urging the Shadow Beast on. We ran past another wall of windows, and a beady green dragon eye stared in at us, chasing after us and swinging its enormous head against the glass. It broke into a thousand lethal shards and Dragon fire bloomed from Lionel's jaws.

I raised my hands to attack him, but the palace shutters slammed in his face before I could and all three of us sprayed water over them before turning them to solid ice to put out the flames.

The Shadow Beast skidded as I tugged on its fur to urge it down another hall, the doors to Lionel's quarters just up ahead, the doorknobs changed for golden Dragon heads. My upper lip curled back at the tacky, egotistical decorations he'd brought into my family home.

The palace opened the doors wide for us and the Shadow Beast was moving so fast that it crashed into Lionel's four poster bed, the wood breaking as we all went tumbling from the animal's back. I threw out air magic to toss the debris away from us and cushion our fall, scrambling upright as my heart beat furiously against my ribs.

I ripped open Lionel's drawers, searching for what we needed in frantic movements, tearing the place apart to find it.

"Stardust," I called to the others and Orion nodded, shooting around the room with his speed and throwing every drawer out until he stopped before me with a pouch in his hand and a grin on his lips.

"Why didn't you say so sooner, beautiful?"

I cracked a laugh, but it was lost as Lionel collided with the side of the building, his talons tearing through the stone wall as the whole structure shuddered.

I raised my hands, casting an air shield in place to stop the bricks from falling and throwing my power into sealing every hole he carved into the place. This was mine and Tory's home, and I wasn't going to let him destroy it. The damage wasn't permanent, it could be fixed, at least that was what I kept telling myself.

More Dragons were throwing themselves against the walls to try and gain entry, and one glimpse out the window showed Lionel's servants and prisoners alike being tossed out of windows here, there and everywhere by the magic of the palace. The prisoners ran for their lives, some of them pausing long enough to fight Lionel's followers while others simply raced for freedom.

"Here!" Gabriel called, and I turned, finding him pointing to the wall. "There's a hidden passage, it will lead us to the roof," he said, a lock of raven hair fluttering into his eyes. "We have a chance to get to the wards above. But we have to go now."

I ran with Orion hot on my heels, opening the passage Gabriel had *seen* there and looking back at the Shadow Beast.

"Come on, beastie. Do the smoke thing." I looked at the huge creature sitting on the wreckage of Lionel's bed, chewing its way through Lionel's expensive suits from a toppled wardrobe.

The beast grunted happily, turning to shadow, and Orion and I ran after my brother into the passage with its ghostly form chasing after us.

We followed Gabriel up a tight stairwell and as he made it to a hatch in the ceiling above us, he swung it wide, letting a violent wind into the passage. A huge, snarling green Dragon face loomed down, blotting out the moonlight, and Gabriel released a blast of water so great that it sent Lionel spinning away from us like a lizard caught in a spin cycle. It covered him all over and Gabriel turned it to ice in the next breath, making Lionel's wings freeze too so he started tumbling from the sky like a dead weight, his roar trapped in his throat.

He hit the ground hard, the ice smashing around him as he fought to get up, crying out to the other Dragons as they swept forward to avenge him.

"Fly!" I yelled.

Gabriel took hold of Orion and took off, racing for the moon while I flew after them, higher and higher as we sought to break through the wards. My gaze lowered to the fleeing rebels far below, Nymphs and Dragons moving to try and intercept them as mayhem broke out.

I cast a silver blade in my hand, slitting my palm open and sending the blood away from me on a tempestuous wind. I sent it to every entrance to the secret passages in the grounds that I knew existed, and the palace answered my plea, opening the doors for the fleeing rebels, only to snap shut in the faces of their enemies.

An elated laugh left me, though it wasn't over yet as a hoard of Dragons turned our way, flying hard in a frantic bid to catch us.

The wind made my eyes water, and I raised my hand above me, desperate to feel the kiss of the wards, Phoenix fire licking my fingertips in case we met any kind of resistance.

Magic tingled in my hands, the kind that was steeped in power, but wasn't a match for my Order. I tore through the wards with a boom that splintered through the sky and Orion tossed the stardust over our heads thinking of fuck knew where, as Lionel roared in utter fury below us.

Just before the stars stole us away, I saw the palace locking itself up tight once and for all and I cast a flaming Phoenix bird out of my fire, sending it out to fly above the palace, singing our victory and perching on the roof in a mark of defiance.

Then all went dark, and I was lost to a galaxy of swirling light, feeling the souls of my brother and mate hugging close to me on either side.

Scorpio
Gemini
Virgo
Cancer
Leo
Taurus
Sagittarius
Capricorn
Aquarius
Libra
Pisces

DARIUS

CHAPTER SEVENTY THREE

My soul shook as that beautiful, powerful, unstoppable mate of mine stepped through the barrier between life and death like it was any other door which she refused to leave closed.

She was here.

I reached out towards the table, a bottle of bourbon appearing between my fingers at the mere thought of it just before I poured myself a glass. My hand was trembling. I could feel every step she took within this place, like ripples in a pond signalling to all who dwelled here that something was coming. Something which didn't belong.

I'd cleared that route for her, what power I still claimed currently pressing out of me, widening the way, keeping all other souls from her path while her parents, my mother, Hamish Grus, Azriel Orion and many others fought to keep them at bay too, helping to buy us this time.

Death was endless. The beauty of the eternal palace which I currently sat in beyond compare, the gilded streets outside it filled with countless bounties, and the harrowed gates past that marking the path to immortal pain.

All Fae who had once lived came to this place on their journey into death, able to linger here within the in-between for as long as they desired. I had met spirits who had been here for millennia, and I had watched newly deceased Fae walk straight past the palace to the flickering gates of the beyond without so much as looking aside.

In death all was possible for those who had earned it with their time, all wishes granted to those housed within the palace and the lands surrounding it. And for those who had earned damnation, the screams from the far side of the harrowed gates made it more than clear that their eternity was filled with precisely what they deserved. I'd heard they too could pass on through a flickering gate of their own, but the horrors which lay deeper into that side of death were enough to make most of them linger in torment on this side.

There had been no question of moving on from this place for me. I'd stumbled into the Eternal Palace and had spent my first weeks here fighting to get back to the other side, to keep my promise to the woman who had come for me now. Then I'd grieved the life I'd lost, I'd held my mother close, and I'd come to accept the truth of this place and what it was to me now.

Because death was eternal. And there was no coming back from it.

Her footsteps drew closer, that bond between us yanking tight and drawing her to me, every strike of her boots on the marble floor like an echo of a heartbeat which thundered through my still chest.

The room I had been gifted here was beautiful, ornate, perfect, and yet there was little which really spoke of me the way I'd seen the rooms that others here did. I knew why. Because none of what mattered most to me was here. Nothing that made me feel alive resided in this place and no substitution of the reality which I'd lost would ever suffice.

I swallowed the rich mouthful of bourbon, the taste so reminiscent of Orion that I could almost see him standing there, a single eyebrow raised as if to say, "Aren't you going to get up?"

But I wasn't. I couldn't. The impossible had come to pass and she was striding straight towards me while I waited here like a coward, knowing I could never give her what she needed, never fulfil that yearning in her shattered heart.

I'd seen it all, every moment of suffering and heartache she had endured. I'd watched her become the creature she needed to be to make this journey, watched her bleed for every sacrifice and felt the agony she had taken upon herself in this pointless hunt.

But I'd been to the Room of Knowledge and looked out of the great orb, at the world through the eyes of the stars themselves, and I knew the truth when I beheld it there. It had destroyed me, that understanding had broken the last rays of hope I held for a solution to our situation, but I knew that this would break me more. To steal a moment in her arms, to hold her close and know how fleeting it would be. Because she couldn't stay here, no matter how selfish I wanted to be over that desire, I knew it couldn't be. She had a world waiting for her and a destiny so great that even the stars weren't certain of it yet. She'd been born to topple mountains and make the stars quake; she'd been born to ruin and rise.

I stood and looked into the shimmering wall behind me, my own personal view of all those I loved who remained among the living.

I'd watched everything from this place, rarely left it, my attention glued here even though I knew it could lead to madness. But I wasn't ready to turn my gaze from the fates of the living. I couldn't focus on my afterlife while so many people I cared for were in peril, fighting against all odds to survive the wrath of my father.

It was nothing but a window really, but when I felt fear or love beyond what I could contain, I could step into it. I could push through that barrier and stand among my loved ones without them seeing me at all. I couldn't truly affect anything, but sometimes when I touched them or bellowed a warning, they felt me there. It wasn't much, just the hint of my soul dancing around them, but I knew that they felt me all the same. It wasn't enough. But it had to be.

Her footsteps drew closer like the ticking hands of a clock, and I swallowed the lump in my throat as I took a step towards the tall, double doors then stopped.

She was here. And that meant I was going to have to face the consequences of my failure in their fullest at last.

I couldn't make myself move from that spot, the sunshine beaming in from the windows, casting one side of my face in the light while the other was left in shadow. Like the two parts of my soul; the man I was when I was hers, burning bright and hot and full of life, and the one I had been in all the years before her, festering in a need for vengeance, drowning in my own failures.

I wasn't sure which of those men I had become in the end, though I supposed I would always be some mixture of both.

The doors flung themselves wide as she reached them, banging against the walls either side of the frame and leaving us there, staring at one another, tension crackling in the space which divided us just as it always had.

And of course, there was no smile there, of course she wasn't pleased to see me in that fairy tale perfect way that most people would have dreamed up for this scenario. She was fury given breath, her green eyes flashing with that deep and resounding rage in her and her full lips pursed with anger as she took me in, standing before a chair which could have been a throne, waiting for her to come to me.

"Hello, Roxy," I said, my voice rough, my gaze drinking her in. She was bloody and battered, the price of her passage into this place weighing heavily upon her shoulders, and the runes she had painted on her flesh glowing slightly, like they were warding off the press of death which ached to have a taste of her.

Those lips parted, a thousand kisses burning through my memory as I watched them, waiting, wondering if after all of it she might still think I was worthy of her.

No words escaped her, not a single one and I almost smiled at that. Roxanya Vega left speechless, no venom left to spit, no rage left to break from her. I thought I'd never see the day.

She took a step towards me, then another. Every inch she closed between us awakening that desperate need in me for her. She was mine, my one good thing, the keeper of my heart and the shackles surrounding my soul.

I'd broken over her grief for me. I'd shattered watching her fall apart. Yet here she was, striding through the barriers of death itself to come for me. Her. Only ever her.

Roxy's eyes moved over me slowly, the doors banging shut behind her as she kept coming for me, taking in the opalescent sheen of my shirt, the golden cloak which was pinned over my shoulders. I'd been hailed a true warrior in the moment of my arrival here, a circlet placed upon my brow in honour of the sacrifice I'd made fighting for those I loved. I appeared as such now, but I felt anything but valiant beneath that penetrating gaze of hers.

She drew closer, the air between us growing thin as I took her in, this beautiful, broken, queen of mine.

Roxanya Vega fell still with less than a foot dividing us, her face turned up to look at me, her eyes telling me that she feared this was some trick, that I might vanish again at any moment, ripping the last of her hope from her and destroying what little strength she'd clung to.

I wanted to reach for her, kiss her, tell her…all the things that words could never encompass. But there was something I needed to do for her before I could attempt any of that.

I drew the glimmering sword from my hip in a fluid movement before placing its tip against the ground between us and dropping to one knee in front of her. A tremor rumbled through the Veil as my knee hit the ground and I clasped the pommel of my sword as I bowed my head before her, my limbs trembling with the magnitude of this action, of what I had known and should have admitted for a long time now.

"I pledge myself and all that I am to you, my Queen," I breathed, emotion wracking my core as those words tumbled from me at last, my place in this world somehow fixing there as if I had found the truth of my own destiny, and all that I had ever needed to be. "I would be your sword to fight your enemies, your shield to protect your people, your monster to own and to wield. I would be yours in any and all of the ways I could be, and I should have told you that a long, long time ago. I am your creature, your servant…yours."

Silence followed my words, and I didn't dare move, didn't dare look at her to gauge the way that promise had been received, even knowing it had come far too late to matter now.

"You once told me that you would never bow," she said, her fingers brushing my jaw in the lightest of touches which set my entire body quaking beneath her. "You told me, that I would have to break you, just as you once tried to break me, and you laughed at the idea of it."

My lips parted, but I had no words. We'd promised each other no more apologies for the time that came before us, but I'd struggled with that oath every day since making it. The memories I had of hurting her tortured me always, and as if my mere thoughts on the subject had summoned them, I heard my own cruel laughter ringing out from behind me. The wall I'd used to watch my loved ones still fighting in the realm of the living also replayed memories when called upon to do so. And apparently it thought now was the time to remind us both of all the damage I had done when we'd met.

I dared to look up at her, needing to know, needing to see what hurt still lined her beautiful features as the worst of me was presented to her once more, as she was reminded of all that I'd done to her.

But she wasn't looking at the wall, her green eyes were entirely fixed on me, and there was so much love there that it cut me apart to look at it. To know how unworthy I was of it.

"My father," I rasped but she shook her head, ebony hair tumbling over one shoulder from the movement and taking the edge from that warrior's visage so that I could see the girl she was beneath it. My girl.

"He has no place here," she said firmly. "And he is not your father. He bears no responsibility for the man you became despite him. He can't have a single piece of credit for that. He can't even have your name anymore."

"My name?" I asked, a frown furrowing my brow and she nodded as she traced the back of her hand along my cheek, the metal of her wedding ring brushing my skin and filling my chest with more pride and love than I had thought anyone capable of.

"You're Darius Vega now. And you weren't built to bow to anyone."

The words I'd once spoken to her resounded through me as she fisted my shirt in her hand and yanked me to my feet.

The sword fell from my grip as I stood for her, and her mouth captured mine as she hauled me to her.

My hands came around her waist as my lips parted for her and I drew every piece of her flush against me, the world fading to less than nothing beyond us as she claimed me right there, in the heart of death, like it meant nothing at all that she had ripped her way into this place to come for me.

She didn't release her hold on my shirt as she pulled me against her, kissing me like everything that made up the entire universe began and ended with the two of us.

That kiss was hello and goodbye, a bittersweet reunion, and a promise of everything we should have had. It was a breath of life into the silent cavity of my chest, a wordless plea for me to return to her, for the world to somehow make sense again purely because we were together.

But it was a lie.

Even as I felt the heat of her skin against mine, there was no denying the coolness that came from me. Even as my lips devoured hers and she released a sound so full of love and hurt that it burnt me, there was something still dividing us. I inhaled her air, and she consumed my soul, but that line remained. It remained, and it grew until our kiss broke apart and we were left staring at each other, facing the fact of our reality.

I opened my mouth to say the words, but she shook her head fiercely, tears gilding those stunning eyes as they saw right through me. Like they'd always seen right through me.

I kept my silence. Just for a little longer. Because I could see that she knew now anyway. She had felt that divide, had realised what still parted us, even with her fighting her way through the doors of death to come for me. Because I couldn't step back into life. There was no path leading that way, not for me.

Until I found you by Stephen Sanchez started playing at little more than a thought from me and I offered her my hand. One more song. The wedding dance we should have had. The beginning we'd been denied.

Roxy hesitated as she looked at my hand and I knew that she knew. One song. A few minutes stolen before it would be over. Before we had to face this goodbye and I would go back to waiting for her while she returned to the life she still needed to live.

She swallowed thickly and her hand slid into mine as she let me steal this moment, like she couldn't bring herself to deny me this one request.

"Roxy," I rasped, the feel of her so hauntingly perfect as I drew her into my arms, the warmth of her fire breathing the echoes of life into my lungs as if it were real, as if we might truly have been standing on the precipice of a future together.

"I hate it when you call me that," she whispered, her eyes tilting up to meet mine as I drew her against my chest, the world blurring around us.

Rose petals fell from the sky, dropping against her skin and coating her in them until she was clad entirely in their blood red colour, her wedding dress appearing on her as I was gifted a moment reliving that unreal memory when she had given herself to me entirely, beyond all reason, utterly mine, no matter how little I had deserved it.

"No, you don't," I growled, feeling the tremor in my flesh as it passed into hers, our souls connecting, tangling, weaving themselves back together as if we had never been ripped apart at all. "From the first moment I called you by that name, you looked at me and you knew me. You knew yourself. We just spent too long lying about the truth of that destiny."

"I'm done with destiny," she hissed, the light around us shuddering as her power flared, pushing against the will of the stars themselves while she used the raw magic she owned to deny them. The foundations of this place and everything beyond us rattled as she shook the heavens for this stolen moment, and I wondered how I had ever tried to deny the strength in her.

The song continued to play around us, and we both knew that its end would be the end of this too. We couldn't keep stealing time that had never been intended for us.

"You shouldn't have come here," I breathed though I couldn't mean it, not really. Not while she was there in my arms, real, and raw, and beautiful, her heart thrumming with all the life we should have lived together, the thump of it against my hollow chest almost making me feel like my own heart still pounded within me, the way it always had for her. "You know I can't leave this place."

"You can," she said fiercely, trying to pull back, but I held her tightly, refusing to let go. Our moments were slipping by one by one, and I knew as well as she did that there was no after. The song would end and so would this, the two of us slipping apart like grains of sand divided by an ocean. There was no power on earth – even one as great as hers – which could deny the laws of all.

"Fuck, I wish I could," I swore to her, drawing her tight against me and inhaling the summer and winter scent of her. It was all things and nothing at all. This essence of immeasurable power which hummed with so much of everything that I was little more than a mortal kneeling before a goddess. "I wish I could come back with you more than any man has ever wished for any fate in all the history of all the world. I'm yours, Roxy, heart and soul and everything beyond, I'm yours. But even that can't free me from this place. What I lost can't be returned. There is no healing the body I once owned and there is no returning through the Veil now that it has closed at my back."

The walls trembled again, the truth she wanted to deny rushing up on us as the song played on and I looked into her green eyes, trying to show her what she was to me, what she had been. My salvation. I would have died a thousand deaths to be gifted this moment in her arms, to look at this perfect creation and see so much love for me burning within her. She had tried to deny death itself for me.

There was only her.

It had been no false declaration. She was my light when I had been so lost in the dark. She was the mirror she made me face, the truth I needed to see. And still she'd loved me. She'd been the only one who ever could have looked at all of the darkness in me, who could have seen beyond what I had done and found something worth loving within it. She'd been forged for me by something so much more powerful than fate. And the only regret I had in death was that I had broken her heart in the end. I hadn't been able to keep my promise. And though I'd tried, I'd fought to get back to her with all I had from the moment I'd found myself here, I knew that there was no going back.

This was goodbye.

And the song was ending.

"I love you, Roxanya Vega, and I wish I could have been worthy of you."

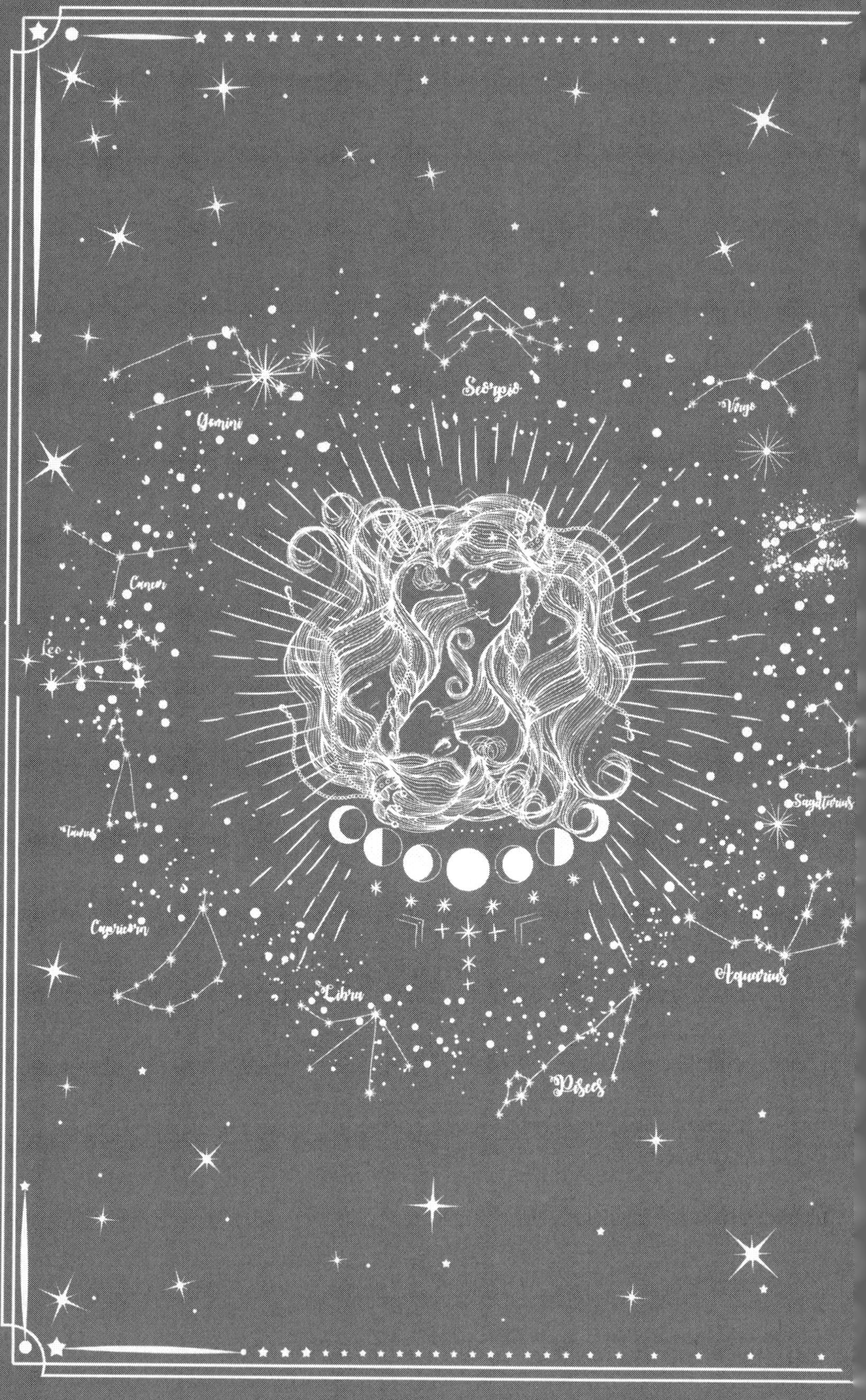
Scorpio
Virgo
Gemini
Cancer
Aries
Leo
Taurus
Sagittarius
Capricorn
Aquarius
Libra
Pisces

Tory

CHAPTER SEVENTY FOUR

The silence which broke at the end of that song was like a strike of lightning through my heart as a deafening boom made the foundation of the Veil rock beneath us and I stumbled back a step.

Darius caught my hand, his eyes full of longing as he tried to hold onto me despite the weight of power which was trying to drive me back. Back the way I had come, back to a world where he wasn't there, and I was so desperately alone.

"No," I gasped, my fingers locking tight around his even as the world flickered and blurred, his hand in mine losing substance before materialising again.

"I'll wait for you," he swore to me. "Right here. I'll wait for you for as long as it takes. And I'll watch over you, Roxy. I'll be there even though you won't see me. I'll never truly leave you. I swear it. I'll wait for you even if eternity passes me by while I do. I won't ever leave you."

"It's not enough," I choked out, my vision blurring with tears as I felt the enormity of my grief coming for me again, like a mouth full of sharp teeth waiting to rip me apart bit by bit. "I won't leave without you."

My words were fierce, furious, and yet they were empty, and we both knew it. I could feel him slipping away. He had nothing to come back to, no heart to beat for him, no way to return. It wasn't like he'd just slipped beyond the Veil and was teetering on the edge of death. It had been weeks. And death had gotten a taste for him now, its hooked claws lodged deep within his chest.

The walls splintered with cracks as I refused to release him and the pain in his eyes mirrored my own as we both fought to hold on.

"Roxy," he began but that was the only word I could hear, his lips moving but his words stolen away as the Veil pressed closer, forcing me back again, trying to push me out.

I shook my head with determination, drawing the dagger from my hip where it had remained as I had found myself in my wedding dress once more. The hilt was cold and the blade still as deadly as it had been on the day that it had torn him from me. The sun steel dagger responsible for piercing his heart.

"Don't!" he roared as he spotted the blade, the intent in my eyes. But I wasn't succumbing to grief. I wasn't surrendering to the only chance we had to remain together because I wasn't going to leave my other half alone in the world of the living.

So death couldn't have me. But it couldn't have him either.

My grip on his hand became insubstantial again but I refused to let go, instead latching on to that thread which connected our souls, that unbreakable link between us which nothing could rip apart. My power rose up in me and I latched myself to that thread.

The sky beyond the windows flashed purple and orange, a storm of pure magic thrashing against the confines of the Veil as my presence here threatened the stability of it all and in the distance I could hear a clash of blades, a roar of raised voices like someone was fighting beyond these walls, but I couldn't spare my attention for that.

"Don't let go," I snarled at Darius and his dark eyes flashed with gold as he took in the power echoing through my words.

He nodded as he realised I wasn't giving in to this fate, that I wasn't going to allow the stars to force me from this path. He knew me. And he knew that I wasn't born to give in any more than he was.

"You are going to fight this," I ordered him. "You will fight it with all you have and if the price of that fight is the end of us both then I will gladly take that over death or life without you."

Darius's jaw locked as he took in that command, the warrior I knew him to be blazing in his expression as he nodded in agreement, his fingers tightening on mine.

"I'll give you all I have," he swore and I nodded.

It would be enough. It had to be.

His fingers bit into mine as magic built within him and a roar powerful enough to shake the stars in the sky erupted from his chest as his Dragon burst from his flesh, clawing its way out of his Fae form instead of transforming it, separating itself from him as his fingers remained locked with mine. I gasped as it tore its way right out of him, leaving the man I loved panting before me as the beast of fire and talons beat its golden wings and began to circle us protectively.

I stared in wonder at the incredible might of his Dragon form, the beast even bigger than I remembered, its rage a potent thing which demanded a moment from the claws of death and took it without waiting for an answer.

My Phoenix cried out to join it from the confines of my soul and a shuddering breath escaped me as I burst into flames, bronze wings tearing from my back before beating once and taking off, leaving my Fae body behind as a bird of flame and fury raced to join the Dragon.

We were surrounded by our beasts, the creatures who resided alongside our souls fighting off the laws of magic for us as we stood between them in an orb of potent power, our hands still locked as one while a wild wind tore at our clothes and hair, almost knocking us from our feet.

The roof of the palace splintered overhead before hurtling away like it had been caught in the fist of a giant, and I looked up at the spiteful stars as they looked right back, their almighty power washing over us, promising their wrath if I didn't stop this now.

I smiled at them as I slit my arm open, and the blood of a true royal spilled from the wound.

I reached for Darius, fisting his shirt right over the place where his heart should have been and ripping the fabric open to reveal the inked skin there.

"Roxy," he growled, catching my wrist as I raised two bloodstained fingers. "What will this cost you?"

"No cost is greater than the loss of you," I replied as the world hissed, the acidic whispers of the stars closing in on us.

Stealer of life.

Twister of destiny.

Beware the cost.

Turn from this path.

Stop before you unbalance the scales.

His ascension will bear a price.

"I don't care," I snarled, and the truth of my words shut them up, the pure honesty I wielded sharper than any blade. Let them come for me. What more could they even take?

Darius's eyes reflected the flames of our Orders, as the beasts who were us and were somehow separate in this place circled and bellowed, fighting off the power of life and death as they bought us the time we needed.

He released my wrist, and I threw myself into the dark power of ether as I summoned it from the ground itself, the air, the flames, the distant rain, all of it flooding towards me and answering my call without so much as a hint of starlight among it.

That magic coiled within me like a serpent ready to strike and when it became unbearable, I released it like a whip, lashing at the sky far above and battering the stars themselves with a many-tailed attack.

They screamed as the ether tore into them and I smiled grimly, finally able to fulfil the curse I'd promised them.

Talons of ether cut into their power and with a flood of my will, I stole a piece of magic from each and every one of them. I stole what they refused to give willingly, and I took pleasure in the horrified screams which rattled the sky itself as I twisted their will to my own and forced them to fuel this magic in me.

My legs gave out, but Darius caught me, holding me upright so I could keep going, so I could fulfil my promise to him and my curse on the stars.

I hissed through the pain in my own chest as I began to paint a rune over the place where his heart should have been, but I didn't slow.

"My soul is his," I said, my words thick with magic as the declaration became an undeniable truth, like it was written into the fabric of the world just as any other law of nature might be. "My heart is his."

Darius gasped as he felt the weight of that power too, his knees almost buckling as he stumbled towards me, but I was there, waiting to catch him and he caught me too, his hands clasping my face between them, his forehead pressing to mine as we held each other up.

"Let them beat as one," I choked out, the power I was wielding catching in my throat, the words burning on my tongue as my body fought to contain this magic. "Let them *be* one," I demanded, painting another line on his skin, the rune I had found hidden in the Book of Ether, so ancient and so powerful that it didn't even have a name. it hadn't even been drawn in one piece, each line separately marked out with instructions on how they should be combined and clear warnings never to attempt it, for the power it held was a force beyond any that our world had ever known.

But I was beyond our world now, in the chokehold of death and clinging to love with a fist of iron. And I had made an oath to the stars to make them pay for their curse on our love, so it was time I showed them just how serious I had been.

"My life is bound to his. His death bound to mine. One heart…." I panted heavily, my legs caving and nothing but Darius's grip on me holding me upright. "One life…" I collapsed as power ripped me apart from the inside out, but he was there, holding me up, gripping me tight and trembling with the effort it took to do so. He was there. And I would never be without him again.

"One path. Together," I hissed, a slash of my finger completing the rune and a scream burst from my lips as pain pierced my heart in an immeasurable wave.

"No!" Darius bellowed, his eyes dropping from my face and forcing me to look down at the sun steel blade which now pierced my chest, mirroring the wound which had stolen him from me, the agony of it wrenching at the anchors of my soul as it tried to rip me away into death too.

I almost succumbed, but as my eyes fell closed, I saw nothing but blue beyond them, my other half fading as I was pulled away from her and every piece of that possibility causing my soul to riot and rebel.

I didn't even know where I found more power, but I drew it into me, my eyes opening once again, meeting his as horror spilled through his gaze and I shook my head in denial.

No. I hadn't bound us in death. I had bound us in life and those motherfuckers knew it.

The power I had summoned exploded out of me, time warping and shifting around us as I refused their latest attempt to thwart me.

The stars' final bid to win this game against me fell to ruin as I looked down at my chest once more and found nothing there, the sun steel blade still gripped in my fist where it had been all along.

The heat of my Phoenix bled through my fingers and the blade turned molten, a puddle of silver dripping to the floor between us as it was destroyed, and the power of our binding sank in.

My heart thundered within my chest, its pace a resounding drum of war which demanded a reply.

I gripped Darius's forearms where he still held me and met his eyes as fear and wonder spilled through them.

"There is only him," I swore and with that vow, my power broke, crashing from me, through him and into the very heart of death itself.

There was a cost to this. A cost which I knew I would be forced to pay, but none could surpass my need for him. Just him. Only ever him.

And as I was hurled from the clutches of death back into the world of the living, a soul was carried with me just as the book had suggested it could be, a single sound meeting my ears which granted the one and only wish I had ever truly had for myself. Someone who saw every broken, sharp edge of me and who loved me for every cut it offered them.

The thump of Darius's heartbeat rang out in perfect synchronicity with my own because it *was* my own. One heart. One life. Never to be parted again.

Scorpio
Gemini
Virgo
Cancer
Aries
Leo
Sagittarius
Taurus
Capricorn
Aquarius
Libra
Pisces

DARCY

CHAPTER SEVENTY FIVE

We landed on mossy ground, and I managed to keep my feet, but still bumped headfirst into Orion's chest, a laugh rumbling through him.

He gripped my arm to steady me, eyes glittering as we shared this moment which was so similar to the first time I'd travelled by stardust.

"Watch it, Vega," he teased, an echo of a time lost to us now.

I fell against him, grabbing Gabriel's arm and yanking him into the fold too as we panted heavily and hugged each other tight. All the fractured pieces of my heart found a way back together after so long in imprisonment, and I didn't even care where we were, only that we weren't under Lavinia's control anymore, and Lionel was far, far away.

"We did it!" I cried, sunlight bursting through my chest and making me almost choke up with it. I looked around at the foggy marsh we'd arrived at, a large stone hut standing to our right which looked long abandoned, but I lost sight of it as Orion scooped me up, spinning me around so fast it was like I was in a tornado.

When we stopped spinning, he kissed me hard, crushing his mouth to mine again and again, speaking between every touch of our mouths. "You. Phenomenal. Fucking. Girl."

Gabriel snatched me from Orion's grip, putting me in a headlock and scrubbing his knuckles against my hair. "You little hellion," he laughed.

I fought to get free with a growl, but when he let me go, I just shoved his chest playfully unable to stop smiling.

"What about you two? You came bounding up that hill riding the freaking Shadow Beast," I said, shaking my head at them and the ghostly grey shadow at my back danced around my shoulders, giving off an aura of excitement.

"Noxy's idea." Orion folded his arms and Gabriel chuckled.

"We didn't have much choice considering the Nymphs were about to fucking annihilate us," Gabriel said then grabbed Orion roughly and clapped him on the back as they embraced.

I looked between them with a dumbass grin on my face and the feeling of an eagle soaring through the centre of me, like my heart had sprouted wings and taken off.

"What is this place?" I looked around again, the fog drawing closer over the wetland.

"It just popped into my head," Orion said. "My father used to bring me here sometimes to collect old bones. It's the site of a long-forgotten battle, so the bones aren't guarded. Though believe me they have sunk deep into the bog and are mostly lost."

"You and your dad had a creepy kind of fun together, didn't you?" I said with a teasing smirk.

"We really did," Orion said wistfully. "We can take shelter in there for a bit." He pointed to the hut, and I led the way into it, casting a fire in the wide hearth. Grass had sprouted between the cracks in the floor and the charred walls spoke of the war that had been fought here long ago, but it was a sanctuary for us now.

An owl hooted indignantly somewhere up in the rafters, clearly annoyed we'd come here and disturbed its nesting spot.

I used earth magic to cast a wooden sofa with a soft bed of moss to cushion it, and I dropped onto it with a sigh of relief. Orion sat beside me, but Gabriel seemed distracted by something, picking up a stick that was resting against the wall by the fireplace.

"Oooh, look at that," he cooed, cocking his head to one side as he examined it. "That's a real nice stick. The grain is just perfect. And look at those nodules..." He ran his fingers over them then tucked the thing into his waistband possessively before moving to sit on my other side.

"Got yourself a nice little stick, did ya?" I questioned teasingly.

"Yes, and I'm going to give it to my wife when we get back to the rebels," he announced, puffing out his chest.

"She'll love that, brother," Orion said encouragingly, neither of them seeming to think Gabriel's stick was amusing. Or cute. And it was definitely cute.

The Shadow Beast materialised, taking up the rest of the space in the hut. It laid down and folded its front paws together, panting furiously and washing hot air over us.

"You did great, boy," I praised. "Or...girl."

The Shadow Beast got up, heading outside and cocking a leg to pee on a tree while Orion frowned at it.

"Definitely a boy," I said. "And he's housetrained - yay!"

I smiled at Orion who gave me a cool look.

"You're free now," he said, wafting the Shadow Beast away as he padded back inside. "Off you go."

I elbowed Orion in the ribs. "He's staying."

"He is not," he insisted.

"Hush, I need to focus. I'll try and find a way to reach our family," Gabriel said, and we fell quiet, looking to him intently as his eyes glazed with visions. But he didn't come back from them after several minutes, and I guessed it wasn't going to be easy. Maybe not even possible. The rebels had to be hiding their movements well or Lionel would have found them long ago, but I trusted Gabriel to find us a path somehow.

I cast a silencing bubble around me and Orion to give Gabriel some quiet, bathing in the heat of my fire as my magic recharged, the feel of doing so after so long without having access to my power giving me a headrush. Everything about this night was impossible, and yet somehow it was real. And my mind couldn't quite catch up with this reality we'd found our way to.

Orion slid his fingers between mine, bringing my hand to his mouth and kissing the back of it. "We really made it, Blue."

I smiled big at him, emotion welling in my chest and nearly overwhelming me. "Now we just need to find the others."

The Shadow Beast shuffled closer, lifting its beautiful umber eyes to mine, its bear-like face kind of adorable now that it wasn't fixed in a snarl.

"Hey there..." I leaned forward, holding out my hand in an offering to pet it, but letting it come to me first.

"Blue," Orion warned, but I ignored him as the beast raised its head, pressing its face to my hand in encouragement.

My heart beat a little harder as I brushed my fingers through its fur, now greyish instead of darkest black.

"You're just a big teddy bear, aren't you?" I said and it let out a little huff of pleasure as I scratched one of its ears.

"It's a dangerous, bloodthirsty creature, and we should leave it here in this marsh the moment we have a route to follow," Orion said, taking hold of my wrist to try and pull my hand away from it.

I gave him a look that could have melted iron and his jaw ticked as he held my gaze, his fingers still tight on me. "Darcy Vega-"

"Lance Orion," I countered. "I'm keeping him, and you're not going to tell me otherwise."

"You're crazy. That thing killed countless people. It almost killed Tory," he said, shaking his head and looking to the huge animal which had caused so much bloodshed in this war. My heart tugged over the memory of Tory broken and dying beneath me, the guilt flooding into the cavity beneath my ribs and stealing my breath.

"Do you blame me for that too?" I whispered, knowing he didn't, but this was exactly why he was a hypocrite if he believed I was innocent, but the Shadow Beast wasn't.

"Of course not," he said passionately. "But we don't know this creature's intentions. It could be working for Lavinia, feeding our location back to her this instant."

"Then why did he help us escape?" I said fiercely. "He wouldn't have done that if he was working for her. And when I broke the collar around his neck, I felt that connection shatter. I burned it away with my Phoenix. There's nothing left of her taint on him."

The animal licked my hand, giving Orion a sidelong glance that seemed to imply it understood what was going on here.

"So how do you plan to walk that thing back among the rebels? They're going to fear it. They'll hate it for what it did at the battle," Orion said, and my smile dropped.

"They'll need time to come around to him. But for now…maybe I can keep him hidden." I thought on how I might do that then willed my earth Element to create a silver ring in my palm, getting a little carried away over being able to wield this power again and growing two beautiful black metal Shadow Beast heads either side of a large, clear gemstone which was hollow inside, with a tiny hole in the centre of it.

"Do you think you can fit in here in your smoke form?" I asked the beast and intelligence brightened his eyes.

He turned to smoke and rushed into the space I'd created for him, turning the clear gemstone grey inside. I turned to Orion triumphantly and he gave me a dry look that said he wasn't pleased I'd just found a solution to a problem he didn't want me to solve.

"Looks like he's coming with us," I said brightly.

"Joy," Orion said sarcastically.

I shifted nearer to him and hissed as the dagger I'd slid through the material of my shorts dug into me. I tugged it free, studying it in the firelight, and scoring my thumb over the crimson garnet stone in its hilt. I wondered if my mother or father's hand had held this dagger once, had admired this very stone that decorated it. Power seemed to vibrate within the beautiful stone, and I bit down on my lip, hope fluttering inside me.

"What do you think?" I whispered, holding it out to Orion and he raised his right arm, sensing what I was wondering. The Guild Mark on his forearm flared to life, the intricate design of the sword glittering beneath his skin, all of the zodiac constellations shining along it like starlight.

"Garnet for Capricorn," he announced with a smile, then he took the blade, placing it down on the wall beside him and tugging me closer by the thigh, hooking my knee over his legs. "Now let me look at you."

He captured my chin, angling my face up towards his as he gazed deep into my eyes, studying them with an air of euphoria about him. I didn't have to ask to know that he was looking at my Elysian rings, and I bathed in the feeling of bliss expanding from him. He was bloody from battle, clothes torn and muscles still tight from fighting, looking like a warrior from some old folklore, woven into existence and given life.

But he wasn't a knight with deeds of virtue to his name. He was my devoted, ruthless Vampire. And he was finally safe. Free at last.

Scorpio
Gemini
Virgo
Cancer
Leo
Sagittarius
Taurus
Capricorn
Aquarius
Libra
Pisces

TORY

CHAPTER SEVENTY SIX

I gasped as I woke, my heart thrashing in alarm as I found myself laying on a bed of moss in a stone chamber beneath the ground, a fire roaring beside me and the red wedding dress I'd been reclothed in still clinging to my frame.

Real.

But then where-

I pushed myself upright, shivering despite the warmth of the fire as I looked around at the dark cave, frowning at the emptiness as I hunted it for him.

I couldn't tell how much time had passed since that power had almost consumed me, but my body was heavy with the feeling of sleep, and my magic rumbled contentedly inside myself, refilled by the fire beside me.

Half a thought had my Phoenix rousing inside my chest, the warmth of its flames flaring through my body and warming me from the inside out as I found it there, back where it belonged, as if I had simply dreamed up the memory of it parting from my body to aid in that dark magic beyond the Veil.

I ran my fingers over the lace of my dress, marvelling in the detail of it, the perfect replica of the one I'd worn to marry the man who I'd walked into death for. It was as if I'd stepped back in time, to a moment that had been stolen from us when war broke out and the worst had come to pass.

But if this was my wedding day, then where was my groom?

I headed to the stone doorway on bare feet, my boots gone along with everything else I'd had with me, and I wondered if they were lost entirely. The Book of Ether alone was an invaluable weapon, and I would mourn the loss of it if it was gone.

I stepped into a stone corridor and realised that despite the darkness of my surroundings, I recognised them, my fingers reaching out to brush along the weathered carvings lining the wall of the ruins we had taken refuge in after escaping the battle so long ago.

I followed the familiar path towards the exit despite the darkness which made it near impossible to see, my stomach fluttering with nerves like I was some blushing bride awaiting her wedding night.

I parted my lips to call out to him, but found I didn't have the words, uncertain what I would say after that cataclysmic reunion, afraid of what he might be feeling now or if he could have been changed by his time away from the living.

Soft grass met my toes as I stepped out onto the mountainside, and I looked up towards the sky where the stars shone dimly. It was as if they were trying to avoid my attention, licking their wounds over what I'd done to them and remembering that I could do more if I was forced to.

I looked away from them and began climbing towards the peak, walking up the mountain towards that beautiful spot where Darius had been laid to rest alongside his mother and Hamish, beneath the Dragon tree his dearest friends had crafted for them.

I stepped into the small clearing, the tokens of grief and small offerings to the dead from the rebels still surrounding the coffins, magic keeping the flowers in bloom, the everflames glowing and the ice sculptures sparkling.

The two coffins sat there in the silence, the larger one closer to me and making my heart hurt as I looked through the ice at the still bodies within, their hands clasped in a final act of love. I hadn't seen them beyond the Veil. I hadn't seen anyone at all aside from him, and I didn't know what to make of that. There were so many Fae I would have liked to have found my way to.

I stepped up to Darius's coffin and sucked in a sharp breath as I took in the jagged crack which splintered through the centre of it, the ice melted away and the place where his body had lain empty.

I'd been expecting it, but that didn't quell the shock I felt at the brutality of that truth.

Where was he?

I turned slowly, scanning the dark view ahead of me and smiling as I spotted an enormous shadow racing across the moon. A shadow with a wingspan to rival an aircraft and a jaw which spat hellfire into the sky as if announcing his return to the entire world and challenging any and all of them to deny it if they dared.

He banked hard, turning towards the mountain again and I broke into a run as I headed out of the small clearing where the coffins lay, sprinting for the ground further down the hillside where there would be room for a Dragon to land.

My feet slipped in the frozen stalks of grass as he swooped towards me, bellowing fire over my head, and making my blood pump faster as I held my ground.

Darius landed in front of me with a boom that threatened to knock the snow from the peak of the mountain, and I smiled up at him as I reached out to stroke his golden nose.

He dipped his head obligingly, my hand skating up between his eyes as he pressed his forehead against my chest and exhaled a cloud of smoke which engulfed me entirely.

He shifted within it and my palm fell to his chest, right over his heart as he appeared before me.

My everything.

"Hello, wife," he purred, the corner of that sinful mouth hooking up.

The sight of him made my heart leap and I gasped in surprise as I felt his own leap beneath my palm in unison with it. The true twin to my own now, bound as one by the magic of ether and starlight alike.

"You know I only married you because you were dying," I replied, unable to help myself as my fingers caressed the scar which had healed over on his chest, the mark of the blade which had killed him remaining even now. A reminder and a blessing.

"Liar, liar," he growled, stepping towards me so I was forced back.

I let him move me, step by step, my hand on his chest, his body towering over mine as I fell into his shadow, liking it far too much in the dark.

"How long has it been since…" I trailed off, not sure how to describe what had happened to us, but he knew what I meant.

"A day and a night – dawn is an hour away, at most," he replied, still backing me up, the intensity of his gaze almost paralysing.

"Did you wake up in that coffin?" I breathed, the thought of it making me recoil, but Darius didn't so much as flinch.

"The return of my magic to my body had melted it away before I came to," he explained. “The power binding us, your heartbeat…that was already in place as well.”

I swallowed thickly, nodding as I took that in, my feet moving from grass to stone as he backed me right into the ruins, his steps sure, that intensity unwavering as his gaze roamed over me from head to foot, like he was a starving man, and I was a freshly made meal.

“So you saw the others there. You saw your mom and Hamish?” I asked softly and his eyes met mine through the dark as he fell still for a moment, their deaths laying heavily on us both.

“I saw them beyond the Veil,” he admitted. “I’ve made my peace with their passing and I…”

I could hardly see him in the darkness, but I could feel his eyes on me, assessing, hesitating, but he didn’t hold back, not now and not ever. We were beyond anything like that now.

“I saw your mother and father too.”

“You spoke with them?” I breathed, my pulse picking up and his matching it where I still held my hand over his heart as he nodded.

“They are so incredibly proud of you, Roxy,” he murmured, the taste of those words on the air making something within me loosen. “They saw what you were doing, what you were planning to attempt and they – my mom, Hamish, Azriel and many others too – they all helped hold the way open for you. They fought back the army of the dead who would have tried to force their way through the rift you carved and made it possible for you to reach me.”

“They…all of them did that for us?” I asked in astonishment, unable to comprehend the idea of a fight waging within death itself over the magic I’d used to get there.

The Book of Ether had been full of warnings against necromancy for that very reason – the press of dead souls always desperate to break back through the Veil, but I’d ignored the warnings then forgotten them entirely when I’d found him at last.

“They did,” he agreed. “Because they can see what it took me so long to accept. They’ve been watching and waiting and hoping for you and Darcy to rise for a long time. And they want to be a part of your army too. Even if only in spirit.”

His words sparked a memory in me which had a smile rising to my lips as I tilted my head back and tried to seek out his eyes in the dark.

“You bowed for me,” I said, the words seeming unreal as I spoke them, the fact of them so unlikely and yet I couldn’t have imagined it.

Darius growled and smoke slid from his lips, the scent of it and the cedar which lined his skin so impossibly perfect that I moaned as I inhaled.

He started walking again, and I kept my palm over his heart, still marvelling at the perfect synchronicity of our pulses, the eternal bond which now linked us as one.

I backed up before him, my breaths growing shallow as the intent in his strides became clear, and he turned me into the room I’d been given when I came here before.

Fire sprung to life in the corners of the stone room, the dull orange glow finally offering me a clear view of this beast of mine as he loomed over me.

I glanced at the stone bed, still cushioned with moss, but he ignored it, stalking me right back to the wall until I was trapped there between it and him, only my hand on his chest maintaining any distance between us.

He placed his palms either side of my head, caging me in and leaning closer, closing the gap between us, only my wedding dress parting our flesh.

I stared at him, this man in the flesh of a god, risen from the dead and haunted by so many demons. He was a stunning creature, his body cut with pure muscle, his bronze skin coated with those magnificent tattoos and his eyes always swirling with that inner darkness which I loved far too much for my own good.

We just stared at each other as the seconds ticked by, the promises passing between our bodies making me hot all over and my breaths come shallowly.

“What are you looking at?” I breathed when he remained there, his gaze roaming over my features and his body so achingly close while not being close enough at all.

“I’m looking at the woman who crossed into death for me,” he replied, his tone rough with a reverence I didn't deserve. "The woman whose heart found it possible to love me even though I could never be worthy of it. You cursed the stars themselves for me and forced them to bend to your will. You risked dark magic and death before your oath was fulfilled, you bound your own heart to mine so that you could haul me back here to you."

"You and me weren't a story that was ready to end," I said, my hand slipping from his chest, past his neck and finally cupping his jaw. The bite of his stubble raked against the scar on my palm as I looked into the roiling gold of his eyes, his Dragon shifting beneath his flesh, watching me, assessing me.

"I have spent my whole life knowing I wasn't ever going to be the noble knight our kingdom needed," he said slowly. "The other Heirs were always much better suited to being valiant than me. I was the one who crossed into the dark, the villain who was needed to absolve the stains my father was leaving in his wake. And with every choice I made to follow that path, I came to accept that no one would ever be able to love me the way you impossibly love me. I gave up on hoping for anything even close to this. I gave up on the idea of love at all. Until you. My beautiful, burning saviour-"

"Don't do that," I interrupted him, my gaze hardening. "Don't place me on some impossible pedestal and make me into the hero in your story. I'm not that, Darius. There will be a price to pay for bringing you back and the universe knows I won't allow for it to be taken from our flesh, but that only means it will be carved from something else. And I don't care. I'm selfish enough not to care about that so long as I have you here with me. I'm selfish enough to bind your heart to mine because that means I will never face losing you again. Our lives are linked and so our souls are bound as one too. If death takes either of us now, it will collect us both and I'm okay with that."

"I don't think that you're my hero, Roxy," he said, his hand shifting from the rock beside me as he took my jaw in his grasp and ran his thumb down over my lips before shifting his grip to my throat. "I think you're *my* villain too."

A smile tugged at the corners of my lips before his mouth took mine in a breath-taking kiss that had my soul rising to the edges of my skin and hunting for a way to get closer to his.

I pushed my fingers into his dark hair and dragged him to me as I parted for him, his tongue captivating mine as his grip on my throat tightened and he crushed me against the wall.

I moaned into his mouth, the ecstasy of this reality consuming me, and I had to fight the tears which were trying to break from my hold. But I didn't want to cry. I wanted to laugh and whoop and sing to the fucking moon and back about this, about him, my own darkness returned, my brutal tormentor, my fearless saviour, my ruinous hellion. All mine, for now and always.

My teeth captured his bottom lip and Darius growled as the tone of our reunion shifted from the pure bliss of our love for one another to the feral need of passion that always burned so hot between us.

He dropped his hands to my thighs and lifted me into his arms, the press of his cock driving against me through the fabric of my wedding dress as his fingers bit into my skin.

His mouth released mine, his lips carving their way from the corner of my mouth to the edge of my jaw then lower, his teeth raking against my skin and making me gasp in pleasure, my fingers digging into his powerful shoulders.

"Do you want me to kneel for you again, my Queen?" he asked against my skin, his fists bunching in the fabric of my dress.

"Yes," I gasped, his words making my heart race and I knew that meant that his was too, our pulses joined in this tumultuous gallop which marked how much we needed this.

Darius fell to my command, and I sucked in a sharp breath as he dropped down before me, his grip on my thighs keeping me pinned to the wall above him until he could hook my legs over his broad shoulders.

I clawed at the fabric of my dress, flames coming to my fingertips as I made to burn it off, but he snatched my wrist into his grasp, pinning me in that reckless gaze of his.

"Don't," he snarled, somehow dominant even while he was on his knees with my legs wrapped around his neck, and I bit my lip as I looked down at him.

"Why not?"

"Because this dress is a reminder of the day when you gave yourself to me entirely. It is a reminder of the day when I died trying to fight for you and you cursed the stars themselves as you swore to undo that wrong. This is the dress of the Queen who owns me heart and soul, and I want to be able to see you in it as often as I can. I want to be able to dress you up in it then peel it back off again to claim you with my tongue and my hands and my cock."

"Who knew the big, bad Dragon Heir would be into wedding roleplay?" I teased and he grinned at me, this feral, wicked grin that promised to destroy any scraps of virtue I might have had left.

"Oh, Roxy. You have no fucking idea."

Darius found the edge of my skirt and shoved it up suddenly, my breath catching as he bared me to him and a fucking whimper escaped me as his mouth dropped to the inside of my right thigh, his tongue skimming the edge of the tattoo I'd gotten for him there. And those words had never rung so true. There was only him. Now and always. Until our hearts stopped beating and we crossed beyond the Veil once more.

He pushed my knees further apart as he began to move his mouth up the inside of my thigh and I shifted against the rock wall unsteadily, but his hands were there before I could slip, gripping my ass and pulling me to him as his mouth descended on me without mercy.

"Fuck," I gasped as he ran his tongue straight over my clit, his lips closing around me and his stubble biting at the soft skin of my thighs.

He used his grip on my ass to angle me better and I could do nothing but grip the heavy folds of my dress so I could watch him destroy me with that sinful mouth.

Darius devoured me like he'd been starving for me, his fingers digging into my ass as he buried his mouth against me and licked and sucked until I was writhing against him, begging for release.

He denied me instantly, dropping his mouth lower and sinking his tongue into me, lapping and tasting while my clit throbbed with need, and I cursed his name.

"Make me come," I snarled at him, managing to fist his hair in my hand and dragging him northward, his dark chuckle letting me know that he was getting exactly what he wanted from me.

"Is that an order from my queen?" he teased, the deep rumble of his voice against my core almost sending me over the edge. "The first she ever gave me. What will the citizens of her kingdom think of that?"

"They'll wonder why you weren't capable of doing it without command," I snarled back at him, then cried out as he shoved my thighs even further apart and descended on me at that challenge.

His tongue was a gift from the heavens, the masterful strokes destroying me in seconds as he gave in and I shattered for him, crying out and praising his name while my hips rocked against his face, and I took and took from him.

I sagged back against the wall, and he was on his feet instantly, planting me down on trembling legs and turning me around so that my back was to him.

I braced my hands against the wall, shivering as his mouth met with the back of my neck and he brushed my hair over my shoulder to expose more of my skin.

I tried to catch my breath as he kissed me there, his fingers slipping down my spine, unfastening the dress button by button, the caress of his fingers moving down my body enough to drive me insane.

The dress fell from me in a pool of red, and for a moment all I could see was blood as I looked down at it, the stain of so much death which had clung to us on our journey to this point.

"I'd kill a thousand enemies if it brought me to this," Darius rumbled in my ear, like he could tell what I was thinking without me needing to voice it. "I'd paint myself in blood and stain my soul beyond repair. Anything to bring me here, anything to have you in my arms like this."

"So would I," I replied, looking over my shoulder at him and as our eyes met, I knew we were thinking the same thing. That that was wrong. That we shouldn't have been so willing to sacrifice the world for the sake of this, but it didn't change the truth. Darius and I had been bad news from the first moment we'd laid eyes on one another, we were toxic, hateful, and limitless. But we were still here, and we wouldn't be turning from each other now or ever.

Perhaps we should have been more concerned about our vicious natures, but as Darius took hold of my chin and kissed me, I knew I didn't care. I didn't want to care. I only wanted him.

His tongue sank into my mouth and his cock drove against my ass, a moan slipping from me as I felt how big he was, my spine arching with a command for more.

His hand moved around my waist, dropping low to explore me, his growl of approval echoing down to my core as he found me drenched for him and instantly sank three fingers into me.

My moan broke our kiss and he smirked at me, leaning in to nip my ear as he fucked me with his hand, filling and stretching me, the heel of his palm grinding against my clit and making my head spin.

I was free falling for him, every nerve ending buzzing at his touch and as his teeth sank into the side of my neck, I came again, my fingernails biting into the rock wall before me as my pussy clenched tight around his fingers and pleasure rocketed through every inch of my being.

His teeth sank in deeper, a feral snarl escaping him as the pain of the bite bled into pleasure which echoed on through me. I could do nothing but grip the wall as he withdrew his fingers and used his knee to widen my legs then drove his cock into me from behind.

"Oh god," I panted, and he took his teeth from my flesh, replacing them with his tongue as he pushed in harder, filling me with his enormous length and pressing me tight to the wall.

He moved his hands to my hips as he began to fuck me, and I could do little more than moan his name as he took me in that savage, wild way, his mouth destroying me, flesh owning me and my body caving to his every desire.

There was something feral and animal in the way he was taking me, like the creature he was at his core just needed to mark me as his, our own mating, sanctioned by no one but us and with no strings attached beyond our everlasting devotion to one another.

He was so big, his body utterly dominating mine, his thick length filling me entirely and striking deep within me so that my core rattled with a promise of more bliss.

His fingers found my clit as I was crushed between him and the wall and I arched into him as he fucked me hard and rough, the need between us having no room for pretty or sweet. That wasn't us. But this was. Brutal, punishing, savage and wild.

I fisted his hair over my shoulder as he pounded into me, my tits scraping against the rock wall and my body managing to find pleasure in that too as my aching nipples gained some relief.

He sucked on my neck hard enough to leave a mark before, licking and kissing the spot which he had no doubt bruised and I moaned loudly as I drew close to the edge once more.

"I'm going to hear that sound every fucking day from now until the end of time," he promised me, his cock so deep inside me that I could hardly draw breath. "And when you come for me, when I own and destroy your body, you will know right down to the core of you who you belong to, won't you, Roxy?"

"Yes," I panted, the time for mocking and teasing long past as he fucked me deep and hard, his fingers moving expertly against my clit. "I'm yours. Always," I swore, and he growled in approval of that.

"Mine," he agreed in a dark promise, his grip on my hip tightening as he thrust deep inside me. "Always."

He sank his teeth into my neck again, pleasure and pain colliding as a snarl rolled from him that was all beast. I cried out as I began to come, my senses overwhelmed by everything about this, about *him*.

Darius slammed into me without mercy, his teeth drawing blood as he bit down even harder and with a ferocious roar he came, forcing my body to comply with his as he swelled and pulsed inside me, filling me with his seed.

My pussy throbbed and clamped tight around the thick length of him, and I gasped as his fingers continued to massage my clit, drawing every last bit of pleasure from me as he took his teeth from my neck.

His body weighed heavily against mine as we panted there, the thump of his heart against my back in perfect rhythm with my own.

"Before the stars ever got to have a say in it, I would have picked you for my own," he told me, his words interspersed with kisses to the side of my face, my jaw, my neck. "My obsession with you has been tormenting me from the moment we met and will continue to torment me for the rest of time. I can't get enough, won't ever get enough."

"Death has made you sentimental," I panted, craning my neck to look over my shoulder at him and I found him watching me with an intensity that stole my breath clean from my lungs.

"I love you, Roxanya Vega," he growled, hands roaming up my sides as he withdrew enough to part our bodies and I instantly missed the feeling of him inside me. "I love this freckle right here…" His mouth dropped to my shoulder as he placed a light kiss against it, and I breathed a laugh. "And I love this one, just here…" He moved his mouth lower, placing it against my shoulder blade where my wing would burst from my skin if I shifted, making the sensitive skin there tingle with pleasure.

"What else?" I teased and he grabbed me suddenly, tossing me over his shoulder and slapping my ass hard enough to make me curse.

"I love that filthy mouth," he admitted before throwing me down on the mossy bed.

My hair tumbled around me where I fell, and I scowled up at him as I pushed myself onto my elbows, but that only seemed to urge him on.

"I love the way you call me an asshole," he said, beating me to it before I could utter the word.

"Well, that's handy, because I'm forced to do it a hell of a lot," I quipped and he grinned, stalking closer.

"I love the way you look right now, just fucked and furious, utterly sated and yet panting for more."

"You have a seriously high opinion of yourself," I said, but his grin only grew as he placed his hands onto the bed either side of my feet and moved onto his knees at the end of it.

"I love these little toes," he teased, kissing my instep, and snatching my ankle into his grasp when I tried to jerk away.

"That tickles," I protested, but he just did it again.

"Look at these feet," he purred, nipping at my instep again and making me moan as he hit some unknown nerve there which sent a spark of energy racing straight to my core. "How do they stomp so loudly and furiously through the kingdom when they're so small?"

"My feet are average sized," I protested, though I guessed compared to his Dragon feet they were fairly small. But that didn't count.

"Mmm…" Darius seemed to consider that before moving on with his inspection of me, and I couldn't help but notice the thickness of his cock, already hardening again as he gave my body so much attention.

It should have been uncomfortable having him look at me like that, I should have felt exposed or uncertain or at the very least vulnerable, but it just felt…right. I had given myself to him entirely, and that meant all of me, flaws included, insecurities be damned.

"Well, I may have found my favourite freckle," he said, placing a kiss to the side of my left knee then raising his eyes to the tattoo on my right thigh beside it. "But the prize for my favourite mark on this sinfully tempting skin of yours, would have to go to that."

"Am I expected to give you a similar assessment when you're done with me?" I taunted and his eyes flashed gold with his Dragon once more.

"Well, that's a problem, Roxy, because I won't ever be done with you," he swore and goddamn him, I fucking blushed.

Darius grinned like the asshole he was, and I smacked his shoulder, striking the flaming tattoo which was inked there, leading down to the Dragon and Phoenix covering his back.

"Do you still claim your tattoo has nothing to do with me?" I asked as he crawled further up my body, kissing every freckle he found and giving me a mouth-watering view of his powerful back, stained with more ink than I even remembered.

"You mean the one I got on your birthday the summer before you came to the academy?" he asked casually, and I gaped at him.

"You got that on my birthday?" I hissed, smacking him again for never having told me that before, and he chuckled against my stomach before kissing the side of my ribs.

"Yeah. There was a boring as fuck memorial service every year where the kingdom would sob over baby pics of the two of you and celebrate the age you would have been."

"Boring?" I hissed and he laughed again, this time moving to my nipple and sucking hard, his hand shifting to grip my other breast and a moan hitching from my throat.

"These I love a lot," Darius growled into my skin before moving his mouth to my other nipple, forcing my spine to arch as I moaned louder, my thighs parting with need. "They're just so-"

"You were telling me about the tattoo you didn't get for me on my birthday," I ground out, though it was seriously tempting to let him continue with his assessment of my tits instead of gaining those answers.

"Right…" Darius moved his mouth to my collar bone, leaving my nipples hard and aching, his words interspersed with kisses as he continued. "So, there was the boring memorial – sorry Roxy, but I spent my whole life attending those kinds of bullshit events and though it was sad and all, I didn't know you and it had been eighteen years, so…"

"I get it, asshole, you didn't care about two dead babies."

"I didn't say I didn't care," he replied firmly. "I just preferred to show that by killing Nymphs in my free time. Isn't that a better testimony to my grief than me standing about paying lip service at a repetitive memorial year after year?"

"Oh, so you're charming me with your bloodlust?"

"Don't pretend it doesn't turn you on."

"Tell me about the tattoo or you won't be finding out what turns me on again today," I insisted as he huffed and moved over me, leaning his weight on his forearm, while brushing a few strands of hair from my face with his free hand.

"I just woke up in the early hours that morning and knew I wanted it. I'm not much of an artist at the best of times but I drew it, exactly as you see it, like the design was caught inside me, desperate to get out. I left without telling anyone where I was going and didn't get back from having it done until that evening. I was expecting to face Father's wrath over missing the memorial service but when I returned, I found everyone in uproar because two incredibly powerful magical signatures had just been discovered in the mortal realm and it turned out you'd come back from the dead."

My lips twitched in amusement, and I reached up to trace my fingers along his jaw. "How bored you must have been before I came along to torment you."

"Just a little," he agreed. "Anyway, like I said: the tattoo has nothing to do with you. So stop being so conceited and thinking my whole life revolves around you."

I slapped his arm and he spanked the side of my ass in reply, making me moan unexpectedly and his eyes darkened with lust.

"So you're just going to stick to your belief that you waking up *on my birthday* and heading out to get your biggest tattoo with no pre-planning at all, had fuck all to do with me – even though it depicts my Order and yours in a dance which looks one step away from violence and another away from love?" I demanded.

"Just a coincidence," he agreed, shrugging infuriatingly and I scowled at him.

"I hate you again," I muttered, and he smirked at me.

"No, baby, you never quite managed to hate me."

"Asshole," I bit out, that infuriating smile only widening at the insult.

"Now. Where was I?" he asked slowly, his fingers moving in my hair. "Oh yes; I love the way your hair feels when it's wrapped tight in my fist."

"And let me guess, you love the way my lips feel wrapped around your cock?" I teased, drawing a growl from him as his gaze roamed over my mouth.

"Undoubtedly," he agreed, his mouth dropping over mine as he claimed a surprisingly sweet kiss from me.

I sighed in contentment as I met the press of his lips against mine and his hand trailed down my side languidly, caressing my skin in a feather light touch before moving between my thighs.

He shifted his mouth to my ear as he moved over me, and my pulse began to hammer at the promise building between us once more.

His fingers caressed my clit then sank lower, feeling the evidence of his claiming mixed with my wetness and I moaned with a need for more as he teased me, the thick length of his cock pressing against my thigh.

"And I really, truly love filling your pretty pussy with my cum and making you scream my name until your throat is raw," he growled.

My gasp cut off with a moan as he rolled on top of me and drove his cock into me with a single, punishing thrust.

His mouth captured mine again and he gripped my wrists, pinning them above me as he took what he wanted and began fucking me again, the fires of hell burning in his eyes and the monster in him shining through with every brutal thrust.

My hips met his with every move, my cries of pleasure echoing off of the cave roof as he destroyed me and rebuilt me all at once, owning me entirely and filling my body with bliss as I fell apart from him time and again, his captive, his obsession, his Queen.

Scorpio
Virgo
Gemini
Cancer
Leo
Sagittarius
Taurus
Capricorn
Aquarius
Libra
Pisces

MILTON

CHAPTER SEVENTY SEVEN

The hunt was getting too close to our trails, the K.U.N.Ts everywhere and Nova analysing everything.

Gary was gone. Dead, most likely. The evidence discovered against him before any of us could do a single thing to stop them coming for him.

I hadn't been able to sleep for the last week, not since we'd all tried to escape in the dead of night, only to find the wards around the academy strengthened beyond all measure. There was no crossing them, no escape beyond the front entrance, and that was heavily guarded 'for our protection.' Students had been banned from leaving the academy grounds whilst a thorough search and investigation was underway to sniff out the rebels among us.

It was that fucking song.

The rage it had invoked in the man who claimed to be our king was beyond anything I could have predicted, and his retaliation had been swift and brutal.

Ever since that day in The Orb, the academy had been put into total lockdown under the guise of protecting us from the nefarious rebels who had supposedly snuck in here to sabotage him that day.

It was utter bullshit designed to placate our parents and anyone else on the outside.

Ever since that day, the K.U.N.Ts had been out in force, Nymphs and Dragon Guild members coming and going to aid in the hunt. Even the FIB had been tasked with discovering who had done it.

Gary had had the software on his Atlas, everything needed to create the song, as well as the original version which he'd spliced together.

We'd thought that we'd dealt with it by smashing it and hurling into the depths of Aqua Lake, but against all odds, some Siren K.U.N.T. had discovered it. The first we knew of that terrible twist of fate had been the thump of boots slamming against the floor of the Jupiter Hall corridor five seconds before the doors had been damn near blasted from their hinges, and our Cardinal Magic lesson had been invaded by a platoon of the FIB.

Honey Highspell had laughed as they pounced on Gary, and only Bernice's hand snatching mine had saved me from joining him in his fate as I leapt to my feet, magic burning in my palms as I thought to save him.

It still gutted me to remember how I'd given in to the plea in her beautiful eyes, guttering my flames and retreating to the back of the room with the rest of our classmates as Gary was beaten and hauled from the room.

"Long live the true Queens!" he'd roared as they dragged him out of sight, nothing but bloodstains marking where he'd been sat mere moments before their arrival.

I'd been caught on those words, playing them over and over in my mind ever since he'd screamed them in that final act of defiance. Had they been the last words he'd ever spoken? Did I have the guilt of his death to lay as a burden upon me now? And was I an absolute piece of shit for half hoping they had been?

Because if they weren't, if he had been taken away from here for interrogation, then I knew it wouldn't be long before they came for the rest of us too. He knew our names, our faces, our crimes. All of it. And though I knew he would hoard those secrets with all he was, I also knew of the brutality the FIB used to extract information. No one could hold out forever against their methods.

That was why we needed a way out. But so far, every attempt we'd made had been thwarted, the wards too strong, the patrols too regular.

We were going to die here.

The thought had kept me from sleep night after night, even the moment of weakness I'd given into mere hours ago hadn't been enough to calm those thrashing fears.

I tightened my hold on Bernice, trying to focus on how it had felt to give in to the desire between us at last. I'd offered her a bell and she had let me fasten the choker which held it around her throat. The tears in her eyes had told me she knew she wouldn't be wearing it for long, that the future we might have hoped for wouldn't come to pass now.

The purity I'd found between her thighs as I drove myself into her had eased the burden on my soul a little. I'd lost myself in the feeling of her body as the bell she wore rang with every thrust of my hips, letting everyone know she'd been claimed at last. And the way she'd mooed as she came for me, loving every inch of me, had made me explode inside her with a bellowing moo of my own. She was my cow now. The first of my herd and even as she lay sated and sleeping in my arms, I couldn't help but feel guilty for that fact.

A bull was supposed to protect his cows. But my horns felt clipped, my hooves shackled in this place.

We'd struck a blow against the tyranny that was rife in this kingdom, but it wasn't enough. I wanted to fight, truly, in the army of the Vega Queens. I wanted to be there when they rose into their power and watch as they cut Lionel Acrux down.

I knew that future wasn't certain, but I'd been dreaming of it every night for months now, aching to see that bastard's head fall from his shoulders into the dirt at their feet.

A screeching sound in the distance had me bolting upright in my bed in Ignis House, Bernice complaining softly as I released her.

I pushed out of the bed, my pulse pounding as I moved towards my window on bare feet, a sense of unease pouring over me.

Dawn was approaching, but as I looked out, the sky was almost entirely dark, the rocky plane of Fire Territory spreading away beneath me towards the north of the school grounds and lit only by a faint glimmer from the waning moon.

I hunted the ground and sky, certain I'd sensed something out there and cracking my window open to get a better look.

There was a scent on the cool breeze which I inhaled deeply, frowning as I analysed the smell of something almost oily mixed with smoke. I was well used to the strange scents which coloured the air at the academy by now, recognising most of them from herbs to Orders to the taint of powerful magic, but nothing about that smell was familiar to me.

A flicker of movement caught my attention between a pair of jutting rocks in the landscape below, and I sucked in a breath laced with fear as I caught sight of eight huge legs, their knees turning back on themselves as a hulking beast of teeth and nightmares scuttled towards the House.

"Bernice?" I hissed, backing away from the window as my heart began to thunder in my chest, and I quickly grabbed some clothes, yanking them on. "Bernice, wake up," I said more forcefully, yanking the covers off of her and exposing her naked body to me as she flinched at the cool air.

My heart ached as I looked at the bell hanging from her throat, and she blinked up at me in surprise. "What is it?"

"I don't fucking know, but I think our time might have run out." I swallowed thickly then snatched my Atlas into my grip, the only plan which I and the rest of the Undercover A.S.S. had been able to fully agree on coming together. We knew our days were limited. There was no way out of here, and it was only a matter of time before the K.U.N.Ts or the FIB or someone else came for us.

We would fight, but we knew we couldn't win, so we'd offer the world the truth of our final stand instead. Each of us kept a chest strap with us at all times, ready to hold our Atlases in place so that we could live stream whatever happened to us out into the world via social media.

I didn't want to die. But if our deaths were coming for us then I wanted them to hold meaning, I wanted the world to see what Lionel Acrux did to those who wouldn't stand by and blindly follow him.

I hurried back to the window as I started the live stream on FaeBook and strapped my Atlas to my chest.

"My name is Milton Hubert," I said to the microphone as Bernice dressed herself behind me and I hunted the darkness for any sign of that thing moving out there again. "And I am currently inside Zodiac Academy."

I didn't say anything else, unwilling to implicate myself in any rebel activities just in case I was wrong and they hadn't come yet, but as the sound of breaking glass echoed through the building below me and the screams of my classmates carried into the air, I was filled with the certainty that it had.

Scorpio
Gemini
Virgo
Cancer
Leo
Sagittarius
Taurus
Capricorn
Aquarius
Libra
Pisces

XAVIER

CHAPTER SEVENTY EIGHT

Tyler Corbin: *Brooooo. You don't even understand the level of snacking I just descended to. I got the munchies after I flew through a rainbow at sunset, but when I tell you this amount of food was unnatural…*

It started with one little chip, but by the stars, that chip led to two and two led to three. Next thing you know, I'm neck deep in fifty flavours of chip, packets torn open, crumbs reaching regions of my body I never knew existed. But things be getting dry. Real dry in my chip pie. So I fetched the dips from the food store. Oh man, I had so many dips. Tzatziki. Hummus. Taramasalata. Sour cream and chive. So I'm stacking those chips, flavour mixing, dipping left and right, but my salt levels are overloading at this point. I'm talking swallowing your uncle Jimbob's jizz after he ate a bucket of salt and dipped his junk in the ocean, salty.

So now I'm thirstier than a fish in a bucket of sand, but some star damned Heptian Toad has gone and got himself stuck in the water pipes in R.U.M.P. Castle, so the water had to be turned off while they rescue him!

So I'm out roaming the island for water, and I'm gonna put this bluntly fam, I am as naked as a #hornyVampire looking for some #Pegavag. I had shamelessly stripped down while eating those chips and I'd rolled in them too, because something has got me acting like a wild man tonight. Tell me, is there some kind of celestial force at work right now that's turned me into a chip feasting phantom? Or did the rainbow fuck me up and jiggle my crazy juice?

Side note: I can't lose my abs, man. I worked my ass off for these. But now I'm drifting in the sea on my back, typing out this post with my cock and balls floating on the surface saluting the moon, and I can't think about anything else except that chip nest waiting for me back in my room. I wanna dive into it headfirst and crunch my way to glory #helpahorseout #chipclop #pegabinge #chipshame #saltysurvivor #dipanddie

Justine Irving: I heard there's sun flares at the moment and my Aunt Grundig said sun flares give you the yum yums – it's probably that Tyler! #sunyum #sunnytummy

Ameira Elias: Wait – there's chips??? Oh I am so DONE with the hierarchy forming here. I've been begging my boyfriend Karl to make me some chips with his earth Element and he told me that only 'healthy' food is being made for the rebels #wheresthesnacks

Melissa Lewis: I saw Karl eating chips the other day – you know everyone gets a chip ration, right? Looks like he had a lot of chips too. Enough for two people...
Ameira Elias: Wait...what???? @KarlLagoon W.T.F.???????
Anna Parker: I just flew over the ocean and wondered what was sparkling down there, winking at me like a diamond. It must have been your #sparkly megaPegapeen and your #shinybrinyhiny

I snorted horsily in amusement, scrolling down to the next post, then frowning as I remembered Tyler's room was my room, and that meant there were gonna be crumbs galore in our bed tonight. *Dammit Tyler.*

It was late, but my mind wouldn't rest so I'd taken a walk out around the island, the wintry night air slipping over my back. I willed heat into my veins with my fire Element to keep the cold at bay, but a different kind of cold took hold of me as I scrolled onto a livestream on FaeBook.

"There are monsters everywhere on campus! They're hunting us!" Milton's voice carried through the speaker, the stream showing him running down a narrow stairway while screams rang around campus.

A horrid creature dove into view, like a giant mealworm with spines around its wide mouth and sharp, needle-like armour all over its body. Milton cast fire, the flames pouring from him, but the thing seemed to be immune to it, writhing towards him up the stairs and forcing him to retreat.

It caught him before he could make it away, and a girl's cry sounded behind him. "Milton!" she yelled in fear.

"Brown Cow down – Brown Cow down!" Milton's live feed cut out as the monster slammed down on his chest, static crackling across the screen and horror blurred my mind.

As I scrolled, I found more feeds, students streaming all over campus and showing fights breaking out in all the Elemental Houses against the monsters.

I took off running back to R.U.M.P. Castle, panic darting through me as I shot a message to the group chat, finding that someone had changed all of our names to some stupid nicknames. It was undeniably Seth.

Twinkle Stud:
Zodiac Academy is under attack!

Batty Betty:
Butter my bagels! We must rally together – meet in the bowels of the mighty R.U.M.P!

Twinkle Stud:
Where's the bowels???

Batty Betty:
The entrance hall, you nincompoop!

Bitey C:
On my way.

Wolfman:
Me too. Heading there from the depths of the butt castle.

Fish Fury:
Gerry I really don't know how you fused this bagel onto my dick but – fuck
this message was deleted

Wolfman:
OH. MY. STARS. Did everyone see that???!!!

Twinkle Stud:
We need to go!!

Bitey C:
I saw everything. And I've been in the entrance hall for ages. Where are you all? Shall I zoom around and grab everyone?

Twinkle Stud:
I'm almost there!

Batty Betty:
I am riding the banister down at this very moment, you fine Vampirious man, with the Flail of Unending Celestial Karma resting upon my shoulder, ready to bring certain doom down upon the skulls of our enemies!

Bitey C:
Has anyone heard from Tory?

Wolfman:
I heard something...

Bitey C:
What did you hear??

Wolfman:
*I heard she's gonna use a breast reduction spell to wither her tits away. Anyone bothered by that?? **eyes emoji***

Batty Betty:
LIES! The bosoms of the true Queens shall never be shrunk!

Wolfman:
Okay FINE it was a lie. But would anyone be bothered by that if she DID shrink her tits???

Bitey C:
Whatever makes her happy.

Wolfman:
Oh I get it. It alllllll makes sense now.

Bitey C:
What does? And is anyone actually going to get here because I could have run fifty laps of the island by now.

Wolfman:
pancake emoji** **wolf emoji

Herald of Truth:
Sorry – just saw this! I'll wake Sofia. We're coming with you this time so I can report it all to The Daily Solaria ASAP.

I shoved my Atlas away as I made it to the drawbridge, running across it and heading inside to find Caleb there, spinning one of his twin blades in his hand.

Geraldine came sliding down the banister behind him in full armour, yodelling as she went. As she made it to the bottom, she leapt off and did a forward roll across the floor before leaping upright and placing her hands on her hips. "What-ho, dear Pegobrother?"

"Er, no ho. Just waiting to go," I said, and she slapped me on the shoulder hard enough to send me stumbling sideways.

Seth stepped through a door to my right, innocently combing his fingers through his hair.

"Hello," he said dramatically, casting a sidelong look at Caleb who scowled at him.

Max came running down the stairs with a strained expression as he hooked his bow over his shoulder. "Gerry, I need a word," he hissed.

"Have a hundred words, Maxy boy. I shall not silence your luscious lips," she said, waving a hand to beckon him into the middle of our group.

"In private," he said through his teeth.

"Is there really a bagel stuck on your cock?" Seth jogged over to Max, resting his chin on his shoulder.

Max batted him away, glancing around like he really wished we weren't all here to witness this.

"Bandicoots," Geraldine laughed. "Are you blushing, you sweet salamander? There's nothing to be embarrassed about, Maxy boy. We are an adventurous duo, you and I. And a little rumpus with a bagel is hardly a shock to the ears of an orgy-bound Wolf such as Seth Capella, and we all know Caleb Altair enjoys a public Pega-pounding-"

"I do not," Caleb barked, eyes flashing in rage.

"We need to get going," I said in concern, thinking of Milton.

Washer came running down the stairs in a pair of Y-fronts which were baggy around the ass but way too tight at the front.

"You dinged my dongler, Miss Grus?" he said, rubbing sleep from his eyes.

"I didn't ding any such thing," Geraldine balked. "But I did send you an urgent message, Brian, for it is time for you to step up and summon the rebels into action. Rally the troops. Arm the people. Raise the army and bring them to Zodiac Academy. We shall forge ahead and begin the battle as we await the arrival of the army!"

"What's happening?" Washer asked in fright, tugging at his Y-fronts to adjust them and I wrinkled my nose.

"The academy is under attack," I said, and Washer gasped.

"I shall rouse the whole legion with my Siren power, sending it deep into their dreams and tugging on the shafts of their souls, squeezing and pulling until they are primed and ready to blow, to spray our enemies with the seed of rebellion," he swore.

I grimaced and Caleb took a pointed step away from Washer before our old professor turned and ran back upstairs.

"Well, he shall do the job, even if he does it disturbingly so," Geraldine muttered.

Tyler appeared on the stairway, holding Sofia's hand as they ran to join us and she placed my metal horn into my grip. I put it on, strapping it tight under my chin, ready to go to war for the rebels and Sofia whinnied fiercely, looking equally prepared to fight.

"I'll open the wards so we can use stardust," Caleb said, pulling a pouch from his pocket it.

"Wait," Max said urgently. "I can't go yet. I..." He looked to Geraldine in desperation.

"There's no time, my dear dolphin. Ignore the crumbles along your codwhacker and I shall free you of the bagel's grasp when the fight is done," Geraldine said, jogging towards the door.

"Gerry!" he snapped at her, and Seth gave him a pitying look.

"Can't you just, break it off?" he whispered, but we could all hear him easily.

“No, she’s done something to it, so it feels as soft as butter, but it’s as hard as stone if I try to break it,” Max hissed.

“Let me take a look.” Seth reached for Max’s pants, but he knocked his hand away.

“No,” Max growled. “Just leave it.”

“What’s going on?” Tyler asked curiously and Max’s back straightened.

“Nothing. Let’s go.” Max marched to the door, walking a little awkwardly and if I hadn’t been so worried about the attack on Zodiac, I would have laughed.

“You can’t go to war with a bagel on your cock. As your bestie, I can’t let you.” Seth ran at Max, Pitball tackling him to the ground and shoving his hand down his pants.

“Seth!” Max shouted, a wave of anger crashing from him into everyone around him and I stamped my foot as the emotion took hold of me.

Seth did some weird twisting motion within Max’s pants then lifted the bagel above his head with a smug look on his face.

“How’d you do that?” Max gasped in relief.

“Believe it or not, this isn’t the strangest object I’ve jangled off a guy’s cock, Max,” Seth said, pushing to his feet and pulling Max after him. “You wouldn’t believe the things some Fae stick their dicks in. Packs of crayons, flower pots, cakes, Pegasex dolls.” He threw a look at Caleb whose expression turned volcanic.

“Fuck you.” He shot out the door after Geraldine and Seth swallowed a whimper, fixing his features into something far colder.

“What’s going on between you two?” I asked and Seth growled at me.

“This shit’s getting bad.” Tyler moved forward, showing us the screen on his Atlas and Seth’s brow furrowed as he took in the live stream on FaeBook.

“Lame Lionel has sent this monster to murder us!” Frank cried through the camera, showing a huge, beetle-like creature raging through the Aer House common room ahead. “Please help us!”

Seth howled in agony and raced outside while the rest of us hurried to follow him. Caleb shot ahead of Geraldine with a burst of speed, raising his hands skyward and using a flood of power to carve a hole in the wards to let us out.

We gathered close around him and he tossed stardust into the air, the stars yanking us away into their grip and the view of the island disappearing into the dark. We were thrown this way and that, the stars seeming to be in a turbulent mood before they spat us out and we crashed violently to the ground.

“Holy fuck, who pissed in the stars’ oatmeal?” Seth cursed, shoving upright, and pulling Caleb with him.

“There’s some weird shit going on. I’m just so hungry, man,” Tyler said. “Even you look appetising right now.”

“Hark!” Geraldine cried, gaining all of our attention as we turned to her and the tall fence that circled Zodiac Academy. “We must stay together this night, forge our path as one and cut down any enemy who crosses us. This academy belongs to the people of Solaria, to the newly Awakened, the children of brawn and might, and it belongs to each and every one of us too. It has been a home to many, a place of solace and safety. But now, a darkness creeps between its halls, and it is time we banish it for good. We must reclaim these grounds, for they are ours!”

I neighed in reply as hollers and howls went up from everyone else, and I moved forward, feeling the zest of the wards tingling against my skin and warning me away.

“We need to break through this,” I said. “I think we should power share.”

I looked over my shoulder at the others and Geraldine stepped forward, slapping her hand into mine. “We are friends through and through, and we must lay our trust in each other now, allow our power to ram into one another, and construct a colossal instrument that can slice through this here barrier and cleave it asunder.”

She offered her hand to Sofia, and she took it, taking hold of Tyler’s hand next. The Heirs fell beyond them, all of us linking up in a line.

“Let us plunge our power into our dear Xavier,” Geraldine said, her magic flooding against my palm and I focused, letting my shields down and allowing it to come in.

I gasped at the feel of her magic merging with mine, the wildness of her twisting into a rumbling, swirling power inside me. Everyone else worked to let down their barriers and suddenly all of their power crashed into me at once, making me neigh in surprise, the shock it all sending my heart galloping.

It was ice and fire and earth, all of it crashing and swirling and begging for an outlet. I channelled it towards the wards and it slammed into it like a bolt of fury, a flash of red light billowing up and away from us, arcing along the wards and bringing them down in a cascading rain of light.

Geraldine released my hands and I whinnied from the thrill of it, dizzy from so much power and stumbling a little.

Seth jogged closer, looking anxious to keep moving as he used his air magic to yank open a gap in the fence. I followed him onto campus where screams and the horrid sounds of some twisted monster carried from somewhere ahead. I steeled myself as my gaze fell on Aer Tower which was standing tall above us in the distance, the turbine at its peak twisting in the wind.

Howls of pain carried from inside and Seth howled in reply, terror lacing that sound. He took off without a word and we all fell in at his back, chasing after him towards the havoc, ready to fight with all the passion in our hearts.

Scorpio
Virgo
Gemini
Cancer
Leo
Sagittarius
Capricorn
Aquarius
Libra
Pisces

DARCY

CHAPTER SEVENTY NINE

Orion had fallen asleep with his head resting in my lap and I mindlessly brushed my fingers through his hair, my gaze fixed on the movements of the flames in the fireplace dancing this way and that. I was in a trance, lost to the heat of that enchanting fire while my magic reserves practically overflowed with how long I'd sat in it.

Gabriel had barely come out of The Sight since we'd arrived here, moving outside at dawn to refuel his magic only to return with vague murmurings about how he was yet to find something tangible. I'd managed to make him eat some fruit I'd grown with earth magic before he'd let The Sight take him again, his exhaustion clear. But he was determined to find a way back to the others, a firm path or clue to lead us to their door.

Orion had been trying to make a connection with Caleb's mind again too, focusing for hours at a time to see if he could re-establish it. But he'd had no luck yet.

Now, night had come once more and Gabriel lay on one of the beds we'd made, the old stone hut restored to something much more liveable. Though we would likely move on tomorrow if Gabriel got no leads by the morning. We'd have to move every couple of days after that in case Vard managed to *see* us, but I didn't like the idea of aimlessly travelling around the kingdom in hopes of one day striking lucky with a vision of our friends. There had to be a way we could find them, a message we could send somehow…

Gabriel rubbed his eyes, pushing to his feet as he came out of the depths of some vision. He was wearing new jeans, a blue shirt tucked into the back of them as he kept his wings out. Orion had disappeared off yesterday with a pinch of stardust to fetch us the clothes and I was now wearing a fitted black jumpsuit and some boots, while he wore jeans and a white t-shirt. It was such a small thing, and yet it felt seriously good to have my own clothes again. But the shine was wearing off of eating food I could easily grow with my earth magic. I wanted chocolate dammit.

"Anything?" I asked as Gabriel walked over to me, but he shook his head, looking dejected.

"I'm sorry," he sighed. "They've hidden themselves too well."

"That's a good thing. If the greatest Seer alive can't find them, then at least that means Lionel can't find them either," I said encouragingly and he cocked his head, looking down at Orion sleeping.

My gaze followed his and my brows pulled together as I painted a little circle over Orion's temple.

"I'm never going to be able to repay him for what he did for me," I whispered, my heart caught in a vice.

Gabriel shifted closer and I glanced up at him, finding his arms folded and an intense look about him. The tattoos on his bare chest seemed to shimmer in the firelight, like they were imbued with a power far greater than I understood.

"You will," he said with complete certainty. "You would go to the sun and back for him. So long as he is with you, he is where he wants to be. Only you have the power to make him happy beyond all imagination."

"But what if the curse of this broken promise stays with me always? What if we can't figure out what it is? Then we'll never be free of the darkness that haunts my every move."

Gabriel's eyes glazed suddenly, and I held my breath the entire time he was stolen away, hoping he might *see* something that could help us.

He blinked, coming back to me and when his eyes met mine again, they were gilded with war. But that flash of darkness in him gave way to a whoop of joy that made my heart lift.

Orion leapt to his feet with a shot of Vampire speed, his fangs bared and his arms swinging before he'd even found an enemy to strike.

Gabriel *saw* it all coming, darting out of Orion's way with ease before wheeling around to look at us with a big smile.

I jumped up onto the couch, heart rioting and adrenaline thundering. "What is it? Did you *see* them?"

"I *saw* the Heirs," Gabriel said excitedly, and I squealed in joy, lunging toward the bag of stardust I'd left on the couch and looking around for our weapons. "Not so fast, little warrior." Gabriel caught me by the arm as I went to run past him towards our gear, and Orion moved closer.

"What is it, Noxy?" Orion asked, his expression becoming serious.

Gabriel's smile dropped too. "I *saw* them fighting a monster at Zodiac Academy in Aer Tower."

"What?" I balked, twisting out of his hold and running for the weapons again. I strapped my mother's Harpy sword at my hip and looked over at the others, finding Gabriel latching the Hydra sword to his belt and Orion casually tossing the garnet gemstone dagger in his hand, clearly waiting for me. *Damn speedy bastards.*

"Ready yet, Blue?" Orion asked with a teasing smirk.

"Lemme just check my Shadow Beast ring." I twisted it around on my middle finger then raised it to swear at him as I joined them. "Yup. All good."

"You're gonna be in trouble for that," Orion growled in my ear as Gabriel took a pinch of stardust from the pouch.

"Ready?" Gabriel asked and Phoenix fire swum in my veins, the heat of it making my heart sing. I was starting to get a taste for battle that seemed wholly Fae, fighting for freedom, justice and vengeance, the sweetest forms of chaos.

"Ready," Orion and I confirmed, and Gabriel tossed the stardust into the air.

A thrill shot through me at the thought of seeing the Heirs again, tangling with my confusion and fear over why there would be a monster at Zodiac Academy.

The stars gleamed around us, whispering together in a language I couldn't understand, like they were conspiring. I didn't like the way their stares pressed into me, as if I was at the heart of their plans, and they had some imminent fate headed my way.

My feet hit solid ground and the three of us shared a fervid look, confirming they had felt the change in the stars too. But we couldn't waste time when the Heirs might need us, or if their fight was already done and they were about to stardust out of here again.

Orion stepped closer to the fence, finding a spot where two bars had been bent apart. "The wards are down. They came this way."

He ducked through onto campus and I followed with my brother at my back, the sound of screams spiralling up into the night. I exhaled slow and a puff of air fogged before me, my fire Element skipping out into my veins to banish the cold.

"We'll fly, and Orion, you run," I directed, letting my wings unfurl from my back, the soft bronze feathers brushing my skin.

Gabriel let his wings out too and we took off while Orion remained below us, shooting across Air Territory, the vast plane of land stretching out around us towards the sea cliffs.

I flew with Gabriel at my back, my gaze fixing on Aer Tower up ahead, highlighted in the lambent moonlight, and happy memories tumbled through me at the sight of my old House. This was the only place that had ever felt like home to me, and now it was under attack, I was damn well going to fight for it.

The sea air flooded over me, bringing the taste of brine to my tongue as I tucked my wings and dropped like a bullet from the sky.

I landed at the door, finding Orion there waiting for us, dagger drawn and danger in his eyes. Gabriel swept down behind me, his eyes glazing for a second before he came back to us.

"They're in the common room," he said, and I raised a hand, casting air at the triangular Elemental symbol above the door, anxious to keep moving.

It opened for us, and I pushed my way inside, running for the stairs. A guttural yowl cut the air apart somewhere above us and my magic tingled against my palms, the three of us staying together as we raced up the spiralling stone stairway towards the fight raging in the common room.

My boots beat against the floor, and sparks of fire snapped against my skin as my Phoenix hungered to come out. My breaths came heavier, but I didn't slow, if anything running faster as I thought of my friends waiting above. Of seeing them again, even if it was right in the midst of battle.

We made it to the top of the stairs and my heart felt like it was going to burst as I threw the door to the common room open, finding a giant creature in the centre of it. It was beetle-like with hardened plates of yellow armour over its hunched back, its six legs ending in taloned feet.

Max was hovering on a gust of air, his bow raised, and all of his arrows but one were already embedded deep in the creature's shell, proving how difficult this horrid creature was to kill. He released his final arrow, aiming true and it flew right between the eyes of the monster, making it slump down dead.

Caleb and Seth were revealed beyond it, panting from the fight, Caleb's twin daggers wet with blood and Seth's metal claws tainted with it too.

I staggered to a halt, the air going out of me and my heart nearly bursting out of my chest at the sight of them.

Seth spotted me first as Gabriel and Orion drew closer at my back, and my friend's jaw dropped, his hand reaching for Caleb's sleeve and tugging insistently.

"No fucking way," Max said as he spotted us and Caleb looked up too, his navy gaze settling on us at last.

"It's Darcy," Seth gasped. "Look. It's Darcy!"

"I see that," Caleb laughed, and Seth broke into a run, leapfrogging over the dead monster and slamming into me so hard that I fell on my ass. He howled his joy, licking my face and laughter tumbled from my throat as I drew him into a tight hug, his earthy scent surrounding me.

"How are you here? What about the curse?" he whimpered.

"It's broken. I'm free," I said earnestly, and he howled with all the happiness in the world vibrating through that single noise. Hell, I'd missed him. I'd missed all of them.

I looked up through the curtain of Seth's hair that had fallen over me, seeing Caleb collide with Orion at full Vampire speed, sending him flying back into a wall and a crack exploded up the middle of it.

"The Death bond?" Caleb begged of him, nose to nose with my mate.

"Gone, brother," Orion said with relief in his voice. "I'll tell you everything soon."

Max came running over, purest joy leaving his body and making my happiness grow and grow. It didn't feel real, but I was damn well gonna claim this moment and brand it to the inside of my mind.

Seth howled again, jumping to his feet and Max swept down on me, picking me up into his strong arms, my feet not even touching the floor as he gave me a bone-crushing hug.

"How?" he asked.

"Long story," I wheezed, but I didn't even care that it felt like my ribs were about to pop; it was so, so good to see him again.

When he released me, I found Caleb hugging Gabriel and Orion tried to escape as Seth sprinted for him with his arms outstretched.

"My moon friend!" he cried, and Orion tried to bat him off as Seth collided with him and licked him straight on the forehead.

Seth whimpered like a dog who hadn't seen his owner for a year and Orion relented, letting Seth clamber onto him like a limpet and hug him tight, nuzzling his face while Orion twitched a grin and clapped Seth on the shoulder.

"Yeah, yeah." Orion pushed him off at last and Seth came hurtling back towards me. "Oh my stars!" he yelled, but instead of slamming into me, he went flying past me, then started circling us all as fast as he could. "By the moon – awooooooo!"

"What's he doing?" I laughed.

"I think he's got the zoomies," Caleb said with a smirk, and Seth continued to race around us until he was panting and pulling Gabriel into a firm hug.

"Oh I missed you so much, Gabriel," Seth said with a choked sob.

"We don't really hang out, like ever," Gabriel said, patting him on the back.

"We're gonna," Seth said, releasing him and giving him an intent look. "Every day. Morning, noon and night."

"O…kay," Gabriel said with a chuckle then Seth took another dive at Orion, but he shot away this time instead of being trapped in second hug.

"How did you get free?" Max asked and Gabriel started answering, but everything else in the world stopped existing to me as the sound of a warbling yodel carried from the floor below us.

I took off without thought, sprinting into the stairwell, taking the steps two at a time. It was impossible. There was no way, no damn way this could be real. But I knew that voice, knew it from every desperate dream I'd had about that girl each night, missing her with all my heart.

I ran like the hounds of hell were at my heels, turning down the first corridor off the stairs and finding Geraldine there in all her armoured glory, spinning her flail like a mad thing. A boy with a K.U.N.T. badge pinned to his shirt went running from her with a scream in his throat.

He staggered past me, flying down the stairs before I could even think to stop him because my mind couldn't move from anything except this implausible reality right in front of me.

"Come back here, you scallywag!" she shrieked, turning my way and I fell totally still.

"Geraldine?" I rasped, shaking my head. Because surely the stars were playing tricks on me. I'd killed her, felt her armour crack beneath the claws of the Shadow Beast, seen her bloody and broken on the ground, so pale that life couldn't have lived on in her. Yet here she was, battle bound and sublime.

A noise left her that was somewhere between a gurgling sink and a baby dolphin, then she fell to her knees, tossing her flail aside and crawling towards me, sobbing and choking out words as she went. "My eyes deceive me! It cannot be, for I have wished upon a waning moon and all the phases fore and after for this very dream to materialise. I have cracked like a pebble in a stone lopper, and this truly cannot be!" She made it to me, grabbing my boot and shrieking, rolling onto her back and staring up at me in wide eyed wonder. "Nay! The stars play tricks upon my eyeballs! My dear lady Darcy lays in chains within the Palace of Souls, captive to the cretin of shadows and her lame Dragoon! Nay – nay!"

I leaned down, gripping her arms and hauling her upright, and she looked at me with tears racing down her cheeks. I realised my own tears were falling and my heart was floating in my chest. "It's me. I got away and my curse is broken. I've missed you so, so much."

Geraldine reached two trembling hands towards my face, feeling my features then throwing her head back with an almighty wail. "Stars, planets, sun and moon! My plea has been answered, my lady of bluest hair and heart of flame has returned!" She fell apart into sobs and I dragged her into the tightest hug I had in me, burying my face against her shoulder. She broke apart, releasing violent hiccups between every sob.

"It-*hic*-can-*hic*-not-*hic*-beeeee!" She shuddered in my arms, and I cried too, the wound of losing her healing over at long last.

"I thought I killed you," I said in horror as we managed to part enough to look at each other again. "I thought the Shadow Beast-"

"Nay," she croaked. "It did not. I rose like a dandelion in a quarry of doom, but do not concern yourself of such a long-ago deed. No blame falls upon your brow, my Queen." She staggered to her knees, bowing her head to me and I caught hold of her shoulders, dragging her back up again.

"Don't do that," I begged, cupping her cheek, and blinking through my tears. "I'm so glad you're okay. And I'm so sorry for what I did."

My heart hurt with the weight of guilt I'd been carrying over her death, but it was easing at finding her alive. It just didn't seem real.

"Do not tangle your tongue on such words, dear Darcy," she said, sniffing heavily. "I do not blame you for the whims of that beast any more than I blame the moon for chasing the sun. It is not your doing. It is a force outside of you and your virtuous soul."

I nodded, needing to hear those words like I needed air to breathe. The door to one of the rooms opened at her back and Xavier, Tyler and Sofia stepped out, dragging a couple of K.U.N.T.s with them and tossing them onto the floor unconscious.

My lips parted and Sofia neighed wildly as she spotted me, charging over, and slamming into me.

"Oh my god, it's so good to see you," I gasped, squeezing her tight and Tyler drove into me next, my legs nearly buckling at the weight of them falling against me.

"Where the hell did you come from?" Tyler cried.

"I got away," I said. "I'll explain everything soon."

"We got away too," Gabriel's voice sounded at my back.

"Look it's Orion and Gabriel!" Seth shouted as they all appeared in the stairwell and Geraldine let out another shriek that almost burst my ear drums.

"Your Orry man and your wing-ed brother," Geraldine screeched, slamming into them, and pulling them both under her arms in a violent sort of hug, knocking their heads together as they gave in to her brutal affection.

Sofia and Tyler released me, and my gaze fell on Xavier, pain racing through my core at the echo of darkness in his eyes. I moved towards him, shaking my head as all words failed me, my legs feeling leaden. Darius, his mom…everything he must have suffered through in the wake of their loss.

"I know," he said before I spoke, tears welling in my eyes again. "You don't have to say it."

I nodded, swallowing the lump in my throat, and just drawing him into a firm hug, thinking of all he'd had taken from him.

"I'm so glad you're alright," I said.

"Ditto," he agreed, and as I released him, he gave me a slanted smile that didn't quite touch his eyes.

"Where's Tory?" I looked around, suddenly aching for my twin with the blazing intensity of every star in the sky, and wondering if she might be in one of these rooms or – or –

"She's not here," Caleb answered, dashing my hope to pieces. "She left a few days ago and didn't tell anyone where she was going."

My heart twisted sharply at that news, and sadness washed over me.

"She'll come back. She always comes back," Seth said encouragingly. "Sometimes she's frownier when she returns, and sometimes she does crazy shit like sending her soul out of her body but-"

"What?" I gasped, horrified at the idea of that.

Seth elbowed Caleb. "Tell her, Cal. Tell her how Tory does weird, dark magic stuff now, but it's okay because her soul did come back that time. And if she's off soul-walking again it's probably completely fine, because…because…" He ran out of steam on that train of thought, whining as he nudged Caleb again.

"Yeah, she'll be fine," Caleb assured us.

Seth looked over my shoulder and I glanced back, finding Frank and a few more of his pack peeking out of a room at the far end of the corridor. "Is it safe now, Alpha?" he asked.

"Just stay there and lock the door tight until it's over. I'll make sure the tower is clear," Seth said with authority and Frank nodded, his eyes darting onto me.

"Oh my stars, it's you," he gasped then snapped the door shut, a tumult of chatter breaking out.

"We should move," Max said, wincing as screams carried across campus.

I drew my sword again as my friends closed in around me, ready to dive into the fray.

"What's happening here?" I asked, the current situation stealing my attention. "What are those monsters and why are they here?"

"It would seem that the false king has sent them, my lady. Here on some gruesome mission to hunt down the rebels who had been working against him from within these fine walls," Geraldine explained.

"They're killing people who stood up to him?" I gasped in disgust and the others nodded in confirmation. "Then we have to help them."

"Yes - it is time to unite as a legion of justice!" Geraldine bellowed, wiping her damp cheeks and stepping closer. "Point me at your enemies, my lady. For I am your weapon forged of havoc and punishment. We shall carve the heads of a thousand monsters from their bodies this very night, and the whole world will shudder with the knowledge of their queen's return. For the night is deep and the dawn is yonder. And between the now and the rising sun, blood waits to be spilled and enemies wait to be slain. We are the knights of the Vega Court, and we are at your service." She spun around on her heel, facing the others. "Listen close and listen well. The stars have returned our queen to us, and it is our duty to fight like the soldiers of the Perrypot and slay the ganderghouls who have come to spread peril across the precious lands of our academy. It is time to take up arms and sing our song of slaughter and misery into the flapping ears of our assailants! There shall not be a single soul in Solaria who does not know of our victory by dawn! Long live the true Queens!"

Scorpio
Virgo
Gemini
Cancer
Aries
Leo
Sagittarius
Taurus
Capricorn
Aquarius
Libra
Pisces

DARIUS

CHAPTER EIGHTY

We hadn't slept, our insatiable need for each other and endless reclaiming of what we'd lost keeping us occupied hour after hour. I gave in to all the hopeless want that had consumed me these months, as I buried myself in the obsession which had kept me sane throughout so many horrors.

Here, in this place, we had stolen time from the world, day turning into night once more as we gave in to lust and greed and passion and slowly healed the ache that had scarred our souls while we'd been parted by the Veil.

I wasn't certain if I was supposed to feel differently now, uncomfortable in my own skin or furious at fate, my father, all of it, but I simply felt content.

The world waited beyond these walls, but as I lay on my back, feasting on my girl as she fucked my face, I just couldn't find it in me to care about that.

I gripped her round ass as I devoured her, growling against her clit and smiling like the asshole I was as she fell apart for me with a cry of pleasure.

Roxy tumbled down onto the bed beside me, punching me in the bicep as I continued to grin at her.

"We said we'd leave first thing," she muttered, her voice drunk with pleasure and my smile only continued to grow as I pushed myself up onto my elbow and looked at what I'd done to her.

"We said we'd leave when we woke, but we haven't slept so…" I reached for her thigh, but she slapped me away with a shake of her head.

"We're in the middle of a war," she reminded me, as if I could have forgotten.

"We were in the middle of something else too-"

"We need to go," she said firmly, not for the first time, but the way her eyes flashed said she might actually mean it now. "We can't. Not…not right now. Later. After you've returned to the others, and they can see you're alive again. I can't just keep hoarding you away in this ruin forever. They're grieving too."

I sighed as I gave in to her demand, licking the taste of her from my lips as I rolled over and got to my feet.

"I guess I'll get dressed then," I said, though I couldn't really feign disappointment in the idea of reuniting with the others after so long. I yearned to see them so much that I felt like a kid waking up on their birthday, excited to rip into my gifts.

I eyed Roxy as I moved towards the exit so I could retrieve the clothes I'd been buried in from my coffin.

The moment I'd woken up in that place, I'd been filled with the desperate need to stretch my wings, so after finding Roxy laying in the grass beside me and relocating her to the bed within the ruins, I'd headed back outside, stripped off, and taken flight.

My Dragon had blasted endless flames into the sky as it was released upon the world of the living once again. I couldn't deny the urge I felt to shift once more as I stepped out into the cold air with Roxy hounding my steps, her wedding dress back on and my smile fighting to make a comeback.

I held a hand out to her and she took it, the simple touch sending electricity pouring through my body as I caressed the scar on her palm.

"I don't actually know how I'm going to be able to find them," she admitted as we stalked up the hill, and I looked down at her as a shaft of moonlight made her black hair glisten with silver. "I lost my pack when we returned from death and my Atlas was inside it, so-"

"Your pack was beside my coffin when I woke," I told her, and she gaped at me before trying to smack me again.

I caught her fist and yanked her closer by it. "Careful baby, or you'll give me ideas," I purred but she just rolled her eyes as she yanked her fist from my hold again.

"Why didn't you mention that before?"

"Because I was more interested in fucking you than checking out your luggage," I replied, drawing a snort of laughter from her.

I turned to face her, catching her cheek in my palm, and looking at the joy which sparked in her eyes as she gazed back at me. It felt unreal. Like we couldn't possibly deserve this after everything we'd sacrificed and yet there we stood, reunited and stronger than ever.

"What?" she asked, blinking at me as I continued to study her and I shrugged, forcing myself to let her go again.

"Just you, Roxy. Only ever you."

"Don't go getting soft on me," she grumbled as she turned away and started up the hill once more, leading the way onto the secluded clifftop where she'd once laid me to rest.

I paused beside my mom's coffin, brushing my fingers against the ice as I looked in at her and Hamish, free from Lionel at last, gone where he could never find them, his soul too rotten and festering to ever be allowed passage into their side of the afterlife.

Roxy found her pack and quickly stripped out of her wedding dress as she exchanged it for a pair of jeans and black crop top.

I moved to join her, picking up my own abandoned clothes and dressing myself in the armour I'd died in, the bloodstain surrounding the hole in it a russet brown against the black.

Roxy noticed it too, raising a hand to cast it away but I caught her fingers in mine to stop her.

"Leave it," I said, amusement touching my words. "Let everyone see the mark of the wound which killed me when they meet me on the battlefield. Let my enemies remember that even death can't defeat me when I come for them."

Roxy rolled her eyes but gave in, grabbing my battle axe from the remains of my coffin and tossing it to me.

"I'm going to call Geraldine," she said, taking her Atlas from her pack at last and switching it on. I noticed the endless trail of missed calls and texts which she'd received while it was off, but she just dismissed them all, hitting dial on Geraldine's number instead of bothering to read any of them.

I moved closer to listen in and on the third ring, Geraldine gasped an answer.

"Oh, my lady!" she cried. "Are you ready to return to the bosom of your dearest compadres?"

"Yeah, I-"

"There is mischief afoot!" Geraldine cut her off and shit, I'd really missed that crazy motherfucker. “Scoundrels and gherkin lovers converge on our once beloved academy this very moment. We have seen the light of truth via the Atlas of video knowledge, and it is so! We headed yonder to defeat the swines, and would welcome your most benevolent and wonderous help in this adventure.”

“Lionel is attacking Zodiac Academy?” Roxy asked in alarm, and I had no fucking idea how she’d come to that conclusion based on the nonsense Geraldine had just spewed, but it seemed she was right as her friend replied.

“It is so! He has set hell hounds of death to hunt within its fine walls and we have come to cleave them from this world. Also your dear and beauteous sis-” Geraldine wailed and a monstrous scream rattled the speaker before the call was abruptly cut off.

“Shit,” Roxy cursed, dropping the Atlas into her pocket, and grabbing some stardust from the pack instead. “Let’s go.”

I picked up her sword belt and cinched it tight around her waist as she snatched a dagger from the pack too. We left the rest of her shit where it was, knowing we’d be better off coming back for it later.

She met my gaze with those wild green eyes and threw the stardust over our heads without another word.

The world bent and twisted around us, the stars hissing curses beneath their breath as their own rules forced them to let us travel, and I couldn’t help but laugh at them before they dumped us unceremoniously at the gates to the academy.

I heard the screams before I spotted anything and Roxy drew her sword as she sprinted for the entrance, a blast of pure energy tearing from her and making the gates crumple in her path. The wards were already down and that was its own testimony to whatever chaos laid within.

My heart began pumping with adrenaline, my grip on my battle axe tightening as I willed the Phoenix fire imbued in it to spark to life, and a war cry escaped my lips.

I wanted to hunt down our enemies and rain carnage upon them, my need for bloodshed rioting through my flesh more potently than I had ever experienced before. My taste for violence spiked and I bared my teeth in a snarl as I hunted for a victim to fall at the swing of my axe.

Roxy looked just as feral as I felt, as she drew her flaming sword in an arc before her, the light of it reflecting in her green eyes.

Screams carried on the wind from the heart of the academy, and I used my axe to point the way before breaking into a sprint with my girl at my side.

We ran like the fires of hell were on our tails, diving into the darkness beneath the trees in The Wailing Wood and my blood pumped hotter, faster, the need for death and brutality a rampant desire which blotted out all else.

“Do you feel that?” Roxy asked, her gaze flashing with excitement as she looked to me, and I swear the need for violence in me pulsed at the look in her eyes.

“I do.” I had been born a warrior, never afraid of death or savagery, but no battle had ever called to me so powerfully before and there was an ache in my limbs which begged me to join the fight.

Perhaps it was my return from death that had me hungering for a kill with such vitriol but whatever it was, I had no time to question it as we sprinted into the academy grounds and took the main path which led through The Wailing Wood towards The Orb and other buildings at the heart of campus.

“There,” Roxy said, pointing with her sword into the darkness beneath the trees and I looked that way as I felt it too, pain and bloodshed and battle.

My pulse was thumping with it, my knowledge of it unquestionable and yet I had no idea how we could be so certain of such a thing.

A repetitive clicking sound broke from the woods to our right and I swung towards it just as a beast fit for hell leapt from the high bough of an ash tree.

I swung my axe up between us, my blade severing one of its four arms before I could even get a good look at it.

The thing shrieked, a flash of pale, bluish skin and huge pincers making me leap back and Roxy cursed as she swung her sword at it too.

The creature was about twice the size of me, insectile in its looks aside from its chest and head which looked disturbingly Fae, the male's mouth stretching wide in a furious cry.

The noise that exploded from him didn't sound like any voice I'd ever heard before though. It was high pitched and full of dread, the shriek it released spilling out around us until my ears rung from it.

I ducked low as it lunged at me with its pincers snapping, a blast of fire exploding against its chest as I threw my power at it, but my magic struck some shield tight to its skin and flared away again.

Roxy jumped back as the beast swung around and I whistled sharply to draw its attention, my heart thrashing with the need for this kill.

The thing lunged and instead of retreating, I launched myself at it, my axe swinging in a two-handed attack as I slipped to one side and swung the weapon straight into its back.

One of its arms slammed into me, knocking me away while my axe remained lodged in its spine, and it shrieked again as blood spilled from it. But it recovered fast and ran at me once more.

I rolled aside as it lunged, pincers slamming into the ground where I'd just been and Roxy took the opportunity to strike at it, her sword punching through the side of its neck and making it howl in pain.

Blood splattered over me, and my heart thundered as a feeling of euphoria swept through my veins, my limbs singing with the power of battle and a hunger for death building within me that screamed for more.

The creature fell to the ground, howling and thrashing and I pounced on it, drawing a dagger from my belt and stabbing it over and over again, the fury in my flesh demanding more even as it fell still beneath me, and I felt its death sweep over me like a breath of ecstasy.

Roxy decapitated the thing with a cry of effort and the bond between us seemed to pull tight, yanking against my soul as the moment of the kill united us.

I shoved to my feet, ripping my axe from the creature's corpse and stalking towards her as her eyes lit with a feral energy that mirrored my own.

I fisted her hair, yanking her head back as I stole a kiss from her, the blood marking her body making her even more desirable as some power beyond the two of us revelled in the death we'd offered up.

She moaned into my mouth as she returned the kiss and I knew she felt it too, this unholy need for violence which was making our joined hearts race with excitement.

Distant screams broke us apart and I turned towards the path, grinning darkly as the fight beckoned us on.

The need for death and carnage ran rampant through my soul, that same, endless desire reflected in her eyes as the world seemed to hum with it.

We didn't have time to question this strange, addictive feeling, and I broke into a sprint.

Roxy's wings exploded from her back, and she took to the sky, a warrior queen on the hunt, swooping between the trees of The Wailing Wood.

I ran beneath her, power crackling in the air as magic built in her free fist, before we reached the buildings that made up the heart of the academy campus.

Students were running, screaming in terror, and racing between the buildings as we paused to take in what was happening, but as a few of them spotted Roxy, their screams turned into cheers of relief.

"The true queens have come!"

"We're saved!"

"It's inside Earth Observatory!"

Her blazing wings cast me into shadow behind her, but as they cried out at her arrival and she hesitated to listen to them, I took in that piece of information and sprinted away towards the screams I could hear coming from the observatory.

My blood pounded mercilessly in my veins as the need for more death consumed me, my muscles burning as I ran faster and faster through the shadows beyond the buildings.

I made it to the back of the observatory just as a great crash ripped through the air and a window far above me shattered.

A shield of heat exploded from me as the glass came raining down, and it fell in molten globules either side of me without so much as touching my skin.

Tarot cards fluttered from the broken window as I began to climb towards the thing which was causing those terrified screams inside the building, my toes and fingers finding purchase between the brickwork while I stowed my axe on my back once more.

I set my attention on the opening above, barely even noticing as some of the cards fluttered down to brush against me, the call of fate ringing in the air between them.

As one touched my cheek, I caught it, looking into the face of the Knight of Swords before he tumbled away towards the ground. Death approaching.

I couldn't deny that.

I hauled myself up to the broken window then into the building itself, fire springing from my fingertips as I took in the darkened room. Six students were contained within an air shield at the centre of the space, their hands connected as they power shared to hold off two of the deformed monsters which were trying to batter their way to them.

The terror in their eyes had me breaking into a run as I drew my axe once more and I couldn't help but notice my boot landing on the Death card like it was welcoming me to the fray.

"You will pay in blood and carnage," a voice hissed on the wind, and I got the feeling the stars were watching this all too closely.

But as I fell into the dance of battle once again, I found I didn't give a fuck about that, because the swing of my axe felt too fucking good.

Scorpio
Gemini
Virgo
Cancer
Leo
Taurus
Sagittarius
Capricorn
Aquarius
Libra
Pisces

TORY

CHAPTER EIGHTY ONE

I sprinted down the path towards Ignis House where explosions of fire were bursting from the shattered glass windows as the students gifted with that Element fought against another one of the monsters somewhere within.

Darius ran a few paces behind me, his footsteps shadowing mine just like they had so often when we'd run along this exact path in the past. Though we'd never sprinted down it while blood-drenched, gripping weapons in our fists and hungering for death before.

My whole body was alight with need for it, my pulse seeming to beat purely towards the next swing of my blade, an opportunity to draw blood or to colour the air with screams.

A flash of fire blasted from a window high above us, the glass building rattling from a fight taking place inside. I shot a grin at Darius before leaping skyward and flying straight for it.

My husband growled as I left him behind, sprinting for the main doors rather than shifting and shredding through his clothes – no doubt because his big scaley Dragon form had zero chance of fitting through that hole anyway, and I guessed he didn't want to end up fighting naked.

Heat flared across my skin as I sped towards the opening the broken window created, and I threw air magic out around myself, banishing my wings at the last moment. My boots hit the floor in the common room, and I skidded on the broken glass that littered it, taking in the scene before me.

Fire flared from all around the circular space, the students gathered there launching it at the monstrous creature in the midst of them.

The thing shrieked as it lunged for a guy I recognised as a senior across the room, and he threw a wave of fire at it with a cry of fear.

The beast didn't so much as flinch, lunging through the flames which licked harmlessly along its alabaster flesh and diving on its prey with a victorious shriek.

Screams sounded through the room as its serrated mouth latched onto the guy's chest and I broke into a run, swinging my blade with a battle cry.

The monster had a long body with eight spindly legs that bent back on themselves at the knees, like a cross between some kind of larva and a spider, but five times as mean.

My boot landed on its thick tail, and I ran straight up its spine, my sword swinging in a vicious arc before I plunged it straight down through its back, hoping to strike lucky and hit a vital organ.

"Tory?" Milton Hubert's voice took me by surprise, and I looked up from my position on the monster's back.

The creature bucked beneath me, releasing the guy it had been eating and sending him crashing into the wall with a wet crack. He groaned in agony and some of the other students ran to help him while I played rodeo with the vicious creature, trying to keep its attention away from them.

I lost sight of Milton as I fought to keep hold of my sword, and the beast reared up, swinging towards me. Its body coiled back on itself, that pit of endless teeth seeking to devour me, and I was forced to jump away as those gnashing jaws snapped at my face.

I hit the ground and rolled across the broken debris of the common room, bits of chairs and tables digging into me, before I leapt to my feet and created a spear out of earth magic.

"You saw our livestreams?" Milton panted as I found him beside me, a cracked Atlas strapped to his chest and blood staining his clothes.

"I had a call with Geraldine. She said we were needed," I replied with a shrug before hurling the spear, watching it fly true and pierce the flesh of the beast before us.

That mostly seemed to piss the thing off, and I threw an air shield out in front of us as it turned and ran our way.

Students screamed, sprinting towards us and diving behind the protection of my shield. I dug my heels in and grunted at the impact of the monster's body colliding with it.

"Fire doesn't hurt it. We've been fighting and fighting, but there are hardly any of us with more than one Element, and it knows exactly who it's searching for," Milton breathed fearfully.

"You were rebelling?" I asked, and he nodded proudly, his hand tightening around the fingers of the girl beyond him and I recognised Bernice with a jolt of surprise.

"This isn't your House," I blurted, and she looked to Milton with a hint of a smile.

"I was staying the night. But since that thing showed up, we've just been trying to survive. But fire only seems to enrage it, and my water doesn't do much either and the K.U.N.T.s have barred the exit-"

"Well, that would explain what's keeping Dari-"

The doors at the far side of the common room burst open and flames erupted all around the huge figure who strode across the threshold, his arrogant swagger knowing no bounds as he casually swung his axe in one fist, his dark gaze seeking me out among the chaos with ease.

"Holy shit, I heard he was dead," Milton gasped in alarm.

I flexed my fingers and tightened my hold on my air magic before wrapping the monster in it, hurling the thing across the room towards my husband.

"He was," I admitted, a laugh breaking from me as I broke into a run, slipping through my air shield before letting it close at my back where the Ignis students were clamouring to take shelter.

Two more spears formed in my hands and Darius swung his axe with deadly abandon, severing one of the thing's legs so it toppled to one side.

I hurled my spears at the monster, the need for death pounding through me as blood splattered the walls. Darius severed another leg while the monster thrashed violently.

"Fire doesn't-" I began but Darius realised that for himself as he hurled a blast of flames at it and the monster leapt straight through them, tackling him to the ground.

I sprang onto the creature's back again, grabbing the hilt of my sword and ripping it free while Darius fought and punched it from beneath.

The beast bucked and I was almost knocked off, but I managed to grab onto its flubbery hide, keeping my position on its back as I raised my hand and formed a battalion of razor-sharp icicles in the air all around us.

With a swipe of my hand, the icicles shot for the beast, bypassing me and Darius and burying themselves in its flesh with brutal efficiency.

The monster shrieked in agony as my attack finally found something vital and Darius managed to roll out from beneath it as it reared up once more.

I dove away as it tried to snap at me, and the moment its sinewy neck was extended, Darius swung his axe up and over his head before cleaving right through it.

Blood splashed the walls and I scrambled away from the decapitated body, the high of the kill leaving me bouncing on the balls of my feet.

"More," I gasped as Darius stalked towards me, the dark look in his eyes saying he wanted to devour me, and the entire world could follow right along after us.

The Ignis students were cheering, sobbing and calling out their eternal thanks to us, but I couldn't look away from the dark soul who was a perfect mirror to my own, my need for him all consuming and our love for one another a force destructive enough to defy death itself.

The twin hammering of our hearts made a tremor run through the core of me, but before he could close that distance, a scream caught my attention from outside in the grounds.

I snapped around so fast that I almost lost my footing, my gaze instantly locking on the distant figure in The Howling Meadow who soared above another two of the gruesome monsters which had been sent to attack the rebels within this school. She was fully shifted, fire coating her body as her Phoenix lit up the sky like a beacon of hope for everyone who could see it.

"Darcy," I gasped in astonishment, my brain struggling to catch up to the truth of what I was seeing as my sister threw her hands out and blasted the monster beneath her with a flash of water magic so powerful that I felt the aftershocks of it carrying through the space dividing us.

Darius appeared at my side, his blood-slicked fingers tightening around mine for half a heartbeat before he released me.

"Go," he commanded, and I met his eyes for an all too brief moment, before breaking into a run and diving headfirst out of the shattered window.

My wings burst from my back the second I had room for them, and I let the fire swallow me, fully shifting into my Order form and racing across campus to join with her, to reunite at last. My other half. My eternal love.

The sun was brightening the sky overhead as it made its way closer to cresting the horizon, but its light paled in comparison to the two Phoenixes who dominated the heavens, the stars fading to irrelevance beyond us as all eyes turned our way.

"The true Queens herald the coming morn!" Geraldine cried so loudly that the entire campus could hear her magically enhanced voice, a cheer going up from all around.

I flew towards the battle raging between our friends and the two monsters that bellowed and roiled between them, magic crackling at my fingertips. They were all there, Geraldine, the Heirs, Xavier, Sofia and Tyler, even Orion and Gabriel too. Our family reunited at last. I didn't know how it was possible that that they'd escaped, that Darcy's power and Order had returned, and Orion somehow still lived, but I didn't care, it only mattered that they were here and we were reunited at last.

Before I could release the magic I'd gathered, a glimmer of light drew my gaze and I looked up as if a ghostly hand had caught my chin and forced my head to rise.

In the distance, just beyond the academy fence, the landscape crawled with movement, monsters like the ones below us lumbering closer in terrifying numbers.

"Darcy!" I yelled, drawing her attention just as she unleashed a fistful of ice onto the monsters beneath us and the closest one screamed in pain.

"Tor!" she gasped, beating her wings hard as she flew towards me, our reunion bringing a smile of purest joy to her fire-kissed features.

I pointed beyond her as she approached, drawing her attention to Lionel's latest weapons which were racing closer with every moment.

"Holy shit," she murmured, and the sounds of battle from below seemed to fade as I felt the weight of destiny drawing in on us.

The stars glimmered brighter in the sky as if they'd found some surge of confidence once more and were looking forward to seeing this fate come to pass.

"Lionel is going to let those things kill every student in the academy in an attempt to take us out," I growled, seeing that scaley bastard's cowardly tactics for precisely what they were. No doubt he'd been hoping for this when he attacked this place, striking at Fae we knew personally and allowing those broadcasts to go out into the world to lure us here. It was a trap. But it wasn't going to work.

"We should form a solid unit, attack them as one," Darcy began but I shook my head.

"It won't work. We need something more powerful. We need to unite our magic against them," I said firmly, countless spells and incantations from the books on ether and dark magic surging through my mind.

"You want to power share?" Darcy asked, offering her hand instantly.

"We need to do more than that," I replied darkly, drawing a dagger from my belt before meeting her eyes. "Do you trust me?"

"Always," she replied without hesitation, and we shared a grim look before I took hold of her hand and began to carve a mark into her palm.

Darcy hissed at the bite of the cut, but didn't try to stop me as I carved the jagged S shape of Eihwaz into her skin, the rune for defence and protection. Next, I cut my own palm open, marking a bloody sideways W onto my flesh. Sowulo for victory.

"Don't hold back," I said firmly.

I took her hand in mine, our blood merging and the power of those runes rocketing through us so hard that we were almost torn apart. Darcy cursed, her grip tightening as she looked to me for an explanation I simply couldn't give her right now.

Caleb and Orion held a chain of ice between them below us and as I watched, they sped in opposite directions around the smaller of the two monstrous creatures, binding it with the chain then yanking it so tight that the thing was cut in two.

I didn't even wait for it to finish dying, the thrill of its demise washing over me. I sent a whip of air magic towards it and stole a shard of bone from its corpse before holding it up and calling on the ether to take it as an offering.

I began a chant which I'd read in the Book of Fire, the words burning on their way out of my throat, and Darcy gasped as the ether began to build around her too.

"Let it in," I hissed, watching her.

I continued to chant that ancient, evil spell, my tongue blistering as I forced the words from my mouth.

The moment Darcy gave herself to the ether, it felt like an explosion igniting the core of the earth, the power merging between us so great that we both began to shake with it.

The pain of the chant lessened as she took on half the burden, and I looked into her eyes as I spat the final word from my lips.

Darcy's pupils dilated as the power between us grew beyond all measure, threatening to consume every piece of us if we didn't release it. As one, we raised our free hands and let it explode.

It was as if a match had been flicked into a pot of Faesine, the world itself bucking with the aftershock of the explosion as it tore from our bodies, our Phoenix flames merging with that blast of power and flying from us along with everything else.

A wave of pure energy tore away from us like we were a stone dropped into a silent pool and had somehow caused a tsunami.

The wall of fire that spilled from our grasp sent screams up all around us, but the only ones it burned were the monsters who had set themselves against us.

I felt the one our friends had been fighting die first, its existence snuffing out like a candle in a strong wind, the power it had held in life gusting through me and raising euphoria beneath my skin.

One after another, those terrible creatures were consumed by our flames, each death more beautiful than the last, a moan of pleasure catching in my throat as I bathed in the exquisite power I was gifted by their ends.

My gaze met Darcy's as we hung there, suspended by the force of our own power as it tore through our enemies one by one. But instead of the pure bliss I was experiencing with so much death, I found only fear and uncertainty in her eyes.

The wind returned to the world first of all, my stomach swooping as we plummeted from the sky, our wings flaring on instinct to catch us as we returned to the ground. We landed between a huge circle of our friends, plus the students and staff from the academy.

They stared at us with utter awe staining their features, Geraldine's jaw hanging slack as the silence stretched.

Until footsteps broke it.

Heavy boots strode between the gathered crowd, making my pulse thunder with recognition as he appeared between the bodies, as gasps of fear, disbelief and utter confusion spilled out around him.

"All hail the true Queens," Darius growled in a low and powerful voice which rang with a clap of magic that seemed to break the spell that had fallen over everyone who was still staring at us in awe.

Darcy inhaled sharply, incredulous at the sight of his return and in the next second, Geraldine screamed, her voice sailing out among the masses. Then the Heirs and Orion all cried out to Darius at once in shock, delight and disbelief. Countless other voices broke out to him too, but his attention didn't waver for one single moment.

I met my husband's eyes as he dropped to one knee before us, placing the head of his axe against the ground and bowing his head low before us.

"I pledge my life to your service."

His words were like a summoning and suddenly they were all there, Caleb falling to his knees at Darius's side, his navy eyes wide with amazement as he looked first to his lost brother, then to Darcy and I who stood shell shocked, hand in hand, in the wake of that terrible power we had just summoned to save us all.

"I pledge my life in your service," Caleb said loudly, silence echoing out once more as the crowd seemed to grow and grow, pressing in on us from all sides as this momentous act unfurled before them.

"I pledge my life in your service," Max echoed, falling to his knees on Darius's other side, his head lowering, and the overwhelming feeling of love and respect that flooded from him almost floored me.

Darcy's hand tightened around mine, the two of us too stunned to do more than just stare at the final Heir as he stepped forward, looking between the two of us and the impossibility of Darius's return before he fell to his knees on Caleb's other side.

"I pledge my life in your service," Seth breathed almost reverently, and I sucked in a sharp breath as heat began to grow in my chest.

The stars flared in defiance overhead as the feeling of that power grew, Geraldine dropping to her knees with a cry of her devotion, followed by Orion who smirked knowingly. Then Gabriel, Xavier, Tyler, Sofia, and the entire school beyond them, every one of them falling to their knees before us.

Only then did I spot our army who had come to fight alongside us, their ranks spreading out beyond us into The Wailing Wood and throughout the entire campus as they dropped to their knees too. The ex-Councillors were among them, hesitating only a fraction of a second before they shared a look of awe and dropped down to their knees as one.

"Long live the true Queens!" Geraldine bayed.

Her words were echoed by everyone just as the sun crested the horizon and we were gilded in the first rays of dawn.

The power surrounding us built further, and I gasped as I felt hands brushing against my cheek, turning to look at Darcy just as a crown of blue flames appeared upon her brow.

The reflection in her green eyes told me a matching crown of red had appeared for me too. We gaped at one another as the truth of our ascension fell over us, our parents' presence seeming closer than ever before as though they had been the ones to crown us.

A thundering pulse grew against my chest and Darcy looked to my throat suddenly, her hand reaching out to touch the Imperial Star which had begun to glow with untold power.

"We can use it," I breathed, my eyes widening with the things that impossible power could offer us.

Darcy stared at the amulet in shock before her gaze lifted back to mine and the smile we exchanged was heady and beautiful, quickly becoming a burst of laughter. The endless sea of our people remained on their knees all around us, our reign beginning with that first light of dawn, the stars practically banished by our denial of the fate they'd been counting on.

We looked out over the people who had just sworn their lives to us, preparing to call them to their feet, but before so much as a single word could escape either of us, a flash of light flared across the sky.

I was blinded by it, a yank in my gut tearing me away from the ground, and as a scream ripped from my throat, the only thing I found to hold onto was my sister's hand in mine.

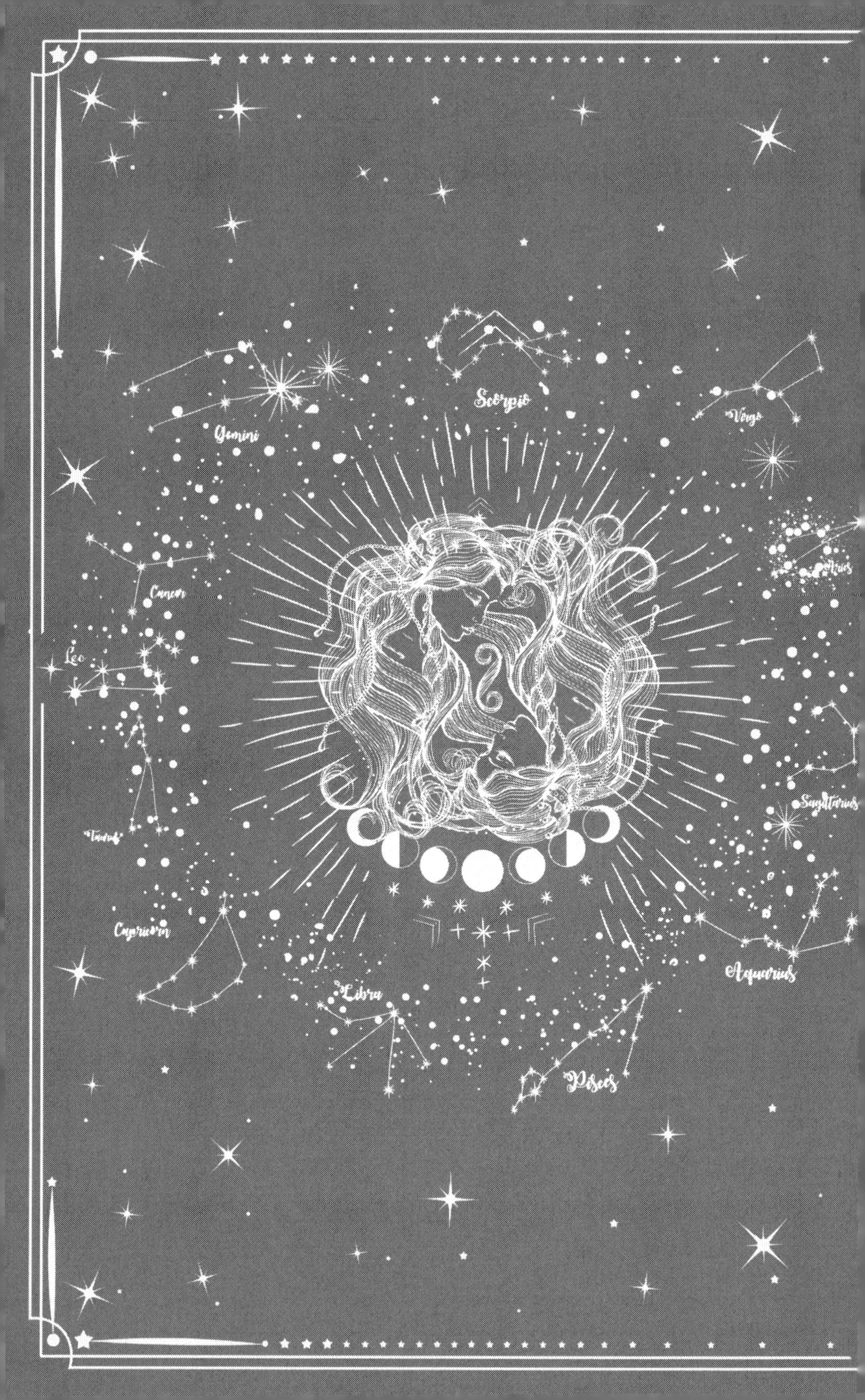
Scorpio
Virgo
Gemini
Cancer
Leo
Sagittarius
Taurus
Capricorn
Aquarius
Libra
Pisces

DARCY

CHAPTER EIGHTY TWO

The sky appeared to crack, sucking Tory and I away into a dark rift that swallowed us down greedily, tasting the sins on our bones.

I could see nothing. Or perhaps I *was* nothing. Because the abyss I was standing in seemed infinitely a part of me, and I could no longer feel my sister's fingers around mine. I tried to feel my body, reaching for Tory too, sure she was here yet entirely not at the same time.

"All you have ever truly possessed lays here with you now," the stars whispered, their words like raindrops falling heavily against me, striking everywhere, and away into eternity. *"Skin and bone and beating heart, all hold no value here, beyond the confines of your world. You are the fire that burned long before you knew of your own existence. One soul severed, light and dark, the perfect balance. But where there is balance, there is unbalance..."*

I tried to answer the voice that held no gender, or any kind of true identity at all. But my own voice was lost, fragments of it scattered around me in the boundless void. I was one with it all, and as I reached into it, I was given a sense of every living thing on earth, like their lives were sparking in this space, with a hungry, almost arrogant need to exist. There was a purpose beneath it, one I couldn't quite grasp, and as I reached for it, the voice spoke again.

"Careful, daughter of the flames. Knowledge such as that cannot be unlearned."

I willed my words to form, pushing them out into the nothingness and forcing them to forge. "Where's my sister?"

"I'm here," she spoke in answer, and the darkness gave way to the sensation of her, like her body was reforming at my side, but I still couldn't feel her.

"Fate changer," the stars hissed at her. *"A cost to bear, a burden worn. Will regrets shatter the foundations of your blood bound choice?"*

"I will never regret bringing Darius back. You stole him before his time, and I will pay whatever price I have to now," Tory spat, her ire tainting the air.

Knowing she had somehow raised Darius from the dead left me both overjoyed, and terrified of what she'd done to achieve it. But I couldn't ask her about it now under the weight of the stars' stares.

"What do you want?" I asked, intention circling in the air like moths around a flame.

"We have an offering," the stars whispered and one by one they appeared from the darkness, like delicate jewels hanging within the canvas of black. The light they emitted was imbued with power, the kind of magic that had no limits, a single drop of it able to give life or snatch it away. *"Once, in a time long lost, there was a star among us who idolised the Fae. Clydinius of the Seventh House."*

I frowned, recognising that as the name of the fallen star the first Phoenix queen had spoken with, the one who had gifted her the Imperial Star.

"He watched them rise, he watched them fall, he saw their love, their wrath, heard their laughter and their mourning cries. But with each passing century, this star grew tired of it all. And a forbidden desire grew within him, a terrible desire not meant for stars."

"What was it?" I breathed, every resounding word spoken creating a pulse in the air.

"Clydinius believed Fae were not worthy of the greatness we gifted them, for it was wasted and spoiled in the hands of your kind, every empire rising only to surely fall. So Clydinius came to the Court of Caelestina where the fates are woven thread by thread, and destiny spins upon a coin of iron. There, he spoke treasonous words, expressing the very desire which could unbalance the bedrock of the world. Clydinius wished for us all to descend from the heavens, to claim a place upon the earth and walk among the Fae as gods. In response to this declaration, Arcturus of the Sixth House cast Clydinius from the sky, where only one fate awaited him. Or so we thought. For we were fooled... Clydinius had wished for this all along, and instead of releasing his powers upon impact with the earth, Clydinius made a deal with a Fae, breaking all the laws of old and blaspheming against the teachings of the Origin."

"The Origin?" Tory questioned.

"The Origin is the beginning and end of all things. She is the giver of life, of fate, of all reality. She is the oldest star in our universe, a creator and destroyer. She set the laws of reality itself."

"But aren't you all supposed to be neutral in every fate you offer?" I accused.

"They're not neutral. They do what they want, whatever entertains them most," Tory growled.

"We seek harmony in all things. We right the tipping of the scales, forever seeking a point of bliss. We have no need nor use for sentiment or feeling. Right or wrong. A star should never be corrupted, it should not be possible within the realms of all that is. But Clydinius was the exception."

"Bullshit," Tory snarled. "You're all the same. If you were about fairness, then we wouldn't have had to go through all of this."

"It is not us who cursed you so," the stars whispered, and I felt the truth of those words ringing to the centre of me, like I'd known it all along and yet I'd never been able to grasp that knowledge until now.

"Clydinius cursed us," I said, seeing the real depths of that truth now. It went beyond these stars, disrupting any plans they might have chosen to lay in place for us. I could feel that intangible power thrumming in the air and almost sensed the binds of the curse anchoring my soul to the single star which had placed it upon our bloodline. We were prisoners to Clydinius's vengeance, and nothing we did in this war would succeed long term unless we could find a way free of it.

"What's the broken promise?" I asked in desperation. "If we keep it, we'll break the curse, right? We can restore the balance."

"Yes, daughter of the flames," they answered. *"Queens crowned, a kingdom kneeling at your feet. A choice lays in your hands now."*

"What choice?" Tory demanded.

The darkness finally shifted, rippling like ink around me before I found myself standing in a memory of the past. I recognised Elvia Vega, the first Phoenix Queen, on her knees before the star, Clydinius.

"The version of this memory you perceived within the Memoriae crystal was altered by Queen Avalon Vega generations after this night," the stars revealed. *"For*

she wished to ensure no Phoenix ever kept the promise made with the fallen star. She wished to pass the power of the Imperial Star down the Vega line to secure their position as royalty forevermore. This, daughter of the flames, is the shard of the memory that was destroyed..."

I was launched forward into Queen Elvia's mind, seeing it all through her eyes once more and feeling Tory's soul joining mine.

My palm tingled painfully where it still lay against the gleaming surface of the fallen star. The brightness made me wince, my eyes hurting and a ringing growing in my ears. I screamed as it intensified, begging to be spared, unsure if I had angered it somehow. But then a part of the star cracked off in my palm, a tremendous blast of magic cutting it clean from the star itself. The light faded and I found a rough, unhewn piece of the star lying in my palm that hummed with unimaginable power, so beautiful it left me speechless.

"Wield my heart, and you will win your war. But when it is done, you will return my heart to me, and use it for one final cast, as only a Fae can."

"What cast?" I breathed, fear knotting in my chest as a terrible sense of foreboding washed over me.

"You will breathe life into my heart when it is returned to me. You will offer me the power to take the form of a Fae and walk among the world."

My throat thickened at the idea of that, the thought of a star living on earth seeming wholly unnatural. But power was licking at my fingers hungrily, and while the heart of the star was clutched in my fist, I couldn't deny the temptation of it. I could win my war, and pass this gift down to my children.

"If you do not return my heart, there will be dire consequences," the star warned, and my body trembled with the omen of devastation that laced its words.

"How long?" I asked. "Until it must be returned?"

"A hundred years, no more. Buy you and your child the glory you crave, then have one of your bloodline offer me what I seek."

I nodded, relief setting in at knowing I could claim this power for so long.

"I will make sure it is returned. And the promise is kept," I vowed, and a snap of power struck me in the chest, binding me body and soul to that promise, leaving me breathless as it sank into my very blood.

"Then it is done," the star hissed.

"Thank you," I breathed, and those words leaving my lips set the earth quaking and the sky singing.

No, not singing. That beautiful, haunting noise that hovered on the edges of my hearing was screams, the stars above trying to defy what had been done, what this star had offered me going against all nature of its kind and mine.

Tory and I were pulled from the memory and fear echoed out around me into the abyss, the stars all glittering mournfully.

"You are in possession of Clydinius's heart," the stars whispered anxiously. *"The Imperial Star longs to return to him, but if you keep the promise, you will bring about a plague upon the earth. There shall be no peace, only blight and death. We fear that Clydinius will seek to become the ultimate power of your world, and while he reigns below, we cannot reign above. All shall be lost. All shall fall."*

"But if we don't return it, if we don't keep the promise, we'll be cursed forever?" I said in horror.

"The Vega curse will prevail," the stars confirmed. *"It shall worsen, you shall never know peace, and all those you love shall suffer at your side. We cannot intervene. The choice lays in your hands. Make the right one, daughters of the flames."*

The darkness receded and I suddenly stood eye to eye with my sister. Just she and I, suspended in a chasm of black with this burden of knowledge pressing down on us, and a blood-bound choice which would seal our fates.

"We've been cursed this whole time because of that fucking star," Tory said fiercely. "I say we use the Imperial Star to kill Lionel, Lavinia and all their screwed-up followers. We're not bringing some psycho star into the world to walk around, and cause fuck knows what havoc."

I shook my head in refusal of that. "We can't wield it. Look what happened to our dad. What happened to all the Phoenixes who tried to use it. It never works out well. Why don't we destroy it instead?"

Tory raised a hand to the rough stone that was clasped in the amulet around her neck as she considered that, and I could see her temptation to wield it, to end Lionel for all he'd done. I desperately wanted that too, but not like this. Not with a piece of that cursed star which had caused our father so much torment.

"We use it first, then we destroy it," Tory said.

"I don't think we should ever use it," I objected. "It could make everything so much worse. When I watched those memories play out in the crystal, the Phoenixes were all killed off. They were consumed by their own flames, turned to ash."

"I'll risk it," Tory said stubbornly, and I grabbed her hand, pulling it away from the star.

"I don't want to risk *you*," I replied firmly, and her gaze softened at that, the grief she'd suffered all too clear in her eyes, and I knew she wouldn't wish that on me.

"I suppose using this lump of rock to kill Lionel might make it seem like we couldn't crush him without it," she admitted, releasing her hold on the amulet. "And I really am looking forward to seeing the look on his face when I cut his head off and prove just how much more powerful than him I am."

I snorted at that beautiful mental image, and for a moment I was just so full of relief to be reunited with my twin that I couldn't help but smile at her.

"We could return it, break our curse and destroy Clydinius the second he materialises," I suggested, and her eyes widened at that.

"Kill a star?" she murmured, a smirk lifting her lips at the idea, and no matter how crazy it sounded, I was all in. It was the only option that led to us breaking our curse.

"If we pull it off, we'll be free of the curse, free of fucking Clyde and-"

"And nothing will stand in our way when we attack Lionel and his army," Tory finished for me.

I stepped toward her, feeling our decision solidifying, and knowing this might be the stupidest, riskiest thing we ever did. But it was an answer to all of our problems.

The stars were screaming, responding to the choice we'd made as our decision resonated out to the edges of the universe. They had no choice but to give into our wishes, unable to touch this fate. It was ours, and ours alone, and this was what we'd decided.

The darkness swirled around us, rivers of colour spilling into it until we were travelling through a swathe of starlight.

We were thrown out of their embrace into the oppressive heat of a jungle I knew well, and the scent of mangoes on the air made my stomach turn at the memory of how many we'd eaten when we'd stayed here at the Palace of Flames. We were no longer shifted into our Orders, and no crowns of fire hung above us either. It was just us, two sisters, nothing more or less. And something about that seemed right for this task.

Tory pushed to her feet, taking my arm and pulling me with her, and we gazed at the dark entrance to the cave before us. Vines hung down over the rocky outcrop above it, and an ancient bronze path led up to its entrance, overgrown with lush foliage and long grass. The rising sun's glow lit the way forward as if its light was solely aimed here and nowhere else in the world.

There was a heavy energy in the air, the kind that made every beat of my heart labour and every breath I took sit wetly in my lungs. We couldn't be far from the Palace of Flames; I could almost feel its proximity to this place.

"At last, the Vega bloodline returns," a voice filled my head that was feminine, then masculine, then something in between. *"Have you come to fulfil the broken promise at last?"*

Tory and I shared a look then she raised her chin and spoke loud and clear to it. "We have."

An excited, expectant power buzzed along the surface of my skin, drawing us closer, begging us to come find its source. Beautiful silver runes ignited on the cavern wall, running away into the dark to guide us onward.

Tory and I shared a look, and we strode side by side into the dark, leaving our hesitations behind us for good.

"We shouldn't shift. This is where I saw all those Phoenixes burst into flames," I said warily, noticing an old pile of bones under a layer of dust.

"Okay," she agreed.

"Twins," the star purred. *"One soul, two halves."*

Tory gasped, raising a hand to the Imperial Star hanging from her throat, and the glow which had been coming from it since the Heirs had all bowed to us turned into a full-on shine, golden light rippling out from it.

"It's beating like a heart," she said thickly.

"That's what it is, I guess," I said, tempted to make her take it off. I knew what Clydinius was capable of with his curse over the Vegas, and I didn't want that thing turning on us.

"Each of you have worn my heart around your throat. I have watched, waited. I have learned much from you and your ancestors," Clydinius said with an eagerness to his voice that was unlike anything I'd heard from other stars before. *"Come closer..."*

We walked ever on, following the glowing runes on the wall, and I glanced at Tory with fear brushing the edges of my soul. This could be it. We could face the star and fail; we might never walk back out of this dark cave, and the truth of that fact sank in deep.

I studied her face, seeing the differences in her, a darkness in her eyes that hadn't been there the last time we'd stood side by side as free Fae. She'd changed in the time since the battle, and my heart ruptured as it didn't fully recognise her anymore. Had I been so blind not to realise we'd reached a crossroads and turned down different paths?

I never would have intentionally chosen to go different ways in life, in fact, part of me just wanted to stay as kids, in a time where all we'd had was each other. But life happened, and now it seemed like we might never be those little girls again, hand in hand, facing the world together and keeping everyone out. We didn't need to do that anymore, and if we survived this night, what were our lives even going to look like now?

My fingers brushed hers but she withdrew, shutting me out, or maybe she didn't even realise she'd done it.

"Tor, you know I love you right?" I said, needing her to know in case a time came where it was too late to ever say it again.

She frowned at me, her eyes searching mine for something she seemed unable to find.

"Yeah, and I love you." She kept walking, moving half a step ahead of me and the air thickened with unspoken words.

"You're angry with me," I stated.

"Let's not do this right now," she said, but I couldn't leave it. We could be walking to our deaths.

"It has to be now," I said, grabbing her arm but she yanked it out of my hold, wheeling towards me with a look that was all fire. "*Tory*."

"Fine. You wanna know why I'm mad? Because you chose Orion over me. And I get it. It's not like I don't understand how much you love him, but it was always us first. And when I had no one in the world, when I was broken and lost and only still breathing at all because I knew I had to hold on for you, I had to come for you, you *still* chose him."

"Lavinia was torturing him," I said, shaking my head in anger. "How could I leave him there when he'd offered up everything for me? What kind of mate would I be?"

"A better mate than a sister, I guess." She turned her back on me and a snarl rolled from my throat.

"You're different. Something's happened to you," I said furiously, chasing her down and not letting her walk away from this.

"A whole hell of a lot has happened, Darcy. And maybe you'd know that if you'd been there. But I broke alone, and I did things I can't ever undo to piece myself back together, to find a way into the land of the dead and drag back the man who left me wrecked in his wake."

"I hate that you went through that, I really do. I want to know everything that happened so I can understand. But right now, I just need you to know I'm sorry I wasn't there. Really, I am. But I had my own shit going on, Tor. And apart from anything else, I was a danger to you. I couldn't control the Shadow Beast."

"I know," she gritted out, then she heaved a sigh, gazing off along the path we were taking together. "Shit's just different now. And maybe it's for the best."

"What's that supposed to mean?" I asked, gripping her wrist as she quickened her pace.

She glanced down to where my hand held onto her, a frown furrowing deep into her brow.

"You and me, we're different. We have different wants, different needs. I'm always going to love you, and you'll always be my twin, but I'm not sure we should depend on each other like we used to. At least, I shouldn't depend on you the way I did... We need to stand strong on our own. Especially if we're going to rule Solaria one day. We have to be independent. We have to bring our own strengths to the throne."

"We're strongest together." I said passionately and her throat bobbed.

"I don't know if that's true anymore. You've got this moral compass inside you that always sets you on the right path. But mine's not like that. Especially not now. It's leading me down a dark road and it's a road I want to go down, because it's the one I think I need to follow if we're going to win this war. And it's one you can't follow me on."

Tory kept walking and refusal burned hot inside me, melting my core, and turning it to solder.

"No," I growled. "Don't walk away from me, Tory. We may be different but we're the same where it counts. We've always found a balance between us, light to each other's dark and dark to each other's light, just like the stars said. We make room for each other and show up for each other, and when peril comes knocking, we stand and take on death itself together. Don't let the world ruin us. We may be different trees but we're growing side by side, our branches intertwined forever. You support me and I support you. That's how it's always going to be. Because that's what sisters do."

Tory turned to me, her eyes blazing with emotion. "Even if my soul is dipped in blood and carnage?"

"I'll always love you as you are right now, and I know you've been through a lot. I want to know this new you."

"Really?" she whispered, and I saw the essence of my sister's soul, how brittle it could be when she turned a magnifying glass on herself. She saw a broken creature with sins to her name, and all the harsh choices she'd had to make. But that wasn't what I saw.

"Really," I said firmly. "When I look at you, I will always see the girl who took on the whole world for me, even when we were skinny little orphans with nothing and no one to love us. We loved each other, and that kind of love is greater than all else. It'll never die, no matter who we become. No matter who else we love now too. At our core, we're still us."

She moved towards me, wrapping me in her arms, a hug from her meaning so much, she had no idea. "The past won't come again, Darcy. These fleeting, fragile seconds. They're all gone when they're gone."

"So let's spend as many of them as we can together and spend as few of them as possible being angry with each other. I know this war will change us, but please... please promise me we'll still be together when it's over."

"I promise," she said, hooking her pinky finger around mine as she released me.

We stayed like that, stealing one of those transient moments, already losing our grip on it, but trying to buy a little more time in its company, stretching the milliseconds out until we had to part. And as we walked down into the depths of the caverns, our hands found each other's and we were just two little girls again, about to take on an enemy that was far bigger than us. But together, we would find a way to defeat it.

We followed the glittering silver runes all the way down into the belly of the cave system, passing bones, gold and treasure that gleamed under layers of dust and cobwebs.

A cavern finally widened in front of us, and we stepped into it, the power of the star even more terrible down here, so vigorous it made my skin prickle, drawing my magic to the edges of my being.

The runes decorated the walls here too, and plants flourished everywhere despite there being no way for sunlight to enter this place, vines climbing up to the ceiling and little wildflowers blooming all over them. At the centre of the cave, still entirely underground, a huge tree stood tall and proud, its roots covering the earthy floor around it.

The runes arrowed towards a round stone door on the far side of the cavern and we strode over to it, taking in the zodiac wheel that framed it. The wheel gleamed with that same silver light of the runes, thrumming expectantly like it was waiting for us to do something.

Tory and I moved as one, reaching for the centre of that door and as our fingers met with it, the Gemini star sign lit up and the door trembled before it opened.

"Come forth, daughters of the flames, twins of Gemini, wielders of the four Elements. You were born to right this wrong of old, and it is time to keep the promise of your elders."

I gritted my teeth as we stepped beyond that door and golden light broke through the shadows, calling to me in a way that dove deep into my desires and tugged hard.

A golden rune illuminated beneath us, then another and another as we moved forward.

"Truth, fortune, honesty, virtue," Tory murmured, clearly recognising their meaning, and I was pretty sure I heard the word death among the list too as she continued. So that was just peachy.

The golden glow brightened into a huge sphere before us and I realised we'd arrived at the star, the enormous rock somehow even bigger than it had seemed in Elvia's memory.

A rough hole was cut into its surface, marking the place where the Imperial Star belonged.

"Return the heart," Clydinius whispered eagerly, that golden light pulsing and flickering.

The power ringing through the air made my ears pop as we drew closer and Tory took the chain from her neck, holding the Imperial Star in her fist. She broke it out of the amulet, removing the concealment spells that had been placed on it too, then moved towards the hole, the thrill in the air skipping against my skin.

I slid my hand around Tory's, bearing this burden with her and ensuring this act was ours as one.

"Ready?" she whispered.

"What's that saying the Oscuras use? A morte..."

"E ritorno," she finished, and we thrust the heart of the star into the hole, fixing it back in place.

"Creatia," I spoke the power word Orion had found in his father's diary, one that could be used to wield the Imperial Star. It meant creation, and surely was the only power word capable of giving a body to this entity.

Light blazed from the hole, threading between our fingers and setting my pulse racing. There was no going back now. We'd done what we'd done, the promise kept.

The moment the power latched inside the star, a force blasted into us that sent us flying onto our backs. I cast an air shield around us as Tory drew her sword, the two of us shoving upright, ready to fight.

The energy in the air was changing, the star pulsing, thrumming, the light erratic and dancing everywhere. It struck against my shield, slicing through it and Tory carved her sword through the light, but it made no difference.

"Shift and you will burn," Clydinius warned, and I kept my Phoenix firmly locked down, raising my hands and blasting fire at it with all I had.

The flames sizzled out against its shining surface and Tory snatched my hand, her magic uniting with mine and making us twice as powerful together. She raised her palm, freezing the star as I leant her my strength, then she tried to crack it like an egg with the whip of a huge vine. Our magic did nothing, and suddenly it was all ebbing away, the well in my chest hollowing out as my magic was sucked into that all-powerful being before us.

"It is too late to fight," Clydinius said, amusement in his tone, his voice becoming more solid, less ethereal. *"The promise is fulfilled."*

Tory cursed, throwing her hand out before her and for a moment a pentagram appeared on the ground that was cast from blazing fire, but a wash of magic tore it apart before I could so much as blink.

I heard the stone door slam shut at our backs and the truth of our reality shuddered through me. Our magic was entirely tapped out and our hands parted as I drew my sword, facing down this enemy.

I ran forward with my sister at my side, slamming my blade against the star, making it shriek in rage. Tory's sword didn't even make it that far as we were blasted away from it again, hitting the far wall and crumpling back to the ground.

The star glowed so brightly I could see nothing at all beyond it, and the piercing, shrill noise in my head made it impossible to move.

We were forced to cover our ears and hunker close together as that horrid sound ripped through every fibre of our bodies. The pain was immobilising, like a thousand rusty knives scraping along the inside of my skin.

Flashes of the future raced through my mind, and I realised I was seeing it all through Clydinius's eyes, his plans for the world. Razing cities to dust, claiming all the treasures of the kingdom for himself and sitting atop a mountain of bones, forged into a throne.

With an abruptness that left my head spinning, it came to an end.

I blinked as the light faded away, finding two girls standing in the cavern, the image of Tory and I, flames flickering between their fingers.

"I am Fae," the false me spoke in reverence, my voice perfectly mimicked by the star.

"True freedom is mine," the fake Tory finished, as if this thing was both of us now, housed in our skins.

We shoved to our feet, charging with battle cries, each of us aimed at the mirrors of ourselves, and swinging our blades in deadly arcs.

But as our swords came tearing towards their bodies, the air shimmered and the star vanished before our eyes, leaving us behind. Reality set in and I looked toward the closed stone door, the walls of the cavern and the ceiling of stone above. We were trapped here without a drop of magic, unable to summon our Orders or else meet a gruesome end. And in the wake of Clydinius's departure, words rang out around us in the voice of the stars, a new fate knitted into existence in response to what we'd done.

When all hope hinges on a promise forged of lies,
Beware the threaded minds of blood and chaos.
Unlikely friends and broken bonds may shift the tide,
Cleave open the walls of the lost in the depths of the unholy night.
Unleash the souls tethered in the tainted dark,
Unite the rising twelve and toll the bells of fate.

Scorpio
Gemini
Virgo
Cancer
Leo
Taurus
Capricorn
Libra
Aquarius
Pisces

VARD

CHAPTER EIGHTY THREE

I strode through the palace of jade green stone which Lionel had tasked his army to build for him, on the outcrops of the Bermanian Mountains at the far east of the kingdom, in the days that had passed since he'd been driven out of The Palace of Souls.

It was cold here. Cold and grey and barren. Which suited me just fine.

I'd been gifted a new lab for my experiments, my grief over the loss of Brownmary and the rest of my wonderful creations still rankling me, yet there were promising subjects among those I'd been given to toy with.

I took my wallet from my pocket and opened it, sighing at the photograph I kept there of my dear Ian Belor. The pinnacle of my success with these trials. He was such a beautiful monster, such a perfect specimen. But it was so hard to recreate that perfection, the varying qualities of my subjects impossible to predict. Not to mention how I liked to tinker with them, the changes I made always a little different from the last.

I pressed my fingers to the photograph and closed my wallet once more, returning it to my pocket as I began to climb the endless stairs of green stone.

The rooms which had been gifted to The Bonded Men took up the lower three levels, and I passed them by on silent feet, not wishing to spend more time than necessary with the oafish Dragons.

I hated them. Every last one. Their superior attitudes clawing at my skin every time I had to endure them. Elitism at its finest. And yet none of them could do the things I could do. None of them came close to my prowess. But still, I went unnoticed, my name a whisper instead of a cry of adoration.

I made it to the opulent upper part of the palace where the King and Queen resided, the silence thankfully stretching, unlike the last time I had been up here, subjected to listening to them fuck like the hellish creatures they were. It never lasted long at least. But I preferred not to bear witness to their coupling all the same.

"Sire?" I called as I looked between the sweeping stairs ahead of me and the vaulted throne room to my right, uncertain of where to find my King.

"This way," a voice came from right behind me and I jerked around as I found that snivelling butler Horace there, his eyes narrowing expectantly.

I had half a mind to break through his mental defences and scramble his brains like a freshly cracked egg.

I resisted the urge and swept after him, my grey robes trailing across the jade stone floor as we passed hastily crafted tapestries and paintings with loose threads and wet paint, each depicting the Dragon King and his Shadow Queen in their glory. There were even a few of their abominable offspring, Tharix's unnerving gaze seeming to pierce me through to my core as I passed by the images of him.

The entire place reeked of fresh magic and desperation. Lionel Acrux and that twisted shadow creature he had taken for a bride playing the part of wedded bliss, now that they had further need of one another.

They wanted the world to buy into this lie of their new palace. They were trying to make everyone believe they had come here by choice, to build a new seat of power within the kingdom. They wanted the people of Solaria to believe that they had not been rattled by the Vega girls who continued to defy them, and they would never admit that they now had no access to The Palace of Souls.

But I knew better. I saw it all.

Horace led me down a smaller corridor than the others, the walls here bare and not covered during the hasty renovations as of yet. With each step I took, the air grew cooler and less welcoming.

"Through there," Horace said abruptly, pointing me on as he stopped, the set of his jaw telling me that he wouldn't go a single step further.

I ignored him as I brushed past his shoulder, raising my chin as I strode down the narrow corridor, before finding an open door beyond it which impossibly led outside. This palace had been built onto the side of the cliff itself and I was deep within the building now, surely deep inside the rocks of the cliff and certainly not anywhere near the sky, but as I stepped out it became clear that there was a gap here, carved into the rocks themselves.

I spotted the King ahead of me, standing before a large precipice, Lavinia clinging to his arm, caressing him possessively while the wind whipped the shadows of her dress around her naked body wildly.

I wetted my lips as I spied her nipple between the shifting shadows, her body lithe and supple beneath them, though only a fool would have wished to sink his cock into her.

Tharix dropped down before me so suddenly that I yelped, stumbling backwards and falling onto my ass as the too handsome face of that demon child loomed over me.

"Whoops," he sneered, and my heart stilled at the seductive voice which spilled from his lips.

"You speak now?" I muttered as I scrambled to my feet, fighting off the terror his presence was trying to stoke in me.

"Mother has been giving me lessons in many things," he purred and as I glanced at Lavinia again, I found both her and Lionel sneering at me.

"You're late," Lionel hissed, his lip curling back as he surveyed me, and I brushed my cloak off as I stepped around Tharix and hurried closer to him.

"I came as soon as I was summoned, my King," I assured him, bowing low while noticing the way he was gripping his wife's ass. Ever since the two of them had run to this place they had been inseparable, both of them as transparent as glass in their attempts to cling to each other's power.

Lavinia was still a thing of horrors, but she was altered since Gwendalina Vega had bound her within her own shadows, cutting off her hold on the rest of them. She was still as beautiful as before, but that depth of power that had once roiled in her eyes was gone, the booming presence she had once commanded now muted. She needed her Acrux King more than ever before and he needed her too. Hence this marital bliss.

"Well don't linger now. I need you to look into the future for me. There is power in this place, great and dreadful power which now belongs entirely to us. Let me know if it is enough," Lionel demanded, pointing me towards that precipice where a turbulent energy thrashed violently in its desperation to break free.

But it couldn't break free. It was a slave now. A gift that the two of them had stolen and would abuse for as long as they saw fit.

I swallowed the lump in my throat as I closed in on the endless drop before them, looking down into the dark where Lavinia's shadows coiled like a pit of vipers.

I couldn't see the thing they had caged within those shadows, no sign at all to say what it was or how it could be possible. But I knew. There was nothing so terrible in this world or the next which might compare.

I drew in a long breath and called upon my gift of The Sight, raising a hand over that great drop and trying not to flinch away. The wind bellowed through the chasm once more, threatening to tip me over the edge. I had no desire to meet what awaited at the foot of that drop in any way beyond this.

At first, The Sight did little more than offer me a few glimpses of futures so uncertain that I couldn't so much as pin down a single detail, and my palms began to sweat as Tharix circled nearer to me.

"Why do we keep this worthless pawn so close, Daddy?" Lavinia asked softly, though she made no attempt to keep her words from me.

"I often wonder the same thing, my love," Lionel muttered, making my pulse race as I pushed on my gift, begging it to offer me something, anything that could be of use to them.

"Tharix is hungry," Lavinia went on in that petulant tone, her hand sliding down Lionel's chest towards his crotch.

I closed my eyes to clear my mind from thinking on what she might convince him to do to me if I failed him again now.

"Ravenous," Tharix agreed, his breath a hot wash over the shell of my ear, and I bit down on a whimper as I begged the stars to listen just this fucking once.

At first there was nothing, an empty, eternal nothing which seemed to mock me in my time of need, and a tremor stole through me as I saw only death in my future.

But then, just as hope was about to abandon me, Tharix's footsteps moving to my other side, like a beacon of light the power of the stars erupted through me, and my lips began to move before I could even understand the words.

"The power of the fallen has awoken, greed and glory blazing as one.
All fates hang in the balance as the flames rise from the hollow,
But the Dragon still may prosper if the paths of the enemy are thwarted.
Beware the one whose name is Nox, and seek the treasures of the ancient ring.
Use the stolen, ally with the might of your maker.
Not all starlight gleams."

Lavinia gasped excitedly as the power of the prophecy released me and I sagged in my own skin, stumbling back from the edge of the precipice.

"The stars favour me still," Lionel purred, his hand clapping down on my shoulder as he beamed smugly and I nodded, though my interpretation wasn't quite so clean cut. "The Dragon will prosper." He chuckled to himself as he and Lavinia began to dissect my words and I backed away, nodding demurely.

I didn't agree with what he believed the stars were promising him, but it mattered not. He was a means to an end, and so long as I remained in his good graces, he offered me all I needed to conduct my experiments. So I stood there in silence as he twisted the words the stars had offered me into his own designs.

And I painted on a smile, just like always.

AUTHOR'S NOTE

This book.

This. Fucking. Book.

I tell you now, we have been on a rollercoaster writing this one. Downs and downs and downs and…wait, maybe it was actually a really long slide? But then there was that time when Leon hugged a random skull, Washer whistled for his life, Xavier took the harness ride of shame, Max got his urchins fondled and Seth gave himself an unplanned nipple transplant, so there were plenty of ups too!

She's a beastie, that's for sure. We went into this one knowing it would be a girthy Brenda, but over 380k words was beyond anything we could have expected – hence the somewhat hectic few weeks it took us to finish up writing her. But here she is, the whale of our collection and you just made it over her humpback, past the fields of death and plunging off what I would like to think of as a not soooo brutal cliff.

All you have to worry about from here on out is whatever the fuck Clyde might be planning, (also fuck yeah, you guys finally met Clyde!!! We have been waiting on that little egg of doom for YEARS and he has at last arrived to the fullness of his best life, ready to wreak havoc and cause untold atrocities) the fact that Lionel and Lavinia are up to something somewhat ominous, Tharix finding his voice and considering a career in death opera, the twins being stuck in that cave of doom – which wasn't inspired by, but does remind me a bit of that Moana/Maui meeting which my son insists on starting that movie with every time – "I want to watch Maui, but not with her on the island, I want to see it from when she gets shut in the cave." He's a boy after his mother's heart…. Not that there will be a handy little scramble hole for the twins to escape through – nothing is ever that easy in Solaria.

But I digress, we were talking about the few things you may be concerned over for book 9. So I guess we should toss in the turbulent sea of the twins' current relationship, the cost of bringing big D back and the constant warnings that have been flying around over Covens. So not much.

On a slightly more serious note, as you've gotten this far into this series with us, you have clearly decided to dive headfirst into the twisted imaginings of our overactive minds, and we can't express to you how much it means to us that you've done so. This life was a dream which we never dared believe could become a reality, but through every person who has taken a chance with us, fallen for our morally corrupt men, leapt feet first into our worlds of carnage and whimsy, let the slow burns eat you alive, cried, raged, screamed and loved with us, we have somehow found ourselves in this wonderful position and we can never express our gratitude to you enough for that.

Writing this book and these characters carved pieces of our souls off with each and every word, and we can only hope you enjoy devouring them just as much as we enjoy bathing in your tears.

If you'd like to come and join our reader community where you'll always get the tea served first, join us here, here, and here.

Love you always, Susanne & Caroline xoxo

ALSO BY
CAROLINE PECKHAM
&
SUSANNE VALENTI

Brutal Boys of Everlake Prep

(Complete Reverse Harem Bully Romance Contemporary Series)

Kings of Quarantine

Kings of Lockdown

Kings of Anarchy

Queen of Quarantine

**

Dead Men Walking

(Reverse Harem Dark Romance Contemporary Series)

The Death Club

Society of Psychos

**

The Harlequin Crew

(R*everse Harem Mafia Romance Contemporary Series)*

Sinners Playground

Dead Man's Isle

Carnival Hill

Paradise Lagoon

Harlequinn Crew Novellas

Devil's Pass

**

Dark Empire

(Dark Mafia Contemporary Standalones)

Beautiful Carnage

Beautiful Savage

**

The Ruthless Boys of the Zodiac

(Reverse Harem Paranormal Romance Series - Set in the world of Solaria)

Dark Fae

Savage Fae

Vicious Fae

Broken Fae

Warrior Fae

Zodiac Academy

(M/F Bully Romance Series- Set in the world of Solaria, five years after Dark Fae)

The Awakening

Ruthless Fae

The Reckoning

Shadow Princess

Cursed Fates

Fated Thrones

Heartless Sky

Sorrow and Starlight

The Awakening - As told by the Boys

Zodiac Academy Novellas

Origins of an Academy Bully

The Big A.S.S. Party

Darkmore Penitentiary

(Reverse Harem Paranormal Romance Series - Set in the world of Solaria, ten years after Dark Fae)

Caged Wolf

Alpha Wolf

Feral Wolf

**

The Age of Vampires

(Complete M/F Paranormal Romance/Dystopian Series)

Eternal Reign

Eternal Shade

Eternal Curse

Eternal Vow

Eternal Night

Eternal Love

**

Cage of Lies

(M/F Dystopian Series)

Rebel Rising

**

Tainted Earth

(M/F Dystopian Series)

Afflicted

Altered

Adapted

Advanced

**

The Vampire Games

(Complete M/F Paranormal Romance Trilogy)

V Games

V Games: Fresh From The Grave

V Games: Dead Before Dawn

*

The Vampire Games: Season Two

(Complete M/F Paranormal Romance Trilogy)

Wolf Games

Wolf Games: Island of Shade

Wolf Games: Severed Fates

*

The Vampire Games: Season Three

Hunter Trials

*

The Vampire Games Novellas

A Game of Vampires

**

The Rise of Issac

(Complete YA Fantasy Series)

Creeping Shadow

Bleeding Snow

Turning Tide

Weeping Sky

Failing Light

Printed by Amazon Italia Logistica S.r.l.
Torrazza Piemonte (TO), Italy

74535687R00415